For the first time in one volume, two action-packed novels of adventure and suspense from Tom Clancy, the unrivalled master of thriller writing.

THE HUNT FOR RED OCTOBER

Silently, beneath the chill Atlantic waters, an ultra-secret Soviet submarine, the *Red October,* is heading west. Captain Marko Ramius is finally putting into action a desperate plan – to defect to the US, taking the *Red October* with him.

The Americans want her. The Soviets want her back. With all-out war only moments away, the superpowers race across the ocean on a terrifying, heart-stopping mission. The most incredible chase in history is on. . .

PATRIOT GAMES

When Jack Ryan foils an Ulster Liberation Army terrorist attack on the Royal Family, his courageous actions not only win him the admiration of an entire nation, they also rouse the enmity and hatred of that nation's most dangerous men.

Now a ULA target himself, Ryan plunges into the murky world of counter-intelligence, where he uncovers connections between the ULA and an international underground network that place him at the forefront of the deadly battle against international terrorism, and pitch him into the most desperate struggle of his life. . .

Works by Tom Clancy

The Hunt for Red October
Red Storm Rising
Patriot Games
The Cardinal of the Kremlin
Clear and Present Danger
The Sum of All Fears

TOM CLANCY

THE HUNT FOR
RED OCTOBER

PATRIOT GAMES

Diamond Books
An Imprint of HarperCollins*Publishers,*
77–85 Fulham Palace Road,
Hammersmith, London W6 8JB

This Diamond Books omnibus edition first published 1992
9 8 7 6 5 4 3 2

ISBN 0 261 66000 4

Printed and bound in Great Britain by
BPC Hazell Books Ltd
A member of
The British Printing Company Ltd

Contents

THE HUNT FOR
RED OCTOBER

First published in Great Britain by Collins 1985
Copyright © 1984 by Jack Ryan Enterprises Ltd

The Author asserts the moral right to
be identified as the author of this work

ACKNOWLEDGEMENTS

For technical information and advice I am especially indebted to Michael Shelton, former naval aviator; Larry Bond, whose naval wargame, 'Harpoon', was adopted for the training of NROTC cadets; Drs Gerry Sterner and Craig Jeschke; and Lieutenant Commander Gregory Young, USN.

For Ralph Chatham,
a sub driver who spoke the truth,
and for all the men who wear dolphins

The First Day

Friday, 3 December

The *Red October*

Captain First Rank Marko Ramius of the Soviet Navy was dressed for the Arctic conditions normal to the Northern Fleet submarine base at Polyarnyy. Five layers of wool and oilskin enclosed him. A dirty harbour tug pushed his submarine's bow around to the north, facing down the channel. The dock that had held his *Red October* for two interminable months was now a water-filled concrete box, one of the many specially built to shelter strategic missile submarines from the harsh elements. On its edge a collection of sailors and dockyard workers watched his ship sail in stolid Russian fashion, without a wave or a cheer.

'Engines ahead slow, Kamarov,' he ordered. The tug slid out of the way, and Ramius glanced aft to see the water stirring from the force of the twin bronze propellers. The tug's commander waved. Ramius returned the gesture. The tug had done a simple job, but done it quickly and well. The *Red October*, a *Typhoon*-class sub, moved under her own power towards the main ship channel of the Kola Fjord.

'There's Purga, Captain.' Gregoriy Kamarov pointed to the ice-breaker that would escort them to sea. Ramius nodded. The two hours required to transit the channel would tax not his seamanship but his endurance. There was a cold north wind blowing, the only sort of north wind in this part of the world. Late autumn had been surprisingly mild, and scarcely any snow had fallen in an area that measures it in metres; then a week before a major winter storm had savaged the Murmansk coast, breaking pieces off the Arctic icepack. The icebreaker was no formality. The *Purga* would butt aside any ice that might have drifted overnight into the channel. It would not do at all for the Soviet Navy's newest missile submarine to be damaged by an errant chunk of frozen water.

The water in the fjord was choppy, driven by the brisk wind. It began to lap over the *October's* spherical bow, rolling back down the flat missile deck which lay before the towering black sail. The water was coated with the bilge oil of numberless ships, filth that would not evaporate in the low temperatures and that left a black ring on the rocky walls of the fjord as though from the bath of a slovenly giant. An altogether apt simile, Ramius thought. The Soviet giant cared little for the dirt it left on the face of the earth, he

1

grumbled to himself. He had learned his seamanship as a boy on inshore fishing boats, and knew what it was to be in harmony with nature.

'Increase speed to one-third,' he said. Kamarov repeated his captain's order over the bridge telephone. The water stirred more as the *October* moved astern of the *Purga*. Captain Lieutenant Kamarov was the ship's navigator, his last duty station having been harbour pilot for the large combatant vessels based on both sides of the wide inlet. The two officers kept a weather eye on the armed icebreaker three hundred metres ahead. The *Purga's* after deck had a handful of crewmen stomping about in the cold, one wearing the white apron of a ship's cook. They wanted to witness the *Red October's* first operational cruise, and besides, sailors will do almost anything to break the monotony of their duties.

Ordinarily it would have irritated Ramius to have his ship escorted out – the channel here was wide and deep – but not today. The ice was something to worry about. And so, for Ramius, was a great deal else.

'So, my Captain, again we go to sea to serve and protect the *Rodina*!' Captain Second Rank Ivan Yurievich Putin poked his head through the hatch – without permission, as usual – and clambered up the ladder with the awkwardness of a landsman. The tiny control station was already crowded enough with the captain, the navigator, and a mute lookout. Putin was the ship's *zampolit* (political officer). Everything he did was to serve the *Rodina* (Motherland), a word that had mystical connotations to a Russian and, along with V. I. Lenin, was the Communist party's substitute for a godhead.

'Indeed, Ivan,' Ramius replied with more good cheer than he felt. 'Two weeks at sea. It is good to leave the dock. A seaman belongs at sea, not tied alongside, overrun with bureaucrats and workmen with dirty boots. And we will be warm.'

'You find this cold?' Putin asked incredulously.

For the hundredth time Ramius told himself that Putin was the perfect political officer. His voice was always too loud, his humour too affected. He never allowed a person to forget what he was. The perfect political officer, Putin was an easy man to fear.

'I have been in submarines too long, my friend. I grow accustomed to moderate temperatures and a stable deck under my feet.' Putin did not notice the veiled insult. He'd been assigned to submarines after his first tour on destroyers had been cut short by chronic seasickness – and perhaps because he did not resent the close confinement aboard submarines, something that many men cannot tolerate.

'Ah, Marko Aleksandrovich, in Gorkiy on a day like this, flowers bloom!'

'And what sort of flowers might those be, Comrade Political Officer?' Ramius surveyed the fjord through his binoculars. At noon the sun was barely over the southeast horizon, casting orange light and purple shadows along the rocky walls.

'Why, snow flowers, of course,' Putin said, laughing loudly. 'On a day like this the faces of the children and the women glow pink, your breath trails behind you like a cloud, and the vodka tastes especially fine. Ah, to be in Gorkiy on a day like this!'

The bastard ought to work for Intourist, Ramius told himself, except that Gorkiy is a city closed to foreigners. He had been there twice. It had struck him as a typical Soviet city, full of ramshackle buildings, dirty streets, and ill-clad citizens. As it was in most Russian cities, winter was Gorkiy's best season. The snow hid all the dirt. Ramius, half Lithuanian, had childhood memories of a better place, a coastal village whose Hanseatic origin had left rows of presentable buildings.

It was unusual for anyone other than a Great Russian to be aboard – much less command – a Soviet naval vessel. Marko's father, Aleksandr Ramius, had been a hero of the Party, a dedicated, believing Communist who had served Stalin faithfully and well. When the Soviets first occupied Lithuania in 1940, the elder Ramius was instrumental in rounding up political dissidents, shop owners, priests, and anyone else who might have been troublesome to the new regime. All were shipped off to fates that now even Moscow could only guess at. When the Germans invaded a year later, Aleksandr fought heroically as a political commissar, and was later to distinguish himself in the Battle of Leningrad. In 1944 he returned to his native land with the spearhead of the Eleventh Guards Army to wreak bloody vengeance on those who had collaborated with the Germans or been suspected of such. Marko's father had been a true Soviet hero – and Marko was deeply ashamed to be his son. His mother's health had been broken during the endless siege of Leningrad. She died giving birth to him, and he was raised by his paternal grandmother in Lithuania while his father strutted through the Party Central Committee in Vilnius, awaiting his promotion to Moscow. He got that, too, and was a candidate member of the Politburo when his life was cut short by a heart attack.

Marko's shame was not total. His father's prominence had made his current goal a possibility, and Marko planned to wreak his own vengeance on the Soviet Union, enough, perhaps, to satisfy the thousands of his countrymen who had died before he was ever born.

'Where we are going, Ivan Yurievich, it will be colder still.'

Putin clapped his captain's shoulder. Was his affection feigned or real? Marko wondered. Probably real. Ramius was an honest man, and he recognized that this short, loud oaf did have some human feelings.

'Why is it, Comrade Captain, that you always seem glad to leave the *Rodina* and go to sea?'

Ramius smiled behind his binoculars. 'A seaman has one country, Ivan Yurievich, but two wives. You never understand that. Now I go to my other wife, the cold, heartless one that owns my soul.' Ramius paused. The smile vanished. 'My only wife, now.'

Putin was quiet for once, Marko noted. The political officer had been there, had cried real tears as the coffin of polished pine rolled into the cremation chamber. For Putin the death of Natalia Bogdanova Ramius had been a cause of grief, but beyond that the act of an uncaring God whose existence he regularly denied. For Ramius it had been a crime committed not by God but the State. An unnecessary, monstrous crime, one that demanded punishment.

'Ice.' The lookout pointed.

'Loose-pack ice, starboard side of the channel, or perhaps something calved off the east-side glacier. We'll pass well clear,' Kamarov said.

'Captain!' The bridge speaker had a metallic voice. 'Message from fleet headquarters.'

'Read it.'

'"Exercise area clear. No enemy vessels in vicinity. Proceed as per orders. Signed, Korov, Fleet Commander."'

'Acknowledged,' Ramius said. The speaker clicked off. 'So, no *Amerikantsi* about?'

'You doubt the fleet commander?' Putin inquired.

'I hope he is correct,' Ramius replied, more sincerely than his political officer would appreciate. 'But you remember our briefings.'

Putin shifted on his feet. Perhaps he was feeling the cold.

'Those American 688-class submarines, Ivan, the *Los Angeleses*. Remember what one of their officers told our spy? That they could sneak up on a whale and bugger it before it knew they were there? I wonder how the KGB got that bit of information. A beautiful Soviet agent, trained in the ways of the decadent West, too skinny, the way the imperialists like their women, blonde hair . . .' The captain grunted amusement. 'Probably the American officer was a boastful boy, trying to find a way to do something similar to our agent, no? And feeling his liquor, like most sailors. Still. The American *Los Angeles* class, and the new British *Trafalgars*, those we must guard against. They are a threat to us.'

'The Americans are good technicians, Comrade Captain,' Putin said, 'but they are not giants. Their technology is not so awesome. *Nasha lutcha*,' he concluded. Ours is better.

Ramius nodded thoughtfully, thinking to himself that *zampoliti* really ought to know something about the ships they supervised, as mandated by Party doctrine.

'Ivan, didn't the farmers around Gorkiy tell you it is the wolf you do not see that you must fear? But don't be overly concerned. With this ship we will teach them a lesson, I think.'

'As I told the Main Political Administration,' Putin clapped Ramius' shoulder again, '*Red October* is in the best of hands.'

Ramius and Kamarov both smiled at that. You son of a bitch! the captain thought, saying in front of my men that *you* must pass on my fitness to

4

command! A man who could not command a rubber raft on a calm day! A pity you will not live to eat those words, Comrade Political Officer, and spend the rest of your life in the gulag for that misjudgement. It would almost be worth leaving you alive.

A few minutes later the chop began to pick up, making the submarine roll. The movement was accentuated by their height above the deck, and Putin made excuses to go below. Still a weak-legged sailor. Ramius shared the observation silently with Kamarov, who smiled agreement. Their unspoken contempt for the *zampolit* was a most un-Soviet thought.

The next hour passed quickly. The water grew rougher as they approached the open sea, and their icebreaker escort began to wallow on the swells. Ramius watched her with interest. He had never been on an icebreaker, his entire career having been in submarines. They were more comfortable, but also more dangerous. He was accustomed to the danger, though, and the years of experience would stand him in good stead now.

'Sea buoy in sight, Captain.' Kamarov pointed. The red lighted buoy was riding actively on the waves.

'Control room, what is the sounding?' Ramius asked over the bridge telephone.

'One hundred metres below the keel, Comrade Captain.'

'Increase speed to two-thirds, come left ten degrees.' Ramius looked at Kamarov. 'Signal our course change to *Purga*, and hope he doesn't turn the wrong way.'

Kamarov reached for the small blinker light stowed under the bridge coaming. The *Red October* began to accelerate slowly, her 30,000-ton bulk resisting the power of her engines. Presently the bow wave grew to a three-metre standing arc of water; man-made combers rolled down the missile deck, splitting against the front of the sail. The *Purga* altered course to starboard, allowing the submarine to pass well clear. Ramius looked aft at the bluffs of the Kola Fjord. They had been carved to this shape millennia before by the remorseless pressure of towering glaciers. How many times in his twenty years of service with the Red Banner Northern Fleet had he looked at the wide, flat U-shape? This would be the last. One way or another, he'd never go back. Which way would it turn out? Ramius admitted to himself that he didn't much care. Perhaps the stories his grandmother had taught him were true, about God and the reward for a good life. He hoped so – it would be good if Natalia were not truly dead. In any case, there was no turning back. He had left a letter in the last mailbag taken off before sailing. There was no going back after that.

'Kamarov, signal to *Purga*: "Diving at – ,"' he checked his watch, '" – 1320 hours. Exercise OCTOBER FROST begins as scheduled. You are released to other assigned duties. We will return as scheduled."'

Kamarov worked the trigger on the blinker light to transmit the message. The *Purga* responded at once, and Ramius read the flashing signal unaided:

'IF THE WHALES DON'T EAT YOU. GOOD LUCK TO *RED OCTOBER*!'

Ramius lifted the phone again, pushing the button for the sub's radio room. He had the same message transmitted to fleet headquarters, Severomorsk. Next he addressed the control room.

'Depth under the keel?'

'One hundred forty metres, Comrade Captain.'

'Prepare to dive.' He turned to the lookout and ordered him below. The boy moved towards the hatch. He was probably glad to return to the warmth below, but took the time for one last look at the cloudy sky, and receding cliffs. Going to sea on a submarine was always exciting, and always a little sad.

'Clear the bridge. Take the conn when you get below, Gregoriy.' Kamarov nodded and dropped down the hatch, leaving the captain alone.

Ramius made one last careful scan of the horizon. The sun was barely visible aft, the sky leaden, the sea black except for the splash of whitecaps. He wondered if he were saying good-bye to the world. If so, he would have preferred a more cheerful view of it.

Before sliding down he inspected the hatch seat, pulling it shut with a chain and making sure the automatic mechanism functioned properly. Next he dropped eight metres down the inside of the sail to the pressure hull, then two more into the control room. A *michman* (warrant officer) shut the second hatch and with a powerful spin turned the locking wheel as far as it would go.

'Gregoriy?' Ramius asked.

'Straight board shut,' the navigator said crisply, pointing to the diving board. All hull-opening indicator lights showed green, safe. 'All systems aligned and checked for dive. The compensation is entered. We are rigged for dive.'

The captain made his own visual inspection of mechanical, electrical, and hydraulic indicators. He nodded, and the *michman* of the watch unlocked the vent controls.

'Dive,' Ramius ordered, moving to the periscope to relieve Vasily Borodin, his *starpom* (executive officer). Kamarov pulled the diving alarm, and the hull reverberated with the racket of a loud buzzer.

'Flood the main ballast tanks. Rig out the diving planes. Ten degrees down-angle on the planes,' Kamarov ordered, his eyes alert to see that every crewman did his job exactly. Ramius listened carefully but did not look. Kamarov was the best young seaman he had ever commanded, and had long since earned his captain's trust.

The *Red October's* hull was filled with the noise of rushing air as vents at the top of the ballast tanks were opened and water entering from the tank floods at the bottom chased the buoying air out. It was a lengthy process, for the submarine had many such tanks, each carefully subdivided by numerous cellular baffles. Ramius adjusted the periscope lens to look down and saw the black water change briefly to foam.

The *Red October* was the largest and finest command Ramius had ever had, but the sub had one major flaw. She had plenty of engine power and a new drive system that he hoped would befuddle American and Soviet submarines alike, but she was so big that she changed depth like a crippled whale. Slow going up, even slower going down.

'Scope under.' Ramius stepped away from the instrument after what seemed a long wait. 'Down periscope.'

Passing forty metres,' Kamarov said.

'Level off at one hundred metres.' Ramius watched his crewmen now. The first dive could make experienced men shudder, and half his crew were farmboys straight from training camp. The hull popped and creaked under the pressure of the surrounding water, something that took getting used to. A few of the younger men went pale but stood rigidly upright.

Kamarov began the procedure for levelling off at the proper depth. Ramius watched with a pride he might have felt for his own son as the lieutenant gave the necessary orders with precision. He was the first officer Ramius had recruited. The control room crew snapped to his command. Five minutes later the submarine slowed her descent at ninety metres and settled the next ten to a perfect stop at one hundred.

'Well done, Comrade Lieutenant. You have the conn. Slow to one-third speed. Have the sonarmen listen on all passive systems.' Ramius turned to leave the control room, motioning Putin to follow him.

And so it began.

Ramius and Putin went aft to the submarine's wardroom. The captain held the door open for the political officer, then closed and locked it behind himself. The *Red October's* wardroom was a spacious affair for a submarine, located immediately forward of the galley, aft of the officer accommodations. Its walls were soundproofed, and the door had a lock because her designers had known that not everything the officers had to say was necessarily for the ears of the enlisted men. It was large enough for all of the *October's* officers to eat as a group – though at least three of them would always be on duty. The safe containing the ship's orders was here, not in the captain's stateroom where a man might use his solitude to try opening it by himself. It had two dials. Ramius had one combination, Putin the other. Which was hardly necessary, since Putin undoubtedly knew their mission orders already. So did Ramius, but not all the particulars.

Putin poured tea as the captain checked his watch against the chronometer on the bulkhead. Fifteen minutes until he could open the safe. Putin's courtesy made him uneasy.

'Two more weeks of confinement,' the *zampolit* said, stirring his tea.

'The Americans do this for two *months*, Ivan. Of course, their submarines are far more comfortable.' Despite her huge bulk, the *October's* crew accommodations would have shamed a gulag jailer. The crew consisted of fifteen officers, housed in fairly decent cabins aft, and a hundred enlisted men whose bunks were stuffed into corners and racks throughout the bow, forward of the missile room. The *October's* size was deceptive. The interior of her double hull was crammed with missiles, torpedoes, a nuclear reactor and its support equipment, a huge backup diesel power plant, and bank of nickle-cadmium batteries outside the pressure hull, which was ten times the size of its American counterparts. Running and maintaining the ship was a huge job for so small a crew, even though extensive use of automation made her the most modern of Soviet naval vessels. Perhaps the men didn't need proper bunks. They would only have four or six hours a day to make use of them. This would work to Ramius' advantage. Half of his crew were draftees on their first operational cruise, and even the more experienced men knew little enough. The strength of his enlisted crew, unlike that of Western crews, resided much more in his eleven *michmanyy* (warrant officers) than in his *glavnyy starshini* (senior petty officers). All of them were men who would do – were specifically trained to do – exactly what their officers told them. And Ramius had picked the officers.

'You want to cruise for two months?' Putin asked.

'I have done it on diesel submarines. A submarine belongs at sea, Ivan. Our mission is to strike fear into the hearts of the imperialists. We do not accomplish this tied up in our barn at Polyarnyy most of the time, but we cannot stay at sea any longer because any period over two weeks and the crew loses efficiency. In two weeks this collection of children will be a mob of numbed robots.' Ramius was counting on that.

'And we could solve this by having capitalist luxuries?' Putin sneered.

'A true Marxist is objective, Comrade Political Officer,' Ramius chided, savouring this last argument with Putin. 'Objectively, that which aids us in carrying out our mission is good, that which hinders us is bad. Adversity is supposed to hone one's spirit and skill, not dull them. Just being aboard a submarine is hardship enough, is it not?'

'Not for you, Marko.' Putin grinned over his tea.

'I am a seaman. Our crewmen are not, most never will be. They are a mob of farmers' sons and boys who yearn to be factory workers. We must adjust to the times, Ivan. These youngsters are not the same as we were.'

'That is true enough,' Putin agreed. 'You are never satisfied, Comrade Captain. I suppose it is men like you who force progress upon us all.'

Both men knew exactly why Soviet missile submarines spent so little of their time – barely fifteen percent of it – at sea, and it had nothing to do with creature comforts. The *Red October* carried twenty-six SS-N-20 Seahawk missiles, each with eight 500-kiloton multiple independently targetable re-entry vehicles – MIRVs – enough to destroy two hundred cities. Land-based bombers could only fly a few hours at a time, then had to return to their bases. Land-based missiles arrayed along the main East-West Soviet rail network were always where paramilitary troops of the KGB could get at them lest some missile regiment commander suddenly came to realize the power at his fingertips. But missile submarines were by definition beyond any control from land. Their entire mission was to disappear.

Given that fact, Marko was surprised that his government had them at all. The crew of such vessels had to be trusted. And so they sailed less often than their Western counterparts, and when they did it was with a political officer aboard to stand next to the commanding officer, a second captain always ready to pass approval on every action.

'Do you think you could do it, Marko, cruise for two months with these farmboys?'

'I prefer half-trained boys, as you know. They have less to unlearn. Then I can train them to be seamen the right way, my way. My personality cult?'

Putin laughed as he lit a cigarette. 'That observation has been made in the past, Marko. But you are our best teacher and your reliability is well known.' This was very true. Ramius had sent hundreds of officers and seamen on to other submarines whose commanders were glad to have them. It was another paradox that a man could engender trust within a society that scarcely recognized the concept. Of course, Ramius was a loyal Party member, the son of a Party hero who had been carried to his grave by three Politburo members. Putin waggled his finger. 'You should be commanding one of our higher naval schools, Comrade Captain. Your talents would better serve the state there.'

'It is a seaman I am, Ivan Yurievich. Only a seaman, not a schoolmaster – despite what they say about me. A wise man knows his limitations.' And a bold one seizes opportunities. Every officer aboard had served with Ramius before, except for three junior lieutenants, who would obey their orders as readily as any wet-nosed *matros* (seaman), and the doctor, who was useless.

The chronometer chimed four bells.

Ramius stood and dialled in his three-element combination. Putin did the same, and the captain flipped the lever to open the safe's circular door. Inside was a manila envelope plus four books of cipher keys and missile-targeting coordinates. Ramius removed the envelope, then closed the door, spinning both dials before sitting down again.

'So, Ivan, what do you suppose our orders tell us to do?' Ramius asked theatrically.

'Our duty, Comrade Captain.' Putin smiled.

'Indeed.' Ramius broke the wax seal on the envelope and extracted the four-page operation order. He read it quickly. It was not complicated.

'So, we are to proceed to grid square 54-90 and rendezvous with our attack submarine *V. K. Konovalov* – that's Captain Tupolev's new command. You know Viktor Tupolev? No? Viktor will guard us from imperialist intruders, and we will conduct a four-day acquisition and tracking drill, with him hunting us – if he can.' Ramius chuckled. 'The boys in the attack submarine directorate still have not figured how to track our new drive system. Well, neither will the Americans. We are to confine our operations to grid square 54-90 and the immediately surrounding squares. That ought to make Viktor's task a bit easier.'

'But you will not let him find us?'

'Certainly not,' Ramius snorted. 'Let? Viktor was once my pupil. You give nothing to an enemy, Ivan, even in a drill. The imperialists certainly won't! In trying to find us, he also practices finding their missile submarines. He will have a fair chance of locating us, I think. The exercise is confined to nine squares, forty thousand square kilometres. We shall see what he has learned since he served with us – oh, that's right, you weren't with me then. That's when I had the *Suslov*.'

'Do I see disappointment?'

'No, not really. The four-day drill with *Konovalov* will be an interesting diversion.' Bastard, he said to himself, you knew beforehand exactly what our orders were – and you do know Viktor Tupolev, liar. It was time.

Putin finished his cigarette and his tea before standing. 'So, again I am permitted to watch the master captain at work – befuddling a poor boy.' He turned towards the door. 'I think – '

Ramius kicked Putin's feet out from under him just as he was stepping away from the table. Putin fell backwards while Ramius sprang to his feet and grasped the political officer's head in his strong fisherman's hands. The captain drove his neck downward to the sharp, metal-edged corner of the wardroom table. It struck the point. In the same instant Ramius pushed down on the man's chest. An unnecessary gesture – with the sickening crackle of bones Ivan Putin's neck broke, his spine severed at the level of the second cervical vertebra, a perfect hangman's fracture.

The political officer had no time to react. The nerves to his body below the neck were instantly cut off from the organs and muscles they controlled. Putin tried to shout, to say something, but his mouth flapped open and shut without a sound except for the exhalation of his last lungful of air. He tried to gulp air down like a landed fish, and this did not work. Then his eyes went up to Ramius, wide in shock – there was no pain, and no emotion but surprise. The captain laid him gently on the tile deck.

Ramius saw the face flash with recognition, then darken. He reached down to take Putin's pulse. It was nearly two minutes before the heart stopped completely. When Ramius was sure that his political officer was dead, he took the teapot from the table and poured two cups' worth on the deck, careful to drip some on the man's shoes. Next he lifted the body to the wardroom table and threw open the door.

'Dr Petrov to the wardoom at once!'

The ship's medical office was only a few steps aft. Petrov was there in seconds, along with Vasily Borodin, who had hurried aft from the control room.

'He slipped on the deck where I spilled my tea,' Ramius gasped, performing closed heart massage on Putin's chest. 'I tried to keep him from falling, but he hit his head on the table.'

Petrov shoved the captain aside, moved the body around, and leapt on the table to kneel astride it. He tore the shirt open, then checked Putin's eyes. Both pupils were wide and fixed. The doctor felt around the man's head, his hands working downward to the neck. They stopped there, probing. The doctor shook his head slowly.

'Comrade Putin is dead. His neck is broken.' The doctor's hands came loose, and he closed the *zampolit's* eyes.

'No!' Ramius shouted. 'He was alive only a minute ago.' The commanding officer was sobbing. 'It's my fault. I tried to catch him, but I failed. My fault!' He collapsed into a chair and buried his face in his hands. 'My fault,' he cried, shaking his head in rage, struggling visibly to regain his composure. An altogether excellent performance.

Petrov placed his hand on the captain's shoulder. 'It was an accident, Comrade Captain. These things happen, even to experienced men. It was not your fault. Truly, Comrade.'

Ramius swore under his breath, regaining control of himself. 'There is nothing you can do?'

Petrov shook his head. 'Even in the finest clinic in the Soviet Union nothing could be done. Once the spinal cord is severed, there is no hope. Death is virtually instantaneous – but also it is quite painless,' the doctor added consolingly.

Ramius drew himself up as he took a long breath, his face set. 'Comrade Putin was a good shipmate, a loyal Party member, and a fine officer.' Out of the corner of his eye he noticed Borodin's mouth twitch. 'Comrades, we will continue our mission! Dr Petrov, you will carry our comrade's body to the freezer. This is – gruesome, I know, but he deserves and will get an honourable military funeral, with his shipmates in attendance, as it should be, when we return to port.'

'Will this be reported to fleet headquarters?' Petrov asked.

'We cannot. Our orders are to maintain strict radio silence.' Ramius handed the doctor a set of operations orders from his pocket. Not those taken from the safe. 'Page three, Comrade Doctor.'

Petrov's eyes went wide reading the operational directive.

'I would prefer to report this, but our orders are explicit: Once we dive, no transmissions of any kind, for any reason.'

Petrov handed the papers back. 'Too bad, our comrade would have looked forward to this. But orders are orders.'

'And we shall carry them out.'

'Putin would have it no other way,' Petrov agreed.

'Borodin, observe: I take the comrade political officer's missile control key from his neck, as per regulations,' Ramius said, pocketing the key and chain.

'I note this, and will so enter it in the log,' the executive officer said gravely.

Petrov brought in his medical orderly. Together they took the body aft to the medical office, where it was zippered into a body bag. The orderly and a pair of sailors then took it forward, through the control room, into the missile compartment. The entrance to the freezer was on the lower missile deck, and the men carried the body through the door. While two cooks removed food to make room for it, the body was set reverently down in the corner. Aft, the doctor and the executive officer made the necessary inventory of personal effects, one copy for the ship's medical file, another for the ship's log, and a third for a box that was sealed and locked up in the medical office.

Forward, Ramius took the conn in a subdued control room. He ordered the submarine to a course of two-nine-zero degrees, west-northwest. Grid square 54-90 was to the east.

The Second Day

Saturday, 4 December

The *Red October*

It was the custom in the Soviet Navy for the commanding officer to announce his ship's operational orders and to exhort the crew to carry them out in true Soviet fashion. The orders were then posted for all to see – and be inspired by – outside the ship's Lenin Room. In large surface ships this was a classroom where political awareness classes were held. In *Red October* it was a closet-sized library near the wardroom where Party books and other ideological material were kept for the men to read. Ramius disclosed their orders the day after sailing to give his men the chance to settle into the ship's routine. At the same time he gave a pep talk. Ramius always gave a good one. He'd had a lot of practice. At 0800 hours when the forenoon watch was set, he entered the control room and took some file cards from an inside jacket pocket.

'Comrades!' he began, talking into the microphone, 'this is the captain speaking. You all know that our beloved friend and comrade, Captain Ivan Yurievich Putin, died yesterday in a tragic accident. Our orders do not permit us to inform fleet headquarters of this. Comrades, we will dedicate our efforts and our work to the memory of our comrade, Ivan Yurievich Putin – a fine shipmate, an honourable Party member, and a courageous officer.

'Comrades! Officers and men of *Red October*! We have orders from the Red Banner Northern Fleet High Command, and they are orders worthy of this ship and this crew!

'Comrades! Our orders are to make the ultimate test of our new silent propulsion system. We are to head *west*, past the North Cape of America's imperialist puppet state, Norway, then to turn southwest towards the Atlantic Ocean. We will pass all of the imperialist sonar nets, and we will *not* be detected! This will be a true test of our submarine and his capabilities. Our own ships will engage in a major exercise to locate us and at the same time to befuddle the arrogant imperialist navies. Our mission, first of all, is to evade detection by anyone. We will teach the Americans a lesson about Soviet technology that they will not soon forget! Our orders are to continue southwest, skirting the American coast to challenge and defeat their newest and best hunter submarines. We will proceed all the way to our socialist brothers in Cuba, and we will be the *first ship* to make use of a new and supersecret nuclear submarine base that we have been building for two years right under their imperialist noses on the south coast of Cuba. A fleet replenishment vessel is already en route to rendezvous with us there.

'Comrades! If we succeed in reaching Cuba undetected by the imperialists – and we will! – the officers and men of Red October will have a week – a week of shore leave to visit our fraternal socialist comrades on the beautiful island of Cuba. I have been there, comrades, and you will find it to be exactly what you have read, a paradise of warm breezes, palm trees and comradely good fellowship.' By which Ramius meant women. 'After this we will return to the Motherland by the same route. By this time, of course, the imperialists will know who and what we are, from their slinking spies and cowardly reconnaissance aircraft. It is intended that they should know this, because we will again evade detection on the trip home. This will let the imperialists know that they may not trifle with the men of the Soviet Navy, that we can approach their coast at the time of our choosing, and that they must respect the Soviet Union!

'Comrades! We will make the first cruise of *Red October* a memorable one!'

Ramius looked up from his prepared speech. The men on watch in the control room were exchanging grins. It was not often that a Soviet sailor was allowed to visit another country, and a visit by a nuclear submarine to a foreign country, even an ally, was nearly unprecedented. Moreover, for Russians the sand of Cuba was as exotic as Tahiti, a promised land of white sand beaches and dusky girls. Ramius knew differently. He had read articles in *Red Star* and other state journals about the joys of duty in Cuba. He had also been there.

Ramius changed cards in his hands. He had given them the good news.

'Comrades! Officers and men of *Red October*!' Now for the bad news that everyone was waiting for. 'This mission will not be an easy one. It demands our best efforts. We must maintain absolute radio silence, and our operating routines must be *perfect*! Rewards only come to those who truly earn them. Every officer and every man aboard, from your commanding officer to the newest *matros*, must do his socialist duty and do it well! If we work together as comrades, as the New Soviet Men we are, we shall succeed. You young comrades new to the sea: Listen to your officers, to your *michmanyy*, and to your *starshini*. Learn your duties well, and carry them out exactly. There are no small jobs on this ship, no small responsibilities. Every comrade depends for his life upon every other. Do your duty, follow your orders, and when we have completed this voyage, you will be true Soviet sailors! That is all.' Ramius released his thumb from the mike switch and set it back in the cradle. Not a bad speech, he decided – a large carrot and a small stick.

In the galley aft a petty officer was standing still, holding a warm loaf of bread and looking curiously at the bulkhead-mounted speaker. That wasn't what their orders were supposed to be, was it? Had there been a change in plans? The *michman* pointed him back to his duties, grinning and chuckling at the prospect of a week in Cuba. He had heard a lot of stories about Cuba and Cuban women and was looking forward to seeing if they were true.

In the control room Ramius mused. 'I wonder if any American submarines are about?'

'Indeed, Comrade Captain,' nodded Captain Second Rank Borodin, who had the watch. 'Shall we engage the caterpillar?'

'Proceed, Comrade.'

'Engines all stop,' Borodin ordered.

'All stop.' The quartermaster, a *starshina* (petty officer), dialled the annunciator to the STOP position. An instant later the order was confirmed by the inner dial, and a few seconds after that the dull rumble of the engines died away.

Borodin picked up the phone and punched the button for engineering. 'Comrade Chief Engineer, prepare to engage the caterpillar.'

It wasn't the official name for the new drive system. It had no name as such, just a project number. The nickname *caterpillar* had been given it by a young engineer who had been involved in the sub's development. Neither Ramius nor Borodin knew why, but as often happens with such names, it had stuck.

'Ready, Comrade Borodin,' the chief engineer reported back in a moment.

'Open doors fore and aft,' Borodin ordered next.

The *michman* of the watch reached up the control board and threw four switches. The status light over each changed from red to green. 'Doors show open, Comrade.'

'Engage caterpillar. Build speed slowly to thirteen knots.'

'Build slowly to one-three knots, Comrade,' the engineer acknowledged.

14

The hull, which had gone momentarily silent, now had a new sound. The engine noises were lower and very different from what they had been. The reactor plant noises, mainly from pumps that circulated the cooling water, were almost imperceptible. The caterpillar did not use a great deal of power for what it did. At the *michman's* station the speed gauge, which had dropped to five knots, began to creep upward again. Forward of the missile room, in a space shoehorned into the crew's accommodations, the handful of sleeping men stirred briefly in their bunks as they noted an intermittent rumble aft and the hum of electric motors a few feet away, separated from them by the pressure hull. They were tired enough even on their first full day at sea to ignore the noise, fighting back to their precious allotments of sleep.

'Caterpillar functioning normally, Comrade Captain,' Borodin reported.

'Excellent. Steer two-six-zero, helm,' Ramius ordered.

'Two-six-zero, Comrade.' The helmsman turned his wheel to the left.

The USS *Bremerton*

Thirty miles to the northeast, the USS *Bremerton* was on a heading of two-two-five, just emerging from under the icepack. A 688-class attack submarine, she had been on an ELINT – electronic intelligence gathering – mission in the Kara Sea when she was ordered west to the Kola Peninsula. The Russian missile boat wasn't supposed to have sailed for another week, and the *Bremerton's* skipper was annoyed at this latest intelligence screw-up. He would have been in place to track the *Red October* if she had sailed as scheduled. Even so, the American sonarmen had picked up on the Soviet sub a few minutes earlier, despite the fact that they were travelling at fourteen knots.

'Conn, sonar.'

Commander Wilson lifted the phone. 'Conn, aye.'

'Contact lost, sir. His screws stopped a few minutes ago and have not restarted. There's some other activity to the east, but the missile sub has gone dead.'

'Very well. He's probably settling down to a slow drift. We'll be creeping up on him. Stay awake, Chief.' Commander Wilson thought this over as he took two steps to the chart table. The two officers of the fire control tracking party who had just been establishing the track for the contact looked up to learn their commander's opinion.

'If it was me, I'd go down near the bottom and circle slowly right about here.' Wilson traced a rough circle on the chart that enclosed the *Red October's* position. 'So let's creep up on him. We'll reduce speed to five knots and see if we can move in and reacquire him from his reactor plant noise.' Wilson turned to the officer of the deck. 'Reduce speed to five knots.'

'Aye, Skipper.'

In the Central Post Office building in Severomorsk a mail sorter watched sourly as a truck driver dumped a large canvas sack on his work table and went back out the door. He was late – well, not really late, the clerk corrected himself, since the idiot had not been on time once in five years. It was a Saturday, and he resented being at work. Only a few years before, the forty-hour week had been started in the Soviet Union. Unfortunately this change had never affected such vital public services as mail delivery. So, here he was, still working a six-day week – and without extra pay! A disgrace, he thought, and had said often enough in his apartment, playing cards with his workmates over vodka and cucumbers.

He untied the drawstring and turned the sack over. Several smaller bags tumbled out. There was no sense in hurrying. It was only the beginning of the month, and they still had weeks to move their quota of letters and parcels from one side of the building to the other. In the Soviet Union every worker is a government worker, and they have a saying: As long as the bosses pretend to pay us, we will pretend to work.

Opening a small mailbag, he pulled out an official-looking envelope addressed to the Main Political Administration of the Navy in Moscow. The clerk paused, fingering the envelope. It probably came from one of the submarines based at Polyarnyy, on the other side of the fjord. What did the letter say? the sorter wondered, playing the mental game that amused mailmen all over the world. Was it an announcement that all was ready for the final attack on the imperialist West? A list of Party members who were late paying their dues, or a requisition for more toilet paper? There was no telling. Submariners! They were all prima donnas – even the farmboy conscripts still picking shit from between their toes paraded around like members of the Party elite.

The clerk was sixty-two. In the Great Patriotic War he had been a tankrider serving in a guards tank corps attached to Konev's First Ukrainian Front. That, he told himself, was a man's job, riding into action on the back of the great battle tanks, leaping off to hunt for the German infantrymen as they cowered in their holes. When something needed doing against those slugs, it was *done*! Now what had become of Soviet fighting men? Living aboard luxury liners with plenty of good food and warm beds. The only warm bed he had ever known was over the exhaust vent of his tank's diesel – and he'd had to fight for that! It was crazy what the world had become. Now sailors acted like czarist princes and wrote tons of letters back and forth and called it work. These pampered boys didn't know what hardship was. And their privileges! Every word they committed to paper was priority mail. Whimpering letters to their sweethearts, most of it, and here he was sorting through it all on a Saturday to see that it got to their womenfolk – even though they couldn't possibly have a reply for two weeks. It just wasn't like the old days.

16

The sorter tossed the envelope with a negligent flick of the wrist towards the surface mailbag for Moscow on the far side of his work table. It missed, dropping to the concrete floor. The letter would be placed aboard the train a day late. The sorter didn't care. There was a hockey game that night, the biggest game of the young season, Central Army against Wings. He had a litre of vodka bet on Wings.

Morrow, England

'Halsey's greatest popular success was his greatest error. In establishing himself as a popular hero with legendary aggressiveness, the admiral would blind later generations to his impressive intellectual abilities and a shrewd gambler's instinct to –' Jack Ryan frowned at his computer. It sounded too much like a doctoral dissertation, and he had already done one of those. He thought of dumping the whole passage from the memory disc but decided against it. He had to follow this line of reasoning for his introduction. Bad as it was, it did serve as a guide for what he wanted to say. Why was it that introductions always seemed to be the hardest part of a history book? For three years now he had been working on *Fighting Sailor*, an authorized biography of Fleet Admiral William Halsey. Nearly all of it was contained on a half-dozen floppy discs lying next to his Apple computer.

'Daddy?' Ryan's daughter was staring up at him.

'And how's my little Sally today?'

'Fine.'

Ryan picked her up and set her on his lap, careful to slide his chair away from the keyboard. Sally was all checked out on games and educational programmes, and occasionally thought that this meant she was able to handle Wordstar also. Once that had resulted in the loss of twenty thousand words of electronically recorded manuscript. And a spanking.

She leaned her head against her father's shoulder.

'You don't look fine. What's bothering my little girl?'

'Well, Daddy, y'see, it's almost Chris'mas, an . . . I'm not sure that Santa knows where we are. We're not where we were last year.'

'Oh, I see. And you're afraid he doesn't come here?'

'Uh huh.'

'Why didn't you ask me before? Of course he comes here. Promise.'

'Promise?'

'Promise.'

'Okay.' She kissed her father and ran out of the room, back to watching cartoons on the telly, as they called it in England. Ryan was glad she had interrupted him. He didn't want to forget to pick up a few things when he flew over to Washington. Where was – oh, yeah. He pulled a disc from his desk drawer and inserted it in the spare disc drive. After clearing the screen, he scrolled up the Christmas list, things he still had to get. With a simple command a copy of the list was made on the adjacent printer. Ryan tore the page off and tucked it in his wallet. Work didn't appeal to him this Saturday morning. He decided to play with his kids. After all, he'd be stuck in Washington for much of the coming week.

The *V. K. Konovalov*

The Soviet submarine *V. K. Konovalov* crept above the hard sand bottom of the Barents Sea at three knots. She was at the southwest corner of grid square 54-90 and for the past ten hours had been drifting back and forth on a north-south line, waiting for the *Red October* to arrive for the beginning of Exercise OCTOBER FROST. Captain Second Rank Viktor Alexievich Tupolev paced slowly around the periscope pedestal in the control room of his small, fast attack sub. He was waiting for his old mentor to show up, hoping to play a few tricks on him. He had served with the Schoolmaster for two years. They had been good years, and while he found his former commander to be something of a cynic, especially about the Party, he would unhesitatingly testify to Ramius' skill and craftiness.

And his own. Tupolev, now in his third year of command, had been one of the Schoolmaster's star pupils. His current vessel was a brand-new *Alfa*, the fastest submarine ever made. A month earlier, while Ramius had been fitting out the *Red October* after her initial shakedown, Tupolev and three of his officers had flown down to see the model sub that had been the test-bed for the prototype drive system. Thirty-two meters long and diesel-electric powered, it was based in the Caspian Sea, far from the eyes of imperialist spies, and kept in a covered dock, hidden from their photographic satellites. Ramius had had a hand in the development of the caterpillar, and Tupolev recognized the mark of the master. It would be a bastard to detect. Not quite impossible, though. After a week of following the model around the north end of the Caspian Sea in an electrically powered launch, trailing the best passive sonar array his country had yet made, he thought he had found a flaw. Not a big one, just big enough to exploit.

Of course there was no guarantee of success. He was not only in competition with a machine, but also with the captain commanding her. Tupolev knew this area intimately. The water was almost perfectly isothermal; there was no thermal layer for a submarine to hide under. They were far enough from the freshwater rivers on the north coast of Russia not to have to worry about pools and walls of variable salinity interfering with their sonar searches. The *Konovalov* had been built with the best sonar systems the Soviet Union had yet produced, copied closely from the French DUUV-23 and a bit improved, the factory technicians said.

Tupolev planned to mimic the American tactic of drifting slowly, with just enough speed to maintain steerage, perfectly quiet and waiting for the *Red October* to cross his path. He would then trail his quarry closely and log each change in course and speed, so that when they compared logs in a few weeks the Schoolmaster would see that his erstwhile student had p!ayed his own winning game. It was about time someone did.

'Anything new on sonar?' Tupolev was getting tense. Patience came hard to him.

'Nothing new, Comrade Captain.' The *starpom* tapped the X on the chart that marked the position of the *Rokossovskiy*, a *Delta*-class missile sub they had been tracking for several hours in the same exercise area. 'Our friend is still cruising in a slow circle. Do you think that *Rokossovskiy* might be trying to confuse us? Would Captain Ramius have arranged for him to be here, to complicate our task?'

The thought had occurred to Tupolev. 'Perhaps, but probably not. This exercise was arranged by Korov himself. Our mission orders were sealed, and Marko's orders should have been also. But then, Admiral Korov is an old friend of our Marko.' Tupolev paused for a moment and shook his head. 'No. Korov is an honourable man. I think Ramius is proceeding this way as slowly as he can. To make us nervous, to make us question ourselves. He will know we are to hunt him and will adjust his plans accordingly. He might try to enter the square from an unexpected direction – or to make us think that he is. You have never served under Ramius, Comrade Lieutenant. He is a fox, that one, an old grey-whiskered fox. I think we will continue to patrol as we are for another four hours. If we have not yet acquired him then, we will cross over to the southeast corner of the square and work our way in to the centre. Yes.'

Tupolev had never expected that this would be easy. No attack submarine commander had ever embarrassed Ramius. He was determined to be the first, and the difficulty of the task would only confirm his own prowess. In one or two more years, Tupolev planned to be the new master.

The Third Day

Sunday, 5 December

The *Red October*

The *Red October* had no time of her own. For her the sun neither rose nor set, and the days of the week had little significance. Unlike surface ships, which changed their clocks to conform with the local time wherever they were, submarines generally adhered to a single time reference. For American subs this was Zulu, or Greenwich mean time. For the *Red October* it was Moscow standard time, which by normal reckoning was actually one hour ahead of standard time to save on utility expenses.

Ramius entered the control room in mid-morning. Their course was now two-five-zero, speed thirteen knots, and the submarine was running thirty metres above the bottom at the west edge of the Barents Sea. In a few more hours the bottom would drop away to an abyssal plain, allowing them to go much deeper. Ramius examined the chart first, then the numerous banks of instruments covering both side bulkheads in the compartment. Last he made some notations in the order book.

'Lieutenant Ivanov!' he said sharply to the junior officer of the watch.

'Yes, Comrade Captain!' Ivanov was the greenest officer aboard, fresh from Lenin's Komsomol School in Leningrad, pale, skinny, and eager.

'I will be calling a meeting of the senior officers in the wardroom. You will now be the officer of the watch. This is your first cruise, Ivanov. How do you like it?'

'It is better than I had hoped, Comrade Captain,' Ivanov replied with greater confidence than he could possibly have felt.

'That is good, Comrade Lieutenant. It is my practice to give junior officers as much responsibility as they can handle. While we senior officers are having our weekly political discussion, *you* are in command of this vessel! The safety of this ship and all his crew is *your* responsibility! You have been taught all you need to know, and my instructions are in the order book. If we detect another submarine or surface ship you will inform me at once and instantly initiate evasion drill. Any questions?'

'No, Comrade Captain.' Ivanov was standing at rigid attention.

'Good.' Ramius smiled. 'Pavel Ilych, you will forever remember this as one of the great moments of your life. I know, I can still remember my first watch. Do not forget your orders or your responsibilities!'

Pride sparkled in the boy's eyes. It was too bad what would happen to him, Ramius thought, still the teacher. On first inspection, Ivanov looked to have the makings of a good officer.

Ramius walked briskly aft to the ship's medical office.

'Good morning, Doctor.'

'Good morning to you, Comrade Captain. It is time for our political meeting?' Petrov had been reading the manual for the sub's new X-ray machine.

'Yes, it is, Comrade Doctor, but I do not wish you to attend. There is something else I want you to do. While the senior officers are at the meeting, I have the three youngsters standing watch in control and the engineering spaces.'

'Oh?' Petrov's eyes went wide. It was his first time on a submarine in several years.

Ramius smiled. 'Be at ease, Comrade. I can get from the wardroom to control in twenty seconds, as you know, and Comrade Melekhin can get to his precious reactor just as fast. Sooner or later our young officers must learn to function on their own. I prefer that they learn sooner. I want you to keep an eye on them. I know that they all have the knowledge to do their duties. I want to know if they have the temperament. If Borodin or I watch over them, they will not act normally. And in any case, this is a medical judgement, no?'

'Ah, you wish me to observe how they react to their responsibilities.'

'Without the pressure of being observed by a senior line 35 officer,' Ramius confirmed. 'One must give young officers room to grow – but not too much. If you observe something that you question, you will inform me at once. There should be no problems. We are in open sea, there is no traffic about, and the reactor is running at a fraction of its total power. The first test for young officers ought to be an easy one. Find some excuse for travelling back and forth, and keep an eye on the children. Ask questions about what they are doing.'

Petrov laughed at that. 'Ah, and also you would have me learn a few things, Comrade Captain? They told me about you at Severomorsk. Fine, it will be as you say. But this will be the first political meeting I have missed in years.'

'From what your file says, you could teach Party doctrine to the Politburo, Yevgeni Konstantinovich.' Which said little about his medical ability, Ramius thought.

The captain moved forward to the wardroom to join his brother officers, who were waiting for him. A steward had left several pots of tea along with black bread and butter to snack on. Ramius looked at the corner of the table. The bloodstain had long since been wiped away, but he could remember exactly what it looked like. This, he reflected, was one difference between himself and the man he had murdered. Ramius had a conscience. Before taking his seat, he turned to lock the door behind him. His officers were all sitting at attention, since the compartment was not large enough for them to stand once the bench seats were folded down.

Sunday was the normal day for the political awareness session at sea. Ordinarily Putin would have officiated, reading some *Pravda* editorials, followed by selected quotations from the works of Lenin and a discussion of the lessons to be learned from the readings. It was very much like a church service.

With the demise of the *zampolit* this duty devolved upon the commanding officer, but Ramius doubted that regulations anticipated the sort of discussion on today's agenda. Each officer in this room was a member of his conspiracy. Ramius outlined their plans – there had been some minor changes which he had not mentioned to anyone. Then he told them about the letter.

'So, there is no going back,' Borodin observed.

'We have all agreed upon our course of action. Now we are committed to it.' Their reactions to his words were just what he expected them to be – sober. As well they might be. All were single; no one left behind a wife or children. All were Party members in good standing, their dues paid up to the end of the year, their Party cards right where they were supposed to be, 'next to their hearts.' And each one shared with his comrades a deep-seated dissatisfaction with, in some cases a hatred of, the Soviet government.

The planning had begun soon after the death of his Natalia. The rage he had almost unknowingly suppressed throughout his life had burst forth with a violence and passion that he had struggled to contain. A lifetime of self-control had enabled him to conceal it, and a lifetime of naval training had enabled him to choose a purpose worthy of it.

Ramius had not yet begun school when he first heard tales from other children about what his father Aleksandr had done in Lithuania in 1940 and after that country's dubious liberation from the Germans in 1944. These were the repeated whisperings of their parents. One little girl told Marko a story that he recounted to Aleksandr, and to the boy's uncomprehending horror her father vanished. For his unwitting mistake Marko was branded an informer. Stung by the name he was given for committing a crime – which the State taught was not a crime at all – whose enormity never stopped pulling at his conscience, he never informed again.

In the formative years of his life, while the elder Ramius ruled the Lithuanian Party Central Committee in Vilnius, the motherless boy was raised by his paternal grandmother, common practice in a country savaged by four years of brutal war. Her only son left home at an early age to join Lenin's Red Guards, and while he was away she kept to the old ways, going to mass every day until 1940 and never forgetting the religious education that had been passed on to her. Ramius remembered her as a silver-haired old woman who told wonderful bedtime stories. Religious stories. It would have been far too dangerous for her to bring Marko to the religious ceremonies that had never been entirely stamped out, but she did manage to have him baptized a Roman Catholic soon after his father had deposited him with her. She never told Marko about this. The risk would have been too great. Roman Catholicism had been brutally suppressed in the Baltic states. It was a religion, and as he grew older Marko learned that Marxism-Leninism was a jealous god, tolerating no competing loyalties.

Grandmother Hilda told him bedtime stories from the Bible, each with a lesson of right and wrong, virtue and reward. As a child he found them merely entertaining, but he never told his father about them because even then he knew that Aleksandr would object. After the elder Ramius again resumed control of his son's life, this religious education faded into Marko's memory, neither fully remembered nor fully forgotten.

As a boy, Ramius sensed more than thought that Soviet Communism ignored a basic human need. In his teens, his misgivings began to take a coherent shape. The Good of the People was a laudable enough goal, but in denying a man's soul, an enduring part of his being, Marxism stripped away the foundation of human dignity and individual value. It also cast aside the objective measure of justice and ethics which, he decided, was the principal legacy of religion to civilized life. From earliest adulthood on, Marko had his own idea about right and wrong, an idea he did not share with the State. It gave him a means of gauging his actions and those of others. It was something he was careful to conceal. It served as an anchor for his soul and, like an anchor, it was hidden far below the visible surface.

Even as the boy was grappling with his first doubts about his country, no one could have suspected it. Like all Soviet children, Ramius joined the Little Octobrists, then the Young Pioneers. He paraded at the requisite battle shrines in polished boots and blood-red scarf, and gravely stood watch over the remains of some unknown soldier while clasping to his chest a deactivated PPSh submachinegun, his back ramrod straight before the eternal flame. The solemnity of such duty was no accident. As a boy Marko was certain that the brave men whose graves he guarded so intensely had met their fates with the same sort of selfless heroism that he saw portrayed in endless war movies at the local cinema. They had fought the hated Germans to protect the women and children and old people behind the lines. And like a nobleman's son of an earlier Russia, he took special pride in being the son of a Party chieftain. The party, he heard a hundred times before he was five, was the Soul of the People; the unity of Party, People, and Nation was the holy trinity of the Soviet Union, albeit with one segment more important than the others. His father fitted easily into the cinematic image of a Party apparatchik. Stern but fair, to Marko he was a frequently absent, gruffly kind man who brought his son what presents he could and saw to it that he had all the advantages the son of a Party secretary was entitled to.

Although outwardly he was the model Soviet child, inwardly he wondered why what he learned from his father and in school conflicted with the other lessons of his youth. Why did some parents refuse to let their children play with him? Why when he passed them did his classmates whisper 'stukach,' the cruel and bitter epithet of informer? His father and the Party taught that informing was an act of patriotism, but for having done it once he was shunned. He resented the taunts of his boyhood peers, but he never once complained to his father, knowing that this would be an evil thing to do.

Something was very wrong – but what? He decided that he had to find the answers for himself. By choice Marko became individual in his thinking, and so unknowingly committed the gravest sin in the Communist pantheon. Outwardly the model of a Party member's son, he played the game carefully and according to all the rules. He did his duty for all Party organizations, and was always the first to volunteer for the menial tasks allotted to children aspiring to Party membership, which he knew was the only path to success or even comfort in the Soviet Union. He became good at sports. Not team sports – he worked at track and field events in which he could compete as an individual and measure the performances of others. Over the years he learned to do the same in all of his endeavours, to watch and judge the actions of his fellow citizens and officers with cool detachment, behind a blank face that concealed his conclusions.

In the summer of his eighth year the course of his life was forever changed. When no one would play with 'the little *stukach*,' he would wander down to the fishing docks of the small village where his grandmother had made her home. A ragtag collection of old wooden boats sailed each morning, always behind a screen of patrol boats manned by MGB – as the KGB was then known – border guards, to reap a modest harvest from the Gulf of Finland. Their catch supplemented the local diet with needed protein and provided a minuscule income for the fishermen. One boat captain was old Sasha. An officer in the czar's navy, he had revolted with the crew of the cruiser *Avrora*, helping to spark the chain of events that changed the face of the world. Marko did not learn until many years later than the crewmen of the *Avrora* had broken with Lenin – and been savagely put down by Red Guards. Sasha had spent twenty years in labour camps for his part in that collective indiscretion and only been released at the beginning of the Great Patriotic War. The *Rodina* had found herself in need of experienced seamen to pilot ships into the ports of Murmansk and Archangel, to which the Allies were bringing weapons, food, and the sundries that allow a modern army to function. Sasha had learned his lesson in the gulag: he did his duty efficiently and well, asking for nothing in return. After the war, he'd been given a kind of freedom for his services, the right to perform back-breaking work under perpetual suspicion.

By the time Marko met him, Sasha was over sixty, a nearly bald man with ropy old muscles, a seaman's eye, and a talent for stories that left the youngster wide-eyed. He'd been a midshipman under the famous Admiral Marakov at Port Arthur in 1906. Probably the finest seaman in Russian history, Marakov's reputation as a patriot and an innovative fighting sailor was sufficiently unblemished that a Communist government would eventually see fit to name a missile cruiser in his memory. At first wary of the boy's reputation, Sasha saw something in him that others missed. The boy without friends and the sailor without a family became comrades. Sasha spent hours telling and retelling the tale of how he had been on the admiral's flagship, the *Petropavlovsk*, and participated in the one Russian victory over the hated Japanese – only to have his battleship sunk and his admiral killed by a mine while returning to port. After this Sasha had led his seamen as naval infantry, winning three decorations for courage under fire. This experience – he waggled his finger seriously at the boy – taught him of the mindless corruption of the czarist regime and convinced him to join one of the first naval soviets when such action meant certain death at the hands of the czar's secret police, the *okhrana*. He told his own version of the October Revolution from the thrilling perspective of an eyewitness. But Sasha was very careful to leave the later parts out.

He allowed Marko to sail with him and taught him the fundamentals of seamanship that decided a boy not yet nine that his destiny lay with the sea. There was a freedom at sea he could never have on land. There was a romance about it that touched the man growing within the boy. There were also dangers, but in a summer-long series of simple, effective lessons, Sasha taught the boy that preparation, knowledge, and discipline can deal with any form of danger; that danger confronted properly is not something a man must fear. In later years Marko would reflect often on the value this summer had held for him, and wonder just how far Sasha's career might have led if other events had not cut it short.

Marko told his father about Sasha towards the end of that long Baltic summer and even took him to meet the old seadog. The elder Ramius was sufficiently impressed with him and what he had done for his son that he arranged for Sasha to have command of a newer, larger boat and moved him up on the list for a new apartment. Marko almost believed that the Party could do a good deed – that he himself had done his first manly good deed. But old Sasha died the following winter, and the good deed came to nothing. Many years later Marko realized that he hadn't known his friend's last name. Even after years of faithful service to the *Rodina*, Sasha had been an unperson.

At thirteen Marko travelled to Leningrad to attend the Nakhimov School. There he decided that he, too, would become a professional naval officer. Marko would follow the quest for adventure that had for centuries called young men to the sea. The Nakhimov School was a special three-year prep school for youngsters aspiring to a career at sea. The Soviet Navy at that time was little more than a coastal defence force, but Marko wanted very much to be a part of it. His father urged him to a life of Party work, promising rapid promotion, a life of comfort and privilege. But Marko wanted to earn whatever he received on his own merits, not to be remembered as an appendage of the 'liberator' of Lithuania. And a life at sea offered romance and excitement that even made serving the State something he could tolerate. The navy had little tradition to build on. Marko sensed that in it there was room to grow, and saw that many aspiring naval cadets were like himself, if not mavericks then as close to mavericks as was possible in a society so closely controlled as his own. The teenager thrived with his first experience of fellowship.

Nearing graduation, his class was exposed to the various components of the Russian fleet. Ramius at once fell in love with submarines. The boats at that time were small, dirty, and smelled from the open bilges that the crews used as a convenient latrine. At the same time submarines were the only offensive arm that the navy had, and from the first Marko wanted to be on the cutting edge. He'd had enough lectures on naval history to know that submarines had twice nearly strangled England's maritime empire and had successfully emasculated the economy of Japan. This had greatly pleased him; he was glad the Americans had crushed the Japanese navy that had so nearly killed his mentor.

He graduated from the Nakhimov School first in his class, winner of the gold-plated sextant for his mastery of theoretical navigation. As leader of his class, Marko was allowed the school of his choice. He selected the Higher Naval School for Underwater Navigation, named for Lenin's Komsomol, VVMUPP, still the principal submarine school of the Soviet Union.

His five years at VVMUPP were the most demanding of his life, the more so since he was determined not to succeed but to excel. He was first in his class in every subject, in every year. His essay on the political significance of Soviet naval power was forwarded to Sergey Georgiyevich Gorshkov, then commander in chief of the Baltic Fleet and clearly the coming man of the Soviet Navy. Gorshkov had seen the essay published in *Morskoi Sbornik (Naval Collections)*, the leading Soviet naval journal. It was a model of progressive Party thought, quoting Lenin six different times.

By this time Marko's father was a candidate member of the Presidium, as the Politburo was then called, and very proud of his son. The elder Ramius was no one's fool. He finally recognized that the Red Fleet was a growing flower and that his son would someday have a position of importance in it. His influence moved his son's career rapidly along.

By thirty, Marko had his first command and a new wife. Natalia Bogdanova was the daughter of another Presidium member whose diplomatic duties had taken him and his family all over the world. Natalia had never been a healthy girl. They had no children, their three attempts each ending in miscarriage, the last of which had nearly killed her. She was a pretty, delicate woman, sophisticated by Russian standards, who polished her husband's passable English with American and British books – politically approved ones to be sure, mainly the thoughts of Western leftists, but also a smattering of genuine literature, including Hemingway, Twain, and Upton Sinclair. Along with his naval career, Natalia had been the centre of his life. Their marriage, punctuated by prolonged absences and joyous returns, made their love even more precious than it might have been.

When construction began on the first class of Soviet nuclear-powered submarines, Marko found himself in the yards learning how the steel sharks were designed and built. He was soon known as a very hard man to please as a junior quality control inspector. His own life, he was aware, would ride on the workmanship of these often drunk welders and fitters. He became an expert in nuclear engineering, spent two years as a *starpom*, and then received his first nuclear command. She was a *November*-class attack submarine, the first crude attempt by the Soviets to make a battleworthy long-range attack boat to threaten Western navies and lines of communication. Not a month later a sister ship suffered a major reactor casualty off the Norwegian coast, and Marko was first to arrive on the scene. As ordered, he successfully rescued the crew, then sank the disabled sub lest Western navies learn her secrets. Both tasks he performed expertly and well, a noteworthy tour de force for a young commander. Good performance was something he had always felt it was important to reward in his subordinates, and the fleet commander at that time felt the same way. Marko soon moved on to a new *Charlie I*-class sub.

It was men like Ramius who went out to challenge the Americans and the British. Marko took few illusions with him. The Americans, he knew, had long experience in naval warfare – their own greatest fighter, Jones, had once served the Russian navy for the Czaritza Catherine. Their submariners were legendary for their craftiness, and Ramius found himself pitted against the last of the war-trained Americans, men who had endured the sweaty fear of underwater combat and utterly defeated a modern navy. The deadly serious game of hide-and-seek he played with them was not an easy one, the less so because they had submarines years ahead of Soviet designs. But it was not a time without a few victories.

Ramius gradually learned to play the game by American rules, training his officers and men with care. His crews were rarely as prepared as he wished – still the Soviet Navy's greatest problem – but where other commanders cursed their men for their failings, Marko corrected the failings of his men. His first *Charlie*-class submarine was called the *Vilnius Academy*. This was partially a slur against his half-Lithuanian blood – though since he had been born in Leningrad of a Great Russian, his internal passport designated him as that – but mainly recognition that officers came to him half-trained and left him ready for advancement and eventual command. The same was true of his conscripted crewmen. Ramius did not permit the low-level terrorism normal throughout the Soviet military. He saw his task as the building of seamen, and he produced a greater percentage of reenlistments than any other submarine commander. A full ninth of the *michmanyy* in the Northern Fleet submarine force were Ramius-trained professionals. His brother submarine commanders were delighted to take aboard his *starshini*, and more than one advanced to officer's school.

After eighteen months of hard work and diligent training Marko and his *Vilnius Academy* were ready to play their game of fox and hounds. He happened upon the USS *Triton* in the Norwegian Sea and hounded her mercilessly for twelve hours. Later he would note with no small satisfaction that the *Triton* was soon thereafter retired, because, it was said, the oversized vessel had proven unable to deal with the newer Soviet designs. The diesel-powered submarines of the British and the Norwegians that he occasionally happened across while snorkeling he dogged ruthlessly, often subjecting them to vicious sonar lashing. Once he even acquired an American missile submarine, managing to maintain contact with her for nearly two hours before she vanished like a ghost into the black waters.

The rapid growth of the Soviet Navy and the need for qualified officers during his early career prevented Ramius from attending the Frunze Academy. This was normally a *sine qua non* of career advancement in all of the Soviet armed services. Frunze, in Moscow near the old Novodevichiy Monastery, was named for a hero of the Revolution. It was the premiere school for those who aspired to high command, and though Ramius had not attended it as a student, his prowess as an operational commander won him an appointment as an instructor. It was something earned solely on merit, for which his highly placed father was not responsible. That was important to Ramius.

The head of the naval section at Frunze liked to introduce Marko as 'our test pilot of submarines.' His classes became a prime attraction not only for the naval officers in the academy but also for the many others who came to hear his lectures on naval history and maritime strategy. At weekends spent at his father's official dacha in the village of Zhukova-1, he wrote manuals for submarine operations and the training of crews, and specifications for the ideal attack submarine. Some of his ideas had been controversial enough to upset his erstwhile sponsor, Gorshkov, by this time commander in chief of the entire Soviet Navy – but the old admiral was not entirely displeased.

Ramius proposed that officers in the submarine service should work in a single class of ship – better yet, the same ship – for years, the better to learn their profession and the capabilities of their vessels. Skilled captains, he suggested, should not be forced to leave their commands for desk-bound promotions. Here he lauded the Red Army's practice of leaving a field commander in his post so long as the man wanted it, and deliberately contrasted his view on this matter with the practice of imperialist navies. He stressed the need for extended training in the fleet, for longer-service enlisted men, and for better living conditions on submarines. For some of his ideas he found a sympathetic ear in the high command. For others he did not, and thus Ramius found himself destined never to have his own admiral's flag. By this time he did not care. He loved his submarines too much ever to leave them for a squadron or even a fleet command.

After finishing at Frunze, he did indeed become a test pilot of submarines. Marko Ramius, now a captain first rank, would take out the first ship of every submarine class to 'write the book' on its strengths and weaknesses, to develop operational routines and training guidelines. The first of the *Alfas* was his, the first of the *Deltas* and *Typhoons*. Aside from one extraordinary mishap on an *Alfa*, his career had been one uninterrupted story of achievement.

Along the way he became the mentor of many young officers. He often wondered what Sasha would have thought as he taught the demanding art of submarine operations to scores of eager young men. Many of them had already become commanding officers themselves; more had failed. Ramius was a commander who took good care of those who pleased him – and took good care of those who did not. Another reason why he had never made admiral was his unwillingness to promote officers whose fathers were as powerful as his own but whose abilities were unsatisfactory. He never played favourites where duty was concerned, and the sons of a half-dozen high Party officials received unsatisfactory fitness reports despite their active performance in weekly Party discussions. Most had become *zampoliti*. It was this sort of integrity that earned him trust in fleet command. When a really tough job was at hand, Ramius' name was usually the first to be considered for it.

Also along the way he had gathered to himself a number of young officers whom he and Natalia virtually adopted. They were surrogates for the family Marko and his wife never had. Ramius found himself shepherding men much like himself, with long-suppressed doubts about their country's leadership. He was an easy man to talk to, once a man had proven himself. To those with political doubts, those with just grievances, he gave the same advice: 'Join the Party.' Nearly all were already Komsomol members, of course, and Marko urged them to take the next step. This was the price of a career at sea, and guided by their own craving for adventure most officers paid that price. Ramius himself had been allowed to join the Party at eighteen, the earliest possible age, because of his father's influence. His occasional talks at weekly Party meetings were perfect recitations of the Party line. It wasn't hard, he'd tell his officers patiently. All you had to do was repeat what the Party said – just change the words around slightly. This was much easier than navigation – one had only to look at the political officer to see that! Ramius became known as a captain whose officers were both proficient and models of political conformity. He was one of the best Party recruiters in the navy.

Then his wife died. Ramius was in port at the time, not unusual for a missile sub commander. He had his own dacha in the woods west of Polyarnyy, his own Zhiguli automobile, the officer car and driver those with his command station enjoyed, and numerous other creature comforts that came with his rank and his parentage. He was a member of the Party elite, so when Natalia had complained of abdominal pain, going to the Fourth Department clinic which served only the privileged had been a natural mistake – there was a saying in the Soviet Union: Floors parquet, docs okay. He'd last seen his wife alive lying on a trolley, smiling as she was wheeled towards the operating room.

The surgeon on call had arrived at the hospital late, and drunk, and allowed himself too much time breathing pure oxygen to sober up before starting the simple procedure of removing an inflamed appendix. The swollen organ burst just as he was retracting tissue to get at it. A case of peritonitis immediately followed, complicated by the perforated bowel the surgeon caused in his clumsy haste to repair the damage.

Natalia was placed on antibiotic therapy, but there was a shortage of medicine. The foreign – usually French – pharmaceuticals used in Fourth Department clinics had run out. Soviet antibiotics, 'plan' medications, were substituted. It was a common practice in Soviet industry for workers to earn bonuses by manufacturing goods over the usual quota, goods that bypassed what quality control existed in Soviet industry. This particular batch of medication had never been inspected or tested. *And the vials had probably been filled with distilled water instead of antibiotics*, Marko learned the next day. Natalia had lapsed into deep shock and coma, dying before the series of errors could be corrected.

The funeral was appropriately solemn, Ramius remembered bitterly. Brother officers from his own command and over a hundred other navy men whom he had befriended over the years were there, along with members of Natalia's family and representatives of the local Party Central Committee. Marko had been at sea when his father died, and because he had known the extent of Aleksandr's crimes, the loss had had little effect. His wife's death, however, was nothing less than a personal catastrophe. Soon after they had married Natalia had joked that every sailor needs someone to return to, that every woman needs someone to wait for. It had been as simple as that – and infinitely more complex, the marriage of two intelligent people who had over fifteen years learned each other's foibles and strengths and grown even closer.

Marko Ramius watched the coffin roll into the cremation chamber to the sombre strain of a classical requiem, wishing that he could pray for Natalia's soul, hoping that Grandmother Hilda had been right, that there was something beyond the steel door and mass of flame. Only then did the full weight of the event strike him: *the State had robbed him of more than his wife, it had robbed him of a means to assuage his grief with prayer, it had robbed him of the hope – if only an illusion – of ever seeing her again.* Natalia, gentle and kind had been his only happiness since that Baltic summer long ago. Now that happiness was gone forever. As the weeks and months wore on he was tormented by her memory; a certain hairstyle, a certain walk, a certain laugh encountered on the streets or in the shops of Murmansk was all it took to thrust Natalia back to the forefront of his consciousness, and when he was thinking of his loss, he was not a professional naval officer.

The life of Natalia Bogdanova Ramius had been lost at the hands of a surgeon who had been drinking while on call – a court-martial offense in the Soviet Navy – but Marko could not have the doctor punished. The surgeon was himself the son of a Party chieftain, his status secured by his own sponsors. Her life might have been saved by proper medication, but there had not been enough foreign drugs, and Soviet pharmaceuticals were untrustworthy. The doctor could not be made to pay, the pharmaceutical workers could not be made to pay – the thought echoed back and forth across his mind, feeding his fury until he decided that the State would be made to pay.

The idea had taken weeks to form and was the product of a career of training and contingency planning. When the construction of the *Red October* was restarted after a two-year hiatus, Ramius knew that he would command her.

He had helped with the designing of her revolutionary drive system and had inspected the model, which had been running on the Caspian Sea for some years in absolute secrecy. He asked for relief from his command so that he could concentrate on the construction and outfitting of the *October* and select and train his officers beforehand, the earlier to get the missile sub into full operation. The request was granted by the commander of the Red Banner Northern Fleet, a sentimental man who had also wept at Natalia's funeral.

Ramius had already known who his officers would be. All graduates of the Vilnius Academy, many the 'sons' of Marko and Natalia, they were men who owed their place and their rank to Ramius; men who cursed the inability of their country to build submarines worthy of their skills; men who had joined the Party as told and then become even more dissatisfied with the Motherland as they learned that the price of advancement was to prostitute one's mind and soul, to become a highly paid parrot in a blue jacket whose every Party recitation was a grating exercise in self-control. For the most part they were men for whom this degrading step had not borne fruit. In the Soviet Navy there were three routes to advancement. A man could become a *zampolit* and be a pariah among his peers. Or he could be a navigation officer and advance to his own command. Or he could be shunted into a speciality in which he would gain rank and pay – but never command. Thus a chief engineer on a Soviet naval vessel could outrank his commanding officer and still be his subordinate.

Ramius looked around the table at his officers. Most had not been allowed to pursue their own career goals despite their proficiency and despite their Party membership. The minor infractions of youth – in one case an act committed at age eight – prevented two from ever being trusted again. With the missile officer, it was because he was a Jew; though his parents had always been committed, believing Communists, neither they nor their son were ever trusted. Another officer's elder brother had demonstrated against the invasion of Czechoslovakia in 1968 and disgraced his whole family. Melekhin, the chief engineer and Ramius' equal in rank, had never been allowed the route to command simply because his superiors wanted him to be an engineer. Borodin, who was ready for his own command, had once accused a *zampolit* of homosexuality; the man he had informed on was the son of the chief *zampolit* of the Northern Fleet. There are many paths to treason.

'And what if they locate us?' Kamarov speculated.

'I doubt that even the Americans can find us when the caterpillar is operating. I am certain that our own submarines cannot. Comrades, I helped design this ship,' Ramius said.

'What will become of us?' the missile officer muttered.

'First we must accomplish the task at hand. An officer who looks too far ahead stumbles over his own boots.'

'They will be looking for us,' Borodin said.

'Of course,' Ramius smiled, 'but they will not know where to look until it is too late. Our mission, comrades, is to avoid detection. And so we shall.'

The Fourth Day

Monday, 6 December

CIA Headquarters

Ryan walked down the corridor on the top floor of the Langley, Virginia, headquarters of the Central Intelligence Agency. He had already passed through three separate security checks, none of which had required him to open his locked briefcase, now draped under the folds of his buff-coloured toggle coat, a gift from an officer in the Royal Navy.

What he had on was mostly his wife's fault, an expensive suit bought on Savile Row. It was English cut, neither conservative nor on the leading edge of contemporary fashion. He had a number of suits like this arranged neatly in his closet by colours, which he wore with white shirts and striped ties. His only jewellery was a wedding band and a university ring, plus an inexpensive but accurate digital watch on a more expensive gold band. Ryan was not a man who placed a great deal of value in appearances. Indeed, his job was to see through these in the search for hard truth.

He was physically unremarkable, an inch over six feet, and his average build suffered a little at the waist from a lack of exercise enforced by the miserable English weather. His blue eyes had a deceptively vacant look; he was often lost in thought, his face on autopilot as his mind puzzled through data or research material for his current book. The only people Ryan needed to impress were those who knew him; he cared little for the rest. He had no ambition to celebrity. His life, he judged, was already as complicated as it needed to be – quite a bit more complicated than most would guess. It included a wife he loved and two children he doted on, a job that tested his intellect, and sufficient financial independence to choose his own path. The path Jack Ryan had chosen was in the CIA. The agency's official motto was, The truth shall make you free. The trick, he told himself at least once a day, was finding that truth, and while he doubted that he would ever reach this sublime state of grace, he took quiet pride in his ability to pick at it, one small fragment at a time.

The office of the deputy director for intelligence occupied a whole corner of the top floor, overlooking the tree-covered Potomac Valley. Ryan had one more security check to pass.

'Good morning, Dr Ryan.'

'Hi, Nancy.' Ryan smiled at her. Nancy Cummings had held her secretarial job for twenty years, had served eight DDIs, and if the truth were known she probably had as good a feel for the intelligence business as the political appointees in the adjacent office. It was the same as with any large business – the bosses came and went, but the good executive secretaries lasted forever.

'How's the family, Doctor? Looking forward to Christmas?'

'You bet – except my Sally's a little worried. She's not sure Santa knows that we've moved, and she's afraid he won't make it to England for her. He will,' Ryan confided.

'It's so nice when they're that little.' She pressed a hidden button. 'You can go right in, Dr Ryan.'

'Thanks, Nancy.' Ryan twisted the electronically protected knob and walked into the DDI's office.

Vice Admiral James Greer was reclining in his high-backed judge's chair reading through a folder. His oversized mahogany desk was covered with neat piles of folders whose edges were bordered with red tape and whose covers bore various code words.

'Hiya, Jack!' he called across the room. 'Coffee?'

'Yes, thank you, sir.'

James Greer was sixty-six, a naval officer past retirement age who kept working through brute competence, much as Hyman Rickover had, though Greer was a far easier man to work for. He was a 'mustang,' a man who had entered the naval service as an enlisted man, earned his way into the Naval Academy, and spent forty years working his way to a three-star flag, first commanding submarines, then as a full-time intelligence specialist. Greer was a demanding boss, but one who took care of those who pleased him. Ryan was one of these.

Somewhat to Nancy's chagrin, Greer liked to make his own coffee with a West Bend drip machine on the shelf behind his desk, where he could just turn around to reach it. Ryan poured himself a cup – actually a navy-style handleless mug. It was traditional navy coffee, brewed strong, with a pinch of salt.

'You hungry, Jack?' Greer pulled a pastry box from a desk drawer. 'I got some sticky buns here.'

'Why thanks, sir. I didn't eat much on the plane.' Ryan took one, along with a paper napkin.

'Still don't like to fly?' Greer was amused.

Ryan sat down in the chair opposite his boss. 'I suppose I ought to be getting used to it. I like the Concorde better than the wide-bodies. You only have to be terrified half as long.'

'How's the family?'

'Fine, thank you, sir. Sally's in first grade – loves it. And little Jack is toddling around the house. These buns are pretty good.'

'New bakery just opened up a few blocks from my place. I pass it on the way in every morning.' The admiral sat upright in his chair. 'So, what brings you over today?'

'Photographs of the new Soviet missile boat, *Red October*,' Ryan said casually between sips.

'Oh, and what do our British cousins want in return?' Greer asked suspiciously.

'They want a peek at Barry Somers' new enhancement gadgets. Not the machines themselves – at first – just the finished product. I think it's a fair bargain, sir.' Ryan knew the CIA didn't have any shots of the new sub. The operations directorate did not have a man at the building yard at Severodvinsk or a reliable man at the Polyarnyy submarine base. Worse, the rows of 'boat barns' built to shelter the missile submarines, modelled on World War II German submarine pens, made satellite photography impossible. 'We have ten frames, low obliques, five each bow and stern, and one from each perspective is undeveloped so that Somers can work on them fresh. We are not committed, sir, but I told Sir Basil that you'd think it over.'

The admiral grunted. Sir Basil Charleston, chief of the British Secret Intelligence Service, was a master of the quid pro quo, occasionally offering to share sources with his wealthier cousins and a month later asking for something in return. The intelligence game was often like a primitive marketplace. 'To use the new system, Jack, we need the camera used to take the shots.'

'I know.' Ryan pulled the camera from his coat pocket. 'It's a modified Kodak disc camera. Sir Basil says it's the coming thing in spy cameras, nice and flat. This one, he says, was hidden in a tobacco pouch.'

'How did you know that – that we need the camera?'

'You mean how Somers uses lasers to –'

'Ryan!' Greer snapped. 'How much do you know?'

'Relax, sir. Remember back in February, I was over to discuss those new SS-20 sites on the Chinese border? Somers was here, and you asked me to drive him out to the airport. On the way out he started babbling about this great new idea he was heading west to work on. He talked about it all the way to Dulles. From what little I understood, I gather that he shoots laser beams through the camera lenses to make a mathematical model of the lens. From that, I suppose, he can take the exposed negative, break down the image into the – original incoming light beams, I guess, then use a computer to run *that* through a computer-generated theoretical lens to make a perfect picture. I probably have it wrong.' Ryan could tell from Greer's face that he didn't.

'Somers talks too goddamned much.'

'I told him that, sir. But once the guy gets started, how the hell do you shut him up?'

'And what do the Brits know?' Greer asked.

'Your guess is as good as mine, sir. Sir Basil asked me about it, and I told him that he was asking the wrong guy – I mean, my degrees are in economics and history, not physics. I told him we needed the camera – but he already knew that. Took it right out of his desk and tossed it to me. I did not reveal a thing about this, sir.'

'I wonder how many other people he spilled to. Geniuses! They operate in their own crazy little worlds. Somers is like a little kid sometimes. And you know the First Rule of Security: The likelihood of a secret's being blown is proportional to the *square* of the number of people who're in on it.' It was Greer's favourite dictum.

His phone buzzed. 'Greer ... Right.' He hung up. 'Charlie Davenport's on the way up, per your suggestion, Jack. Supposed to be here half an hour ago. Must be the snow.' The admiral jerked a hand towards the window. There were two inches on the ground, with another inch expected by nightfall. 'One flake hits this town and everything goes to hell.'

Ryan laughed. That was something Greer, a down-easter from Maine, never could seem to understand.

'So, Jack, you say this is worth the price?'

'Sir, we've wanted these pictures for some time, what with all the contradictory data we've been getting on the sub. It's your decision and the judge's but, yes, I think they're worth the price. These shots are very interesting.'

'We ought to have our own men in that damned yard,' Greer grumped. Ryan didn't know how Operations had screwed that one up. He had little interest in field operations. Ryan was an analyst. How the data came to his desk was not his concern, and he was careful to avoid finding out. 'I don't suppose Basil told you anything about their man?'

Ryan smiled, shaking his head. 'No, sir, and I did not ask.' Greer nodded his approval.

'Morning, James!'

Ryan turned to see Rear Admiral Charles Davenport, director of naval intelligence, with a captain trailing in his wake.

'Hi, Charlie. You know Jack Ryan, don't you?'

'Hello, Ryan.'

'We've met,' Ryan said.

'This is Captain Casimir.'

Ryan shook hands with both men. He'd met Davenport a few years before while delivering a paper at the Naval War College in Newport, Rhode Island. Davenport had given him a hard time in the question-and-answer session. He was supposed to be a bastard to work for, a former aviator who had lost flight status after a barrier crash and, some said, still bore a grudge. Against whom? Nobody really knew.

'Weather in England must be as bad as here, Ryan.' Davenport dropped his bridge coat on top of Ryan's. 'I see you stole a Royal Navy overcoat.'

Ryan was fond of his toggle coat. 'A gift, sir, and quite warm.'

'Christ, you even talk like a Brit. James, we gotta bring this boy home.'

'Be nice to him, Charlie. He's got a present for you. Grab yourself some coffee.'

Casimir scurried over to fill a mug for his boss, then sat down at his right hand. Ryan let them wait a moment before opening his briefcase. He took out four folders, keeping one and handing the others around.

'They say you've been doing some fairly good work, Ryan,' Davenport said. Jack knew him to be a mercurial man, affable one moment, brittle the next. Probably to keep his subordinates off balance. 'And – Jesus Christ!' Davenport had opened his folder.

'Gentlemen, I give you *Red October*, courtesy of the British Secret Intelligence Service,' Ryan said formally.

The folders had the photographs arranged in pairs, four each of four-by-four prints. In the back were ten-by-ten blowups of each. The photos had been taken from a low-oblique angle, probably from the rim of the graving dock that had held the boat during her post-shakedown refit. The shots were paired, fore and aft, fore and aft.

'Gentlemen, as you can see, the lighting wasn't all that great. Nothing fancy here. It was a pocket camera loaded with 400-speed colour film. The first pair was processed normally to establish light levels. The second was pushed for greater brightness using normal procedures. The third pair was digitally enhanced for colour resolution, and the fourth was digitally enhanced for line resolution. I have undeveloped frames of each view for Barry Somers to play with.'

'Oh?' Davenport looked up briefly. 'That's right neighbourly of the Brits. What's the price?' Greer told him. 'Pay up. It's worth it.'

'That's what Jack says.'

'Figures,' Davenport chuckled. 'You know he really is working for them.'

Ryan bristled at that. He liked the English, liked working with their intelligence community, but he knew what country he came from. Jack took a deep breath. Davenport liked to goad people, and if he reacted Davenport would win.

'I gather that Sir John Ryan is still well connected on the other side of the ocean?' Davenport said, extending the prod.

Ryan's knighthood was an honorary one. It was his reward for having broken up a terrorist incident that had erupted around him in St James's Park, London. He'd been a tourist at the time, the innocent American abroad, long before he'd been asked to join the CIA. The fact that he had unknowingly prevented the assassination of two very prominent figures had gotten him more publicity than he'd ever wanted, but it had also brought him in contact with a lot of people in England, most of them worth the time.

Those connections had made him valuable enough that the CIA asked him to be part of a joint American-British liaison group. That was how he had established a good working relationship with Sir Basil Charleston.

'We have lots of friends over there, sir, and some of them were kind enough to give you these,' Ryan said coolly.

Davenport softened. 'Okay, Jack, then you do me a favour. You see whoever gave us these gets something nice in his stocking. They're worth plenty. So, exactly what do we have here?'

To the unschooled observer, the photographs showed the standard nuclear missile submarine. The steel hull was blunt at one end, tapered at the other. The workmen standing on the floor of the dock provided scale – she was huge. There were twin bronze propellers at the stern, on either side of a flat appendage which the Russians called a beaver tail, or so the intelligence reports said. With the twin screws the stern was unremarkable except in one detail.

'What are these doors for?' Casimir asked.

'Hmm. She's a big bastard.' Davenport evidently hadn't heard. 'Forty feet longer than we expected, by the look of her.'

'Forty-four, roughly.' Ryan didn't much like Davenport, but the man did know his stuff. 'Somers can calibrate that for us. And more beam, two metres more than the other *Typhoons*. She's an obvious development of the *Typhoon* class, but –'

'You're right, Captain,' Davenport interrupted. 'What are those doors'?'

'That's why I came over.' Ryan had wondered how long this would take. He'd caught onto them in the first five seconds. 'I don't know, and neither do the Brits.'

The *Red October* had two doors at the bow and stern, each about two metres in diameter, though they were not quite circular. They had been closed when the photos were shot and only showed up well on the number four pair.

'Torpedo tubes? No – four of them are inboard.' Greer reached into his drawer and came out with a magnifying glass. In an age of computer-enhanced imagery it struck Ryan as charmingly anachronistic.

'You're the sub driver, James,' Davenport observed.

'Twenty years ago, Charlie.' He'd made the switch from line officer to professional spook in the early sixties. Captain Casimir, Ryan noted, wore the wings of a naval aviator and had the good sense to remain quiet. He wasn't a 'nuc.'

'Well, they can't be torpedo tubes. They have the normal four of them at the bow, inboard of these openings . . . must be six or seven feet across. How about launch tubes for the new cruise missile they're developing?'

'That's what the Royal Navy thinks. I had a chance to talk it over with their intelligence chaps. But I don't buy it. Why put an anti-surface-ship weapon on a strategic platform? We don't, and we deploy our boomers a lot further forward than they do. The doors are symmetrical through the boat's axis. You can't launch a missile out of the stern, sir. The openings barely clear the screws.'

'Towed sonar array,' Davenport said.

'Granted they could do that, if they trail one screw. But why two of them?' Ryan asked.

Davenport gave him a nasty look. 'They love redundancies.'

'Two doors forward, two aft. I can buy cruise missile tubes. I can buy a towed array. But both sets of doors exactly the same size?' Ryan shook his head. 'Too much of a coincidence. I think it's something new. That's what interrupted her construction for so long. They figured something new for her and spent the last two years rebuilding the *Typhoon* configuration to accommodate it. Note also that they added six more missiles for good measure.'

'Opinion,' Davenport observed.

'That's what I'm paid for.'

'Okay, Jack, what do you think it is?' Greer asked.

'Beats me, sir. I'm no engineer.'

Admiral Greer looked his guests over for a few seconds. He smiled and leaned back in his chair. 'Gentlemen, we have what? Ninety years of naval experience in this room, plus this young amateur.' He gestured at Ryan. 'Okay, Jack, you've set us up for something. Why did you bring this over personally?'

'I want to show these to somebody.'

'Who?' Greer's head cocked suspiciously to one side.

'Skip Tyler. Any of you fellows know him?'

'I do,' Casimir nodded. 'He was a year behind me at Annapolis. Didn't he get hurt or something?'

'Yeah,' Ryan said. 'Lost his leg in an auto accident four years ago. He was up for command of the *Los Angeles* and a drunk driver clipped him. Now he teaches engineering at the Academy and does a lot of consulting work with Sea Systems Command – technical analysis, looking at their ship designs. He has a doctorate in engineering from MIT, and he knows how to think unconventionally.'

'How about his security clearance?' Greer asked.

'Top secret or better, sir, because of his Crystal City work.'

'Objections, Charlie?'

Davenport frowned. Tyler was not part of the intelligence community. 'Is this the guy who did the evaluation of the new *Kirov*?'

'Yes, sir, now that I think about it,' Casimir said. 'Him and Saunders over at Sea Systems.'

'That was a nice piece of work. It's okay with me.'

'When do you want to see him?' Greer asked Ryan.

'Today, if it's all right with you, sir. I have to run over to Annapolis anyway, to get something from the house, and – well, do some quick Christmas shopping.'

'Oh? A few dolls?' Davenport asked.

Ryan turned to look the admiral in the eye. 'Yes, sir, as a matter of fact. My little girl wants a Skiing Barbie doll and some Jordache doll outfits. Didn't you ever play Santa, Admiral?'

Davenport saw that Ryan wasn't going to back off anymore. He wasn't a subordinate to be browbeaten. Ryan could always walk away. He tried a new tack. 'Did they tell you over there that *October* sailed last Friday?'

'Oh?' They hadn't. Ryan was caught off guard. 'I thought she wasn't scheduled to sail until this Friday.'

'So did we. Her skipper is Marko Ramius. You heard about him?'

'Only secondhand stuff. The Brits say he's pretty good.'

'Better than that,' Greer noted. 'He's about the best sub driver they have, a real charger. We had a considerable file on him when I was at DIA. Who's bird-doggin' him for you Charlie?'

'*Bremerton* was assigned to it. She was out of position doing some ELINT work when Ramius sailed, but she was ordered over. Her skipper's Bud Wilson. Remember his dad?'

Greer laughed out loud. 'Red Wilson? Now there was one spirited submarine driver! His boy any good?'

'So they say. Ramius is about the best the Soviets have, but Wilson's got a 688 boat. By the end of the week, we'll be able to start a new book on *Red October*.' Davenport stood. 'We gotta head back, James.' Casimir hurried to get the coats. 'I can keep these?'

'I suppose, Charlie. Just don't go hanging them on the wall, even to throw darts at. And I guess you want to get moving, too, Jack?'

'Yes, sir.'

Greer lifted his phone. 'Nancy, Dr Ryan will need a car and a driver in fifteen minutes. Right.' He set the receiver down and waited for Davenport to leave. 'No sense getting you killed out there in the snow. Besides, you'd probably drive on the wrong side of the road after a year in England. Skiing Barbie, Jack?'

'You had all boys, didn't you, sir? Girls are different.' Ryan grinned. 'You've never met my little Sally.'

'Daddy's girl?'

'Yep. God help whoever marries her. Can I leave these photographs with Tyler?'

'I hope you're right about him, son. Yes, he can hold onto them – if and only if he has a good place to keep them.'

'Understood, sir.'

'When you get back – probably be late, the way the roads are. You're staying at the Marriott?'

'Yes, sir.'

Greer thought that over. 'I'll probably be working late. Stop by here before you bed down. I may want to go over a few things with you.'

'Will do, sir. Thanks for the car.' Ryan stood.

'Go buy your dolls, son.'

Greer watched him leave. He liked Ryan. The boy was not afraid to speak his mind. Part of that came from having money and being married to more money. It was a sort of independence that had advantages. Ryan could not be bought, bribed, or bullied. He could always go back to writing history books full time. Ryan had made money on his own in four years as a stock-broker, betting his own money on high-risk issues and scoring big before leaving it all behind – because, he said, he hadn't wanted to press his luck. Greer didn't believe that. He thought Jack had been bored – bored with making money. He shook his head. The talent that had enabled him to pick winning stocks Ryan now applied to the CIA. He was rapidly becoming one of Greer's star analysts, and his British connections made him doubly valuable. Ryan had the ability to sort through a pile of data and come out with the three or four facts that meant something. This was too rare a thing at the CIA. The agency still spent too much of its money collecting data, Greer thought, and not enough collating it. Analysts had none of the supposed glamour – a Hollywood-generated illusion – of a secret agent in a foreign land. But Jack knew how to analyse reports from such men and data from technical sources. He knew how to make a decision and was not afraid to say what he thought, whether his bosses liked it or not. This sometimes grated the old admiral, but on the whole he liked having subordinates whom he could respect. The CIA had too many people whose only skill was kissing ass.

The US Naval Academy

The loss of his left leg above the knee had not taken away Oliver Wendell Tyler's roguish good looks or his zest for life. His wife could testify to this. Since leaving the active service four years before, they had added three children to the two they already had and were working on a sixth. Ryan found him sitting at a desk in an empty classroom in Rickover Hall, the US Naval Academy's science and engineering building. He was grading papers.

'How's it goin', Skip?' Ryan leaned against the door frame. His CIA driver was in the hall.

'Hey, Jack! I thought you were in England.' Tyler jumped to his foot – his own phrase – and hobbled over to grab Ryan's hand. His prosthetic leg ended in a square rubber-coated band instead of a pseudo-foot. It flexed at the knee, but not by much. Tyler had been a second-squad All American offensive tackle sixteen years before, and the rest of his body was as hard as the aluminium and fibreglass in his left leg. His handshake could make a gorilla wince. 'So, what are you doing here?'

'I had to fly over to get some work done and do a little shopping. How's Jean and your . . . five?'

'Five and two-thirds.'

'Again? Jean ought to have you fixed.'

'That's what she said, but I've had enough things disconnected.' Tyler laughed. 'I guess I'm making up for all those monastic years as a nuc. Come on over and grab a chair.'

Ryan sat on the corner of the desk and opened his briefcase. He handed Tyler a folder.

'Got some pictures I want you to look at.'

'Okay.' Tyler flipped it open. 'Whose – a Russian! Big bastard. That's the basic *Typhoon* configuration. Lots of modifications, though. Twenty-six missiles instead of twenty. Looks longer. Hull's flattened out some, too. More beam?'

'Two or three metres' worth.'

'I heard you were working with the CIA. Can't talk about that, right?'

'Something like that. And you never saw these pictures Skip. Understood?'

'Right.' Tyler's eyes twinkled. 'What do you want me not to look at them for?'

Ryan pulled the blowups from the back of the folder. 'These doors, bow and stern.'

'Uh-huh.' Tyler set them down side by side. 'Pretty big. They're two metres or so, paired fore and aft. They look symmetrical through the long axis. Not cruise missile tubes, eh?'

'On a boomer? You put something like that on a strategic missile sub?'

'The Russkies are a funny bunch, Jack, and they design things their own way. This is the same bunch that built the *Kirov* class with a nuclear reactor *and* an oil-fired steam plant. Hmm . . . twin screws. The aft doors can't be for a sonar array. They'd foul the screws.'

'How 'bout if they trail one screw?'

'They do that with surface ships to conserve fuel, and sometimes with their attack boats. Operating a twin-screw missile boat on one wheel would probably be tricky on this baby. The *Typhoon's* supposed to have handling problems, and boats that handle funny tend to be sensitive to power settings. You end up jinking around so much that you have trouble holding course. You notice how the doors converge at the stern?'

'No, I didn't.'

Tyler looked up. 'Damn! I should have realized it right off the bat. It's a propulsion system. You shouldn't have caught me marking papers, Jack. It turns your brain to jelly.'

'Propulsion system?'

'We looked at this – oh, must have been twenty some years ago – when I was going to school here. We didn't do anything with it, though. It's too inefficient.'

'Okay, tell me about it.'

'They called it a tunnel drive. You know how out West they have lots of hydroelectric power plants? Mostly dams. The water spills onto wheels that turn generators. Now there's a few new ones that kind of turn that around. They tap into underground rivers, and the water turns impellers, and they turn the generators instead of a modified mill wheel! An impeller is like a propeller, except the water drives it instead of the other way around. There's some minor technical differences, too, but nothing major. Okay so far?

'With this design, you turn that around. You suck water in the bow and your impellers eject it out the stern, and that moves the ship.' Tyler paused, frowning. 'As I recall you have to have more than one per tunnel. They looked at this back in the early sixties and got to the model stage before dropping it. One of the things they discovered is that one impeller doesn't work as well as several. Some sort of back pressure thing. It was a new principle, something unexpected that cropped up. They ended up using four, I think, and it was supposed to look something like the compressor sets in a jet engine.'

'Why did we drop it?' Ryan was taking rapid notes.

'Mostly efficiency. You can only get so much water down the pipes no matter how powerful your motors are. And the drive system took up a lot of room. They partially beat that with a new kind of electric induction motor, I think, but even then you'd end up with a lot of extraneous machinery inside the hull. Subs don't have that much room to spare, even this monster. The top speed limit was supposed to be about ten knots, and that just wasn't good enough, even though it did virtually eliminate cavitation sounds.'

'Cavitation?'

'When you have a propeller turning in the water at high speed, you develop an area of low pressure behind the trailing edge of the blade. This can cause water to vaporize. That creates a bunch of little bubbles. They can't last long under the water pressure, and when they collapse the water rushes forward to pound against the blades. That does three things. First, it makes noise, and us sub drivers hate noise. Second, it can cause vibration, something else we don't like. The old passenger liners, for example, used to flutter several inches at the stern, all from cavitation and slippage. It takes a hell of a lot of force to vibrate a 50,000-ton ship; that kind of force breaks things. Third, it tears up the screws. The big wheels only used to last a few years. That's why back in the old days the blades were bolted onto the hub instead of being cast in one piece. The vibration is mainly a surface ship problem, and the screw degradation was eventually conquered by improved metallurgical technology.

'Now, this tunnel drive system avoids the cavitation problem. You still have cavitation, but the noise from it is mainly lost in the tunnels. That makes good sense. The problem is that you can't generate much speed without making the tunnels too wide to be practical. While one team was working on this, another was working on improved screw designs. Your typical sub screw today is pretty large, so it can turn more slowly for a given speed. The slower the turning speed, the less cavitation you get. The problem is also mitigated by depth. A few hundred feet down, the higher water pressure retards bubble formation.'

'Then why don't the Soviets copy our screw designs?'

'Several reasons, probably. You design a screw for a specific hull and engine combination, so copying ours wouldn't automatically work for them. A lot of this work is still empirical, too. There's a lot of trial and error in this. It's a lot harder, say, than designing an airfoil, because the blade cross-section changes radically from one point to another. I suppose another reason is that their metallurgical technology isn't as good as ours – same reason that their jet and rocket engines are less efficient. These new designs place great value on high-strength alloys. It's a narrow specialty, and I only know the generalities.'

'Okay, you say that this is a silent propulsion system, and it has a top speed limit of ten knots?' Ryan wanted to be clear on this.

'Ballpark figure. I'd have to do some computer modelling to tighten that up. We probably sti!l have the data laying around at the Taylor Laboratory.' Tyler referred to the Sea Systems Command design facility on the north side of the Severn River. 'Probably still classified, and I'd have to take it with a big grain of salt.'

'How come?'

'All this work was done twenty years ago. They only got up to fifteen-foot models – pretty small for this sort of thing. Remember that they had already stumbled across one new principle, that back-pressure thing. There might have been more out there. I expect they tried some computer models, but even if they did, mathematical modelling techniques back then were dirt-simple. To duplicate this today I'd have to have the old data and programmes from Taylor, check it all over, then draft a new programme based on this configuration.' He tapped the photographs. 'Once that was done, I'd need access to a big league mainframe computer to run it.'

'But you could do it'?'

'Sure. I'd need exact dimensions on this baby, but I've done this before for the bunch over at Crystal City. The hard part's getting the computer time. I need a big machine.'

'I can probably arrange access to ours.'

Tyler laughed. 'Probably not good enough, Jack. This is specialised stuff. I'm talking about a Cray-2, one of the biggies. To do this you have to mathematically simulate the behaviour of millions of little parcels of water, the water flow over – and through, in this case – the whole hull. Same sort of thing NASA has to do with the Space Shuttle. The actual work is easy enough – it's the *scale* that's tough. They're simple calculations, but you have to make millions of them per second. That means a big Cray, and there's only a few of them around. NASA has one in Houston, I think. The navy has a few in Norfolk for ASW work – you can forget about those. The air force has one in the Pentagon, I think, and all the rest are in California.'

'But you could do it?'

'Sure.'

'Okay, get to work on it, Skip, and I'll see if we can get you the computer time. How long?'

'Depending on how good the stuff at Taylor is, maybe a week. Maybe less.'

'How much do you want for it?'

'Aw, come on, Jack!' Tyler waved him off.

'Skip, it's Monday. You get us this data by Friday and there's twenty thousand dollars in it. You're worth it, and we want this data. Agreed?'

'Sold.' They shook hands. 'Can I keep the pictures?'

'I can leave them if you have a secure place to keep them. Nobody gets to see them, Skip. Nobody.'

'There's a nice safe in the superintendent's office.'

'Fine, but be doesn't see them.' The superintendent was a former submariner.

'He won't like it,' Tyler said. 'But okay.'

'Have him call Admiral Greer if he objects. This number.' Ryan handed him a card. 'You can reach me here if you need me. If I'm not in, ask for the admiral.'

'Just how important is this?'

'Important enough. You're the first guy who's come up with a sensible explanation for these hatches. That's why I came here. If you can model this for us, it'll be damned useful. Skip, one more time: This is highly sensitive. If you let anybody see these, it's my ass.'

'Aye aye, Jack. Well, you've laid a deadline on me, I better get down to it. See you.' After shaking hands, Tyler took out a lined pad and started listing the things he had to do. Ryan left the building with his driver. He remembered a Toys-R-Us right up Route 2 from Annapolis, and he wanted to get that doll for Sally.

CIA Headquarters

Ryan was back at the CIA by eight that evening. It was a quick trip past the security guards to Greer's office.

'Well, did you get your Surfing Barbie?' Greer looked up.

'Skiing Barbie,' Ryan corrected. 'Yes, sir. Come on, didn't you ever play Santa?'

'They grew up too fast, Jack. Even my grandchildren are all past that stage.' He turned to get some coffee. Ryan wondered if he ever slept. 'We have something more on *Red October*. The Russians seem to have a major ASW exercise running in the northeast Barents Sea. Half a dozen ASW search aircraft, a bunch of frigates, and an *Alfa*-class attack boat, all running around in circles.'

44

'Probably an acquisition exercise. Skip Tyler says those doors are for a new drive system.'

'Indeed.' Greer sat back. 'Tell me about it.'

Ryan took out his notes and summarised his education in submarine technology. 'Skip says he can generate a computer simulation of its effectiveness,' he concluded.

Greer's eyebrows went up. 'How soon?'

'End of the week, maybe. I told him if he had it done by Friday we'd pay him for it. Twenty thousand sound reasonable?'

'Will it mean anything?'

'If he gets the background data he needs, it ought to, sir. Skip's a very sharp cookie. I mean, they don't give doctorates away at MIT, and he was in the top five of his Academy class.'

'Worth twenty thousand dollars of our money?' Greer was notoriously tight with a buck.

Ryan knew how to answer this. 'Sir, if we followed normal procedure on this, we'd contract one of the Beltway Bandits –' Ryan referred to the consulting firms that dotted the beltway around Washington, D.C. ' – they'd charge us five or ten times as much, and we'd be lucky to have the data by Easter. This way we might just have it while the boat's still at sea. If worst comes to worst, sir, I'll foot the bill. I figured you'd want this data fast, and it's right up his alley.'

'You're right.' It wasn't the first time Ryan had short-circuited normal procedure. The other times had worked out fairly well. Greer was a man who looked for results. 'Okay, the Soviets have a new missile boat with a silent drive system. What does it all mean?'

'Nothing good. We depend on our ability to track their boomers with our attack boats. Hell, that's why they agreed a few years back to our proposal about keeping them five thousand miles from each other's coasts, and why they keep their missile subs in port most of the time. This could change the game a bit. By the way, *October's* hull, I haven't seen what it's made of.'

'Steel. She's too big for a titanium hull, at least for what it would cost. You know what they have to spend on their *Alfas*?'

'Too much for what they got. You spend that much money for a super-strong hull, then put a noisy power plant in it. Dumb.'

'Maybe. I wouldn't mind having that speed, though. Anyway, if this silent drive system really works, they might be able to creep up onto the continental shelf.'

'Depressed-trajectory shot,' Ryan said. This was one of the nastier nuclear war scenarios in which a sea-based missile was fired from within a few hundred miles of its target. Washington is a bare hundred air miles from the Atlantic Ocean. Though a missile on a low, fast flight path loses much of its accuracy, a few of them can be launched to explode over Washington in less than five minutes' time, too little for a president to react. If the Soviets were able to kill the president that quickly, the resulting disruption of the chain of command would give them ample time to take out the land-based missiles – there would be no one with authority to fire. This scenario is a grand-strategic version of a simple mugging, Ryan thought. A mugger doesn't attack his victim's arms – he goes for the head. 'You think *October* was built with that in mind?'

'I'm sure the thought occurred to them,' Greer observed. 'It would have occurred to us. Well, we have *Bremerton* up there to keep an eye on her, and if this data turns out to be useful we'll see if we can come up with an answer. How are you feeling?'

'I've been on the go since five thirty London time. Long day, sir.'

'I expect so. Okay, we'll go over the Afghanistan business tomorrow morning. Get some sleep, son.'

'Aye aye, sir.' Ryan got his coat. 'Good night.'

It was a fifteen-minute drive to the Marriott. Ryan made the mistake of turning the TV on to the beginning of Monday Night Football. Cincinnati was playing San Francisco, the two best quarterbacks in the league pitted against one another. Football was something he missed living in England, and he managed to stay awake nearly three hours before fading out with the television on.

SOSUS Control

Except for the fact that everyone was in uniform, a visitor might easily have mistaken the room for a NASA control centre. There were six wide rows of consoles, each with its own TV screen and typewriter keyboard supplemented by lighted plastic buttons, dials, headphone jacks, and analogue and digital controls. Senior Chief Oceanographic Technician Deke Franklin was seated at console fifteen.

The room was SOSUS (sonar surveillance system) Atlantic Control. It was in a fairly nondescript building, uninspired government layer cake, with windowless concrete walls, a large air-conditioning system on a flat roof, and an acronym-coded blue sign on a well-tended but now yellowed lawn. There were armed marines inconspicuously on guard inside the three entrances. In the basement were a pair of Cray-2 supercomputers tended by twenty acolytes, and behind the building was a trio of satellite ground stations, all up- and down-links. The men at the consoles and the computers were linked electronically by satellite and landline to the SOSUS system.

Throughout the oceans of the world, and especially astride the passages that Soviet submarines had to cross to reach the open sea, the United States and other NATO countries had deployed gangs of highly sensitive sonar receptors. The hundreds of SOSUS sensors received and forwarded an unimaginably vast amount of information, and to help the system operators classify and analyse it a whole new family of computers had to be designed, the supercomputers. SOSUS served its purpose admirably well. Very little could cross a barrier without being detected. Even the ultraquiet American and British attack submarines were generally picked up. The sensors, lying on the bottom of the sea, were periodically updated; many now had their own signal processors to presort the data they forwarded, lightening the load on the central computers and enabling more rapid and accurate classification of targets.

Chief Franklin's console received data from a string of sensors planted off the coast of Iceland. He was responsible for an area forty nautical miles across, and his sector overlapped the ones east and west so that, theoretically, three operators were constantly monitoring any segment of the barrier. If he got a contact, he would first notify his brother operators, then type a contact report into his computer terminal, which would in turn be displayed on the master control board in the control room at the back of the floor. The senior duty officer had the frequently exercised authority to prosecute a contact with a wide range of assets, from surface ships to antisubmarine aircraft. Two world wars had taught American and British officers the necessity of keeping their sea lines of communication – SLOCs – open.

Although this quiet, tomblike facility had never been shown to the public, and though it had none of the drama associated with military life, the men on duty here were among the most important in the service of their country. In a war, without them, whole nations might starve.

Franklin was leaning back in his swivel chair, puffing contemplatively on an old briar pipe. Around him the room was dead quiet. Even had it not been, his five-hundred-dollar headphones would have effectively sealed him off from the outside world. A twenty-six year chief, Franklin had served his entire career on destroyers and frigates. To him, submarines and submariners were the enemy, regardless of what flag they might fly or what uniform they might wear.

An eyebrow went up, and his nearly bald head cocked to one side. The pulls on the pipe grew irregular. His right hand reached forward to the control panel and switched off the signal processors so that he could get the sound without computerised interference. But it was no good. There was too much background noise. He switched the filters back on. Next he tried some changes in his azimuth controls. The SOSUS sensors were designed to give bearing checks through the selective use of individual receptors, which he could manipulate electronically, first getting one bearing, then using a neighbouring gang to triangulate for a fix. The contact was very faint, but not too far from the line, he judged. Franklin queried his computer terminal. The USS *Dallas* was up there. *Gotcha*! he said with a thin smile. Another noise came through, a low-frequency rumble that only lasted a few seconds before fading out. Not all that quiet, though. Why hadn't he heard it before switching the reception azimuth? He set his pipe down and began making adjustments on his control board.

'Chief?' A voice came over his headphones. It was the senior duty officer.
'Yes, Commander?'

'Can you come back to control? I have something I want you to hear.'

'On the way, sir.' Franklin rose quietly. Commander Quentin was a former destroyer skipper on a limited duty after a winning battle with cancer. Almost a winning battle, Franklin corrected himself. Chemotherapy had killed the cancer – at the cost of nearly all his hair, and turning his skin into a sort of transparent parchment. Too bad, he thought, Quentin was a pretty good man.

The control room was elevated a few feet from the rest of the floor so that its occupants could see over the whole crew of duty operators and the main tactical display on the far wall. It was separated from the floor by glass, which allowed them to speak to one another without disturbing the operators. Franklin found Quentin at his command station, where he could tap into any console on the floor.

'Howdy, Commander.' Franklin noted that the officer was gaining some weight back. It was about time. 'What do you have for me, sir?'

'On the Barents Sea net.' Quentin handed him a pair of phones. Franklin listened for several minutes, but he didn't sit down. Like many people he had a gut suspicion that cancer was contagious.

'Damned if they ain't pretty busy up there. I read of a pair of *Alfas*, a *Charlie*, a *Tango*, and a few surface ships. What gives, sir?'

'There's a *Delta* there, too, but she just surfaced and killed her engines.'

'Surfaced, Skipper?'

'Yep. They were lashing her pretty hard with active sonar, then a 'can queried her on a gertrude.'

'Uh-huh. Acquisition game, and the sub lost.'

'Maybe.' Quentin rubbed his eyes. The man looked tired. He was pushing himself too hard, and his stamina wasn't half what it should have been. 'But the *Alfas* are still pinging, and now they're headed west, as you heard.'

'Oh.' Franklin pondered that for a moment. 'They're looking for another boat, then. The *Typhoon* that was supposed to have sailed the other day, maybe?'

'That's what I thought – except she headed west, and the exercise area is northeast of the fjord. We lost her the other day on SOSUS. *Bremerton's* up sniffing around for her now.'

'Cagey skipper,' Franklin decided. 'Cut his plant all the way back and just drifting.'

'Yeah,' Quentin agreed. 'I want you to move down to the North Cape barrier supervisory board and see if you can find her, Chief. She'll still have her reactor working, and she'll be making some noise. The operators we have on that sector are a little young. I'll take one and switch him to your board for a while.'

'Right, Skipper,' Franklin nodded. That part of the team was still green, used to working on ships. SOSUS required more finesse. Quentin didn't have to say that he expected Franklin to check in on the whole North Cape team's boards and maybe drop a few small lessons as he listened in on their channels.

'Did you pick up on *Dallas*?'

'Yes, sir. Real faint, but I think I got her crossing my sector, headed north-west for Toll Booth. If we get an Orion down there, we might just get her locked in. Can we rattle their cage a little?'

Quentin chuckled. He didn't much care for submariners either. 'No, NIFTY DOLPHIN is over, Chief. We'll just log it and let the skipper know when he comes back home. Nice work, though. You know her reputation. We're not supposed to hear her at all.'

'That'll be the day!' Franklin snorted.

'Let me know what you find, Deke.'

'Aye aye, Skipper. You take care of yourself, hear?'

The Fifth Day

Tuesday, 7 December

Moscow

It was not the grandest office in the Kremlin, but it suited his needs. Admiral Yuri Ilych Padorin showed up for work at his customary seven o'clock after the drive from his six-room apartment in the Kutuzovskiy Prospekt. The large office windows overlooked the Kremlin walls; except for those he would have had a view of the Moscow River, now frozen solid. Padorin did not miss the view, though he had won his spurs commanding river gunboats forty years before, running supplies across the Volga into Stalingrad. Padorin was now the chief political officer of the Soviet Navy. His job was men, not ships.

On the way in he nodded curtly to his secretary, a man of forty. The yeoman leaped to his feet and followed his admiral into the inner office to help him off with his greatcoat. Padorin's navy-blue jacket was ablaze with ribbons and the gold star medal of the most coveted award in the Soviet military, Hero of the Soviet Union. He had won that in combat as a freckled boy of twenty, shuttling back and forth on the Volga. Those were good days, he told himself, dodging bombs from the German Stukas and the more random artillery fire with which the Fascists had tried to interdict his squadron . . . Like most men he was unable to remember the stark terror of combat.

It was a Tuesday morning, and Padorin had a pile of mail waiting on his desk. His yeoman got him a pot of tea and a cup – the usual Russian glass cup set in a metal holder, sterling silver in this case. Padorin had worked long and hard for the perks that came with this office. He settled in his chair and read first through the intelligence dispatches, information copies of data sent each morning and evening to the operational commands of the Soviet Navy. A political officer had to keep current, to know what the imperialists were up to so that he could brief his men on the threat.

Next came the official mail from within the People's Commissariat of the Navy and the Ministry of Defense. He had access to all of the correspondence from the former, while that from the latter had been carefully vetted since the Soviet armed services share as little information as possible. There wasn't too much mail from either place today. The usual Monday afternoon meeting had covered most of what had to be done that week, and nearly everything Padorin was concerned with was now in the hands of his staff for disposition. He poured a second cup of tea and opened a new pack of unfiltered cigarettes, a habit he'd been unable to break despite a mild heart attack three years earlier. He checked his desk calendar – good, no appointments until ten.

Near the bottom of the pile was an official-looking envelope from the Northern Fleet. The code number at the upper left corner showed that it came from the *Red October*. Hadn't he just read something about that?

Padorin rechecked his ops dispatches. So, Ramius hadn't turned up in his exercise area? He shrugged. Missile submarines were supposed to be elusive, and it would not have surprised the old admiral at all if Ramius were twisting a few tails. The son of Aleksandr Ramius was a prima donna who had the troubling habit of seeming to build his own personality cult: he kept some of the men he trained and discarded others. Padorin reflected that those rejected for line service had made excellent *zampoliti*, and appeared to have more line knowledge than was the norm. Even so, Ramius was a captain who needed watching. Sometimes Padorin suspected that he was too much a sailor and not enough a Communist. On the other hand, his father had been a model Party member and a hero of the Great Patriotic War. Certainly he had been well thought of, Lithuanian or not. And the son? Years of letter-perfect performance, as many years of stalwart Party membership. He was known for his spirited participation at meetings and occasionally brilliant essays. The people in the naval branch of the GRU, the Soviet military intelligence agency, reported that the imperialists regarded him as a dangerous and skilled enemy. Good, Padorin thought, the bastards ought to fear our men. He turned his attention back to the envelope.

Red October, now there was a fitting name for a Soviet warship! Named not only for the revolution that had forever changed the history of the world but also for the Red October Tractor Plant. Many was the dawn when Padorin had looked west to Stalingrad to see if the factory still stood, a

50

symbol to the Soviet fighting men struggling against the Hitlerite bandits. The envelope was marked Confidential and his yeoman had not opened it as he had the other routine mail. The admiral took his letter opener from the desk drawer. It was a sentimental object, having been his service knife years before. When his first gunboat had been sunk under him, one hot August night in 1942, he had swum to shore and been pounced on by a German infantryman who hadn't expected resistance from a half-drowned sailor. Padorin had surprised him, sinking the knife in his chest and breaking off half the blade as he stole his enemy's life. Later a machinist had trimmed the blade down. It was no longer a proper knife, but Padorin wasn't about to throw this sort of souvenir away.

'Comrade Admiral,' the letter began – but the type had been scratched out and replaced with a hand-written 'Uncle Yuri.' Ramius had jokingly called him that years back when Padorin was chief political officer of the Northern Fleet. 'Thank you for your confidence, and for the opportunity you have given me with command of this magnificent ship!' Ramius ought to be grateful, Padorin thought. Performance or not, you don't give this sort of command to –

What? Padorin stopped reading and started over. He forgot the cigarette smoldering in his ashtray as he reached the bottom of the first page. A joke. Ramius was known for his jokes – but he'd pay for this one. This was going too fucking far! He turned the page.

'*This is no joke, Unle Yuri – Marko.*'

Padorin stopped and looked out of the window. The Kremlin wall at this point was a beehive of niches for the ashes of the Party faithful. He couldn't have read the letter correctly. He started to read it again. His hands began to shake.

He had a direct line to Admiral Gorshkov, with no yeomen or secretaries to bar the way.

'Comrade Admiral, this is Padorin.'

'Good morning, Yuri,' Gorshkov said pleasantly.

'I must see you immediately. I have a situation here.'

'What sort of situation?' Gorshkov asked warily.

'We must discuss it in person. I am coming over now.' There was no way he'd discuss this over the phone; he knew it was tapped.

The USS *Dallas*

Sonarman Second Class Ronald Jones, his division officer noted, was in his usual trance. The young college dropout was hunched over his instrument table, body limp, eyes closed, face locked into the same neutral expression he wore when listening to one of the many Bach tapes on his expensive personal cassette player. Jones was the sort who categorized his tapes by their flaws, a ragged piano tempo, a botched flute, a wavering French horn.

He listened to sea sounds with the same discriminating intensity. In all the navies of the world, submariners were regarded as a curious breed, and submariners themselves looked upon sonar operators as odd. Their eccentricities, however, were among the most tolerated in the military service. The executive officer liked to tell a story about a sonar chief he'd served with for two years, a man who had patrolled the same areas in missile submarines for virtually his whole career. He became so familiar with the humpback whales that summered in the area that he took to calling them by name. On retiring, he went to work for the Woods Hole Oceanographic Institute, where his talent was regarded not so much with amusement as awe.

Three years earlier, Jones had been asked to leave the California Institute of Technology in the middle of his junior year. He had pulled one of the ingenious pranks for which Cal Tech students were justly famous, only it hadn't worked. Now he was serving his time in the navy to finance his return. It was his announced intention to get a doctorate in cybernetics and signal processing. In return for an early out, after receiving his degree he would go to work for the Naval Research Laboratory. Lieutenant Thompson believed it. On joining the *Dallas* six months earlier, he had read the files of all his men. Jones' IQ was 158, the highest on the boat by a fair margin. He had a placid face and sad brown eyes that women found irresistible. On the beach Jones had enough action to wear down a squad of marines. It didn't make much sense to the lieutenant. He'd been the football hero at Annapolis. Jones was a skinny kid who listened to Bach. It didn't figure.

The USS *Dallas*, a 688-class attack submarine, was forty miles from the coast of Iceland, approaching her patrol station, code-named Toll Booth. She was two days late getting there. A week earlier, she had participated in the NATO war game NIFTY DOLPHIN, which had been postponed several days because the worst North Atlantic weather in twenty years had delayed other ships detailed to it. In that exercise the *Dallas*, teamed with HMS *Swiftsure,* had used the foul weather to penetrate and ravage the simulated enemy formation. It was yet another top performance for the *Dallas* and her skipper, Commander Bart Mancuso, one of the youngest submarine commanders in the U.S. Navy. The mission had been followed by a courtesy call at the *Swiftsure's* Royal Navy base in Scotland, and the American sailors were still shaking off hangovers from the celebration . . . Now they had a different mission, a new development in the Atlantic submarine game. For three weeks, the *Dallas* was to report on traffic in and out of Red Route One.

Over the past fourteen months, newer Soviet submarines had been using a strange, effective tactic for shedding their American and British shadowers. Southwest of Iceland the Russian boats would race down the Reykjanes Ridge, a finger of underwater highlands pointing to the deep Atlantic basin. Spaced at intervals from five miles to half a mile, these mountains with their knife-edged ridges of brittle igneous rock rivalled the Alps in size. Their peaks were about a thousand feet beneath the stormy surface of the North Atlantic. Before the late sixties submarines could barely approach the peaks, much less probe their myriad valleys. Throughout the seventies Soviet naval survey vessels had been seen patrolling the ridge – in all seasons, in all weather, quartering and requartering the area in thousands of cruises. Then, fourteen months before the *Dallas'* present patrol, the USS *Los Angeles* had been tracking a Soviet *Victor II*-class attack submarine. The *Victor* had skirted the Icelandic coast and gone deep as she approached the ridge. The *Los Angeles* had followed. The *Victor* proceeded at eight knots until she passed between the first pair of seamounts, informally known as Thor's Twins. All at once she went to full speed and moved southwest. The skipper of the *Los Angeles* made a determined effort to track the *Victor* and came away from it badly shaken. Although the 688-class submarines were faster than the older *Victors*, the Russian submarine had simply not slowed down – for fifteen hours, it was later determined.

At first it had not been all that dangerous. Submarines had highly accurate inertial navigation systems able to fix their positions to within a few hundred yards from one second to another. But the *Victor* was skirting cliffs as though her skipper could see them, like a fighter dodging down a canyon to avoid surface-to-air missile fire. The *Los Angeles* could not keep track of the cliffs. At any speed over twenty knots both her passive and active sonar, including the echofathometre, became almost useless. The *Los Angeles* thus found herself navigating completely blind. It was, the skipper later reported, like driving a car with the windows painted over, steering with a map and a stopwatch. This was theoretically possible, but the captain quickly realized that the inertial navigation system had a built-in error factor of several hundred yards; this was aggravated by gravitational disturbances, which affected the 'local vertical,' which in turn affected the inertial fix. Worst of all, his charts were made for surface ships. Objects below a few hundred feet had been known to be misplaced by miles – something that mattered to no one until recently. The interval between mountains had quickly become less than his cumulative navigational error – sooner or later his submarine would drive into a mountainside at over thirty knots. The captain backed off. The *Victor* got away.

Initially it was theorized that the Soviets had somehow staked out one particular route, that their submarines were able to follow it at high speed. Russian skippers were known to pull some crazy stunts, and perhaps they were trusting to a combination of initial systems, magnetic and gyro compasses attuned to a specific track. This theory had never developed much of a following, and in a few weeks it was known for certain that the Soviet submarines speeding through the ridge were following a multiplicity of tracks. The only thing American and British subs could do was stop periodically to get a sonar fix of their positions, then race to catch up. But the Soviet subs never slowed, and the 688s and *Trafalgars* kept falling behind.

The *Dallas* was on Toll Booth station to monitor passing Russian subs, to watch the entrance to the passage the U.S. Navy was now calling Red Route One, and to listen for any external evidence of a new gadget that might enable the Soviets to run the ridge so boldly. Until the Americans could copy it, there were three unsavoury alternatives: they could continue losing contact with the Russians; they could station valuable attack subs at the known exits from the route; or they could set up a whole new SOSUS line.

Jones' trance lasted ten minutes – longer than usual. He ordinarily had a contact figured out in far less time. The sailor leaned back and lit a cigarette.

'Got something, Mr Thompson.'

'What is it?' Thompson leaned against the bulkhead.

'I don't know.' Jones picked up a spare set of phones and handed them to his officer. 'Listen up, sir.'

Thompson himself was a masters candidate in electrical engineering, an expert in sonar system design. His eyes screwed shut as he concentrated on the sound. It was a very faint low-frequency rumble – or swish. He couldn't decide. He listened for several minutes before setting the headphones down, then shook his head.

'I got it a half hour ago on the lateral array,' Jones said. He referred to a subsystem of the BQQ-5 multifunction submarine sonar. Its main component was an eighteen-foot-diameter dome located in the bow. The dome was used for both active and passive operations. A new part of the system was a gang of passive sensors which extended two hundred feet down both sides of the hull. This was a mechanical analogue to the sensory organs on the body of a shark. 'Lost it, got it back, lost it, got it back,' Jones went on. 'It's not screw sounds, not whales or fish. More like water going through a pipe, except for that funny rumble that comes and goes. Anyway, the bearing is about two-five-zero. That puts it between us and Iceland, so it can't be too far away.'

'Let's see what it looks like. Maybe that'll tell us something.'

Jones took a double-plugged wire from a hook. One plug went into a socket on his sonar panel, the other into the jack on a nearby oscilloscope. The two men spent several minutes working with the sonar controls to isolate the signal. They ended up with an irregular sine wave which they were only able to hold a few seconds at a time.

'Irregular,' Thompson said.

'Yeah, it's funny. It sounds regular, but it doesn't look regular. Know what I mean, Mr Thompson?'

'No, you've got better ears.'

'That's cause I listen to better music, sir. That rock stuff'll kill your ears.'

Thompson knew he was right, but an Annapolis graduate doesn't need to hear that from an enlisted man. His vintage Janis Joplin tapes were his own business. 'Next step.'

'Yessir.' Jones took the plug from the oscilloscope and moved it into a panel to the left of the sonar board, next to a computer terminal.

During her last overhaul, the *Dallas* had received a very special toy to go along with her BQQ-5 sonar system. Called the BC-10, it was the most powerful computer yet installed aboard a submarine. Though only about the size of a business desk, it cost over five million dollars and ran at eighty million operations per second. It used newly developed sixty-four-bit chips and made use of the latest processing architecture. Its bubble memory could easily accommodate the computing needs of a whole squadron of submarines. In five years every attack sub in the fleet would have one. Its purpose, much like that of the far larger SOSUS system, was to process and analyse sonar signals; the BC-10 stripped away ambient noise and other naturally produced sea sounds to classify and identify man-made noise. It could identify ships by name from their individual acoustical signatures, much as one could identify the finger or voice prints of a human.

As important as the computer was its programming software. Four years before, a PhD candidate in geophysics who was working at Cal Tech's geophysical laboratory had completed a programme of six hundred thousand steps designed to predict earthquakes. The problem the programme addressed was one of signal versus noise. It overcame the difficulty seismologists had discriminating between random noise that is constantly monitored on seismographs and genuinely unusual signals that foretell a seismic event.

The first Defense Department use of the programme was in the Air Force Technical Applications Command (AFTAC), which found it entirely satisfactory for its mission of monitoring nuclear events throughout the world in accordance with arms control treaties. The Navy Research Laboratory also redrafted it for its own purposes. Though inadequate for seismic predictions, it worked very well indeed in analysing sonar signals. The programme was known in the navy as the signal algorythmic processing system (SAPS).

'SAPS SIGNAL INPUT,' Jones typed into the video display terminal (VDT).

'READY,' the BC-10 responded at once.

'RUN.'

'WORKING.'

For all the fantastic speed of the BC-10, the six hundred thousand steps of the programme, punctuated by numerous GOTO loops, took time to run as the machine eliminated natural sounds with its random profile criteria and then locked into the anomalous signal. It took twenty seconds, an eternity in computer time. The answer came up on the VDT. Jones pressed a key to generate a copy on the adjacent matrix printer.

'Hmph.' Jones tore off the page. '"ANOMALOUS SIGNAL EVALUATED AS MAGMA DISPLACEMENT." That's SAPS' way of saying take two aspirin and call me at end of the watch.'

Thompson chuckled. For all the ballyhoo that had accompanied the new system, it was not all that popular in the fleet. 'Remember what the papers said when we were in England? Something about seismic activity around Iceland, like when that island poked up back in the sixties.'

Jones lit another cigarette. He knew the student who had originally drafted this abortion they called SAPS. One problem was that it had a nasty habit of analysing the wrong signal – and you couldn't tell it was wrong from the result. Besides, since it had been originally designed to look for seismic events, Jones suspected it of a tendency to interpret anomalies as seismic events. He didn't like the built-in bias, which he felt the research laboratory had not entirely removed. It was one thing to use computers as a tool, quite another to let them do your thinking for you. Besides, they were always discovering new sea sounds that nobody had ever heard before, much less classified.

'Sir, the frequency is all wrong for one thing – nowhere near low enough. How 'bout I try an' track in on this signal with the R-15?' Jones referred to the towed array of passive sensors that the *Dallas* was trailing behind her at low speed.

Commander Mancuso came in just then, the usual mug of coffee in his hand. If there was one frightening thing about the captain, Thompson thought, it was his talent for showing up when something was going on. Did he have the whole boat wired?

'Just wandering by,' he said casually. 'What's happening this fine day?' The captain leaned against the bulkhead. He was a small man, only five eight, who had fought a battle against his waistline all his life and was now losing because of the good food and lack of exercise on a submarine. His dark eyes were surrounded by laugh lines that were always deeper when he was playing a trick on another ship.

Was it day? Thompson wondered. The six-hour one-in-three rotating watch cycle made for a convenient work schedule, but after a few changes you had to press the button on your watch to figure out what day it was, else you couldn't make the proper entry in the log.

'Skipper, Jones picked up a funny signal on the lateral. The computer says it's magma displacement.'

'And Jonesy doesn't agree with that.' Mancuso didn't have to make it a question.

'No, sir, Captain, I don't. I don't know what it is, but for sure it ain't that.'

'You against the machine again?'

'Skipper, SAPS works pretty well most of the time, but sometimes it's a real *kludge*.' Jones' epithet was the most pejorative curse of electronics people. 'For one thing, the frequency is all wrong.'

'Okay, what do you think?'

'I don't know, Captain. It isn't screw sounds, and it isn't any naturally produced sound that I've heard. Beyond that . . .' Jones was struck by the informality of the discussion with his commanding officer, even after three years on nuclear subs. The crew of the *Dallas* was like one big family, albeit one of the old frontier families, since everybody worked pretty damned hard. The captain was the father. The executive officer, everyone would readily agree, was the mother. The officers were the older kids, and the enlisted men were the younger kids. The important thing was, if you had something to say, the captain would listen to you. To Jones, this counted for a lot.

Mancuso nodded thoughtfully. 'Well, keep at it. No sense letting all this expensive gear go to waste.'

Jones grinned. Once he had told the captain in precise detail how he could convert this equipment into the world's finest stereo rig. Mancuso had pointed out that it would not be a major feat, since the sonar gear in this room alone cost over twenty million dollars.

'Christ!' The junior technician bolted upright in his chair. 'Somebody just stomped on the gas.'

Jones was the sonar watch supervisor. The other two watchstanders noted the new signal, and Jones switched his phones to the towed array jack while the two officers kept out of the way. He took a scratch pad and noted the time before working on his individual controls. The BQR-15 was the most sensitive sonar rig on the boat, but its sensitivity was not needed for this contact.

'Damn,' Jones muttered quietly.

'*Charlie*,' said the junior technician.

Jones shook his head. '*Victor*. *Victor* class for sure. Doing turns for thirty knots – burst of cavitation noise, he's digging big holes in the water, and he doesn't care who knows it. Bearing zero-five-zero. Skipper, we got good water around us, and the signal is real faint. He's not close.' It was the closest thing to a range estimate Jones could come up with. Not close meant anything over ten miles. He went back to working his controls. 'I think we know this guy. This is the one with a bent blade on his screw, sounds like he's got a chain wrapped around it.'

'Put it on speaker,' Mancuso told Thompson. He didn't want to disturb the operators. The lieutenant was already keying the signal into the BC-10.

The bulkhead-mounted speaker would have commanded a four-figure price in any stereo shop for its clarity and dynamic perfection; like everything else on the 688-class sub, it was the very best that money could buy. As Jones worked on the sound controls they heard the whining chirp of propeller cavitation, the thin screech associated with a bent propeller blade, and the deeper rumble of a *Victor*'s reactor plant at full power. The next thing Mancuso heard was the printer.

'*Victor I*-class, number six,' Thompson announced.

'Right,' Jones nodded. '*Vic*-six, bearing still zero-five-zero.' He plugged the mouthpiece into his headphones. 'Conn, sonar, we have a contact. A *Victor* class, bearing zero-five-zero, estimated target speed thirty knots.'

Mancuso leaned out into the passageway to address Lieutenant Pat Mannion, officer of the deck. 'Pat, man the fire-control tracking party.'

'Aye, Cap'n.'

'Wait a minute!' Jones' hand went up. 'Got another one!' He twiddled some knobs. 'This one's a *Charlie* class. Damned if he ain't digging holes, too. More easterly, bearing zero-seven-three, doing turns for about twenty-eight knots. We know this guy, too. Yeah, *Charlie II*, number eleven.' Jones slipped a phone off one ear and looked at Mancuso. 'Skipper, the Russkies have sub races scheduled for today?'

'Not that they told me about. Of course, we don't get the sports page out here,' Mancuso chuckled, swirling the coffee around in his cup and hiding his real thoughts. What the hell was going on? 'I suppose I'll go forward and take a look at this. Good work, guys.'

He went a few steps forward into the attack centre. The normal steaming watch was set. Mannion had the conn, with a junior officer of the deck and seven enlisted men. A first-class firecontrolman was entering data from the target motion analyser into the Mark 117 fire control computer. Another officer was entering control to take charge of the tracking exercise. There was nothing unusual about this. The whole watch went about its work alertly but with the relaxed demeanour that came with years of training and experience. While the other armed services routinely had their components run exercises against allies or themselves in emulation of Eastern Bloc tactics, the navy had its attack submarines play their games against the real thing – and constantly. Submariners typically operated on what was effectively an at-war footing.

'So we have company,' Mannion observed.

'Not that close,' Lieutenant Charles Goodman noted. 'These bearings haven't changed a whisker.'

'Conn, sonar.' It was Jones' voice. Mancuso took it.

'Conn, aye. What it is, Jonesy?'

'We got another one, sir. *Alfa 3*, bearing zero-five-five. Running flat out. Sounds like an earthquake, but faint sir.'

'*Alfa 3*? Our old friend, the *Politovskiy*. Haven't run across her in a while. Anything else you can tell me?'

'A guess, sir. The sound on this one warbled, then settled down, like she was making a turn. I think she's heading this way – that's a little shaky. And we have some more noise to the northeast. Too confused to make any sense of just now. We're working on it.'

'Okay, nice work, Jonesy. Keep at it.'

'Sure thing, Captain.'

Mancuso smiled as he set the phone down, looking over at Mannion. 'You know, Pat, sometimes I wonder if Jonesy isn't part witch.'

Mannion looked at the paper tracks that Goodman was drawing to back up the computerised targeting process. 'He's pretty good. Problem is, he thinks we work for him.'

'Right now we are working for him.' Jones was their eyes and ears, and Mancuso was damned glad to have him.

'Chuck?' Mancuso asked Lieutenant Goodman.

'Bearing still constant on all three contacts, sir.' Which probably meant they were heading for the *Dallas*. It also meant that they could not develop the range data necessary for a fire control solution. Not that anyone wanted to shoot but this was the point of the exercise.

'Pat, let's get some sea room. Move us about ten miles east,' Mancuso ordered casually. There were two reasons for this. First, it would establish a base line from which to compute probable target range. Second, the deeper water would make for better acoustical conditions, opening up to them the distant sonar convergence zones. The captain studied the chart as his navigator gave the necessary orders, evaluating the tactical situation.

Bartolomeo Mancuso was the son of a barber who closed his shop in Cicero, Illinois, every fall to hunt deer on Michigan's Upper Peninsula. Bart had accompanied his father on these hunts, shot his first deer at the age of twelve and every year thereafter until entering the Naval Academy. He had never bothered after that. Since becoming an officer on nuclear submarines he had learned a much more diverting game. Now he hunted people.

Two hours later an alarm bell went off on the ELF radio in the sub's communications room. Like all nuclear submarines, the *Dallas* was trailing a lengthy wire antenna attuned to the extremely low-frequency transmitter in the central United States. The channel had a frustratingly narrow data band width. Unlike a TV channel, which transmitted thousands of bits of data per frame, thirty frames per second, the ELF radio passed on data slowly, about one character every thirty seconds. The duty radioman waited patiently while the information was recorded on tape. When the message was finished, he ran the tape at high speed and transcribed the message, handing it to the communications officer who was waiting with his code book.

The signal was actually not a code but a 'one-time-pad' cipher. A book, published every six months and distributed to every nuclear submarine, was filled with randomly generated transpositions for each letter of the signal. Each scrambled three-letter group in this book corresponded to a preselected word or phrase in another book. Deciphering the message by hand took under three minutes, and when that was completed it was carried to the captain in the attack centre.

NHG	JPR	YTR
FROM COMSUBLANT	TO LANTSUBS AT SEA	STANDBY
OPY TBD	QEQ	GER
POSSIBLE MAJOR	REDEPLOYMENT ORDER	LARGE-SCALE
MAL	ASF	NME
UNEXPECTED	REDFLEET OPERATION	IN PROGRESS
TYQ	ORV	
NATURE UNKNOWN	NEXT ELF MESSAGE	
HWZ		
COMMUNICATE SSIX		

COMSUBLANT – commander of the Submarine Force in the Atlantic – was Mancuso's big boss, Vice Admiral Vincent Gallery. The old man was evidently contemplating a reshuffling of his entire force, no minor affair. The next wake-up signal, AAA – encrypted, of course – would alert them to go to periscope-antenna depth to get more detailed instructions from SSIX, the submarine satellite information exchange, a geosynchronous communications satellite used exclusively by submarines.

The tactical situation was becoming clearer, though its strategic implications were beyond his ability to judge. The ten-mile move eastward had given them adequate range information for their initial three contacts and another *Alfa* which had turned up a few minutes later. The first of the contacts, *Vic* 6, was now within torpedo range. A Mark 48 was locked in on her, and there was no way that her skipper could know the *Dallas* was here. *Vic* 6 was a deer in his sights – but it wasn't hunting season.

Though not much faster than the *Victors* and *Charlies*, and ten knots slower than the smaller *Alfas*, the *Dallas* and her sisters could move almost silently at nearly twenty knots. This was a triumph of engineering and design, the product of decades of work. But moving without being detected was useful only if the hunter could at the same time detect his quarry. Sonars lost effectiveness as their carrier platform increased speed. The *Dallas'* BQQ-5 retained twenty percent effectiveness at twenty knots, nothing to cheer about. Submarines running at high speed from one point to another were blind and unable to harm anyone. As a result, the operating pattern of an attack submarine was much like that of a combat infantryman. With a rifleman it was called dash-and-cover; with a sub, sprint-and-drift. After detecting a target, a sub would race to a more advantageous position, stop to reacquire her prey, then dash again until a firing position had been achieved. The sub's quarry would be moving too, and if the submarine could gain position in front of it, she had then only to lie in wait like a great hunting cat to strike.

The submariner's trade required more than skill. It required instinct, and an artist's touch; monomaniacal confidence, and the aggressiveness of a professional boxer. Mancuso had all of these things. He had spent fifteen years learning his craft, watching a generation of commanders as a junior officer, listening carefully at the frequent round-table discussions which made submarining a very human profession, its lessons passed on by verbal tradition. Time on shore had been spent training in a variety of computerised simulators, attending seminars, comparing notes and ideas with his peers. Aboard surface ships and ASW aircraft he learned how the 'enemy' – the surface sailors – played his own hunting game.

Submariners lived by a simple motto: there are two kinds of ships, submarines . . . and targets. What would *Dallas* be hunting? Mancuso wondered. Russian subs? Well, if that was the game and the Russians kept racing around like this, it ought to be easy enough. He and the *Swiftsure* had just bested a team of NATO ASW-experts, men whose countries depended on their ability to keep the sea-lanes open. His boat and his crew were performing as well as any man could ask. In Jones he had one of the ten best sonar operators in the fleet. Mancuso was ready, whatever the game might be. As on the opening day of hunting season, outside considerations were dwindling away. He was becoming a weapon.

CIA Headquarters

It was 4.45 in the morning, and Ryan was dozing fitfully in the back of a CIA Chevy taking him from the Marriott to Langley. He'd been over for what? twenty hours? About that, enough time to see his boss, see Skip, get the presents for Sally, and check the house. The house looked to be in good shape. He had rented it to an instructor at the Naval Academy. He could have gotten five times the rent from someone else, but he didn't want any wild parties in his home. The officer was a Bible-thumper from Kansas, and made an acceptable custodian.

Five and a half hours of sleep in the past – thirty? Something like that; he was too tired to look at his watch. It wasn't fair. Sleeplessness murders judgment. But it made little sense telling himself that, and telling the admiral would make less.

He was in Greer's office five minutes later.

'Sorry to have to wake you up, Jack.'

'Oh, that's all right, sir,' Ryan returned the lie. 'What's up?'

'Come on over and grab some coffee. It's going to be a long day.'

Ryan dropped his topcoat on the sofa and walked over to pour a mug of navy brew. He decided against Coffee Mate or sugar. Better to endure it naked and get the caffeine full force. 'Any place I can shave around here, sir?'

'Head's behind the door, over in the corner.' Greer handed him a yellow sheet torn from a telex machine. 'Look at this.'

TOP SECRET
102200Z*****38976

NSA SIGINT BULLETIN

REDNAV OPS

MESSAGE FOLLOWS

AT 083145Z NSA MONITOR STATIONS [DELETED] [DELETED] AND [DELETED] RECORDED AN ELF BROADCAST FROM REDFLEET ELF FACILITY SEMIPOLIPINSK XX MESSAGE DURATION 10 MINUTES XX 6 ELEMENTS XX

ELF SIGNAL IS EVALUATED AS 'PREP' BROADCAST TO REDFLEET SUBMARINES AT SEA XX

AT 090000Z AN 'ALL SHIPS' BROADCAST WAS MADE BY REDFLEET HEADQUARTERS CENTRAL COMMO STATION TULA AND SATELLITES THREE AND FIVE XX BANDS USED: HF VHF UHF XX MESSAGE DURATION 39 SECONDS WITH 2 REPEATS IDENTICAL CONTENT MADE AT 091000Z AND 092000Z XX 475 5-ELEMENT CIPHER GROUPS XX

SIGNAL COVERAGE AS FOLLOWS: NORTHERN FLEET AREA BALTIC FLEET AREA AND MED SQUADRON AREA XX NOTE FAR EAST FLEET NOT REPEAT NOT AFFECTED BY THIS BROADCAST XX

NUMEROUS ACKNOWLEDGEMENT SIGNALS EMANATED FROM ADDRESSES IN AREAS CITED ABOVE XX ORIGIN AND TRAFFIC ANALYSIS TO FOLLOW XX NOT COMPLETED AT THIS TIME XX BEGINNING AT 1OOOOOZ NSA MONITOR STATIONS [DELETED] [DELETED] AND [DELETED] RECORDED INCREASED HF AND VHF TRAFFIC AT REDFLEET BASES POLYARNYY SEVEROMORSK PECHENGA TALLINN KRONSTADT AND EASTERN MED AREA XX ADDITIONAL HF AND VHF TRAFFIC FROM REDFLEET ASSETS AT SEA XX AMPLIFICATION TO FOLLOW XX

EVALUATION: A MAJOR UNPLANNED REDFLEET OPERATION HAS BEEN ORDERED WITH FLEET ASSETS REPORTING AVAILABILITY AND STATUS XX

END BULLETIN

NSA SENDS

1022152

BREAKBREAK

Ryan looked at his watch. 'Fast work by the boys at NSA, and fast work by our duty watch officers, getting everybody up.' He drained his mug and went over for a refill. 'What's the word on signal traffic analysis?'

'Here.' Greer handed him a second telex sheet.

Ryan scanned it. 'That's a lot of ships. Must be nearly everything they have at sea. Not much on the ones in port, though.'

'Landline,' Greer observed. 'The ones in port can phone fleet ops, Moscow. By the way, that *is* every ship they have at sea in the Western Hemisphere. Every damned one. Any ideas?'

'Let's see, we have that increased activity in the Barents Sea. Looks like a medium-sized ASW exercise. Maybe they're expanding it. Doesn't explain the increased activity in the Baltic and Med, though. Do they have a war game laid on?'

'Nope. They just finished CRIMSON STORM a month ago.'

Ryan nodded. 'Yeah, they usually take a couple of months to evaluate that much data – and who'd want to play games up there at this time of the year?'

The weather's supposed to be a bitch. Have they ever run a major game in December?'

'Not a big one, but most of these acknowledgements are from submarines, son, and subs don't care a whole lot about the weather.'

'Well, given some other preconditions, you might call this ominous. No idea what the signal said, eh?'

'No. They're using computer-based ciphers, same as us. If the spooks at the NSA can read them, they're not telling me about it.' In theory the National Security Agency came under the titular control of the director of Central Intelligence. In fact it was a law unto itself. 'That's what traffic analysis is all about, Jack. You try to guess intentions by who's talking to whom.'

'Yes, sir, but when everybody's talking to everybody – '

'Anything else on alert? Their army? Voyska PVO?' Ryan referred to the Soviet air defense network.

'Nope, just the fleet. Subs, ships, and naval aviation.'

Ryan stretched. 'That makes it sound like an exercise, sir. We'll want a little more data on what they're doing, though. Have you talked to Admiral Davenport?'

'That's the next step. Haven't had time. I've only been in long enough to shave myself and turn the coffee on.' Greer sat down and set his phone receiver in the desk speaker before punching in the numbers.

'Vice Admiral Davenport.' The voice was curt.

'Morning, Charlie, James here. Did you get that NSA – 976?'

'Sure did, but that's not what got me up. Our SOSUS net went berserk a few hours ago.'

'Oh?' Greer looked at the phone, then at Ryan.

'Yeah, nearly every sub they have at sea just put the pedal to the metal, and all at about the same time.'

'Doing what exactly, Charlie?' Greer prompted.

'We're still figuring that out. It looks like a lot of boats are heading into the North Atlantic. Their units in the Norwegian Sea are racing southwest. Three from the western Med are heading that way, too, but we haven't got a clear picture yet. We need a few more hours.'

'What do they have operating off our coast, sir?' Ryan asked.

'They woke you up, Ryan? Good. Two old *Novembers*. One's a raven conversion doing an ELINT job off the cape. The other one's sitting off King's Bay making a damned nuisance of itself.'

Ryan smiled to himself. An American or allied ship was a *she*; the Russians used the male pronoun for a ship; and the intelligence community usually referred to a Soviet ship as *it*.

'There's a *Yankee* boat,' Davenport went on, 'a thousand miles south of Iceland, and the initial report is that it's heading north. Probably wrong. Reciprocal bearing, transcription error, something like that. We're checking. Must be a goof, because it was heading south earlier.'

Ryan looked up. 'What about their other missile boats?'

'Their *Deltas* and *Typhoons* are in the Barents Sea and the Sea of Okhotsk, as usual. No news on them. Oh, we have attack boats up there, of course, but Gallery doesn't want them to break radio silence, and he's right. So all we have at the moment is the report on the stray *Yankee*.'

'What are we doing, Charlie?' Greer asked.

'Gallery has a general alert out to his boats. They're standing by in case we need to redeploy. NORAD has gone to a slightly increased alert status, they tell me.' Davenport referred to the North American Aerospace Defense Command. 'CINCLANT and CINCPAC fleet staffs are up and running around in circles, like you'd expect. Some extra P-3s are working out of Iceland. Nothing much else at the moment. First we have to figure out what they're up to.'

'Okay, keep me posted.'

'Roger, if we hear anything I'll let you know, and I trust – '

'We will.' Greer killed the phone. He shook a finger at Ryan. 'Don't you go to sleep on me, Jack.'

'On top of this stuff?' Ryan waved his mug.

'You're not concerned, I see.'

'Sir, there's nothing to be concerned about yet. It's what, one in the afternoon over there now? Probably some admiral, maybe old Sergey himself, decided to toss a drill at his boys. He wasn't supposed to be all that pleased with how CRIMSON STORM worked out, and maybe he decided to rattle a few cages – ours included, of course. Hell, their army and air force aren't involved, and it's for damned sure that if they were planning anything nasty the other services would know about it. 'We'll have to keep an eye on this, but so far I don't see anything to – ' Ryan almost said lose sleep over ' – sweat about.'

'How old were you at Pearl Harbour?'

'My father was nineteen, sir. He didn't marry until after the war, and I wasn't the first little Ryan.' Jack smiled. Greer knew all this. 'As I recall you weren't all that old yourself.'

'I was a seaman second on the old *Texas*.' Greer had never made it into that war. Soon after it started he'd been accepted by the Naval Academy. By the time he had graduated from there and finished training at submarine school, the war was almost over. He reached the Japanese coast on his first cruise the day after the war ended. 'But you know what I mean.'

'Indeed I do, sir, and that's why we have the CIA, DIA, NSA, and NRO, among others. If the Russkies can fool all of us, maybe we ought to read up on our Marx.'

'All those subs heading into the Atlantic . . .'

'I feel better with word that the *Yankee* is heading north. They've had enough time to make that a hard piece of data. Davenport probably doesn't want to believe it without confirmation. If Ivan was looking to play hardball, that *Yankee*'d be heading south. The missiles on those old boats can't reach very far. Sooo – we stay up and watch. Fortunately, sir, you make a decent cup of coffee.'

'How does breakfast grab you?'

'Might as well. If we can finish up on the Afghanistan stuff maybe I can fly back tomorr – tonight.'

'You still might. Maybe this way you'll learn to sleep on the plane.'

Breakfast was sent up twenty minutes later. Both men were accustomed to big ones, and the food was surprisingly good. Ordinarily CIA cafeteria food was government-undistinguished, and Ryan wondered if the night crew, with fewer people to serve, might take the time to do their job right. Or maybe they had sent out for it. The two men sat around until Davenport phoned at quarter to seven.

'It's definite. All the boomers are heading towards port. We have good tracks on two *Yankees*, three *Deltas*, and a *Typhoon*. *Memphis* reported in when her *Delta* took off for home at twenty knots after being on station for five days, and then Gallery queried *Queenfish*. Same story – looks like they're all headed for the barn. Also we just got some photos from a Big Bird pass over the fjord – for once it wasn't covered with clouds – and we have a bunch of surface ships with bright infrared signatures, like they're getting steam up.'

'How about *Red October*?' Ryan asked.

'Nothing. Maybe our information was bad, and she didn't sail. Wouldn't be the first time.'

'You don't suppose they've lost her?' Ryan wondered aloud.

Davenport had already thought of that. 'That would explain the activity up north, but what about the Baltic and Med business?'

'Two years ago we had that scare with *Tullibee*,' Ryan pointed out. 'And the CNO was so furious he threw an all-hands rescue drill on both oceans.'

'Maybe,' Davenport conceded. The blood in Norfolk was supposed to have been ankle deep after that fiasco. The USS *Tullibee*, a small one-of-a-kind attack sub, had long carried a reputation for bad luck. In this case it had spilled over onto a lot of others.

'Anyway, it looks a whole lot less scary than it did two hours back. They wouldn't be recalling their boomers if they were planning anything against us, would they?' Ryan said.

'I see that Ryan still has your crystal ball, James.'

'That's what I pay him for, Charlie.'

'Still, it is odd,' Ryan commented. 'Why recall all of the missile boats? Have they ever done this before? What about the ones in the Pacific?'

'Haven't heard about those yet,' Davenport replied. 'I've asked CINCPAC for data, but they haven't gotten back to me yet. On the other question, no, they've never recalled all their boomers at once, but they do occasionally reshuffle all their positions at once. That's probably what this is. I said they're heading towards port, not into it. We won't know that for a couple of days.'

'What if they're afraid they've lost one?' Ryan ventured.

'No such luck,' Davenport scoffed. 'They haven't lost a boomer since that *Golf* we lifted off Hawaii, back when you were in high school, Ryan. Ramius is too good a skipper to let that happen.'

So was Captain Smith of the *Titanic*, Ryan thought.

'Thanks for the info, Charlie.' Greer hung up. 'Looks like you were right, Jack. Nothing to worry about yet. Let's get that data on Afghanistan in here – and just for the hell of it, we'll look at Charlie's pictures of their Northern Fleet when we're finished.'

Ten minutes later a messenger arrived with a cart from central files. Greer was the sort who liked to see the raw data himself. This suited Ryan. He'd known of a few analysts who had based their reports on selective data and been cut off at the knees for it by this man. The information on the cart was from a variety of sources, but to Ryan the most significant were tactical radio intercepts from listening posts on the Pakistani border, and, he gathered, from inside Afghanistan itself. The nature and tempo of Soviet operations did not indicate a backing off, as seemed to be suggested by a pair of recent articles in *Red Star* and some intelligence sources inside the Soviet Union. They spent three hours reviewing the data.

'I think Sir Basil is placing too much stock in political intelligence and too little in what our listening posts are getting in the field. It would not be unprecedented for the Soviets not to let their field commanders know what's going on in Moscow, of course, but on the whole I do not see a clear picture,' Ryan concluded.

The admiral looked at him. 'I pay you for answers, Jack.'

'Sir, the truth is that Moscow moved in there by mistake. We know that from both military and political intelligence reports. The tenor of the data is pretty clear. From where I sit, I don't see that *they* know what they want to do. In a case like this the bureaucratic mind finds it most easy to do nothing. So, their field commanders are told to continue the mission, while the senior party bosses fumble around looking for a solution and covering their asses for getting into the mess in the first place.'

'Okay, so we know that we don't know.'

'Yes, sir. I don't like it either, but saying anything else would be a lie.'

The admiral snorted. There was a lot of that at Langley, intelligence types giving answers when they didn't even know the questions. Ryan was still new enough to the game that when he didn't know, he said so. Greer wondered if that would change in time. He hoped not.

After lunch a package arrived by messenger from the National Reconnaissance Office. It contained the photographs taken earlier in the day on two successive passes by a KH-II satellite. They'd be the last such photos for a while because of the restrictions imposed on orbital mechanics and the generally miserable weather on the Kola Peninsula. The first set of visible light shots taken an hour after the FLASH signal had gone out from Moscow showed the fleet at anchor or tied to the docks. On infrared a number of them were glowing brightly from internal heat, indicating that their boilers or gas-turbine engines were operating. The second set of photos had been taken on the next orbital pass at a very low angle.

Ryan scrutinized the blowups. 'Wow! *Kirov, Moska, Kiev,* three *Karas,* five *Krestas,* four *Krivaks*, eight *Udaloys*, and five *Sovremennys.*'

'Search and rescue exercise, eh?' Greer gave Ryan a hard look. 'Look at the bottom here. Every fast oiler they have is following them out. That's most of the striking force of the Northern Fleet right there, and if they need oilers, they figure to be out for a while.'

'Davenport could have been more specific. But we still have their boomers heading back in. No amphibious ships in this photo, just combatants. Only the new ones, too, the ones with range and speed.'

'And the best weapons.'

'Yeah,' Ryan nodded. 'And all scrambled in a few hours. Sir, if they had this planned in advance, we'd have known about it. This must have been laid on today. Interesting.'

'You've picked up the English habit of understatement, Jack.' Greer stood up to stretch. 'I want you to stay over an extra day.'

'Okay sir.' He looked at his watch. 'Mind if I phone the wife? I don't want her to drive out to the airport for a plane I'm not on.'

'Sure, and after you're finished that, I want you to go down and see someone at DIA who used to work for me. See how much operational data they're getting on this sortie. If this is a drill, we'll know soon enough, and you can still take your Surfing Barbie home tomorrow.'

It was a Skiing Barbie, but Ryan didn't say so.

The Sixth Day

Wednesday, 8 December

CIA Headquarters

Ryan had been to the office of the director of central intelligence several times before to deliver briefings and occasional personal messages from Sir Basil Charleston to his highness, the DCI. It was larger than Greer's, with a better view of the Potomac Valley, and appeared to have been decorated by a professional in a style compatible with the DCI's origins. Arthur Moore was a former judge of the Texas State Supreme Court, and the room reflected his southwestern heritage. He and Admiral Greer were sitting on a sofa near the picture windows. Greer waved Ryan over and passed him a folder.

The folder was made of red plastic and had a snap closure. Its edges were bordered with white tape and the cover had a simple white paper label bearing the legends EYES ONLY Δ and WILLOW. Neither notation was unusual. A computer in the basement of the Langley headquarters selected random names at the touch of a key; this prevented a foreign agent from inferring anything from the name of an operation. Ryan opened the folder and looked first at the index sheet. Evidently there were only three copies of the WILLOW document, each initialled by its owner. This one was initialled by the DCI himself. A CIA document with only three copies was unusual enough that Ryan, whose highest clearance was NEBULA, had never encountered one. From the grave looks of Moore and Greer, he guessed that these were two of the Δ-cleared officers; the other, he assumed, was the deputy director of operations (DDO), another Texan named Robert Ritter.

Ryan turned the index sheet. The report was a xeroxed copy of something that had been typed on a manual machine, and it had too many strikeovers to have been done by a real secretary. If Nancy Cummings and the other elite executive secretaries had not been allowed to see this . . . Ryan looked up.

'It's all right, Jack,' Greer said. 'You've just been cleared for 'WILLOW.'

Ryan sat back, and despite his excitement began to read the document slowly and carefully.

The agent's code name was actually CARDINAL. The highest ranking agent-in-place the CIA had ever had, he was the stuff that legends are made of. CARDINAL had been recruited more than twenty years earlier by Oleg Penkovskiy. Another legend – a dead one – Penkovskiy had at the time been a colonel in the GRU, the Soviet military intelligence agency, a larger and more active counterpart to America's Defense Intelligence Agency (DIA). His position had given him access to daily information on all facets of the Soviet military, from the Red Army's command structure to the operational status of intercontinental missiles. The information he smuggled out through his British contact, Greville Wynne, was supremely valuable, and Western countries had come to depend on it – too much. Penkovskiy was discovered during the Cuban Missile Crisis in 1962. It was his data, ordered and delivered under great pressure and haste, that told President Kennedy that Soviet strategic systems were not ready for war. This information enabled the president to back Khrushchev into a corner from which there was no easy exit. The famous blink ascribed to Kennedy's steady nerves was, as in many such events throughout history, facilitated by his ability to see the other man's cards. This advantage was given him by a courageous agent whom he would never meet. Penkovskiy's response to the FLASH request from Washington was too rash. Already under suspicion, this finished him. He paid for his treason with his life. It was CARDINAL who first learned that he was being watched more closely than was the norm for a society where everyone is watched. He warned Penkovskiy – too late. When it became clear that the colonel could not be extracted from the Soviet Union, he himself urged CARDINAL to betray him. It was the final ironic joke of a brave man that his own death would advance the career of an agent whom he had recruited.

CARDINAL's job was necessarily as secret as his name. A senior adviser and confidant of a Politburo member, CARDINAL often acted as his representative within the Soviet military establishment. He thus had access to political and military intelligence of the highest order. This made his information extraordinarily valuable – and, paradoxically, highly suspect. Those few experienced CIA case officers who knew of him found it impossible to believe that he had not been 'turned' somewhere along the line by one of the thousands of KGB counterintelligence officers whose sole duty it is to watch everyone and everything. For this reason CARDINAL-coded material was generally cross-checked against the reports of other spies and sources. But he had outlived many small-fry agents.

The name CARDINAL was known in Washington only to the top three CIA executives. On the first day of each month a new code name was chosen for his data, a name made known only to the highest echelon of CIA officers and analysts. This month it was WILLOW. Before being passed on, grudgingly, to outsiders, CARDINAL data was laundered as carefully as Mafia income to disguise its source. There were also a number of security measures that protected the agent and were unique to him. For fear of cryptographic exposure of his identity, CARDINAL material was hand delivered, never transmitted by radio or landline. CARDINAL himself was a very careful man – Penkovskiy's fate had taught him that. His information was conveyed through a series of intermediaries to the chief of the CIA's Moscow station. He had outlived twelve station chiefs; one of these, a retired field officer, had a brother who was a Jesuit. Every morning the priest, an instructor in philosophy and theology at Fordham University in New York, said mass for the safety and the soul of a man whose name he would never know. It was as good an explanation as any for CARDINAL's continued survival.

Four separate times he had been offered extraction from the Soviet Union. Each time he had refused. To some this was proof that he'd been turned, but to others it was proof that like most successful agents CARDINAL was a man driven by something he alone knew – and therefore, like most successful agents, he was probably a little crazy.

The document Ryan was reading had been in transit for twenty hours. It had taken five for the film to reach the American embassy in Moscow, where it was delivered at once to the station chief. An experienced field officer and former reporter for the *New York Times*, he worked under the cover of press attaché. He developed the film himself in his private darkroom. Thirty minutes after its arrival, he inspected the five exposed frames through a magnifying glass and sent a FLASH-priority dispatch to Washington saying that a CARDINAL signal was en route. Next he transcribed the message from the film to flash paper on his own portable typewriter, translating from the Russian as he went. This security measure erased both the agent's handwriting and, by the paraphrasing automatic to translation, any personal peculiarities of his language. The film was then burned to ashes, the report folded into a metal container much like a cigarette case. This held a small pyrotechnic charge that would go off if the case were improperly opened or suddenly shaken; two CARDINAL signals had been lost when their cases were accidentally dropped. Next the station chief took the case to the embassy's courier-in-residence, who had already been booked on a three-hour Aeroflot flight to London. At Heathrow Airport the courier sprinted to make connections with a Pan Am 747 to New York's Kennedy International, where he connected with the Eastern shuttle to Washington's National Airport. By eight that morning the diplomatic bag was in the State Department. There a CIA officer removed the case, drove it immediately to Langley, and handed it to the DCI. It was opened by an instructor from the CIA's technical services branch. The DCI made three copies on his personal Xerox machine and burned the flash paper in his ashtray. These security measures had struck a few of the men who had succeeded to the office of the DCI as laughable. The laughs had never outlasted the first CARDINAL report.

When Ryan finished the report he referred back to the second page and read it through again, shaking his head slowly. The WILLOW document was the strongest reinforcement yet of his desire not to know how intelligence information reached him. He closed the folder and handed it back to Admiral Greer.

'Christ, sir.'

'Jack, I know I don't have to say this – but what you have just read, nobody, not the president, not Sir Basil, not God if He asks, *nobody* learns of it without the authorisation of the director. Is that understood?' Greer had not lost his command voice.

'Yes, sir.' Ryan bobbed his head like a schoolboy.

Judge Moore pulled a cigar from his jacket pocket and lit it, looking past the flame into Ryan's eyes. The judge, everyone said, had been a hell of a field officer in his day. He'd worked with Hans Tofte during the Korean War and had been instrumental in bringing off one of the CIA's legendary missions, the disappearance of a Norwegian ship that had been carrying a cargo of medical personnel and supplies for the Chinese. The loss had delayed a Chinese offensive for several months, saving thousands of American and allied lives. But it had been a bloody operation. All of the Chinese personnel and all of the Norwegian crewmen had vanished. It was a bargain in the simple mathematics of war, but the morality of the mission was another matter. For this reason, or perhaps another, Moore had soon thereafter left government service to become a trial lawyer in his native Texas. His career had been spectacularly successful, and he'd advanced from wealthy courtroom lawyer to distinguished appellate judge. He had been recalled to the CIA three years earlier because of his unique combination of absolute personal integrity and experience in black operations. Judge Moore hid a Harvard law degree and a highly ordered mind behind the facade of a West Texas cowboy, something he had never been but simulated with ease.

'So, Dr Ryan, what do you think of this?' Moore said as the deputy director of operations came in. 'Hi, Bob, come on over here. We just showed Ryan here the WILLOW file.'

'Oh?' Ritter slid a chair over, neatly trapping Ryan in the corner. 'And what does the admiral's fair-haired boy think of that?'

'Gentlemen, I assume that you all regard this information as genuine,' Ryan said cautiously, getting nods. 'Sir, if this information was hand delivered by the Archangel Michael, I'd have trouble believing it – but since you gentlemen say it's reliable . . .' They wanted his opinion. The problem was, his conclusion was too incredible. Well, he decided, I've gotten this far by giving my honest opinions . . .

Ryan took a deep breath and gave them his evaluation.

'Very well, Dr Ryan,' Judge Moore nodded sagaciously. 'First I want to hear what else it might be, then I want you to defend your analysis.'

'Sir, the most obvious alternative doesn't bear much thinking about. Besides, they've been able to do it since Friday and they haven't done it,' Ryan said, keeping his voice low and reasonable. Ryan had trained himself to be objective. He ran through the four alternatives he had considered, careful to examine each in detail. This was no time to allow personal views to intrude on his thinking. He spoke for ten minutes.

'I suppose there's one more possibility, Judge,' he concluded. 'This could be disinformation aimed at blowing this source. I cannot evaluate that possibility.'

'The thought has occurred to us. All right, now that you've gone this far, you might as well give your operational recommendation.'

'Sir, the admiral can tell you what the navy'll say.'

'I sorta figured that one out, boy,' Moore laughed. 'What do you think?'

'Judge, setting up the decision tree on this will not be easy – there are too many variables, too many possible contingencies. But I'd say yes. If it's possible, if we can work out the details, we ought to try. The biggest question is the availability of our own assets. Do we have the pieces in place?'

Greer answered. 'Our assets are slim. One carrier, *Kennedy*. I checked. *Saratoga's* in Norfolk with an engineering casualty. On the other hand, HMS *Invincible* was just over here for that NATO exercise, sailed from Norfolk Monday night. Admiral White, I believe, commanding a small battle group.'

'Lord White, sir?' Ryan asked. 'The Earl of Weston?'

'You know him?' Moore asked.

'Yes, sir. Our wives are friendly. I shot grouse with him in Scotland last September. He makes noises like a good operator, and I hear he has a good reputation.'

'You're thinking we might want to borrow their ships, James?' Moore asked. 'If so, we'll have to tell them about this. But we have to tell our side first. There's a meeting of the National Security Council at one this afternoon. Ryan, you will prepare the briefing papers and deliver the briefing yourself.'

Ryan blinked. 'That's not much time, sir.'

'James here says you work well under pressure. Prove it.' He looked at Greer. 'Get a copy of his briefing papers and be ready to fly to London. That's the president's decision. If we want their boats, we'll have to tell them why. That means briefing the prime minister, and that's your job. Bob, I want you to confirm this report. Do what you have to do, but do not get WILLOW involved.'

'Right,' Ritter replied.

Moore looked at his watch. 'We'll meet back here at 3:30 depending on how the meeting goes. Ryan, you have ninety minutes. Get cracking.'

What am I being measured for? Ryan wondered. There was talk in the CIA that Judge Moore would be leaving soon for a comfortable ambassadorship, perhaps to the Court of St James's, a fitting reward for a man who had worked long and hard to reestablish a close relationship with the British. If the judge left, Admiral Greer would probably move into this office. He had the virtues of age – he wouldn't be around that long – and of friends on Capitol Hill. Ritter had neither. He had complained too long and too openly about congressmen who leaked information on his operations and his field agents, getting men killed in the process of demonstrating their importance on the local cocktail circuit. He also had an ongoing feud with the chairman of the Select Intelligence Committee.

With that sort of reshuffling at the top and this sudden access to new and fantastic information . . . What does it mean for me? Ryan asked himself. They couldn't want him to be the next DDI. He knew he didn't have anything like the experience required for that job – though maybe in another five or six years . . .

Reykjanes Ridge

Ramius inspected his status board. The *Red October* was heading southwest on track eight, the westernmost surveyed route on what Northern Fleet submariners called Gorshkov's Railroad. His speed was thirteen knots. It never occurred to him that this was an unlucky number, an Anglo-Saxon superstition. They would hold this course and speed for another twenty hours. Immediately behind him, Kamarov was seated at the submarine's gravitometer board, a large rolled chart behind him. The young lieutenant was chain-smoking, and looked tense as he ticked off their position on the chart. Ramius did not disturb him. Kamarov knew his job, and Borodin would relieve him in another two hours.

Installed in the *Red October's* keel was a highly sensitive device called a gradiometer, essentially two large lead weights separated by a space of one hundred yards. A laser-computer system measured the space between the weights down to a fraction of an angstrom. Distortions of that distance or lateral movement of the weights indicated variations in the local gravitational field. The navigator compared these highly precise local values to the values of his chart. With careful use of gravitometers in the ship's inertial navigation system, he could plot the vessel's location to within a hundred metres, half the length of the ship.

The mass-sensing system was being added to all the submarines that could accommodate it. Younger attack boat commanders, Ramius knew, had used it to run the Railroad at high speed. Good for the commander's ego, Ramius judged, but a little hard on the navigator. He felt no need for recklessness. Perhaps the letter had been a mistake . . . No, it prevented second thoughts. And the sensor suites on attack submarines simply were not good enough to detect the *Red October* so long as he maintained his silent routine. Ramius was certain of this; he had used them all. He would get where he wanted to go, do what he wanted to do, and nobody, not his own countrymen, not even the Americans, would be able to do a thing about it. That's why earlier he had listened to the passage of an *Alfa* thirty miles to his east and smiled.

The White House

Judge Moore's CIA car was a Cadillac limousine that came with a driver and a security man who kept an Uzi submachinegun under the dashboard. The driver turned right off Pennsylvania Avenue onto Executive Drive. More a parking lot than a street, this served the needs of senior officials and reporters who worked at the White House and the Executive Office Building, 'Old State,' that shining example of Institutional Grotesque that towered over the executive mansion. The driver pulled smoothly into a vacant VIP slot and jumped out to open the doors after the security man had swept the area with his eyes. The judge got out first and went ahead, and as Ryan caught up he found himself walking on the man's left, half a step behind. It took a moment to remember that this instinctive action was exactly what the marine corps had taught him at Quantico was the proper way for a junior officer to accompany his betters. It forced Ryan to consider just how junior he was.

'Ever been in here before, Jack?'

'No, sir, I haven't.'

Moore was amused. 'That's right, you come from around here. Now, if you came from farther away, you'd have made the trip a few times.' A marine guard held the door open for them. Inside a Secret Service agent signed them in. Moore nodded and walked on.

'Is this to be in the Cabinet Room, sir?'

'Uh-uh. Situation Room, downstairs. It's more comfortable and better equipped for this sort of thing. The slides you need are already down there, all set up. Nervous?'

'Yes, sir, I sure am.'

Moore chuckled. 'Settle down, boy. The president has wanted to meet you for some time now. He liked that report on terrorism you did a few years back, and I've shown him some more of your work, and the one on Russian missile submarine operations, and the one you just did on management practices in their arms industries. All in all, I think you'll find he's a pretty regular guy. Just be ready when he asks questions. He'll hear every word you say, and he has a way of hitting you with good ones when he wants.' Moore turned to descend a staircase. Ryan followed him down three flights, then they came to a door which led to a corridor. The judge turned left and walked to yet another door, this one guarded by another Secret Service agent.

'Afternoon, Judge. The president will be down shortly.'

'Thank you. This is Dr Ryan. I'll vouch for him.'

'Right.' The agent waved them in.

It was not nearly as spectacular as Ryan had expected. The Situation Room was probably no larger than the Oval Office upstairs. There was expensive-looking wood panelling over what were probably concrete walls. This part of the White House dated back to the complete rebuilding job done under Truman. Ryan's lectern was to his left as he went in. It stood in front and slightly to the right of a roughly diamond-shaped table, and behind it was the projection screen. A note on the lectern said the slide projector in the middle of the table was ready loaded and focused, and gave the order of the slides, which had been delivered from the National Reconnaissance Office.

Most of the people were already here, all of the Joint Chiefs of Staff and the secretary of defence. The secretary of state, he remembered, was still shuttling back and forth between Athens and Ankara trying to settle the latest Cyprus situation. This perennial thorn in NATO's southern flank had flared up a few weeks earlier when a Greek student had run over a Turkish child with his car and been killed by a gang minutes later. By the end of the day fifty people had been injured, and the putatively allied countries were once more at each other's throats. Now two American aircraft carriers were cruising the Aegean as the secretary of state laboured to calm both sides. It was bad enough that two young people had died, Ryan thought, but not something to get a country's army mobilised for.

Also at the table were General Thomas Hilton, chairman of the Joint Chiefs of Staff, and Jeffrey Pelt, the president's national security adviser, a pompous man Ryan had met years before at Georgetown University's Centre for Strategic and International Studies. Pelt was going through some papers and dispatches. The chiefs were chatting amicably among themselves when the commandant of the marine corps looked up and spotted Ryan. He got up and walked over.

'You Jack Ryan?' General David Maxwell asked.

'Yes, sir.' Maxwell was a short, tough fireplug of a man whose stubbly haircut seemed to spark with aggressive energy. He looked Ryan over before shaking hands.

'Pleased to meet you, son. I liked what you did over in London. Good for the corps.' He referred to the terrorist incident in which Ryan had very nearly been killed. 'That was good, quick action you took, Lieutenant.'

'Thank you, sir. I was lucky.'

'Good officer's supposed to be lucky. I hear you got some interesting news for us.'

'Yes sir. I think you will find it worth your time.'

'Nervous?' The general saw the answer and smiled thinly. 'Relax, son. Everybody in this damned cellar puts his pants on the same way as you.' He backhanded Ryan to the stomach and went back to his seat. The general whispered something to Admiral Daniel Foster, chief of naval operations. The CNO looked Ryan over for a moment before going back to what he was doing.

The president arrived a minute later. Everyone in the room stood as he walked to his chair, on Ryan's right. He said a few quick things to Dr Pelt, then looked pointedly at the DCI.

'Gentlemen, if we can bring this meeting to order, I think Judge Moore has some news for us.'

'Thank you, Mr President. Gentlemen, we've had an interesting development today with respect to the Soviet naval operation that started yesterday. I have asked Dr Ryan here to deliver the briefing.'

The president turned to Ryan. The younger man could feel himself being appraised. 'You may proceed.'

Ryan took a sip of ice water from a glass hidden in the lectern. He had a wireless control for the slide projector and a choice of pointers. A separate high-intensity light illuminated his notes. The pages were full of errors and scribbled corrections. There had not been time to edit the copy.

'Thank you, Mr President. Gentlemen, my name is Jack Ryan, and the subject of this briefing is recent Soviet naval activity in the North Atlantic. Before I get to that it will be necessary for me to lay a little groundwork. I trust you will bear with me for a few minutes, and please feel free to interrupt with questions at any time.' Ryan clicked on the slide projector. The overhead lights near the screen dimmed automatically.

'These photographs come to us courtesy of the British,' Ryan said. He now had everyone's attention. 'The ship you see here is the Soviet fleet ballistic missile submarine *Red October*, photographed by a British agent in her dock at their submarine base at Polyarnyy, near Murmansk in northern Russia. As you can see, she is a very large vessel, about 650 feet long, a beam of roughly 85 feet, and an estimated submerged displacement of 32,000 tons. These figures are roughly comparable to those of a World War I battleship.'

Ryan lifted a pointer. 'In addition to being considerably larger than our own *Ohio*-class Trident submarines, *Red October* has a number of technical differences. She carries twenty-six missiles instead of our twenty-four. The earlier *Typhoon*-class vessels, from which she was developed, only have twenty. *October* carries the new SS-N-20 sea-launched ballistic missile, the Seahawk. It's a solid-fuel missile with a range of about six thousand nautical miles, and it carries eight multiple independently targetable re-entry vehicles, MIRV's, each with an estimated yield of five hundred kilotons. It's the same RV carried by their SS-18s, but there are less of them per launcher.

'As you can see, the missile tubes are located forward of the sail instead of aft, as in our subs. The forward diving planes fold into slots in the hull here; ours go on the sail. She has twin screws; ours have one propeller. And finally, her hull is oblate. Instead of being cylindrical like ours, it is flattened out markedly top and bottom.'

Ryan clicked to the next slide. It showed two views superimposed, bow over stern. 'These frames were delivered to us undeveloped. They were processed by the National Reconnaissance Office. Please note the doors here at the bow and here at the stern. The British were a little puzzled by these, and that's why I was permitted to bring the shots over earlier this week. We weren't able to figure out their function at the CIA either, and it was decided to seek the opinion of an outside consultant.'

'Who decided?' the secretary of defence demanded angrily. 'Hell, I haven't even seen them yet!'

'We only got them Monday, Bert,' Judge Moore replied soothingly. 'These two on the screen are only four hours old. Ryan suggested an outside expert, and James Greer approved it. I concurred.'

'His name is Oliver W. Tyler. Dr Tyler is a former naval officer who is now associate professor of engineering at the Naval Academy and a paid consultant to Sea Systems Command. He's an expert in the analysis of Soviet naval technology. Skip – Dr Tyler – concluded that these doors are the intake and exhaust vents for a new silent propulsion system. He is currently developing a computer model of the system, and we hope to have this information by the end of the week. The system itself is rather interesting.' Ryan explained Tyler's analysis briefly.

'Okay, Dr Ryan.' The president leaned forward. 'You've just told us that the Soviets have built a missile submarine that's supposed to be hard for our men to locate. I don't suppose that's news. Go on.'

'*Red October's* captain is a man named Marko Ramius. That is a Lithuanian name, although we believe his internal passport designates his nationality as Great Russian. He is the son of a high Party official, and as good a submarine commander as they have. He's taken out the lead ship of every Soviet submarine class for the past ten years.

'*Red October* sailed last Friday. We do not know exactly what her orders were, but ordinarily their missile subs – that is, those with the newer long-range missiles – confine their activities to the Barents Sea and adjacent areas in which they can be protected from our attack boats by land-based ASW aircraft, their own surface ships, and attack submarines. About noon local time on Sunday, we noted increased search activity in the Barents Sea. At the time we took this to be a local ASW exercise, and by late Monday it looked to be a test of *October's* new drive system.

'As you all know, early yesterday saw a vast increase in Soviet naval activity. Nearly all of the blue-water ships assigned to their Northern Fleet are now at sea, accompanied by all of their fast fleet-replenishment vessels. Additional fleet auxiliaries sailed from the Baltic Fleet bases and the western Mediterranean. Even more disquieting is the fact that nearly every nuclear submarine assigned to the Northern Fleet – their largest – appears to be heading into the North Atlantic. This includes three from the Med, since submarines there come from the Northern Fleet, not the Black Sea Fleet. Now we think we know why all this happened.' Ryan clicked to the next slide. This one showed the North Atlantic, from Florida to the Pole, with Soviet ships marked in red.

'The day *Red October* sailed, Captain Ramius evidently posted a letter to Admiral Yuri llych Padorin. Padorin is chief of the Main Political Administration of their navy. We do not know what that letter said, but here we can see its results. This began to happen not four hours after that letter was opened. Fifty-eight nuclear-powered submarines and twenty-eight major surface combatants all headed our way. This is a remarkable reaction in four hours. This morning we learned what their orders are.

'Gentlemen, these ships have been ordered to locate *Red October*, and if necessary, to sink her.' Ryan paused for effect. 'As you can see, the Soviet surface force is here, about halfway between the European mainland and Iceland. Their submarines, these in particular, are all heading southwest towards the US coast. Please note, there is no unusual activity on the Pacific side of either country – except we have information that Soviet fleet ballistic missile submarines in *both* oceans are being recalled to port.

'Therefore, while we do not know exactly what Captain Ramius said, we can draw some conclusions from these patterns of activity. It would appear that they think he's heading in our direction. Given his estimated speed as something between ten and thirty knots, he could be anywhere from here, below Iceland, to here, just off our coast. You will note that in either case he has successfully avoided detection by all four of these SOSUS barriers –'

'Wait a minute. You say they have issued orders to their ships to sink one of their own submarines?'

'Yes, Mr President.'

The president looked at the DCI. 'This is reliable information, Judge?'

'Yes, Mr President, we believe it to be solid.'

'Okay, Dr Ryan, we're all waiting. What's this Ramius fellow up to?'

'Mr President, our evaluation of this intelligence data is that *Red October* is attempting to defect to the United States.'

The room went very quiet for a moment. Ryan could hear the whirring of the fan in the slide projector as the National Security Council pondered that. He held his hands on the lectern to keep them from shaking under the stare of the ten men in front of him.

'That's a very interesting conclusion, Doctor.' The president smiled. 'Defend it.'

'Mr President, no other conclusion fits the data. The really crucial thing, of course, is the recall of their other missile boats. They've never done that before. Add to that the fact that they have issued orders to sink their newest and most powerful missile sub, and that they are chasing in this direction, and one is left with the conclusion that they think she has left the reservation and is heading this way.'

'Very well. What else could it be?'

'Sir, he could have told them that he's going to fire his missiles. At us, at them, the Chinese, or just about anyone else.'

'And you don't think so?'

'No, Mr President. The SS-N-20 has a range of six thousand miles. That means he could have hit any target in the Northern Hemisphere from the moment he left the dock. He's had six days to do that, but he has not fired. Moreover, if he had threatened to launch his birds, he would have to consider the possibility that the Soviets would enlist our assistance to locate and sink him. After all, if our surveillance systems detect the launch of nuclear-armed missiles in any direction, things could get very tense, very quickly.'

'You know he could fire his birds in both directions and start World War III,' the secretary of defence observed.

'Yes, Mr Secretary. In that case we'd be dealing with a total madman – more than one, in fact. On our missile boats there are five officers, who must all agree and act in unison to fire their missiles. The Soviets have the same number. For political reasons their nuclear warhead security procedures are even more elaborate than ours. Five or more people, all of whom wish to end the world?' Ryan shook his head. 'That seems most unlikely, sir, and again, the Soviets would be well advised to inform us and enlist our aid.'

'Do you really think they would inform us?' Dr Pelt asked. His tone indicated what he thought.

'Sir, that's more a psychological question than a technical one, and I deal principally with technical intelligence. Some of the men in this room have met their Soviet counterparts and are better equipped to answer that than I am. My answer to your question, however, is yes. That would be the only rational thing for them to do, and while I do not regard the Soviets as entirely rational by our standards, they are rational by their own. They are not given to this sort of high-stakes gambling.'

'Who is?' the president observed. 'What else might it be?'

'Several things, sir. It could simply be a major naval exercise aimed at testing their ability to close our sea lines of communication and our ability to respond, both on short notice. We reject this possibility for several reasons. It's too soon after their autumn naval exercise, CRIMSON STORM, and they are only using nuclear submarines; no diesel-powered boats seem to be involved. Clearly speed is at a premium in their operation. And as a practical matter, they do not run major exercises at this time of year.'

'And why is that?' the president asked.

Admiral Foster answered for Ryan. 'Mr President, the weather up there at this time of the year is extremely bad. Even we don't schedule exercises under these conditions.'

'I seem to recall we just ran a NATO exercise, Admiral,' Pelt noted.

'Yes, sir, south of Bermuda, where the weather's a lot nicer. Except for an antisub exercise off the British Isles, all of NIFTY DOLPHIN was held on our side of the lake.'

'Okay, let's get back to what else their fleet might be up to,' the president ordered.

'Well, sir, it might not be an exercise at all. It could be the real thing. This could be the beginning of a conventional war against NATO, its first step being interdiction of the sea lines of communication. If so, they've achieved complete strategic surprise and are now throwing it away by operating so overtly that we cannot fail to notice or react forcefully. Moreover, there is no corresponding activity whatever in their other armed services. Their army and air force – except for maritime surveillance aircraft – and the Pacific Fleet are engaged in routine training operations.

'Finally, this could be an attempt to provoke or divert us, drawing our attention to this while they are preparing to spring a surprise somewhere else. If so, they're going about it in a strange way. If you try to provoke somebody, you don't do it in his front yard. The Atlantic, Mr President, is still our ocean. As you can see from this chart, we have allies on both sides of the ocean, and we can establish air superiority over the entire Atlantic if we so choose. Their navy is numerically large, larger than ours in some critical areas, but they cannot project force as well as we can – not yet, anyway – and certainly not right off our coast.' Ryan took a sip of water.

'So, gentlemen, we have a Soviet missile submarine at sea when all the others, in both oceans, are being recalled. We have their fleet at sea with orders to sink that sub, and evidently they are chasing it in our direction. As I said, this is the only conclusion that fits the data.'

'How many men on the sub, Doctor?' the president asked.

'We believe 110 or so, sir.'

'So, 110 men all decide to defect to the United States at one time. Not an altogether bad idea,' the president observed wryly, 'but hardly a likely one.'

Ryan was ready for that. 'There is precedent for this, sir. On November 8, 1975, the *Storozhevoy*, a Soviet *Krivak*-class missile frigate, attempted to run from Riga, Latvia, to the Swedish island of Gotland. The political officer aboard, Valery Sablin, led a mutiny of the enlisted personnel. They locked their officers in their cabins and raced away from the dock. They came close to making it. Air and fleet units attacked them and forced them to halt within fifty miles of Swedish territorial waters. Two more hours and they would have made it. Sablin and twenty-six others were court-martialled and shot. More recently we have had reports of mutinous episodes on several Soviet vessels – especially submarines. In 1980 an *Echo*-class Soviet attack submarine surfaced off Japan. The captain claimed to have had a fire aboard, but photographs taken by naval reconnaissance aircraft – ours and Japanese – did not show smoke or fire-damaged debris being jettisoned from the submarine. However, the crewmen on deck did show sufficient evidence of trauma to support the conclusion that a riot had taken place aboard. We have had similar, sketchier reports for some years now. While I admit this is an extreme example, our conclusion is decidedly not without precedent.'

Admiral Foster reached inside his jacket and came out with a plastic-tipped cigar. His eyes sparkled behind the match. 'You know, I could almost believe this.'

'Then I wish you'd tell us all why, Admiral,' the president said, 'because I still don't.'

'Mr President, most mutinies are led by officers, not enlisted men. The reason for this is simply that the enlisted men do not know how to navigate the ship. Moreover, officers have the advantages and educational background to know that successful rebellion is a possibility. Both of these factors would be even more true in the Soviet Navy. What if just the officers are doing this?'

'And the rest of the crew is going along with them?' Pelt asked. 'Knowing what would happen to them and their families?'

Foster puffed a few times on his cigar. 'Ever been to sea, Dr Pelt? No? Let's imagine for the moment that you're taking a world cruise, on the *Queen Elizabeth 2*, say. One fine day you're in the middle of the Pacific Ocean – but how do you know exactly where you are? You don't know. You know what the officers tell you. Oh, sure, if you know a little astronomy, you might be able to estimate your latitude to within a few hundred miles. With a good watch and some knowledge of spherical trigonometry you might even guess your longitude to within a few hundred. Okay? That's on a ship that you can see from.

'These guys are on a submarine. You can't see a whole lot. Now, what if the officers – not even all the officers – are doing this? How will the crew know what's going on?' Foster shook his head. 'They won't. They can't. Even our guys might not, and our men are trained a lot better than theirs. Their seamen are nearly all conscripts, remember. On a nuclear submarine you are absolutely cut off from the outside world. No radios except for ELF and VLF – and that's all encrypted; messages have to come through the communications officer. So, he has to be in on it. Same thing with the boat's navigator. They use inertial navigation systems, same as us. We have one of theirs, from that *Gold* we lifted off Hawaii. In their machine the data is also encrypted. The quartermaster reads the numbers off the machine, and the navigator gets their position from a book. In the Red Army, on *land*, maps are classified documents. Same thing in their navy. The enlisted men don't get to see charts and are not encouraged to know where they are. This would be especially true on missile submarines, right?

'On top of all that, these guys are working sailors, nucs. When you're at sea, you have a job to do, and you do it. On their ships, that means from fourteen to eighteen hours a day. These kids are all draftees with very simple training. They're taught to perform one or two tasks – and to follow their orders exactly. The Soviets train people to do their jobs by rote, with as little thinking as possible. That's why on major repair jobs you see officers holding tools. Their men will have neither the time nor the inclination to question their officers about what's going on. You do your job, and depend on everybody else to do his. That's what discipline at sea is all about.' Foster tapped his cigar ash into an ashtray. 'Yes, sir, you get the officers together, maybe not even all of them, and this would work. Getting ten or twelve dissidents together is a whole lot easier than assembling a hundred.'

'Easier, but hardly easy, Dan,' General Hilton objected. 'For Christ's sake, they have at least one political officer aboard, plus moles from their intelligence outfits. You really think a Party hack would go along with this?'

'Why not? You heard Ryan – that frigate's mutiny was led by the political officer.'

'Yeah, and since then they have shaken up that whole directorate,' Hilton responded.

'We have defecting KGB types all the time, all good Party members,' Foster said. Clearly he liked the idea of a defecting Russian sub.

The president took all this in, then turned to Ryan. 'Dr Ryan, you have managed to persuade me that your scenario is a theoretical possibility. Now, what does the CIA think we ought to do about it?'

'Mr President, I'm an intelligence analyst, not – '

'I know very well what you are, Dr Ryan. I've read enough of your work. I can see you have an opinion. I want to hear it.'

Ryan didn't even look at Judge Moore. 'We grab her, sir.'

'Just like that?'

'No, Mr President, probably not. However, Ramius could surface off the Virginia Capes in a day or two and request political asylum. We ought to be prepared for that contingency, sir, and my opinion is that we should welcome him with open arms.' Ryan saw nods from all the chiefs. Finally somebody was on his side.

'You've stuck your neck out on this one,' the president observed kindly.

'Sir, you asked me for an opinion. It will probably not be that easy. These *Alfas* and *Victors* appear to be racing for our coast, almost certainly with the intention of establishing an interdiction force – effectively a blockade of our Atlantic cost.'

'*Blockade*,' the president said, 'an ugly word.'

'Judge,' General Hilton said, 'I suppose it's occurred to you that this is a piece of disinformation aimed at blowing whatever highly placed source generated this report?'

Judge Moore affected a sleepy smile. 'It has, General. If this is a sham, it's a damned elaborate one. Dr Ryan was directed to prepare this briefing on the assumption that this data is genuine. If it is not, the responsibility is mine.' God bless you, Judge, Ryan said to himself, wondering just how gold-plated the WILLOW source was. The judge went on, 'In any case, gentlemen, we will have to respond to this Soviet activity whether our analysis is accurate or not.'

'Are you getting confirmation of this, Judge?' the president asked.

'Yes, sir, we are working on that.'

'Good.' The president was sitting straight, and Ryan noted his voice become crisper. 'The judge is correct. We have to react to this, whatever they're really up to. Gentlemen, the Soviet Navy is heading for our coast. What are we doing about it?'

Admiral Foster answered first. 'Mr President, our fleet is putting to sea at this moment. Everything that'll steam is out already, or will be by tomorrow night. We've recalled our carriers from the South Atlantic, and we are redeploying our nuclear submarines to deal with this threat. We began this morning to saturate the air over their surface force with P-3C Orion patrol aircraft, assisted by British Nimrods operating out of Scotland. General?' Foster turned to Hilton.

'At this moment we have E-3A Sentry AWACS-type aircraft circling them along with Dan's Orions, both accompanied by F-15 Eagle fighters out of Iceland. By this time Friday we'll have a squadron of B-52s operating from Loring Air Force Base in Maine. These will be armed with Harpoon air-to-surface missiles, and they'll be orbiting the Soviets in relays. Nothing aggressive, you understand,' Hilton smiled. 'Just to let them know we're interested. If they continue to come this way, we will redeploy some tactical air assets to the East Coast, and, subject to your approval, we can activate some national guard and reserve squadrons quietly.'

'Just how will you do that quietly?' Pelt asked.

'Dr Pelt, we have a number of guard outfits scheduled to run through our Red Flag facility at Nellis in Nevada starting this Sunday, a routine training rotation. They go to Maine instead of Nevada. The bases are pretty big, and they belong to SAC.' Hilton referred to the Strategic Air Command. 'They have good security.'

'How many carriers do we have handy?' the president asked.

'Only one at the moment, sir, *Kennedy*. *Saratoga* stripped a main turbine last week, and it'll take a month to replace. *Nimitz* and *America* are both in the South Atlantic right now, *America* coming back from the Indian Ocean, *Nimitz* heading out to the Pacific. Bad luck. Can we recall a carrier from the eastern Med?'

'No.' The president shook his head. 'This Cyprus thing is still too sensitive. Do we really need to? If anything . . . untoward happens, can we handle their surface force with what we have at hand?'

'Yes, sir!' General Hilton said at once. 'Dr Ryan said it: the Atlantic is our ocean. The air force alone will have over five hundred aircraft designated for this operation, and another three or four hundred from the navy. If any sort of shooting match develops, that Soviet fleet will have an exciting and short life.'

'We will try to avoid that, of course,' the president said quietly. 'The first press reports surfaced this morning. We had a call from Bud Wilkins of the *Times* right before lunch. If the American people find out too soon what the scope of this is . . . Jeff?'

'Mr President, let's assume for the moment that Dr Ryan's analysis is correct. I don't see what we can do about it,' Pelt said.

'What?' Ryan blurted. 'I, ah, beg your pardon, sir.'

'We can't exactly steal a Russian missile sub.'

'Why not!' Foster demanded. 'Hell, we have enough of their tanks and aircraft.' The other chiefs agreed.

'An aircraft with a crew of one or two is one thing, Admiral. A nuclear-powered submarine with twenty-six rockets and a crew of over a hundred is something else. Naturally, we can give asylum to the defecting officers.'

'So, you're saying that if the thing does come sailing into Norfolk,' Hilton joined in, 'we give it back! Christ, man, it carries two hundred warheads! They just might use those goddamned things against us someday, you know. Are you sure you want to give them back?'

'That's a billion-dollar asset, General,' Pelt said diffidently .

Ryan saw the president smile. He was said to like lively discussions. 'Judge, what are the legal ramifications?'

'That's admiralty law, Mr President.' Moore looked uneasy for once. 'I've never had an admiralty practice, takes me all the way back to law school. Admiralty is *jus gentium* – the same legal codes theoretically apply to all countries. American and British admiralty courts routinely cite each other's rulings. But as for the rights that attach to a mutinous crew – I have no idea.'

'Judge, we are not dealing with mutiny or piracy,' Foster noted. 'The correct term is *barratry*, I believe. Mutiny is when the crew rebels against lawful authority. Gross misconduct of the officers is called barratry. Anyway, I hardly think we need to attach legal folderol to a situation involving nuclear weapons.'

'We might, Admiral,' the president mused. 'As Jeff said, this is a highly valuable asset, legally their property, and they will know we have her. I think we are agreed that not all the crew is likely to be in on this. If so, those not party to the mutiny – barratry, whatever – will want to return home after it's all over. And we'll have to let them go, won't we?'

'Have to?' General Maxwell was doodling on a pad. 'Have to?'

'General,' the president said firmly, 'we will not, repeat *not*, be party to the imprisonment or murder of men whose only desire is to return to home and family. Is that understood?' He looked around the table. 'If they know we have her, they'll want her back. And they will know we have her from the crewmen who want to return home. In any case, big as this thing is, how could we hide her?'

'We might be able to,' Foster said neutrally, 'but as you say, the crew is a complication. I presume we'll have the chance to look her over?'

'You mean conduct a quarantine inspection, check her for seaworthiness, maybe make sure they're not smuggling drugs into the country?' The president grinned. 'I think we might arrange that. But we are getting ahead of ourselves. There's a lot of ground to cover before we get to that point. What about our allies?'

'The English just had one of their carriers over here. Could you use her, Dan?' General Hilton asked.

'If they let us borrow her, yes. We just finished that ASW exercise south of Bermuda, and the Brits acquitted themselves well. We could use *Invincible*, the four escorts, and the three attack boats. The force is being recalled at high speed because of this.'

'Do they know of this development, Judge?' the president asked.

'Not unless they've developed it themselves. This information is only a few hours old.' Moore did not reveal that Sir Basil had his own ear in the Kremlin. Ryan didn't know much about it himself, had only heard some disconnected rumblings. 'With your permission, I have asked Admiral Greer to be ready to fly to England to brief the prime minister.'

'Why not just send – '

Judge Moore was shaking his head. 'Mr President, this information – let's say it's only delivered by hand.' Eyebrows went up all around the table.

'When is he leaving?'

'This evening, if you wish. There are a couple of VIP flights leaving Andrews tonight. Congressional flights.' It was the usual end-of-session junket season. Christmas in Europe, on fact-finding missions.

'General, do we have anything quicker?' the president asked Hilton.

'We can scratch up a VC-141. Lockheed JetStar, almost as fast as a -135, and we can have it up in half an hour.'

'Do it.'

'Yes, sir, I'll call that in right now.' Hilton rose and walked to a phone in the corner.

'Judge, tell Greer to pack his bags. I'll have a cover letter waiting for him on the plane to give to the prime minister. Admiral, you want the *Invincible*?'

'Yes, sir.'

'I'll get her for you. Next, what do we tell our people at sea?'

'If *October* just sails in, it won't be necessary, but if we have to communicate with her – '

'Excuse me, Judge,' Ryan said, 'that is rather likely – that we'll have to. They'll probably have these attack boats on the coast before she gets here, If so, we'll have to warn her off if only to save the defecting officers. They are out to locate and sink her.'

'We haven't detected her. What makes you think they can?' Foster asked, miffed at the suggestion.

'They did build her, Admiral. So they might know things about her that will enable them to locate her more easily than us.

'Makes sense,' the president said. 'That means somebody goes out to brief the fleet commanders. We can't broadcast this, can we, Judge?'

'Mr President, this source is too valuable to compromise in any way. That's all I can say here, sir.'

'Very well, somebody flies out. Next thing is, we'll have to talk to the Soviets about this. For the moment they can say that they're operating in home waters. When will they pass Iceland?'

'Tomorrow night, unless they change course,' Foster answered.

'Okay, we give it a day, for them to call this off and for us to confirm this report. Judge, I want something to back up this fairy tale in twenty-four hours. If they haven't turned back by midnight tomorrow, I'll call Ambassador Arbatov into my office Friday morning.' He turned to the chiefs. 'Gentlemen, I want to see contingency plans for dealing with this situation by tomorrow afternoon. We will meet here tomorrow at two. One more thing: *no leaks*! This information does not go beyond this room without my personal approval. If this story breaks to the press, I'll have heads on my desk. Yes, General?'

'Mr President, in order to develop those plans,' Hilton said after sitting back down, 'we have to work through our field commanders and some of our own operations people. Certainly we'll need Admiral Blackburn.' Blackburn was CINCLANT, commander in chief of the Atlantic.

'Let me think that one over. I'll be back to you in an hour. How many people at the CIA know about this?'

'Four, sir. Ritter, Greer, Ryan, and myself, sir. That's all.'

'Keep it that way.' The president had been bedevilled by security leaks for months.

'Yes, Mr President.'

'Meeting is adjourned.'

The president stood. Moore walked around the table to keep him from leaving at once. Dr Pelt stayed also as the rest filed out of the room. Ryan stood outside the door.

'That was all right.' General Maxwell grabbed his hand. He waited until everyone else was a few yards down the hall before going on. 'I think you're crazy, son, but you sure put a burr under Dan Foster's saddle. No, even better: I think he got a hard-on.' The little general chuckled. 'And if we get the sub, maybe we can change the president's mind and arrange for the crew to disappear. The judge did that once, you know.' It was a thought that chilled Ryan as he watched Maxwell swagger down the hall.

'Jack, you want to come back in here a minute?' Moore's voice called.

'You're an historian, right?' the president asked, reviewing his notes. Ryan hadn't even noticed him holding a pen.

'Yes, Mr President. That's what my graduate degree's in.' Ryan shook his hand.

'You have a fine sense of the dramatic, Jack. You would have made a decent trial lawyer.' The president had made his reputation as a hard-driving state's attorney. He had survived an unsuccessful Mafia assassination attempt early in his career which hadn't hurt his political ambitions one bit. 'Damned nice briefing.'

'Thank you, Mr President.' Ryan beamed.

'The judge tells me you know the commander of that British task force.'

It was like a sandbag hitting his head. 'Yes, sir. Admiral White. I've been shooting with him, and our wives are good friends. They're close to the Royal Family.'

'Good. Somebody has to fly out to brief our fleet commander, then go on to talk to the Brits, if we get their carrier, as I expect we will. The judge says we ought to let Admiral Davenport go out with you. So, you fly out to *Kennedy* tonight, then on to *Invincible*.'

'Mr President, I –'

'Come now, Dr Ryan,' Pelt smiled thinly. 'You are uniquely suited to this. You already have access to the intelligence, you know the British commander, and you're a naval intelligence specialist. You fit. Tell me, how eager do you think the navy is about getting this *Red October*?'

'Of course they're interested in it, sir. To get a chance to look at it, better yet to run it, take it apart, and run it some more. It would be the intelligence coup of all time.'

'That's true. But maybe they're a little too eager.'

'I don't understand what you mean, sir,' Ryan said, though he understood it just fine. Pelt was the president's favourite. He was not the Pentagon's favourite.

'They might take a chance that we might not want them to take.'

'Dr Pelt, if you're saying that a uniformed officer would – '

'He's not saying that. At least not exactly. What he's saying is that it might be useful for me to have somebody out there who can give me an independent, civilian point of view.'

'Sir, you don't know me.'

'I've read a lot of your reports.' The chief executive was smiling. It was said he could turn dazzling charm on and off like a spotlight. Ryan was being blinded, knew it, and couldn't do a thing about it. 'I like your work. You have a good feel for things, for facts. Good judgment. Now, one reason I got to where I am is good judgment, too, and I think you can handle what I have in mind. The question is, will you do it, or won't you?'

'Do what, exactly, sir?'

'After you get out there, you stay put for a few days, and report directly to me. Not through channels, directly to me. You'll get the cooperation you need. I'll see to that.'

Ryan didn't say anything. He'd just become a spy, a field officer, by presidential fiat. Worse, he'd be spying on his own side.

'You don't like the idea of reporting on your own people, right? You won't be, not really. Like I said, I want an independent, civilian opinion. We'd prefer to send an experienced case officer out, but we want to minimize the number of people involved in this. Sending Ritter or Greer out would be far too obvious, whereas you, on the other hand, are a relative – '

'Nobody?' Jack asked.

'As far as they're concerned, yes,' Judge Moore replied. 'The Soviets have a file on you. I've seen parts of it. They think you're an upper-class drone, Jack.'

I am a drone, Ryan thought, unmoved by the implicit challenge. *In this company I sure as hell am.*

'Agreed, Mr President. Please forgive me for hesitating. I've never been a field officer before.'

'I understand.' The president was magnanimous in victory. 'One more thing. If I understand how submarines operate, Ramius could just have taken off, not saying anything. Why tip them off? Why the letter? The way I read this, it's counterproductive.'

It was Ryan's turn to smile. 'Ever meet a sub driver, sir? No? How about an astronaut?'

'Sure. I've met a bunch of the Shuttle pilots.'

'They're the same breed of cat, Mr President. As to why he left the letter, there's two parts to that. First, he's probably mad about something, exactly what we'll find out when we see him. Second, he figures he can pull this off regardless of what they try to stop him with – and he wants them to know that. Mr President, the men who drive subs for a living are aggressive, confident, and very, very smart. They like nothing better than making somebody else, a surface ship operator for example, look like an idiot.'

'You just scored another point, Jack. The astronauts I've met, on most things they're downright humble, but they think they're gods when it comes to flying. I'll keep that in mind. Jeff, let's get back to work. Jack, keep me posted.'

Ryan shook his hand again. After the president and his senior adviser left, he turned to Judge Moore. 'Judge, what the hell did you tell him about me?'

'Only the truth, Jack.' Actually, the judge had wanted this operation to be run by one of the CIA's senior case officers. Ryan had not been part of his scheme, but presidents have been known to spoil many carefully laid plans. The judge took his philosophically. 'This is a big move up in the world for you, if you do your job right. Hell, you might even like it.'

Ryan was sure he wouldn't, and he was right.

CIA Headquarters

He didn't speak the whole way back to Langley. The director's car pulled into the basement parking garage, where they got out and entered a private elevator that took them directly to Moore's office. The elevator door was disguised as a wall panel, which was convenient but melodramatic, Ryan thought. The DCI went right to his desk and lifted a phone.

'Bob, I need you in here right now.' He glanced at Ryan, standing in the middle of the room. 'Looking forward to this, Jack?'

'Sure, Judge,' Ryan said without enthusiasm.

'I can see how you feel about this spying business, but the whole thing could develop into an extremely sensitive situation. You ought to be damned flattered you're being trusted with it.'

Ryan caught the between-the-lines message just as Ritter breezed in.

'What's up, Judge?'

'We're laying an operation on. Ryan is flying out to the *Kennedy* with Charlie Davenport to brief the fleet commanders on this *October* business. The president bought it.'

'Guess so. Greer left for Andrews just before you pulled in. Ryan gets to fly out, eh?'

'Yes. Jack, the rule is this: you can brief the fleet commander and Davenport, that's all. Same for the Brits, just the boss-sailor. If Bob can confirm WILLOW, the data can be spread out, but only as much as is absolutely necessary. Clear?'

'Yes, sir. I suppose somebody has told the president that it's hard to accomplish anything if nobody knows what the hell is going on. Especially the guys who're doing the work.'

'I know what you're saying, Jack. We have to change the president's mind on that. We will, but until we do, remember – he is the boss. Bob, we'll need to rustle something up so he'll fit in.'

'Naval officer's uniform? Let's make him a commander, three stripes, usual ribbons.' Ritter looked Ryan over. 'Say a forty-two long. We can have him outfitted in an hour, I expect. This operation have a name?'

'That's next.' Moore lifted his phone again and tapped in five numbers. 'I need two words . . . Uh-huh, thank you.' He wrote a few things down. 'Okay, gentlemen, we're calling this Operation MANDOLIN. You, Ryan, are Magi. Ought to be easy to remember, given the time of year. We'll work up a series of code words based on those while you're being fitted. Bob, take him down there yourself. I'll call Davenport and have him arrange the flight.'

Ryan followed Ritter to the elevator. It was going too fast, everyone was being too clever, he thought. This Operation MANDOLIN was racing forward before they knew what the hell they were going to do, much less how. And the choice of his code name struck Ryan as singularly inappropriate. He wasn't anyone's wise man. The name should have been something more like 'Halloween.'

The Seventh Day

Thursday, 9 December

The North Atlantic

When Samuel Johnson compared sailing in a ship to 'being in jail, with the chance of being drowned,' at least he had the consolation of travelling to his ship in a safe carriage, Ryan thought. Now he was going to sea, and before he got to his ship Ryan stood the chance of being smashed to red pulp in a plane crash. Jack sat hunched in a bucket seat on the port side of a Grumman Greyhound, known to the fleet without affection as a COD (for carrier onboard delivery), a flying delivery truck. The seats, facing aft, were too close together, and his knees jutted up against his chin. The cabin was far more amenable to cargo than to people. There were three tons of engine and electronics parts stowed in crates aft – there, no doubt, so that the impact of a plane crash on the valuable equipment would be softened by the four bodies in the passenger section. The cabin was not heated. There were no windows. A thin aluminium skin separated him from a two-hundred-knot wind that shrieked in time with the twin turbine engines. Worst of all, they were flying through a storm at five thousand feet, and the COD was jerking up and down in hundred-foot gulps like a berserk roller coaster. The only good thing was the lack of lighting, Ryan thought – at least nobody can see how green my face is. Right behind him were two pilots, talking away loudly so they could be heard over the engine noise. The bastards were enjoying themselves!

'The noise lessened somewhat, or so it seemed. It was hard to tell. He'd been issued foam-rubber ear protectors along with a yellow, inflatable life preserver and a lecture on what to do in the event of a crash. The lecture had been perfunctory enough that it took no great intellect to estimate their chances of survival if they did crash on a night like this. Ryan hated flying. He had once been a marine second lieutenant, and his active career had ended after only three months when his platoon's helicopter had crashed on Crete during a NATO exercise. He had injured his back, nearly been crippled for life, and ever since regarded flying as something to be avoided. The COD, he thought, was bouncing more down than up. It probably meant they were close to the *Kennedy*. The alternative did not bear thinking about. They were only ninety minutes out of Oceana Naval Air Station at Virginia Beach. It felt like a month, and Ryan swore to himself that he'd never be afraid on a civilian airliner again.

The nose dropped about twenty degrees, and the aircraft seemed to be flying right at something. They were landing, the most dangerous part of carrier flight operations. He remembered a study conducted during the Vietnam War in which carrier pilots had been fitted with portable electro-cardiographs to monitor stress, and it had surprised a lot of people that the most stressful time for carrier pilots wasn't while they were being shot at – it was while they were landing, particularly at night.

Christ, you're full of happy thoughts! Ryan told himself. He closed his eyes. One way or another, it would be over in a few seconds.

The deck was slick with rain and heaving up and down, a black hole surrounded by perimeter lights. The carrier landing was a controlled crash. Massive landing gear struts and shock absorbers were needed to lessen the bone-crushing impact. The aircraft surged forward only to be jerked to a halt by the arresting wire. They were down. They were safe. Probably. After a moment's pause, the COD began moving forward again. Ryan heard some odd noises as the plane taxied and realised that they came from the wings folding up. The one danger he had not considered was flying on an aircraft whose wings were supposed to collapse. It was, he decided, just as well. The plane finally stopped moving, and the rear hatch opened.

Ryan flipped off his seatbelts and stood rapidly, banging his head on the low ceiling. He didn't wait for Davenport. With his canvas bag clutched to his chest he darted out of the rear of the aircraft. He looked around, and was pointed to the *Kennedy's* island structure by a yellow-shirted deck crewman. The rain was falling heavily, and he felt rather than saw that the carrier was indeed moving on the fifteen-foot seas. He ran towards an open, lighted hatch fifty feet away. He had to wait for Davenport to catch up. The admiral didn't run. He walked with a precise thirty-inch step, dignified as a flag officer should be, and Ryan decided that he was probably annoyed that his semisecret arrival prohibited the usual ceremony of bosun's pipes and side boys. There was a marine standing inside the hatch, a corporal, resplendent in striped blue trousers, khaki shirt and tie, and snow-white pistol belt. He saluted, welcoming both aboard.

'Corporal, I want to see Admiral Painter.'

'The admiral's in flag quarters, sir. Do you require escort?'

'No, son, I used to command this ship. Come along, Jack.' Ryan got to carry both bags.

'Gawd, sir, you actually used to do this for a living?' Ryan asked.

'Night carrier landings? Sure, I've done a couple of hundred. What's the big deal?' Davenport seemed surprised at Ryan's awe. Jack was sure it was an act.

The inside of the *Kennedy* was much like the interior of the USS *Guam*, the helicopter assault ship Ryan had been assigned to during his brief military career. It was the usual navy maze of steel bulkheads and pipes, everything painted the same shade of cave-grey. The pipes had some coloured bands and stencilled acronyms which probably meant something to the men who ran the ship. To Ryan they might as well have been neolithic cave paintings. Davenport led him through a corridor, around a corner, down a 'ladder' made entirely of steel and so steep he almost lost his balance, down another passageway, and around another corner. By this time Ryan was thoroughly lost. They came to a door with a marine stationed in front. The sergeant saluted perfectly, and opened the door for them.

Ryan followed Davenport in – and was amazed. Flag quarters on the USS *Kennedy* might have been transported as a block from a Beacon Hill mansion. To his right was a wall-sized mural large enough to dominate a big living room. A half-dozen oils, one of them a portrait of the ship's namesake, President John Fitzgerald Kennedy, dotted the other walls, themselves covered with expensive-looking panelling. The deck was covered in thick crimson wool, and the furniture was pure civilian, French provincial, oak and brocade. One could almost imagine they were not aboard a ship at all, except that the ceiling – 'overhead' – had the usual collection of pipes, all painted grey. It was a decidedly odd contrast to the rest of the room.

'Hi ya, Charlie!' Rear Admiral Joshua Painter emerged from the next room, drying his hands with a towel. 'How was it coming in?'

'Little rocky,' Davenport allowed, shaking hands. 'This is Jack Ryan.'

Ryan had never met Painter but knew him by reputation. A Phantom pilot during the Vietnam War, he had written a book, *Paddystrikes*, on the conduct of the air campaigns. It had been a truthful hook, not the sort of thing that wins friends. He was a small, feisty man who could not have weighed more than a hundred thirty pounds. He was also a gifted tactician and a man of puritanical integrity.

'One of yours, Charlie?'

'No, Admiral, I work for James Greer. I am not a naval officer. Please accept my apologies. I don't like pretending to be what I'm not. The uniform was the CIA's idea.' This drew a frown.

'Oh? Well, I suppose that means you're going to tell me what Ivan's up to. Good, I hope to hell somebody knows. First time on a carrier? How did you like the flight in?'

'It might be a good way to interrogate prisoners of war,' Ryan said as offhandedly as he could. The two flag officers had a good laugh at his expense, and Painter called for some food to be sent in.

The double doors to the passageway opened several minutes later and a pair of stewards – 'mess management specialists' – came in, one bearing a tray of food, the other two pots of coffee. The three men were served in a style appropriate to their rank. The food, served on silver-trimmed plates, was simple but appetizing to Ryan, who hadn't eaten in twelve hours. He dished cole slaw and potato salad onto his plate and selected a pair of corned-beef-on-ryes.

'Thank you. That's all for now,' Painter said. The stewards came to attention before leaving. Okay, let's get down to business.'

Ryan gulped down half a sandwich. 'Admiral, this information is only twenty hours old.' He took the briefing folders from his bag and handed them around. His delivery took twenty minutes, during which he managed to consume the two sandwiches and a goodly portion of his cole slaw and spill coffee on his hand-written notes. The two flag officers were a perfect audience, not interrupting once, only darting a few disbelieving looks at him.

'God Almighty,' Painter said when Ryan finished. Davenport just stared poker-faced as he contemplated the possibility of examining a Soviet missile sub from the inside. Jack decided he'd be a formidable opponent over cards. Painter went on, 'Do you really believe this?'

'Yes, sir, I do.' Ryan poured himself another cup of coffee. He would have preferred a beer to go with his corned beef. It hadn't been bad at all, and good kosher corned beef was something he'd been unable to find in London.

Painter leaned back and looked at Davenport. 'Charlie, you tell Greer to teach this lad a few lessons – like how a bureaucrat ain't supposed to stick his neck this far out on the block. Don't *you* think this is a little far-fetched?'

'Josh, Ryan here's the guy who did the report last June on Soviet missile-sub patrol patterns.'

'Oh? That was a nice piece of work. It confirmed something I've been saying for two or three years.' Painter rose and walked to the corner to look out at the stormy sea. 'So, what are we supposed to do about all this?'

'The exact details of the operation have not been determined. What I expect is that you will be directed to locate *Red October* and attempt to establish communications with her skipper. After that? We'll have to figure a way to get her to a safe place. You see, the president doesn't think we'll be able to hold onto her once we get her – if we get her.'

'What?' Painter spun around and spoke a tenth of a second before Davenport did. Ryan explained for several minutes.

'Dear God above! You give me one impossible task, then you tell me that if we succeed in it, we gotta give the goddamned thing back to them!'

'Admiral, my recommendation – the president asked me for one – was that we keep the submarine. For what it's worth, the Joint Chiefs are on your side, too, along with the CIA. As it is, though, if the crewmen want to go back home we have to send them back, and then the Soviets will know we have the boat for sure. As a practical matter, I can see the other side's point. The vessel is worth a pile of money, and it is their property. And how would we hide a 30,000-ton submarine?'

'You hide a submarine by sinking it,' Painter said angrily. 'They're designed to do that, you know. "Their property!" We're not talking about a damned passenger liner. That's something designed to kill people – our people!'

'Admiral, I am on your side,' Ryan said quietly. 'Sir, you said we've given you an impossible task. Why?'

'Ryan, finding a boomer that does not want to be found is not the easiest thing in the world. We practice against our own. We damned near always fail, and you say this one's already passed all the northeast SOSUS lines. The Atlantic's a rather large ocean, and a missile sub's noise footprint is very small.'

'Yes, sir.' Ryan noted to himself that he might have been overly optimistic about their chances for success.

'What sort of shape are you in, Josh?' Davenport asked.

'Pretty good, really. The exercise we just ran, NIFTY DOLPHIN, worked out all right. Our part of it,' Painter corrected himself. '*Dallas* raised some hell on the other side. My ASW crews are functioning very well. What sort of help are we getting?'

'When I left the Pentagon, the CNO was checking the availability of P-3s out on the Pacific, so you'll probably be seeing more of those. Everything that'll move is putting to sea. You're the only carrier, so you've got overall tactical command, right? Come on, Josh, you're our best ASW operator.'

Painter poured some coffee for himself. 'Okay, we have one carrier deck. *America* and *Nimitz* are still a good week away. Ryan, you said you're flying out to *Invincible*. We get her, too, right?'

'The president was working on that. Want her?'

'Sure. Admiral White has a good nose for ASW, and his boys really lucked out during DOLPHIN. They killed two of our attack boats, and Vince Gallery was some kind of pissed about that. Luck's a big part of this game. That would give us two decks instead of one. I wonder if we can get some more S-3s?' Painter referred to the Lockheed Vikings, carrier-borne antisubmarine aircraft.

'Why?' Davenport asked.

'I can transfer my F-18s to shore, and that'll give us room for twenty more Vikings. I don't like losing the striking power, but what we're going to need is more ASW muscle. That means more S-3s. Jack, you know that if you're wrong, that Russkie surface force is going to be a handful to deal with. You know how many surface-to-surface missiles they're packing?'

'No, sir.' Ryan was certain it was too many.

'We're one carrier, and that makes us their primary target. If they start shooting at us, it'll get awful lonesome – then it'll get awful exciting.' The phone rang. 'Painter here . . . Yes. Thank you. Well, *Invincible* just turned around. Good, they're giving her to us along with two tin cans. The rest of the escorts and the three attack subs are still heading home.' He frowned. 'I can't really fault them for that. That means we have to give them some escorts, but it's a good trade. I want that flight deck.'

'Can we chopper Jack out to her?' Ryan wondered if Davenport knew what the president had ordered him to do. The admiral seemed interested in getting him off the *Kennedy*.

Painter shook his head. 'Too far for a chopper. Maybe they can send a Harrier back for him.'

'The Harrier's a fighter, sir,' Ryan commented.

'They have an experimental two-seat version set up for ASW patrolling. It's supposed to work reasonably well outside their helo perimeter. That's how they bagged one of our attack boats, caught her napping.' Painter finished off the last of his coffee.

'Okay, gentlemen, let's get ourselves down to ASW control and try to figure a way to run this circus act. CINCLANT will want to hear what I have in mind. I suppose I'd better decide for myself. We'll also call *Invincible* and have them send a bird back to ferry you out, Ryan.'

Ryan followed the two admirals out of the room. He spent two hours watching Painter move ships around the ocean like a chess master with his pieces.

The USS *Dallas*

Bart Mancuso had been on duty in the attack centre for more than twenty hours. Only a few hours of sleep separated this stretch from the previous one. He had been eating sandwiches and drinking coffee, and two cups of soup had been thrown in by his cooks for variety's sake. He examined his latest cup of freeze-dried without affection.

'Cap'n?' He turned. It was Roger Thompson, his sonar officer.

'Yes, what is it?' Mancuso pulled himself away from the tactical display that had occupied his attention for several days. Thompson was standing at the rear of the compartment. Jones was standing beside him holding a clipboard and what looked like a tape machine.

'Sir, Jonesy has something I think you ought to look at.'

Mancuso didn't want to be bothered – extended time on duty always taxed his patience. But Jones looked eager and excited. 'Okay, come on over to the chart table.'

The *Dallas*' chart table was a new gadget wired into the BC-10 and projected onto a TV-type glass screen four feet square. The display moved as the *Dallas* moved. This made paper charts obsolete, though they were kept anyway. Charts can't break.

'Thanks, Skipper,' Jones said, more humbly than usual. 'I know you're kinda busy, but I think I got something here. That anomalous contact we had the other day's been bothering me. I had to leave it after the ruckus the other Russkie subs kicked up, but I was able to come back to it three times to make sure it was still there. The fourth time it was gone, faded out. I want to show you what I worked up. Can you punch up our course track for back then on this baby, sir?'

The chart table was interfaced through the BC-10 into the ship's inertial navigation system, SINS. Mancuso punched the command in himself. It was getting so that you couldn't flush the head without a computer command . . . The *Dallas*' course track showed up as a convoluted red line, with tick marks displayed at fifteen-minute intervals.

'Great!' Jones commented. 'I've never seen it do that before. That's all right. Okay.' Jones pulled a handful of pencils from his back pocket. 'Now, I got the contact first at 0915 or so, and the bearing was about two-six-nine.' He set a pencil down, eraser at *Dallas*' position, point directed west towards the target. 'Then at 0930 it was bearing two-six-zero. At 9048, it was two-five-zero. There's some error built into these, Cap'n. It was a tough signal to lock in on, but the errors should average out. Right about then we got all this other activity, and I had to go after them, but I came back to it about 1000, and the bearing was two-four-two.' Jones set down another pencil on the due-east line traced when the *Dallas* had moved away from the Icelandic coast. 'At 1015 it was two-three-four, and at 1030 is was two-two-seven. These last two are shaky, sir. The signal was real faint, and I didn't have a very good lock on it.' Jones looked up. He appeared nervous.

'So far, so good. Relax, Jonesy. Light up if you want.'

'Thanks, Cap'n.' Jones fished out a cigarette and lit it with a butane lighter. He had never approached the captain quite this way. He knew Mancuso to be a tolerant, easygoing commander – if you had something to say. He was not a man who liked his time wasted, and it was sure as hell he wouldn't want it wasted now. 'Okay, sir, we gotta figure he couldn't be too far away from us, right? I mean, he had to be between us and Iceland. So let's say he was about halfway between. That gives him a course about like this.' Jones set down some more pencils.

'Hold it, Jonesy. Where does the course come from?'

'Oh, yeah.' Jones flipped open his clipboard. 'Yesterday morning, night, whatever it was, after I got off watch, it started bothering me, so I used the move we made offshore as a baseline to do a little course track for him. I know how, Skipper: I read the manual. It's easy, just like we used to do at Cal Tech to chart star motion. I took an astronomy course in my freshman year.'

Mancuso stifled a groan. It was the first time he had ever heard this called easy, but on looking at Jones' figures and diagrams, it appeared that he had done it right. 'Go on.'

Jones pulled a Hewlitt Packard scientific calculator from his pocket and what looked like a National Geographic map liberally coated with pencil marks and scribblings. 'You want to check my figures, sir?'

'We will, but I'll trust you for now. What's the map?'

'Skipper, I know it's against the rules an' all, but I keep this as a personal record of the tracks the bad guys use. It doesn't leave the boat, sir, honest. I may be a little off, but all this translates to a course of about two-two-zero and a speed of ten knots. And *that* aims him right at the entrance of Route One. Okay?'

'Go on.' Mancuso had already figured that one. Jonesy was on to something.

'Well, I couldn't sleep after that, so I skipped back to sonar and pulled the tape on the contact. I had to run it through the computer a few times to filter out all the crap – sea sounds, the other subs, you know – then I rerecorded it at ten times normal speed.' He set his cassette recorder on the chart table. 'Listen to this, Skipper.'

The tape was scratchy, but every few seconds there was a *thrum*. Two minutes of listening seemed to indicate a regular interval of about five seconds. By this time Lieutenant Mannion was looking over Thompson's shoulder, listening, and nodding speculatively.

'Skipper, that's gotta be a man-made sound. It's just too regular for anything else. At normal speed it didn't make much sense, but once I speeded it up, I had the sucker.'

'Okay, Jonesy, finish it,' Mancuso said.

'Captain, what you just heard was the acoustical signature of a Russian submarine. He was heading for Route One, taking the inshore track off the Icelandic coast. You can bet money on that, Skipper.'

'Roger?'

'He sold me, Captain,' Thompson replied.

Mancuso took another look at the course track, trying to figure an alternative. There wasn't any. 'Me, too. Roger, Jonesy makes sonarman first class today. I want to see the paper work done by the turn of the next watch, along with a nice letter of commendation for my signature. Ron,' he poked the sonarman in the shoulder, 'that's all right. Damned well done!'

'Thanks, Skipper.' Jones' smile stretched from ear to ear.

'Pat, please call Lieutenant Butler to the attack centre.'

Mannion went to the phone to call the boat's chief engineer.

'Any idea what it is, Jonesy?' Mancuso turned back.

The sonarman shook his head. 'It isn't screw sounds. I've never heard anything like it.' He ran the tape back and played it again.

Two minutes later, Lieutenant Earl Butler came into the attack centre. 'You rang, Skipper?'

'Listen to this, Earl.' Mancuso rewound the tape and played it a third time.

Butler was a graduate of the University of Texas and every school the navy had for submarines and their engine systems. 'What's that supposed to be?'

'Jonesy says it's a Russian sub. I think he's right.'

'Tell me about the tape,' Butler said to Jones.

'Sir, it's speeded up ten times, and I washed it through the BC-10 five times. At normal speed it doesn't sound like much of anything.' With uncharacteristic modesty, Jones did not point out that it had sounded like something to him.

'Some sort of harmonic? I mean, if it was a propeller, it'd have to be a hundred feet across, and we'd be hearing one blade at a time. The regular interval suggests some sort of harmonic.' Butler's face screwed up. 'But a harmonic what?'

'Whatever it was, it was headed right here.' Mancuso tapped Thor's Twins with his pencil.

'That makes him a Russian, all right,' Butler agreed. 'Then they're using something new. Again.'

'Mr Butler's right,' Jones said. 'It does sound like a harmonic rumble. The other funny thing is, well, there was this background noise, kinda like water going through a pipe. I don't know, it didn't pick up on this. I guess the computer filtered it off. It was real faint to start with – anyway, that's outside my field.'

'That's all right. You've done enough for one day. How do you feel?' Mancuso asked.

'A little tired, Skipper. I've been working on this for a while.'

'If we get close to this guy again, you think you can track him down?' Mancuso knew the answer.

'You bet, Cap'n! Now that we know what to listen for, you bet I'll bag the sucker!'

Mancuso looked at the chart table. 'Okay, if he was heading for the Twins, and then ran the route at, say twenty-eight or thirty knots, and then settled down to his base course and speed of about ten or so . . . that puts him about here now. Long ways off. Now, if we run at top speed . . . forty-eight hours will put us here, and that'll put us in front of him. Pat?'

'That's about right, sir,' Lieutenant Mannion concurred. 'You're figuring he ran the route at full speed, then settled down – makes sense. He wouldn't need the quiet drive in that damned maze. It gives him a free shot for four or five hundred miles, so why not uncrank his engines? That's what I'd do.'

'That's what we'll try to do, then. We'll radio in for permission to leave Toll Booth station and track this character down. Jonesy, running at max speed means you sonarmen will be out of work for a while. Set up the contact tape on the simulator and make sure the operators all know what this guy sounds like, but get some rest. All of you. I want you at a hundred per-cent when we try to reacquire this guy. Have yourself a shower. Make that a Hollywood shower – you've earned it – and rack out. When we do go after this character, it'll be a long, tough hunt.'

'No sweat, Captain. We'll get him for you. Bet on it. You want to keep my tape, sir?'

'Yeah.' Mancuso ejected the tape and looked up in surprise. 'You sacrificed a Bach for this?'

'Not a good one, sir. I have a Christopher Hogwood of this piece that's much better.'

Mancuso pocketed the tape. 'Dismissed, Jonesy. Nice work.'

'A pleasure, Cap'n.' Jones left the attack centre counting the extra money for jumping a rate.

'Roger, make sure your people are well rested over the next two days. When we do go after this guy, it's going to be a bastard.'

'Aye, Captain.'

'Pat, get us up to periscope depth. We're going to call this one into Norfolk right now. Earl, I want you thinking about what's making that noise.'

'Right, Captain.'

While Mancuso drafted his message, Lieutenant Mannion brought the *Dallas* to periscope-antenna depth with an upward angle on the diving planes. It took five minutes to get from five hundred feet to just below the stormy surface. The submarine was subject to wave action, and while it was very gentle by surface ship standards, the crew noted her rocking. Mannion raised the periscope and ESM (electronic support measures) antenna, the latter used for the broad-band receiver designed to detect possible radar emissions. There was nothing in view – he could see about five miles – and the ESM instruments showed nothing except for aircraft sets, which were too far away to matter. Next Mannion raised two more masts. One was a reedlike UHF (ultrahigh frequency) receiving antenna. The other was new, a laser transmitter. This rotated and locked onto the carrier wave signal of the Atlantic SSIX, the communications satellite used exclusively by submarines. With the laser, they could send high-density transmissions without giving away the sub's position.

'All ready, sir,' the duty radioman reported.

'Transmit.'

The radioman pressed a button. The signal, sent in a fraction of a second, was received by photovoltaic cells, read over to a UHF transmitter, and shot back down by a parabolic dish antenna towards Atlantic Fleet Communications headquarters. At Norfolk another radioman noted the reception and pressed a button that transmitted the same signal up to the satellite and back to the *Dallas*. It was a simple way to identify garbles.

The *Dallas* operator compared the received signal with the one he'd just sent. 'Good copy, sir.'

Mancuso ordered Mannion to lower everything but the ESM and UHF antennae.

Atlantic Fleet Communications

In Norfolk the first line of the dispatch revealed the page and line of the one-time-pad cipher sequence, which was recorded on computer tape in the maximum security section of the communications complex. An officer typed the proper numbers into his computer terminal, and an instant later the machine generated a clear text. The officer checked it again for garbles. Satisfied there were none, he took the printout to the other side of the room where a yeoman was seated at a telex. The officer handed him the dispatch.

The yeoman keyed up the proper addressee and transmitted the message by dedicated landline to COMSUBLANT Operations, half a mile away. The landline was fibre optic, located in a steel conduit under a paved street. It was checked three times a week for security purposes. Not even the secrets of nuclear weapons performance were as closely guarded as day-to-day tactical communications.

COMSUBLANT Operations

A bell went off in the operations room as the message came up on the 'hot' printer. It bore a Z prefix, which indicated FLASH-priority status.

Z090414ZDEC

TOP SECRET THEO

FM: USS DALLAS

TO: COMSUBLANT

INFO: CINCLANTFLT

//NOOOOO//

REDFLEET SUBOPS
1. REPORT ANOMALOUS SONAR CONTACT ABOUT O900Z 7DEC AND LOST AFTER INCREASE IN REDFLEET SUB ACTIVITY. CONTACT SUBSEQUENTLY EVALUATED AS REDFLEET SSN/SSBN TRANSITING ICELAND INSHORE TRACK TOWARDS ROUTE ONE. COURSE SOUTHWEST SPEED TEN DEPTH UNKNOWN .
2. CONTACT EVIDENCED UNUSUAL REPEAT UNUSUAL ACOUSTICAL CHARACTERISTICS. SIGNATURE UNLIKE ANY KNOWN REDFLEET SUBMARINE.
3. REQUEST PERMISSION TO LEAVE TOLL BOOTH TO PURSUE AND INVESTIGATE. BELIEVE A NEW DRIVE SYSTEM WITH UNUSUAL SOUND CHARACTERISTICS BEING USED THIS SUB. BELIEVE GOOD PROBABILITY CAN LOCATE AND IDENTIFY.

A lieutenant junior grade took the dispatch to the office of Vice Admiral Vincent Gallery. COMSUBLANT had been on duty since the Soviet subs had started moving. He was in an evil mood.

'A FLASH priority from *Dallas*, sir.'

'Uh-huh.' Gallery took the yellow form and read it twice. 'What do you suppose this means?'

'No telling, sir. Looks like he heard something, took his time figuring it out, and wants another crack at it. He seems to think he's onto something unusual.'

'Okay, what do I tell him? Come on, mister. You might be an admiral yourself someday and have to make decisions.' An unlikely prospect, Gallery thought.

'Sir, *Dallas* is in an ideal position to shadow their surface force when it gets to Iceland. We need her where she is.'

'Good textbook answer.' Gallery smiled up at the youngster, preparing to cut him off at the knees. 'On the other hand, *Dallas* is commanded by a fairly competent man who wouldn't be bothering us unless he really thought he had something. He doesn't go into specifics, probably because it's too complicated for a tactical FLASH despatch, and also because he thinks that we know his judgment is good enough to take his word on something. "New drive system with unusual sound characteristics." That may be a crock, but he's the man on the scene, and he wants an answer. We tell him yes.'

'Aye aye, sir,' the lieutenant said, wondering if the skinny old bastard made decisions by flipping a coin when his back was turned.

The *Dallas*

Z090432ZDEC

TOP SECRET

FM: COMSUBLANT

TO: USS DALLAS

A. USS DALLAS Z090414ZDEC

B. COMSUBLANT INST 2000.5

OPAREA ASSIGNMENT N04220

1. REQUEST REF A GRANTED.
2. AREAS BRAVO ECHO GOLF REF B ASSIGNED FOR UNRESTRICTED OPS 090500Z TO 140001Z. REPORT AS NECESSARY.
VADM GALLERY SENDS.

'Hot damn!' Mancuso chuckled. That was one nice thing about Gallery. When you asked him a question, by God, you got an answer, yes or no, before you could rig your antenna in. Of course, he reflected, if it turned out that Jonesy was wrong and this was a wild-goose chase, he'd have some explaining to do. Gallery had handed more than one sub skipper his head in a bag and set him on the beach.

Which was where he was headed regardless, Mancuso knew. Since his first year at Annapolis all he had ever wanted was command of his own attack boat. He had that now, and he knew that the rest of his career would be downhill. In the rest of the navy your first command was just that, a first command. You could move up the ladder and command a fleet at sea eventually, if you were lucky and had the right stuff. Not submariners, though. Whether he did well with the *Dallas* or poorly, he'd lose her soon enough. He had this one and only chance. And afterwards, what? The best he could hope for was command of a missile boat. He'd served on those before and was sure that commanding one, even a new *Ohio*, was about as exciting as watching paint dry. The boomer's job was to stay hidden. Mancuso wanted to be the hunter, that was the exciting end of the business. And after commanding a missile boat? He could get a 'major surface command,' perhaps a nice oiler – it would be like switching mounts from Secretariat to Elsie the Cow. Or he could get a squadron command and sit in an office on board a tender, pushing paper. At best in that position he'd go to sea once a month, his main purpose being to bother sub skippers who didn't want him there. Or he could get a desk job in the Pentagon – what fun! Mancuso understood why some of the astronauts had cracked up after coming back from the moon. He, too, had worked many years for this command, and in another year his boat would be gone. He'd have to give the *Dallas* to someone else. But he did have her now.

'Pat, let's lower all masts and take her down to twelve hundred feet.'

'Aye aye, sir. Lower the masts,' Mannion ordered. A petty officer pulled on the hydraulic control levers.

'ESM and UHF masts lowered, sir,' the duty electrician reported.

'Very well. Diving officer, make your depth twelve hundred feet.'

'Twelve hundred feet, aye,' the diving officer responded. 'Fifteen degrees down-angle on the planes.'

'Fifteen degrees down, aye.'

'Let's move her, Pat.'

'Aye, Skipper. All ahead full.'

'All ahead full, aye.' The helmsman reached up to turn the annunciator.

Mancuso watched his crew at work. They did their jobs with mechanistic precision. But they were not machines. They were men. His.

In the reactor spaces aft, Lieutenant Butler had his enginemen acknowledge the command and gave the necessary orders. The reactor coolant pumps went to fast speed. An increased amount of hot, pressurized water entered the exchanger, where its heat was transferred to the steam on the outside loop. When the coolant returned to the reactor it was cooler than it had been and therefore denser. Being denser, it trapped more neutrons

101

in the reactor pile, increasing the ferocity of the fission reaction and giving off yet more power. Farther aft, saturated steam in the 'outside' or non-radioactive loop of the heat exchange system emerged through clusters of control valves to strike the blades of the high-pressure turbine. The *Dallas'* huge bronze screw began to turn more quickly, driving her forward and down.

The engineers went about their duties calmly. The noise in the engine spaces rose noticeably as the systems began to put out more power, and the technicians kept track of this by continuously monitoring the banks of instruments under their hands. The routine was quiet and exact. There was no extraneous conversation, no distraction. Compared to a submarine's reactor spaces, a hospital operating room was a den of libertines.

Forward, Mannion watched the depth gauge go below six hundred feet. The diving officer would wait until they got to nine hundred feet before starting to level off, the object being to zero the dive out exactly at the ordered depth. Commander Mancuso wanted the *Dallas* below the thermocline. This was the border between differing temperatures. Water settled in isothermal layers of uniform stratification. The relatively flat boundary where warmer surface water met colder deep water was a semi-permeable barrier which tended to reflect sound waves. Those waves that did manage to penetrate the thermocline were mostly trapped below it. Thus, though the *Dallas* was now running below the thermocline at over thirty knots and making as much noise as she was capable of, she would still be difficult to detect with surface sonar. She would also be largely blind, but then there was not much down there to run into.

Mancuso lifted the microphone for the PA system. 'This is the captain speaking. We have just started a speed run that will last forty-eight hours. We are heading towards a point where we hope to locate a Russian sub that went past us two days ago. This Russkie is evidently using a new and rather quiet propulsion system that nobody's run across before. We're going to try and get ahead of him and track on him as he passes us again. This time we know what to listen for, and we'll get a nice clear picture of him. Okay, I want everyone on this boat to be well rested. When we get there, it'll be a long, tough hunt. I want everybody at a hundred per-cent. This one will probably be interesting.' He switched off the microphone. 'What's the movie tonight?'

The diving officer watched the depth gauge stop moving before answering. As chief of the boat, he was also manager of the *Dallas'* cable TV system, three video-cassette recorders in the mess room which led to televisions in the wardroom, and various other crew accommodations. 'Skipper, you got a choice. *Return of the Jedi* or two football tapes: Oklahoma-Nebraska and Miami-Dallas. Both those games were played while we were on the exercise, sir. It'll be like watching them live.' He laughed. 'Commercials and all. The cooks are already making the popcorn.'

'Good. I want everybody nice and loose.' Why couldn't they ever get Navy tapes, Mancuso wondered. Of course, Army had creamed them this year . . .

'Morning, Skipper.' Wally Chambers, the executive officer, came into the attack centre. 'What gives?'

'Come on back to the wardroom, Wally. I want you to listen to something.' Mancuso took the cassette from his shirt pocket and led Chambers aft.

The V. K. Konovalov

Two hundred miles northeast of the *Dallas*, in the Norwegian Sea, the *Konovalov* was racing southwest at forty-one knots. Captain Tupolev sat alone in the wardroom rereading the dispatch he'd received two days before. His emotions alternated between rage and grief. The Schoolmaster had done *that*! He was dumbfounded.

But what was there to do? Tupolev's orders were explicit, the more so since, as his *zampolit* had pointed out, he was a former pupil of the traitor Ramius. He, too, could find himself in a very bad position. If the slug succeeded.

So, Marko had pulled a trick on everyone, not just the *Konovalov*. Tupolev had been slinking around the Barents Sea like a fool while Marko had been heading the other way. Laughing at everyone, Tupolev was sure. Such treachery, such a hellish threat against the *Rodina*. It was inconceivable – and all too conceivable. All the advantages Marko had. A four-room apartment, a dacha, his own Zhiguli. Tupolev did not yet have his own automobile. He had earned his way to a command, and now it was all threatened by – this! He'd be lucky to keep what he had.

I have to kill a friend, he thought. Friend? Yes, he admitted to himself, Marko had been a good friend and a fine teacher. Where had he gone wrong?

Natalia Bogdanova.

Yes, that had to be it. A big stink, the way that had happened. How many times had he had dinner with them, how many times had Natalia laughed about her fine, strong, big sons? He shook his head. A fine woman killed by a damned incompetent fool of a surgeon. Nothing could be done about it, he was the son of a Central Committee member. It was an outrage the way things like that still happened, even after three generations of building social-ism. But nothing was sufficient to justify this madness.

Tupolev bent over the chart he'd brought back. He'd be on his station in five days, in less time if the engine plant held together and Marko wasn't in too much of a hurry – and he wouldn't be. Marko was a fox, not a bull. The other *Alfas* would get there ahead of his, Tupolev knew, but it didn't matter. He had to do this himself. He'd get ahead of Marko and wait. Marko would try to slink past, and the *Konovalov* would be there. And the *Red October* would die.

The North Atlantic

The British Sea Harrier FRS.4 appeared a minute early. It hovered briefly off the *Kennedy's* port beam as the pilot sized up his landing target, the wind, the sea conditions. Maintaining a steady thirty-knot forward speed to compensate for the carrier's forward speed, he side-slipped his fighter neatly on the right, then dropped it gently amidships, slightly forward of the *Kennedy's* island structure, exactly in the centre of the flight deck. Instantly a gang of deck crewmen raced for the aircraft, three carrying heavy metal chocks, another a metal ladder which he set up by the cockpit, whose canopy was already coming open. A team of four snaked a fuelling hose towards the aircraft, eager to demonstrate the speed with which the US Navy services aircraft. The pilot was dressed in an orange coverall and yellow life jacket. He set his helmet on the back of the front seat and came down the ladder. He watched briefly to be sure his fighter was in capable hands before sprinting to the island. He met Ryan at the hatch.

'You Ryan? I'm Tony Parker. Where's the loo?' Jack gave him the proper directions and the pilot darted off, leaving Ryan standing there in the flight suit, holding his bag and feeling stupid. A white plastic flight helmet dangled from his other hand as he watched the crewmen fueling the Harrier. He wondered if they knew what they were doing.

Parker was back in three minutes. 'Commander,' he said 'there's one thing they've never put in a fighter, and that's a bloody toilet. They fill you up with coffee and tea and send you off, and you've no place to go.'

'I know the feeling. Anything else you have to do?'

'No, sir. Your admiral chatted with me on the radio when I was flying in. Looks like your chaps have finished fuelling my bird. Shall we be off?'

'What do I do with this?' Ryan held up his bag, expecting to have to told it in his lap. His briefing papers were inside the flight suit, tucked against his chest.

'We put it in the boot, of course. Come along, sir.'

Parker walked out to the fighter jauntily. The dawn was a feeble one. There was a solid overcast at one or two thousand feet. It wasn't raining, but looked as though it might. The sea, still rolling at about eight feet, was a grey, crinkled surface dotted with whitecaps. Ryan could feel the *Kennedy* moving, surprised that something so huge could be made to move at all. When they got to the Harrier, Parker took the duffle in one hand and reached for a recessed handle on the underside of the fighter. Twisting and pulling the lever, he revealed a cramped space about the size of a small refrigerator. Parker stuffed the bag into it, slamming the door shut behind it, making sure the locking lever was fully engaged. A deck crewman in a yellow shirt conferred with the pilot. Aft a helicopter was revving its engines, and a Tomcat fighter was taxiing towards a midships catapult. On top of this a thirty-knot wind was blowing. The carrier was a noisy place.

Parker waved Ryan up the ladder. Jack, who liked ladders about as much as he liked flying, nearly fell into his seat. He struggled to get situated properly, while a deck crewman strapped him into the four-point restraint system. The man put the helmet on Ryan's head and pointed to the jack for its intercom system. Maybe American crews really did know something about Harriers. Next to the plug was a switch. Ryan flipped it.

'Can you hear me, Parker?'

'Yes, Commander. All settled in?'

'I suppose.'

'Right.' Parker's head swivelled to check the engine intakes. 'Starting the engine.'

The canopies stayed up. Three crewmen stood close by with large carbon dioxide extinguishers, presumably in case the engine exploded. A dozen others were standing by the island, watching the strange aircraft as the Pegasus engine screamed to life. Then the canopy came down.

'Ready, Commander?'

'If you are.'

The Harrier was not a large fighter, but it was certainly the loudest. Ryan could feel the engine noise ripple through his body as Parker adjusted his thrust-vector controls. The aircraft wobbled, dipped at the nose, then rose shakily into the air. Ryan saw a man by the island point and gesture to them. The Harrier slid to port, moving away from the island as it gained in height.

'That wasn't too bad,' Parker said. He adjusted the thrust controls, and the Harrier began true forward flight. There was little feeling of acceleration, but Ryan saw that the *Kennedy* was rapidly falling behind. A few seconds later they were beyond the inner ring of escorts.

'Let's get on top of this muck,' Parker said. He pulled back on the stick and headed for the clouds. In seconds they were in them, and Ryan's field of view was reduced from five miles to five feet in an instant.

Jack looked around his cockpit, which had flight controls and instruments. Their airspeed showed one hundred fifty knots and rising, altitude four hundred feet. This Harrier had evidently been a trainer, but the instrument panel had been altered to include the read-out instruments for a sensor pod that could be attached to the belly. A poor man's way of doing things, but from what Admiral Painter said it had evidently worked well enough. He figured the TV-type screen was the FLIR readout, which monitored a forward-looking infra-red heat sensor. The airspeed gauge now said three hundred knots, and the climb indicator showed a twenty-degree angle of attack. It felt like more than that.

'Should be hitting the top of this soon,' Parker said. 'Now!'

The altimetre showed twenty-six thousand feet when Ryan was blasted by pure sunlight. One thing about flying that he never got used to was that no matter how awful the weather was on the ground, if you flew high enough you could always find the sun. The light was intense, but the sky's colour was noticeably deeper than the soft blue seen from the ground. The ride became airliner smooth as they escaped the lower turbulence. Ryan fumbled with his visor to shield his eyes.

'That better, sir?'

'Fine, Lieutenant. It's better than I expected.'

'What do you mean, sir?' Parker inquired.

'I guess it beats flying on a commercial bird. You can see more. That helps.'

'Sorry we don't have any extra fuel, or I'd show you some aerobatics. The Harrier will do almost anything you ask of her.

'That's all right.'

'And your admiral,' Parker went on conversationally, 'said that you don't fancy flying.'

Ryan's hands grabbed the armrests as the Harrier went through three complete revolutions before snapping back to level flight. He surprised himself by laughing. 'Ah, the British sense of humour.'

'Orders from your admiral, sir,' Parker semi-apologized. 'We wouldn't want you to think the Harrier's another bloody bus.'

Which admiral, Ryan wondered, Painter or Davenport? Probably both. The top of the clouds was like a rolling field of cotton . He'd never appreciated that before, looking through a foot-square window on an airliner. In the back seat he almost felt as if he were sitting outside.

'May I ask a question, sir?'

'Sure.'

'What's the flap?'

'What do you mean?

'I mean, sir, that they turned my ship around. Then I get orders to ferry a VIP from *Kennedy* to *Invincible*.'

'Oh, okay. Can't say, Parker. I'm delivering some messages to your boss. I'm just the mailman,' Ryan lied. Roll that one three times.

'Excuse me, Commander, but you see, my wife is expecting a child, our first, soon after Christmas. I hope to be there, sir.'

'Where do you live?'

'Chatham, that's –'

'I know. I live in England myself at the moment. Our place is in Marlow, upriver from London. My second kid got started over there.'

'Born there?'

'Started there. My wife say's it's those strange hotel beds, do it to her every time. If I were a betting men, I'd give you good odds, Parker. First babies are always late anyway.'

'You say you live in Marlow?'

'That's right, we built a house there earlier this year.'

'Jack Ryan – John Ryan? The same chap who –'

'Correct. You don't have to tell anybody that, Lieutenant.'

'Understood, sir. I didn't know you were a naval officer.'

'That's why you don't have to tell anyone.'

'Yes, sir. Sorry for the stunt earlier.'

'That's all right. Admirals must have their little laughs. I understand you guys just ran an exercise with our guys.'

'Indeed we did, Commander. I sank one of your submarines, the *Tullibee*. My systems operator and I, that is. We caught her near the surface at night with our FLIR and dropped noisemakers all round her. You see, we didn't let anyone know about our new equipment. All's fair, as you know. I understand her commander was bloody furious. I'd hoped to meet him in Norfolk, but he didn't arrive until the day we sailed.'

'You guys have a good time in Norfolk?'

'Yes, Commander. We were able to get in a day's shooting on your Chesapeake Bay, the Eastern Shore, I believe you call it.'

'Oh yeah? I used to hunt there. How was it?'

'Not bad. I got my three geese in half an hour. Bag limit was three – stupid.'

'You called in and blasted three geese in a half hour this late in the season?'

'That is how I earn my modest living, Commander, shooting,' Parker commented.

'I was up for a grouse shoot with your admiral last September. They made me use a double. If you show up with my kind of gun – I use a Remington automatic – they look at you like you're some kind of terrorist. I got stuck with a pair of Purdeys that didn't fit. Got fifteen birds. Seemed an awful lazy way to hunt, though, with one guy loading my gun for me, and another platoon of ghillies driving the game. We just about annihilated the bird population, too.'

'We have more game per acre than you do.'

'That's what the admiral said. How far to *Invincible*?'

'Forty minutes.'

Ryan looked at the fuel gauges. They were half empty already. In a car he'd be thinking about a fill-up. All that fuel gone in half an hour. Well, Parker didn't seem excited.

The landing on HMS *Invincible* was different from the COD's arrival on the *Kennedy*. The ride became rocky as Parker descended through the clouds, and it occurred to Ryan that they were on the leading edge of the same storm he'd endured the night before. The canopy was coated with rain, and he heard the impact of thousands of raindrops on the airframe – or was it hail? Watching the instruments, he saw that Parker levelled out at a thousand feet, while they were still in clouds, then descended more slowly, breaking into the clear at a hundred feet. The *Invincible* was scarcely half the *Kennedy's* size. He watched her bobbing actively on the fifteen-foot seas. Parker used the same technique as before. He hovered briefly on the carrier's port side, then slid to the right, dropping the fighter twenty feet onto a painted circle. The landing was hard, but Ryan was able to see it coming. The canopy came up at once.

'You can get out here,' Parker said. 'I have to taxi to the elevator.'

A ladder was already in place. He unbuckled and got out. A crewman had already retrieved his bag. Ryan followed him to the island and was met by an ensign – a sublieutenant, the British call the rank.

'Welcome aboard, sir.' The youngster couldn't be more than twenty, Ryan thought. 'Let me help you out of the flight suit.'

The sublieutenant stood by as Ryan unzipped and took off his helmet, Mae West, and coverall. He retrieved his cap from the bag. In the process he bounced off the bulkhead a few times. The *Invincible* seemed to be corkscrewing in a following sea. A bow wind and a following sea? In the North Atlantic in winter, nothing was too crazy. The officer took his bag, and Ryan held onto the briefing material.

'Lead on, *left*enant,' Ryan gestured. The youngster shot up a series of three ladders, leaving Jack panting behind, thinking about the jogging he wasn't getting in. The combination of the ship's motion and an inner ear badly scrambled from the day's flying made him dizzy, and he found himself bumping into things. How did professional pilots do it?

'Here's the flag bridge, sir.' The sublieutenant held the door open.

'Hello, Jack!' boomed the voice of Vice Admiral John White, eighth Earl of Weston. He was a tall, well-built man of fifty with a florid complexion set off by a white scarf at his neck. Jack had first met him earlier in the year, and since then his wife Cathy and the Countess, Antonia, had become close friends, members of the same circle of amateur musicians. Cathy Ryan played classical piano. Toni White, an attractive woman of forty-four, owned a Guarnieri del Jesu violin. Her husband was a man whose peerage was treated as a convenient after-thought. His career in the Royal Navy had been built entirely on merit. Jack walked over to take his hand.

'Good day, Admiral.'

'How was your flight?'

'Different. I've never been in a fighter before, much less one with ambitions to mate with a hummingbird,' Ryan smiled. The bridge was overheated, and it felt good.

'Jolly good. Let's go aft to my sea cabin.' White dismissed the sublieutenant, who handed Jack his bag before withdrawing. The admiral led him aft through a short passageway and left into a small compartment.

It was surprisingly austere, considering that the English liked their comforts and that White was a peer. There were two curtained portholes, a desk, and a couple of chairs. The only human touch was a colour photograph of his wife. The entire port wall was covered with a chart of the North Atlantic.

'You look tired, Jack.' White waved him to the upholstered chair.

'I am tired. I've been on the go since – hell, since 6:00 A.M. yesterday. I don't know about time changes, I think my watch is still on European time.'

'I have a message for you.' White pulled a slip of paper from his pocket and handed it over.

'Greer to Ryan. WILLOW confirmed,' Ryan read. 'Basil sends regards. Ends.' Somebody had confirmed WILLOW. Who? Maybe Sir Basil, maybe Ritter. Ryan would not quote odds on that one.

Jack tucked it in his pocket. 'This is good news, sir.'

'Why the uniform?'

'Not my idea, Admiral. You know who I work for, right? They figured I'd be less conspicuous this way.'

'At least it fits.' The admiral lifted a phone and ordered refreshments sent to them. 'How's the family, Jack?'

'Fine, thank you, sir. The day before I came over Cathy and Toni were playing over at Nigel Ford's place. I missed it. You know, if they get much better, we ought to have a record cut. There aren't too many violin players better than your wife.'

A steward arrived with a plateful of sandwiches. Jack had never figured out the British taste for cucumbers on bread.

'So, what's the flap?'

'Admiral, the significance of the message you just gave me is that I can tell this to you and three other officers. This is very hot stuff, sir. You'll want to make your choices accordingly.'

'Hot enough to turn my little fleet around.' White thought it over before lifting the phone and ordering three of his officers to the cabin. He hung up. 'Captain Carstairs, Captain Hunter, and Commander Barclay – they are, respectively, *Invincible's* commanding officer, my fleet operations officer, and my fleet intelligence officer.'

'No chief of staff?'

'Flew home, death in the family. Something for your coffee?' White extracted what looked like a brandy bottle from a desk drawer.

'Thank you, Admiral.' He was grateful for the brandy. The coffee needed the help. He watched the admiral pour a generous amount, perhaps with the ulterior motive of making him speak more freely. White had been a British sailor longer than he'd been Ryan's friend.

The three officers arrived together, two carrying folding metal chairs.

'Admiral,' Ryan began, 'you might want to leave that bottle out. After you hear this story, we might all need a drink.' He passed out his two remaining briefing folders and talked from memory. His delivery took fifteen minutes.

'Gentlemen,' he concluded, 'I must insist that this information be kept strictly confidential. For the moment no one outside this room may learn it.'

'That is too bad,' Carstairs said. 'This makes for a bloody good sea story.'

'And our mission?' White was holding the photographs. He poured Ryan another shot of brandy, gave the bottle a brief look, then stowed it back in the desk.

'Thank you, Admiral. For the moment our mission is to locate *Red October*. After that we're not sure. I imagine just locating her will be hard enough.'

'An astute observation, Commander Ryan,' Hunter said.

'The good news is that Admiral Painter has requested that CINCLANT assign you control of several US Navy vessels, probably three 10152-class frigates, and a pair of FFG7 *Perrys*. They all carry a chopper or two.'

'Well, Geoffrey?' White asked.

'It's a start,' Hunter agreed.

'They'll be arriving in a day or two. Admiral Painter asked me to express his confidence in your group and its personnel.'

'A whole fucking Russian missile submarine . . .' Barclay said almost to himself. Ryan laughed.

'Like the idea, Commander?' At least he had one convert.

'What if the sub is heading for the UK? Does it then become a British operation?' Barclay asked pointedly.

'I suppose it would, but from the way I read the map, if Ramius was heading for England, he'd already be there. I saw a copy of the president's letter to the prime minister. In return for your assistance, the Royal Navy gets the same access to the data we develop as our guys get. We're on the same side gentlemen. The question is, can we do it?'

'Hunter?' the admiral asked.

'If this intelligence is correct . . . I'd say we have a good chance, perhaps as good as fifty percent. On one hand, we have a missile submarine attempting to evade detection. On the other, we have a great deal of ASW arrayed to locate her, and she will be heading towards one of only a few discrete locations. Norfolk, of course, Newport, Groton, King's Bay, Port Everglades, Charleston. A civilian port such as New York is less likely, I think. The problem is, what with Ivan sending all his *Alfas* racing to your coast, they will get there ahead of *October*. They may have a specific port target in mind. We'll know that in another day. So, I'd say they have an equal chance. They'll be able to operate far enough off your coast that your government will have no viable legal reason to object to whatever they do. If anything, I'd say the Soviets have the advantage. They have both a clearer idea of the submarine's capabilities and a simpler overall mission. That more than balances their less capable sensors.'

'Why isn't Ramius coming on faster?' Ryan asked. 'That's the one thing I can't figure. Once he clears the SOSUS lines off Iceland, he's clear into the deep basin – so why not crack his throttles wide open and race for our coast?'

'At least two reasons,' Barclay answered. 'How much operational intelligence data do you see?'

'I handle individual assignments. That means I hop around a lot from one thing to another. I know a good deal about their boomers, for example, but not as much about their attack boats.' Ryan didn't have to explain he was CIA.

'Well, you know how compartmentalised the Sovs are. Ramius probably doesn't know where their attack submarines are, not all of them. So, if he were to race about, he'd run the off chance of blundering into a stray *Victor* and being sunk without ever knowing what was happening. Second, what if the Soviets did enlist American assistance, saying perhaps that a missile sub had been taken over by a mutinous crew of Maoist counter-revolutionaries – and then your navy detects a missile submarine racing down the North Atlantic towards the American coast? What would your president do?'

'Yeah,' Ryan nodded. 'We'd blow it the hell out of the water.'

'There you have it. Ramius is in the trade of stealth, and he'll likely stick to what he knows,' Barclay concluded. 'Fortunately or unfortunately, he's jolly good at it.'

'How soon will we have performance data on this quiet drive system?' Carstairs wanted to know.

'Next couple of days, we hope.'

'Where does Admiral Painter want us?' White asked.

'The plan he submitted to Norfolk puts you on the right flank. He wants *Kennedy* inshore to handle the threat from their surface force. He wants your force farther out. You see, Painter thinks there's a chance that Ramius will come straight south from the G-l-U-K gap into the Atlantic basin and just sit for a while. The odds favour his not being detected there, and if the Soviets send the fleet after him, he's got the time and supplies to sit out there longer than they can maintain a force off our coast – both for technical and political reasons. Additionally, he wants your striking power out here to threaten their flank. It has to be approved by the commander in chief of the Atlantic Fleet, and a lot of details remain to be worked out. For example, Painter requested some E-3 Sentries to support you out here.'

'A month in the middle of the North Atlantic in winter?' Carstairs winced. He had been the *Invincible's* executive officer during the war around the Falklands and had ridden in the violent South Atlantic for endless weeks.

'Be happy for the E-3s.' The admiral smiled. 'Hunter, I want to see plans for using all these ships the Yanks are giving us, and how we can cover a maximum area. Barclay, I want to see your evaluation of what our friend Ramius will do. Assume he's still the clever bastard we've come to know and love.'

'Aye aye, sir.' Barclay stood with the others.

'Jack, how long will you be with us?'

'I don't know, Admiral. Until they recall me to the *Kennedy*, I guess. From where I sit, this operation was laid on too fast. Nobody really knows what the hell we're supposed to do.'

'Well, why don't you let us see to this for a while? You look exhausted. Get some sleep.'

'True enough, Admiral.' Ryan was beginning to feel the brandy.

'There's a cot in the locker over there. I'll have someone set it up for you, and you can sleep in here for the time being. If anything comes in for you, we'll get you up.'

'That's kind of you, sir.' Admiral White was a good guy, Jack thought, and his wife was something very special. In ten minutes, Ryan was on the cot and asleep.

The *Red October*

Every two days the *starpom* collected the radiation badges. This was part of a semiformal inspection. After seeing to it that every crewman's shoes were spit shined, every bunk was properly made, and every footlocker was arranged according to the book, the executive officer would take the two-day-old badges and hand the sailors new ones, usually along with some terse advice to square themselves away as New Soviet Men ought. Borodin had this procedure down to a science. Today, as always, the trip from one compartment to another took two hours. When he was finished, the bag on his left hip was full of old badges, and the one on his right was depleted of new ones. He took the badges to the ship's medical office.

'Comrade Petrov, I have a gift for you.' Borodin set the leather bag on the physician's desk.

'Good.' The doctor smiled up at the executive officer. 'With all the healthy young men I have little to do but read my journals.'

Borodin left Petrov to his task. First the doctor set the badges out in order. Each bore a three-digit number. The first digit identified the badge series, so that if any radiation were detected there would be a time reference. The second digit showed where the sailor worked, the third where he slept. This system was easier to work with than the old one, which had used individual numbers for each man.

The developing process was cookbook-simple. Petrov could do it without a thought. First he switched off the white overhead light and replaced it with a red one. Then he locked his office door. Next he took the development rack from its holder on the bulkhead, broke open the plastic holders, and transferred the film strips to spring clips on the rack.

Petrov took the rack into the adjacent laboratory and hung it on the handle of the single filing cabinet. He filled three large square basins with chemicals. Though a qualified physician, he had forgotten most of his inorganic chemistry and didn't remember exactly what the developing chemicals were. Basin number one was filled from bottle number one. Basin two was filled from bottle two, and basin three, he remembered, was filled with water. Petrov was in no hurry. The midday meal was not for two more hours, and his duties were truly boring. The last two days he had been reading his medical texts on tropical diseases. The doctor was looking forward to visiting Cuba as much as anyone aboard. With luck a crewman would come down with some obscure malady, and he'd have something interesting to work on for once.

Petrov set the lab timer for seventy-five seconds and submerged the film strips in the first basin as he pressed the start button. He watched the timer under the red light, wondering if the Cubans still made rum. He had been there, too, years before, and acquired a taste for the exotic liquor. Like any good Soviet citizen, he loved his vodka but had the occasional hankering for something different.

The timer went off and he lifted the rack, shaking it carefully over the tank. No sense getting the chemical – silver nitrate? something like that – on his uniform. The rack went into the second tank, and he set the timer again. Pity the orders had been so damned secret – he could have brought his tropical uniform. He'd sweat like a pig in the Cuban heat. Of course, none of those savages ever bothered to wash. Maybe they had learned something in the past fifteen years? He'd see.

The timer dinged again, and Petrov lifted the rack a second time, shaking it and setting it in the water-filled basin. Another boring job completed. Why couldn't a sailor fall down a ladder and break something? He wanted to use his East German X-ray machine on a live patient. He didn't trust the Germans, Marxists or not, but they did make good medical equipment, including his X-ray, autoclave, and most of his pharmaceuticals. Time. Petrov lifted the rack and held it up against the X-ray reading plate, which he switched on.

'*Nichevo!*' Petrov breathed. He had to think. His badge was fogged. Its number was 3-4-8: third badge series, frame fifty-four (the medical office galley section), aft (officers') accommodation.

Though only two centimetres across, the badges were made with variable sensitivity. Ten vertically segmented columns were used to quantify the exposure level. Petrov saw that his was fogged all the way to segment four. The engine room crewmen's were fogged to segment five, and the torpedomen, who spent all their time forward, showed contamination only in segment one.

'Son of a bitch.' He knew the sensitivity levels by heart. He took the manual down to check them anyway. Fortunately, the segments were logarithmic. His exposure was twelve rads. Fifteen to twenty-five for the engineers. Twelve to twenty-five rads in two days, not enough to be dangerous. Not really life threatening, but . . . Petrov went back into his office, careful to leave the films in the lab. He picked up the phone.

'Captain Ramius? Petrov here. Could you come aft to my office, please?'

'On the way, Comrade Doctor.'

Ramius took his time. He knew what the call was about. The day before they sailed, while Petrov had been ashore procuring drugs for his cupboard, Borodin had contaminated the badges with the X-ray machine.

'Yes, Petrov?' Ramius closed the door behind him.

'Comrade Captain, we have a radiation leak.'

'Nonsense. Our instruments would have detected it at once.'

Petrov got the films from the lab and handed them to the captain. 'Look here.'

Ramius held them up to the light, scanning the film strips top to bottom. He frowned. 'Who knows of this?'

'You and I, Comrade Captain.'

'You will tell no one – no one.' Ramius paused. 'Any chance that the films were – that they have something wrong, that you made an error in the developing process?'

Petrov shook his head emphatically. 'No, Comrade Captain. Only you, Comrade Borodin, and I have access to these. As you know, I tested random samples from each batch three days before we sailed.' Petrov wouldn't admit that, like everyone, he had taken the samples from the top of the box they were stored in. They weren't really random.

'The maximum exposure I see here is . . . ten to twenty?' Ramius understated it. 'Whose numbers?'

'Bulganin and Surzpoi. The torpedomen forward are all under three rads.'

'Very well. What we have here, Comrade Doctor, is a possible minor – minor, Petrov – leak in the reactor spaces. At worst a gas leak of some sort. This has happened before, and no one has ever died from it. The leak will be found and fixed. We will keep this little secret. There is no reason to get the men excited over nothing.'

Petrov nodded agreement, knowing that men had died in 1970 in an accident on the submarine *Voroshilov*, more in the icebreaker *Lenin*. Both accidents were a long time ago, though, and he was sure Ramius could handle things. Wasn't he?

The Pentagon

The E ring was the outermost and largest of the Pentagon's rings, and since its outside windows offered something other than a view of sunless court-yards, this was where the most senior defence officials had their offices. One of these was the office of the director of operations for the Joint Chiefs of Staff, the J-3. He wasn't there. He was down in a sub-basement room known colloquially as the Tank because its metal walls were dotted with electronic noisemakers to foil other electronic devices.

He had been there for twenty-four hours, though one would not have known this from his appearance. His green trousers were still creased, his khaki shirt still showed the folds made by the laundry, its collar starched plywood-stiff, and his tie was held neatly in place by a gold marine corps tiepin. Lieutenant General Edwin Harris was neither a diplomat nor a service academy gradu-ate, but he was playing peacemaker. An odd position for a marine.

'God damn it!' It was the voice of Admiral Blackburn, CINCLANT. Also present was his own operations officer, Rear Admiral Pete Stanford. 'Is this any way to run an operation?'

The Joint Chiefs were all there, and none of them thought so.

'Look, Blackie, I told you where the orders come from.' General Hilton, chairman of the Joint Chiefs of Staff, sounded tired.

'I understand that, General, but this is largely a submarine operation, right? I gotta get Vince Gallery in on this, and you should have Sam Dodge working up at this end. Dan and I are both fighter jocks, Pete's an ASW expert. We need a sub driver in on this.'

'Gentlemen,' Harris said calmly, 'for the moment the plan we have to take to the president need only deal with the Soviet threat. Let's hold this story about the defecting boomer in abeyance for the moment, shall we?'

'I agree,' Stanford nodded. 'We have enough to worry about right here.'

The attention of the eight flag officers turned to the map table. Fifty-eight Soviet submarines and twenty-eight surface warships, plus a gaggle of oiler and replenishment ships, were unmistakably heading for the American coast. To face this, the US Navy had one available carrier. The *Invincible* did not rate as such. The threat was considerable. Among them the Soviet vessels carried over three hundred surface-to-surface cruise missiles. Though principally designed as antiship weapons, the third of them believed to carry nuclear warheads were sufficient to devastate the cities on the East Coast. From a position off New Jersey, these missiles could range from Norfolk to Boston.

'Josh Painter proposes that we keep *Kennedy* inshore,' Admiral Blackburn said. 'He wants to run the ASW operation from his carrier, transferring his light attack squadrons to shore and replacing them with S-3s. He wants *Invincible* out on their seaward flank.'

'I don't like it,' General Harris said. Neither did Pete Stanford, and they had agreed earlier that the J-3 would launch the counterplan. 'Gentlemen, if we're only going to have one deck to use, we damned well ought to have a carrier and not an oversized ASW platform.'

'We're listening, Eddie,' Hilton said.

'Let's move *Kennedy* out here.' He moved the counter to a position west of the Azores. 'Josh keeps his attack squadrons. We move *Invincible* inshore to handle the ASW work. It's what the Brits designed her for, right? They're supposed to be good at it. *Kennedy* is an offensive weapon, her mission is to threaten them. Okay, if we deploy like this, she is the threat. From over here she can range against their surface force from outside their surface-to-surface missile perimeter – '

'Better yet,' Stanford interjected, pointing to some vessels on the map, 'threaten this service force here. If they lose these oilers, they ain't going home. To meet that threat they'll have to redeploy themselves. For starters, they'll have to move *Kiev* offshore to give themselves some kind of air

115

defense against *Kennedy*. We can use the spare S-3s from shore bases. They can still patrol the same area.' He traced a line about five hundred miles off the coast.

'Leaves *Invincible* kind of naked, though,' the CNO, Admiral Forster, noted.

'Josh was asking about some E-3 coverage for the Brits.' Blackburn looked at the air force chief of staff, General Claire Barnes.

'You want help, you get help,' Barnes said. 'We'll have a Sentry operating over *Invincible* at dawn tomorrow, and if you move her inshore we can maintain that round the clock. I'll throw in a wing of F-16s if you want.'

'What do you want in return, Max?' Foster asked. Nobody called him Claire.

'The way I see this, you have *Saratoga's* air wing sitting around doing nothing. Okay, by Saturday I'll have five hundred tactical fighters deployed from Dover to Loring. My boys don't know much about antiship stuff. They'll have to learn in a hurry. I want you to send your kids to work with mine, and I also want your Tomcats. I like the fighter-missile combination. Let one squadron work out of Iceland, the other out of New England to track the Bears Ivan's starting to send our way. I'll sweeten that. If you want, we'll send some tankers to Lajes to help keep *Kennedy's* birds flying.'

'Blackie?' Foster asked.

'Deal,' Blackburn nodded. 'The only thing that bothers me is that *Invincible* doesn't have all that much ASW capacity.'

'So we get more,' Stanford said. 'Admiral, what say we take *Tarawa* out of Little Creek, team her with *New Jersey's* group, with a dozen ASW choppers aboard and seven or eight Harriers?'

'I like it,' Harris said quickly. 'Then we have two baby carriers with a noteworthy striking force right in front of their groups, *Kennedy* playing stalking tiger to their east, and a few hundred tactical fighters to the west. They have to come into a three-way box. This actually gives us more ASW patrolling capacity than we'd have otherwise.'

'Can *Kennedy* handle her mission alone out there?' Hilton asked.

'Depend on it,' Blackburn replied. 'We can kill any one, maybe any two of these four groups in an hour. The ones nearest shore will be your job, Max.'

'How long did you two characters rehearse this?' General Maxwell, commandant of the marine corps, asked the operations officers. Everyone chuckled.

The *Red October*

Chief Engineer Melekhin cleared the reactor compartment before beginning the check for the leak. Ramius and Petrov were there also, plus the engineering duty officers and one of the young lieutenants, Svyadov. Three of the officers carried Geiger counters.

116

The reactor room was quite large. It had to be to accommodate the massive, barrel-shaped steel vessel. The object was warm to the touch despite being inactive. Automatic radiation detectors were in every corner of the room, each surrounded by a red circle. More were hanging on the fore and aft bulkheads. Of all the compartments on the submarine, this was the cleanest. The deck and bulkheads were spotless white-painted steel. The reason was obvious: the smallest leak of reactor coolant had to be instantly visible even if all the detectors failed.

Svyadov climbed an aluminium ladder affixed to the side of the reactor vessel to run the detachable probe from his counter over every welded pipe joint. The speaker-annunciator on the hand-held box was turned to maximum so that everyone in the compartment could hear it, and Svyadov had an earpiece plugged in for even greater sensitivity. A youngster of twenty-one, he was nervous. Only a fool would feel entirely safe looking for a radiation leak. There is a joke in the Soviet Navy: How do you tell a sailor from the Northern Fleet? He glows in the dark. It had been a good laugh on the beach, but not now. He knew that he was conducting the search because he was the youngest, least experienced, and most expendable officer. It was an effort to keep his knees from wobbling as he strained to reach all over and around the reactor piping.

The counter was not entirely silent, and Svyadov's stomach cringed at each click generated by the passage of a random particle through the tube of ionized gas. Every few seconds his eyes flickered to the dial that measured intensity. It was well inside the safe range, hardly registering at all. The reactor vessel was a quadruple-layer design, each layer several centimetres of tough stainless steel. The three inner spaces were filled with a barium-water mixture, then a barrier of lead, then polyethylene, all designed to prevent the escape of neutrons and gamma particles. The combination of steel, barium, lead and plastic successfully contained the dangerous elements of the reaction, allowing only a few degrees of heat to escape, and the dial showed, much to his relief, that the radiation level was less than that on the beach at Sochi. The highest reading was made next to a light bulb. This made the lieutenant smile.

'All readings in normal range, comrades,' Svyadov replied.

'Start over,' Melekhin ordered, 'from the beginning.'

Twenty minutes later Svyadov, now sweating from the warm air that gathered at the top of the compartment, made an identical report. He came down awkwardly, his arms and legs tired.

'Have a cigarette,' Ramius suggested. You did well, Svyadov.'

'Thank you, Comrade Captain. It's warm up there from the lights and the coolant pipes.' The lieutenant handed the counter to Melekhin. The lower dial showed a cumulative count, well within the safe range.

'Probably some contaminated badges,' the chief engineer commented sourly. 'It would not be the first time. Some joker in the factory or at the yard supply office – something for our friends in the GRU to check into. "Wreckers!" A joke like this ought to earn somebody a bullet.'

'Perhaps,' Ramius chuckled. 'Remember the incident on *Lenin*?' He referred to the nuclear-powered icebreaker that had spent two years tied to the dock, unusable because of a reactor mishap. 'A ship's cook had some badly crusted pans, and a madman of an engineer suggested that he use live steam to get them cleaned. So the idiot walked down to the steam generator and opened an inspection valve, with his pots under it?'

Melekhin rolled his eyes. 'I remember it! I was a staff engineering officer then. The Captain had asked for a Kazakh cook – '

'He liked horsemeat with his kasha,' Ramius said.

' – and the fool didn't know the first thing about a ship. Killed himself and three other men, contaminated the whole fucking compartment for twenty months. The captain only got out of the gulag last year.'

'I bet the cook got his pans cleaned, though,' Ramius observed.

'Indeed, Marko Aleksandrovich – they may even be safe to use in another fifty years.' Melekhin laughed raucously.

That was a hell of a thing to say in front of a young officer, Petrov thought. There was nothing, nothing at all funny about a reactor leak. But Melekhin was known for his heavy sense of humour, and the doctor imagined that twenty years of working on reactors allowed him and the captain to view the potential dangers phlegmatically. Then, there was the implicit lesson in the story: never let someone who does not belong into the reactor spaces.

'Very well,' Melekhin said, 'now we check the pipes in the generator room. Come, Svyadov, we still need your young legs.'

The next compartment aft contained the heat exchanger/steam generator, turboalternators, and auxiliary equipment. The main turbines were in the next compartment, now inactive while the electrically driven caterpillar was operating. In any case, the steam that turned them was supposed to be clean. The only radioactivity was in the inside loop. The reactor coolant, which carried short-lived but dangerous radioactivity, never flashed to steam. This was in the outside loop and boiled from uncontaminated water. The two water supplies met but never mixed inside the heat exchanger, the most likely site for a coolant leak because of its more numerous fittings and valves.

The more complex piping required a full fifty minutes to check. These pipes were not as well insulated as those forward. Svyadov nearly burned himself twice, and his face was bathed in perspiration by the time he finished his first sweep.

'Readings all safe again, comrades.'

'Good,' Melekhin said. 'Come down and rest a moment before you check it again.'

Svyadov almost thanked his chief for that, but this would not have done at all. As a young, dedicated officer and member of the Komsomol, no exertion was too great. He came down carefully, and Melekhin handed him another cigarette. The chief engineer was a grey-haired perfectionist who took decent care of his men.

'Why, thank you, Comrade,' Svyadov said.

Petrov got a folding chair. 'Sit, Comrade Lieutenant, rest your legs.'

The lieutenant sat down at once, stretching his legs to work out the knots. The officers at VVMUPP had told him how lucky he was to draw this assignment. Ramius and Melekhin were the two best teachers in the fleet, men whose crews appreciated their kindness along with their competence.

'They really should insulate those pipes,' Ramius said. Melekhin shook his head.

'Then they'd be too hard to inspect.' He handed the counter to his captain.

'Entirely safe,' the captain read off the cumulative dial. 'You get more exposure tending a garden.'

'Indeed,' Melekhin said. 'Coal miners get more exposure than we do, from the release of radon gas in the mines. Bad badges, that's what it has to be. Why not take out a whole batch and check it?'

'I could, Comrade,' Petrov answered. 'But then, due to the extended nature of our cruise, we'd have to run for several days without any. Contrary to regulations, I'm afraid.'

'You are correct. In any case the badges are only a backup to our instruments.' Ramius gestured to the red-circled detectors all over the compartment.

'Do you really want to recheck the piping?' Melekhin asked.

'I think we should,' Ramius said.

Svyadov swore to himself, looking down at the deck.

'There is no extravagance in the pursuit of safety,' Petrov quoted doctrine. 'Sorry, Lieutenant.' The doctor was not a bit sorry. He had been genuinely worried, and was now feeling a lot better.

An hour later the second check had been completed. Petrov took Svyadov forward for salt tablets and tea to rehydrate himself. The senior officer left, and Melekhin ordered the reactor plant restarted.

The enlisted men filed back to their duty stations, looking at one another. Their officers had just checked the 'hot' compartments with radiation instruments. The medical orderly had looked pale while earlier and refused to say anything. More than one engine attendant fingered his radiation badge and checked his wristwatch to see how long it would be before he went off duty.

The Eighth Day

Friday, 10 December

HMS *Invincible*

Ryan awoke in the dark. The curtains were drawn on the cabin's two small portholes. He shook his head a few times to clear it and began to assess what

119

was going on around him. The *Invincible* was moving on the seas, but not as much as before. He got up to look out of a porthole and saw the last red glow of sunset aft under scudding clouds. He checked his watch and did some clumsy mental arithmetic, concluding that it was six in the evening, local time. That translated to about six hours of sleep. He felt pretty good, considering. A minor headache from the brandy – so much for the theory that good stuff doesn't give you a hangover – and his muscles were stiff. He did a few sit-ups to work out the knots.

There was a small bathroom – head, he corrected himself – adjoining the cabin. Ryan splashed some water on his face and washed his mouth out, not wanting to look in the mirror. He decided he had to. Counterfeit or not, he was wearing his country's uniform and he had to look presentable. It took a minute to get his hair in place and the uniform arranged properly. The CIA had done a nice job of tailoring, given such short notice. Finished, he went out of the door towards the flag bridge.

'Feeling better, Jack?' Admiral White pointed him to a tray full of cups. It was only tea, but it was a start.

'Thank you, Admiral. Those few hours really helped. I guess I'm in time for dinner.'

'Breakfast,' White corrected him with a laugh.

'What – uh, pardon me, Admiral?' Ryan shook his head again. He was still a little groggy.

'That's a sun*rise*, Commander. Change in orders, we're heading west again, *Kennedy's* moving east at high speed, and we're to take station inshore.'

'Who said, sir?'

'CINCLANT. I gather Joshua was not at all pleased. You are to remain with us for the moment, and under the circumstances it seemed the reasonable thing to let you sleep. You did appear to need it.'

Must have been eighteen hours, Ryan thought. No wonder he felt stiff.

'You do look much better,' Admiral White noted from his leather swivel chair. He got up, took Ryan's arm, and guided him aft. 'Now for breakfast. I've been waiting for you. Captain Hunter will brief you on our revised orders. Weather's clearing up for a few days, they tell me. Escort assignments are being reshuffled. We're to operate in conjunction with your *New Jersey* group. Our antisubmarine operations begin in earnest in another twelve hours. It's a good thing you got that extra sleep, lad. You'll bloody need it.'

Ryan ran his hand over his face. 'Can I shave, sir?'

'We still permit beards. Let it wait until after breakfast.'

Flag quarters on HMS *Invincible* were not quite to the standard of those on the *Kennedy* – but close. White had a private dining area. A steward in a white livery served them expertly, setting a third place for Hunter, who appeared within a few minutes. When they started talking, the steward was excused.

'We rendezvous with a pair of your *Knox*-class frigates in two hours. We already have them on radar. Two more 1052s, plus an oiler and two *Perrys* will join us in another thirty-six hours. They were on their way home from the Med. With our own escorts, a total of nine warships. A noteworthy collection, I think. We'll be working five hundred miles offshore with the *New Jersey* – *Tarawa* force two hundred miles to our west.'

'*Tarawa*? What do we need a regiment of marines for?' Ryan asked.

Hunter explained briefly. 'Not a bad idea, that. The funny thing is, with *Kennedy* racing for the Azores, that rather leaves us guarding the American coast.' Hunter grinned. 'This may be the first time the Royal Navy has ever done that – certainly since it belonged to us.'

'What are we up against?'

'The first of the *Alfas* will be on your coast tonight, four of them ahead of all the others. The Soviet surface force passed Iceland last night. It's divided into three groups. One is built around their carrier *Kiev*, two cruisers and four destroyers; the second, probably the force flag, is built around *Kirov*, with three additional cruisers and six destroyers; and the third is centred on *Moskva*, three more cruisers and seven destroyers. I gather that the Soviets will want to use the *Kiev* and *Moskva* groups inshore, with *Kirov* guarding them out to sea – but *Kennedy's* relocation will make them rethink that. Regardless, the total force carries a considerable number of surface-to-surface missiles, and potentially, we are very exposed. To help out with that, your air force has an E-3 Sentry detailed to arrive here in an hour to exercise with our Harriers, and when we get farther west, we'll have additional land-based air support. On the whole our position is hardly an enviable one, but Ivan's is rather less so. So far as the question of finding *Red October* is concerned?' Hunter shrugged. 'How we conduct our search will depend on how Ivan deploys. At the moment we're conducting some tracking drills. The lead *Alfa* is eighty miles northwest of us, steaming at forty-plus knots, and we have a helicopter in pursuit – which is roughly what it amounts to,' the fleet operations officer concluded. 'Will you join us below?'

'Admiral?' Ryan wanted to see *Invincible's* combat information centre.

'Certainly.'

Thirty minutes later Ryan was in a darkened, quiet room whose walls were a solid bank of electronic instruments and glass plotting panels. The Atlantic Ocean was full of Russian submarines.

The White House

The Soviet ambassador entered the Oval Office a minute early, at 10:59 A.M. He was a short, overweight man with a broad Slavic face and eyes that would have done a professional gambler proud. They revealed nothing. He was a career diplomat, having served in a number of posts throughout the Western world, and a thirty-year member of the Communist party's Foreign Department.

'Good morning, Mr President, Dr Pelt.' Alexei Arbatov nodded politely to both men. The president, he noted at once, was seated behind his desk. Every other time he'd been here the president had come around the desk to shake hands, then sat down beside him.

'Help yourself to some coffee, Mr Ambassador,' Pelt offered. The special assistant to the president for national security affairs was well known to Arbatov. Jeffrey Pelt was an academic from the Georgetown University's Centre for Strategic and International Studies – an enemy, but a well-mannered, *kulturny* enemy. Arbatov had a fondness for the niceties of formal behaviour. Today, Pelt was standing at his boss's side, unwilling to come too close to the Russian bear. Arbatov did not get himself any coffee.

'Mr Ambassador,' Pelt began, 'we have noted a troubling increase in Soviet naval activity in the North Atlantic.'

'Oh?' Arbatov's eyebrows shot up in a display of surprise that fooled no one, and he knew it. 'I have no knowledge of this. As you know, I have never been a sailor.'

'Shall we dispense with the bullshit, Mr Ambassador?' the president said. Arbatov did not permit himself to be surprised by the vulgarity. It made the American president seem very Russian, and like Soviet officials he seemed to need a professional like Pelt around to smooth the edges. 'You currently have nearly a hundred naval vessels operating in the North Atlantic or heading in that direction. Chairman Narmonov and my predecessor agreed years ago that no such operation would take place without prior notification. The purpose of this agreement, as you know, was to prevent acts that might appear to be unduly provocative to one side or the other. This agreement has been kept – until now.

'Now, my military advisers tell me that what is going on looks very much like a war exercise, indeed, could be the precursor to a war. How are we to tell the difference? Your ships are now passing east of Iceland, and will soon be in a position from which they can threaten our trade routes to Europe. This situation is at the least unsettling, and at the most a grave and wholly unwarranted provocation. The scope of this action has not yet been made public. That will change, and when it does, Alex, the American people will demand action on my part.' The president paused, expecting a response but getting only a nod.

Pelt went on for him. 'Mr Ambassador, your country has seen fit to cast aside an agreement which for years has been a model of East-West cooperation. How can you expect us to regard this as anything other than a provocation?'

'Mr President, Dr Pelt, truly I have no knowledge of this.' Arbatov lied with the utmost sincerity. 'I will contact Moscow at once to ascertain the facts. Is there any message you wish me to pass along?'

'Yes. As you and your superiors in Moscow will understand,' the president said, 'we will deploy our ships and aircraft to observe yours. Prudence requires this. We have no wish to interfere with whatever legitimate operations your forces may be engaged in. It is not our intention to make a provocation of our own, but under the terms of our agreement we have the right to know what is going on, Mr Ambassador. Until we do, we are unable to issue the proper orders to our men. It would be well for your government to consider that having so many of your ships and our ships, your aircraft and our aircraft in close proximity is an inherently dangerous situation. Accidents can happen. An action by one side or the other which at another time would seem harmless might seem to be something else entirely. Wars have begun in this way, Mr Ambassador.' The president leaned back to let that thought hang in the air for a moment. When he went on, he spoke more gently. 'Of course, I regard this possibility as remote, but is it not irresponsible to take such chances?'

'Mr President, you make your point well, as always, but as you know, the sea is free for the passage of all, and – '

'Mr Ambassador,' Pelt interrupted, 'consider a simple analogy. Your next-door neighbour begins to patrol his front yard with a loaded shotgun while your children are at play in your own front yard. In this country such action would be technically legal. Even so, would it not be a matter of concern?'

'So it would, Dr Pelt, but the situation you describe is very different – '

Now the president interrupted. 'Indeed it is. The situation at hand is far more dangerous. It is the breach of an agreement, and I find that especially disquieting. I had hoped that we were entering a new era of Soviet-American relations. We have settled our trade differences. We have just concluded a new grain agreement. You had a major part in that. We have been moving forward, Mr Ambassador – is this at an end?' The president shook his head emphatically. 'I hope not, but the choice is yours. The relationship between our countries can only be based on trust.

'Mr Ambassador, I trust that I have not alarmed you. As you know, it is my habit to speak plainly. I personally dislike the greasy dissimulation of diplomacy. At times like this, we must communicate quickly and clearly. We have a dangerous situation before us, and we must work together, rapidly, to resolve it. My military commanders are greatly concerned, and I need to know – today – what your naval forces are up to. I expect a reply by seven this evening. Failing that I will be on the direct line to Moscow to demand one.'

Arbatov stood. 'Mr President, I will transmit your message within the hour. Please keep in mind, however, the time differential between Washington and Moscow – '

'I know that a weekend has just begun, and that the Soviet Union is a worker's paradise, but I expect that some of your country's managers may still be at work. In any case, I will detain you no further. Good day.'

Pelt led Arbatov out, then came back and sat down.

'Maybe I was just a little tough on him,' the president said.

'Yes, sir.' Pelt thought that he had been too damned tough. He had little affection for the Russians but he too liked the niceties of diplomatic exchange. 'I think we can say that you succeeded in getting your message across.'

'He knows.'

'He knows. But he doesn't know we know.'

'We think,' the president grimaced. 'What a crazy goddamned game this is! And to think I had a nice, safe career going for me putting mafiosi in jail . . . Do you think he'll snap at the bait I offered?'

'"Legitimate operations?" Did you see his hands twitch at that? He'll go after it like a marline after a squid.' Pelt walked over to pour himself half a cup of coffee. It pleased him that the china service was gold trimmed. 'I wonder what they'll call it: Legitimate operations . . . probably a rescue mission. If they call it a fleet exercise they admit to violating the notification protocol. A rescue operation justifies the level of activity, the speed with which it was laid on, and the lack of publicity. Their press never reports this sort of thing. As a guess, I'd say they'll call it a rescue, say a submarine is missing, maybe even to the point of calling it a missile sub.'

'No, they won't go that far. We also have that agreement about keeping our missile subs five hundred miles offshore. Arbatov probably has his instructions on what to tell us already, but he'll play for all the time he can. It's also vaguely possible that he's in the dark. We know how they compartmentalise information. You suppose we're reading too much into his talent for obfuscation?'

'I think not, sir. It is a principle of diplomacy,' Pelt observed, 'that one must know something of the truth in order to lie convincingly.'

The president smiled. 'Well, they've had enough time to play this game. I hope my belated reaction will not disappoint them.'

'No, sir. Alex must have half expected you to kick him out the door.'

'The thought's occurred to me more than once. His diplomatic charm has always been lost on me. That's the one thing about the Russians – they remind me so much of the mafia chieftains I used to prosecute. The same smattering of culture and good manners, and the same absence of morality.' The president shook his head. He was talking like a hawk again. 'Stay close, Jeff. I have George Farmer coming in here in a few minutes, but I want you around when our friend comes back.'

Pelt walked back to his office pondering the president's remark. It was, he admitted to himself, crudely accurate. The most wounding insult to an educated Russian was to be called *nekulturny*, uncultured – the term didn't translate adequately – yet the same men who sat in the gilt boxes at the Moscow State Opera weeping at the end of a performance of *Boris Gudunov* could immediately turn around and order the execution or imprisonment of a hundred men without blinking. A strange people, made more strange by their political philosophy. But the president had too many sharp edges, and

Pelt wished he'd learn to soften them. A speech in front of the American Legion was one thing, a discussion with the ambassador of a foreign power was something else.

CIA Headquarters

'CARDINAL's in trouble, Judge.' Ritter sat down.

'No surprise there.' Moore removed his glasses and rubbed his eyes. Something Ryan had not seen was the cover note from the station chief in Moscow saying that to get his latest signal out, CARDINAL had by-passed half the courier chain that ran from the Kremlin to the US embassy. The agent was getting bold in his old age. 'What does the station chief say exactly?'

'CARDINAL's supposed to be in the hospital with pneumonia. Maybe it's true, but . . .'

'He's getting old, and it is winter over there, but who believes in coincidences?' Moore looked down at his desk. 'What do you suppose they'd do if they've turned him?'

'He'd die quietly. Depends on who turned him. If it was the KGB, they might want to make something out of it, especially since our friend Andropov took a lot of their prestige with him when he left. But I don't think so. Given who his sponsor is, it would raise too much of a ruckus. Same thing if the GRU turns him. No, they'd grill him for a few weeks, then quietly do away with him. A public trial would be too counterproductive.'

Judge Moore frowned. They sounded like doctors discussing a terminally ill patient. He didn't even know what CARDINAL looked like. There was a photograph somewhere in the file, but he had never seen it. It was easier that way. As an appellate court judge he had never had to look a defendant in the eye; he'd just reviewed the law in a detached way. He tried to keep his stewardship of the CIA the same way. Moore knew that this might be perceived as cowardly, and was very different from what people expect of a DCI – but even spies got old, and old men developed consciences and doubts that rarely troubled the young. It was time to leave the 'Company.' Nearly three years, it was enough. He'd accomplished what he was supposed to do.

'Tell the station chief to lay off. No inquiries of any kind directed at CARDINAL. If he's really sick, we'll be hearing from him again. If not, we'll know that soon enough, too.'

'Right.'

Ritter had succeeded in confirming CARDINAL's report. One agent had reported that the fleet was sailing with additional political officers, another that the surface force was commanded by an academic sailor and crony of Gorshkov, who had flown to Sveromorsk and boarded the *Kirov* minutes before the fleet had sailed. The naval architect who was believed to have designed the *Red October* was supposed to have gone with him. A British

125

agent had reported that detonators for the various weapons carried by the surface ships had been hastily taken aboard from their usual storage depots ashore. Finally, there was an unconfirmed report that Admiral Korov, commander of the Northern Fleet, was not at his command post; his whereabouts were unknown. Together the information was enough to confirm the WILLOW report, and more was still coming in.

The US Naval Academy

'Skip?'

'Oh, howdy, Admiral. Will you join me?' Tyler waved to a vacant chair across the table.

'I got a message from the Pentagon for you.' The superintendent of the Naval Academy, a former submarine officer, sat down. 'You have an appointment tonight at 1930 hours. That's all they said.'

'Great!' Tyler was just finishing his lunch. He'd been working on the simulation programme nearly around the clock since Monday. The appointment meant that he would have access to the air force's Cray-2 tonight. His programme was just about ready.

'What's this all about anyway?'

'Sorry, sir, I can't say. You know how it is.'

The White House

The Soviet ambassador was back at four in the afternoon. To avoid press notice he had been taken into the Treasury building across the street from the White House and brought through a connecting tunnel which few knew existed. The president hoped that he had found this unsettling. Pelt hustled in to be there when Arbatov arrived.

'Mr President,' Arbatov reported, standing at attention. The president had not known that he had any military experience. 'I am instructed to convey to you the regrets of my government that there has not been time to inform you of this. One of our nuclear submarines is missing and presumed lost. We are conducting an emergency rescue operation.'

The president nodded soberly, motioning the ambassador to a chair. Pelt sat next to him.

'This is somewhat embarrassing, Mr President. You see, in our navy as in yours, duty on a nuclear submarine is a posting of the greatest importance, and consequently those selected for it are among our best educated and trusted men. In this particular case several members of the crew – the officers, that is – are sons of high Party officials. One is even the son of a Central Committee member – I cannot say which, of course. The Soviet Navy's great effort to find her sons is understandable, though I admit a bit undisciplined.' Arbatov feigned embarrassment beautifully, speaking as

126

though he were confiding a great family secret. 'Therefore, this has developed into what your people call an "all hands" operation. As you undoubtedly know, it was undertaken virtually overnight.'

'I see,' the president said sympathetically. 'That makes me feel a little better, Alex. Jeff, I think it's late enough in the day. How about you fix us all a drink. Bourbon, Alex?'

'Yes, thank you, sir.'

Pelt walked over to a rosewood cabinet against the wall. The ornate antique contained a small bar, complete with an ice bucket which was stocked every afternoon. The president often liked to have a drink or two before dinner, something else that reminded Arbatov of his countrymen. Dr Pelt had had ample experience playing presidential bartender. In a few minutes he came back with three glasses in his hands.

'To tell you the truth, we rather suspected this was a rescue operation,' Pelt said.

'I don't know how we get our young men to do this sort of work.' The president sipped at his drink. Arbatov worked hard on his. He had said frequently at local cocktail parties that he preferred American bourbon to his native vodka. Maybe it was true. 'We've lost a pair of nuclear boats, I believe. How many does this make for you, three, four?'

'I don't know, Mr President. I expect your information on this is better than my own.' The president noted that he had just told the truth for the first time today. 'Certainly I can agree with you that such duty is both dangerous and demanding.'

'How many men aboard, Alex?' the president asked.

'I have no idea. A hundred more or less, I suppose. I've never been aboard a naval vessel.'

'Mostly kids, probably, just like our crews. It is indeed a sad commentary on both our countries that our mutual suspicions must condemn so many of our best young men to such hazards, when we know that some won't be coming back. But – how can it be otherwise?' The president paused, turning to look out the windows. The snow was melting on the South Lawn. It was time for his next line.

'Perhaps we can help,' the president offered speculatively. 'Yes, perhaps we can use this tragedy as an opportunity to reduce those suspicions by some small amount. Perhaps we can make something good come from this to demonstrate that our relations really have improved.'

Pelt turned away, fumbling for his pipe. In their many years of friendship he could never understand how the president got away with so much. Pelt had met him at Washington University, when he was majoring in political science, the president in prelaw. Back then the chief executive had been president of the dramatics society. Certainly amateur theatrics had helped his legal career. It was said that at least one Mafia don had been sent up the river by sheer rhetoric. The president referred to it as his sincere act.

'Mr Ambassador, I offer you the assistance and the resources of the United States in the search for your missing countrymen.'

'That is most kind of you, Mr President, but – '

The president held his hand up. 'No buts, Alex. If we cannot cooperate in something like this, how can we hope to cooperate in more serious matters? If memory serves, last year when one of our navy patrol aircraft crashed off the Aleutians, one of your fishing vessels' – it had been an intelligence trawler – 'picked up the crew, saved their lives. Alex, we owe you a debt for that, a debt of honour, and the United States will not be said to be ungrateful.' He paused for effect. 'They're probably all dead, you know. I don't suppose there's more chance of surviving a sub accident than of surviving a plane crash. But at least the crew's families will know. Jeff, don't we have some specialised submarine rescue equipment?'

'With all the money we give the navy? We damned well ought to. I'll call Foster about it.'

'Good,' the president said. 'Alex, it is too much to expect that our mutual suspicions will be allayed by something so small as this. Your history and ours conspire against us. But let's make a small beginning with this. If we can shake hands in space or over a conference table in Vienna, maybe we can do it here also. I will give the necessary instructions to my commanders as soon as we're finished here.'

'Thank you, Mr President.' Arbatov concealed his uneasiness.

'And please convey my respects to Chairman Narmonov and my sympathy for the families of your missing men. I appreciate his effort, and yours, in getting this information to us.'

'Yes, Mr President.' Arbatov rose. He left after shaking hands. What were the Americans really up to? He'd warned Moscow: call it a rescue mission and they'd demand to help. It was their stupid Christmas season, and Americans were addicted to happy endings. It was madness not to call it something else – to hell with the protocol.

At the same time he was forced to admire the American president. A strange man, very open, yet full of guile. A friendly man most of the time, yet always ready to seize the advantage. He remembered stories his grandmother had told, about how gypsies switched babies. The American president was very Russian.

'Well,' the president said after the doors closed, 'now we can keep a nice close eye on them, and they can't complain. They're lying and we know it – but they don't know we know. And we're lying, and they certainly suspect it, but not why we're lying. Gawd! and I told him this morning that not knowing was dangerous! Jeff, I've been thinking about this. I do not like the fact that so much of their navy is operating off our coast. Ryan was right, the Atlantic is our ocean. I want the air force and the navy to cover them like a goddamned blanket! That's our ocean, and I damned well want them to know it.' The president finished off his drink. 'On the question of the sub,

I want our people to have a good look at it, and whoever of the crew wants to defect, we take care of. Quietly, of course.'

'Of course. As a practical matter, having the officers is as great a coup as having the submarine.'

'But the navy will still want to keep it.'

'I just don't see how we can do that, not without eliminating the crewmen, and we can't do that.'

'Agreed.' The president buzzed his secretary. 'Get me General Hilton.'

The Pentagon

The air force's computer centre was in a sub-basement of the Pentagon. The room temperature was well below seventy degrees. It was enough to make Tyler's leg ache where it met the metal-plastic prosthesis. He was used to that.

Tyler was sitting at a control console. He had just finished a trial run of his programme, named MORAY after the vicious eel that inhabits oceanic reefs. Skip Tyler was proud of his programming ability. He'd taken the old dinosaur programme from the files of the Tayler Lab, adapted it to the common Defense Department computer language, AD – named for Lady Ada Lovelace, daughter of Lord Byron – and then tightened it up. For most people this would have been a month's work. He'd done it in four days, working almost around the clock not only because the money was an attractive incentive but also because the project was a professional challenge. He ended the job quietly satisfied that he could still meet an impossible deadline with time to spare. It was eight in the evening. MORAY had just run through a one-variable-value test and not crashed. He was ready.

He'd never seen the Cray-2 before, except in photographs, and he was pleased to have a chance to use it. The -2 was five units of raw electrical power, each one roughly pentagonal in shape, about six feet high and four across. The largest unit was the main-frame processor bank; the other four were memory banks, arrayed around it in a cruciform configuration. Tyler typed in the command to load his variable sets. For each of the *Red October's* main dimensions – length, beam, height – he input ten discrete numerical values. Then came six subtly different values for her hull form, block and prismatic coefficients. There were five sets of tunnel dimensions. This aggregated to over thirty thousand possible permutations. Next he keyed in eighteen power variables to cover the range of possible engine systems. The Cray-2 absorbed this information and placed each number in its proper slot. It was ready to run.

'Okay,' he announced to the system operator, an air force master sergeant.

'Roge.' The sergeant typed 'XQT' into his terminal. The Cray-2 went to work.

Tyler walked over to the sergeant's console.

'That's a right lengthy programme you've input, sir.' The sergeant laid a ten-dollar bill on the top of the console. 'Betcha my baby can run it in ten minutes.'

'Not a chance.' Tyler laid his own bill next to the sergeant's. 'Fifteen minutes, easy.'

'Split the difference?'

'Alright. Where's the head around here?'

'Out the door, sir, turn right, go down the hall and it's on the left.'

Tyler moved towards the door. It annoyed him that he could not walk gracefully, but after four years the inconvenience was a minor one. He was alive – that's what counted. The accident had occurred on a cold, clear night in Groton, Connecticut, only a block from the shipyard's main gate. On Friday at three in the morning he was driving home after a twenty-hour day getting his new command ready for sea. The civilian yard worker had had a long day also, stopping off at a favourite watering hole for a few too many, as the police established afterwards. He got into his car, started it, and ran a red light, ramming Tyler's Pontiac broadside at fifty miles per hour. For him the accident was fatal. Skip was luckier. It was at an intersection, and he had the green light; when he saw the front end of the Ford not a foot from his left-side door, it was far too late. He did not remember going through a pawnshop window, and the next week, when he hovered near death at the Yale-New Haven hospital, was a complete blank. His most vivid memory was of waking up, eight days later he was to learn, to see his wife, Jean, holding his hand. His marriage up to that point had been a troubled one, not an uncommon problem for nuclear submarine officers. His first sight of her was not a complimentary one – her eyes were bloodshot, her hair was tousled – but she had never looked quite so good. He had never appreciated just how important she was. A lot more important than half a leg.

'Skip? Skip Tyler!'

The former submariner turned awkwardly to see a naval officer running towards him.

'Johnnie Coleman! How the hell are you!'

It was Captain Coleman now, Tyler noted. They had served together twice, a year on the *Tecumseh*, another on the *Shark*. Coleman, a weapons expert, had commanded a pair of nuclear subs.

'How's the family, Skip?'

'Jean's fine. Five kids now, and another on the way.'

'Damn!' They shook hand with enthusiasm. 'You always were a randy bugger. I hear you're teaching at Annapolis.'

'Yeah, and a little engineering stuff on the side.'

'What are you doing here?'

'I'm running a programme on the air force computer. Checking a new ship configuration for Sea Systems Command.' It was an accurate enough cover story. 'What do they have you doing?'

130

'OP-02's office. I'm chief of staff for Admiral Dodge.'

'Indeed?' Tyler was impressed. Vice Admiral Sam Dodge was the current OP-02. The office of the deputy chief of naval operations for submarine warfare had administrative control of all aspects of submarine operations. 'Keeping you busy?'

'You know it! The crap's really hit the fan.'

'What do you mean'?' Tyler hadn't seen the news or read a paper since Monday.

'You kidding?'

'I've been working on this computer programme twenty hours a day since Monday, and I don't get ops dispatches anymore.' Tyler frowned. He had heard something the other day at the Academy but not paid any attention to it. He was the sort who could focus his whole mind on a single problem.

Coleman looked up and down the corridor. It was late on a Friday evening, and they had it entirely to themselves. 'Guess I can tell you. Our Russian friends have some sort of major exercise laid on. Their whole Northern Fleet's at sea, or damned near. They have subs all over the place.'

'Doing what?'

'We're not sure. Looks like they might have a major search and rescue operation. The question is, after what? They have four *Alfas* doing a max speed run for our coast right now, with a gaggle of *Victors* and *Charlies* charging in behind them. At first we were worried that they wanted to block the trade routes, but they blitzed right past those. They're definitely heading for our coast, and whatever they're up to we're getting tons of information.'

'What do they have moving?' Tyler asked.

'Fifty-eight nuclear subs, and thirty or so surface ships.'

'Gawd! CINCLANT must be going ape!'

'You know it, Skip. The fleet's at sea, all of it. Every nuke we have is scrambling for a redeployment. Every P-3 Lockheed ever made is either over the Atlantic or heading that way.' Coleman paused. 'You're still cleared, right?'

'Sure, for the work I do for the Crystal City gang. I had a piece of the evaluation of the new *Kirov*.'

'I thought that sounded like your work. You always were a pretty good engineer. You know, the old man still talks about that job you did for him on the old *Tecumseh*. Maybe I can get you in to see what's happening. Yeah, I'll ask him.'

Tyler's first cruise after graduating from nuc school in Idaho had been with Dodge. He'd done a tricky repair job on some ancillary reactor equipment two weeks earlier than estimated with a little creative effort and some back-channel procurement of spare parts. This had earned him and Dodge a flowery letter of commendation.

'I bet the old man would love to see you. When will you be finished down here?'

'Maybe half an hour.'

'You know where to find us?'

'Have they moved OP-02?'

'Same place. Call me when you're finished. My extension is 78730. Okay? I gotta get back.'

'Right.' Tyler watched his old friend disappear down the corridor, then proceeded on his way to the men's room, wondering what the Russians were up to. Whatever it was, it was enough to keep a three-star admiral and his four-striped captain working on a Friday night in Christmas season.

'Eleven minutes, 53.18 seconds, sir,' the sergeant reported, pocketing both bills.

The computer printout was over two hundred pages of data. The cover sheet plotted a rough-looking bell curve of speed solutions, and below it was the noice prediction curve. The case-by-case solutions were printed individually on the remaining sheets. The curves were predictably messy. The speed curve showed the majority of solutions in the ten to twelve-knot range, the total range going from seven to eighteen knots. The noise curve was surprisingly low.

'Sergeant that's one hell of a machine you have here.'

'Believe it, sir. And reliable. We haven't had an electronic fault all month.'

'Can I use a phone?'

'Sure, take your pick, sir.'

'Okay, Sarge.' Tyler picked up the nearest phone. 'Oh, and dump the programme.'

'Okay.' He typed in some instructions. 'MORAY is . . . gone. Hope you kept a copy, sir.'

Tyler nodded and dialled the phone.

'OP-02A, Captain Coleman.'

'Johnnie, this is Skip.'

'Great! Hey, the old man wants to see you. Come right up.'

Tyler placed the printout in his briefcase and locked it. He thanked the sergeant one more time before hobbling out the door, giving the Cray-2 one last look. He'd have to get in here again.

He could not find an operating elevator and had to struggle up a gently sloped ramp. Five minutes later he found a marine guarding the corridor.

'You Commander Tyler, sir?' the guard asked. 'Can I see some ID, please?'

Tyler showed the corporal his Pentagon pass, wondering how many one-legged former submarine officers there might be.

'Thank you, Commander. Please go down the corridor. You know the room, sir?'

'Sure. Thanks, Corporal.'

Vice Admiral Dodge was sitting on the corner of a desk reading over some message flimsies. Dodge was a small, combative man who'd made his mark commanding three separate boats, then pushing the *Los Angeles*-class attack submarines through their lengthy development programme. Now he was 'Grand Dolphin,' the senior admiral who fought all the battles with Congress.

'Skip Tyler! You're looking good, laddy.' Dodge gave Tyler's leg a furtive glance as he came over to take his hand. 'I hear you're doing a great job at the Academy.'

'It's all right, sir. They even let me scout the occasional ballgame.'

'Hmph, shame they didn't let you scout Army.'

Tyler hung his head theatrically. 'I did scout Army, sir. They were just too tough this year. You heard about their middle linebacker, didn't you?'

'No, what about him?' Dodge asked.

'He picked armour as his duty assignment, and they gave him an early trip to Fort Knox – not to learn about tanks. To *be* a tank.'

'Ha!' Dodge laughed. 'Johnnie says you have a bunch of new kids.'

'Number six is due the end of February,' Tyler said proudly.

'Six? You're not a Catholic or a Mormon, are you? What's with all this bird hatching?'

Tyler gave his former boss a wry look. He'd never understood that prejudice in the nuclear navy. It came from Rickover, who had invented the disparaging term *bird hatching* for fathering more than one child. What the hell was wrong with having kids?

'Admiral, since I'm not a nuc anymore, I have to do *something* on nights and weekends.' Tyler arched his eyebrows lecherously. 'I hear the Russkies are playing games.'

Dodge was instantly serious. 'They sure are. Fifty-eight attack boats – every nuclear boat in the Northern Fleet – heading this way with a big surface group, and most of their service forces tagging along.'

'Doing what?'

'Maybe you can tell me. Come on back to my inner sanctum.' Dodge led Tyler into a room where he saw another new gadget, a projection screen that displayed the North Atlantic from the Tropic of Cancer to the polar ice pack. Hundreds of ships were represented. The merchantmen were white, with flags to identify their nationality; the Soviet ships were red, and their shapes depicted their ship type; the American and allied ships were blue. The ocean was getting crowded.

'Christ.'

'You got that one right, lad.' Dodge nodded grimly. 'How are you cleared?'

'Top secret and some special things, sir. I see everything we have on their hardware, and I do a lot of work with Sea Systems on the side.'

'Johnnie said you did the evaluation of the new *Kirov* they just sent out to the Pacific – not bad, by the way.'

'These two *Alfas* heading for Norfolk?'

'Looks like it. And they're burning a lot of neutrons doing it.' Dodge pointed. 'That one's heading to Long Island Sound as though to block the entrance to New London, and that one's heading to Boston, I think. These *Victors* are not far behind. They already have most of the British ports staked out. By Monday they'll have two or more subs off every major port we have.'

'I don't like the looks of this, sir.'

'Neither do I. As you see, we're nearly a hundred percent at sea ourselves. The interesting thing, though – what they're doing just doesn't figure. I – '

Captain Coleman came in.

'I see you let the prodigal son in, sir,' Coleman said.

'Be nice to him, Johnnie. I seem to remember when he was a right fair sub driver. Anyway, at first it looked like they were going to block the SLOCs, but they went right past. What with these *Alfas*, they might be trying to blockade our coast.'

'What about out west?'

'Nothing. Nothing at all, just routine activity.'

'That doesn't make any sense,' Tyler objected. 'You don't ignore half the fleet. Of course, if you're going to war you don't announce it by kicking every boat to max power either.'

'The Russians are a funny bunch, Skip,' Coleman pointed out.

'Admiral, if we start shooting at them – '

'We hurt 'em,' Dodge said. 'With all the noise they're making we have good locations on near all of 'em. They have to know that, too. That's the one thing that makes me believe they're not up to anything really bad. They're smart enough not to be that obvious – unless that's what they want us to think.'

'Have they said anything?' Tyler asked.

'Their ambassador says they've lost a boat, and since it has a bunch of big shots' kids aboard, they laid on an all-hands rescue mission. For what that's worth.'

Tyler set his briefcase down and walked closer to the screen. 'I can see the pattern for a search and rescue, but why blockade our ports?' He paused, thinking rapidly as his eyes scanned the top of the display. 'Sir. I don't see any boomers up here.'

'They're in port – all of 'em, on both oceans. The last *Delta* tied up a few hours ago. That's funny, too,' Dodge said, looking at the screen again.

'All of them sir?' Tyler asked as offhandedly as he could. Something had just occurred to him. The display screen showed the *Bremerton* in the Barents Sea but not her supposed quarry. He waited a few seconds for an answer. Getting none, he turned to see the two officers observing him closely.

'Why do you ask, son?' Dodge said quietly. In Sam Dodge, gentleness could be a red warning flag.

Tyler thought this one over for a few seconds. He'd given Ryan his word. Could he phrase his answer without compromising it and still find out what he wanted? Yes, he decided. There was an investigative side to Skip Tyler's character, and once he was onto something, his psyche compelled him to run it down.

'Admiral, do they have a missile sub at sea, a brand new one?'

Dodge stood very straight. Even so he still had to look up at the younger man. When he spoke, his voice was glacial. 'Exactly where did you get that information, Commander?'

Tyler shook his head. 'Admiral, I'm sorry, but I can't say. It's compartmented, sir. I think this is something you ought to know, and I'll try to get it to you.'

Dodge backed off to try a different tack. 'You used to work for me, Skip.' The admiral was unhappy. He'd bent a rule to show something to his former subordinate because he knew him well and was sorry that he had not received the command he had worked so hard for. Tyler was technically a civilian, even though his suits were still navy blue. What made it really bad was that he knew something himself. Dodge had given him some information, and Tyler wasn't giving any back.

'Sir, I gave my word,' Skip apologized. 'I will try to get this to you. That's a promise, sir. May I use a phone?'

'Outer office,' Dodge said flatly. There were four telephones within sight.

Tyler went out and sat at a secretary's desk. He took his notebook from a coat pocket and dialled the number on the card Ryan had left him.

'Acres,' a female voice answered.

'Could I speak to Dr Ryan, please?'

'Dr Ryan is not here at the moment.'

'Then . . . give me Admiral Greer, please.'

'One moment, please.'

'James Greer?' Dodge was behind him. 'Is that who you're working for?'

'This is Greer. Your name Skip Tyler?'

'Yes, sir.'

'You have that information for me?'

'Yes, sir, I do.'

'Where are you?'

'In the Pentagon, sir.'

'Okay, I want you to drive right up here. You know how to find the place? The guards at the main gate will be waiting for you. Get moving, son.' Greer hung up.

'You're working for the CIA?' Dodge asked.

'Sir – I can't say. If you will excuse me, sir, I have some information to deliver.'

'*Mine*?' the admiral demanded.

'No, sir. I already had it when I came in here. That's the truth, Admiral. And I will try to get this back to you.'

'Call me.' Dodge ordered. 'We'll be here all night.'

CIA Headquarters

The drive up the George Washington Parkway was easier than he expected. The decrepit old highway was crowded with shoppers but moved along at a steady crawl. He got off at the right exit and presently found himself at the guard post for the main highway entrance to the CIA. The barrier was down.

'Your name Tyler, Oliver W.?' the guard asked. 'ID please.' Tyler handed him his Pentagon pass.

'Okay, Commander. Pull your car right to the main entrance. Somebody will be there to meet you.'

It was another two minutes to the main entrance through mostly empty parking lots glazed with ice from yesterday's melted snow. The armed guard who was waiting for him tried to help him out of the car. Tyler didn't like to be helped. He shrugged him off. Another man was waiting for him under the canopied main entrance. They were waved right through to the elevator.

He found Admiral Greer sitting in front of his office fireplace, seemingly half asleep. Skip didn't know that the DDI had only returned from England a few hours earlier. The admiral came to and ordered his plain-clothes security officer to withdraw. 'You must be Skip Tyler. Come on over and sit down.'

'That's quite a fire you have going there, sir.'

'I shouldn't bother. Looking at a fire makes me go to sleep. Of course, I could use a little sleep right now. So, what do you have for me?'

'May I ask where Jack is?'

'You may ask. He's away.'

'Oh.' Tyler unlocked his briefcase and removed the printout. 'Sir, I ran the performance model of this Russian sub. May I ask her name?'

Greer chuckled. 'Okay, you've earned that much. Her name is *Red October*. You'll have to excuse me, son. I've had a busy couple of days, and being tired makes me forget my manners. Jack says you're pretty sharp. So does your personnel file. Now, you tell me. What'll she do?'

'Well, Admiral, we have a wide choice of data here, and – '

'The short version, Commander. I don't play with computers. I have people who do that for me.'

'From seven to eighteen knots, the best bet is ten to twelve. With that speed range, you can figure a radiated noise level about the same as that of a *Yankee* doing six knots, but you'd have to factor reactor plant noise into that also. Moreover, the character of the noise will be different from what we're used to. These multiple impeller models don't put out normal propulsion noises. They seem to generate an irregular harmonic rumble. Did Jack tell you about this? It results from a back-pressure wave in the tunnels. This fights the water flow, and that makes the rumble. Evidently there's no way around it. Our guys spent two years trying to find one. What they got was a new principle of hydrodynamics. The water almost acts like air in a jet engine at idle or low speed, except that water doesn't compress like air does. So, our guys will be able to detect something, but it will be different. They're going to have to get used to a wholly new acoustical signature. Add to that the lower signal intensity, and you have a boat that will be harder to detect than anything they have at this time.'

'So that's what all this says.' Greer rifled through the pages.

'Yes, sir. You'll want to have your own people look through it. The model – the programme, that is – could stand a little improvement. I didn't have much time. Jack said you wanted this in a hurry. May I ask a question, sir?'

'You can try.' Greer leaned back, rubbing his eyes.

'Is, ah, *Red October* at sea? That's it, isn't it? They're trying to locate her right now?' Tyler asked innocently.

'Uh huh, something like that. We couldn't figure what these doors meant. Ryan said you might be able to, and I suppose he was right. You've earned your money, Commander. This data might just enable us to find her.'

'Admiral, I think *Red October* is up to something, maybe even trying to defect to the United States.'

Greer's head came around. 'Whatever makes you think that?'

'The Russkies have a major fleet operation in progress. They have subs all over the Atlantic, and it looks like they're trying to blockade our coast. The story is a rescue job for a lost boat – and today I hear that all of their other missile boats have been recalled to port.' Tyler smiled. 'That's kind of an odd set of coincidences, sir.'

Greer turned and stared at the fire. He had just joined the DIA when the army and air force had pulled off the daring raid on the Song Tay prison camp twenty miles west of Hanoi. The raid had been a failure because the North Vietnamese had removed all of the captured pilots a few weeks before, something that aerial photographs could not determine. But everything else had gone perfectly. After penetrating hundreds of miles into hostile territory, the raiding force appeared entirely by surprise and caught many of the camp guard literally with their pants down. The Green Berets did a letter-perfect job of getting in and out. In the process they killed several hundred enemy troops, themselves sustaining a single casualty, a broken ankle. The most impressive part of the mission, however, was its secrecy. Operation KINGPIN had been rehearsed for months, and despite this its nature and objective had not been guessed by friend or enemy – until the day of the raid itself. On that day a young air force captain of intelligence went into his general's office to ask if a deep-penetration raid into North Vietnam had been laid on for the Song Tay prisoner-of-war camp. His astonished commander proceeded to grill the captain at length, only to learn that the bright young officer had seen enough disjointed bits and pieces to construct a clear picture of what was about to happen. Events like this gave security officers peptic ulcers.

'*Red October*'s going to defect, isn't she?' Tyler persisted.

If the admiral had had more sleep he might have bluffed it out. As it was, his response was a mistake. 'Did Ryan tell you this?'

'Sir, I haven't spoken with Jack since Monday. That's the truth, sir.'

'Then where did you get this other information?' Greer snapped.

'Admiral, I used to wear the blue suit. Most of my friends still do. I hear things,' Tyler evaded. 'The whole picture dropped into place an hour ago. The Russkies have never recalled all of their boomers at once. I know, I used to hunt them.'

Greer sighed. 'Jack thinks the same as you. He's out with the fleet right now. Commander, if you tell that to anyone, I'll have your other leg mounted overtop that fireplace. Do you understand me?'

'Aye aye, sir. What are we going to do with her?' Tyler smiled to himself, thinking that as a senior consultant to Sea Systems Command, he'd sure as hell get a chance to look at a for-real Russian submarine.

'Give her back. After we've had a chance to look her over, of course. But there's a lot of things that could happen to prevent our ever seeing her.'

It took Skip a moment to grasp what he'd just been told. 'Give her back! Why, for Christ's sake?'

'Commander, just how likely do you think this scenario is? Do you think the whole crew of a submarine has decided to come over to us all at once?' Greer shook his head. 'Smart money is that it's only the officers, maybe not all of them, and that they're trying to get over here without the crew's knowing what they're up to.'

'Oh.' Tyler considered that. 'I suppose that does make sense – but why give her back? This isn't Japan. If somebody landed a MiG-25 here we wouldn't give it back.'

'This is not like holding onto a stray fighter plane. The boat is worth a billion dollars, more if you throw in the missiles and warheads. And legally, the president says, it's their property. So if they find out we have her, they'll ask for her back, and we'll have to give her back. Okay, how will they know we have her? Those crew members who don't want to defect will ask to go home. Whoever asks, we send.'

'You know, sir, that whoever does want to go back will be in a whole shitload of trouble – excuse me, sir.'

'A shitload and a half.' Tyler hadn't known that Greer was a mustang and could swear like a real sailor. 'Some will want to stay, but most won't. They have families. Next you'll ask me if we might arrange for the crew to disappear.'

'The thought has occurred to me,' Tyler said.

'It's occurred to us, too. But we won't. Murder a hundred men? Even if we wanted to, there's no way we could conceal it in this day and age. Hell, I doubt even the Soviets could. Besides that, this simply is not the sort of thing you do in peacetime. That's one difference between us and them. You can take those reasons in any order you want.'

'So, except for the crew, we'd keep her . . .'

'Yes, if we could hide her. And if a pig had wings, it could fly.'

138

'Lots of places to hide her, Admiral. I can think of a few right here on the Chesapeake, and if we could get her round the Horn, there's a million little atolls we could use, and they all belong to us.'

'But the crew will know, and when we send them home they'll tell their bosses,' Greer explained patiently. 'And Moscow will ask for her back, Oh, sure, we'll have a week or so to conduct, uh, safety and quarantine inspections, to make sure they weren't trying to smuggle cocaine into the country.' The admiral laughed. 'A British admiral suggested we invoke the old slave-trading treaty. Somebody did that back in World War II, to put the grab on a German blockade runner right before we got into it. So, we'll get a ton of intelligence regardless.'

'Better to keep her, and run her, and take her apart . . .' Tyler said quietly, staring into the orange-white flames on the oak logs. How do we keep her? he wondered. An idea began to rattle around in his head. 'Admiral, what if we could get the crew off without them knowing that we have the submarine?'

'Your full name is Oliver Wendell Tyler? Well, son, if you were named after Harry Houdini instead of a justice of the Supreme Court, I – ' Greer looked into the engineer's face. 'What do you have in mind?'

While Tyler explained Greer listened intently.

'To do this, sir, we'll have to get the navy in on it right quick. Specifically, we'll need the cooperation of Admiral Dodge, and if my speed figures for this boat are anything like accurate, we'll have to move smartly.'

Greer rose and walked around the couch a few times to get his circulation going. 'Interesting. The timing would be almost impossible, though.'

'I didn't say it would be easy, sir, just that we *could* do it.'

'Call home, Tyler. Tell your wife you won't be making it home. If I don't get any sleep tonight, neither do you. There's coffee behind my desk. First I have to call the judge, then we'll talk to Sam Dodge.'

The USS *Pogy*

'*Pogy*, this is Black Gull 4. We're getting low on fuel. Have to return to the barn,' the Orion's tactical coordinator reported, stretching after ten hours at his control console. 'Anything you want us to get you? Over.'

'Yeah, have a couple of cases of beer sent out,' Commander Wood replied. It was the current joke between P-3C and submarine crews. 'Thanks for the data. We'll take it from here. Out.'

Overhead, the Lockheed Orion increased power and turned southwest. The crewmen aboard would each hoist an extra beer or two at dinner, saying it was for their friends on the submarine.

'Mr Dyson, take her two hundred feet. One-third speed.'

The officer of the deck gave the proper orders as Commander Wood moved over to the plot.

The USS *Pogy* was three hundred miles northeast of Norfolk, awaiting the arrival of two Soviet *Alfa*-class submarines which several relays of antisubmarine patrol aircraft had tracked all the way from Iceland. The *Pogy* was named for a distinguished World War II fleet submarine, named in turn for an undistinguished game fish. She had been at sea for eighteen hours, and was fresh from an extended overhaul at the Newport News shipyard. Nearly everything aboard was either straight from manufacturers' crates or had been completely worked over by the skilled shipfitters on the James River. This was not to say that everything worked properly. Many items had failed in one way or another on the post-overhaul shakedown the previous week, a fact less unusual than lamentable, Commander Wood thought. The *Pogy*'s crew was new, too. Wood was on his first deployment as a commanding officer after a year of desk duty in Washington, and too many of the enlisted men were green, just out of sub school at New London, still getting accustomed to their first cruise on a submarine. It takes time for men used to blue skies and fresh air to learn the regime inside a thirty-two-feet-diameter steel pipe. Even the experienced men were making adjustments to their new boat and officers.

The *Pogy* had met her top speed of thirty-three knots on post-overhaul trials. This was fast for a ship but slower than the speed of the *Alfas* she was listening to. Like all American submarines, her long suit was stealth. The *Alfas* had no way of knowing she was there and that they would be easy targets for her weapons, the more so since the patrolling Orion had fed the *Pogy* exact range information, something that ordinarily takes time to deduce from a passive sonar plot.

Lieutenant Commander Tom Reynolds, the executive officer and fire control coordinator, stood casually over the tactical plot. 'Thirty-six miles to the near one, and forty on the far one.' On the display they were labelled Pogy-Bait 1 and 2. Everyone found the use of this service epithet amusing.

'Speed forty-two?' Wood asked.

'Yes, Captain.' Reynolds had handled the radio exchange until Black Gull 4 had announced its intention to return to base. 'They're driving those boats for all they're worth. Right for us. We have hard solutions on both . . . zap! What do you suppose they're up to?'

'The word from CINCLANT is that their ambassador says they're on a SAR mission for a lost boat.' His voice indicated what he thought of that.

'Search and rescue, eh?' Reynolds shrugged. 'Well, maybe they think they lost a boat off Point Comfort, 'cause if they don't slow down real fast, that's where they'll end up. I've never heard of *Alfas* operating this close to our coast. Have you, Sir?'

'Nope.' Wood frowned. The thing about the *Alfas* was that they were fast and noisy. Soviet tactical doctrine seemed to call for them mainly in defensive roles: as 'interceptor submarines' they could protect their own missile subs, and with their high speed they could engage American attack

140

submarines, then evade counter-attack. Wood didn't think the doctrine was sound, but that was all right with him.

'Maybe they want to blockade Norfolk,' Reynolds suggested.

'You might have a point there,' Wood said. 'Well, in any case, we'll just sit tight and let them burn right past us. They'll have to slow as they cross the continental shelf line, and we'll tag along behind them, nice and quiet.'

'Aye,' Reynolds said.

If they had to shoot, both men reflected, they'd find out just how tough the *Alfa* really was. There had been much talk about the strength of the titanium used for her hull, whether it really would withstand the force of several hundred pounds of high explosive in direct contact. A new shaped-charge warhead for the Mark 48 torpedo had been developed for just this purpose and for handling the equally tough *Typhoon* hull. Both officers set this thought aside. Their assigned mission was to track and shadow.

The *E. S. Politovskiy*

Pogy-Bait 2 was known to the Soviet Navy as the *E. S. Politovskiy*. This *Alfa*-class attack sub was named for the chief engineering officer of the Russian fleet who had sailed all the way around the world to meet his appointment with destiny in the Tsushima Straits. Evgeni Sigismondavich Politovskiy had served the czar's navy with skill and a devotion to duty equal to that of any officer in history, but in his diary, which was discovered years later in Leningrad, the brilliant officer had decried in the most violent terms the corruption and excesses of the czarist regime, giving a grim counterpoint to the selfless patriotism he had shown as he sailed knowingly to his death. This made him a genuine hero for Soviet seamen to emulate, and the State had named its greatest engineering achievement in his memory. Unfortunately the *Politovskiy* had enjoyed no better luck than he had enjoyed in the face of Togo's guns.

The *Politovskiy's* acoustical signature was labelled *Alfa* 3 by the Americans. This was incorrect; she had been the first of the *Alfas*. The small, spindle-shaped attack submarine had reached forty-three knots three hours into her initial builder's trials. Those trials had been cut short only a minute later by an incredible mishap: a fifty-ton right whale had somehow blundered in her path, and the *Politovskiy* had rammed the unfortunate creature broadside. The impact had smashed ten square metres of bow plating, annihilated the sonar dome, knocked a torpedo tube askew, and nearly flooded the torpedo room. This did not count shock damage to nearly every interior system from electronic equipment to the galley stove, and it was said that if anyone but the famous Vilnius headmaster had been in command, the submarine would surely have been lost. A two-metre segment of the whale's rib was now a permanent fixture at the officer's club in Severomorsk, dramatic testament to the strength of Soviet submarines; in fact the damage had taken over a year to repair, and by the time the *Politovskiy* sailed again there were already two other *Alfas* in service. Two days after sailing on her next shakedown, she suffered another major casualty, the total failure of her high-pressure turbine. This had taken six months to replace. There had been three more minor incidents since, and the submarine was forever marked as a bad luck ship.

Chief Engineer Vladimir Petchukocov was a loyal Party member and a committed atheist, but he was also a sailor an-l therefore profoundly superstitious. In the old days, his ship would have been blessed on launching and thereafter every time she sailed. It would have been an impressive ceremony, with a bearded priest, clouds of incense, and evocative hymns. He had sailed without any of that and found himself wishing otherwise. He needed some luck. Petchukocov was having trouble with his reactor.

The *Alfa* reactor plant was small. It had to fit into a relatively small hull. It was also powerful for its size, and this one had been running at one hundred percent rated power for just over four days. They were racing for the American coast at 42.3 knots, as fast as the eight-year-old plant would permit. The *Politovskiy* was due for a comprehensive overhaul: new sonar, new computers, and a redesigned reactor control suite were all planned for the coming months. Petchukocov thought it irresponsible – reckless – to push his submarine so hard, even if everything were functioning properly. No *Alfa* plant on a submarine had ever been pushed this hard, not even a new one. And on this one, things were beginning to come apart.

The primary high-pressure reactor coolant pump was beginning to vibrate ominously. This was particularly worrying to the engineer. There was a backup, but the secondary pump had a lower rated power, and using it meant losing eight knots of speed. The *Alfa* plant achieved its high power not with a sodium-cooled system – as the Americans thought – but by running at a far higher pressure than any reactor system afloat and using a revolutionary heat exchange system that boosted the plant's overall thermal efficiency to forty-one percent, well in excess of that for any other submarine. But the price of this was a reactor that at full power was redlined on every monitor gauge – and in this case the red lines were not mere symbolism. They signified genuine danger.

This fact, added to the vibrating pump, had Petchukocov seriously concerned; an hour earlier he had pleaded with the captain to reduce power for a few hours so that his skilled crew of engineers could make repairs. It was probably only a bad bearing, after all, and they had spares. The pump had been designed so that it would be easy to fix. The captain had wavered, wanting to grant the request, but the political officer had intervened, pointing out that their orders were both urgent and explicit: they had to be on station as quickly as possible; to do otherwise would be 'politically unsound.' And that was that.

Petchukocov bitterly remembered the look in his captain's eyes. What was the purpose of a commanding officer if his every order had to be approved by a political flunky? Petchukocov had been a faithful Communist since joining the Octobrists as a boy – but damn it! what was the point of having specialists and engineers? Did the Party really think that physical laws could be overturned by the whim of some apparatchik with a heavy desk and a dacha in the Moscow suburbs? The engineer swore to himself.

He stood alone at the master control board. This was located in the engine room, aft of the compartment that held the reactor and the heat exchange/steam generator, the latter placed right at the submarine's centre of gravity. The reactor was pressurized to twenty kilograms per square centimetre, about twenty-eight hundred pounds per square inch. Only a fraction of this pressure came from the pump. The higher pressure caused a higher boiling point for the coolant. In this case, the water was heated to over 900° Celsius, a temperature sufficient to generate steam, which gathered at the top of the reactor vessel; the steam bubble applied pressure to the water beneath, preventing the generation of more steam. The steam and water regulated one another in a delicate balance. The water was dangerously radioactive as a result of the fission reaction taking place within the uranium fuel rods. The function of the control rods was to regulate the reaction. Again, the control was delicate. At most the rods could absorb just less than one percent of the neutron flux, but this was enough either to permit the reaction or to prevent it.

Petchukocov could recite all this data in his sleep. He could draw a wholly accurate schematic diagram of the entire engine plant from memory and could instantly grasp the significance of the slightest change in his instrument readings. He stood perfectly straight over the control board, his eyes tracing the myriad dials and gauges in a regular pattern, one hand poised over the SCRAM switch, the other over the emergency cooling controls.

He could hear the vibration. It had to be a bad bearing getting worse as it wore more and more unevenly. If the crankshaft bearing went bad, the pump would seize, and they'd have to stop. This would be an emergency, though not really a dangerous one. It would mean that repairing the pump – if they could repair it at all – would take days instead of hours, eating up valuable time and spare parts. That was bad enough. What was worse, and what Petchukocov did not know, was that the vibration was generating pressure waves in the coolant.

To make use of the newly developed heat exchanger, the *Alfa* plant had to move water rapidly through its many loops and baffles. This required a high-pressure pump which accounted for one hundred fifty pounds of the total system pressure – almost ten times what was considered safe in Western reactors. With the pump so powerful, the whole engine room complex, normally very noisy at high speed, was like a boiler factory and the pump's vibration was disturbing the performance of the monitor instruments. It was making the needles on his gauges waver, Petchukocov noted. He was right, and wrong. The pressure gauges were really wavering because of the thirty-pound overpressure waves pulsing through the system. The chief engineer did not recognize this for what it was. He had been on duty too many hours.

Within the reactor vessel, these pressure waves were approaching the frequency at which a piece of equipment resonated. Roughly halfway down the interior surface of the vessel was a titanium fitting, part of the backup cooling system. In the event of a coolant loss, and *after* a successful SCRAM, valves inside and outside the vessel would open, cooling the reactor either with a mixture of water and barium, or, as a last measure, with seawater which could be vented in and out of the vessel – at the cost of ruining the entire reactor. This had been done once, and though it had been costly, the action of a junior engineer had prevented the loss of a *Victor*-class attack sub by catastrophic meltdown.

Today the inside valve was closed, along with the corresponding through-hull fitting. The valves were made of titanium because they had to function reliably after prolonged exposure to high temperature, and also because titanium was very corrosion-resistant – high-temperature water was murderously corrosive. What had not been fully considered was that the metal was also exposed to intense nuclear radiation, and this particular titanium alloy was not completely stable under extended neutron bombardment. The metal had become brittle over the years. The minute waves of hydraulic pressure were beating against the clapper in the valve. As the pump's frequency of vibration changed it began to approach the frequency at which the clapper vibrated. This caused the clapper to snap harder and harder against its retaining ring. The metal at its edges began to crack.

A *michman* at the forward end of the compartment heard it first, a low buzz coming through the bulkhead. At first he thought it was feedback noise from the PA speaker, and he waited too long to check it. The clapper broke free and dropped out of the valve nozzle. It was not very large, only ten centimetres in diameter and five millimetres thick. This type of fitting is called a butterfly valve, and the clapper looked just like a butterfly, suspended and twirling in the water flow. If it had been made of stainless steel it would have been heavy enough to fall to the bottom of the vessel. But it was made of titanium, which was both stronger than steel and very much lighter. The coolant flow moved it up, towards the exhaust pipe.

The outward-moving water carried the clapper into the pipe, which had a fifteen-centimeter inside diameter. The pipe was made of stainless steel, two-meter sections welded together for easy replacement in the cramped quarters. The clapper was borne along rapidly towards the heat exchanger. Here the pipe took a forty-five-degree downward turn and the clapper jammed momentarily. This blocked half of the pipe's channel, and before the surge of pressure could dislodge the clapper too many things happened. The moving water had its own momentum. On being blocked, it generated a back-pressure wave within the pipe. Total pressure jumped momentarily to thirty-four hundred pounds. This caused the pipe to flex a few millimeters. The increased pressure, lateral displacement of a weld joint, and cumulative effect of years of high-temperature erosion of the steel damaged the joint.

A hole the size of a pencil point opened. The escaping water flashed instantly into steam, setting off alarms in the reactor compartment and neighbouring spaces. It ate at the remainder of the weld, rapidly expanding the failure until reactor coolant was erupting as though from a horizontal fountain. One jet of steam demolished the adjacent reactor-control wiring conduits.

What had just begun was a catastrophic loss-of-coolant accident.

The reactor was fully depressurized within three seconds. Its many gallons of coolant exploded into steam, seeking release into the surrounding compartment. A dozen alarms sounded at once on the master control board, and in the blink of an eye Vladimir Petchukocov faced his ultimate nightmare. The engineer's automatic trained reaction was to jam his finger on the SCRAM switch, but the steam in the reactor vessel had disabled the rod control system, and there wasn't time to solve the problem. In an instant, Petchukocov knew that his ship was doomed. Next he opened the emergency coolant controls, admitting seawater into the reactor vessel. This automatically set off alarms throughout the hull.

In the control room forward, the captain grasped the nature of the emergency at once. The *Politovskiy* was running at one hundred fifty metres. He had to get her to the surface immediately, and he shouted orders to blow all ballast and make full rise on the diving planes.

The reactor emergency was regulated by physical laws. With no reactor coolant to absorb the heat of the uranium rods, the nuclear reaction actually stopped – there was no water to attenuate the neutron flux. This was no solution, however, since the residual decay heat was sufficient to melt everything in the compartment. The cold water admitted into the vessel drew off the heat but also slowed down too many neutrons, keeping them in the reactor core. This caused a runaway reaction that generated even more heat, more than any amount of coolant could control. What had started as a loss-of-coolant accident became something worse: a cold-water accident. It was now only a matter of minutes before the entire core melted, and the *Politovskiy* had that long to get to the surface.

Petchukocov stayed at his post in the engine room, doing what he could. His own life, he knew, was almost certainly lost. He had to give his captain time to surface the boat. There was a drill for this sort of emergency, and he barked orders to implement it. It only made things worse.

His duty electrician moved along the electrical control panels switching from main power to emergency, since residual steam power in the turbo-alternators would die in a few more seconds. In a moment the submarine's power completely depended on standby batteries.

In the control room power was lost to the electrically controlled trim tabs on the trailing edge of the diving planes, which automatically switched back to electrohydraulic control. This powered not just the small trim tabs but the diving planes as well. The control assemblies moved instantly to a fifteen-degree up-angle – and she was still moving at thirty-nine knots. With all her ballast tanks now blasted free of water by compressed air, the submarine was very light, and she rose like a climbing aircraft. In seconds the astonished control room crew felt their boat rise to an up-angle that was forty-five degrees and getting worse. A moment later they were too busy trying to stand to come to grips with the problem. Now the *Alfa* was climbing almost vertically at thirty miles per hour. Every man and unsecured item aboard fell sternward.

In the motor control room aft, a crewman crashed against the main electrical switchboard, short-circuiting it with his body, and all power aboard was lost. A cook who had been inventorying survival gear in the torpedo room forward struggled into the escape trunk as he fought his way into an exposure suit. Even with only a year's experience, he was quick to understand the meaning of the hooting alarms and unprecedented actions of his boat. He yanked the hatch shut and began to work the escape controls as he had been taught in submarine school.

The *Politovskiy* soared through the surface of the Atlantic like a broaching whale, coming three quarters of her length out of the water before crashing back.

The USS *Pogy*

'Conn, sonar.'

'Conn, aye, Captain speaking.'

'Skipper, you better hear this. Something just went crazy on Bait 2,' *Pogy*'s chief reported. Wood was in the sonar room in seconds, putting on earphones plugged into a tape recorder which had a two-minute offset. Commander Wood heard a whooshing sound. The engine noises stopped. A few seconds later there was an explosion of compressed air, and a staccato of hull-popping noises as the submarine changed depth rapidly.

'What's going on?' Wood asked quickly.

The *E.S. Politovskiy*

In the *Politovskiy*'s reactor, the runaway fission reaction had virtually annihilated both the incoming seawater and the uranium fuel rods. Their debris settled on the after wall of the reactor vessel. In a minute there was a metre-wide puddle of radioactive slag, enough to form its own critical mass. The reaction continued unabated, this time directly attacking the tough stainless steel of the vessel. Nothing manmade could long withstand five thousand degrees of direct heat. In ten seconds the vessel wall failed. The uranium mass dropped free, against the aft bulkhead.

Petchukocov knew he was dead. He saw the paint on the forward bulkhead turn black, and his last impression was of a dark mass surrounded with a blue glow. The engineer's body vaporized an instant later, and the mass of slag dropped to the next bulkhead aft.

Forward, the submarine's nearly vertical angle in the water eased. The high-pressure air in the ballast tanks spilled out of the bottom floods and the tanks filled with water, dropping the angle of the boat and submerging her. In the forward part of the submarine men were screaming. The captain struggled to his feet, ignoring his broken leg, trying to get control, to get his men organised and out of the submarine before it was too late, but the luck of Evgeni Sigismondavich Politovskiy would plague his namesake one last time. Only one man escaped. The cook opened the escape trunk hatch and got out. Following what he had learned during the drill, he began to seal the hatch so that men behind him could use it, but a wave slapped him off the hull as the sub slid backwards.

In the engine room, the changing angle dropped the melted core to the deck. The hot mass attacked the steel deck first, burning through that, then the titanium of the hull. Five seconds later the engine room was vented to the sea. The *Politovskyi*'s largest compartment filled rapidly with water. This destroyed what little reserve buoyancy the ship had, and the acute down-angle returned. The *Alfa* began her last dive.

The stern dropped just as the captain began to get his control room crew to react to orders again. His head struck an instrument console. What slim hopes his crew had died with him. The *Politovskiy* was falling backwards, her propeller windmilling the wrong way as she slid to the bottom of the sea.

The *Pogy*

'Skipper, I was on the *Chopper* back in sixty-nine,' the *Pogy*'s chief said, referring to a horrifying accident on a diesel-powered submarine.

'That's what it sounds like,' his captain said. He was now listening to direct sonar input. There was no mistaking it. The submarine was flooding. They had heard the ballast tanks refill; this could only mean interior compartments were filling with water. If they had been closer, they might have heard the screams of men in that doomed hull. Wood was just as happy he couldn't. The continuing rush of water was dreadful enough. Men were dying, Russians, his enemy, but men not unlike himself, and there was not a thing that could be done about it.

Bait 1, he saw, was proceeding, unmindful of what had happened to her trailing sister.

The *E.S. Politovskiy*

It took nine minutes for the *Politovskiy* to fall the two thousand feet to the ocean floor. She impacted savagely on the hard sand bottom at the edge of the continental shelf. It was a tribute to her builders that her interior bulkheads held. All the compartments from the reactor room aft were flooded and half the crew killed in them, but the forward compartments were

147

dry. Even this was more curse than blessing. With the aft air storage banks unusable and only emergency battery power to run the complex environmental control systems, the forty men had only a limited supply of air. They were spared a rapid death from the crushing North Atlantic only to face a slower one from asphyxiation.

The Ninth Day

Saturday, 11 December

The Pentagon

A female yeoman first class held the door open for Tyler. He walked in to find General Harris standing alone over the large chart table pondering the placement of tiny ship models.

'You must be Skip Typer.' Harris looked up.

'Yes, sir.' Tyler was standing as rigidly at attention as his prosthetic leg allowed. Harris came over quickly to shake hands.

'Greer says you used to play ball.'

'Yes, General, I played right tackle at Annapolis. Those were good years.' Tyler smiled, flexing his fingers. Harris looked like an iron-pumper.

'Okay, if you used to play ball, you can call me Ed.' Harris poked him in the chest. 'Your number was seventy-eight, and you made All American, right?'

'Second string, sir. Nice to know somebody remembers.'

'I was temporary duty at the Academy for a few months back then, and I caught a couple of games. I never forget a good offensive lineman. I made All Conference at Montana – long time ago. What happened to the leg?'

'Drunk driver clipped me. I was the lucky one. The drunk didn't make it.'

'Serves the bastard right.'

Tyler nodded agreement, but remembered that the drunken shipfitter had had his own wife and family, according to the police. 'Where is everybody?'

'The chiefs are at their normal – well, normal for a weekday, not a Saturday – intelligence briefing. They ought to be down in a few minutes. So, you're teaching engineering at Annapolis now, eh?'

'Yes, sir. I got a doctorate in that along the way.'

'Name's Ed, Skip. And this morning you're going to tell us how we can hold onto that maverick Russian sub?'

'Yes, sir – Ed.'

'Tell me about it, but let's get some coffee first.' The two men went to a table in the corner with coffee and doughnuts. Harris listened to the younger man for five minutes, sipping his coffee and devouring a couple of jam doughnuts. It took a lot of food to support his frame.

'Son of a gun,' the J-3 observed when Tyler finished. He walked over to the chart. 'That's interesting. Your idea depends a lot on sleight of hand. We'd have to keep them away from where we're pulling this off. About here, you say?' He tapped the chart.

'Yes, General. The thing is, the way they seem to be operating we can do this to seaward of them – '

'And do a double shuffle. I like it. Yeah, I like it, but Dan Foster won't like losing one of our own boats.'

'I'd say it's worth the trade.'

'So would I,' Harris agreed. 'But they're not my boats After we do this, where do we hide her – if we get her?'

'General, there are some nice places right here on the Chesapeake Bay. There's a deep spot on the York River and another on the Patuxent, both owned by the navy, both marked Keep Out on the charts. Nice thing about subs, they're supposed to be invisible. You just find a deep enough spot and flood your tanks. That's temporary, of course. For a more permanent spot, maybe Truk or Kwajalein in the Pacific. Nice and far from any place.'

'And the Soviets would never notice the presence of a sub tender and three hundred submarine technicians there all of a sudden? Besides, those islands don't really belong to us anymore, remember?'

Tyler hadn't expected this man to be a dummy. 'So, what if they do find out in a few months? What will they do, announce it to the whole world? I don't think so. By that time we'll have all the information we want, and we can always produce the defecting officers in a nice news conference. How would that look for them? Anyway, it figures that after we've had her for a while, we'll break her up. The reactor'll go to Idaho for tests. The missiles and warheads will get taken off. The electronics gear will be taken to California for testing, and the CIA, NSA, and navy will have gunfights over the crypto gear. The stripped hulk will be taken to a nice deep spot and scuttled. No evidence. We don't have to keep this a secret forever, just for a few months.'

Harris set his cup down. 'You'll have to forgive me for playing devil's advocate. I see you've thought this out. Fine, I think it's worth a hard look. It means coordinating a lot of hardware, but it doesn't really interfere with what we're already doing. Okay, you have my vote.'

The Joint Chiefs arrived three minutes later. Tyler had never seen so many stars in one room.

'You wanted to see all of us, Eddie?' Hilton asked.

'Yes, General. This is Dr Skip Tyler.'

Admiral Foster came over first to take his hand. 'You got us that performance data on *Red October* that we were just briefed on. Good work, Commander.'

'Dr Tyler thinks we should hold onto her if we get her,' Harris said deadpan. 'The president won't let us.'

'Gentlemen, what if I told you that there was a way to send the crewmen home without them knowing that we have her? That's the issue, right? We have to send the crewmen back to Mother Russia. I say there's a way to do that, and the remaining question is where to hide her.'

'We're listening,' Hilton said suspiciously.

'Well, sir, we'll have to move quickly to get everything in place. We'll need *Avalon* from the West Coast. *Mystic* is already aboard the *Pigeon* in Charleston. We need both of them, and we need an old boomer of our own that we can afford to do without. That's the hardware. The real trick, however, is the timing – and we have to find her. That may be the hardest part.'

'Maybe not,' Foster said. 'Admiral Gallery reported this morning that *Dallas* may be onto her. Her report dovetails nicely with your engineering model. We'll know more in a few days. Go on.'

Tyler explained. It took ten minutes since he had to answer questions and use the chart to diagram time and space constraints. When he was finished, General Barnes was at the phone calling the commander of the Military Airlift Command. Foster left the room to call Norfolk, and Hilton was on his way to the White House.

The *Red October*

Except for those on watch, every officer was in the wardroom. Several pots of tea were on the table, all untouched, and again the door was locked.

'Comrades,' Petrov reported, 'the second set of badges was contaminated, worse than the first.'

Ramius noted that Petrov was rattled. It wasn't the first set of badges, or the second. It was the third and fourth since sailing. He had chosen his ship's doctor well.

'Bad badges,' Melekhin growled. 'Some bastard of a trickster in Severomorsk – or perhaps an imperialist spy playing a typical enemy trick on us. When they catch the son of a bitch, I will shoot him myself – whoever he is! This sort of thing is treasonous!'

'Regulations require that I report this,' Petrov noted. 'Even though the instruments show safe levels.'

'Your adherence to the rules is noted, Comrade Doctor. You have acted correctly,' Ramius said. 'And now regulations stipulate that we make yet another check. Melekhin, I want you and Borodin to do it personally. First check the radiation instruments themselves. If they are working properly, we

150

will be certain that the badges are defective – or have been tampered with. If so, my report on this incident will demand someone's head.' If was not unknown for drunken shipyard workers to be sent to the gulag. 'Comrades, in my opinion there is nothing at all to concern us. If there were a leak, Comrade Melekhin would have discovered it days ago. We all have work to do.'

They were all back in the wardroom half an hour later. Passing crewmen noticed this, and already the whispering started.

'Comrades,' Melekhin announced, 'we have a major problem.'

The officers, especially the younger ones, looked a little pale. On the table was a Geiger counter stripped into a score of small parts. Next to it was a radiation detector taken off the reactor room bulkhead, its inspection cover removed.

'Sabotage,' Melekhin hissed. It was a word fearsome enough to make any Soviet citizen shudder. The room went deathly still, and Ramius noted that Svyadov was holding his face under rigid control.

'Comrades, mechanically speaking these instruments are quite simple. As you know, this counter has ten different settings. We can choose from ten sensitivity ranges, using the same instrument to detect a minor leak or to quantify a major one. We do that by dialling this selector, which engages one of ten electrical resistors of increasing value. A child could design this, or maintain and repair it.' The chief engineer tapped the underside of the selector dial. 'In this case the proper resistors have been clipped off, and new ones soldered on. Settings one to eight have the same impedance value. All of our counters were inspected by the same dockyard technician three days before we sailed. Here is his inspection sheet.' Melekhin tossed it on the table contemptuously.

'Either he or another spy sabotaged this and all the other counters I've looked at. It would have taken a skilled man no more than an hour. In the case of this instrument.' The engineer turned the fixed detector over. 'You see that the electrical parts have been disconnected, except for the test circuit, which was rewired. Borodin and I removed this from the forward bulkhead. This is skilled work; whoever did this is no amateur. I believe that an imperialist agent has sabotaged our ship. First he disabled our radiation monitor instruments, then he probably arranged a low-level leak in our hop piping. It would appear, comrades, that Comrade Petrov was correct. We may have a leak. My apologies, Doctor.'

Petrov nodded jerkily. Compliments like this he could easily forego.

'Total exposure, Comrade Petrov?' Ramius asked.

'The greatest is for the enginemen, of course. The maximum is fifty rads for Comrades Melekhin and Svyadov. The other engine crewmen run from twenty to forty-five rads, and the cumulative exposure drops rapidly as one moves forward. The torpedomen have only five rads or so, mostly less. The officers exclusive of engineers run from ten to twenty-five.' Petrov paused, telling himself to be more positive. 'Comrades, these are not lethal doses. In fact, one can tolerate a dose of up to a hundred rads without any near-term physiological effects, and one can survive several hundred. We do face a serious problem here, but it is not yet a life-threatening emergency.'

'Melekhin?' the captain asked.

'It is my engine plant, and my responsibility. We do not yet *know* that we have a leak. The badges could still be defective or sabotaged. This could all be a vicious psychological trick played on us by the main enemy to damage our morale. Borodin will assist me. We will personally repair these and conduct a thorough inspection of all reactor systems. I am too old to have children. For the moment, I suggest that we deactivate the reactor and proceed on battery. The inspection will take us four hours at most. I also recommend that we reduce reactor watches to two hours. Agreed, Captain?'

'Certainly, Comrade. I know that there is nothing you cannot repair.'

'Excuse me, Comrade Captain,' Ivanov spoke up. 'Should we report this to fleet headquarters?'

'Our orders are not to break radio silence,' Ramius said.

'If the imperialists were able to sabotage our instruments . . . What if they knew our orders beforehand and are attempting to make us use the radio so they can locate us?' Borodin asked.

'A possibility,' Ramius replied. 'First we will determine if we have a problem, then its severity. Comrades we have a fine crew and the best officers in the fleet. We will see to our own problems, conquer them, and continue our mission. We all have a date in Cuba that I intend to meet – to hell with imperialist plots!'

'Well said,' Melekhin concurred.

'Comrades, we will keep this secret. There is no reason to excite the crew over what may be nothing, and at most is something we can handle on our own.' Ramius ended the meeting.

Petrov was less sure, and Svyadov was trying very hard not to shake. He had a sweetheart at home and wanted one day to have children. The young lieutenant had been painstakingly trained to understand everything that went on in the reactor systems and to know what to do if things went awry. And it was some consolation to know that most of the solutions to reactor problems to be found in the book had been written by some of the men in this room. Even so, something that could neither be seen nor felt was invading his body, and no rational person would be happy with that.

The meeting adjourned. Melekhin and Borodin went aft to the engineering stores. A *michman* electrician came with them to get the proper parts. He noted that they were reading from the maintenance manual for a radiation detector. When he went off duty an hour later, the whole crew knew that the reactor had been shut down yet again. The electrician conferred with his bunkmate, a missile maintenance technician. Together they discussed the reason for working on a half dozen Geiger counters and other instruments, and their conclusion was an obvious one.

The submarine's bosun overheard the discussion and pondered the conclusion himself. He had been on nuclear submarines for ten years. Despite this he was not an educated man and regarded any activity in the reactor spaces as something to the left of witchcraft. It worked the ship, how he did not know, though he was certain that there was something unholy about it. Now he began to wonder if the devils he never saw inside that steel drum were coming loose. Within two hours the entire crew knew that something was wrong and that their officers had not yet figured out a way to deal with it.

The cooks bringing food forward from the galley to the crew spaces were seen to linger in the bow as long as they could. Men standing watch in the control room shifted on their feet more than usual, Ramius noted, hurrying forward at the change of watch.

The USS *New Jersey*

It took some getting used to, Commodore Zachary Eaton reflected. When his flagship was built, he was sailing boats in a bathtub. Back then the Russians were allies, but allies of convenience, who shared a common enemy instead of a common goal. Like the Chinese today, he judged. The enemy then had been the Germans and the Japanese. In his twenty-six-year career, he had been to both countries many times, and his first command, a destroyer, had been homeported at Yokosuka. It was a strange world.

There were several nice things about his flagship. Big as she was, her movement on the ten-foot seas was just enough to remind him that he was at sea, not at a desk. Visibility was about ten miles, and somewhere out there, about eight hundred miles away, was the Russian fleet. His battleship was going to meet them just like in the old old days, as if the aircraft carrier had never come along. The destroyers *Caron* and *Stump* were in sight, five miles off either bow. Further forward, the cruisers *Biddle* and *Wainwright* were doing radar picket duty. The surface action group was marking time instead of proceeding forward as he would have preferred. Off the New Jersey coast, the helicopter assault ship *Tarawa* and two frigates were racing to join up, bringing ten AV-8B Harrier attack fighters and fourteen ASW helicopters to supplement his air strength. This was useful, but not of critical concern to Eaton. The *Saratoga*'s air wing was now operating out of Maine, along with a goodly collection of air force birds working hard to learn the maritime strike business. HMS *Invincible* was two hundred miles to his east, conducting aggressive ASW patrols, and eight hundred miles east of that force was the *Kennedy*, hiding under a weather front off the Azores. It slightly irked the commodore that the Brits were helping out. Since when did the US Navy need help defending the American coast? Not that they didn't owe us the favour, though.

The Russians had split into three groups, with the carrier *Kiev* eastern-most to face the *Kennedy*'s battle group. His expected responsibility was the *Moskva* group, with the *Invincible* handling the *Kirov*'s. Data on all three was being fed to him continuously and digested by his operations staff down in flag plot. What were the Soviets up to? he wondered.

He knew the story that they were searching for a lost sub, but Eaton believed that as much as if they'd explained that they had a bridge they wanted to sell. Probably, he thought, they want to demonstrate that they can trail their coats down our coast whenever they want, to show that they have a seagoing fleet and to establish a precedent for doing this again.

Eaton did not like that.

He did not much care for his assigned mission either. He had two tasks that were not fully compatible. Keeping an eye on their submarine activity would be difficult enough. The *Saratoga*'s Vikings were not working his area, despite his request, and most of the Orions were working farther out, closer to the *Invincible*. His own ASW assets were barely adequate for local defense, much less active sub hunting. The *Tarawa* would change that, but also change his screening requirements. His other mission was to establish and maintain sensor contact with the *Moskva* group and to report at once any unusual activity to CINCLANTFLT, the commander in chief of the Atlantic Fleet. This made sense, sort of. If their surface ships did anything untoward. Eaton had the means to deal with them. It was being decided now how closely he should shadow them.

The problem was whether he should be nearby or far away. Near meant twenty miles – gun range. The *Moskva* had ten escorts, none of which could possibly survive more than two of his sixteen-inch projectiles. At twenty miles he had the choice of using full-sized or subcalibre rounds, the latter guided to their targets by a laser designator installed atop the main director tower. Tests the previous year had determined that he could maintain a steady firing rate of one round every twenty seconds, with the laser shifting fire from one target to another until there were no more. But this would expose the *New Jersey* and her escorts to torpedo and missile fire from the Russian ships.

Backing farther off, he could still fire sabot rounds from fifty miles, and they could be directed to the target by a laser designator aboard the battlewagon's helicopter. This would expose the chopper to surface-to-air missile fire and to Soviet helicopters suspected of having air-to-air missile capability. To help out with this, the *Tarawa* was bringing a pair of Apache attack helicopters, which carried lasers, air-to-air missiles, and their own air-to-surface missiles; they were antitank weapons expected to work well against small warships.

His ships would be exposed to missile fire, but he didn't fear for his flagship. Unless the Russians were carrying nuclear warheads, their antiship missiles would not be able to damage his ship gravely – the *New Jersey* had upwards of a foot of class B armour plate. They would, however, play hell with his radar and communications gear, and worse, they would be lethal to his thin-hulled escorts. His ships carried their own antiship missiles, Harpoons and Tomahawks, though not as many as he would have liked.

And what about a Russian sub hunting them? Eaton had been told of none, but you never knew where one might be hiding. Oh well – he couldn't worry about everything. A submarine could sink the *New Jersey*, but she would have to work at it. If the Russians were really up to something nasty, they'd get the first shot, but Eaton would have enough warning to launch his own missiles and get off a few rounds of gunfire while calling for air support – none of which would happen, he was sure.

He decided that the Russians were on some sort of fishing expedition. His job was to show them that the fish in these waters were dangerous.

Naval Air Station, North Island, California

The oversized tractor-trailer crept at two miles per hour into the cargo bay of the C-5A Galaxy transport under the watchful eyes of the aircraft's loadmaster, two flight officers, and six naval officers. Oddly, only the latter, none of whom wore aviator's wings, were fully versed in the procedure. The vehicle's centre of gravity was precisely marked, and they watched the mark approach a particular number engraved on the cargo bay floor. The work had to be done exactly. Any mistake could fatally impair the aircraft's trim and imperil the lives of the flight crew and passengers.

'Okay, freeze it right there,' the senior officer called. The driver was only too glad to stop. He left the keys in the ignition, set all the brakes, and put the truck in gear before getting out. Someone else would drive it out of the aircraft on the other side of the country. The loadmaster and six airmen immediately went to work, snaking steel cables to eyebolts on the truck and trailer to secure the heavy load. Shifting cargo was something else an aircraft rarely survived, and the C-5A did not have ejection seats.

The loadmaster saw to it that his ground crewmen were properly at work before walking over to the pilot. He was a twenty-five-year sergeant who loved the C-5s despite their blemished history.

'Cap'n, what the hell is this thing?'

'It's called a DSRV, Sarge, deep submergence rescue vehicle.'

'Says *Avalon* on the back, sir,' the sergeant pointed out.

'Yeah, so it has a name. It's sort of a lifeboat for submarines. Goes down to get the crew out if something screws up.'

'Oh.' The sergeant considered that. He'd flown tanks, helicopters, general cargo, once a whole battalion of troops on his – he thought of the aircraft as his – Galaxy before. This was the first time he had ever flown a ship. If it had a name, he reasoned, it was a ship. Damn, the Galaxy could do anything! 'Where we takin' it, sir?'

'Norfolk Naval Air Station, and I've never been there either.' The pilot watched the securing process closely. Already a dozen cables were attached. When a dozen more were in place, they'd put tension on the cables to prevent the minutest shift. 'We figure a trip of five hours, forty minutes, all on internal fuel. We got the jet stream on our side today. Weather's supposed to be okay until we hit the coast. We lay over for a day, then come back Monday morning.'

'Your boys work pretty fast,' said the senior naval officer, Lieutenant Ames, coming over.

'Yes, Lieutenant, another twenty minutes.' The pilot checked his watch. 'We ought to be taking off on the hour.'

'No hurry, Captain. If this thing shifts in flight, I guess it would ruin our whole day. Where do I send my people?'

'Upper deck forward. There's room for fifteen or so just aft of the flight deck.' Lieutenant Ames knew this but didn't say so. He'd flown with his DSRV across the Atlantic several times and across the Pacific once, every time on a different C-S.

'May I ask what the big deal is?' the pilot inquired.

'I don't know,' Ames said. 'They want me and my baby in Norfolk.'

'You really take that little bitty thing underwater, sir?' the loadmaster asked.

'That's what they pay me for. I've had her down to forty-eight hundred feet, almost a mile.' Ames regarded his vessel with affection.

'A mile *under* water, sir? Jesus – uh, pardon me, sir, but I mean, isn't that a little hairy – the water pressure, I mean?'

'Not really. I've been down to twenty thousand aboard *Trieste*. It's really pretty interesting down there. You see all kinds of strange fish.' Though a fully qualified submariner, Ames' first love was research. He had a degree in oceanography and had commanded or served in all of the navy's deep-submergence vehicles except the nuclear-powered NR-I. 'Of course, the water pressure would do bad things to you if anything went wrong, but it would be so fast you'd never know it. If you fellows want a check ride, I could probably arrange it. It's a different world down there.'

'That's okay, sir.' The sergeant went back to swearing at his men.

'You weren't serious,' the pilot observed.

'Why not? It's no big deal. We take civilians down all the time, and believe me, it's a lot less hairy than riding this damned white whale during a mid-air refuelling.'

'Uh-huh,' the pilot noted dubiously. He'd done hundreds of those. It was entirely routine, and he was surprised that anyone would find it dangerous. You had to be careful, of course, but, hell, you had to he careful driving every morning. He was sure that an accident on this pocket submarine wouldn't leave enough of a man to make a decent meal for a shrimp. It takes all kinds, he decided. 'You don't go to sea by yourself in that, do you?'

'No, ordinarily we work off a submarine rescue ship, *Pigeon* or *Ortolan*. We can also operate off a regular submarine. That gadget you see there on the trailer is our mating collar. We can nest on the back of a sub at the after escape trunk, and the sub takes us where we need to go.'

'Does this have to do with the flap on the East Coast?'

'That's a good bet, but nobody's said anything official to us. The papers say the Russians have lost a sub. If so, we might go down to look at her, maybe rescue any survivors. We can take off twenty or twenty-five men at a time, and our mating collar is designed to fit Russians subs as well as our own.'

'Same size?'

'Close enough,' Ames cocked an eyebrow. 'We plan for all kinds of contingencies.'

'Interesting.'

The North Atlantic

The YAK-36 Forger had left the *Kiev* half an hour before, guided first by gyro-compass and now by the ESM pod on the fighter's stubby rudder fin. Senior Lieutenant Viktor Shavrov's mission was not an easy one. He was to approach the American E-3A Sentry radar surveillance aircraft, one of which had been shadowing his fleet for three days now. The AWACS (airborne warning and control system) aircraft had been careful to circle well beyond SAM range, but had stayed close enough to maintain constant coverage of the Soviet fleet, reporting every manoeuvre and radio transmission to their command base. It was like having a burglar watching one's apartment and being unable to do anything about it.

Shavrov's mission was to do something about it. He couldn't shoot, of course. His orders from Admiral Stralbo in the *Kirov* had been explicit about that. But he was carrying a pair of Atoll heat-seeking missiles which he would be sure to show the imperialists. He and his admiral expected that this would teach them a lesson: the Soviet Navy did not like having imperialist snoopers about, and accidents had been known to happen. It was a mission worthy of the effort it took.

This effort was considerable. To avoid detection by the airborne radar Shavrov had to fly as low and slow as his fighter could operate, a bare twenty metres above the rough Atlantic; this way he would get lost in the sea return. His speed was two hundred knots. This made for excellent fuel economy, though his mission was at the ragged edge of his fuel load. It also made for very rough flying as his fighter bounced through the roiled air at the wave tops. There was a low-hanging mist that cut visibility to a few kilometres. So much the better, he thought. The nature of the mission had chosen him, rather than the other way around. He was one of the few Soviet pilots experienced in low-level flying. Shavrov had not become a sailor-pilot by himself. He'd started flying attack helicopters for frontal aviation in Afghanistan, graduating to fixed-wing aircraft after a year's bloody apprenticeship. Shavrov was an expert in nap-of-the-earth flying, having learned it by necessity, hunting the bandits and counter-revolutionaries that hid in the towering mountains like hydrophobic rats. This skill had made him attractive to the fleet, which had transferred him to sea duty without his having had much say in the matter. After a few months he had no complaints, his perks and extra pay being more attractive than his former frontal aviation base on the Chinese border. Being one of the few hundred carrier-qualified Soviet airmen had softened the blow of missing his chance to fly the new MiG-27, though with luck, if the new full-sized carrier were ever finished, he'd have the chance to fly the naval version of that wonderful bird. Shavrov could wait for that, and with a few successful missions like this one he might have his squadron command.

He stopped daydreaming – the mission was too demanding for that. This was real flying. He'd never flown against Americans, only against the weapons they gave to the Afghan bandits. He had lost friends to those weapons, some of whom had survived their crashes only to be done to death by the Afghan savages in ways that would have made even a German puke. It would be good to teach the imperialists a lesson personally.

The radar signal was growing stronger. Beneath his ejection seat a tape recorder was making a continuous record of the signal characteristics of the American aircraft so that the scientific people would he able to devise a means of jamming and foiling the vaunted American flying eye. The aircraft was only a converted 707, a glorified passenger plane, hardly a worthy opponent for a crack fighter pilot! Shavrov checked his chart. He'd have to find it soon. Next he checked his fuel. He'd dropped his last external tank a few minutes earlier and all he had now was his internal fuel. The turbofan was guzzling fuel, something he had to keep an eye on. He planned to have only five or ten minutes of fuel left when he returned to his ship. This did not trouble him. He already had over a hundred carrier landings.

There! His hawk's eyes caught the glint of sun off metal at one o'clock high. Shavrov eased back on his stick and increased power gently, bringing his Forger into a climb. A minute later he was at two thousand metres. He could see the Sentry now, its blue paint blending neatly into the darkening sky. He was coming up beneath its tail, and with luck the empennage would shield him from the rotating radar antenna. Perfect! He'd blaze by her a few times, letting the flight crew see his Atolls, and –

It took Shavrov a moment to realize that he had a wingman.

Two wingmen.

Fifty metres to his left and right, a pair of American F-15 Eagle fighters. The visored face of one pilot was staring at him.

'YAK-106, YAK-106, please acknowledge.' The voice on his SSB (single side band) radio circuit spoke flawless Russian. Shavrov did not acknowledge. They had read the number off his engine intake housing before he had known they were there.

'106, 106, this is the Sentry aircraft you are now approaching. Please identify yourself and your intentions. We get a little anxious when a stray fighter comes our way, so we've had three following you for the past hundred kilometres.'

Three? Shavrov turned his head around. A third Eagle with four Sparrow missiles was hanging fifty metres from his tail, his 'six.'

'Our men compliment you on your ability to fly low and slow, 106.'

Lieutenant Shavrov was shaking with rage as he passed four thousand metres, still eight thousand from the American AWACS. He had checked his six every thirty seconds on the way in. The Americans must have been riding back there, hidden in the mist, and vectored in on him by instructions from the Sentry. He swore to himself and held course. He'd teach that AWACS a lesson!

'Break off, 106.' It was a cool voice, without emotion except perhaps a trace of irony. '106, if you do not break off, we will consider your mission to be hostile. Think about it, 106. You are beyond radar coverage of your own ships, and you are not yet within missile range of us.'

Shavrov looked to his right. The Eagle was breaking off – so was the one to the left. Was it a gesture, taking the heat off of him and expecting some courtesy in return? Or where they clearing the way for the one behind him – he checked, still there – to shoot? There was no telling what these imperialist criminals would do; he was at least a minute from the fringe of their missile range. Shavrov was anything but a coward. Neither was he a fool. He moved his stick, curving his fighter a few degrees to the right.

'Thank you, 106,' the voice acknowledged. 'You see, we have some trainee operators aboard. Two of them are women, and we don't want them to get rattled their first time out.' Suddenly it was too much. Shavrov thumbed the radio switch on his stick.

'Shall I tell you what you can do with your women, Yankee'!'

'You are *nekulturny*, 106,' the voice replied softly. 'Perhaps the long overwater flight has made you nervous. You must be about at the limit of your internal fuel. Bastard of a day to fly, what with all these crazy, shifting winds. Do you need a position check, over?'

'Negative, Yankee!'

'Course back to *Kiev* is one-eight-five, true. Have to be careful using a magnetic compass this far north, you know. Distance to *Kiev* is 318.6 kilometres. Warning – there is a rapidly moving cold front coming in from the southwest. That's going to make flying a little rough in a few hours. Do you require an escort back to *Kiev*?'

'Pig!' Shavrov swore to himself. He switched his radio off, cursing himself for his lack of discipline. He had allowed the Americans to wound his pride. Like most fighter pilots, he had a surfeit of that.

'106, we did not copy your last transmission. Two of my Eagles are heading that way. They will form up on you and see that you get home safely. Have a happy day, Comrade. Sentry-November, out.

159

The American lieutenant turned to his colonel. He couldn't keep a straight face any longer. 'God, I thought I'd strangle talking like that.' He sipped some Coke from a plastic cup. 'He really thought he'd sneak up on us.'

'In case you didn't notice, he did get within a mile of Atoll range, and we don't have authorisation to shoot at him until he flips one at us – which might wreck our day,' the colonel grumped. 'Nice job twisting his tail, Lieutenant.'

'A pleasure, Colonel.' The operator looked at his screen. 'Well, he's heading back to momma, with Cobras 3 and 4 on his six. He's going to be one unhappy Russkie when he gets home. If he gets home. Even with those drop tanks, he must be near his range limit.' He thought for a moment. 'Colonel, if they do this again, how 'bout we offer to take the guy home with us?'

'Get a Forger – what for? I suppose the navy'd like to have one to play with, they don't get much of Ivan's hardware, but the Forger's a piece of junk.'

Shavrov was tempted to firewall his engine but restrained himself. He'd already shown enough personal weakness for one day. Besides, his YAK could only break Mach 1 in a dive. Those Eagles could do it straight up, and they had plenty of fuel. He saw that they both carried FAST-pack conformal fuel cells. They could cross whole oceans with those. Damn the Americans and their arrogance! Damn his own intelligence officer for telling him he could sneak up on the Sentry! Let the air-to-air armed Backfires go after them. They could handle that damned overbred passenger bus, could get to it faster than its fighter guardians could react.

The Americans, he saw, were not lying about the weather front. A line of cold weather squawls racing northeast was just on the horizon as he approached the *Kiev*. The Eagles backed off as he approached the formation. One American pilot pulled alongside briefly to wave goodbye. His head bobbed at Shavrov's return gesture. The Eagles paired up and turned back north.

Five minutes later he was aboard the *Kiev*, still pale with rage. As soon as the wheels were chocked he jumped to the carrier deck, stomping off to see his squadron commander.

The Kremlin

The city of Moscow was justly famous for its subway system. For a pittance, people could ride nearly anywhere they wanted on a modern, safe, garishly decorated electric railway system. In case of war, the underground tunnels could serve as a bomb shelter for the citizens of Moscow. This secondary use was the result of the efforts of Nikita Khrushchev, who when construction was begun in the mid-thirties had suggested to Stalin that the system be driven deep. Stalin had approved. The shelter consideration had been decades ahead of its time; nuclear fission had then only been a theory, fusion hardly thought of at all.

On a spur of the line running from Sverdlov Square to the old airport, which ran near the Kremlin, workers bored a tunnel that was later closed off with a ten-metre-thick steel and concrete plug. The hundred-metre-long space was connected to the Kremlin by a pair of elevator shafts, and over time it had been converted to an emergency command centre from which the Politburo could control the entire Soviet empire. The tunnel was also a convenient means of going unseen from the city to a small airport from which Politburo members would be flown to their ultimate redoubt, beneath the granite monolith at Zhiguli. Neither command post was a secret to the West – both had existed far too long for that – but the KGB confidently reported that nothing in the Western arsenals could smash through the hundreds of feet of rock which in both places separated the Politburo from the surface.

This fact was of little comfort to Admiral Yuri llych Padorin. He found himself seated at the far end of a ten-metre-long conference table looking at the grim faces of the ten Politburo members, the inner circle that alone made the strategic decisions affecting the fate of his country. None of them were officers. Those in uniform reported to these men. Up the table to his left was Admiral Sergey Gorshkov, who had disassociated himself from this affair with consummate skill, even producing a letter in which he had opposed Ramius' appointment to command the *Red October*. Padorin, as chief of the Main Political Administration, had successfully blocked Ramius' transfer, pointing out that Gorshkov's candidate for command was occasionally late in paying his Party dues and did not speak up at the regular meetings often enough for an officer of his rank. The truth was that Gorshkov's candidate was not so proficient an officer as Ramius, whom Gorshkov had wanted for his own operations staff, a post that Ramius had successfully evaded for years.

Party General Secretary and President of the Union of Soviet Socialist Republics Andre Narmonov shifted his gaze to Padorin. His face gave nothing away. It never did, unless he wished it to – which was rare enough. Narmonov had succeeded Andropov when the latter had suffered a heart attack. There were rumours about that, but in the Soviet Union there are always rumours. Not since the days of Laventri Beria had the security chieftain come so close to power, and senior Party officials had allowed themselves to forget that. It would not be forgotten again. Bringing the KGB to heel had taken a year, a necessary measure to secure the privileges of the Party elite from the supposed reforms of the Andropov clique.

Narmonov was the apparatchik par excellence. He had first gained prominence as a factory manager, an engineer with a reputation for fulfilling his quota early, a man who produced results. He had risen steadily by using his own talents and those of others, rewarding those he had to, ignoring those he could. His position as general secretary of the Communist Party was not entirely secure. It was still early in his stewardship of the Party, and he depended on a loose coalition of colleagues – not friends, these men did not make friends. His succession to this chair had resulted more from ties within the Party structure than from personal ability, and his position would depend on consensus rule for years, until such time as his will could dictate policy.

Narmonov's dark eyes, Padorin could see, were red from tobacco smoke. The ventilation system down here had never worked properly. The general secretary squinted at Padorin from the other end of the table as he decided what to say, what would please the members of this cabal, these ten old, passionless men.

'Comrade Admiral,' he began coldly, 'we have heard from Comrade Gorshkov what the chances are of finding and destroying this rebellious submarine before it can complete its unimaginable crime. We are not pleased. Nor are we pleased with the fantastic error in judgement that gave command of our most valuable ship to this slug. What I want to know from you, Comrade, is what happened to the *zampolit* aboard, and what security measures were taken by your office to prevent this infamy from taking place!'

There was no fear in Narmonov's voice, but Padorin knew it had to be there. This 'fantastic error' could ultimately be laid at the chairman's feet by members who wanted another in that chair – unless he were able somehow to separate himself from it. If this meant Padorin's skin, that was the admiral's problem. Narmonov had had men flayed before.

Padorin had prepared himself for this over several days. He was a man who had lived through months of intensive combat operations and had several boats sunk from under him. If his body was softer now, his mind was not. Whatever his fate might be, Padorin was determined to meet it with dignity. If they remember me as a fool, he thought, it will be as a coura- geous fool. He had little left to live for in any case. 'Comrade General Secretary,' he began, 'the political officer aboard *Red October* was Captain Ivan Yurievich Putin, a stalwart and faithful Party member. I cannot imagine – '

'Comrade Padorin,' Defense Minister Ustinov interrupted, 'we presume that you also could not imagine the unbelievable treachery of this Ramius. You now expect us to trust your judgement on this man also?'

'The most disturbing thing of all,' added Mikhail Alexandrov, the Party theoretician who had replaced the dead Mikhail Suslov and was even more determined than the departed ideologue to be simon-pure on Party doctrine, 'is how tolerant the Main Political Administration has been towards this renegade. It is amazing, particularly in view of his obvious efforts to construct his own personality cult throughout the submarine service, even in the polit- ical arm, it would seem. Your criminal willingness to overlook this – this *obvious* aberration from Party policy – does not make your judgement appear very sound.'

'Comrades, you are correct in judging that I erred badly in approving Ramius for command, and also that we allowed him to select most of *Red October*'s senior officers. At the same time, we chose some years ago to do things in this way, to keep officers associated with a single ship for many years, and to give the captain great sway over their careers. This is an operational question, not a political one.'

'We have already considered that,' Narmonov replied. 'It is true that in this case there is enough blame for more than one man.' Gorshkov didn't move, but the message was explicit: his effort to separate himself from this scandal had failed. Narmonov didn't care how many heads it took to prop up his chair.

'Comrade Chairman,' Gorshkov objected, 'the efficiency of the fleet – '

'Efficiency?' Alexandrov said. 'Efficiency? This Lithuanian half-breed is *efficiently* making fools of our fleet with his chosen officers while our remaining ships blunder about like newly castrated cattle.' Alexandrov alluded to his first job on a state farm. A fitting beginning, it was generally thought, for the man who held the position of chief idealogue was as popular in Moscow as the plague, but the Politburo had to have him or one like him. The ideological chieftain was always the kingmaker. Whose side was he on now – in addition to his own?'

'The most likely explanation is that Putin was murdered,' Padorin continued. 'He alone of the officers left behind a wife and family.'

'That's another question, Comrade Admiral.' Narmonov seized this issue. 'Why is it that none of these men are married? Didn't that tell you something? Must we of the Politburo supervise everything? Can't you think for yourselves?'

As if you want us to, Padorin thought. 'Comrade General Secretary, most of our submarine commanders prefer young, unmarried officers in their wardrooms. Duty at sea is demanding, and single men have fewer distractions. Moreover, each of the senior officers aboard is a Party member in good standing with a praiseworthy record. Ramius has been treacherous, there is no denying that, and I would gladly kill the son of a bitch with my own hands – but he has deceived more good men than there are in this room.'

'Indeed,' Alexandrov observed. 'And now that we are in this mess, how do we get out of it?'

Padorin took a deep breath. He'd been waiting for this. 'Comrades, we have another man aboard *Red October*, unknown to either Putin or Captain Ramius, an agent of the Main Political Administration.'

'What?' Gorshkov said. And why did I not know of this?'

Alexandrov smiled. 'That's the first intelligent thing we've heard today. Go on.'

'This individual is covered as an enlisted man. He reports directly to our office, bypassing all operational and political channels. His name is Igor Loginov. He is twenty-four, a – '

'*Twenty-four!*' Narmonov shouted. 'You trust a child with this responsibility?'

'Comrade, Loginov's mission is to blend in with the conscripted crewmen, to listen in on conversations, to identify likely traitors, spies, and saboteurs.

In truth he looks younger still. He serves alongside young men, and he must be young himself. He is, in fact, a graduate of the higher naval school for political officers at Kiev and the GRU intelligence academy. He is the son of Arkady Ivanovich Loginov, chief of the Lenin Steel Plant at Kazan. Many of you here know his father.' Narmonov was among those who nodded, a flickering of interest in his eyes. 'Only an elite few are chosen for this duty. I have met and interviewed this boy myself. His record is clear, he is a Soviet patriot without question.'

'I know his father,' Narmonov confirmed. 'Arkady Ivanovich is an honourable man who has raised several good sons. What are this boy's orders?'

'As I said, Comrade General Secretary, his ordinary duties are to observe the crewmen and report on what he sees. He's been doing this for two years, and he is good at it. He does not report to the *zampolit* aboard, but only to Moscow or to one of my representatives. In a genuine emergency, his orders are to report to the *zampolit*. If Putin is alive – and I do not believe this, comrades – he would be part of the conspiracy, and Loginov would know not to do this. In a true emergency, therefore, his orders are to destroy the ship and make his escape.'

'This is possible?' Narmonov asked. 'Gorshkov?'

'Comrades, all of our ships carry powerful scuttling charges, submarines especially.'

'Unfortunately,' Padorin said, 'these are generally not armed, and only the captain can activate them. Ever since the incident on *Storozhevoy*, we in the Main Political Administration have had to consider that an incident such as this one was indeed a possibility, and that its most damaging manifestation would involve a missile-carrying submarine.'

'Ah,' Narmonov observed, 'he is a missile mechanic.'

'No, Comrade, he is a ship's cook,' Padorin replied.

'Wonderful! He spends all his day boiling potatoes!' Narmonov's hands flew up in the air, his hopeful demeanour gone in an instant, replaced with palpable wrath. 'You wish your bullet now, Padorin?'

'Comrade Chairman, this is a better cover assignment than you may imagine.' Padorin did not flinch, wanting to show these men what he was made of. 'On *Red October* the officers' accommodations and galley are aft. The crew's quarters are forward – the crew eat there since they do not have a separate messroom – with the missile room in between. As a cook he must travel back and forth many times each day, and his presence in any particular area will not be thought unusual. The food freezer is located adjacent to the lower missile deck forward. It is not our plan that he should activate the scuttling charges. We have allowed for the possibility that the captain could disarm them. Comrades, these measures have been carefully thought out.'

'Go on,' Narmonov grunted.

'As Comrade Gorshkov explained earlier, *Red October* carries twenty-six Seahawk missiles. These are solid-fuel rockets, and one has a range-safety package installed.

'Range safety?' Narmonov was puzzled.

Up to this point the military officers at the meeting, none of them Politburo members, had kept their peace. Padorin was surprised when General V. M. Vishenkov, commander of the Strategic Rocket Forces, spoke up. 'Comrades, these details were worked out through my office some years ago. As you know, when we test our missiles, we have safety packages aboard to explode them if they go off course. Otherwise they might land on one of our own cities. Our operational missiles do not ordinarily carry them – for the obvious reason, the imperialist might learn a way to explode them in flight.'

'So, our young GRU comrade will blow up the missile. What of the warheads?' Narmonov asked. An engineer by training, he could always be distracted by a technical discourse, always impressed by a clever one.

'Comrade,' Vishenkov went on, 'the missile warheads are armed by accelerometers. Thus they cannot be armed until the missile reaches its full programmed speed. The Americans use the same system, and for the same reason, to prevent sabotage. These safety systems are absolutely reliable. You could drop one of the re-entry vehicles from the top of the Moscow television transmitter onto a steel plate and it would not fire.' The general referred to the massive TV tower whose construction Narmonov had personally supervised while head of the Central Communications Directorate. Vishenkov was a skilled political operator.

'In the case of a solid-fuel rocket,' Padorin continued, recognizing his debt to Vishenkov, wondering what he'd ask for in return, and hoping he'd live long enough to deliver, 'a safety package ignites all of the missile's three stages simultaneously.'

'So the missile just takes off?' Alexandrov asked.

'No, Comrade Academician. The upper stage might, if it could break through the missile tube hatch, and this would flood the missile room, sinking the submarine. But even if it did not, there is sufficient thermal energy in either of the first stages to reduce the entire submarine to a puddle of molten iron, twenty times what is necessary to sink it. Loginov has been trained to bypass the alarm system on the missile tube hatch, to activate the safety package, set a timer, and escape.'

'Not just to destroy the ship?' Narmonov asked.

'Comrade General Secretary,' Padorin said, 'it is too much to ask a young man to do his duty, knowing that it means certain death. We would be unrealistic to expect this. He must have at least the possibility of escape, otherwise human weakness might lead to failure.'

'This is reasonable,' Alexandrov said. 'Young men are motivated by hope, not fear. In this case, young Loginov would hope for a considerable reward.'

'And get it,' Narmonov said. 'We will make every effort to save this young man, Gorshkov.'

'If he is truly reliable,' Alexandrov noted.

'I know that my life depends on this, Comrade Academician,' Padorin said, his back still straight. He did not get a verbal answer, only nods from half the heads at the table. He had faced death before and was at the age where it remains the last thing a man need face.

The White House

Arbatov came into the Oval Office at 4:50 P.M. He found the president and Dr Pelt sitting in easy chairs across from the chief executive's desk.

'Come on over, Alex. Coffee?' The president pointed to a tray on the corner of his desk. He was not drinking today, Arbatov noted.

'No, thank you, Mr President. May I ask – '

'We think we found your sub, Alex,' Pelt answered. 'They just brought these dispatches over, and we're checking them now.' The adviser held up a ring binder of message forms.

'Where is it, may I ask?' The ambassador's face was deadpan.

'Roughly three hundred miles northeast of Norfolk. We have not located it exactly. One of our ships noted an underwater explosion in the area – no, that's not right. It was recorded on a ship, and when the tapes were checked a few hours later, they thought they heard a submarine explode and sink. Sorry, Alex,' Pelt said. 'I should have known better than to read through all this stuff without an interpreter. Does your navy talk in its own language, too?'

'Officers do not like for civilians to understand them.' Arbatov smiled. 'This has doubtless been true since the first man picked up a stone.'

'Anyway, we have ships and aircraft searching the area now.'

The president looked up. 'Alex, I talked to the chief of naval operations, Dan Foster, a few minutes ago. He said not to expect any survivors. The water there's over a thousand feet deep, and you know what the weather is like. They said it's right on the edge of the continental shelf.'

'The Norfolk Canyon, sir,' Pelt added.

'We are conducting a thorough search,' the president continued. 'The navy is bringing in some specialised rescue equipment, search gear, all that sort of thing. If the submarine is located, we'll get somebody down to them on the chance there might be survivors. From what the CNO tells me it is just possible that there might be if the interior partitions – bulkheads, I think he called them – are intact. The other question is their air supply, he said. Time is very much against us, I'm afraid. All this fantastically expensive equipment we buy them, and they can't locate one damned object right off our coast.'

Arbatov made a mental record of these words. It would make a worthwhile intelligence report. The president occasionally let –

'By the way, Mr Ambassador, what exactly was your submarine doing there?'

'I have no idea, Dr Pelt.'

'I trust it was not a missile sub,' Pelt said. 'We have an agreement to keep those five hundred miles offshore. The wreck will of course be inspected by our rescue craft. Were we to learn that it is indeed a missile sub . . .'

'Your point is noted. Still, those are international waters.'

The president turned and spoke softly. 'So is the Gulf of Finland, Alex, and, I believe, the Black Sea.' He let this observation hang in the air for a moment. 'I sincerely hope that we are not heading back to that kind of situation. Are we talking about a missile submarine, Alex?'

'Truly, Mr President, I have no idea. Certainly I should hope not.'

The president could see how carefully the lie was phrased. He wondered if the Russians would admit that there was a captain out there who had disregarded his orders. No, they would probably claim a navigation error.

'Very well. In any case, we will be conducting our own search and rescue operation. We'll know soon enough what sort of vessel we're talking about.' The president looked suddenly uneasy. 'One more thing Foster talked about. If we find bodies – pardon the crudity on a Saturday afternoon – I expect that you will want them returned to your country.'

'I have had no instructions on this,' the ambassador answered truthfully, caught off guard.

'It was explained to me in too much detail what a death like this does to a man. In simple terms, they're crushed by the water pressure, not a very pretty thing to see, they tell me. But they were men, and they deserve some dignity even in death.'

Arbatov conceded the point. 'If this is possible, then, I believe that the Soviet people would appreciate this humanitarian gesture.'

'We'll do our best.'

And the American best, Arbatov remembered, included a ship named the *Glomar Explorer*. This notorious exploration ship had been built by the CIA for the specific purpose of recovering a Soviet *Golf*-class missile submarine from the floor of the Pacific Ocean. She had been placed in storage, no doubt to await the next such opportunity. There would be nothing the Soviet Union could do to prevent the operation, a few hundred miles off the American coast, three hundred miles from the United States' largest naval base.

'I trust that the precepts of international law will be observed, gentlemen. That is, with respect to the vessel's remains and the crew's bodies.'

'Of course, Alex.' The president smiled, gesturing to a memorandum on his desk. Arbatov struggled for control. He'd been led down this path like a schoolboy, forgetting that the American president had been a skilled courtroom tactician – not something that life in the Soviet Union prepares a man for – and knew all about legal tricks. Why was this bastard so easy to underestimate?

The president was also struggling to control himself. It was not often that he saw Alex flustered. This was a clever opponent, not easily caught off balance. Laughing would spoil it.

The memorandum from the attorney general had arrived only that morning. It read:

Mr President,

Pursuant to your request, I have asked the chief of our admiralty law department to review the question of international law regarding the ownership of sunken or derelict vessels, and the law of salvage pertaining to such vessels. There is a good deal of case law on the subject. One simple example is *Dalmas v Stathos* (84FSuff. 828, 1949 A.M.C. 770 [S.D.N.Y. 1949]):

No problem of foreign law is here involved, for it is well settled that 'salvage is a question arising out of the *jus gentium* and does not ordinarily depend on the municipal law of particular countries.'

The international basis for this is the Salvage Convention of 1910 (Brussels), which codified the transnational nature of admiralty and salvage law. This was ratified by the United Sates in the Salvage Act of 1912, 37 Stat. 242, (1912), 46 U.S.C.A.§§727-731; and also in 37 Stat. 1658 (1913).

'International law will be observed, Alex,' the president promised. 'In all particulars.' And whatever we get, he thought, will be taken to the nearest port, Norfolk, where it will be turned over to the receiver of wrecks, an overworked federal official. If the Soviets want anything back, they can bring action in admiralty court, which means the federal district court sitting in Norfolk, where, if the suit were successful – *after* the value of the salved property was determined, and *after* the US Navy was paid a proper fee for its salvage effort, also determined by the court – the wreck would be returned to its rightful owners. Of course, the federal district court in question had, at last check, an eleven-month backlog of cases.

Arbatov would cable Moscow on this. For what good it would do. He was certain the president would take perverse pleasure in manipulating the grotesque American legal system to his own advantage, all the time pointing out that, as president, he was constitutionally unable to interfere with the working of the courts.

Pelt looked at his watch. It was about time for the next surprise. He had to admire the president. For a man with only limited knowledge of international affairs only a few years earlier, he'd learned fast. This outwardly simple, quiet-talking man was at his best in face to face situations, and after a lifetime's experience as a prosecutor, he still loved to play the game of negotiation and tactical exchange. He seemed able to manipulate people with frighteningly casual skill. The phone rang and Pelt got it, right on cue.

'This is Dr Pelt speaking. Yes, Admiral – where? When? Just one? I see ... Norfolk?' Thank you, Admiral, that is very good news. I will inform the president immediately. Please keep us advised.' Pelt turned around. 'We got one, alive, by God!'

'A survivor off the lost sub?' The president stood.

'Well, he's a Russian sailor. A helicopter picked him up an hour ago, and they're flying him to the Norfolk base hospital. They picked him up 290 miles northeast of Norfolk, so I guess that makes it fit. The men on the ship say he's in pretty bad shape, but the hospital is ready for him.'

The president walked to his desk and lifted the phone. 'Grace, ring me Dan Foster right now ... Admiral, this is the president. The man they picked up, how soon to Norfolk? Another two hours?' He grimaced. 'Admiral, you get on the phone to the naval hospital, and you tell them that I say they are to do everything they can for that man. I want him treated like he was my own son, is that clear? Good. I want hourly reports on his condition. I want the best people we have in on this, the very best. Thank you, Admiral.' He hung up. 'All right!'

'Maybe we were too pessimistic, Alex,' Pelt chirped up.

'Will we be allowed to see our man?' Arbatov asked at once.

'Certainly,' the president answered. 'You have a doctor at the embassy, don't you?'

'Yes, we do, Mr President.'

'Take him down, too. He'll be extended every courtesy. I'll see to that. Jeff, are they searching for other survivors?'

'Yes, Mr President. There's a dozen aircraft in the area right now, and two more ships on the way.'

'Good!' The president clapped his hands together, enthusiastic as a kid in a toystore. 'Now, if we can find some more survivors, maybe we can give your country a meaningful Christmas present, Alex. We will do everything we can, you have my word on that.'

'That is very kind of you, Mr President. I will communicate this happy news to my country at once.'

'Not so fast, Alex.' The chief executive held his hand up. 'I'd say this calls for a drink.'

The Tenth Day

Sunday 12 December

SOSUS Control

At SOSUS Control in Norfolk, the picture was becoming increasingly difficult. The United States simply did not have the technology to keep track of submarines in the deep ocean basins. The SOSUS receptors were principally laid at shallow-water choke points, on the bottom of undersea ridges and highlands. The strategy of the NATO countries was a direct consequence of this technological limitation. In a major war with the Soviets, NATO would use the Greenland-Iceland-United Kingdom SOSUS barrier as a huge tripwire, a burglar alarm system. Allied submarines and ASW patrol aircraft would try to seek out, attack, and destroy Soviet submarines as they approached it, before they could cross the lines.

The barrier had never been expected to halt more than half of the attacking submarines, however, and those that succeeded in slipping through would have to be handled differently. The deep ocean basins were simply too wide and too deep – the average depth was over two miles – to be littered with sensors as the shallow choke points were. This was a fact that cut both ways. The NATO mission would be to maintain the Atlantic Bridge and continue transoceanic trade, and the obvious Soviet mission would be to interdict this trade. Submarines would have to spread out over the vast ocean to cover the many possible convoy routes. NATO strategy behind the SOSUS barriers, then, was to assemble large convoys, each ringed with destroyers, helicopters, and fixed-wing aircraft. The escorts would try to establish a protective bubble about a hundred miles across. Enemy submarines would not be able to exist within that bubble, if in it they would be hunted down and killed – or merely driven off long enough for the convoy to speed past. Thus while SOSUS was designed to neutralize a huge, fixed expanse of sea, deep-basin strategy was founded on mobility, a moving zone of protection for the vital North Atlantic shipping.

This was an altogether sensible strategy, but one that could not be tested under realistic conditions, and, unfortunately, one that was largely useless at the moment. With all of the Soviet *Alfas* and *Victors* already on the coast, and the last of the *Charlies, Echoes,* and *Novembers* just arriving on their stations, the master screen Commander Quentin was staring at was no longer filled with discrete little red dots but rather with large circles. Each dot or circle designated the position of a Soviet submarine. A circle represented an estimated position, calculated from the speed with which a sub could move without giving off enough noise to be localized by the many sensors being employed. Some circles were ten miles across, some as much as fifty; an area anywhere from seventy-eight to two thousand square miles had to be searched if the submarine were again to be pinned down. And there were just too damned many of the boats.

Hunting the submarines was principally the job of the P-3C Orion. Each Orion carried sonobuoys, air-deployable active and passive sonar sets that were dropped from the belly of the aircraft. On detecting something, a sonobuoy reported to its mother aircraft and then automatically sank lest it fall into unfriendly hands. The sonobuoys had limited electrical power and thus limited range. Worse, their supply was finite. The sonobuoy inventory was already being depleted alarmingly, and soon they would have to cut back on expenditures. Additionally, each P-3C carried FLIRs, forward-looking infra-red scanners, to identify the heat signature of a nuclear sub, and MADs, magnetic anomaly detectors that located the disturbance in the earth's magnetic field caused by a large chunk of ferrous metal like a submarine. MAD gear could only detect a magnetic disturbance six hundred yards to the left and right of an aircraft's course track, and to do this the aircraft had to fly low, consuming fuel and limiting the crew's visual search range. FLIR had roughly the same limitation.

Thus the technology used to localize a target first detected by SOSUS, or to 'delouse' a discrete piece of ocean preparatory to the passage of a convoy, simply was not up to a random search of the deep ocean.

Quentin leaned forward. A circle had just changed to a dot. A P-3C had just dropped an explosive sounding charge and localized an *Echo*-class attack sub five hundred miles south of the Grand Banks. For an hour they had a near-certain shooting solution on that *Echo*; her name was written on the Orion's Mark 46 ASW torpedoes.

Quentin sipped at his coffee. His stomach rebelled at the additional caffeine, remembering the abuse of four months of hellish chemotherapy. If there were to be a war, this was one way it might start. All at once, their submarines would stop, perhaps just like this. Not sneaking to kill convoys in mid-ocean but attacking them closer to shore, the way the Germans had done . . . and all the American sensors would be in the wrong place. Once stopped the dots would grow to circles, ever wider, making the task of finding the subs all the more difficult. Their engines quiet, the boats would be invisible traps for the passing merchant vessels and warships racing to bring life-saving supplies to the men in Europe. Submarines were like cancer. Just like the disease that he had only barely defeated. The invisible, malignant vessels would find a place, stop to infect it, and on his screen the malignancies would grow until they were attacked by the aircraft he controlled from this room. But he could not attack them now. Only watch.

'PK EST 1 HOUR – RUN,' he typed into his computer console.

'23,' the computer answered at once.

Quentin grunted. Twenty-four hours earlier the PK, probability of a kill, had been forty – forty probable kills in the first hour after getting a shooting authorization. Now it was barely half that, and this number had to be taken with a large grain of salt, since it assumed that everything would work, a happy state of affairs found only in fiction. Soon, he judged, the number would be under ten. This did not include kills from friendly submarines that were trailing the Russians under strict orders not to reveal their positions. His sometime allies in the *Sturgeons*, *Permits*, and *Los Angeleses* were playing their own ASW game by their own set of rules. A different breed. He tried to think of them as friends, but it never quite worked. In his twenty years of naval service submarines had always been the enemy. In war they would be useful enemies, but in a war it was widely recognized that there was no such thing as a friendly submarine.

A B-52

The bomber crew knew exactly where the Russians were. Navy Orions and air force Sentries had been shadowing them for days now, and the day before, he'd been told, the Soviets had sent an armed fighter from the *Kiev* to the nearest Sentry. Possibly an attack mission, probably not, it had in any case been a provocation.

Four hours earlier the squadron of fourteen had flown out of Plattsburg, New York, at 0330, leaving behind black trails of exhaust smoke hidden in the predawn gloom. Each aircraft carried a full load of fuel and twelve missiles whose total weight was far less that the -52's design bomb load. This made for good, long range.

Which was exactly what they needed. Knowing where the Russians were was only half the battle. Hitting them was the other. The mission profile was simple in concept, rather more difficult in execution. As had been learned in missions over Hanoi – in which the B-52 had participated and sustained SAM (surface-to-air missile) damage – the best method of attacking a heavily defended target was to converge from all points of the compass at once, 'like the enveloping arms of an angry bear,' the squadron commander had put it at the briefing, indulging his poetic nature. This gave half the squadron relatively direct courses to their target; the other half had to curve around, careful to keep well beyond effective radar coverage; all had to turn exactly on cue.

The B-52s had turned ten minutes earlier, on command from the Sentry quarterbacking the mission. The pilot had added a twist. His course to the Soviet formation took his bomber right down a commercial air route. On making his turn, he had switched his IFF transponder from its normal setting to international. He was fifty miles behind a commercial 747, thirty miles ahead of another, and on Soviet radar all three Boeing products would look exactly alike – harmless.

It was still dark down on the surface. There was no indication that the Russians were alerted yet. Their fighters were only supposed to be VFR (visual flight rules) capable, and the pilot imagined that taking off and landing on a carrier in the dark was pretty risky business, doubly so in bad weather.

'Skipper,' the electronic warfare officer called on the intercom, 'we're getting L- and S-band emissions. They're right where they're supposed to be.'

'Roger. Enough for a return off us?'

'That's affirm, but they probably think we're flying Pan Am. No fire control stuff yet, just routine air search.'

'Range to target?'

'One-three-zero miles.'

It was almost time. The mission profile was such that all would hit the 125-mile circle at the same moment.

'Everything ready?'

'That's a roge.'

The pilot relaxed for another minute, waiting for the signal from the entry.

'FLASHLIGHT, FLASHLIGHT, FLASHLIGHT.' The signal came over the digital radio channel.

'That's it! Let 'em know we're here,' the aircraft commander ordered.

'Right.' The electronic warfare officer flipped the clear plastic cover off his set of toggle switches and dials controlling the aircraft's jamming systems. First he powered up his systems. This took a few seconds. The -52's electronics were all old seventies-vintage equipment, else the squadron would not be part of the junior varsity. Good learning tools, though, and the lieutenant was hoping to move up to the new B-1Bs now beginning to come off the Rockwell assembly line in California. For the past ten minutes the ESM pods on the bomber's nose and wingtips had been recording the Soviet radar signals, classifying their exact frequencies, pulse repetition rates, power, and the individual signature characteristics of the transmitters. The lieutenant was brand new to this game. He was a recent graduate of electronic warfare school, first in his class. He considered what he should do first, then selected a jamming mode, not his best, from a range of memorized options.

The *Nikolayev*

A hundred and twenty-five miles away on the *Kara*-class cruiser *Nikolayev* a radar *michman* was examining some blips that seemed to be in a circle around his formation. In an instant his screen was covered with twenty ghostly splotches tracing crazily in various directions. He shouted the alarm, echoed a second later by a brother operator. The officer of the watch hurried over to check the screen.

By the time he go there the jamming mode had changed and six lines like the spokes of a wheel were rotating slowly around a central axis.

'Plot the strobes,' the officer ordered.

Now there were blotches, lines, and sparkles.

'More than one aircraft, Comrade.' The *michman* tried flipping through his frequency settings.

'Attack warning!' another *michman* shouted. His ESM receiver had just reported the signals of aircraft search-radar sets of the type used to acquire targets for air-to-surface missiles.

The B-52

'We got hard targets,' the weapons officer on the -52 reported. 'I got a lock on the first three birds.'

'Roger that,' the pilot acknowledged. 'Hold for ten more seconds.'

'Ten seconds,' the officer replied. 'Cutting switches . . . *now*.'

'Okay, kill the jamming.'

'ECM systems off.'

The *Nikolayev*

'Missile acquisition radars have ceased,' the combat information centre officer reported to the cruiser's captain, just now arrived from the bridge. Around them the *Nikolayev*'s crew was racing to battle stations. 'Jamming has also ceased.'

'What is out there?' the captain asked. Out of a clear sky his beautiful clipper-bowed cruiser had been threatened – and now all was well?

'At least eight enemy aircraft in a circle around us.'

The captain examined the now normal S-band air search screen. There were numerous blips, mainly civilian aircraft. The half circle of others had to be hostile, though.

'Could they have fired missiles?'

'No, Comrade Captain, we would have detected it. They jammed our search radars for thirty seconds and illuminated us with their own search systems for twenty. Then everything stopped.'

'So, they provoke us and now pretend nothing has happened?' the captain growled. 'When will they be within SAM range?'

'This one and these two will be within range in four minutes if they do not change course.'

'Illuminate them with our missile control systems. Teach the bastards a lesson.'

The officer gave the necessary instructions, wondering who was being taught what. Two thousand feet above one of the B-52s was an EC-135 whose computerized electronic sensors were recording all signals from the Soviet cruiser and taking them apart, the better to know how to jam them. It was the first good look at the new SA-N-8 missile system.

Two F-14 Tomcats

The double-zero code number on its fuselage marked the Tomcat as the squadron commander's personal bird; the black ace of spades on the twin-rudder tail indicated his squadron, Fighting 41, 'The Black Aces.' The pilot was Commander Robby Jackson, and his radio call sign was Spade 1.

Jackson was leading a two-plane section under the direction of one of the *Kennedy*'s E-2C Hawkeyes, the navy's more diminutive version of the air force's AWACS and close brother to the COD, a twin-prop aircraft whose radome makes it look like an aeroplane being terrorized by a UFO. The weather was bad – depressingly normal for the North Atlantic in December – but was supposed to improve as they headed west. Jackson and his wingman, Lieutenant (j.g.) Bud Sanchez, were flying through nearly solid clouds, and they had eased their formation out somewhat. In the limited visibility both remembered that each Tomcat had a crew of two and a price of over thirty million dollars.

They were doing what the Tomcat does best. An all-weather interceptor, the F-14 has transoceanic range, Mach 2 speed, and a radar computer fire control system that can lock on to and attack six separate targets with long-range Phoenix air-to-air missiles. Each fighter was now carrying two of those along with a pair each of AIM-9M Sidewinder heat-seekers. Their prey was a flight of YAK-36 Forgers, the bastard V/STOL fighters that operated from the carrier *Kiev*. After harassing the Sentry the previous day, Ivan had decided to close with the *Kennedy* force, no doubt guided in with data from a reconnaissance satellite. The Soviet aircraft had come up short, their range being fifty miles less than they needed to sight the *Kennedy*. Washington decided that Ivan was getting a little too obnoxious on this side of the ocean. Admiral Painter had been given permission to return the favour, in a friendly sort of way.

Jackson figured that he and Sanchez could handle this, even outnumbered. No Soviet aircraft, least of all the Forger, was equal to the Tomcat – certainly not while I'm flying it, Jackson thought.

'Spade 1, your target is at your twelve o'clock and level, distance now twenty miles,' reported the voice of Hummer 1, the Hawkeye a hundred miles aft. Jackson did not acknowledge.

'Got anything, Chris?' he asked his radar intercept officer, Lieutenant Commander Christiansen.

'An occasional flash, but nothing I can use.' They were tracking the Forgers with passive systems only, in this case an infra-red sensor.

Jackson considered illuminating their targets with his powerful fire control radar. The Forgers' ESM pods would sense this at once, reporting to their pilots that their death warrant had been written but not yet signed. 'How about *Kiev*?'

'Nothing. The *Kiev* group is under total EMCON.'

'Cute,' Jackson commented. He guessed that the SAC raid on the *Kirov-Nikolayev* group had taught them to be more careful. It was not generally known that warships often made no use whatever of their radar systems, a protective measure called EMCON, for emission control. The reason was that a radar beam could be detected at several times the distance at which it generated a return signal to its transmitter and could thus tell an enemy more than it told its operators. 'You suppose these guys can find their way home without help?'

'If they don't, you know who's gonna get blamed.' Christiansen chuckled.

'That's a roge,' Jackson agreed.

'Okay, I got infra-red acquisition. Clouds must be thinning out some.' Christiansen was concentrating on his instruments, oblivious of the view out of the canopy.

'Spade 1, this is Hummer 1, your target is twelve o'clock, at your level, range now ten miles.' The report came over the secure radio circuit.

Not bad, picking up the Forgers' heat signature through this slop, Jackson thought, especially since they had small, inefficient engines.

'Radar coming on, Skipper,' Christiansen advised. '*Kiev* has an S-band air search just come on. They have us for sure.'

'Right.' Jackson thumbed his mike switch. 'Spade 2, illuminate targets – now.'

'Roger, lead,' Sanchez acknowledged. No point hiding now.

Both fighters activated their powerful AN/AWG-9 radars. It was now two minutes to intercept.

The radar signals, received by the ESM threat-receivers on the Forgers' tail fins, set off a musical tone in the pilot headsets which had to be turned off manually, and lit up a red warning light on each control panel.

The Kingfisher Flight

'Kingfisher flight, this is *Kiev*,' called the carrier's air operations officer. 'We show two American fighters closing in on you at high speed from the rear.'

'Acknowledged.' The Russian flight leader checked his mirror. He'd hoped to avoid this, though he hadn't expected to. His orders were to take no action unless fired upon. They had just broken into the clear. Too bad, he'd have felt safer in the clouds.

The pilot of Kingfisher 3, Lieutenant Shavrov, reached down to arm his four Atolls. Not this time, Yankee, he thought.

The Tomcats

'One minute, Spade 1, you ought to have visual any time,' Hummer 1 called in.

'Roger . . . Tallyho!' Jackson and Sanchez broke into the clear. The Forgers were a few miles ahead, and the Tomcats' 250-knot speed advantage was eating that distance up rapidly. The Russian pilots are keeping a nice, tight formation, Jackson thought, but anybody can drive a bus.

'Spade 2, let's go to burners on my mark. Three, two, one – mark!'

Both pilots advanced their engine controls and engaged their afterburners, which dumped raw fuel into the tail pipes of their new F-110 engines. The fighters leapt forward with a sudden double thrust and went quickly through Mach 1.

The Kingfisher Flight

'Kingfisher, warning, warning, the *Amerikantsi* have increased speed,' *Kiev* cautioned.

Kingfisher 4 turned in his seat. He saw the Tomcats a mile aft, twin dart-like shapes racing before trails of black smoke. Sunlight glinted off one canopy, and it almost looked like the flashes of a –

'They're attacking!'

'What?' The flight leader checked his mirror again. 'Negative, negative – hold formation!'

The Tomcats screeched fifty feet overhead, the sonic booms they trailed sounding just like explosions. Shavrov acted entirely on his combat-trained instincts. He jerked back on his stick and triggered his four missiles at the departing American fighters.

'Three, what did you do?' the Russian flight leader demanded.

'They were attacking us, didn't you hear?' Shavrov protested.

The Tomcats

'Oh shit! Spade Flight, you have four Atolls after you,' the voice of the Hawkeye's controller said.

'Two, break right,' Jackson ordered. 'Chris, activate countermeasures.' Jackson threw his fighter into a violent evasive turn to the left. Sanchez broke the other way.

In the seat behind Jackson's, the radar intercept officer flipped switches to activate the aircraft's defence systems. As the Tomcat twisted in mid-air, a series of flares and balloons were ejected from the tail section, each an infra-red or radar lure for the pursuing missiles. All four were targeted on Jackson's fighter.

'Spade 2 is clear, Spade 2 is clear. Spade 1, you still have four birds in pursuit,' the voice from the Hawkeye said.

'Roger.' Jackson was surprised at how calmly he took it. The Tomcat was doing over eight hundred miles per hour and accelerating. He wondered how much range the Atoll had. His rearward-looking radar warning light flicked on.

'Two, get after them!' Jackson ordered.

'Roger, lead.' Sanchez swept into a climbing turn, fell off into a hammer-head, and· dived at the retreating Soviet fighters.

When Jackson turned, two of the missiles lost lock and kept going straight into open air. A third, decoyed into hitting a flare, exploded harmlessly. The fourth kept its infra-red seeker head on Spade 1's glowing tail pipes and bored right in. The missile struck the Spade 1 at the base of its starboard rudder fin.

The impact tossed the fighter completely out of control. Most of the explosive force was spent as the missile blasted through the boron surface into open air. The fin was blown completely off, along with the right-side stabilizer. The left fin was badly holed by fragments, which smashed through the back of the fighter's canopy, hitting Christiansen's helmet. The right engine's fire warning lights came on at once.

Jackson heard the *oomph* over his intercom. He killed every engine switch on the right side and activated the in-frame fire extinguisher. Next he chopped power to his port engine, still on afterburner. By this time the Tomcat was in an inverted spin. The variable-geometry wings angled out to low-speed configuration. This gave Jackson aileron control, and he worked quickly to get back to normal attitude. His altitude was four thousand feet. There wasn't much time.

'Okay, baby,' he coaxed. A quick burst of power gave him back aerodynamic control, and the former test pilot snapped his fighter over – too hard. It went through two complete rolls before he could catch it in level flight. 'Gotcha! You with me, Chris?'

Nothing. There was no way he could look around, and there were still four hostile fighters behind him.

'Spade 2, this is lead.'

'Roger, lead.' Sanchez had the four Forgers bore-sighted. They had just fired at his commander.

Hummer 1

On Hummer 1, the controller was thinking fast. The Forgers were holding formation, and there was a lot of Russian chatter on the radio circuit.

'Spade 2, this is Hummer 1, break off, I say again, break off, do not, repeat do not fire. Acknowledge. Spade 2, Spade 1 is at your nine o'clock, two thousand feet below you.' The officer swore and looked at one of the enlisted men he worked with.

'That was too fast, sir, just too fuckin' fast. We got tapes of the Russkies. I can't understand it, but it sounds like *Kiev* is right pissed.'

'They're not the only ones,' the controller said, wondering if he had done the right thing calling Spade 2 off. It sure as hell didn't feel that way.

The Tomcats

Sanchez' head jerked in surprise. 'Roger, breaking off.' His thumb came off the switch. 'Goddammit!' He pulled his stick back, throwing the Tomcat into a savage loop. 'Where are you, lead?'

Sanchez brought his fighter under Jackson's and did a slow circle to survey the visible damage.

'Fire's out, Skipper. Right side rudder and stabilizer are gone. Left side fin – shit, I can see through it, but it looks like it oughta hold together. Wait a minute. Chris is slumped over, Skipper. Can you talk to him?'

'Negative, I've tried. Let's go back home.'

Nothing would have pleased Sanchez more than to blast the Forgers right out of the sky, and with his four missiles he could have done this easily. But like most pilots, he was highly disciplined.

'Roger, lead.'

'Spade 1, this is Hummer 1, advise your condition, over.'

'Hummer 1, we'll make it unless something else falls off. Tell them to have docs standing by. Chris is hurt. I don't know how bad.'

It took an hour to get to the *Kennedy*. Jackson's fighter flew badly, would not hold course in any specific attitude. He had to adjust trim constantly. Sanchez reported some movement in the aft cockpit. Maybe it was just the intercom shot out, Jackson thought hopefully.

Sanchez was ordered to land first so that the deck would be cleared for Commander Jackson. On the final approach the Tomcat started to handle badly. The pilot struggled with his fighter, planting it hard on the deck and catching the number one wire. The right-side landing gear collapsed at once, and the thirty-million-dollar fighter slid sideways into the barrier that had been erected. A hundred men with fire-fighting gear raced towards it from all directions.

The canopy went up on emergency hydraulic power. After unbuckling himself Jackson fought his way around and tried to grab for his backseater. They had been friends for many years.

Chris was alive. It looked like a quart of blood had poured down the front of his flight suit, and when the first orderly took the helmet off, he saw that it was still pumping out. The second orderly corpsman pushed Jackson out of the way and attached a cervical collar to the wounded airman. Christiansen was lifted gently and lowered on to a stretcher whose bearers ran towards the island. Jackson hesitated a moment before following it.

Norfolk Naval Medical Center

Captain Randall Tait of the Navy Medical Corps walked down the corridor to meet the Russians. He looked younger than his forty-five years because his full head of black hair showed not the first sign of grey. Tait was a Mormon, educated at Brigham Young University and Stanford Medical School, who had joined the navy because he had wanted to see more of the world than one could from an office at the foot of the Wasatch Mountains. He had accomplished that much, and until today had also avoided anything resembling diplomatic duty. As the new chief of the Department of Medicine at Bethesda Naval Medical Center he knew that couldn't last. He had flown down to Norfolk only a few hours earlier to handle the case. The Russians had driven down, and taken their time doing it.

'Good morning, gentlemen. I'm Dr Tait.' They shook hands all around, and the lieutenant who had brought them up walked back to the elevator.

'Dr Ivanov,' the shortest one said. 'I am physician to the embassy.'

'Captain Smirnov.' Tait knew him to be assistant naval attaché, a career intelligence officer. The doctor had been briefed on the helicopter trip down by a Pentagon intelligence officer who was now drinking coffee in the hospital commissary.

'Vasily Petchkin, Doctor. I am second secretary to the embassy.' This one was a senior KGB officer, a 'legal' spy with a diplomatic cover. 'May we see our man?'

'Certainly. Will you follow me please?' Tait led them back down the corridor. He'd been on the go for twenty hours. This was part of the territory as chief of service at Bethesda. He got all the hard calls. One of the first things a doctor learns is how not to sleep.

The whole floor was set up for intensive care, Norfolk Naval Medical Center having been built with war casualties in mind. Intensive Care Unit Number Three was a room twenty-five feet square. The only windows were on the corridor wall, and the curtains had been drawn back. There were four beds, only one occupied. The young man in it was almost totally concealed. The only thing not hidden by the oxygen mask covering his face was an unruly clump of wheat-coloured hair. The rest of his body was fully draped. An IV stand was next to the bed, its two bottles of fluid merging in a single line that led under the covers. A nurse dressed like Tait in surgical greens was standing at the foot of the bed, her green eyes locked on the electrocardiograph readout over the patient's head, dropping momentarily to make a notation on his chart. On the far side of the bed was a machine whose function was not immediately obvious. The patient was unconscious.

'His condition?' Ivanov asked.

'Critical,' Tait replied. 'It's a miracle he got here alive at all. He was in the water for at least twelve hours, probably more like twenty. Even accounting for the fact that he was wearing a rubber exposure suit, given the ambient air and water temperatures there's just no way he ought to have been alive. On admission his core temperature was 23.8°C.' Tait shook his head. 'I've read about worse hypothermia cases in the literature, but this is by far the worst I've ever seen.'

'Prognosis?' Ivanov looked into the room.

Tait shrugged. 'Hard to say. Maybe as good as fifty-fifty, maybe not. He's still extremely shocked. He's a fundamentally healthy person. You can't see it from here, but he's in superb physical shape, like a track and field man. He has a particularly strong heart; that's probably what kept him alive long enough to get here. We have the hypothermia pretty much under control now. The problem is, with hypothermia so many things go wrong at once. We have to fight a number of separate but connected battles against different systemic enemies to keep them from overwhelming his natural defences. If anything's going to kill him, it'll be the shock. We're treating that with electrolytes, the normal routine, but he's going to be on the edge for several days at least, I – '

Tait looked up. Another man was pacing down the hall. Younger than Tait, and taller, he had a white lab coat over his greens. He carried a metal chart.

'Gentlemen, this is Doctor – Lieutenant – Jameson. He's the physician of record on the case. He admitted your man. What do you have, Jamie?'

'The sputum sample showed pneumonia. Bad news. Worse, his blood chemistry isn't getting any better, and his white count is *dropping*.'

'Great.' Tait leaned against the window frame and swore to himself.

'Here's the printout from the blood analyser.' Jameson handed the chart over.

'May I see this, please?' Ivanov came around.

'Sure.' Tait flipped the metal cloud chart open and held it so that everyone could see it. Ivanov had never worked with a computerized blood analyser, and it took several seconds for him to orient himself.

'This is not good.'

'Not at all,' Tait agreed.

'We're going to have to jump on that pneumonia, hard,' Jameson said. 'This kid's got too many things going wrong. If the pneumonia really takes hold . . . ' He shook his head.

'Keflin?' Tait asked.

'Yeah.' Jameson pulled a vial from his pocket. 'As much as he'll handle. I'm guessing that he had a mild case before he got dumped in the water, and I hear that some penicillin-resistant strains have been cropping up in Russia. You use mostly penicillin over there, right?' Jameson looked down at Ivanov.

'Correct. What is this keflin?'

'It's a big gun, a synthetic antibiotic, and it works well on resistant strains.'

'Right now, Jamie,' Tait ordered.

Jameson walked around the corner to enter the room. He injected the antibiotic into a 100cc piggyback IV bottle and hung it on a stand.

'He's so young,' Ivanov noted. 'He treated our man initially?'

'His name's Albert Jameson. We call him Jamie. He's twenty-nine, graduated Harvard third in his class, and he's been with us ever since. He's board-certified in internal medicine and virology. He's as good as they come.' Tait suddenly realized how uncomfortable he was dealing with the Russians. His education and years of naval service taught him that these men were the enemy. That didn't matter. Years before he had sworn an oath to treat patients without regard to outside considerations. Would they believe this,

181

or did they think he'd let their man die because he was a Russian? 'Gentlemen, I want you to understand this: we're giving your man the very best care we can. We're not holding anything back. If there's a way to give him back to you alive, we'll find it. But I can't make any promises.'

The Soviets could see that. While waiting for instructions from Moscow, Petchkin had checked up on Tait and found him to be, though a religious fanatic, an efficient and honourable physician, one of the best in government service.

'Has he said anything?' Petchkin asked, casually.

'Not since I've been here. Jamie said that right after they started warming him up he was semiconscious and babbled for a few minutes. We taped it, of course, and had a Russian-speaking officer listen to it. Something about a girl with brown eyes, didn't make any sense. Probably his sweetheart – he's a good-looking kid, he probably has a girl at home. It was totally incoherent, though. A patient in his condition has no idea what's going on.'

'Can we listen to the tape?' Petchkin said.

'Certainly. I'll have it sent up.'

Jameson came around the corner. 'Done. A gram of keflin every six hours. Hope it works.'

'How about his hands and feet?' Smirnov asked. The captain knew something about frostbite.

'We're not even bothering with that,' Jameson answered. 'We have cotton around the digits to prevent maceration. If he survives the next few days, we'll get blebs and maybe have some tissue loss, but that's the least of our problems. You guys know what his name is?' Petchkin's head snapped around. He wasn't wearing any dogtags when he arrived. His clothes didn't have the ship's name. No wallet, no identification, not even any coins in the pockets. It doesn't matter very much for his initial treatment, but I'd feel better if you could pull his medical records. It would be good to know if he has any allergies or underlying medical conditions. We don't want him to go into shock from an allergic reaction to drug treatment.'

'What was he wearing?' Smirnov asked.

'A rubber exposure suit,' Jameson answered. 'The guys who found him left it on him, thank God. I cut it off him when he arrived. Under that, shirt, pants, handkerchief. Don't your guys wear dogtags?'

'Yes,' Smirnov responded. 'How did you find him?'

'From what I hear, it was pure luck. A helicopter off a frigate was patrolling and spotted him in the water. They didn't have any rescue gear aboard, so they marked the spot with a dye marker and went back to their ship. A bosun volunteered to go in after him. They loaded him and a raft cannister into the chopper and flew him back, with the frigate hustling down south. The bosun kicked out the raft, jumped in after it – and landed on it. Bad luck. He broke both his legs, but he did get your sailor into the raft. The tincan picked them up an hour later and they were both flown directly here.'

'How is your man?'

'He'll be all right. The left leg wasn't too bad, but the right tibia was badly splintered,' Jameson went on. 'He'll recover in a few months. Won't be doing much dancing for a while, though.'

The Russians thought the Americans had deliberately removed their man's identification. Jameson and Tait suspected that the man had disposed of his tags, possibly hoping to defect. There was a red mark on the neck that indicated forcible removal.

'If it is permitted,' Smirnov said, 'I would like to see your man, to thank him.'

'Permission granted, Captain,' Tait nodded. 'That would be kind of you.'

'He must be a brave man.'

'A sailor doing his job. Your people would do the same thing.' Tait wondered if this were true. 'We have our differences, gentlemen, but the sea doesn't care about that. The sea – well, she tries to kill us all regardless what flag we fly.'

Petchkin was back looking through the window, trying to make out the patient's face.

'Could we see his clothing and personal effects?' he asked.

'Sure, but it won't tell you much. He's a cook. That's all we know,' Jameson said.

'A cook?' Petchkin turned around.

'The officer who listened in on the tape – obviously he was an intelligence officer, right? He looked at the number on his shirt and said it made him a cook.' The three-digit number indicated that the patient had been a member of the port watch, and that his battle station was damage control. Jameson wondered why the Russians numbered all their enlisted men. To be sure they didn't trespass? Petchkin's head, he noticed, was almost touching the glass pane.

'Dr Ivanov, do you wish to attend the case?' Tait asked.

'Is this permitted?'

'It is.'

'When will he be released?' Petchkin inquired. 'When may we speak with him?'

'Released?' Jameson snapped. 'Sir, the only way he'll be out of here in less than a month will be in a box. So far as consciousness is concerned, that's anyone's guess. That's one very sick kid you have in there.'

'But we must speak to him!' the KGB agent protested.

Tait had to look up at the man. 'Mr Petchkin, I understand your desire to communicate with your man – but he is my patient now. We will do nothing, repeat *nothing*, that might interfere with his treatment and recovery. I got orders to fly down here to handle this. They tell me those orders came from the White House. Fine. Doctors Jameson and Ivanov will assist me, but that patient is now my responsibility, and my job is to see to it that he walks out of this hospital alive and well. Everything else is secondary to that objective. You will be extended every courtesy. But I make the rules here.' Tait paused. Diplomacy was not something he was good at. 'Tell you what, you want to sit in there yourselves in relays, that's fine with me. But you have to follow the rules. That means you scrub, change into sterile clothing, and follow the instructions of the duty nurse. Fair enough?'

Petchkin nodded. American doctors think they are gods, he said to himself.

Jameson, busy re-examining the blood analyser printout, had ignored the sermon. 'Can you gentlemen tell us what kind of sub he was on?'

'No,' Petchkin said at once.

'What are you thinking, Jamie?'

'The dropping white count and some of these other indicators are consistent with radiation exposure. The gross symptoms would have been masked by the overlying hypothermia.' Suddenly Jameson looked at the Soviets. 'Gentlemen, we have to know this, was he on a nuclear sub?'

'Yes,' Smirnov answered, 'he was on a nuclear-powered submarine.'

'Jamie, take his clothing to radiology. Have them check the buttons, zipper, anything metal for evidence of contamination.'

'Right.' Jameson went to collect the patient's effects.

'May we be involved in this?' Smirnov asked.

'Yes, sir,' Tait responded, wondering what sort of people these were. The guy had to come off a nuclear submarine, didn't he? Why hadn't they told him at once? Didn't they want him to recover?

Petchkin pondered the significance of this. Didn't they know he had come off a nuclear-powered sub? Of course – he was trying to get Smirnov to blurt out that the man was off a missile submarine. They were trying to cloud the issue with this story about contamination. Nothing that would harm the patient, but something to confuse their class enemies. Clever. He'd always thought the Americans were clever. And he was supposed to report to the embassy in an hour – report what? How was he supposed to know who the sailor was?

Norfolk Naval Shipyard

The USS *Ethan Allen* was about at the end of her string. Commissioned in 1961, she had served her crews and her country for over twenty years, carrying Polaris sea-launched ballistic missiles in endless patrols through sunless seas. Now she was old enough to vote, and this was very old for a submarine. Her missile tubes had been filled with ballast and sealed months before. She had only a token maintenance crew while the Pentagon bureaucrats debated her future. There had been talk of a complicated cruise missile system to make her into a SSGN like the new Russian Oscars. This was judged too expensive. *Ethan Allen*'s was generation-old technology. Her S5W reactor was too dated for much more use. Nuclear radiation had bombarded the metal vessel and its internal fittings with many billions of neutrons. Recent examination of test strips had revealed that over a period of time the character of the metal had changed, becoming dangerously brittle. The system had at most another three years of useful life. A new reactor would be too expensive. The *Ethan Allen* was doomed by her senescence.

The maintenance crew was made up of members of her last operational team, mainly old-timers looking forward to retirement, with a leavening of kids who needed education in repair skills. The *Ethan Allen* could still serve as a school, especially a repair school since so much of her equipment was worn out.

Admiral Gallery had come aboard early that morning. The chiefs had regarded that as particularly ominous. He had been her first skipper many years before, and admirals always seemed to visit their early commands – right before they were scrapped. He'd recognized some of the senior chiefs and asked them if the old girl had any life in her. To a man, the chiefs said yes. A ship becomes more than a machine to her crew. Each of a hundred ships, built by the same men at the same yard to the same plans, will have her own special characteristics – most of them bad, really, but after her crew becomes accustomed to them they are spoken of affectionately, particularly in retrospect. The admiral had toured the entire length of the *Ethan Allen*'s hull, pausing to run his gnarled, arthritic hands over the periscope he had used to make certain that there really was a world outside the steel hull, to plan the rare 'attack' against a ship hunting his sub – or a passing tanker, just for practice. He'd commanded the *Ethan Allen* for three years, alternating his gold crew with another officer's blue crew, working out of Holy Loch Scotland. Those were good years, he told himself, a damned sight better than sitting at a desk with a lot of vapid aides running around. It was the old navy game, up or out: just when you got something that you were really good at, something you really liked, it was gone. It made good organizational sense. You had to make room for the youngsters coming up – but, God! to be young again, to command one of the new ones that now he only had the opportunity to ride a few hours at a time, a courtesy to the skinny old bastard in Norfolk.

She'd do it, Gallery knew. She'd do fine. It was not the end he would have preferred for *his* fighting ship, but when you came down to it, a decent end for a fighting ship was something rare. Nelson's *Victory*, the *Constitution* in Boston harbour, the odd battleship kept mummified by her namesake state – they'd had honourable treatment. Most warships were sunk as targets or broken up for razor blades. The *Ethan Allen* would die for a purpose. A crazy purpose, perhaps crazy enough to work, he said to himself as he returned to COMSUBLANT headquarters.

Two hours later a truck arrived at the dock where the *Ethan Allen* lay dormant. The chief quartermaster on deck at the time noted that the truck came from Oceana Naval Air Station. Curious, he thought. More curiously, the officer who got out was wearing neither dolphins nor wings. He saluted the quarterdeck first, then the chief who had the deck while *Ethan Allen*'s remaining two officers supervised a repair job on the engine spaces. The officer from the naval air station made arrangements for a work gang to load the sub with four bullet-shaped objects, which went through the deck hatches. They were large, barely able to fit through the torpedo and capsule loading hatches, and it took some handling to get them emplaced. Next came plastic pallets to set them on and metal straps to secure them. They look like bombs, the chief electrician thought as the younger men did the donkey work. But they couldn't be that; they were too light; obviously made of ordinary sheet metal. An hour later a truck with a pressurized tank on its loadbed arrived. The submarine was cleared of her personnel and carefully ventilated. Then three men snaked a hose to each of the four objects. Finished, they ventilated the hull again, leaving gas detectors near each object. By this time, the crew noted, their dock and the one next to it were being guarded by armed marines so that no one could come over and see what was happening to the *Ethan Allen*.

When the loading, or filling, or whatever, was finished, a chief went below to examine the metal shells more carefully. He wrote down the stenciled acronym PPB76A/J6713 on a pad. A chief yeoman looked the designation up in a catalogue and did not like what he found – Pave Pat Blue 76. Pave Pat Blue 76 was a bomb, and the *Ethan Allen* had four of them aboard. Nothing nearly so powerful as the missile warheads she had once carried, but a lot more ominous, the crew agreed. The smoking lamp was out by mutual accord before anyone made an order of it.

Gallery came back soon thereafter and spoke with all of the senior men individually. The youngsters were sent ashore with their personal gear and an admonition that they had not seen, felt, heard, or otherwise noticed anything unusual on the *Ethan Allen*. She was going to be scuttled at sea. That was all. Some political decision in Washington – and if you tell *that* to anyone, start thinking about a twenty-year tour at McMurdo Sound, as one man put it.

It was a tribute to Vincent Gallery that each of the old chiefs stayed aboard. Partly it was a chance for one last cruise on the old girl, a chance to say goodbye to a friend. Mostly it was because Gallery said it was important, and the old-timers remembered that his word had been good once.

The officers showed up at sundown. The lowest-ranking among them was a lieutenant commander. Two four-striped captains would be working the reactor, along with three senior chiefs. Two more four-stripers would handle the navigation, a pair of commanders the electronics. The rest would be spread around to handle the plethora of specialized tasks necessary to the operation of a complex warship. The total complement, not even a quarter the size of a normal crew, might have caused some adverse comment on the part of the senior chiefs, who didn't consider just how much experience these officers had.

One officer would be working the diving planes, the chief quartermaster was scandalized to learn. The chief electrician he discussed this with took it in his stride. After all, he noted, the real fun was driving the boats, and officers only got to do that at New London. After that all they got to do was walk around and look important. True, the quartermaster agreed, but could they handle it? If not, the electrician decided, they would take care of things – what else were chiefs for but to protect officers from their mistakes? After that they argued good-naturedly over who would be chief of the boat. Both men had nearly identical experience and time in rate.

The USS *Ethan Allen* sailed for the last time at 2345 hours. No tug helped her away from the dock. The skipper eased her deftly away from the dock with gentle engine commands and strains on his lines that his quartermaster could only admire. He'd served with the skipper before, on the *Skipjack* and the *Will Rogers*. 'No tugs, no nothin',' he reported to his bunkmate later. 'The old man knows his shit.' In an hour they were past the Virginia Capes and ready to dive. Ten minutes later they were gone from sight. Below, on a course of one-one-zero, the small crew of officers and chiefs settled into the demanding routine of running their old boomer shorthanded. The *Ethan Allen* responded like a champ, steaming at twelve knots, her old machinery hardly making any noise at all.

The Eleventh Day

Monday, 13 December

An A-10 Thunderbolt

It was a lot more fun than flying DC-9s. Major Andy Richardson had over ten thousand hours in those and only six hundred or so in his A-10 Thunderbolt II strike fighter, but he much preferred the smaller of the twin-engine aircraft. Richardson belonged to the 175th Tactical Fighter Group of the Maryland Air National Guard. Ordinarily his squadron flew out of a small military airfield east of Baltimore. But two days earlier, when his outfit had been activated, the 175th and six other national guard and reserve air groups had crowded the already active SAC base at Loring Air Force Base in Maine. They had taken off at midnight and had refuelled in midair only half an hour earlier, a thousand miles out over the North Atlantic. Now

Richardson and his flight of four were skimming a hundred feet over the black waters at four hundred knots.

A hundred miles behind the four fighters, ninety aircraft were following at thirty thousand feet in what would look very much to the Soviets like an alpha strike, a weighted attack mission of armed tactical fighters. It was exactly that – and also a feint. The real mission belonged to the low-level team of four.

Richardson loved the A-10. She was called with back-handed affection the Warthog or just plain Hog by the men who flew her. Nearly all tactical aircraft had pleasing lines conferred on them by the need in combat for speed and manoeuvrability. Not the Hog, which was perhaps the ugliest bird ever built for the US Air Force. Her twin turbofan engines hung like afterthoughts at the twin-rudder tail, itself a throwback to the thirties. Her slablike wings had not a whit of sweepback and were bent in the middle to accommodate the clumsy landing gear. The undersides of the wings were studded with many hard points so ordnance could be carried, and the fuselage was built around the aircraft's primary weapon, the GAU-8 thirty-millimetre rotary cannon designed specifically to smash Soviet tanks.

For tonight's mission, Richardson's flight had a full load of depleted-uranium slugs for their Avenger cannons and a pair of Rockeye cluster bomb cannisters, additional antitank weapons. Directly beneath the fuselage was a LANTIRN (low-altitude navigation and targeting infra-red for night) pod; all the other ordnance stations save one were occupied by fuel tanks.

The 175th had been the first national guard squadron to receive LANTIRN. It was a small collection of electronic and optical systems that enabled the Hog to see at night while flying at minimum altitude searching for targets. The systems projected a heads-up display (HUD) on the fighter's windshield, in effect turning night to day and making this mission profile marginally less hazardous. Beside each LANTIRN pod was a smaller object which, unlike the cannon shells and Rockeyes, was intended for use tonight.

Richardson didn't mind – indeed, he relished – the hazards of the mission. Two of his three comrades were, like him, airline pilots, the third a crop duster, all experienced men with plenty of practice in low-level tactics. And their mission was a good one.

The briefing, conducted by a naval officer, had taken over an hour. They were paying a visit to the Soviet Navy. Richardson had read in the papers that the Russians were up to something, and when he had heard at the briefing that they were sending their fleet to trail its coat this close to the American coast, he had been shocked at their boldness. It had angered him to learn that one of their crummy little day fighters had back-shot a navy Tomcat the day before, nearly killing one of its officers. He wondered why the navy was being cut out of the response. Most of the *Saratoga*'s air group was visible on the concrete pads at Loring, sitting alongside the B-52s, A-6E Intruders, and F-18 Hornets with their ordnance carts a few feet away. He guessed that his mission was only the first act, the delicate part. While Soviet eyes were locked on the alpha strike hovering at the edge of their SAM range, his flight of four would dash in under radar cover to the fleet flagship, the nuclear-powered battle cruiser *Kirov*. To deliver a message.

It was surprising that guardsmen had been selected for this mission. Nearly a thousand tactical aircraft were now mobilized on the East Coast, about a third of them reservists of one kind or another, and Richardson guessed that that was part of the message. A very difficult tactical operation was being run by second-line airmen, while the regular squadrons sat ready on the runways of Loring, and McGuire, and Dover, and Pease, and several other bases from Virginia to Maine, fuelled, briefed, and ready. Nearly a thousand aircraft! Richardson smiled. There wouldn't be enough targets to go around.

'Linebacker Lead, this is Sentry-Delta. Target bearing zero-four-eight, range fifty miles. Course is one-eight-five, speed twenty.'

Richardson did not acknowledge the transmission over the encrypted radio link. The flight was under EMCON. Any electronic noise might alert the Soviets. Even his targeting radar was switched off, and only passive infra-red and low-light television sensors were operating. He looked quickly left and right. Second-line flyers, hell! he said to himself. Every man in the flight had at least four thousand hours, more than most regular pilots would ever have, more than most of the astronauts, and their birds were maintained by people who tinkered with aeroplanes because they liked to. The fact of the matter was that his squadron had better aircraft-availability rates than any regular squadron and had had fewer accidents than the wet-nosed hotdogs who flew the Warthogs in England and Korea. They'd show the Russkies that.

He smiled to himself. This sure beat flying his DC-9 from Washington to Providence and Hartford and back every day for US Air! Richardson, who had been an air force fighter pilot, had left the service eight years earlier because he craved the higher pay and flashy lifestyle of a commercial airline pilot. He'd missed Vietnam, and commercial flying did not require anything like this degree of skill; it lacked the *rush* of skimming at treetop level.

So far as he knew, the Hog had never been used for maritime strike missions – another part of the message. It was no surprise that she'd be good at it. Her antitank munitions would be effective against ships. Her cannon slugs and Rockeye clusters were designed to shred armoured battle tanks, and he had no doubts what they would do to thin-hulled warships. Too bad this wasn't for real. It was about time somebody taught Ivan a lesson.

A radar sensor light blinked on his threat receiver; S-band radar, it was probably meant for surface search, and was not powerful enough for a return yet. The Soviets did not have any aerial radar platforms, and their ship-carried sets were limited by the earth's curvature. The beam was just over his head; he was getting the fuzzy edge of it. They would have avoided detection better still by flying at fifty feet instead of a hundred, but orders were not to.

'Linebacker flight, this is Sentry-Delta. Scatter and head in,' the AWACS commanded.

The A-10s separated from their interval of only a few feet to an extended attack formation that left miles between the aircraft. The orders were for them to scatter at thirty miles' distance. About four minutes. Richardson checked his digital clock; the Linebacker flight was right on time. Behind them, the Phantoms and Corsairs in the alpha strike would be turning towards the Soviets, just to get their attention. He ought to be seeing them soon . . .

The HUD showed small bumps on the projected horizon – the outer screen of destroyers, the *Udaloys* and *Sovremennys*. The briefing officer had shown them silhouettes and photos of the warships.

Beep! his threat receiver chirped. An X-band missile guidance radar had just swept over his aircraft and lost it, and was now trying to regain contact. Richardson flipped on his ECM (electronic countermeasures) jamming systems. The destroyers were only five miles away now. Forty seconds. Stay dumb, comrades, he thought.

He began to manoeuvre his aircraft radically, jinking up, down, left, right, in no particular pattern. It was only a game, but there was no sense in giving Ivan an easy time. If this had been for real, his Hogs would be blazing in behind a swarm of antiradar missiles and would be accompanied by Wild Weasel aircraft trying to scramble and kill Soviet missile control systems. Things were moving very fast now. A screening destroyer loomed in his path, and he nudged his rudder to pass clear of her by a quarter mile. Two miles to the *Kirov* – eighteen seconds.

The HUD system painted an intensified image. The *Kirov*'s pyramidal mast-stack-radar structure was filling his windshield. He could see blinking signal lights all around the battle cruiser. Richardson gave more right rudder. They were supposed to pass within three hundred yards of the ship, no more, no less. His Hog would blaze past the bow, the others past the stern and either beam. He didn't want to cut it too close. The major checked to be certain that his bomb and cannon controls were locked in the safe position. No sense getting carried away. About now in a real attack he'd trigger his cannon and a stream of solid slugs would lance the light armour of the *Kirov*'s forward missile magazines, exploding the SAM and cruise missiles in a huge fireball and slicing through the superstructure as if it were thin as newsprint.

At five hundred yards, the captain reached down to arm the flare pod, attached next to the LANTIRN.

Now! He flipped the switch, which deployed half a dozen high-intensity magnesium parachute flares. All four Linebacker aircraft acted within seconds. Suddenly the *Kirov* was inside a box of blue-white magnesium light. Richardson pulled back on his stick, banking into a climbing turn past the battle cruiser. The brilliant light dazzled him, but he could see the graceful lines of the Soviet warship as she was turning hard on the choppy seas, her men running along the deck like ants.

If we were serious, you'd all be dead now – get the message?

Richardson thumbed his radio switch. 'Linebacker Lead to Sentry-Delta,' he said in the clear. 'Robin Hood, repeat Robin Hood. Linebacker flight, this is lead, form up on me. Let's go home.'

'Linebacker flight, this is Sentry-Delta. Outstanding!' the controller responded. 'Be advised that *Kiev* has a pair of Forgers in the air, thirty miles east, heading your way. They'll have to hustle to catch up. Will advise. Out.'

Richardson did some fast arithmetic in his head. They probably could not catch up, and even if they did, twelve Phantoms from the 107th Fighter Interceptor Group were ready for it.

'Hot damn, lead!' Linebacker 4, the crop duster, moved gingerly into his slot. 'Did you see those turkeys pointing up at us? God damn, did we rattle their cage!'

'Heads up for Forgers,' Richardson cautioned, grinning ear to ear inside his oxygen mask. *Second-line flyers, hell!*

'Let 'em come,' Linebacker 4 replied. 'Any of those bastards closes me and my thirty, it'll be the last mistake he ever makes!' Four was a little too aggressive for Richardson's liking, but the man did know how to drive his Hog.

'Linebacker flight, this is Sentry-Delta. The Forgers have turned back. You're in the clear. Out.'

'Roger that, out. Okay, flight, lets settle down and head home. I guess we've earned our pay for the month.' Richardson looked to make sure he was on an open frequency. 'Ladies and gentlemen, this is Captain Barry Friendly,' he said, using the in-house US Air public relations joke that had become a tradition in the 175th. 'I hope you have enjoyed your flight, and thank you for flying Warthog Air.'

The *Kirov*

On the *Kirov*, Admiral Stralbo raced from the combat information centre to the flag bridge, too late. They had acquired the low-level raiders only a minute from the outer screen. The box of flares was already behind the battle cruiser, several still burning in the water. The bridge crew, he saw, was rattled.

'Sixty to seventy seconds before they were on us, Comrade Admiral,' the flag captain reported, 'we were tracking the orbiting attack force and these four – we think four – raced in under our radar coverage. We had missile lock on two of them despite their jamming.'

Stralbo frowned. That performance was not nearly good enough. If the strike had been real, the *Kirov* would have been badly damaged at least. The Americans would gladly trade a pair of fighters for a nuclear-powered cruiser. If all American aircraft attacked like this . . .

'The arrogance of the Americans is fantastic!' The fleet *zampolit* swore.

'It was foolish to provoke them,' Stralbo observed sourly. 'I knew that something like this would happen, but I expected it from *Kennedy*.'

'That was a mistake, a pilot error,' the political officer replied.

'Indeed, Vasily. And *this* was no mistake! They just sent us a message, telling us that we are fifteen hundred kilometres from their shore without useful air cover, and that they have over five hundred fighters waiting to pounce on us from the west. In the meantime *Kennedy* is stalking us to the east like a rabid wolf. We are not in an attractive position.'

'The Americans would not be so brash.'

'Are you sure of that, Comrade Political Officer? Sure? What if one of their aircraft commits a "pilot error"? And sinks one of our destroyers? And what if the American president gets on the direct link to Moscow to apologize before we can even report it? They swear it was an accident and promise to punish the stupid pilot – then what? You think the imperialists are so predictable this close to their own coastline? I do not. I think they are praying for the smallest excuse to pounce on us. Come to my cabin. We must consider this.'

The two men went aft. Stralbo's cabin was a spartan affair. The only decoration on the wall was a print of Lenin speaking to Red Guards.

'What is our mission, Vasily?' Stralbo asked.

'To support our submarines, help them to conduct the search –'

'Exactly. Our mission is to support, not to conduct offensive operations. The Americans do not want us here. Objectively, I can understand this. With all our missiles we are a threat to them.'

'But our orders are not to threaten them,' the *zampolit* protested. 'Why would we want to strike their homeland?'

'And, of course, the imperialists recognize that we are peaceful socialists! Come now, Vasily, these are our enemies! Of *course* they do not trust us. Of course they wish to attack us, given the smallest excuse. They are already interfering with our search, pretending to help. They do not want us here – and in allowing ourselves to be provoked by their aggressive actions, we fall into their trap.' The admiral stared down at his desk. 'Well, we shall change that. I will order the fleet to discontinue anything that may appear the least bit aggressive. We will end all air operations beyond normal local patrolling. We will not harass their nearby fleet units. We will use only normal navigational radars.'

'And?'

'And we will swallow our pride and be as meek as mice. Whatever provocation they make, we will not react to it.'

'Some will call this cowardice, Comrade Admiral,' the *zampolit* warned.

Stralbo had expected that. 'Vasily, don't you see? In pretending to attack us they have already victimized us. They force us to activate our newest and most secret defence systems so they can gather intelligence on our radars and fire control systems. They examine the performance of our fighters and helicopters, the manoeuvrability of our ships, and most of all, our command and control. We shall put an end to that. Our primary mission is too important. If they continue to provoke us, we will act as though our mission is indeed peaceful – which it is as far as they are concerned – and protest our innocence. And we make them the aggressors. If they continue to provoke us, we shall watch to see what their tactics are, and give them nothing in return. Or would you prefer that they prevent us from carrying out our mission?'

The *zampolit* mumbled his consent. If they failed in their mission, the charge of cowardice would be a small matter indeed. If they found the renegade submarine, they'd be heroes regardless of what else happened.

The *Dallas*

How long had he been on duty? Jones wondered. He could have checked easily enough by punching the button on his digital watch, but the sonarman didn't want to. It would be too depressing. Me and my big mouth – *you bet, Skipper*, my ass! he swore to himself. He'd detected the sub at a range of about twenty miles, maybe, had just barely gotten her – and the fuckin' Atlantic Ocean was three thousand miles across, at least sixty footprint diameters. He'd need more than luck now.

Well, he did get a Hollywood shower out of it. Ordinarily a shower on a freshwater-poor ship meant a few seconds of wetting down and a minute or so of lathering, followed by a few more seconds of rinsing the suds off. It got you clean but was not very satisfying. This was an improvement over the old days, the oldtimers liked to say. But back then, Jones often responded, the sailors had to pull oars – or run off diesel and batteries, which amounted to the same thing. A Hollywood shower is something a sailor starts thinking about after a few days at sea. You leave the water running, a long, continuous stream of wonderfully warm water. Commander Mancuso was given to awarding this sensuous pastime in return for above-average performance. It gave people something tangible to work for. You couldn't spend extra money on a sub, and there was no beer or women.

Old movies – they were making an effort on that score. The boat's library wasn't bad, when you had time to sort through the jumble. And the *Dallas* had a pair of Apple computers and a few dozen game programs for amusement. Jones was the boat champion at Choplifter and Zork. The computers were also used for training purposes, of course, for practice exams and programmed learning texts that ate up most of the use time.

The *Dallas* was quartering an area east of the Grand Banks. Any boat transiting Route One tended to come through here. They were moving at five knots, trailing out the BQR-15 towed-array sonar. They'd had all kinds of contacts. First, half the submarines in the Russian Navy had whipped by

193

at high speed, many trailed by American boats. An *Alfa* had burned past them at over forty knots, not three thousand yards away. It would have been so easy, Jones had thought at the time. The *Alfa* had been making so much – noise that one could have heard it with a glass against the hull, and he'd had to turn his amplifiers down to minimum to keep the noise from ruining his ears. A pity they couldn't have fired. The set up had been so simple, the firing solution so easy that a kid with an old-fashioned sliderule could have done it. That *Alfa* had been meat on the table. The *Victor*s came running next, and the *Charlies* and *Novembers* last of all. Jones had been listening to surface ships away to the west, a lot of them doing twenty knots or so, making all kinds of noise as they pounded through the waves. They were way far off, and not his concern.

They had been trying to acquire this particular target for over two days, and Jones had had only an odd hour of sleep here and there. Well, that's what they pay me for, he reflected bleakly. This was not unprecedented, he'd done it before, but he'd be happy when the labour ended.

The large-aperture towed array was at the end of a thousand-foot cable. Jones referred to the use of it as trolling for whales. In addition to being their most sensitive sonar rig, it protected the *Dallas* against intruders shadowing her. Ordinarily a submarine's sonar will work in any direction except aft – an area called the cone of silence, or the baffles. The BQR-15 changed that. Jones had heard all sorts of things on it, subs and surface ships all the time, low-flying aircraft on occasion. Once, during an exercise off Florida, it had been the noise of diving pelicans that he could not figure out until the skipper had raised the periscope for a look. Then off Bermuda they had encountered mating humpbacks, and a very impressive noise that was. Jones had a personal copy of the tape of them for use on the beach: some women found it interesting, in a kinky sort of way. He smiled to himself.

There was a considerable amount of surface noise. The signal processors filtered most of it out, and every few minutes Jones switched them off his channel, getting the sound unimpeded to make sure that they weren't filtering too much out. Machines were dumb; Jones wondered if SAPS might be letting some of that anomalous signal get lost inside the computer chips. That was a problem with computers, really a problem with programming: you'd tell the machine to do something, and it would go and do it to the wrong thing. Jones often amused himself working up programs. He knew a few people from college who drew up game programs for personal computers; one of them was making good money with Sierra On-Line Systems . . .

Daydreaming again, Jonesy, he chided himself. It wasn't easy listening to nothing for hours on end. It would have been a good idea, he thought, to let sonarmen read on duty. He had better sense than to suggest it. Mr Thompson might go along, but the skipper and all the senior officers were ex-reactor types with the usual rule of iron: You shall watch every instrument with absolute concentration all the time. Jones didn't think this was very smart.

It was different with sonarmen. They burned out too easily. To combat this Jones had his music tapes and his games. He could lose himself in any sort of diversion, especially Choplifter. A man had to have something, he reasoned, to lose his mind in, at least once a day. And something on duty in some cases. Even truck drivers, hardly the most intellectual of people, had radios and tape players to keep from becoming mesmerized. But sailors on a nuclear sub costing the best part of a billion . . .

Jones leaned forward, pressing the headphones tight against his head. He tore a page of doodles from his scratch pad and noted the time on a fresh sheet. Next he made some adjustments on his gain controls, already near the top of the scale, and flipped off the processors again. The cacophony of surface noise nearly took his head off. Jones tolerated this for a minute, working the manual muting controls to filter out the worst of the high-frequency noise. Aha! Jones said to himself. Maybe SAPS is messing me up a little – too soon to tell for sure.

When Jones had first been checked out on this gear in sonar school he'd had a burning desire to show it to his brother, who had a masters in electrical engineering and worked as a consultant in the recording industry. He had eleven patents to his name. The stuff on the *Dallas* would have knocked his eyes out. The navy's systems for digitalizing sound were years ahead of any commercial technique. Too bad it was all classified right alongside nuclear stuff . . .

'Mr Thompson,' Jones said quietly, not looking around, 'can you ask the skipper if maybe we can swing more easterly and drop down a knot or two?'

'Skipper.' Thompson went out into the passageway to relay the request. New course and engine orders were given in fifteen seconds. Mancuso was in sonar ten seconds after that.

The skipper had been sweating this. It had been obvious two days ago that their erstwhile contact had not acted as expected, had not run the route, or had never slowed down. Commander Mancuso had guessed wrong on something – had he also guessed wrong on their visitor's course? And what did it mean if their friend had not run the route? Jones had figured that one out long before. It made her a boomer. Boomer skippers never go fast.

Jones was sitting as usual, hunched over his table, his left hand up commanding quiet as the towed array came around to a precise east-west azimuth at the end of its cable. His cigarette burned away unnoticed in the ashtray. A reel-to-reel tape recorder was operating continuously in the sonar room, its tapes changed hourly and kept for later analysis on shore. Next to it was another whose recordings were used aboard the *Dallas* for re-examination of contacts. He reached up and switched it on, then turned to see his captain looking down at him. Jones' face broke into a thin, tired smile.

'Yeah,' he whispered.

Mancuso pointed to the speaker. Jones shook his head. 'Too faint, Cap'n. I just barely got it now. Roughly north, I think, but I need some time on that.' Mancuso looked at the intensity needle Jones was tapping. It was down to zero – almost. Every fifty seconds or so it twitched, just a little. Jones was making furious notes. 'The goddamned SAPS filters are blanking part of this out!!!!! We need smoother amplifiers and better manual filter controls!!' he wrote.

Mancuso told himself that this was faintly ridiculous. He was watching Jones as he had watched his wife when she'd had Dominic, and he was timing the twitches on a needle as he had timed his wife's contractions. But there was no thrill to match this. The comparison he used to explain it to his father was the thrill you get on the first day of hunting season, when you hear the leaves rustle and you know it's not a man making the noise. But it was better than that. He was hunting men, men like himself in a vessel like his own . . .

'Getting louder, Skipper.' Jones leaned back and lit a cigarette. 'He's heading our way. I make him three-five-zero, maybe more like three-five-three. Still real faint, but that's our boy. We got him.' Jones decided to risk an impertinence. He'd earned a little tolerance. 'We wait or we chase, sir?'

'We wait. No sense spooking him. We let him come in nice and close while we do our famous imitation of a hole in the water, then we tag along behind him to wax his tail for a while. I want another tape of this set up, and I want the BC-10 to run a SAPS scan. Use the instruction to bypass the processing algorythms. I want this contact analysed, not interpreted. Run it every two minutes. I want his signature recorded, digitalised, folded, spindled, and mutilated. I want to know everything there is about him, his propulsion noises, his plant signature, the works. I want to know exactly who he is.'

'He's a Russkie, sir,' Jones observed.

'But which Russkie?' Mancuso smiled.

'Aye, Cap'n.' Jones understood. He'd be on duty another two hours, but the end was in sight. Almost. Mancuso sat down and lifted a spare set of headphones, stealing one of Jones' cigarettes. He'd been trying to break the habit for a month. He'd have a better chance on the beach.

HMS *Invincible*

Ryan was now wearing a Royal Navy uniform. This was temporary. Another mark of how fast this job had been laid on was that he had only the one uniform and two shirts. All of his wardrobe was now being cleaned and in the interim he had on a pair of English-made trousers and a sweater. Typical, he thought – nobody even knows I'm here. They had forgotten him. No messages from the president – not that he'd ever expected one – and Painter and Davenport were only too glad to forget that he was ever on the *Kennedy*. Greer and the judge were probably going over some damned fool thing or another, maybe chuckling to themselves about Jack Ryan having a pleasure cruise at government expense.

It was not a pleasure cruise. Jack had rediscovered his vulnerability to seasickness. The *Invincible* was off Massachusetts, waiting for the Russian surface force and hunting vigorously after the red subs in the area. They were steaming in circles on an ocean that would not settle down. Everyone was busy – except him. The pilots were up twice a day or more, exercising with their US Air Force and Navy counterparts working from shore bases. The ships were practising surface warfare tactics. As Admiral White had said at breakfast, it had developed into a jolly good extension of NIFTY DOLPHIN. Ryan didn't like being a supernumerary. Everyone was polite, of course. Indeed, the hospitality was nearly overpowering. He had access to the command centre and when he watched to see how the Brits hunted subs down everything was explained to him in sufficient detail that he actually understood about half of it.

At the moment he was reading alone in White's sea cabin, which had become his permanent home aboard. Ritter had thoughtfully tucked a CIA staff study into his duffle bag. Entitled 'Lost Children: A Psychological Profile of East Bloc Defectors,' the three-hundred-page document had been drafted by a committee of psychologists and psychiatrists who worked with the CIA and other intelligence agencies helping defectors settle into American life – and, he was sure, helping spot security risks in the CIA. Not that there were many of those, but there were two sides to everything the Company did.

Ryan admitted to himself that this was pretty interesting stuff. He had never really thought about what makes a defector, figuring that there were enough things happening on the other side of the Iron Curtain to make any rational person want to take whatever chance he got to run west. But it was not that simple, he read, not that simple at all. Everyone who came over was a fairly unique individual. While one might recognize the inequities of life under Communism and yearn for justice, religious freedom, a chance to develop as an individual, another might simply want to get rich, having read about how greedy capitalists exploit the masses and decided that being an exploiter has its good points. Ryan found this interesting if cynical.

Another defector type was the fake, the imposter, someone planted on the CIA as a living piece of disinformation But this kind of character could cut both ways. He might ultimately turn out to be a genuine defector. America, Ryan smiled, could be pretty seductive to someone used to the grey life in the Soviet Union. Most of the plants, however, were dangerous enemies. For this reason a defector was never trusted. Never. A man who had changed countries once could do it again. Even the idealists had doubts, great pangs of conscience at having deserted their motherland. In a footnote a doctor commented that the most wounding punishment for Aleksander Solzhenitsyn was exile. As a patriot, being alive far from his home was more of a torment than living in a gulag. Ryan found that curious, but enough so to be true.

The rest of the document addressed the problem of getting them settled.

197

Not a few Soviet defectors had committed suicide after a few years. Some had simply been unable to cope with freedom, the way that long-term prison inmates often fail to function without highly structured control over their lives and commit new crimes hoping to return to their safe environment. Over the years the CIA had developed a protocol for dealing with this problem, and a graph in an appendix showed that the severe maladjustment cases were trending dramatically down. Ryan took his time reading. While getting his doctorate in history at Georgetown University he had used a little free time to audit some psychology classes. He had come away with the gut suspicion that shrinks didn't really know much of anything, that they got together and agreed on random ideas they would all use . . . He shook his head. His wife occasionally said that, too. A clinical instructor in opthalmic surgery on an exchange programme at Guy's Hospital in London, Caroline Ryan regarded everything as cut and dried. If someone had eye trouble, she would either fix it or not fix it. A mind was different, Jack decided after reading through the document a second time, and each defector had to be treated as an individual, handled carefully by a sympathetic case officer who had both the time and inclination to look after him properly. He wondered if he'd be good at it.

Admiral White walked in. 'Bored, Jack?'

'Not exactly, Admiral. When do we make contact with the Soviets?'

'This evening. Your chaps have given them a very rough time over that Tomcat incident.'

'Good. Maybe people will wake up before something really bad happens.'

'You think it will?' White sat down.

'Well, Admiral, if they really are hunting a missing sub, yes. If not, then they're here for another purpose entirely, and I've guessed wrong. Worse than that, I'll have to live with that misjudgment – or die with it.'

Norfolk Naval Medical Center

Tait was feeling better. Dr Jameson had taken over for several hours, allowing him to curl up on a couch in the doctor's lounge for five hours. That was the most sleep he ever seemed to get in one shot, but it was sufficient to make him look indecently chipper to the rest of the floor staff. He made a quick phone call and some milk was sent up. As a Mormon, Tait avoided everything with caffeine – coffee, tea, even cola drinks – and though this type of self-discipline was unusual for a physician, to say nothing of a uniformed officer, he scarcely thought about it except on rare occasions when he pointed out its longevity benefits to his brother practitioners. Tait drank his milk and shaved in the restroom, emerging ready to face another day.

'Any word on the radiation exposure, Jamie?'

The radiology lab had struck out. 'They brought a nucleonics officer over from a sub tender, and he scanned the clothes. There was a possible twenty-rad contamination, not enough for frank physiological effects. I think what it might have been was that the nurse took the sample from the back of his hand. The extremities might still have been suffering from the vascular shutdown. That could explain the depleted white count. Maybe.'

'How is he otherwise?'

'Better. Not much, but better. I think maybe the keflin's taking hold.' The doctor flipped open the chart. 'White count is coming back. I put a unit of white blood into him two hours ago. The blood chemistry is approaching normal limits. Blood pressure is one hundred over sixty-five, heart rate is ninety-four. Temperature ten minutes ago was 100.8 – it's been fluctuating for several hours.

'His heart looks pretty good. In fact, I think he's going to make it, unless something unexpected crops up.' Jameson reminded himself that in extreme hypothermia cases the unexpected can take a month or more to appear.

Tait examined the chart, remembering what he had been like years ago. A bright young doc, just like Jamie, certain that he could cure the world. It was a good feeling. A pity that experience – in his case, two years at Danang – beat that out of you. Jamie was right, though; there was enough improvement here to make the patient's chances appear measurably better.

'What are the Russians doing?' Tait asked.

'Petchkin has the watch at the moment. When it came his turn, and he changed into scrubs – you know he has that Captain Smirnov holding on to his clothes, like he expects us to steal them or something?'

Tait explained that Petchkin was a KGB agent.

'No kidding? Maybe he has a gun tucked away.' Jameson chuckled. 'If he does, he'd better watch it. We got three marines up here with us.'

'Marines? What for?'

'Forgot to tell you. Some reporter found out we had a Russkie up here and tried to bluff his way on to the floor. A nurse stopped him. Admiral Blackburn found out and went ape. The whole floor's sealed off. What's the big secret anyway?'

'Beats me, but that's the way it is. What do you think of this Petchkin guy?'

'I don't know. I've never met any Russians before. They don't smile a whole lot. The way they're taking turns watching the patient, you'd think they expect us to make off with him.'

'Or maybe that he'll say something they don't want us to hear?' Tait wondered. 'Did you get the feeling that they might not want him to make it? I mean, when they didn't want to tell us about what his sub was?'

Jameson thought about that. 'No. The Russians are supposed to make a secret of everything, aren't they? Anyway, Smirnov did come through with it.'

'Get some sleep, Jamie.'

'Aye, Cap'n.' Jameson walked off towards the lounge.

We asked them what kind of a sub, the captain thought, meaning whether it was a nuke or not. What if they thought we were asking if it was a missile sub? That makes sense, doesn't it? Yeah. A missile sub right off our coast, and all this activity in the North Atlantic. Christmas season. Dear God! If they were going to do it, they'd do it right now, wouldn't they? He walked down the hall. A nurse came out of the room with a blood sample to be taken down to the lab. This was being done hourly, and it left Petchkin alone with the patient for a few minutes.

Tait walked around the corner and saw Petchkin through the window, sitting in a chair at the corner of the bed and watching his countryman, who was still unconscious. He had on green scrubs. Made to be put on in a hurry, these were reversible, with a pocket on both sides so a surgeon didn't have to waste a second to see if they were inside out. As Tait watched, Petchkin reached for something through the low collar.

'Oh, God!' Tait raced around the corner and shot through the swinging door. Petchkin's look of surprise changed to amazement as the doctor batted a cigarette and lighter from his hand, then to outrage as he was lifted from his chair and flung towards the door. Tait was the smaller of the two, but his sudden burst of energy was sufficient to eject the man from the room. 'Security!' Tait screamed.

'What is the meaning of this?' Petchkin demanded. Tait was holding him in a bearhug. Immediately he heard feet racing down the hall from the lobby.

'What is it, sir?' A breathless marine lance corporal with a .45 Colt in his right hand skidded to a halt on the tile floor.

'This man just tried to kill my patient!'

'*What!*' Petchkin's face was crimson.

'Corporal, your post is now at that door. If this man tries to get into that room, you will stop him any way you have to. Understood?'

'Aye aye, sir!' The corporal looked at the Russian. 'Sir, would you please step away from the door?'

'What is the meaning of this outrage!'

'Sir, you will step away from the door, right now.' The marine holstered his pistol.

'What is going on here?' It was Ivanov, who had sense enough to ask this question in a quiet voice from ten feet away.

'Doctor, do you want your sailor to survive or not?' Tait asked, trying to calm himself.

'What – of course we wish him to survive. How can you ask this?'

'Then why did Comrade Petchkin just try to kill him?'

'I did not do such a thing!' Petchkin shouted.

'What did he do, exactly?' Ivanov asked.

Before Tait could answer, Petchkin spoke rapidly in Russian, then switched to English. 'I was reaching for a smoke, that is all. I have no weapon. I wish to kill no one. I only wish to have a cigarette.'

'We have No Smoking signs all over the floor, except in the lobby – you didn't see them? You were in a room in intensive care, with a patient on hundred-per cent oxygen, the air and bedclothes saturated with oxygen, and you were going to flick your goddamned Bic!' The doctor rarely used profanity. 'Oh sure, you'd get burned some, and it would look like an accident – and that kid would be dead! I know what you are, Petchkin, and I don't think you're that stupid. Get off my floor!'

The nurse, who had been watching this, went into the patient's room. She came back out with a pack of cigarettes, two loose ones, a plastic butane lighter, and a curious look on her face.

Petchkin was ashen. 'Dr Tait, I assure you that I had no such intention. What are you saying would happen?'

'Comrade Petchkin,' Ivanov said slowly in English, 'there would be an explosion and fire. You cannot have a flame near oxygen.'

'*Nichevo!*' Petchkin finally realized what he had done. He had waited for the nurse to leave – medical people never let you smoke when you ask. He didn't know the first thing about hospitals, and as a KGB agent he was accustomed to doing whatever he wanted. He started speaking to Ivanov in Russian. The Soviet doctor looked like a parent listening to a child's explanation for a broken glass. His response was spirited.

For his part, Tait began to wonder if he hadn't over-reacted – anyone who smoked was an idiot to begin with.

'Dr Tait,' Petchkin said finally, 'I swear to you that I had no idea of this oxygen business. Perhaps I am a fool.'

'Nurse,' Tait turned, 'we will not leave this patient unattended by our personnel at any time – never. Have an orderly come to pick the blood samples and anything else. If you have to go to the head, get relief first.'

'Yes, Doctor.'

'No more screwing around, Mr Petchkin. Break the rules again, sir, and you're off the floor for good. Do you understand?'

'It will be as you say, Doctor, and allow me, please, to apologize.'

'You stay put,' Tait said to the marine. He walked away shaking his head angrily, mad at the Russians, embarrassed with himself, wishing he were back at Bethesda where he belonged, and wishing he knew how to swear coherently. He took the service elevator down to the first floor and spent five minutes looking for the intelligence officer who had flown down with him. Ultimately he found him in a game room playing Pac Man. They conferred in the hospital administrator's vacant office.

'You really thought he was trying to kill the guy?' the commander asked incredulously.

'What was I supposed to think?' Tait demanded. 'What do you think?'

'I think he just screwed up. They want that kid alive – no, first they want him talking – more than you do.'

'How do you know that?'

'Petchkin calls their embassy every hour. We have the phones tapped, of course. How do you think?'

'What if it's a trick?'

'If he's that good an actor he belongs in the movies. You keep that kid alive, Doctor, and leave the rest to us. Good idea to have the marine close, though. That'll rattle 'em a bit. Never pass up a chance to rattle 'em. So, when will he be conscious?'

'No telling. He's still feverish, and very weak. Why do they want him to talk?' Tait asked.

'To find out what sub he was on. Petchkin's KGB contact blurted that out on the phone – sloppy! *Very* sloppy! They must be real excited about this.'

'Do we know what sub it was?'

'Sure,' the intelligence officer said mischievously.

'Then what's going on, for Lord's sake!'

'Can't say, Doc.' The commander smiled as if he knew, though he was as much in the dark as anyone.

Norfolk Naval Shipyard

The USS *Scamp* sat at the dock while a large overhead crane settled the *Avalon* on its support rack. The captain watched impatiently from atop the sail. He and his boat had been called in from hunting a pair of *Victor*s, and he did not like it one bit. The attack boat skipper had only run a DSRV exercise a few weeks before, and right now he had better things to do than play mother whale to this damned useless toy. Besides, having the minisub perched on his after escape trunk would knock ten knots off his top speed. And there'd be four more men to bunk and feed. The *Scamp* was not all that large.

At least they'd get good food out of this. The *Scamp* had been out five weeks when the recall order arrived. Their supply of fresh vegetables was exhausted, and they availed themselves of the opportunity to have fresh food trucked down to the dock. A man tires quickly of three-bean salad. Tonight they'd have real lettuce, tomatoes, fresh corn instead of canned. But that didn't make up for the fact that there were Russians out there to worry about.

'All secure?' the captain called down to the curved after deck.

'Yes, Captain. We're ready when you are,' Lieutenant Ames answered.

'Engine room,' the captain called down on intercom, 'I want you ready to answer bells in ten minutes.'

'Ready now, Skipper.'

A harbour tug was standing by to help manoeuvre them from the dock. Ames had their orders, something else that the captain didn't like. Surely they would not be doing any more hunting, not with that damned *Avalon* strapped on.

The *Red October*

'Look here, Svyadov,' Melekhin pointed, 'I will show you how a saboteur thinks.'

The lieutenant came over and looked. The chief engineer was pointing at an inspection valve on the heat exchanger. Before he got an explanation, Melekhin went to the bulkhead phone.

'Comrade Captain, this is Melekhin. I have found it. I require the reactor to be stopped for an hour. We can operate the caterpillar on batteries, no?'

'Of course, Comrade Chief Engineer,' Ramius said, 'proceed.'

Melekhin turned to the assistant engineering officer. 'You will shut the reactor down and connect the batteries to the caterpillar motors.'

'At once, Comrade.' The officer began to work the controls.

The time taken to find the leak had been a burden on everyone. Once they had discovered that the Geiger counters were sabotaged and Melekhin and Borodin had repaired them, they had begun a complete check of the reactor spaces, a devilishly tricky task. There had never been a question of a major steam leak, else Svyadov would have gone looking for it with a broomstick – even a tiny leak could easily shave off an arm. They reasoned that it had to be a small leak in the low-pressure part of the system. Didn't it? It was the not knowing that had troubled everyone.

The check made by the chief engineer and executive officer had lasted no less than eight hours, during which the reactor had again been shut down. This cut all electricity off throughout the ship except for emergency lights and the caterpillar motors. Even the air systems had been curtailed. That had set the crew muttering to themselves.

The problem was, Melekhin could still not find the leak, and when the badges had been developed a day earlier, there was nothing on them! How was this possible?

'Come, Svyadov, tell me what you see.' Melekhin came back over and pointed.

'The water test valve.' Opened only in port, when the reactor was cold, it was used to flush the cooling system and to check for unusual water contamination. The thing was grossly unremarkable, a heavy-duty valve with a large wheel. The spout underneath it, below the pressurized part of the pipe, was threaded rather than welded.

'A large wrench, if you please, Lieutenant.' Melekhin was drawing the lesson out, Svyadov thought. He was the slowest of teachers when he was trying to communicate something important. Svyadov returned with a metre-long pipe wrench. The chief engineer waited until the plant was closed down, then double-checked a gauge to make sure the pipes were depressurized. He was a careful man. The wrench was set on the fitting, and he turned it. It came off easily.

'You see, Comrade Lieutenant, the threads on the pipe actually go up on to the valve casing. Why is this permitted?'

'The threads are on the outside of the pipe, Comrade. The valve itself bears the pressure. The fitting which is screwed on is merely a directional spigot. The nature of the union does not compromise the pressure loop.'

'Correct. A screw fitting is not strong enough for the plant's total pressure.' Melekhin worked the fitting all the way off with his hands. It was perfectly machined, the threads still bright from the original engine work. 'And there is the sabotage.'

'I don't understand.'

'Someone thought this one over very carefully, Comrade Lieutenant.' Melekhin's voice was half admiration, half rage. 'At normal operating pressure, cruising speed, that is, the system is pressurized to eight kilograms per square centimetre, correct?'

'Yes, Comrade, and at full power the pressure is ninety per cent higher.' Svyadov knew all this by heart.

'But we rarely go to full power. What we have here is a dead-end section of the steam loop. Now, here a small hole has been drilled, not even a millimetre. Look.' Melekhin bent over to examine it himself. Svyadov was happy to keep his distance. 'Not even a millimetre. The saboteur took the fitting off, drilled the hole, and put it back. The tiny hole permits a minuscule amount of steam to escape, but only very slowly. The steam cannot go up, because the fitting sits against this flange. Look at this machine work! It is perfect, you see, perfect! The steam, therefore, cannot escape upward. It can only force its way down the threads, around and around, ultimately escaping inside the spout. Just enough. Just enough to contaminate this compartment by a tiny amount.' Melekhin looked up. 'Someone was a very clever man. Clever enough to know exactly how this system works. When we reduced power to check for the leak before, there was not enough pressure remaining in the loop to force the steam down the threads, and we could not find the leak. There is only enough pressure at normal power levels – but if you suspect a leak, you power-down the system. And if we had gone to maximum power, who can say what might have happened?' Melekhin shook his head in admiration. 'Someone was very, very clever. I hope I meet him. Oh, I hope I meet this clever man. For when I do, I will take a pair of large steel pliers – ,' Melekhin's voice lowered to a whisper, ' – and I will crush his balls! Get me the small electric welding set, Comrade. I can fix this myself in a few minutes.'

Captain First Rank Melekhin was as good as his word. He wouldn't let anyone near the job. It was his plant, and his responsibility. Svyadov was just as happy for that. A tiny bead of stainless steel was worked into the fault, and Melekhin filed it down with jeweller's tools to protect the threads. Then he brushed rubber-based sealant on to the threads and worked the fitting back into place. The whole procedure took twenty-eight minutes by Svyadov's watch. As they had told him in Leningrad, Melekhin was the best engineer in submarines.

'A static pressure test, eight kilograms,' he ordered the assistant engineering officer.

The reactor was reactivated. Five minutes later the pressure went all the way to normal power. Melekhin held a counter under the spout for ten minutes – and got nothing, even on the number two setting. He walked to the phone to tell the captain the leak was fixed.

Melekhin had the enlisted men let back into the compartment to return the tools to their places.

'You see how it is done, Lieutenant?'

'Yes, Comrade. Was that one leak sufficient to cause all of our contamination?'

'Obviously.'

Svyadov wondered about this. The reactor spaces were nothing but a collection of pipes and fittings, and this bit of sabotage could not have taken long. What if other such time bombs were hidden in the system?

'Perhaps you worry too much, Comrade,' Melekhin said. 'Yes, I have considered this. When we get to Cuba, I will have a full-power static test made to check the whole system, but for the moment I do not think this is a good idea. We will continue the two-hour watch cycle. There is the possibility that one of our own crewmen is the saboteur. If so, I will not have people in these spaces long enough to commit more mischief. You will watch the crew closely.'

The Twelfth Day

Tuesday, 14 December

The *Dallas*

'*Crazy Ivan!*' Jones shouted loudly enough to be heard in the attack centre. 'Turning to starboard!'

'Skipper!' Thompson repeated the warning.

'All stop!' Mancuso ordered quickly. 'Rig ship for ultra-quiet!'

A thousand yards ahead of the *Dallas*, her contact had just begun a radical turn to the right. She had been doing so about every two hours since they had regained contact, though not regularly enough for the *Dallas* to settle into a comfortable pattern. Whoever is driving that boomer knows his business, Mancuso thought. The Soviet missile submarine was making a complete circle so her bow-mounted sonar could check for anyone hiding in her baffles.

Countering this manoeuvre was more than just tricky – it was dangerous, especially the way Mancuso did it. When the *Red October* changed course, her stern, like those of all ships, moved in the direction opposite the turn. She was a steel barrier directly in the *Dallas'* path for as long as it took her to move through the first part of the turn, and the 7,000-ton attack submarine took a lot of space to stop.

The exact number of collisions that had occurred between Soviet and American submarines was a closely guarded secret; that there had been such collisions was not. One characteristically Russian tactic for forcing Americans to keep their distance was a stylized turn called the Crazy Ivan in the US Navy.

The first few hours they had trailed this contact, Mancuso had been careful to keep his distance. He had learned that the submarine was not turning quickly. She was, rather, manoeuvring in a leisurely manner, and seemed to ascend fifty to eighty feet as she turned, banking almost like an aircraft. He suspected that the Russian skipper was not using his full manoeuvrability – an intelligent thing for a captain to do, keeping some of his performance in reserve as a surprise. These facts allowed the *Dallas* to trail very closely indeed and gave Mancuso a chance to chop his speed and drift forwards so that he barely avoided the Russian's stern. He was getting good at it – a little too good, his officers were whispering. The last time they had not missed the Russian's screws by more than a hundred fifty yards. The contact's large turning circle was taking her completely around the *Dallas* as the latter sniffed at her prey's tail.

Avoiding collision was the most dangerous part of the manoeuvre, but not the only part. The *Dallas* also had to remain invisible to her quarry's passive sonar systems. For her to do so the engineers had to cut power in their S6G reactor to a tiny fraction of its total output. Fortunately the reactor was able to run on such low power without the use of a coolant pump, since coolant could be transferred by normal convection circulation. When the steam turbines halted, all propulsion noises stopped entirely. In addition, a strict silent ship routine was enforced. No activity on the *Dallas* that might generate noise was permitted, and the crew took it seriously enough that even ordinary conversations in the mess were muted.

'Speed coming down,' Lieutenant Goodman reported. Mancuso decided that the *Dallas* would not be part of a ramming this time and went aft to sonar.

'Target is still turning right,' Jones reported quietly. 'Ought to be clear now. Distance to the stern, maybe two hundred yards, maybe a shade less . . . Yeah, we're clear now, bearing is changing more rapidly. Speed and engine noises are constant. A slow turn to the right.' Jones caught the captain out of the corner of his eye and turned to hazard an observation. 'Skipper, this guy is real confident in himself. I mean, *real* confident.'

'Explain,' Mancuso said, figuring he knew the answer.

'Cap'n, he's not chopping speed the way we do, and we turn a lot sharper than this. It's almost like – like he's doing this out of habit, y'know? Like he's in a hurry to get somewhere, and really doesn't think anybody can track – wait . . . Yeah, okay, he's just about reversed course now, bearing off the starboard bow, say half a mile . . . Still doing the slow turn. He'll go right around us again. Sir, if he knows anybody's back here, he's playing it awful cool. What do you think, Frenchie?'

Chief Sonarman Laval shook his head. 'He don't know we're here.' The chief didn't want to say anything else. He thought Mancuso's close tailing was reckless. The man had balls, playing with a 688 like this, but one little screw-up and he'd find himself with a pail and shovel, on the beach.

'Passing down the starboard side. No pinging.' Jones took out his calculator and punched in some numbers. 'Sir, this angular turn rate at this speed makes the range about a thousand yards. You suppose his funny drive system goofs up his rudders any?'

'Maybe.' Mancuso took a spare set of phones and plugged them in to listen.

The noise was the same. A swish, and every forty or fifty seconds an odd, low-frequency rumble. This close they could also hear the gurgling and throbbing of the reactor pump. There was a sharp sound, maybe a cook moving a pan on a metal grate. No silent ship drill on this boat. Mancuso smiled to himself. It was like being a cat burglar, hanging this close to an enemy submarine – no, not an enemy, not exactly – hearing everything. In better acoustical conditions they could have heard conversations. Not well enough to understand them, of course, but as if they were at a dinner party listening to the gabble of a dozen couples at once.

'Passing aft and still circling. His turning radius must be a good thousand yards,' Mancuso observed.

'Yes, Cap'n, about that,' Jones agreed.

'He just can't be using all his rudder, and you're right, Jonesy, he is very damned casual about this. Hmph, the Russians are all supposed to be paranoid – not this boy.' So much the better, Mancuso thought.

If he were going to hear the *Dallas* it would be now, with the bow-mounted sonar pointed almost directly at them. Mancuso took off his headphones to listen to his boat. The *Dallas* was a tomb. The words *Crazy Ivan* had been passed, and within seconds his crew had responded. How do you reward a whole crew? Mancuso wondered. He knew he worked them hard, sometimes too hard – but damn! Did they deliver!

'Port beam,' Jones said. 'Exactly abeam now, speed unchanged, travelling a little straighter, maybe, distance about eleven hundred, I think.' The sonarman took a handkerchief from his back pocket and used it to wipe his hands.

There's tension all right, but you'd never know it listening to the kid, the captain thought. Everyone in his crew was acting like a professional.

'He's passed us. On the port bow, and I think the turn has stopped. Betcha he's settled back down on one-nine-zero.' Jones looked up with a grin. 'We did it again, Skipper.'

'Okay. Good work, you men.' Mancuso went back to the attack centre. Everyone was waiting expectantly. The *Dallas* was dead in the water, drifting slowly downward with her slight negative trim.

'Let's get the engines turned back on. Build her up slowly to thirteen knots.' A few seconds later an almost imperceptible noise began as the reactor plant increased power. A moment after that the speed gauge twitched upwards. The *Dallas* was moving again.

'Attention, this is the captain speaking,' Mancuso said into the sound-powered communications system. The electrically powered speakers were turned off, and his word would be relayed by watchstanders in all compartments. 'They circled us again without picking us up. Well done, everybody. We can all breathe again.' He placed the handset back in its holder. 'Mr Goodman, let's get back on her tail.'

'Aye, Skipper. Left five degrees rudder, helm.'

'Left five degrees rudder, aye.' The helmsman acknowledged the order, turning his wheel as he did so. Ten minutes later the *Dallas* was back astern of her contact.

A constant fire control solution was set up on the attack director. The Mark 48 torpedoes would barely have sufficient distance to arm themselves before striking the target in twenty-nine seconds.

Ministry of Defence, Moscow

'And how are you feeling, Misha?'

Mikhail Semyonovich Filitov looked up from a large pile of documents. He looked flushed and feverish still. Dmitri Ustinov, the defence minister, worried about his old friend. He should have stayed in the hospital another few days as the doctors had advised. But Misha had never been one to take advice, only orders.

'I feel good, Dmitri. Any time you walk out of a hospital you feel good – even if you are dead,' Filitov smiled.

'You still look sick,' Ustinov observed.

'Ah! At our age you always look sick. A drink, Comrade Defence Minister?' Filitov hoisted a bottle of Stolychnaya vodka from a desk drawer.

'You drink too much, my friend,' Ustinov chided.

'I do not drink enough. A bit more antifreeze and I would not have caught cold last week.' He poured two tumblers half full and held one out to his guest. 'Here, Dmitri, it is cold outside.'

Both men tipped their glasses, took a gulp of the clear liquid, and expelled their breath with an explosive *pah*.

'I feel better already.' Filitov's laugh was hoarse. 'Tell me, what became of that Lithuanian renegade?'

'We're not sure,' Ustinov said.

'Still? Can you tell me now what his letter said?'

Ustinov took another swallow before explaining. When he finished the story Filitov was leaning forward at his desk, shocked.

'Mother of God! And he has still not been found? How many heads?'

'Admiral Korov is dead. He was arrested by the KGB, of course, and died of a brain haemorrhage soon thereafter.'

'A nine-millimetre haemorrhage, I trust,' Filitov observed coldly. 'How many times have I said it? What goddamned use is a navy? Can we use it against the Chinese? Or the NATO armies that threaten us – no! How many rubles does it cost to build and fuel those pretty barges for Gorshkov and what do we get for it – nothing! Now he loses one submarine, and the whole fucking fleet cannot find it. It is a good thing that Stalin is not alive.'

Ustinov agreed. He was old enough to remember what happened then to anyone who reported results short of total success. 'In any case, Padorin may have saved his skin. There is one extra element of control on the submarine.'

'Padorin!' Filitov took another gulp of his drink. 'That eunuch! I've only met him, what, three times. A cold fish, even for a commissar. He never laughs, even when he drinks. Some Russian he is. Why is it, Dmitri, that Gorshkov keeps so many old farts like that around?'

Ustinov smiled into his drink. 'The same reason I do, Misha.' Both men laughed.

'So, how will Comrade Padorin save our secrets and keep his skin? Invent a time machine?'

Ustinov explained to his old friend. There weren't many men whom the defence minister could speak to and feel comfortable with. Filitov drew the pension of a full colonel of tanks and still wore the uniform proudly. He had faced combat for the first time on the fourth day of the Great Patriotic War, as the Fascist invaders were driving east. Lieutenant Filitov had met them southeast of Brest Litovsk with a troop of T-34/76 tanks. A good officer, he had survived his first encounter with Guderian's panzers, retreated in good order, and fought a constant mobile action for days before being caught in the great encirclement at Minsk. He had fought his way out of that trap, and later another at Vyasma, and had commanded a battalion spearheading Zhukov's counterblow from the suburbs of Moscow. In 1942 Filitov had taken part in the disastrous counter-offensive towards Kharkov but again escaped, this time on foot, leading the battered remains of the regiment from that dreadful cauldron on the Dnieper River. With another regiment later that year he had led the drive that shattered the Italian Army on the flank of Stalingrad and encircled the Germans. He'd been wounded twice in that campaign. Filitov had acquired the reputation of a commander who was both good and lucky. That luck had run out at Kursk, where he had battled the troopers of SS division *Das Reich*. Leading his men into a furious tank battle, Filitov and his vehicle had run straight into an ambush of eighty-eight-millimetre guns. That he had survived at all was a miracle. His chest still bore the scars from the burning tank, and his right arm was next to useless. This was enough to retire a charging tactical commander who had won the gold star of the Hero of the Soviet Union no less than three times, and a dozen other decorations.

After months of being shuttled from one hospital to another, he had become a representative of the Red Army in the armament factories that had been moved to the Urals east of Moscow. The drive that made him a premiere combat soldier would come to serve the State even better behind the lines. A born organizer, Filitov learned to run roughshod over factory bosses to streamline production, and he cajoled design engineers to make the small but often crucial changes in their products that would save crews and win battles.

It was in these factories that Filitov and Ustinov first met, the scarred combat veteran and the gruff apparatchik detailed by Stalin to produce enough tools to drive the hated invaders back. After a few clashes, the young Ustinov came to recognize that Filitov was totally fearless and would not be bullied on a question involving quality control or fighting efficiency. In the midst of one disagreement, Filitov had practically dragged Ustinov into the turret of a tank and taken it through a combat training course to make his point. Ustinov was the sort who only had to be shown something once, and they soon became fast friends. He could not fail to admire the courage of a soldier who could say no to the people's commissar of armaments. By mid-1944 Filitov was a permanent part of his staff, a special inspector – in short, a hatchet man. When there was a problem at a factory, Filitov saw that it was settled, quickly. The three gold stars and the crippling injuries were usually enough to persuade the factory bosses to mend their ways – and if not, Misha had the booming voice and vocabulary to make a sergeant major wince.

Never a high Party official, Filitov gave his boss valuable input from people in the field. He still worked closely with the tank design and production teams, often taking a prototype or randomly chosen production model through a test course with a team of picked veterans to see for himself how well things worked. Crippled arm or not, it was said that Filitov was among the best gunners in the Soviet Union. And he was a humble man. In 1965 Ustinov thought to surprise his friend with general's stars and was somewhat angered by Filitov's reaction – he had not earned them on the field of battle, and that was the only way a man could earn stars. A rather impolitic remark, as Ustinov wore the uniform of a marshal of the Soviet Union, earned for his Party work and industrial management, it nevertheless demonstrated that Filitov was a true New Soviet Man, proud of what he was and mindful of his limitations.

It is unfortunate, Ustinov thought, that Misha has been so unlucky otherwise. He had been married to a lovely woman, Elena Filitova, who had been a minor dancer with the Kirov when the youthful officer had met her. Ustinov remembered her with a trace of envy; she had been the perfect soldier's wife. She had given the State two fine sons. Both were now dead. The elder had died in 1956, still a boy, an officer cadet sent to Hungary because of his political reliability and killed by counter-revolutionaries before his seventeenth birthday. He was a soldier who had taken a soldier's chance. But the younger had been killed in a training accident, blown to pieces by a faulty breech mechanism in a brand-new T-55 tank in 1959. That had been a disgrace. And Elena had died soon thereafter, of grief more than anything else. Too bad.

Filitov had not changed all that much. He drank too much, like many soldiers, but he was a quiet drunk. In 1961 or so, Ustinov remembered, he had taken to cross-country skiing. It made him healthier and tired him out, which was probably what he really wanted, along with the solitude. He was still a fine listener. When Ustinov had a new idea to float before the Politburo, he usually tried it out on Filitov first to get his reaction. Not a sophisticated man, Filitov was an uncommonly shrewd one who had a soldier's instinct for finding weaknesses and exploiting strengths. His value as a liaison officer was unsurpassed. Few men living had three gold stars won on the field of battle. That got him attention, and it still made officers far his senior listen to him. 'So, Dmitri Fedorovich, do you think this would work? Can one man destroy a submarine?' Filitov asked. 'You know rockets, I don't.'

'Certainly. It's merely a question of mathematics. There is enough energy in a rocket to melt the submarine.'

'And what of our man?' Filitov asked. Always the combat soldier, he would be the type to worry about a brave man alone in enemy territory.

'We will do our best, of course, but there is not much hope.'

'He must be rescued, Dmitri! Must! You forget, young men like that have a value beyond their deeds, they are not mere machines who perform their duties. They are symbols for our other young officers, and alive they are worth a hundred new tanks or ships. Combat is like that, Comrade. We have forgotten this – and look what has happened in Afghanistan!'

'You are correct, my friend, but – only a few hundred kilometres from the American coast, if that much?'

'Gorshkov talks so much about what his navy can do, let him do this!' Filitov poured another glass. 'One more, I think.'

'You are not going skiing again, Misha.' Ustinov noted that he often fortified himself before driving his car to the woods east of Moscow. 'I will not permit it.'

'Not today, Dmitri, I promise – though I think it would do me good. Today I will go to the *banya* to take steam and sweat the rest of the poisons from this old carcass. Will you join me?'

'I have to work late.'

'The *banya* is good for you,' Filitov persisted. It was a waste of time, and both knew it. Ustinov was a member of the 'nobility' and would not mingle in the public steam baths. Misha had no such pretensions.

The *Dallas*

Exactly twenty-four hours after reacquiring the *Red October*, Mancuso called a conference of his senior officers in the wardroom. Things had settled down somewhat. Mancuso had even managed to squeeze in a couple of four-hour naps and was feeling vaguely human again. They now had time to build an accurate sonar picture of the quarry, and the computer was refining a signature classification that would be out to the other fleet attack boats in a matter of weeks. From trailing they had a very accurate model of the propulsion system's noise characteristics, and from the bihourly circling they had also built a picture of the boat's size and power plant specifications.

The executive officer, Wally Chambers, twirled a pencil in his fingers like a baton. 'Jonesy's right. It's the same power plant that the *Oscars* and *Typhoons* have. They've quietened it down, but the gross signature characteristics are virtually identical. Question is, what's it turning? It sounds like the propellers are ducted somehow, or shrouded. A directional prop with a collar around it, maybe, or some sort of tunnel drive. Didn't we try that once?'

'Long time ago,' Lieutenant Butler, the engineering officer, said. 'I heard a story about it while I was at Arco. It didn't work out, but I don't remember why. Whatever it is, it's really knocked down on the propulsion noises. That rumble though . . . It's some sort of harmonic all right – but a harmonic what? You know, except for that we'd never have picked it up in the first place.'

'Maybe,' Mancuso said. 'Jonesy says that the signal processors have tended to filter this noise out, almost as though the Soviets know what SAPS does and have tailored a system to beat it. But that's hard to believe.' There was general agreement on this point. Everyone knew the principles on which SAPS operated, but there were probably not fifty men in the country who could really explain the nuts and bolts details.

'We're agreed she's a boomer?' Mancuso asked.

Butler nodded. 'No way you could fit that power plant into an attack hull. More important, she acts like a boomer.'

'Could be an *Oscar*,' Chamber suggested.

'No. Why send an *Oscar* this far south? *Oscar*'s an antiship platform. Uh-uh, this guy's driving a boomer. He ran the route at the speed he's running now – and that's acting like a missile boat,' Lieutenant Mannion noted. 'What are they up to with all this other activity? That's the real question. Maybe trying to sneak up on our coast – just to see if they can do it. It's been done before, and all this other activity makes for a hell of a diversion.'

They all considered that. The trick had been tried before by both sides. Most recently, in 1978, a Soviet *Yankee*-class missile sub had closed to the edge of the continental shelf off the coast of New England. The evident objective had been to see if the United States could detect it or not. The navy had succeeded, and then the question had been whether or not to react and let the Soviets know.

'Well, I think we can leave the grand strategy to the folks on the beach. Let's phone this one in. Lieutenant Mannion, tell the OOD to get us to periscope depth in twenty minutes. We'll try to slip away and back without his noticing.' Mancuso frowned. This was never easy.

A half an hour later the *Dallas* radioed her message.

ZI40925ZDEC
TOP SECRET THEO
FR: USS DALLAS
TO: COMSUBLANT
INFO: CINCLANTFLT
A. USS DALLAS Z090414ZDEC
I. ANOMALOUS CONTACT REACQUIRED 0538Z 13DEC. CURRENT POSITION LAT 42° 35' LONG 49° 12'. COURSE 194 SPEED 13 DEPTH 600. HAVE TRACKED 24 HOURS WITHOUT COUNTERDETECTION. CONTACT EVALUATED AS REDFLEET SSBN GROSS SIZE, ENGINE CHARACTERISTICS INDICATIVE TYPHOON CLASS. HOWEVER CONTACT USING NEW DRIVE SYSTEM NOT REPEAT NOT PROPELLERS. HAVE ESTABLISHED DETAILED SIGNATURE PROFILE. 2. RETURNING TO TRACKING OPERATIONS. REQUEST ADDITIONAL OPAREA ASSIGNMENTS. AWAIT REPLY 1030Z.

COMSUBLANT Operations

'Bingo!' Gallery said to himself. He walked back to his office, careful to close the door before lifting the scrambled line to Washington.

'Sam, this is Vince. Listen up: *Dallas* reports she is tracking a Russian boomer with a new kind of quiet drive system, about six hundred miles southeast of the Grand Banks, course one-nine-four, speed thirteen knots.'

'All right! That's Mancuso?' Dodge said.

'Bartolomeo Vito Mancuso, my favourite Guinea,' Gallery confirmed. Getting him this command had not been easy because of his age. Gallery had gone the distance for him. 'I told you the kid was good, Sam.'

'Jesus, you see how close they are to the *Kiev* group?' Dodge was looking at his tactical display.

'They are cutting it close,' Gallery agreed. '*Invincible*'s not too far away, though, and I have *Pogy* out there, too. We moved her off the shelf when

213

we called *Scamp* back in. I figure *Dallas* will need help. The question is how obvious do we want to be.'

'Not very. Look, Vince, I have to talk to Dan Foster about this.'

'Okay. I have to reply to *Dallas* in, hell, in fifty-five minutes. You know the score. He has to break contact to reach us, then sneak back. Hustle, Sam.'

'Right, Vince.' Dodge switched buttons on his phone. 'This is Admiral Dodge. I need to talk to Admiral Foster right now.'

The Pentagon

'Ouch. Between *Kiev* and *Kirov*. Nice.' Lieutenant General Harris took a marker from his pocket to represent the *Red October*. It was a sub-shaped piece of wood with a Jolly Roger attached. Harris had an odd sense of humour. 'The president says we can try and keep her?' he asked.

'If we can get her to the place we want at the time we want,' General Hilton said. 'Can *Dallas* signal her?'

'Good trick, General.' Foster shook his head. 'First things first. Let's get *Pogy* and *Invincible* there for starters, then we figure out how to warn him. From this course track, Christ, he's heading right for Norfolk. You believe the balls on this guy? If worse comes to worse, we can always try to escort him in.'

'Then we'd have to give the boat back,' Admiral Dodge objected.

'We have to have a fall-back position, Sam. If we can't warn him off, we can try and run a bunch of ships through with him to keep Ivan from shooting.'

'The law of the sea is your bailiwick, not mine,' General Barnes, the air force chief of staff, commented. 'But from where I sit doing that could be called anything from piracy to an overt act of war. Isn't this exercise complicated enough already?'

'Good point, General,' Foster said.

'Gentlemen, I think we need time to consider this. Okay, we still have time, but right now let's tell *Dallas* to sit tight and track the bugger,' Harris said. 'And report any changes in course or speed. I figure we have about fifteen minutes to do that. Next we can get *Pogy* and *Invincible* staked out on their path.'

'Right, Eddie.' Hilton turned to Admiral Foster. 'If you agree, let's do that right now.'

'Send the message, Sam,' Foster ordered.

'Aye aye.' Dodge went to the phone and ordered Admiral Gallery to send the reply.

Z141030ZDEC
TOP SECRET
FR: COMSUBLANT

214

TO: USS DALLAS

A. USS DALLAS Z140925ZDEC

1. CONTINUE TRACKING. REPORT ANY CHANGES IN COURSE OR SPEED. HELP ON THE WAY.

2. ELF TRANSMISSION 'G' DESIGNATES FLASH OPS DIRECTIVE READY FOR YOU.

3. YOUR OPAREA UNRESTRICTED. BRAVO ZULU DALLAS KEEP IT UP. VADM GALLERY SENDS.

'Okay, let's look at this,' Harris said. 'What the Russians are up to never has figured, has it?'

'What do you mean, Eddie?' Hilton asked.

'Their force composition for one thing. Half these surface platforms are anti-air and anti-surface, not primary ASW assets. And why bring *Kirov* along at all? Granted she makes a nice force flag, but they could do the same thing with *Kiev*.'

'We talked about that already,' Foster observed. 'They ran down the list of what they had that could travel this far at a high speed of advance and took everything that would steam. Same with the subs they sent, half of them are antisurface SSGNs with limited utility against submarines. The reason, Eddie, is that Gorshkov wants every platform here he can get. A half-capable ship is better than nothing. Even one of the old *Echoes* might get lucky, and Sergey is probably hitting the knees every night praying for luck.'

'Even so, they've split their surface groups into three forces, each with anti-air and anti-surface elements, and they're kind of thin on ASW hulls. Nor have they sent their ASW aircraft to stage out of Cuba. Now that is curious,' Harris pointed out.

'It would blow their cover story. You don't look for a dead sub with aircraft – well, they might, but if they started using a wing of Bears out of Cuba, the president would go ape,' Foster said. 'We'd harass them so much they'd never accomplish anything. For us this would be a technical operation, but they factor politics into everything they do.'

'Fine, but that still doesn't explain it. What ASW ships and choppers they do have are pinging away like mad. You might look for a dead sub that way, but *October* ain't dead, is she?'

'I don't understand, Eddie,' Hilton said.

'How would you look for a stray sub, given these circumstances?' Harris asked Foster.

'Not like this,' Foster said after a moment. 'Using surface, active sonar would warn the boat off long before they could get a hard contact. Boomers are fat on passive sonar. She'd hear them coming and skedaddle out of the way. You're right, Eddie. It's a sham.'

'So what the hell are their surface ships up to?' Barnes asked, puzzled.

215

'Soviet naval doctrine is to use surface ships to support submarine operations,' Harris explained. 'Gorshkov is a decent tactical theoretician, and occasionally a very innovative gent. He said years ago that for submarines to operate effectively they have to have outside help, air or surface assets in direct or proximate support. They can't use air this far from home without staging out of Cuba, and at best finding a boat in open ocean that doesn't want to be found would be a difficult assignment.

'On the other hand, they know where she's heading, a limited number of discrete areas, and those are staked out with fifty-eight submarines. The purpose of the surface forces, therefore, is not to participate in the hunt itself – though if they got lucky, they wouldn't mind. The purpose of the surface forces is to keep us from interfering with their submarines. They can do that by staking out the areas we're likely to be with their surface assets and watching what we're doing.' Harris paused for a moment. 'That's smart. We have to cover them, right? And since they're on a "rescue" mission, we have to do more or less what they're doing, so we ping away also, and they can use our own ASW expertise against us for their own purposes. We play right into their hands.'

'Why?' Barnes asked again.

'We're committed to helping in the search. If we find their boat, they're close enough to find out, acquire, localize, and shoot – and what can we do about it? Not a thing.

'Like I said, they figure to locate and shoot with their submarines. A surface acquisition would be pure luck, and you don't plan for luck. So, the primary objective of the surface fleets is to ride shotgun for, and draw our forces away from, their subs. Secondarily they can act as beaters, driving the game to the shooters – and again, since we're pinging, we're helping them. We're providing an additional stalking horse.' Harris shook his head in grudging admiration. 'Not too shabby, is it? If *Red October* hears them coming, she runs a little harder for whatever port the skipper wants, right into a nice, tight trap. Dan, what are the chances they can bag her coming into Norfolk, say?'

Foster looked down at the chart. Russian submarines were staked out on every port from Maine to Florida. 'They have more subs than we have ports. Now we know that this guy can be picked up, and there's only so much area to cover off each port, even outside the territorial limit . . . You're right, Eddie. They have too good a chance of making the kill. Our surface groups are too far away to do anything about it. Our subs don't know what's happening, we have orders not to tell them, and even if we could, how could they interfere? Fire at the Russian subs before they could shoot – and start a war?' Foster let out a long breath. 'We gotta warn him off.'

'How?' Hilton asked.

'Sonar, a gertrude message maybe,' Harris suggested.

Admiral Dodge shook his head. 'You can hear that through the hull. If we continue to assume that only the officers are in on this, well, the crew might figure out what's happening, and there's no predicting the consequences. Think we can use *Nimitz* and *America* to force them off the coast? They'll be close enough to enter the operation soon. Damn! I don't want this guy to get this close, then get blown away right off our coast.'

'Not a chance,' Harris said. 'Ever since the raid on *Kirov* they've been acting too docile. That's pretty cute, too. I bet they had that figured out. They know that having so many of their ships operating off our coast is bound to provoke us, so they make the first move, we up the ante, and they just plain fold – so now if we keep leaning on them, we're the bad guys. They're just doing a rescue operation, not threatening anybody. The *Post* reported this morning that we have a Russian survivor in the Norfolk naval hospital. Anyway, the good news is that they've miscalculated *October*'s speed. These two groups will pass her left and right, and with their seven-knot speed advantage they'll just pass her by.'

'Disregard the surface groups entirely?' Maxwell asked.

'No,' Hilton said, 'that tells them we are no longer buying the cover story. They'd wonder why – and we still have to cover their surface groups. They're a threat whether they're acting like honest merchants or not.'

'What we can do is pretend to release *Invincible*. With *Nimitz* and *America* ready to enter the game, we can send her home. As they pass *October* we can use that to our advantage. We put *Invincible* to seaward of their surface groups as though she's heading home and interpose her on *October*'s course. We still have to figure out a way to communicate with her, though. I can see how to get the assets in place, but that hurdle remains, gentlemen. For the moment, are we agreed to position *Invincible* and *Pogy* for the intercept?'

The *Invincible*

'How far is she from us?' Ryan asked.

'Two hundred miles. We can be there in ten hours.' Captain Hunter marked the position on the chart. 'USS *Pogy* is coming east, and she ought to be able to rendezvous with *Dallas* an hour or so after we do. This will put us about a hundred miles east of this surface group when *October* arrives. Bloody hell, *Kiev* and *Kirov* are a hundred miles east and west of her.'

'You suppose her captain knows it?' Ryan looked at the chart, measuring the distances with his eyes.

'Unlikely. He's deep, and their passive sonars are not as good as ours. Sea conditions are against it also. A twenty-knot surface wind can play havoc with sonar, even that deep.'

'We have to warn him off.' Admiral White looked at the ops dispatch. '"Without using acoustical devices."'

'How the hell do you do that? You can't reach down that far with a radio,' Ryan noted. 'Even I know that. My God, this guy's come four thousand miles, and he's going to get killed within sight of his objective.'

'How to communicate with a submarine?'

Commander Barclay straightened up. 'Gentlemen, we are not trying to communicate with a submarine, we are trying to communicate with a man.'

'What are you thinking?' Hunter asked.

'What do we know about Marko Ramius?' Barclay's eyes narrowed.

'He's a cowboy, typical submarine commander, thinks he can walk on water,' Captain Carstairs said.

'Who spent most of his time in attack submarines,' Barclay added. 'Marko's bet his life that he could sneak into an American port undetected by anyone. We have to shake that confidence to warn him off.'

'We have to talk to him first,' Ryan said sharply.

'And so we shall,' Barclay smiled, the thought now fully formed in his mind. 'He's a former attack submarine commander. He'll still be thinking about how to attack his enemies, and how does a sub commander do that?'

'Well?' Ryan demanded.

Barclay's answer was the obvious one. They discussed his idea for another hour, then Ryan transmitted it to Washington for approval. A rapid exchange of technical information followed. The *Invincible* would have to make the rendezvous in daylight, and there was not time for that. The operation was set back twelve hours. The *Pogy* joined formation with the *Invincible*, standing as sonar sentry twenty miles to her east. An hour before midnight, the ELF transmitter in northern Michigan transmitted a message: 'G.' Twenty minutes later, the *Dallas* approached the surface to get her orders.

The Thirteenth Day

Wednesday, 15 December

The *Dallas*

'Crazy Ivan,' Jones called out again, 'turning to port!'

'Okay, all stop,' Mancuso ordered, holding a dispatch in his hand which he had been rereading for hours. He was not pleased with it.

'All stop, sir,' the helmsman responded.

'All back full.'

'All back full, sir.' The helmsman dialled in the command and turned, his face a question.

Throughout the *Dallas* the crew heard noise, too much noise as poppet valves opened to vent steam on to the reverse turbine blades, trying to spin the propeller the wrong way. It made for instant vibration and cavitation noises aft.

'Right full rudder.'

'Right full rudder, aye.'

'Conn, sonar, we are cavitating,' Jones spoke over the intercom.

'Very well, sonar!' Mancuso answered sharply. He did not understand his new orders, and things he didn't understand made him angry.

'Speed down to four knots,' Lieutenant Goodman reported.

'Rudder amidships, all stop.'

'Rudder amidships aye, all stop aye,' the helmsman responded at once. He didn't want the captain barking at him. 'Sir, my rudder is amidships.'

'Jesus!' Jones said in the sonar room. 'What's the skipper doin'?'

Mancuso was in sonar a second later. 'Still doing the turn to port, Cap'n. He's astern of us 'cause of the turn we made,' Jones observed as neutrally as he could. It was close to an accusation, Mancuso noticed.

'Flushing the game, Jonesy,' Mancuso said coolly.

You're the boss, Jones thought, smart enough not to say anything else. The captain looked as though he was going to snap somebody's head off, and Jones had just used up a month's worth of tolerance. He switched his phones to the towed array plug.

'Engine noises diminishing, sir. He's slowing down,' Jones paused. He had to report the next part. 'Sir, it's a fair guess he heard us.'

'He was supposed to,' Mancuso said.

The *Red October*

'Captain, an enemy submarine,' the *michman* said urgently.

'Enemy?' Ramius asked.

'American. He must have been trailing us, and he had to back down to avoid a collision when we turned. Definitely an American, broad on the port bow, range under a kilometre, I think.' He handed Ramius his phones.

'688,' Ramius said to Borodin. 'Damn! He must have stumbled across us in the past two hours. Bad luck.'

The *Dallas*

'Okay, Jonesy, yankee-search him.' Mancuso gave the order for an active sonar search personally. The *Dallas* had slewed further around before coming to a near halt.

Jones hesitated for a moment, still reading the reactor plant noise on his passive systems. Reaching, he powered up the active transducers in the BQQ-5's main sphere at the bow.

Ping! A wave front of sound energy was directed at the target.

Pong! The wave was reflected back off the hard steel hull and returned to the *Dallas*.

'Range to target, 1,050 yards,' Jones said. The returning pulse was processed through the BC-10 computer and showed some rough details. 'Target configuration is consistent with a *Typhoon*-class boomer. Angle on the bow seventy or so. No doppler. He's stopped.' Six more pings confirmed this.

'Secure pinging,' Mancuso said. There was some small satisfaction in learning that he had evaluated the contact correctly. But not much.

Jones killed power to the system. What the hell did I have to do that for? he wondered. He'd already done everything but read the number off her stern.

The *Red October*

Every man on the *October* knew now that they had been found. The lash of the sonar waves had resounded through the hull. It was not a sound a submariner liked to hear. Certainly not on top of a troublesome reactor, Ramius thought. Perhaps he could make use of this . . .

The *Dallas*

'Somebody on the surface,' Jones said suddenly. 'Where the hell did they come from? Skipper, there was nothing, *nothing*, a minute ago, and now I'm getting engine sounds. Two, maybe more – make that two 'cans . . . and something bigger. Like they were sitting up there waiting for us. A minute ago they were sitting still. Damn! I didn't hear a *thing*.'

The *Invincible*

'We timed that rather nicely,' Admiral White said.

'Lucky,' Ryan observed.

'Luck is part of the game, Jack.'

HMS *Bristol* was the first to pick up the sound of the two submarines and of the turn the *Red October* had made. Even at five miles the subs were barely readable. The Crazy Ivan manoeuvre had terminated three miles away, and the surface ships had been able to get good position fixes by reading off the *Dallas*' active sonar emissions.

'Two helicopters en route, sir,' Captain Hunter reported. 'They'll be on station in another minute.'

'Signal *Bristol* and *Fife* to stay to windward of us. I want *Invincible* between them and the contact.'

'Aye aye, sir.' Hunter relayed the order to the communications room. The destroyermen on the escorts would find that order peculiar, using a carrier to screen destroyers.

A few seconds later a pair of Sea King helicopters stopped and hovered fifty feet over the surface, letting down dipping sonars at the end of a cable as they struggled to hold position. These sonars were far less powerful than ship-carried sonars and had distinctive characteristics. The data they developed was transmitted by digital link to the *Invincible*'s command centre.

The *Dallas*

'Limeys,' Jones said at once. 'That's a helicopter set, the 195, I think. That means the big ship off to the south is one of their baby carriers, sir, with a two-can escort.'

Mancuso nodded. 'HMS *Invincible*. She was over our side of the lake for NIFTY DOLPHIN. That means the Brit varsity, their best ASW operators.'

'The big one's moving this way, sir. Turns indicate ten knots. The choppers – two of them – have both of us. No other subs around that I hear.'

The *Invincible*

'Positive sonar contact,' said the metal speaker. 'Two submarines, range two miles from *Invincible*, bearing zero-two-zero.'

'Now for the hard part,' Admiral White said.

Ryan and the four Royal Navy officers who were privy to the mission were on the flag bridge, with the fleet ASW officer in the command centre below, as the *Invincible* steamed slowly north, slightly to the left of the direct course to the contacts. All five swept the contact area with powerful binoculars.

'Come on, Captain Ramius,' Ryan said quietly. 'You're supposed to be a hotshot. Prove it.'

The *Red October*

Ramius was back in his control room scowling at his chart. A stray American *Los Angeles* stumbling on to him was one thing, but he had run into a small task force. English ships, at that. Why? Probably an exercise. The Americans and the English often worked together, and pure accident had walked *October* right into them. Well. He'd have to evade before he could get on with what he wanted to do. It was that simple. Or was it? A hunter submarine, a carrier, and two destroyers after him. What else? He would have to find out if he were going to lose them all. This would take the best part of a day. But now he'd have to see what he was up against. Besides, it would show them that he was confident, that he could hunt *them* if he wished.

'Borodin, bring the ship to periscope depth. Battle stations.'

The *Invincible*

'Come up, Marko,' Barclay urged. 'We have a message for you, old boy.'

'Helicopter three reports contact is coming up,' the speaker said.

White lifted a phone. 'Recall one of the helicopters.'

The distance to the *Red October* was down to a mile and a half. One of the Sea Kings lifted up and circled around, reeling in its sonar transducer.

'Contact depth is five hundred feet, coming up slowly.'

The *Red October*

Borodin was pumping water slowly from the *October*'s trim tanks. The missile submarine increased speed to four knots, and most of the force required to change her depth came from the diving planes. The *starpom* was careful to bring her up slowly, and Ramius had her heading directly towards the *Invincible*.

The *Invincible*

'Hunter, are you up on your Morse?' Admiral White inquired.

'I believe so, Admiral,' Hunter answered. Everyone was getting excited. What a chance this was!

Ryan swallowed hard. In the past few hours, while the *Invincible* had been lying still on the rolling sea, his stomach had really gone bad. The pills the ship's doctor had given him helped, but now the excitement was making it worse. There was an eighty-foot sheer drop from the flag bridge to the sea. Well, he thought, if I have to puke, there's nothing in the way. Screw it.

The *Dallas*

'Hull popping noises, sir,' Jones said. 'Think he's heading up.'

'Up?' Mancuso wondered for a second. 'Yeah, that fits. He's a cowboy. He wants to see what he's up against before he tries to evade. That fits. I bet he doesn't know where we've been the past two days.' The captain went forward to the attack centre.

'Looks like he's going up, Skipper,' Mannion said, watching the attack director. 'Dumb.' Mannion had his own opinion of submarine captains depending on their periscopes. Too many of them spent too much time looking out at the world. He wondered how much of this was an implicit reaction to the enforced confinement of submarining, something just to make sure that there really was a world up there, to make sure the instruments were correct. Entirely human, Mannion thought, but it could make you vulnerable . . .

'We go up, too, Skipper?'

'Yeah, slow and easy.'

The *Invincible*

The sky was half-filled with white, fleecy clouds, their undersides grey with the threat of rain. A twenty-knot wind was blowing from the south-west, and a six-foot sea was running, its dark waves streaked with whitecaps. Ryan saw the *Bristol* and *Fife* holding station to windward. Their captains, no doubt, were muttering a few choice words at this disposition. The American escorts, which had been detached the previous day, were now sailing to rendezvous with the USS *New Jersey*.

White was talking into the phone again. 'Commander, I want to know the instant we get a radar return from the target area. Train every set aboard on to that patch of ocean. I also want to know of any, repeat any, sonar signals from that area . . . That is correct. Depth of target? Very well. Recall the second helicopter, I want both on station to windward.'

They had agreed that the best method of passing the message would be to use a blinker light. Only someone placed in the direct line of sight would be able to read the signal. Hunter moved to the light, holding a sheet of paper Ryan had given him. The yeomen and signalmen normally stationed here were gone.

The *Red October*

'Thirty metres, Comrade Captain,' Borodin reported. The battle watch was set in the control centre.

'Periscope,' Ramius said calmly. The oiled metal tube hissed upward on hydraulic pressure. The captain handed his cap to the junior officer of the watch as he bent to look into the eyepiece. 'So, we have here three imperialist ships. HMS *Invincible*. Such a name for a ship!' He scoffed for his audience. 'Two escorts, *Bristol*, and a County-class cruiser.'

The *Invincible*

'Periscope, starboard bow!' the speaker announced.

'I see it!' Barclay's hand shot out to point. 'There it is!'

Ryan strained to find it. 'I got it.' It was like a small broomstick sitting vertically in the water, about a mile away. As the waves rolled past, the bottom-most visible part of the periscope flared out.

'Hunter,' White said quietly. To Ryan's left the captain began jerking his hand on the lever that controlled the light shutters.

The *Red October*

Ramius didn't see it at first. He was making a complete circle of the horizon, checking for any other ships or aircraft. When he finished the circuit, the flashing light caught his eye. Quickly he tried to interpret the signal. It took him a moment to realize it was pointed right at him.

AAA AAA AAA RED OCTOBER CAN YOU READ THIS CAN YOU READ THIS PLEASE PING US ONE TIME ON ACTIVE SONAR IF YOU CAN READ THIS PLEASE PING US ONE TIME ON ACTIVE SONAR IF YOU CAN READ THIS AAA AAA AAA RED OCTOBER RED OCTOBER CAN YOU READ THIS CAN YOU READ THIS

The message kept repeating. The signal was jerky and awkward. Ramius didn't notice this. He translated the English signal in his head, at first thinking it was a signal to the American submarine. His knuckles went white on the periscope hand grips as he translated the message in his mind.

'Borodin,' he said finally, after reading the message a fourth time, 'we set up a practice firing solution on *Invincible*. Damn, the periscope rangefinder is sticking. A single ping, Comrade. Just one, for range.'

Ping!

The *Invincible*

'One ping from the contact area, sir, sound Soviet,' the speaker reported.

White lifted his phone. 'Thank you. Keep us informed.' He set it back down. 'Well, gentlemen . . . '

'He did it!' Ryan sang out. 'Send the rest, for Christ's sake!'

'At once.' Hunter grinned like a madman.

RED OCTOBER RED OCTOBER YOUR WHOLE FLEET IS CHASING AFTER YOU YOUR WHOLE FLEET IS CHASING AFTER YOU YOUR PATH IS BLOCKED BY NUMEROUS VESSELS NUMEROUS ATTACK SUBMARINES ARE WAITING TO ATTACK YOU REPEAT NUMEROUS ATTACK SUBMARINES ARE WAITING TO ATTACK YOU PROCEED TO RENDEZVOUS 33N 75W WE HAVE SHIPS THERE WAITING FOR YOU REPEAT PROCEED TO RENDEZVOUS 33N 75W WE HAVE SHIPS THERE WAITING FOR YOU IF YOU UNDERSTAND AND AGREE PLEASE PING US AGAIN ONE TIME

The *Red October*

'Distance to target, Borodin?' Ramius asked, wishing he had more time as the message was repeated again and again.

'Two thousand metres, Comrade Captain. A nice, fat target for us if we . . . ' The *starpom*'s voice trailed off as he saw the commander's face.

They know our name, Ramius was thinking, *they know our name! How can this be? They knew where to find us – exactly! How? What can the*

Americans have? How long has the Los Angeles *been trailing us? Decide – you must decide!*

'Comrade, one more ping on the target, just one.'

The *Invincible*

'One more ping, Admiral.'

'Thank you.' White looked at Ryan. 'Well, Jack, it would seem that your intelligence estimate was indeed correct. Jolly good.'

'Jolly good my ass, my Lord Earl! I was right! Son of a *bitch!*' Ryan's hands flew up in the air, his seasickness forgotten. He calmed down. The occasion called for more decorum. 'Excuse me, Admiral. We have some things to do.'

The *Dallas*

Whole fleet is chasing after you . . . . Proceed to 33N 75W. What the hell is going on? Mancuso wondered, catching the end of the second signal.

'Conn, sonar. Getting hull popping noises from the target. His depth is changing. Engine noise increasing.'

'Down scope.' Mancuso lifted the phone. 'Very well, sonar. Anything else, Jones?'

'No, sir. The helicopters are gone, and there aren't any emissions from the surface ships. What gives, sir?'

'Beats me.' Mancuso shook his head as Mannion brought the *Dallas* back in pursuit of the *Red October*. What the hell was happening here? the captain wondered. Why was a Brit carrier signalling to a Russian submarine, and why were they sending her to a rendezvous off the Carolinas? Whose subs were blocking her path? It couldn't be. No way. It just couldn't be . . .

The *Invincible*

Ryan was in the *Invincible*'s communications room. 'MAGI TO OLYMPUS,' he typed into the special encoding device the CIA had sent out with him, 'PLAYED MY MANDOLIN TODAY. SOUNDED PRETTY GOOD. I'M PLANNING A LITTLE CONCERT, AT THE USUAL PLACE. EXPECT GOOD CRITICAL REVIEWS. AWAITING INSTRUCTIONS.' Ryan had laughed before at the code words he was supposed to use for this. He was laughing now, for a different reason.

The White House

'So,' Pelt observed, 'Ryan expects the mission will be successful. Everything's going according to plan, but he didn't use the code group for certain success.'

The president leaned back comfortably. 'He's honest. Things can always go wrong. You have to admit, though, things do look good.'

'This plan the chiefs came up with is crazy, sir.'

'Perhaps, but you've been trying to poke a hole in it for several days now, and you haven't succeeded. The pieces will all fall in place shortly.'

The president was being clever, Pelt saw. The man liked being clever.

The *Invincible*

'OLYMPUS TO MAGI. I LIKE OLD-FASHIONED MANDOLIN MUSIC. CONCERT APPROVED,' the message said.

Ryan sat back comfortably, sipping at his brandy. 'Well, that's good. I wonder what the next part of the plan is?'

'I expect that Washington will let us know. For the moment,' Admiral White said, 'we'll have to move back west to interpose ourselves between *October* and the Soviet fleet.'

The *Avalon*

Lieutenant Ames surveyed the scene through the tiny port on the *Avalon*'s bow. The *Alfa* lay on her port side. She had obviously hit stern first, and hard. One blade was snapped off the propeller, and the lower rudder fin was smashed. The whole stern might have been knocked off true; it was hard to tell in the low visibility.

'Moving forward slowly,' he said, adjusting the controls. Behind him an ensign and a senior petty officer were monitoring instruments and preparing to deploy the manipulator arm, attached before they sailed, which carried a television camera and floodlights. These gave them a slightly wider field of view than the navigation ports permitted. The DSRV crept forward at one knot. Visibility was under twenty yards, despite the million candles of illumination from the bow lights.

The sea floor at this point was a treacherous slope of alluvial silt dotted with boulders. It appeared that the only thing that had prevented the *Alfa* from sliding farther down was her sail, driven like a wedge into the bottom.

'Holy gawd!' The petty officer saw it first. There was a crack in the *Alfa*'s hull – or was there?

'Reactor accident,' Ames said, his voice detached and clinical. 'Something burned through the hull. Lord, and that's titanium! Burned right through, from the inside out. There's another one, two burn-throughs. This one's bigger, looks like a good yard across. No mystery what killed her, guys: That's two compartments open to the sea.' Ames looked over to the depth gauge: 1,880 feet. 'Getting all this on tape?'

'Aye, Skipper,' the electrician first class answered. 'Crummy way to die. Poor bastards.'

'Yeah, depending on what they were up to.' Ames manoeuvred the *Avalon* around the *Alfa*'s bow, working the directional propeller carefully and adjusting trim to cruise down the other side, actually the top of the dead sub. 'See any evidence of a hull fracture?'

'No,' the ensign answered, 'just the two burn-throughs. I wonder what went wrong.'

'A for-real China Syndrome. It finally happened to somebody.' Ames shook his head. If there was anything the navy preached about reactors, it was safety. 'Get the transducer against the hull. We'll see if anybody's alive in there.'

'Aye.' The electrician worked the waldo controls as Ames tried to keep the *Avalon* dead still. Neither task was easy. The DSRV was hovering, nearly resting on the sail. If there were survivors, they had to be in the control room or forward. There could be no life aft.

'Okay, I got contact.'

All three men listened intently, hoping for something. Their job was search and rescue, and as submariners themselves they took it seriously.

'Maybe they're asleep.' The ensign switched on the locater sonar. The high-frequency waves resonated through both vessels. It was a sound fit to wake the dead, but there was no response. The air supply in the *Politovskiy* had run out a day before.

'That's that,' Ames said quietly. He manoeuvred upward as the electrician rigged in the manipulator arm, looking for a spot to drop a sonar transponder. They would be back again when the topside weather was better. The navy would not pass up this chance to inspect an *Alfa*, and the *Glomar Explorer* was sitting unused somewhere on the West Coast. Would she be activated? Ames would not bet against that.

'*Avalon*, *Avalon*, this is *Scamp* – ,' the voice on the gertrude was distorted but readable, ' – return at once. Acknowledge.'

'*Scamp*, this is *Avalon*. On the way.'

The *Scamp* had just received an ELF message and gone briefly to periscope depth for a FLASH operational order. 'PROCEED AT BEST SPEED TO 33N 75W.' The message didn't say why.

CIA Headquarters

'CARDINAL is still with us,' Moore told Ritter.

'Thank God for that.' Ritter sat down.

'There's a signal en route. This time he didn't try to kill himself getting it to us. Maybe being in the hospital scared him a little. I'm extending another offer to extract him.'

'Again?'

'Bob, we have to make the offer.'

'I know. I had one sent myself a few years back, you know. The old bastard just doesn't want to quit. You know how it goes, some people thrive on the

227

action. Or maybe he hasn't worked out his rage yet . . . I just got a call from Senator Donaldson.' Donaldson was the chairman of the Select Committee on Intelligence.

'Oh?'

'He wants to know what we know about what's going on. He doesn't buy the cover story about a rescue mission, and thinks we know something different.'

Judge Moore leaned back. 'I wonder who planted that idea in his head?'

'Yeah. I have a little idea we might try. I think it's time and this is a dandy opportunity.'

The two senior executives discussed this for an hour. Before Ritter left for the Hill, they cleared it with the president.

Washington, DC

Donaldson kept Ritter waiting in his outer office for fifteen minutes while he read the paper. He wanted Ritter to know his place. Some of the DDO's remarks about leaks from the Hill had touched a sore spot with the senator from Connecticut, and it was important for appointed and civil service officials to understand the difference between themselves and the elected representatives of the people.

'Sorry to keep you waiting, Mr Ritter.' Donaldson did not rise, nor did he offer to shake hands.

'Quite all right, sir. Took the chance to read a magazine. Don't get to do that much, what with the schedule I work.' They fenced with each other for the first moment.

'So, what are the Soviets up to?'

'Senator, before I address that subject, I must say this: I had to clear this meeting with the president. This information is for you alone, no one else may hear it, sir. No one. That comes from the White House.'

'There are other men on my committee, Mr Ritter.'

'Sir, if I do not have your word, as a gentleman,' Ritter added with a smile, 'I will not reveal this information. Those are my orders. I work for the executive branch, Senator. I take my orders from the president.' Ritter hoped his recording device was getting all of this.

'Agreed,' Donaldson said reluctantly. He was angry because of the foolish restrictions, but pleased that he was getting to hear this. 'Go on.'

'Frankly, sir, we're not sure exactly what's going on.' Ritter said.

'Oh, so you've sworn me to secrecy so that I can't tell anyone that, again, the CIA doesn't know what the hell is going on?'

'I said we don't know exactly what's happening. We do know a few things. Our information comes mainly from the Israelis, and some from the French. From both channels we have learned that something has gone very wrong with the Soviet Navy.'

'I gathered that. They've lost a sub.'

'At least one, but that's not what's going on. Someone, we think, has played a trick on the operations directorate of the Soviet Northern Fleet. I can't say for sure, but I think it was the Poles.'

'Why the Poles?'

'I don't know for sure that it is, but both the French and Israelis are well connected with the Poles, *and* the Poles have a long-standing beef with the Soviets. I do know – at least I think I know – that whatever this is did not come from a Western intelligence agency.'

'So, what's happening?' Donaldson demanded.

'Our best guess is that someone has committed at least one forgery, possibly as many as three, all aimed at raising hell in the Soviet Navy – but whatever it was, it's gotten far out of hand. A lot of people are working hard to cover their asses, the Israelis say. As a guess, I think they managed to alter a submarine's operational orders, then forged a letter from her skipper threatening to fire his missiles. The amazing thing is that the Soviets went for it.' Ritter frowned. 'We may have it all backwards, though. All we really know for sure is that somebody, probably the Poles, has played a fantastic dirty trick on the Russians.'

'Not us?' Donaldson asked pointedly.

'No, sir, absolutely not! If we tried something like that – even if we succeeded, which isn't likely – they might try the same thing with us. You could start a war that way, and you know the president would never authorize it.'

'But someone at the CIA might not care what the president thinks.'

'Not in my department! It would be my head. Do you really think we could run an operation like this and then successfully conceal it? Hell, Senator, I *wish* we could.'

'Why the Poles, and why are they able to do it?'

'We've been hearing for some time about a dissident faction inside their intelligence community, one that does not especially love the Soviets. You can pick any number of reasons why. There's the fundamental historical enmity, and the Russians seem to forget that the Poles are Polish first, Communists second. My own guess is that it's this business with the pope, even more than the martial law thing. We know that our old friend Andropov initiated a replay of the Henry II/Becket business. The pope has given Poland a great deal of prestige, done things for the country that even Party members feel good about. Ivan went and spat on their whole country when he did that – you wonder that they're mad? As to their ability, people seem to overlook just what a class act their intelligence service always has been. They're the ones who made the Enigma breakthrough in 1939, not the the Brits. They're damned effective, and for the same reason as the Israelis. They have enemies to the east and the west. That sort of thing breeds good agents. We know for certain that they have a lot of people inside Russia, guest workers paying Narmonov off for the economic supports given to their country. We also know that a lot of Polish engineers are working in Soviet shipyards. I admit it's funny, neither country has much of a maritime tradition, but the Poles build lots of Soviet merchant hulls. Their yards are more efficient than the Russian ones, and lately they've been giving technical help, mainly in quality control, to the naval building yards.'

'So, the Polish intelligence service has played a trick on the Soviets,' Donaldson summarized. 'Gorshkov was one of the guys who took a hard line on intervention, wasn't he?'

'True, but he's probably just a target of opportunity. The real aim of this has to be to embarrass Moscow. The fact that this operation attacks the Soviet Navy has no significance in itself. The objective is to raise hell in their senior military channels, and they all come together in Moscow. God, I wish I knew what was really happening! From the five per-cent we do know, this operation has to be a real masterpiece, the sort of thing legends are made of. We're working on it, trying to find out. So are the Brits, and the French, and the Israelis – Benny Herzog of the Mossad is supposed to be going ape. The Israelis do pull this kind of trick on their neighbours, regularly. They say officially that they don't know anything beyond what they've told us. Maybe so. Or maybe they gave the Poles some technical help – hard to say. It's certain that the Soviet Navy is a strategic threat to Israel. But we need more time on that. The Israeli connection looks a little too pat at this point.'

'But you don't know what's happening, just the how and why.'

'Senator, it's not that easy. Give us some time. At the moment we may not even want to know. To summarize, somebody has laid a colossal piece of disinformation on the Soviet Navy. It was probably aimed at merely shaking them up, but it has clearly gotten out of hand. How or why it happened, we do not know. You can bet, however, that whoever initiated this operation is working very hard to cover his tracks.' Ritter wanted the senator to get this right.

'If the Soviets find out who did it, their reaction will be nasty – depend on it. In a few weeks we might know more. The Israelis owe us for a few things, and eventually they'll let us in on it.'

'For a couple more F-15s and a company of tanks,' Donaldson observed.

'Cheap at the price.'

'But if we're not involved in this, why the secrecy?'

'You gave me your word, Senator,' Ritter reminded him. 'For one thing, if word leaked out, would the Soviets believe we're not involved? Not likely! We're trying to civilize the intelligence game. I mean, we're still enemies, but having the various intelligence services in conflict uses up too many assets, and it's dangerous to both sides. For another, well, if we ever do find out how all this happened, we just might want to make use of it ourselves.'

'Those reasons are contradictory.'

Ritter smiled. 'The intelligence game is like that. If we find out who did this, we can use that information to our advantage. In any case, Senator, you gave me your word, and I will report that to the president on my return to Langley.'

'Very well.' Donaldson rose. The interview was at an end. 'I trust you will keep us informed of future developments.'

'That's what we have to do, sir.' Ritter stood.

'Indeed. Thank you for coming down. ' They did not shake hands this time either.

Ritter walked into the hall without passing through the anteroom. He stopped to look down into the atrium of the Hart building. It reminded him of the local Hyatt. Uncharacteristically, he took the stairs instead of the elevator down to the first floor. With luck he had just settled a major score. His car was waiting for him outside, and he told the driver to head for the FBI building.

'Not a CIA operation?' Peter Henderson, the senator's chief aide, asked.

'No. I believe him,' Donaldson said. 'He's not smart enough to pull something like that.'

'I don't know why the president doesn't get rid of him,' Henderson commented. 'Of course, the kind of person he is, maybe it's better that he's incompetent.' The senator agreed.

When he returned to his office, Henderson adjusted the venetian blinds on his window, though the sun was on the other side of the building. An hour later the driver of a passing Black & White taxicab looked up at the window and made a mental note.

Henderson worked late that night. The Hart building was nearly empty with most of the senators out of town. Donaldson was there only because of personal business and to keep an eye on things. As chairman of the Select Committee on Intelligence he had more duties than he would have liked at this time of year. Henderson took the elevator down to the main lobby, looking every inch the senior congressional aide – a three-piece grey suit, an expensive leather attaché case, his hair just so, and his stride jaunty as he left the building. A Black & White cab came around the corner and stopped to let out a fare. Henderson got in.

'Watergate,' he said. Not until the taxi had driven a few blocks did he speak again.

Henderson had a modest one-bedroom apartment in the Watergate complex, an irony that he himself had considered many times. When he got to his destination he did not tip the driver. A woman got in as he walked to the main entrance. Taxis in Washington are very busy in the early evening.

'Georgetown University, please,' she said, a pretty young woman with auburn hair and an armload of books.

'Night school?' the driver asked, checking the mirror.

'Exams,' the girl said, her voice a trace uneasy. 'Psych.'

'Best thing to do with exams is relax,' the driver advised.

Special Agent Hazel Loomis fumbled with her books. Her purse dropped to the floor. 'Oh, damn.' She bent over to pick it up, and while doing so retrieved a miniature tape recorder that another agent had left under the driver's seat.

It took fifteen minutes to get to the university. The fare was $3.85. Loomis gave the driver a five and told him to keep the change. She walked across the campus and entered a Ford which drove straight to the J. Edgar Hoover Building. A lot of work had gone into this – and it had been so easy!

'Always is, when the bear walks into your sight.' The inspector who had been running the case turned left on to Pennsylvania Avenue. 'The problem is finding the damned bear in the first place.'

The Pentagon

'Gentlemen, you have been asked here because each of you is a career intelligence officer with a working knowledge of submarines and Russian,' Davenport said to the four officers seated in his office. 'I have need of officers with your qualifications. This is a volunteer assignment. It could involve a considerable element of danger – we cannot be sure at this point. The only other thing I can say is that this will be a dream job for an intelligence officer – but the sort of dream that you'll never be able to tell anyone about. We're all used to that, aren't we?' Davenport ventured a rare smile. 'As they say in the movies, if you want in, fine; if not, you may leave at this point, and nothing will ever be said. It is asking a lot to expect men to walk into a potentially dangerous assignment blind-folded.'

Of course nobody left; the men who had been called here were not quitters. Besides, something would be said, and Davenport had a good memory. These were professional officers. One of the compensations for wearing a uniform and earning less money than an equally talented man can make in the real world is the off chance of being killed.

'Thank you, gentlemen. I think you will find this worth your while.' Davenport stood and handed each man a manila envelope. 'You will soon have the chance to examine a Soviet missile submarine – from the inside.' Four pairs of eyes blinked in unison.

33N 75W

The USS *Ethan Allen* had been on station now for more than thirty hours. She was cruising in a five-mile circle at a depth of two hundred feet. There was no hurry. The submarine was making just enough speed to maintain steerage way, her reactor producing only ten per cent of rated power. The chief quartermaster was assisting in the galley.

232

'First time I've ever done this in a sub,' one of the *Allen*'s officers who was acting as ship's cook noted, stirring an omelette.

The quartermaster sighed imperceptibly. They ought to have sailed with a proper cook, but theirs had been a kid, and every enlisted man aboard now had over twenty years of service. The chiefs were all technicians, except the quarter-master, who could handle a toaster on a good day.

'You cook much at home, sir?'

'Some. My parents used to have a restaurant down at Pass Christian. This is my mama's special Cajun omelette. Shame we don't have any bass. I can do some nice things with bass and a little lemon. You fish much, Chief?'

'No, sir.' The small complement of officers and senior chiefs was working in an informal atmosphere, and the quartermaster was a man accustomed to discipline and status boundaries. 'Commander, can I ask what the hell we're doing?'

'Wish I knew, Chief. Mostly we're waiting for something.'

'But what, sir?'

'Damned if I know. You want to hand me those ham cubes? And could you check the bread in the oven? Ought to be about done.'

The *New Jersey*

Commodore Eaton was perplexed. His battle group was holding twenty miles south of the Russians. If it hadn't been dark he could have seen the *Kirov*'s towering superstructure on the horizon from his perch on the flag bridge. Her escorts were in a single broad line ahead of the battle cruiser, pinging away in the search for a submarine.

Since the air force had staged its mock attack the Soviets had been acting like sheep. This was out of character to say the least. The *New Jersey* and her escorts were keeping the Russian formation under constant observation, and a pair of Sentry aircraft were watching for good measure. The Russian redeployment had switched Eaton's responsibility to the *Kirov* group. This suited him. His main battery turrets were trained in, but the guns were loaded with eight-inch guided rounds and the fire control stations were fully manned. The *Tarawa* was thirty miles south, her armed strike force of Harriers sitting ready to move at five-minute notice. The Soviets had to know this, even though their ASW helicopters had not come within five miles of an American ship for two days. The Bear and Backfire bombers which were passing overhead in shuttle rounds to Cuba – only a few, and those returning to Russia as quickly as they could be turned around – could not fail to report what they saw. The American vessels were in extended attack formation, the missiles on the *New Jersey* and her escorts being fed continuous information from the ships' sensors. And the Russians were ignoring them. Their only electronic emissions were routine navigation radars. Strange.

The *Nimitz* was now within air range after a five-thousand-mile dash from the South Atlantic; the carrier and her nuclear-powered escorts, the *California, Bainbridge*, and *Truxton*, were now only four hundred miles to the south, and the *America* battle group half a day behind them. The *Kennedy* was five hundred miles to the east. The Soviets would have to consider the danger of three carrier air wings at their backs and hundreds of land-based air force birds gradually shifting south from one base to another. Perhaps this explained their docility.

The Backfire bombers were being escorted in relays all the way from Iceland, first by navy Tomcats from the *Saratoga*'s air wing, then by air force Phantoms operating in Maine, which handed the Soviet aircraft off to Eagles and Fighting Falcons as they worked down the coast almost as far south as Cuba. There was not much doubt how seriously the United States was taking this, though American units were no longer actively harassing the Russians. Eaton was glad they weren't. There was nothing more to be gained from harassment, and anyway, if it had to, his battle group could switch from a peace to a war footing in about two minutes.

The Watergate Apartments

'Excuse me, I just moved in down the hall, and my phone isn't hooked up yet. Would you mind if I made a call?'

Henderson arrived at that decision quickly enough. Five three or so, auburn hair, grey eyes, adequate figure, a dazzling smile, and fashionably dressed. 'Sure, welcome to the Watergate. Come on in.'

'Thank you. I'm Hazel Loomis. My friends call me Sissy.' She held out her hand.

'Pete Henderson. The phone's in the kitchen. I'll show you.' Things were looking up. He'd just ended a lengthy relationship with one of the senator's secretaries. It had been hard on both of them.

'I'm not disturbing anything, am I? You don't have anyone here, do you?'

'No, just me and the TV. Are you new to DC? The night life isn't all it's cracked up to be. At least, not when you have to go to work the next day. Who do you work for – I take it you're single?'

'That's right. I work for DARPA, as a computer programmer. I'm afraid I can't talk about it very much.'

All sorts of good news, Henderson thought. 'Here's the phone.'

Loomis looked around quickly as though evaluating the job the decorator had done. She reached into her purse and took out a dime, handing it to Henderson. He laughed.

'The first call is free, and believe me, you can use my phone whenever you want.'

'I just knew' she said, punching the buttons, 'that this would be nicer than living in Laurel. Hello, Kath? Sissy. I just got moved in, haven't even got my phone hooked up yet . . . Oh, a guy down the hall was kind enough to let me use his phone . . . Okay, see you tomorrow for lunch. Bye, Kathy.'

Loomis looked around. 'Who decorated for you?'

'Did it myself. I minored in art at Harvard, and I know some nice shops in Georgetown. You can find some good bargains if you know where to look.'

'Oh, I'd just *love* to have my place look like this! Could you show me around?'

'Sure, the bedroom first?' Henderson laughed to show that he had no untoward intentions – which of course he did, though he was a patient man in such matters. The tour, which lasted several minutes, assured Loomis that the apartment was indeed empty. A minute later there was a knock at the door. Henderson grumbled good-naturedly as he went to answer it.

'Pete Henderson?' The man asking the question was dressed in a business suit. Henderson had on jeans and a sport shirt.

'Yes?' Henderson backed up, knowing what this had to be. What came next, though, surprised him.

'You're under arrest, Mr Henderson,' Sissy Loomis said, holding up her ID card. 'The charge is espionage. You have the right to remain silent, you have the right to speak with an attorney. If you give up the right to remain silent, everything you say will be recorded and may be used against you. If you do not have an attorney or cannot afford one, we will see to it that an attorney is appointed to represent you. Do you understand these rights, Mr Henderson?' It was Sissy Loomis' first espionage case. For five years she had specialized in bank robbery stakeouts, often working as a teller with a .357 magnum revolver in her cash drawer. 'Do you wish to waive these rights?'

'No, I do not.' Henderson's voice was raspy.

'Oh, you will,' the inspector observed. 'You will.' He turned to the three agents who had accompanied him. 'Take this place apart. Neatly, gentlemen, and quietly. We don't want to wake anyone. You, Mr Henderson, will come with us. You can change first. We can do this the easy way or the hard way. If you promise to cooperate, no cuffs. But if you try to run – you don't want to do that, believe me.' The inspector had been in the FBI for twenty years and had never even drawn his service revolver in anger, while Loomis had already shot and killed two men. He was old-time FBI, and couldn't help but wonder what Mr Hoover would think of that, not to mention the new Jewish director.

The *Red October*

Ramius and Kamarov conferred over the chart for several minutes, tracing alternate course tracks before agreeing on one. The enlisted men ignored this. They had never been encouraged to know about charts. The captain walked to the aft bulkhead and lifted the phone.

'Comrade Melekhin,' he ordered, waiting a few seconds. 'Comrade, this is the captain. Any further difficulties with the reactor systems?'

'No, Comrade Captain.'

'Excellent. Hold things together another two days.' Ramius hung up. It was thirty minutes to the turn of the next watch.

Melekhin and Kirill Surzpoi, the assistant engineer, had the duty in the engine room. Melekhin monitored the turbines and Surzpoi handled the reactor systems. Each had a *michman* and three enlisted men in attendance. The engineers had had a very busy cruise. Every gauge and monitor in the engine spaces, it seemed, had been inspected, and many had been entirely rebuilt by the two senior officers, who had been helped by Valintin Bugayev, the electronics officer and on-board genius who was also handling the political awareness classes for the crewmen. The engine room crewmen were the most rattled on the vessel. The supposed contamination was common knowledge – there are no long-lived secrets on a submarine. To ease their load ordinary seamen were supplementing the engine watches. The captain called this a good chance for the cross-training he believed in. The crew thought it was a good way to get poisoned. Discipline was being maintained, of course. This was owing partly to the trust the men had in their commanding officer, partly to their training, but mostly to their knowledge of what would happen if they failed to carry out their orders immediately and enthusiastically.

'Comrade Melekhin,' Surzpoi called, 'I am showing pressure fluctuation on the main loop, number six gauge.'

'Coming.' Melekhin hurried over and shoved the *michman* out of the way when he got to the master control panel. 'More bad instruments! The others show normal. Nothing important,' the chief engineer said blandly, making sure everyone could hear. The whole compartment watch saw the chief engineer whisper something to his assistant. The younger one shook his head slowly, while two sets of hands worked the controls.

A loud two-phase buzzer and a rotating red alarm light went off.

'SCRAM the pile!' Melekhin ordered.

'SCRAMing.' Surzpoi stabbed his finger on the master shutdown button.

'You men, get forward!' Melekhin ordered next. There was no hesitation. 'No, you, connect battery power to the caterpillar motors, quickly!'

The warrant officer raced back to throw the proper switches, cursing his change of orders. It took forty seconds.

'Done, Comrade!'

'*Go!*'

The warrant officer was the last man out of the compartment. He made certain that the hatches were dogged down tight before running to the control room.

'What is the problem?' Ramius asked calmly.

'Radiation alarm in the heat-exchange room!'

236

'Very well, go forward and shower with the rest of your watch. Get control of yourself.' Ramius patted the *michman* on the arm. 'We have had these problems before. You are a trained man. The crewmen look to you for leadership.'

Ramius lifted the phone. It was a moment before the other end was picked up. 'What has happened, Comrade?' The control room crew watched their captain listen to the answer. They could not help but admire his calm. Radiation alarms had sounded throughout the hull. 'Very well. We do not have too many hours of battery power left, Comrade. We must go to snorkeling depth. Stand by to activate the diesel. Yes.' He hung up.

'Comrades, you will listen to me.' Ramius' voice was under total control. 'There has been a minor failure in the reactor control systems. The alarm you heard was not a major radiation leak, but rather a failure of the reactor rod control systems. Comrades Melekhin and Surzpoi successfully executed an emergency reactor shutdown, but we cannot operate the reactor properly without the primary controls. We will, therefore, complete our cruise on diesel power. To ensure against any *possible* radiation contamination, the reactor spaces have been isolated, and all compartments, engineering spaces first, will be vented with surface air when we snorkel. Kamarov, you will go aft to work the environmental controls. I will take the conn.'

'Aye, Comrade Captain!' Kamarov went aft.

Ramius lifted the microphone to give this news to the crew. Everyone was waiting for something. Forward, some crewmen muttered among themselves that *minor* was a word suffering from overuse, that nuclear submarines did not run on diesel and ventilate with surface air for the hell of it.

Finished with his terse announcement, Ramius ordered the submarine to approach the surface.

The *Dallas*

'Beats me, Skipper.' Jones shook his head. 'Reactor noises have stopped, pumps are cut way back, but he's running at the same speed, just like before. On battery, I guess.'

'Must be a hell of a battery system to drive something that big this fast,' Mancuso observed.

'I did some computations on that a few hours ago.' Jones held up his pad. 'This is based on the *Typhoon* hull, with a nice slick hull coefficient, so it's probably conservative.'

'Where did you learn to do this, Jonesy?'

'Mr Thompson looked up the hydrodynamic stuff for me. The electrical end is fairly simple. He might have something exotic – fuel cells, maybe. If not, if he's running ordinary batteries, he has enough raw electrical power to crank every car in LA.'

Mancuso shook his head. 'Can't last forever.'

Jones held up his hand. 'Hull creaking . . . Sounds like he's going up some.'

The *Red October*

'Raise snorkel,' Ramius said. Looking through the periscope he verified that the snorkel was up. 'Well, no other ships in view. That is good news. I think we have lost our imperialist hunters. Raise the ESM antenna. Let's be sure no enemy aircraft are lurking about with their radars.'

'Clear, Comrade Captain.' Bugayev was manning the ESM board. 'Nothing at all, not even airliner sets.'

'So, we have indeed lost our rat pack.' Ramius lifted the phone again. 'Melekhin, you may open the main induction and vent the engine spaces, then start the diesel.' A minute later everyone aboard felt the vibration as the *October*'s massive diesel engine cranked on battery power. This sucked up all the air from the reactor spaces, replacing it with air drawn through the snorkel and ejecting the 'contaminated' air into the sea.

The engine continued to crank for two minutes, and throughout the hull men waited for the rumble that would mean the engine had caught and could generate power to run the electric motors. It didn't catch. After another thirty seconds the cranking stopped. The control room phone buzzed. Ramius lifted it.

'What is wrong with the diesel, Comrade Chief Engineer?' the captain asked sharply. 'I see. I'll send men back – oh. Stand by.' Ramius looked around, his mouth a thin, bloodless line. The junior engineering officer, Svyadov, was standing at the back of the compartment. 'I need a man who knows diesel engines to help Comrade Melekhin.'

'I grew up on a State farm,' Bugayev said. 'I started playing with tractor engines as a boy.'

'There is an additional problem . . . '

Bugayev nodded knowingly. 'So I gather, Comrade Captain, but we need the diesel, do we not?'

'I will not forget this, Comrade,' Ramius said quietly.

'Then you can buy me some rum in Cuba, Comrade.' Bugayev smiled courageously. 'I wish to meet a Cuban comrade, preferably one with long hair.'

'May I accompany you, Comrade?' Svyadov asked anxiously. He had just been going on watch, approaching the reactor room hatch, when he'd been knocked aside by escaping crewmen.

'Let us assess the nature of the problem first,' Bugayev said, looking at Ramius for confirmation.

'Yes, there is plenty of time. Bugayev, report to me yourself in ten minutes.'

'Aye aye, Comrade Captain.'

'Svyadov, take charge of the lieutenant's station.' Ramius pointed to the ESM board. 'Use the opportunity to learn some new skills.'

The lieutenant did as he was ordered. The captain seemed very preoccupied. Svyadov had never seen him like this before.

The Fourteenth Day

Thursday, 16 December

A Super Stallion

They were travelling at one hundred fifty knots, two thousand feet over the darkened sea. The Super Stallion helicopter was old. Built towards the end of the Vietnam War, she had first seen service clearing mines off Haiphong harbour. That had been her primary duty, pulling a sea sled and acting as a flying minesweeper. Now, the big Sikorski was used for other purposes, mainly long-range heavy-lift missions. The three turbine engines perched atop the fuselage packed a considerable amount of power and could carry a platoon of armed combat troops a great distance.

Tonight, in addition to her normal flight crew of three, she was carrying four passengers and a heavy load of fuel in the outrigger tanks. The passengers were clustered in the aft corner of the cargo area, chatting among themselves or trying to over the racket of the engines. Their conversation was animated. The intelligence officers had dismissed the danger implicit in their mission – no sense dwelling on that – and were speculating on what they might find aboard an honest-to-God Russian submarine. Each man considered the stories that would result, and decided it was a shame that they would never be able to tell them. None voiced this thought, however. At most a handful of people would ever know the entire story; the others would only see disjointed fragments that later might be thought parts of any number of other operations. Any Soviet agent trying to determine what this mission had been would find himself in a maze with dozens of blank walls.

The mission profile was a tight one. The helicopter was flying on a specific track to HMS *Invincible*, from which they would fly to the USS *Pigeon* aboard a Royal Navy Sea King. The Stallion's disappearance from Oceana Naval Air Station for only a few hours would be viewed merely as a matter of routine.

The helicopter's turboshaft engines, running at maximum cruising power, were gulping down fuel. The aircraft was now four hundred miles off the US coast and had another eighty miles to go. Their flight to the *Invincible* was not direct; it was a dog-leg course intended to fool whoever might have noticed their departure on radar. The pilots were tired. Four hours is a long time to sit in a cramped cockpit, and military aircraft are not known for their creature comforts. The flight instruments glowed a dull red. Both men were especially careful to watch their artificial horizon; a solid overcast denied them a fixed reference point aloft, and flying over water at night was mesmerizing. It was by no means an unusual mission, however. The pilots had done this many times, and their concern was not unlike that of an experienced driver on a slick road. The dangers were real, but routine.

'Juliet 6, your target is bearing zero-eight-zero, range seventy-five miles,' the Sentry called in.

'Thinks we're lost?' Commander John Marcks wondered over the intercom.

'Air force,' his co-pilot replied. 'They don't know much about flying over water. They think you get lost without roads to follow.'

'Uh-huh,' Marcks chuckled. 'Who do you like in the Eagles game tonight?'

'Oilers by three and a half.'

'Six and a half. Philly's fullback is still hurt.'

'Five.'

'Okay, five bucks. I'll go easy on you.' Marcks grinned. He loved to gamble. The day after Argentina had attacked the Falklands, he'd asked if anyone in the squadron wanted to take Argentina and seven points.

A few feet above their heads and a few feet aft, the engines were racing at thousands of RPM, turning gears to drive the seven-bladed main rotor. They had no way of knowing that a fracture was developing in the transmission casing, near the fluid test port.

'Juliet 6, your target has just launched a fighter to escort you in. Will rendezvous in eight minutes. Approaching you at eleven o'clock, angels three.'

'Nice of them,' Marcks said.

Harrier 2

Lieutenant Parker was flying the Harrier that would escort the Super Stallion. A sub-lieutenant sat in the back seat of the Royal Navy aircraft. Its purpose was not actually to escort the chopper to the *Invincible*; it was to make a last check for any Soviet submarines that might notice the Super Stallion in flight and wonder what it was doing.

'Any activity on the water?' Parker asked.

'Not a glimmer.' The sub-lieutenant was working the FLIR package, which was sweeping left and right over their course track. Neither man knew what was going on, though both had speculated at length, incorrectly, on what it was that was chasing their carrier all over the bloody ocean.

'Try looking for the helicopter,' Parker said.

'One moment . . . There. Just south of our track.' The sub-lieutenant pressed a button and the display came up on the pilot's screen. The thermal image was mainly of the engines clustered atop the aircraft inside the fainter, dull-green glow of the hot rotor tips.

'Harrier 2-0, this is Sentry Echo. Your target is at your one o'clock, distance twenty miles, over.'

'Roger, we have him on our IR box. Thank you, out,' Parker said. 'Bloody useful things, those Sentries.'

'The Sikorski's running for all she's worth. Look at that engine signature.'

The Super Stallion

At this moment the transmission casing fractured. Instantly the gallons of lubricating oil became a greasy cloud behind the rotor hub, and the delicate gears began to tear at one another. An alarm light flashed on the control panel. Marcks and the co-pilot instantly reached down to cut power to all three engines. There was not enough time. The transmission tried to freeze, but the power of the three engines tore it apart. What happened was the next thing to an explosion. Jagged pieces burst through the safety housing and ripped the forward part of the aircraft. The rotor's momentum twisted the Stallion savagely around, and it dropped rapidly. Two of the men in the back, who had loosened their seatbelts, jerked out of their seats and rolled forward.

'MAYDAY MAYDAY MAYDAY, this is Juliet 6,' the co-pilot called. Commander Marcks' body was slumped over the controls, a dark stain on the back of his neck. 'We're goin' in, we're goin' in. MAYDAY MAYDAY MAYDAY.'

The co-pilot was trying to do something. The main rotor was windmilling slowly – too slowly. The automatic decoupler that was supposed to allow it to autorotate and give him a vestige of control had failed. His controls were nearly useless, and he was riding the point of a blunt lance towards a black ocean. It was twenty seconds before they hit. He fought with his airfoil controls and tail rotor in order to jerk the aircraft around. He succeeded, but it was too late.

Harrier 2-0

It was not the first time Parker had seen men die. He had taken a life himself after sending a Sidewinder missile up the tailpipe of an Argentine Dagger fighter. That had not been pleasant. This was worse. As he watched, the Super Stallion's humpbacked engine cluster blew apart in a shower of sparks. There was no fire as such, for what good it did them. He watched and tried

241

to will the nose to come up – and it did, but not enough. The Stallion hit the water hard. The fuselage snapped apart in the middle. The front end sank in an instant, but the after part wallowed for a few seconds like a bathtub before beginning to fill with water. According to the picture supplied by the FLIR package, no one got clear before it sank.

'Sentry, Sentry, did you see that, over?'

'Roger that, Harrier. We're calling a SAR mission right now. Can you orbit?'

'Roger, we can loiter here.' Parker checked his fuel. 'Nine-zero minutes. I – stand by.' Parker nosed his fighter down and flicked on his landing lights. This lit up the low-light TV system. 'Did you see that, Ian?' he asked his backseater.

'I think it moved.'

'Sentry, Sentry, we have a possible survivor in the water. Tell *Invincible* to get a Sea King down here straightaway. I'm going down to investigate. Will advise.'

'Roger that, Harrier 2-0. Your captain reports a helo spooling up right now. Out.'

The Royal Navy Sea King was there in twenty-five minutes. A rubber-suited paramedic jumped in the water to get a collar on the one survivor. There were no others, and no wreckage, only a slick of jet fuel evaporating slowly into the cold air. A second helicopter continued the search as the first raced back to the carrier.

The *Invincible*

Ryan watched from the bridge as the medics carried the stretcher into the island. Another crewman appeared a moment later with a briefcase.

'He had this, sir. He's a lieutenant commander, name of Dwyer. One leg and several ribs broken. He's in a bad way, Admiral.'

'Thank you.' White took the case. 'Any possibility of other survivors?'

The sailor shook his head. 'Not a good one, sir. The Sikorski must have sunk like a stone.' He looked at Ryan. 'Sorry, sir.'

Ryan nodded. 'Thanks.'

'Norfolk on the radio, Admiral,' a communications officer said.

'Let's go, Jack.' Admiral White handed him the briefcase and led him to the communications room.

'The chopper went in. We have one survivor being worked on right now,' Ryan said over the radio. It was silent for a moment.

'Who is it?'

'Name's Dwyer. They took him right to sick bay, Admiral. He's out of action. Tell Washington. Whatever this operation is supposed to be, we have to rethink it.'

'Roger. Out,' Admiral Blackburn said.

'Whatever we decide to do,' Admiral White observed, 'it will have to be fast. We must get our helo off to the *Pigeon* in two hours to have her back before dawn.'

Ryan knew exactly what that would mean. There were only four men at sea who both knew what was going on and were close enough to do anything. He was the only American among them. The *Kennedy* was too far away. The *Nimitz* was close enough, but using her would mean getting the data to her by radio, and Washington was not enthusiastic about that. The only other alternative was to assemble and dispatch another intelligence team. There just wasn't enough time.

'Let's get this case open, Admiral. I need to see what this plan is.' They picked up a machinist's mate on the way to White's cabin. He proved to be an excellent locksmith.

'Dear God!' Ryan breathed, reading the contents of the case. 'You better see this.'

'Well,' White said a few minutes later, 'that is clever.'

'It's cute, all right,' Ryan said. 'I wonder what genius thought it up. I know I'm going to be stuck with this. I'll ask Washington for permission to take a few officers along with me.'

Ten minutes later they were back in communications. White had the compartment cleared. Then Jack spoke over the encrypted voice channel. Both hoped the scrambling device worked.

'I hear you fine, Mr President. You know what happened to the helicopter.'

'Yes, Jack, most unfortunate. I need you to pinch-hit for us.'

'Yes, sir, I anticipated that.'

'I can't order you, but you know what the stakes are. Will you do it?'

Ryan closed his eyes. 'Affirmative.'

'I appreciate it, Jack.'

Sure you do. 'Sir, I need your authorization to take some help with me, a few British officers.'

'One,' the president said.

'Sir, I need more than that.'

'One.'

'Understood, sir. We'll be moving in an hour.'

'You know what's supposed to happen?'

'Yes, sir. The survivor had the ops orders with him. I've already read them over.'

'Good luck, Jack.'

'Thank you, sir. Out.' Ryan flipped off the satellite channel and turned to Admiral White. 'Volunteer once, just one time, and see what happens.'

'Frightened?' White did not appear amused.

'Damned right I am. Can I borrow an officer? A guy who speaks Russian if possible. You know what this may involve.'

'We'll see. Come on.'

Five minutes later they were back in White's cabin awaiting the arrival of four officers. All turned out to be lieutenants, all under thirty.

'Gentlemen,' the admiral began, 'this is Commander Ryan. He needs an officer to accompany him on a voluntary basis for a mission of some importance. Its nature is secret and most unusual, and there may be some danger involved. You four have been asked here because of your knowledge of Russian. This is all I can say.'

'Going to talk to a Sov submarine?' the oldest of them chirped up. 'I'm your man. I have a degree in the language and my first posting was aboard HMS *Dreadnought*.'

Ryan weighed the ethics of accepting the man before telling him what was involved. He nodded, and White dismissed the others.

'I'm Jack Ryan.' He extended his hand.

'Owen Williams. So, what are we up to?'

'The submarine is named *Red October* – '

'*Krazny Oktyabr*.' Williams smiled.

'And she's attempting to defect to the United States.'

'Indeed? So that's what we've been mucking about for. Jolly decent of her CO. Just how certain are we of this?'

Ryan took several minutes to detail the intelligence information. 'We blinkered instructions to him, and he seems to have played along. But we won't know for sure until we get aboard. Defectors have been known to change their minds, it happens a lot more often than you might imagine. Still want to come along?'

'Miss a chance like this? Exactly how do we get aboard, Commander?'

'The name's Jack. I'm CIA, not navy.' He went on to explain the plan.

'Excellent. Do I have time to pack some things?'

'Be back here in ten minutes,' White said.

'Aye aye, sir.' Williams drew to attention and left.

White was on the phone. 'Send Lieutenant Sinclair to see me.' The admiral explained that he was the commander of the *Invincible*'s marine detachment. 'Perhaps you might need another friend along.'

The other friend was an FN nine-millimetre automatic pistol with a spare clip and a shoulder holster that disappeared nicely under his jacket. The mission orders were shredded and burned before they left.

Admiral White accompanied Ryan and Williams to the flight deck. They stood at the hatch, looking at the Sea King as its engines screeched into life.

'Good luck, Owen.' White shook hands with the youngster, who saluted and moved off.

'My regards to your wife, Admiral.' Ryan took his hand.

'Five and a half days to England. You'll probably see her before I do. Be careful, Jack.'

244

Ryan smiled crookedly. 'It's my intelligence estimate, isn't it? If I'm right, it'll just be a pleasure cruise – assuming the helicopter doesn't crash on me.'

'The uniform looks good on you, Jack.'

Ryan hadn't expected that. He drew himself to attention and saluted as he'd been taught at Quantico. 'Thank you, Admiral. Be seeing you.'

White watched him enter the chopper. The crew chief slid the door shut, and a moment later the Sea King's engines increased power. The helicopter lifted unevenly for a few feet before its nose dipped to port and began a climbing turn to the south. Without flying lights the dark shape was lost to sight in less than a minute.

33N 75W

The *Scamp* rendezvoused with the *Ethan Allen* a few minutes after midnight. The attack sub took up station a thousand yards astern of the old missile boat, and both cruised in an easy circle as their sonar operators listened to the approach of a diesel-powered vessel, the USS *Pigeon*. Three of the pieces were now in place. Three more were to come.

The *Red October*

'There is no choice,' Melekhin said. 'I must continue to work on the diesel.'

'Let us help you,' Svyadov said.

'And what do you know of diesel fuel pumps?' Melekhin asked in a tired but kind voice. 'No, Comrade. Surzpoi, Bugayev, and I can handle it alone. There is no reason to expose you also. I will report back in an hour.'

'Thank you, Comrade.' Ramius clicked the speaker off. 'This cruise has been a troublesome one. Sabotage. Never in my career has something like this happened! If we cannot fix the diesel . . . We have only a few hours more of battery power, and the reactor requires a total overhaul and safety inspection. I swear to you, Comrades, if we find the bastard who did this to us . . . '

'Shouldn't we call for help?' Ivanov asked.

'This close to the American coast, and perhaps an imperialist submarine still on our tail? What sort of "help" might we get, eh? Comrades, perhaps our problem is no accident, have you considered that? Perhaps we have become pawns in a murderous game.' He shook his head. 'No, we cannot risk this. The Americans must not get their hands on this submarine!'

CIA Headquarters

'Thank you for coming on such short notice, Senator. I apologize for getting you up so early.' Judge Moore met Donaldson at the door and led him into his capacious office. 'You know Director Jacobs, don't you?'

'Of course, and what brings the heads of the FBI and the CIA together at dawn?' Donaldson asked with a smile. This had to be good. Heading the Select Committee was more than a job, it was fun, real fun to be one of the few people who were really in the know.

The third person in the room, Ritter, helped a fourth person out of a high-backed chair that had blocked him from view. It was Peter Henderson, Donaldson saw to his surprise. His aide's suit was rumpled as though he'd been up all night. Suddenly it wasn't fun anymore.

Judge Moore waxed solicitous. 'You know Mr Henderson, of course.'

'What is the meaning of this?' Donaldson asked, his voice more subdued than anyone expected.

'You lied to me, Senator,' Ritter said. 'You promised that you would not reveal what I told you yesterday, knowing all the time that you'd tell this man – '

'I did no such thing.'

'– who then told a fellow KGB agent,' Ritter went on. 'Emil?'

Jacobs set his coffee down. 'We've been on to Mr Henderson for some time. It was his contact that had us stumped. Some things are just too obvious. A lot of people in DC have regular cab pickup. Henderson's contact was a cab driver. We finally got it right.'

'The way we found out about Henderson was through you, Senator,' Moore explained. 'We had a very good agent in Moscow a few years ago, a colonel in their Strategic Rocket Forces. He'd been giving us good information for five years, and we were about to get him and his family out. We try to do that, you know; you can't run agents forever, and we really owed this man. But I made the mistake of revealing his name to your committee. One week later, he was gone – vanished. He was eventually shot, of course. His wife and three daughters were sent to Siberia. Our information is that they live in a lumber settlement east of the Urals. Typical sort of place, no plumbing, lousy food, no medical facilities available, and since they're the family of a convicted traitor, you can probably imagine what sort of hell they must endure. A good man dead, and a family destroyed. Try thinking about that, Senator. This is a true story, and these are real people.

'We didn't know at first who had leaked it. It had to be you, or one of two others, so we began to leak information to individual committee members. It took six months, but your name came up three times. After that we had Director Jacobs check out all of your staffers. Emil?'

'When Henderson was an assistant editor of the Harvard *Crimson*, in 1970, he was sent to Kent State to do a piece on the shooting. You remember, the "Days of Rage" thing after the Cambodian incursion and that awful screw-up with the national guard. I was in on that, too, as luck would have it. Evidently it turned Henderson's stomach. Understandable. But not his reaction. When he graduated and joined your staff, he started talking with his old activist friends about his job. This led to a contact from the Russians, and they asked for some information. That was during the Christmas bombing – he really didn't like that. He delivered. It was low-level stuff at first, nothing they couldn't have got a few days later from the *Post*. That's how it works. They offered the hook, and he nibbled at it. A few years later, of course, they struck the hook nice and hard and he couldn't get away. We all know how the game works.

'Yesterday we planted a tape recorder in his taxi. You'd be amazed how easy it was. Agents get lazy, too, just like the rest of us. To make a long story short, we have you on tape promising not to reveal the information to anyone, and we have Henderson here spilling that data not three hours later to a known KGB agent, also on tape. You have violated no laws, Senator, but Mr Henderson has. He was arrested at nine last night. The charge is espionage, and we have the evidence to make it stick.'

'I had no knowledge whatever of this,' Donaldson said.

'We hadn't the slightest thought that you might,' Ritter said.

Donaldson faced his aide. 'What do you have to say for yourself?'

Henderson didn't say anything. He thought about saying how sorry he was, but how to explain his emotions? The dirty feeling of being an agent for a foreign power, juxtaposed with the thrill of fooling a whole legion of government spooks. When he was caught these emotions changed to fear at what would happen to him, and relief that it was all over.

'Mr Henderson has agreed to work for us,' Jacobs said helpfully. 'As soon as you leave the Senate, that is.'

'What does that mean?' Donaldson asked.

'You've been in the Senate, what? Thirteen years, isn't it? You were originally appointed to fill out an unexpired term, if memory serves,' Moore said.

'You might try asking my reaction to blackmail,' the senator observed.

'Blackmail?' Moore held his hands out. 'Good Lord, Senator, Director Jacobs has already told you that you have broken no laws, and you have my word that the CIA will not leak a word of this. Now, whether or not the Justice Department decides to prosecute Mr Henderson is not in our hands. "Senate Aide Convicted of Treason: Senator Donaldson Professes No Knowledge of Aide's Action."'

Jacobs went on, 'Senator, the University of Connecticut has offered you the chair in their school of government for some years now. Why not take it?'

'Or Henderson goes to prison. You put that on my conscience?'

'Obviously he cannot go on working for you, and it should be equally obvious that if he is fired after so many years of exemplary service in your office, it will be noticed. If, on the other hand, you decide to leave public life, it would not be too surprising if he were not able to get a job of equivalent stature with another senator. So, he will get a nice job in the General Accounting Office, where he will still have access to all sorts of secrets. Only from now on,' Ritter said, 'we decide which secrets he passes along.'

'No statute of limitations on espionage,' Jacobs pointed out.

'If the Soviets find out,' Donaldson said, and stopped. He didn't really care, did he? Not about Henderson, not about the fictitious Russian. He had an image to save, losses to cut.

'You win, Judge.'

'I thought you'd see it our way. I'll tell the president. Thanks for coming in, Senator. Mr Henderson will be a little late to the office this morning. Don't feel too badly about him, Senator. If he plays ball with us, in a few years we might just let him off the hook. It's happened before, but he'll have to earn it. Good morning, sir.'

Henderson would play along. His alternative was life in a maximum security penitentiary. After listening to the tape of his conversation in the cab, he'd made his confession in front of a court stenographer and a television camera.

The *Pigeon*

The ride to the *Pigeon* had been mercifully uneventful. The catamaran-hull rescue ship had a small helicopter platform aft, and the Royal Navy helicopter had hovered two feet above it, allowing Ryan and Williams to jump down. They were taken immediately to the bridge as the helicopter buzzed back northeast to her home.

'Welcome aboard, gentlemen,' the captain said agreeably. 'Washington says you have orders for me. Coffee?'

'Do you have tea?' Williams asked.

'We can probably find some.'

'Let's go someplace we can talk in private,' Ryan said.

The *Dallas*

The *Dallas* was now in on the plan. Alerted by another ELF transmission, Mancuso had brought her to antenna depth briefly during the night. The lengthy EYES ONLY message had been decrypted by hand in his cabin. Decryption was not Mancuso's strong point. It took him an hour as Chambers conned the *Dallas* back to trail her contact. A crewman passing the captain's cabin heard a muted *damn* through the door. When Mancuso reappeared, his mouth couldn't keep from twitching into a smile. He was not a good card player either.

The *Pigeon*

The *Pigeon* was one of the navy's two modern submarine rescue ships designed to locate and reach a sunken nuclear sub quickly enough to save her crew. She was outfitted with a variety of sophisticated equipment, chief among them the DSRV. This vessel, the *Mystic*, was hanging on its rack between the *Pigeon*'s twin catamaran hulls. There was also a 3-d sonar operating at low power, mainly as a beacon, while the *Pigeon* cruised in slow circles a few miles south of the *Scamp* and *Ethan Allen*. Two Perry-class frigates were twenty miles north, operating in conjunction with three Orions to sanitize the area.

'*Pigeon*, this is *Dallas*, radio check, over.'

'*Dallas*, this is *Pigeon*. Read you loud and clear, over,' the rescue ship's captain replied on the secure radio channel.

'The package is here. Out.'

'Captain, on *Invincible* we had an officer send the message with a blinker light. Can you handle the blinker light?' Ryan asked.

'To be part of this? Are you kidding?'

The plan was simple enough, just a little too cute. It was clear that the *Red October* wanted to defect. It was even possible that everyone aboard wanted to come over – but hardly likely. They were going to get everyone off the *Red October* who might want to return to Russia, then pretend to blow up the ship with one of the powerful scuttling charges Russian ships are known to carry. The remaining crewmen would then take their boat northwest into Pamlico's Sound to wait for the Soviet fleet to return home, sure that the *Red October* had been sunk and with the crew to prove it. What could possibly go wrong? A thousand things.

The *Red October*

Ramius looked through his periscope. The only ship in view was the USS *Pigeon*, though his ESM antenna reported surface radar activity to the north, a pair of frigates standing guard over the horizon. So, this was the plan. He watched the blinker light, translating the message in his mind.

Norfolk Naval Medical Center

'Thanks for coming down, Doc.' The intelligence officer had taken over the office of assistant hospital administrator. 'I understand our patient woke up.'

'About an hour ago,' Tait confirmed. 'He was conscious for about twenty minutes. He's asleep now.'

'Does this mean he'll make it?'

'It's a positive sign. He was reasonably coherent, so there's no evident brain damage. I was a little worried about that. I'd have to say the odds are in his favour now, but these hypothermia cases have a way of souring on you in a hurry. He's a sick kid, that hasn't changed.' Tait paused. 'I have a question for you, Commander: Why aren't the Russians happy?'

'What makes you think that?'

'Kind of hard to miss. Besides, Jamie found a doctor on staff who understands Russian, and we have him attending the case.'

'Why didn't you let me know about that?'

'The Russians don't know either. That was a medical judgment, Commander. Having a physician around who speaks the patient's language is simply good medical practice.' Tait smiled, pleased with himself for having thought up his own intelligence ploy while at the same time adhering to proper medical ethics and naval regulations. He took a file card from his pocket. 'Anyway, the patient's name is Andre Katyskin. He's a cook, like we thought, from Leningrad. The name of his ship was the *Politovskiy*.'

'My compliments, Doctor.' The intelligence officer acknowledged Tait's manoeuvre, though he wondered why it was that amateurs had to be so damned clever when they butted into things that didn't concern them.

'So why are the Russians unhappy?' Tait did not get an answer. 'And why don't you have a guy up there? You knew all along, didn't you? You knew what ship he escaped from, and you knew why she sank . . . So, if they wanted most of all to know what ship he came from, and if they don't like the news they got – does that mean they have *another* missing sub out there?'

CIA Headquarters

Moore lifted his phone. 'James, you and Bob get in here right now!'

'What is it, Arthur?' Greer asked a minute later.

'The latest from CARDINAL.' Moore handed xeroxed copies of a message to both men. 'How quick can we get word out?'

'That far out? Means a helicopter, a couple of hours at least. We have to get this out quicker than that,' Greer urged.

'We can't endanger CARDINAL, period. Draw up a message and get the navy or air force to relay it by hand.' Moore didn't like it, but he had no choice.

'It'll take too long!' Greer objected loudly.

'I like the boy, too, James. Talking about it doesn't help. Get moving.'

Greer left the room cursing like the fifty-year sailor he was.

The *Red October*

'Comrades. Officers and men of *Red October*, this is the captain speaking.' Ramius' voice was subdued, the crewmen noticed. The incipient panic that had started a few hours earlier had driven them to the brittle edge of riot. 'Efforts to repair our engines have failed. Our batteries are nearly flat. We are too far from Cuba for help, and we cannot expect help from the *Rodina*. We do not have enough electrical power even to operate our environmental control systems for more than a few hours. We have no choice, we must abandon ship.

'It is no accident that an American ship is now close to us, offering what they call assistance. I will tell you what has happened, comrades. An imperialist spy has sabotaged our ship, and somehow they knew what our orders were. They were waiting for us, comrades, waiting and hoping to get their dirty hands on our ship. They will not. The crew will be taken off. They will not get our *Red October*! The senior officers and I will remain behind to set off the scuttling charges. The water here is five thousand metres deep. They will not have our ship. All crewmen except those on duty will assemble in their quarters. That is all.' Ramius looked around the control room. 'We have lost, comrades. Bugayev, make the necessary signals to Moscow and to the American ship. We will then dive to a hundred metres. We will take no chance that they will seize our ship. I take full responsibility for this – disgrace! Mark this well, comrades. The fault is mine alone.'

The *Pigeon*

'Signal received: "SSS,"' the radioman reported.

'Ever been on a submarine before, Ryan?' Cook asked.

'Nope. I hope it's safer 'n flying.' Ryan tried to make a joke of it. He was deeply frightened.

'Well, let's get you down to *Mystic*.'

The *Mystic*

The DSRV was nothing more than three metal spheres welded together with a propeller on the back and some boiler plating all around to protect the pressure-bearing parts of the hull. Ryan was first through the hatch, then Williams. They found seats and waited. A crew of three was already at work.

The *Mystic* was ready for operation. On command, the *Pigeon*'s winches lowered her to the calm water below. She dived at once, her electric motors hardly making any noise. Her low-power sonar system immediately acquired the Russian submarine, half a mile away, at a depth of three hundred feet. The operating crew had been told that this was a straightforward rescue mission. They were experts. The *Mystic* was hovering over the missile sub's forward escape trunk within ten minutes.

The directional propellers worked them carefully into place and a petty officer made certain that the mating skirt was securely fastened. The water in the skirt between *Mystic* and *Red October* was explosively vented into a low-pressure chamber on the DSRV. This established a firm seal between the two vessels, and the residual water was pumped out.

'Your ball now, I guess.' The lieutenant motioned Ryan to the hatch in the floor of the middle segment.

'I guess.' Ryan knelt by the hatch and banged a few times with his hand. No response. Next he tried a wrench. A moment later three clangs echoed back, and Ryan turned the locking wheel in the centre of the hatch. When he pulled the hatch up, he found another that had already been opened from below. The lower perpendicular hatch was shut. Ryan took a deep breath and climbed down the ladder of the white painted cylinder, followed by Williams. After reaching the bottom Ryan knocked on the lower hatch.

The *Red October*

It opened at once.

'Gentlemen, I am Commander Ryan, United States Navy. Can we be of assistance?'

The man he spoke to was shorter and heavier than himself. He wore three stars on his shoulder boards, an extensive set of ribbons on his breast, and a broad gold stripe on his sleeve. So, this was Marko Ramius . . .

'Do you speak Russian?'

'No, sir, I do not. What is the nature of your emergency?'

'We have a major leak in our reactor system. The ship is contaminated aft of the control room. We must evacuate.'

At the words *leak* and *reactor* Ryan felt his skin crawl. He remembered how positive he had been that his scenario was correct. On land, nine hundred miles away, in a nice, warm office, surrounded by friends – well, not enemies. The looks he was getting from the twenty men in this compartment were lethal.

'Dear God! Okay, let's get moving then. We can take off twenty-five men at a time, sir.'

'Not so fast, Commander Ryan. What will become of my men?' Ramius asked loudly.

'They will be treated as our guests, of course. If they need medical attention, they will get it. They will be returned to the Soviet Union as quickly as we can arrange it. Did you think we'd put them in prison?'

Ramius grunted and turned to speak with the others in Russian. On the flight from the *Invincible* Ryan and Williams had decided to keep the latter's knowledge of Russian secret for a while, and Williams was now dressed in an American uniform. Neither thought a Russian would notice the different accent.

'Dr Petrov,' Ramius said, 'you will take the first group of twenty-five. Keep control of the men, Comrade Doctor! Do not let the Americans speak to them as individuals, and let no man wander off alone. You will behave correctly, no more, no less.'

'Understood, Comrade Captain.'

Ryan watched Petrov count the men off as they passed through the hatch and up the ladder. When they were finished, Williams secured first the *Mystic*'s hatch and then the one on the *October*'s escape truck. Ramius had a *michman* check it. They heard the DSRV disengage and motor off.

The silence that ensued was as long as it was awkward. Ryan and Williams stood in one corner of the compartment, Ramius and his men opposite them. It made Ryan think back to high school dances where boys and girls gathered in separate groups and there was a no-man's-land in the middle. When an officer fished out a cigarette, he tried breaking the ice.

'May I have a cigarette, sir?'

Borodin jerked the pack, and a cigarette came part way out. Ryan took it, and Borodin lit it with a paper match.

'Thanks. I gave it up, but underwater in a sub with a bad reactor, I don't think it's too dangerous, do you? Ryan's first experience with a Russian cigarette was not a happy one. The black coarse tobacco made him dizzy, and it added an acrid smell to the air around them, which was already thick with the odour of sweat, machine oil, and cabbage.

'How did you come to be here?' Ramius asked.

'We were heading towards the coast of Virginia, Captain. A Soviet submarine sank there last week.'

'Oh?' Ramius admired the cover story. 'A Soviet submarine?'

'Yes, Captain. The boat was what we call an *Alfa*. That's all I know for sure. They picked up a survivor and he's in the Norfolk naval hospital. May I ask your name, sir?'

'Marko Aleksandrovich Ramius.'

'Jack Ryan.'

'Owen Williams.' They shook hands all around.

'You have a family, Commander Ryan?' Ramius asked.

'Yes, sir. A wife, a son, and a daughter. You, sir?'

'No, no family.' He turned and addressed a junior officer in Russian. 'Take the next group. You heard my instructions to the doctor?'

'Yes, Comrade Captain!' the young man said.

They heard the *Mystic*'s electric motors overhead. A moment later came the metallic clang of the mating collar gripping the escape trunk. It had taken forty minutes but it had seemed like a week. God, what if the reactor really was bad? Ryan thought.

The *Scamp*

Two miles away, the *Scamp* had halted a few hundred yards from the *Ethan Allen*. Both submarines were exchanging messages on their gertrudes. The *Scamp*'s sonarmen had noted the passage of the three submarines an hour earlier. The *Pogy* and *Dallas* were now between the *Red October* and the other two American subs, their sonar operators listening intently for any interference, any vessel that might come their way. The transfer area was far enough offshore to miss the coastal traffic of commercial freighters and tankers, but that might not keep them from meeting a stray vessel from another port.

The *Red October*

When the third set of crewmen left under the control of Lieutenant Svyadov, a cook at the end of the line broke away, explaining that he wanted to retrieve his cassette tape machine, something he had saved months for. No one noticed when he didn't return, not even Ramius. His crewmen, even the experienced *michmanyy*, jostled one another to get out of their submarine. There was only one more group to go.

The *Pigeon*

On the *Pigeon*, the Soviet crewmen were taken to the crew's mess. The American sailors were observing their Russian counterparts closely, but no words passed. The Russians found the tables set with a meal of coffee, bacon, eggs, and toast. Petrov was happy for that. It was no problem keeping control of the men when they ate like wolves. With a junior officer acting as interpreter, they asked for and got plenty of additional bacon. The cooks had orders to stuff the Russians with all the food they could eat. It kept everyone busy as a helicopter landed from shore with twenty new men, one of whom raced to the bridge.

The *Red October*

'Last group,' Ryan murmured to himself. The *Mystic* mated again. The last round trip had taken an hour. When the pair of hatches was opened, the lieutenant from the DSRV came down.

'Next trip will be delayed, gentlemen. Our batteries have about had it. It'll take ninety minutes to recharge. Any problem?'

'It will be as you say,' Ramius replied. He translated for his men and then ordered Ivanov to take the next group. 'The senior officers will stay behind. We have work to do.' Ramius took the young officer's hand. 'If something happens, tell them in Moscow that we have done our duty.'

'I will do that, Comrade Captain.' Ivanov nearly choked on his answer.

Ryan watched the sailors leave. The *Red October*'s escape trunk hatch was closed, then the *Mystic*'s. One minute later there was a clanging sound as the minisub lifted free. He heard the electric motors whirring off, fading rapidly away and felt the green-painted bulkheads closing in on him. Being on an aeroplane was frightening, but at least the air didn't threaten to crush you. Here he was underwater, three hundred miles from shore in the world's largest submarine with only ten men aboard who knew how to run her.

'Commander Ryan,' Ramius said, drawing himself to attention, 'my officers and I request political asylum in the United States – and we bring you this small present.' Ramius gestured towards the steel bulkheads.

Ryan had already framed his reply. 'Captain, on behalf of the president of the United States, it is my honour to grant your request. Welcome to freedom, gentlemen.'

No one knew that the intercom system in the compartment had been switched on. The indicator light had been unplugged hours before. Two compartments forward the cook listened, telling himself that he had been right to stay behind, wishing he had been wrong. Now what will I do? he wondered. His duty. That sounded easy enough – but would he remember how to carry it out?

'I don't know what to say about you guys,' Ryan shook everyone's hand again. 'You pulled it off. You really pulled it off!'

'Excuse me, Commander,' Kamarov said. 'Do you speak Russian?'

'Sorry, Lieutenant Williams here does, but I do not. A group of Russian-speaking officers was supposed to be here in my place, but their helicopter crashed at sea last night.' Williams translated this. Four of the officers had no knowledge of English.

'And what happens now?'

'In a few minutes, a missile submarine will explode two miles from here. One of ours, an old one. I presume that you told your men you were going to scuttle – Jesus, I hope you didn't say what you were really doing?'

'And have a war aboard my ship?' Ramius laughed. 'No, Ryan. Then what?'

'When everybody thinks *Red October* has sunk, we'll head northwest to the Ocracoke Inlet and wait. USS *Dallas* and *Pogy* will be escorting us. Can these few men operate the ship?'

'These men can operate any ship in the world!' Ramius said it in Russian first. His men grinned. 'So, you think that our men will not know what has become of us?'

'Correct. *Pigeon* will see an underwater explosion. They have no way of knowing it's in the wrong place, do they? You know that your navy has many ships operating off our coast right now? When they leave, well, then we'll figure out where to keep this present permanently. I don't know where that will be. You men, of course, will be our guests. A lot of our people will want to talk with you. For the moment, you can be sure that you will be treated very well – better than you can imagine.' Ryan was sure that the CIA would give each a considerable sum of money. He didn't say so, not wanting to insult this kind of bravery. It had surprised him to learn that defectors rarely expect to receive money, almost never ask for any.

'What about political education?' Kamarov asked.

Ryan laughed. 'Lieutenant, somewhere along the line somebody will take you aside to explain how our country works. That will take about two hours. After that you can immediately start telling us what we do wrong – everybody else in the world does, why shouldn't you? But I can't do that now. Believe this, you will love it, probably more than I do. I have never lived in a country that was not free, and maybe I don't appreciate my home as much as I should. For the moment, I suppose you have work to do.'

'Correct,' Ramius said. 'Come, my new comrades, we will put you to work also.'

Ramius led Ryan aft through a series of watertight doors. In a few minutes he was in the missile room, a vast compartment with twenty-six dark-green tubes towering through two decks. The business end of a boomer, with two-hundred-plus thermonuclear warheads. The menace in this room was enough to make hair bristle at the back of Ryan's neck. These were not academic abstractions, these were real. The upper deck he walked on was a grating. The lower deck, he could see, was solid. After passing through this and another compartment they were in the control room. The interior of the submarine was ghostly quiet; Ryan sensed why sailors are superstitious.

'You will sit here.' Ramius pointed Ryan to the helmsman's station on the port side of the compartment. There was an aircraft-style wheel and a gang of instruments.

'What do I do?' Ryan asked, sitting.

'You will steer the ship, Commander. Have you never done this before?'

'No, sir. I've never been on a submarine before.'

'But you are a naval officer.'

Ryan shook his head. 'No, captain. I work for the CIA.'

'CIA?' Ramius hissed the acronym as if it were poisonous.

'I know, I know.' Ryan dropped his head on the wheel. 'They call us the Dark Forces. Captain, this is one Dark Force who's probably going to wet his pants before we're finished here. I work at a desk, and believe me on this if nothing else – there's nothing I'd like better than to be home with my wife and kids right now. If I had half a brain, I would have stayed in Annapolis and kept writing my books.'

'Books? What do you mean?'

'I'm an historian, Captain. I was asked to join the CIA a few years ago as an analyst. Do you know what that is? Agents bring in their data, and I figure out what it means. I got into this mess by mistake – shit, you don't believe me, but it's true. Anyway, I used to write books on naval history.'

'Tell me your books,' Ramius ordered.

'*Opinions and Decisions*, *Doomed Eagles*, and a new one coming out next year, *Fighting Sailor*, a biography of Admiral Halsey. My first one was about the Battle of Leyte Gulf. It was reviewed in *Morskoi Sbornik*, I understand. It dealt with the nature of tactical decisions made under combat conditions. There's supposed to be a dozen copies at the Frunze library.'

Ramius was quiet for a moment. 'Ah, I know this book. Yes, I read parts of it. You were wrong, Ryan. Halsey acted stupidly.'

'You will do well in my country, Captain Ramius. You are already a book critic. Captain Borodin, can I trouble you for a cigarette?' Borodin tossed him a full pack and matches. Ryan lit one. It was terrible.

The *Avalon*

The *Mystic*'s fourth return was the signal for the *Ethan Allen* and *Scamp* to act. The *Avalon* lifted off her bed and motored the few hundred yards to the old missile boat. Her captain was already assembling his men in the torpedo room. Every hatch, door, manhole, and drawer had been opened all over the boat. One of the officers was coming forward to join the others. Behind him trailed a black wire that led to each of the bombs aboard. This he connected to a timing device.

'All ready, Captain.'

The *Red October*

Ryan watched Ramius order his men to their posts. Most went aft to run the engines. Ramius had the good manners to speak in English, repeating himself in Russian for those who did not understand their new language.

'Kamarov and Williams, you will go forward and secure all hatches.' Ramius explained for Ryan's benefit. 'If something goes wrong – it won't, but if it does – we do not have enough men to make repairs. So, we seal the entire ship.'

It made sense to Ryan. He set an empty cup on the control pedestal to serve as an ashtray. He and Ramius were alone in the control room.

'When are we to leave?' Ramius asked.

'Whenever you are ready, sir. We have to get to Ocracoke Inlet at high tide, about eight minutes after midnight. Can we make it?'

Ramius consulted his chart. 'Easily.'

Kamarov led Williams through the communications room forward of control. They left the watertight door there open, then went forward to the missile room. Here they climbed down a ladder and walked forward on the lower missile deck to the forward missile room bulkhead. They proceeded through the door into the stores compartments, checking each hatch as they went. Near the bow they went up another ladder into the torpedo room, dogging the hatch down behind them, and proceeded aft through the torpedo storage and crew spaces. Both men sensed how strange it was to be aboard a ship with no crew, and they took their time, Williams twisting his head to look at everything and asking Kamarov questions. The lieutenant was happy to answer them in his mother language. Both men were competent officers, sharing a romantic attachment to their profession. For his part, Williams was greatly impressed by the *Red October* and said as much several times. A great deal of attention had been paid to small details. The deck was tiled. The hatches were lined with thick rubber gaskets. They hardly made any noise at all as they moved about checking watertight integrity, and it was obvious that more than mere lip service had been paid to making this submarine a quiet one.

Williams was translating a favourite sea story into Russian as they opened the hatch to the missile room's upper deck. When he stepped through the hatch behind Kamarov, he remembered that the missile room's bright overhead lights had been left on. Hadn't they?

Ryan was trying to relax and failing at it. The seat was uncomfortable, and he recalled the Russian joke about how they were shaping the New Soviet Man – with airliner seats that contorted an individual into all kinds of impossible shapes. Aft, the engine room crew had begun powering up the reactor. Ramius was speaking over the intercom phone with his chief engineer, just before the sound of moving reactor coolant increased to generate steam for the turboalternators.

Ryan's head went up. It was as though he felt the sound before hearing it. A chill crawled up the back of his neck before his brain told him what the sound had to be.

'What was that?' he said automatically, knowing already what it was.

'What?' Ramius was ten feet aft, and the caterpillar engines were now turning. A strange rumble reverberated through the hull.

'I heard a shot – no, several shots.'

Ramius looked amused as he came a few steps forward. 'I think you hear the sounds of the caterpillar engines, and I think it is your first time on a submarine boat, as you said. The first time is always difficult. It was so even for me.'

Ryan stood up. 'That may be, Captain, but I know a shot when I hear it.' He unbuttoned his jacket and pulled out the pistol.

'You will give me that.' Ramius held out his hand. 'You may not have a pistol on my submarine!'

'Where are Williams and Kamarov?' Ryan wavered.

Ramius shrugged. 'They are late, yes, but this is a big ship.'

'I'm going forward to check.'

'You will stay at your post!' Ramius ordered. 'You will do as I say!'

'Captain, I just heard something that sounded like gunshots, and I am going forward to check it out. Have you ever been shot at? I have. I have the scars on my shoulder to prove it. You'd better take the wheel, sir.'

Ramius picked up a phone and punched a button. He spoke in Russian for a few seconds and hung up. 'I will go to show you that my submarine has no souls – ghosts, yes? Ghosts, no ghosts.' He gestured to the pistol. 'And you are no spy, eh?'

'Captain, believe what you want to believe, okay? It's a long story, and I'll tell it to you someday.' Ryan waited for the relief that Ramius had evidently called for. The rumble of the tunnel drive made the sub sound like the inside of a drum.

An officer whose name he did not remember came into the control room. Ramius said something that drew a laugh – which stopped when the officer saw Ryan's pistol. It was obvious that neither Russian was happy he had one.

'With your permission, Captain?' Ryan gestured forward.

'Go on, Ryan.'

The watertight door between control and the next space had been left open. Ryan entered the radio room slowly, eyes tracing left and right. It was clear. He went forward to the missile room door, which was dogged tight. The door, four feet or so high and about two across, was locked in place with a central wheel. Ryan turned the wheel with one hand. It was well oiled. So were the hinges. He pulled the door open slowly and peered around the hatch coaming.

'Oh, shit,' Ryan breathed, waving the captain forward. The missile compartment was a good two hundred feet long, lit only by six or eight small glow lights. Hadn't it been brightly lit before? At the far end was a splash of bright light, and the far hatch had two shapes sprawled on the gratings next to it. Neither moved. The light Ryan saw them by was flickering next to the missile tube.

'Ghosts, Captain?' he whispered.

'It is Kamarov.' Ramius said something else under his breath in Russian.

Ryan pulled the slide back on his FN automatic to make sure a round was in the chamber. Then he stepped out of his shoes.

'Better let me handle this. Once upon a time I was a lieutenant in the marines.' And my training at Quantico, he thought to himself, had damned little to do with this. Ryan entered the compartment.

The missile room was almost a third of the submarine's length and two decks high. The lower deck was solid metal. The upper one was made of metal grates. Sherwood Forest, this place was called on American missile boats. The term was apt enough. The missile tubes, a good nine feet in diameter and painted a darker green than the rest of the room, looked like the trunks of enormous trees. He pulled the hatch shut behind him and moved to his right.

The light seemed to be coming from the farthest missile tube on the starboard side of the upper missile deck. Ryan stopped to listen. Something was happening there. He could hear a low rustling sound, and the light was moving as though it came from a hand-held work lamp. The sound was travelling down the smooth sides of the interior hull plating.

'Why me?' he whispered to himself. He'd have to get past thirteen missile tubes to get to the source of that light, cross over two hundred feet of open deck.

He moved around the first one, pistol in his right hand at waist level, his left hand tracing the cold metal of the tube. Already he was sweating into the checkered hard-rubber pistol grips. That, he told himself, is why they're checkered. He got between the first and second tubes, looked to port to make sure nobody was there, and got ready to move forward. Twelve to go.

The deck grating was welded out of eighth-inch metal bars Already his feet hurt from walking on it. Moving slowly and carefully around the next circular tube, he felt like an astronaut orbiting the moon and crossing a continuous horizon. Except on the moon there wasn't anybody waiting to shoot you.

A hand came down on his shoulder. Ryan jumped and whirled around. Ramius. He had something to say, but Ryan put his fingertips on the man's lips and shook his head. Ryan's heart was beating so loudly that he could have used it for sending Morse code, and he could hear his own breathing – so why the hell hadn't he heard Ramius?

Ryan gestured his intention to go around the outboard side of each missile. Ramius indicated that he would go around the inboard sides. Ryan nodded. He decided to button his jacket and turn the collar up. It would make him a harder target. Better a dark shape than one with a white triangle on it. Next tube.

Ryan saw that words were painted on the tubes, with other inscriptions forged on to the metal itself. The letters were in Cyrillic and probably said No Smoking or Lenin Lives or something similarly useless. He saw and heard everything with great acuity, as though someone had taken sandpaper to all his senses to make him fantastically alert. He edged around the next tube, his fingers flexing nervously on the pistol grip, wanting to wipe the sweat from his eyes. There was nothing here; the port side was okay. Next one . . .

It took five minutes to get halfway down the compartment, between the sixth and seventh tubes. The noise from the forward end of the compartment was more pronounced now. The light was definitely moving. Not by much, but the shadow of the number one tube was jittering ever so slightly. It had to be a work light plugged into a wall socket or whatever they called that on a ship. What was he doing? Working on a missile? Was there more than one man? Why didn't Ramius do a head count getting his crew into the DSRV?

Why didn't *I*? Ryan swore to himself. Six more to go.

As he went around the next tube he indicated to Ramius that there was probably one man all the way at the far end. Ramius nodded curtly, having already reached that conclusion. For the first time he noticed that Ryan's shoes were off, and, thinking that was a good idea, he lifted his left foot to take off a shoe. His fingers, which felt awkward and stiff, fumbled with the shoe. It fell on a loose piece of grating with a clatter. Ryan was caught in the open. He froze. The light at the far end shifted, then went dead still. Ryan darted to his left and peered around the edge of the tube. Five more to go. He saw part of a face – and a flash.

He heard the shot and cringed as the bullet hit the after bulkhead with a *clang*. Then he drew back for cover.

'I will cross to the other side,' Ramius whispered.

'Wait till I say.' Ryan grabbed Ramius' upper arm and went back to the starboard side of the tube, pistol in front. He saw the face and this time he fired first, knowing he'd miss. At the same moment he pushed Ramius left.

The captain raced to the other side and crouched behind a missile tube.

'We have you,' Ryan said aloud.

'You have nothing.' It was a young voice, young and very scared.

'What are you doing?' Ryan asked.

'What do you think, Yankee?' This time the taunt was more effective.

Probably figuring a way to set off a warhead, Ryan decided. A happy thought.

'Then you will die too,' Ryan said. Didn't the police try to reason with barricaded suspects? Didn't a New York cop say on TV once, 'We try to bore them to death?' But those were criminals. What was Ryan dealing with? A sailor who stayed behind? One of Ramius' own officers who'd had second thoughts? A KGB agent? A GRU agent covered as a crewman?

'Then I will die,' the voice agreed. The light moved. Whatever he was doing, he was trying to get back to it.

Ryan fired twice as he went around the tube. Four to go. His bullets clanged uselessly as they hit the forward bulkhead. There was a remote chance that a carom shot – no . . . He looked left and saw that Ramius was still with him, shading to the port side of the tubes. He had no gun. Why hadn't he gotten himself one?

Ryan took a deep breath and leaped around the next tube. The guy was waiting for this. Ryan dived to the deck, and the bullet missed him.

'Who are you?' Ryan asked, raising himself on his knees and leaning against the tube to catch his breath.

'A Soviet patriot! You are the enemy of my country, and you shall not have this ship!'

He was talking too much, Ryan thought. Good. Probably. 'You have a name?'

'My name is of no account.'

'How about a family?' Ryan asked.

'My parents will be proud of me.'

A GRU agent. Ryan was certain. Not the political officer. His English was too good. Probably some kind of backup for the political officer. He was up against a trained field officer. Wonderful. A trained agent, and just like he said, a patriot. Not a fanatic, a man trying to do his duty. He was scared, but he'd do it.

And blow this whole fucking ship up, with me on it.

Still, Ryan knew he had an edge. The other guy had something he had to do. Ryan only had to stop him or delay him long enough. He went to the starboard side of the tube and looked around the edge with just his right eye. There was no light at all at his end of the compartment – another edge. Ryan could see him more easily than he could see Ryan.

'You don't have to die, my friend. If you just set the gun down . . . ' And *what*? End up in a federal prison? More likely just disappear. Moscow could not learn that the Americans had their sub.

'And CIA will not kill me, eh?' the voice sneered, quavering. 'I am no fool. If I am to die, it will be to my purpose, my friend!'

Then the light clicked off. Ryan had wondered how long that would take. Did it mean that he was finished whatever the hell he was doing? If so, in an instant they'd all be gone. Or maybe the guy just realized how vulnerable the light made him. Trained field officer or not, he was a kid, a frightened kid, and probably had as much to lose as Ryan had. Like hell, Ryan thought, I have a wife and two kids, and if I don't get to him fast, I'll sure as hell lose them.

Merry Christmas, kids, your daddy just got blown up. Sorry there's no body to bury, but you see . . . It occurred to Ryan to pray briefly – but for what? For help in killing another man? *It's like this, Lord* . . .

'Still with me, Captain?' he called out.

'*Da.*'

That would give the GRU agent something to worry about. Ryan hoped the captain's presence would force the man to shade more to the port side of his tube. Ryan ducked and rushed around the port side of his. Three to go. Ramius followed suit on his side. He drew a shot, but Ryan heard it miss.

He had to stop, to rest. He was hyperventilating. It was the wrong time for that. He had been a marine lieutenant – for three whole months before the chopper crash – and he was supposed to know what to do! He had *led* men. But it was a whole lot easier to lead forty men with rifles than it was to fight all by himself.

Think!

'Maybe we can make a deal,' Ryan suggested.

'Ah, yes, we can decide which ear the shot comes in.'

'Maybe you'd like being an American.'

'And my parents, Yankee, what of them?'

'Maybe we can get them out,' Ryan said from the starboard side of his tube, moving left as he waited for a reply. He jumped again. Now there were two missile tubes separating him from his friend in the GRU, who was probably trying to crosswire the warheads and make half a cubic mile of ocean turn to plasma.

'Come, Yankee, we will die together. Now only one *puskatel* separates us.'

Ryan thought quickly. He couldn't remember how many times he'd fired, but the pistol held thirteen rounds. He'd have enough. The extra clip was useless. He could toss it one way and move the other, creating a diversion. Would it work? Shit! It worked in the movies. It was for damned sure that doing nothing wasn't going to work.

Ryan took the gun in his left hand and fished in his coat pocket for the spare clip with his right. He put the clip in his mouth while he switched the gun back. A poor highwayman's shift . . . He took the clip in his left hand. Okay. He had to toss the clip right and move left. Would it work? Right or wrong, he didn't have a hell of a lot of time.

At Quantico he was taught to read maps, evaluate terrain, call in air and artillery strikes, manoeuvre his squads and fire teams with skill – and here he was, stuck in a goddamned steel pipe three hundred feet under water, shooting it out with pistols in a room with two hundred hydrogen bombs!

It was time to do something. He knew what that had to be – but Ramius moved first. Out the corner of his eye he caught the shape of the captain running towards the forward bulkhead. Ramius leaped at the bulkhead and flicked a light switch on as the enemy fired at him. Ryan tossed the clip to the right and ran forward. The agent turned to his left to see what the noise was, sure that a cooperative move had been planned.

As Ryan covered the distance between the last two missile tubes he saw Ramius go down. Ryan dived past the number one missile tube. He landed on his left side, ignoring the pain that set his arm on fire as he rolled to line up his target. The man was turning as Ryan jerked off six shots. Ryan didn't hear himself screaming. Two rounds connected. The agent was lifted off the deck and twisted halfway around from the impact. His pistol dropped from his hand and he fell limp to the deck.

Ryan was shaking too badly to get up at once. The pistol, still tight in his hand, was aimed at his victim's chest. He was breathing hard and his heart was racing. Ryan closed his mouth and tried to swallow a few times; his mouth was as dry as cotton. He got slowly to his knees. The agent was still alive, lying on his back, eyes open and still breathing. Ryan had to use his hand to stand up.

He'd been hit twice, Ryan saw, once in the upper left chest and once lower down, about where the liver and spleen are. The lower wound was a wet red circle which the man's hands clutched. He was in his early twenties, if that, and his clear blue eyes were staring at the overhead while he tried to say something. His face was rigid with pain as he mouthed words, but all that came out was an unintelligible gurgle.

'Captain,' Ryan called, 'you okay?'

'I am wounded, but I think I shall live, Ryan. Who is it?'

'How the hell should I know?'

The blue eyes fixed on Jack's face. Whoever he was, he knew death was coming for him. The pain on the face was replaced by something else. Sadness, an infinite sadness . . . He was still trying to speak. A pink froth gathered at the corners of his mouth. Lung shot. Ryan moved closer, kicking the gun clear and kneeling down beside him.

'We could have made a deal,' he said quietly.

The agent tried to say something, but Ryan couldn't understand it. A curse, a call for his mother, something heroic? Jack would never know. The eyes went wide with pain one last time. The last breath hissed out through the bubbles and the hands on the belly went limp. Ryan checked for a pulse at the neck. There was none.

'I'm sorry.' Ryan reached down to close the victim's eyes. He was sorry – why? Tiny beads of sweat broke out all over his forehead, and the strength he had drawn upon in the shootout deserted him. A sudden wave of nausea overpowered him. 'Oh, Jesus, I'm – ' He dropped to all fours and threw up violently, his vomit spilling through the grates on to the lower deck ten feet below. For a whole minute his stomach heaved, well past the time he was dry. He had to spit several times to get the worst of the taste from his mouth before standing.

Dizzy from the stress and the quart of adrenalin that had been pumped into his system, he shook his head a few times, still looking at the dead man at his feet. It was time to come back to reality.

Ramius had been hit in the upper leg. It was bleeding. Both his hands, covered with blood, were placed on the wound, but it didn't look that bad. If the femoral artery had been cut, the captain would already have been dead.

Lieutenant Williams had been hit in the head and chest. He was still breathing but unconscious. The head wound was only a crease. The chest wound, close to the heart, made a sucking noise. Kamarov was not so lucky. A single shot had gone straight through the top of his nose, and the back of his head was a bloody wreckage.

'Jesus, why didn't somebody come and help us!' Ryan said when the thought hit him.

'The bulkhead doors are closed, Ryan. There is the – how do you say it?'

Ryan looked where the captain pointed. It was the intercom system. 'Which button?' The captain held up two fingers. 'Control room, this is Ryan. I need help here, your captain has been shot.'

The reply came in excited Russian, and Ramius responded loudly to make himself heard. Ryan looked at the missile tube. The agent had been using a work light, just like an American one, a light bulb in a metal holder with wire across the front. A door into the missile tube was open. Beyond it a smaller hatch, evidently leading into the missile itself, was also open.

'What was he doing, trying to explode the warheads?'

'Impossible,' Ramius said, in obvious pain. 'The rocket warheads – we call this special safe. The warheads cannot – not fire.'

'So what was he doing?' Ryan went over to the missile tube. A sort of rubber bladder was lying on the deck. 'What's this?' He hefted the gadget in his hand. It was made of rubber or rubberized fabric with a metal or plastic frame inside, a metal nipple on one corner, and a mouthpiece.

'He was doing something to the missile, but he had an escape device to get off the sub,' Ryan said. 'Oh, Christ! A timing device.' He bent down to pick up the work light and switched it on, then stood back and peered into the missile compartment. 'Captain, what's in here?'

'That is – the guidance compartment. It has a computer that tells the rocket how to fly. The door – ,' Ramius' breaths were coming hard, ' – is a hatch for the officer.'

Ryan peered into the hatch. He found a mass of multi-coloured wires and circuit boards connected in a way he'd never seen before. He poked through the wires half expecting to find a ticking alarm clock wired to some dynamite sticks. He didn't.

Now what should he do? The agent had been up to something – but what? Did he finish? How could Ryan tell? He couldn't. One part of his brain screamed at him to do something, the other part said that he'd be crazy to try.

Ryan put the rubber-coated handle of the light between his teeth and reached into the compartment with both hands. He grabbed a double handful of wires and yanked back. Only a few broke loose. He released one bunch and concentrated on the other. A clump of plastic and copper spaghetti came loose. He did it again for the other bunch. 'Aaah!' he gasped, receiving an electric shock. An eternal moment followed while he waited to be blown up. It passed. There were more wires to pull. In under a minute he'd ripped out every wire he could see along with a half-dozen small breadboards. Next he smashed the light against everything he thought might break until the compartment looked like his son's toybox – full of useless fragments.

He heard people running into the compartment. Borodin was in front. Ramius motioned him over to Ryan and the dead agent.

'Sudets?' Borodin said. 'Sudets?' He looked at Ryan. 'This is cook.'

Ryan took the pistol from the deck. 'Here's his recipe file. I think he was a GRU agent. He was trying to blow us up. Captain Ramius, how about we launch this missile – just jettison the goddamned thing, okay?'

'A good idea, I think.' Ramius' voice had become a hoarse whisper. 'First close the inspection hatch, then we – can fire from the control room.'

Ryan used his hand to sweep the fragments away from the missile hatch, and the door slid neatly back into place. The tube hatch was different. It was a pressure-bearing one and much heavier, held in place by two spring-loaded latches. Ryan slammed it three times. Twice it rebounded, but the third time it stuck.

Borodin and another officer were already carrying Williams aft. Someone had set a belt on Ramius' leg wound. Ryan got him to his feet and helped him walk. Ramius grunted in pain every time he had to move his left leg.

'You took a foolish chance, Captain,' Ryan observed.

'This is my ship – and I do not like the dark. It was my fault! We should have made a careful counting as the crew left.'

They arrived at the watertight door. 'Okay, I'll go through first.' Ryan stepped through and helped Ramius through backward. The belt had loosened, and the wound was bleeding again.

'Close the hatch and lock it,' Ramius ordered.

It closed easily. Ryan turned the wheel three times, then got under the captain's arm again. Another twenty feet and they were in the control room. The lieutenant at the wheel was ashen.

Ryan sat the captain in a chair on the port side. 'You have a knife, sir?'

Ramius reached in his trouser pocket and came out with a folding knife and something else. 'Here, take this. It's the key for the rocket warheads. They cannot fire unless this is used. You keep it.' He tried to laugh. It had been Putin's, after all.

Ryan flipped it around his neck, opened the knife, and cut the captain's trousers all the way up. The bullet had gone clean through the meaty part of the thigh. He took a clean handkerchief from his pocket and held it against the entrance wound. Ramius handed him another handkerchief. Ryan placed this against the half-inch exit wound. Next he set the belt across both, drawing it as tight as he could.

'My wife might not approve, but that will have to do.'

'Your wife?' Ramius asked.

'She's a doc, an eye surgeon to be exact. The day I got shot she did this for me.' Ramius' lower leg was growing pale. The belt was too tight, but Ryan didn't want to loosen it just yet. 'Now, what about the missile?'

Ramius gave an order to the lieutenant at the wheel, who relayed it through the intercom. Two minutes later three officers entered the control room. Speed was cut to five knots, which took several minutes. Ryan worried about the missile and whether or not he had destroyed whatever boobytrap the agent had installed. Each of the three newly arrived officers took a key from around his neck. Ramius did the same, giving his second key to Ryan. He pointed to the starboard side of the compartment.

'Rocket control.'

Ryan should have guessed as much. Arrayed throughout the control room were five panels, each with three rows of twenty-six lights and a key slot under each set.

'Put your key in number one, Ryan.' Jack did, and the others inserted their keys. The red light came on and a buzzer sounded.

The missile officer's panel was the most elaborate. He turned a switch to flood the missile tube and open the number one hatch. The red panel lights began to blink.

'Turn your key, Ryan,' Ramius said.

'Does this fire the missile?' Christ, what if that happens? Ryan wondered.

'No no. The rocket must be armed by the rocket officer. This key explodes the gas charge.'

Could Ryan believe him? Sure he was a good guy and all that, but how could Ryan know he was telling the truth?

'Now!' Ramius ordered. Ryan turned his key at the same instant as the others. The amber light over the red light blinked on. The one under the green cover stayed off.

The *Red October* shuddered as the number one SS-N-20 was ejected upward by the gas charge. The sound was like a truck's air brake. The three officers withdrew their keys. Immediately the missile officer shut the tube hatch.

The *Dallas*

'What?' Jones said. 'Conn, sonar, the target just flooded a tube – a missile tube? God almighty!' On his own, Jones powered up the under-ice sonar and began high-frequency pinging.

'What the hell are you doing?' Thompson demanded. Mancuso was there a second later.

'What's going on?' the captain snapped. Jones pointed at his display.

'The sub just launched a missile, sir. Look, Cap'n, two targets. But it's just hangin' there, no missile ignition. God!'

The *Red October*

Will it float? Ryan wondered.

It didn't. The Seahawk missile was pushed upward and to starboard by the gas charge. It stopped fifty feet over her deck as the *October* cruised past. The guidance hatch that Ryan had closed was not fully sealed. Water filled the compartment and flooded the warhead bus. The missile in any case had a sizable negative buoyancy, and the added mass in the nose tipped it over. The nose-heavy trim gave it an eccentric path, and it spiralled down like a seedpod from a tree. At ten thousand feet water pressure crushed the seal over the missile blast cones, but the Seahawk, otherwise undamaged, retained its shape all the way to the bottom.

The *Ethan Allen*

The only thing still operating was the timer. It had been set for thirty minutes, which had allowed the crew plenty of time to board the *Scamp*, now leaving the area at ten knots. The old reactor had been completely shut down. It was stone cold. Only a few emergency lights remained on from residual battery power. The timer had three redundant firing circuits, and all went off within a millisecond of one another, sending a signal down the detonator wires.

They had put four Pave Pat Blue bombs on the *Ethan Allen*. The Pave Pat Blue was a FAE (fuel-air explosive) bomb. Its blast efficiency was roughly five times that of an ordinary chemical explosive. Each bomb had a pair of gas-release valves, and only one of the eight valves failed. When they burst open, the pressurized propane in the bomb casings expanded violently outwards. In an instant the atmospheric pressure in the old submarine tripled as her every part was saturated with an explosive air-gas mixture. The four bombs filled the *Ethan Allen* with the equivalent of twenty-five tons of TNT evenly distributed throughout the hull.

The squibs fired almost simultaneously, and the results were catastrophic: the *Ethan Allen*'s strong steel hull burst as if it were a balloon. The only item not totally destroyed was the reactor vessel, which fell free of the shredded wreckage and dropped rapidly to the ocean floor. The hull itself was blasted into a dozen pieces, all bent into surreal shapes by the explosion. Interior equipment formed a metallic cloud within the shattered hull, and everything fluttered downwards, expanding over a wide area during the three-mile descent to the hard sand bottom.

The *Dallas*

'Holy shit!' Jones slapped the headphones off and yawned to clear his ears. Automatic relays within the sonar system protected his ears from the full force of the explosion, but what had been transmitted was enough to make him feel as though his head had been hammered flat. The explosion was heard through the hull by everyone aboard.

'Attention all hands, this is the captain speaking. What you just heard is nothing to worry about. That's all I can say.'

'Gawd, Skipper!' Mannion said.

'Yeah, let's get back on the contact.'

'Aye, Cap'n.' Mannion gave his commander a curious look.

The White House

'Did you get the word to him in time?' the president asked.

'No, sir.' Moore slumped into his chair. 'The helicopter arrived a few minutes too late. It may be nothing to worry about. You'd expect that the captain would know enough to get everyone off except for his own people. We're concerned, of course, but there isn't anything we can do.'

'I asked him personally to do this, Judge. Me.'

Welcome to the real world, Mr President, Moore thought. The chief executive had been lucky – he'd never had to send men to their deaths. Moore reflected that it was something easy to consider beforehand, less easy to get used to. He had affirmed death sentences from his seat on an appellate bench, and that had not been easy – even for men who had richly deserved their fates.

'Well, we'll just have to wait and see, Mr President. The source this data comes from is more important than any one operation.'

'Very well. What about Senator Donaldson?'

'He agreed to our suggestion. This aspect of the operation has worked out very well indeed.'

'Do you really expect the Russians to buy it?' Pelt asked.

'We've left some nice bait, and we'll jerk the line a little to get their attention. In a day or two we'll see if they nibble at it. Henderson is one of their all-stars – his code name is Cassius – and their reaction to this will tell us just what sort of disinformation we can pass through him. He could turn out to be very useful, but we'll have to watch out for him. Our KGB colleagues have a very direct method for dealing with doubles.'

'We don't let him off the hook unless he earns it,' the president said coldly.

Moore smiled. 'Oh, he'll earn it. We own Mr Henderson.'

The Fifteenth Day

Friday, 17 December

Ocracoke Inlet

There was no moon. The three-ship procession entered the inlet at five knots, just after midnight to take advantage of the extra-high spring tide. The *Pogy* led the formation since she had the shallowest draft, and the *Dallas* trailed the *Red October*. The coast guard stations on either side of the inlet were occupied by naval officers who had relieved the 'coasties.'

Ryan had been allowed atop the sail, a humanitarian gesture from Ramius that he much appreciated. After eighteen hours inside the *Red October* Jack had felt confined, and it was good to see the world – even if it was nothing but dark empty space. The *Pogy* showed only a dim red light that disappeared if it was looked at for more than a few seconds. He could see the water's feathery wisps of foam and the stars playing hide-and-seek through the clouds. The west wind was a harsh twenty knots coming off the water.

Borodin was giving terse, monosyllabic orders as he conned the submarine up a channel that had to be dredged every few months despite the enormous jetty which had been built to the north. The ride was an easy one, the two or three feet of chop not mattering a whit to the missile sub's 30,000-ton bulk. Ryan was thankful for this. The black water calmed, and when they entered sheltered waters a Zodiac-type rubber boat zoomed towards them.

'Ahoy *Red October*!' a voice called in the darkness. Ryan could barely make out the grey lozenge shape of the Zodiac. It was ahead of a tiny patch of foam formed by the sputtering outboard motor.

'May I answer, Captain Borodin?' Ryan asked, getting a nod. 'This is Ryan. We have two casualties aboard. One's in bad shape. We need a doctor and a surgical team right away! Do you understand?'

'Two casualties, and you need a doc, right.' Ryan thought he saw a man holding something to his face, and thought he heard the faint crackle of a radio. It was hard to tell in the wind. 'Okay. We'll have a doc flown down right away, *October*. *Dallas* and *Pogy* both have medical corpsmen aboard. You want 'em?'

'Damn straight!' Ryan replied at once.

'Okay. Follow *Pogy* two more miles and stand by.' The Zodiac sped forward, reversed course, and disappeared in the darkness.

'Thank God for that,' Ryan breathed.

'You are be – believer?' Borodin asked.

'Yeah, sure.' Ryan should not have been surprised by the question. 'Hell, you gotta believe in something.'

'And why is that, Commander Ryan?' Borodin was examining the *Pogy* through oversized night glasses.

Ryan wondered how to answer. 'Well, because if you don't, what's the point of life? That would mean Sartre and Camus and all those characters were right – all is chaos, life has no meaning. I refuse to believe that. If you want a better answer, I know a couple priests who'd be glad to talk to you.'

Borodin did not respond. He spoke an order into the bridge microphone, and they altered course a few degrees to starboard.

The *Dallas*

A half mile aft, Mancuso was holding a light-amplifying night scope to his eyes. Mannion was at his shoulder, struggling to see.

'Jesus Christ,' Mancuso whispered.

'You got that one right, Skipper,' Mannion said, shivering in his jacket.

'I'm not sure I believe it either. Here comes the Zodiac.' Mannion handed his commander the portable radio used for docking.

'Do you read?'

'This is Mancuso.'

'When our friend stops, I want you to transfer ten men to her, including your orderly. They report two casualties who need medical attention. Pick good men, Commander, they'll need help running the boat – just make damned sure they're men who don't talk.'

'Acknowledged. Ten men including the medic. Out.' Mancuso watched the raft speed off to the *Pogy*. 'Want to come along, Pat?'

'Bet your ass, uh, sir. You planning to go?' Mannion asked.

Mancuso was judicious. 'I think Chambers is up to handling *Dallas* for a day or so, don't you?'

On shore, a naval officer was on the phone to Norfolk. The coast guard station was crowded, almost entirely with officers. A fibreglass box sat next to the phone so that they could communicate with CINCLANT in secrecy. They had been here only two hours and would soon leave. Nothing could appear out of the ordinary. Outside, an admiral and a pair of captains watched the dark shapes through starlight scopes. They were as solemn as men in a church.

Cherry Point, North Carolina

Commander Ed Noyes was resting in the doctor's lounge of the naval hospital at the US Marine Corps Air Station, Cherry Point, North Carolina. A qualified flight surgeon, he had the duty for the next three nights so that he'd have four days off over Christmas. It had been a quiet night. This was about to change.

'Doc?'

Noyes looked up to see a marine captain in MP livery. The doctor knew him. Military police delivered a lot of accident cases. He set down his *New England Journal of Medicine.*

'Hi, Jerry. Something coming in?'

'Doc, I got orders to tell you to pack everything you need for emergency surgery. You got two minutes, then I take you to the airfield.'

'What for? What kind of surgery?' Noyes stood.

'They didn't say, sir, just that you fly out somewhere, alone. The orders come from topside, that's all I know.'

'Damn it, Jerry, I have to know what sort of surgery it is so I know what to take!'

'So take everything, sir. I gotta get you to the chopper.'

Noyes swore and went into the trauma receiving room. Two more marines were waiting there. He handed them four sterile sets, prepackaged instrument trays. He wondered if he'd need some drugs and decided to grab an armful, along with two units of plasma. The captain helped him on with his coat, and they moved out the door to a waiting jeep. Five minutes later they pulled up to a Sea Stallion whose engines were already screaming.

'What gives?' Noyes asked the colonel of intelligence inside, wondering where the crew chief was.

'We're heading out over the sound,' the colonel explained. 'We have to let you down on a sub that has some casualties aboard. There's a pair of orderlies to assist you, and that's all I know, okay?' It had to be okay. There was no choice in the matter.

The Stallion lifted off at once. Noyes had flown in them often enough. He had two hundred hours piloting helicopters, another three hundred in fixed-wing aircraft. Noyes was the kind of doctor who'd discovered too late that flying was as attractive a calling as medicine. He went up at every opportunity, often giving pilots special medical care for their dependents to get backseat time in an F-4 Phantom. The Sea Stallion, he noted, was not cruising. It was running flat out.

Pamlico Sound

The *Pogy* came to a halt about the time the helicopter left Cherry Point. The *October* altered course to starboard again and halted even with her to the

271

north. The *Dallas* followed suit. A minute after that the Zodiac reappeared at the *Dallas*' side, then approached the *Red October* slowly, almost wallowing with her cargo of men.

'Ahoy *Red October*!'

This time Borodin answered. He had an accent but his English was understandable. 'Identify.'

'This is Bart Mancuso, commanding officer of USS *Dallas*. I have our ship's medical representative aboard and some other men. Request permission to come aboard, sir.'

Ryan saw the *starpom* grimace. For the first time Borodin really had to face up to what was happening, and he would have been less than human to accept it without some kind of struggle.

'Permission is – yes.'

The Zodiac edged right up to the curve of the hull. A man leaped aboard with a line to secure the raft. Ten men clambered off, one breaking away to climb up the submarine's sail.

'Captain? I'm Bart Mancuso. I understand you have some hurt men aboard.'

'Yes,' Borodin nodded, 'the captain and a British officer, both shot.'

'Shot?' Mancuso was surprised.

'Worry about that later,' Ryan said sharply. 'Let's get your doc working on them, okay?'

'Sure, where's the hatch?'

Borodin spoke into the bridge mike, and a few seconds later a circle of light appeared on deck at the foot of the sail.

'We haven't got a physician, we have an independent duty orderly. He's pretty good, and *Pogy*'s man will be here in another couple minutes. Who are you, by the way?'

'He is a spy,' Borodin said with palpable irony.

'Jack Ryan.'

'And you, sir?'

'Captain Second Rank Vasily Borodin. I am – the first officer, yes? Come over into the station, Commander. Please excuse me, we are all very tired.'

'You're not the only ones.' There wasn't that much room. Mancuso perched himself on the coaming. 'Captain, I want you to know we had a bastard of a time tracking you. You are to be complimented for your professional skill.'

The compliment did not elicit the anticipated response from Borodin. 'You were able to track us. How?'

'I brought him along, you can meet him.'

'And what are we to do?'

'Orders from shore are to wait for the doc to arrive and dive. Then we sit tight until we get orders to move. Maybe a day, maybe two. I think we could all use the rest. After that, we get you to a nice safe place, and I will personally buy you the best damned Italian dinner you ever had.' Mancuso grinned. 'You get Italian food in Russia?'

'No, and if you are accustomed to good food, you may find *Krazny Oktyabr* not to your liking.'

'Maybe I can fix that. How many men aboard?'

'Twelve. Ten Soviet, the Englishman, and the spy.' Borodin glanced at Ryan with a thin smile.

'Okay.' Mancuso reached into his coat and came out with a radio. 'This is Mancuso.'

'We're here, Skipper,' Chambers replied.

'Get some food together for our friends. Six meals for twenty-five men. Send a cook over with it. Wally, I want to show these men some good chow. Got it?'

'Aye, aye, Skipper. Out.'

'I got some good cooks, Captain. Shame this wasn't last week. We had lasagna, just like momma used to make. All that was missing was the Chianti.'

'They have vodka,' Ryan observed.

'Only for spies,' Borodin said. Two hours after the shoot-out Ryan had had the shakes badly, and Borodin had sent him a drink from the medical stores. 'We are told that your submarine men are greatly pampered.'

'Maybe so,' Mancuso nodded. 'But we stay out sixty or seventy days at a time. That's hard enough, don't you think?'

'How about we go below?' Ryan suggested. Everyone agreed. It was getting cold.

Borodin, Ryan, and Mancuso went below to find the Americans on one side of the control room and the Soviets on the other, just like before. The American captain broke the ice.

'Captain Borodin, this is the man who found you. Come here, Jonesy.'

'It wasn't very easy, sir,' Jones said. 'Can I get to work? Can I see your sonar room?'

'Bugayev.' Borodin waved the ship's electronics officer over. The captain-lieutenant led the sonarman aft.

Jones took one look at the equipment and muttered, 'Kludge.' The face plates all had louvres on them to let out the heat. God, did they use vacuum tubes? Jones wondered. He pulled a screwdriver from his pocket to find out.

'You speak English, sir?'

'Yes, a little.'

'Can I see the circuit diagrams for these, please?'

Bugayev blinked. No enlisted men, and only one of his *michmanyy*, had ever asked for them. Then he took the binder of schematics from its shelf on the forward bulkhead.

Jones matched the code number of the set he was checking with the right section of the binder. Unfolding the diagram, he noted with relief that ohms were ohms, all over the world. He began tracing his finger along the page, then pulled the cover panel off to look inside the set.

'Kludge, megakludge to the max!' Jones was shocked enough to lapse into Valspeak.

'Excuse me, what is this "kludge?"'

'Oh, pardon me, sir. That's an expression we use in the navy. I don't know how to say it in Russian. Sorry.' Jones stifled a grin as he went back to the schematic. 'Sir, this one here's a low-powered high-frequency set, right? You use this for mines and stuff?'

It was Bugayev's turn to be shocked. 'You have been trained in Soviet equipment?'

'No, sir, but I've heard a lot of it.' Wasn't this obvious? Jones wondered. 'Sir, this is a high-frequency set, but it doesn't draw a lot of power. What else is it good for? A low-power FM set you use for mines, for work under ice, and for docking, right?'

'Correct.'

'You have a gertrude, sir?'

'Gertrude?'

'Underwater telephone, sir, for talking to other subs.' Didn't this guy know anything?

'Ah, yes, but it is located in control, and it is broken.'

'Uh-huh.' Jones looked over the diagram again. 'I think I can rig a modulator on this baby, then, and make it into a gertrude for ya. Might be useful. You think your skipper would want that, sir?'

'I will ask.' He expected Jones to stay put, but the young sonarman was right behind him when he went to control. Bugayev explained the suggestion to Borodin while Jones talked to Mancuso.

'They got a little FM set that looks just like the old gertrudes in sonar school. We have a spare modulator in stores, and I can probably rig it up in thirty minutes, no sweat,' the sonarman said.

'Captain Borodin, do you agree?' Mancuso asked.

Borodin felt as if he were being pushed too fast, even though the suggestion made perfectly good sense. 'Yes, have your man do it.'

'Skipper, how long we gonna be here?' Jones asked.

'A day or two, why?'

'Sir, this boat looks kinda thin on creature comforts, you know? How 'bout I grab a TV and a tape machine? Give 'em something to look at, you know, sort of give 'em a quick look at the USA?'

Mancuso laughed. They wanted to learn everything they could about this boat, but they had plenty of time for that, and Jones' idea looked like a good way to ease the tension. On the other hand, he didn't want to incite a mutiny on his own sub. 'Okay, take the one from the wardroom.'

'Right, Skipper.'

The Zodiac delivered the *Pogy*'s orderly a few minutes later, and Jones took the boat back to the *Dallas*. Gradually the officers were beginning to engage in conversation. Two Russians were trying to talk to Mannion and were looking at his hair. They had never met a black man before.

'Captain Borodin, I have orders to take something out of the control room that will identify – I mean, something that comes from this boat.' Mancuso pointed. 'Can I take that depth gauge? I can have one of my men rig a substitute.' The gauge, he saw, had a number.

'For what reason?'

'Beats me, but those are my orders.'

'Yes,' Borodin replied.

Mancuso ordered one of his chiefs to perform the job. The chief pulled a crescent wrench from his pocket and removed the nut holding the needle and dial in place.

'This is a little bigger than ours, Skipper, but not by much. I think we have a spare. I can flip it backwards and scribe in the markings, okay?'

Mancuso handed his radio over. 'Call it in and have Jonesy bring the spare back with him.'

'Aye, Cap'n.' The chief put the needle back in place after setting the dial on the deck.

The Sea Stallion did not attempt to land, though the pilot was tempted. The deck was almost large enough to try. As it was, the helicopter hovered a few feet over the missile deck, and the doctor leaped into the arms of two seamen. His supplies were tossed down a moment later. The colonel remained in the back of the chopper and slid the door shut. The bird turned slowly to move back southwest, its massive rotor raising spray from the waters of Pamlico Sound.

'Was that what I think it was?' the pilot asked over the intercom.

'Wasn't it backwards? I thought missile subs had the missiles aft of the sail. Those were in front of the sail, weren't they? I mean, wasn't that the rudder sticking up behind the sail?' the co-pilot responded quizzically.

'It was a Russian sub!' the pilot said.

'*What?*' It was too late to see, they were already two miles away. 'Those were our guys on the deck. They weren't Russians.'

'Son of a *bitch!*' the major swore wonderingly. And he couldn't say a thing. The colonel of division intelligence had been damned specific about that: 'You don't see nothin', you don't hear nothin', you don't think nothin', and you goddamned well don't ever say nothin'.'

'I'm Doctor Noyes,' the commander said to Mancuso in the control room. He had never been on a submarine before, and when he looked around he saw a compartment full of instruments all in a foreign language. 'What ship is this?'

'*Krazny Oktyabr*,' Borodin said, coming over. In the centrepiece of his cap there was a gleaming red star.

'What the hell is going on here?' Noyes demanded.

'Doc,' Ryan took him by the arm, 'you have two patients aft. Why not let's worry about them?'

Noyes followed him aft to sick bay. 'What's going on here?' he persisted more quietly.

'The Russians just lost a submarine,' Ryan explained, 'and now she belongs to us. And if you tell anybody – '

'I read you, but I don't believe you.'

'You don't have to believe me. What kind of cutter are you?'

'Thoracic.'

'Good,' Ryan turned into sick bay, 'you have a gunshot wound victim who needs you bad.'

Williams was lying naked on the table. A sailor came in with an armful of medical supplies and set them on Petrov's desk. The *October*'s medical locker had a supply of frozen plasma, and the two orderlies already had two units running into the lieutenant. A chest tube was in, draining into a vacuum bottle.

'We got a nine-millimetre in this man's chest,' one of the corpsmen said after introducing himself and his partner. 'He's had a chest tube in the last ten hours, they tell me. The head looks worse than it is. Right pupil is a little brown, but no big deal. The chest is bad, sir. You'd better take a listen.'

'Vitals?' Noyes fished in his bag for a stethoscope.

'Heart is 110 and thready. Blood pressure's eighty over forty.'

Noyes moved his stethoscope around Williams' chest, frowning. 'Heart's in the wrong place. We have a left tension pneumothorax. There must be a quart of fluid in there, and it sounds like he's heading for congestive failure.' Noyes turned to Ryan. 'You get out of here. I've got a chest to crack.'

'Take care of him, Doc. He's a good man.'

'Aren't they all,' Noyes observed, stripping off his jacket. 'Let's get scrubbed, people.'

Ryan wondered if a prayer would help. Noyes looked and talked like a surgeon. Ryan hoped he was. He went aft to the captain's cabin, where Ramius was sleeping with the drugs he'd been given. The leg had stopped bleeding, and evidently one of the orderlies had checked on it. Noyes could work on him next. Ryan went forward.

Borodin felt he had lost control and didn't like it, though it was something of a relief. Two weeks of constant tension plus the nerve-wrenching change in plans had shaken the officer more than he would have believed. The situation was now unpleasant – the Americans were trying to be kind, but they were so damned overpowering! At least the *Red October*'s officers were not in danger.

Twenty minutes later the Zodiac was back again. Two sailors went topside to unload a few hundred pounds of frozen food, then helped Jones with his electronic gear. It took several minutes to get everything squared away, and the seamen who took the food forward came back shaken after finding two stiff bodies and a third frozen solid. There had not been time to move the two recent casualties.

'Got everything, Skipper,' Jones reported. He handed the depth gauge dial to the chief.

'What is all of this?' Borodin asked.

'Captain, I got the modulator to make the gertrude.' Jones held up a small box. 'This other stuff is a little colour TV, a video cassette recorder, and some movie tapes. The skipper thought you gentlemen might want something to relax with, to get to know us a little, you know?'

'Movies?' Borodin shook his head. 'Cinema movies?'

'Sure,' Mancuso chuckled. 'What did you bring, Jonesy?'

'Well, sir, I got *E.T.*, *Star Wars*, *Big Jake,* and *Hondo*.' Clearly Jones wanted to be careful what parts of America he introduced the Russians to.

'My apologies, Captain. My crewman has limited taste in movies.'

At the moment Borodin would have settled for *The Battleship Potemkin*. The fatigue was really hitting him hard.

The cook bustled aft with an armload of groceries. 'I'll have coffee in a few minutes, sir,' he said to Borodin on his way to the galley.

'I would like something to eat. None of us has eaten in a day,' Borodin said.

'Food!' Mancuso called aft.

'Aye, Skipper. Let me figure this galley out.'

Mannion checked his watch. 'Twenty minutes, sir.'

'We have everything we need aboard?'

'Yes, sir.'

Jones bypassed the pulse control on the sonar amplifier and wired in the modulator. It was even easier than he'd expected. He had taken a radio microphone from the *Dallas* along with everything else and now connected it to the sonar set before powering the system up. He had to wait for the set to warm up. Jones hadn't seen this many tubes since he'd gone out on TV repair jobs with his father, and that had been a long time ago.

'*Dallas*, this is Jonesy, do you copy?'

'Aye.' The reply was scratchy, like a taxicab radio.

'Thanks. Out.' He switched off. 'It works. That was pretty easy, wasn't it?'

Enlisted man, hell! And not even trained on Soviet equipment! the *October*'s electronics officer thought. It never occurred to him that this piece of equipment was a near copy of an obsolete American FM system. 'How long have you been a sonarman?'

'Three and a half years, sir. Since I dropped out of college.'

'You learn all this in three years?' the officer asked sharply.

Jones shrugged. 'What's the big deal, sir? I've been foolin' with radios and stuff since I was a kid. You mind if I play some music, sir?'

Jones had decided to be especially nice. He had only one tape of a Russian composer, the Nutcracker Suite, and had brought that along with four Bachs. Jones liked to hear music while he prayed over circuit diagrams. The young sonarman was in Hog Heaven. All the Russian sets he had listened to for three years – now he had their schematics, their hardware, and the time to figure them all out. Bugayev continued to watch in amazement as Jones' fingers did their ballet through the manual pages to the music of Tchaikovsky.

'Time to dive, sir,' Mannion said in control.

'Very well. With your permission, Captain Borodin, I will assist with the vents. All hatches and openings are . . . shut.' The diving board used the same light-array system as American boats, Mancuso noticed.

Mancuso took stock of the situation one last time. Butler and his four most senior petty officers were already tending to the nuclear tea kettle aft. The situation looked pretty good, considering. The only thing that could really go badly wrong would be for the *October*'s officers to change their minds. The *Dallas* would be keeping the missile sub under constant sonar observation. If she moved, the *Dallas* had a ten-knot speed advantage with which to block the channel.

'The way I see it, Captain, we are rigged for dive,' Mancuso said.

Borodin nodded and sounded the diving alarm. It was a buzzer, just like on American boats. Mancuso, Mannion and a Russian officer worked the complex vent controls. The *Red October* began her slow descent. In five minutes she was resting on the bottom, with seventy feet of water over the top of her sail.

The White House

Pelt was on the phone to the Soviet embassy at three in the morning. 'Alex, this is Jeffrey Pelt.'

'How are you, Dr Pelt? I must offer my thanks and that of the Soviet people for your action to save our sailor. I was informed a few minutes ago that he is now conscious, and that he is expected to recover fully.'

'Yes, I just learned that myself. What's his name, by the way?' Pelt wondered if he had awakened Arbatov. It didn't sound like it.

'Andre Katyskin, a cook petty officer from Leningrad.'

'Good. Alex, I am informed that USS *Pigeon* has rescued nearly the entire crew of another Soviet submarine off the Carolinas. Her name, evidently, was *Red October*. That's the good news, Alex. The bad news is that the vessel exploded and sank before we could get them all off. Most of the officers, and two of our officers, were lost.'

'When was this?'

'Very early yesterday morning. Sorry about the delay, but *Pigeon* had trouble with the radio, as a result of the underwater explosion, they say. You know how that sort of thing can happen.'

'Indeed.' Pelt had to admire the response, not a trace of irony. 'Where are they now?'

'The *Pigeon* is sailing to Charleston, South Carolina. We'll have your crewmen flown directly to Washington from there.'

'And this submarine exploded? You are sure?'

'Yeah, one of the crewmen said they had a major reactor accident. It was just good luck that *Pigeon* was there. She was heading to the Virginia coast to look at the other one you lost. I think your navy needs a little work, Alex,' Pelt observed.

'I will pass that along to Moscow, Doctor,' Arbatov responded dryly. 'Can you tell us where this happened?'

'I can do better than that. We have a ship taking a deep-diving research sub down to look for the wreckage. If you want, you can have your navy fly a man to Norfolk, and we'll fly him out to check it for you. Fair enough?'

'You say you lost two officers?' Arbatov played for time, surprised at the offer.

'Yes, both rescue people. We did get a hundred men off, Alex,' Pelt said defensively. 'That's something.'

'Indeed it is, Dr Pelt. I must cable Moscow for instructions. I will be back to you. You are at your office?'

'Correct. Bye, Alex.' He hung up and looked at the president. 'Do I pass, boss?'

'Work a little bit on the sincerity, Jeff.' The president was sprawled in a leather chair, a robe over his pyjamas. 'They'll bite?'

'They'll bite. They sure as hell want to confirm the destruction of the sub. Question is, can we fool 'em?'

'Foster seems to think so. It sounds plausible enough.'

'Hmph. Well, we have her, don't we?' Pelt observed.

'Yep. I guess that story about the GRU agent was wrong, or else they kicked him off with everybody else. I want to see that Captain Ramius. Jeez! Pulling a reactor scare, no wonder he got everybody off the ship!'

The Pentagon

Skip Tyler was in the CNO's office trying to relax in a chair. The coast guard station on the inlet had had a low-light television, the tape from which had been flown by helicopter to Cherry Point and from there by Phantom jet fighter to Andrews. Now it was in the hands of a courier whose automobile was just pulling up at the Pentagon's main entrance.

'I have a package to hand deliver to Admiral Foster,' an ensign announced a few minutes later. Foster's flag secretary pointed him to the door.

'Good morning, sir! This is for you, sir.' The ensign handed Foster the wrapped cassette.

'Thank you. Dismissed.'

Foster inserted the cassette in the tape player atop his office television. The set was already on, and the picture appeared in several seconds.

Tyler was standing beside the CNO as it focused. 'Yep.'

'Yep,' Foster agreed.

The picture was lousy – no other word for it. The low-light television system did not give a very sharp picture since it amplified all of the ambient light equally. This tended to wash out many details. But what they saw was enough: a very large missile submarine whose sail was much further aft than the sails on anything a Western country made. She dwarfed the *Dallas* and *Pogy*. They watched the screen without a word for the next fifteen minutes. Except for the wobbly camera, the picture was about as lively as a test pattern.

'Well,' Foster said as the tape ended, 'we got us a Russian boomer.'

'How 'bout that?' Tyler grinned.

'Skip, you were up for command of *Los Angeles*, right?'

'Yes, sir.'

'We owe you for this, Commander, we owe you a lot. I did some checking the other day. An officer injured in the line of duty does not necessarily have to retire unless he is demonstrably unfit for duty. An accident while returning from working on your boat is line of duty, I think, and we've had a few ship commanders who were short a leg. I'll go to the president myself on this, son. It will mean a year's work getting back in the groove, but if you still want your command, by God, I'll get it for you.'

Tyler sat down for that. It would mean being fitted for a new leg, something he'd been considering for months, and a few weeks getting used to it. Then a year – a good year – relearning everything he needed to know before he could go to sea . . . He shook his head. 'Thank you, Admiral. You don't know what that means to me – but, no. I'm past that now. I have a different life, and different responsibilities now, and I'd just be taking someone else's slot. Tell you what, you let me get a look at that boomer, and we're even.'

'That I can guarantee.' Foster had hoped he'd respond that way, had been nearly sure of it. It was too bad, though. Tyler, he thought, would have been a good candidate for his own flag except for the leg. Well, nobody ever said the world was fair.

The *Red October*

'You guys seem to have things under control,' Ryan observed. 'Does anybody mind if I flake out somewhere?'

'Flake out?' Borodin asked.

'Sleep.'

'Ah, take Dr Petrov's cabin, across from the medical office.'

On his way aft Ryan looked in Borodin's cabin and found the vodka bottle that had been liberated. It didn't have much taste, but it was smooth enough. Petrov's bunk was not very wide or very soft. Ryan was past caring. He took a long swallow and lay down in his uniform, which was already so greasy and dirty as to be beyond hope. He was asleep in five minutes.

The *Sea Cliff*

The air-purifier system was not working properly, Lieutenant Sven Johnsen thought. If his sinus cold had lasted a few more days he might not have noticed. The *Sea Cliff* was just passing ten thousand feet, and they couldn't tinker with the system until they surfaced. It was not dangerous – the environmental control systems had as many built-in redundancies as the Space Shuttle – just a nuisance.

'I've never been so deep,' Captain Igor Kaganovich said conversationally. Getting him here had been complicated. It had required a Helix helicopter from the *Kiev* to the *Tarawa*, then a U.S. Navy Sea King to Norfolk. Another helicopter had taken him to the USS *Austin*, which was heading for 33N 75W at twenty knots. The *Austin* was a landing ship dock, a large vessel whose aft end was a covered well. She was usually used for landing craft, but today she carried the *Sea Cliff*, a three-man submarine that had been flown down from Woods Hole, Massachusetts.

'Does take some getting used to,' Johnsen agreed, 'but when you get down to it, five hundred feet, ten thousand feet, doesn't make much difference. A hull fracture would kill you just as fast, just down here there'd be less residue for the next boat to try and recover.'

'Keep thinking those happy thoughts, sir,' machinist's mate First Class Jesse Overton said. 'Still clear on sonar?'

'Right, Jess.' Johnsen had been working with the machinist's mate for two years. The *Sea Cliff* was their baby, a small, rugged research submarine used mainly for oceanographic tasks, including the emplacement or repair of SOSUS sensors. On the three-man sub there was little place for bridge discipline. Overton was not well educated or very articulate – at least not politely articulate. His skill at manoeuvring the minisub was unsurpassed, however, and Johnsen was just as happy to leave that job to him. It was the lieutenant's task to manage the mission at hand.

'Air system needs some work,' Johnsen observed.

'Yeah, the filters are about due for replacement. I was going to do that next week. Coulda' done it this morning, but I figured the backup control wiring was more important.'

'Guess I have to go along with you on that. Handling okay?'

'Like a virgin.' Overton's smile was reflected in the thick Lexan view port in front of the control seat. The *Sea Cliff*'s awkward design made her clumsy to manoeuvre. It was as though she knew what she wanted to do, just not quite how she wanted to do it. 'How wide's the target area?'

'Pretty wide. *Pigeon* says after the explosion the pieces spread from hell to breakfast.'

'I believe it. Three miles down, and a current to spread it around.'

'The boat's name is *Red October*, Captain? A *Victor*-class attack submarine, you said?'

'That is your name for the class,' Kaganovich said.

'What do you call them?' Johnsen asked. He got no reply. What was the big deal? he wondered. What did the name of the class matter to anybody?

'Switching on locator sonar.' Johnsen activated several systems, and the *Sea Cliff* pulsed with the sound of the high-frequency sonar mounted on her belly. There's the bottom.' The yellow screen showed bottom contours in white.

'Anything sticking up, sir?' Overton asked.

'Not today, Jess.'

A year before they had been operating a few miles from this spot and nearly been impaled on a Liberty ship, sunk around 1942 by a German U-boat. The hulk had been sitting up at an angle, propped up by a massive boulder. That near collision would surely have been fatal, and it had taught both men caution.

'Okay, I'm starting to get some hard returns. Directly ahead, spread out like a fan. Another five hundred feet to the bottom.'

'Right.'

'Hmph. There's one big piece, 'bout thirty feet long, maybe nine or ten across, eleven o'clock, three hundred yards. We'll go for that one first.'

'Coming left, lights coming on now.'

A half-dozen high-intensity floodlights came on, at once surrounding the submersible in a globe of light. It did not penetrate more than ten yards in the water, which ate up the light energy.

'There's the bottom, just where you said, Mr Johnsen,' Overton said. He halted the powered descent and checked for buoyancy. Almost exactly neutral, good. 'This current's going to be tough on battery power.'

'How strong is it?'

'Knot an' a half, maybe more like two, depending on bottom contours. Same as last year. I figure we can manoeuvre an hour, hour an' a half, tops.'

Johnsen agreed. Oceanographers were still puzzling over this deep current, which seemed to change direction from time to time in no particular pattern. Odd. There were a lot of odd things in the ocean. That's why Johnsen got his oceanography degree, to figure some of the buggers out. It sure beat working for a living. Being three miles down wasn't work, not to Johnsen.

'I see somethin', a flash off the bottom right in front of us. Want me to grab it?'

'If you can.'

They couldn't see it yet on any of the *Sea Cliff*'s three TV monitors, which looked straight ahead, forty-five degrees left and right of the bow.

'Okay.' Overton put his right hand on the waldo control. This was what he was really best at.

'Can you see what it is?' Johnsen asked, fiddling with the TV.

'Some kinda instrument. Can you kill the number one flood, sir?' It's dazzlin' me.'

'Wait one.' Johnsen leaned forwards to kill the proper switch. The number one floodlight provided illumination for the bow camera, which went immediately blank.

'Okay, baby, now let's just hold steady . . .' The machinist's mate's left hand worked the directional propeller controls; his right was poised in the waldo glove. Now he was the only one who could see the target. Overton's reflection was grinning at itself. His right hand moved rapidly.

'Gotcha!' he said. The waldo took the depth-gauge dial a diver had magnetically affixed to the *Sea Cliff*'s bow prior to setting out from the *Austin*'s dock bay. 'You can hit the light again, sir.'

Johnsen flicked it on, and Overton manoeuvred his catch in front of the bow camera. 'Can ya see what it is?'

'Looks like a depth gauge. Not one of ours, though,' Johnsen observed. 'Can you make it out, Captain?'

'*Da*,' Kaganovich said at once. He let out a long breath, trying to sound unhappy. 'It is one of ours. I cannot read the number, but it is Soviet.'

'Put it in the basket, Jess,' Johnsen said.

'Right.' He manoeuvred the waldo, placing the dial in a basket welded on the bow, then getting the manipulator arm back to its rest position. 'Getting some silt. Let's pick up a little.'

As the *Sea Cliff* got too close to the bottom the wash from her propellers stirred up the fine alluvial silt. Overton increased power to get back to a twenty-foot height.

'That's better. See what the current is doin', Mr Johnsen? Good two knots. Gonna cut our bottom time.' The current was wafting the cloud to port, rather quickly. 'Where's the big target?'

'Dead ahead, about a hundred yards. Let's make sure we see what that is.'

'Right. Going forward . . . There's something, looks like a butcher knife. We want it?'

'No, let's keep going.'

'Okay, range?'

'Sixty yards. Ought to be seeing it soon.'

The two officers saw it on TV the same time Overton did. Just a spectral image at first, it faded like an after-image in one's eye. Then it came back.

Overton was the first to react. 'Damn!'

It was more than thirty feet long and appeared perfectly round. They approached from its rear and saw the main circle and within it four smaller cones that stuck out a foot or so.

'That's a missile, Skipper, a whole fuckin' Russkie nuclear missile!'

'Hold position, Jess.'

'Aye aye.' He backed off on the power controls.

'You said she was a *Victor*,' Johnsen said to the Soviet.

'I was mistaken.' Kaganovich's mouth twitched.

'Let's take a closer look, Jess.'

The *Sea Cliff* moved forward, up the side of the rocket body. The Cyrillic lettering was unmistakable, though they were too far off to make out the serial numbers. There was a new treasure for Davey Jones, an SS-N-20 Seahawk, with its eight five-hundred-kiloton MIRVs.

Kaganovich was careful to note the markings on the missile body. He'd been briefed on the Seahawk immediately before flying from the *Kiev*. As an intelligence officer, he ordinarily knew more about American weapons than their Soviet counterparts.

How convenient, he thought. The Americans had allowed him to ride in one of their most advanced research vessels whose internal arrangements he had already memorized, and they had accomplished his mission for him. The *Red October* was dead. All he had to do was get that information to Admiral Stralbo on the *Kirov* and the fleet could leave the American coast. Let them come to the Norwegian Sea to play their nasty games! See who would win them up there!

'Position check, Jess. Mark the sucker.'

'Aye.' Overton pressed a button to deploy a sonar transponder that would respond only to a coded American sonar signal. This would guide them back to the missile. They would return later with their heavy-lift rig to put a line on the missile and haul it to the surface.

'That is the property of the Soviet Union,' Kaganovich pointed out. 'It is in – under international waters. It belongs to my country.'

'Then you can fuckin' come and get it!' snapped the American seaman. He must be an officer in disguise, Kaganovich thought. 'Beg pardon, Mr Johnsen.'

'We'll be back for it,' Johnsen said.

'You'll never lift it. It is too heavy,' Kaganovich objected.

'I suppose you're right.' Johnsen smiled.

Kaganovich allowed the Americans their small victory. It could have been worse. Much worse. 'Shall we continue to search for more wreckage?'

'No, I think we'll go back up,' Johnsen decided.

'But your orders – '

'My orders, Captain Kaganovich, were to search for the remains of a *Victor*-class attack submarine. We found the grave of a boomer. You lied to us, Captain, and our courtesy to you ends at this point. You got what you wanted, I guess. Later we'll be back for what we want.' Johnsen reached up and pulled the release handle for the iron ballast. The metal slab dropped free. This gave the *Sea Cliff* a thousand pounds of positive buoyancy. There was no way to stay down now, even if they wanted to.

'Home, Jess.'

'Aye aye, Skipper.'

The ride back to the surface was a silent one.

The USS *Austin*

An hour later, Kaganovich climbed to the *Austin*'s bridge and requested permission to send a message to the *Kirov*. This had been agreed upon beforehand, else the *Austin*'s commanding officer would have refused. Word on the dead sub's identity had spread fast. The Soviet officer broadcast a series of code words, accompanied by the serial number from the depth-gauge dial. These were acknowledged at once.

Overton and Johnsen watched the Russian board the helicopter, carrying the depth-gauge dial.

'I didn't like him much, Mr Johnsen. *Keptin Kaganobitch*. The name sounds like a terminal stutter. We snookered him, didn't we?'

'Remind me never to play cards with you, Jess.'

The *Red October*

Ryan woke up after six hours to music that seemed dreamily familiar. He lay in his bunk for a minute trying to place it, then slipped his feet into his shoes and went forward to the wardroom.

It was *E.T.* Ryan arrived just in time to see the credits scrolling up the thirteen-inch TV set sitting on the forward end of the wardroom table. Most of the Russian officers and three Americans had been watching it. The Russians were all dabbing their eyes. Jack got a cup of coffee and sat at the end of the table.

'You like it?'

'It was magnificent!' Borodin proclaimed.

Lieutenant Mannion chuckled. 'Second time we ran it.'

One of the Russians started speaking rapidly in his native language. Borodin translated for him. 'He asks if all American children act with such – Bugayev, *svobodno?*'

'Free,' Bugayev translated, incorrectly but close enough.

Ryan laughed. 'I never did, but the movie was set in California – people out there are a little crazy. The truth is, no, kids don't act like that – at least I've never seen it, and I have two. At the same time, we do raise our kids to be a lot more independent than Soviet parents do.'

Borodin translated, and then gave the Russian response. 'So, all American children are not such hooligans?'

'Some are. America is not perfect, gentlemen. We make lots of mistakes.' Ryan had decided to tell the truth insofar as he could.

Borodin translated again. The reactions around the table were a little dubious.

'I have told them this movie is a child's story and should not be taken too seriously. This is so?'

'Yes, sir,' Mancuso, who had just come in, said. 'It's a kid's story, but I've seen it five times. Welcome back, Ryan.'

'Thank you, Commander. I take it you have things under control.'

'Yep. I guess we all needed the chance to unwind. I'll have to write Jonesy another commendation letter. This really was a good idea.' He waved at the television. 'We have lots of time to be serious.'

Noyes came in. 'How's Williams?' Ryan asked.

'He'll make it.' Noyes filled his cup. 'I had him open for three and a half hours. The head wound was superficial – bloody as hell, but head wounds are like that. The chest was a close one, though. The bullet missed the pericardium by a whisker. Captain Borodin, who gave that man first aid?'

The *starpom* pointed to a lieutenant. 'He does not speak English.'

'Tell him that Williams owes him his life. Putting that chest tube in was the difference. He would have died without it.'

'You're sure he'll make it?' Ryan persisted.

'Of course he'll make it, Ryan. That's what I do for a living. He'll be a sick boy for a while, and I'd feel better if we had him in a real hospital, but everything's under control.'

'And Captain Ramius?' Borodin asked.

'No problem. He's still sleeping. I took my time sewing it up. Ask him where he got his first aid training.'

Borodin did. 'He says he likes to read medical books.'

'How old is he?'

'Twenty-four.'

'Tell him if he ever wants to study medicine, I'll tell him how to get started. If he knows how to do the right thing at the right time, he might just be good enough to do it for a living.'

The young officer was pleased by this comment and asked how much money a doctor could make in America.

'I'm in the service, so I don't make very much. Forty-eight thousand a year, counting flight pay. I could do a lot better on the outside.'

'In the Soviet Union,' Borodin pointed out, 'doctors are paid about the same as factory workers.'

'Maybe that explains why your docs are no good,' Noyes observed.

'When will the captain be able to resume command?' Borodin asked.

'I'm going to keep him down all day,' Noyes said. 'I don't want him to start bleeding again. He can start moving around tomorrow. Carefully. I don't want him on that leg too much. He'll be fine, gentlemen. A little weak from the blood loss but he'll recover fully.' Noyes made his pronouncements as though he were quoting physical laws.

'We thank you, Doctor,' Borodin said.

Noyes shrugged. 'It's what they pay me for. Now can I ask a question? What the hell is going on here?'

Borodin laughed, translating the question for his comrades. 'We will all become American citizens.'

'And you're bringing a sub along with you, eh? Son of a gun. For a while there I thought this was some sort of – I don't know, something. This is quite a story. Guess I can't tell it to anybody, though.'

'Correct, Doctor,' Ryan smiled.

'Too bad,' Noyes muttered as he headed back to sick bay.

Moscow

'So, Comrade Admiral, you report success to us?' Narmonov asked.

'Yes, Comrade General Secretary,' Gorshkov nodded, surveying the conference table in the underground command centre. All of the inner circle were here, along with the military chiefs and the head of the KGB. 'Admiral Stralbo's fleet intelligence officer, Captain Kaganovich, was permitted by the Americans to view the wreckage from aboard one of their deep-submergence research vessels. The craft recovered a fragment of wreckage, a depth-gauge dial. These objects are numbered, and the number was immediately relayed to Moscow. It was positively from *Red October*. Kaganovich also inspected a missile blasted loose from the submarine. It was definitely a Seahawk. *Red October* is dead. Our mission is accomplished.'

'By chance, Comrade Admiral, not by design,' Mikhail Alexandrov pointed out. 'Your fleet failed in its mission to *locate* and destroy the submarine. I think Comrade Gerasimov has some information for us.'

Nikolay Gerasimov was the new KGB chief. He had already given his report to the political members of this group and was eager to release it to these strutting peacocks in uniform. He wanted to see their reactions. The KGB had scores to settle with these men. Gerasimov summarized the report he had from agent Cassius.

'Impossible!' Gorshkov snapped.

'Perhaps,' Gerasimov conceded politely. 'There is a strong probability that this is a very clever piece of disinformation. It is now being investigated by our agents in the field. There are, however, some interesting details which support this hypothesis. Permit me to review them, Comrade Admiral.

'First, why did the Americans allow our man aboard one of their most sophisticated research submarines? Second, why did they cooperate with us at all, saving our sailor from the *Politovskiy* and telling us about it? They let us see our man immediately. Why? Why not keep our man, use him, and dispose of him? Sentimentality? I think not. Third, at the same time they

287

picked this man up their air and fleet units were harassing our fleet in the most blatant and aggressive manner. This suddenly stopped, and a day later they were tripping over their own feet in their efforts to assist in our "search and rescue."'

'Because Stralbo wisely and courageously decided to refrain from reacting to their provocations,' Gorshkov replied.

Gerasimov nodded politely again. 'Perhaps so. That was an intelligent decision on the admiral's part. It cannot be easy for a uniformed officer to swallow his pride so. On the other hand, I speculate that it is also possible that about this time the Americans received this information which Cassius passed on to us. I further speculate that the Americans were fearful of our reaction were we to suspect that they had perpetrated this entire affair as a CIA operation. We know now that several imperialist intelligence services are inquiring as to the reason for this fleet operation.

'Over the past two days we have been doing some fast checking of our own. We find,' Gerasimov consulted his notes, 'that there are twenty-nine Polish engineers at the Polyarnyy submarine yard, mainly in quality control and inspection posts, that mail and message-handling procedures are very lax, and that Captain Ramius did not, as he supposedly threatened in his letter to Comrade Padorin, sail his submarine into New York harbour, but was rather in a position a thousand kilometres south when the submarine was destroyed.'

'That was an obvious piece of disinformation on Ramius' part,' Gorshkov objected. 'Ramius was both baiting us and deliberately misleading us. For that reason we deployed our fleet at all of the American ports.'

'And never did find him,' Alexandrov noted quietly. 'Go on, Comrade.'

Gerasimov continued. 'Whatever port he was supposedly heading for, he was over five hundred kilometres from any of them, and we are certain that he could have reached any of them on a direct course. In fact, Comrade Admiral, as you reported in your initial briefing, he could have reached the American coast within seven days of leaving port.'

'To do that, as I explained at length last week, would have meant travelling at maximum speed. Missile submarine commanders prefer not to do this,' Gorshkov said.

'I can understand it,' Alexandrov observed, 'in view of the fate of the *Politovskiy*. But you would expect a traitor to the *Rodina* to run like a thief.'

'Into the trap we set,' Gorshkov replied.

'Which failed,' Narmonov commented.

'I do not claim that this story is true, nor do I claim it is even a likely one at this point,' Gerasimov said, keeping his voice detached and clinical, 'but there is sufficient circumstantial evidence supporting it that I must recommend an in-depth investigation by the Committee for State Security touching on all aspects of this affair.'

'Security in my yards is a naval and GRU matter,' Gorshkov said.

'No longer.' Narmonov announced the decision reached two hours earlier. 'The KGB will investigate this shameful business along two lines. One group will investigate the information from our agent in Washington. The other will proceed on the assumption that the letter from – allegedly from – Captain Ramius was genuine. If this was a traitorous conspiracy, it could only have been possible because Ramius was able under current regulations and practices to choose his own officers. The Committee for State Security will report to us on the desirability of continuing this practice, on the current degree of control ship captains have over the careers of their officers, and over Party control of the fleet. I think we will begin our reforms by allowing officers to transfer from one ship to another with greater frequency. If officers stay in one place too long, obviously they may develop confusion in their loyalties.'

'What you suggest will destroy the efficiency of my fleet!' Gorshkov pounded on the table. It was a mistake.

'The People's fleet, Comrade Admiral,' Alexandrov corrected. 'The Party's fleet.' Gorshkov knew where that idea came from. Narmonov still had Alexandrov's support. That made the comrade general secretary's position secure, and that meant the positions of other men around this table were not. Which men?

Padorin's mind revolted at the suggestion from the KGB. What did those bastard spies know about the navy? Or the Party? They were all corrupt opportunists. Andropov had proven that, and the Politburo was now letting this whelp Gerasimov attack the armed services, which safeguarded the nation against the imperialists, had saved it from Andropov's clique, and had never been anything but the stalwart servants of the Party. But it does all fit, doesn't it? he thought. Just as Khrushchev had deposed Zhukov, the man who made his succession possible when Beria was done away with, so these bastards would now play the KGB against the uniformed men who had made their positions safe in the first place . . .

'As for you, Comrade Padorin,' Alexandrov went on.

'Yes, Comrade Academician.' For Padorin there was no apparent escape. The Main Political Administration had passed final approval on Ramius' appointment. If Ramius were indeed a traitor, then Padorin stood condemned for gross misjudgment, but if Ramius had been an unknowing pawn, then Padorin along with Gorshkov had been duped into precipitous action.

Narmonov took his cue from Alexandrov. 'Comrade Admiral, we find that your secret provisions to safeguard the security of the submarine *Red October* were successfully implemented – unless, that is, Captain Ramius was blameless and scuttled the ship himself along with his officers and the Americans who were doubtless trying to steal it. In either case, pending the KGB's inspection of the parts recovered from the wreck, it would appear that the submarine did not fall into enemy hands.'

Padorin blinked several times. His heart was beating fast, and he could feel a twinge of pain in his left chest. Was he being let off? Why? It took him a second to understand. He was the political officer, after all. If the Party was seeking to re-establish political control over the fleet – no, to reassert what never had been lost – then the Politburo could not afford to depose the Party's representative in high command. This would make him the vassal of these men, Alexandrov especially. Padorin decided that he could live with that.

And it made Gorshkov's position extremely vulnerable. Though it would take some months, Padorin was sure that the Russian fleet would have a new chief, one whose personal power would not be sufficient to make policy without Politburo approval. Gorshkov had become too big, too powerful, and the Party chieftains did not wish to have a man with so much personal prestige in high command.

I have my head, Padorin thought to himself, amazed at his good fortune.

'Comrade Gerasimov,' Narmonov went on, 'will be working with the political security section of your office to review your procedures and to offer suggestions for improvements.'

So, now he became the KGB's spy in high command? Well, he had his head, his office, his dacha, and his pension in two years. It was a small price to pay. Padorin was more than content.

The Sixteenth Day

Saturday, 18 December

The East Coast

The USS *Pigeon* arrived at her dock in Charleston at four in the morning. The Soviet crewmen, quartered in the crew's mess, had become a handful for everyone. As much as the Russian officers had worked to limit contact between their charges and their American rescuers, this had never really been possible. To state it simply, they had been unable to block the call of nature. The *Pigeon* had stuffed her visitors with good navy chow, and the nearest head was a few yards aft. On the way to and from the facilities, the *Red October*'s crewmen met with American soldiers, some of whom were Russian-speaking officers disguised as enlisted men, others of whom were

Russian language specialists in the enlisted rates flown out just as the last load of Soviets had arrived aboard. The fact that they were aboard a putatively hostile vessel and had found friendly Russian-speaking men had been overpowering for many of the young conscripts. Their remarks had been recorded on hidden tape machines for later examination in Washington. Petrov and the three junior officers had been slow to catch on, but when they did they took to escorting the men to the toilet in relays, like protective parents. What they were not able to prevent was an intelligence officer in a bosun's uniform making an offer of asylum: anyone who wished to remain in the United States would be permitted to do so. It took ten minutes for the information to spread through the crew.

When it came time for the American crewmen to eat, the Russian officers could hardly prohibit contact, and it turned out that the officers themselves got very little to eat, so busy were they patrolling the mess tables. To the bemused surprise of their American counterparts, they were forced to decline repeated invitations to the *Pigeon*'s wardroom.

The *Pigeon* docked carefully. There was no hurry. As the gangway was set in place, the band on the dock played a selection of Soviet and American airs to mark the cooperative nature of the rescue mission. The Soviets had expected that their arrival would be a quiet one given the time of day. They were mistaken in this. When the first Soviet officer was halfway down the gangway, he was dazzled by fifty high-intensity television lights and the shouted questions of television reporters routed out of bed to meet the rescue ship and so have a bright piece of Christmas season news for the morning network broadcasts. The Russians had never encountered anything like Western newsmen before, and the resulting cultural collision was total chaos. Reporters singled out the officers, blocking their paths to the consternation of marines trying to keep control of things. To a man the officers pretended not to know a word of English, only to find that an enterprising reporter had brought along a Russian language professor from the University of South Carolina in Columbia. Petrov found himself stumbling through politically acceptable platitudes in front of a half-dozen cameras and wishing the entire affair were the bad dream it seemed to be. It took an hour to get every Russian sailor aboard the three buses chartered for the purpose and off to the airport. Along the way cars and vans filled with news crews raced alongside the buses, continuing to annoy the Russians with camera lights and further shouted questions that no one could understand. The scene at the airport was not much different. The air force had sent down a VC-135 transport, but before the Russians could board it they again had to jostle their way through a sea of reporters. Ivanov found himself confronted with a Slavic language expert whose Russian was marred by a horrendous accent. Boarding took another half hour.

A dozen air force officers got everyone seated and passed out cigarettes and liquor miniatures. By the time the VIP transport reached twenty thousand feet, it was a very happy flight. An officer spoke to them over the intercom system, explaining what was to happen. Medical checks would be made of everyone. The Soviet Union would be sending a plane for them the next day, but everyone hoped their stay might be extended a day or two so that they might experience American hospitality in full. The flight crew outdid itself telling their passengers the history of every landmark, town, village, interstate highway, and truck stop on the flight route, proclaiming through the interpreter the wish of all Americans for peaceful, friendly relations with the Soviet Union, expressing the professional admiration of the US Air Force for the courage of the Soviet seamen, and mourning the deaths of the officers who had courageously lingered behind, allowing their men to go first. The whole affair was a masterpiece of duplicity aimed at overwhelming them, and it began to succeed.

The aircraft flew low over the Washington suburbs while approaching Andrews Air Force Base. The interpreter explained that they were flying over middle-class homes that belonged to ordinary workers in government and local industry. Three more buses awaited them on the ground, and instead of driving on the beltway around Washington, DC, the buses drove directly through town. American officers on each bus apologized for the traffic jams, telling the passengers that nearly every American family has one car, many two or more, and that people only use public transportation to avoid the nuisance of driving. The *nuisance* of driving one's own car, the Soviet seamen thought in amazement. Their political officers might later tell them that this was a total lie, but who could deny the thousands of cars on the road? Surely this could not all be a sham staged for the benefit of a few sailors on an hour's notice? Driving through southeast DC they noted that black people owned cars – scarcely had room to park them all! The bus continued down the Mall, with the interpreters voicing the hope that they would be allowed to see the many museums open to everyone. The Air and Space Museum, it was mentioned, had a moon rock brought back by the Apollo astronauts . . . The Soviets saw the joggers in the Mall and the thousands of people casually strolling around. They jabbered among themselves as the buses turned north to Bethesda through the nicer sections of northwest Washington.

At Bethesda they were met by television crews broadcasting live over all three networks and by friendly, smiling US Navy doctors and orderlies who led them into the hospital for medical checks.

Ten embassy officials were there, wondering how to control the group but politically unable to protest the attention given their men in the spirit of détente. Doctors had been brought in from Walter Reed and other government hospitals to give each man a quick and thorough medical examination, particularly to check for radiation poisoning. Along the way each man found himself alone with a U.S. Navy officer, who asked politely if that individual might wish to stay in the United States, pointing out that each man making this decision would be required to make his intentions known in person to a representative of the Soviet embassy – but that if he wished to do so, he would be permitted to stay. To the fury of the embassy officials, four men made this decision, one recanting after a confrontation with the naval attaché. The Americans had been careful to have each meeting videotaped so that later accusations of intimidation could be refuted at once.

When the medical checks were completed – thankfully, radiation exposure levels had been slight – the men were again fed and bedded down.

Washington, DC

'Good morning, Mr Ambassador,' the president said. Arbatov noted that again Dr Pelt was standing at his master's side behind the large antique desk. He had not expected this meeting to be a pleasant one.

'Mr President, I am here to protest the attempted kidnapping of our seamen by the United States government.'

'Mr Ambassador,' the president responded sharply, 'in the eyes of a former district attorney, kidnapping is a vile and loathsome crime, and the government of the United States of America will not be accused of such a thing – certainly not in this office! We have not, do not, and never will kidnap people. Is that clear to you, sir?'

'Besides which, Alex,' Pelt said less forcefully, 'the men to whom you refer would not be alive were it not for us. We lost two good men rescuing your servicemen. You might at least express some appreciation for our efforts to save your crew, and perhaps make a gesture of sympathy for the Americans who lost their lives in the process.'

'My government notes the heroic effort of your two officers, and does wish to express its appreciation and that of the Soviet people for the rescue. Even so, gentlemen, deliberate efforts have been made to entice some of those men to betray their country.'

'Mr Ambassador, when your trawler rescued the crew of our patrol plane last year, officers of the Soviet armed forces offered money, women, and other enticements to our crewmen if they would give out information or agree to stay behind in Vladivostok, correct? Don't tell me that you have no knowledge of this. You know that's how the game is played. At the time we did not object to this, did we? No, we were sufficiently grateful that those six men were still alive, and now, of course, all of them are back at work. We remain grateful for your country's humanitarian concern for the lives of ordinary American citizens. In this case, each officer and enlisted man was told that he could stay if he wished to do so. No force of any kind was used. Each man wishing to remain here was required by us to meet with an official of your embassy so as to give a fair chance to explain to him the error of his ways. Surely this is fair, Mr Ambassador. We made no offers of money or women. We do not buy people, and we damned well do not – ever – kidnap

293

people. Kidnappers are people I put in jail. I even managed to have one executed. Don't you ever accuse me of that again,' the president concluded righteously.

'My government insists that all of our men be returned to their homeland,' Arbatov persisted.

'Mr Ambassador, any person in the United States, regardless of his nationality or the manner of his arrival, is entitled to the full protection of our law. Our courts have ruled on this many times, and under our law no man or woman may be compelled to do something against his will without due process. The subject is closed. Now, I have a question for you. What was a ballistic missile submarine doing three hundred miles from the American coast?'

'A missile submarine, Mr President?'

Pelt lifted a photograph from the president's desk and handed it to Arbatov. Taken from the tape recorder on the *Sea Cliff*, it showed the SS-N-20 sea-launched ballistic missile

'The name of the submarine is – was *Red October*,' Pelt said. 'It exploded and sank three hundred miles from the coast of South Carolina. Alex, we have an agreement between our two countries that no such vessel will approach either country to within five hundred miles – eight hundred kilometres. We want to know what that submarine was doing there. Don't try to tell us that this missile is some kind of fabrication – even if we had wanted to do such a foolish thing, we wouldn't have had the time. That's one of your missiles, Mr Ambassador, and the submarine carried nineteen more just like it.' Pelt deliberately mis-stated the number. 'And the government of the United States asks the government of the Soviet Union how it came to be there, in violation of our agreement, while so many other of your ships are so close to our Atlantic coast.'

'That must be the lost submarine,' Arbatov offered.

'Mr Ambassador,' the president said softly, 'the submarine was not lost until Thursday, seven days after you told us about it. In short, Mr Ambassador, your explanation of last Friday does not coincide with the facts we have physically established.'

'What accusation are you making?' Arbatov bristled.

'Why, none, Alex,' the president said. 'If that agreement is no longer operative, then it is no longer operative. I believe we discussed that possibility last week also. The American people will know later today what the facts are. You are sufficiently familiar with our country to imagine their reaction. I will have an explanation. For the moment, I see no further reason for your fleet to be off our coast. The "rescue" has been successfully concluded, and the further presence of the Soviet fleet can only be a provocation. I want you and your government to consider what my military commanders are telling me right now – or if you prefer, what your commanders would be telling General Secretary Narmonov if the situation were

294

reversed. I will have an explanation. Without one I can reach one of only a few conclusions – and those are conclusions I would prefer not to choose from. Send that message to your government, and tell them that since some of your men have opted to stay here, we'll probably find out what was really happening in short order. Good day.'

Arbatov left the office, turning left to leave by the west entrance. A marine guard held the door open, a polite gesture that stopped short of his eyes. The ambassador's driver, waiting outside in a Cadillac limousine, held the door open for him. The driver was chief of the KGB's political intelligence section at that organization's Washington station.

'So,' he said, checking traffic on Pennsylvania Avenue before making a left turn.

'So, the meeting went exactly as I had predicted, and now we can be absolutely certain why they are kidnapping our men,' Arbatov replied.

'And that is, Comrade Ambassador?' the driver prompted. He did not let his irritation show. Only a few years before this Party hack would not have dared temporize with a senior KGB officer. It was a disgrace, what had happened to the Committee for State Security since the death of Comrade Andropov. But things would be set right again. He was certain of that.

'The president all but accused us of sending the submarine deliberately to their shore in violation of our secret 1979 protocol. They are holding our men to interrogate them, to take their heads apart so that they can learn what the submarine's orders were. How long will that take CIA? A day? Two?' Arbatov shook his head angrily. 'They may know already – a few drugs, a woman, perhaps, to loosen their tongues. The president also invited Moscow to imagine what the Pentagon hotheads are telling him to think! And telling him to do. No mystery there, is there? They will say we were rehearsing a surprise nuclear attack – perhaps even executing one! As if we were not working harder than they to achieve peaceful coexistence! Suspicious fools, they are fearful about what has happened, and even more angry.'

'Can you blame them, Comrade?' the driver asked, taking all of this in, filing, analysing, composing his independent report to Moscow Centre.

'And he said that there was no further reason for our fleet to be off their coast.'

'How did he say this? Was it a demand?'

'His words were soft. Softer than I expected. This concerns me. They are planning something, I think. Rattling a sabre makes noise, drawing it does not. He demands an explanation for this entire affair. What do I tell him? What *was* happening?'

'I suspect that we will never know.' The senior agent did know – the original story, that is, incredible as it was. That the navy and the GRU could allow such a fantastic error to take place had amazed him. The story from agent Cassius was scarcely less mad. The driver had passed it on to Moscow himself. Was it possible that the United States and the Soviet Union were both victims of a third party? An operation gone awry, and the Americans trying to find out who was responsible and how it was done so that they might try to do it themselves? That part of the story made sense, but did the rest? He frowned at the traffic. He had orders from Moscow Centre: if this was a CIA operation, he was supposed to find out immediately. He didn't believe it was. If so the CIA was being unusually effective in covering it. Was it possible to cover such a complex operation? He didn't think so. Regardless, he and his colleagues would be working for several weeks to penetrate any cover there was, to find out what was being said in Langley and in the field, while other KGB sections did the same throughout the world. If the CIA had penetrated the Northern Fleet's high command he'd find out. Of that he was confident. He could almost wish they had done so. The GRU would be responsible for the disaster, and would be disgraced after profiting from the KGB's loss of prestige a few years back. If he was reading the situation correctly, the Politburo was turning the KGB loose on the GRU and the military, allowing Moscow Centre to initiate its own independent investigation of the affair. Regardless of what was found, the KGB would come out ahead and deflate the armed services. One way or another, his organization would discover what had taken place, and if it was damaging to his rivals, so much the better . . .

When the door closed behind the Soviet ambassador, Dr Pelt opened a side door to the Oval Office. Judge Moore came in.

'Mr President, it's been a while since I've had to do things like hide in closets.'

'You really expect this to work?' Pelt said.

'Yes, I do now.' Moore settled comfortably into a leather chair.

'Isn't this a little shaky, Judge?' Pelt asked. 'I mean running an operation this complex?'

'That's the beauty of it, Doctor, we're not running anything. The Soviets will be doing that for us. Oh, sure, we'll have a lot of our people prowling around Eastern Europe asking a lot of questions. So will Sir Basil's fellows. The French and the Israelis already are, because we've asked them if they know what's happening with the stray missile sub. The KGB will find out quickly enough and wonder why the four main Western intelligence agencies are all asking the same questions – instead of pulling into their shells like they'd expect them to if this were our operation.

'You have to appreciate the dilemma the Soviets face, a choice between two equally unattractive scenarios. On the other hand, they can choose to believe that one of their most trusted professional officers has committed high treason on an unprecedented scale. You've seen our file on Captain Ramius. He's the Communist version of an eagle scout, a genuine New Soviet Man. Add to that the fact that a defection conspiracy necessarily involves a number of equally trusted officers. The Soviets have a mind block against believing that individuals of this type will ever leave the Workers' Paradise. That seems paradoxical, I admit, given the strenuous efforts they expend to keep people from leaving their country, but it's true. Losing a ballet dancer or a KGB agent is one thing – losing the son of a Politburo member, an officer with nearly thirty years of unblemished service, is quite another. Moreover, a naval captain has a lot of privileges; you might call his defection the equivalent of a self-made millionaire leaving New York to live in Moscow. They simply will not believe it.

'On the other hand, they can believe the story we planted through Henderson, which is also unattractive but is supported by a good deal of circumstantial evidence, especially our efforts to entice their crewmen to defect. You saw how furious they are about that. The way they think, this is a gross violation of the rules of civilized behaviour. The president's forceful reaction to our discovery that this was a missile submarine is also evidence that favours Henderson's story.'

'So what side will they come down on?' the president asked.

'That, sir, is a question of psychology more than anything else, and Soviet psychology is very hard for us to read. Given the choice between the collective treason of ten men and an outside conspiracy, my opinion is that they will prefer the latter. For them to believe that this really was a defection – well, it would force them to re-examine their own beliefs. Who likes to do that?' Moore gestured grandly. 'The latter alternative means that their security has been violated by outsiders, but being a victim is more palatable than having to recognize the intrinsic contradictions of their own governing philosophy. On top of that we have the fact that the KGB will be running the investigation.'

'Why?' Pelt asked, caught up in the judge's plot.

'In either case, a defection or a penetration of naval operational security, the GRU would have been responsible. Security of the naval and military forces is their bailiwick, the more so with the damage done to the KGB after the departure of our friend Andropov. The Soviets can't have an organization investigating itself – not in their intelligence community! So, the KGB will be looking to take its rival service apart. From the KGB's perspective, outside instigation is the far more attractive alternative; it makes for a bigger operation. If they confirm Henderson's story and convince everyone that it's true – and they will, of course – it makes them look all that much better for having uncovered it.'

'They will confirm the story?'

'Of course they will! In the intelligence business if you look hard enough for something, you find it, whether it's really there or not. Lord, we owe this Ramius fellow more than he will ever know. An opportunity like this doesn't come along once in a generation. We simply can't lose.'

'But the KGB will emerge stronger,' Pelt observed. 'Is that a good thing?'

Moore shrugged. 'Bound to happen eventually. Unseating and possibly killing Andropov gave the military services too much prestige, just like with Beria back in the fifties. The Soviets depend on political control of their military as much as we do – more. Having the KGB take their high command apart gets the dirty work done for them. It had to happen anyway, so it's just as well that we can profit by it. There's only a few more things we have to do.'

'Such as?' the president asked.

'Our friend Henderson will leak information in a month or so saying that we had a submarine tracking *Red October* all the way from Iceland.'

'But why?' Pelt objected. 'Then they'll know that we were lying, that all the excitement over the missile sub was a lie.'

'Not exactly, Doctor,' Moore said. 'Having a missile sub this close to our coast remains a violation of the agreement and from their point of view we have no way of knowing why she was there – until we interrogate the crewmen remaining behind, who will probably tell us little of value. The Soviets will expect that we have not been completely truthful with them on this affair. The fact that we were trailing their sub and were ready to destroy it at any time gives them the evidence of our duplicity that they'll be looking for. We'll also say that *Dallas* monitored the reactor incident on sonar and that will explain the proximity of our rescue ship. They know, well, they certainly suspect, that we have concealed something. This will mislead them about what it was we really concealed. The Russians have a saying for this. They call it wolf meat. And they will launch an extensive operation to penetrate our operation, whatever it is. But they will find nothing. The only people in the CIA who know what is really going on are Greer, Ritter, and myself. Our operations people have orders to *find out* what was going on, and that's all that can leak out.'

'What about Henderson, and how many of our people know about the submarine?' the president asked.

'If Henderson spills anything to them he'll be signing his own death warrant. The KGB deals severely with double agents, and would not believe that we tricked him into delivering false information. He knows it, and we'll be keeping a close eye on him in any case. How many of our people know about the sub? A hundred perhaps, and the number will increase somewhat – but remember that they think we now have two dead Soviet subs off our coast, and they have every reason to believe that whatever Soviet sub equipment turns up in our labs has been recovered from the ocean floor. We will, of course, be reactivating the *Glomar Explorer* for just that purpose. They'd be suspicious if we didn't. Why disappoint them? Sooner or later they just might figure the whole story out, but by that time the stripped hulk will be at the bottom of the sea.'

'So, we can't keep this a secret forever?' Pelt asked.

'Forever's a long time. We have to plan for the possibility. For the immediate future the secret should be fairly safe, what with only a hundred people in on it. In a year, minimum, more likely two or three, they may have accumulated enough data to suspect what has happened, but by that time there won't be much physical evidence to point to. Moreover, if the KGB discovers the truth, will they *want* to report it? Were the GRU to find out, they certainly would, and the resulting chaos within their intelligence community would also work to our benefit.' Moore took a cigar from a leather holder. 'As I said, Ramius has given us a fantastic opportunity on several levels. And the beauty of it is that we don't have to do much of anything. The Russians will be doing all the legwork, looking for something that isn't there.'

'What about the defectors, Judge?' the president asked.

'They, Mr President, will be taken care of. We know how to do this, and we rarely have a complaint about the CIA's hospitality. We'll take some months to debrief them, and at the same time we'll be preparing them for life in America. They'll get new identities, reeducation, cosmetic surgery if necessary, and they'll never have to work another day as long as they live – but they will want to work. Almost all of them do. I expect the navy will find places for them, paid consultants for their submarine warfare department, that sort of thing.'

'I want to meet them,' the president said impulsively.

'That can be arranged, sir, but it will have to be discreet,' Moore cautioned.

'Camp David, that ought to be secure enough. And Ryan, Judge, I want him taken care of.'

'Understood, sir. We're bringing him along rather quickly already. He has a big future with us.'

Tyuratam, USSR

The reason *Red October* had been ordered to dive long before dawn was orbiting the earth at a height of eight hundred kilometres. The size of a Greyhound bus, Albatross 8 had been sent aloft eleven months earlier by a heavy-lift booster from the Cosmodrome at Tyuratam. The massive satellite, called a RORSAT, for radar ocean reconnaissance satellite, was specifically designed for maritime surveillance.

Albatross 8 passed over Pamlico Sound at 1131 local time. Its on-board programming was designed to trace thermal receptors over the entire visible horizon, interrogating everything in sight and locking on any signature that fitted its acquisition parameters. As it continued on its orbit and passed over elements of the US fleet, the *New Jersey*'s jammers were aimed upward to scramble its signal. The satellite's tape systems dutifully recorded this. The jamming would tell the operators something about American electronic warfare systems. As Albatross 8 crossed the pole, the parabolic dish on its front tracked in on the carrier signal of another bird, the *Iskra* communications satellite.

When the reconnaissance satellite located its higher flying cousin, a laser side-link transmitted the contents of the Albatross' tape bank. The *Iskra* immediately relayed this to the ground station at Tyuratam. The signal was also received by a fifteen-metre dish located in western China which was operated by the US National Security Agency in cooperation with the Chinese, who used the data received for their own purposes. The Americans transmitted it via their own communications satellite to NSA headquarters at Fort Meade, Maryland. At almost the same time the digital signal was examined by two teams of experts five thousand miles apart.

'Clear weather,' a technician moaned. '*Now* we get clear weather!'

'Enjoy it while you can, Comrade.' His neighbour at the next console was watching data from a geosynchronous weather satellite that monitored the Western Hemisphere. Knowing the weather over a hostile country can have great strategic value. 'There's another cold front approaching their coast. Their winter has been like ours. I hope they are enjoying it.'

'Our men at sea will not.' The technician mentally shuddered at the thought of being at sea in a major storm. He'd taken a Black Sea cruise the previous summer and become hopelessly seasick. 'Aha! What is this? Colonel!'

'Yes, Comrade? The colonel supervising the watch came over quickly.

'See here, Comrade Colonel.' The technician traced a finger on the TV screen. 'This is Pamlico Sound, on the central coast of the United States. Look here, Comrade.' The thermal image of the water on the screen was black, but as the technician adjusted the display it changed to green with two white patches, one larger than the other. Twice the large one split into two segments. The image was of the surface of the water, and some of the water was half a degree warmer than it should have been. The differential was not constant, but it did return enough to prove that something was adding heat to the water.

'Sunlight, perhaps?' the colonel asked.

'No, Comrade, the clear sky gives even sunlight to the entire area,' the technician said quietly. He was always quiet when he thought he was on to something. 'Two submarines, perhaps three, thirty metres under the water.'

'You are certain?'

The technician flipped on a switch to display the radar picture, which showed only the corduroy pattern of small waves.

'There is nothing *on* the water to generate this heat, Comrade Colonel. Therefore it must be something *under* the water. The time of year is wrong for mating whales. It can only be nuclear submarines, probably two, perhaps three. I speculate, Colonel, that the Americans have been sufficiently frightened by the deployment of our fleet to seek shelter for their missile submarines. Their missile sub base is only a few hundred kilometres south. Perhaps one of their *Ohio*-class boats has taken shelter here and is being protected by a hunter sub, as ours are.'

'Then he will soon move out. Our fleet is being recalled.'

'Too bad, it would be good to track him. This is a rare opportunity, Comrade Colonel.'

'Indeed. Well done, Comrade Academician.' Ten minutes later the data had been transmitted to Moscow.

Soviet Naval High Command, Moscow

'We will make use of this opportunity, Comrade,' Gorshkov said. 'We are now recalling our fleet, and we will allow several submarines to remain behind to gather electronic intelligence. The Americans will probably lose several in the shuffle.'

'Quite likely,' the chief of fleet operations said.

'The *Ohio* will go south, probably to their submarine base at Charleston or Kings Bay. Or north to Norfolk. We have *Konovalov* at Norfolk, and *Shabilikov* off Charleston. Both will stay in place for several days, I think. We must do something right to show the politicians that we have a real navy. Being able to track on an *Ohio* would be a beginning.'

'I'll have the orders out in fifteen minutes, Comrade.' The chief of operations thought this was a good idea. He had not liked the report of the Politburo meeting that he'd gotten from Gorshkov – though if Sergey were on his way out, he would be in a good place to take over the job . . .

The *New Jersey*

The RED ROCKET message had arrived in Eaton's hand only moments before: Moscow had just transmitted a lengthy operational order via satellite to the Soviet fleet. Now the Russians were in a real fix, the commodore thought. Around them were three carrier battle groups – the *Kennedy*, *America*, and *Nimitz* – all under Josh Painter's command. Eaton had them in sight, and had operational control of the *Tarawa* to augment his own surface action group. The commodore turned his binoculars on the *Kirov*.

'Commander, bring the group to battle stations.'

'Aye.' The group operations officer lifted the tactical radio mike. 'Blue Boys, this is Blue King. Amber Light, Amber Light, execute. Out.'

Eaton waited four seconds for the *New Jersey*'s general quarters alarm to sound. The crew raced to their guns.

'Range to *Kirov*?'

'Thirty-seven thousand six hundred yards, sir. We've been sneaking in a laser range every few minutes. We're dialed in, sir,' the group operations officer reported. 'Main battery turrets are still loaded with sabots, and gunnery's been updating the solution every thirty seconds.'

A phone buzzed next to Eaton's command chair on the flag bridge.

'Eaton.'

'All stations manned and ready, Commodore,' the battleship's captain reported. Eaton looked at his stopwatch.

'Well done, Captain. We've got the men drilled very well indeed.'

In the *New Jersey*'s combat information centre the numerical displays showed the exact range to the *Kirov*'s mainmast. The logical first target is always the enemy flagship. The only question was how much punishment the *Kirov* could absorb – and what would kill her first, the gun rounds or the Tomahawk missiles. The important part, the gunnery officer had been saying for days, was to kill the *Kirov* before any aircraft could interfere. The *New Jersey* had never sunk a ship all on her own. Forty years was a long time to wait.

'They're turning,' the group operations officer said.

'Yep, let's see how far.'

The *Kirov*'s formation had been on a westerly course when the signal arrived. Every ship in the circular array turned to starboard, all together. Their turns stopped when they reached a heading of zero-four-zero.

Eaton set his glasses down in the holder. 'They're going home. Let's inform Washington and keep the men at stations for a while.'

Dulles International Airport

The Soviets outdid themselves getting their men away from the United States. An Aeroflot Illyushin IL-62 was taken out of regular international service and sent directly from Moscow to Dulles. It landed at sunset. A near copy of the British VC-10, the four-engine aircraft taxied to the remotest service area for refueling. Along with some other passengers who did not leave the plane to stretch their legs, a spare flight crew was brought along so that the plane could immediately return home. A pair of mobile lounges drove from the terminal building two miles to the waiting aircraft. Inside them the crewmen of the *Red October* looked out at the snow-dusted countryside, knowing this was their final look at America. They were quiet, having been roused from bed in Bethesda and taken by bus to Dulles only an hour earlier. This time no reporters harassed them.

The four officers, nine *michmanyy*, and the remaining enlisted crew were split into distinct groups as they boarded. Each group was taken to a separate part of the aircraft. Each officer and *michman* had his own KGB interrogator, and the debriefing began as the aircraft started its takeoff roll. By the time the Illyushin reached cruising altitude most of the crewmen were asking themselves why they had not opted to remain behind with their traitorous countrymen. These interviews were decidedly unpleasant.

'Did Captain Ramius act strangely?' a KGB major asked Petrov.

'Certainly not!' Petrov answered quickly, defensively. 'Didn't you know our submarine was sabotaged? We were lucky to escape with our lives!'

'Sabotaged? How?'

'The reactor systems. I am the wrong one to ask on this, I am not an engineer, but it was I who detected the leaks. You see, the radiation film badges showed contamination, but the engine room instruments did not. Not only was the reactor tampered with, but all of the radiation-sensing instruments were disabled. I saw this myself. Chief Engineer Melekhin had to rebuild several to locate the leaking reactor piping. Svyadov can tell this better. He saw it himself.'

The KGB officer was scribbling notes. 'And what was your submarine doing so close to the American coast?'

'What do you mean? Don't you know what our orders were?'

'What were your orders, Comrade Doctor?' The KGB officer stared hard into Petrov's eyes.

The doctor explained, concluding, 'I saw the orders. They were posted for all to see, as is normal.'

'Signed by whom?'

'Admiral Korov. Who else?'

'Did you not find those orders a little strange?' the major asked angrily.

'Do you question your orders, Comrade Major?' Petrov summoned up some spine. '*I* do not.'

'What happened to your political officer?'

In another space Ivanov was explaining how the *Red October* had been detected by American and British ships. 'But Captain Ramius evaded them brilliantly! We would have made it except for that damned reactor accident. You must find who did that to us, Comrade Captain. I wish to see him die myself!'

The KGB officer was unmoved. 'And what was the last thing the captain said to you?'

'He ordered me to keep control of my men, not to let them speak with Americans any more than necessary, and he said that the Americans would never get their hands on our ship.' Ivanov's eyes filled with tears at the thought of his captain and his ship, both lost. He was a proud and privileged young Soviet man, the son of a Party academician. 'Comrade, you and your people must find the bastards who did this to us.'

'It was very clever,' Svyadov was recounting a few feet away. 'Even Comrade Melekhin only found it on his third attempt, and he swore vengeance on the men who did it. I saw it myself,' the lieutenant said, forgetting that he never had, really. He explained in detail, to the point of drawing a diagram of how it had been done. 'I don't know about the final accident. I was just coming on duty then. Melekhin, Surzpoi, and Bugayev worked for hours attempting to engage our auxiliary power systems.' He shook his head. 'I tried to join them, but Captain Ramius forbade it. I tried again, against orders, but Comrade Petrov prevented me.'

Two hours over the Atlantic the senior KGB interrogators met aft to compare notes.

'So, if this captain was acting, he was devilishly good at it,' the colonel in charge of the initial interrogations summarized. 'His orders to his men were impeccable. The mission orders were announced and posted as is normal – '

'But who among these men knows Korov's signature? And we can't very well ask Korov, can we?' a major said. The commander of the Northern Fleet had died of a cerebral haemorrhage two hours into his first interrogation in the Lubyanka, much to everyone's disappointment. 'It could have been forged in any case. Do we have a secret submarine base in Cuba? And what of the death of the *zampolit*?'

'The doctor is sure it was an accident,' another major answered. 'The captain thought he had struck his head, but he had actually broken his neck. I feel they should have radioed for instructions, though.'

'A radio silence order,' the colonel said. 'I checked. This is entirely normal for missile submarines. Was this Captain Ramius skilled in unarmed combat? Might he have murdered the *zampolit*?'

'A possibility,' mused the major who had questioned Petrov. 'He was not trained in such things, but it is not hard to do.'

The colonel did not know whether to agree. 'Do we have any evidence that the crew thought a defection was being attempted?' All heads shook negatively. 'Was the submarine's operational routine otherwise normal?'

'Yes, Comrade Colonel,' a young captain said. 'The surviving navigation officer, Ivanov, says that the evasion of imperialist surface and sub forces was effected perfectly – exactly in accordance with established procedures, but executed brilliantly by this Ramius fellow over a period of twelve hours. I have not even suggested that treason might be involved. Yet.' Everyone knew that these sailors would be spending time in the Lubyanka until each head had been picked clean.

'Very well,' the colonel said, 'up to this point we have no indication of treason by the officers of the submarine? I thought not. Comrades, you will continue your interrogations in a gentler fashion until we arrive in Moscow. Allow your charges to relax.'

The atmosphere on the aircraft gradually became more pleasant. Snacks were served, and vodka to loosen the tongues and encourage comradely good fellowship with the KGB officers, who were drinking water. The men all knew that they would be imprisoned for some time, and this fate was accepted with what to a Westerner would be surprising fatalism. The KGB would be working for weeks to reconstruct every event on the submarine from the time the last line was cast off at Polyarnyy to the moment the last man entered the *Mystic*. Other teams of agents were already working worldwide to learn if what happened to the *Red October* was a CIA plot or the plot of some other intelligence service. The KGB would find its answer, but the colonel in charge of the case was beginning to think the answer did not lie with these seamen.

Noyes allowed Ramius to walk the fifteen feet from sick bay to the wardroom under supervision. The patient did not look very good, but this was largely because he needed a wash and a shave, like everyone else aboard. Borodin and Mancuso assisted him into his seat at the head of the table.

'So, Ryan, how are you today?'

'Good, thank you, Captain Ramius.' Ryan smiled over his coffee. In fact he was hugely relieved, having for the past several hours been able to leave the question of running the sub to the men who actually knew something about it. Though he was counting the hours until he could get out of the *Red October*, for the first time in two weeks he was neither seasick nor terrified. 'How is your leg, sir?'

'Painful. I must learn not to be shot again. I do not remember saying to you that I owe you my life, as all of us do.'

'It was my life, too,' Ryan replied, a little embarrassed.

'Good morning, sir!' It was the cook. 'May I fix you some breakfast, Captain Ramius?'

'Yes, I am very hungry.'

'Good! One US Navy breakfast. Let me get some fresh coffee, too.' He disappeared into the passageway. Thirty seconds later he was back with fresh coffee and a place setting for Ramius. 'Ten minutes on the breakfast, sir.'

Ramius poured a cup of coffee. There was a small envelope in the saucer. 'What is this?'

'Coffee Mate,' Mancuso chuckled. 'Cream for your coffee, Captain.'

Ramius tore open the packet, staring suspiciously inside before dumping the contents into the cup and stirring.

'When do we leave?'

'Sometime tomorrow,' Mancuso answered. The *Dallas* was going to periscope depth periodically to receive operational orders and relaying them to the *October* by gertrude. 'We learned a few hours ago that the Soviet fleet is heading back northeast. We'll know for sure by sundown. Our guys are keeping a close eye on them.'

'Where do we go?' Ramius asked.

'Where did you tell them you were going?' Ryan wanted to know. 'What exactly did your letter say?'

'You know about the letter – how?'

'We know – that is, I know about the letter, but that's all I can say, sir.'

'I told Uncle Yuri that we were sailing to New York to make a present of this ship to the president of the United States.'

'But you didn't head for New York,' Mancuso objected.

'Certainly not. I wished to enter Norfolk. Why go to a civilian port when a naval base is so close? You say I should tell Padorin the truth?' Ramius shook his head. 'Why? Your coast is so large.'

Dear Admiral Padorin, I'm sailing for New York . . . No wonder they went ape! Ryan thought.

'We go to Norfolk or Charleston?' Ramius asked.

'Norfolk, I think,' Mancuso said.

'Didn't you know they'd send the whole fleet after you?' Ryan snapped. 'Why send the letter at all?'

'So they will know,' Ramius answered. 'So they will know. I did not expect that anyone would locate us. There you surprised us.'

The American skipper tried not to smile. 'We detected you off the coast of Iceland. You were luckier than you imagine. If we'd sailed from England on schedule, we'd have been fifteen miles closer inshore, and we would have had you cold. Sorry, Captain, but our sonars and sonar operators are very good. You can meet the man who first tracked you later. He's working with your man Bugayev at the moment.'

'*Starshina*,' Borodin said.

'Not an officer?' Ramius asked.

'No, just a very good operator,' Mancuso said, surprised. Why would anyone want an officer to stand watch on sonar gear?

The cook came back in. His idea of the standard US Navy breakfast was a large platter with a slab of ham, two eggs over easy, a pile of hash browns, and four slices of toast, with a container of apple jelly.

'Let me know if you want more, sir,' the cook said.

'This is a normal breakfast?' Ramius asked Mancuso.

'Nothing unusual about it. I prefer waffles myself. Americans eat big breakfasts.' Ramius was already attacking his. After two days without a normal meal and all the blood loss from his leg wound, his body was screaming for food.

'Tell me, Ryan,' Borodin was lighting a cigarette, 'what is it in America that we will find most amazing?'

Jack motioned to the captain's plate. 'Food stores.'

'Food stores?' Mancuso asked.

'While I was sitting on *Invincible* I read over a CIA report on people who come over to our side.' Ryan didn't want to say *defectors*. Somehow the word sounded demeaning. 'Supposedly the first thing that surprises people, people from your part of the world, is going through a supermarket.'

'Tell me about them,' Borodin ordered.

'A building about the size of a football field – well, maybe a little smaller than that. You go in the front door and get a shopping cart. The fresh fruits and vegetables are on the right, and you gradually work your way left through the other departments. I've been doing that since I was a kid.'

'You say fresh fruits and vegetables? What about now, in winter?'

'What about winter?' Mancuso said. 'Maybe they cost a little more, but you can always get fresh produce. That's the one thing we miss on the boats. Our supply of fresh produce and milk only lasts us about a week.'

'And meat?' Ramius asked.

'Anything you want,' Ryan answered. 'Beef, pork, lamb, turkey, chicken. American farmers are very efficient. The United States feeds itself and has plenty left over. You know that, the Soviet Union buys our grain. Hell, we pay farmers not to grow things, just to keep the surplus under control.' The four Russians were doubtful.

'What else?' Borodin asked.

'What else will surprise you? Nearly everyone has a car. Most people own their own homes. If you have money, you can buy nearly anything you want. The average family in America makes something like twenty thousand dollars a year, I guess. These officers all make more than that. The fact of the matter is that in our country if you have some brains – and all of you men do – and you are willing to work – and all of you men are – you will live a comfortable life even without any help. Besides, you can be sure that the CIA will take good care of you. We wouldn't want anybody to complain about our hospitality.'

'And what will become of my men?' Ramius asked.

'I can't say exactly, sir, since I've never been involved in this sort of thing myself. I would guess that you will be taken to a safe place to relax and unwind. People from the CIA and the navy will want to talk to you at length. That's no surprise, right? I told you this before. A year from now you will be doing whatever you choose to do.'

'And anybody who wants to take a cruise with us is welcome to,' Mancuso added.

Ryan wondered how true this was. The navy would not want to let any of these men on a 688-class boat. It might give one of them information valuable enough to enable him to return home and keep his head.

'How does a friendly man become a CIA spy?' Borodin asked.

'I am not a spy, sir,' Ryan said again. He couldn't blame them for not believing him. 'Going through graduate school I got to know a guy who mentioned my name to a friend of his in the CIA, Admiral James Greer. Back a few years ago I was asked to join a team of academics that was called in to check up on some of the CIA's intelligence estimates. At the time I was happily engaged writing books on naval history. At Langley – I was there for two months during the summer – I did a paper on international terrorism. Greer liked it, and two years ago he asked me to go to work there full time. I accepted. It was a mistake,' Ryan said, not really meaning it. Or did he? 'A year ago I was transferred to London to work on a joint intelligence evaluation team with the British Secret Service. My normal job is to sit at a desk and figure out the stuff that field agents send in. I got myself roped into this because I figured out what you were up to, Captain Ramius.'

'Was your father a spy?' Borodin asked.

'No, my dad was a police officer in Baltimore. He and my mother were killed in a plane crash ten years ago.'

307

Borodin expressed his sympathy. 'And you, Captain Mancuso, what made you a sailor?'

'I wanted to be a sailor since I was a kid. My dad's a barber. I decided on submarines at Annapolis because I thought it looked interesting.'

Ryan was watching something he had never seen before, men from two different places and two very different cultures trying to find common ground. Both sides were reaching out, seeking similarities of character and experience, building a foundation for understanding. This was more than interesting. It was touching. Ryan wondered how difficult it was for the Soviets. Probably harder than anything he had ever done – their bridges were burned. They had cast themselves away from everything they had known, trusting that what they found would be better. Ryan hoped they would succeed and make their transition from Communism to freedom. In the past two days he had come to realize what courage it took for men to defect. Facing a gun in a missile room was a small matter compared with walking away from one's whole life. It was strange how easily Americans put on their freedoms. How difficult would it be for these men who had risked their lives to adapt to something that men like Ryan so rarely appreciated? It was people like these who had built the American Dream, and people like these who were needed to maintain it. It was odd that such men should come from the Soviet Union. Or perhaps not so odd, Ryan thought, listening to the conversation going back and forth in front of him.

The Seventeenth Day

Sunday, 19 December

The *Red October*

'Eight more hours,' Ryan whispered to himself. That's what they had told him. An eight-hour run to Norfolk. He was back at the rudder diving-plane controls by his own request. Operating them was the only thing he knew how to do, and he had to do something. The *October* was still badly short-handed. Nearly all of the Americans were helping out in the reactor and engine spaces aft. Only Mancuso, Ramius, and himself were in control. Bugayev, with the help of Jones, was monitoring the sonar equipment a few feet away, and the medical people were still worrying over Williams in sick bay. The cook was shuttling back and forth with sandwiches and coffee, which Ryan found disappointing, probably because he had been spoiled by Greer's.

Ramius was half sitting on the rail that surrounded the periscope pedestal. The leg wound was not bleeding, but it had to be hurting more than the man admitted since he was letting Mancuso check the instruments and handle the navigation.

'Rudder amidships,' Mancuso ordered.

'Midships.' Ryan turned the wheel back to the right to centre it, checking his rudder angle indicator. 'Rudder is amidships, steady on course one-two-zero.'

Mancuso frowned at his chart, nervous at being forced to pilot the massive submarine in so cavalier a manner. 'You have to be careful around here. The sandbar keeps building up from the southerly littoral drift, and they have to dredge it every few months. The storms this area's been having can't have helped much.' Mancuso went back to look through the periscope.

'I am told this is a dangerous area,' Ramius said.

'The graveyard of the Atlantic,' Mancuso confirmed. 'A lot of ships have died along the Outer Banks. Weather and current conditions are bad enough. The Germans are supposed to have had a hell of a time here during the war. Your charts don't show it, but there's hundreds of wrecks spotted on the bottom.' He went back to the chart table. 'Anyway, we give this place a nice wide berth, and we don't turn north till about here.' He traced a line on the chart.

'These are your waters,' Ramius agreed.

They were in a loose three-boat formation. The *Dallas* was leading them out to sea, the *Pogy* was trailing. All three boats were travelling flooded-down, their decks nearly awash, with no one on their bridge stations. All visual navigation was being done by periscope. No radar sets were operating. None of the three boats was making any electronic noise. Ryan glanced casually at the chart table. They were beyond the inlet proper, but the chart was marked with sandbars for several more miles.

Nor were they using the *Red October*'s caterpillar drive system. It had turned out to be almost exactly what Skip Tyler had predicted. There were two sets of tunnel impellers, a pair about a third of the way back from the bow and three more just aft of midships. Mancuso and his engineers had examined the plans with great interest, then commented at length on the quality of the caterpillar design.

For his part, Ramius had not wanted to believe that he had been detected so early on. Mancuso had ultimately produced Jones with his personal map to show the *October*'s estimated course off Iceland. Though a few miles off the ship's log, it was too close to have been a coincidence.

'Your sonar must be better than we expected,' Ramius grumbled a few feet from Ryan's control station.

'It is pretty good,' Mancuso allowed. 'Better yet, there's Jonesy – he's the best sonarman I've ever had.'

'So young, and so smart.'

'We get a lot of them that way,' Mancuso smiled. 'Never as many as we'd like, of course, but our kids are all volunteers. They know what they're getting into. We're picky about who we take, and then we train the hell out of 'em.'

'Conn, sonar.' It was Jones' voice. '*Dallas* is diving, sir.'

Very well.' Mancuso lit a cigarette as he went to the intercom phone. He punched the button for engineering. 'Tell Mannion we need him forward. We'll be diving in a few minutes. Yeah.' He hung up and went back to the chart.

'You have them for more than three years, then?' Ramius asked.

'Oh, yeah. Hell, otherwise we'd be letting them go right after they're fully trained, right?'

Why couldn't the Soviet Navy get and retain people like this? Ramius thought. He knew the answer all too well. The Americans fed their men decently, gave them a proper mess room, paid them decently, gave them trust – all the things he had fought twenty years for.

'You need me to work the vents?' Mannion said, coming in.

'Yeah, Pat, we'll dive in another two or three minutes.'

Mannion gave the chart a quick look on his way to the vent manifold.

Ramius hobbled to the chart. 'They tell us that your officers are chosen from the bourgeois classes to control ordinary sailors from the working class.'

Mannion ran his hands over the vent controls. There sure were enough of them. He'd spent two hours the previous day figuring the complex system out. 'That's true, sir. Our officers do come from the ruling class. Just look at me,' he said deadpan. Mannion's skin was about the colour of coffee grounds, his accent pure South Bronx.

'But you are a black man,' Ramius objected, missing the jibe.

'Sure, we're a real ethnic boat.' Mancuso looked through the periscope again. 'A Guinea skipper, a black navigator, and a crazy sonarman.'

'I heard that, sir!' Jones called out rather than use the intercom speaker. 'Gertrude message from *Dallas*. Everything looks okay. They're waiting for us. Last gertrude message for a while.'

'Conn, aye. We're clear, finally. We can dive whenever you wish, Captain Ramius,' Mancuso said.

'Comrade Mannion, vent the ballast tanks,' Ramius said. The *October* had never actually surfaced and was still rigged for dive. 'Aye aye, sir.' The lieutenant turned the topmost rank of master switches on the hydraulic controls.

Ryan winced. The sound made him think of a million toilets being flushed at once.

'Five degrees down on the planes, Ryan,' Ramius said.

'Five degrees down, aye.' Ryan pushed forward on the yoke. 'Planes five degrees down.'

'She's slow going down,' Mannion observed, watching the hand-painted depth-gauge replacement. 'So durn big.'

'Yeah,' Mancuso said. The needle passed twenty metres.

'Planes to zero,' Ramius said.

'Planes to zero angle, aye.' Ryan pulled back on the control. It took thirty seconds for the submarine to settle. She seemed very slow to respond to the controls. Ryan had thought that submarines were as responsive as aircraft.

'Make her a little light, Pat. Enough that it takes a degree of down to hold her level,' Mancuso said.

'Uh-huh.' Mannion frowned, checking the depth gauge. The ballast tanks were now fully flooded, and the balancing act would have to be done with the much smaller trim tanks. It took him five minutes to get the balance exactly right.

'Sorry, gentlemen. I'm afraid she's too big to dial in quick,' he said, embarrassed with himself.

Ramius was impressed but too annoyed to show it. He had expected the American captain to take longer than this to do it himself. Trimming a strange sub so expertly on his first try . . .

'Okay, now we can come around north,' Mancuso said. They were two miles past the last charted bar. 'Recommend new course zero-zero-eight, Captain.'

'Ryan, rudder left ten degrees,' Ramius ordered. 'Come to zero-zero-eight.'

'Okay, rudder left ten degrees,' Ryan responded, keeping one eye on the rudder indicator, the other on the gyro compass repeater. 'Come to oh-oh-eight.'

'Caution, Ryan. He turns slowly, but once turning you must use much backward – '

'Opposite,' Mancuso corrected politely.

'Yes, opposite rudder to stop him on proper course.'

'Right.'

'Captain, do you have rudder problems?' Mancuso asked. 'From tracking you it seemed that your turning circle was rather large.'

'With the caterpillar it is. The flow from the tunnels strikes the rudder very hard, and it flutters if you use too much rudder. On our first sea trials, we had damage from this. It comes from – how do you say – the come-together of the two caterpillar tunnels.'

'Does this affect operations with the propellers?' Mannion asked.

'No, only with the caterpillar.'

Mancuso didn't like that. It didn't really matter. The plan was a simple, direct one. The three boats would make a straight dash to Norfolk. The two American attack boats would leapfrog forwards at thirty knots to sniff out the areas ahead while the *October* plodded along at a constant twenty.

Ryan began to ease his rudder as the bow came around. He waited too long. Despite five degrees of right rudder, the bow swung right past the intended course, and the gyro repeater clicked accusingly on every third degree until it stopped at zero-zero-one. It took another two minutes to get back on the proper course.

'Sorry about that. Steady on zero-zero-eight,' he finally reported.

Ramius was forgiving. 'You learn fast, Ryan. Perhaps one day you will be a true sailor.'

'No thanks! The one thing I've learned on this trip is that you guys earn every nickle you get.'

'Don't like subs?' Mannion chuckled.

'No place to jog.'

'True. Unless you still need me, Captain, I'm ready to go aft. The engine room's awful shorthanded,' Mannion said.

Ramius nodded. Was he from the ruling class? the captain wondered.

The V.K. Konovalov

Tupolev was heading back west. The fleet order had instructed everyone but his *Alfa* and one other to return home at twenty knots. Tupolev was to move west for two and a half hours. Now he was on a reciprocal heading at five knots, about the top speed the *Alfa* could travel without making much noise. The idea was that his sub would be lost in the shuffle. So, an *Ohio* was heading for Norfolk – or Charleston more probably. In any case, Tupolev would circle quietly and observe. The *Red October* was destroyed. That much he knew from the ops order. Tupolev shook his head. How could Marko have done such a thing? Whatever the answer, he had paid for his treason with his life.

The Pentagon

'I'd feel better if we had some more air cover,' Admiral Foster said, leaning against the wall.

'Agreed, sir, but we can't be so obvious, can we?' General Harris asked.

A pair of P-3Bs was now sweeping the track from Hatteras to the Virginia Capes as though on a routine training mission. Most of the other Orions were far out at sea. The Soviet fleet was already four hundred miles offshore. The three surface groups had rejoined and were now ringed by their submarines. The *Kennedy, America,* and *Nimitz* were five hundred miles to their east, and the *New Jersey* was dropping back. The Russians would be watched all the way home. The carrier battle groups would be following them all the way to Iceland, keeping a discreet distance and maintaining air groups at the fringe of their radar coverage continuously, just to let them know that the United States still cared. Aircraft based on Iceland would track them the rest of the way home.

HMS *Invincible* was now out of the operation and about halfway home. American attack subs were returning to normal patrol patterns, and all Soviet subs were reported to be off the coast, though this data was sketchy. They were travelling in loose packs and the noise generated made tracking difficult for the patrolling Orions, which were short of sonobuoys. Still and all, the operation was about over, the J-3 judged.

'You heading for Norfolk, Admiral?' Harris asked.

'Thought I might get together with CINCLANT, a postaction conference, you understand,' Foster said.

'Aye aye, sir,' Harris said.

The *New Jersey*

She was travelling at twelve knots, with a destroyer fueling on either beam. Commodore Eaton was in the flag plot. It was all over and nothing had happened, thank God. The Soviets were now a hundred miles ahead, within Tomahawk range but well beyond everything else. All in all, he was satisfied. His force had operated successfully with the *Tarawa*, which was now headed south to Mayport, Florida. He hoped they'd be able to do this again soon. It had been a long time since a flag officer on a battleship had had a carrier respond to his command. They had kept the *Kirov* force under continuous surveillance. If there had been a battle Eaton was convinced that they'd have handled Ivan. More importantly, he was certain that Ivan knew it. All they awaited now was the order to return to Norfolk. It would be nice to be back home for Christmas. He figured his men had earned it. Many of the battleship's men were old-timers, and nearly everyone had a family.

The *Red October*

Ping. Jones noted the time on his pad and called out, 'Captain, just got a ping from *Pogy*.'

The *Pogy* was now ten miles ahead of the *October* and *Dallas*. The idea was that after she got ahead and listened for ten minutes, a single ping from her active sonar would signal that the ten miles to the *Pogy* and the twenty or more miles beyond her were clear. The *Pogy* would drift slowly to confirm this, and a mile to the *October*'s east the *Dallas* went to full speed to leapfrog ten miles beyond the other attack sub.

Jones was experimenting with the Russian sonar. The active gear, he'd found, was not too bad. The passive systems he didn't want to think about. When the *Red October* had been lying still in Pamlico Sound, he'd been unable to track in on the American subs. They had also been still, with their reactors only turning generators, but they had been no more than a mile away. He was disappointed that he'd not been able to locate them.

313

The officer with him, Bugayev, was a friendly enough guy. At first he'd been a little standoffish – as if he were a lord and I were a serf, Jones thought – until he'd seen how the skipper treated him. This surprised Jones. From what little he knew of Communism, he had expected everyone to be fairly equal. Well, he decided, that's what I get from reading *Das Kapital* in a freshman poli-sci course. It made a lot more sense to look at what Communism built. Garbage, mostly. The enlisted men didn't even have their own mess room. Wasn't that some crap! Eating your meals in your bunk rooms!

Jones had taken an hour – when he was supposed to be sleeping – to explore the submarine. Mr Mannion had joined him. They started in the bunkroom. The individual footlockers didn't lock – probably so that officers could rifle through them. Jones and Mannion did just that. There was nothing of interest. Even the sailor porn was junk. The poses were just plain dumb, and the women – well, Jones had grown up in California. Garbage. It was not at all hard for him to understand why the Russians wanted to defect.

The missile had been interesting. He and Mannion opened an inspection hatch to examine the inside of the missile. Not too shabby, they thought. There was a little too much loose wiring, but that probably made testing easier. The missile seemed awfully big. So, he thought, that's what the bastards have been aiming at us. He wondered if the navy would hold on to a few. If it was ever necessary to flip some at old Ivan, might as well include a couple of his own. Dumb idea, Jonesy, he said to himself. He didn't ever want those goddamned things to fly. One thing was for sure: everything on this bucket would be stripped off, tested, taken apart, tested again – and he was the navy's number one expert on Russian sonar. Maybe he'd be present during the analysis . . . It might be worth staying in the navy a few extra months for.

Jones lit a cigarette. 'Want one of mine, Mr Bugayev?' He held his pack out to the electronics officer.

'Thank you, Jones. You were in university?' The lieutenant took the American cigarette that he'd wanted but been too proud to ask for. It was dawning on him slowly that this enlisted man was his technical equal. Though not a qualified watch officer, Jones could operate and maintain sonar gear as well as anyone he'd known.

'Yes, sir.' It never hurt to call officers sir, Jones knew. Especially the dumb ones. 'California Institute of Technology. Five semesters completed, A average. I didn't finish.'

'Why did you leave?'

Jones smiled. 'Well, sir, you gotta understand that Cal Tech is, well, kinda a funny place. I played a little trick on one of my professors. He was working with strobe lights for high-speed photography, and I rigged a little switch to work the room lights off the strobe. Unfortunately there was a short in the switch, and it started this little electrical fire.' Which had burned out a lab, destroying three months of data and fifteen thousand dollars of equipment. 'That broke the rules.'

'What did you study?'

'I was headin' for a degree in electrical engineering, with a strong minor in cybernetics. Three semesters to go. I'll get it, then my masters, then my doctorate, and then I'll go back to work for the navy as a civilian.'

'Why are you a sonar operator?' Bugayev sat down. He had never spoken like this with an enlisted man.

'Hell, sir, it's fun! When something's going on – you know, a war game, tracking another sub, like that – I am the skipper. All the captain does is react to the data I give him.'

'And you like your commander?'

'Sure thing! He's the best I've had – I've had three. My skipper's a good guy. You do your job okay, and he doesn't hassle you. You got something to say to him, and he listens.'

'You say you will go back to college. How do you pay for it? They tell us that only the ruling class sons go to university.'

'That's crap, sir. In California if you're smart enough to go, you go. In my case, I've been saving my money – you don't spend much on a sub, right? – and the navy pitches in, too. I got enough to see me all the way through my masters. What's your degree in?'

'I attended a higher naval school. Like your Annapolis. I would like to get a proper degree in electronics,' Bugayev said, voicing his own dream.

'No sweat. I can help you out. If you're good enough for Cal Tech, I can tell you who to talk to. You'd like California. That is the place to live.'

'And I wish to work on a real computer,' Bugayev went on, wistful.

Jones laughed quietly. 'So, buy yourself one.'

Buy a computer?'

'Sure, we got a couple of little ones, Apples, on *Dallas*. Cost you about, oh, two thousand for a nice system. That's a lot less than what a car goes for.'

'A computer for two thousand dollars?' Bugayev went from wistful to suspicious, certain that Jones was leading him on.

'Or less. For three grand you can get a really nice rig. Hell, you tell Apple who you are, and they'll probably give it to you for free, or the navy will. If you don't want an Apple, there's the Commodore, TRS-80, Atari. All kinds. Depends on what you want to use it for. Look, just one company, Apple, has sold over a million of 'em. They're little, sure, but they're real computers.'

'I have never heard of this – Apple?'

'Yeah, Apple. Two guys started the company back when I was in junior high. Since then they've sold a million or so, like I said – and they are some kinda rich! I don't have one myself – no room on a sub – but my brother has his own computer, an IBM-PC. You still don't believe me, do you?'

'A working man with his own computer? It is hard to believe.' He stabbed out the cigarette. American tobacco was a little bland, he thought.

'Well, sir, then you can ask somebody else. Like I said, *Dallas* has a couple of Apples, just for the crew to use. There's other stuff for fire control, navigation, and sonar, of course. We use the Apples for games – you'll love computer games, for sure. You've never had fun till you've tried Choplifter – and other things, education programs, stuff like that. Honest, Mr Bugayev, you can walk into most any shopping centre and find a place to buy a computer. You'll see.'

'How do you use a computer with your sonar?'

'That would take a while to explain, sir, and I'd probably have to get permission from the skipper.' Jones reminded himself that this guy was still the enemy, sort of.

The *V.K. Konovalov*

The *Alfa* drifted slowly at the edge of the continental shelf, about fifty miles southeast of Norfolk. Tupolev ordered the reactor plant chopped back to about five per cent of total output, enough to operate the electrical systems and little else. It also made his submarine almost totally quiet. Orders were passed by word of mouth. The *Konovalov* was on a strict silent ship routine. Even ordinary cooking was forbidden. Cooking meant moving metal pots on metal grates. Until further notice, the crew was on a diet of cheese sandwiches. They spoke in whispers when they spoke at all. Anyone who made noise would attract the attention of the captain, and everyone aboard knew what that meant.

SOSUS Control

Quentin was reviewing data sent by digital link from the two Orions. A crippled missile boat, the USS *Georgia*, was heading into Norfolk after a partial turbine failure, escorted by a pair of attack boats. They had been keeping her out, the admiral had said, because of all the Russian activity on the coast, and the idea now was to get her in, fixed, and out as quickly as possible. The *Georgia* carried twenty-four Trident missiles, a noteworthy fraction of the country's total deterrent force. Repairing her would be a high priority item now that the Russians were gone. It was safe to bring her in, but they wanted the Orions first to check and see if any Soviet submarines had lingered behind in the general confusion.

A P-3B was cruising at nine hundred feet about fifty miles southeast of Norfolk. The FLIR showed nothing, no heat signature on the surface, and the MAD gear detected no measurable disturbance in the earth's magnetic field, though one aircraft's flight path took her within a hundred yards of the *Alfa*'s position. The *Konovalov*'s hull was made of non-magnetic titanium. A sonobuoy dropped seven miles to the south of her position also failed to pick up the sound of her reactor plant. Data was being transmitted continuously to Norfolk, where Quentin's operations staff entered it into his computer. The problem was, not all of the Soviet subs had been accounted for.

Well, the commander thought, that figures. Some of the boats had taken the opportunity to creep away from their charted loci. There was the odd chance, he had reported, that one or two strays were still out there, but there was no evidence of this. He wondered what CINCLANT had working. Certainly he had seemed awfully pleased with something, almost euphoric. The operation against the Soviet fleet had been handled pretty well, what he'd seen of it, and there was that dead *Alfa* out there. How long until the *Glomar Explorer* came out of mothballs to go and get that? He wondered if he'd get a chance to look the wreck over. What an opportunity!

Nobody was taking the current operation all that seriously. It made sense. If the *Georgia* were indeed coming in with a sick engine she'd be coming slow, and a slow *Ohio* made about as much noise as a virgin whale determined to retain her status. And if CINCLANTFLT were all that concerned about it, he would not have detailed the delousing operation to a pair of P-3s piloted by reservists. Quentin lifted the phone and dialled CINCLANTFLT Operations to tell them again that there was no indication of hostile activity.

The *Red October*

Ryan checked his watch. It had been five hours already. A long time to sit in one chair, and from a quick glance at the chart it appeared that the eight-hour estimate had been optimistic – or he'd misunderstood them. The *Red October* was tracing up the shelf time and would soon begin to angle west for the Virginia Capes. Maybe it would take another four hours. It couldn't be too soon. Ramius and Mancuso looked pretty tired. Everybody was tired. Probably the engine room people most of all – no, the cook. He was ferrying coffee and sandwiches to everyone. The Russians seemed especially hungry.

The *Dallas*/The *Pogy*

The *Dallas* passed the *Pogy* at thirty-two knots, leapfrogging again, with the *October* a few miles aft. Lieutenant Commander Wally Chambers, who had the conn, did not like being blind on the speed run of thirty-five minutes despite word from the *Pogy* that everything was clear.

The *Pogy* noted her passage and turned to allow her lateral array to track on the *Red October*.

'Noisy enough at twenty knots,' the *Pogy*'s sonar chief said to his companions. '*Dallas* doesn't make that much at thirty.'

The *V. K. Konovalov*

'Some noise to the south,' the *michman* said.

'What exactly?' Tupolev had been hovering at the door for hours, making life unpleasant for the sonarmen.

'Too soon to say, Comrade Captain. Bearing is not changing, however. It is heading this way.'

Tupolev went back to the control room. He ordered power reduced further in the reactor systems. He considered killing the plant entirely, but reactors took time to start up and there was no telling yet how distant the contact might be. The captain smoked three cigarettes before going back to sonar. It would not do at all to make the *michman* nervous. The man was his best operator.

'One propeller, Comrade Captain, an American, probably a *Los Angeles*, doing thirty-five knots. Bearing has changed only two degrees in fifteen minutes. He will pass close aboard, and – wait . . . His engines have stopped.' The forty-year-old warrant officer pressed the headphones against his ears. He could hear the cavitation sounds diminish, then stop entirely as the contact faded away to nothing. 'He has stopped to listen, Comrade Captain.'

Tupolev smiled. 'He will not hear us, Comrade. Racing and stopping. Can you hear anything else? Might he be escorting something?'

The *michman* listened to the headphones again and made some adjustments on his panel. 'Perhaps . . . there is a good deal of surface noise, Comrade, and I – wait. There seems to be some noise. Our last target bearing was one-seven-one, and this new noise is . . . one-seven-five. Very faint, Comrade Captain – a ping, a single ping on active sonar.'

'So.' Tupolev leaned against the bulkhead. 'Good work, Comrade. Now we must be patient.'

The *Dallas*

Chief Laval pronounced the area clear. The BQQ-5's sensitive receptors revealed nothing, even after the SAPS system had been used. Chambers manoeuvred the bow around so that the single ping would go out to the *Pogy*, which in turn fired off her own ping to the *Red October* to make sure the signal was received. It was clear for another ten miles. The *Pogy* moved out at thirty knots, followed by the US Navy's newest boomer.

The *V. K. Konovalov*

'Two more submarines. One single screw, the other twin screw, I think. Still faint. The single-screw submarine is turning much more rapidly. Do the Americans have twin-screw submarines, Comrade Captain?'

'Yes, I believe so.' Tupolev wondered about this. The difference in signature characteristics was not all that pronounced. They'd see in any case. The

Konovalov was creeping along at two knots, one hundred and fifty metres beneath the surface. Whatever was coming seemed to be coming right for them. Well, he'd teach the imperialists something after all.

The *Red October*

'Can anybody spell me at the wheel?' Ryan asked.

'Need a stretch?' Mancuso asked, coming over.

'Yeah. I could stand a trip to the head, too. The coffee's about to bust my kidneys.'

'I'll relieve you, sir.' The American captain moved into Ryan's seat. Jack headed aft to the nearest head. Two minutes later he was feeling much better. Back in the control room, he did some knee bends to get circulation back in his legs, then looked briefly at the chart. It seemed strange, almost sinister, to see the US coast marked in Russian.

'Thank you, Commander.'

'Sure.' Mancuso stood.

'It is certain that you are no sailor, Ryan.' Ramius had been watching him without a word.

'I have never claimed to be one, Captain,' Ryan said agreeably. 'How long to Norfolk?'

'Oh, another four hours, tops,' Mancuso said. 'The idea's to arrive after dark. They have something to get us in unseen, but I don't know what.'

'We left the sound in daylight. What if somebody saw us then?' Ryan asked.

'I didn't see anything, but if anybody was there, all he'd have seen was three sub conning towers with no numbers on them.' They had left in daylight to take advantage of a "window" in Soviet satellite coverage.

Ryan lit another cigarette. His wife would give him hell for this, but he was tense from being on the submarine. Sitting at the helmsman's station left him with nothing to do but stare at the handful of instruments. The sub was easier to hold level than he had expected, and the only radical turn he had attempted showed how eager the sub was to change course in any direction. Thirty-some-thousand tons of steel, he thought – no wonder.

The *Pogy*/The *Red October*

The *Pogy* stormed past the *Dallas* at thirty knots and continued for twenty minutes, stopping eleven miles beyond her – and three miles from the *Konovalov*, whose crew was scarcely breathing now. The *Pogy*'s sonar, though lacking the new BC-10/SAPS signal-processing system, was otherwise state of the art, but it was impossible to hear something that made no noise at all, and the *Konovalov* was silent.

The *Red October* passed the *Dallas* at 1500 hours after receiving the latest all-clear signal. Her crew was tired and looking forward to arriving at Norfolk two hours after sundown. Ryan wondered how quickly he could fly back to London. He was afraid that the CIA would want to debrief him at length. Mancuso and the crewmen of the *Dallas* wondered if they'd get to see their families. They weren't counting on it.

The *V. K. Konovalov*

'Whatever it is, it is big, very big, I think. His course will take him within five kilometres of us.'

'An *Ohio*, as Moscow said,' Tupolev commented.

'It sounds like a twin-screw submarine, Comrade Captain,' the *michman* said.

'The *Ohio* has one propeller. You know that.'

'Yes, Comrade. In any case, he will be with us in twenty minutes. The other attack submarine is moving at thirty-plus knots. If the pattern holds, he will proceed fifteen kilometres beyond us.'

'And the other American?'

'A few kilometres seaward, drifting slowly, like us. I do not have an exact range. I could raise him on active sonar, but that – '

'I am aware of the consequences,' Tupolev snapped. He went back to the control room.

'Tell the engineers to be ready to answer bells. All men at battle stations?'

'Yes, Comrade Captain,' the *starpom* replied. 'We have an excellent firing solution on the American hunter sub – the one moving, that is. The way he runs at full speed makes it easy for us. The other we can localize in seconds.'

'Good, for a change.' Tupolev smiled. 'You see what we can do when circumstances favour us?'

'And what shall we do?'

'When the big one passes us, we will close and ream his asshole. They have played their games. Now we shall play ours. Have the engineers increase power. We will need full power shortly.'

'It will make noise, Comrade,' the *starpom* cautioned.

'True, but we have no choice. Ten per cent power. The *Ohio* cannot possibly hear that, and perhaps the near hunter sub won't either.'

The *Pogy*

'Where did that come from?' The sonar chief made some adjustments on his board. 'Conn, sonar, I got a contact, bearing two-three-zero.'

'Conn, aye,' Commander Wood answered at once. 'Can you classify?'

'No, sir. It just came up. Reactor plant and steam noises, real faint, sir. I can't quite read the plant signature . . .' He flipped the gain controls to maximum. 'Not one of ours. Skipper, I think maybe we got us an *Alfa* here.'

'Oh, great! Signal *Dallas* right now!'

The chief tried, but the *Dallas*, running at thirty-two knots, missed the five rapid pings. The *Red October* was now eight miles away.

The *Red October*

Jones' eyes suddenly screwed shut. 'Mr Bugayev, tell the skipper I just heard a couple of pings.'

'Couple?'

'More 'n one, but I didn't get a count.'

The *Pogy*

Commander Wood made his decision. The idea had been to send the sonar signals on a highly directional, low-power basis so as to minimize the chance of revealing his own position. But the *Dallas* hadn't picked that up.

'Max power, Chief. Hit *Dallas* with everything.'

'Aye aye.' The chief flipped his power controls to full. It took several seconds until the system was ready to send a hundred-kilowatt blast of energy.

Ping ping ping ping ping!

The *Dallas*

'Wow!' Chief Laval exclaimed. 'Conn, sonar, danger signal from *Pogy*!'

'All stop!' Chambers ordered. 'Quiet ship.'

'All stop.' Lieutenant Goodman relayed the orders a second later. Aft, the reactor watch reduced steam demand, increasing the temperature in the reactor. This allowed neutrons to escape out of the pile, rapidly slowing the fission reaction.

'When speed gets to four knots, go to one-third speed,' Chambers told the officer of the deck as he went aft to the sonar room. 'Frenchie, I need data in a hurry.'

'Still going too fast, sir,' Laval said.

The *Red October*

'Captain Ramius, I think we should slow down,' Mancuso said judiciously.

'The signal was not repeated,' Ramius disagreed. The second directional signal had missed them, and the *Dallas* had not relayed the danger signal yet because she was still travelling too fast to locate the *October* and pass it along.

'Okay, sir. *Dallas* has killed power.'

Wood chewed on his lower lip. 'All right, let's find the bastard. Yankee search, Chief, max power.' He went back to control. 'Man battle stations.' An alarm went off two seconds later. The *Pogy* had already been at increased readiness, and within forty seconds all stations were manned, with the executive officer, Lieutenant Commander Tom Reynolds, as fire control coordinator. His team of officers and technicians were waiting for data to feed into the Mark 117 fire control computer.

The sonar dome in the *Pogy*'s bow was blasting sound energy into the water. Fifteen seconds after it started the first return signal appeared on Chief Palmer's screen.

'Conn, sonar, we have a positive contact, bearing two-three-four, range six thousand yards. Classify probable *Alfa* class from his plant signature,' Palmer said.

'Get me a solution!' Wood said urgently.

'Aye.' Reynolds watched the data input as another team of officers was making a paper and pencil plot on the chart table. Computer or not, there had to be a backup. The data paraded across the screen. The *Pogy*'s four torpedo tubes contained a pair of Harpoon antiship missiles and two Mark 48 torpedos. Only the torpedoes were useful at the moment. The Mark 48 was the most powerful torpedo in the inventory; wire-guided – and able to home in with its own active sonar – it ran at over fifty knots and carried a half-ton warhead. 'Skipper, we got a solution for both fish. Running time four minutes, thirty-five seconds.'

'Sonar, secure pinging,' Wood said.

'Aye aye. Pinging secured, sir.' Palmer killed power to the active systems. 'Target elevation-depression angle is near zero, sir. He's about at our depth.'

'Very well, sonar. Keep on him.' Wood now had his target's position. Further pinging would only give it a better idea of his own.

The *Dallas*

'*Pogy* was pinging something. They got a return, bearing one-nine-one, about,' Chief Laval said. 'There's another sub out there. I don't know what. I can read some plant and steam noises, but not enough for a signature.'

The *Pogy*

'The boomer's still movin', sir,' Chief Palmer reported.

'Skipper,' Reynolds looked up from the paper tracks, 'her course takes her between us and the target.'

'Terrific. All ahead one-third, left twenty degrees rudder.' Wood moved to the sonar room while his orders were carried out. 'Chief, power up and stand by to ping the boomer hard.'

'Aye aye, sir.' Palmer worked his controls. 'Ready, sir.'

'Hit him straight on. I don't want him to miss this time.'

Wood watched the heading indicator on the sonar plot swing. The *Pogy* was turning rapidly, but not rapidly enough to suit him. The *Red October* – only he and Reynolds knew that she was Russian, though the crew was speculating like mad – was coming in too fast.

'Ready, sir.' 'Hit it.'

Palmer punched the impulse control.

Ping ping ping ping ping!

The *Red October*

'Skipper,' Jones yelled. 'Danger signal!'

Mancuso jumped to the annunciator without waiting for Ramius to react. He twisted the dial to All Stop. When this was done he looked at Ramius. 'Sorry, sir.'

'All right.' Ramius scowled at the chart. The phone buzzed a moment later. He took it and spoke in Russian for several seconds before hanging up. 'I told them that we have a problem but we do not know what it is.'

'True enough.' Mancuso joined Ramius at the chart. Engine noises were diminishing, though not quickly enough to suit the American. The *October* was quiet for a Russian sub, but this was still too noisy for him.

'See if your sonarman can locate anything,' Ramius suggested.

'Right.' Mancuso took a few steps aft. 'Jonesy, find what's out there.'

'Aye, Skipper, but it won't be easy on this gear.' He already had the sensor arrays working in the direction of the two escorting attack subs. Jones adjusted the fit of his headphones and started working on the amplifier controls. No signal processors, no SAPS, and the transducers weren't worth a damn! But this wasn't the time to get excited. The Soviet systems had to be manipulated electromechanically, unlike the computer-controlled ones he was used to. Slowly and carefully, he altered the directional receptor gangs in the sonar dome forward, his right hand twirling a cigarette pack, his eyes shut tight. He didn't notice Bugayev sitting next to him, listening to the same input.

The *Dallas*

'What do we know, Chief?' Chambers asked.

'I got a bearing and nothing else. *Pogy*'s got him all dialled in, but our friend powered back his engine right after he got lashed, and he faded out on me. *Pogy* got a big return off him. He's probably pretty close, sir.'

Chambers had only moved up to his executive officer's posting four months earlier. He was a bright, experienced officer and a likely candidate for his own command, but he was only thirty-three years old and had only been back in submarines for those four months. The year and a half prior to that he'd been a reactor instructor in Idaho. The gruffness that was part of his job as Mancuso's principal on-board disciplinarian also shielded more insecurity than he would have cared to admit. Now his career was on the line. He knew exactly how important this mission was. His future would ride on the decisions he was about to make.

'Can you localize with one ping?'

The sonar chief considered this for a second. 'Not enough for a shooting solution, but it'll give us something.'

'One ping, do it.'

'Aye.' Laval worked on his board briefly, triggering the active elements.

The *V. K. Konovalov*

Tupolev winced. He had acted too soon. He should have waited until they were past – but then if he had waited that long, he would have had to move, and now he had all three of them hovering nearby, almost still.

The four submarines were moving only fast enough for depth control. The Russian *Alfa* was pointed southeast, and all four were arrayed in a roughly trapezoidal fashion, open end seaward. The *Pogy* and the *Dallas* were to the north of the *Konovalov*, the *Red October* was southeast of her.

The *Red October*

'Somebody just pinged her,' Jones said quietly. 'Bearing is roughly north-west, but she isn't making enough noise for us to read her. Sir, if I had to make a bet, I'd say she was pretty close.'

'How do you know that?' Mancuso asked.

'I heard the pulse direct – just one ping to get a range, I think. It was from a BQQ-5. Then we heard the echo off the target. The maths works out a couple of different ways, but smart money is he's between us and our guys, and a little west. I know it's shaky, sir, but it's the best we got.'

'Range ten kilometres, perhaps less,' Bugayev commented.

'That's kinda shaky, too, but it's as good a starting place as any. Not a whole lot of data. Sorry, Skipper. Best we can do,' Jones said.

Mancuso nodded and returned to control.

'What gives?' Ryan asked. The plane controls were pushed all the way forward to maintain depth. He had not grasped the significance of what was going on.

'There's a hostile submarine out there.'

'What information do we have?' Ramius asked.

'Not much. There's a contact northwest, range unknown, but probably not very clear. I know for sure it's not one of ours. Norfolk said this area was cleared. That leaves one possibility. We drift?'

'We drift,' Ramius echoed, lifting the phone. He spoke a few orders.

The *October*'s engines were providing the power to move the submarine at a fraction over two knots, barely enough to maintain steerage way and not enough to maintain depth. With her slight positive buoyancy, the *October* was drifting upward a few feet per minute despite the plane setting.

The *Dallas*

'Let's move back south. I don't like the idea of having that *Alfa* closer to our friend than we are. Come right to one-eight-five, two-thirds,' Chambers said finally.

'Aye aye,' Goodman said. 'Helm, right fifteen degrees rudder, come to new course one-eight-five. All ahead two thirds.'

'Right fifteen degrees rudder, aye.' The helmsman turned the wheel. 'Sir, my rudder is right fifteen degrees, coming to new course one-eight-five.'

The *Dallas*' four torpedo tubes were loaded with three Mark 48s and a decoy, an expensive MOSS (mobile submarine simulator). One of her torpedoes was targeted on the *Alfa*, but the firing solution was vague. The 'fish' would have to do some of the tracking by itself. The *Pogy*'s two torpedoes were almost perfectly dialled in.

The problem was that neither boat had authority to shoot. Both attack submarines were operating under the normal rules of engagement. They could fire in self-defence only and defend the *Red October* only by bluff and guile. The question was whether the *Alfa* knew what the *Red October* was.

The *Konovalov*

'Steer for the *Ohio*,' Tupolev ordered. 'Bring speed to three knots. We must be patient, comrades. Now that the Americans know where we are they will not ping us again. We will move from our place quietly.'

The *Konovalov*'s bronze propeller turned more quickly. By shutting down some non-essential electrical systems, the engineers were able to increase speed without increasing reactor output.

The *Pogy*

On the *Pogy*, the nearest attack boat, the contact faded, degrading the directional bearing somewhat. Commander Wood debated whether or not to get another bearing with active sonar but decided against it. If he used active sonar his position would be like that of a policeman looking for a burglar in a dark building with a flashlight. Sonar pings could well tell his target more than they told him. Using passive sonar was the normal routine in such a case.

Chief Palmer reported the passage of the *Dallas* down their port side. Both Wood and Chambers decided not to use their underwater telephones to communicate. They could not afford to make any noise now.

The *Red October*

They had been creeping along for a half hour now. Ryan was chain-smoking at his station, and his palms were sweating as he struggled to maintain his composure. This was not the sort of combat he had been trained for, being trapped inside a steel pipe, unable to see or hear anything. He knew that there was a Soviet submarine out there, and he knew what her orders were. If her captain realized who they were – then what? The two captains, he thought, were amazingly cool.

'Can your submarines protect us?' Ramius asked.

'Shoot at a Russian sub?' Mancuso shook his head. 'Only if he shoots first – at them. Under the normal rules, we don't count.'

'*What?*' Ryan was stunned.

'You want to start a war?' Mancuso smiled, as though he found this situation amusing. 'That's what happens when warships from two countries start exchanging shots. We have to smart our way out of this.'

'Be calm, Ryan,' Ramius said. 'This is our usual game. The hunter submarine tries to find us, and we try not to be found. Tell me, Captain Mancuso, at what range did you hear us off Iceland?'

'I haven't examined your chart closely, Captain,' Mancuso mused. 'Maybe twenty miles, thirty or so kilometres.'

'And then we were travelling at thirteen knots – noise increases faster than speed. I think we can move east, slowly, without being detected. We use the caterpillar, move at six knots. As you know, Soviet sonar is not so efficient as American. Do you agree, Captain?'

Mancuso nodded. 'She's your boat, sir. May I suggest northeast? That ought to put us behind our attack boats inside an hour, maybe less.'

'Yes.' Ramius hobbled over to the control board to open the tunnel hatches, then went back to the phone. He gave the necessary orders. In a minute the caterpillar motors were engaged and speed was increasing slowly.

'Rudder right ten, Ryan,' Ramius said. 'And ease the plane controls.'

'Rudder right ten, sir, easing the planes, sir.' Ryan carried the orders out, glad that they were doing something.

'Your course is zero-four-zero, Ryan,' Mancuso said from the chart table.

'Zero-four-zero, coming right through three-five-zero.' From the helmsman's seat he could hear the water swishing down the portside tunnel. Every minute or so there was an odd rumble that lasted three or four seconds. The speed gauge in front of him passed through four knots.

'You are frightened, Ryan?' Ramius chuckled.

Jack swore to himself. His voice had wavered. 'I'm a little tired, too.'

'I know it is difficult for you. You do well for a new man with no training. We will be late to Norfolk, but we shall get there, you will see. Have you been on a missile boat, Mancuso?'

'Oh, sure. Relax, Ryan. This is what boomers do. Somebody comes lookin' for us, we just disappear.' The American commander looked up from the chart. He considered marking it up more but decided not to. There were some very interesting notations on this coastal chart – like programmed missile-firing positions. Fleet intelligence would go ape over this sort of information.

The *Red October* was moving northeast at six knots now. The *Konovalov* was coming southeast at three. The *Pogy* was heading south at two, and the *Dallas* south at fifteen. All four submarines were now within a six-mile-diameter circle, all converging on about the same point.

The *V. K. Konovalov*

Tupolev was enjoying himself. For whatever reason, the Americans had chosen to play a conservative game that he had not expected. The smart thing, he thought, would have been for one of the attack boats to close in and harass him, allowing the missile sub to pass clear with the other escort. Well, at sea nothing was ever quite the same twice. He sipped at a cup of tea as he selected a sandwich.

His sonar *michman* noted an odd sound in his sonar set. It only lasted a few seconds, then was gone. Some far-off seismic rumble, he thought at first.

The *Red October*

They had risen because of the *Red October*'s positive trim, and now Ryan had five degrees of down-angle on the diving planes to get back down to a hundred metres. He heard the captains discussing the absence of a thermocline. Mancuso explained that it was not unusual for the area, particularly after violent storms. They agreed that it was unfortunate. A thermal layer would have helped their evasion.

Jones was at the aft entrance of the control room, rubbing his ears. The Russian phones were not very comfortable. 'Skipper, I'm getting something to the north, comes and goes. I haven't gotten a bearing lock on it.'

'Whose?' Mancuso asked.

'Can't say, sir. The active sonar isn't too bad, but the passive stuff just isn't up to the drill, Skipper. We're not blind, but close to it.'

'Okay, if you hear something, sing out.'

'Aye aye, Captain. You got some coffee out here? Mr Bugayev sent me for some.'

'I'll have a pot sent in.'

'Right.' Jones went back to work.

'Comrade Captain, I have a contact, but I do not know what it is,' the *michman* said over the phone.

Tupolev came back, munching on his sandwich. *Ohios* had been acquired so rarely by the Russians – three times to be exact, and in each case the quarry had been lost within minutes – that no one had a feel for the characteristics of the class.

The *michman* handed the captain a spare set of phones. 'It may take a few minutes, Comrade. It comes and goes.'

The water off the American coast, though nearly isothermal, was not entirely perfect for sonar systems. Minor currents and eddies set up moving walls that reflected and channelled sound energy on a nearly random basis. Tupolev sat down and listened patiently. It took five minutes for the signal to come back.

The *michman*'s hand waved. 'Now, Comrade Captain.'

His commanding officer looked pale.

'Bearing?'

'Too faint, and too short to lock in – but three degrees on either bow, one-three-six to one-four-two.'

Tupolev tossed the headphones on the table and went forward. He grabbed the political officer by the arm and led him quickly to the wardroom.

'It's *Red October*!'

'Impossible. Fleet Command said that his destruction was confirmed by visual inspection of the wreckage.' The *zampolit* shook his head emphatically.

'We have been tricked. The caterpillar acoustical signature is unique, Comrade. The Americans have him, and he is out there. We must destroy him!'

'No. We must contact Moscow and ask for instructions.'

The *zampolit* was a good Communist, but he was a surface ship officer who didn't belong on submarines, Tupolev thought.

'Comrade Zampolit, it will take several minutes to approach the surface, perhaps ten or fifteen to get a message to Moscow, thirty more for Moscow to respond at all – and then they will request *confirmation!* An hour in all, two, three? By that time *Red October* will be gone. Our original orders are operative, and there is no time to contact Moscow.'

'But what if you are wrong?'

'I am not wrong, Comrade!' the captain hissed. 'I will enter my contact report in the log, and my recommendations. If you forbid this, I will log that also! I am right, Comrade. It will be your head, not mine. Decide!'

'You are certain?'

'*Certain!*'

'Very well.' The *zampolit* seemed to deflate. 'How will you do this?'

'As quickly as possible, before the Americans have a chance to destroy us. Go to your station, Comrade.' The two men went back to the control room. The *Konovalov*'s six bow torpedo tubes were loaded with Mark C 533-millimetre wire-guided torpedoes. All they needed was to be told where to go.

'Sonar, search forward on all active systems!' the captain ordered.

The *michman* pushed the button.

The *Red October*

'Ouch.' Jones' head jerked around. 'Skipper, we're being pinged. Port side, midships, maybe a little forward. Not one of ours, sir.'

The *Pogy*

'Conn, sonar, the *Alfa*'s got the boomer! The *Alfa* bearing is one-nine-two.'

'All ahead two-thirds,' Wood ordered immediately.

'All ahead two-thirds, aye.'

The *Pogy*'s engines exploded into life, and soon her propeller was thrashing the black water.

The *V. K. Konovalov*

'Range seven thousand, six hundred metres. Elevation angle zero,' the *michman* reported. So, this was the submarine they had been sent to hunt, he thought. He had just donned a headset that allowed him to report directly to the captain and fire control officer.

The *starpom* was the chief fire control supervisor. He quickly entered the data into the computer. It was a simple problem of target geometry. 'We have a solution for torpedoes one and two.'

'Prepare to fire.'

'Flooding tubes.' The *starpom* flipped the switches himself, reaching past the petty officer. 'Outer torpedo tube doors are open.'

'Recheck firing solution!' Tupolev said.

The *Pogy*

The *Pogy*'s sonar chief was the only man to hear the transient noise.

'Conn, sonar, *Alfa* contact – she just flooded tubes, sir! Target bearing is one-seven-nine.'

The *V. K. Konovalov*

'Solution confirmed, Comrade Captain,' the *starpom* said.

'Fire one and two,' Tupolev ordered.

'Firing one . . . Firing two.' The *Konovalov* shuddered twice as compressed air charges ejected the electrically powered torpedoes.

The *Red October*

Jones heard it first. 'High-speed screws port side!' he said loudly and clearly. 'Torpedoes in the water port side!'

'*Ryl nalyeva!*' Ramius ordered automatically.

'*What?*' Ryan asked.

'Left, rudder left!' Ramius pounded his fist on the rail.

'Left full, do it!' Mancuso said.

'Left full rudder, aye.' Ryan turned the wheel all the way and held it down. Ramius was spinning the annunciator to flank speed.

The *Pogy*

'Two fish running,' Palmer said. 'Bearing is changing right to left. I say again, torpedo bearing changing right to left rapidly on both fish. They're targeted on the boomer.'

The *Dallas*

The *Dallas* heard them, too. Chambers ordered flank speed and a turn to port. With torpedoes running his options were limited, and he was doing what American practice taught, heading someplace else – very fast.

The *Red October*

'I need a course!' Ryan said.

'Jonesy, give me a bearing!' Mancuso shouted.

'Three-two-zero, sir. Two fish heading in,' Jones responded at once, working his controls to nail the bearing down. This was no time to screw up.

'Steer three-two-zero, Ryan,' Ramius ordered, 'if we can turn so fast.'

Thanks a lot, Ryan thought angrily, watching the gyrocompass click through three-five-seven. The rudder was hard over, and with the sudden increase in power from the caterpillar motors, he could feel feedback flutter through the wheel.

'Two fish heading in, bearing is three-two-zero, I say again bearing is constant,' Jones reported, much cooler than he felt. 'Here we go, guys . . .'

The *Pogy*

Her tactical plot showed the *October*, the *Alfa*, and the two torpedoes. The *Pogy* was four miles north of the action.

'Can we shoot?' the exec asked.

'At the *Alfa?*' Wood shook his head emphatically. 'No, dammit. It wouldn't make a difference anyway.'

The *V. K. Konovalov*

The two Mark C torpedoes were charging at forty-one knots, a slow speed for this range, so that they could be more easily guided by the *Konovalov*'s sonar systems. They had a projected six-minute run, with one minute already completed.

The *Red October*

'Okay, coming through three-four-five, easing the rudder off,' Ryan said.

Mancuso kept quiet now. Ramius was using a tactic that he didn't particularly agree with, turning into the fish. It offered a minimum target profile, but it gave them a simpler geometric intercept solution. Presumably Ramius knew what Russian fish could do. Mancuso hoped so.

'Steady on three-two-zero, Captain,' Ryan said, eyes locked on the gyro repeater as though it mattered. A small voice in his brain congratulated him for going to the head an hour earlier.

'Ryan, down, maximum down on the diving planes.'

'All the way down.' Ryan pushed the yoke to the stops. He was terrified, but even more frightened of fouling up. He had to assume that both commanders knew what they were about. There was no choice for him. Well, he thought, he did know one thing. Guided torpedoes can be tricked. Like radar signals that are aimed at the ground, sonar pulses can be obscured, especially when the sub they are trying to locate is near the bottom or the surface, areas where the pulses tend to be reflected. If the *October* dived she could lose herself in an opaque field – presuming she got there fast enough.

The *V. K. Konovalov*

'Target aspect has changed, Comrade Captain. Target is now smaller,' the *michman* said.

Tupolev considered this. He knew everything there was on Soviet combat doctrine – and knew that Ramius had written a good deal of it. Marko would do what he taught all of us to do, Tupolev thought. Turn into the oncoming weapons to minimize target cross-section and dive for the bottom to become lost in the confused echoes. 'Target will be attempting to dive into the bottom-capture field. Be alert.'

'Aye, Comrade. Can he reach the bottom quickly enough?' the *starpom* asked.

Tupolev racked his brain for the *October*'s handling characteristics. 'No, he cannot dive that deep in so short a time. We have him.' Sorry, my old friend, but I have no choice, he thought.

The *Red October*

Ryan cringed each time the sonar lash echoed through the double hull. 'Can't you jam that or something?' he demanded.

'Patience, Ryan,' Ramius said. He had never faced live warheads before but had exercised this problem a hundred times in his career. 'Let him know he has us first.'

'Do you carry decoys?' Mancuso asked.

'Four of them, in the torpedo room, forward – but we have no torpedomen.'

Both captains were playing the cool game, Ryan noted bitterly from inside his terrified little world. Neither was willing to show fright before his peer. But they were both trained for this.

'Skipper,' Jones called, 'two fish, bearing constant at three-two-zero – they just went active. I say again, the fish are now active – shit! they sound just like 48s. Skipper, they sound like Mark 48 fish.'

Ramius had been waiting for this. 'Yes, we stole the torpedo sonar from you five years ago, but not your torpedo engines. *Bugayev!*'

In the sonar room, Bugayev had powered up the acoustical jamming gear as soon as the fish were launched. Now he carefully timed his jamming pulses to coincide with those from the approaching torpedoes. The pulses were dialled into the same carrier frequency and pulse repetition rate. The timing had to be precise. By sending out slightly distorted return echoes, he could create ghost targets. Not too many, nor too far away. Just a few, close by, and he might be able to confuse the fire control operators on the attacking *Alfa*. He thumbed the trigger switch carefully, chewing on an American cigarette.

The *V. K. Konovalov*

'Damn! He's jamming us.' The *michman*, noting a pair of new pips, showed his first trace of emotion. The fading pip from the true contact was now bordered with two new ones, one north and closer, the other south and farther away. 'Captain, the target is using Soviet jamming equipment.'

'You see?' Tupolev said to the *zampolit*. 'Use caution now,' he ordered his *starpom*.

The *Red October*

'Ryan, up on all planes!' Ramius shouted.

'All the way up.' Ryan yanked back, pulling the yoke hard against his belly and hoping that Ramius knew what the hell he was doing.

'Jones, give us time and range.'

'Aye.' The jamming gave them a sonar picture plotted on the main scopes. 'Two fish, bearing three-two-zero. Range to number one is 2,000 yards, to number two is 2,300 – I got a depression angle on number one! Number one fish is heading down a little, sir.' Maybe Bugayev wasn't so dumb after all, Jones thought. But they had two fish to sweat . . .

The *Pogy*

The *Pogy*'s skipper was enraged. The goddamned rules of engagement prevented him from doing a goddamned thing, except, maybe –

'Sonar, ping the sonuvabitch! Max power, blast the sucker!'

The *Pogy*'s BQQ-5 sent timed wave fronts of energy lashing at the *Alfa*. The *Pogy* couldn't shoot, but maybe the Russian didn't know that, and maybe this lashing would interfere with their targeting sonar.

The *Red October*

'Any time now – one of the fish has capture, sir. I don't know which.' Jones moved the phones off one ear, his hand poised to slap the other off. The homing sonar on one torpedo was now tracking them. Bad news. If these were like Mark 48s . . . Jones knew all too well that those things didn't miss much. He heard the change in the Doppler shift of the propellers as they passed beneath the *Red October*. 'He missed, sir. Number one missed under us. Number two is heading in, ping interval is shortening.' He reached over and patted Bugayev on the shoulder. Maybe he really was the on-board genius that the Russians said he was.

The *V. K. Konovalov*

The second Mark C torpedo was cutting through the water at forty-one knots. This made the torpedo-target closing speed about fifty-five. The guidance and decision loop was a complex one. Unable to mimic the computer homing system on the American Mark 48, the Soviets had the torpedo's targeting sonar report back to the launching vessel through an insulated wire. The *starpom* had a choice of sonar data with which to guide the torpedoes, that from the sub-mounted sonar or that from the torpedoes themselves. The first fish had been duped by the ghost images that the jamming had duplicated on the torpedo sonar frequency. For the second, the *starpom* was using the lower-frequency bow sonar. The first one had missed low, he knew now. That meant that the target was the middle pip. A quick frequency change by the *michman* cleared the sonar picture for a few seconds before the jamming mode was altered. Coolly and expertly, the *starpom* commanded the second torpedo to select the centre target. It ran straight and true.

The five-hundred-pound warhead struck the target a glancing blow aft of midships, just forward of the control room. It exploded a millisecond later.

The *Red October*

The force of the explosion hurled Ryan from his chair, and his head hit the deck. He came to from a moment's unconsciousness with his ears ringing in the dark. The shock of the explosion had shorted out a dozen electrical switchboards, and it was several seconds before the red battle lights clicked on. Aft, Jones had flipped his headphones off just in time, but Bugayev, trying to the last second to spoof the incoming torpedo, had not. He was rolling in agony on the deck, one eardrum ruptured, totally deafened. In the engine spaces men were scrambling back to their feet. Here the lights had stayed on, and Melekhin's first action was to look at the damage-control status board.

The explosion had occurred on the outer hull, a skin of light steel. Inside it was a water-filled ballast tank, a beehive of cellular beams seven feet across. Located beyond the tank were high-pressure air flasks. Then came the *October*'s battery bank and the inner pressure hull. The torpedo had impacted in the centre of a steel plate on the outer hull, several feet from any weld joints. The force of the explosion had torn a hole twelve feet across, shredded the interior ballast tank beams, and ruptured a half-dozen air flasks, but already much of its force had been dissipated. The final damage was done to thirty of the large nickel-cadmium battery cells. Soviet engineers had placed these here deliberately. They had known that such a placement would make them difficult to service, difficult to recharge, and worst of all expose them to seawater contamination. All this had been accepted in light of their secondary purpose as additional armour for the hull. The *October*'s batteries saved her. Had it not been for them, the force of the explosion would have been spent on the pressure hull. Instead it was greatly reduced by the layered defensive system which had no Western counterpart. A crack had developed at a weld joint on the inner hull, and water was spraying into the radio room as though from a high-pressure hose, but the hull was otherwise secure.

In control, Ryan was soon back in his seat trying to determine if his instruments still worked. He could hear water splashing into the next compartment forward. He didn't know what to do. He did know it would be a bad time to panic, much as his brain screamed for the release.

'What do I do?'

'Still with us?' Mancuso's face looked satanic in the red lights.

'No, goddammit, I'm dead – what do I do?'

'Ramius?' Mancuso saw the captain holding a flashlight taken from a bracket on the aft bulkhead.

'Down, dive for the bottom.' Ramius took the phone and called engineering to order the engines stopped. Melekhin had already given the order.

Ryan pushed his controls forward. In a goddamned submarine that's got a goddamned hole punched in it, they tell you to go *down!* he thought.

The *V. K. Konovalov*

'A solid hit, Comrade Captain,' the *michman* reported. 'His engines stopped. I hear hull creaking noises, his depth is changing.' He tried some additional pings but got nothing. The explosion had greatly disturbed the water. There were rumbling echoes of the initial explosion reverberating through the sea. Trillions of bubbles had formed, creating an 'ensonified zone' around the target that rapidly obscured it. His active pings were reflected back by the cloud of bubbles, and his passive listing ability was greatly reduced by the recurring rumbles. All he knew for sure was that one torpedo had hit, probably the second. He was an experienced man trying to decide what was noise and what was signal, and he had reconstructed most of the events correctly.

The *Dallas*

'Score one for the bad guys,' the sonar chief said. The *Dallas* was running too fast to make proper use of her sonar, but the explosion was impossible to miss. The whole crew heard it through the hull.

In the attack centre Chambers plotted their position two miles from where the *October* had been. The others in the compartment looked at their instruments without emotion. Ten of their shipmates had just been hit, and the enemy was on the other side of the wall of noise.

'Slow to one-third,' Chambers ordered.

'All ahead one-third,' the officer of the deck repeated.

'Sonar, get me some data,' Chambers said.

'Working on it, sir.' Chief Laval strained to make sense of what he heard. It took a few minutes as the *Dallas* slowed to under ten knots. 'Conn, sonar, the boomer took one hit. I don't hear her engines . . . but there ain't no breakup noises. I say again, sir, no breakup noises.'

'Can you hear the *Alfa?*'

'No, sir, too much crud in the water.'

Chamber's face screwed into a grimace. You're an officer, he told himself, they pay you to think. First, what's happening? Second, what do you do about it? Think it through, then act.

'Estimated distance to target?'

'Something like nine thousand yards, sir,' Lieutenant Goodman said, reading the last solution off the fire control computer. 'She'll be on the far side of the ensonified zone.'

'Make your depth six hundred feet.' The diving officer passed this on to the helmsman. Chambers considered the situation and decided on his course of action. He wished Mancuso and Mannion were here. The captain and navigator were the other two members of what passed for the *Dallas'* tactical management committee. He needed to exchange some ideas with other experienced officers – but there weren't any.

'Listen up. We're going down. The disturbance from the explosion will stay fairly steady. If it moves at all, it'll go up. Okay, we'll go under it. First we want to locate the boomer. If she isn't there, then she's on the bottom. It's only nine hundred feet here, so she could be on the bottom with a live crew. Whether or not she's on the bottom, we gotta get between her and the *Alfa*.' And, he thought on, if the *Alfa* shoots then, I kill the fucker, and rules of engagement be damned. They had to trick this guy. But how? And where was the *Red October*?

The *Red October*

She was diving more quickly then expected. The explosion had also ruptured a trim tank, causing more negative buoyancy than they had at first allowed for.

The leak in the radio room was bad, but Melekhin had noted the flooding on his damage control board and reacted immediately. Each compartment had its own electrically powered pump. The radio room pump, supplemented by a master-zone pump that he had also activated, was managing, barely, to keep up with the flooding. The radios were already destroyed, but no one was planning to send any messages.

'Ryan, all the way up, and come right full rudder,' Ramius said.

'Right full rudder, all the way up on the planes,' Ryan said. 'We going to hit the bottom?'

'Try not to,' Mancuso said. 'It might spring the leak worse.'

'Great,' Ryan growled back.

The *October* slowed her descent, arcing east below the ensonified zone. Ramius wanted it between himself and the *Alfa*. Mancuso thought that they might just survive after all. In that case he'd have to give this boat's plans a closer look.

The *Dallas*

'Sonar, give me two low-powered pings for the boomer. I don't want anybody else to hear this, Chief.'

'Aye.' Chief Laval made the proper adjustments and sent the signals out. 'All right! Conn, sonar, I got her! Bearing two-zero-three, range two thousand yards. She is not, repeat *not*, on the bottom, sir.'

'Left fifteen degrees rudder, come to two-zero-three,' Chambers ordered.

'Left fifteen degrees rudder, aye!' the helmsman sang out. 'New course two-zero-three. Sir, my rudder is left fifteen degrees.'

'Frenchie, tell me about the boomer!'

'Sir, I got . . . pump noises, I think . . . little, bearing is now two-zero-one. I can track her on passive, sir.'

'Thompson, plot the boomer's course. Mr Goodman, we still have that MOSS ready for launch?'

'Aye aye,' responded the torpedo officer.

The *V. K. Konovalov*

'Did we kill him?' the *zampolit* asked.

'Probably,' Tupolev answered, wondering if he had or not. 'We must close to be certain. Ahead slow.'

'Ahead slow.'

The *Pogy*

The *Pogy* was now within two thousand yards of the *Konovalov*, still pinging her mercilessly.

'He's moving, sir. Enough that I can read passive,' Sonar Chief Palmer said.

'Very well, secure pinging,' Wood said.

'Aye, pinging secured.'

'We got a solution?'

'Locked in tight,' Reynolds answered. 'Running time is one minute eighteen seconds. Both fish are ready.'

'All ahead one-third.'

'All ahead one-third, aye.' The *Pogy* slowed. Her commanding officer wondered what excuse he might find for shooting.

The *Red October*

'Skipper, that was one of our sonars that pinged us, off north-north-east. Low-power ping, sir, must be close.'

'Think you can raise her on gertrude?'

'Yes, sir!'

'Captain?' Mancuso asked. 'Permission to communicate with my ship?'

'Yes.'

'Jones, raise her right now.'

'Aye. This is Jonesy calling Frenchie, do you copy?' The sonarman frowned at the speaker. 'Frenchie, answer me.'

The *Dallas*

'Conn, sonar, I got Jonesy on the gertrude.'

Chambers lifted the control room gertrude phone. 'Jones, this is Chambers. What is your condition?'

Mancuso took the mike away from his man. 'Wally, this is Bart,' he said. 'We took one midships, but she's holding together. Can you run interference for us?'

'Aye aye! Starting right now, out.' Chambers replaced the phone. 'Goodman, flood the MOSS tube. Okay, we'll go in behind the MOSS. If the *Alfa* shoots at it, we take her out. Set it to run straight for two thousand yards, then turn south.'

'Done. Outer door open, sir.'

'Launch.'

'MOSS away, sir.'

The decoy ran forward at twenty knots for two minutes to clear the *Dallas*, then slowed. It had a torpedo body whose forward portion carried a powerful sonar transducer that ran off a tape recorder and broadcast the recorded sounds of a 688-class submarine. Every four minutes it changed over from loud operation to silent. The *Dallas* trailed a thousand yards behind the decoy, dropping several hundred feet below its course track.

The *Konovalov* approached the wall of bubbles carefully, with the *Pogy* trailing to the north.

'Shoot at the decoy, you son of a bitch,' Chambers said quietly. The attack centre crew heard him and nodded grim agreement.

The *Red October*

Ramius judged that the ensonified zone was now between him and the *Alfa*. He ordered the engines turned back on and the *Red October* proceeded on a north-easterly course.

The *V. K. Konovalov*

'Left ten degrees rudder,' Tupolev ordered quietly. 'We'll come around the dead zone to the north and see if he is still alive when we turn back. First we must clear the noise.'

'Still nothing,' the *michman* reported. 'No bottom impact, no collapse noises . . . New contact, bearing one-seven-zero . . . Different sound, Comrade Captain, one propeller . . . Sounds like an American.'

'What heading?'

'South, I think. Yes, south . . . The sound's changing. It is American.'

'An American sub is decoying. We ignore it.'

'Ignore it?' the *zampolit* said.

'Comrade, if you were heading north and were torpedoed, would you then head south? Yes, you would – but not Marko. It is too obvious. This American is decoying to try to take us away from him. Not too clever, this one. Marko would do better. And he would go north. I know him, I know how he thinks. He is now heading north, perhaps northeast. They would not decoy if he was dead. Now we know that he is alive but crippled. We will find him and finish him,' Tupolev said calmly, fully caught up in the hunt for *Red October*, remembering all he had been taught. He would prove now that he was the new master. His conscience was still. Tupolev was fulfilling his destiny.

'But the Americans – '

'Will not shoot, Comrade,' the captain said with a thin smile. 'If they could shoot, we would already be dead from the one to the north. They cannot shoot without permission. They must *ask* for permission, as we must – but we already have the permission, and the advantage. We are now where the torpedo struck him, and when we clear the disturbance we will find him again. Then we will have him.'

The *Red October*

They couldn't use the caterpillar. One side was smashed by the torpedo hit. The *October* was moving at six knots, driven by her propellers, which made more noise than the other system. This was much like the normal drill of protecting a boomer. But the exercise always presupposed that the escorting attack boats could shoot to make the bad guy go away . . .

'Left rudder, reverse course,' Ramius ordered.

'What?' Mancuso was astounded.

'Think, Mancuso,' Ramius said, looking to be sure that Ryan carried out the order. Ryan did, not knowing why.

'Think, Commander Mancuso,' Ramius repeated. 'What has happened? Moskva ordered a hunter sub to remain behind, probably a *Politovskiy*-class boat, the *Alfa* you call him. I know all their captains. All young, all, ah, aggressive? Yes, aggressive. He must know we are not dead. If he knows this, he will pursue us. So, we go back like a fox and let him pass.'

Mancuso didn't like this. Ryan could tell without looking.

'We cannot shoot. Your men cannot shoot. We cannot run from him – he is faster. We cannot hide – his sonar is better. He will move east, use his speed to contain us and his sonar to locate us. By moving west, we have the best chance to escape. This he will not expect.'

Mancuso still didn't like it, but he had to admit it was clever. Too damned clever. He looked back down at the chart. It wasn't his boat.

The *Dallas*

'The bastard went right past. Either ignored the decoy or flat didn't hear it. He's abeam of us, we'll be in his baffles soon,' Chief Laval reported.

Chambers swore quietly. 'So much for that idea. Right fifteen degrees rudder.' At least the *Dallas* had not been heard. The submarine responded rapidly to the controls. 'Let's get behind him.'

The *Pogy*

The *Pogy* was now a mile off the *Alfa*'s port quarter. She had the *Dallas* on sonar and noted her change of course. Commander Wood simply did not know what to do next. The easiest solution was to shoot, but he couldn't. He contemplated shooting on his own. His every instinct told him to do just this. The *Alfa* was hunting Americans . . . But he couldn't give in to his instinct. Duty came first.

There was nothing worse than overconfidence, he reflected bitterly. The assumption behind this operation had been that there wouldn't be anybody around, and even if there were the attack subs would be able to warn the boomer off well in advance. There was a lesson in this, but Wood didn't care to think about it just now.

The *V. K. Konovalov*

'Contact,' the *michman* said into the microphone. 'Ahead, almost dead ahead. Using propellers and going at slow speed. Bearing zero-four-four, range unknown.'

'Is it *Red October*?' Tupolev asked.

'I cannot say, Comrade Captain. It could be an American. He's coming this way, I think.'

'Damn!' Tupolev looked around the control room. Could they have passed the *Red October*? Might they already have killed him?

The *Dallas*

'Does he know we're here, Frenchie?' Chambers asked, back in sonar.

'No way, sir.' Laval shook his head. 'We're directly behind him. Wait a minute . . .' The chief frowned. 'Another contact, far side of the *Alfa*. That's gotta be our friend, sir. Jesus! I think he's heading this way. Using his wheels, not that funny thing.'

'Range to the *Alfa*?'

'Under three thousand yards, sir.'

'All ahead two thirds! Come left ten degrees!' Chambers ordered. 'Frenchie, ping, but use the under-ice sonar. He may not know what that is. Make him think we're the boomer.'

'Aye aye, sir!'

The *V. K. Konovalov*

'High-frequency pinging aft!' the *michman* called out. 'Does not sound like an American sonar, Comrade.'

Tupolev was suddenly puzzled. Was it an American to seaward? The other one on his port quarter was certainly American. It had to be the *October*.

340

Marko was still the fox. He had lain still, letting them go past, so that he could shoot at them!

'All ahead full, left full rudder!'

The *Red October*

'Contact!' Jones sang out. 'Dead ahead. Wait . . . It's an *Alfa!* She's close! Seems to be turning. Somebody pinging her on the other side. Christ, she's real close. Skipper, the *Alfa* is not a point source. I got signal separation between the engine and the screw.'

'Captain,' Mancuso said. The two commanders looked at one another and communicated a single thought as if by telepathy. Ramius nodded.

'Get us range.'

'Jonesy, ping the sucker!' Mancuso ran aft.

'Aye.' The systems were full powered. Jones loosed a single ranging ping. 'Range fifteen hundred yards. Zero elevation angle, sir. We're level with her.'

'Mancuso, have your man give us range and bearing!' Ramius twisted the annunciator handle savagely.

'Okay, Jonesy, you're our fire control. Track the mother.'

The *V. K. Konovalov*

'One active sonar ping to starboard, distance unknown, bearing zero-four-zero. The seaward target just ranged on us,' the *michman* said.

'Give me a range,' Tupolev ordered.

'Too far aft of the beam, Comrade. I am losing him aft.'

One of them was the *October* – but which? Could he risk shooting at an American sub? No!

'Solution to the forward target?'

'Not a good one,' the *starpom* replied. 'He's manoeuvring and increasing speed.'

The *michman* concentrated on the western target. 'Captain, contact forward is not, repeat not Soviet. Forward contact is American.'

'*Which* one?' Tupolev screamed.

'West and northwest are both American. East target unknown.'

'Keep the rudder at full.'

'Rudder is full,' the helmsman responded, holding the wheel over.

'The target is behind us. We must lock on and shoot as we turn. Damn, we are going too fast. Slow to one-third speed.'

The *Konovalov* was normally quick to turn, but the power reduction made her propeller act like a brake, slowing the manoeuvre. Still, Tupolev was doing the right thing. He had to point his torpedo tubes near the bearing of the target, and he had to slow rapidly enough for his sonar to give him accurate firing information.

The *Red October*

'Okay, the *Alfa* is continuing her turn, now heading right to left . . . Propulsion sounds are down some. She just chopped power,' Jones said, watching the screen. His mind was working furiously computing course, speed, and distance. 'Range is now twelve hundred yards. She's still turning. We doin' what I think?'

'Looks that way.'

Jones set the active sonar on automatic pinging. 'Have to see what this turn does, sir. If she's smart she'll burn off south and get clear first.'

'Then pray he ain't smart,' Mancuso said from the passageway. 'Steady as she goes!'

'Steady as she goes,' Ryan said, wondering if the next torpedo would kill them.

'Her turn is continuing. We're on her port beam now, maybe her port bow.' Jones looked up. 'She's going to get around first. Here come the pings.'

The *Red October* accelerated to eighteen knots.

The *V. K. Konovalov*

'I have him,' the *michman* said. 'Range one thousand metres, bearing zero-four-five. Angle zero.'

'Set it up,' Tupolev ordered his exec.

'It will have to be a zero-angle shot. We're swinging too rapidly,' the *starpom* said. He set it up as quickly as he could. The submarines were now closing at over forty knots. 'Ready for tube five only! Tube flooded, door – open. Ready!'

'Shoot!'

'Fire five!' The *starpom*'s finger stabbed the button.

The *Red October*

'Range down to nine hundred – high-speed screws dead ahead! We have one torpedo in the water dead ahead. One fish, heading right in!'

'Forget it, track the *Alfa*!'

'Aye, okay, the *Alfa*'s bearing two-two-five, steadying down. We need to come left a little, sir.'

'Ryan, come left five degrees, your course is two-two-five.'

'Left five rudder, coming to two-two-five.'

'The fish is closing rapidly, sir,' Jones said.

'Screw it! Track the *Alfa*.'

'Aye. Bearing is still two-two-five. Same as the fish.'

The combined speed ate up the distance between the submarines rapidly. The torpedo was closing in on the *October* faster still, but it had a safety device built in. To prevent them from blowing up their own launch platform, torpedoes could not arm until they were five hundred to a thousand yards from the boat that launched them. If the *October* closed the *Alfa* fast enough, she could not be hurt.

The *October* was now passing twenty knots.

'Range to the *Alfa* is seven hundred fifty yards, bearing two-two-five. The torpedo is close, sir, a few more seconds.' Jones cringed, staring at the screen.

Klonk!

The torpedo struck the *Red October* dead centre in her hemispherical bow. The safety lock still had another hundred metres to run. The impact broke it into three pieces, which were batted aside by the accelerating missile submarine.

'A dud!' Jones laughed. 'Thank you, God! Target still bearing two-two-five, range is seven hundred yards.'

The *V. K. Konovalov*

'No explosion?' Tupolev wondered.

'The safety locks!' The *starpom* swore. 'He'd had to set it up too fast.'

'Where is the target?'

'Bearing zero-four-five, Comrade. Bearing is constant,' the *michman* replied, 'closing rapidly.'

Tupolev blanched. 'Left full rudder, all ahead flank!'

The *Red October*

'Turning, turning left to right,' Jones said. 'Bearing is now two-three-zero, spreading out a little. Need a little right rudder, sir.'

'Ryan, come right five degrees.'

'Rudder is right five,' Jack answered.

'No, rudder ten right!' Ramius countermanded his order. He had been keeping a track with pencil and paper. And he knew the *Alfa*.

'Right ten degrees,' Ryan said.

'Near-field effect, range down to four hundred yards, bearing is two-two-five to the centre of the target. Target is spreading out left and right, mostly left,' Jones said rapidly. 'Range . . . three hundred yards. Elevation angle is zero, we are level with the target. Range two hundred fifty, bearing two-two-five to target centre. We can't miss, Skipper.'

'We're gonna hit!' Mancuso called out.

Tupolev should have changed depth. As it was he depended on the *Alfa*'s acceleration and manoeuvrability, forgetting that Ramius knew exactly what these were.

'Contact spread way the hell out – instantaneous return, sir!'

'Brace for impact!'

Ramius had forgotten the collision alarm. He yanked at it only seconds before impact.

343

The *Red October* rammed the *Konovalov* just aft of midships at a thirty-degree angle. The force of the collision ruptured the *Konovalov*'s titanium pressure hull and crumpled the *October*'s bow as if it were a beer can.

Ryan had not braced hard enough. He was thrown forward, and his face struck the instrument panel. Aft, Williams was catapulted from his bed and caught by Noyes before his head hit the deck. Jones' sonar systems were wiped out. The missile submarine bounded up and over the top of the *Alfa*, her keel grating across the upper deck of the smaller vessel as the momentum carried her forward and upward.

The *V. K. Konovalov*

The *Konovalov* had had full watertight integrity set. It did not make a difference. Two compartments were instantly vented to the sea, and the bulkhead between the control room and the after compartments failed a moment later from hull deformation. The last thing that Tupolev saw was a curtain of white foam coming from the starboard side. The *Alfa* rolled to port, turned by the friction of the *October*'s keel. In a few seconds the submarine was upside down. Throughout her length men and gear tumbled about like dice. Half the crew were already drowning. Contact with the *October* ended at this point, when the *Konovalov*'s flooded compartments made her drop stern first toward the bottom. The political officer's last conscious act was to yank at the disaster beacon handle, but it was to no avail: the sub was inverted, and the cable fouled on the sail. The only marker on the *Konovalov*'s grave was a mass of bubbles.

The *Red October*

'We still alive?' Ryan's face was bleeding profusely.

'Up, up on the planes!' Ramius shouted.

'All the way up.' Ryan pulled back with his left hand holding his right over the cuts.

'Damage report,' Ramius said in Russian.

'Reactor system is intact,' Melekhin answered at once. 'The damage control board shows flooding in the torpedo room – I think. I have vented high-pressure air into it, and the pump is activated. Recommend we surface to assess damage.'

'*Da!*' Ramius hobbled to the air manifold and blew all tanks.

The *Dallas*

'Jesus,' the sonar chief said, 'somebody hit somebody. I got breakup noises going down and hull-popping noises going up. Can't tell which is which, sir. Both engines are dead.'

'Get us up to periscope depth quick!' Chambers ordered.

The *Red October*

It was 1654 local time when the *Red October* broke the surface of the Atlantic Ocean for the first time, forty-seven miles southeast of Norfolk. There was no other ship in sight.

'Sonar is wiped out, Skipper.' Jones was switching off his boxes. 'Gone, crunched. We got some piddly-ass lateral hydrophones. No active stuff, not even the gertrude.'

'Go forward, Jonesy. Nice work.'

Jones took the last cigarette from his pack. 'Any time, sir – but I'm gettin' out next summer, depend on it.'

Bugayev followed him forward, still deafened and stunned from the torpedo hit.

The *October* was sitting still on the surface, down by the bow and listing twenty degrees to port from the vented ballast tanks.

The *Dallas*

'How about that,' Chambers said. He lifted the microphone. 'This is Commander Chambers. They killed the *Alfa!* Our guys are safe. Surfacing the boat now. Stand by the fire and rescue party!'

The *Red October*

'You okay, Commander Ryan?' Jones turned his head carefully. 'Looks like you broke some glass the hard way, sir.

'You don't worry till it stops bleeding,' Ryan said drunkenly.

'Guess so.' Jones held his handkerchief over the cuts. 'But I sure hope you don't always drive this bad, sir.'

'Captain Ramius, permission to lay to the bridge and communicate with my ship?' Mancuso asked.

'Go, we may need help with the damage.'

Mancuso got into his jacket, checking to make sure his small docking radio was still in the pocket where he had left it. Thirty seconds later he was atop the sail. The *Dallas* was surfacing as he made his first check of the horizon. The sky had never looked so good.

He couldn't recognize the face four hundred yards away, but it had to be Chambers.

'*Dallas*, this is Mancuso.'

'Skipper, this is Chambers. You guys okay?'

'Yes! But we may need some hands. The bow's all stove in and we took a torpedo midships.'

'I can see it, Bart. Look down.'

'Jesus!' The jagged hole was awash, half out of the water, and the submarine was heavily down by the bow. Mancuso wondered how she could float at all, but it wasn't the time to question why.

'Come over here, Wally, and get the raft out.'

'On the way. Fire and rescue is standing by, I – there's our other friend,' Chambers said.

The *Pogy* surfaced three hundred yards directly ahead of the *October*.

'*Pogy* says the area's clear. Nobody here but us. Heard that one before?' Chambers laughed mirthlessly. 'How about we radio in?'

'No, let's see if we can handle it first.' The *Dallas* approached the *October*. Within minutes Mancuso's command submarine was seventy yards to port, and ten men on a raft were struggling across the chop. Up to this time only a handful of men aboard the *Dallas* had known what was going on. Now everyone knew. He could see his men pointing and talking. What a story they had.

Damage was not as bad as they had feared. The torpedo room had not flooded – a sensor damaged by the impact had given a false reading. The forward ballast tanks were permanently vented to the sea, but the submarine was so big and her ballast tanks so subdivided that she was only eight feet down at the bow. The list to port was only a nuisance. In two hours the radio room leak had been plugged, and after a lengthy discussion among Ramius, Melekhin, and Mancuso it was decided that they could dive again if they kept their speed down and did not go below thirty metres. They'd be late getting to Norfolk.

The Eighteenth Day

Monday, 20 December

The *Red October*

Ryan again found himself atop the sail thanks to Ramius, who said that he had earned it. In return for the favour, Jack had helped the captain up the ladder to the bridge station. Mancuso was with them. There was now an American crew below in the control room, and the engine room complement had been supplemented so that there was something approaching a normal steaming watch. The leak in the radio room had not been fully contained, but it was above the waterline. The compartment had been pumped out, and the *October*'s list had eased to fifteen degrees. She was still down by the bow, which was partially compensated for when the intact ballast tanks were blown dry. The crumpled bow gave the submarine a decidedly asymmetrical wake, barely visible in the moonless, cloud-laden sky. The *Dallas* and the *Pogy* were still submerged, somewhere aft, sniffing for additional interference as they neared Capes Henry and Charles.

Somewhere farther aft an LNG (liquefied natural gas) carrier was approaching the passage, which the coast guard had closed to all normal traffic in order to allow the floating bomb to travel without interference all the way to the LNG terminal at Cove Point, Maryland – or so the story went. Ryan wondered how the navy had persuaded the ship's skipper to fake engine trouble or somehow delay his arrival. They were six hours late. The navy must have been nervous as all hell until they had finally surfaced forty minutes earlier and been spotted immediately by a circling Orion.

The red and green buoy lights winked at them, dancing on the chop. Forward he could see the lights of the Chesapeake Bay Bridge-Tunnel, but there were no moving automobile lights. The CIA had probably staged a messy wreck to shut it down, maybe a tractor-trailer or two full of eggs or gasoline. Something creative.

'You've never been to America before,' Ryan said, just to make conversation.

'No, never to a Western country. Cuba once, many years ago.'

Ryan looked north and south. He figured they were inside the capes now. 'Well, welcome home, Captain Ramius. Speaking for myself, sir, I'm damned glad you're here.'

'And happier that you are here,' Ramius observed.

Ryan laughed out loud. 'You can bet your ass on that. Thanks again for letting me up here.'

'You have earned it, Ryan.'

'The name's Jack, sir.'

'Short for John, is it?' Ramius asked. 'John is the same as Ivan, no?'

'Yes, sir, I believe it is.' Ryan didn't understand why Ramius' face broke into a smile.

'Tug approaching.' Mancuso pointed.

The American captain had superb eyesight. Ryan didn't see the boat through his binoculars for another minute. It was a shadow, darker than the night, perhaps a mile away.

'*Sceptre*, this is tug *Paducah*. Do you read? Over.'

Mancuso took the docking radio from his pocket. '*Paducah*, this is *Sceptre*. Good morning, sir.' He was speaking in an English accent.

'Please form up on me, Captain, and follow us in.'

'Jolly good, *Paducah*. Will do. Out.'

HMS *Sceptre* was the name of an English attack submarine. She must be somewhere remote, Ryan thought, patrolling the Falklands or some other faraway location so that her arrival at Norfolk would be just another routine occurrence, not unusual and difficult to disprove. Evidently they were thinking about some agent's being suspicious of a strange sub's arrival.

The tug approached to within a few hundred yards, then turned to lead them in at five knots. A single red tuck light showed.

'I hope we don't run into any civilian traffic,' Mancuso said.

'But you said the harbour entrance was closed,' Ramius said.

'Might be some guy in a little sailboat out there. The public has free passage through the yard to the Dismal Swamp Canal, and they're damned near invisible on radar. They slip through all the time.'

'This is crazy.'

'It's a free country, Captain,' Ryan said softly. 'It will take you some time to understand what free really means. The word is often misused, but in time you will see just how wise your decision was.'

'Do you live here, Captain Mancuso?' Ramius asked.

'Yes, my squadron is based in Norfolk. My home is in Virginia Beach, down that way. I probably won't get there anytime soon. They're going to send us right back out. Only thing they can do. So, I miss another Christmas at home. Part of the job.'

'You have a family?'

'Yes, Captain. A wife and two sons. Michael, eight, and Dominic, four. They're used to having daddy away.'

'And you, Ryan?'

'Boy and a girl. Guess I will be home for Christmas. Sorry, Commander. You see, for a while there I had my doubts. After things get settled down some I'd like to get this whole bunch together for something special.'

'Big dinner bill,' Mancuso chuckled.

'I'll charge it to the CIA.'

'And what will the CIA do with us?' Ramius asked.

'As I told you, Captain, a year from now you will be living your own lives, wherever you wish to live, doing whatever you wish to do.'

'Just so?'

'Just so. We take pride in our hospitality, sir, and if I ever get transferred back from London, you and your men are welcome in my home at any time.'

'Tug's turning to port.' Mancuso pointed. The conversation was taking too maudlin a turn for him.

'Give the order, Captain,' Ramius said. It was, after all, Mancuso's harbour.

'Left five degrees rudder,' Mancuso said into the microphone.

'Left five degrees rudder, aye,' the helmsman responded. 'Sir, my rudder is left five degrees.'

'Very well.'

The *Paducah* turned into the main channel, past the *Saratoga*, which was sitting under a massive crane, and headed towards a mile-long line of piers in the Norfolk Naval Shipyard. The channel was totally empty, just the *October* and the tug. Ryan wondered if the *Paducah* had a normal complement of enlisted men or a crew made entirely of admirals. He would not have given odds either way.

Norfolk, Virginia

Twenty minutes later they were at their destination. The Eight-Ten Dock was a new dry dock built to service the *Ohio*-class fleet ballistic missile submarines, a huge concrete box over eight hundred feet long, larger than it had to be, covered with a steel roof so that spy satellites could not see if it were occupied or not. It was in the maximum security section of the base, and one had to pass several security barriers of armed guards – marines, not the usual civilian guards – to get near the dock, much less into it.

'All stop,' Mancuso ordered.

'All stop, aye.'

The *Red October* had been slowing for several minutes, and it was another two hundred yards before she came to a complete halt. The *Paducah* curved around to starboard to push her bow round. Both captains would have preferred to power their own way in, but the damaged bow made manoeuvring tricky. The diesel-powered tug took five minutes to line the bow up properly, headed directly into the water-filled box. Ramius gave the engine command himself, the last for this submarine. She eased forward through the black water, passing slowly under the wide roof. Mancuso ordered his men topside to handle the lines tossed them by the handful of sailors on the rim of the dock, and the submarine came to a halt exactly in its centre. Already the gate they had passed through was closing, and a canvas cover the size of a clipper's mainsail was being drawn across it. Only when cover was securely in place were the overhead lights switched on. Suddenly a group of thirty or so officers began screaming like fans at a ballgame. The only thing left out was the band.

'Finished with the engines,' Ramius said in Russian to the crew in the manoeuvring room, then switched to English with a trace of sadness in his voice. 'So. We are here.'

The overhead travelling crane moved down towards them and stopped to pick up the brow, which it brought around and laid carefully on the missile deck forward of the sail. The brow was hardly in place when a pair of officers with gold braid nearly to their elbows walked – ran – across it. Ryan recognized the one in front. It was Dan Foster.

The chief of naval operations saluted the quarterdeck as he got to the edge of the gangway, then looked up at the sail. 'Request permission to come aboard, sir.'

'Permission is – '

'Granted,' Mancuso prompted.

'Permission is granted,' Ramius said loudly.

Foster jumped aboard and hurried up the exterior ladder on the sail. It wasn't easy, since the ship still had a sizeable list to port. Foster was puffing as he reached the control station.

'Captain Ramius, I'm Dan Foster.' Mancuso helped the CNO over the bridge coaming. The control station was suddenly crowded. The American admiral and the Russian captain shook hands, then Foster shook Mancuso's. Jack came last.

'Looks like the uniform needs a little work, Ryan. So does the face.'

'Yeah, well, we ran into some trouble.'

'So I see. What happened?'

Ryan didn't wait for the explanation. He went below without excusing himself. It wasn't his fraternity. In the control room the men were standing around exchanging grins, but they were quiet, as if they feared the magic of the moment would evaporate all too quickly. For Ryan it already had. He looked for the deck hatch and climbed up through it, taking with him everything he'd brought aboard. He walked up the gangway against traffic. No one seemed to notice him. Two hospital corpsmen were carrying a stretcher, and Ryan decided to wait on the dock for Williams to be brought out. The British officer had missed everything, having only been fully conscious for the past three hours. As Ryan waited he smoked his last Russian cigarette. The stretcher, with Williams tied on to it, was manhandled out. Noyes and the medical orderlies from the subs tagged along.

'How are you feeling?' Ryan walked alongside the stretcher toward the ambulance.

'Alive,' Williams said, looking pale and thin. 'And you?'

'What I feel under my feet is solid concrete. Thank God for that!'

'And what he's going to feel is a hospital bed. Nice meeting you, Ryan,' the doctor said briskly. 'Let's move it, people.' The orderlies loaded the stretcher into an ambulance parked just inside the oversized doors. A minute later it was gone.

'You Commander Ryan, sir?' a marine sergeant asked after saluting.

Ryan returned the salute. 'Yes.'

'I have a car waiting for you, sir. Will you follow me, please?'

'Lead on, Sergeant.'

The car was a grey navy Chevy that took him directly to the Norfolk Naval Air Station. Here Ryan boarded a helicopter. By now he was too tired to care if it were a sleigh with reindeer attached. During the thirty-five minute trip to Andrews Air Force Base Ryan sat alone in the back, staring into space. He was met by another car at the base and driven straight to Langley.

CIA Headquarters

It was four in the morning when Ryan finally entered Greer's office. The admiral was there, along with Moore and Ritter. The admiral handed him something to drink. Not coffee, Wild Turkey bourbon whisky. All three senior executives took his hand.

'Sit down, boy,' Moore said.

'Damned well done,' Greer smiled.

'Thank you.' Ryan took a long pull on the drink. 'Now what?'

'Now we debrief you,' Greer answered.

'No, sir. Now I fly the hell home.'

Greer's eyes twinkled as he pulled a folder from a coat pocket and tossed it in Ryan's lap. 'You're booked out of Dulles at 7:05 A.M. First flight to London. And you really should wash up, change your clothes, and collect your Skiing Barbie.'

Ryan tossed the rest of the drink off. The sudden slug of whisky made his eyes water, but he was able to refrain from coughing.

'Looks like that uniform got some hard use,' Ritter observed.

'So did the rest of me.' Jack reached inside the jacket and pulled out the automatic pistol. 'This got some use, too.'

'The GRU agent? He wasn't taken off with the rest of the crew?' Moore asked.

'You *knew* about him? You knew and you didn't get word to me, for Christ's sake!'

'Settle down, son,' Moore said. 'We missed connections by half an hour. Bad luck, but you made it. That's what counts.'

Ryan was too tired to scream, too tired to do much of anything. Greer took out a tape recorder and a yellow pad full of questions.

'Williams, the British officer, is in a bad way,' Ryan said, two hours later. 'The doc says he'll make it, though. The sub isn't going anywhere. Bow's all crunched in, and there's a pretty nice hole where the torpedo got us. They were right about the *Typhoon*, Admiral, the Russians built that baby strong, thank God. You know, there may be people left alive on that *Alfa* . . .'

'Too bad,' Moore said.

Ryan nodded slowly. 'I figured that. I don't know that I like it, sir, leaving men to die like that.'

'Nor do we,' Judge Moore said, 'nor do we, but if we were to rescue someone from her, well, then everything we've – everything you've been through would be for nothing. Would you want that?'

'It's a chance in a thousand anyway,' Greer said.

'I don't know,' Ryan said, finishing off his third drink and feeling it. He had expected Moore to be uninterested in checking the *Alfa* for signs of life. Greer had surprised him. So, the old seaman had been corrupted by this affair – or just by being at the CIA – into forgetting the seaman's code. And what did this say about Ryan? 'I just don't know.'

'It's a war, Jack,' Ritter said, more kindly than usual, 'a real war. You did well, boy.'

'In a war you do well to come home alive,' Ryan stood, 'and that, gentlemen, is what I plan to do, right now.'

'Your things are in the head.' Greer checked his watch. 'You have time to shave if you want.'

'Oh, almost forgot.' Ryan reached inside his collar to pull out the key. He handed it to Greer. 'Doesn't look like much, does it? You can kill fifty million people with that. "My name is Ozymandias, king of kings! Look on my works, ye mighty, and despair!"' Ryan headed for the washroom, knowing he had to be drunk to quote Shelley.

They watched him disappear. Greer switched off the tape machine, looking at the key in his hand. 'Still want to take him to see the president?'

'No, not a good idea,' Moore said. 'Boy's half smashed, not that I blame him a bit. Get him on the plane, James. We'll send a team to London tomorrow or the next day to finish the debriefing.'

'Good.' Greer looked into his empty glass. 'Kind of early in the day for this, isn't it?'

Moore finished off his third. 'I suppose. But then it's been a fairly good day, and the sun's not even up yet. Let's go, Bob. We have an operation of sorts to run.'

Norfolk Naval Shipyard

Mancuso and his men boarded the *Paducah* before dawn and were ferried back to the *Dallas*. The 688-class attack submarine sailed immediately and was back underwater before the sun rose. The *Pogy*, which had never entered port, would complete her deployment without her orderly aboard. Both submarines had orders to stay out thirty more days, during which their crewmen would be encouraged to forget everything they had seen, heard, or wondered about.

The *Red October* sat alone with the dry dock draining around her, guarded by twenty armed marines. This was not unusual in the Eight-Ten Dock. Already a select group of engineers and technicians was inspecting her. The first items taken off were her cipher books and machines. They would be in National Security Agency headquarters at Fort Meade before noon.

Ramius, his officers, and their personal gear were taken by bus to the same airfield Ryan had used. An hour later they were in a CIA safe house in the rolling hills south of Charlottesville, Virginia. They went immediately to bed except for two men, who stayed awake watching cable television, already amazed at what they saw of life in the United States.

Dulles International Airport

Ryan missed the dawn. He boarded a TWA 747 that left Dulles on time, at 7:05 A.M.. The sky was overcast, and when the aircraft burst through the cloud layer into sunlight, Ryan did something he had never done before. For the first time in his life, Jack Ryan fell asleep on an aeroplane.

PATRIOT GAMES

For Wanda

When bad men combine, the good must associate; else they will fall one by one, an unpitied sacrifice in a contemptible struggle.

Edmund Burke

Behind all the political rhetoric being hurled at us from abroad, we are bringing home one unassailable fact – [terrorism is] a crime by any civilized standard, committed against innocent people, away from the scene of political conflict, and must be dealt with as a crime. . .

[I]n our recognition of the nature of terrorism as a crime lies our best hope of dealing with it. . .

[L]et us use the tools that we have. Let us invoke the cooperation we have the right to expect around the world, and with that cooperation let us shrink the dark and dank areas of sanctuary until these cowardly marauders are held to answer as criminals in an open and public trial for the crimes they have committed and receive the punishment they so richly deserve.

William H. Webster,
Director, Federal Bureau of Investigation,
October 15, 1985

1

A Sunny Day in London Town

Ryan was nearly killed twice in half an hour. He left the taxi a few blocks short of his destination. It was a fine, clear day, the sun already low in the blue sky. Ryan had been sitting for hours in a series of straight-back wooden chairs, and he wanted to walk a bit to work the kinks out. Traffic was relatively light on the streets and sidewalks. That surprised him, but he looked forward to the evening rush hour. Clearly these streets had not been laid out with automobiles in mind, and he was sure that the afternoon chaos would be something to behold. Jack's first impression of London was that it would be a fine town to walk in, and he moved at his usual brisk pace, unchanged since his stint in the Marine Corps, marking time unconsciously by tapping the edge of his clipboard against his leg.

Just short of the corner the traffic disappeared, and he moved to cross the street early. He automatically looked left, right, then left again as he had since childhood, and stepped off the curb –

And was nearly crushed by a two-storey red bus that screeched past him with a bare two feet to spare.

'Excuse me, sir.' Ryan turned to see a police officer – they call them constables over here, he reminded himself – in uniform complete to the Mack Sennett hat. 'I'd cross at the lights if I were you, sir. And keep an eye out for the painted signs on the road to look right or left. We don't want to lose too many tourists to the traffic.'

'How do you know I'm a tourist?' He would now, from Ryan's accent.

The cop smiled patiently. 'Because you looked the wrong way, sir, and you dress like an American. Please be careful, sir. Good day.' The bobby moved off with a friendly nod, leaving Ryan to wonder what there was about his brand-new three-piece suit that marked him as an American.

Chastened, he walked to the corner. Painted lettering on the road warned him to LOOK RIGHT, along with an arrow for the dyslexic. He waited for the lights to change, and was careful to stay within the painted lines. Jack remembered that he'd have to pay close attention to the traffic, especially when he rented the car Friday. England was one of the last places in the world where the people drove on the wrong side of the road. He was sure it would take some getting used to.

But they did everything else well enough, he thought comfortably, already drawing universal observations one day into his first trip to Britain. Ryan was a practiced observer, and one can draw many conclusions from a few glances. He was walking in a business and professional district. The other people on the sidewalk were better dressed than their American counterparts would be – aside from the punks with their spiked orange and purple hair, he thought. The architecture here was a hodgepodge ranging from Octavian Augustus to Mies van der Rohe, but most of the buildings had an old, comfortable look that in Washington or Baltimore would long since have been replaced with an unbroken row of new and soulless glass boxes. Both aspects of the town dovetailed nicely with the good manners he'd encountered so far. It was a working vacation for Ryan, but first impressions told him that it would be a very pleasant one nonetheless.

There were a few jarring notes. Many people seemed to be carrying umbrellas. Ryan had been careful to check the day's weather forecast before setting out on his research trip. A fair day had been accurately predicted – in fact it had been called a hot day, though temperatures were only in the upper sixties. A warm day for this time of year, to be sure, but 'hot'? Jack wondered if they called it Indian summer here. Probably not. Why the umbrellas, though? Didn't people trust the local weather service? Was *that* how the cop knew I was an American?

Another thing he ought to have anticipated was the plethora of Rolls-Royces on the streets. He hadn't seen more than a handful in his entire life, and while the streets were not exactly crowded with them, there were quite a few. He himself usually drove around in a five-year-old VW Rabbit. Ryan stopped at a news-stand to purchase a copy of *The Economist*, and had to fumble with the change from his cab fare for several seconds in order to pay the patient dealer, who doubtless also had him pegged for a Yank. He paged through the magazine instead of watching where he was going as he went down the street, and presently found himself halfway down the wrong block. Ryan stopped dead and thought back to the city map he'd inspected before leaving the hotel. One thing Jack could not do was remember street names, but he had a photographic memory for maps. He walked to the end of the block, turned left, proceeded two blocks, then right, and sure enough there was St James's Park. Ryan checked his watch; he was fifteen minutes early. It was downhill past the monument to a Duke of York, and he crossed the street near a longish classical building of white marble.

Yet another pleasant thing about London was the profusion of green spaces. The park looked big enough, and he could see that the grass was tended with care. The whole autumn must have been unseasonably warm. The trees still bore plenty of leaves. Not many people around, though. Well, he shrugged, it's Wednesday. Middle of the week, the kids were all in school, and it was a normal business day. So much the better, he thought. He'd deliberately come over after the tourist season. Ryan did not like crowds. The Marine Corps had taught him that, too.

'*Daddee*!' Ryan's head snapped around to see his little daughter running towards him from behind a tree, heedless as usual of her safety. Sally arrived with her customary thump against her tall father. Also as usual, Cathy Ryan trailed behind, never quite able to keep up with their little white tornado. Jack's wife did look like a tourist. Her Canon 35mm camera was draped over one shoulder, along with the camera case that doubled as an oversized purse when they were on vacation.

'How'd it go, Jack?'

Ryan kissed his wife. Maybe the Brits don't do that in public either, he thought. 'Great, babe. They treated me like I owned the place. Got all my notes tucked away.' He tapped his clipboard. 'Didn't you get anything?' Cathy laughed.

'The shops here deliver.' She smiled in a way that told him she'd parted with a fairish bit of the money they had allocated for shopping. 'And we got something really nice for Sally.'

'Oh?' Jack bent over to look his daughter in the eye. 'And what might that be?'

'It's a surprise, Daddy.' The little girl twisted and giggled like a true four-year-old. She pointed to the park. 'Daddy, they got a lake with swans and peccalins!'

'Pelicans,' Jack corrected.

'Big white ones!' Sally loved peccalins.

'Uh-huh,' Ryan observed. He looked up to his wife. 'Get any good pictures?'

Cathy patted her camera. 'Oh, sure. London is already Canonized – or would you prefer that we spent the whole day shopping?' Photography was Cathy Ryan's only hobby, and she was good at it.

'Ha!' Ryan looked down the street. The pavement here was reddish, not black, and the road was lined with what looked like beech trees. The Mall, wasn't it? He couldn't remember, and would not ask his wife, who'd been to London many times. The palace was larger than he'd expected, but it seemed a dour building, three hundred yards away, hidden behind a marble monument of some sort. Traffic was a little thicker here, but moved briskly. 'What do we do for dinner?'

'Catch a cab back to the hotel?' She looked at her watch. 'Or we can walk.'

'They're supposed to have a good dining room. Still early, though. These civilized places make you wait until eight or nine.' He saw another Rolls go by in the direction of the palace. He was looking forward to dinner, though not really to having Sally there. Four-year-olds and four-star restaurants didn't go well together. Brakes squealed off to his left. He wondered if the hotel had a baby-sitting –

B O O M !

Ryan jumped at the sound of an explosion not thirty yards away. *Grenade*, something in his mind reported. He sensed the whispering sound of fragments in the air and a moment later heard the chatter of automatic weapons fire. He spun around to see the Rolls turned crooked in the road. The front end seemed lower than it should be, and its path was blocked by a black sedan. There was a man standing at its right front fender, firing an AK–47 rifle into the front end, and another man was racing around to the car's left rear.

'*Get down!*' Ryan grabbed his daughter's shoulder and forced her to the ground behind a tree, yanking his wife roughly down beside her. A dozen cars were stopped raggedly behind the Rolls, none closer than fifty feet, and these shielded his family from the line of fire. Traffic on the far side was blocked by the sedan. The man with the Kalashnikov was spraying the Rolls for all he was worth.

'Sonuvabitch!' Ryan kept his head up, scarcely able to believe what he saw. 'It's the goddamned IRA – they're killing somebody right –' Ryan moved slightly to his left. His peripheral vision took in the faces of people up and down the street, turning and staring, in each face the black circle of a shock-opened mouth. *This is really happening!* he thought, *right in front of me, just like that, just like some Chicago gangster movie. Two bastards are committing murder. Right here. Right now. Just like that.* 'Son of a *bitch!*'

Ryan moved farther left, screened by a stopped car. Covered by its front fender, he could see one man standing at the left rear of the Rolls, just standing there, his pistol hand extended as though expecting someone to bolt from the passenger door. The bulk of the Rolls screened Ryan from the AK gunner, who was crouched down to control his weapon. The near gunman had his back to Ryan. He was no more than fifty feet away. He didn't move, concentrating on the passenger door. His back was still turned. Ryan would never remember making any conscious decision.

He moved quickly around the stopped car, head down, keeping low and accelerating rapidly, his eyes locked on his target – the small of the man's back – just as he'd been taught in high school football. It took only a few seconds to cover the distance, with Ryan's mind reaching out, willing the man to stay dumb just a moment longer. At five feet Ryan lowered his shoulder and drove off both legs. His coach would have been proud.

The blind-side tackle caught the gunman perfectly. His back bent like a bow and Ryan heard bones snap as his victim pitched forward and down. A satisfying *klonk* told him that the man's head had bounced off the bumper on the way to the pavement. Ryan got up instantly – winded but full of adrenalin – and crouched beside the body. The man's pistol had dropped from his hand and lay beside the body. Ryan grabbed it. It was an automatic of some sort he had never handled. It looked like a 9mm Makarov or some other East Bloc military issue. The hammer was back and the safety catch off. He fitted the gun carefully in his right hand – his left hand didn't seem

360

to be working right, but Ryan ignored that. He looked down at the man he'd just tackled and shot him once in the hip. Then he brought the gun up to eye level and moved to the right rear corner of the Rolls. He crouched lower still and peeked around the edge of the bodywork.

The other gunman's AK was lying on the street and he was firing into the car with his own pistol, something else in his other hand. Ryan took a deep breath and stepped from behind the Rolls, levelling his automatic at the man's chest. The other gunman turned his head first, then swivelled off-balance to bring his own gun around. Both men fired at the same instant. Ryan felt a fiery thump in his left shoulder and saw his own round take the man in the chest. The 9mm slug knocked the man backwards as though from a hard punch. Ryan brought his own pistol from recoil and squeezed off another round. The second bullet caught the man under the chin and exploded out the back of his head in a wet, pink cloud. Like a puppet with severed strings, the gunman fell to the pavement without a twitch. Ryan kept his pistol centred on the man's chest until he saw what had happened to his head.

'Oh, God!' The surge of adrenalin left him as quickly as it had come. Time slowed back down to normal, and Ryan found himself suddenly dizzy and breathless. His mouth was open and gasping for air. Whatever force had been holding his body erect seemed to disappear, leaving his frame weak, on the verge of collapse. The black sedan backed up a few yards and accelerated past him, racing down the street, then turning left up a side street. Ryan didn't think to take the number. He was stunned by the flashing sequence of events with which his mind had still not caught up.

The one he'd shot twice was clearly dead, his eyes open and surprised at fate, a foot-wide pool of blood spreading back from his head. Ryan was chilled to see a grenade in his gloved left hand. He bent down to ensure that the cotter pin was still in place on the wooden stick handle, and it was a slow, painful process to straighten up. Next he looked to the Rolls.

The first grenade had torn the front end to shreds. The front wheels were askew, and the tyres flat on the road. The driver was dead. Another body was slumped over in the front seat. The thick windshield had been blasted to fragments. The driver's face was – gone, a red spongy mass. There was a red smear on the glass partition separating the driver's seat from the passenger compartment. Jack moved around the car and looked in the back. He saw a man lying prone on the floor, and under him the corner of a woman's dress. He tapped the pistol butt against the glass. The man stirred for a moment, then froze. At least he was alive.

Ryan looked at his pistol. It was empty, the slide locked back on a dry clip. His breath was coming in shudders now. His legs were wobbling under him and his hands were beginning to shake convulsively, which gave his wounded shoulder brief, sharp waves of intense pain. He looked around and saw something to make him forget that –

A soldier was running towards him, with a police officer a few yards behind. One of the palace guards, Jack thought. The man had lost his bearskin hat but still had an automatic rifle with a half-foot of steel bayonet perched on the muzzle. Ryan quickly wondered if the rifle might be loaded and decided it might be expensive to find out. This was a guardsman, he told himself, a professional soldier from a crack regiment who'd had to prove he had real balls before they sent him to the finishing school that made windup toys for tourists to gawk at. Maybe as good as a Sea Marine. *How did you get here so fast?*

Slowly and carefully, Ryan held the pistol out at arm's length. He thumbed the clip-release button, and the magazine clattered down to the street. Next he twisted the gun so that the soldier could see it was empty. Then he set it down on the pavement and stepped away from it. He tried to raise his hands, but the left one wouldn't move. The guardsman all the time ran smart, head up, eyes tracing left and right but never leaving Ryan entirely. He stopped ten feet away with his rifle at low-guard, its bayonet pointed right at Jack's throat, just like it said in the manual. His chest was heaving, but the soldier's face was a blank mask. The policeman hadn't caught up, his face bloody as he shouted into a small radio.

'At ease, Trooper,' Ryan said as firmly as he could. It was not impressive. 'We got two bad guys down. I'm one of the good guys.' The guardsman's face didn't change a whit. The boy was a pro, all right. Ryan could hear his thinking – how easy to stick the bayonet right out his target's back. Jack was in no shape to avoid that first thrust.

'*DaddeeDaddeeDaddee!*' Ryan turned his head and saw his little girl racing past the stalled cars towards him. The four-year-old stopped a few feet away from him, her eyes wide with horror. She ran forward to wrap both arms around her father's leg and screamed up at the guardsman: '*Don't you hurt my daddy!*'

The soldier looked from father to daughter in amazement as Cathy approached more carefully, hands in the open.

'Soldier,' she announced in her voice of professional command, 'I'm a doctor, and I'm going to treat that wound. So you can put that gun down, right now!'

The police constable grabbed the guardsman's shoulder and said something Jack couldn't make out. The rifle's angle changed fractionally as the soldier relaxed ever so slightly. Ryan saw more cops running to the scene, and a white car with its siren screaming. The situation, whatever it was, was coming under control.

'You lunatic.' Cathy surveyed the wound dispassionately. There was a dark stain on the shoulder of Ryan's new suit jacket that turned the gray wool to purple-crimson. His whole body was shaking now. He could barely stand and the weight of Sally hanging on his leg was forcing him to weave. Cathy grabbed his right arm and eased him down to the pavement, sitting him back against the side of the car. She moved his coat away from the wound and probed gently at his shoulder. It didn't feel gentle at all. She reached around to his back pocket for a handkerchief and pressed it against the centre of the wound.

'That doesn't feel right,' she remarked to no one.

'Daddy, you're all bloody!' Sally stood an arm's length away, her hands fluttering like the wings of a baby bird. Jack wanted to reach out to her, to tell her everything was all right, but the three feet of distance might as well have been a thousand miles – and his shoulder was telling him that things were definitely not all right.

There were now about ten police officers around the car, many of them panting for breath. Three had handguns out, and were scanning the gathering crowd. Two more red-coated soldiers appeared from the west. A police sergeant approached. Before he could say anything Cathy looked up to bark an order.

'Call an ambulance *right now!*'

'On the way, mum,' the Sergeant replied with surprising good manners. 'Why don't you let us look after that?'

'I'm a doctor,' she answered curtly. 'You have a knife?'

The Sergeant turned to remove the bayonet from the first guardsman's rifle and stooped down to assist. Cathy held the coat and vest clear for him to cut away, then both cut the shirt free from his shoulder. She tossed the handkerchief clear. It was already blood-sodden. Jack started to protest.

'Shut up, Jack.' She looked over to the Sergeant and jerked her chin towards Sally. 'Get her away from here.'

The Sergeant gestured for a guardsman to come over. The Private scooped Sally up in his arms. He took her a few feet away, cradling her gently to his chest. Jack saw his little girl crying pitifully, but somehow it all seemed to be very far away. He felt his skin go cold and moist – shock?

'Damn,' Cathy said gruffly. The Sergeant handed her a thick bandage. She pressed it against the wound and it immediately went red as she tried to tie it in place. Ryan groaned. It felt as though someone had taken an axe to his shoulder.

'Jack, what the hell were you trying to do?' she demanded through clenched teeth as she fumbled with the cloth ties.

Ryan snarled back, the sudden anger helping to block out the pain. 'I didn't try – I fucking did it!' The effort required to say that took half his strength away with it.

'Uh-huh,' Cathy grunted. 'Well, you're bleeding like a pig, Jack.'

More men ran in from the other direction. It seemed that a hundred sirens were converging on the scene with men – some in uniform, some not – leaping out to join the party. A uniformed policeman with more ornate epaulettes began to shout orders at the others. The scene was impressive. A separate, detached part of Ryan's brain catalogued it. There he was, sitting against the Rolls, his shirt soaked red as though blood had been poured from a pitcher. Cathy, her hands covered with her husband's blood, was still trying to arrange the bandage correctly. His daughter was gasping out tears in the arms of a burly young soldier who seemed to be singing to her in a language that Jack couldn't make out. Sally's eyes were locked on him, full of desperate anguish. The detached part of his mind found all this very amusing until another wave of pain yanked him back to reality.

The policeman who'd evidently taken charge came up to them after first checking the perimeter. 'Sergeant, move him aside.'

Cathy looked up and snapped angrily: 'Open the other side, dammit, I got a bleeder here!'

'The other door's jammed, ma'am. Let me help.' Ryan heard a different kind of siren as they bent down. The three of them moved him aside a foot or so, and the senior officer made to open the car door. They hadn't moved him far enough. When the door swung open, its edge caught Ryan's shoulder. The last thing he heard before passing out was his own scream of pain.

Ryan's eyes focused slowly, his consciousness a hazy, variable thing that reported items out of place and out of time. For a moment he was inside a vehicle of some sort. The lateral movements of its passage rippled agony through his chest, and there was an awful atonal sound in the distance, though not all that far away. He thought he saw two faces he vaguely recognized. Cathy was there, too, wasn't she – no, there were some people in green. Everything was soft and vague except the burning pain in his shoulder and chest, but when he blinked his eyes all were gone. He was someplace else again.

The ceiling was white and nearly featureless at first. Ryan knew somehow that he was under the influence of drugs. He recognized the feelings, but could not remember why. It required several minutes of lazy concentration for him to determine that the ceiling was made of white acoustic tiles on a white metal framework. Some of the tiles were waterstained and served to give him a reference. Others were translucent plastic for the soft fluorescent lighting. There was something tied under his nose, and after a moment he began to feel a cool gas tracing into his nostrils – oxygen? His other senses began to report in one at a time. Expanding radially down from his head, they began to explore his body and reported reluctantly to his brain. Some unseen things were taped to his chest. He could feel them pulling at the hairs that Cathy liked to play with when she was drunk. His left shoulder felt . . . didn't really feel at all. His whole body was far too heavy to move even an inch.

A hospital, he decided after several minutes. *Why am I in a hospital. . . ?* It took an indeterminate period of concentration for Jack to remember why he was here. When it came to him, it was just as well that he could contemplate the taking of a human life from within the protective fog of drugs.

I was shot, too, wasn't I? Ryan turned his head slowly to the right. A bottle of IV fluids was hanging on a metal stand next to the bed, its rubber hose trailing down under the sheet where his arm was tied down. He tried to feel the prick of the catheter that had to be inside the right elbow, but couldn't. His mouth was cottony dry. *Well, I wasn't shot on the right side.* . . . Next he tried to turn his head to the left. Something soft but very firm prevented it. Ryan wasn't able to care very much about it. Even his curiosity for his condition was a tenuous thing. For some reason his surroundings seemed much more interesting than his own body. Looking directly up, he saw a TV-like instrument, along with some other electronic stuff, none of which he could make out at the acute angle. *EKG readout? Something like that*, he decided. It all figured. He was in a surgical recovery room, wired up like an astronaut while the staff decided if he'd live or not. The drugs helped him to consider the question with marvellous objectivity.

'Ah, you're awake.' A voice other than the distant, muffled tone of the PA system. Ryan dropped his chin to see a nurse of about fifty. She had a Bette Davis face crinkled by years of frowns. He tried to speak to her, but his mouth seemed glued shut. What came out was a cross between a rasp and a croak. The nurse disappeared while he tried to decide what exactly the sound was.

A man appeared a minute or so later. He was also in his fifties, tall and spare, dressed in surgical greens. There was a stethoscope hanging from his neck, and he seemed to be carrying something that Ryan couldn't quite see. He seemed rather tired, but wore a satisfied smile.

'So,' he said, 'you're awake. How are you feeling?' Ryan managed a full-fledged croak this time. The doctor – ? – gestured to the nurse. She came forward to give Ryan a sip of water through a glass straw.

'Thanks.' He sloshed the water around his mouth. It was not enough to swallow. His mouth tissues seemed to absorb it all at once. 'Where am I?'

'You're in the surgical recovery unit of St Thomas's Hospital, recovering from surgery on your upper left arm and shoulder. I'm your surgeon, Charles Scott. My team and I have been working on you for, oh, about six hours now, and it would appear that you will probably live,' he added judiciously. He seemed to regard Ryan as a successful piece of work.

Rather slowly and sluggishly Ryan thought to himself that the English sense of humour, admirable as it might otherwise be, was a little too dry for this sort of situation. He was composing a reply when Cathy came into view. The Bette Davis nurse moved to head her off.

'I'm sorry, Mrs Ryan, but only medical person –'

'I'm a doctor.' She held up her plastic ID card. The man took it.

'Wilmer Eye Institute, Johns Hopkins Hospital.' The surgeon extended his hand and gave Cathy a friendly, colleague-to-colleague smile. 'How do you do, Doctor? My name is Charles Scott.'

'That's right,' Ryan confirmed groggily. 'She's the surgeon doctor. I'm the historian doctor.' No one seemed to notice.

'Sir Charles Scott? Professor Scott?'

'The same.' A benign smile. *Everyone likes to be recognized*, Ryan thought as he watched from his back.

'One of my instructors knows you – Professor Knowles.'

'Ah, and how is Dennis?'

'Fine, Doctor. He's associate professor of orthopaedics now.' Cathy shifted gears smoothly, back to medical professional. 'Do you have the X-rays?'

'Here.' Scott held up a manila envelope and extracted a large film. He held it up in front of a lighting panel. 'We took this prior to going in.'

'Damn.' Cathy's nose wrinkled. She put on the half-glasses she used for close work, the ones Jack hated. He watched her head move slowly from side to side. 'I didn't know it was *that* bad.'

Professor Scott nodded. 'Indeed. We think the collarbone was broken before he was shot, then the bullet came crashing through here – just missed the brachial plexus, so we expect no serious nerve damage – and did all this damage.' He traced a pencil across the film. Ryan couldn't see any of it from the bed. 'Then it did this to the top of the humerus before stopping here, just inside the skin. Bloody powerful thing, the nine millimetre. As you can see, the damage was quite extensive. We had quite a time finding all these fragments and fitting them back in their proper places, but – we were able to accomplish this.' Scott held a second film up next to the first. Cathy was quiet for several seconds, her head swivelling back and forth.

'That is nice work, Doctor!'

Sir Charles' smile broadened a notch. 'From a Johns Hopkins surgeon, yes, I think I'll accept that. Both these pins are permanent, this screw also, I'm afraid, but the rest should heal rather nicely. As you can see, all the large fragments are back where they belong, and we've every reason to expect a full recovery.'

'How much impairment?' A detached question. Cathy could be maddeningly unemotional about her work.

'We're not sure yet,' Scott said slowly. 'Probably a little, but it shouldn't be severe. We can't guarantee a complete restoration of function – the damage was far too extensive for that.'

'You mind telling me something?' Ryan tried to sound angry, but it hadn't come out right.

'What I mean, Mr Ryan, is that you'll probably have some permanent loss of the use of your arm – precisely how much we can't determine as yet – and from now on you'll have a permanent barometer. Henceforth, whenever the weather is about to change for the worse, you'll know it before anyone else.'

'How long in this cast?' Cathy wanted to know.

'At least a month.' The surgeon seemed apologetic. 'It is awkward, I know, but the shoulder must be immobilized for at least that long. After that we'll have to re-evaluate the injury and we can probably revert to a normal cast for another . . . oh, another month or so, I expect. I presume he heals well, no allergies. Looks to be in good health, decent physical shape.'

366

'Jack's in good physical shape, except for a few loose marbles in his head,' Cathy nodded, an edge on her weary voice. 'He jogs. No allergies except ragweed, and he heals rapidly.'

'Yeah,' Ryan confirmed. 'Her teethmarks go away in under a week, usually.' He thought this uproariously funny, but no one laughed.

'Good,' Sir Charles said. 'So, Doctor, you can see that your husband is in good hands. I'll leave the two of you together for five minutes. After that, I want him to get some sleep, and you look as though you could do with some too.' The surgeon moved off with Bette Davis in his wake.

Cathy moved closer to him, changing yet again from cool professional to concerned wife. Ryan told himself for perhaps the millionth time how lucky he was to have this girl. Caroline Ryan had a small, round face, short butterblonde hair, and the world's prettiest blue eyes. Behind those eyes was a person with intelligence at least the equal of his own, someone he loved as much as a man could. He would never understand how he'd won her. Ryan was painfully aware that on his best day his own undistinguished features, a heavy beard and a lantern jaw, made him look like a dark-haired Dudley Do-Right of the Mounties. She played pussycat to his crow. Jack tried to reach out for her hand, but was foiled by straps. Cathy took his.

'Love ya, babe,' he said softly.

'Oh, Jack.' Cathy tried to hug him. She was foiled by the cast that he couldn't even see. 'Jack, why the hell did you do that?'

He had already decided how to answer that. 'It's over and I'm still alive, okay? How's Sally?'

'I think she's finally asleep. She's downstairs with a policeman.' Cathy did look tired. 'How do you think she is, Jack? Dear God, she saw you killed almost. You scared us both to death.' Her china-blue eyes were rimmed in red, and her hair looked terrible, Jack saw. Well, she never was able to do much of anything with her hair. The surgical caps always ruined it.

'Yeah, I know. Anyway, it doesn't look like I'll be doing much more of that for a while,' he grunted. 'Matter of fact, it doesn't look like I'll be doing much of anything for a while.' That drew a smile. It was good to see her smile.

'Fine. You're supposed to conserve your energy. Maybe this'll teach you a lesson – and don't tell me about all those strange hotel beds going to waste.' She squeezed his hand. Her smile turned impish. 'We'll probably work something out in a few weeks. How do I look?'

'Like hell.' Jack laughed quietly. 'I take it the doc was a somebody?'

He saw his wife relax a little. 'You might say that. Sir Charles Scott is one of the best orthopods in the world. He trained Professor Knowles – he did a super job on you. You're lucky to have an arm at all, you know – my God!'

'Easy, babe. I'm going to live, remember?'

'I know, I know.'

'It's going to hurt, isn't it?'

Another smile. 'Just a bit. Well. I've got to put Sally down. I'll be back tomorrow.' She bent down to kiss him. Skin full of drugs, oxygen tube, dry mouth, and all, it felt good. *God*, he thought, *God, how I love this girl.* Cathy squeezed his hand one more time and left.

The Bette Davis nurse came back. It was not a satisfactory trade.

'I'm "Doctor" Ryan, too, you know,' Jack said warily.

'Very good, Doctor. It's time for you to get some rest. I'll be here to look after you all night. Go to sleep now. Doctor Ryan.'

On this happy note Jack closed his eyes. Tomorrow would be a real bitch, he was sure. It would keep.

2

Cops and Royals

Ryan awoke at 6:35 A.M. He knew that because it was announced by a radio disc-jockey whose voice faded to an American Country and Western song of the type which Ryan avoided at home by listening to all-news radio stations. The singer was admonishing mothers not to allow their sons to become cowboys, and Ryan's first muddled thought of the day was, *Surely they don't have that problem over here . . . do they?* His mind drifted along on this tangent for half a minute, wondering if the Brits had C&W bars with sawdust on the floors, mechanical bull rides, and office workers who strutted around with pointy-toed boots and five-pound belt buckles. . . . *Why not?* he concluded. *Yesterday I saw something right out of a Dodge City movie.*

Jack would have been just as happy to slide back into sleep. He tried closing his eyes and willing his body to relax, but it was no use. The flight from Dulles had left early in the morning, barely three hours after he'd awakened. He hadn't slept on the plane – it was something he simply could not do – but flying always exhausted him, and he'd gone to bed soon after arriving at the hotel. Then how long had he been unconscious in the hospital? Too long, he realized. Ryan was all slept out. He would have to begin facing the day.

Someone off to his right was playing a radio just loudly enough to hear. Ryan turned his head and was able to see his shoulder –

Shoulder, he thought, *that's why I'm here. But* where's here? It was a different room. The ceiling was smooth plaster, recently painted. It was dark, the only illumination coming from a light on the table next to the bed, perhaps enough to read by. There seemed to be a painting on the wall – at least a rectangle darker than the wall, which wasn't white. Ryan took this in, consciously delaying his examination of his left arm until no excuses remained. He turned his head slowly to the left. He saw his arm first of all. It was sticking up at an angle, wrapped in a plaster and fibreglass cast that went all the way to his hand. His fingers stuck out like an afterthought, about the same shade of gray as the plaster-gauze wrappings. There was a metal ring at the back of the wrist, and in the ring was a hook whose chain led to a metal frame that arced over the bed like a crane.

First things first. Ryan tried to wiggle his fingers. It took several seconds before they acknowledged their subservience to his central nervous system. Ryan let out a long breath and closed his eyes to thank God for that. About where his elbow was a metal rod angled downwards to join the rest of the cast, which, he finally appreciated, began at his neck and went diagonally to his waist. It left his arm sticking out entirely on its own and made Ryan look like half a bridge. The cast was not tight on his chest, but touched almost everywhere, and already he had itches where he couldn't scratch. The surgeon had said something about immobilizing the shoulder, and, Ryan thought glumly, he hadn't been kidding. His shoulder ached in a distant sort of way with the promise of more to come. His mouth tasted like a urinal, and the rest of his body was stiff and sore. He turned his head the other way.

'Somebody over there?' he asked softly.

'Oh, hello.' A face appeared at the edge of the bed. Younger than Ryan, mid-twenties or so, and lean. He was dressed casually, his tie loose in his collar, and the edge of a shoulder holster showed under his jacket. 'How are you feeling, sir?'

Ryan attempted a smile, wondering how successful it was. 'About how I look, probably. Where am I, who are you – first, is there a glass of water in this place?'

The policeman poured ice water from a plastic jug into a plastic cup. Ryan reached out with his right hand before he noticed that it wasn't tied down as it had been the last time he awoke. He could now feel the place where the IV catheter had been. Jack greedily sucked the water from the straw. It was only water, but no beer ever tasted better after a day's yardwork. 'Thanks, pal.'

'My name is Anthony Wilson. I'm supposed to look after you. You're in the VIP suite of St Thomas's Hospital. Do you remember why you're here, sir?'

'Yeah, I think so,' Ryan nodded. 'Can you unhook me from this thing? I have to go. ' The other reminder of the IV.

'I'll ring the sister – here.' Wilson squeezed the button that was pinned to the edge of Ryan's pillow.

Less than fifteen seconds later a nurse came through the door and flipped on the overhead lights. The blaze of light dazzled Jack for a moment before he saw it was a different nurse. Not Bette Davis, this one was young and pretty, with the eager, protective look common to nurses. Ryan had seen it before, and hated it.

'Ah, you're awake,' she observed brightly. 'How are you feeling?'

'Great,' Ryan grumped. 'Can you unhook me? I have to go to the john.'

'You're not supposed to move just yet, Doctor Ryan. Let me fetch you something.' She disappeared out the door before he could object. Wilson watched her leave with an appraising look. Cops and nurses, Ryan thought. His dad had married a nurse; he'd met her after bringing a gunshot victim into the emergency room.

The nurse – her name tag said KITTIWAKE – returned in under a minute bearing a stainless steel bottle as though it were a priceless gift. Which under the circumstances, it was, Ryan admitted to himself. She lifted the covers on the bed and suddenly Jack realized that his hospital gown was not really on, but just tied loosely around his neck – worse, the nurse was about to make the necessary adjustments for him to use the bottle. Ryan's right hand shot downwards under the covers to take it away from her. He thanked God for the second time this morning that he was able, barely, to reach down far enough.

'Could you, uh, excuse me for a minute?' Ryan willed the girl out of the room, and she went, smiling her disappointment. He waited for the door to close completely before continuing. In deference to Wilson he stifled his sigh of relief. Kittiwake was back through the door after counting to sixty.

'Thank you.' Ryan handed her the receptacle and she disappeared out the door. It had barely swung shut when she was back again. This time she stuck a thermometer in his mouth and grabbed his wrist to take his pulse. The thermometer was one of the new electronic sort, and both tasks were completed in fifteen seconds. Ryan asked for the score, but got a smile instead of an answer. The smile remained fixed as she made the entries on his chart. When this task was fulfilled, she made a minor adjustment in the covers, beaming at Ryan. *Little Miss Efficiency*, Ryan told himself. *This girl is going to be a real pain in the ass*.

'Is there anything I might get you, Doctor Ryan?' she asked. Her brown eyes belied the wheat-coloured hair. She was cute. She had that dewy look. Ryan was unable to remain angry with pretty women, and hated them for it. Especially young nurses with that dewy look.

'Coffee?' he asked hopefully.

'Breakfast is not for another hour. Can I fetch you a cup of tea?'

'Fine.' It wasn't, but it would get rid of her for a little while. Nurse Kittiwake breezed out the door with her ingenuous smile.

'*Hospitals*!' Ryan snarled when she was gone.

'Oh, I don't know,' Wilson observed, the image of Nurse Kittiwake fresh in his mind.

'You ain't the one getting your diapers changed.' Ryan grunted and leaned back into the pillow. It was useless to fight it, he knew. He smiled in spite of himself. *Useless to fight it.* He'd been through this twice before, both times with young, pretty nurses. Being grumpy only made them all the more eager to be overpoweringly nice – they had time on their side, time and patience enough to wear anyone down. He sighed out his surrender. It wasn't worth the waste of energy. 'So, you're a cop, right? Special Branch?'

'No, sir. I'm with C-13, Anti-Terrorist Branch.'

'Can you fill me in on what happened yesterday? I kinda missed a few things.'

'How much do you remember, Doctor?' Wilson slid his chair closer. Ryan noted that he remained halfway facing the door, and kept his right hand free.

'I saw – well, I *heard* an explosion, a hand grenade, I think- and when I turned I saw two guys shooting hell out of a Rolls-Royce. IRA, I guess. I took two of them out, and another one got away in a car. The cavalry arrived, and I passed out and woke up here.'

'Not IRA. ULA – Ulster Liberation Army, a Maoist offshoot of the Provos. Nasty buggers. The one you killed was John Michael McCrory, a very bad boy from Londonderry – one of the chaps who escaped from the Maze last July. This is the first time he's surfaced since. And the last' – Wilson smiled coldly – 'We haven't identified the other one yet. That is, not as of when I came on duty three hours ago.'

'ULA?' Ryan shrugged. He remembered hearing the name, though he couldn't talk about that. 'The guy I – killed. He had an AK, but when I came around the car he was using a pistol. How come?'

'The idiot jammed it. He had two full magazines taped end to end, like you see all the time in the movies, but like they trained us specifically *not* to do in the paras. We reckon he bashed it, probably when he came out of the car. The second magazine was bent at the top end – wouldn't feed the rounds properly, you see. Damn good luck for you. You *knew* you were going after a chap with a Kalashnikov?' Wilson examined Ryan's face closely.

Jack nodded. 'Doesn't sound real smart, does it?'

'You were a bloody fool.' Wilson said this just as Kittiwake came through the door with a tea tray. The nurse flashed the cop an emphatically disapproving look as she set the tray on the bedstand and wheeled it over. Kittiwake arranged things just so, and poured Ryan a cup with delicacy. Wilson had to do his own.

'So who was in the car, anyway?' Ryan asked. He noted strong reactions.

'You didn't know?' Kittiwake was dumbfounded.

'There wasn't much time to find out.' Ryan dropped two packets of brown sugar into his cup. His stirring stopped abruptly when Wilson answered his question.

'The Prince and Princess of Wales. And their new baby.'

Ryan's head snapped around. 'What?'

'You really didn't know?' the nurse asked.

'You're serious,' Ryan said quietly. *They wouldn't kid about this, would they?*

'Too bloody right, I'm serious,' Wilson went on, his voice very even. Only his choice of words betrayed how deeply the affair disturbed him. 'Except for you, they would all three be quite dead, and that makes you a bloody hero, Doctor Ryan.' Wilson sipped his tea neat and fished out a cigarette.

Ryan set his cup down. 'You mean you let them drive around here without a police or secret service – whatever you call it – without an escort?'

'Supposedly it was an unscheduled trip. Security arrangements for the Royals are not my department in any case. I would speculate, however, that those whose department it is will be rethinking a few things,' Wilson commented.

'They weren't hurt?'

'No, but their driver was killed. So was their security escort from DPG – Diplomatic Protection Group – Charlie Winston. I knew Charlie. He had a wife, and four kids.'

Ryan observed that the Rolls should have had bulletproof glass.

Wilson grunted. 'It *did* have bulletproof glass. Actually plastic, a complex polycarbonate material. Unfortunately, no one seems to have read what it said on the box. The guarantee is only for a year. Turns out that sunlight breaks the material down somehow or other. The windshield was no more use than ordinary safety glass. Our friend McCrory put thirty rounds into it, and it just shattered, killing the driver first. The inside partition, thank God, had not been exposed to sunlight, and remained intact. The last thing Charlie did was push the button to put it up. That probably saved them, too – didn't do Charlie much good, though. He had enough time to draw his automatic, but we don't think he was able to get off a single shot.'

Ryan thought back. There had been blood in the back of the Rolls – not just blood. The driver's head had been blown apart, and his brains had scattered into the passenger compartment. Jack winced thinking about it. The escort had probably leaned over to push the button before defending himself. . . . *Well*, Jack thought, *that's what they pay them for. What a hell of a way to earn a living*.

'It was fortunate that you intervened when you did. They both had hand grenades, you know.'

'Yeah, I saw one.' Ryan sipped away the last of his tea. 'What the hell was I thinking about?' *You weren't thinking at all, Jack*. That's *what you were thinking about*.

Kittiwake saw Ryan go pale. 'You feel quite all right?' she asked.

'I guess.' Ryan grunted in wonderment. 'Dumb as I was, I must feel pretty good – I ought to be dead.'

'Well, that definitely will not happen here.' She patted his hand. 'Please ring if you need anything.' Another beaming smile and she left.

Ryan was still shaking his head. 'The other one got away?'

Wilson nodded. 'We found the car near a tube station a half mile away. Stolen, of course. No real problem for him to get clean away. Disappear into the underground. Go to Heathrow, perhaps, and catch a plane to the continent – Brussels, say – then a plane to Ulster or the Republic, and a car the rest of the way home. That's one route; there are others, and it's impossible to cover them all. He was drinking beer last night, watching the news coverage on television in his favourite pub, most likely. Did you get a look at him?'

'No, just a shape. I didn't even think to get the tag number – dumb. Right after that the redcoat came running up to me.' Ryan winced again. 'Christ, I thought he'd put that pigsticker right through me. For a second there I could see it all – I do something right, then get wasted by a good guy.'

Wilson laughed. 'You don't know how lucky you were. The current guard force is from the Welsh Guards.'

'So?'

'His Royal Highness's own regiment, as it were. He's their colonel-in-chief. There you were with a pistol – how would you expect him to react?' Wilson stubbed out his cigarette. 'Another piece of good luck, your wife and daughter came running up to you, and the soldier decides to wait a bit, just long enough for things to sort themselves out. Then our chap catches up with him and tells him to stand easy. And a hundred more of my chaps come swooping in.

'I hope you can appreciate this, Doctor. Here we were with three men dead, two others wounded, a Prince and Princess looking as though they'd been shot – your wife examined them on the scene, by the way, and pronounced them fit just before the ambulance arrived – a baby, a hundred witnesses each with his own version of what had just taken place. A bloody Yank – an Irish-American to boot! – whose wife claims he's the chap in the white hat.' Wilson laughed again. 'Total chaos!

'First order of business, of course, was to get the Royals to safety. The police and guardsmen handled that, probably praying by this time that someone would make trouble. They're still in an evil mood, they tell me, angrier even than from the bandstand bombing incident. Not hard to understand. Anyway, your wife flatly refused to leave your side until you were under doctor's care here. Quite a forceful woman, they tell me.'

'Cathy's a surgeon,' Ryan explained. 'When she plays doc, she's used to having her own way. Surgeons are like that.'

'After she was quite satisfied we drove her down to the Yard. Meanwhile we had a merry time identifying you. They called your Legal Attaché at the American Embassy and he ran a check through your FBI, plus a backup check through the Marine Corps.' Ryan stole a cigarette from Wilson's pack. The policeman lit it with a butane lighter. Jack gagged on the smoke, but he needed it. Cathy would give him hell for it, he knew, but one thing at a time. 'Mind you, we never really thought you were one of them. Have to be a maniac to bring the wife and child along on this sort of job. But we have to be careful.'

Ryan nodded agreement, briefly dizzy from the smoke. *How'd they know to check through the Corps . . . oh, my Marine Corps Association card. . . .*

'In any event things are pretty well sorted out. Your government are sending us everything we need – probably here by now, in fact.' Wilson checked his watch.

'My family's all right?'

Wilson smiled in rather an odd way. 'They're being very well looked after, Doctor Ryan. You have my word on that.'

'The name's Jack.'

'Fine. I'm Tony.' They finally got around to shaking hands. 'And as I said, you're a bloody hero. Care to see what the press have to say?' He handed Ryan a *Daily Mirror* and a *Times*.

'Dear God!'

The tabloid *Mirror*'s front page was almost entirely a colour photograph of himself, sitting unconscious against the Rolls. His chest was a scarlet mass.

THANK GOD THEY'RE SAFE

A bold attempt to assassinate Their Royal Highnesses the Prince and Princess of Wales within sight of Buckingham Palace was thwarted today by the courage of an American tourist.

John Patrick Ryan, an historian and formerly a lieutenant in the United States Marines, dashed barehanded into a pitched battle on The Mall as over a hundred Londoners watched in shocked disbelief. Ryan, 31, successfully disabled one gunman and, taking his weapon, shot another dead. Ryan himself was seriously wounded in the exchange. He was taken by ambulance to St Thomas's Hospital, where emergency surgery was successfully performed by Sir Charles Scott.

A third terrorist is reported to have escaped the scene, by running east on The Mall, then turning north on Marlborough Road.

Senior police officials were unanimous in their opinion that, but for Ryan's courageous intervention, Their Royal Highnesses would certainly have been slain.

Ryan turned the page to see more headlines and another colour photograph of himself in happier circumstances. It was his graduation photo from Quantico, and he had to smile at himself, resplendent, then, in blue high-necked blouse, two shiny gold bars, and the Mamaluke sword. It was one of the few decent photographs ever taken of him.

'Where did they get this?'

'Oh, your Marine friends were most helpful. In fact, one of your Marine ships – helicopter carrier, or something like that – is at Portsmouth right now. I understand your former colleagues are getting all the free beer they can swill.'

Ryan laughed at that. Next he picked up the *Times*, whose headline was marginally less lurid.

The Prince and Princess of Wales escaped certain death this afternoon. Three, possibly four terrorists armed with hand grenades and Kalashnikov assault rifles lay in wait for their Rolls-Royce; only to have their carefully-laid plans foiled by the bold intervention of J. P. Ryan, formerly a second lieutenant in the United States Marine Corps, and now an historian. . . .

Ryan flipped to the editorial page. The lead item, signed by the publisher, screamed for vengeance while praising Ryan, America, and the United States Marine Corps, and thanked Divine Providence with a flourish worthy of a Papal Encyclical.

'Reading about yourself?' Ryan looked up. Sir Charles Scott was standing at the foot of his bed with an aluminium chart.

'First time I ever made the papers.' Ryan set them down.

'You've earned it, and it would seem the sleep did you some good. How do you feel?'

'Not bad, considering. How am I?' Ryan asked.

'Pulse and temperature normal – almost normal. Your colour isn't bad at all. With luck we might even avoid postoperative infection, though I wouldn't want to give odds on that,' the doctor said. 'How badly does it hurt?'

'It's there, but I can live with it,' Ryan answered cautiously.

'It's only two hours since your last medication. I trust you're not one of those thickheaded fools who won't take painkillers?'

'Yes, I am,' Ryan said. He went on slowly. 'Doctor, I've been through this twice before. The first time, they gave me too much of the stuff, and coming off was – I'd just as soon not go through that again, if you know what I mean.'

Ryan's career in the Marine Corps had ended after a mere three months with a helicopter crash on the shores of Crete during a NATO exercise. The resulting back injury had sent Ryan to Bethesda Naval Medical Center, outside Washington, where the doctors had been a little too generous with their pain medications, and Ryan had taken two weeks to get over them. It was not an experience he wanted to repeat.

Sir Charles nodded thoughtfully. 'I think so. Well, it's your arm.' The nurse came back in as he made some notations on the chart. 'Rotate the bed a bit.'

Ryan hadn't noticed that the rack from which his arm hung was actually circular. As the head of the bed came up, his arm dropped to a more comfortable angle. The doctor looked over his glasses at Ryan's fingers.

'Would you wiggle them, please?' Ryan did so. 'Good, that's very good. I didn't think there'd be any nerve damage. Doctor Ryan, I'm going to prescribe something mild, just enough to keep the edge off it. I want you to take what I prescribe.' Scott's head came around to face Ryan directly. 'I've never yet got a patient addicted to drugs, and I don't propose to start with you. Don't be pigheaded: pain, discomfort will delay your recovery – unless, that is, you *want* to remain in hospital for several months?'

'Message received, Sir Charles.'

'Right.' The surgeon smiled. 'If you should feel the need for something stronger, I shall be here all day. Just ring Nurse Kittiwake here.' The girl beamed in anticipation.

'How about something to eat?'

'You think you can keep something down?'

If not, Kittiwake will probably love to help me throw up. 'Doc, in the last thirty-six hours I've had a continental breakfast and a light lunch.'

'Very well. We'll try some soft foods.' He made another notation on the chart and flashed a look to Kittiwake: *Keep an eye on him.* She nodded.

'Your charming wife told me that you're quite obstinate. We'll see about that. Still you are doing rather nicely. You can thank your physical condition for that – and my outstanding surgical skill, of course.' Scott chuckled to himself. 'After breakfast someone will help you freshen up for your more, ah, official visitors. Oh, don't expect to see your family soon. They were quite exhausted last night. I gave your wife something to help her sleep; I hope she took it. Your little daughter was all done in.' Scott gave Ryan a serious look. 'I wasn't misleading you earlier. Discomfort *will* slow your recovery. Do what I tell you and we'll have you out of that bed in a week, and discharged in two – perhaps. But you must do exactly as I say.'

'Understood, sir. And thanks. Cathy said you did a good job on the arm.'

Scott tried to shrug it off. The smile showed only a little. 'One must take proper care of one's guests. I'll be back late this afternoon to see how you're progressing.' He left, mumbling instructions to the nurse.

The police arrived in force at 8:30. By this time Ryan had been able to eat his hospital breakfast and wash up. Breakfast had been a huge disappointment, with Wilson collapsing in laughter at Ryan's comment on its appearance – but Kittiwake had been so downcast from this that Ryan had felt constrained to eat all of it, even the stewed prunes that he'd loathed since childhood. Only after finishing had he realized that her demeanour had probably been a sham, a device to get him to eat all the slop. *Nurses*, he reminded himself, *are tricky.* At eight an orderly had arrived to help him clean up. Ryan shaved himself, with the orderly holding the mirror and clucking every time he nicked himself. Four nicks – Ryan customarily used an electric shaver, and hadn't faced a bare blade in years. By 8:30 Ryan felt and looked human again. Kittiwake had brought in a second cup of coffee. It wasn't very good, but it was still coffee.

There were three police officers, very senior ones, Ryan thought, from the way Wilson snapped to his feet and scurried about to arrange chairs for them before excusing himself out the door.

James Owens appeared to be the most senior, and inquired as to Ryan's condition – politely enough that he probably meant it. He reminded Ryan of his own father, a craggy, heavyset man, and, judging from his large, gnarled hands, one who had earned his way to commander's rank after more than a few years of walking the streets and enforcing the law the hard way.

Chief Superintendent William Taylor was about forty, younger than his Anti-Terrorist Branch colleague, and neater. Both senior detectives were well dressed, and both had the red-rimmed eyes that came from an uninterrupted night's work.

David Ashley was the youngest and best-dressed of the three. About Ryan's size and weight, perhaps five years older. He described himself as a representative of the Home Office, and he looked a great deal smoother than either of the others.

'You're quite certain you're up to this?' Taylor asked.

Ryan shrugged. 'No sense waiting.'

Owens took a cassette tape recorder from his portfolio and set it on the bedstand. He plugged in two microphones, one facing Ryan, the other towards the officers. He punched the record button and announced the date, time, and place.

'Doctor Ryan,' Owens asked formally, 'do you know that this interview is being recorded.'

'Yes, sir.'

'And do you have any objection to this?'

'No, sir. May I ask a question?'

'Certainly,' Owens answered.

'Am I being charged with anything? If so, I would like to contact my embassy and have an attor –' Ryan was more than a little uneasy to be the focus of so much high-level police attention, but was cut off by the chuckles of Mr Ashley. He noted that the other police officers deferred to him for the answer.

'Doctor Ryan, you may just have things the wrong way round. For the record, sir, we have no intention whatever of charging you with anything. Were we to do so, I dare say we'd be looking for new employment by day's end.'

Ryan nodded, not showing his relief. He'd not yet been sure of this, sure only that the law doesn't have to make sense. Owens began reading his questions from a yellow pad.

'Can you give us your name and address, please?'

'John Patrick Ryan. Our mailing address is Annapolis, Maryland. Our home is at Peregrine Cliff, about ten miles south of Annapolis on the Chesapeake Bay.'

'And your occupation?' Owens checked off something on his pad.

'I guess you could say I have a couple of jobs. I'm an instructor in history at the US Naval Academy in Annapolis. I lecture occasionally at the Naval War College in Newport, and from time to time I do a little consulting work on the side.'

'That's all?' Ashley inquired with a friendly smile – or was it friendly? Ryan asked himself. Jack wondered just how much they'd managed to find out about him in the past – what? fifteen hours or so – and exactly what Ashley was hinting at. *You're no cop*, Ryan thought. *What exactly are you?* Regardless, he had to stick to his cover story, that he was a part-time consultant to the Mitre Corporation.

'And the purpose of your visit to this country?' Owens went on.

'Combination vacation and research trip. I'm gathering data for a new book, and Cathy needed some time off. Sally is still a pre-schooler, so we decided to head over now and miss the tourist season.' Ryan took a cigarette from the pack Wilson had left behind. Ashley lit it from a gold lighter. 'In my coat – wherever that is – you'll find letters of introduction to your Admiralty and the Royal Naval College at Dartmouth.'

'We have the letters,' Owens replied. 'Quite illegible now, I'm afraid, and I fear your suit is ruined as well. What the blood didn't get to, your wife and our sergeant finished off with a knife. So when did you arrive in Britain?'

'It's still Thursday, right? Well, we got in Tuesday night from Dulles International outside Washington. Arrived about seven-thirty, got to the hotel about nine-thirty or so, had a snack sent up, and went right to sleep. Flying always messes me up – jet lag, whatever. I conked right out.' That was not exactly true, but Ryan didn't think they needed to know *everything*.

Owens nodded. They had already learned why Ryan hated flying. 'And yesterday?'

'I woke up about seven, I guess, had breakfast and a paper sent up, then just kinda lazed around until about eight-thirty. I arranged to meet Cathy and Sally in the park around four, then caught a cab to the Admiralty building – close, as it turned out, I could have walked it. As I said, I had a letter of introduction to see Admiral Sir Alexander Woodson, the man in charge of your naval archives – he's retired, actually. He took me down to a musty sub-sub-basement. He had the stuff I wanted all ready for me.

'I came over to look at some signal digests. Admiralty signals between London and Admiral Sir James Somerville. He was commander of your Indian Ocean fleet in the early months of 1942, and that's one of the things I'm writing about. So I spend the next three hours reading over faded carbon copies of naval dispatches and taking notes.'

'On this?' Ashley held up Ryan's clipboard. Jack snatched it from his hands.

'Thank God !' Ryan exclaimed. 'I was sure it got lost.' He opened it and set it up on the bedstand, then typed in some instructions. 'Ha! It still works!'

'What exactly is that thing?' Ashley wanted to know. All three got out of their chairs to look at it.

'This is my baby.' Ryan grinned. On opening the clipboard he revealed a typewriter-style keyboard and a yellow Liquid Crystal Diode display. Outwardly it looked like an expensive clipboard, about an inch thick and bound in leather. 'It's a Cambridge Datamaster Model-C Field Computer. A friend of mine makes them. It has an MC-68000 microprocessor, and two megabytes of bubble memory.'

'Care to translate that?' Taylor asked.

'Sorry. It's a portable computer. The microprocessor is what does the actual work. Two megabytes means that the memory stores up to two million characters – enough for a whole book – and since it uses bubble memory, you don't lose the information when you switch it off. A guy I went to school with set up a company to make these little darlings. He hit on me for some startup capital. I use an Apple at home, this one's just for carrying around.'

'We knew it was some sort of computer, but our chaps couldn't make it work,' Ashley said.

'Security device. The first time you use it, you input your user's code and activate the lockout. Afterwards, unless you type in the code, it doesn't work – period.'

'Indeed?' Ashley observed. 'How foolproof is it?'

'You'd have to ask Fred. Maybe you could read the data right off the bubble chips. I don't know how computers work. I just use 'em,' Ryan explained. 'Anyway, here are my notes.'

'Getting back to your activities of yesterday,' Owens said, giving Ashley a cool look. 'We now have you to noon.'

'Okay. I broke for lunch. A guy on the ground floor directed me to a – a pub, I guess, two blocks away. I don't remember the name of the place. I had a sandwich and a beer while I played with this thing. That took about half an hour. I spent another hour at the Admiralty building before I checked out. Left about quarter of two, I suppose. I thanked Admiral Woodson – very good man. I caught a cab to – don't remember the address, it was on one of my letters. North of – Regent's Park, I think. Admiral Sir Roger De Vere. He served under Somerville. He wasn't there. His housekeeper said he got called out of town suddenly due to a death in the family. So I left a message that I'd been there and flagged another cab back downtown. I decided to get out a few blocks early and walk the rest of the way.'

'Why?' Taylor asked.

'Mainly I was stiff from all the sitting – in the Admiralty building, the flight, the cab. I needed a stretch. I usually jog every day, and I get restless when I miss it.'

'Where did you get out?' Owens asked.

'I don't know the name of the street. If you show me a map I can probably point it out.' Owens nodded for him to go on. 'Anyway, I nearly got run over by a double-decker bus, and one of your uniformed cops told me not to jaywalk –' Owens looked surprised at that and scribbled some notes. Perhaps they hadn't learned of that encounter. 'I picked up a magazine at a street stand and met Cathy about, oh, three-forty or so. They were early, too.'

'And how had she spent her day?' Ashley inquired. Ryan was certain that they had this information already.

'Shopping, mainly. Cathy's been over here a few times, and likes to shop in London. She was last here about three years ago for a surgical convention, but I couldn't make the trip.'

'Left you with the little one?' Ashley smiled thinly again. Ryan sensed that Owens was annoyed with him.

'Grandparents. That was before her mom died. I was doing comps for my doctorate at Georgetown, couldn't get out of it. As it was I got my degree in two and a half years, and I sweated blood that last year between the university and seminars at the Center for Strategic and International Studies. This was supposed to be a vacation.' Ryan grimaced. 'The first real vacation since our honeymoon.'

'What were you doing when the attack took place?' Owens got things back on track. All three inquisitors seemed to lean forward in their seats.

'Looking the wrong way. We were talking about what we'd do for dinner when the grenade went off.'

'You knew it was a grenade?' Taylor asked.

Ryan nodded. 'Yeah. They make a distinctive sound. I hate the damned things, but that's one of the little toys the Marines trained me to use at Quantico. Same thing with the machine-gunner. At Quantico we were exposed to East Bloc weapons. I've handled the AK–47. The sound it makes is different from our stuff, and that's a useful thing to know in combat. How come they didn't both have AKs?'

'As near as we can work out,' Owens said, 'the man you wounded disabled the car with a rifle-launched antitank grenade. Forensic evidence points to this. His rifle, therefore, was probably one of the new AK-74s, the small-calibre one, fitted to launch grenades. Evidently he didn't have time to remove the grenade-launcher assembly and decided to press on with his pistol. He had a stick grenade as well, you know.' Jack didn't know about the rifle grenade, but the type of hand-grenade he'd seen suddenly leaped out of his memory.

'The antitank kind?' Ryan asked.

'You know about that, do you?' Ashley responded.

'I used to be a Marine, remember? Called the RKG-something, isn't it? Supposed to be able to punch a hole in a light armoured vehicle or rip up a truck pretty good.' *Where the hell did they get those little rascals – and why didn't they use them. . . ? You're missing something, Jack.*

'Then what?' Owens asked.

'First thing, I got my wife and kid down on the deck. The traffic stopped pretty quick. I kept my head up to see what was happening.'

'Why?' Taylor inquired.

'I don't know,' Ryan said slowly. 'Training, maybe. I wanted to see what the hell was going on – call it stupid curiosity. I saw the one guy hosing down the Rolls and the other one hustling around the back, like he was trying to bag anyone who tried to jump out of the car. I saw that if I moved to my left I could get closer. I was screened by the stopped cars. All of a sudden I was within fifty feet or so. The AK gunner was screened behind the Rolls, and the pistolero had his back to me. I saw that I had a chance, and I guess I took it.'

'Why?' It was Owens this time, very quiet.

'Good question. I don't know, I really don't.' Ryan was silent for half a minute. 'It made me mad. Everyone I've met over here so far has been pretty nice, and all of a sudden I see these two cocksuckers committing murder right the hell in front of me.'

'Did you guess who they were?' Taylor asked.

'Doesn't take much imagination, does it? That pissed me off, too. I guess that's it – anger. Maybe that's what motivates people in combat,' Ryan mused. 'I'll have to think about that. Anyway, like I said, I saw the chance and I took it.

'It was easy – I was very lucky.' Owens' eyebrows went up at that understatement. 'The guy with the pistol was dumb. He should have checked his back. Instead he just kept looking at his kill zone – very dumb. You always "check-six." I blindsided him.' Ryan grinned. 'My coach would have been proud – I really stuck him good. But I guess I ought to have had my pads on, 'cause the doc says I broke something up here when I hit him. He went down pretty hard. I got his gun and shot him – you want to know why I did that, right?'

'Yes,' Owens replied.

'I didn't want him to get up.'

'He was unconscious – he didn't wake up for two hours, and had nasty concussion when he did.'

If I'd known he had that grenade, I wouldn't have shot him in the ass! 'How was I supposed to know that?' Ryan asked reasonably. 'I was about to go up against a somebody with a light machine gun, and I didn't need a bad guy behind me. So I neutralized him. I could have put one through the back of his head – at Quantico when they say "neutralize," they mean *kill*. My dad was the cop. Most of what I know about police procedures comes from watching TV, and I *know* most of that's wrong. All I knew was that I couldn't afford to have him come at me from behind. I can't say I'm especially proud of it, but at the time it seemed like a good idea.

'I moved around the right-rear corner of the car and looked around. I saw the guy was using a pistol. Your man Wilson explained that to me – that was lucky, too. I wasn't real crazy about taking an AK on with a dinky little handgun. He saw me come around. We both fired about the same time – I just shot straighter, I guess.'

Ryan stopped. He hadn't meant it to sound like that. *Is that how it was? If you don't know, who does?* Ryan had learned that in a crisis, time compresses and dilates – seemingly at the same time. *It also fools your memory, doesn't it? What else could I have done?* He shook his head.

'I don't know,' he said again. 'Maybe I should have tried something else. Maybe I should have said, "Drop it!" or "Freeze!" like they do on TV – but there just wasn't time. Everything was *right now* – him or me – do you know what I mean? You don't . . . you don't reason all this out when you only have half a second of decision time. I guess you go on training and instinct. The only training I've had was in the Green Machine, the Corps. They don't teach you to arrest people – Christ's sake, I didn't *want* to kill anybody, I just didn't have a hell of a choice in the matter.' Ryan paused for a moment.

'Why didn't he – quit, run away, something! He saw I had him. He must have known I had him cold.' Ryan slumped back into the pillow. Having to articulate what had happened brought it back all too vividly. *A man is dead because of you, Jack. All the way dead. He had his instincts, too, didn't he? But yours worked better – so why doesn't that make you feel good?*

'Doctor Ryan,' Owens said calmly, 'the three of us have personally interviewed six people, all of whom had a clear view of the incident. From what they have told us, you've just related the circumstances to us with remarkable clarity. Given the facts of the matter, I – we – don't see that you had any choice at all. It's as certain as such things possibly can be that you did precisely the right thing. And your second shot didn't matter, if that's troubling you. Your first went straight through his heart.'

Jack nodded. 'Yeah, I could see that. The second shot was completely automatic, like my hand did it without being told. The gun came back down and zap! No thought at all . . . funny how your brain works. It's like one part does the doing and another part does the watching and advising. The "watching" part saw the first round go right through his ten-ring, but the "doing" part kept going till he went down. I might have tried to squeeze off another round for all I know, but the gun was empty.'

'The Marines taught you to shoot very well indeed,' Taylor observed.

Ryan shook his head. 'Dad taught me when I was a kid. The Corps doesn't make a big deal about pistols anymore – they're just for show. If the bad guys get that close, it's time to leave. I carried a rifle. Anyway, the guy was only fifteen feet away.' Owens made some more notes.

'The car took off a few seconds later. I didn't get much of a look at the driver. It could have been a man or a woman. He or she was white, that's all I can say. The car went whippin' up the street and turned, last I saw of it.'

'It was one of our London taxis – did you notice that?' Taylor asked.

Ryan blinked. 'Oh, you're right. I didn't really think about that – that's dumb! Hell, you have a million of the damned things around. No wonder they used one of those.'

'Eight thousand six hundred and seventy-nine, to be exact,' Owens said. 'Five thousand nine hundred and nineteen of which are painted black.'

A light flashed in Ryan's head. 'Tell me, was this an assassination attempt or were they trying to kidnap them?'

'We're not sure about that. You might be interested to know that Sinn Fein, the political wing of the Provisional IRA, have released a statement completely disowning the incident.'

'You believe that?' Ryan asked. With pain medications still coursing through his system, he didn't quite notice how skilfully Taylor had parried his question.

'Yes, we are leaning in that direction. Even the Provos aren't this crazy, you know. Something like this has far too high a political price. They learned that much from killing Lord Mountbatten – wasn't even the IRA who did that, but INLA, the Irish National Liberation Army. Anyway it cost them a lot of money from their American sympathizers,' Taylor said.

'I see from the papers that your fellow citizens are pretty worked up about this.'

'Indeed they are, Doctor Ryan. It's rather remarkable how terrorists can always seem to find a way to shock us, no matter what horrors have gone before,' Owens noted. His voice was wholly professional, but Ryan sensed that the chief of Anti-Terrorist Branch was willing to rip the head right off the surviving terrorist with his bare hands. They looked strong enough to do just that. 'So what happened next?'

'I made sure the guy I shot – the second one – was dead. Then I checked the car. The driver – well, you know about that, and the security officer. One of your people, Mr Owens?'

'Charlie was a friend of mine. He's been with the Royal Family's security detail for three years now. . . .' Owens spoke almost as though the man were still alive, and Ryan wondered if they had ever worked together. Police make especially close friendships, he knew.

'Well, you guys know the rest. I hope somebody gives that redcoat a pat on the head. Thank God he took the time to think it all out – at least long enough for your guy to show up and calm him down. Would have been embarrassing for everybody if he'd stuck that bayonet out my back.'

Owens grunted agreement. 'Indeed it would.'

'Was that rifle loaded?' Ryan asked.

'If it was,' Ashley replied, 'why didn't he shoot?'

'A crowded street isn't the best place to use a high-powered rifle, even if you're sure of your target,' Ryan answered. 'It was loaded, wasn't it?'

'We cannot discuss security matters,' Owens said.

I knew it was loaded, Ryan told himself. 'Where the hell did he come from, anyway? The Palace is a good ways off.'

'Clarence House – the white building adjoining St James's Palace. The terrorists picked a bad time – or perhaps a bad place – for their attack. There's a guard post at the southwest corner of the building. The guard changes every two hours. When the attack took place, the change was just under way. That meant that four soldiers were there at the time, not just one. The police on duty at the palace heard the explosion and gunfire. The Sergeant in charge ran to the gate to see what was going on and yelled for a guardsman to follow.'

'He's the one who sounded the alarm, right? That's how the rest of them arrived so fast?'

'Charlie Winston,' Owens said. 'The Rolls has an electronic attack alarm – you don't need to tell anyone that. That alerted headquarters. Sergeant Price acted entirely on his own initiative. Unfortunately for him, the guardsman was a hurdler – the lad runs track and field – and vaulted the barriers there. Price tried to do the same, but fell down and broke his nose. He had a devil of a time catching up, plus sending out his own alarm by portable radio.'

'Well, I'm glad he caught up when he did. That trooper scared the hell out of me. I hope your Sergeant gets a pat on the head, too.'

'The Queen's Police Medal for starters, and the thanks of Her Majesty,' Ashley said. 'One thing that has confused us, Doctor Ryan. You left the military with a physical disability, yet you showed nothing of this yesterday.'

'You know that after I left the Corps, I went into the brokerage business. I made something of a name for myself, and Cathy's father came down to talk to me. That's when I met Cathy. I passed on the invitation to move to New York, but Cathy and I hit it right off. One thing led to another, and pretty soon we were engaged. I wore a back brace then, because every so often my back would go bad on me. Well, it happened again right after we got engaged, and Cathy took me into Johns Hopkins to have one of her teachers check me out. One was Stanley Rabinowisz, professor of neurosurgery there. He ran me through three days of tests and said he could fix me good as new.

'It turned out that the docs at Bethesda had goofed my myelogram. No reflection on them, they were sharp young docs, but Stan's about the best there is. Good as his word, too. He opened me up that Friday, and two months later I *was* almost as good as new,' Ryan said. 'Anyway, that's the story of Ryan's back. I just happened to fall in love with a pretty girl who was studying to be a surgeon.'

'Your wife is certainly a most versatile and competent woman,' Owens agreed.

'And you found her pushy,' Ryan observed.

'No, Doctor Ryan. People under stress are never at their best. Your wife also examined Their Royal Highnesses on the scene, and that was most useful to us. She refused to leave your side until you were under competent medical care; one can hardly fault her for that. She did find our identification procedures a touch longwinded, I think, and she was quite naturally anxious about you. We might have moved things along more quickly –'

'No need to apologize, sir. My dad was a cop. I know the score. I understand you had trouble identifying us.'

'Just over three hours – a timing problem, you see. We had your passport out of your coat, and your driving licence, which, we were glad to see, had your photograph. Our initial request to your Legal Attaché was just before five, and that made it noon in America. Lunchtime, you see. He called the FBI's Baltimore field office, who in turn called their Annapolis office. The identification business is fairly straightforward – first they had to find some lads at your Naval Academy who knew who you were, when you came over, and so forth. Next they found the travel agent who booked your flight and hotel. Another agent went to your motor vehicle registration agency. Many of these people were off eating lunch, and that must have cost us roughly an hour. Simultaneously he – the Attaché – sent a query to your Marine Corps. Within three hours we had a fairly complete history on you – including fingerprints. We had those from your travel documents and the hotel registration, and they matched your military records, of course.'

'Three hours, eh?' *Dinnertime here, and lunchtime at home, and they did it all in three hours. Damn.*

'While all that was going on we had to interview your wife several times to make sure she'd told us everything she'd seen –'

'And she gave it to you exactly the same way every time, right?' Ryan asked.

'Right,' Owens said. He smiled. 'That's quite remarkable, you know.'

Ryan grinned. 'Not for Cathy. Some things, medicine especially, she's a real machine. I'm surprised she didn't hand you a roll of film.'

'She said that herself,' Owens replied. 'The photographs in the paper are from a Japanese tourist – that's a cliché, isn't it? – several hundred yards away with a telephoto lens. You might be interested to know that your Marine Corps thinks rather highly of you, by the way.' Owens consulted his notes. 'Tied for first in your class at Quantico, and your fitness reports were excellent.'

'So, you're satisfied I'm a good guy?'

'We were convinced of that from the first moment,' Taylor said. 'We must be thorough in major criminal cases, however, and this one obviously had more than its share of complications.'

'There's one thing that bothers me,' Jack said. There was more than one, but his brain was working too slowly to classify them all.

'What's that?' Owens asked.

'What the hell were they – The Royals, you call them? – doing out on the street with only one guard – wait a minute.' Ryan's head cocked to one side. He went on, speaking rather slowly as his mind struggled to arrange his thoughts. 'That ambush was planned – this wasn't any accidental encounter. But the bad guys caught 'em on the fly. . . . They had to hit a particular car in a particular place. Somebody timed this one out. There were some more people involved in this, weren't there?' Ryan heard a lot of silence for a moment. It was all the answer he needed. 'Somebody with a radio . . . those characters had to know that they were coming, the route they'd take, and exactly when they got into the kill zone. Even then it wouldn't be all that easy, 'cause you have to worry about traffic. . . .'

'Just an historian, Doctor Ryan?' Ashley asked.

'They teach you how to do ambushes in the Marines. If you want to ambush a specific target . . . first, you have to have intelligence information; second, you choose your ground; third, you put your own security guys out to tell you when the target is coming – that's just the bare-bones requirements. Why here – why St James's Park, The Mall?' *The terrorist is a political creature. The target and the place are chosen for political effect*, Ryan told himself. 'You didn't answer my question before: was this an assassination or an attempted kidnapping?'

'We are not entirely sure,' Owens answered.

Ryan looked over his guests. He'd just touched an open nerve. *They disabled the car with an antitank rifle-grenade, and both of them had the hand-thrown kind, too. If they just wanted to kill . . . the grenades would defeat any armour on the car, why use guns at all? No, if this was a straight assassination attempt, they would not have taken so long, would they? You just fibbed to me, Mr Owens. This was definitely a kidnap attempt and you know it.*

'Why just the one security officer in the car, then? You have to protect your people better than that.' *What was it Tony said? An unscheduled trip? The first requirement for a successful ambush is good* intelligence. . . . *You can't pursue this, idiot!* The Commander solved the problem for Jack.

'Well, I believe we covered everything we need for now. We'll probably be back tomorrow,' Owens said.

'How are the terrorists – the one I wounded, I mean?'

'He has not been terribly cooperative. Won't speak to us at all, not even to tell us his name – old story dealing with this lot. We only identified him a few hours ago. No previous criminal record at all – his name appeared as a possible player in two minor cases, but nothing more than that. He's recovering quite nicely, and in three weeks or so,' Taylor said coldly, 'he should be taken before the Queen's Bench, tried before a jury of twelve good men and true, convicted, and sentenced to spend the remainder of his natural life in a secure prison.'

'Only three weeks?' Ryan asked.

'The case is clear-cut,' Owens said. 'We have three photographs from our Japanese friend that show this lad holding his gun behind the car, and nine good eyewitnesses. There will be no mucking about with this lad.'

'And I'll be there to see it,' Ryan observed.

'Of course. You will be our most important witness, Doctor. A formality, but a necessary one. And no claim of lunacy like the chap who tried to kill your President. This boy is a university graduate and he comes from a good family. '

Ryan shook his head. 'Ain't that a hell of a thing? But most of the really bad ones are, aren't they?'

'You know about terrorists?' Ashley asked.

'Just things I've read,' Ryan answered quickly. *That was a mistake, Jack. Cover it.* 'Officer Wilson said the ULA were Maoists.'

'That's right, ' Taylor said.

'That really is crazy. Hell, even the Chinese aren't Maoists anymore, at least the last time I checked they weren't. Oh – what about my family?'

Ashley laughed. 'About time you asked, Doctor. We couldn't very well leave them at the hotel, could we? It was arranged for them to be put up at a highly secure location.'

'You needn't be concerned,' Owens agreed. 'They are quite safe. My word on it.'

'Where, exactly?' Ryan wanted to know.

'A security matter, I'm afraid,' Ashley said. The three inquisitors shared an amused look. Owens checked his watch and shot a look to the others.

'Well,' Owens said. He switched off the tape recorder. 'We don't want to trouble you further the day after surgery. We will probably be back to check a few additional details. For the moment, sir, you have the thanks of all of us at the Yard for doing our job for us.'

'How long will I have Mr Wilson here?'

'Indefinitely. The ULA are likely to be somewhat annoyed with you,' Owens said. 'And it would be most embarrassing for us if they were to make an attempt on your life and find you unprotected. We don't regard this as likely, mind, but we must be careful.'

'I can live with that,' Ryan agreed. *I make a hell of a target here, don't I? A third-grader could kill me with a Popsicle stick.*

'The press want to see you,' Taylor said.

'I'm thrilled.' *Just what I need*, Ryan thought. 'Could you hold them off a bit?'

'Simple enough,' Owens agreed. 'Your medical condition doesn't permit it at the moment. But you should get used to the idea that you're now something of a public figure.'

'Like hell!' Ryan snorted. 'I like being obscure.' *Then you should have stayed behind the tree, dumbass! Just what have you got yourself into?*

'You can't refuse to see them indefinitely, you know,' Taylor said gently.

387

Jack let out a long breath. 'You're correct, of course. But not today. Tomorrow is soon enough.' *Let the hubbub die down some first*, Ryan thought stupidly.

'One can't stay in the shadows for ever, Doctor Ryan,' Ashley said, standing. The others took their cue from him.

The cops and Ashley – Ryan now had him pegged as some kind of spook, intelligence or counterintelligence – took their leave. Wilson came back in, with Kittiwake trailing behind.

'Did they tire you out?' the nurse asked.

'I think I'll live,' Ryan allowed. Kittiwake thrust a thermometer in his mouth to make sure.

Forty minutes after the police had left, Ryan was typing happily away on his computer-toy, reviewing notes and drafting some fresh copy. Cathy Ryan's most frequent (and legitimate) complaint about her husband was that while he was reading – or worse, writing – the world could end around him without his taking notice. This was not entirely true. Jack did notice Wilson jumping to attention out the corner of his eye, but he did not look up until he had finished the new paragraph. When he did, he saw that his new visitors were Her Majesty, the Queen of the United Kingdom of Great Britain and Northern Ireland, and her husband, the Duke of Edinburgh. His first coherent thought was a mental curse that no one had warned him. His second, that he must look very funny with his mouth hanging open.

'Good morning, Doctor Ryan,' the Queen said agreeably. 'How are you feeling?'

'Uh, quite well, thank you, uh, Your Majesty. Won't you, uh, please sit down?' Ryan tried to sit more erect in his bed, but was halted by a flash of pain from his shoulder. It helped to centre his thoughts and reminded him that his medication was nearly due.

'We have no wish to impose,' she said. Ryan sensed that she didn't wish to leave right away, either. He took a second to frame his response.

'Your Majesty, a visit from a head of state hardly qualifies as an imposition. I would be most grateful for your company.' Wilson hustled to get two chairs and excused himself out the door as they sat.

The Queen was dressed in a peach-coloured suit whose elegant simplicity must have made a noteworthy dent even in her clothing budget. The Duke was in a dark blue suit which finally made Ryan understand why his wife wanted him to buy some clothes over here.

'Doctor Ryan,' she said formally, 'on our behalf, and that of our people, we wish to express to you our most profound gratitude for your action of yesterday. We are very much in your debt.'

Ryan nodded soberly. He wondered just how awful he looked. 'For my own part, ma'am, I am glad that I was able to be of service – but the truth of the matter is that I didn't really do all that much. Anyone could have done the same thing. I just happened to be the closest.'

'The police say otherwise,' the Duke observed. 'And after viewing the scene myself, I am inclined to agree with them. I'm afraid you're a hero whether you like it or not.' Jack remembered that this man had once been a professional naval officer – probably a good one. He had the look.

'Why did you do it, Doctor Ryan?' the Queen asked. She examined his face closely.

Jack made a quick guess. 'Excuse me, ma'am, but are you asking why I took the chance, or why an Irish-American would take the chance?' Jack was still ordering his own thoughts, examining his own memories. *Why* did *you do it? Will you ever know?* He saw that he'd guessed right and went on quickly.

'Your Majesty, I cannot speak to your Irish problem. I'm an American citizen, and my country has enough problems of its own without having to delve into someone else's. Where I come from we – that is, Irish-Americans – have made out pretty well. We're in all the professions, business, and politics, but your prototypical Irish-American is still a basic police officer or firefighter. The cavalry that won the West was a third Irish, and there are still plenty of us in uniform – especially the Marine Corps, as a matter of fact. Half of the local FBI office lived in my old neighbourhood. They had names like Tully, Sullivan, O'Connor, and Murphy. My dad was a police officer for half his life, and the priests and nuns who educated me were mostly Irish, probably.

'Do you see what I mean, Your Majesty? In America we are the forces of order, the glue that holds society together – so what happens?

'Today, the most famous Irishmen in the world are the maniacs who leave bombs in parked cars, or assassins who kill people to make some sort of political point. I don't like that, and I know my dad wouldn't like it. He spent his whole working life taking animals like that off the street and putting them in cages where they belong. We've worked pretty hard to get where we are – too hard to be happy about being thought of as the relatives of terrorists.' Jack smiled. 'I guess I understand how Italians feel about the Mafia. Anyway, I can't say that all this stuff paraded through my head yesterday, but I did kind of figure what was going on. I couldn't just sit there like a dummy and let murder be committed before my eyes and not do *something*. So I saw my chance and I took it.'

The Queen nodded thoughtfully. She regarded Ryan with a warm, friendly smile for a few moments and turned to look at her husband. The two communicated without words. They'd been married long enough for that, Ryan thought. When she turned back, he could see that a decision had been reached.

'So, then. How shall we reward you?'

'Reward, ma'am?' Ryan shook his head. 'Thank you very much, but it's not necessary. I'm glad I was able to help. That's enough.'

'No, Doctor Ryan, it is not enough. One of the nicer things about being Queen is that one is permitted to recognize meritorious conduct, then to reward it properly. The Crown cannot appear to be ungrateful.' Her eyes sparkled with some private joke. Ryan found himself captivated by the woman's humanity. He'd read that some people found her to be less than intelligent. He already knew they were far off the mark. There was an active brain behind those eyes, and an active wit as well. 'Accordingly, it has been decided that you shall be invested as a Knight Commander of the Victorian Order.'

'What – er, I beg your pardon, ma'am?' Ryan blinked a few times as his brain tried to catch up with his ears.

'The Victorian Order has only recently been established. Its purpose is to reward those who have rendered personal service to the Crown. Obviously you qualify. This is the first case for many years that an heir to the throne has been saved from almost certain death. As an historian yourself, you might be interested to learn that our own scholars are in disagreement as to when was our most recent precedent – in any event, you will henceforth be known as Sir John Ryan.'

Again Jack thought that he must look rather funny with his mouth open.

'Your Majesty, American law –'

'We know,' she interrupted smoothly. 'The Prime Minister will be discussing this with your President later today. We believe that in view of the special nature of this case, and in the interest of Anglo-American relations, the matter will be settled amicably.'

'There is ample precedent for this,' the Duke went on. 'After the Second World War a number of American officers were accorded similar recognition. Your Fleet Admiral Nimitz, for example, became a Knight Commander of the Bath, along with Generals Eisenhower, Bradley, Patton, and a number of others.

'For the purposes of American law, it will probably be considered honorary – but for our purposes it will be quite real.'

'Well.' Ryan fumbled for something to say. 'Your Majesty, insofar as this does not conflict with laws of my country, I will be deeply honoured to accept.' The Queen beamed.

'That's settled, then. Now, how are you feeling – really feeling?'

'I've felt worse, ma'am. I have no complaints – I just wish I'd moved a little faster.'

The Duke smiled. 'Being wounded makes you appear that much more heroic – nothing like a little drama.'

Especially if it's someone else's shoulder, my Lord Duke, Ryan thought. A small bell went off in his head. 'Excuse me, this knighthood, does it mean that my wife will be called –'

'Lady Ryan? Of course.' The Queen flashed her warm smile again.

Jack grinned broadly. 'You know, when I left Merrill Lynch, Cathy's father was madder than – he was very angry with me, said I'd never amount to anything writing history books. Maybe this will change his mind.' He was sure that Cathy would not mind the title – *Lady Ryan*. No, she wouldn't mind that one little bit.

'Not so bad a thing after all?'

'No, sir, and please forgive me if I gave that impression. I'm afraid you caught me a little off balance.' Ryan shook his head. *This whole damned affair has me a lot off balance.* 'Might I ask a question, sir?'

'Certainly.'

'The police wouldn't tell me where they're keeping my family.' This drew a hearty laugh. The Queen answered.

'It is the opinion of the police that there might exist the possibility of a reprisal against you or your family. Therefore it was decided that they should be moved to a more secure location. Under the circumstances, we decided that they might most easily be moved to the Palace – it was the least thing we could do. When we left, your wife and daughter were fast asleep, and we left strict instructions that they should not be disturbed.'

'The Palace?'

'We have ample room for guests, I assure you,' the Queen replied.

'Oh, Lord!' Ryan muttered.

'You have an objection?' the Duke asked.

'My little girl, she –'

'Olivia?' the Queen said, rather surprised. 'She's a lovely child. When we saw her last night she was sleeping like an angel.'

'Sally' – Olivia had been a peace offering to Cathy's family that hadn't worked; it was the name of her grandmother – 'is a little angel, asleep, but when she wakes up she's more like a little tornado, and she's very good at breaking things. Especially valuable things.'

'What a dreadful thing to say!' Her Majesty feigned shock. 'That lovely little girl. The police told us that she broke hearts throughout Scotland Yard last evening. I fear you exaggerate, Sir John.'

'Yes, ma'am.' There was no arguing with a queen.

3

Flowers and Families

Wilson had been mistaken in his assessment. The escape had taken longer than anyone at the Yard had thought. Six hundred miles away, a Sabena flight was landing outside of Cork. The passenger in seat 23-D of the Boeing 737 was entirely unremarkable; his sandy hair was cut medium-close, and he was dressed like a middle-level executive in a neat but rumpled suit that gave the entirely accurate impression of a man who'd spent a long day on the job and got too little sleep before catching a flight home. An experienced traveller to be sure, with one carry-on flight bag. If asked, he could have given a convincing discourse on the wholesale fish business in the accent of Southwestern Ireland. He could change accents as easily as most men changed shirts; a useful skill, since TV news crews had made the patois of his native Belfast recognizable the world over. He read the London *Times* on the flight, and the topic of discussion in his seat row, as with the rest of the aircraft, was the story which covered the front page.

'A terrible thing, it is,' he'd agreed with the man in 23-E, a Belgian dealer in machine tools who could not have known how an event might be terrible in more than one way.

All the months of planning, the painstakingly gathered intelligence, the rehearsals carried out right under the Brit noses, the three escape routes, the radiomen – all for nothing because of this bloody meddler. He examined the photo on the front page.

Who are you, Yank? he wondered, *John Patrick Ryan. Historian – a bloody academic! Ex-Marine – trust a damned bootneck to stick his nose where it doesn't belong!* John Patrick Ryan. *You're a bloody Catholic, aren't you? Well, Johnny nearly put paid on your account. . . . Too bad about Johnny. Good man Johnny was, dependable, loved his guns, and true to the Cause.*

The plane finally came to a stop at the jetway. Forward, the stewardess opened the door, and the passengers rose to get their bags from the overhead stowage. He got his, and joined the slow movement forward. He tried to be philosophical about it. In his years as a 'player', he'd seen operations go awry for the most ridiculous of reasons. But this op was so important. So *much* planning. He shook his head as he tucked the paper under his arm. *We'll just have to try again, that's all. We can afford to be patient.* One failure, he told himself, didn't matter in the great scheme of things. The other side had been lucky this time. *We only have to be lucky once.* The men in the H-blocks weren't going anywhere.

What about Sean? A mistake to have taken him along. He'd helped plan the operation from the beginning. Sean knows a great deal about the Organization. He set that worry aside as he stepped off the aircraft. *Sean would never talk. Not Sean, not with his girl in her grave these past five years, from a para's stray bullet.*

He wasn't met, of course. The other men who had been part of the operation were already back, their equipment left behind in rubbish bins, wiped clean of fingerprints. Only he had the risk of exposure, but he was sure that this Ryan fellow hadn't got a good look at his face. He thought back again to be sure. No. The look of surprise on his face, the look of pain he'd seen there. The American couldn't have got much of a look – if he had, an identikit composite picture would be in the press already, complete with the moppy wig and fake glasses.

He walked out of the terminal building to the parking lot, his travel bag slung over his shoulder, searching in his pocket for the keys that had set off the airport metal detector in Brussels – what a laugh that was! He smiled for the first time in nearly a day. It was a clear, sunny day, another glorious Irish fall it was. He drove his year-old BMW – a man with a business cover had to have a full disguise, after all – down the road to the safehouse. He was already planning two more operations. Both would require a lot of time, but time was the one thing he had in unlimited quantity.

It was easy enough to tell when it was time for another pain medication. Ryan was unconsciously flexing his left hand at the far end of the cast. It didn't reduce the pain, but did seem to move it about somewhat as the muscles and tendons changed place slightly. It bothered his concentration however much he tried to shut it out. Jack remembered all the TV shows in which the detective or otherwise employed hero took a round in the shoulder but recovered fully in time for the last commercial. The human shoulder – his, at any rate – was a solid collection of bones that bullets – *one* bullet – all too easily broke. As the time for another medication approached it seemed that he could feel every jagged edge of every broken bone grating against its neighbour as he breathed, and even the gentle tapping of his right-hand fingers on the keyboard seemed to ripple across his body to the focus of his pain until he had to stop and watch the wall clock – for the first time he wanted Kittiwake to appear with his next instalment of chemical bliss.

Until he remembered his fear. The pain of his back injury had made his first week at Bethesda a living hell. He knew that his present injury paled by comparison, but the body does not remember pain, and the shoulder was *here and now*. He forced himself to remember that pain medications had made his back problem almost tolerable . . . except that the doctors had gotten just a little too generous with his dosages. More than the pain, Ryan dreaded withdrawal from morphine sulphate. That had lasted a week, the wanting that seemed to draw his entire body into some vast empty place, someplace where his innermost self found itself entirely alone and *needing* . . . Ryan shook his head. The pain rippled through his left arm and shoulder and he forced himself to welcome it. *I'm not going to go through that again. Never again.*

The door opened. It wasn't Kittiwake – the med was still fourteen minutes away. Ryan had noticed a uniform outside the door when it had opened before. Now he was sure. A thirtyish uniformed officer came in with a floral arrangement and he was followed by another who was similarly loaded. A scarlet and gold ribbon decorated the first, a gift from the Marine Corps, followed by another from the American Embassy.

'Quite a few more to come, sir,' one uniformed officer said.

'The room isn't all that big. Can you give me the cards and spread these around some? I'm sure there's people around who'd like them.' *And who wants to live in a jungle?* Within ten minutes Ryan had a pile of cards, notes, and telegrams. He found that reading the words of others was better than reading his own when it came to blocking out the ache of his damaged shoulder.

Kittiwake arrived. She gave the flowers only a fleeting glance before administering Ryan's medication, and hustled out with scarcely a word. Ryan learned why five minutes later.

His next visitor was the Prince of Wales. Wilson snapped to his feet again, and Jack wondered if the kid's knees were tiring of this. The medication was already working. His shoulder was drifting farther away, but along with this came a slight feeling of lightheadedness as from a couple of stiff drinks. Maybe that was part of the reason for what happened next.

'Howdy.' Jack smiled. 'How are you feeling, sir?'

'Quite well, thank you.' The answering smile contained no enthusiasm. The Prince looked very tired, his thin face stretched an extra inch or so, with a lingering sadness around the eyes. His shoulders drooped within the conservative grey suit.

'Why don't you sit down, sir?' Ryan invited. 'You look as though you had a tougher night than I did.'

'Yes, thank you, Doctor Ryan.' He made another attempt to smile. It failed. 'And how are you feeling?'

'Reasonably well, Your Highness. And how is your wife – excuse me, how is the Princess doing?'

The Prince's words did not come easily, and he had trouble looking up to Ryan from his chair. 'We both regret that she couldn't come with me. She's still somewhat disturbed – in shock, I believe. She had a very . . . bad experience.'

Brains splattered over her face. I suppose you might call that a bad experience. 'I saw. I understand that neither of you was physically injured, thank God. I presume your child also?'

'Yes, all thanks to you, Doctor.'

Jack tried another one-armed shrug. The gesture didn't hurt so much this time. 'Glad to help, sir – I just wish I hadn't got myself shot in the process.' His attempt at levity died on his lips. He'd said the wrong thing in the wrong way. The Prince looked at Jack very curiously for a moment, but then his eyes went flat again.

'We would all have been killed except for you, you know – and on behalf of my family and myself – well, thank you. It's not enough just to say that –' His Highness went on, then halted again and struggled to find a few more words. 'But it's the best I can manage. I wasn't able to manage very much yesterday, come to that,' he concluded, staring quietly at the foot of the bed.

Aha! Ryan thought. The Prince stood and turned to leave. *What do I do now?*

'Sir, why don't you sit down and let's talk this one over for a minute, okay?'

His Highness turned back. For a moment he looked as though he would say something, but the drawn face changed again and turned away.

'Your Highness, I really think . . .' *No effect. I can't let him go out of here like this. Well, if good manners won't work* – Jack's voice became sharp.

'*Hold it!*' The Prince turned with a look of great surprise. '*Sit down, goddammit!*' Ryan pointed to the chair. *At least I have his attention now. I wonder if they can take a knighthood back. . .*

By this time the Prince flushed a bit. The colour gave his face life that it had lacked. He wavered for a moment, then sat with reluctance and resignation.

'Now,' Ryan said heatedly, 'I think I know what's eating at you, sir. You feel bad because you didn't do a John Wayne number yesterday and handle those gunmen all by yourself, right?' The Prince didn't nod or make any other voluntary response, but a hurt expression around his eyes answered the question just as surely.

'Aw, crap!' Ryan snorted. In the corner, Tony Wilson went pale as a ghost. Ryan didn't blame him.

'You oughta have better sense. . . sir,' Ryan added hastily. 'You've been through the service schools, right? You've qualified as a pilot, parachuted out of airplanes, and even had command of your own ship?' He got a nod. Time to step it up. 'Then you've got no excuse, you damned well ought to have better sense than to think like that! You're not really that dumb, are you?'

'What exactly do you mean?' *A trace of anger*, Ryan thought. *Good.*

'Use your head. You've been trained to think this sort of thing out, haven't you? Let's critique the exercise. Examine what the tactical situation was yesterday. You were trapped in a stopped car with two or three bad guys outside holding automatic weapons. The car is armour-plated, but you're stuck. What can you do? The way I see it, you had three choices:

'One. You can just freeze, just sit there and wet your pants. Hell, that's what most normal people would do, caught by surprise like that. That's probably the normal reaction, But you didn't do that.

'Two. You can try to get out of the car and *do something*, right?'

'Yes, I should have.'

'Wrong!' Ryan shook his head emphatically. 'Sorry, sir, but that's not a real good idea. The guy I tackled was waiting for you to do just that. That guy could have put a nine-millimetre slug in your head before you had both feet on the pavement. You look like you're in pretty good shape. You probably move pretty good – but ain't nobody yet been able to outrun a bullet, sir! That choice might have gotten you killed, and the rest of your family along with you.

'Three. Your last choice, you tough it out and pray the cavalry gets there in time. You know you're close to home. You know there's cops and troops around. So you know that time is on your side if you can survive for a couple of minutes. In the meantime you try to protect your family as best you can. You get them down on the floor of the car and get overtop of them so the only way the terrorists can get them is to go through you first. And *that*, my friend, is what you did.' Ryan paused for a moment to let him absorb this.

'You did *exactly* the right thing, dammit!' Ryan leaned forward until his shoulder pulled him back with a gasp. It wasn't all that much of a pain medication. 'Jesus, this hurts. Look, sir, you were stuck out in the open – with a lousy set of alternatives. But you used your head and took the best one you had. From where I sit, you could not have done any better than you did. So there is nothing, repeat *nothing*, for you to feel bad about. And if you don't believe me, ask Wilson. He's a cop.' The Prince turned his head.

The Anti-Terrorist Branch officer cleared his throat. 'Excuse me, Your Royal Highness, but Doctor Ryan is quite correct. We were discussing this, this problem yesterday, and we reached precisely the same conclusion.'

Ryan looked over to the cop. 'How long did you fellows kick the idea around, Tony?'

'Perhaps ten minutes,' Wilson answered.

'That's six *hundred* seconds, Your Highness. But you had to think and act in – what? Five? Maybe three? Not much time to make a life-and-death decision, is it? Mister, I'd say you did damned well. All that training you've picked up along the line worked. And if you were evaluating someone else's performance instead of your own, you'd say the same thing, just like Tony and his friends did.'

'But the press –'

'Oh, screw the press!' Ryan snapped back, wondering if he'd gone too far. 'What do reporters know about anything? They don't *do* anything, for crying out loud, they just report what other people do. You can fly an airplane, you've jumped out of them – flying scares the hell out of me; I don't even want to think about jumping out of one – and commanded a ship. Plus you ride horses and keep trying to break your neck – and now, finally, you're a father, you got a kid of your own now, right? Isn't that enough to prove to the world that you've got balls? You're not some dumb kid, sir. You're a trained pro. Start acting like one.'

Jack could see his mind going over what he'd just been told. His Highness was sitting a little straighter now. The smile that began to form was an austere one, but at least it had some conviction behind it.

'I am not accustomed to being addressed so forcefully.'

'So cut my head off.' Ryan grinned. 'You looked like you needed a little straightening out – but I had to get your attention first, didn't I? I'm not going to apologize, sir. Instead, why don't you look in that mirror over there. I bet the guy you see now looks better than the one who shaved this morning.'

'You really believe what you said?'

'Of course. All you have to do is look at the situation from the outside, sir. The problem you had yesterday was tougher than any exercise I had to face at Quantico, but you gutted it out. Listen, I'll tell you a story.

'My first day at Quantico, first day of the officer's course. They line us up, and we meet our Drill Instructor, Gunnery Sergeant Willie King – humongous black guy, we called him Son of Kong. Anyway, he looks us up and down and says, "Girls, I got some good news, and I got some bad news. The good news is, if you prove that you're good enough to get through this here course, you ain't got nothin' left to prove as long as you live." And he waits for a couple of seconds. "The bad news is, you gotta prove it to *me*!" '

'You were top in your class,' the Prince said. He'd been briefed, too.

'I was third in that one. I tied for first in the Basic Officer's Course later on. Yeah, I did okay. That course was a gold-plated sonuvabitch. The only easy thing was sleeping – by the time your day was finished, falling asleep was easy enough. But, you know, Son of Kong was almost right.

'If you make it through Quantico, you know you've done something. After that there was only one more thing left for me to prove, and the Corps didn't have anything to do with that.' Ryan paused for a moment. 'Her name is Sally. Anyway, you and your family are alive, sir. Okay, I helped – but so did you. And if any reporter-expert says different, you still have the Tower of London, right? I remember that stuff in the press about your wife last year. Damn, if anybody'd talked that way about Cathy I'd have changed his voice for him.'

'Changed his voice?' His Highness asked.

'The *hard* way!' Ryan laughed. 'I guess that's a problem with being important – you can't shoot back. Too bad. People in that business could use some manners, and people in your business are entitled to some privacy, just like the rest of us.'

'And what of your manners, Sir John?' A real smile now.

'*Mea maxima culpa*, my Lord Prince, you got me there.'

'Still, we might not be here except for you.'

'I couldn't just sit there and watch some people get murdered. If situations had been reversed, I'll bet you'd have done the same thing I did.'

'You really think so?' His Highness was surprised.

'Sir, are you kidding? Anybody dumb enough to jump out of an airplane is dumb enough to try anything.'

The Prince stood and walked over to the mirror on the wall. Clearly he liked what he saw there. 'Well,' he murmured to the mirror. He turned back to voice his last self-doubt.

'And if you had been in my place?'

'I'd probably just've wet my pants,' Ryan replied. 'But you have an advantage over me, sir. You've thought about this problem for a few years, right? Hell, you practically grew up with it, and you've been through basic training – Royal Marines, too, maybe?'

'Yes, I have.'

Ryan nodded. 'Okay, so you had your options figured out beforehand, didn't you? They caught you by surprise, sure, but the training shows. You did all right. Honest. Sit back down, and maybe Tony can pour us some coffee.'

Wilson did so, though he was clearly uneasy to be close to the heir. The Prince of Wales sipped at his cup while Ryan lit up one of Wilson's cigarettes. His Highness looked on disapprovingly.

'That's not good for you, you know,' he pointed out.

Ryan just laughed. 'Your Highness, since I arrived in this country, I nearly got run over by one of those two-storey buses, I almost got my head blown off by a damned Maoist, then I nearly get myself shish-kabobed by one of your redcoats.' Ryan waved the cigarette in the air. 'This is the *safest* damned thing I've done since I got here! What a vacation this's turned out to be.'

'You do have a point,' the Prince admitted. 'And quite a sense of humour, Doctor Ryan.'

'I guess the valium – or whatever they're giving me – helps. And the name's Jack.' He held out his hand. The Prince took it.

'I was able to meet your wife and daughter yesterday – you were unconscious at the time. I gather that your wife is an excellent physician. Your little daughter is quite wonderful.'

'Thanks. How do you like being a daddy?'

'The first time you hold your newborn child . . .'

'Yeah,' Jack said. 'Sir, that's what it's all about.' He stopped talking abruptly.

Bingo, Ryan thought. *A four-month-old baby. If they kidnap the Prince and Princess, well, no government can cave in to terrorism. The politicians and police have to have a contingency plan already set up for this, don't they? They'd take this town apart one brick at a time, but they wouldn't – couldn't – negotiate anything, and that was just too bad for the grown-ups, but a little baby. . . damn, there's a bargaining chip! What kind of people would –*

'Bastards,' Ryan whispered to himself. Wilson blanched, but the Prince suspected what Jack was thinking about.

'I'm sorry?'

'They weren't trying to kill you. Hell, I bet you weren't even the real objective. . .' Ryan nodded slowly. He searched his mind for the data he'd seen on the ULA. There hadn't been much – it hadn't been his area of focus in any case – a few titbits of shadowy intelligence reports, mixed with a lot of pure conjecture. 'They didn't want to kill you at all, I bet. And when you covered the wife and kid, you burned their plan . . . maybe, or maybe you just – yeah, maybe you just threw them a curve, and that blew their timing a little bit.'

'What do you mean?' the Prince asked.

'Goddamned medications slow your brain down,' Ryan said mainly to himself. 'Have the police told you what the terrorists were up to?'

His Highness sat upright in the chair. 'I can't –'

'You don't have to,' Ryan cut him off. 'Did they tell you that what you did definitely – *definitely* – saved all of you?'

'No, but –'

'Tony?'

'They told me you were a very clever chap, Jack,' Wilson said. 'I'm afraid I can't comment further. Your Royal Highness, Doctor Ryan may be correct in his assessment.'

'What assessment?' The Prince was puzzled.

Ryan explained. It only took a few minutes.

'How did you arrive at this conclusion, Jack?'

Ryan's mind was still churning through the hypothesis. 'Sir, I'm an historian. My business is figuring things out. Before that I was a stockbroker – doing essentially the same thing. It's not all that hard when you think about it. You look for apparent inconsistencies and then you try to figure out why they're not really inconsistent.' He concluded, 'It's all speculation on my part, but I'm willing to bet that Tony's colleagues are pursuing it.' Wilson didn't say anything. He cleared his throat – which was answer enough.

The Prince looked deep into his coffee cup. His face was that of a man who had recovered from fear and shame. Now he contemplated cold anger at what might have been.

'Well, they've had their chance, haven't they?'

'Yes, sir. I imagine if they ever try again, it'll be a lot harder. Right, Tony?'

'I seriously doubt that they will ever try again,' Wilson replied. 'We should develop some good intelligence from this incident. The ULA have stepped over an invisible line. Politically, success might have enhanced their position, but they didn't succeed, did they? This will harm them, harm their "popular" support. Some people who know them will now consider talking – not to us, you understand, but some of what they say will get to us in due course. They were outcasts before, they will be outcasts even more now.'

Will they learn from this? Ryan wondered. *If so, what will they have learned? There's a question.* Jack knew that it had only two possible answers, and that those answers were diametrically opposed. He made a mental note. He'd follow up on this when he got home. It wasn't a merely academic exercise now. He had a bullet hole in his shoulder to prove that.

The Prince rose to his feet. 'You must excuse me, Jack. I'm afraid I have rather a full day ahead.'

'Going back out, eh?'

'If I hide, they've won. I understand that fact better now than when I came in here. And I have something else to thank you for.'

'You would have figured it out sooner or later. Better it should be sooner, don't you think?'

'We must see more of each other.'

'I'd like that, sir. Afraid I'm stuck here for a while, though.'

'We are travelling out of the country soon – the day after tomorrow. It's a state visit to New Zealand and the Solomon Islands. You may be gone before we get back.'

'Is your wife up to it, Your Highness?'

'I think so. A change of scenery, the doctor said, is just the ticket. She had a very bad experience yesterday, but' – he smiled – 'I think it was harder on me than on her.'

I'll buy that, Ryan thought. *She's young, she'll bounce back, and at least she has something good to remember. Putting your body between your family and the bullets ought to firm up any relationship.* 'Hey, she sure as hell knows you love her, sir.'

'I do, you know,' the Prince said seriously.

'It's the customary reason to get married, sir,' Jack replied, 'even for us common folk.'

'You're a most irreverent chap, Jack.'

'Sorry about that.' Ryan grinned. So did the Prince.

'No, you're not.' His Highness extended his hand. 'Thank you, Sir John, for many things.'

Ryan watched him leave with a brisk step and a straight back.

'Tony, you know the difference between him and me? I can say that I used to be a Marine, and that's enough. But that poor guy's got to prove it every damned day, to everybody he meets. I guess that's what you have to do when you're in the public eye all the time.' Jack shook his head. 'There's no way in hell they could pay me enough to take his job.'

'He's born to it,' Wilson said.

Ryan thought about that. 'That's one difference between your country and mine. You think people are born to something. We know that they have to grow into it. It's not the same thing, Tony.'

'Well, you're part of it now, Jack.'

'I think I should go. ' David Ashley looked at the telex in his hand. The disturbing thing was that he'd been requested by name. The Provisional IRA knew who he was, and they knew that he was the Security Service executive on the case. *How the hell did they know* that!

'I agree,' James Owens said. 'If they're this anxious to talk with us, they might be anxious enough to tell us something useful. Of course, there is an element of risk. You could take someone with you.'

Ashley thought about that one. There was always the chance that he'd be kidnapped, but . . . The strange thing about the Provisional IRA was that they did have a code of conduct. Within their own definitions, they were honourable. They assassinated their targets without remorse, but they wouldn't deal in drugs. Their bombs would kill children, but they'd never kidnapped one. Ashley shook his head.

'No, people from the Service have met with them before and there's never been a problem. I'll go alone.' He turned for the door.

'Daddy!' Sally ran into the room and stopped cold at the side of the bed as she tried to figure a way to climb high enough to kiss her father. She grabbed the side rails and set one foot on the bedframe as if it were the monkey bars at her nursery school and sprang upwards. Her diminutive frame bent over the edge of the mattress as she scrambled for a new foothold, and Ryan pulled her up.

'Hi, Daddy.' Sally kissed him on the cheek.

'And how are you today?'

'Fine. What's that, Daddy?' She pointed.

'It's called a cast,' Cathy Ryan answered. 'I thought you had to go to the bathroom.'

'Okay.' Sally jumped back off the bed.

'I think it's in there,' Jack said. 'But I'm not sure.'

'I thought so,' Cathy said after surveying Jack's attachment to the bed. 'Okay, come on, Sally.'

A man had entered behind his family, Ryan saw. Late twenties, very athletic, and nicely dressed, of course. He was also rather good-looking, Jack reflected.

'Good afternoon, Doctor Ryan,' he said. 'I'm William Greville.'

Jack made a guess. 'What regiment?'

'Twenty-second, sir.'

'Special Air Service?' Greville nodded, a proud but restrained smile on his lips.

'When you care enough to send the very best,' Jack muttered. 'Just you?'

'And a driver, Sergeant Michaelson, a policeman from the Diplomatic Protection Group.'

'Why you and not another cop?'

'I understand your wife wishes to see a bit of the countryside. My father is something of an authority on various castles, and Her Majesty thought that your wife might wish to have an, ah, escort familiar with the sights. Father has dragged me through nearly every old house in England, you see.'

'Escort' is the right word, Ryan thought, remembering what the 'Special Air Service' really was. The only association they had with airplanes was jumping out of them – or blowing them up.

Greville went on. 'I am also directed by my colonel to extend an invitation to our regimental mess.'

Ryan gestured at his suspended arm. 'Thanks, but that might have to wait a while.'

'We understand. No matter, sir. Whenever you have the chance, we'll be delighted to have you in for dinner. We wanted to extend the invitation before the bootnecks, you see.' Greville grinned. 'What you did was more our sort of op, after all. Well, I had to extend the invitation. You want to see your family, not me.'

'Take good care of them . . . Lieutenant?'

'Captain,' Greville corrected. 'We will do that, sir.' Ryan watched the young officer leave as Cathy and Sally emerged from the bathroom.

'What do you think of him?' Cathy asked.

'His daddy's a count, Daddy!' Sally announced. 'He's nice.'

'What?'

'His father's Viscount-something-or-other,' his wife explained as she walked over. 'You look a lot better.'

'So do you, babe.' Jack craned his neck up to meet his wife's kiss.

'Jack, you've been smoking.' Even before they'd gotten married, Cathy had bullied him into stopping.

Her damned sense of smell, Jack thought. 'Be nice, I've had a hard day.'

'Wimp!' she observed disgustedly.

Ryan looked up at the ceiling. *To the whole world I'm a hero, but I smoke a couple of cigarettes and to Cathy that makes me a wimp.* He concluded that the world was not exactly overrun with justice.

'Gimme a break, babe.'

'Where'd you get them?'

'I have a cop babysitting me in here – he had to go someplace a few minutes ago.'

Cathy looked around for the offending cigarette pack so that she could squash it. Jack had it stashed under his pillow. Cathy Ryan sat down. Sally climbed into her lap.

'How do you feel?'

'I know it's there, but I can live with it. How'd you make out last night?'

'You know where we are now, right?'

'I heard.'

'It's like being Cinderella.' Caroline Muller Ryan, MD, grinned.

John Patrick Ryan, PhD, wiggled the fingers of his left hand. 'I guess I'm the one who turned into the pumpkin. I guess you're going to make the trips we planned. Good.'

'Sure you don't mind?'

'Half the reason for the vacation was to get you away from hospitals, Cathy, remember? No sense taking all the film home unused, is it?'

'It'd be a lot more fun with you.'

Jack nodded. He'd looked forward to seeing the castles on the list, too. Like many Americans, Ryan could not have abided the English class system, but that didn't stop him from being fascinated with its trappings. *Or something like that*, he thought. His knighthood, he knew, might change that perspective if he allowed himself to dwell on it.

'Look on the bright side, babe. You've got a guide who can tell you every-thing you ever wanted to know about Lord Jones's castle on the coast of whatever. You'll have plenty of time for it, too.'

'Yeah,' she said, 'the police said we'd be staying over a while longer than we planned. I'll have to talk to Professor Lewindowski about that.' She shrugged. 'They'll understand.'

'How do you like the new place? Better than the hotel?'

'You're going to have to see – no, you'll have to *experience* it.' She laughed. 'I think hospitality is the national sport over here. They must teach it in the schools, and have quarterly exams. And guess who we're having dinner with tonight?'

'I don't have to guess.'

'Jack, they're so *nice*.'

'I noticed. Looks like you're really getting the VIP treatment.'

'What's the Special Air Service – he's some kind of pilot?'

'Something like that,' Jack said diffidently. Cathy might feel uncomfortable sitting next to a man who had to be carrying a gun. And was trained to use it with as little compunction as a wolf might use his teeth. 'You're not asking how I feel.'

'I got hold of your chart on the way in,' Cathy explained.

'And?'

'You're doing okay, Jack. I see you can move your fingers. I was worried about that.'

'How come?'

'The brachial plexus – it's a nerve junction inside your shoulder. The bullet missed it by about an inch and a half. That's why you can move your fingers. The way you were bleeding, I thought the brachial artery was cut, and that runs right next to the nerves. It would have put your arm out of business for good. But' – she smiled – 'you lucked out. Just broken bones. They hurt but they heal.'

Doctors are so wonderfully objective, Ryan told himself, even the ones you marry. *Next thing, she'll say the pain is good for me.*

'Nice thing about pain,' Cathy went on. 'It tells you the nerves are working.'

Jack closed his eyes and shook his head. He opened them when he felt Cathy take his hand.

'Jack, I'm so proud of you.'

'Nice to be married to a hero?'

'You've always been a hero to me.'

'Really?' She'd never said *that* before. What was heroic about being an historian? Cathy didn't know the other stuff he did, but that wasn't especially heroic either.

'Ever since you told Daddy to – well, you know. Besides, I love you, remember?'

'I seem to recall a reminder of that the other day.'

Cathy made a face. 'Better get your mind off that for a while.'

'I know.' Ryan made a face of his own. 'The patient must conserve his energy – or something. Whatever happened to that theory about how a happy attitude speeds recovery?'

'That's what I get for letting you read my journals. Patience, Jack.'

Nurse Kittiwake came in, saw the family, and made a quick exit.

'I'll try to be patient,' Jack said, and looked longingly at the closing door.

'You turkey,' Cathy observed. 'I know you better than that.'

She did, Jack knew. He couldn't even make that threat work. *Oh, well – that's what you get for loving your wife.*

Cathy stroked his face. 'What did you shave with this morning, a rusty nail?'

'Yeah – I need my razor. Maybe my notes, too?'

'I'll bring them over or have somebody do it.' She looked up when Wilson came back in.

'Tony, this is Cathy, my wife, and Sally, my daughter. Cathy, this is Tony Wilson. He's the cop who's babysitting me.'

'Didn't I see you last night?' Cathy never forgot a face – so far as Jack could tell, she never forgot much of anything.

'Possibly, but we didn't speak – rather a busy time for all of us. You are well, Lady Ryan?'

'Excuse me?' Cathy asked. 'Lady Ryan?'

'They didn't tell you?' Jack chuckled.

'Tell me what?'

Jack explained. 'How do you like being married to a knight?'

'Does that mean you have to have a horse, Daddy?' Sally asked hopefully. 'Can I ride it?'

'Is it legal, Jack?'

'They told me that the Prime Minister and the President would discuss it today.'

'My God,' Lady Ryan said quietly. After a moment, she started smiling.

'Stick with me, kid.' Jack laughed.

'What about the horse, Daddy!' Sally insisted.

'I don't know yet. We'll see.' He yawned. The only practical use Ryan acknowledged for horses was running at tracks – or maybe tax shelters. *Well, I already have a sword*, he told himself.

'I think Daddy needs a nap,' Cathy observed. 'And I have to buy something for dinner tonight.'

'Oh, God!' Ryan groaned. 'A whole new wardrobe.'

Cathy grinned. 'Whose fault is that, Sir John?'

They met at Flanagan's Steakhouse on O'Connell Street in Dublin. It was a well-regarded establishment whose tourist trade occasionally suffered from being too close to a McDonald's. Ashley was nursing a whiskey when the second man joined him. A third and fourth took a booth across the room and watched. Ashley had come alone. This wasn't the first such meeting, and Dublin was recognized – most of the time – as neutral ground. The two men on the other side of the room were to keep a watch for members of the Garda, the Republic's police force.

'Welcome to Dublin, Mr Ashley,' said the representative of the Provisional Wing of the Irish Republican Army.

'Thank you, Mr Murphy,' the counterintelligence officer answered. 'The photograph we have on file doesn't do you justice.'

'Young and foolish, I was. And very vain. I didn't shave very much then,' Murphy explained. He picked up the menu that had been waiting for him. 'The beef here is excellent, and the vegetables are always fresh. This place is full of bloody tourists in the summer – those who don't want chips – driving prices up as they always do. Thank God they're all back home in America now, leaving so much money behind in this poor country.'

'What information do you have for us?'

'Information?'

'You asked for the meeting, Mr Murphy,' Ashley pointed out.

'The purpose of the meeting is to assure you that we had no part in that bloody fiasco yesterday.'

'I could have read that in the papers – I did, in fact.'

'It was felt that a more personal communiqué was in order, Mr Ashley.'

'Why should we believe you?' Ashley asked, sipping at his whiskey. Both men kept their voices low and level, though neither man had the slightest doubt as to what they thought of each other.

'Because we are not as crazy as that,' Murphy replied. The waiter came, and both men ordered. Ashley chose the wine, a promising Bordeaux. The meal was on his expense account. He was only forty minutes off the flight from London's Gatwick airport. The request for a meeting had been made before dawn in a telephone call to the British Ambassador in Dublin.

'Is that a fact?' Ashley said after the waiter left, staring into the cold blue eyes across the table.

'The Royal Family are strictly off limits. As marvellous a political target as they all are' – Murphy smiled – 'we've known for some time that an attack on them would be counterproductive.'

'Really?' Ashley pronounced the word as only an Englishman can do it. Murphy flushed angrily at this most elegant of insults.

'Mr Ashley, we are enemies. I would as soon kill you as have dinner with you. But even enemies can negotiate, can't they, now?'

'Go on.'

'We had no part of it. You have my word.'

'Your word as a Marxist-Leninist?' Ashley inquired with a smile.

'You are very good at provoking people, Mr Ashley.' Murphy ventured his own smile. 'But not today. I am here on a mission of peace and understanding.'

Ashley nearly laughed out loud, but caught himself and grinned into his drink.

'Mr Murphy, I would not shed a single tear if our lads were to catch up with you, but you are a worthy adversary, I'll say that. And a charming bastard.'

Ah, the English sense of fair play, Murphy reflected. *That's why we'll win eventually, Mr Ashley.*

No, you won't. Ashley had seen that look before.

'How can I make you believe me?' Murphy asked reasonably.

'Names and addresses,' Ashley answered quietly.

'No. We can't do that and you know it.'

'If you wish to establish some sort of quid pro quo, that's how you must go about it.'

Murphy sighed. 'Surely you know how we are organized. Do you think we can punch out a bloody computer command and print out our roster? We're not even sure ourselves who they are. Some men, they just drop out. Many come south and simply vanish, more afraid of us than of you, they are – and with reason,' Murphy added. 'The one you have alive, Sean Miller – we've never even heard the name.'

'And Kevin O'Donnell?'

'Yes, he's probably the leader. He dropped off the earth four years ago, as you well know, after – ah, you know the story as well as I.'

Kevin Joseph O'Donnell, Ashley reminded himself. *Thirty-four now. Six feet, one hundred and sixty pounds, unmarried – this data was old and therefore suspect. The all-time Provo champion at 'own-goals.' Kevin had been the most ruthless chief of security the Provos had ever had, thrown out after it had been proven that he'd used his power as counterintelligence boss to purge the Organization of political elements he disapproved of. What was the figure – ten, fifteen, solid members that he'd had killed or maimed before the Brigade Commander'd found him out? The amazing thing,* Ashley thought, *was that he'd escaped alive at all.* But Murphy was wrong on one thing. Ashley didn't know what had finally tipped the Brigade that O'Donnell was an outlaw.

'I fail to see why you feel the urge to protect him and his group.' He knew the reason, but why not prod the man when he had the chance?

'And if we turn "grass," what becomes of the Organization?' Murphy asked.

'Not my problem, Mr Murphy, but I do see your point. Still and all, if you want us to believe you –'

'Mr Ashley, you demonstrate the basis of the entire problem we have, don't you? Had your country ever dealt with Ireland in mutual good faith, surely we would not be here now, would we?'

The intelligence officer reflected on that. It took no more than a couple of seconds, so many times had he examined the historical basis of the Troubles. Some deliberate policy acts, mixed with historical accidents – who could have known that the onset of the crisis that erupted into World War I would prevent a solution to the issue of 'Home [or "Rome"] Rule,' that the Conservative Party of the time would use this issue as a hammer that would eventually crush the Liberal Party – and who was there to blame now? They were all dead and forgotten, except by hard-core academics who knew that their studies mattered for nothing. It was far too late for that. *Is there a way out of this bloody quagmire?* he wondered. Ashley shook his head. That was not his brief. That was something for politicians. The same sort, he reminded himself, who'd built the Troubles, one small brick at a time.

'I'll tell you this much, Mr Ashley –' The waiter showed up with dinner. It was amazing how quick the service was here. The waiter uncorked the wine with a flourish, allowing Ashley to smell the cork and sample a splash in his glass. The Englishman was surprised at the quality of the restaurant's cellar.

'This much you will tell me . . .' Ashley said after the waiter left.

'They get very good information. So good, you wouldn't believe it. And their information comes from your side of the Irish Sea, Mr Ashley. We don't know who, and we don't know how. The lad who found out died, four years ago, you see.' Murphy sampled the broccoli. 'There, I told you the vegetables were fresh.'

'Four years?'

Murphy looked up. 'You don't know the story, then? That is a surprise, Mr Ashley. Yes. His name was Mickey Baird. He worked closely with Kevin. He's the lad who – well, you can guess. He was talking with me over a jar in Derry and said that Kevin had a bloody good new intelligence source. Next day he was dead. The day after, Kevin managed to escape us by an hour. We haven't seen him since. If we find Kevin again, Mr Ashley, we'll do your work for you, and leave the body for your SAS assassins to collect. Would that be fair enough, now? We can't exactly tout to the enemy, but he's on our list, too, and if you manage to find the lad, and you don't wish to bring him in yourselves, we'll handle the job for you – assuming, of course, that you don't interfere with the lads who do the work. Can we agree on that?'

'I'll pass that along,' Ashley said. 'If I could approve it myself, I would. Mr Murphy, I think we can believe you on this.'

'Thank you, Mr Ashley. That wasn't so painful, was it?' Dinner was excellent.

4

Players

Ryan tried to blink away the blue dots that swirled around his eyes as the television crews set up their own lights. Why the newspaper photographers couldn't wait for the powerful TV lights, he didn't know, and didn't bother asking. Everyone was kind enough to ask how he felt – but nothing short of respiratory arrest would have gotten them out of the room in any case.

It could have been worse, of course. Dr Scott had told the newspeople rather forcefully that his patient needed rest to recover speedily, and Nurse Kittiwake was there to glower at the intruders. So press access to Ryan was being limited to no more than the number of people who would fit into his room. This included the TV crew. It was the best sort of bargain Jack could get. The cameramen and sound technicians took up space that would otherwise be occupied by more inquisitorial reporters.

The morning papers – Ryan had been through the *Times* and the *Daily Telegraph* – had carried reports that Ryan was a former (or current) employee of the Central Intelligence Agency, something that was technically not true, and that Jack had not expected to become public in any case. He found himself remembering what the people at Langley said about leaks, and how pleased they'd been with his offhand invention of the Canary Trap. *A pity they couldn't use it in my case*, Ryan told himself wryly. *I really need this complication to my life, don't I? For crying out loud, I turned their offer* down. *Sort of.*

'All ready here,' the lighting technician said. A moment later he proved this was true by turning on the three klieg lights that brought tears to Jack's squinted eyes.

'They are awfully bright, aren't they?' a reporter sympathized, while the still photographers continued to snap-and-whir away with their strobe-equipped Nikons.

'You might say that,' Jack replied. A two-headed mike was clipped to his robe.

'Say something, will you?' the sound man asked.

'And how are you enjoying your first trip to London, Doctor Ryan?'

'Well, I better not hear any complaints about how American tourists are staying away due to panic over the terrorism problem!' Ryan grinned. *You jerk.*

'Indeed,' the reporter laughed. 'Okay?'

The cameraman and sound man pronounced themselves ready.

Ryan sipped at his tea and made certain that the ashtray was out of sight. One print journalist shared a joke with a colleague. A TV correspondent from NBC was there, along with the London correspondent of the *Washington Post*, but all the others were British. Everything would be pooled with the rest of the media, it had been agreed. There just wasn't room here for a proper press conference. The camera started rolling tape.

They ran through the usual questions. The camera turned to linger on his arm, hanging from its overhead rack. They'd run that shot with the voice-over of Jack's story on when he was shot, he was sure. Nothing like a little drama, as he'd already been told. He wiggled his fingers for the camera.

'Doctor Ryan, there are reports in the American and British press that you are an employee of the Central Intelligence Agency.'

'I read that this morning. It was as much a surprise to me as it was to anyone else.' Ryan smiled. 'Somebody made a mistake. I'm not good-looking enough to be a spy.'

'So you deny that report?' asked the *Daily Mirror*.

'Correct. It's just not true. I teach history at the Naval Academy, in Annapolis. That ought to be easy enough to check out. I just gave an exam last week. You can ask my students.' Jack waved his left hand at the camera again.

'The report comes from some highly placed sources,' observed the *Post*.

'If you read a little history, you'll see that highly placed folks have been known to make mistakes. I think that's what happened here. I teach. I write books. I lecture – okay, I did give a lecture at CIA once, but that was just a repeat of one I delivered at the Naval War College and one other symposium. It wasn't even classified. Maybe that's where the report comes from. Like I said, check it out. My office is in Leahy Hall, at the Naval Academy. I think somebody just goofed.' *Somebody goofed, all right.* 'I can get you guys a copy of the lecture. It's no big deal.'

'How do you like being a public figure, now?' one of the Brit TV people asked.

Thanks for changing the subject. 'I think I can live without it. I'm not a movie star, either – again, not good-looking enough.'

'You're far too modest, Doctor Ryan,' a female reporter observed.

'Please be careful how you say that. My wife will probably see this.' There was general laughter. 'I suppose I'm good-looking enough for her. That's enough. With all due respect, ladies and gentlemen, I'll be perfectly glad to descend back into obscurity.'

'Do you think that likely?'

'That depends on how lucky I am, ma'am. And on whether you folks will let me.'

'What do you think we should do with the terrorist, Sean Miller?' the *Times* asked.

'That's for a judge and jury to decide. You don't need me for that.'

'Do you think we should have capital punishment?'

'We have it where I live. For your country, that ,is a question for your elected representatives. We both live in democracies, don't we? The people you elect are supposed to do what the voters ask them to do.' *Not that it always works that way, but that's the theory. . . .*

'So you support the idea?' the *Times* persisted.

'In appropriate cases, subject to strict judicial review, yes. Now you're going to ask me about this case, right? It's a moot point. Anyway, I'm no expert on criminal justice. My dad was a cop but I'm just a historian.'

'And what of your perspective, as an Irish-American, on the Troubles?' the *Telegraph* wanted to know.

'We have enough problems of our own in America without having to borrow yours.'

'So you say we should solve it, then?'

'What do you think? Isn't that what problems are for?'

'Surely you have a suggestion. Most Americans do.'

'I think I teach history. I'll let other people make it. It's like being a reporter.' Ryan smiled. 'I get to criticize people long after they make their decisions. That doesn't mean I know what to do today.'

'But you knew what to do on Tuesday,' the *Times* pointed out. Ryan shrugged.

'Yeah, I guess I did,' Ryan said on the television screen.

'You clever bastard,' Kevin Joseph O'Donnell muttered into a glass of Guinness. His base of operations was much farther from the border than any might have suspected. Ireland is a small country, and distances are but relative things – particularly to those with all the resources they need. His former colleagues in the Provisional IRA had extensive safehouses along the border, convenient to a quick trip across from either direction. Not for O'Donnell. There were numerous practical reasons. The Brits had their informers and intelligence people there, always creeping about – and the SAS raiders, who were not averse to a quick snatch – or a quiet kill – of persons who had made the mistake of becoming too well known. The border could be a convenience to either side. A more serious threat was the Provisional IRA itself, which also watched the border closely. His face, altered as it was with some minor surgery and a change in hair colour, might still be recognizable to a former colleague. But not here. And the border wasn't all that far a drive in a country barely three hundred miles long.

He turned away from the television and gazed out the leaded-glass windows to the darkness of the sea. He saw the running lights of a car ferry inbound from Le Havre. The view was always a fine one. Even in the limited visibility of an ocean storm, one could savour the fundamental force of nature as the grey waves battered the rocky cliff. Now, the clear, cold air gave him a view to the star-defined horizon, and he spied another merchant ship heading eastwards for an unknown port. It pleased O'Donnell that this stately house on the headlands had once belonged to a British lord. It pleased him more that he'd been able to purchase it through a dummy corporation; that there were few questions when cash and a reputable solicitor were involved. So vulnerable this society – all societies were when you had the proper resources . . . and a competent tailor. So shallow they were. So lacking in political awareness. *One must know who one's enemies are*, O'Donnell told himself at least ten times every day. Not a liberal 'democratic' society, though. Enemies were people to be dealt with, compromised with, to be civilized, brought into the fold, co-opted.

Fools, self-destructive, ignorant fools who earned their own destruction.

Someday they would all disappear, just as one of those ships slid beneath the horizon. History was a science, an inevitable process. O'Donnell was sure of that.

He turned again to stare into the fire burning under the wide, stone mantel. There had once been stag heads hanging over it, perhaps the lord's favourite fowling piece – from Purdey's, to be sure. And a painting or two. Of horses, O'Donnell was sure – they had to be paintings of horses. The country gentleman who had built this house, he mused, would have been someone who'd been given everything he had. No ideology would have intruded in his empty, useless head. He would have sat in a chair very like this one and sipped his malt whiskey and stared into the fire – his favourite dog at his feet – while he chatted about the day's hunting with a neighbour and planned the hunting for the morrow. *Will it be birds again, or fox, Bertie? Haven't had a good fox hunt in weeks, time we did it again, don't you think?* Or something like that, he was sure. O'Donnell wondered if there was a seasonal aspect to it, or had the lord just done whatever suited his mood. The current owner of the country house never hunted animals. What was the point of killing something that could not harm you or your cause, something that had no ideology? Besides, that was something the Brits did, something the local gentry still did. He didn't hunt the local Irish gentry, they weren't worth his contempt, much less his action. At least, not yet. *You don't hate trees*, he told himself. *You ignore the things until you have to cut them down.* He turned back to the television.

That Ryan fellow was still there, he saw, talking amiably with the press idiots. Bloody hero. *Why did you stick your nose in where it doesn't belong?* Reflex, sounds like, O'Donnell judged. *Bloody meddling fool. Don't even know what's going on, do you? None of you do.*

Americans. The Provo fools still like to talk it up with your kind, telling their lies and pretending that they represent Ireland. What do you Yanks know about anything? *Oh, but we can't afford to offend the Americans*, the Provos still said. Bloody Americans, with all their money and all their arrogance, all their ideas on right and wrong, their childish vision of Irish destiny. Like children dressed up for First Communion. So pure. So naive. So useless with their trickle of money – for all that the Brits complained about NORAID, O'Donnell knew that the Provisional IRA had not netted a million dollars from America in the past three years. All the Americans knew of Ireland came from a few movies, some half-remembered songs for St Paddy's Day, and the occasional bottle of whiskey. What did they know of life in Ulster, of the imperialist oppression, the way all Ireland was still enslaved to the decaying British Empire, which was, in turn, enslaved to the American one? What did they know about anything? *But we can't offend the Americans.* The leader of the ULA finished off his beer and set it on the end table.

The Cause didn't require much, not really. A clear ideological objective. A few good men. Friends, the right friends, with access to the right resources. That was all. Why clutter things up with bloody Americans? And a public political wing – Sinn Fein electing people to Parliament, what rubbish! They were waiting, *hoping* to be co-opted by the Brit imperialists. Valuable political targets declared off-limits. And people wondered why the Provos were getting nowhere. Their ideology was bankrupt, and there were too many people in the Brigade. When the Brits caught some, a few were bound to turn tout and inform on their comrades. The kind of commitment needed for this sort of job demanded an elite few. O'Donnell had that, all right. *And you need to have the right plan*, he told himself with a wispy smile. O'Donnell had his plan. This Ryan fellow hadn't changed that, he reminded himself.

'Bastard's bloody pleased with himself, isn't he?'

O'Donnell turned to see a fresh bottle of Guinness offered. He took it and refilled his glass. 'Sean should have watched his back. Then this bloody hero would be a corpse.' *And the mission would have been successful. Damn!*

'We can still do something about that.'

O'Donnell shook his head. 'We don't waste our energy on the insignificant. The Provos have been doing that for ten years and look where it has got them.'

'What if he is CIA? What if we've been infiltrated and he was there –'

'Don't be a bloody fool,' O'Donnell snapped. 'If they'd been tipped, every peeler in London would have been there in plain clothes waiting for us.' *And I would have known beforehand*, he didn't say. Only one other member of the Organization knew of his source, and he was in London. 'It was luck, good for them, bad for us. Just luck. We were lucky in your case, weren't we, Michael?' Like any Irishman he still believed in luck. Ideology would never change that.

The younger man thought of his eighteen months in the H-Blocks at Long Kesh prison, and was silent. O'Donnell shrugged at the television as the news programme changed to another story. Luck. That was all. Some monied Yank with too long a nose who'd been very lucky. Any random event, like a punctured tyre, a defective radio battery, or a sudden rainstorm, could have made the operation fail, too. And his advantage over the other side was that they had to be lucky all the time. O'Donnell only had to be lucky once. He considered what he had just seen on the television and decided that Ryan wasn't worth the effort.

Mustn't offend the Americans, he thought to himself again, this time with surprise. *Why? Aren't they the enemy, too? Kevin, me boy, now you're thinking like those idiots in the Provisional IRA. Patience is the most important quality in the true revolutionary. One must wait for the proper moment – and then strike decisively.*

He waited for his next intelligence report.

The rare book shop was in the Burlington Arcade, the century-old promenade of shops off the most fashionable part of Piccadilly. It was sandwiched between one of London's custom tailors – this one catered mainly to the tourists who used the arcade to shelter from the elements – and a jeweller. It had the sort of smell that draws bibliophiles as surely as the scent of nectar draws a bee, the musty, dusty odour of dried-out paper and leather binding. The shop's owner-operator was contrastingly young, dressed in a suit whose shoulders were sprinkled with dust. He started every day by running a feather duster over the shelves, and the books were ever exuding new quantities of it. He had grown to like it. The store had an ambience that he dearly loved. The store did a small but lucrative volume of business, depending less on tourists than on a discreet number of regular customers from the upper reaches of London society. The owner, a Mr Dennis Cooley, travelled a great deal, often flying out on short notice to participate in an auction of some deceased gentleman's library, leaving the shop to the custody of a young lady who would have been quite pretty if she'd worked at it a little harder. Beatrix was off today.

Mr Cooley had an ancient teak desk in keeping with the rest of the shop's motif, and even a cushionless swivel chair to prove to the customers that nothing in the shop was modern. Even the bookkeeping was done by hand. No electronic calculators here. A battered ledger book dating back to the 1930s listed thousands of sales, and the shop's book catalogue was made of simple filing cards in small wooden boxes, one set listing books by title, and another by author. All writing was done with a gold-nibbed fountain pen. A no-smoking sign was the only modern touch. The smell of tobacco might have ruined the shop's unique aroma. The store's stationery bore the 'by appointment to' crests of four Royal Family members. The arcade was but a ten-minute uphill walk from Buckingham Palace. The glass door had a hundred-year-old silver bell hanging on the top of the frame. It rang.

'Good morning, Mr Cooley.'

'And to you, sir,' Dennis answered one of his regulars as he stood. He had an accent so neutral that his customers had him pegged as a native of three different regions. 'I have the first-edition Defoe. The one you called about earlier this week. Just came in yesterday.'

'Is this the one from that collection in Cork you spoke about?'

'No, sir. I believe it's originally from the estate of Sir John Claggett, near Swaffham Prior. I found it at Hawstead's in Cambridge.'

'A first edition?'

'Most certainly, sir.' The book dealer did not react noticeably. The code phrase was both constant and changing. Cooley made frequent trips to Ireland, both north and south, to purchase books from the estates of deceased collectors or from dealers in the country. When the customer mentioned any county in the Irish Republic, he indicated the destination for his information. When he questioned the edition of the book, he also indicated its importance.

Cooley pulled the book off the shelf and set it on his desk. The customer opened it with care, running his finger down the title page.

'In an age of paperbacks and half-bound books. . .'

'Indeed.' Cooley nodded. Both men's love for the art of bookbinding was genuine. Any good cover becomes more real than its builders expect. 'The leather is in remarkable shape.' His visitor grunted agreement.

'I must have it. How much?'

The dealer didn't answer. Instead Cooley removed the card from the box and handed it to his customer. He gave the card only a cursory look.

'Done.' The customer sat down in the store's only other chair and opened his briefcase. 'I have another job for you. This is an early copy of *The Vicar of Wakefield*. I found it last month in a little shop in Cornwall.' He handed the book over. Cooley needed only a single look at its condition.

'Scandalous.'

'Can your chap restore it?'

'I don't know. . .' The leather was cracked, some of the pages had been dog-eared, and the binding was frayed almost to nonexistence.

'I'm afraid the attic in which they found it had a leaky roof,' the customer said casually.

'Oh?' *Is the information that important?* Cooley looked up. 'A tragic waste.'

'How else can you explain it?' The man shrugged.

'I'll see what I can do. He's not a miracle worker, you know.' *Is it that important?*

'I understand. Still, the best you can arrange.' *Yes, it's that important.*

'Of course, sir.' Cooley opened his desk drawer and withdrew the cashbox.

This customer always paid cash. Of course. He removed the wallet from his suit coat and counted out the fifty-pound notes. Cooley checked the amount, then placed the book in a stout cardboard box, which he tied with string. No plastic bags for this shop. Seller and buyer shook hands. The transfer was complete. The customer walked south towards Piccadilly, then turned right, heading west towards Green Park and downhill to the Palace.

Cooley took the envelope that had been hidden in the book and tucked it away in a drawer. He finished making his ledger entry, then called his travel agent to book a flight to Cork, where he would meet a fellow dealer in rare books and have lunch at the Old Bridge restaurant before catching a flight home. Beatrix would have to manage the shop tomorrow. It did not occur to him to open the envelope. That was not his job. The less he knew, the less he was vulnerable if he were caught. Cooley had been trained by professionals, and the first rule pounded into his head had been *need-to-know*. He ran the intelligence operation, and he needed to know how to do that. He didn't always need to know what specific information he gathered.

414

'Hello, Doctor Ryan.' It was an American voice, with a South Bay Boston accent that Jack remembered from his college days. It sounded good. The man was in his forties, a wiry, athletic frame, with thinning black hair. He had a flower box tucked under his arm. Whoever he was, the cop outside had opened the door for him.

'Howdy. Who might you be?'

'Dan Murray. I'm the Legal Attaché at the embassy. FBI,' he explained. 'Sorry I couldn't get down sooner, but things have been a little busy.' Murray showed his ID to the cop sitting in with Ryan – Tony Wilson was off duty. The cop excused himself. Murray took his seat.

'Lookin' good, ace.'

'You could have left the flowers at the main desk.' Ryan gestured around the room. Despite all his efforts to spread the flowers about, he could barely see the walls for all the roses.

'Yeah, I figured that. How's the grub?'

'Hospital food is hospital food.'

'Figure that, too.' Murray removed the red ribbon and opened the box. 'How does a Whopper and fries grab you? You have a choice of vanilla or chocolate shakes.'

Jack laughed – and grabbed.

'I've been over here three years,' Murray said. 'Every so often I have to hit the fast-food joints to remind myself where I come from. You can get tired of lamb. The local beer's pretty good, though. I'd have brought a few of those but – well, you know.'

'You just made a friend for life, Mr Murray, even without the beer.'

'Dan.'

'Jack.' Ryan was tempted to wolf down the burger for fear of having a nurse come through the door and throw an immediate institutional fit. *No*, he decided, *I'll enjoy this one*. He selected the vanilla shake. 'The local guys say you broke records identifying me.'

'No big deal.' Murray poked a straw into the chocolate one. 'By the way, I bring you greetings from the Ambassador – he wanted to come over, but they have a big-time party for later tonight. And my friends down the hall send their regards, too.'

'Who down the hall?'

'The people you have never worked for.' The FBI agent raised his eyebrows.

'Oh.' Jack swallowed a few fries. 'Who the hell broke that story?'

'Washington. Some reporter was having lunch with somebody's aide – doesn't really matter whose, does it? They all talk too much. Evidently he remembered your name in the back of the final report and couldn't keep his trap shut. Apologies from Langley, they told me to tell you. I saw the TV stuff. You dodged that pretty good.'

'I told the truth – barely. All my checks came through Mitre Corporation. Some sort of bookkeeping thing, and Mitre had the consulting contract.'

'I understand all your time was at Langley, though.'

'Yeah, a little cubbyhole on the third floor with a desk, a computer terminal, and a scratchpad. Ever been there?'

Murray smiled. 'Once or twice. I'm in the terrorism business, too. The Bureau has a much nicer decorator. Helps to have a PR department, don't you know?' Murray affected a caricatured London accent. 'I saw a copy of the report. Nice work. How much of it did you do?'

'Most. It wasn't all that hard. I just came up with a new angle to look at it from.'

'It's been passed along to the Brits – I mean, it came over here two months ago for the Secret Intelligence Service. I understand they liked it.'

'So their cops know.'

'I'm not sure – well, you can probably assume they do now. Owens is cleared all the way on this stuff.'

'And so's Ashley.'

'He's a little on the snotty side, but he's damned smart. He's "Five. " '

'What?' Ryan didn't know that one.

'He's in MI-5, the Security Service. We just call it Five. Has a nice insider feel that way.' Murray chuckled.

'I figured him for something like that. The other two started as street cops. It shows.'

'It struck a few people as slightly curious – the guy who wrote *Agents and Agencies* gets stuck in the middle of a terrorist op. That's why Ashley showed up.' Murray shook his head. 'You wouldn't believe all the coincidences you run into in my business. Like you and me.'

'I know you come from New England – oh, don't tell me. Boston College?'

'Hey, I always wanted to be an FBI agent. It was either BC or Holy Cross, right?' Murray grinned. That in-house FBI joke went back two generations, and was not without a few grains of truth. Ryan leaned back and sucked the shake up the straw. It tasted wonderful.

'How much do we know about these ULA guys?' Jack asked. 'I never saw very much at Langley.'

'Not a hell of a lot. The boss-man's a chap named Kevin O'Donnell. He used to be in the Provisional IRA. He started throwing rocks in the streets and supposedly worked his way up to head counterintelligence man. The Provos are pretty good at that. Have to be. The Brits are always working to infiltrate the Organization. The word is that he got a little carried away cleansing the ranks, and barely managed to skip out before they gave him Excedrin Headache number three-five-seven. Just plain disappeared and hasn't been spotted since. A few sketchy reports, like maybe he spent some time in Libya, like maybe he's back in Ulster with a new face, like maybe he has a lot of money – want to guess where from? – to throw around. All we know for sure is that he's one malignant son of a bitch.

'His organization?' Murray set the milk shake down. 'It's gotta be small, probably less than thirty. We think he had part of the breakout from Long Kesh last summer. Eleven hard-core Provos got out. The RUC bagged one of 'em two days later and he said that six of the eleven went south, probably to Kevin's outfit. He was a little pissed by that. They were supposed to come back to the Provisional IRA fold, but somebody convinced them to try something different. Some very bad boys – they had a total of fifteen murders among them. The one you killed is the only one to show up since.'

'Are they that good?' Ryan asked.

'Hey, the Provisional IRA are the best terrorists in the world, unless you count those bastards in Lebanon, and those are mostly family groups. Hell of a way to describe them, isn't it? But they are the best. Well organized, well trained, and they *believe*, if you know what I mean. They really care about what they're doing. The level of commitment these characters have to the Cause is something you have to see to believe.'

'You've been in on it?'

'Some. I've been able to sit in on interrogations – the other side of the two-way mirror, I mean. One of these guys wouldn't talk – wouldn't even give 'em his name! – for a week. Just sat there like a sphinx. Hey, I've chased after bank robbers, kidnappers, mob guys, spies, you name it. These fellows are real pros – and that's the Provisional IRA, maybe five hundred real members, not even as big as a New York Mafia family, and the RUC – that's the Royal Ulster Constabulary, the local cops – is lucky to convict a handful in a year. They have a law of *omertà* up there that would impress the old-time Sicilians. But at least the cops have a handle on who the bastards are. The ULA – we got a couple of names, a few pictures, and that's it. It's almost like the Islamic Jihad bums. You only know them from what they do.'

What do they do?' Ryan asked.

'They seem to specialize in high-risk, high-profile operations. It took over a year to confirm that they exist at all; we thought they were a special-action group of the Provisional IRA. They're an anomaly within the terrorist community. They don't make press releases, they don't take public credit for what they do. They go for the big-time stuff and they cover their tracks like you wouldn't believe. It takes resources to do that. Somebody is bankrolling them in a pretty big way. They've been identified for nine jobs we're sure of, maybe two others. They've only had three operations go bad – quite a track record. They missed killing a judge in Londonderry because the RPG round was a dud – it still took his bodyguard out. They tried to hit a police barracks last February. Somebody saw them setting up and phoned in – but the bastards must have been monitoring the police radio. They skipped before the cavalry arrived. The cops found an eighty-two-millimetre mortar and a box of rounds – high-explosive and white phosphorus, to be exact. And you got in the way of the last one.

'These suckers are getting pretty bold,' Murray said. 'On the other hand, we got one now.'

'We?' Ryan said curiously. 'It's not our fight.'

'We're talking terrorists, Jack. Everybody wants them. We swap information back and forth with the Yard every day. Anyway, the guy they have in the can right now, they'll keep talking at him. They have a hook on this one. The ULA is an outcast outfit. He is going to be a pariah and he knows it. His colleagues from Provisional IRA and INLA won't circle wagons around him. He'll go to a maximum-security prison, probably to one on the Isle of Wight, populated with some real bad boys. Not all of them are political types, and the ordinary robbers and murderers will probably – well, it's funny how patriotic these guys are. Spies, for example, have about as much fun in the joint as child molesters. This guy went after the Royal Family, the one thing over here that everybody loves. We're talking some serious hard time with this kid. You think the guards are going to bust their ass looking out for his well-being? He's going to learn a whole new sport. It's called *survival*. After he has a taste of it, people will talk to him. Sooner or later that kid's going to have to decide just how committed he is. He just might break down a little. Some have. That's what we play for, anyway. The bad guys have the initiative, we have organization and procedures. If they make a mistake, give us an opportunity, we can act on it.'

Ryan nodded. 'Yeah, it's all intelligence.'

'That's right. Without the right information we're crippled. All we can do is plod along and hope for a break. But give us one solid fact and we'll bring the whole friggin' world down on 'em. It's like taking down a brick wall. The hard part's getting that first brick loose.'

'And where do they get their information?'

'They told me you tumbled to that,' Murray observed with a smile.

'I don't think it was a chance encounter. Somebody had to tip them. They hit a moving target making an unscheduled trip.'

'How the hell did you know that?' the agent demanded.

'Doesn't matter, does it? People talk. Who knew that they were coming in?'

'That is being looked at. The interesting thing is what they were coming in for. Of course, that could just be a coincidence. The Prince gets briefed on political and national security stuff, same as the Queen does. Something happened with the Irish situation, negotiations between London and Dublin. He was coming in for the briefing. All I can tell you.'

'Hey, if you checked me out, you know how I'm cleared,' Ryan sniffed.

Murray grinned. 'Nice try, ace. If you weren't cleared TS, I wouldn't have told you this much. We're not privy to it yet anyway. Like I said, it might just have been a coincidence, but you guessed right on the important part.

It was an unscheduled trip and somebody got the word out for the ambush. Only way it could have happened. You will consider that classified information, Doctor Ryan. It doesn't go past that door.' Murray was affable. He was also very serious about his job.

Jack nodded agreement. 'No problem. It was a kidnap, too, wasn't it?'

The FBI agent grimaced and shook his head. 'I've handled about a half-dozen kidnappings and closed every case with a conviction. We only lost one hostage – they killed that kid the first day. Those two were executed. I watched,' Murray said coldly. 'Kidnapping is a high-risk crime all the way down the line. They have to be at a specific place to get their money – that's usually what gets 'em caught. We can track people like you wouldn't believe, then bring in the cavalry hard and fast. In this case . . . we're talking some impressive bargaining chips, and there would not be a money transfer – the public release of some "political" prisoners is the obvious objective. The evidence does lean that way, except that these characters have never done one of those. It makes the escape procedures a lot more complex, but these ULA characters have always had their escape routes well planned beforehand. I'd say you're probably right, but it's not as clear-cut as you think. Owens and Taylor aren't completely sure, and our friend isn't talking. Big surprise.'

'They've never made a public announcement, you said? Was this supposed to be their break into the big time? Their first public announcement, they might as well do it with something spectacular,' Ryan said thoughtfully.

'That's a fair guess.' Murray nodded. 'It certainly would have put them on the map. Like I said, our intel on these chaps is damned thin; almost all of it's secondhand stuff that comes through the Provisional IRA – which is why we thought they were actually part of it. We haven't exactly figured what they're up to. Every one of their operations has – how do I say this? There seems to be a pattern there, but nobody's ever figured it out. It's almost as though the political fallout isn't aimed at us at all, but that doesn't make any sense – not that it *has* to make sense,' the agent grunted. 'It's not easy trying to psychoanalyse the terrorist mind.'

'Any chance they'll come after me, or –'

Murray shook his head. 'Unlikely, and the security's pretty tight. You know who they have taking your wife and kid around?'

'SAS – I asked.'

'That youngster's on their Olympic pistol team, and I hear that he has some field experience that never made the papers. The DPG escort is also one of the varsity, and they'll have a chase car everywhere they go. The security on you is pretty impressive, too. You have some big-league interest in your safety. You can relax. And after you get home it's all behind you. None of these groups has *ever* operated in the US. We're too important to them. NORAID means more to them psychologically than financially. When they fly to Boston, it's like crawling back into the womb, all the beers people buy for them, it tells them that they're the good guys. No, if they started raising hell out our side of the pond – I don't think they could take being persona non grata in Boston. It's the only real weak point the Provisional IRA and the rest have, and unfortunately it's not one that we can exploit all that well. We've pretty much cut down on the weapons pipeline, but, hell, they get most of their stuff from the other side now. Or they make their own. Like explosives. All you need is a bag of ammonia-based fertilizer and you can make a respectable bomb. You can't arrest a farmer for carrying fertilizer in his truck, can you? It's not as sexy as some good plastique, but it's a hell of a lot easier to get. For guns and heavier stuff – anybody can get AK-47s and RPGs, they're all over the place. No, they depend on us for moral support, and there's quite a few people who'll give it, even in Congress. Remember the fight over the extradition treaty? It's amazing. These bastards kill people.

'Both sides.' Murray paused for a moment. 'The Protestant crazies are just as bad. The Provisionals waste a prod. Then the Ulster Volunteer Force sends a car through a Catholic neighbourhood and pops the first convenient target. A lot of the killing is purely random now. Maybe a third of the kills are people who were walking down the wrong street. The process feeds on itself, and there's not much of a middle ground left anymore. Except the cops – I know, the RUC used to be the bad guys, too, but they've just about ended that crap. The Law has got to be the Law for everyone – but that's too easy to forget sometimes, like in Mississippi back in the sixties, and that's essentially what happened in Northern Ireland. Sir Jack Hermon is trying to turn the RUC into a professional police force. There are plenty of people left over from the bad old days, but the troops are coming around. They must be. The cops are taking casualties from both sides, the last one was killed by prods. They firebombed his house.' Murray shook his head. 'It's amazing. I was just over there two weeks ago. Their morale's great, especially with the new kids. I don't know how they do it – well, I do know. They have their mission, too. The cops and the courts have to re-establish justice, and the people have to see that they're doing it. They're the only hope that place has, them and a few of the church leaders. Maybe common sense'll break out someday, but don't hold your breath. It's going to take a long time. Thank God for Tom Jefferson and Jim Madison, bub. Sometimes I wonder how close we came to that sectarian stuff. It's like a Mafia war that everybody can play in.'

'Well, Judge?' Admiral James Greer hit the off switch on the remote control as the Cable News Network switched topics. The Director of Central Intelligence tapped his cigar on the cut-glass ashtray.

'We know he's smart, James, and it looks like he knows how to handle himself with reporters, but he's impetuous,' Judge Arthur Moore said.

'Come on, Arthur. He's young. I want somebody in here with some fresh ideas. You going to tell me now that you didn't like his report? First time at bat, and he turns out something that good!'

Judge Moore smiled behind his cigar. It was drizzling outside the seventh-floor window of the office of the Deputy Director, Intelligence, of the Central Intelligence Agency. The rolling hills of the Potomac Valley prevented his seeing the river, but he could spy the hills a mile or so away on the far side. It was a far prettier view than that of the parking lots.

'Background check?'

'We haven't done a deep one yet, but I'll bet you a bottle of your favourite bourbon that he comes up clean.'

'No bet, James!' Moore had already seen Jack's service record from the Marine Corps. Besides, he hadn't come to the Agency. They had gone to him and he'd turned them down on the first offer. 'You think he can handle it, eh?'

'You really ought to meet the kid, Judge. I had him figured out the first ten minutes he was in here last July.'

'You arranged the leak?'

'Me? Leak?' Admiral Greer chuckled. 'Nice to know how he can handle himself, though, isn't it? Didn't even blink when he fielded the question. The boy takes his clearance seriously, and' – Greer held up the telex from London – 'he's asking good questions. Emil says his man Murray was fairly impressed, too. It's just a damned shame to waste him teaching history.'

'Even at your alma mater?'

Greer smiled. 'Yes, that does hurt a little. I want him, Arthur. I want to teach him, I want to groom him. He's our kind of people.'

'But he doesn't seem to think so.'

'He will.' Greer was quietly positive.

'Okay, James. How do you want to approach him?'

'No hurry. I want a very thorough background check done first – and who knows? Maybe he'll come to us.'

'No chance,' Judge Moore scoffed.

'He'll come to us requesting information on this ULA bunch,' Greer said.

The Judge thought about that one. One thing about James Greer, Moore knew, was his ability to see into things and people as though they were made of crystal. 'That makes sense.'

'You bet it does. It'll be a while – the Attaché says he has to stay over for the trial and all – but he'll be in this office two weeks after he gets back, asking for a chance to research this ULA outfit. If he does, I'll pop the offer – if you agree, Arthur. I also want to talk to Emil Jacobs at FBI and compare files on these ULA characters.'

'Okay.'

They turned to other matters.

5

Perqs and Plots

The day Ryan was released from the hospital was the happiest in his life, at least since Sally had been born at Johns Hopkins, four years before. It was after six in the evening when he finally finished dressing himself – the cast made that a very tricky exercise – and plopped down in the wheelchair. Jack had groused about that, but it was evidently a rule as inviolable in British hospitals as in American ones: patients are not allowed to walk out – somebody might think they were cured. A uniformed policeman pushed him out of the room into the hall. Ryan didn't look back.·

Virtually the whole floor staff was lined up in the hall, along with a number of the patients Ryan had met the past week and a half as he'd relearned how to walk up and down the drab corridors – with a ten-degree list from the heavy cast. Jack flushed red at the applause, the more so when people reached out to shake his hand. *I'm not an Apollo astronaut*, he thought. *The Brits are supposed to be more dignified than this.*

Nurse Kittiwake gave a little speech about what a model patient he was. *What a pleasure and an honour* . . . Ryan blushed again when she finished, and gave him some flowers, to take to his lovely wife, she said. Then she kissed him, on behalf of everyone else. Jack kissed back. It was the least he could do, he told himself, and she really was a pretty girl. Kittiwake hugged him, cast and all, and tears started running out of her eyes. Tony Wilson was at her side and gave Jack a surreptitious wink. That was no surprise. Jack shook hands with another ten or so people before the cop got him into the lift.

'Next time you guys find me wounded in the street,' Ryan said, 'let me die there.'

The policeman laughed. 'Bloody ungrateful fellow you are.'

'True.'

The lift opened at the lobby and he was grateful to see that it had been cleared except for the Duke of Edinburgh and a gaggle of security people.

'Good evening, My Lord.' Ryan tried to stand, but was waved back down.

'Hello, Jack! How are you feeling?' They shook hands, and for a moment he was afraid that the Duke himself would wheel him out the door. That would have been intolerable, but the police officer resumed his pushing as the Duke walked alongside. Jack pointed forward.

'Sir, I will improve at least fifty percent when we make it through that door.'

'Hungry?'

'After hospital food? I just might eat one of your polo horses.'

The Duke grinned. 'We'll try to do a little better than that.'

Jack noticed seven security people in the lobby. Outside was a Rolls-Royce . . . and at least four other cars, along with a number of people who did not look like ordinary passersby. It was too dark to see anyone prowling the roofs, but they'd be there, too. *Well*, Ryan thought, *they've learned their lessons on security. Still a damned shame, though, and it means the terrorists have won a victory. If they make society change, even a little, they've won something. Bastards.* The cop brought him right to the Rolls.

'Can I get up now?' The cast was so heavy that it ruined his balance. Ryan stood a little too fast and nearly smashed into the car, but caught himself with an angry shake of the head before anyone had to grab for him. He stood still for a moment, his left arm sticking out like the big claw on a fiddler crab, and tried to figure how to get into the car. It turned out that the best way was to stick the cast in first, then rotate clockwise as he followed it. The Duke had to enter from the other side, and it turned out to be rather a snug fit. Ryan had never been in a Rolls before, and found that it wasn't all that spacious.

'Comfortable?'

'Well – I'll have to be careful not to punch a window out with this damned thing.' Ryan leaned back and shook his head with an eyes-closed smile.

'You really are glad to be out of hospital.'

'My Lord, on that you can wager one of your castles. This makes three times I've been in the body and fender shop, and that's enough.' The Duke motioned for the driver to pull out. The convoy moved slowly into the street, two lead cars and two chase cars surrounding the Rolls-Royce. 'Sir, may I ask what's happening this evening?'

'Very little, really. A small party in your honour, with just a few close friends.'

Jack wondered what 'a few close friends' meant. Twenty? Fifty? A hundred? He was going to dinner at . . . *Scotty, beam me up!* 'Sir, you know that you've really been too kind to us.'

'Bloody rubbish. As well as the debt we owe you – not exactly what one would call a small debt, Jack. As well as that, it's been entirely worthwhile to meet some new people. I even finished your book Sunday night. I thought it was excellent; you must send me a copy of your next one. And the Queen and your wife have got on marvellously together. You are a very lucky chap to have a wife like that – and that little imp of a daughter. She's a gem, Jack, a thoroughly wonderful little girl.'

Ryan nodded. He often wondered what he had done to be so lucky. 'Cathy says that she's seen about every castle in the realm, and thanks a lot for the people you put with her. It made me feel a lot better about having them run all over the place.' The Duke waved his hand dismissively. It wasn't worth talking about. 'How did the research go on your new book?'

'Quite well, sir.' The one favourable result of his being in the hospital was that he'd had the time to sift through all of it in detail. His computer had two hundred new pages of notes stored in its bubble chips, and Ryan had a new perspective on judging the actions of others. 'I guess I've learned one thing from my little escapade. Sitting in front of a keyboard isn't quite the same as looking into the front end of a gun. Decisions are a little different from that perspective.' Ryan's tone made a further statement.

The Duke laughed. 'I shouldn't think that anyone will fault yours.'

'Maybe. The thing is, my decision was made on pure instinct. If I'd known what I was doing – what if I had done the *wrong* thing on instinct?' He looked out the window. 'Here I am, supposed to be an expert on naval history, with special emphasis on how decisions are made under stress, and I'm still not satisfied with my own. Damn.' Jack concluded quietly: 'Sir, you don't forget killing somebody. You just don't.'

'You oughtn't to dwell on it, Jack.'

'Yes, sir.' Ryan turned back from the window. The Duke was looking at him much the same way his father had, years before. 'A conscience is the price of morality, and morality is the price of civilization. Dad used to say that many criminals don't have a conscience, not much in the way of feelings at all. I guess that's what makes us different from them.'

'Exactly. Your introspection is a fundamentally healthy thing, but you shouldn't overdo it. Put it behind you, Jack. It was my impression of Americans that you prefer to look to the future rather than the past. If you can't do that professionally, at least try to do it personally.'

'Understood, sir. Thank you.' *Now if I could just make the dreams stop.* Nearly every night Jack relived the shoot-out on The Mall. Almost three weeks now. Something else they didn't tell you about on TV. The human mind has a way of punishing itself for killing a fellow man. It remembers and relives the incident again and again. Ryan hoped it would stop someday.

The car turned left onto Westminster Bridge. Jack hadn't known exactly where the hospital was, just that it was close to a railway station and close enough to Westminster to hear Big Ben toll the hours. He looked up at the Gothic stonework. 'You know, besides the research I wanted to do, I actually wanted to see part of your country, sir. Not much time left for that.'

'Jack, do you really think we will let you return to America without experiencing British hospitality?' The Duke was greatly amused. 'We are quite proud of our hospitals, of course, but tourists don't come here to see those. Some small arrangements have been made.'

'Oh.'

Ryan had to think a moment to figure where they were, but the maps he'd studied before coming over came back to him. It was called Birdcage Walk – he was only three hundred yards from where he'd been shot . . . there was the lake that Sally liked. He could see Buckingham Palace past the head of the security officer in the left front seat. Knowing that he was going there was one thing, but now the building loomed in front of him and the emotional impact started to take hold.

They entered the Palace grounds at the northeast gate. Jack hadn't seen the Palace before except from a distance. The perimeter security didn't seem all that impressive, but the Palace's hollow-square design hid nearly everything from outside view. There could easily be a company of armed troops inside – and who could tell? More likely civilian police, Ryan knew, backed up by a lot of electronic hardware. But there would be some surprises hidden away, too. After the scares in the past, and this latest incident, he imagined that this place was as secure as the White House – or even better, given greater space in and around the buildings.

It was too dark to make out many details, but the Rolls pulled through an archway into the building's courtyard, then under a canopy, where a sentry snapped to present-arms in the crisp three-count movement the Brits used. As the car stopped, a footman in livery pulled the door open.

Getting out was the reverse of getting in. Ryan turned counterclockwise, stepped out backwards, and pulled his arm out behind. The footman grabbed his arm to help. Jack didn't want the help, but this wasn't a good time to object.

'You'll need a little practice on that,' the Duke observed.

'I think you're right, sir.' Jack followed him to the door, where another servant did his duty.

'Tell me, Jack – the first time we visited you, you seemed far more intimidated by the presence of the Queen than by me. Why's that?'

'Well, sir, you used to be a naval officer, right?'

'Of course.' The Duke turned and looked rather curious.

Ryan grinned. 'Sir, I work at Annapolis. The Academy crawls with naval officers, and remember I used to be a Marine. If I let myself get intimidated by every swabbie who crossed my path, the Corps would come and take my sword back.'

'You cheeky bugger!' They both had a laugh.

Ryan had expected to be impressed by the Palace. Even so, it was all he could manage to keep from being overwhelmed. Half the world had once been run from this house, and in addition to what the Royal Family had acquired over the centuries had come gifts from all over the world. Everywhere he looked the wide corridors were decorated with too many masterpieces of painting and sculpture to count. The walls were mainly covered with ivory-coloured silk brocaded with gold thread. The carpets, of course, were imperial scarlet over marble or parquet hardwood. The money manager that Jack had once been tried to calculate the value of it all. He overloaded after about ten seconds. The paintings alone were so valuable that any attempt to sell them off would distort the world market in fine art. The gilt frames alone. . . . Ryan shook his head, wishing he had the time to examine every painting. *You could live here five years and not have time to appreciate it all.* He almost fell behind, but managed to control his gawking and kept pace with the older man. Ryan's discomfiture was growing. To the Duke this was home – perhaps one so large as to be something of a nuisance, but nonetheless home, routine. The Rubens masterpieces on the wall were part of the scenery, as familiar to him as the photographs of wife and kids on any man's office desk. To Ryan the impact of where he was, an impact made all the more crushing by the trappings of wealth and power, made him want to shrink away to nothingness. It was one thing to take his chance on the street – the Marines, after all, had prepared and trained him for that – but . . . *this*.

Get off it, Jack, he told himself. *They're a royal family, but they're not your royal family.* This didn't work. They were *a* royal family. That was enough to lacerate most of his ego.

'Here we are,' the Duke said after turning right through an open door. 'This is the Music Room.'

It was about the size of the living/dining room in Ryan's house, the only thing he had seen thus far that could be so compared with any part of his $300,000 home on Peregrine Cliff. The ceiling was higher here, domed with gold-leaf trim. There were about thirty people, Ryan judged, and the moment they entered all conversation stopped. Everyone turned to stare at Ryan – Jack was sure they'd seen the Duke before – and his grotesque cast. He had a terrible urge to slink away. He needed a drink.

'If you'll excuse me for a moment, Jack, I must be off. Back in a few minutes.'

Thanks a lot, Ryan thought as he nodded politely. *Now what do I do?*

'Good evening, Sir John,' said a man in the uniform of a vice admiral of the Royal Navy. Ryan tried not to let his relief show. Of course, he'd been handed off to another custodian. He realized belatedly that lots of people came here for the first time. Some would need a little support while they got used to the idea of being in a palace, and there would be a procedure to take care of them. Jack took a closer look at the man's face as they shook hands. There was something familiar about it. 'I'm Basil Charleston.'

Aha! 'Good evening, sir.' His first week at Langley he'd seen the man, and his CIA escort had casually noted that this was 'B.C.' or just 'C,' the chief of the British Secret Intelligence Service, once known as MI-6. *What are you doing here?*

'You *must* be thirsty.' Another man arrived with a glass of champagne. 'Hello. I'm Bill Holmes.'

'You gentlemen work together?' Ryan sipped at the bubbling wine.

'Judge Moore told me you were a clever chap,' Charleston observed.

'Excuse me? Judge who?'

'Nicely done, Doctor Ryan,' Holmes smiled as he finished off his glass. 'I understand that you used to play football – the American kind, that is. You were on the junior varsity team, weren't you?'

'Varsity and junior varsity, but only in high school. I wasn't big enough for college ball,' Ryan said, trying to mask his uneasiness. 'Junior Varsity' was the project name under which he'd been called in to consult with CIA.

'And you wouldn't happen to know anything about the chap who wrote *Agents and Agencies*?' Charleston smiled. Jack went rigid.

'Admiral, I cannot talk about that without –'

'Copy number sixteen is sitting on my desk. The good judge told me to tell you that you were free to talk about the "smoking word-processor."'

Ryan let out a breath. The phrase must have come originally from James Greer. When Jack had made the Canary Trap proposal to the Deputy Director, Intelligence, Admiral James Greer had made a joke about it, using those words. Ryan was free to talk. Probably. His CIA security briefing had not exactly covered this situation.

'Excuse me, sir. Nobody ever told me that I was free to talk about that.'

Charleston went from jovial to serious for a moment. 'Don't apologize, lad. One is supposed to take matters of classification seriously. That paper you wrote was an excellent bit of detective work. One of our problems, as someone doubtless told you, is that we take in so much information now that the real problem is making sense of it all. Not easy to wade through all the muck and find the gleaming nugget. For the first time in the business, your report was first-rate. What I didn't know about was this thing the Judge called the Canary Trap. He said you could explain it better than he.' Charleston waved for another glass. A footman, or some sort of servant, came over with a tray. 'You know who I am, of course.'

'Yes, Admiral. I saw you last July at the Agency. You were getting out of the executive elevator on the seventh floor when I was coming out of the DDI's office, and somebody told me who you were.'

'Good. Now you know that all of this remains in the family. What the devil is this Canary Trap?'

'Well, you know about all the problems CIA has with leaks. When I was finishing off the first draft of the report, I came up with an idea to make each one unique.'

'They've been doing that for years,' Holmes noted. 'All one must do is misplace a comma here and there. Easiest thing in the world. If the newspeople are foolish enough to print a photograph of the document, we can identify the leak.'

'Yes, sir, and the reporters who publish the leaks know that, too. They've learned not to show photographs of the documents they get from their sources, haven't they?' Ryan answered. 'What I came up with was a new twist on that. *Agents and Agencies* has four sections. Each section has a summary paragraph. Each of those is written in a fairly dramatic fashion.'

'Yes, I noticed that,' Charleston said. 'Didn't read like a CIA document at all. More like one of ours. We use people to write our reports, you see, not computers. Do go on.'

'Each summary paragraph has six different versions, and the mixture of those paragraphs is unique to each numbered copy of the paper. There are over a thousand possible permutations, but only ninety-six numbered copies of the actual document. The reason the summary paragraphs are so – well, lurid, I guess – is to entice a reporter to quote them verbatim in the public media. If he quotes something from two or three of those paragraphs, we know which copy he saw and therefore who leaked it. They've got an even more refined version of the trap working now. You can do it by computer. You use a thesaurus programme to shuffle through synonyms, and you can make every copy of the document totally unique.'

'Did they tell you if it worked?' Holmes asked.

'No, sir. I had nothing to do with the security side of the Agency.' *And thank God for that.*

'Oh, it worked.' Sir Basil paused for a moment. 'That idea is bloody simple – and bloody brilliant! Then there was the substantive aspect of the paper. Did they tell you that your report agreed in nearly every detail with an investigation we ran last year?'

'No, sir, they didn't. So far as I know, all the documents I worked with came from our own people.'

'Then you came up with it entirely on your own? Marvellous.'

'Did I goof up on anything?' Ryan asked the Admiral.

'You should have paid a bit more attention to that South African chap. That's more our patch, of course, and perhaps you didn't have enough information to fiddle with. We're giving him a very close look at the moment.'

Ryan finished off his glass and thought about that. There had been a good deal of information on Mr Martens . . . *What did I miss?* He couldn't ask that, not now. Bad form. But he could ask –

'Aren't the South African people –'

'I'm afraid the cooperation they give us isn't quite as good now as it once was, and Erik Martens is quite a valuable chap for them. One can hardly blame them, you know. He does have a way of procuring what their military need, and that rather limits the pressure his government are willing to put on him,' Holmes pointed out. 'There is also the Israeli connection to be considered. They occasionally stray from the path, but we – SIS and CIA – have too many common interests to rock the boat severely.' Ryan nodded. The Israeli defence establishment had orders to generate as much income as possible, and this occasionally ran contrary to the wishes of Israel's allies. *I remember Martens' connections, but I must have missed something important . . . what?*

'Please don't take this as criticism,' Charleston said. 'For a first attempt your report was excellent. The CIA must have you back. It's one of the few Agency reports that didn't threaten to put me to sleep. If nothing else, perhaps you might teach their analysts how to write. Surely they asked if you wanted to stay on?'

'They asked, sir. I didn't think it was a very good idea for me.'

'Think again,' Sir Basil suggested gently. 'This Junior Varsity idea was a good one, like the Team-B programme back in the seventies. We do it as well – get some outside academics into the shop – to take a new look at all the data that cascades in through the front door. Judge Moore, your new DCI, is a genuine breath of fresh air. Splendid chap. Knows the trade quite well, but he's been away from it long enough to have some new ideas. You are one of them, Doctor Ryan. You belong in the business, lad.'

'I'm not so sure about that, sir. My degree's history and –'

'So is mine,' Bill Holmes said. 'One's degree doesn't matter. In the intelligence trade we look for the right sort of mind. You appear to have it. Ah, well, we can't recruit you, can we? I would be rather disappointed if Arthur and James don't try again. Do think about it.'

I have, Ryan didn't say. He nodded thoughtfully, mulling over his own thoughts. *But I like teaching history.*

'The hero of the hour!' Another man joined the group.

'Good evening, Geoffrey,' Charleston said. 'Doctor Ryan, this is Geoffrey Watkins of the Foreign Office.'

'Like David Ashley of the "Home Office"?' Ryan shook the man's hand.

'Actually I spend much of my time right here,' Watkins said.

'Geoff's the liaison officer between the Foreign Office and the Royal Family. He handles briefings, dabbles in protocol, and generally makes a nuisance of himself,' Holmes explained with a smile. 'How long now, Geoff?'

Watkins frowned as he thought that over. 'Just over four years, I think. Seems like only last week. Nothing like the glamour one might expect. Mainly I carry the dispatch box and try to hide in corners.' Ryan smiled. He could identify with that.

'Nonsense,' Charleston objected. 'One of the best minds in the Office, else they wouldn't have kept you here.'

Watkins made an embarrassed gesture. 'It does keep me rather busy.'

'It must,' Holmes observed. 'I haven't seen you at the tennis club in months.'

'Doctor Ryan, the Palace staff have asked me to express their appreciation for what you have done.' He droned on for a few more seconds. Watkins was an inch under Ryan's height and pushing forty. His neatly trimmed black hair was going gray at the sides, and his skin was pale in the way of people who rarely saw the sun. He looked like a diplomat. His smile was so perfect that he must have practiced it in front of a mirror. It was the sort of smile that could have meant anything. Or more likely, nothing. There was interest behind those blue eyes, though. As had happened many times in the past few weeks, this man was trying to decide what Dr John Patrick Ryan was made of. The subject of the investigation was getting very tired of this, but there wasn't much Jack could do about it.

'Geoff is something of an expert on the Northern Ireland situation,' Holmes said.

'No one's an "expert,"' Watkins said with a shake of his head. 'I was there at the beginning, back in 1969. I was in uniform then, a subaltern with – well, that hardly matters now, does it? How do you think we should handle the problem, Doctor Ryan?'

'People have been asking me that question for three weeks, Mr Watkins. How the hell should I know?'

'Still looking for ideas, Geoff?' Holmes asked.

'The right idea is out there somewhere,' Watkins said, keeping his eyes on Ryan.

'I don't have it,' Jack said. 'And even if someone did, how would you know? I teach history, remember, I don't make it.'

'Just a history teacher, and these two chaps descend on you?'

'We wanted to see if he really works for the CIA, as the papers say,' Charleston responded.

Jack took the signal from that. Watkins wasn't cleared for everything, and was not to know about his past association with the Agency – not that he couldn't draw his own conclusions, Ryan reminded himself. Regardless, rules were rules. *That's why I turned Greer's offer down*, Jack remembered. *All those idiot rules. You can't talk to anybody about this or that, not even to your wife. Security. Security. Security . . . Crap! Sure,* some *things have to stay secret, but if nobody gets to see them, how is anyone supposed to make use of them – and what good is a secret you can't use?*

'You know, it'll be nice to get back to Annapolis. At least the mids believe I'm a teacher!'

'Quite,' Watkins noted. *And the head of SIS is asking you for an opinion on Trafalgar. What exactly are you, Ryan?* After leaving military service in 1972 and joining the Foreign Office, Watkins had often played the foreign service officer's embassy game: *Who's the spook?* He was getting mixed signals from Ryan, and this made the game all the more interesting. Watkins loved games. All sorts.

'How do you keep yourself busy now, Geoff?' Holmes asked.

'You mean, aside from the twelve-hour days? I do manage to read the occasional book. I just started going through *Moll Flanders* again.'

'Really?' Holmes asked. 'I just started *Robinson Crusoe* a few days ago. One sure way of getting one's mind off the world is to return to the classics.'

'Do you read the classics, Doctor Ryan?' Watkins asked.

'Used to. Jesuit education, remember? They don't let you avoid the old stuff.' *Is* Moll Flanders *a classic?* Jack wondered. *It's not in Latin or Greek, and it's not Shakespeare. . . .*

'"Old stuff." What a terrible attitude!' Watkins laughed.

'Did you ever try to read Virgil in the original?' Ryan asked. *'Arma virumque cano, trojae qui primus ab oris. . . ?'*

'Geoff and I were at Winchester together,' Holmes explained. *'Contiquere omnes, intenteque ora tenebant. . . .'* Both public school graduates had a good chuckle.

'Hey, I got good marks in Latin, I just don't remember any of it,' Ryan said defensively.

'Another colonial philistine,' Watkins observed.

Ryan decided that he didn't like Mr Watkins. The foreign service officer was deliberately hitting him to get reactions, and Ryan had long since tired of this game. Ryan was happy with what he was, and didn't need a bunch of amateur pshrinks, as he called them, to define his personality for him.

'Sorry. Where I live we have slightly different priorities.'

'Of course,' Watkins replied. The smile hadn't changed a whit. This surprised Jack, though he wasn't sure why.

'You live not far from the Naval Academy, don't you? Wasn't there some sort of incident there recently?' Sir Basil asked. 'I read about it in some report somewhere. I never did get straight on the details.'

'It wasn't really terrorism – just your basic crime. A couple of midshipmen saw what looked like a drug deal being made in Annapolis, and called the police. The people who got arrested were members of a local motorcycle gang. A week later, some of the gang members decided to take the mids out. They got past the Jimmy Legs – the civilian security guards – about three in the morning and sneaked into Bancroft Hall. They must have assumed that it was just another college dorm – not hardly. The kids standing midwatch spotted them, got the alarm out, and then everything came apart. The intruders got themselves lost – Bancroft has a couple of miles of corridors – and cornered. It's a federal case since it happened on government property, and the FBI takes a very dim view of people who try to tamper with witnesses. They'll be gone for a while. The good news is that the Marine guard force at the Academy has been beefed up, and it's a lot easier to get in and out now.'

'Easier?' Watkins asked. 'But –'

Jack smiled. 'With Marines on the perimeter, they leave a lot more gates open – a Marine guard beats a locked gate any day.'

'Indeed. I –' Something caught Charleston's eye. Ryan was facing the wrong way to see what it was, but the reactions were plain enough. Charleston and Holmes began to disengage, with Watkins making his way off first. Jack turned in time to see the Queen appear at the door, coming past a servant.

The Duke was at her side, with Cathy trailing a diplomatically defined distance behind and to the side. The Queen came first to him.

'You are looking much better.'

Jack tried to bow – he thought he was supposed to – without endangering the Queen's life with his cast. The main trick was standing still, he'd learned. The weight of the thing tended to induce a progressive lean to the left. Moving around helped him stay upright.

'Thank you, Your Majesty. I feel much better. Good evening, sir.'

One thing about shaking hands with the Duke, you knew there was a man at the other end. 'Hello again, Jack. Do try to be at ease. This is completely informal. No receiving line, no protocol. Relax.'

'Well, the champagne helps.'

'Excellent,' the Queen observed. 'I think we'll let you and Caroline get reacquainted for the moment.' She and the Duke moved off.

'Easy on the booze, Jack.' Cathy positively glowed in a white cocktail dress so lovely that Ryan forgot to wonder what it had cost. Her hair was nicely arranged and she had make-up on, two things that her profession regularly denied her. Most of all, she was Cathy Ryan. He gave his wife a quick kiss, audience and all.

'All these people –'

'Screw 'em,' Jack said quietly. 'How's my favourite girl?'

Her eyes sparkled with the news, but her voice was deadpan-professional: 'Pregnant.'

'You sure – *when*?'

'I'm sure, darling, because, A, I'm a doctor, and B, I'm two weeks late. As to when, Jack, remember when we got here, as soon as we put Sally down to bed. . . . It's those strange hotel beds, Jack.' She took his hand. 'They do it every time.'

There wasn't anything for Jack to say. He wrapped his good arm around her shoulders and squeezed as discreetly as his emotions would allow. If she was two weeks late – well, he knew Cathy to be as regular as her Swiss watch. *I'm going to be a daddy – again!*

'We'll try for a boy this time,' she said.

'You know that's not important, babe.'

'I see you've told him.' The Queen returned as quietly as a cat. The Duke, Jack saw, was talking to Admiral Charleston. About what? he wondered. 'Congratulations, Sir John.'

'Thank you, Your Majesty, and thank you for a lot of things. We'll never be able to repay you for all your kindness.'

The Christmas-tree smile again. 'It is we who are repaying you. From what Caroline tells me, you will now have at least one positive reminder of your visit to our country.'

'Indeed, ma'am, but more than one.' Jack was learning how the game was played.

'Caroline, is he always so gallant?'

'As a matter of fact, ma'am, no. We must have caught him at a weak moment,' Cathy said. 'Or maybe being over here is a civilizing influence.'

'That is good to know, after all the horrid things he said about your little Olivia. Do you know that she refused to go to bed without kissing me goodnight? Such a lovely, charming little angel. And *he* called her a menace!'

Jack sighed. It wasn't hard for him to get the picture. After three weeks in this environment, Sally was probably doing the cutest curtsies in the history of Western Civilization. By this time the Palace staff was probably fighting for the right to look after her. Sally was a true daddy's girl. The ability to manipulate the people around her came easily. She'd practiced on her father for years.

'Perhaps I exaggerated, ma'am.'

'Scandalous.' The Queen's eyes flared with amusement. 'She has not broken a single thing. Not one. And I'll have you know that she's turning into the best equestrienne we have seen in years.'

'Excuse me?'

'Riding lessons,' Cathy explained.

'You mean on a horse?'

'What else would she ride?' the Queen asked.

'Sally, on a horse?' Ryan looked at his wife. He didn't like that idea very much.

'And doing splendidly.' The Queen sprang to Cathy's defence. 'It's quite safe, Sir John. Riding is a fine skill for a child to learn. It teaches discipline, coordination, and responsibility.'

Not to mention a fabulous way to break her pretty little neck, Ryan thought. Again he remembered that one does not argue with a queen, especially under her own roof.

'You could even try to ride yourself,' the Queen said. 'Your wife rides.'

'We have enough land now, Jack,' Cathy said. 'You'd love it.'

'I'd fall off,' Ryan said bleakly.

'Then you climb back on again until you get it right,' said a woman with over fifty years of riding behind her.

It's the same with a bike, except you don't fall as far off a bike, and Sally's too little for a bike, Ryan told himself. He got nervous watching Sally move her Hotwheel trike around the driveway. *For God's sake, she's so little the horse wouldn't even know if she was there or not.* Cathy read his mind.

'Children do have to grow up. You can't protect her from everything,' his wife pointed out.

'Yes, dear, I know.' *The hell I can't. That's my job.*

A few minutes later everyone headed out of the room for dinner. Ryan found himself in the Blue Drawing Room, a breathtaking pillared hall, and then passed through mirrored double doors into the State Dining Room.

The contrast was incredible. From a room of muted blue they entered one ablaze with scarlet, fabric-covered walls. Overhead the vaulted ceiling was ivory and gold, and over the snow-white fireplace was a massive portrait – of whom? Ryan wondered. It had to be a king, of course, probably 18th or

19th century, judging by his white . . . pantyhose, or whatever they'd called them then, complete with garter. Over the door they'd entered was the royal cipher of Queen Victoria, VR, and he wondered how much history had passed through – or been made right in this single room.

'You will sit at my right hand, Jack,' the Queen said.

Ryan took a quick look at the table. It was wide enough that he didn't have to worry about clobbering Her Majesty with his left arm. That wouldn't do.

The worst thing about the dinner was that Ryan would be forever unable to remember – and too proud to ask Cathy – what it was. Eating one-handed was something he'd had a lot of practice at, but never had he had such an audience, and Ryan was sure that everyone was watching him. After all, he was a Yank and would have been something of a curiosity even without his arm. He constantly reminded himself to be careful, to go easy on the wine, to watch his language. He shot the occasional glance at Cathy, sitting at the other end of the table next to the Duke and clearly enjoying herself. It made her husband slightly angry that she was more at ease than he was. *If there was ever a pig in the manger*, Ryan thought while chewing on something he immediately forgot, *it's me.* He wondered if he would be here now, had he been a rookie cop or a private in the Royal Marines who just happened to be at the right place. Probably not, he thought. *And why is that?* Ryan didn't know. He did know that something about the institution of nobility went against his American outlook. At the same time, being knighted – even honorarily – was something he liked. It was a contradiction that troubled him in a way he didn't understand. All this attention was too seductive, he told himself. *It'll be good to get away from it. Or will it?* He sipped at a glass of wine. *I know I don't belong here, but do I want to belong here? There's a good question.* The wine didn't give him an answer. He'd have to find it somewhere else.

He looked down the table to his wife, who did seem to fit in very nicely. She'd been raised in a similar atmosphere, a monied family, a big house in Westchester County, lots of parties where people told one another how important they all were. It was a life he'd rejected, and that she had walked away from. They were both happy with what they had, each with a career, but did her ease with this mean that she missed . . . Ryan frowned.

'Feeling all right, Jack?' the Queen asked.

'Yes, ma'am, please excuse me. I'm afraid it will take me a while to adjust to all of this.'

'Jack,' she said quietly, 'the reason everyone likes you – and we all do, you know – is because of who and what you are. Try to keep that in mind.'

It struck Ryan that this was probably the kindest thing he'd ever been told. Perhaps nobility was supposed to be a state of mind rather than an institution. His father-in-law could learn from that, Ryan thought. His father-in-law could learn from a lot of things.

434

Three hours later Jack followed his wife into their room. There was a sitting room off to the right. In front of him the bed had already been turned down. He pulled the tie loose from his collar and undid the button, then let out a long, audible breath.

'You weren't kidding about turning into pumpkins.'

'I know,' his wife said.

Only a single dim light was lit, and his wife switched it off. The only illumination in the room was from distant streetlights that filtered through the heavy curtains. Her white dress stood out in the darkness, but her face showed only the curve of her lips and the sparkle of her eyes as she turned away from the light. Her husband's mind filled in the remaining details. Jack wrapped his good arm around his wife and cursed the monstrosity of plaster that encased his left side as he pulled her in close. She rested her head on his healthy shoulder, and his cheek came down to the softness of her fine blonde hair. Neither said anything for a minute or two. It was enough to be alone, together in the quiet darkness.

'Love ya, babe.'

'How are you feeling, Jack?' The question was more than a simple inquiry.

'Not bad. Pretty well rested. The shoulder doesn't hurt very much anymore. Aspirin takes care of the aches.' This was an exaggeration, but Jack was used to the discomfort.

'Oh, I see how they did it.' Cathy was exploring the left side of his jacket. The tailors had put press studs on the underside so that it would not so much conceal the cast as make it look dressed. His wife undid the studs quickly and pulled the coat off. The shirt went next.

'I am able to do this myself, you know.'

'Shut up, Jack. I don't want to have to wait all night for you to undress.' He next heard the sound of a long zipper.

'Can I help?'

There was laughter in the darkness. 'I might want to wear this dress again. And be careful where you put that arm.'

'I haven't crunched anyone yet.'

'Good. Let's try to keep a perfect record.' A whisper of silk. She took his hand. 'Let's get you sitting down.'

After he sat on the edge of the bed, the rest came easy. Cathy sat beside him. He felt her, cool and smooth at his side, a hint of perfume in the air. He reached around her shoulder, down to the soft skin of her abdomen.

It's happening right now, growing away while we sit here. 'You're going to have my baby,' Jack said softly. *There really is a God, and there really are miracles.*

Her hand came across his face. 'That's right. I can't have anything to drink after tonight – but I wanted to enjoy tonight.'

'You know, I really do love you.'

'I know,' she said. 'Lie back.'

6

Trials and Troubles

Preliminary testimonies lasted for about two hours while Ryan sat on a marble bench outside Old Bailey's number two courtroom. He tried to work on his computer, but he couldn't seem to keep his mind on it, and found himself staring around the hundred-sixty-year-old building.

Security was incredibly tight. Outside, numerous uniformed police constables stood about in plain sight, small zippered pistol cases dangling from their hands. Others, uniformed and not, stood on the buildings across Newgate Street like falcons on the watch for rabbits. Except rabbits don't carry machine guns and RPG-7 bazookas, Ryan thought. Every person who entered the building was subjected to a metal detector sensitive enough to *ping* on the foil inside a cigarette pack, and nearly everyone was given a pat-down search. This included Ryan, who was surprised enough at the intimacy of the search to tell the officer that he went a bit far for a first date. The grand hall was closed off to anyone not connected with the case, and less prominent trials had been switched among the building's nineteen courtrooms to accommodate *Crown v Miller.*

Ryan had never been in a courtroom before. He was amused by the fact that he'd never even had a speeding ticket, his life had been so dull until now. The marble floor – nearly everything in sight was marble – gave the hall the aspect of a cathedral, and the walls were decorated with aphorisms such as Cicero's THE WELFARE OF THE PEOPLE IS THE HIGHEST LAW, a phrase he found curiously – or at least potentially – expedient in what was certainly designed as a temple to the idea of law. He wondered if the members of the ULA felt the same way, and justified their activities in accordance with their view of the welfare of the people. *Who doesn't?* Jack asked himself. *What tyrant ever failed to justify his crimes?* Around him were a half-dozen other witnesses. Jack didn't talk with them. His instructions were quite specific: even the appearance of conversation might give cause to the defence lawyers to speculate that witnesses had coached one another. The prosecution team had bent every effort to make their case a textbook example of correct legal procedure.

The case was being handled on a contradictory basis. The ambush had taken place barely four weeks ago, and the trial was already under way – an unusually speedy process even by British standards. Security was airtight. Admittance to the public gallery (visitors entered from another part of the building) was being strictly controlled. But at the same time, the trial was being handled strictly as a criminal matter. The name 'Ulster Liberation Army' had not been mentioned. The prosecutor had not once used the word terrorist. The police ignored – publicly – the political aspects of the case. Two men were dead, and this was a trial for murder – period. Even the press was playing along, on the theory that there was no more contemptuous way to treat the defendant than to call him a simple criminal, and not sanctify him as a creature of politics. Jack wondered about additional political or intelligence-related motives in this treatment, but no one was talking along those lines, and the defence counsel certainly couldn't defend his client better by calling him a member of a terrorist group. In the media, and in the courtroom, this was a case of murder.

The truth was different, of course, and everyone knew it. But Ryan knew enough about the law to remember that lawyers rarely concern themselves with truth. The rules were far more important. There would therefore be no official speculation on the goal of the criminals, and no involvement of the Royal Family, aside from depositions that they could not identify the living conspirator and hence had no worthwhile evidence to offer.

It didn't matter. From the press coverage of the evidence it seemed clear enough that the trial was as airtight as was possible without a videotape of the entire event. Similarly, Cathy was not to testify. In addition to forensic experts who had testified the day before, the Crown had eight eyewitnesses. Ryan was number two. The trial was expected to last a maximum of four days. As Owens had told him in the hospital, there would be no mucking about with this lad.

'Doctor Ryan? Would you please follow me, sir?' The VIP treatment continued here also. An usher in short sleeves and tie came over and led him into the courtroom through a side door. A police officer took his computer after opening the door. 'Showtime,' Ryan whispered to himself.

Old Bailey Number 2 was an extravagance of 19th-century woodworking. The large room was panelled with so much solid oak that the construction of a similar room in America would draw a protest from the Sierra Club for all the trees it required. The actual floorspace was surprisingly small, scarcely as much as the dining room in his house, a similarity made all the more striking by a table set in the centre. The judge's bench was a wooden fortress adjacent to the witness box. The Honorable Mr Justice Wheeler sat in one of the five high-backed chairs behind it. He was resplendent in a scarlet robe and sash, and a horsehair wig, called a 'peruke,' Ryan had been told, that fell to his narrow shoulders and clearly looked like something from another age. The jury box was to Ryan's left. Eight women and four men sat in two even rows, each face full of anticipation. Above them was the public gallery, perched like a choir loft and angled so that Ryan could barely see the people there. The barristers were to Ryan's right, across the small floorspace, wearing black robes, 18th-century cravats, and their own, smaller wigs. The net effect of all this was a vaguely religious atmosphere that made Ryan slightly uneasy as he was sworn.

William Richards, QC, the prosecutor, was a man of Ryan's age, similar in height and build. He began with the usual questions: your name, place of residence, profession, when did you arrive, for what purpose? Richards predictably had a flair for the dramatic, and by the time the questions carried them to the shooting, Ryan could sense the excitement and anticipation of the audience without even looking at their faces.

'Doctor Ryan, could you describe in your own words what happened next?'

Jack did exactly this for ten minutes, without interruption, all the while half-facing the jury. He tried to avoid looking into their faces. It seemed an odd place to get stage fright, but this was precisely what Ryan felt. He focused his eyes on the oak panels just over their heads as he ran through the events. It was almost like living it again, and Ryan could feel his heart beating faster as he concluded.

'And, Doctor Ryan, can you identify for us the man whom you first attacked?' Richards finally asked.

'Yes, sir.' Ryan pointed. 'The defendant, right there, sir.'

It was Ryan's first really good look at him. His name was Sean Miller – not a particularly Irish name to Ryan's way of thinking. He was twenty-six, short, slender, dressed neatly in a suit and tie. He was smiling up at someone in the visitors' gallery, a family member perhaps, when Ryan pointed. Then his gaze shifted, and Ryan examined the man for the first time. What sort of person, Jack had wondered for weeks, could plan and execute such a crime? What was missing in him, or what terrible thing lived in him that most civilized people had the good fortune to lack? The thin, acne-scarred face was entirely normal. Miller could have been an executive trainee at Merrill Lynch or any other business concern. Jack's father had spent his life dealing with criminals, but their existence was a puzzlement to Ryan. *Why are you different? What makes you what you are?* Ryan wanted to ask, knowing that even if there were an answer the question would remain. Then he looked at Miller's eyes. He looked for . . . something, a spark of life, humanity – something that would say this was indeed another human being. It could only have been two seconds, but for Ryan the moment seemed to linger into minutes as he looked into those pale gray eyes and saw. . . .

Nothing. Nothing at all. And Jack began to understand a little.

'The record will show,' the Lord Justice intoned to the court reporter, 'that the witness identified the defendant, Sean Miller.'

'Thank you, My Lord,' Richards concluded.

Ryan took the opportunity to blow his nose. He'd acquired a head cold over the preceding weekend.

'Are you quite comfortable, Doctor Ryan?' the judge inquired. Jack realized that he'd been leaning on the wooden rail.

'Excuse me, your hon – My Lord. This cast is a little tiring.' Every time Sally came past her father, she had taken to singing, 'I'm a little teapot. . . .'

'Usher, a stool for the witness,' the judge ordered.

The defence team was seated adjacent to the prosecution, perhaps fifteen feet farther away in the same row of seats, green leather cushions on the oak benches. In a moment the usher arrived with a simple wooden stool, and Ryan settled down on it. What he really needed was a hook for his left arm, but he was gradually becoming used to the weight. It was the constant itching that drove him crazy, but there was nothing anybody could do about that.

The counsel for the defence rose with elegant deliberation. His name was Charles Atkinson, more commonly known as Red Charlie, a lawyer with a penchant for radical causes and radical crimes. He was supposed to be an embarrassment to the Labour Party, which he had served until recently in Parliament. Red Charlie was about thirty pounds overweight, his wig askew atop a florid, strangely thin face for the ample frame. Defending terrorists must have paid well enough, Ryan thought. *There's a question Owens must be looking into*, Ryan told himself. *Where is your money coming from, Mr Atkinson?*

'May it please Your Lordship,' he said formally to the bench. He walked slowly towards Ryan, a sheaf of notes in his hand.

'Doctor Ryan – or should I say Sir John?'

Jack waved his hand. 'Whatever is convenient to you, sir,' he answered indifferently. They had warned him about Atkinson. *A very clever bastard*, they'd said. Ryan had known quite a few clever bastards in the brokerage business.

'You were, I believe, a *left*enant in the United States Marine Corps?'

'Yes, sir, that is correct.'

Atkinson looked down at his notes, then over at the jury. 'Bloodthirsty mob, the US Marines,' he muttered.

'Excuse me, sir? Bloodthirsty?' Ryan asked. 'No, sir. Most of the Marines I know are beer drinkers.'

Atkinson spun back at Ryan as a ripple of laughter came down from the gallery. He gave Jack a thin, dangerous smile. They'd warned Jack most of all to beware his word games and tactical skill in the courtroom. *To hell with it*, Ryan told himself. He smiled back at the barrister. *Go for it, asshole. . . .*

'Forgive me, Sir John. A figure of speech. I meant to say that the US Marines have a reputation for aggressiveness. Surely this is true?'

'Marines are light infantry troops who specialize in amphibious assault. We were pretty well trained, but when you get down to it we weren't all that different from any other kind of soldier. It's just a matter of specialization in a particularly tough field,' Ryan answered, hoping to throw him a little off balance. Marines were supposed to be arrogant, but that was mostly movie stuff. If you're really good, they'd taught him at Quantico, you don't have to be arrogant. Just letting people know you're a Marine was usually enough.

'Assault troops?'

'Yes, sir. That's basically correct.'

'So, you commanded assault troops, then?'

'Yes, sir.'

'Try not to be too modest, Sir John. What sort of man is selected to lead such troops. Aggressive? Decisive? Bold? Certainly he would have more of these qualities than the average foot soldier?'

'As a matter of fact, sir, in my edition of *The Marine Officer's Guide*, the foremost of the qualities that the Corps looks for in an officer is *integrity*.' Ryan smiled again. Atkinson hadn't done his homework on that score. 'I commanded a platoon, sure, but as my captain explained to me when I came aboard, my principal job was to carry out the orders he gave me, and to lean on my gunny – my platoon sergeant – for his practical experience. The job I was in was supposed to be as much a learning experience as a command slot. I mean, in business it's called an entry-level position. You don't start shaking the world your first day on the job in any business.'

Atkinson frowned a bit. This was not going as he'd expected.

'Ah, then, Sir John, a *left*enant of American Marines is really a leader of Boy Scouts. Surely you don't mean that?' he asked, a sarcastic edge on his voice.

'No, sir. Excuse me, I did not mean to give that impression, but we're not a bunch of hyperaggressive barbarians either. My job was to carry out orders, to be as aggressive as the situation called for, and to exercise some amount of judgment, like any officer. But I was only there three months, and I was still learning how to be an officer when I was injured. Marines follow orders. Officers give orders, of course, but a second lieutenant is the lowest form of officer. You take more than you give. I guess you've never been in the service,' Ryan tagged on the barb at the end.

'So, what sort of training *did* they give you?' Atkinson demanded, either angry or feigning it.

Richards looked up to Ryan, a warning broadcast from his eyes. He'd emphasized several times that Jack shouldn't cross swords with Red Charlie.

'Really, basic leadership skills. They taught us how to lead men in the field,' Ryan replied. 'How to react to a given tactical situation. How to employ the platoon's weapons, and to a lesser extent, the weapons in a rifle company. How to call in outside support from artillery and air assets –'

'To react?'

'Yes, sir, that is part of it.' Ryan kept his answers as long as he thought he could get away with, careful to keep his voice even, friendly, and informative. 'I've never been in anything like a combat situation – unless you count this thing we're talking about, of course – but our instructors were very clear about telling us that you don't have time to think very much when bullets are flying. You have to know what to do, and you have to do it fast – or you get your own people killed.'

'Excellent, Sir John. You were trained to react quickly and decisively to tactical stimuli, would you say that was correct?'

'Yes, sir.' Ryan thought he saw the ambush coming.

'So, in the unfortunate incident before this court, when the initial explosion took place, you have testified that you were looking in the wrong direction?'

'I was looking away from the explosion, yes, sir.'

'How soon afterwards did you turn to see what was happening?'

'Well, sir, as I said earlier, the first thing I did was to get my wife and daughter down under cover. Then I looked up. How long did that take?' Ryan cocked his head. 'At least one second, sir, maybe as many as three. Sorry, but as I said earlier, it's hard to recall that sort of thing – you don't have a stopwatch on yourself, I mean.'

'So, when you *finally* did look up, you had not seen what had immediately transpired?'

'Correct, sir.' *Okay, Charlie, ask the next question.*

'You did not, therefore, see my client fire his pistol, nor throw a hand grenade?'

Cute, Ryan thought, surprised that he'd try this ploy. *Well, he has to try something, doesn't he?* 'No, sir. When I first saw him, he was running around the corner of the car, from the direction of the other man, the one who was killed – the one with the rifle. A moment later he was at the right-rear corner of the Rolls, facing away from me, with the pistol in his right hand, pointed forward and down, as if –'

'Assumption on your part,' Atkinson interrupted. 'As if what? It could have been any one of several things. But what things? How could you tell what he was doing there? You did not see him get out of the car, which later drove off. For all you know he might have been another pedestrian racing to the rescue, just as you did, mightn't he?'

Jack was supposed to be surprised by this.

'Assumption, sir? No, I'd call it a judgment. For him to have been racing to the rescue as you suggest, he would have had to come from across the street. I doubt that anyone could have reacted anywhere near fast enough to do that at all, not to mention the fact that there was a guy there with a machine gun to make you think twice about it. Also, the direction I saw him running from was directly away from the guy with the AK-47. If he was running to the rescue, why away from him? If he had a gun, why not shoot him? At the time I never considered this possibility, and it seems pretty unlikely now, sir.'

'Again, a *conclusion*, Sir John,' Atkinson said as though to a backward child.

'Sir, you asked me a question, and I tried to answer it, with the reasons to back up my answer.'

'And you expect us to believe that all this flashed through your mind in a brief span of seconds?' Atkinson turned back to the jury.

'Yes, sir, it did,' Ryan said with conviction. 'That's all I can say – it did.'

'I don't suppose you've been told that my client has never before been arrested, or accused of any crime?'

'I guess that makes him a first offender.'

'It's for the jury to decide that,' the lawyer snapped back. 'You did not see him fire a single shot, did you?'

'No, sir, but his automatic had an eight-shot clip, and there were only three rounds in it. When I fired my third shot, it was empty.'

'So what? For all you know someone else could have fired that gun. You did not see him fire, did you?'

'No, sir.'

'So it might have been dropped by someone in the car. My client might have picked it up and, I repeat, been doing the same thing you were doing – this could all be true, but you have no way of knowing this, do you?'

'I cannot testify about things I didn't see, sir. However, I *did* see the street, the traffic, and the other pedestrians. If your client did what you say, where did he come from?'

'Precisely – you don't know, do you?' Atkinson said sharply.

'When I saw your client, sir, he was coming from the direction of the stopped car.' Jack gestured to the model on the evidence table. 'For him to have come off the sidewalk, then gotten the gun, and then appeared where I saw him – there's just no way unless he's an Olympic-class sprinter.'

'Well, we'll never know, will we – you made sure of that. You reacted precipitously, didn't you? You reacted as you were trained to by the US Marines, never stopping to assess the situation. You raced into the fray quite recklessly, attacked my client and knocked him unconscious, then tried to kill him.'

'No, sir, I did not try to kill your client. I've already –'

'*Then why did you shoot an unconscious, helpless man*?'

'My Lord,' prosecutor Richards said, standing up, 'we have already asked that question.'

'The witness may answer on further reflection,' Justice Wheeler intoned. No one would say that this trial was unfair.

'Sir, I did not know he was unconscious, and I didn't know how long it would be before he got up. So, I shot to disable him. I just didn't want him to get back up for a while.'

'I'm sure that's what they said at My Lai.'

'That wasn't the Marines, Mr Atkinson,' Ryan shot back.

The lawyer smiled up at Jack. 'I suppose your chaps were better trained at keeping quiet. Indeed, perhaps you yourself have been trained in such things. . . .'

'No, sir, I have not.' *He's making you angry, Jack.* He took his handker-chief out and blew his nose again. The two deep breaths helped. 'Excuse me, I'm afraid the local weather has given me a bit of a head cold. What you just said – if the Marines trained people in that sort of stuff, the newspapers would have plastered it on their front pages years ago. No, moral issues aside for the moment, the Corps has a much better sense of public relations than that, Mr Atkinson.'

'*Indeed.*' The barrister shrugged. 'And what about the Central Intelligence Agency?'

'Excuse me?'

'What of the press reports that you've worked for the CIA?'

'Sir, the only times I've been paid by the US government,' Jack said, choosing his words very carefully, 'the money came from the Navy Department, first as a Marine, then later – now, that is, as an instructor at the United States Naval Academy. I have never been employed by any other government agency, period.'

'So you are not an agent of the CIA? I remind you that you are under oath.'

'No, sir. I am not now, and I never have been any kind of agent – unless you count being a stockbroker. I don't work for the CIA.'

'And these news reports?'

'I'm afraid that you'll have to ask the reporters. I don't know where that stuff comes from. I teach history. My office is in Leahy Hall on the Naval Academy grounds. That's kind of a long way from Langley.'

'Langley? You know where the CIA is, then?'

'Yes, sir. It's on record that I have delivered a lecture there. It was the same lecture I delivered the month before at the Naval War College at Newport, Rhode Island. My paper dealt with the nature of tactical decision-making. I have never worked for the Central Intelligence Agency, but I did, once, give a lecture there. Maybe that's where all these reports started.'

'I think you're lying, Sir John,' Atkinson observed.

Not quite, Charlie. 'I can't help what you think, sir. I can only answer your questions truthfully.'

'And you never wrote an official report for the government entitled *Agents and Agencies*?'

Ryan did not allow himself to react. *Where did you get that bit of data, Charlie?* He answered the question with great care.

'Sir, last year – that is, last summer, at the end of the last school year – I was asked to be a contract consultant to a private company that does government work. The company is the Mitre Corporation, and I was hired on a temporary basis as part of one of their consulting contracts with the US government. The work involved was classified, but it obviously had nothing at all to do with this case.'

'Obviously? Why don't you let the jury decide that?'

'Mr Atkinson,' Justice Wheeler said tiredly, 'are you suggesting that this work in which the witness was involved has a direct connection with the case before the court?'

'I think we might wish to establish that, My Lord. It is my belief that the witness is misleading the court.'

'Very well.' The judge turned. 'Doctor Ryan, did this work in which you were engaged have anything whatever to do with a case of murder in the city of London, or with any of the persons involved in this case?'

'No, sir.'

'You are quite certain?'

'Yes, sir.'

'Are you now or have you ever been an employee of any intelligence or security agency of the American government?'

'Except for the Marine Corps, no, sir.'

'I remind you of your oath to tell the truth – the whole, complete truth. Have you misled the court in any way, Doctor Ryan?'

'No, sir, absolutely not.'

'Thank you, Doctor Ryan. I believe that question is now settled.' Mr Justice Wheeler turned back to his right. 'Next question, Mr Atkinson.'

The barrister had to be angry at that, Ryan thought, but he didn't let it show. He wondered if someone had briefed the judge.

'You say that you shot my client *merely* in the hope that he would not get up?'

Richards stood. 'My Lord, the witness has already –'

'If His Lordship will permit me to ask the next question, the issue will be more clear,' Atkinson interrupted smoothly.

'Proceed.'

'Doctor Ryan, you said that you shot my client in the hope that he would not get up. Do the US Marine Corps teach one to shoot to disable, or to kill?'

'To kill, sir.'

'And you are telling us, therefore, that you went against your training?'

'Yes, sir. It is pretty clear that I was not on a battlefield. I was on a city street. It never occurred to me to kill your client.' *I wish it had, then I probably wouldn't be here*, Ryan thought, wondering if he really meant it.

'So you reacted in accordance with your training when you leaped into the fray on The Mall, but then you *disregarded* your training a moment later? Do you think it reasonable that all of us here will believe *that*?'

Atkinson had finally succeeded in confusing Ryan. Jack had not the slightest idea where this was leading.

'I haven't thought of it that way, sir, but, yes, you are correct,' Jack admitted. 'That is pretty much what happened.'

'And next you crept to the corner of the car, saw the second person whom you had seen earlier, and instead of trying to disable him, you shot him dead without warning. In this case, it is clear that you reverted again to your Marine training, and shot to kill. Don't you find this inconsistent?'

Jack shook his head. 'Not at all, sir. In each case I used the force necessary to – well, the force I had to use, as I saw things.'

'I think you are wrong, Sir John. I think that you reacted like a hotheaded officer of the United States Marines throughout. You raced into a situation of which you had no clear understanding, attacked an innocent man, and tried then to kill him while he lay helpless and unconscious on the street. Next you coldly gunned down someone else without the first thought of trying to disarm him. You did not know then, and you do not know now what was really happening, do you?'

'No, sir, I do not believe that was the case at all. What was I supposed to have done with the second man?'

Atkinson saw an opening and used it. 'You just told the court that you only wished to disable my client – when in fact you tried to kill him. How do you expect us to believe that when your next action had not the first thing to do with such a *peaceful* solution?'

'Sir, when I saw McCrory, the second gunman, for the first time, he had an AK-47 assault rifle in his hands. Going up against a light machine gun with a pistol –'

'But by this time you saw that he didn't have the Kalashnikov, didn't you?'

'Yes, sir, that's true. If he'd still had it – I don't know, maybe I wouldn't have stepped around the car, maybe I would have shot from cover, from behind the car, that is.'

'Ah, I see!' Atkinson exclaimed. 'Instead, here was your chance to confront and kill the man in true cowboy fashion.' His hands went up in the air. 'Dodge City on The Mall!'

'I wish you'd tell me what you think I should have done,' Jack said with some exasperation.

'For someone able to shoot straight through the heart on his first shot, why not shoot the gun from his hand, Sir John?'

'Oh, I see.' Atkinson had just made a mistake. Ryan shook his head and smiled. 'I wish you'd make up your mind.'

'What?' The barrister was caught by surprise.

'Mr Atkinson, a minute ago you said that I tried to kill your client. I was at arms-length range, but I *didn't* kill him. So I'm a pretty lousy shot. But you expect me to be able to hit a man in the hand at fifteen or twenty feet. It doesn't work that way, sir. I'm either a good shot or a bad shot, sir, but not both. Besides, that's just TV stuff, shooting a gun out of somebody's hand. On TV the good guy can do that, but TV isn't real. With a pistol, you aim for the centre of your target. That's what I did. I stepped out from behind the car to get a clear shot, and I aimed. If McCrory had not turned his gun towards me – I can't say for sure, but probably I would not have shot. But he did turn and fire, as you can see from my shoulder – and I did

445

return fire. It is true that I might have done things differently. Unfortunately I did not. I had – I didn't have much time to take action. I did the best I could. I'm sorry the man was killed, but that was his choice, too. He saw I had the drop on him, but he turned and fired – and he fired first, sir.'

'But you never said a word, did you?'

'No, I don't think I did,' Jack admitted.

'Don't you wish you'd done things differently?'

'Mr Atkinson, if it makes you feel any better, I have gone over that again and again for the past four weeks. If I'd had more time to think, perhaps I would have done something different. But I'll never know, because I didn't have more time.' Jack paused. 'I suppose the best thing for all concerned would be if all this had never happened. But I didn't make it happen, sir. He did.' Jack allowed himself to look at Miller again.

Miller was sitting in a straight-back wooden chair, his arms crossed in front of him, and head cocked slightly to the left. A smile started to take shape at one corner of his mouth. It didn't go very far, and wasn't supposed to. It was a smile for Ryan alone . . . or maybe not me alone, Jack realized. Sean Miller's gray eyes didn't blink – he must have practiced that – as they bored in on him from thirty feet away. Ryan returned the stare, careful to keep his face without expression, and while the court reporter finished up his transcription of Jack's testimony, and the visitors in the overhead gallery shared whispered observations, Ryan and Miller were all alone, testing each other's wills. *What's behind those eyes?* Jack wondered again. No weakling, to be sure. This was a game – Miller's game that he'd practiced before, Ryan thought with certainty. There was strength in there, like something one might encounter in a predatory animal. But there was nothing to mute the strength. There was none of the softness of morality or conscience, only strength and will. With four police constables around him, Sean Miller was as surely restrained as a wolf in a cage, and he looked at Ryan as a wolf might from behind the bars, without recognition of his humanity. He was a predator, looking at a . . . thing – and wondering how he might reach it. The suit and the tie were camouflage, as had been his earlier smile at his friends in the gallery. He wasn't thinking about them now. He wasn't thinking about what the court would decide. He wasn't thinking about prison, Jack knew. He was thinking only about something named Ryan, something he could see just out of his reach. In the witness box, Jack's right hand flexed in his lap as though to grasp the pistol which lay in sight on the evidence table a few feet away.

This wasn't an animal in a cage, after all. Miller had intelligence and education. He could think and plan, as a human could, but he would not be restrained by any human impulses when he decided to move. Jack's academic investigation of terrorists for the CIA had dealt with them as abstractions, robots that moved about and did things, and had to be neutralized one way or another. He'd never expected to meet one. More important, Jack had never expected to have one look at him in this way. Didn't he know that Jack was just doing his civic duty?

You could care less about that. I'm something that got in your way. I hurt you, killed your friend, and defeated your mission. You want to get even, don't you? A wounded animal will always seek out its tormentor, Jack told himself. *And this wounded animal has a brain. This one has a memory.* Out of sight to anyone else, he wiped a sweaty hand on his pants. *This one* is thinking.

Ryan was frightened in a way that he'd never known before. It lasted several seconds before he reminded himself that Miller was surrounded by four cops, that the jury would find him guilty, that he would be sentenced to prison for the remainder of his natural life, and that prison life would change the person or thing that lived behind those pale gray eyes.

And I used to be a Marine, Jack told himself. *I'm not afraid of you. I can handle you, punk. I took you out once, didn't I?* He smiled back at Sean Miller, just a slight curve at the corner of his own mouth. *Not a wolf – a weasel. Nasty, but not that much to worry about,* he told himself. Jack turned away as though from an exhibit in the zoo. He wondered if Miller had seen through his quiet bravado.

'No further questions,' Atkinson said.

'The witness may step down,' Mr Justice Wheeler said.

Jack stood up from the stool and turned to find the way out. As he did so, his eyes swept across Miller one last time, long enough to see that the look and the smile hadn't changed.

Jack walked back out to the grand hall as another witness passed in the other direction. He found Dan Murray waiting for him.

'Not bad,' the FBI agent observed, 'but you want to be careful locking horns with a lawyer. He almost tripped you up.'

'You think it'll matter?'

Murray shook his head. 'Nah. The trial's a formality, the case is airtight.'

'What'll he get?'

'Life. Normally over here "life" doesn't mean any more than it does stateside – six or eight years. For this kid, "life" means *life*. Oh, there you are, Jimmy.'

Commander Owens came down the corridor and joined them. 'How did our lad perform?'

'Not an Oscar winner, but the jury liked him,' Murray said.

'How can you tell that?'

'That's right, you've never been through this, have you? They sat perfectly still, hardly even breathed while you were telling your story. They believed everything you said, especially the part about how you've thought and worried about it. You come across as an honest guy.'

'I am,' Ryan said. 'So?'

'Not everybody is,' Owens pointed out. 'And juries are actually quite good at noticing it. That is, some of the time.'

Murray nodded. 'We both have some good – well, not so good – stories about what a jury can do, but when you get down to it, the system works pretty well. Commander Owens, why don't we buy this gentleman a beer?'

'A fine idea, Agent Murray.' Owens took Ryan's arm and led him to the staircase.

'That kid's a scary little bastard, isn't he?' Ryan said. He wanted a professional opinion.

'You noticed, eh?' Murray observed. 'Welcome to the wonderful world of the international terrorist. Yeah, he's a tough little son of a bitch, all right. Most of 'em are, at first.'

'A year from now he'll have been changed a bit. He's a hard one, mind, but the hard ones are often rather brittle,' Owens said. 'They sometimes crack. Time is very much on our side, Jack. And even if he doesn't, that's one less to worry about.'

'A very confident witness,' the TV news commentator said. 'Doctor Ryan fended off a determined attack by the defence counsel, Charles Atkinson, and identified defendant Sean Miller quite positively in the second day of The Mall Murder trial in Old Bailey Number Two.' The picture showed Ryan walking down the hill from the courthouse with two men in attendance. The American was gesturing about something, then laughed as he passed the TV news camera.

'Our old friend Owens. Who's the other one?' O'Donnell asked.

'Daniel E. Murray, FBI representative at Grosvenor Square,' replied his intelligence officer.

'Oh. Never saw his face. So that's what he looks like. Going out for a jar, I'll wager. The hero and his coat-holders. Pity we wouldn't have had a man with an RPG right there....' They'd scouted James Owens once, trying to figure a way to assassinate him, but the man always had a chase car and never used the same route twice. His house was always watched. They could have killed him, but the getaway would have been too risky, and O'Donnell was not given to sending his men on suicide missions. 'Ryan goes home either tomorrow or the next day.'

'Oh?' The intelligence officer hadn't learned that. *Where does Kevin get all his special information. . . ?*

'Too bad, isn't it? Wouldn't it be grand to send him home in a coffin, Michael?'

'I thought you said he was not a worthwhile target,' Mike McKenney said.

'Ah, but he's a proud one, isn't he? Crosses swords with our friend Charlie and prances out of the Bailey for a pint of beer. Bloody American, so sure of everything.' *Wouldn't it be nice to . . .* Kevin O'Donnell shook his head. 'We have other things to plan. Sir John can wait, and so can we.'

'I practically had to hold a gun on somebody to get to do this,' Murray said over his shoulder. The FBI agent was driving his personal car, with a Diplomatic Protection Group escort on the left front seat, and a chase car of C-13 detectives trying to keep up.

Keep your eyes on the damned road, Ryan wished as hard as he could. His exposure to London traffic to this point had been minimal, and only now did he appreciate that the city's speed limit was considered a matter of contempt by the drivers. Being on the wrong side of the road didn't help either.

'Tom Hughes – he's the Chief Warder – told me what he had planned, and I figured you might want an escort who talks right.'

And drives right, Ryan thought as they passed a truck – lorry – on the wrong side. *Or was it the right side? How do you tell?* He could tell that they'd missed the lorry's rearlights by about eighteen inches. English roads were not impressive for their width.

'Damned shame you didn't get to see very much.'

'Well, Cathy did, and I caught a lot of TV.'

'What did you watch?'

'Jack laughed. 'I caught a lot of the replays of the cricket championships.'

'Did you ever figure out the rules?' Murray asked, turning his head again.

'It has rules?' Ryan asked incredulously. 'Why spoil it with rules?'

'They say it does, but damn if I ever figured them out. But we're getting even now.'

'How's that?'

'Football is becoming pretty popular over here. Our kind, I mean. I gave Jimmy Owens a big runaround last year on the difference between offside and illegal procedure.'

'You mean encroachment and false start, don't you?' the DPG man inquired.

'See? They're catching on.'

'You mean I could have gotten football on TV, and nobody told me!'

'Too bad, Jack,' Cathy observed.

'Well, here we are.' Murray stood on the brakes as he turned downhill towards the river. Jack noticed that he seemed to be heading the wrong way down a one-way street, but at least he was going more slowly now. Finally the car stopped. It was dark. The sunset came early this time of year.

'Here's your surprise.' Murray jumped out and got the door, allowing Ryan to repeat his imitation of a fiddler crab exiting from a car. 'Hi, there, Tom!'

Two men approached, both in Tudor uniforms of blue and red. The one in the lead, a man in his late fifties, came directly to Ryan.

'Sir John, Lady Ryan, welcome to Her Majesty's Tower of London. I am Thomas Hughes, this is Joseph Evans. I see that Dan managed to get you here on time.' Everyone shook hands.

'Yeah, we didn't even have to break mach-1. May I ask what the surprise is?'

'But then it wouldn't be a surprise,' Hughes pointed out. 'I had hoped to conduct you around the grounds myself, but there's something I must attend to. Joe will see to your needs, and I'll rejoin you shortly.' The Chief Warder walked off with Dan Murray in his wake.

'Have you been to the Tower before?' Evans asked. Jack shook his head.

'I have, when I was nine,' Cathy said. 'I don't remember very much.'

Evans motioned for them to come along with him. 'Well, we'll try to implant the knowledge more permanently this time.'

'You guys are all soldiers, right?'

'Actually, Sir John, we are all ex-sergeant majors – well, two of us were warrant officers. I was sergeant major in 1 Para when I retired. I had to wait four years to get accepted here. There is quite a bit of interest in this job, as you might imagine. The competition is very keen.'

'So, you were what we call a command sergeant-major, sir?'

'Yes, I think that's right.'

Ryan gave a quick look to the decorations on Evans' coat – it looked more like a dress, but he had no plans to say that.

Those ribbons didn't mean that Evans had come out of the dentist's office with no cavities. It didn't take much imagination to figure what sort of men got appointed to this job. Evans didn't walk; he marched with the sort of pride that took thirty years of soldiering to acquire.

'Is your arm troubling you, sir?'

'My name's Jack, and my arm's okay.'

'I had a cast just like that one back in 'sixty-eight, I think it was. Training accident,' Evans said with a rueful shake of his head. 'Landed on a stone fence. Hurt like the very devil for weeks.'

'But you kept jumping.' *And did your push-ups one-handed, didn't you?*

'Of course.' Evans stopped. 'Right, now this imposing edifice is the Middle Tower. There used to be an outer structure right there where the souvenir shop is. They called it the Lion Tower, because that's where the royal menagerie was kept until 1834.'

The speech was delivered as perfectly as Evans had done, several times per day, for the past four years. *My first castle*, Jack thought, looking at the stone walls.

'Was the moat for-real?'

'Oh, yes, and a very unpleasant one at that. The problem, you see, was that it was designed so that the river would wash in and out every day, thereby keeping it fresh and clean. Unfortunately the engineer didn't do his sums quite right, and once the water came in, it stayed in. Even worse, everything that got thrown away by the people living here was naturally enough thrown into the moat – and stayed there, and rotted. I suppose it served a tactical purpose, though. The smell of the moat alone must have been sufficient to keep all but the most adventurous chaps away. It was finally drained in 1843, and now it serves a really useful purpose – the children can play football there. On the far side are swings and jungle gyms. Do you have children?'

'One and a ninth,' Cathy answered.

'Really?' Evans smiled in the darkness. 'Bloody marvellous! I suppose that's one Yank who will be forever – at least a little – British! Moira and I have two, both of them born overseas. Now this is the Byward Tower.'

'These things all had drawbridges, right?' Jack asked.

'Yes, the Lion and Middle towers were essentially islands with twenty or so feet of smelly water around them. You'll also notice that the path into the grounds has a right-angle turn. The purpose of that, of course, was to make life difficult for the chaps with the battering ram.'

Jack looked at the width of the moat and the height of the walls as they passed into the Tower grounds proper. 'So nobody ever took this place?'

Evans shook his head. 'There has never been a serious attempt, and I wouldn't much fancy trying today.'

'Yeah,' Ryan agreed. 'You sweat having somebody come in and bomb the place?'

'That's happened. I'm sorry to say, in the White Tower, over ten years ago – terrorists. Security is somewhat tighter now,' Evans said.

In addition to the Yeoman Warders there were uniformed guards like those Ryan had encountered on The Mall, wearing the same red tunics and bearskin hats, and carrying the same kind of modern rifle. It was rather an odd contrast to Evans' period uniform, but no one seemed to notice.

'You know, of course, that this facility served many purposes over the years. It was the royal prison, and as late as World War Two, Rudolf Hess was kept here. Now, do you know who was the first Queen of England to be executed here?'

'Anne Boleyn,' Cathy answered.

'Very good. They teach our history in America?' Evans asked.

'*Masterpiece Theatre*,' Cathy explained. 'I saw the TV show.'

'Well, then you know that all the private executions were carried out with an axe – except hers. King Henry had a special executioner imported from France; he used a sword instead of an axe.'

'He didn't want it to hurt?' Cathy asked with a twisted smile. 'Nice of him.'

'Yes, he was a considerate chap, wasn't he? And this is Traitor's Gate. You might be interested to know that it was originally called the Water Gate.'

Ryan laughed. 'Lucky for you guys too, eh?'

'Indeed. Prisoners were taken through this gate by boat to Westminster for trial.'

'Then back here for their haircuts?'

'Only the really important ones. Those executions – they were private instead of public – were done on the Tower Green. The public executions were carried out elsewhere.' Evans led them through the gate in the Bloody

Tower, after explaining its history. Ryan wondered if anyone had ever put all this place's history into one book, and if so, how many volumes it required.

The Tower Green was far too pleasant to be the site of executions. Even the signs to keep people off the grass said *Please*. Two sides were lined with Tudor-style (of course) houses, but the northern edge was the site where the scaffolding was erected for the high-society executions. Evans went through the procedure, which included having the executioner pay the headsman – in advance – in the hope that he'd do a proper job.

'The last woman to be executed here,' Evans went on, 'was Jane, Viscountess Rochford, 13 February, 1542.'

'What did she do?' Cathy asked.

'What she didn't do, actually. She neglected to tell King Henry the Eighth that his fifth wife, Catherine Howard, was, uh, amorously engaged with someone other than her husband,' Evans said delicately.

'That was a real historic moment,' Jack chuckled. 'That's the last time a woman was ever executed for keeping her mouth *shut*.'

Cathy smiled at her husband. 'Jack, how about I break your other arm?'

'And what would Sally say?'

'She'd understand,' his wife assured him.

'Sergeant major, isn't it amazing how women stick together?'

'I did not survive thirty-one years as a professional soldier by being so foolish as to get involved in domestic disputes,' Evans said sensibly.

I lose, Ryan told himself The remainder of the tour lasted about twenty minutes. The Yeoman led them downhill past the White Tower, then left towards an area roped off from the public. A moment later Ryan and his wife found themselves in another of the reasons that men applied for the job.

The Yeoman Warders had their own little pub hidden away in the 14th-century stonework. Plaques from every regiment in the British Army – and probably gifts from many others – lined the walls. Evans handed them off to yet another man. Dan Murray reappeared, a glass in his hand.

'Jack, Cathy, this is Bob Hallston.'

'You must be thirsty,' the man said.

'You could talk me into a beer,' Jack admitted. 'Cathy?'

'Something soft.'

'You're sure?' Hallston asked.

'I'm not a temperance worker, I just don't drink when I'm pregnant,' Cathy explained.

'Congratulations!' Hallston took two steps to the bar and returned with a glass of lager for Jack, and what looked like ginger ale for his wife. 'To your health, and your baby's.'

Cathy beamed. There was something about pregnant women, Jack thought. His wife wasn't just pretty anymore. She glowed. He wondered if it was only for him.

452

'I understand you're a doctor?'

'I'm an ophthalmic surgeon.'

'And you teach history, sir?'

'That's right. I take it you work here, too.'

'Correct. There are thirty-nine of us. We are the ceremonial guardians of the Sovereign. We have invited you here to thank you for doing our job, and to join us in a small ceremony that we do every night.'

'Since 1240,' Murray said.

'The year 1240?' Cathy asked.

'Yeah, it's not something they cooked up for the tourists. This is the real thing,' Murray said. 'Right, Bob?'

'Quite real. When we lock up for the night, this museum collection becomes the safest place in England.'

'I'll buy that,' Jack tossed off half his beer. 'And if they get past those kids out there, the bad guys have you fellows to worry about.'

'Yes.' Hallston smiled. 'One or two of us might remember our basic skills. I was in the original SAS, playing hare and hounds with Rommel in the Western Desert. Dreadful place, the desert. Left me with a permanent thirst.'

They never lose it, Ryan thought. They never lose the look, not the real professionals. They get older, add a few pounds, mellow out a little, but beneath all that you can still see the discipline and the essential toughness that makes them different. And the pride, the understated confidence that comes from having done it all, and not having to talk about it very much, except among themselves. It never goes away.

'Do you have any Marines in here?'

'Two,' Hallston said. 'We try to keep them from holding hands.'

'Right! Be nice, I used to be a Marine.'

'No one's perfect,' Hallston sympathized.

'So, what's this Key Ceremony?'

'Well, back in the year 1240, the chap whose job it was to lock up for the night was set upon by some ruffians. Thereafter, he refused to do his duty without a military escort. Every night since, without interruption, the Chief Warder locks the three principal gates, then places the keys in the Queen's House on the Tower Green. There's a small ceremony that goes along with this. We thought that you and your wife might like to see it.' Hallston sipped his beer. 'You were in court today, I understand. How did it go?'

'I'm glad it's behind me. Dan says I did all right.' Ryan shrugged. 'When Mr Evans showed us the block topside – I wonder if it still works,' Ryan said thoughtfully, remembering the look on that young face. *Is Miller sitting in his cell right now, thinking about me?* Ryan drank the last of his beer. *I'll bet he is.*

'Excuse me?'

'That Miller kid. It's a shame you can't take him up there for a short haircut.'

Hallston smiled coldly. 'I doubt anyone here would disagree with you. We might even find a volunteer to swing the axe.'

'You'd have to hold a lottery, Bob.' Murray handed Ryan another glass. 'You still worrying about him, Jack?'

'I've never seen anybody like that before.'

'He's in jail, Jack,' Cathy pointed out.

'Yeah, I know.' *So why are you still thinking about him?* Jack asked himself. *The hell with it. The hell with him.* 'This is great beer, Sar-major.'

'That's the real reason they apply for the job,' Murray chuckled.

'One of the reasons.' Hallston finished his glass. 'Almost time.'

Jack finished off his second glass with a gulp. Evans reappeared, now wearing street clothes, and led them back out to the chilled night air. It was a clear night, with a three-quarters moon casting muted shadows on the stone battlements. A handful of electric lights added a few isolated splashes of light. Jack was surprised how peaceful it was for being in the centre of a city, like his own home over the Chesapeake. Without thinking, he took his wife's hand as Evans led them west towards the Bloody Tower. A small crowd was already there, standing by Traitor's Gate, and a Warder was giving them instructions to be as quiet as possible, and not, of course, to take any photographs. A sentry was posted there, plus four other men under arms, their breath illuminated by the blue-white floodlights. It was the only sign of life. Otherwise they might have been made of stone.

'Right about now,' Murray whispered.

Jack heard a door close somewhere ahead. It was too dark to see very much, and the few lights that were turned on only served to impair his night vision. He heard the sound of jingling keys first of all, like small bells rattling to the measured tread of a walking man. Next he saw a point of light. It grew into a square lantern with a candle inside, carried by Tom Hughes, the Chief Warder. The sound of his footsteps was as regular as a metronome as he approached, his back ramrod-straight from a lifetime of practice. A moment later the four soldiers formed up on him, the warder between them, and they marched off, back into the tunnel-like darkness to the fading music of the rattling keys and cleated shoes clicking on the pavement, leaving the sentry at the Bloody Tower.

Jack didn't hear the gates close, but a few minutes later the sound of the keys returned, and he glimpsed the returning guards in the irregular splashes of light. For some reason the scene was overpoweringly romantic. Ryan reached around his wife's waist and pulled her close. She looked up.

Love you, he said with his lips as the keys approached again. Her eyes answered.

To their right, the sentry snapped to on-guard: 'Halt! Who goes there?' His words reverberated down the corridor of ancient stone.

The advancing men stopped at once, and Tom Hughes answered the challenge: 'The keys!'

'Whose keys?' the sentry demanded.

'Queen Anne's keys!'

'Pass, Queen Anne's keys!' The sentry brought his rifle to present-arms.

The sentries, with Hughes in their midst, resumed their march and turned left, up the slope to the Tower Green. Ryan and his wife followed close behind. At the steps that capped the upward slope waited a squad of riflemen. Hughes and his escort stopped. The squad on the steps came to present-arms, and the Chief Warder removed his uniform bonnet.

'God preserve Queen Anne!'

'Amen!' the guard force replied.

Behind them, a bugler stood. He blew Last Post. The notes echoed against the stones in a way that denoted the end of day, and when necessary, the end of life. Like the circular waves that follow a stone's fall into the water, the last mournful note lingered until it faded to nothingness in the still air. Ryan bent down to kiss his wife. It was a magical moment that they would not soon forget.

The Chief Warder proceeded up the steps to secure the keys for the night, and the crowd withdrew.

'Every night since 1240, eh?' Jack asked.

'The ceremony was interrupted during the Blitz. A German bomb fell into the Tower grounds while things were under way. The warder was bowled over by the blast, and the candle in his lantern was extinguished. He had to relight it before he could continue,' Evans said. That the man had been wounded was irrelevant. Some things are more important than that. 'Shall we return to the pub?'

'We don't have anything like this at home,' Cathy said quietly.

'Well, America isn't old enough, is she?'

'It would be nice if we had something like this, maybe at Bunker Hill or Fort McHenry,' Jack said quietly.

Murray nodded agreement. 'Something to remind us why we're here.'

'Tradition is important,' Evans said. 'For a soldier, tradition is often the reason one carries on when there are so many reasons not to. It's more than just yourself, more than just your mates – but it's not just something for soldiers, is it? It is true – or should be true – of any professional community.'

'It is,' Cathy said. 'Any good medical school beats that into your head. Hopkins sure did.'

'So does the Corps,' Jack agreed. 'But we don't express it as well as you just did.'

'We've had more practice.' Evans opened the door to the pub. 'And better beer to aid in our contemplation.'

'Now, if you guys could only learn how to fix beef properly. . . .' Jack said to Murray.

'That's telling 'em, ace,' the FBI agent chuckled.

'Another beer for a brother Marine.' A glass was handed to Ryan by another of the warders. 'Surely you've had enough of this para prima donna by now.'

'Bert's one of the Marines I told you about,' Evans explained.

'I never say bad things about somebody who buys the drinks,' Ryan told Bert.

'That is an awfully sensible attitude. Are you sure you were only a lieutenant?'

'Only for three months.' Jack explained about the helicopter crash.

'That *was* bad luck. Bloody training accidents,' Evans said. 'More dangerous than combat.'

'So you guys work as tour guides here?'

'That's part of it,' the other warder said. 'It's a good way to keep one's hand in, and also to educate the odd lieutenant. Just last week I spoke to one of the Welsh Guards chaps – he was having trouble getting things right, and I gave him a suggestion.'

'The one thing you really miss,' Evans agreed. 'Teaching those young officers to be proper soldiers. Who says the best diplomats work at Whitehall?'

'I never got the feeling that I was completely useless as a second lieutenant,' Jack observed with a smile.

'All depends on one's point of view,' the other yeoman said. 'Still and all, you might have worked out all right, judging by what you did on The Mall.'

'I don't know, Bert. A lieutenant with a hero complex is not the sort of chap you want to be around. They keep doing the damnedest things. But I suppose the ones who survive, and learn, do work out as you say. Tell me, Lieutenant Ryan, what have you learned?'

'Not to get shot. The next time I'll just shoot from cover.'

'Excellent.' Bob Hallston rejoined them. 'And don't leave one alive behind you,' he added. The SAS wasn't noted for leaving people alive by accident.

Cathy didn't like this sort of talk. 'Gentlemen, you can't just kill people like that.'

'The Lieutenant took rather a large chance, ma'am, not the sort of chance that one will walk away from very often. If there is ever a next time – and there won't be, of course. But if there is, you can act like a policeman or a soldier, but not both. You're very lucky to be alive, young man. You have that arm to remind you just how lucky you are. It is good to be brave, Lieutenant. It is better to be smart, and much less painful for those around you,' Evans said. He looked down at his beer. 'Dear God, how *many* times have I said that!'

'How many times have we all said it?' Bert said quietly. 'And the pity is, so many of them didn't listen. Enough of that. This lovely lady doesn't want to hear the ramblings of tired old men. Bob tells me that you are expecting another child. In two months, I shall be a grandfather for the first time.'

'Yes, he can hardly wait to show us the pictures.' Evans laughed. 'A boy or a girl this time?'

'Just so all the pieces are attached and they all work.' There was general agreement on the point. Ryan finished off his third beer of the evening. It was pretty strong stuff, and he was getting a buzz from it. 'Gentlemen, if any of you come to America, and happen to visit the Washington area, I trust you will let us know.'

'And the next time you are in London, the bar is open,' Tom Hughes said. The Chief Warder was back in civilian clothes, but carrying his uniform bonnet, a hat whose design went back three or four centuries. 'And perhaps you'll find room in your home for this. Sir John, with the thanks of us all.'

'I'll take good care of this.' Ryan took the hat, but couldn't bring himself to put it on. He hadn't earned that right.

'Now, I regret to say that if you don't leave now, you'll be stuck here all night. At midnight all the doors are shut, and that is that.'

Jack and Cathy shook hands all around, then followed Hughes and Murray out the door.

The walk between the inner and outer walls was still quiet, the air still cold, and Jack found himself wondering if ghosts walked the Tower Grounds at night. It was almost –

'What's that?' He pointed to the outer wall. A spectral shape *was* walking up there.

'A sentry,' Hughes said. 'After the Ceremony of the Keys, the guards don their pattern-disruptive clothing.' They passed the sentry at the Bloody Tower, now dressed in camouflage fatigues, with web gear and ammo pouches.

'Those rifles are loaded now, aren't they?' Jack asked.

'Not very much use otherwise, are they? This is a very safe place,' Hughes replied.

Nice to know that some places are, Ryan thought. *Now why did I think that?*

7

Speedbird Home

The Speedway Lounge at Heathrow Airport's Terminal 4 was relaxing enough, or would have been had Jack not been nervous about flying. Beyond the floor-to-ceiling windows he could see the Concorde he'd be taking home in a few minutes. The designers had given their creation the aspect of a living creature, like some huge, merciless bird of prey, a thing of fearful beauty. It sat there at the end of the jetway atop its unusually high landing gear, staring at Ryan impassively over its daggerlike nose.

'I wish the Bureau would let me commute back and forth on that baby,' Murray observed.

'It's pretty!' Sally Ryan agreed.

It's just another goddamned airplane, Jack told himself. *You can't see what holds it up.* Jack didn't remember whether it was Bernoulli's Principle or the Venturi Effect, but he knew that it was something *inferred*, not actually seen, that enabled aircraft to fly. He remembered that something had interrupted the Principle or Effect over Crete and nearly killed him, and that nineteen months later that same something had reached up and killed his parents five thousand feet short of the runway at Chicago's O'Hare International Airport. Intellectually he knew that his Marine helicopter had died of a mechanical failure, and that commercial airliners were simpler and easier to maintain than CH-46s. He also knew that bad weather had been the main contributing factor in his parents' case – and the weather here was clear – but to Ryan there was something outrageous about flying, something unnatural.

Fine, Jack. Why not go back to living in caves and hunting bear with a pointed stick? What's natural about teaching history, or watching TV, or driving a car? Idiot.

But I hate to fly, Ryan reminded himself.

'There has never been an accident in the Concorde,' Murray pointed out. 'And Jimmy Owens's troops gave the bird a complete checkout.' The possibility of a bomb on that pretty white bird was a real one. The explosives experts from C-13 had spent over an hour that morning making sure that nobody had done that, and now police dressed as British Airways ground crewmen stood around the airliner. Jack wasn't worried about a bomb. Dogs could find bombs.

'I know,' Jack replied with a wan smile. 'Just a basic lack of guts on my part.'

'It's only lack of guts if you don't go, ace,' Murray pointed out. He was surprised that Ryan was so nervous, though he concealed it well, the FBI agent thought. Murray enjoyed flying. An Air Force recruiter had almost convinced him to become a pilot, back in his college days.

No, it's lack of brains if I do, Jack told himself. *You really are a wimp*, another part of his brain informed him. *Some Marine you turned out to be!*

'When do we blast off, Daddy?' Sally asked.

'One o'clock.' Cathy told her daughter. 'Don't bother Daddy.'

Blast off, Jack thought with a smile. *Damnit, there is* nothing *to be afraid of and you know it!* Ryan shook his head and sipped at his drink from the complimentary bar. He counted four security people in the lounge, all trying to look inconspicuous. Owens was taking no chances on Ryan's last day in

England. The rest was up to British Airways. He wasn't even being billed for the extra cost. Ryan wondered if that was good luck or bad.

A disembodied female voice announced the flight. Jack finished off the drink and rose to his feet.

'Thanks for everything, Dan.'

'Can we go now, Daddy?' Sally asked brightly. Cathy took her daughter's hand.

'Wait a minute !' Murray stooped down to Sally. 'Don't I get a hug and a kiss?'

'Okay.' Sally obliged with enthusiasm. 'G'bye, Mr M'ray.'

'Take good care of our hero,' the FBI man told Cathy.

'He'll be all right,' she assured him.

'Enjoy the football, ace!' Murray nearly crushed Jack's hand. 'That's the one thing I really miss.'

'I can send you tapes.'

'It's not the same. Back to teaching history, eh?'

'That's what I do,' Ryan said.

'We'll see,' Murray observed cryptically. 'How the hell do you walk with that thing on?'

'Badly,' Ryan chuckled. 'I think the doc installed some lead weights, or maybe he left some tools in there by mistake. Well, here we are.' They reached the entrance to the jetway.

'Break a leg.' Murray smiled and moved off.

'Welcome aboard, Sir John,' a flight attendant said. 'We have you in 1-D. Have you flown Concorde before?'

'No.' It was all Jack could muster. Ahead of him, Cathy turned and grinned. The tunnel-like jetway looked like the entrance to the grave.

'Well, you are in for the thrill of your life!' the stewardess assured him.

Thanks a lot! Ryan nearly choked at the outrage, and remembered that he couldn't strangle her with one hand. Then he laughed. There wasn't anything else to do.

He had to duck to avoid crunching his head at the door. It was tiny inside; the cabin was only eight or nine feet across. He looked forward quickly and saw the flight crew in impossibly tight quarters – getting into the pilot's left seat must have been like putting on a boot, it seemed so cramped. Another attendant was hanging up coats. He had to wait until she saw him, and walked sideways, his plaster-encased arm leading the way into the passenger cabin.

'Right here,' his personal guide said.

Jack got into the right-side window seat in the front row. Cathy and Sally were already in their seats on the other side. Jack's cast stuck well over seat 1-C. No one could have sat there. It was just as well that British Airways wasn't charging the difference between this and their L-1011 tickets; there would have been an extra seat charge. He immediately tried to snap on his seat belt and found that it wasn't easy with only one hand. The stewardess was ready for this, and handled it for him.

'You're quite comfortable?'

'Yes.' Jack lied. *I am quite terrified.*

'Excellent. Here is your Concorde information kit.' She pointed towards a gray vinyl folder. 'Would you like a magazine?'

'No, thank you, I have a book in my pocket.'

'Fine. I'll be back after we take off, but if you need anything, please ring.'

Jack pulled the seat belt tighter as he looked forward and left at the airplane's door. It was still open. He could still escape. But he knew he wouldn't do that. He leaned back. The seat was gray, too, a little on the narrow side but comfortable. His placement in the front row gave him all the legroom he needed. The airplane's inside wall – or whatever they called it – was off-white, and he had a window to look out of. Not a very large one, about the size of two paperback books, but better than no window at all. He looked around. The flight was about three-quarters full. These were seasoned travellers, and wealthy ones. Business types mostly, Jack figured, many were reading their copies of the *Financial Times*. And none of them were afraid of flying. You could tell from their impassive faces. It never occurred to Jack that his face was set exactly the same.

'Ladies and gentlemen, this is Captain Nigel Higgins welcoming you aboard British Airways Flight 189, Concorde Service to Washington, DC, and Miami, Florida. We'll begin taxiing in approximately five minutes. Weather at our first stop, Washington's Dulles International Airport, is excellent, clear, with a temperature of fifty-six degrees. We will be in the air a total of three hours and twenty-five minutes. Please observe that the no-smoking sign is lighted, and we ask that while you are seated you keep your seat belts fastened. Thank you,' the clipped voice concluded.

The door had been closed during the speech, Ryan noted sourly. A clever distraction, as their only escape route was eliminated. He leaned back and closed his eyes, resigning himself to fate. One nice thing about being up front was that no one could see him except Cathy – Sally had the window seat – and his wife understood, or at least pretended to. Soon the cabin crew was demonstrating how to put on and inflate life jackets stowed under the seats. Jack watched without interest. Concorde's perfect safety record meant that no one had the first idea on how to ditch one safely, and his position near the nose, so far from the delta-shaped wing, ensured that if they hit the water he'd be in the part of the fuselage that broke off and sank like a cement block. Not that this would matter. The impact itself would surely be fatal.

Asshole, if this bird was dangerous, they would have lost one by now.

The whine of the jet turbines came next, triggering the acid glands in Jack's stomach. He closed his eyes again. *You can't run away.* He commanded himself to control his breathing and relax. That was strangely easy. Jack had never been a white-knuckled flier. He was more likely to be limp.

Some unseen tractor-cart started pushing the aircraft backwards. Ryan looked out of the window and watched the scenery move slowly forward. Heathrow was quite a complex. Aircraft from a dozen airlines were visible, mainly sitting at the terminal buildings like ships at a dock. *Wish we could take a ship home*, he thought, forgetting that he'd been one seasick Marine on Guam, years ago. The Concorde stopped for a few seconds, then began moving under its own power. Ryan didn't know why the landing gear was so high, but this factor imparted an odd sort of movement as they taxied. The captain came on the intercom again and said something about taking off on afterburners, but Ryan didn't catch it, instead watching a Pan Am 747 lift off. The Concorde was certainly prettier, Ryan thought. It reminded him of the models of fighter planes he'd assembled as a kid. *We're going first class.*

The plane made a sweeping turn at the end of the runway and stopped, bobbing a little on the nose gear. *Here we go.*

'Departure positions,' the intercom announced. Somewhere aft the cabin crew strapped into their jump seats. In 1-D, Jack fitted himself into his seat much like a man awaiting electrocution. His eyes were open now, watching out the window.

The engine sounds increased markedly, and Speedbird started to roll. A few seconds later the engine noise appeared to pick up even more, and Ryan was pressed back into the fabric and vinyl chair. *Damn*, he told himself. The acceleration was impressive, about double anything he'd experienced before. He had no way of measuring it, but an invisible hand was pressing him backwards while another pushed at his cast and tried to turn him sideways. The stew had been right. It was a thrill. The grass was racing by his window, then the nose came up sharply. A final bump announced that the main gear was off the ground. Jack listened for its retraction into the airframe, but the sheer power of the takeoff blocked it out. Already they were at least a thousand feet off the ground and rocketing upwards at what seemed an impossible angle. He looked over to his wife. Wow, Cathy mouthed at him. Sally had her nose against the plastic inside window.

The angle of climb eased off slightly. Already the cabin attendants were at work, with a drink cart. Jack got himself a glass of champagne. He wasn't in a celebrating mood, but bubbly wines always affected him fast. Once Cathy had offered to prescribe some Valium for his flying jitters. Ryan had an ingrained reluctance to take drugs. But booze was different, he told himself. He looked out the window. They were still going up. The ride was fairly smooth, no bumps worse than going over the tar strip on a concrete highway.

Jack felt every one, mindful of the fact that he was several thousand feet over – he checked – still the ground.

He fished the paperback out of his pocket and started reading. This was his one sure escape from flying. Jack slouched to his right, his head firmly wedged into the place where the seat and white plastic wall met. He was able to rest his left arm on the aisle seat, and that took the weight off the place on his waist where the cast dug in hard. His right elbow was planted on the armrest, and Ryan made himself a rigid part of the airframe as he concentrated on his book. He'd selected well for the flight, one of Alistair Horne's books on the Franco-German conflicts. He soon found another reason to hate his cast. It was difficult to read and turn pages one-handed. He had to set the book down first to do it.

A brief surge of power announced that first one, then the other pair of afterburners had been activated on the Concorde's Olympus engines. He felt the new acceleration, and the aircraft began to climb again as she passed through mach-1, and the airliner gave meaning to her call sign prefix: 'Speedbird.' Jack looked out the window – they were over water now. He checked his watch: less than three hours to touchdown at Dulles. *You can put up with anything for three hours, can't you?*

Like you have a choice. A light caught his eye. *How did I miss that before?* On the bulkhead a few feet from his head was a digital speed readout. It now read 1024, the last number changing upwards rapidly.

Damn! I'm going a thousand miles per hour. What would Robby say about this? I wonder how Robby's doing. . . . He found himself mesmerized by the number. Soon it was over 1300. The rate of change dropped off nearly to zero, and the display stopped at 1351. *One thousand three hundred fifty-one miles per hour.* He did the computation in his head: nearly two thousand feet per second, almost as fast as a bullet, about twenty miles per minute. *Damn.* He looked out the window again. *But why is it still noisy? If we're going supersonic, how come the sound isn't all behind us? I'll ask Robby. He'll know.*

The puffy, white, fair-weather clouds were miles below and sliding by at a perceptible rate nevertheless. The sun glinted off the waves, and they stood out like shiny blue furrows. One of the things that annoyed Jack about himself was the dichotomy between his terror of flying and his fascination with what the world looked like from up here. He pulled himself back to the book and read of a period when a steam locomotive was the leading edge of human technology, travelling at a thirtieth of what he was doing now. *This may be terrifying, but at least it gets you from place to place.*

Dinner arrived a few minutes later. Ryan found that the champagne had given him an appetite. Jack was rarely hungry on an airplane, but much to his surprise he was now. The menu carried on the annoying, and baffling, English habit of advertising their food in French, as if language had any effect on taste. Jack soon found that the taste needed no amplification. Salmon gave way to a surprisingly good steak – something the Brits have trouble with – a decent salad, strawberries and cream for dessert, and a small plate of cheese. A good port replaced the champagne, and Ryan found that forty minutes had slipped by. Less than two hours to home.

'Ladies and gentlemen, this is the captain speaking. We are now cruising at fifty-three thousand feet, with a ground speed of thirteen hundred fifty-five miles per hour. As we burn off fuel, the aircraft will float up to a peak altitude of roughly fifty-nine thousand feet. The outside air temperature is sixty degrees below zero Celsius, and the aircraft skin temperature is about one hundred degrees Celsius, this caused by friction as we pass through the air. One side effect of this is that the aircraft expands, becoming roughly eleven inches longer in midflight –'

Metal fatigue! Ryan thought bleakly. *Did you have to tell me that?* He touched the window. It felt warm, and he realized that one could boil water on the outside aluminium skin. He wondered what effect that had on the airframe. *Back to the 19th century*, he commanded himself again. Across the aisle his daughter was asleep, and Cathy was immersed in a magazine.

The next time Jack checked his watch there was less than an hour to go. The captain said something about Halifax, Nova Scotia, to his right. Jack looked but saw only a vague dark line on the northern horizon. *North America – we're getting there.* That was good news. As always, his tension and the airliner seat conspired to make his back stiff, and the cast didn't help at all. He felt a need to stand up and walk a few steps, but that was something he tried not to do on airplanes. The steward refilled his port glass, and Jack noticed that the angle of the sun through the window had not changed since London. They were staying even, the aircraft keeping up with the earth's rotation as it sped west. They would arrive at Dulles at about noon, the pilot informed them. Jack looked at his watch again: forty minutes. He stretched his legs and went back to the book.

The next disturbance was when the cabin crew handed out customs and immigration forms. As he tucked his book away, Jack watched his wife go to work listing all the clothes she'd bought. Sally was still asleep, curled up with an almost angelic peace on her face. They made landfall a minute later somewhere over the coast of New Jersey, heading west into Pennsylvania before turning south again. The aircraft was lower now. He'd missed the transonic deceleration, but the cumulus clouds were much closer than they'd been over the ocean. *Okay, Captain Higgins, let's get this bird back on the ground in one solid piece.* He found a silver luggage tag that he was evidently supposed to keep. In fact, he decided to keep the whole package, complete with a certificate that identified him as a Concorde passenger – *or veteran*, he thought wryly. *I survived the British Airways Concorde.*

Dumbass, if you'd flown the L-1011 to Baltimore, you'd still be over the ocean.

They were low enough to see roads now. The majority of aircraft accidents came at landing, but Ryan didn't see it that way. They were nearly home. His fear was nearly at an end. That was good news as he looked out the window at the Potomac. Finally the Concorde took a large nose-high angle again, coming in awfully fast, Jack thought, as she dropped gently towards the ground. A second later he saw the airport perimeter fence. The heavy bumps on the airliner's main gear followed at once. They were down. They were safe. Anything that happened now was a vehicle accident, not an aircraft one, he told himself. Ryan felt safe in cars, mainly because he was in control. *Car – where's our car? We're landing at the wrong airport. . . .*

The seat belt sign came off a moment after the aircraft stopped, and the forward door was opened. Home. Ryan stood and stretched. It was good to be stationary. Cathy had their daughter in her lap, running a brush through her hair as Sally rubbed the sleep from her eyes.

'Okay, Jack?'

'Are we home *already*?' Sally asked.

Her father assured her that they were. He walked forward. The stewardess who'd led him aboard asked if he'd enjoyed the ride, and Jack replied, truthfully, that he had. *Now that it's over.* He found a seat in the mobile lounge, and his family joined him.

'Next time we go across, that's how we do it,' Ryan announced quietly.

'Why? Did you like it?' Cathy was surprised.

'You better believe I like it. You only have to be up there half as long.' Jack laughed, mainly at himself. As with every flight he took, being back on the ground alive carried its own thrill. He had survived what was patently an unnatural act, and the exhilaration of being alive, and home, gave him a quiet glow of his own. The stride of passengers off an airplane is always jauntier than the stride on. The lounge pulled away. The Concorde looked very pretty indeed as they drew away from it and turned towards the terminal.

'How much money did you spend on clothes?' Jack asked as the lounge stopped at the arrival gate. His wife just handed him the form. 'That much?'

'Well, why not?' Cathy grinned. 'I can pay for it out of *my* money, can't I?'

'Sure, babe.'

'And that's three suits for you, too, Jack,' his wife informed him.

'What? How did you –'

'When the tailor set you up for the tux, I had him do three suits. Your arms are the same length, Jack. They'll fit, as soon as we get that damned cast off you, that is.'

Another nice thing about the Concorde: the airliner carried so few people, compared to a wide-body, that getting the luggage back was a snap. Cathy got a trolley – which Sally insisted on pushing – while Jack retrieved their bags. The last obstacle was customs, where they paid over three hundred dollars' worth of penance for Cathy's purchases. Less than thirty minutes after leaving the aircraft, Jack proceeded to his left out the door, helping Sally with the luggage trolley.

'Jack!' It was a big man, taller than Jack's six-one, and broader across the shoulders. He walked badly due to a prosthetic leg that extended above where he had once had a left knee, a gift from a drunken driver. His artificial left foot was a squared-off aluminium band instead of something that looked human. Oliver Wendell Tyler found it easier to walk on. But his hand

464

was completely normal, if rather large. He grabbed Ryan's and squeezed. 'Welcome home, buddy!'

'How's it goin', Skip?' Jack disengaged his hand from the grip of a former offensive tackle and mentally counted his fingers. Skip Tyler was a close friend who never fully appreciated his strength.

'Good. Hi, Cathy.' His wife got a kiss. 'And how's Sally?'

'Fine.' She held up her arms, and got herself picked up as desired. Only briefly, though; Sally wriggled free to get back to the luggage trolley.

'What are you doing here?' Jack asked. *Oh, Cathy must have called....*

'You remember where you parked your car?' Dr Tyler inquired. 'Jean and I retrieved it for you, and dropped it off home. We decided we'd pick you up in ours – more room. She's getting it now.'

'Taking a day off, eh?'

'Something like that. Hell, Jack, Billings has been covering your classes for a couple of weeks. Why can't I take an afternoon off?' A skycap approached them, but Tyler waved him off.

'How's Jean?' Cathy asked.

'Six more weeks.'

'It'll be a little longer for us,' Cathy announced.

'Really?' Tyler's face lit up. 'Outstanding!'

It was cool, with a bright autumn sun as they left the terminal. Jean Tyler was already pulling up with the Tyler family's full-size Chevy wagon. Dark-haired, tall, and willowy, Jean was pregnant with their third and fourth children. The sonogram had confirmed the twins right before the Ryans had left for England. Her otherwise slender frame would have seemed grotesque with the bulge of the babies except for the glow on her face. Cathy went right to her as she got out of the car and said something. Jack knew what it was immediately – their wives immediately hugged: Me, too. Skip wrenched the tailgate open and tossed the luggage inside like so many sheets of paper.

'I gotta admire your timing, Jack. You made it back almost in time for Christmas break,' Skip observed as everyone got in the car.

'I didn't exactly plan it that way,' Jack objected.

'How's the shoulder?'

'Better'n it was, guy.'

'I believe it,' Tyler laughed as he pulled away from the terminal. 'I was surprised they got you on the Concorde. How'd you like it?'

'It's over a lot faster.'

'Yeah, that's what they say.'

'How are things going at school?'

'Ah, nothing ever changes. You heard about The Game?' Tyler's head came around.

'No, as a matter of fact.' *How did I ever forget about that?*

'Absolutely great. Five points down with three minutes left, we recover a fumble on our twelve. Thompson finally gets it untracked and starts hitting sideline patterns – boom, boom, boom, eight-ten yards a pop. Then he pulls a draw play that gets us to the thirty. Army changes its defence, right? So we go to a spread. I'm up in the press box, and I see their strong-side safety is favouring the outside – figures we gotta stop the clock – and we call a post for the tight end. Like a charm! Thompson couldn't have *handed* him the ball any better! Twenty-one to nineteen. What a way to end the season.'

Tyler was an Annapolis graduate who'd made second-string All-American at offensive tackle before entering the submarine service. Three years before, when he'd been on the threshold of his own command a drunk driver had left him without half his leg. Amazingly, Skip hadn't looked back. After taking his doctorate in engineering from MIT, he'd joined the faculty at Annapolis, where he was also able to scout and do a little coaching in the football programme. Jack wondered how much happier Jean was now. A lovely girl who had once worked as a legal secretary, she must have resented Skip's enforced absences on submarine duty. Now she had him home – surely he wasn't straying far; it seemed that Jean was always pregnant – and they were rarely separated. Even when they walked in the shopping malls, Skip and Jean held hands. If anyone found it humorous, he kept his peace about it.

'What are you doing about a Christmas tree, Jack?'

'I haven't thought about it,' Ryan admitted.

'I found a place where we can cut 'em fresh. I'm going over tomorrow. Wanna come?'

'Sure. We have some shopping to do, too,' he added quietly.

'Boy, you've really been out of it. Cathy called last week. Jean and I finished up the, uh, the important part. Didn't she tell you?'

'No.' Ryan turned to see his wife smile at him. *Gotcha!* 'Thanks, Skip.'

'Ah.' Tyler waved his hand as they pulled onto the DC beltway. 'We're going up to Jean's family's place – last chance for her to travel before the twins arrive. And Professor Billings says you have a little work waiting for you.'

A little, Ryan thought. *More like two months' worth.*

'When are you going to be able to start back to work?'

'It'll have to wait until he gets the cast off,' Cathy answered for Jack. 'I'll be taking Jack to Baltimore tomorrow to see about that. We'll get Professor Hawley to check him out.'

'No sense hurrying with that kind of injury,' Skip acknowledged. He had ample personal experience with that sort of thing. 'Robby says hi. He couldn't make it. He's down at Pax River today on a flight simulator, learning to be an airedale again. Rob and Sissy are doing fine, they were just over the house night before last. You picked a good weather day, too. Rained most of last week.'

Home, Jack told himself as he listened. Back to the mundane, day-to-day crap that grates on you so much – until somebody takes it away from you.

466

It was so nice to be back to a situation where rain was a major annoyance, and one's day was marked by waking up, working, eating, and going back to bed. Catching things on television, and football games. The comics in the daily paper. Helping his wife with the wash. Curling up with a book and a glass of wine after Sally was put to bed. Jack promised himself that he'd never find this a dull existence again. He'd just spent over a month on the fast track, and was grateful that he'd left it three thousand miles behind him.

'Good evening, Mr Cooley.' Kevin O'Donnell looked up from his menu.

'Hello, Mr Jameson. How nice to see you,' the book dealer replied with well-acted surprise.

'Won't you join me?'

'Why, yes. Thank you.'

'What brings you into town?'

'Business. I'm staying overnight with friends at Cobh.' This was true; it also told O'Donnell – known locally as Michael Jameson – that he had the latest message with him.

'Care to look at the menu?' O'Donnell handed it over. Cooley inspected it briefly, closed it, and handed it back. No one could have seen the transfer. 'Jameson' let the small envelope inside the folder drop to his lap. The conversation which ensued over the next hour drifted through various pleasantries. There were four Garda in the next booth, and in any case Mr Cooley did not concern himself with operational matters. His job was that of contact agent and cutout. A weak man, O'Donnell thought, though he'd never told this to anyone. Cooley didn't have the right qualities for real operations; he was better suited to the role of intelligence. Not that he'd ever asked, and surely the smaller man had passed through training well enough. His ideology was sound, but O'Donnell had always sensed within him a weakness of character that accompanied his cleverness. No matter. Cooley was a man with no record in any police station. He'd never even thrown a rock, much less a cocktail, at a Saracen. He'd preferred to watch and let his hate fester without an emotional release. Quiet, bookish, and unobtrusive, Dennis was perfect for his job. If Cooley was unable to shed blood, O'Donnell knew, he was also unlikely to shed tears. *You bland little fellow, you can organize a superb intelligence-gathering operation, and so long as you don't have to do any of the wet-work yourself, you can – you have helped cause the death of . . . ten or twelve, wasn't it? Did the man have any emotions at all?* Probably not, the leader judged. Perfect. He had his own little Himmler, O'Donnell told himself – or maybe Dzerzhinsky would be a more apt role model. Yes, 'Iron Feliks' Dzerzhinsky: that malignant, effective little man. It was only the round, puffy face that reminded him of the Nazi Himmler – and a man couldn't choose his looks, could he? Cooley had a future in the organization. When the time came, they'd need a real Dzerzhinsky.

They finished their talking over after-dinner coffee. Cooley picked up the bill. He insisted: business was excellent. O'Donnell pocketed the envelope and left the restaurant. He resisted the urge to read the report. Kevin was a man to whom patience came hard, and as a consequence he forced himself to it. Impatience had ruined more operations than the British Army ever had, he knew. Another lesson from his early days with the Provos. He drove his BMW through the old streets at the legal limit, leaving the town behind as he entered the narrow country roads to his home on the headlands. He did not take a direct route, and kept an eye on his mirror. O'Donnell knew that his security was excellent. He also knew that continued vigilance was the reason it remained so. His expensive car was registered to his corporation's head office in Dundalk. It was a real business, with nine blue-water trawlers that dragged purse-seine nets through the cold northern waters that surrounded the British Isles. The business had an excellent general manager, a man who had never been involved in the Troubles and whose skills allowed O'Donnell to live the life of a country gentleman far to the south. The tradition of absentee ownership was an old one in Ireland – like O'Donnell's home, a legacy from the English.

It took just under an hour to reach the private driveway marked by a pair of stone pillars, and another five minutes to reach the house over the sea. Like any common man, O'Donnell parked his car in the open; the carriage house that was attached to the manor had been converted to offices by a local contractor. He went at once to his study. McKenney was waiting for him there, reading a recent edition of Yeats's poetry. Another bookish lad, though he did not share Cooley's aversion to the sight of blood. His quiet, disciplined demeanour concealed an explosive capacity for action. A man very like O'Donnell himself, Michael was. Like the O'Donnell of ten or twelve years before, his youth needed tempering; hence his assignment as chief of intelligence so that he could learn the value of deliberation, of gathering all the information he could get before he committed himself to action. The Provos never really did that. They used tactical intelligence, but not the strategic kind – a fine explanation, O'Donnell thought, for the mindlessness of their overall strategy. Another of the reasons he had left the Provisionals – but he would return to the fold. Or more properly, the fold would return to him. Then he would have his army. Kevin already had his plan, though not even his closest associates knew it – at least not all of it.

O'Donnell sat in the leather chair behind the desk and took the envelope from his coat pocket. McKenney discreetly went to the corner bar and got his superior a glass of whiskey. With ice, a taste Kevin had acquired in hotter climes several years before. He set the glass on the desk, and O'Donnell took it, sipping off a tiny bit without a word.

There were six pages to the document, and O'Donnell read through the single-spaced pages as slowly and deliberately as McKenney had just been doing with the words of Yeats. The younger man marvelled at the man's patience. For all his reputation as a fighter capable of ruthless action, the chief of the ULA often seemed a creature made of stone, the way he would assemble and process data. Like a computer, but a malignant one. He took fully twenty minutes to go through the six pages.

'Well, our friend Ryan is back in America, where he belongs. Flew home on Concorde, and his wife arranged for a friend to meet them at the airport. Next Monday I expect he'll be back teaching those fine young men and women at their Naval Academy.' O'Donnell smiled at the humour of his words. 'His Highness and his lovely bride will be back home two days late. It seems that their aircraft developed electrical problems, and a new instrument had to be flown in all the way from England – or so the public story will go. In reality, it would seem that they like New Zealand so much that they wanted some additional time to enjoy their privacy. Security on their arrival will be impressive.

'In fact, looking this over, it would seem that their security for the next few months at least will be impenetrable.'

McKenney snorted. 'No security's impenetrable. We've proven that ourselves.'

'Michael, we do not wish to kill them. Any fool can do that,' he said patiently. 'Our objective demands that we take them alive.'

'But –'

Would they never learn? 'No buts, Michael. If I wanted to kill them, they would already be dead, and this Ryan bastard along with them. It's easy to kill, but that won't get us what we want.'

'Yes, sir.' McKenney nodded his submission. 'And Sean?'

'They will be processing him in Brixton Prison for another two weeks or so – our friends in C-13 don't want him far from their reach for the moment.'

'Does that mean that Sean –'

'Most unlikely,' O'Donnell cut him off. 'Still and all, I think the Organization is stronger with him than without him, don't you?'

'But how will we know?'

'There is a great deal of high-level interest in our comrade,' O'Donnell half-explained.

McKenney nodded thoughtfully. He concealed his annoyance that the Commander would not share his intelligence source with his own intelligence chief. McKenney knew how valuable the information was, but where it came from was the deepest of all the ULA's secrets. The younger man shrugged it off. He had his own information sources, and his skill at using their information was growing on a daily basis. Having always to wait so long to act on it chafed on him, but he admitted to himself – grudgingly at first, but with increasing conviction – that full preparation had allowed several tricky operations to go perfectly. Another operation that had not gone so well had landed him in the H-Blocks of Long Kesh prison. The lesson he'd learned from this miscued op was that the revolution needed more competent hands. He'd come to hate the Provisional IRA leadership's ineffectiveness even more than he did the British Army. The revolutionary often had more to fear from friends than enemies.

'Anything new with our colleagues?' O'Donnell asked.

'Yes, as a matter of fact,' McKenney answered brightly. *Our colleagues* were the Provisional Wing of the Irish Republican Army. 'One of the cells of the Belfast Brigade is going to go after a pub, day after tomorrow. Some UVF lads have been using it of late – not very smart of them, is it?'

'I think we can let that one pass,' O'Donnell judged. It would be a bomb, of course, and it would kill a number of people, some of whom might be members of the Ulster Volunteer Force, whom he regarded as the reactionary forces of the ruling bourgeoisie – no more than thugs, since they lacked any ideology at all. So much the better that some UVF would be killed, but really any prod would suffice, since then other UVF gunmen would slink into a Catholic neighbourhood and kill one or two people on the street. And the detectives of the RUC's Criminal Investigation Division would investigate, as always, and no one would admit to have seen much of anything, as usual, and the Catholic neighbourhoods would retain their state of revolutionary instability. Hate was such a useful asset. Even more than fear, hate was what sustained the Cause. 'Anything else?'

'The bombmaker, Dwyer, has dropped out of sight again,' McKenney went on.

'The last time that happened . . . yes, England, wasn't it? Another campaign?'

'Our man doesn't know. He's working on it, but I've told him to be careful.'

'Very good.' O'Donnell would think about this one. Dwyer was one of the best Provisional IRA bombers, a genius with delayed fuses, someone Scotland Yard's C-13 branch wanted as badly as they wanted anyone. Dwyer's capture would be a serious blow to the Provisional IRA leadership . . . . 'We want our lad to be very careful indeed, but it would be useful to know where Dwyer is.'

McKenney got the message loud and clear. It was too bad about Dwyer, but that colleague had picked the wrong side. 'And the Belfast brigadier?'

'No.' The chief shook his head.

'But he'll slip away again. We needed a month to –'

'No, Michael. Timing – remember the importance of timing. The operation is an integrated whole, not a mere collection of events.' The commander of the Provisional IRA's Belfast Brigade – *Brigade, less than two hundred men*, O'Donnell thought wryly – was the most wanted man in Ulster. Wanted by more than one side, though for the moment the Commander perforce had to let the Brits have him. *Too bad. I would dearly love to make you pay personally for casting me out, Johnny Doyle, for putting a price on my head. But on this I, too, must be patient. After all, I want more than your head.* 'You might also keep in mind that our lads have their own skins to protect. The reason timing is so important is that what we have planned can only work once. That's why we must be patient. We must wait for exactly the right moment.'

What right moment? *What plan?* McKenney wanted to know. Only weeks before, O'Donnell had announced that 'the moment' was at hand, only to call things off with a last-second telephone call from London. Sean Miller knew, as did one or two others, but McKenney didn't even know who those privileged fellows were. If there was anything the commander believed in, it was security. The intelligence officer acknowledged its importance, but his youth chafed at the frustration of knowing the importance of what was happening without knowing *what it was*.

'Difficult, isn't it, Mike?'

'Yes, sir, it is,' McKenney admitted with a smile.

'Just keep in mind where impatience has got us,' the leader said.

8

Information

'I guess that about covers it, Jimmy. Thanks from the Bureau for tracking that guy down.'

'I really don't think he's the sort of tourist we need, Dan,' Owens replied. A Floridian who'd embezzled three million dollars from an Orlando bank had made the mistake of stopping off in Britain on his way to another European country, one with slightly different banking laws. 'I think the next time we'll let him do some shopping on Bond Street before we arrest him, though. You can call that a fee – a fee for apprehending him.'

'Ha!' The FBI representative closed the last folder. It was six o'clock local time. Dan Murray leaned back in his chair. Behind him, the brick Georgian buildings across the street paled in the dusk. Men were discreetly patrolling the roofs there, as with all the buildings on Grosvenor Square. The American Embassy was not so much heavily guarded as minorly fortified, so many terrorist threat warnings had come and gone over the past six years. Uniformed police officers stood in front of the building, where North Audley Street was closed off to traffic. The pavement was decorated with concrete 'flowerpots' that a tank could surmount only with difficulty, and the rest of the building had a sloped concrete glacis to fend off car bombs. Inside, behind bullet-resistant glass, a Marine corporal stood guard beside a wall safe containing a .357 Magnum Smith & Wesson revolver. *A hell of a thing*, Murray thought. *A hell of a thing*. The wonderful world of the international terrorist.

Murray hated working in a building that seemed part of the Maginot Line, hated wondering if there might be some Iranian, or Palestinian, or Libyan, or whatever madman of a terrorist, with an RPG-7 rocket launcher in a building across the street from his office. It wasn't fear for his life. Murray had put his life at risk more than once. He hated the injustice, the insult to his profession, that there were people who would kill their fellow men as a part of some form of political expression. *But they're not madmen at all, are they? The behavioural specialists say that they're not. They're romantics – believers, people willing to commit themselves to an ideal, and to commit any crime to further it.* Romantics!

'Jimmy, remember the good old days when we hunted bank bandits who were just in the business for a fast buck?'

'I've never done any of those. I was mainly concerned with ordinary thievery until they set me to handling murders. But terrorism does make you nostalgic for the day of the common thug. I can even remember when *they* were fairly civilized.' Owens refilled his glass with port. A growing problem for the Metropolitan Police was that the criminal use of firearms was no longer so rare as it had once been, this new tool made more popular by the evening news reports on terrorism within the UK. And while the streets and parks of London were far safer than their American counterparts, they were not as safe as they'd only recently been. The times were changing in London, too, and Owens didn't like it at all.

The phone rang. Murray's secretary had just left for the night, and the agent lifted it.

'Murray. Hi, Bob. Yeah, he's right here. Bob Highland for you, Jimmy.' He handed the phone over.

'Commander Owens here.' The officer sipped at his port, then set the glass down abruptly and waved for a pen and pad. 'Where exactly? And you've already – good, excellent. I'm coming straightaway.'

'What gives?' Murray asked quickly.

'We've just had a tip on a certain Dwyer. Bomb factory in a flat on Tooley Street.'

'Isn't that right across the river from the Tower?'

'Too bloody right. I'm off.' Owens rose and grabbed for his coat.

'You mind if I tag along?'

'Dan, you must remember –'

'To keep out of the way.' Murray was already on his feet. One hand unconsciously checked his left hip, where his service revolver would be, had the agent not been in a foreign country. Owens had never carried a gun. Murray wondered how you could be a cop and not be armed with something. Together they left Murray's office and trotted up the corridor, turning left for the lifts. Two minutes later they were in the Embassy's basement parking garage. The two officers from Owens' chase car were already in their vehicle, and the Commander's driver followed them out.

Owens was on the radio the instant the car hit the street, with Murray in the back seat.

'You have people rolling?' Murray asked.

'Yes. Bob will have a team there in a few minutes. Dwyer, by God! The description fits perfectly.' As much as he tried to hide it, Owens was as excited as a kid on Christmas morning.

'Who tipped you?'

'Anonymous. A male voice, claimed to have seen wiring, and something that was wrapped up in small blocks, when he looked in the window.'

'l love it ! Peeping Tom cues the cops – probably afraid his wife'll find out what he's been up to. Well, you take what you get.' Murray grinned. He'd had cases break on slimmer stuff than this.

The evening traffic was curb-to-curb, and the police siren could not change that. It took fully twenty frustrating minutes to travel the five miles to Tooley Street, with Owens listening to the radio, his fist beating softly on the front door's armrest while his men arrived at the suspect house. Finally the car darted across Tower Bridge and turned right. The driver parked it on the pavement alongside two other police cars.

It was a three-storey building of drab, dirty brick, in a working class neighbourhood. Next door was a small pub with its daily menu scrawled on a blackboard. Several patrons were standing at the door, pints in their fists as they watched the police, and more stood across the street. Owens ran to the door. A plainclothes detective was waiting for him.

'All secure, sir. We have the suspect in custody. Top floor, in the rear.'

The Commander trotted up the stairs with Murray on his heels. Another detective met him on the top-floor landing. Owens walked the last thirty feet with a cruel, satisfied smile on his face.

'It's all over, sir,' Highland said. 'Here's the suspect.'

Maureen Dwyer was stark naked, spread-eagled on the floor. Around her was a puddle of water, and a trail of wet footprints coming from the adjacent bathroom.

'She was taking a bath,' Highland explained. 'And she'd left her pistol on the kitchen table. No trouble at all.'

'Do you have a female detective on the way?'

'Yes, sir. I'm surprised she's not here already.'

'Traffic is bloody awful,' Owens noted.

'Any evidence of a companion?'

'No, sir. None at all.' Highland answered. 'Only this.'

473

The bottom drawer of the only bureau in the shabby apartment was lying on the floor. It contained several blocks of what looked like plastic explosive, some blasting caps, and what were probably electronic timers. Already a detective was doing a written inventory while another was busily photographing the entire room with a Nikon camera and strobe. A third was breaking open an evidence kit. Everything in the room would be tagged, dropped in a clear plastic bag, and stored for use in yet another terrorist trial in the Old Bailey. There were smiles of satisfaction everywhere – except for Maureen Dwyer's face, which was pressed to the floor. Two detectives stood over the girl, their service revolvers holstered as they watched the naked, wet figure without a trace of sympathy.

Murray stood in the doorway to keep out of everyone's way while his eyes took in the way Owens' detectives handled the scene. There wasn't much to criticize. The suspect was neutralized, the area secured, and now evidence was being collected; everything was going by the book. He noted that the suspect was kept stationary. A woman officer would perform a cavity search to ensure that she wasn't 'holding' something that might be dangerous. This was a little hard on Miss Dwyer's modesty, but Murray didn't think a judge would object. Maureen Dwyer was a known bomber, with at least three years' work behind her. Nine months before, she'd been seen leaving the site of a nasty one in Belfast that minutes later had killed four people and maimed another three. No, there wouldn't be all that much sympathy for Miss Dwyer. After another several minutes, a detective took the sheet off the bed and draped it over her, covering her from her knees to her shoulders. Through it all, the suspect didn't move. She was breathing rapidly, but made no sound.

'This is interesting,' one man said. He pulled a suitcase from under the bed. After checking it for booby traps, he opened it and extracted a theatrical make-up case complete with four wigs.

'Goodness, I could use one of those myself.' The female detective squeezed past Murray and approached Owens. 'I came as fast as I could, Commander.'

'Carry on.' Owens smiled. He was too happy to let something this minor annoy him.

'Spread 'em, dearie. You know the drill.' The detective put on a rubber glove for her search. Murray didn't watch. This was one thing he'd always been squeamish about. A few seconds later, the glove came off with a snapping sound. A detective handed Dwyer some clothes to put on. Murray watched the suspect dress herself as unselfconsciously as if she'd been alone – no, he thought, alone she'd show more emotion. As soon as her clothes were on, a police officer snapped steel handcuffs on her wrists. The same man informed Dwyer of her rights, not very differently from the way American cops did it. She did not acknowledge the words. Maureen Dwyer looked about at the police, no expression at all on her face, not even anger, and was taken out without having said a single word.

That's a cold piece of work, Murray told himself. Even with her hair wet, with no make-up, she was pretty enough, he thought. Nice complexion. It wouldn't hurt her to knock off eight or ten pounds, but in nice clothes that wouldn't matter very much. *You could pass her on the street, or sit next to her in a bar and offer to buy her a drink, and you'd never suspect that she was carrying two pounds of high explosives in her bag. Thank God we don't have anything like that at home.* . . . He wondered how well the Bureau would do against such a threat. Even with all their resources, the scientific and forensic experts who back up the special agents in the field, this was no easy crime to deal with. For any police force, the name of the game was wait for the bad guys to make a mistake. You had to play for the breaks, just like a football team waited for a turnover. The problem was, the crooks kept getting better, kept learning from their mistakes. It was like any sort of competition. Both sides became increasingly sophisticated. But the criminals always had the initiative. The cops were always playing catchup ball.

'Well, Dan, any criticism? Do we measure up to FBI standards?' Owens inquired with the slightest amount of smugness.

'Don't give me that crap, Jimmy!' Murray grinned. Things were settled down now. The detectives were fully engaged in cataloguing the physical evidence in the confidence that they already had a solid criminal case. 'I'd say you have this one pretty cold. You know how lucky you are not to have our illegal-search-and-seizure rules?' *Not to mention some of our judges.*

'Finished,' the photographer said.

'Excellent,' replied Sergeant Bob Highland, who was running the crime scene.

'How'd you get here so fast, Bob?' Murray wanted to know. 'You take the tube, or what?'

'Why didn't I think of that?' Highland laughed. 'Perhaps we caught the traffic right. We were here within eleven minutes. You weren't that far behind us. We booted the door and had Dwyer in custody in under five seconds. Isn't it amazing how easy it can be – if you have the bloody information you need!'

'Can I come in now?'

'Certainly.' Owens waved him into the apartment.

Murray went right to the bureau drawer with the explosives. The FBI man was an expert on explosive devices. He and Owens crouched over the collection.

'Looks like Czech,' Murray muttered.

'It is,' another detective said. 'From Skoda works, you can tell from the wrapping. These are American, though. California Pyronetics, model thirty-one electronic detonator.' He tossed one – in a plastic bag – to Murray.

'Damn! They're turning up all over the place – a shipment of these little babies got hijacked a year and a half ago. They were heading for an oil field in Venezuela, and got taken outside Caracas,' Murray explained. He gave the small black device a closer look. 'The oil field guys love 'em. Safe, reliable, and damned near foolproof. This is as good as the stuff the Army uses. State of the art.'

'Where else have they turned up?' Owens asked.

'We're sure about three or four. The problem is, they're so small that it's not always possible to identify what's left. A bank in Puerto Rico, a police station in Peru – those were political. The other one – maybe two – were drug related. Until now they've all been on the other side of the Atlantic. As far as I know, this is the first time they've showed up here. These detonators have lot numbers. You'll want to check them against the stolen shipment. I can get a telex off tonight, have you an answer inside an hour.'

'Thank you, Dan.'

Murray counted five one-kilo blocks of explosive. The Czech plastique had a good reputation for quality. It was as potent as the stuff Du Pont made for American military use. One block, properly placed, could take a building down. With the Pyronetics timers, Miss Dwyer could have placed five separate bombs, set them for delayed detonation – as much as a month – and been a thousand miles away when they went off.

'You saved some lives tonight, gentlemen. Good one.' Murray looked up. The apartment had a single window facing to the rear. The window had a pull-down blind that was all the way down, and some cheap, dirty curtains. Murray wondered what this flat cost to rent. Not much, he was sure. The heat was turned way up, and the room was getting stuffy. 'Anybody mind if I let some air in here?'

'Excellent idea, Dan,' Owens answered.

'Let me do it, sir.' A detective with gloves on put up the blind and then the window. Everything in the room would be dusted for fingerprints also, but opening the window wouldn't harm anything. A breeze cooled things off in an instant.

'That's better.' The FBI representative took a deep breath, scarcely noticing the smell of diesel exhaust from the London cabs. . . .

Something was wrong.

It hit Murray as a surprise. Something *was* wrong. *What?* He looked out the window. To the left was a – probably a warehouse, a blank four-storey wall. Past it on the right, he could see the outline of the Tower of London, standing over the River Thames. That was all. He turned his head to see Owens, also staring out the window. The Commander of C-13 turned his head and looked at Murray, a question on his face also.

'Yes,' Owens said.

'What was it that guy on the phone said?' Murray muttered.

Owens' head bobbed. 'Exactly. Sergeant Highland?'

'Yes, Commander?'

'The voice on the phone. What exactly did it say, and what exactly did it sound like?' Owens kept looking out the window.

'The voice had . . . a Midlands accent, I should think. A man's voice. He said that he was looking in the window, and saw explosives and some wires. We have it all on tape, of course.'

Murray reached through the open window and ran a finger along the outside surface of the glass. It came back dirty. 'It sure wasn't a window-washer who called in.' He leaned out the window. There was no fire escape.

'Someone atop the warehouse, perhaps – no,' Owens said at once. 'The angle isn't right, unless she had the material spread out on the floor. That is rather odd.'

'Break-in? Maybe someone got in here, saw the stuff, and decided to call in like a good citizen?' Murray asked. 'That doesn't sound very likely.'

Owens shrugged. 'No telling, is there? A boyfriend she dumped – I think for the moment we can be content with counting our blessings, Dan. There are five bombs that will never hurt anyone. Let's get out of everyone's way and send the telex off to Washington. Sergeant Highland, gentlemen, this was well done! Congratulations to you all for some splendid police work. Carry on.'

Owens and Murray left the building quietly. Outside they found a small crowd being restrained by about ten uniformed constables. A TV news crew was on the scene with its bright lights. These were enough to keep them from seeing across the street. This block had three small pubs. In the doorway of one stood a soft-looking man with a pint of bitter in his hand. He showed no emotion, not even curiosity, as he looked across the street. His memory recorded the faces he saw. His name was Dennis Cooley.

Murray and Owens drove to New Scotland Yard headquarters, where the FBI agent made his telex to Washington. They didn't discuss the one anomaly that the case had unexpectedly developed, and Murray left Owens to his work. C-13 had broken yet another bomb case – and done so in the best way, without a single casualty. It meant that Owens and his people would have a sleepless night of paperwork, and preparing reports for the Home Office bureaucracy, and press releases for Fleet Street, but that was something they would gladly accept.

Ryan's first day back at work was easier than he had expected. His prolonged absence had forced the History Department to reassign his classes, and in any case it was almost time for Christmas break, and nearly all of the mids were looking forward to being home for the holidays. Class routine was slightly relaxed, and even the plebes enjoyed a respite from the upperclassmen's harassment in the wake of the win over Army. For Ryan, the result was a fairish collection of letters and documents piled on his In tray, and a quiet day with which to deal with them. He'd arrived in his office at 7:30; by quarter to five he'd dealt with most of his paperwork, and Ryan felt that he'd delivered an honest day's work. He was finishing a series of test questions

477

for the semester's final exam when he smelled cheap cigar smoke and heard a familiar voice.

'Did you enjoy your vacation, boy?' Lieutenant Commander Robert Jefferson Jackson was leaning against the door frame.

'It had a few interesting moments, Robby. The sun over – or under – the yardarm yet?'

'Damn straight!' Jackson set his white cap on top of Ryan's filing cabinet and collapsed unceremoniously into the leather chair opposite his friend's desk.

Ryan closed the file folder on his draft exam and shoved it into a desk drawer. One of the personal touches in his office was a small refrigerator. He opened it and took out a two-litre bottle of 7-Up, along with an empty bottle of Canada Dry ginger ale, then removed a bottle of Irish whiskey from his desk. Robby got two cups from the table by the door and handed them to Jack. Ryan mixed two drinks to the approximate colour of ginger ale. It was against Academy policy to have alcohol in one's office – a stance Ryan found curious, given the naval orientation of the institution – but drinking 'ginger ale' was a winked-upon subterfuge. Besides, everyone recognized that the Officer and Faculty Club was only a minute's walk away. Jack handed one drink over and replaced everything but the empty ginger ale bottle.

'Welcome home, pal!' Robby held his drink up.

'Nice to be back.' The two men clicked their cups together.

'Glad you made it, Jack. You kind of worried us. How's the arm?' Jackson gestured with his cup.

'Better than it was. You oughta see the cast I started out with. They took it off at Hopkins last Friday. I learned one thing today, though, driving a stick shift through Annapolis with one arm is a bitch.'

'I'll bet,' Robby chuckled. 'Damn if you 'ain't crazy, boy.'

Ryan nodded agreement. He'd met Jackson the previous March at a faculty tea. Robby wore the gold wings of a naval aviator. He'd been assigned to the nearby Patuxent River Naval Air Test Center, Maryland, as an instructor in the test pilot school until a faulty relay had unexpectedly blasted him clear of the Buckeye jet trainer he'd been flying one fine, clear morning. Unprepared for the event, he'd broken his leg badly. The injury had been serious enough to take him off flight status for six months, and the Navy had assigned him to temporary duty as an instructor in Annapolis, where he was currently in the engineering department. It was an assignment which Jackson regarded as one step above pulling oars in a galley.

Jackson was shorter than Ryan, and much darker. He was the fourth son of a Baptist preacher in southern Alabama. When they'd first met, the officer was still in a cast, and Jackson had asked Ryan if he might want to try his hand at kendo. It was something that Ryan had never tried, the Japanese fencing sport in which bamboo staves are used in place of samurai swords. Ryan had used pugil sticks in the Marines and figured it wouldn't be too different. He'd accepted the invitation, thinking that his longer reach would be a decisive advantage, particularly on top of Jackson's reduced mobility. It hadn't occurred to him that Jackson would first have asked a brother officer for a kendo match. In fact, Ryan later learned, he had. He'd also learned by then that Robby had the blinding quickness and killer instinct of a rattlesnake. By the time the bruises had faded, they were fast friends.

For his part, Ryan had introduced the pilot to the smoky flavour of good Irish whiskey, and they'd evolved the tradition of an afternoon drink or two in the privacy of Jack's office.

'Any news on campus?' Ryan asked.

'Still teachin' the boys and girls,' Jackson said comfortably.

'And you've started to like it?'

'Not exactly. The leg's finally back in battery, though. I've been spending my weekends down at Pax River to prove I still know how to fly. You know, you made one hell of a flap hereabouts.'

'When I was shot?'

'Yeah, I was in with the superintendent when the call came in. The soop put it on speaker, and we got this FBI guy askin' if we got a nutcase teacher in London playing cops and robbers. I said, sure, I know the jerk, but they wanted somebody in the History Department to back me up – mainly they wanted the name of your travel agent, I suppose. Anyway, everybody was out to lunch, and I had to track Professor Billings down in the O Club, and the superintendent did some runnin' around, too. You almost ruined the boss's last golf day with the Governor.'

'Damned near ruined my day, too.'

'Was it like they said in the papers?'

'Probably. The Brit papers got it pretty straight.'

Jackson nodded as he tapped the cigar on Ryan's ashtray. 'You're lucky you didn't come home parcel post, boy,' he said.

'Don't you start, Robby. One more guy tells me I'm a hero, and I'll flatten him –'

'Hero? Hell, no! If all you honkies were that dumb, my ancestors would have imported yours.' The pilot shook his head emphatically. 'Didn't anybody ever tell you that hand-to-hand stuff is *dangerous*?'

'If you'd been there, I bet you'd have done the same –'

'No chance! God Almighty, is there anything dumber than a Marine? This hand-to-hand stuff, Jeez, you get blood on your clothes, mess up the shine on your shoes. No way, boy! When I do my killin', it'll be with cannon shells and missiles – you know, the civilized way.' Jackson grinned. 'The safe way.'

'Not like flying an airplane that decides to blast you loose without warning you first,' Ryan scoffed.

'I dinged my leg some, sure, but when I got my Tomcat strapped to my back, I'm hummin' along at six hundred-plus knots. Anybody who wants to put a bullet in me, fella, he can do it, but he's gonna have to work at it.'

Ryan shook his head. He was hearing a safety lecture from someone who just happened to be in the most dangerous business there was – a carrier aviator *and* a test pilot.

'How's Cathy and Sally?' Robby asked, more seriously. 'We meant to come over Sunday, but we had to drive up to Philadelphia on short notice.'

'It was kinda tough on them, but they came through all right.'

'You got a family to worry about, Jack,' Jackson pointed out. 'Leave that rescue stuff to the professionals. The funny thing about Robby, Jack knew, was his caution. For all the down-home bantering about his life as a fighter pilot, Jackson never took a risk he didn't have to. He'd known pilots who had. Many were dead. There was not a single man wearing those gold wings who had not lost a friend, and Jack wondered how deeply that had affected Jackson over the years. Of one thing he was sure, though Robby was in a dangerous business, like all successful gamblers he thought things over before he moved his chips. Wherever his body went, his mind had already gone.

'It's all over, Rob. It's all behind me, and there won't be a next time.'

'We'll put a big roger on that. Who else am I gonna drink with? So how'd you like it over there?'

'I didn't see very much, but Cathy had a great time, all things considered. I think she saw every castle in the country – plus the new friends we made.'

'That must have been right interesting,' Robby chuckled. The flyer stubbed out his cigar. They were cheap, crooked, evil-smelling little things, and Jack figured that Jackson puffed on them only as part of the Image of the Fighter Pilot. 'Not hard to understand why they took a liking to you.'

'They took a liking to Sally, too. They got her started riding horses,' Jack added sourly.

'Oh yeah? So what are they like?'

'You'd like 'em,' Ryan assured him.

Jackson smiled. 'Yeah, I imagine I would. The Prince used to drive Phantoms, so he must be a right guy, and his dad's supposed to know his way around a cockpit, too. I hear you took the Concorde back. How'd you like it?'

'I meant to ask you about that. How come it was so noisy? I mean, if you're doing mach-2-plus, why isn't all the noise behind you?'

Jackson shook his head sadly. 'What's the airplane made out of?'

'Aluminium, I suppose.'

'You suppose the speed of sound is faster in metal than it is in air, maybe?' Jackson asked.

'Oh. The sound travels through the body of the airplane.'

'Sure, engine noise, noise from the fuel pumps, various other things.'

'Okay.' Ryan filed that away.

'You didn't like it, did you?' Robby was amused at his friend's attitude towards flying.

'Why does everybody pick on me for that?' Ryan asked the ceiling.

'Because it's so funny, Jack. You're the last person in the world who's afraid to fly.'

'Hey, Rob, I do it, okay? I get aboard, and strap in, and do it.'

'I know. I'm sorry.' Jackson eased off. 'It's just that it's so easy to needle you on this – I mean, what are friends for? You done good, Jack. We're proud of you. But for Christ's sake, be careful, okay? This hero shit gets people killed.'

'I hear you.'

'Is it true about Cathy?' Robby asked.

'Yep. The doc confirmed it the same day they took the cast off.'

'Way to go, pop! I'd say that calls for another – a light one.' Robby held his cup out, and Jack poured. 'Looks like the bottle's about had it, too.'

'It's my turn to buy the next one, isn't it?'

'It's been so long, I don't remember,' Robby admitted. 'But I'll take your word for it.'

'So they have you back in airplanes?'

'Next Monday they'll let me back in a Tomcat,' Jackson replied. 'And come summer, it's back to the work they pay me for.'

'You got orders?'

'Yeah, you're looking at the prospective XO of VF-41.' Robby held his cup up in the air.

The Executive Officer of Fighter Squadron 41, Ryan translated. 'That's all right, Rob!'

'Yeah, it's not bad, considering I've been a black shoe for the past seven months.'

'Right out on carriers?'

'No, we'll be on the beach for a while, down at Oceana, Virginia. The squadron's deployed now on *Nimitz*. When the boat comes back for refit, the fighters stay on the beach for refresher training. Then we'll probably redeploy on *Kennedy*. They're reshuffling the squadron assignments. Jack, it'll be good to strap that fighter back on! I've been here too long.'

'We're gonna miss you and Sissy.'

'Hey, we don't leave till summer – they're making me finish out the school year – and Virginia Beach isn't all that far away. Come on down and visit, for crying out loud. You don't have to fly, Jack. You can drive,' Jackson pointed out.

'Well, you'll probably be around for the new kid.'

'Good.' Jackson finished off his drink.

'Are you and Sissy going anywhere for Christmas?'

'Not that I know of. I can't, really; most of the holidays I'm gonna be flying down at Pax.'

'Okay, come on over to our place for dinner – three-ish.'

'Cathy's family isn't –'

'No,' Ryan said as he tucked everything back where it belonged. Robby shook his head.

'Some folks just don't catch on,' the pilot observed.

'Well, you know how it is. I don't worship at the temple of the Almighty Dollar anymore.'

'But you managed to do a job on the collection basket.'

Jack grinned. 'Yeah, you might say that.'

'That reminds me. There's a little outfit outside Boston that's gonna hit it big.'

'Oh?' Jack's ears perked up.

'It's called Holoware, Ltd, I think. They came up with new software for the computers on fighter planes – really good stuff, cuts a third off the processing time, generates intercept solutions like magic. It's set up on the simulator down at Pax, and the Navy's going to buy it real soon.'

'Who knows?'

Jackson laughed as he got his things. 'The company doesn't know yet. Captain Stevens down at Pax just got the word from the guys out at Topgun. Bill May out there – I used to fly with Bill – ran the stuff for the first time a month ago, and he liked it so much that he almost got the Pentagon boys to cut through all the bullshit and just buy the stuff. It got hung up, but DCNO-Air is on it now, and they say Admiral Rendall is really hot for it. Thirty more days, and that little company is going to get a Christmas present. A little late,' Robby said, 'but it'll fill one big stocking. Just for the hell of it, I checked the paper this morning, and sure enough, they're listed on the American Exchange. You might want to check it out.'

'What about you?'

The pilot shook his head. 'I don't play the market, but you still fool around there, right?'

'A little. Is this classified or anything?' Jack asked.

'Not that I know of. The classified part is how the software is written, and they got a real good classification system on that – nobody understands it. Maybe Skip Tyler could figure it out, but I never will. You have to be a nuc to think in ones and zeros. Pilots don't think digital. We're analog.' Jackson chuckled. 'Gotta run. Sissy's got a recital tonight.'

'Night, Rob.'

'Low and slow, Jack.' Robby closed the door behind him. Jack leaned back in his chair for a moment. He smiled to himself, then rose and packed some papers into his briefcase.

'Yeah,' he said to himself. 'Just to show him that I still know how.'

Ryan got his coat on and left the building, walking downhill past the Preble Memorial. His car was parked on Decatur Road. Jack drove a five-year-old VW Rabbit. It was a very practical car for the narrow streets of Annapolis, and he refused to have a Porsche like his wife used for commuting back and forth to Baltimore. It was dumb, he'd told Cathy about a thousand times, for two people to have three cars. A Rabbit for him, a 911 for her, and a station wagon for the family. Dumb. Cathy's suggestion that he should sell the Rabbit and drive the wagon was, of course, unacceptable. The little gas engine fired up at once. It sounded too noisy. He'd have to check the muffler. Jack pulled out, turning right, as always, onto Maryland Avenue through Gate Three in the grimly undecorous perimeter wall that surrounded the Academy. A Marine guard saluted him on the way out. Ryan was surprised by that – they'd never done it before.

Driving wasn't easy. When he shifted, Ryan twisted his left hand inside the sling to grab the wheel while his right hand worked the gearshift. The rush-hour traffic didn't help. Several thousand state workers were disgorging themselves from various government buildings, and the crowded streets gave Ryan plenty of opportunity to stop and restart from first gear. His Rabbit had five, plus reverse, and by the time he got to the Central Avenue light he was asking himself why he hadn't got the Rabbit with an automatic. Fuel efficiency was the answer – *is this worth an extra two miles per gallon?* Ryan laughed at himself as he headed east towards the Chesapeake Bay, then right onto Falcon's Nest Road.

There was rarely any traffic back here. Falcon's Nest Road came to a dead end not too far down from Ryan's place, and on the other side of the road were several farms, also dormant at the beginning of winter. The stubby remains of cornstalks lay in rows on the brown, hard fields. He turned left into his driveway. Ryan had thirty acres on Peregrine Cliff. His nearest neighbour, an engineer named Art Palmer, was half a mile away through heavily wooded slopes and across a murky stream. The cliffs on the western shore of the Chesapeake Bay were nearly fifty feet high where Jack lived – those farther south got a little higher, but not much – and made of crumbly sandstone. They were a paleontologist's delight. Every so often a team from a local college or museum would scour at the base and find fossilized shark teeth that had once belonged to a creature as large as a midget submarine, along with the bones of even more unlikely creatures that had lived here a hundred million years earlier.

The bad news was that the cliffs were prone to erosion. His house was built a hundred feet back from the edge, and his daughter was under strict orders – twice enforced with a spanking – not to go anywhere near the edge. In an attempt to protect the cliff face, the state environmental-protection people had persuaded Ryan and his neighbours to plant kudzu, a prolific weed from the American South. The weed had thoroughly stabilized the cliff face, but it was now attacking the trees near the cliff, and Jack periodically had to go after them with a weed-eater to save the trees from being smothered. But that wasn't a problem this time of year.

Ryan's lot was half open and half wooded. The part near the road had once been farmed, though not easily, as the ground was not flat enough to drive a tractor across it safely. As he approached his house, the trees began, some gnarled old oaks, and other deciduous trees whose leaves were gone now, leaving skeletal branches to reach out into the thin, cold air. As he approached the carport, he saw that Cathy was already home, her Porsche and the family wagon parked in the carport. He had to leave his Rabbit in the open.

'Daddy!' Sally yanked open the door and ran out without her jacket to meet her father.

'It's too cold out here,' Jack told his daughter.

'No, it isn't,' Sally replied. She grabbed his briefcase and carried it with two hands, puffing as she climbed up the three steps into the house.

Ryan got out of his coat and hung it in the entry closet. As with everything else, it was hard to do with one hand. He was cheating a little now. As with steering the car, he was starting to use his left hand, careful to avoid putting any strain on his shoulder. The pain was completely gone now, but Ryan was sure that he could bring it back quickly enough if he did something dumb. Besides which, Cathy would yell at him. He found his wife in the kitchen. She was looking at the pantry and frowning.

'Hi, honey.'

'Hi, Jack. You're late.'

'So are you.' Ryan kissed his wife. Cathy smelled his breath. Her nose crinkled.'

'How's Robby?'

'Fine – and I just had two very light ones.'

'Uh-huh.' She turned back to the pantry. 'What do you want for dinner?'

'Surprise me,' Jack suggested.

'You're a big help! I ought to let you fix it.'

'It's not my turn, remember?'

'I knew I should have stopped at the Giant,' Cathy groused.

'How was work?'

'One one procedure. I assisted Bernie on a cornea transplant, then I had to take the residents around for rounds. Dull day. Tomorrow'll be better. Bernie says hi, by the way. How does franks and beans grab you?'

Jack laughed. Ever since they came back, their diet had consisted mainly of basic American staples, and it was a little late for something fancy.

'Okay. I'm going to change and punch up something on the computer for a few minutes.'

'Careful with the arm, Jack.'

Five times a day she warns me. Jack sighed. *Never marry a doctor.* The Ryan home was a deckhouse design. The living/dining room had a cathedral ceiling that peaked sixteen feet over the carpeted floor with an enormous wood beam. A wall of triple-paned windows faced the bay, with a large deck beyond the sliding glass doors. Opposite the glass was a massive brick fireplace that reached through the roof. The master bedroom was half a level above the living room, with a window that enabled one to look down into it. Ryan trotted up the steps. The house design accommodated large closets.

Ryan selected casual clothes, and went through the annoying ritual of changing himself one-handed. He was still experimenting, trying to find an efficient way to do it.

Finished, he went back down, and curved around the stairs to the next level down, his library. It was a large one. Jack read a lot, and also purchased books he didn't have time to read, banking against the time when he would. He had a large desk up against the windows on the bay side of the house. Here was his personal computer, an Apple, and all of its peripheral equipment. Ryan flipped it on and started typing in instructions. Next he put his modem on line and placed a call into CompuServe. The time of day guaranteed easy access, and he selected MicroQuote II from the entry menu.

A moment later he was looking at Holoware, Ltd's stock performance over the past three years. The stock was agreeably unimpressive, fluctuating from two dollars to as much as six, but that was two years back – it was a company which had once held great promise, but somewhere along the way investors had lost confidence. Jack made a note, then exited the programme and got into another, Disclosure II, to look at the company's SEC filings and last annual report. *Okay*, Ryan told himself. The company was making money, but not very much. One problem with hi-tech issues was that so many investors wanted big returns very quickly, or they'd move on to something else, forgetting that things didn't necessarily happen that way. This company had found a small though somewhat precarious niche, and was ready to try something bold. Ryan made a mental estimate of what the Navy contract would be worth and compared it with the company's total revenues. . . .

'Okay!' he told himself before exiting the system completely and shutting his computer down. Next he called his broker. Ryan worked through a discount brokerage firm that had people on duty around the clock. Jack always dealt with the same man.

'Hi, Mort, it's Jack. How's the family?'

'Hello again, Doctor Ryan. Everything's fine with us. What can we do for you tonight?'

'An outfit called Holoware, one of the hi-tech bunch on Highway 128 outside Boston. It's on the AMEX.'

'Okay.' Ryan heard tapping on a keyboard. Everyone used computers. 'Here it is. Going at four and seven-eighths, not a very active issue . . . until lately. There has been some modest activity over the past month.'

'What kind?' Ryan asked. This was another sign to look for.

'Oh, I see. The company is buying itself back a little. No big deal, but they're buying their own stock out.'

Bingo! Ryan smiled to himself. *Thank you, Robby. You gave me a tip on a real live one.* Jack asked himself if this constituted trading on inside information. His initial tip might be called that, but his decision to buy was based on confirmation made legally, on the basis of his experience as a stock trader. *Okay, it's legal.* He could do whatever he wanted.

'How much do you think you can get for me?'

'It's not a very impressive stock.'

'How often am I wrong, Mort?'

'How much do you want?'

'At least twenty-K, and if there's more, I want all of it you can find.' There was no way he'd get hold of more than fifty thousand shares, but Ryan made a snap decision to grab all he could. If he lost, it was only money, and it had been over a year since he'd last had a hunch like this one. If they got the Navy contract, that stock would increase in value tenfold. The company must have had a tip, too. Buying back their own stock on the slim resources they had would, if Ryan was guessing right, dramatically increase the firm's capital, enabling a rapid expansion of operations. Holoware was betting on the future, and betting big.

There was five seconds of silence on the phone.

'What do you know, Jack?' the broker asked finally.

'I'm playing a hunch.'

'Okay . . . twenty-K plus . . . I'll call you at ten tomorrow. You think I should. . . ?'

'It's a toss of the dice, but I think it's a good toss.'

'Thanks. Anything else?'

'No. I have to go eat dinner. Good night, Mort.'

'See ya.' Both men hung up. At the far end of the phone, the broker decided that he'd go in for a thousand shares, too. Ryan was occasionally wrong, but when he was right, he tended to be very right.

'Christmas Day,' O'Donnell said quietly. 'Perfect.'

'Is that the day they're moving Sean?' McKenney asked.

'He leaves London by van at four in the morning. That's bloody good news. I was afraid they'd use a helicopter. No word on the route they'll use. . . .' He read on. 'But they're going to take him across on the Lymington ferry at eight-thirty Christmas morning. Excellent timing, when you think about it. Too early for heavy traffic. Everyone'll be opening their presents and getting dressed for church. The van might even have the ferry to itself – who'd expect a prisoner transfer on Christmas Day?'

'So, we are going to break Sean out, then?'

'Michael, our men do us little good when they're inside, don't they? You and I are flying over tomorrow morning. I think we'll drive down to Lymington and look at the ferry.'

9

A Day for Celebration

'God, it'll be nice to have two arms again,' Ryan observed.

'Two more weeks, maybe three,' Cathy reminded him. 'And keep your hand still inside the damned sling!'

'Yes, dear.'

It was about two in the morning, and things were going badly – and well. Part of the Ryan family tradition – a tradition barely three years old, but a tradition nevertheless – was that after Sally was in bed and asleep, her parents would creep down to the basement storage area – a room with a padlocked door – and bring the toys upstairs for assembly. The previous two years, this ceremony had been accompanied by a couple of bottles of champagne. Assembling toys was a wholly different sort of exercise when the assemblers were half blasted. It was their method of relaxing into the Christmas spirit.

So far things had gone well. Jack had taken his daughter to the seven o'clock children's mass at St Mary's, and got her to bed a little after nine. His daughter had slid her head around the fireplace wall only twice before a loud command from her father had banished her to her bedroom for good, her arm clasping an overly talkative AG Bear to her chest. By midnight it was decided that she was asleep enough for her parents to make a little noise. This had begun the toy trek, as Cathy called it. Both parents removed their shoes to minimize noise on the hardwood steps and went downstairs. Of course, Jack forgot the key to the padlock, and had to climb back upstairs to the master bedroom to search for it. Five minutes later the door was opened and the two of them made four trips each, setting up a lavish pile of multicoloured boxes near the tree, next to Jack's tool kit.

'You know what the two most obscene words in the English language are, Cathy?' Ryan asked nearly two hours later.

'"Assembly required,"' his wife answered with a giggle. 'Honey, last year I said that.'

'A small Phillips.' Jack held his hand out. Cathy smacked the screwdriver into his hand like a surgical instrument. Both of them were sitting on the rug, fifteen feet from the eight-foot tree. Around them was a crescent of toys, some in boxes, some already assembled by the now-exasperated father of a little girl.

'You ought to let me do that.'

'This is man's work,' her husband said. He sat the screwdriver down and sipped at a glass of champagne.

'You chauvinist pig! If I let you do this by yourself, you wouldn't be finished by Easter.'

She was right, Jack told himself. Doing it half-drunk wasn't all that hard. Doing it one-handed was hard but not insurmountable. Doing it one-handed *and* half-drunk was.... The damned screws didn't want to stay in the plastic, and the instructions for putting a V-8 engine together had to be easier than this!

'Why is it that a doll needs a house?' Jack asked plaintively. 'I mean, the friggin' doll's already *in* a house, isn't she?'

'It must be hard, being a chauvinist pig. You dodos just don't understand anything,' Cathy noted sympathetically. 'I guess men never get over baseball bats – all those simple, one-piece toys.'

Jack's head turned slowly. 'Well, the least you could do is have another glass of wine.'

'One's the weekly limit, Jack. I did have a big glass,' she reminded him.

'And made me drink the rest.'

'You bought the bottle, Jack.' She picked it up. 'Big one, too.'

Ryan turned back to the Barbie Doll house. He thought he remembered when the Barbie Doll had been invented, a simple, rather curvy doll, but still just a damned doll, something that girls played with. It hadn't occurred to him then that he might someday have a little girl of his own. *The things we do for our kids*, he told himself. Then he laughed quietly at himself. *Of course we do, and we enjoy it. Tomorrow this will be a funny memory, like the Christmas morning last year when I nearly put this very screwdriver through the palm of my hand.* If he didn't enlist his wife's assistance, Ryan told himself, Santa would be planning next year's flight before he finished. Jack took a deep breath and swallowed his pride.

'Help.'

Cathy checked her watch. 'That took about forty minutes longer than I expected.'

'I must be slowing down.'

'Poor baby, having to drink all that champagne all by himself.' She kissed him on the forehead. 'Screwdriver.'

He handed it to her. Cathy took a quick look at the plans. 'No wonder, you dummy. You're using a short screw when you're supposed to use a long one.'

'I keep forgetting that I'm married to a high-priced mechanic.'

'That's real Christmas spirit, Jack.' She grinned as she turned the screw into place.

'A very pretty, smart, and extremely lovable high-priced mechanic.' He ran a finger down the back of her neck.

'That's a *little* better.'

'Who's better with tools than I am, one-handed.'

Her head turned to reveal the sort of smile a wife saves only for the husband she loves. 'Give me another screw, Jack, and I'll forgive you.'

488

'Don't you think you should finish the doll's house first?'

'Screw, dammit!' He handed her one. 'You have a one-track gutter, but I forgive you anyway.'

'Thanks. If it didn't work, though, I had something else planned.'

'Oh, did Santa come for me, too?'

'I'm not sure. I'll check in a few minutes.'

'You didn't do bad, considering,' his wife said, finishing off the orange plastic roof. 'That's it, isn't it?'

'Last one,' Jack confirmed. 'Thanks for the assist, babe.'

'Did I ever tell you what – no, I didn't. It was one of the ladies-in-waiting. I never did find out what they were waiting for. Anyway, this one countess . . . she was right out of *Gone With the Wind*,' Cathy said with a chuckle. It was his wife's favourite epithet for useless women. 'She asked me if I did needlepoint.'

Not the sort of thing you ask my wife. Jack grinned at the windows. 'And you said . . .'

'Only on eyeballs.' A sweet, nasty smile.

'Oooh. I hope that wasn't over lunch.'

'Jack! You know me better than that. She was nice enough, and she played a pretty good piano.'

'Good as yours?'

'No.' His wife smiled at him. Jack reached out to squeeze the tip of her nose.

'Caroline Ryan, MD, liberated woman, instructor in ophthalmic surgery, world-famous player of classical piano, wife and mother, takes no crap off anybody.'

'Except her husband.'

'When's the last time I ever won an exchange with you?' Jack asked.

'Jack, we're not in competition. We're in love.' She leaned towards him.

'I won't argue with you on that,' he said quietly before kissing his wife's offered lips. 'How many people do you suppose are still in love after all the time we've been married?'

'Just the lucky ones, you old fart. "All the time we've been married"!'

Jack kissed her again and rose. He walked carefully around the sea of toys towards the tree and returned with a small box wrapped in green Christmas paper. He sat down beside his wife, his shoulder against hers as he dropped the box in her lap.

'Merry Christmas, Cathy.'

She opened the box as greedily as a child, but neatly, using her nails to slit the paper. She found a white cardboard box, and inside it, a felt-covered one. This she opened slowly.

It was a necklace of fine gold, more than a quarter-inch wide, designed to fit closely around the neck. You could tell the price by the workmanship and the weight. Cathy Ryan took a deep breath. Her husband held his. Figuring out women's fashions was not his strongest point. He'd got advice from Cissy Jackson, and a very patient clerk at the jewellery store. *Do you like it?*

'I better not swim with this on.'

'But you won't have to take it off when you scrub,' Jack said. 'Here.' He took it from the box and put it around her neck. He managed to clasp it one-handed on the first try.

'You practiced.' One hand traced over the necklace while her eyes looked deeply into his. 'You practiced, just so you could put it on me yourself, didn't you?'

'For a week at the office.' Jack nodded. 'Wrapping it was a bitch, too.'

'It's wonderful. Oh, Jack!' Both her arms darted around his neck, and he kissed the base of hers.

'Thanks, babe. Thanks for being my wife. Thanks for having my kids. Thanks for letting me love you.'

Cathy blinked away a tear or two. They gave her blue eyes a gleam that made him happier than any man on earth. *Let me count the ways. . . .*

'Just something I saw,' he explained casually, lying. It was something he'd seen after looking for nine hours, through seven stores in three shopping malls. 'And it just said to me, "I was made for her."'

'Jack, I didn't get you anything like –'

'Shut up. Every morning I wake up, and see you next to me, I get the best present there is.'

'You are a sentimental jerk right out of some book – but I don't mind.'

'You do like it?' he asked carefully.

'You dummy – I love it!' They kissed again. Jack had lost his parents years before. His sister lived in Seattle, and most of the rest of his relations were in Chicago. Everything he loved was in this house: a wife, a child – and a third of another. He'd made his wife smile on Christmas, and now this year went into the ledger book as a success.

About the time Ryan started assembling the doll's house, four identical blue vans left the Brixton Prison at five-minute intervals. For each, the first thirty minutes involved driving through the side streets of suburban London. In each, a pair of police officers sat looking out the small windows in the rear doors, watching to see if there might be a car trailing the truck on its random path through the city.

They'd picked a good day for it. It was a fairly typical morning for the English winter. The vans drove through patches of fog and cold rain. There was a moderate storm blowing in from the Channel, and best of all, it was dark. The island's northern latitude guaranteed that the sun would not be up for some hours yet, and the dark blue vans were invisible in the early morning.

Security was so strict that Sergeant Bob Highland of C-13 didn't even know that he was in the third van to leave the jail. He did know that he was sitting only a few feet from Sean Miller, and that their destination was the small port of Lymington. They had a choice of three ports to take them to the Isle of Wight, and three different modes of transport: ordinary ferry, hovercraft, and hydrofoil. They might also have chosen a Royal Navy helicopter out of Gosport, but Highland needed only a quick look at the starless sky to rule that one out. *Not a good idea*, he thought to himself. Besides, security is airtight. Not more than thirty people knew that Miller was being moved this morning. Miller himself hadn't known until three hours before, and he still didn't know what prison he was heading to. He'd only learn when he got to the island.

Embarrassments to the British prison system had accumulated over the years. The old, forbidding structures that inhabited such desolate places as Dartmoor in Devon had turned out to be amazingly easy to escape from, and as a result two new maximum-security facilities, Albany and Parkhurst, had been built on the Isle of Wight. There were many advantages to this. An island by definition was easier to secure, and this one had only four regular entry points. More importantly, this island was a clannish place even by English standards, and any stranger on the loose would at least be noticed, and might even be commented upon. The new prisons were somewhat more comfortable than those constructed in the previous century. It was an accident, but one to which Highland did not object. Along with the better living conditions for the prisoners came facilities designed to make escape very difficult – nothing made them impossible, but these new prisons had television cameras to cover every inch of wall, electronic alarms in the most unlikely of places, and guards armed with automatic weapons.

Highland stretched and yawned. With luck he'd get home by early afternoon and still salvage something of Christmas Day with his family.

'I don't see anything at all to concern us,' the other constable said, his nose against the small glass rectangle in the door. 'Only a handful of vehicles on the street, and none are following us.'

'I shouldn't complain,' Highland observed. He turned around to look at Miller.

The prisoner sat all the way forward on the left-hand bench. His hands were manacled, a chain running from the cuffs to a similar pair on his ankles. With luck and a little assistance, a man so restrained might be able to keep pace with a crawling infant, but he'd have little chance of outracing a two-year-old. Miller just sat there, his head back against the wall of the van, his eyes closed as the vehicle bounced and jolted over the road. He looked to be asleep, but Highland knew better. Miller had withdrawn into himself again, lost in some kind of contemplation.

What are you thinking about, Mr Miller? the policeman wanted to ask. It wasn't that he'd failed to ask questions. Almost every day since the incident on The Mall, Highland and several other detectives had sat across a rugged wood table from this young man and tried to start some kind of conversation.

He was a strong one, Highland admitted to himself. He had spoken but one unnecessary word, and that only nine days before. A jailer with more indignation than professionalism had used the excuse of a plumbing problem in Miller's cell to move him temporarily to another. In the other were two ODCs, as they were called: Ordinary Decent Criminals, as opposed to the political kind that C-13 dealt with. One was awaiting sentencing for a series of vicious street robberies, the other for the gun-murder of a shop owner in Kensington. Both knew who Miller was, and hated him enough to look at the small young man as a way to atone for the crimes which they little regretted in any case. When Highland had shown up for yet another fruitless interrogation session, he'd found Miller facedown on the floor of the cell, his pants gone, and the robber sodomizing him so brutally that the policeman had actually felt sympathy for the terrorist.

The Ordinary Decent Criminals had withdrawn at Highland's command, and when the cell door was opened, Highland had himself picked Miller up and helped him to the dispensary. And there Miller had actually spoken to him as though to another human being. A single word from the puffy, split lips: 'Thanks.'

Cop rescues terrorist, Highland thought to himself, *some headline that would be*. The jailer had pleaded innocence, of course. There was a problem with the plumbing in Miller's cell – somehow the work order had got mislaid, you see – and the jailer had been called to quell a disturbance elsewhere. Hadn't heard a sound from that end of the cell block. Not a sound. Miller's face had been beaten to a bloody pulp, and certainly he'd have no toilet problems for a few more days. His sympathy for Miller had been short-lived. Highland was still angry with the jailer. It was his professionalism that was offended. What the jailer had done was, quite simply, wrong, and potentially the first step on a path that could lead back to the rack and hot pincers. The law was not so much designed to protect society from the criminals, but more profoundly to protect society from itself. This was a truth that not even all policemen understood fully, but it was the single lesson that Highland had learned from five years in the Anti-Terrorist Branch. It was a hard lesson to believe when you'd seen the work of the terrorists.

Miller's face still bore some of the marks, but he was a young man and he was healing quickly. Only for a brief few minutes had he been a victim, a human victim. Now he was an animal again. Highland was hard-pressed to think of him as a fellow man – but that was what his professionalism was for. *Even for the likes of you.* The policeman looked back out the rear window.

It was a boring drive, as it had to be with no radio, no conversation, only vigilance for something that almost certainly wasn't out there. Highland wished that he'd put coffee in his thermos instead of tea. They watched the truck pass out of Woking, then Aldershot and Farnham. They were in the estate country of Southern England now. All around them were stately homes belonging to the horse crowd, and the less stately homes of those whom they employed. It was a pity it was dark, Highland thought, this could be a very pleasant drive. As it was, the fog hung in the numerous valleys, and rain pelted the flat metal top of the van, and the van's driver had to be especially careful as he negotiated the narrow, twisting roads that characterize the English countryside. The only good news was the near-total absence of traffic. Here and there Highland saw a solitary light over some distant door, but there was little more than that.

An hour later, the van used the M27 motorway to bypass Southampton, then turned south on to an A road for Lymington. Every few miles they passed through a small village. There were the beginnings of life here and there. Early church services were under way already, but the real travelling wouldn't start until the sun was up, and that was still over two hours off. The weather was worsening. They were only a few miles from the coast now, and the wind was gusting at thirty miles per hour. It blew away the fog, but also drove sheets of cold rain and rocked the van on its wheels.

'Miserable bloody day to take a boat ride,' the other cop in the back commented.

'Only supposed to be thirty minutes,' Highland said, his own stomach already queasy at the thought. Born in a nation of seamen, Bob Highland detested travelling on the water.

'On a day like this? An hour, more like.' The man started humming 'A Life on the Ocean Wave' while Highland started regretting the large breakfast he'd fixed before leaving home.

Nothing for it, he told himself. *After we deliver young Mr Miller, it's home for Christmas and two days off. I've bloody earned it.* Thirty minutes later they arrived in Lymington.

Highland had been there once before, but he remembered more than he could see. The wind off the water was now a good forty miles per hour, a full gale out of the southwest . He remembered from the map that most of the boat ride to the Isle of Wight was in sheltered waters – a relative term, but something to depend on nonetheless. The ferry *Cenlac* waited at the dock for them. Only half an hour before, the boat's captain had been told that a special passenger was en route. That explained the four armed officers who stood or sat in various places around the ferry. A low-profile operation, to be sure, and it didn't interfere with the ferry's other passengers, many of them carrying bundles whose identity didn't need to be guessed at.

The Lymington to Yarmouth ferry cast off her lines at 8:30 exactly. Highland and the other officer remained in the van while the driver and another armed constable who'd ridden in front stood outside. *Another hour*, he told himself, *then a few more minutes to deliver Miller to the prison, and then a leisurely drive back to London. I might even stretch out and get a few winks.* Christmas Dinner was scheduled for four in the afternoon – his contemplation of that event stopped abruptly.

The *Cenlac* entered the Solent. If these waters were sheltered, Highland didn't want to think what the open ocean was like. The *Cenlac* wasn't all that large, and the ferry lacked the weatherly lines of a blue-water craft. The channel gale was broad on her starboard beam, as were the seas, and the boat was already taking fifteen-degree rolls.

'Bloody hell,' the Sergeant observed to himself. He looked at Miller. The terrorist's demeanour hadn't changed a whit. He sat there like a statue, head still against the van's wall, eyes still closed, hands in his lap. Highland decided to try the same thing. There was nothing to be gained by staring out the back window. There wasn't any traffic to worry about now. He sat back and propped his feet on the left-side bench. Somewhere he'd once read that closing one's eyes was an effective defence against motion sickness. He had nothing to fear from Miller. Highland was not carrying a gun, of course, and the keys to the prisoner's manacles were in the driver's pocket. So he did close his eyes, and let his inner ear come to terms with the rolling motion of the ferry without the confusion that would come from staring at the unmoving interior of the truck. It helped a little. His stomach soon started to inform him of its dissatisfaction with the current scheme of things, but it didn't get too bad. Highland hoped that the rougher seas farther out wouldn't change this. They wouldn't.

The sound of automatic weapons fire jerked his head up a moment later. The screams came next, from women and children, followed by the rough shouts of men. Somewhere a car horn started blaring and didn't stop. More guns started. Highland recognized the short bark of some detective's service automatic – answered at once by the staccato of a submachine gun. It couldn't have lasted more than a minute. The *Cenlac*'s own horn started blowing short, loud notes, then stopped after a few seconds while the car's horn kept going. The screams diminished. No longer shrill cries of alarm, they were now the deeper cries of comprehended terror. A few more bursts of machine-gun fire crashed out, then stopped. Highland feared the silence more than the noise. He looked out the window and saw nothing but a car and the dark sea beyond. There would be more, and he knew what it would be. Uselessly his hand went inside his jacket for the pistol that wasn't there.

How did they know – how did the bastards know we'd be here!

Now came more shouts, the sound of orders that would not be disobeyed by anyone who wanted to live through this Christmas Day. Highland's hands balled into fists. He turned to look again at Miller. The terrorist was staring at him now. The sergeant would have preferred a cruel smile to the empty expression he saw on that young, pitiless face.

The metal door shook to the impact of an open hand.

'Open the bloody door or we'll blow it off!'

'What do we do?' the other cop asked.

'We open the door.'

'But –'

'But *what*? Wait for them to hold a gun at some baby's head? They've won.' Highland twisted the handles. Both doors were yanked open.

There were three men there, ski masks pulled down over their faces. They held automatic weapons.

'Let's see your guns,' the tall one said. Highland noted the Irish accent, not that he was very surprised by it.

'We are both unarmed,' the Sergeant answered. He held both hands up.

'Out. One at a time, and flat on the deck.' The voice didn't bother to make any threats.

Highland stepped out of the truck and got to his knees, then was kicked down on to his face. He felt the other cop come down beside him.

'Hello, Sean,' another voice said. 'You didn't think we'd forget you, did you now?'

Still Miller didn't say anything, Highland thought in wonderment. He listened to the flat jingle of his chains as he hobbled out of the van. He saw the shoes of a man step to the doors, probably to help him down.

The driver must be dead, Highland thought. The gunmen had his keys. He heard the manacles come off, then a pair of hands lifted Miller to his feet. Miller was rubbing his wrists, finally showing a little emotion. He smiled at the deck before looking at the Sergeant.

There wasn't much point in looking at the terrorist. Around them he saw at least three men dead. One of the black-clad gunmen pulled a shattered head off a car's wheel, and the horn finally stopped. Twenty feet away a man was grasping at a bloody stomach and moaning, a woman – probably his wife – trying to minister to him. Others lay about on the deck in small knots, each watched by an armed terrorist as their hands sweated on the backs of their necks. There was no unnecessary noise from the gunmen, Highland noted. They were trained men. All the noise came from the civilians. Children were crying, and their parents were faring better than the childless adults. Parents had to be brave to protect their kids, while the single had only their own lives to fear for. Several of these were whimpering.

'You are Robert Highland,' the tall one said quietly. 'Sergeant Highland of the famous C-13?'

'That's right,' the policeman answered. He knew that he was going to die. It seemed a terrible thing to die on Christmas Day. But if he was going to die, there was nothing left to lose. He wouldn't plead, he wouldn't beg. 'And who might you be?'

'Sean's friends, of course. Did you really think that we'd abandon him to your kind?' The voice sounded educated despite the simple diction. 'Do you have anything to say?'

Highland wanted to say something, but he knew that nothing would really matter. He wouldn't even entertain them with a curse – and it came to him that he understood Miller a little better now. The realization shocked him out of his fear. Now he knew why Miller hadn't spoken. *What damned fool things go through your head at a time like this*, he thought. It was almost funny, but more than that it was disgusting.

'Get on with it and be on your way.'

He could only see the tall one's eyes, and was robbed of the satisfaction he might have had from seeing the man's reactions. Highland became angry at that. Now that death was certain, he found himself enraged by the irrelevant. The tall one took an automatic pistol from his belt and handed it to Miller.

'This one's yours, Sean.'

Sean took the gun in his left hand and looked one last time at Highland. *I might as well be a rabbit for all that little fucker cares.*

'I should have left you in that cell,' Highland said, his own voice now devoid of emotion.

Miller considered that for a moment, waiting for a fitting reply to spring from his brain as he held the gun at his hip. A quote from Josef Stalin came to mind. He raised his gun. 'Gratitude, Mr Highland . . . is a disease of dogs.' He fired two rounds from a distance of fifteen feet.

'Come on,' O'Donnell said from behind his mask. Another black-clad man appeared on the vehicle deck. He trotted to the leader.

'Both engines are disabled.'

O'Donnell checked his watch. Things had gone almost perfectly. A good plan, it was – except for the bloody weather. Visibility was under a mile, and –

'There it is, coming up aft,' one man called.

'Patience, lads.'

'Just who the hell are you?' the cop at their feet asked.

O'Donnell fired a short burst for an answer, correcting this oversight. Another chorus of screams erupted, then trailed quickly away into the shriek of the winds. The leader took a whistle from inside his sweater and blew it. The assault group formed up on the leader. There were seven of them, plus Sean. Their training showed, O'Donnell noted with satisfaction. Every man of them stood facing outward around him, gun at the ready in case one of these terrified civilians might be so foolish as to try something. The ferry's captain stood on the ladder sixty feet away, clearly worrying about his next hazard, handling his craft in a storm without engine power. O'Donnell had considered killing all aboard and sinking the boat, but rejected the idea as counterproductive. Better to leave survivors behind to tell the tale, otherwise the Brits might not know of his victory.

'Ready!' the man at the stern announced.

One by one the gunmen moved aft. There was an eight-foot sea rolling, and it would get worse farther out beyond the shelter of Sconce Point. It was a hazard that O'Donnell could accept more readily than the *Cenlac*'s captain.

'Go!' he ordered.

The first of his men jumped into the ten-metre Zodiac. The man at the controls of the small boat took alee from the ferry and used the power of his twin outboards to hold her in close. The men had all practiced that in three-foot seas, and despite the more violent waves, things went easily. As each man jumped aboard, he rolled to starboard to clear a path for the next. It took just over a minute. O'Donnell and Miller went last, and as they hit the rubber deck, the boat moved alee, and the throttles cracked open to full power. The Zodiac raced up the side of the ferry, out of her wind shadow, and then southwest towards the English Channel. O'Donnell looked back at the ferry. There were perhaps six people watching them pull away. He waved to them.

'Welcome back to us, Sean,' he shouted to his comrade.

'I didn't tell them a bloody thing,' Miller replied.

'I know that.' O'Donnell handed the younger man a flask of whiskey. Miller lifted it and swallowed two ounces. He'd forgotten how good it could taste, and the cold sheets of rain made it all the better.

The Zodiac skimmed over the wavetops, almost like a hovercraft, driven by a pair of hundred-horsepower engines. The helmsman stood at his post 'midships, his knees bent to absorb the mild buffeting as he piloted the craft through the wind and rain towards the rendezvous. O'Donnell's fleet of trawlers gave him a wide choice of seamen, and this wasn't the first time he'd used them in an operation. One of the gunmen crawled around to pass out life jackets. In the most unlikely event that someone saw them they would look like a team from the Royal Marines' Special Boat Service, running an exercise on Christmas morning. O'Donnell's operations always covered the angles, were always planned down to the last detail. Miller was the only man he'd ever had captured; and now his perfect record was re-established. The gunmen were securing their weapons in plastic bags to minimize corrosion damage. A few were talking to each other, but it was impossible to hear them over the howl of wind and outboard motors.

Miller had hit the boat pretty hard. He was rubbing his backside.

'Bloody faggots!' he snarled. It was good to be able to talk again.

'What's that?' O'Donnell asked over the noise. Miller explained for a minute. He was sure it had all been Highland's idea, something to soften him up, make him grateful to the cop. That was why both his shots had gone into Highland's guts. There was no sense in letting him die fast. But Miller didn't tell his boss that. That sort of thing was not professional. Kevin might not approve.

'Where's that Ryan bastard?' Sean asked.

'Home in America.' O'Donnell checked his watch and subtracted six hours. 'Fast asleep in his bed, I bet.'

'He set us back a year, Kevin,' Miller pointed out. 'A whole bloody year!'

'I thought you'd say that. Later, Sean.'

The younger man nodded and took another swig of whiskey. 'Where are we going?'

'Somewhere warmer than this!'

The *Cenlac* drifted before the wind. As soon as the last terrorist had left, the Captain had sent his crew below to check for bombs. They'd found none, but the Captain knew that could just mean they were hidden, and a ship was the perfect place to hide anything. His engineer and another sailor were trying to repair one of his diesels while his three deckhands rigged a sea anchor that now streamed over the stern to steady the ferry on the rolling seas. The wind drove the boat closer to land. That did give them more moderate seas, but to touch the coast in this weather was death for all aboard. He thought he might launch one of his lifeboats, but even that entailed dangers that he prayed he might yet avoid.

He stood alone in the pilothouse and looked at his radios – smashed. With them he could call for help, a tug, a merchantman, anything that could put a line on his bow and pull him to safe harbour. But all three of his radio transmitters were wrecked beyond repair by a whole clip of machine gun bullets.

Why did the bastards leave us alive? he asked himself in quiet, helpless rage. His engineer appeared at the door.

'Can't fix it. We just don't have the tools we need. The bastards knew exactly what to break.'

'They knew exactly what to do, all right,' the Captain agreed.

'We're late for Yarmouth. Perhaps –'

'They'll write it off to the weather. We'll be on the rocks before they get their fingers out.' The Captain turned and opened a drawer. He withdrew a flare pistol and a plastic box of star shells. 'Two-minute intervals. I'm going to see to the passengers. If nothing happens in . . . forty minutes, we launch the boats.'

'But we'll kill the wounded getting them in –'

'We'll lose bloody everyone if we don't!' The Captain went below.

One of the passengers was a veterinarian, it turned out. Five people were wounded, and the doctor was trying to treat them, assisted by a member of the crew. It was wet and noisy on the vehicle deck. The ferry was rolling twenty degrees, and a window had been smashed by the seas. One of his deck crew was struggling to put canvas over the hole. The Captain saw that he would probably succeed, then went to the wounded.

'How are they?'

The veterinarian looked up, the anguish plain on his face. One of his patients was going to die, and the other four. . . .

'We may have to move them to the lifeboats soon.'

'It'll kill them. I –'

'Radio,' one of them said through his teeth.

'Lie still,' the doctor said.

'Radio,' he persisted. The man's hands were clasping bandages to his abdomen, and it was all he could do not to scream out his agony.

498

'The bastards wrecked them,' the Captain said. 'I'm sorry – we don't have one.'

'The truck – a radio in the fucking truck!'

'What?'

'Police,' Highland gasped. 'Police van – prisoner transport . . . *radio*. . . .'

'Holy Jesus!' He looked at the van – the radio might not work from inside the ferry. The Captain ran back to the pilothouse and gave an order to his engineer.

It was an easy enough task. The engineer used his tools to remove the VHF radio from the truck. He was able to hook it up to one of the ferry's antennas, and the Captain was using it within five minutes.

'Who is this?' the police dispatcher asked.

'This is the *Cenlac*, you bloody fool. Our marine radios are out. We are disabled and adrift, three miles south of Lisle Court, and we need assistance at once!'

'Oh. Very well. Stand by.' The desk sergeant in Lymington was no stranger to the sea. He lifted his telephone and ran his finger down a list of emergency numbers till he found the right one. Two minutes later he was back to the ferry.

'We have a tugboat heading towards you right now. Please confirm your position three miles south of Lisle Court.'

'That is correct, but we are drifting northeast. Our radar is still operating. We can guide the tug in. For Christ's sake, tell him to hurry. We have wounded aboard.'

The Sergeant bolted upright in his chair. 'Say again – repeat your last.'

The Captain explained in as few words as possible now that help was en route to his ship. Ashore, the Sergeant called his superior, then the local superintendent. Another call went to London. Fifteen minutes later, a Royal Navy flight crew was warming up a Sea King rescue helicopter at Gosport. They flew first to the naval hospital at Portsmouth to pick up a doctor and a medical orderly, then reversed course into the teeth of the gale. It took twenty dreadful minutes to find her, the pilot fighting his aircraft through the buffeting winds while the co-pilot used the look-down radar to pick the ferry's profile out from the sea return on the scope. That was the easy part.

He had to give his aircraft more than forty knots of forward speed just to hold her steady over the boat – and the wind never stayed the same for more than a few seconds, veering a few degrees in direction, changing ten knots in speed as he struggled with the controls to maintain something like a hover over her. Aft, the crew chief wrapped the rescue sling around the doctor first, holding him at the open door. Over the intercom, the pilot told the chief to lower away. At least they had a fairly large target. Two crewmen waited on the top deck of the ferry to receive the doctor. They'd never done it before, but the helicopter crew had, dropping him rapidly to ten feet over the rocking deck, then more easily the last few feet. One crewman tackled the doctor and detached the collar. The medical orderly came next, cursing fate and nature all the way down. He too arrived safely, and the helicopter shot upwards to get away from the dangerous surface.

'Surgeon Lieutenant Dilk, doctor.'

'Welcome. I'm afraid my practice is usually limited to horses and dogs,' the vet replied at once. 'One sucking chest, the other three are belly wounds. One died – I did my best, but –' there wasn't much else to say. 'Fucking murderers!'

The sound of a diesel horn announced the arrival of the tugboat. Lieutenant Dilk didn't bother looking while the Captain and crew caught the messenger line and hauled in a towing wire. Together, the doctors administered morphine and worked to stabilize the wounded.

The helicopter was already gone southwest, a grimmer purpose to their second mission for the day. Another helicopter, this one with armed Marines aboard, was lifting off from Gosport while the first searched the surface with radar and eyes for a black ten-metre zodiac-type rubber boat. Orders had come from the Home Office with record speed, and for once they were orders that men in uniform were trained and equipped to handle: *Locate and destroy*.

'The radar's hopeless,' the co-pilot reported over the intercom.

The pilot nodded agreement. On a calm day they'd have a good chance to pick the rubber boat out, but the return from the confused seas and the flying spray made radar detection impossible.

'They can't have gone too far, and visibility isn't all that bad from up here. We'll do a quartering search and eyeball the bastards.'

'Where do we start?'

'Off the Needles, then inwards to Christchurch Bay, then we'll work west if we have to. We'll catch the bastards before they make land and have the bootnecks meet them on the beach. You heard the orders.'

'Indeed.' The co-pilot activated his tactical navigation display to set up the search pattern. Ninety minutes later it was plain that they'd searched in the wrong place. Surprised – baffled – the helicopters returned to Gosport empty-handed. The pilot went into the ready shack and found two very senior police officers.

'Well?'

'We searched from the Needles to Poole Bay – we didn't miss a thing.' The pilot traced his flight path on the chart. 'That type of boat can make perhaps twenty knots in these sea conditions – at most, and then only with an expert crew. We shouldn't have missed them.' The pilot sipped at a mug of tea. He stared at the chart and shook his head in disbelief. 'No *way* we could have missed them! Not with two machines up.'

'What if they went seaward, what if they went south?'

'But where? Even if they carried enough fuel to cross the Channel, which

I doubt, only a madman would try it. There will be twenty-foot seas out there, and the gale is still freshening. Suicide,' the pilot concluded.

'Well, we know that they're not madmen, they're too damned smart for that. No way they could have got past you, made land before you caught up with them?'

'Not a chance. None.' The flyer was emphatic.

'Then where the hell are they?'

'I'm sorry, sir, but I haven't a clue. Perhaps they sank.'

'Do you believe that?' the cop demanded.

'No, sir.'

Commander James Owens turned away. He looked out the windows. The pilot was right; the storm was worsening. The phone rang.

'For you, sir.' A petty officer held it up.

'Owens, Yes?' His face changed from sadness to rage and back. 'Thank you. Please keep us posted. That was the hospital. Another of the wounded died. Sergeant Highland's in surgery now. One of the bullets hit his spine. That's a total of nine dead, I believe. Gentlemen, is there anything you can suggest to us? I'd be quite willing to hire a gypsy fortune teller at the moment.'

'Perhaps they made south from the Needles, then curved east and landed on the Isle of Wight.'

Owens shook his head. 'We have people there. Nothing.'

'Then they might have rendezvoused with a ship. There is the usual amount of traffic in the Channel.'

'Any way to check that?'

The pilot shook his head. 'No. There's a ship-traffic-control radar at Dover Strait, but not here. We can't board every ship, can we?'

'Very well. Gentlemen, thank you for your efforts, particularly getting your surgeon out as quickly as you did. I was told that your action saved several lives.' Commander Owens walked out of the building. Those left behind marvelled at his self-control. Outside, the senior detective looked up into the leaden sky and swore a mental curse at fortune, but he was too consumed by anger to show what he felt. Owens was a man accustomed to concealing what he thought and felt. Emotions, he often lectured his men, had no place in police work. Of course that was false, and like many cops Owens only succeeded in turning his rage inwards. That accounted for the packet of antacid pills always in his coat pocket, and the quiet spells at home that his wife had learned to live with. He reached in his shirt pocket for a cigarette that wasn't there, then snorted to himself – *how did you ever break that habit, Jimmy?* He stood alone in the car park for a moment, as though the cold rain would dampen his anger. But it only gave him a chill, and he couldn't afford that. He'd have to answer for this, answer to the Commissioner of the Metropolitan Police, answer to the Home Office. Someone – *not me, thank God* – would also have to answer to the Crown.

That thought hammered home. He had failed *them*. He'd failed them twice. He had failed to detect and prevent the original attack on The Mall, and only the incredible luck of that Yank's intervention had saved the day. Then, when everything had subsequently gone right, this failure. Nothing like this had ever happened before. Owens was responsible. It had all happened on his watch. He had personally set up the transport scheme. The method was of his choosing. He had established the security procedures. Picked the day. Picked the routes. Picked the men, all dead now, except for Bob Highland.

How did they know? Owens demanded of himself. *They knew when, they knew where. How did they know? Well*, he told himself, *that's one place to start looking*. The number of people who had this information was known to Owens. Somehow it had been leaked. He remembered the report Ashley had brought back from Dublin. 'So good you would not believe it,' that Provisional IRA bastard had said of O'Donnell's intelligence source. Murphy was wrong, the detective thought. Everyone will believe it now.

'Back to London,' he told the driver.

'Great day, Jack,' Robby observed on the couch.

'Not bad at all,' Ryan agreed. *Of course the house looks like a Toys 'R' Us that got nuked....*

In front of them, Sally was playing with her new toys. She particularly liked the doll's house, Jack was gratified to see. His daughter was winding down, having got her parents up at seven that morning. Jack and Cathy were winding down also after only five hours of sleep. That was a little tough on a pregnant wife, Jack had thought an hour earlier, and he and Robby had cleared away the dishes, now being processed by the dishwasher in the kitchen. Now their wives were on the other couch talking while the menfolk sipped at some brandy.

'Not flying tomorrow?'

Jackson shook his head. 'The bird went tits-up, take another day or so to fix. Besides, what's Christmas without a good brandy? I'll be back in the simulator tomorrow, and regs don't prevent me from drinking before I do that. I don't strap in until three tomorrow, I ought to be fairly sober by then.' Robby'd had one glass of wine with dinner, and had limited himself to only one Hennessy.

'God, I need a stretch.' Jack stood up and beckoned his friend to the stairs.

'How late were you up last night, sport?'

'I think we hit the sack a little after two.'

Robby checked to see that Sally was out of earshot. 'Being Santa is a bitch, isn't it? If you can put all those toys together, maybe I ought to turn you loose on my broke airplane.'

'Wait till I have both arms back.' Jack pulled his arm out of the sling and moved it around as they went down to the library level.

'What's Cathy say about that?'

'What docs always say – hell, if you get well too soon, they lose money!' He moved his wrist around. 'This thing knots up like you wouldn't believe.'

'How's it feel?'

'Pretty good. I think I might get full use back. At least I haven't had it quit on me yet.' Jack checked his watch. 'Want to catch the news?'

'Sure.'

Ryan flipped on the small TV on his deck. Cable had finally made it down his road, and he was already hooked on CNN. It was so nice to get the national and world news whenever you wanted. Jack dropped into his swivel chair while Robby selected another in the corner. It was a few minutes short of the hourly headlines. Jack left the sound down.

'How's the book coming?'

'Getting there. I have all the information in line finally. Four more chapters to write, and two I have to change around some, and it's done.'

'What did you change?'

'Turned out that I got bum data. You were right about that deck-spotting problem on the Japanese carriers.'

'I didn't think that sounded right,' Robby replied. 'They were pretty good, but they weren't that good – I mean, we took 'em at Midway, didn't we?'

'What about today?'

'The Russians? Hey, Jack, anybody wants to fool with me and my Tomcat better have his will fixed up. They don't pay me to lose, son.' Jackson grinned like a sleepy lion.

'Nice to see such confidence.'

'There's better pilots than me,' Robby admitted. 'Three, as a matter of fact. Ask me again in a year, when I'm back in the groove.'

'Oh, yeah!' Jack laughed. The laugh died when he saw the picture on the TV screen. 'That's him – I wonder why –' He turned the sound up.

' . . . killed, including four police officers. An intensive land, sea, and air search is under way for the terrorists who snatched their convicted comrade while en route to a British prison on the Isle of Wight. Sean Miller was convicted only three weeks before in the daring attack on the Prince and Princess of Wales within sight of Buckingham Palace. Two police officers and one of the terrorists were killed before the attack was broken up by American tourist Jack Ryan of Annapolis, Maryland.'

The picture changed to show the weather on the Channel and a Royal Navy helicopter, evidently searching for something. It changed again to a file tape of Miller being taken out of the Old Bailey. Just before he was put in the police van, Miller turned to face the camera, and now weeks later his eyes stared again into those of John Patrick Ryan.

'Oh, my God . . .' Jack muttered.

10

Plans and Threats

'You shouldn't blame yourself, Jimmy,' Murray said. 'And Bob's going to make it. That's something.'

'Certainly,' Owens replied sardonically. 'There's even a fifty-percent chance that he'll learn to walk again. What of the others, Dan? Five good men gone, and four civilians along with them.'

'And maybe the terrorists, too,' Murray pointed out.

'You don't believe that any more than I do!'

It had come as a piece of blind luck. A Royal Navy mine-hunter ship conducting a long term sonar survey of the English Channel had found a new object on the bottom and immediately sent a camera sled down to classify it. The videotape showed the remains of a ten-metre zodiac-type inflatable boat, with two hundred-horse outboard motors. It had clearly sunk as the result of an explosion near the gas tanks, but there was no evidence of the men who'd been aboard, or their weapons. The vessel's skipper had immediately grasped the importance of the discovery and informed his superiors. A salvage crew was preparing now to go out and raise the wreck.

'It's a possibility. One of them might have screwed up, the boat blew, the bad guys get dumped in the drink. . . .'

'And the bodies?'

'Fish food.' Murray smirked. 'Makes a nice image, doesn't it?'

'You're so fond of punting, Dan. Just what percentage of your salary would you bet on that hypothesis?' Owens wasn't in the mood for humour. Murray could see that the head of C-13 still looked on this as a very personal defeat.

'Not very much,' the FBI representative conceded. 'So you think a ship picked them up.'

'It's the only thing that makes the least bit of sense. Nine merchant vessels were close enough to have been involved. We have the list.'

So did Murray. It had been already forwarded to Washington, where the FBI and CIA would both work on it. 'But why not recover the boat, too?'

'Obvious, isn't it? What if one of our helicopters saw them doing it? Or it might have been too difficult for the weather conditions. Or they might just not have wished to trouble themselves. They do have ample financial resources, don't they?'

'When will the Navy raise the wreck?'

'If the weather holds, day after tomorrow,' Owens said. That was the one thing to be happy about. Then they'd have physical evidence. Everything made in the world carried trademarks and serial numbers. Somewhere there would be records of sale. That was how many successful investigations had started – a single sales slip in a single shop had often led to the conviction of the most dangerous criminals. From the videotape, the outboards on the boat looked like American Mercury motors. The Bureau had already been alerted to run that lead down as soon as the engine numbers were in. Murray had already learned that Mercury motors were a favourite all over the world. It would make matters harder, but it was still something; and something was always better than nothing. The resources of the Metropolitan Police and the Bureau were designed for precisely such a task.

'Any breaks on the leak?' Murray asked. This touched the rawest nerve of all.

'He'd better pray we don't find him,' Owens said quietly. There was as yet no danger that this would happen. There had been a total of thirty-one people who'd known the time and route for the prisoner transfer, and five of them were dead – even the driver of the van hadn't known beforehand. That left twenty-six, ranging from a few members of C-13, two more high officials in the Metropolitan Police, ten in the Home Office, a few more in MI-5, the Security Service, and various others. Every one of them had a top-drawer security clearance. *Not that a clearance matters a damn*, Owens told himself again. *By definition a leak had to come from some bastard with a top-drawer clearance*.

But this was different. This was treason – it was worse than treason – a concept that Owens hadn't even thought possible until the last week. Whoever had leaked this had also to have been involved in the attack on the Royal Family. To betray national security secrets to a foreign power was sufficiently heinous to make the Commander think in unprofessional terms. But deliberately to endanger the Royal Family itself was so incomprehensible a crime that Owens had scarcely been able to believe it possible. This wasn't someone of dubious mental state. This was a person with intelligence and considerable skill at dissimulation, someone who had betrayed a trust both personal and national. There had been a time in his country when such people died by torture. It was not a fact that Owens was proud of, but now he understood why it had happened, how easily one might countenance such punishment. The Royal Family served so many functions for the United Kingdom, was so greatly loved by the people. And someone, probably someone very close to them, was quite willing to betray them to a small band of terrorists. Owens wanted that person. Wanted to see him dead, wanted to watch him die. There could be no other punishment for this kind of crime.

His professionalism returned after the few seconds of grim revelry. *We won't find the bastard by wishing him dead. Finding him means police work – careful, painstaking, thorough investigation.* Owens knew how to do that. Neither he nor the elite team of men on the investigation would rest until they succeeded. But none of them doubted that they would ultimately succeed.

'That's two breaks you have, Jimmy,' Murray said after reading his friend's mind. It wasn't hard to do. Both men had handled hard cases, and police differ little over the world.

'Indeed,' Owens said, almost smiling. 'They ought not to have tipped their hand. They should have bent every effort to protect their source. We can compare the lists of who knew that His Highness was coming in that afternoon, and who knew that young Mr Miller was going to Lymington.'

'And the telephone operators who put the calls through,' Murray reminded him. 'And the secretaries and co-workers who might have overheard, and the girlfriends, or boyfriends, who might have heard during some horizontal conversation.'

'Thank you ever so much for that, Dan. One needs encouragement at a time like this.' The Englishman walked over to Murray's cabinet and found a bottle of whiskey – a Christmas present, still unopened on New Year's Eve. 'You're right that they should have protected their intel source. I know you'll get him, Jimmy. I will put some money down on that.'

Owens poured the drinks. It was gratifying to see that the American had finally learned to drink his whiskey decently. In the past year Owens had broken Murray of the need to put ice in everything. It was shameful to contaminate single-malt Scotch whiskey. He frowned at another recurring thought. 'What does that tell us about Sean Miller?'

Murray stretched his arms out. 'More important than you thought, maybe? Maybe they were afraid you'd break information out of him. Maybe they just wanted to keep their perfect record. Maybe something else?'

Owens nodded. In addition to the close working relationship Scotland Yard had with the FBI, Owens valued the opinions of his colleague. Though both were experienced cops, Murray could always be trusted to have a slightly different slant on things. Two years before Owens had been surprised to learn how valuable this might be. Though he never had thought about it, Murray had used his colleague's brain the same way on several occasions.

'So what might that make Miller?' Owens wondered aloud.

'Who can say? Chief of operations?' Murray waved his glass.

'Too young for that.'

'Jimmy, the guy who dropped the atomic bomb on Hiroshima was a full colonel in the Air Force, and twenty-nine years old. Hell, how old is this O'Donnell character?'

'That's what Bob Highland thinks.' Owens stared into his glass for a moment, frowning again.

'Bob's a smart kid, too. God, I hope you can put him back on the street.'

'If not, we can still use him in the office,' Commander Owens said positively. 'He does have a fine brain for the business of investigations – too good to be lost now. Well, I must be off. New Year's Eve, Dan. What do we drink to?'

'That's obvious. A successful investigation. You're going to get that source, Jimmy, and he's going to give you the information you need.' Murray held his glass up. 'To a closed case.'

Yes.' Both men emptied their glasses.

'Jimmy, do yourself a favour and give it a night off. Clear the old head out and start fresh in the morning.'

Owens smiled. 'I'll try.' He picked up his overcoat and walked towards the door. 'One last thing. It hit me on the drive over. These chaps, the ULA, have broken all the rules, haven't they?'

'That's true enough,' Murray replied as he locked up his files.

'There's only one rule they haven't broken.'

Murray turned. 'Oh? What's that?'

'They've never done anything in America.'

'None of them do that.' Murray dismissed the idea.

'None have had much of a reason before.'

'So?'

'Dan, the ULA might have a reason now – and they've never been reticent about breaking the rules. It's just a feeling, no more than that.' Owens shrugged. 'Well. Good night, and a happy new year to you, Special Agent Murray.'

They shook hands ceremonially. 'And to you, Commander Owens. Give my love to Emily.'

Dan saw him to the door, locked it, and returned to his office to make sure all his secure files were locked up properly. It was pitch dark outside at – he checked his watch – quarter to six.

'Jimmy, why did you say that?' Murray asked the darkness. He sat back down in his swivel chair.

No Irish terrorist group had ever operated in the United States. Sure, they raised money there, in the Irish neighbourhoods and saloons of Boston and New York, made the odd speech about their vision for the future of a free, united Ireland – never bothering to say that as committed Marxist-Leninists, their vision of Ireland was of another Cuba. They had always been shrewd enough to know that Irish-Americans might not feel comfortable with that little detail. And there was the gun-running. That was largely something in the past. The Provisional IRA and INLA currently got most of their weapons on the open world market. There were also reports that some of their people had got training in Soviet military camps – you couldn't tell a man's nationality from a satellite photograph, nor could you recognize a specific face. These reports had never been confirmed sufficiently to be released to the press. The same was true of the camps in Libya, and Syria, and Lebanon. Some people, fair-skinned people, were being trained there – but who? The intelligence got a little confused on this point. It was different with the European terrorists. The Arabs who got caught often sang like canaries, but the captured members of the Provisional IRA and INLA, and the Red Army Faction, and *Action-Directe* of France, and all the other shadowy groups gave up their information far more grudgingly. A cultural thing, or maybe they could simply be more certain that their captors would not – could not – use interrogation measures still common in the Middle East. They'd all been raised under democratic rules, and knew precisely the weaknesses of the societies they sought to topple. Murray thought of them as strengths, but recognized the inconveniences that they imposed on law-enforcement professionals. . . .

The bottom line was still that Provisional IRA and INLA had never committed a violent crime in America. Never. Not once.

But Jimmy's right. The ULA has never hesitated to break a rule. The Royal Family was off-limits to everyone else, but not the ULA. The Provisional IRA and INLA never hesitated to advertise its operations – every terrorist group advertises its operations. But not the ULA. He shook his head. There wasn't any evidence to suggest that they'd break this rule. It was simply the one thing that they hadn't done . . . yet. Not the sort of thing to start an investigation with.

'But what are they up to?' he said aloud. Nobody knew that. Even their name was an anomaly. Why did they call themselves the *Ulster* Liberation Army? The nationalist movement always focused on its Irishness, it was an Irish nationalist movement, but the *ULA*'s very name was a regional expression. 'Ulster' was invariably the prefix of the reactionary *Protestant* groups. Terrorists didn't have to make all that much sense in what they did, but they did have to make *some* sense. Everything about the ULA was an anomaly. They did the things no one else would do, called themselves something no one else would.

They did the things no one else would. That's what was chewing on Jimmy, Murray knew. Why did they operate that way? There had to be a reason. For all the madness of their actions, terrorists were rational by their own standards. However twisted their reasoning appeared to an outsider, it did have its own internal logic. The Provisional IRA and INLA had such logic. They had even announced their rationales, and their actions could be seen to fit with what they said: to make Northern Ireland ungovernable. If they succeeded, the British would finally have enough of it and leave. Their objective, therefore, was to sustain a low-level conflict indefinitely and wait for the other side to walk away. It did make conceptual sense.

But the ULA has never said what it's up to. Why not? Why should their objective be a secret? Hell, why should the existence of a terrorist group be a secret – if they're running operations, how can it be a secret? Then why have they never even announced their existence, except within the Provisional

IRA/INLA community itself? This can't be completely unreasoned action, he reminded himself. *They can't be acting completely without reason and still be as effective as they've been.*

'Damn!' The answer was there. Murray could feel it floating at the edge of his consciousness, but his mind couldn't quite reach that far. The agent left his office. Two Marines were already patrolling the corridors, checking that the doors were locked. Dan waved to them on the way to the lift, his mind still trying to assemble the pieces into a unified picture. He wished that Owens hadn't left so soon. He wanted to talk this one over with Jimmy. Maybe the two of them could make sense of it all. No, he told himself, not 'maybe.' They'd find it. It was there, waiting to be found.

I bet Miller knew, Murray thought.

'What a dreadful place,' Sean Miller said. The sunset was magnificent, almost like one at sea. The sky was clear of the usual urban pollution, and the distant dunes gave a crisp, if crenelated, line for the sun to slide behind. The odd thing was the temperature range, of course. The noon temperature had reached ninety-two – and the locals thought of this as a cool day! – but now as the sun sank, a cool wind came up, and soon the temperature would drop to freezing. The sand couldn't hold the heat, and with the clear, dry air, it would just radiate away, back to the stars.

Miller was tired. It had been that sort of day: refresher training. He hadn't touched a weapon in nearly two months. His reactions were off, his marksmanship abysmal, his physical condition little better. He'd actually gained a few pounds on prison food, something that had come as quite a surprise. In a week he'd have that run off. The desert was good for that. Like most men born in the higher latitudes, Miller had trouble tolerating this sort of climate. His physical activity made him thirsty, but he found it difficult to eat when it was so hot. So he drank water and allowed his body to turn in on itself. He'd lose the weight and harden his body more quickly here than anywhere else. But that didn't make him like the place.

Four more of their men were here also, but the remainder of the rescue force had immediately flown home via Rome and Brussels, putting a new string of entry stamps on their 'travel' passports.

'It's not Ireland,' O'Donnell agreed. His nose crinkled at the smell of dust, and his own sweat. Not like home. No smell of the mist over the peat, or coke fires on the hearths, or the alcoholic ambience of the local pub.

That was an annoying development: no alcohol. The locals had got another attack of Allah and decided that even the fellow members of the international revolutionary community could not break God's law. *What a bloody nuisance.*

It wasn't much of a camp. Six buildings, one of them a garage. An unused helicopter pad, a road half-covered with sand from the last storm. One deep well for water. A firing range. Nothing else. In the past as many as fifty people had cycled through here at a time. Not now. This was the ULA's own camp, well separated from camps used by other groups. Every one of them had learned the importance of security. On a blackboard in hut number 1 was a schedule provided by other fair-skinned friends that gave the passover times for American reconnaissance satellites; everyone knew when to be out of sight, and the camp's vehicles were under cover.

Two headlights appeared on the horizon, heading south towards the camp. O'Donnell noted their appearance, but said nothing about it. The horizon was far away. He put his arms into the sleeves of his jacket to ward off the gathering chill as he watched the lights slide left and right, their conical beams tracing over the dunes. The driver was taking his time, Kevin saw. The lights weren't bouncing about. The climate made it hard for a man to push himself hard. Things would get done tomorrow, God willing. *Insh'Allah*, a Latin colleague had once told him, meant the same thing as *mañana* – but without the urgency.

The vehicle was a Toyota Land Cruiser, the four-wheel-drive that had replaced the Land-Rover in most places. The driver took it right into the garage before getting out. O'Donnell checked his watch. The next satellite pass was in thirty minutes. Close enough. He rose and walked into hut number 3. Miller followed, waving to the man who'd just come into the camp. A uniformed soldier from the camp's permanent force closed the garage door, and otherwise ignored them.

'Glad to see you got out, Sean,' the visitor said. He carried a small satchel.

'Thank you, Shamus.'

O'Donnell held open the door. He was not one to stand on ceremony.

'Thank you, Kevin.'

'You're just in time for dinner,' the chief of the ULA said.

'Well, you can't always be lucky,' Shamus Padraig Connolly said. He looked around the inside of the hut. 'No wogs about?'

'Not in here,' O'Donnell assured him.

'Good.' Connolly opened his satchel and brought out two bottles. 'I thought you might like a drop of the pure.'

'How did you get it past the bastards?' Miller asked.

'I heard about the new rule. I told them I was bringing in a gun, of course.' Everyone laughed as Miller fetched three glasses and ice. You always used ice in this place.

'When are you supposed to arrive at the camp?' O'Donnell referred to the one forty miles away used by the Provisional IRA.

'I'm having some car trouble, and staying the night with our uniformed friends. The bad news is that they've confiscated my whiskey.'

'Bloody heathens!' Miller laughed. The three men toasted one another.

'How was it inside, Sean?' Connolly asked. The first round of drinks was already gone.

'Could have been worse. A week before Kevin came for me, I had a bad time with some thugs – the peelers put them up to it, of course, and they had a merry time. Bloody faggots. Aside from that, ah, it is so entertaining to sit there and watch them talk and talk and talk like a bunch of old women.'

'You didn't think that Sean would talk, did you?' O'Donnell asked reprovingly. The smile covered his feelings – of course they had all worried about that; they had worried most of all what might happen when the Provisional IRA and INLA lads in Parkhurst Prison got hold of him.

'Good lad!' Connolly refilled the glasses.

'So, what's the news from Belfast?' the chief asked.

'Johnny Doyle is not very pleased with having lost Maureen. The men are becoming restless – not much, mind, but there is talk. Your op in London, Sean, in case you've not been told, had glasses filled and raised throughout the Six Counties.' That most citizens in Northern Ireland, Protestant and Catholic, had been disgusted by the operation mattered not to Connolly. His small community of revolutionaries was the entire world.

'You don't get drunk for a failure,' Miller observed sourly. *That bastard Ryan!*

'But it was a brilliant attempt. It's clear enough that you were unlucky, no more than that, and we are all slaves to fortune.'

O'Donnell frowned. His guest was too poetic for Kevin's way of thinking, despite the fact, as Connolly was fond of pointing out, that Mao himself had written poetry.

'Will they try to spring Maureen?'

Connolly laughed at that one. 'After what you did with Sean here? Not bloody likely. How ever did you pull that off, Kevin?'

'There are ways.' O'Donnell let it go at that. His intelligence source was under strict orders not to do a thing for two months. Dennis's bookshop was closed so far as he was concerned. The decision to use him to get information for the rescue operation hadn't come easy. That was the problem with good intelligence, his teachers had hammered into his head years before. The really valuable stuff was always a risk to the source itself. It was a paradox. The most useful material was often too dangerous to use, but at the same time intelligence information that could not be used had no value at all.

'Well, you've got everyone's attention. The reason I'm here is to brief our lads on your operation.'

'Really!' Kevin laughed. 'And what does Mr Doyle think of us?'

The visitor crooked a comically accusing finger. 'You are a counterrevolutionary influence whose objective is to wreck the movement. The op on The Mall has had serious repercussions on the other side of the Atlantic. We'll – excuse me, *they'll* be sending some of their lads to Boston in another month or so to set things right, to tell the Yanks that they had nothing to do with it,' Connolly said.

'Money – we don't need their bloody money!' Miller objected. 'And they can put their "moral support" up –'

'Mustn't offend the Americans,' Connolly pointed out.

O'Donnell raised his glass for a toast: 'The devil with the bloody Americans.'

As he drank off the last of his second whiskey, Miller's eyes snapped open sharply enough to make a *click*.

'Kevin, we won't be doing much in the UK for a while. . . .'

'Nor in the Six Counties,' O'Donnell said thoughtfully. 'This is a time to lie low, I think. We'll concentrate on our training for the moment and await our next opportunity.'

'Shamus, how effective might Doyle's men be in Boston?'

Connolly shrugged his shoulders. 'Get enough alcohol into them and they'll believe anything they're told, and toss their dollars into the hat as always.'

Miller smiled for a moment. He refilled his own glass this time as the other two talked on. His own mind began assembling a plan.

Murray had had a number of assignments in the Bureau over his many years of service, ranging from junior agent involved in chasing down bank robbers to instructor in investigation procedures at the FBI Academy at Quantico, Virginia. One thing he'd always told the youngsters in the classroom was the importance of intuition. Law enforcement was still as much art as science. The Bureau had immense scientific resources to process evidence, had written procedures for everything, but when you got down to it, there was never a substitute for the mind of an experienced agent. It was mostly experience, Murray knew, the way you fitted evidence together, the way you got a feel for the mind of your target and tried to predict his next move. But more than experience, there was intuition. The two qualities worked together until you couldn't separate them in your own mind.

That's the hard part, Murray told himself on the drive home from the embassy. *Because intuition can run a little wild if there's not enough evidence to hold on to.*

'You will learn to trust your instincts,' Murray told the traffic, quoting from his memorized class notes. 'Instinct is never a substitute for evidence and procedure, but it can be a very useful tool in adapting one to another – oh, Dan, you would have made a hell of a Jesuit.' He chuckled to himself, oblivious of the stare he was getting from the car on his right.

If it's so damned funny, why does it bother you?

Murray's instinct was ringing a quiet but persistent bell. Why had Jimmy said that? Obviously it was bothering him, too – but what the hell was it?

The problem was, it wasn't just one thing. He saw that now. It was several things, and they were interrelated like some kind of three-dimensional crossword puzzle. He didn't know the number of blanks, and he didn't have any of the clues to the words, but he did know roughly the way they fitted together. That was something. Given time, it might even be enough, but –

'Damn!' His hands gripped tight on the steering wheel as good humour again gave way to renewed frustration. He could talk it over with Owens tomorrow or the next day, but the bell told him that it was more urgent than that.

Why is it so damned urgent? There is no evidence of anything to get excited about.

Murray reminded himself that the first case that he'd broken more or less on his own, ten months after hitting the street as a special agent, had begun with a feeling like this one. In retrospect the evidence had seemed obvious enough once he'd put the right twist on it, but that twist hadn't occurred to anyone else. And with Murray himself it had begun as nothing more than the same sort of intellectual headache he was suffering through in his car. Now he was really mad at himself.

Fact: The ULA broke all the rules. Fact: No Irish terrorist organization had ever run an operation in the US. There were no more Facts. If they ran an op in America . . . well, they were undoubtedly mad at Ryan, but they hadn't made a move against him over here, and that would have been a hell of a lot easier than staging one in the US. What if Miller really was their chief of operations – no, Murray told himself, terrorists don't usually take things personally. It's unprofessional, and the bastards are professional. They'd have to have a better reason than that.

Just because you don't know what the reason is doesn't mean they don't have one, Danny. Murray found himself wondering if his intuition hadn't transformed itself into paranoia with increasing age. *What if there's more than one reason to do it?*

'There's a thought,' he said to himself. One could be an excuse for the other – but what's the *it* that they want to do? *Motive*, all the police procedure manuals said, was the main thing to look for. Murray didn't have a clue on their motive. 'I could go crazy doing this.'

Murray turned left off Kensington Road, into the upscale neighbourhood of flats where he had his official residence. Parking was the usual problem. Even when he'd been assigned to the counterespionage section of the New York City Field Office, parking hadn't been this bad. He found a space perhaps two feet longer than his car and spent nearly five minutes fitting the car into it.

Murray hung his coat on the peg beside the door and walked right into the living room. His wife found him dialling the phone, a ferocious scowl on his face. She wondered what was wrong.

It took a few seconds for the overseas call to go into the proper office.

'Bill, this is Dan Murray . . . we're fine,' his wife heard him say. 'I want

513

you to do something. You know that guy Jack Ryan? Yeah, that's the one. Tell him – hell, how do I say this? Tell him that maybe he should watch his back. . . . I know that, Bill. . . . I can't say, something's bothering me, and I can't – something like that, yeah. . . . I know they've never done it before, Bill, but it's still bothering me. . . . No, nothing specific that I can point to, but Jimmy Owens brought it up, and now he's got me worrying about it. Oh, you got the report already? Good, then you know what I mean.'

Murray leaned back and stared at the ceiling for a moment. 'Call it feeling, or instinct – call it anything you want, it's bothering me. I want somebody to act on it. . . . Good man. How's the family? Oh, yeah? Great! Well, I guess it'll be a happy new year for you. Okay. Take care. 'Bye.' He set the phone down. 'Well, that feels a little better,' he said quietly to himself.

'The party starts at nine,' his wife said. She was used to his bringing work home. He was used to having her remind him of his social obligations.

'I guess I better get dressed, then.' Murray rose and kissed his wife. He did feel better now. He'd done *something* – probably no more than having people in the Bureau wonder what was happening to him over here, but he could live with that. 'Bill's oldest is engaged. He's going to marry her off to a young agent in the D.C. Field Office.'

'Anyone we know?'

'New kid.'

'We have to leave soon.'

'Okay, okay.' He walked to the master bedroom and started to change for the big embassy party.

11

Warnings

'As you see, ladies and gentlemen, the decision Nelson made in this case had the long-term effect of finally putting an end to the stultifying influence of the Royal Navy's formal tactics.' Ryan closed his note folder. 'There is nothing like a decisive victory to teach people a lesson. Questions?'

It was Jack's first day back at teaching class. The room had forty students, all third classmen (that title included the six female mids in the class), or sophomores in civilian terms, taking Ryan's introductory course in naval history. There were no questions. He was surprised. Jack knew he was a pretty good teacher, but not that good. After a moment, one of the students stood up. It was George Winton, a football player from Pittsburgh.

'Doctor Ryan,' he said stiffly, 'I've been asked to make a presentation on behalf of the class.'

'Uh-oh.' Jack took half a step backwards and scanned the body of students theatrically for the advancing threat.

Mid/3 Winton walked forward and produced a small box from behind his back. There was a typed sheet on the top. The young man stood at attention.

'Attention to orders: For service above and beyond the duty of a tourist – even a brainless Marine – the class awards Doctor John Ryan the Order of the Purple Target, in the hope that he will duck the next time, lest he become a part of history rather than a teacher of it.'

Winton opened the box and produced a purple ribbon three inches across on which was inscribed in gold: SHOOT ME. Below it was a brass bull's-eye of equal size. The mid pinned it to Ryan's shoulder so that the target portion almost covered where he'd been shot. The class stood and applauded as Ryan shook hands with the class spokesman.

Jack fingered the 'decoration' and looked up at his class. 'Did my wife put you up to this?' They started converging on him.

'Way to go, Doc!' said an aspiring submarine driver.

'Semper fi!' echoed a would-be Marine.

Ryan held up his hands. He was still getting used to the idea of having his left arm back. The shoulder ached now that he was really using it, but the surgeon at Hopkins had told him that the stiffness would gradually fade away, and the net impairment to his left shoulder would be less than five percent.

'Thank you, people, but you still have to take the exam next week!'

There was general laughter as the kids filed out of the room to their next class. This was Ryan's last for the day. He gathered up his books and notes and trailed out of the room for the walk uphill to his office in Leahy Hall.

There was snow on the ground this frigid January day. Jack had to watch for patches of ice on the brick pavement. Around him the campus of the Naval Academy was a beautiful place. The immense quadrangle bordered by the chapel to the south, Bancroft Hall to the east, and classroom buildings on the other sides, was a glistening white blanket with pathways shovelled from one place to another. The kids – Jack thought of them as kids – marched about as they always did, a little too earnest and serious for Jack's liking. They saved their smiles for places where no outsiders might notice. Each of them had his (or her) shoes spit-shined, and they moved about with straight backs, books tucked under the left arm so as not to interfere with saluting. There was a lot of that here. At the top of the hill, at Gate no. 3, a Marine lance corporal stood with the 'Jimmy Legs' civilian guard. A normal day at the office, Jack told himself. It was a good place to work. The mids were easily the equal of the students of any school in the country, always ready with questions, and, once you earned their trust, capable of some astonishing horseplay. This was something a visitor to the Academy might never suspect, so serious was the kids' public demeanour.

Jack got into the steam-heated warmth of Leahy Hall and bounded up the steps to his office, laughing to himself at the absurd award that dangled from his shoulder. He found Robby sitting opposite his desk.

'What in the hell is that?' the pilot inquired. Jack explained as he set his books down. Robby started laughing.

'It's nice to see the kids can unwind a little, even in exam season. So what's new with you?' Jack asked his friend.

'Well, I'm a Tomcat driver again,' Robby announced. 'Four hours over the weekend. Oh, man! Jack. I'm telling you, I had that baby talking to me. Took her offshore, had her up to mach one-point-four, did a mid-air refuelling, then I came back for some simulated carrier landings, and – it was good, Jack,' the pilot concluded. 'Two more months and I'll be back where I belong.'

'That long, Rob?'

'Flying this bird is not supposed to be easy or they wouldn't need people of my calibre to do it,' Jackson explained seriously.

'It must be hard to be so humble.'

Before Robby could respond, there came a knock on the opened door and a man stuck his head in. 'Doctor Ryan?'

'That's right. Join us.'

'I'm Bill Shaw, FBI.' The visitor came all the way in and held up his ID card. About Robby's height, he was a slender man in his mid-forties with eyes so deep set that they almost gave him the look of a raccoon, the kind of eyes that got that way from sixteen-hour days. A sharp dresser, he looked like a very serious man. 'Dan Murray asked me to come over to see you.'

Ryan rose to take his hand. 'This is Lieutenant Commander Jackson.'

'Howdy.' Robby shook his hand, too.

'I hope I'm not interrupting anything.'

'Not at all – we're both finished teaching for the day. Grab a chair. What can I do for you?'

Shaw looked at Jackson but didn't say anything.

'Well, if you guys have to talk, I can mosey on over to the O-Club –'

'Relax, Rob. Mr Shaw, you're among friends. Can I offer you anything?'

'No, thank you.' The FBI agent pulled the straight-back chair from next to the door. 'I work in the counter-terrorism unit at FBI headquarters. Dan asked me to – well, you know that the ULA rescued their man Miller from police custody.'

Now Ryan was completely serious. 'Yeah – I caught that on TV. Any idea where they took him to?'

Shaw shook his head. 'They just disappeared.'

'Quite an operation,' Robby noted. 'They escaped to seaward, right? Some ship pick them up maybe?' This drew a sharp look. 'You notice my uniform, Mr Shaw? I earn my living out there on the water.'

'We're not sure, but that is a possibility.'

'Whose ships were out there?' Jackson persisted. This wasn't a law-enforcement problem to Robby. It was a naval matter.

'That's being looked at.'

Jackson and Ryan traded a look. Robby fished out one of his cigars and lit it.

'I got a call the last week from Dan. He's a little – I wish to emphasize this, only a little – concerned that the ULA might . . . well, they don't have much of a reason to like you, Doctor Ryan.'

'Dan said that none of these groups has ever operated over here,' Ryan said cautiously.

'That's entirely correct.' Shaw nodded. 'It's never happened. I imagine Dan explained why this is true. The Provisional IRA continues to get money from over here, I am sorry to say, not much, but some. They still get some weapons. There is even reason to believe that they have some surface-to-air missiles –'

'What the hell!' Jackson's head snapped around.

'There have been several thefts of Redeye missiles – the man-portable one the Army's phasing out now. They were stolen from a couple of National Guard armouries. This isn't new. The RUC has captured M-60 machine guns that got over to Ulster the same way. These weapons were either stolen or bought from some supply sergeants who forgot who they were working for. We've convicted several of them in the past year, and the Army's setting up a new system to keep track of things. Only one missile has turned up. They – the Provisional IRA – tried to shoot down a British Army helicopter a few months back. It never made the papers over here, mainly because they missed, and the Brits were able to hush it up.

'Anyway,' Shaw went on, 'if they were to conduct actual terrorist operations over here, the money and the weapons would probably dry up quite a bit. The Provisional IRA knows that, and it stands to reason that the ULA does, too.'

'Okay,' Jack said. 'They've never operated over here. But Murray asked you to come here and warn me. How come?'

'There isn't any reason. If this had come from anyone except Dan, I wouldn't even be here, but Dan's a very experienced agent, and he's a little bit concerned that maybe you should be made aware of his – it's not even enough to be a suspicion, Doctor Ryan. Call it insurance, like checking the tyres on your car before a long drive.'

'Then what the hell are you telling me?' Ryan said testily.

'The ULA has dropped out of sight – that's not saying much, of course. I guess it's the way they dropped out of sight. They pulled a pretty bold operation, and' – he snapped his fingers – 'disappeared back under their rock.'

'Intel,' Jack muttered.

'What's that?' Shaw asked.

'It happened again. The thing in London that I got in the way of, it resulted from very good intelligence information. This did, too, didn't it? They were moving Miller secretly, but the bad guys penetrated Brit security, didn't they?'

'I honestly don't know the specifics, but I'd say you probably had that one figured out pretty well,' Shaw conceded.

Jack picked up a pencil in his left hand and started twirling it. 'Do we know anything about what we're up against here?'

'They're professionals. That's bad news for the Brits and the RUC, of course, but it's good news for you.'

'How's that?' Robby asked.

'Their disagreement with Doctor Ryan here is more or less a "personal" matter. To take action against him would be unprofessional.'

'In other words,' the pilot said, 'when you tell Jack that there's nothing for him to really worry about, you're betting on the "professional" conduct of terrorists.'

'That's one way to put it, Commander. Another way is to say that we have long experience dealing with this type of person.'

'Uh-huh.' Robby stabbed out his cigar. 'In mathematics that's called inductive reasoning. It's a conclusion inferred, rather than deduced from specific evidence. In engineering we call it a WAG.'

'WAG?' Shaw shook his head.

'A Wild-Ass Guess.' Jackson turned to stare into the FBI man's eyes. 'Like most operational intelligence reports – you can't tell the good ones from the bad ones until it's too damned late. Excuse me, Mr Shaw, I'm afraid that we operators aren't always impressed with the stuff we get from the intelligence community.'

'I knew it was a mistake to come here,' Shaw observed. 'Look, Dan told me over the phone that he doesn't have a single piece of evidence to suggest that there is any chance something unusual will happen. I've spent the last couple of days going over what we have on this outfit, and there just isn't any real evidence. He's responding to instinct. When you're a cop, you learn to do that.'

Robby nodded at that one. Pilots trust their instinct, too. Now, his were telling him something.

'So,' Jack leaned back. 'What should I do?'

'The best defence against terrorists – what the security schools teach business executives, for example – is to avoid patterns. Take a slightly different route to work every day. Alter your time of departure somewhat. When you drive in, keep an eye on the mirror. If you see the same vehicle three or more days in a row, take the tag number and call me. I'll be glad to have it run through the computer – no big deal. It's probably nothing to be worried about, just be a little bit more alert. With luck, in a few days or weeks we'll be able to call you and tell you to forget the whole thing. What I am almost certainly doing is alarming you unnecessarily, but you know the rule about how it's better to be safe than sorry, right?'

'And if you get any information the other way?' Jack asked.

'I'll be on the phone to you five minutes later. The Bureau doesn't like the idea of having terrorists operate here. We work damned hard to keep it from happening, and we've been very effective so far.'

'How much of that is luck?' Robby asked.

'Not as much as you think,' Shaw replied. 'Well, Doctor Ryan, I'm really sorry to have worried you about what is probably nothing at all. Here's my card. If there is anything we can do for you, don't hesitate to call me.'

'Thank you, Mr Shaw.' Jack took the card and watched the man leave. He was silent for a few seconds. Then he flipped open his phone list and dialled 011-44-1-499-9000. It took a few seconds for the overseas call to get through.

'American Embassy,' the switchboard operator answered after the first ring.

'Legal Attaché, please.'

'Thank you. Wait, please.' Jack waited. The operator was back in fifteen seconds. 'No answer. Mr Murray has gone home for the day – no, excuse me, he's out of town for the remainder of the week. Can I take a message?'

Jack frowned for a moment. 'No, thank you. I'll call back next week.'

Robby watched his friend hang up. Jack drummed his fingers on the phone and again remembered what Sean Miller's face had looked like. *He's three thousand miles away, Jack*, Ryan told himself. 'Maybe,' he breathed aloud.

'Huh?'

'I never told you about the one I . . . captured, I guess.'

'The one they sprung? The one we saw on TV?'

'Rob, you ever seen – how do I say it? You ever see somebody that you're just automatically afraid of?'

'I think I know what you mean,' Robby said to avoid the question. Jackson didn't know how to answer that. As a pilot, he'd known fear often enough, but always there was training and experience to deal with it. There was no *man* in the world he'd ever been afraid of.

'At the trial, I looked at him, and I just knew that –'

'He's a terrorist, and he kills people. That would bother me, too.' Jackson stood up and looked out the window. 'Jesus, and they call 'em professionals! *I'm* a professional. I have a code of conduct, I train, I practice, I adhere to standards and rules.'

'They're real good at what they do,' Jack said quietly. 'That's what makes them dangerous. And this ULA outfit is unpredictable. That's what Dan Murray told me.' Jackson turned away from the window.

'Let's go see somebody.'

'Who?'

'Just come along, boy.' Jackson's voice had the ring of command when he wanted it to. He set his white officer's cap on his head just so.

They took the stairs down and walked east, past the chapel and Bancroft Hall's massive, prisonlike bulk. Ryan liked the Academy campus except for that. He supposed it was necessary for all the mids to experience the corporate identity of military life, but Jack would not have cared to live that way as a college student. The odd mid snapped a salute at Robby, who returned each with panache as he proceeded in total silence with Jack trying to keep up. Ryan could almost hear the thoughts whirring through the aviator's head. It took five minutes to reach the new LeJeune Annexe across from the Halsey field house.

The large glass and marble edifice contrasted with Bancroft's stolid gray stone. The United States Naval Academy was a government complex, and hence exempt from the normal standards of architectural good taste. They entered the ground floor past a gaggle of midshipmen in jogging suits, and Robby led him down a staircase into the basement. Jack had never been here before. They ended up in a dimly lit corridor whose block walls led to a dead end. Ryan imagined he heard the crack of small-bore pistol fire, and it was confirmed when Jackson opened a heavy steel door to the Academy's new pistol range. They saw a lone figure standing in the centre lane, a .22 automatic steady in his extended right hand.

Sergeant Major Noah Breckenridge was the image of the Marine non-commissioned officer. Six-three, the only fat on his two-hundred-pound frame was in the hot dogs he'd had for lunch in the adjacent Dalgren Hall. He was dressed in a short-sleeved khaki shirt. Ryan had seen but never met him, though Breckenridge's reputation was well known. In twenty-eight years as a Marine, he had been everywhere a Marine can go, done everything a Marine can do. His 'salad bar' of decorations covered five even rows, topmost among them the Navy Cross, which he'd won while a sniper in Vietnam, part of 1st Force Recon. Beneath the ribbons were his marksmanship medals – 'shooting iron' – the least of which was a 'Master' rating. Breckenridge was known for his weapons proficiency. Every year he went to the national championships at Camp Perry, Ohio, and in two of the past five years he had won the President's Cup for his mastery of the .45 Colt automatic. His shoes were so shiny that one could determine only with difficulty that the underlying leather was actually black. His brass shone like stainless steel, and his hair was cut so close that if any gray were in there, the casual observer could never have seen it. He had begun his career as an ordinary rifleman, been an Embassy Marine and a Sea Marine. He had taught marksmanship at the sniper school, been a drill instructor at Parris Island and an officer instructor at Quantico.

When the Marine detail at the Academy had been augmented, Breckenridge had been the divisional Sergeant Major at Camp LeJeune, and it was said that when he left Annapolis, he would complete his thirty-year tour of duty as Sergeant Major of the Corps, with an office adjoining that of the Commandant. His presence at Annapolis was no accident. As he walked about the campus, Breckenridge was himself an eloquent and unspoken challenge to whichever midshipman might still be undecided on his career goals: *Don't even think about being a Marine officer unless you are fit to command a man like this.* It was the sort of challenge that few mids could walk away from. The Marine force that backed up the civilian guards was technically under the command of a captain. In fact, as was so often the case with the Corps, the Captain had the good sense to let Breckenridge run things. The traditions of the Corps were not passed on by officers, but rather by the professional NCOs who were the conservators of it all.

As Ryan and Jackson watched, the Sergeant Major took a fresh pistol from a cardboard box and slipped a clip into it. He fired two rounds, then checked his target through a spotting scope. Frowning, he pulled a tiny screwdriver from his shirt pocket and made an adjustment to the sights. Two more rounds, check, another adjustment. Two more shots. The pistol was now perfectly sighted, and went back into the manufacturer's box.

'How's it going, Gunny?' Robby asked.

'Good afternoon, Commander,' Breckenridge said agreeably. His southern Mississippi accent spilled across the naked concrete floor. 'And how are you today, sir?'

'No complaints. I got somebody I want you to meet. This here's Jack Ryan.'

They shook hands. Unlike Skip Tyler, Breckenridge was a man who understood and disciplined his strength.

'Howdy. You're the guy was in the papers.' Breckenridge examined Ryan like a fresh boot.

'That's right.'

'Pleased to meet you, sir. I know the guy who ran you through Quantico.'

Ryan laughed. 'And how is Son of Kong?'

'Willie's retired now. He runs a sporting goods store down in Roanoke. He remembers you. Says you were pretty sharp for a college boy, and I imagine you remember mosta what he taught you.' Breckenridge gazed down at Jack with a look of benign satisfaction, as though Ryan's action in London was renewed proof that everything the Marine Corps said and did, everything to which he had dedicated his life, really meant something. He would not have believed otherwise in any case, but incidents like this further enhanced his belief in the image of the Corps. 'If the papers got things straight, you did right well, Lieutenant.'

'Not all that well, Sergeant Major –'

'Gunny,' Breckenridge corrected. 'Everybody calls me Gunny.'

'After it was all over,' Ryan went on, 'I shook like a baby's rattle.'

Breckenridge was amused by this. 'Hell, sir, we all do that. What counts is gettin' the job done. What comes after don't matter a damn. So, what can I do for you gentlemen? You want a few rounds of small-bore practice?'

Jackson explained what the FBI agent had said. The Sergeant Major's face darkened, the jaw set. After a moment he shook his head.

'You're sweatin' this, eh? Can't say that I blame you, Lieutenant. "Terrorists!"' he snorted. 'A "terrorist" is a punk with a machine gun. That's all, just a well-armed punk. It doesn't take much to shoot somebody in the back or hose down an airport waiting room. So. Lieutenant, you'll be thinkin' about carrying some protection, right? And maybe something at home.'

'I don't know . . . but I guess you're the man to see.' Ryan hadn't thought about it yet, but it was clear that Robby had.

'How'd you do at Quantico?'

'I qualified with the .45 automatic and the M-16. Nothing spectacular, but I qualified.'

'Do you remember any shootin' now, sir?' Breckenridge asked with a frown. Just qualifying wasn't a very hopeful sign to a serious marksman.

'I usually get my quota of ducks and geese. I missed out this season, though,' Jack admitted.

'Uplands game?'

'I had two good afternoons after dove in September. I'm a pretty fair wing-shot, Gunny. I use a Remington 1100 automatic, 12-gauge.'

Breckenridge nodded. 'Good for a start. That's your at-home gun. Nothing beats a shotgun at close range – short of a flamethrower, that is.' The Sergeant Major smiled. 'You have a deer/slug barrel? No? Well, you're gonna get one of those. It's twenty inches or so, with a cylinder bore and rifle-type sights. You pull the magazine plug, and you got five-round capacity. Now most people'll tell you to use double-ought buck, but I like number four better. More pellets, and you're not giving any range away. You can still hit out to eighty, ninety yards, and that's all you'll ever need. The important thing is, anything you hit with buckshot's goin' down – period.' He paused. 'As a matter of fact, I might be able to get you some flechette rounds.'

'What's that?' Ryan asked.

'It's an experimental thing they foolin' with down at Quantico for military police use, and maybe at the embassies. Instead of lead pellets, you shoot sixty or so darts, about three-caliber diameter, like little arrows. You gotta see what those little buggers do to believe it. Nasty. So that'll take care of home. Now, you gonna want to carry a handgun with you?'

Ryan thought about that. It would mean getting a permit. He thought he could apply to the state police for one . . . or maybe to a certain federal agency. Already his mind was mulling over *that* question.

'Maybe,' he said finally.

'Okay. Let's do a little experiment.' Breckenridge walked into his office. He returned a minute later with a cardboard box.

'Lieutenant, this here's a High-Standard target pistol, a .22 built on a .45 frame.' The Sergeant Major handed it over. Ryan took it, ejected the magazine, and pulled the slide back to make sure the pistol was unloaded.

Breckenridge watched and nodded approvingly. Jack had been taught range safety by his father twenty years before. After that he fitted the weapon in his hand, then sighted down the range to get used to the feel. Every gun is a little different. This was a target pistol, with nice balance and pretty good sights.

'Feels okay,' Ryan said. 'Little lighter than a Colt, though.'

'This'll make it heavier.' Breckenridge handed over a loaded clip. 'That's five rounds. Insert the clip in the weapon, but do not chamber a round until I tell you, sir.' The Sergeant Major was accustomed to giving orders to officers, and knew how to do so politely. 'Step to lane four. Relax. It's a nice day in the park, okay?'

'Yeah. That's how this whole mess started,' Ryan observed wryly.

The Gunny walked over to the switch panel and extinguished most of the lights in the room.

'Okay, Lieutenant, let's keep the weapon pointed down-range and at the floor, if you please, sir. Chamber your first round, and relax.'

Jack pulled the slide back with his left hand, then let it snap forward. He didn't turn around. He told himself to relax and play the game. He heard a cigarette lighter snap shut. Maybe Robby was lighting up one of his cigars.

'I saw a picture of your little girl in the papers, Lieutenant. She's a pretty little thing.'

'Thank you, Gunny. I've seen one of yours on campus, too. Cute, but not very little. I heard she's engaged to a mid.'

'Yes, sir. That's my little baby,' Breckenridge said, like a father rather than a Marine. 'The last of my three. She'll be married –'

Ryan nearly jumped out of his skin as a string of firecrackers began exploding at his feet. He started to turn when Breckenridge screamed at him:

'There, there, there's your target!'

A light snapped on to illuminate a silhouette target fifty feet away. One small part of Ryan's mind knew this was a test – but most of him didn't care. The .22 came up and seemed to aim itself at the paper target. He loosed all five rounds in under three seconds. The noise was still echoing when his trembling hands set the automatic down on the table.

'Jesus Christ, Sar-major!' Ryan nearly screamed.

The rest of the lights came back on. The room stank of gunpowder, and paper fragments from the firecrackers littered the floor. Robby, Jack saw, was standing safely at the entrance to the Gunny's office, while Breckenridge was right behind him, ready to grab Ryan's gun hand if he did anything foolish.

'One of the other things I do is moonlight as an instructor for the Annapolis City Police. You know, it's a real pain in the ass trying to figure a way to simulate the stress of combat conditions. This here's what I came up with. Okay, let's get a look at the target.' Breckenridge punched a button, and a hidden electric motor turned the pulley for lane four.

'Damn!' Ryan growled, looking at the target.

'Not so bad,' Breckenridge judged. 'We got four rounds on the paper. Two snowbirds. Two in the black, both in the chest. Your target is on the ground, Lieutenant, and he's hurt pretty bad.'

'Two rounds out of five – must be the last two. I settled down on them and took some more time.'

'I noticed that.' Breckenridge nodded. 'Your first round was high and to the left, missed the card. Your next two came in here and here. The last two were on the money fairly well. That's not too bad, Lieutenant.'

'I did a hell of a lot better in London.' Ryan was not convinced. The two holes outside the black target silhouette mocked at him, and one round hadn't even found the target at all. . . .

'In London, if the TV got it right, you had a second or two to figure out what you were gonna do,' the Gunny said.

'That's pretty much the way it was,' Ryan admitted.

'You see, Lieutenant, that's the real important part. That one or two seconds makes all the difference, because you have a little time to think things over. The reason so many cops get killed is because they don't have that little bit of time to think it out – but the crooks have done that already. That one second lets you figure what's happening, select your target, and decide what you're gonna do about it. Now, what I just made you do was go through all three steps, all at once. Your first round went wild. The second and third were better, and your last two were good enough to put the target on the ground. That's not bad, son. That's about as well as a trained cop does – but you gotta do better than that.'

'What do you mean?'

'A cop's job is to keep the peace. Your job is just staying alive, and that's a little easier. That's the good news. The bad news is, those bad guys ain't gonna give you two seconds to think unless you make them, or you're real lucky.' Breckenridge waved for the men to follow him into his office. The Sergeant Major plopped down in his cheap swivel chair. Like Jackson, he was a cigar smoker. He lit up something better than what Robby smoked, but it still stank up the room.

'Two things you gotta do. One, I want to see you here every day for a box of .22; that's every day for a month, Lieutenant. You have to learn to shoot better. Shootin' is just like golf. You want to be good at it, you gotta do it every day. You have to work at it, and you need somebody to teach you right.' The Gunny smiled. 'That's no problem; I'll teach you right. The second thing, you have to buy time for yourself if the bad guys come lookin' for you.'

'The FBI told him to drive like the embassy guys do,' Jackson offered.

'Yeah, that's good for starters. Same as in Nam – you don't settle into patterns. What if they try to hit you at home?'

'Pretty isolated, Gunny,' Robby said.

524

'You got an alarm?' Breckenridge asked Ryan.

'No, but I can fix that pretty easy,' Ryan said.

'It's a good idea. I don't know the layout of your place, but if you can buy yourself a few seconds, and you got that shotgun. Lieutenant, you can make 'em wish they never came calling – at least you can hold them off till the police come. Like I said, the name of the game's just staying alive. Now, what about your family?'

'My wife's a doc, and she's pregnant. My little girl – well, you saw her on TV, I guess.'

'Does your wife know how to shoot?'

'I don't think she's ever touched a gun in her life.'

'I teach a class in firearms safety for women – part of the work I do with the local police.'

Ryan wondered how Cathy would react to all this. He put that one off. 'What sort of handgun you think I oughta get?'

'If you come by tomorrow, I'll try you out on a couple of 'em. Mainly you want something you're comfortable with. Don't go out and get a .44 Magnum, Okay? I like automatics, myself. The springs eat up a lot of the recoil, so they're easier to get comfortable with. You want to buy something that's fun to shoot, not something that beats up on your hand and wrist. Me, I like the .45 Colt, but I been shooting that little baby for twenty-some years.' Breckenridge grabbed Ryan's right hand and flexed it around roughly. 'I think I'll start you off on a 9-millimetre Browning. Your hand looks big enough to hold it right – the Browning's got a thirteen-shot clip, you need a fair-sized hand to control it proper. Got a nice safety, too. If you have a kid in the house, Lieutenant, you'd better think about safety, okay?'

'No problem,' Ryan said. 'I can keep it where she can't reach it – we got a big closet, and I can keep them there, seven feet off the floor. Can I practice with a big-bore handgun in here?'

The Sergeant Major laughed. 'That backstop we got used to be the armour plate on a heavy cruiser. Mainly we use .22's in here, but my guards practice with .45's all the time. Sounds to me like you know shotgunnin' pretty good. Once you have that skill with a pistol too, you'll be able to do it with any gun you pick up. Trust me, sir, this is what I do for a living.'

'When do you want me here?'

'Say about four, every afternoon?'

Ryan nodded. 'Okay.'

'About your wife – look, just bring her over some Saturday maybe. I'll sit her down and talk to her about guns. Lots of women, they're just afraid of the noise – and there's all that crap on TV. If nothing else, we'll get her used to shotgunning. You say she's a doc, so she's gotta be pretty smart. Hell, maybe she'll like it. You'd be surprised how many of the gals I teach really get into it.'

Ryan shook his head. Cathy had never once touched his shotgun, and whenever he cleaned it, kept Sally out of the room. Jack hadn't thought much about it, and hadn't minded having Sally out of the way. Little kids and firearms were not a happy mixture. At home he usually had the Remington disassembled and the ammunition locked away in the basement. How would Cathy react to having a loaded gun in the house?

What if you start carrying a gun around? How will she react to that? What if the bad guys are interested in going after them, too. . . ?

'I know what you're thinkin', Lieutenant,' Breckenridge said. 'Hey, the Commander said the FBI didn't think any of this crap was gonna happen, right?'

'Yeah.'

'So what you're doin' is buyin' insurance, okay?'

'He said that, too,' Ryan replied.

'Look – we get intel reports here, sir. Yeah, that's right. Ever since those bike bums broke in, we get stuff from the cops and the FBI, and from some other places – even the Coast Guard. Some of their guys come here for firearms training, 'cause of the drug stuff they got 'em doing now. I'll keep an ear out, too,' Breckenridge assured him.

Information – it's all a battle for information. You have to know what's happening if you're going to do anything about it. Jack turned back to look at Jackson while he made a decision that he'd been trying to avoid ever since he got back from England. He still had the number in his office.

'And if they tell you those bike bums are coming back?' Ryan asked with a smile.

'They'll wish they didn't,' the Sergeant Major said seriously. 'This is a US Navy reservation, guarded by the United States Marine Corps.'

And that's the name of that tune, Ryan thought. 'Well, thanks, Gunny. I'll get out of your way.'

Breckenridge saw them to the door. 'Sixteen hundred tomorrow, Lieutenant. How about you, Commander Jackson?'

'I'll stick to missiles and cannons, Gunny. Safer that way. G'night.'

'Good night, sir.'

Robby walked Jack back to his office. They had to pass on the daily drinks. Jackson had to do some shopping on the way home. After his friend left, Jack stared at his telephone for several minutes. Somehow he'd managed to avoid doing this for several weeks despite his wish to track down information on the ULA. But it wasn't just curiosity anymore. Ryan flipped open his telephone book and turned to the 'G' page. He was able to call the D.C. area direct, though his finger hesitated before it jabbed down on each button.

'This is Mrs Cummings,' a voice answered after the first ring. Jack took a deep breath.

'Hello, Nancy, this is Doctor Ryan. Is the boss in?'

'Let me check. Can you hold for a second?'

'Yes.'

They didn't have one of the new musical hold buttons there, Ryan noted. There was just the muted chirp of electronic noise for him to listen to. *Am I doing the right thing?* he wondered. He admitted to himself that he didn't know.

'Jack?' a familiar voice said.

'Hello, Admiral.'

'How's the family?'

'Fine, thank you, sir.'

'They came through all the excitement all right?'

'Yes, sir.'

'And I understand that your wife's expecting another baby. Congratulations.'

And how did you know that, Admiral? Ryan did not ask. He didn't have to. The DDI was supposed to know everything, and there were at least a million ways he might have found out.

'Thank you, sir.'

'So, what can I do for you?'

'Admiral, I . . .' Jack hesitated. 'I want to look into this ULA bunch.'

'Yeah, I thought you might. I have here on my desk a report from the FBI's terrorism unit about them, and we've been coordinating lately with the SIS. I'd like to see you back here, Jack. Maybe even on a more permanent basis. Have you thought our offer over any more since we last spoke?' Greer inquired innocently.

'Yes, sir, I have, but . . . well, I am committed to the end of the school year.' Jack temporized. He didn't want to have to face that particular question. If forced, he'd just say no, and that would kill his chance to get into Langley.

'I understand. Take your time. When do you want to come over?'

Why are you making it so easy? 'Could I come over tomorrow morning? My first class isn't until two in the afternoon.'

'No problem. Be at the main gate at eight in the morning. They'll be waiting for you. See ya.'

'Goodbye, sir.' Jack hung up.

Well, that was easy. Too easy, Jack thought. *What's he up to?* Ryan dismissed the thought. He wanted to look at what CIA had. They might have stuff the FBI didn't; at the least he'd get a look at more data than he had now, and Jack wanted to do that.

Nevertheless the drive home was a troubled one. Jack watched his rearview mirror after remembering that he'd left the Academy the same way he always did. The hell of it was, he *did* see familiar cars. That was a problem with making your commute about the same time every day. There were at least twenty cars that he had learned to recognize. There was someone's secretary driving her Camaro Z-28. She had to be a secretary. She was dressed too well to be anything else. Then there was the young lawyer in his

BMW – the car made him a lawyer, Ryan thought, wondering how he had ever assigned tags to his fellow commuters. *What if a new one shows up?* he wondered. *Will you be able to tell which one is a terrorist?* Fat chance, he knew. Miller, for all the danger that lay on his face, would look ordinary enough with a jacket and tie, just another state employee fighting his way up Route 2 into Annapolis. . . .

'Paranoid, all this is paranoid.' Ryan murmured to himself. Pretty soon he'd check the rear seat in his car before he got in, to see if someone might be lurking back there like on TV, with a pistol or garotte! He wondered if the whole thing might be a stupid, paranoid waste of time. What if Dan Murray just had a bug up his ass or was simply being cautious? The Bureau probably taught its men to be cautious on these things, he was sure. Do I scare Cathy over this? What if that's all there is to it?

What if it's not?

That's why I'm going to go to Langley tomorrow, Ryan answered himself.

They sent Sally to bed at 8:30, dressed in her bunny-rabbit sleeper, the flannel pyjamas with feet that keep kids warm through the night. She was getting a little old for that, Jack thought, but his wife insisted on them, since their daughter had a habit of kicking the blankets on the floor in the middle of the night.

'How was work today?' his wife asked.

'The mids gave me a medal,' he said, and explained on for a few minutes. Finally he pulled the Order of the Purple Target out of his briefcase. Cathy found it amusing. The smiling stopped when he related the visit from Mr Shaw of the FBI. Jack ran through the information, careful to include everything the agent had said.

'So, he doesn't really think it'll be a problem?' she asked hopefully.

'We can't ignore it.'

Cathy turned away for a moment. She didn't know what to make of this new information. *Of course*, her husband thought. *Neither do I.*

'So what are you going to do?' she asked finally.

'For one thing I'm going to call an alarm company and have the house wired. Next, I've already put my shotgun back together, and it's loaded –'

'No, Jack, not in this house, not with Sally around,' Cathy said at once.

'It's on the top shelf in my closet. It's loaded, but it doesn't have a round chambered. She can't possibly get to it, not even with a stool to stand on. It stays loaded, Cathy. I'm also going to start practicing some with it, and maybe get a pistol, too. And' – he hesitated – 'I want you to start shooting, too.'

'No! I'm a doctor, Jack. I don't use guns.'

'They don't bite,' Jack said patiently. 'I just want you to meet a guy I know who teaches women to shoot. Just meet the guy.'

'No.' Cathy was adamant. Jack took a deep breath. It would take an hour to persuade her, that was the usual time required for her common sense to overcome her prejudices. The problem was, he didn't want to spend an hour on the subject right now.

'So you're going to call the alarm company tomorrow morning?' she asked.

'I have to go somewhere.'

'Where? You don't have any classes until after lunch.'

Ryan took a deep breath. 'I'm going over to Langley.'

'What's at Langley?'

'The CIA,' Jack answered simply.

'What?'

'Remember last summer? I got that consulting money from Mitre Corporation?'

'Yeah.'

'All the work was at CIA headquarters.'

'But – you said over in England that you never –'

'That's where the checks came from. That's who I was working for. But CIA was where I was working *at*.'

'You lied?' Cathy was astounded. 'You lied in a courtroom?'

'No. I said that I was never employed by CIA, and I wasn't.'

'But you never told me.'

'You didn't need to know,' Jack replied. *I knew this wasn't a good idea. . . .*

'I'm your wife, dammit! What were you doing there?'

'I was part of a team of academics. Every few years they bring in outsiders to look at some of their data, just as sort of a check on the regular people who work there. I'm not a spy or anything. I did all the work sitting at a little desk in a little room on the third floor. I wrote a report, and that was that.' There was no sense in explaining the rest to her.

'What was the report about?'

'I can't say.'

'Jack!' She was really mad now.

'Look, babe, I signed an agreement that I would never discuss the work with anybody who wasn't cleared – I gave my word, Cathy.' That calmed her down a bit. She knew that her husband was a real stickler for keeping his word. It was actually one of the things she loved about him. It annoyed her that he used this as a defence, but she knew that it was a wall she couldn't breach. She tried another tack.

'So why are you going back?'

'I want to see some information they have. You ought to be able to figure out what that information is.'

'About the ULA people, then.'

'Well, let's just say that I'm not worried about the Chinese right now.'

'You really are worried about them, aren't you?' She was starting to worry, finally.

529

'Yeah, I guess I am.'

'But why? You said the FBI said they weren't –'

'I don't know – hell, yes, I *do* know. It's that Miller bastard, the one at the trial. He wants to kill me.' Ryan looked down at the floor. It was the first time he'd said it aloud.

'How do you know that?'

'Because I saw his face, Cathy. I saw it, and I'm scared – not just for me.'

'But Sally and I –'

'Do you really think he cares about that?' Ryan snapped angrily. 'These bastards kill people they don't even know. They almost do it for fun. They want to change the world into something they like, and they don't give a damn who's in the way. *They just don't care.*'

'So why go to the CIA? Can they protect you – us – I mean. . . .'

'I want a better feel for what these guys are all about.'

'But the FBI knows that, don't they?'

'I want to see the information for myself. I did pretty good when I worked there,' Jack explained. 'They even asked me to, well, to take a permanent position there. I turned them down.'

'You never told me any of this,' Cathy grumped.

'You know now.' Jack went on for a few minutes, explaining what Shaw had told him. Cathy would have to be careful driving to and from work. She finally started smiling again. She drove a six-cylinder bomb of a Porsche 911. Why she never got a speeding ticket was always a source of wonderment to her husband. Probably her looks didn't hurt, and maybe she flashed her Hopkins ID card, with a story that she was heading to emergency surgery. However she did it, she was in a car with a top speed of over a hundred twenty miles per hour and the manoeuvrability of a jackrabbit. She'd been driving Porsches since her sixteenth birthday, and Jack admitted to himself that she knew how to make the little green sports car streak down a country road – enough to make him hold on pretty tight. This, Ryan told himself, was probably a better defence than carrying a gun.

'So, you think you can remember to do that?'

'Do I really have to?'

'I'm sorry I got us into this. I never – I never knew that anything like this would happen. Maybe I just should have stayed put.'

Cathy ran her hand across his neck. 'You can't change it now. Maybe they're wrong. Like you said, probably they're just acting paranoid.'

'Yeah.'

12

Homecoming

Ryan left home well before seven. First he drove to US Route 50 and headed west towards D.C. The road was crowded, as usual, with the early morning commuters heading to the federal agencies that had transformed the District of Columbia from a picturesque plot of real estate into a pseudo-city of transients. He got off onto 195, the beltway that surrounds the town, heading north through even thicker traffic whose more congested spots were reported on by a radio station's helicopter. It was nice to know why the traffic was moving at fifteen miles per hour on a road designed for seventy.

He wondered if Cathy was doing what she was supposed to do. The problem was that there weren't that many roads for her to use to get to Baltimore. The nursery school that Sally attended was on Ritchie Highway, and that precluded use of the only direct alternate route. On the other hand, Ritchie Highway was always a crowded and fast-moving road, and intercepting her wouldn't be easy there. In Baltimore itself, she had a wide choice of routes into Hopkins, and she promised to switch them around. Ryan looked out at the traffic in front of him and swore a silent curse. Despite what he'd told Cathy, he didn't worry overly much about his family. He was the one who'd got in the way of the terrorists, and if their motivation was really personal, then he was the only target. Maybe. Finally he crossed the Potomac River and got on the George Washington Parkway. Fifteen minutes later he took the CIA exit.

He stopped his Rabbit at the guard post. A uniformed security officer came out and asked his name, though he'd already checked Ryan's licence plate against a computer-generated list on his clipboard. Ryan handed his driver's licence to the guard, who scrupulously checked the photograph against Jack's face before giving him a pass.

'Sir, the visitors' parking lot is to the left, then the second right –'

'Thanks, I've been here before.'

'Very well, sir.' The guard waved him on.

The trees were bare. CIA headquarters was built behind the first rank of hills overlooking the Potomac Valley, in what had once been a lush forest. Most of the trees remained, to keep people from seeing the building. Jack took the first left and drove uphill on a curving road. The visitor's car park was also attended by a guard – this one was a woman – who waved him to an open slot and made another check of Ryan before directing him towards the canopied main entrance. To his right was 'the Bubble,' an igloo-shaped theatre that was connected to the building by a tunnel. He'd once delivered a talk there, a paper on naval strategy. Before him, the CIA building was a seven-storey structure of white stone, or maybe pre-stressed concrete. He'd never checked that closely. As soon as he got inside, the ambience of spook-central hit him like a club. He saw eight security officers, all in civilian clothes now, their jackets unbuttoned to suggest the presence of sidearms. What they really carried was radios, but Jack was sure that men with guns were only a few feet away. The walls had cameras that fed into some central monitoring room – Ryan didn't know where that was; in fact, the only parts of the building he actually knew were the path to his erstwhile cubbyhole of an office, from there to the men's room, and the route to the cafeteria. He'd been to the top floor several times, but each time he'd been escorted since his security pass didn't clear him for that level.

'Doctor Ryan.' A man approached. He looked vaguely familiar, but Jack couldn't put a name on the face. 'I'm Marty Cantor – I work upstairs.'

The name came back as they shook hands. Cantor was Admiral Greer's executive assistant, a preppy type from Yale. He gave Jack a security pass.

'I don't have to go through the visitor room?' Jack waved to his left.

'All taken care of. You can follow me.'

Cantor led him to the first security checkpoint. He took the pass from the chain around his neck and slid it into a slot. A small gate with orange and yellow stripes, like those used for parking garages, snapped up, then down again as Ryan stuck his card in the slot. A computer in a basement room checked the electronic code on the pass and decided that it could safely admit Ryan to the building. The gate went back up. Already Jack was uncomfortable here. *Just like before*, he thought, *like being in a prison – no, security in a prison is nothing compared to this.* There was something about this place that made Jack instantly paranoid.

Jack slung the pass around his neck. He gave it a quick look. It had a colour photograph, taken the previous year, and a number, but no name. None of the CIA passes had names on them. Cantor led off at a brisk walk to the right, then left towards the lifts. Ryan noticed the kiosk where you could buy a Coke and a Snickers bar. It was staffed by blind workers, yet another of the oddly sinister things about the CIA. Blind people were less likely to be security risks, he supposed, though he wondered how they drove in to work every day. The building was surprisingly shabby, the floor tiles never quite shiny, the walls a drab shade of yellow-beige; even the murals were second-rate. It surprised a lot of people that the Agency spent little on the outward trappings of importance. The previous summer Jack had learned that the people here took a perverse pride in the place's seediness.

Everywhere people walked about with anonymous haste. They walked so fast in the building that most corners had hubcap-shaped mirrors to warn you of possible collision with a fellow spook . . . or to alert you that someone might be lurking and listening around the corner.

Why did you come here?

Jack shook the thought off as he entered the lift. Cantor pushed the button for the seventh floor. The door opened a minute later to expose yet another drab corridor. Ryan vaguely remembered the way now. Cantor turned left, then right, as Ryan watched people walking about with a speed that would impress a recruiter for the Olympic Team's heel-and-toe crew. He had to smile at it until he realized that none of them were smiling. A serious place, the Central Intelligence Agency.

The executive row of CIA had its own private corridor – this one had a rug – that paralleled the main one and led to offices facing the east. As always, there were people just standing about and watching. They inspected Ryan and his pass, but showed no reaction, which was good enough news for Jack. Cantor took his charge to the proper door and opened it.

Admiral James Greer was in civilian clothes, as usual, leaning back in a high-backed swivel chair, reading an inevitable folder and sipping at inevitable coffee. Ryan had never seen him otherwise. He was in his middle sixties, a tall, patrician-looking man whose voice could be as courtly or harsh as he wished. His accent was that of Maine, and for all his sophistication, Ryan knew him to be a farmer's son who'd earned his way into the Naval Academy, then spent forty years in uniform, first as a submarine officer, then as a full-time intelligence specialist. Greer was one of the brightest people Ryan had ever met. And one of the trickiest. Jack was convinced that this gray-haired old gentleman could read minds. Surely that was part of the job description for the Deputy Director, Intelligence, of the Central Intelligence Agency. All the data gathered by spies and satellites, and God only knew what else, came across his desk. If Greer didn't know it, it wasn't worth knowing. He looked up after a moment.

'Hello, Doctor Ryan.' The Admiral rose and came over. 'I see you're right on time.'

'Yes, sir. I remembered what a pain the commute was last summer.' Without being asked, Marty Cantor got everyone coffee as they sat on chairs around a low table. One nice thing about Greer was that he always had good coffee, Jack remembered.

'How's the arm, son?' the Admiral asked.

'Almost normal, sir. I can tell you when it's going to rain, though. They say that may go away eventually, but it's like arthritis.'

'And how's your family?'

The man doesn't miss a trick, Jack thought. But Jack had one of his own. 'A little tense at the moment, sir. I broke the news to Cathy last night. She's not real happy about it, but then neither am I.' *Let's get down to business, Admiral.*

'So what exactly can we do for you?' Greer's demeanour changed from pleasant old gentleman to professional intelligence officer.

'Sir, I know this is asking a lot, but I'd like to see what the Agency has on these ULA characters.'

'Not a hell of a lot.' Cantor snorted. 'These boys cover their tracks like real pros. They're being bankrolled in a pretty big way – that's inferred, of course, but it has to be true.'

'Where does your data come from?'

Cantor looked over to Greer and got a nod. 'Doctor, before we go any further, we have to talk about classification.'

Resignedly: 'Yeah. What do I have to sign?'

'We'll take care of that before you leave. We'll show you just about every-thing we've got. What you have to know now is that this stuff is classified SI-codeword.'

'Well, that's no surprise.' Ryan sighed. Special-Intelligence-Codeword was a level of classification higher than top secret. People had to be individually cleared for the data, which was identified by a special codeword. Even the codeword itself was secret. Ryan had only twice before seen data of this sensitivity. *But now they're going to lay it all out in front of me*, he thought as he looked at Cantor. *Greer must really want me back to open a door like this.* 'So, like I said, where does it come from?'

'Some from the Brits – actually from the Provisional IRA via the Brits. Some new stuff from the Italians –'

Italians?' Ryan was surprised for a moment, then realized what the impli-cations of that were. 'Oh. Okay, yeah, they have a lot of people down in sand-dune country, don't they?'

'One of them ID'd your friend Sean Miller last week. He was getting off a certain ship that was, miraculously enough, in the English Channel on Christmas Day,' Greer said.

'But we don't know where he is?'

'He and an unknown number of associates headed south.' Cantor smiled. 'Of course the whole country is south of the Med, so that's not much of a help.'

'The FBI has everything we have, and so do the Brits,' Greer said. 'It's not much to go on, but we do have a team sifting through it.'

'Thanks for letting me take a look, Admiral.'

'We're not doing this out of charity, Doctor Ryan,' the Admiral pointed out. 'I'm hoping that you might find something useful. And this thing has a price for you, too. If you want in, you will be an Agency employee by the end of the day. We can even arrange for you to have a federal pistol permit.'

'How did you know –'

'It's my job to know, sonny.' The old man grinned at him. Ryan didn't think this situation was the least bit funny, but he granted the Admiral his points.

'When can I start?'

'How does your schedule look?'

'I can work on that,' Jack said cautiously. 'I can be here Tuesday morning, and maybe work one full day per week, plus two half-days. In the mornings.

534

Most of my classes are in the afternoon. Semester break is coming up, and then I can give you a full week.'

'Very well. You can work out the details with Marty. Go take care of the paperwork. Nice to see you again, Jack.'

Jack shook his hand once more. 'Thank you, sir.'

Greer watched the door close before he went back to the desk. He waited a few seconds for Ryan and Cantor to clear the corridor, then walked out to the corner office that belonged to the Director of Central Intelligence.

'Well?' Judge Arthur Moore asked.

'We got him,' Greer reported.

'How's the clearance procedure going?'

'Clean. He was a little too sharp doing his stock deals a few years back, but, hell, he was supposed to be sharp.'

'Nothing illegal?' Judge Moore asked. The Agency didn't need someone who might be investigated by the SEC. Greer shook his head.

'Nah, just very smart.'

'Fine. But he doesn't see anything but this terrorist stuff until the clearance procedures are complete.'

'Okay, Arthur!'

'And I don't have Deputy Directors to do our recruiting,' the DCI pointed out.

'You're taking this awfully hard. Does a bottle of bourbon put that much of a dent in your bank account?'

The Judge laughed. The day after Miller had been sprung from British custody, Greer had made the gentlemanly bet. Moore didn't like losing at anything – he'd been a trial lawyer before becoming a jurist – but it was nice to know that his DDI had a head for prognostication.

'I'm having Cantor get him a gun permit, too,' Greer added.

'You sure that's a good idea?'

'I think so.'

'So it's decided, then?' Miller asked quietly.

O'Donnell looked over at the younger man, knowing why the plan had been formulated. It was a good plan, he admitted to himself, an effective plan. It had elements of brilliance in its daring. But Sean had allowed personal feelings to influence his judgment. That wasn't so good.

He turned towards the window. The French countryside was dark, thirty thousand feet below the airliner. All those peaceful people, sleeping in their homes, safe and secure. They were on a red-eye flight, and the plane was nearly empty. The stewardess dozed a few rows aft, and there was no one about to hear what they were saying. The whine of the jet engines would keep any electronic listening device from working, and they'd been very careful to cover their tracks. First the flight to Bucharest, then to Prague, then to Paris, and now the flight home to Ireland, with only French entry stamps on their passports. O'Donnell was a careful man, to the point of carrying notes on his fictitious business meetings in France. They'd get through customs easily enough, O'Donnell was sure. It was late, and the clerks at passport control were scheduled to go home right after this flight arrived.

Sean had a completely new passport, with the proper stamps, of course. His eyes were now brown, courtesy of some contact lenses, his hair changed in colour and style, a neatly trimmed beard changing the shape of his face. Sean hated the beard for its itching. O'Donnell smiled at the darkness. Well, he'd have to get used to that.

Sean didn't say anything else. He sat back and pretended to read through the magazine he'd found in the seat pocket. The pretended patience was gratifying to his chief. The young man had gone through his refresher training (O'Donnell thought in military terms for this sort of thing) with a passion, trimming off the excess weight, reacquainting himself with his weapons, conferring with the intelligence officers from other fair-skinned nations, and living through their critique of the failed operation in London. These 'friends' had not acknowledged the luck factor, and pointed out that another car of men had been needed to ensure success. Through all of it, Sean had kept his peace and listened politely. And now he waited patiently for the decision on his proposed operation. Perhaps the young man had learned something in that English jail.

'Yes.'

Ryan signed the form, acknowledging receipt of the cartful of information. He was back in the same cubbyhole office he'd had the previous summer, a windowless, closet-sized room on the third floor of CIA's main building. His desk was about the smallest size made – in federal prison workshops – for office use, and the swivel chair was a cheap one. CIA chic.

The messenger stacked the documents on the corner of Ryan's desk and wheeled the cart back out of the room. Jack went to work. He took the top off a Styrofoam cup of coffee bought at the kiosk around the corner, dumped in the whole container of creamer and two envelopes of sugar, and stirred it with a pencil as he often did. It was a habit his wife loathed.

The pile was about nine inches high. The files were in oversized envelopes, each of which had an alpha-numeric code stamped on in block figures. The file folders he removed from the top envelope were trimmed with red tape so as to look important – the visual clues were designed to be noticed, to stand out visually. Such files had to be locked up in secure cabinets every night, never left on a desk where someone might take an unauthorized look at them. The papers inside each were held in place with Acco fasteners, and all had numbers. The cover of the first file had its codeword neatly typed on a paper label: FIDELITY. Ryan knew that the code names were assigned at random by a computer, and he wondered how many such files and names there were, if the dictionary of the English language that resided in the computer's memory had been seriously depleted by the elimination of words for the thousands of secret files that sat in cabinets throughout the building. He hesitated for a moment before opening it, as though doing so would irrevocably commit him to employment at CIA; as though the first step on that path had not already been taken. . . .

Enough of that, he told himself, and opened the file. It was the first official CIA report on the ULA, barely a year old.

'Ulster Liberation Army,' the title of the report read. 'Genesis of an Anomaly.'

'Anomaly.' That was the word Murray had used, Ryan remembered. The first paragraph of the report stated with disarming honesty that the information contained in the following thirty single-spaced pages was more speculation than fact, based principally on data extracted from convicted Provisional IRA members – specifically on denials they'd made. *That wasn't our operation*, some of them had said after being caught for another. Ryan frowned. Not exactly the most reliable of evidence. The two men who'd done the report, however, had done a superb job of cross-referencing. The most unlikely story, heard from four separate sources, changed to something else. It was particularly true since the Provisional IRA was, technically speaking, a professional outfit. Jack knew from his own research the previous year that the Provisional Wing of the Irish Republican Army was superbly organized, along the classic cellular lines. It was just like any intelligence agency. With the exception of a handful of top people, the specifics of any particular operation were compartmentalized: known only to those who really needed to know. 'Need-to-know' was the catch phrase in any intelligence agency.

Therefore, if the details of an operation are widely known, the report argued, *it can only be because it was not a Provisional IRA op. Otherwise they would not have known or talked about the details, even among themselves.* This was twisted logic, Jack thought, but fairly convincing nonetheless. The theory held insofar as the Provisional IRA's main rival, the less well organized Irish National Liberation Army, the gang that had killed Lord Louis Mountbatten, had often had its operations identified in the same way. The rivalry between Provisional IRA and INLA had turned vicious often enough, though the latter, with its lack of internal unity and generally amateurish organization, was not nearly as effective.

It was barely a year since the ULA had emerged from the shadows to take some kind of shape. For the first year they'd operated, it was thought by the British that they were a Provisional IRA Special Action Group, a Provo hit squad, a theory broken when a captured Provisional IRA member had indignantly denied complicity in what had turned out to be a ULA assassination. The authors of the report then examined suspected ULA operations, pointing to operational patterns. These, Ryan saw, were quite real. For one thing, they involved more people, on average, than Provisional IRA ops.

That's interesting.... Ryan walked out of the room, heading down the corridor to the kiosk, where he bought a pack of cigarettes. In under a minute he was back to his office, fumbling with the cipher lock on the door.

More people per operation. Ryan lit one of the low-tar smokes. That was a violation of ordinary security procedures. The more people involved in an operation, the greater the risk of its being blown. What did this mean? Ryan examined three separate operations, looking for his own patterns.

It was clear after ten minutes of examination. The ULA was more of a military organization than Provisional IRA. Instead of the small, independent groups typical of urban terrorists, the ULA organized itself more on classic military lines. The Provisional IRA often depended on a single 'cowboy' assassin, less often on the special action groups. There were many cases Ryan knew of, where the one 'designated hitter' – a term popular in CIA the previous year – had his own special gun, and lay in wait like a deer hunter, often for days, to kill a specific target. But the ULA was different. For one thing they didn't generally go for individual targets. They relied, it seemed, on a reconnaissance team and an assault team that worked in close cooperation – the operative word here was 'seemed', Ryan read, since this, again, was something inferred from scanty evidence. When they did something, they usually got away cleanly. Planning and resources.

Classic military lines. That implied a great deal of confidence by the ULA in its people – and in its security. Jack started making notes. The actual facts in the report were thin – he counted six – but the analysis was interesting. The ULA showed a very high degree of professionalism in its planning and execution of operations, more so than the Provisional IRA, which was itself proficient enough. Instead of a small number of really sharp operatives, it appeared that weapons expertise was uniform throughout the small organization. The uniformity of expertise was interesting.

Military training? Ryan wrote down. *How good? Where done? What source?* He looked at the next report. It was dated some months after 'Genesis' and showed a greater degree of institutional interest. CIA had begun to take a closer look at the ULA, starting seven months previously. *Right after I left here*, Jack noted. *Coincidence.*

This one concentrated on Kevin O'Donnell, the suspected leader of the ULA. The first thing Ryan saw was a photograph taken from a British intelligence-gathering team. The man was fairly tall, but otherwise ordinary. The photo was dated years before, and the next thing Jack read was that the man had reportedly had plastic surgery to change his face. Jack studied the photo anyway. He'd been at a funeral for a Provisional IRA member killed by the Ulster Defence Regiment. The face was solemn enough, with a hardness around the eyes. He wondered how much he could draw from a single photo of a man at a funeral for a comrade, and set the picture aside to read the biography of the man.

A working-class background. His father had been a truck driver. His mother had died when he was nine. Catholic schools, of course. A copy of his college transcript showed him to be bright enough. O'Donnell had graduated from university with honours, and his degree was in political science. He'd taken every course on Marxism that the institution had offered, and been involved on the fringes of civil-rights groups in the late sixties and early seventies. This had earned him attention from the RUC and British intelligence agencies. Then, after graduating, he'd dropped out of sight for a year, reappearing in 1972 after the Bloody Sunday fiasco when British Army paratroopers had got out of control and fired into a crowd of demonstrators, killing fourteen people, none of whom had been proven to have a gun.

'There's a coincidence,' Ryan whispered to himself. The paratroopers still claimed that they'd been fired upon from someone in the crowd and merely returned fire to defend themselves. An official government report done by the British backed this up – of course, what else could they say? Ryan shrugged. It might even have been true. The biggest mistake the English had ever made was to send troops into Northern Ireland. What they'd needed was good cops to re-establish law and order, not an army of occupation. But with the RUC out of control then, and supplemented by the B-Special thugs, there hadn't been a real alternative. So soldiers had been sent in, to a situation for which they were unsuited by training . . . and vulnerable to provocation.

Ryan's antennae twitched at that.

Political-science major, heavy course-load in Marxism. O'Donnell had dropped out of sight, then reappeared about a year later immediately after the Bloody Sunday disaster, and soon thereafter was identified by an informer as the Provisional IRA's chief of internal security. He didn't get that job on the basis of college classwork. He'd had to work to earn that. Terrorism, like any other profession, has its apprenticeship. Somehow this Kevin Joseph O'Donnell had earned his spurs. *How did you do that? Were you one of the guys who stage-managed the provocations? If so, where did you learn how, and does that missing year have anything to do with it? Were you trained in urban insurgency tactics . . . in the Crimea maybe. . . ?*

Too much of a coincidence, Jack told himself. The idea of Soviet training for the hard-core members of the Provisional IRA and INLA had been bandied about so much that it had lost credibility. Besides, it didn't have to be something that dramatic. They might just have figured out the proper tactics for themselves, or read them in books. There were plenty of books on the subject of how to be an urban guerrilla. Jack had read several of them.

He flipped forward in time to O'Donnell's second disappearance. Here the information from British sources was fairly complete for once. O'Donnell had been remarkably effective as chief of internal security. Nearly half the people he'd killed really had been informers of one sort or another, not a bad percentage in this sort of business. He found a couple of new pages at the end of the report, and read the information that David Ashley had gathered a few months before in Dublin. . . . *He got a little carried away.* . . . O'Donnell had used his position to eliminate Provos whose politics didn't

539

quite agree with his. It had been discovered, and he'd vanished for a second time. Again the data was speculative, but it tracked with what Murray had told him in London. O'Donnell *had* gone somewhere.

Surely he'd convinced someone to provide his nascent organization with financing, training, and support. *His nascent organization*, Ryan thought. *Where had it come from?* There was a lapse of two years before O'Donnell's disappearance from Ulster and the first positively identified operation of the ULA. Two complete years. The Brit intel data suggested plastic surgery. Where? Who paid for it? *He didn't do that in some jerkwater third-world country*, Ryan told himself. He wondered if Cathy could ask her colleagues at Hopkins about the availability of good facecutters. *Two years to change his face, get financial backing, recruit his troops, establish a base of operations, and begin to make his impact. . . . Not bad*, Ryan thought with grudging admiration. All that in two years.

Another year before the name of the outfit surfaces. . . .

Ryan turned when he heard someone working the lock on his office door. It was Marty Cantor.

'I thought you stopped smoking.' He pointed at the cigarette.

Ryan crushed it out. 'So does my wife. Have you seen all this stuff?'

'Yeah.' Cantor nodded. 'The boss had me run through it over the weekend. What do you think?'

'I think this O'Donnell character is one formidable son of a bitch. He's got his outfit organized and trained like a real army. It's small enough that he knows every one of them. His ideological background tells me he's a careful recruiter. He has an unusually high degree of trust in his troops. He's a political animal, but he knows how to think and plan like a soldier. Who trained him?'

'Nobody knows,' Cantor replied. 'I think you can overestimate that factor, though.'

'I know that,' Ryan agreed. 'What I'm looking for is . . . flavour, I guess. I'm trying to get a feel for how he thinks. It would also be nice to know who's bankrolling him.' Ryan paused, and something else leaped into his mind. 'What are the chances that he has people inside the Provisional IRA?'

'What do you mean?'

'He runs for his life when he finds out that the Provisional IRA leadership is out for his ass. Two years later, he's back in business with his own organization. Where did the troops come from?'

'Some pals from inside the Provisional IRA, obviously,' Cantor said.

'Sure.' Jack nodded. 'People he knew to be reliable. But we also know that he's a counterintelligence type, right?'

'What do you mean?' Cantor hadn't been down this road yet.

'Who's the main threat to O'Donnell?'

'Everybody wants him –'

'Who wants to kill him?' Jack refocused the question. 'The Brits don't have capital punishment – but the Provisional IRA does.'

'So?'

'So if you were O'Donnell, and you recruited people from inside the Provisional IRA, and you knew that the Provisional IRA was interested in having your head on a wall plaque, you think you'd leave people inside to cue you in?'

'Makes sense,' Cantor said thoughtfully.

'Next, who is the ULA's political target?'

'We don't know that.'

'Don't give that crap, Marty!' Ryan snapped. 'Most of the information in these documents comes from inside the Provos, doesn't it? How the hell do these people know what the ULA is up to? How does the data get to them?'

'You're pushing, Jack,' Cantor warned. 'I've seen the data, too. It's mainly negative. The Provos who had the information sweated out of them mainly said that certain operations weren't theirs. The conclusion that ULA did 'em is inferential – circumstantial. I don't think that this stuff is as clear as you do.'

'No, the two guys who did this report make a good case for putting the ULA fingerprint on these ops. What the ULA has is its own *style*, Marty! We can identify that, can't we?'

'You've constructed a circular argument,' Cantor pointed out. 'O'Donnell comes from the Provos, therefore he must have recruited from there, therefore he must have people in there, et cetera. Your basic arguments are logical, but try to remember that they're based on a very shaky foundation. What if the ULA really is a special-action group of the Provisionals? Isn't it in their interest to have something like that?' Cantor was a splendid devil's advocate, one of the reasons he was Greer's executive assistant.

'Okay, there is some truth to that,' Ryan admitted. 'Still, everything I say makes sense, assuming that the ULA is real.'

'Granted that it's logical. But not proven.'

'So it's the first logical thing we have for these characters. What else does that tell us?'

Cantor grinned. 'Let me know when you figure it out.'

'Can I talk to anybody about this?'

'Like who – I just want to ask before I say no.'

'The Legal Attaché in London – Dan Murray,' Ryan said. 'He's supposed to be cleared all the way on this material, isn't't he?'

'Yeah, he is, and he works with our people. Okay, you can talk with him. That keeps it in the family.'

'Thanks.'

Five minutes later Cantor was sitting across from Admiral Greer's desk.

'He really knows how to ask the right questions.'

'So what did he tumble to?' the Admiral asked.

'The same questions that Emil Jacobs and his team have been asking: What's O'Donnell up to? Does he have the Provisional IRA infiltrated? If so, why?'

'And Jack says. . . ?'

'Same as Jacobs and the FBI evaluation: O'Donnell is a counterintelligence type by training. The Provos want his hide on the barn door, and the best way to keep his hide where it belongs is to have people inside to warn him if they get too close.'

The Admiral nodded agreement, then looked away for a moment. That was only part of an answer, his instincts told him. There had to be more. 'Anything else?'

'The training stuff. He hasn't sifted through all the data yet. I think we should give him some time. But you were right, sir. He's pretty sharp.'

Murray lifted his phone and pushed the right button without paying much attention. 'Yeah?'

'Dan? This is Jack Ryan,' the voice on the phone said.

'How's it going, teacher?'

'Not bad. Something I want to talk over with you.'

'Shoot.'

'I think the ULA has the Provisional IRA infiltrated.'

'What?' Murray snapped upright in his chair. 'Hey, ace, I can't –' He looked at the telephone. The line he was talking on was – 'What the hell are you doing on a secure line?'

'Let's say that I'm back in government service,' Ryan replied coyly.

'Nobody told me.'

'So what do you think?'

'I think it's a possibility. Jimmy came up with the idea about three months back. The Bureau agrees that it makes sense. There is no objective evidence to support the theory, but everybody thinks it's a logical – I mean, it would be a smart thing for our friend Kevin to do, if he can. Remember that the Provisional IRA has very good internal security, Jack.'

'You told me that most of what we know about the ULA comes from Provisional IRA sources. How do they get the info?' Ryan asked rapidly.

'What? You lost me.'

'How does the Provisional IRA find out what the ULA is doing?'

'Oh, okay. That we don't know.' It was something that bothered Murray, and James Owens, but cops deal all the time with anonymous information sources.

'Why would they be doing that?'

'Telling the Provos what they're up to? We have no idea. If you have a suggestion, I'm open to it.'

'How about recruiting new members for his team?' Ryan asked.

'Why don't you think that one over for a few seconds,' Murray replied immediately. Ryan had just rediscovered the flat earth theory.

There was a moment of silence. 'Oh – then he'd risk being infiltrated by the Provisionals.'

'Very good, ace. If O'Donnell's got them infiltrated as a security measure to protect himself, why invite members of the group that wants his ass into his own fold? If you want to kill yourself, there're simpler ways, Jack.' Murray had to laugh. He could hear Ryan deflate over the phone.

'Okay, I guess I had that coming. Thanks.'

'Sorry to rain on your parade, but we buried that idea a couple of months ago.'

'But he must have recruited his people from the Provisionals to begin with,' Ryan objected belatedly. He cursed himself for being so slow, but remembered that Murray had been an expert on this subject for years.

'Yeah, I'll buy that, but he kept the numbers very low,' Murray said. 'The bigger the organization gets, the greater the risk that the Provos will infiltrate – and destroy him. Hey, they really want his ass on a platter, Jack.' Murray stopped short of revealing the deal David Ashley had cut with the Provisional IRA. CIA didn't know about that yet.

'How's the family?' he asked, changing the subject.

'Fine.'

'Bill Shaw says he talked to you last week. . . .' Murray said.

'Yeah. That's why I'm here now. You've got me looking over my shoulder, Dan. Anything else that you've cued in on?'

It was Murray's turn to deflate. 'The more I think about it, the more it looks like I got worried over nothing. No evidence at all, Jack. It was just instinct, you know, like from an old woman. Sorry. I think I just overreacted to something Jimmy said. Hope I didn't worry you too much.'

'Don't sweat it,' Jack replied. 'Well, I have to clear out of here. See ya.'

'Yeah. 'Bye, Jack.' Murray replaced the phone in the holder and went back to his paperwork.

Ryan did much the same. He had to leave by noon in order to make his first class of the day. The messenger came back with his cart and took the files away, along with Jack's notes, which, of course, were also classified. He left the building a few minutes later, his mind still sifting through the data he'd read.

What Jack didn't know was that in the new annexe to the CIA headquarters building was the headquarters of the National Reconnaissance Office. This was a joint CIA-Air Force agency that managed the data from satellites and, to a lesser degree, high-altitude reconnaissance aircraft.

The new generation of satellites used television-type scanning cameras instead of photographic film. One consequence of this was that they could be used almost continuously instead of husbanding their film for coverage of the Soviet Union and its satellites. This allowed the NRO to assemble a much better data base on world trends and events, and had generated scores of new projects for hundreds of new analysts – explaining the newly built annexe behind the original CIA building.

One junior analyst's brief was coverage on camps suspected to be used for the training of terrorists. The project had not yet shown enough results to be treated more importantly, though the data and photographs were passed on to the Task Force on Combating Terrorism. TFCT used the satellite photos, as was the norm in government circles. The staffers *ooh*ed and *ahh*ed over the clarity of the shots, were briefed on the new charge-coupled devices that enabled the cameras to get high-resolution pictures despite atmospheric disturbances, noted that, despite all the hoopla, you really couldn't read the numbers on a licence plate – and promptly forgot about them as anything more than pictures of camps where terrorists might be training. Photo reconnaissance interpretation had always been a narrow field for experts only. The analysis work was simply too technical.

And as was so often the case, here was the rub. The junior analyst was better described as a technician. He collected and collated data, but didn't really analyse it. That was someone else's job, for when the project was finished. In this particular case the data being processed noted infra-red energy. The camps he examined on a daily basis – there were over two hundred – were mainly in deserts. That was remarkably good luck. While everyone knew that deserts suffer from blistering daylight heat, it was less appreciated that they can get quite cold at night – falling below freezing in many cases. So the technician was trying to determine the occupancy of the camps from the number of buildings that were heated during the cool nights. These showed up remarkably well on the infra-red: bright blobs of white on a cold, black background.

A computer stored the digital signals from the satellite. The technician called up the camps by code number, noted the number of heated buildings in each, and transferred the data to a second data file. Camp 11-5-18, located at 28° 32' 47" North Latitude, 19° 07' 52" East Longitude, had six buildings, one of which was a garage. This one had at least two vehicles in it; though the building was unheated, the thermal signatures of two internal-combustion engines radiated clearly through the corrugated steel roofs. Of the other five buildings, only one had its heater on, the technician noted. The previous week – he checked – three had been warm. The warm one now, the data sheet said, was occupied by a small guard and maintenance group, thought to be five men. It evidently had its own kitchen, since one part of the building was always a little warmer than the rest. Another building was a full-sized dining hall. That and the dormitories were now empty. The technician made the appropriate notations, and the computer assigned them to a simple line graph that peaked when occupancy was high and fell when it was low.

The technician didn't have the time to check the patterns on the graph, but he assumed, wrongly, that someone else did.

'You remember, Lieutenant,' Breckenridge said. 'Deep breath, let it half out, and squeeze gently.'

The 9mm Browning automatic had excellent sights. Ryan centred them on the circular target and did what the Gunny said. He did it right. The flash and sound of the shot came almost as a surprise to him. The automatic ejected the spent round and was ready to fire again as Jack brought the pistol down from recoil. He repeated the procedure four more times. The pistol locked open on the empty clip and Ryan set it down. Next he took off the muff-type ear protectors. His ears were sweaty.

'Two nines, three tens, two of them in X-ring.' Breckenridge stood away from the spotting scope. 'Not as good as the last time.'

'My arm's tired,' Ryan explained. The pistol weighed almost forty ounces. It didn't seem like much weight until you had to hold it stone-steady at arm's length for an hour.

'You can get some wrist weights – you know, like joggers use. It'll build up your forearm and wrist muscles.' Breckenridge slipped five rounds into the clip of Ryan's pistol and stepped to the line to aim at a fresh target.

The Sergeant Major fired all five in under three seconds. Ryan looked in the spotting scope. There were five holes within the target's X-ring, clustered like the petals on a flower.

'Damn, I forgot how much fun a nice Browning could be.' He ejected the clip and reloaded. 'The sights are right on, too.'

'I noticed,' Jack replied lamely.

'Don't feel too bad, Lieutenant,' Breckenridge said. 'I've been doin' this since you were in diapers.' Five more rounds and the centre was effectively removed from the target, fifty feet away.

'Why are we doing round targets anyway?' Jack asked.

'I want you to get used to the idea of placing your shots exactly where you want them to go,' the Gunny explained. 'We'll sweat the fancy stuff later. For now we'll work on basic skills. You look a little looser today, Lieutenant.'

'Yeah, well, I talked to the FBI guy who originated the warning. Now he says he might have overreacted – maybe I did, too.'

Breckenridge shrugged. 'You never been in combat, Lieutenant. I have. One thing you learn: the first twitch you have is usually right. Keep that in mind.'

Jack nodded, not believing it. He'd accomplished much today. His look at the ULA data told him a lot about the organization but there was not the first inkling that they had ever operated at all in America. The Provisional IRA had plenty of American connections, but no one believed that the ULA did. Even if they planned to do something here, Ryan judged, they'd need the connections. It was possible that O'Donnell might call on some of his previous Provisional IRA friends, but that seemed most unlikely. He was a dangerous man, but only on his own turf. And America wasn't his turf. That's what the data said. Jack knew that this was too broad a conclusion to base on one day's work, of course. He'd keep looking – it seemed that his investigation would last two or three weeks, the way he was going. If nothing else, he wanted to look into the relationship between O'Donnell and the Provos. He did have a feeling that something odd was going on, just as Murray evidently did, and he wanted to examine the data fully, in the hope of coming up with a plausible theory. He owed CIA something for its courtesy.

The storm was magnificent. Miller and O'Donnell stood by the leaded-glass windows and watched as the Atlantic gale beat the sea to foaming waves that slammed against the base of the cliff on which the house stood. The crash of the breaking waves provided the bass notes, while the wind howled and whistled through the trees and raindrops beat their tattoo against the house itself.

'Not a day to be sailing, Sean,' O'Donnell said as he sipped at a whiskey.

'When do our colleagues go to America?'

'Three weeks. Not much time. Do you still want to do it?' The chief of the ULA thought the timing marginal for what Sean planned.

'This is not an opportunity to be missed, Kevin,' Miller answered evenly.

'Do you have another motive?' O'Donnell asked. Better to get it in the open, he decided.

'Consider the ramifications. The Provisionals go over to proclaim their innocence and –'

'Yes, I know. It's a fine opportunity. Very well. When do you want to leave?'

'Wednesday morning. We must move quickly. Even with our contacts, it won't be easy.'

13

Visitors

The two men hunched over the blow-up of the map, flanked by several eight-by-ten photographs.

'This is going to be the hard one,' Alex said. 'This one I can't help you with.'

'What's the problem?' Sean could see it, but by asking the question he could also gauge the skill of his new associate. He'd never worked with a black before, and though he'd met Alex and members of his group the year before, both were unknown quantities, at least in an operational sense.

'He always comes out by Gate Three, here. This street, as you see, is a dead end. He has to go straight west or turn north coming out. He has done both. This street here is wide enough to do the job from a car, but this one – too narrow, and it leads the wrong way. That means the only sure spot is right here, at the corner. Traffic lights here and here.' Alex pointed. 'Both these streets are narrow and always have cars parked on both sides. This building is apartments. These are houses – expensive ones. There isn't much pedestrian traffic here, oddly enough. One man can probably get by. Two or more, uh-uh.' He shook his head. 'And it's a white area. A black man would be conspicuous. Your guy has to wing this one alone, pal, and he's gotta be on foot. Probably inside this door is the best place, but he'll have to be on his toes or the target will get away.'

'How does he get out?' Sean asked.

'I can park a car around this corner, or this one. Timing for that is not a concern. We can wait all day for the right slot. We have a choice of escape routes. That's no problem either. At rush hour the streets are crowded. That actually works for us. The cops will have trouble responding, and we can use a car that looks ordinary, like a state-owned one. They can't stop all of them. Getaway is easy. The problem is your man. He has to be right here.'

'Why not catch him in his car at a different place?'

Alex shook his head. 'Too hard. The roads are too crowded to be sure, and it'd be too easy to lose him. You've seen the traffic, Sean, and he never goes exactly the same way twice. If you want my opinion, you should split the operation, do it one part at a time.'

'No.' Miller was adamant. 'We'll do it the way I want.'

'Okay, man, but I'm telling you, this man is exposed.'

Miller thought that one over for a moment. Finally he smiled. 'I have just the right man for it.'

'The other part?'

Alex switched maps. 'Easy. The target can take any route at all, but they all come to this place here at exactly four forty-five. We've checked six days in the past two weeks, never been off by more than five minutes. We'll do the job right along here, close to the bridge. Anybody could handle this one. We can even rehearse it for you.'

'When?'

'This afternoon good enough?' Alex smiled.

'Indeed. Escape route?'

'We'll show you. We might as well make it a real rehearsal.'

'Excellent.' Miller was well pleased. Getting here had been complicated enough. Not difficult, just complicated, involving six separate flights. It hadn't been without humour, though. Sean Miller was travelling on a British passport at the moment, and the immigration clerk at Miami had taken his Belfast accent for Scottish. It hadn't occurred to him that to an American ear there isn't much difference between a brogue and a burr. *If that's the skill level in American law-enforcement officials*, Miller told himself, *this op should go easily enough.*

They'd do the run-through today. If it looked good he'd summon the team, and they'd go in. . . four days, he judged. The weapons were already in place.

'Conclusions?' Cantor asked.

Ryan picked up a sixty-page sheaf of paper. 'Here's my analysis, for what it's worth – not much,' Jack admitted. 'I didn't turn up anything new. The reports you already have are pretty good, given the lack of real evidence to go on. The ULA is a really kinky bunch. On one hand their operations don't seem to have a real purpose that we can discern – but this kind of skill. . . . They're too professional to be operating without an objective, dammit!'

'True enough,' Cantor said. They were in his office, across the hall from the DDI's. Admiral Greer was out of town. 'You come up with anything at all?'

'I've mapped their operations geographically and against time. No pattern there that I can see. The only visible pattern is in the type of operation, and the execution, but that doesn't mean anything. They like high-profile targets, but – hell, what terrorist doesn't? That's the whole point of being a terrorist, going after the really big game, right? They mostly use East Bloc weapons, but most of the groups do. We infer that they're well financed. That's logical, given the nature of their activity, but again there isn't any substantive evidence to confirm it.

'O'Donnell has a real talent for dropping out of sight, both personally and professionally. There are three whole years we can't account for, one before he turned up around the time of Bloody Sunday and two years after the Provos tried to punch his ticket. They're both complete blanks. I talked to my wife about the plastic surgery angle –'

'What?' Cantor didn't react favourably to that.

'She doesn't know why I wanted the information. Give me a break, Marty. I'm married to a surgeon, remember? One of her classmates is a reconstructive surgeon, and I had Cathy ask her where you can get a new face. Not many places that can really do it – I was surprised. I have a list of where they are in here. Two are behind the Curtain. It turns out that some of the real pioneering work was done in Moscow before World War Two. Hopkins people have been to the institute – it's named for the guy, but I can't recall the name – and they found a few odd things about the place.'

'Like what?' Cantor asked.

'Like two floors that you can't get onto. Annette DiSalvi – Cathy's class-mate – was there two years ago. The top two floors of the place can be reached only by special elevators, and the stairways have barred gates. Odd sort of thing for a hospital. I thought that was a funny bit of information. Maybe it'll be useful to somebody else.'

Cantor nodded. He knew something about this particular clinic, but the closed floors were something new. It was amazing, he thought, how new bits of data could turn up so innocently. He also wondered why a surgical team from John Hopkins had been allowed into the place. He made a mental note to check that out.

'Cathy says this "getting a new face" thing isn't what it's cracked up to be. Most of the work is designed to correct damage from trauma – car accidents and things like that. The job isn't so much to change as to repair. There is a lot of cosmetic work – I mean aside from nose jobs and face-lifts – but that you can accomplish almost as well with a new hair style and a beard. They can change chins and cheekbones pretty well, but if the work is too exten-sive it leaves scars. This place in Moscow is good, Annette says, almost as good as Hopkins or even UCLA. A lot of the best reconstructive surgeons are in California,' Jack explained. 'Anyway, we're not talking a face-lift or a nose job here. Extensive facial surgery involves multiple procedures and takes several months. If O'Donnell was gone for two years, a lot of the time was spent in the body shop.'

'Oh.' Cantor got the point. 'He really is a fast worker, then?'

Jack grinned. 'That's what I was really after. He was out of sight for two years. At least six months of that time must have been spent in some hospi-tal or other. So in the other eighteen months, he recruited his people, set up a base of operations, started collecting operational intelligence, and ran his first op.'

'Not bad,' Cantor said thoughtfully.

'Yeah. So he had to have recruited people from in the Provos. They must have brought some stuff with them, too. I'll bet that his initial operations were things the Provisional IRA had already looked at and set aside for one reason or another. That's why the Brits thought they were actually part of the Provisional IRA to begin with, Marty.'

'You said you didn't find anything important,' Cantor said. 'This sounds like pretty sharp analysis to me.'

'Maybe. All I did was reorder stuff you already had. Nothing new is in here, and I still haven't answered my own question. I don't have much of an idea what they're really up to.' Ryan's hand flipped through the pages of manuscript. His voice showed his frustration. Jack was not accustomed to failure. 'We still don't know where these bastards are coming from. They're up to something, but damned if I know what it is.'

'American connections?'

'None – none at all that we know of. That makes me feel a lot better. There's no hint of a contact with American organizations, and lots of reasons for them not to have any. O'Donnell is too slick to play with his old Provisional IRA contacts.'

'But his recruiting –' Cantor objected. Jack cut him off.

'Over here, I mean. As chief of internal security, he could know who was who in Belfast and Londonderry. But the American connections to the Provisionals all run through Sinn Fein, the Provos' political wing. He'd have to be crazy to trust them. Remember, he did his best to restructure the political leanings in the outfit and failed.'

'Okay. I see what you mean. Possible connections with other groups?'

Ryan shook his head. 'No evidence. I wouldn't bet against contact with some of the European groups, maybe some of the Islamic ones even, but not over here. O'Donnell's a smart cookie. To come over here means too many complications – hey, they don't like me, I can dig that. The good news is that the FBI's right. We're dealing with professionals. I am not a politically significant target. Coming after me has no political value, and these are political animals,' Jack observed confidently. 'Thank God.'

'Did you know that the Provisional IRA – well, Sinn Fein – has a delegation coming over day after tomorrow?'

'What for?'

'The thing in London hurt them in Boston and New York. They've denied involvement about a hundred times, and they have a bunch coming over for a couple of weeks to tell the local Irish communities in person.'

'Aw, crap!' Ryan snarled. 'Why not keep the bastards out of the friggin' country?'

'Not that easy. The people coming over aren't on the Watch List. They've been here before. They're clean, technically. We live in a free democracy, Jack. Remember what Oliver Wendell Holmes said: the Constitution was written for people of fundamentally differing views – or something like that. The short name is Freedom of Speech.'

Ryan had to smile. The outside view of the Central Intelligence Agency people was often one of bumbling fascists, threats to American freedom, corrupt but incompetent schemers, a cross between the Mafia and the Marx brothers. In fact, Ryan had found them to be politically moderate – more so than he was. If the truth ever got out, of course, the press would think it was a sinister ruse. Even he found it very odd.

'I hope somebody will keep an eye on them,' Jack observed.

'The FBI will have people in every bar, swilling their John Jameson and singing "The Men Behind the Wire." And keeping an eye on everything. The Bureau's pretty good at that. They've just about ended the gun-running. The word's gotten out on that – must be a half-dozen people who got sent up the river for sending guns and explosives over.'

'Fine. So now the bad guys use Kalashnikovs, or Armalites made in Singapore.'

'That,' Cantor said, 'is not our responsibility.'

'Well, this here's all that I was able to come up with, Marty. Unless there's other data around, that's all I can give you.' Jack tossed the report in Cantor's lap.

'I'll read this over and get back to you. Back to teaching history?'

'Yep.' Ryan stood and got his coat from the back of the chair. He paused. 'What if something about these guys turns up in a different place?'

'This is the only compartment you can see, Jack –'

'I know that. What I'm asking is, the way this place is set up, how do you connect things from different compartments?'

'That's why we have supervisory oversight teams, and computers,' Cantor answered. *Not that the system always works.* . . .

'If anything new turns up –'

'It's flagged,' Cantor said. 'Both here and at the FBI. If we get any sort of twitch on these fellows, you'll be warned the day we get it.'

'Fair enough.' Ryan made sure his pass was hanging in plain view before going out into the corridor. 'Thanks – and please thank the Admiral for me. You guys didn't have to do this. I wouldn't feel this good if somebody else had told me what I saw for myself. I owe you.'

'You'll be hearing from us,' Cantor promised him.

Ryan nodded and went out the door. He'd be hearing from them, all right. They'd make the offer again, and he'd turn it down again – with the greatest reluctance, of course.

He'd gone out of his way to be humble and polite with Cantor. In truth, he thought his sixty-page report did a pretty good job of organizing what data they did have on the ULA. That squared matters. He didn't really think he owed anybody.

Caroline Muller Ryan, MD, FACS, lived a very controlled and structured life. She liked it that way. In surgery she always worked with the same team of doctors, nurses, and technicians. They knew how she liked to work, how she liked her instruments arranged. Most surgeons had their peculiarities, and the ophthalmic specialists were unusually fastidious. Her team tolerated it because she was one of the best technical surgeons of her age group and also one of the easiest to like. She rarely had problems with her temper, and got along well with her nurses – something that female doctors often had trouble with. Her current problem was her pregnancy, which forced her to limit her exposure to certain operating-room chemicals. Her swelling abdomen was beginning to alter her stance at the table – actually eye surgeons usually sit, but the principle was the same. Cathy Ryan had to reach a little farther now, and joked about it constantly.

These traits carried over to her personal life. She drove her Porsche with mechanistic precision, always shifting the gears at exactly the right RPM setting, taking corners on a line as regular as a Formula One driver's. Doing things the same way every time wasn't a rut for Cathy Ryan; it was perfection. She played the piano that way also. Sissy Jackson, who played and taught professionally, had once remarked that her playing was too perfect, lacking in soul. Cathy took that as a compliment. Surgeons don't autograph their work; they do it the right way, every time.

Which was why she was annoyed with life at the moment. It was a minor annoyance having to take a slightly different route to work every day – in fact it was something of a challenge, since she gave herself the goal of not allowing it to affect her schedule. Driving to and from work never took more than fifty-seven minutes, nor less than forty-nine (unless she came in on a weekend, when different traffic rules applied). She always picked up Sally at exactly quarter to five. Taking new routes, mainly inside Baltimore, threatened to change this segment of her life, but there weren't many driving problems that a Porsche 911 couldn't solve.

Her route this day was down state Route 3, then across a secondary road. That brought her out onto Ritchie Highway, six miles above the Giant Steps Nursery School. She caught the light just right and took the turn in second gear, working quickly up to third, then fourth. The feline growl of the six-cylinder engine reached through the sound insulation as a gentle purr. Cathy Ryan loved her Porsche. She'd never driven anything else until after she was married – a station wagon was useful for shopping and family drives, unfortunately – and wondered what she'd do when her second child arrived. That, she sighed, would be a problem. It depended on where the sitter was, she decided. Or maybe she could finally convince Jack to get a nanny. Her husband was a little too working-class in that respect. He'd resisted the idea of hiring a part-time maid to help with the housework – that was all the more crazy since Cathy knew her husband tended to be something of a slob, slow to hang up his clothing. Getting the maid had changed that a little. Now, nights before the maid was due in, Jack scurried around picking things up so that she wouldn't think the Ryans were a family of slovens. Jack could be so funny. *Yes*, she thought, *we'll get a nanny. After all, Jack's a knight now.* Cathy smiled at the traffic. Pushing him in the right direction wouldn't be all that hard. Jack was very easy to manipulate. She changed lanes and darted past a dump truck in third gear. The Porsche made it so easy to accelerate around things.

She turned right into the Giant Steps car park two minutes later. The sports car bumped over the uneven driveway and she brought it to a stop in the usual spot. Cathy locked the car on getting out, of course. Her Porsche was six years old, but meticulously maintained. It had been her present to herself on getting through her intern year at Hopkins. There wasn't a single scratch on the British Racing Green finish, and only a Hopkins parking sticker marred the gleaming chrome bumper.

'Mommy!' Sally met her at the door.

Cathy bent to pick her up. It was getting harder to bend over, and harder still to stand up with Sally around her neck. She hoped that their daughter would not feel threatened by the arrival of the baby. Some kids were, she knew, but she had already explained to the little girl what was going on, and Sally seemed to like the idea of a new brother or sister.

'So what did my big girl do today?' Dr Ryan asked. Sally liked being called a Big Girl, and this was Cathy's subterfuge for ensuring that sibling rivalry would be minimized by the arrival of a 'little' boy or girl.

Sally wriggled free to drop back to the floor, and held up a finger painting done on what looked like wide-carriage computer paper. It was a credible abstract work of purple and orange. Together, mother and daughter went to the back and got her coat and lunch box. Cathy made sure that Sally's coat was zipped and the hood up – it was only a few degrees above freezing outside, and they didn't want Sally to get another cold. It took a total of five minutes from the time Cathy stopped the car until she was back out the door, walking towards it again.

She didn't really notice the routineness of her daily schedule. Cathy unlocked the door, got Sally into her seat, and made sure the seat belt was fastened snugly before closing and locking the door and going around to the left side of the car.

She looked up briefly. Across Ritchie Highway was a small shopping centre, a 7-Eleven Store, a cleaners, a video store, and a hardware dealer. There was a blue van parked at the 7-Eleven again. She'd noticed it twice the previous week. Cathy shrugged it off. 7-Eleven was a convenience store, and lots of people made it a regular stop on the way home.

'Hello, Lady Ryan,' Miller said inside the van. The two windows in the rear doors – they reminded Miller of the police transport van; he smiled to himself at that – were made of coated glass so that an outsider couldn't see in. Alex was in the store getting a six-pack of Cokes, as he'd done on a fairly regular basis the previous two weeks.

Miller checked his watch: She'd arrived at 4:46 and was leaving at 4.52. Next to him, a man with a camera was shooting away. Miller raised binoculars. The green Porsche would be easy to spot, plus it had a customized licence plate, CR-SRGN. Alex had explained how licence plates in Maryland could be bought to individual specifications, and Sean wondered who'd be using that code next year. Surely there was another surgeon with the CR.

Alex got back in and started the engine. The van left the car park just as the target's Porsche did. Alex did his own driving. He went north on Ritchie Highway, hung a quick U-turn, and raced south to keep the Porsche in sight. Miller joined him in the right-side seat.

'She takes this road south to Route 50, across the Severn River bridge, then gets off 50 onto Route 2. We want to hit her before she does that. We'll proceed, take the same exit, and switch cars where I showed you. Too bad,' Alex said. 'I was beginning to like this here van.'

'You can buy another with what we're paying you.'

A grin split the black face. 'Yeah, I 'spect so. Have a better interior on the next one, too.' He turned right, taking the exit onto Route 50. It was a divided, multilane highway. Traffic was moderate to heavy. Alex explained that this was normal.

'No problem getting the job done,' he assured Miller.

'Excellent,' Miller agreed. 'Good work, Alex.' *Even if you do have a big mouth.*

Cathy always drove more sedately with Sally aboard. The little girl craned her neck to see over the dashboard, her left hand fiddling with the seat belt buckle as it usually did. Her mother was relaxing now. It generally took her about this length of time to settle down from a hard day – there were few easy ones – at the Wilmer Eye Institute. It wasn't stress so much. She'd had two procedures today and would have two more the next day. She loved her work. There were a lot of people now who could see only because of her professional skill, and the satisfaction of that was not something easily communicated, even to Jack. The price of it was that her days were rarely easy ones. The minute precision demanded by ophthalmic surgery denied her coffee – she couldn't risk the slight tremor in her hands that might come from caffeine – and imposed a degree of concentration on her that few professions demanded. There were more difficult medical skills, but not many. This was the main reason she drove her 911. It was as though in pushing through the air, or taking a tight corner at twenty-five in second gear, the car drained the excess energy from the driver and spread it into the environment. She almost always got home in a good mood. Tonight would be better still since it was Jack's turn to fix dinner. If the car had been built with a brain, it would have noticed the reduced pressure on accelerator and brakes as they took the Route 2 exit. It was being pampered now, like a faithful horse that had jumped all the fences properly.

'Okay?' Alex asked, keeping west on Route 50 towards Washington.

The other man in the back handed Miller the clipboard with the new time notation. There was a total of seven entries, all but the last complete with photographs. Sean looked at the numbers. The target was on a beautifully regular schedule.

'Fine,' he said after a moment.

'I can't give you a precise spot for the hit – traffic can make things go a little funny. I'd say we should try on the east side of the bridge.'

'Agreed.'

Cathy Ryan walked into her house fifteen minutes later. She unzipped Sally's coat and watched her little – 'big' – girl struggle out of the sleeves, a skill she was just beginning to acquire. Cathy took it and hung it up before getting out of her coat. Mother and daughter then proceeded to the kitchen, where they heard the unmistakable noise of a husband trying to fix dinner and a television turned to the *MacNeil-Lehrer Report*.

'Daddy, look what I did!' Sally said first.

'Oh, great!' Jack took the picture and examined it with great care. 'I think we'll hang this one up.' All of them got hung up. The art gallery in question was the front of the family refrigerator. A magnetized holder gave the finger painting a semi-permanent place over the ice and cold-water dispenser. Sally never noticed that there was a new hanging spot every day. Nor did she know that every such painting was saved, tucked away in a box in the foyer closet.

'Hi, babe.' Jack kissed his wife next. 'How were things today?'

'Two cornea replacements. Bernie assisted on the second one – it was a bear. Tomorrow, I'm scheduled for a vitrectomy. Bernie says hi, by the way.'

'How's his kid?' Jack asked.

'Just an appendectomy, she'll be climbing the monkey bars next week,' Cathy replied, surveying the kitchen. She often wondered if having Jack fix dinner was worth the wreckage he made of her room. It appeared that he was fixing pot roast, but she wasn't sure. It wasn't that Jack was a bad cook – with some things he was pretty good – he was just so damned sloppy about it. Never kept his utensils neat. Cathy always had her knives, forks, and everything else arranged like a surgical instrument tray. Jack would just set them anywhere and spent half of his time looking for where they were.

Sally left the room and found a TV that didn't have a news show on.

'Good news,' Jack said.

'Oh?'

'I finished up at CIA today.'

'So what are you smiling about?'

'There just isn't anything I see to make me suspect that we have anything to worry about.' Jack explained for several minutes, keeping within the bounds of classification – mostly. 'They've never operated over here. They don't have any contacts over here that we know of. The real thing is that we're not good targets for them.'

'Why?'

'We're not political. The people they go after are soldiers, police, judges, mayors, stuff like that –'

'Not to mention the odd prince,' Cathy observed.

'Yeah, well, we're not one of those either, are we?'

'So what are you telling me?'

'They're a scary bunch. That Miller kid – well, we've talked about that. I'll feel a little better when they have him back in the can. But these guys are pros. They're not going to mount an op three thousand miles from home for revenge.'

Cathy took his hand. 'You're sure?'

'Sure as I can be. The intelligence biz isn't like mathematics, but you get a feel for the other guy, the way his head works. A terrorist kills to make a political point. We ain't political fodder.'

Cathy gave her husband a gentle smile. 'So I can relax now?'

'I think so. Still, keep an eye on the mirror.'

'And you're not going to carry that gun anymore,' she said hopefully.

'Babe, I like shooting. I forgot what fun a pistol can be. I'm going to keep shooting at the Academy, but, no, I won't be wearing it anymore.'

'And the shotgun?'

'It hasn't hurt anybody.'

'I don't *like* it, Jack. At least unload it, okay?' She walked off to the bedroom to change.

'Okay.' It wasn't that important. He'd keep the box of shells right next to the gun, on the top shelf of the closet. Sally couldn't reach it. Even Cathy had to stretch. It would be safe there. Jack reconsidered all his actions over the past three and a half weeks and decided that they had been worthwhile, really. The alarm system on the house wasn't such a bad idea, and he liked his new 9mm Browning. He was getting pretty good scores. If he kept at it for a year, maybe he could give Breckenridge a run for his money.

He checked the oven. Another ten minutes. Next he turned up the TV. The current segment on the *MacNeil-Lehrer News Hour* was – *I'll be damned.*

'Joining us from our affiliate WGBH in Boston is Padraig – did I pronounce that right? – O'Neil, a spokesman for Sinn Fein and an elected member of the British Parliament. Mr O'Neil, why are you visiting America at this time?'

'I and many of my colleagues have visited America many times, to inform the American people of the oppression inflicted upon the Irish people by the British government, the systematic denial of economic opportunity and basic civil rights, the total abrogation of the judicial process, and the continuing brutality of the British army of occupation against the people of Ireland,' O'Neil said in a smooth and reasonable voice. He had done all this before.

'Mr O'Neil,' said someone from the British Embassy in Washington, 'is the political front-man for the Provisional Wing of the so-called Irish Republican Army. This is a terrorist organization that is illegal both in Northern Ireland and in the Irish Republic. His mission in the United States is, as always, to raise money so that his organization can buy arms and explosives. This source of income for the IRA was damaged by the cowardly attack against the Royal Family in London last year, and his reason for being here is to persuade Irish-Americans that the IRA had no part in that.'

'Mr O'Neil,' MacNeil said, 'how do you respond to that?'

The Irishman smiled at the camera as benignly as Bob Keeshan's Captain Kangaroo. 'Mr Bennett, as usual, skirts over the legitimate political issues here. Are Northern Ireland's Catholics denied economic and political opportunity – yes, they are. Have the legal processes in Northern Ireland been subverted for political reasons by the British government – yes, they have. Are we any closer to a political settlement of this dispute that goes back, in its modern phase, to 1969 – no, I regret to say we are not. If I am a terrorist, why have I been allowed into your country? I am, in fact, a member of the British Parliament, elected by the people of my parliamentary district.'

'But you don't take your seat in Parliament,' MacNeil objected.

'And join the government that is killing my constituents?'

'Jesus,' Ryan said, 'what a mess.' He turned the TV off.

'Such a reasonable man,' Miller said. Alex's house was outside the D.C. beltway. 'Tell your friends how reasonable you are, Paddy. And when you get to the pubs tonight, be sure to tell your friends that you have never hurt anyone who was not a genuine oppressor of the Irish people.' Sean watched the whole segment, then placed an overseas call to a pay phone outside a Dublin pub.

The next morning – only five hours later in Ireland – four men boarded a plane for Paris. Neatly dressed, they looked like young executives travelling with their soft luggage to business appointments overseas. At Charles de Gaulle International Airport they made connections to a flight to Caracas. From there they flew Eastern Air Lines to Atlanta, and another Eastern flight to National Airport, just down the Potomac from the memorial to Thomas Jefferson. The four were jet-lagged out and sick of airliner seats when they arrived. They took an airport limousine to a local hotel to sleep off their travel shock. The young businessmen checked out the next morning and were met by a car.

14

Second Chances

There ought to be a law against Mondays, Ryan thought. He stared at what had to be the worst way to start any day: a broken shoelace that dangled from his left fist. Where were the spares? he asked himself. He couldn't ask Cathy; she and Sally had left the house ten minutes before on the way to

Giant Steps and Hopkins. Damn. He started rummaging through his dresser drawers. Nothing. The kitchen. He walked downstairs and across the house to the kitchen drawer that held everything that wasn't someplace else. Hidden beneath the notepads and magnets and scissors he found a spare pair – no, one white lace for a sneaker. He was getting warmer. Several minutes of digging later, he found something close enough. He took one and left the other. After all, shoelaces broke one at a time.

Next Jack had to select a tie for the day. That was never easy, though at least he didn't have his wife around to tell him he'd picked the wrong one. He was wearing a gray suit, and picked a dark blue tie with red stripes. Ryan was still wearing white, button-down shirts made mostly of cotton. Old habits die hard. The suit jacket slid on neatly. It was one of the suits Cathy had bought in England. It was painful to admit that her taste in clothing was far better than his. That London tailor wasn't too bad, either. He smiled at himself in the mirror – *you handsome devil!* – before heading downstairs. His briefcase was waiting on the foyer table, full of the draft quizzes he'd be giving today. Ryan took his overcoat from the closet, checked to see his keys were in the right pocket, got the briefcase, and went out the door.

'Oops!' He unlocked the door and set the burglar alarm before going back outside.

Sergeant Major Breckenridge walked down the double line of Marines, and his long-practiced eyes didn't miss a thing. One private had lint on his blue, high-necked blouse. Another's shoes needed a little more work, and two needed haircuts; you could barely see their scalps under the quarter-inch hair. All in all, there wasn't much to be displeased with. Every one would have passed a normal inspection, but this wasn't a normal post, and normal rules didn't apply. Breckenridge was not a screamer. He'd got past that. His remonstrations were more fatherly now. They carried the force of a command from God nevertheless. He finished the inspection and dismissed the guard detail. Several marched off to their gate posts. Others rode in pick-ups to the more remote posts to relieve the current watch standers at eight o'clock exactly. Each Marine wore his dress blues and a white pistol belt. Their pistols were kept at the posts. They were unloaded, in keeping with the peaceful nature of their duty, but full clips of .45 ACP cartridges were always nearby, in keeping with the nature of the Marines.

Did I really look forward to this? It took all of Ryan's energy just to think that question of himself. But he didn't have any further excuses. In London his injuries had prevented him from doing it. The same had been true of the first few weeks at home. Then he'd spent the early mornings travelling to CIA. That had been his last excuse. None were left.

558

Rickover Hall, he told himself. *I'll stop when I get to Rickover Hall*. He had to stop soon. Breathing the cold air off the river was like inhaling knives. His nose and mouth were like sandpaper and his heart threatened to burst from his chest. Jack hadn't jogged in months, and he was paying the price for his sloth.

Rickover Hall seemed a thousand miles away, though he knew it was only a few hundred more yards. As recently as the previous October, he'd been able to make three circuits of the grounds and come away with nothing more than a good sweat. Now he was only at the halfway mark of his first lap, and death seemed amazingly attractive. His legs were already rubbery with fatigue. His stride was off; Ryan was weaving slightly, a sure sign of a runner who was beyond his limit.

Another hundred yards. About fifteen seconds more, he told himself. All the time he'd spent on his back, all the time sitting down, all the cigarettes he'd sneaked at CIA were punishing him now. The runs he'd had to do at Quantico had been nothing like this. *You were a lot younger then*, Ryan's mind pointed out gleefully.

He turned his head left and saw that he was lined up on the building's east wall. Ryan leaned back and slowed to a walk, hands supported on his hips as his chest heaved to catch up on the oxygen it needed.

'You okay, Doc?' A mid stopped – his legs still pumping in double-time – to look Jack over. Ryan tried to hate him for his youth and energy, but couldn't summon enough energy.

'Yeah, just out of training,' Jack gasped out over three breaths.

'You gotta work back into it slowly, sir,' the twenty-year-old pointed out, and sped off, leaving his history teacher scornfully in his dust. Jack started laughing at himself, but it gave him a coughing fit. The next one to pass him was a girl. Her grin really made things worse.

Don't sit down. Whatever you do, don't sit down.

He turned and moved away from the seawall. Just walking on his wobbly legs was an effort. He took the towel from around his neck to wipe the sweat from his face before he got too much of a chill. Jack held the towel taut between his hands and stretched his arms high. He'd caught his breath now. A renewed supply of oxygen returned to his limbs, and most of the pain left. The rubberiness would go next, he knew. In another ten minutes he'd feel pretty good. Tomorrow he'd make it a little farther – to the Nimitz Library, he promised himself. By May he wouldn't have the mids – at least not the girls – racing past him. Well, not all of the girls, anyway. He was spotting a minimum of ten years to the midshipmen, something that would only get worse. Jack had already passed thirty. Next stop: forty.

Cathy Ryan was in her greens, scrubbing at the special basin outside the surgical suite. The elastic waistband of the pants was high, above the curve of her abdomen, and that made the pants overly short, like the clamdiggers that had been fashionable in her teenage years. A green cap was over her hair, and she wondered yet again why she bothered to brush it out every morning. By the time the procedure was finished, her hair would look like the snaky locks of the Medusa.

'Game time,' she said quietly to herself. She hit the door-opening switch with her elbow, keeping her hands high, just like it was done in the movies. Bernice, the circulating nurse, had her gloves ready, and Cathy reached her hands into the rubber until the tops of the gloves came far up on her forearms. Because of this, she was rarely able to wear her engagement ring, though her simple wedding band posed no problem. 'Thanks.'

'How's the baby?' Bernice asked. She had three of her own.

'At the moment he's learning to jog.' Cathy smiled behind her mask. 'Or maybe he's lifting weights.'

'Nice necklace.'

'Christmas present from Jack.'

Dr Terri Mitchell, the anesthesiologist, hooked the patient up to her various monitors and went to work as the surgeons looked on. Cathy gave the instruments a quick look, knowing that Lisa-Marie always got things right. She was one of the best scrub nurses in the hospital and was picky on the doctors she'd work with.

'All ready, Doctor?' Cathy asked the resident. 'Okay, people, let's see if we can save this lady's eyesight.' She looked at the clock. 'Starting at eight forty-one.'

Miller assembled the submachine gun slowly. He had plenty of time. The weapon had been carefully cleaned and oiled after being test fired the night before at a quarry twenty miles north of Washington. This one would be his personal weapon. Already he liked it. The balance was perfect, the folding stock, when extended, had a good, solid feel to it. The sights were easy to use, and the gun was fairly steady on full-automatic fire. All in all, a nice combination of traits for such a small, deadly weapon. He palmed back the bolt and squeezed the trigger to get a better feel for where it broke. He figured it to be about twelve pounds – perfect, not too light and not too heavy. Miller left the bolt closed on an empty chamber and loaded the magazine of thirty 9mm rounds. Then he folded the stock and tried the hanging hook inside his topcoat. A standard modification to the Uzi, it allowed a person to carry it concealed. That probably wouldn't be necessary, but Miller was a man who planned for all the contingencies. He'd learned that lesson the hard way.

'Ned?'

'Yes, Sean?' Eamonn Clark, known as Ned, hadn't stopped going over the maps and photographs of his place since arriving in America. One of the most experienced assassins in Ireland, he was one of the men the ULA had broken from Long Kesh Prison the previous year. A handsome young man, Clark had spent the previous day touring the Naval Academy grounds, carrying his own camera as he'd photographed the statue of Tecumseh . . . and carefully examined Gate Three. Ryan would drive straight uphill, giving him roughly fifteen seconds to get ready. It would demand vigilance, but Ned had the necessary patience. Besides, they knew the target's schedule. His last class ended at three that afternoon and he hit the gate at a predictable time. Alex was even now parking the getaway car on King George Street. Clark had misgivings, but kept them to himself. Sean Miller had masterminded the prison break that had made him a free man. This was his first real operation with the ULA. Clark decided that he owed them loyalty. Besides, his look at the Academy's security had not impressed him. Ned Clark knew that he was not the brightest man in the room, but they needed a man able to work on his own, and he did know how to do that. He'd proven this seven times.

Outside the house were three cars, the van and two station wagons. The van would be used for the second part of the operation, while the station wagons would take everyone to the airport when the operation was finished.

Miller sat down in an overstuffed chair and ran over the entire operation in his mind. As always, he closed his eyes and visualized every event, then he inserted variables. What if the traffic were unusually heavy or unusually light? What if . . .

One of Alex's men came through the front door. He tossed Miller a Polaroid.

'Right on time?' Sean Miller asked.

'You got it, man.'

The photograph showed Cathy Ryan leading her daughter by the hand into – what was the name of the place? Oh, yes, Giant Steps. Miller smiled at that. Today would be a giant step indeed. Miller leaned back again, eyes closed, to make sure.

'But there wasn't a threat,' a mid objected.

'That's correct. Which is to say we know that *now*. But how did it look to Spruance? He knew what the Japanese fleet had in surface ships. What if they *had* come east, what if the recall order had never been issued?' Jack pointed to the diagram he'd drawn on the blackboard. 'There would have been contact at about oh-three-hundred hours. Who do you think would have won that one, mister?'

'But he blew his chance for a good air strike the next day,' the midshipman persisted.

'With what? Let's look at the losses in the air groups. With all the torpedo craft lost, just what losses do you think he could have inflicted?' Jack asked.

'But –'

'You remember the Kenny Rogers song: You have to know when to walk away, and know when to run. Buck fever is a bad thing in a hunter. In an admiral commanding a fleet it can be disastrous. Spruance looked at his information, looked at his capabilities, and decided to call it a day. A secondary consideration was – what?'

'To cover Midway?' another mid asked.

'Right. What if they had carried on with the invasion? That was gamed out at Newport once and the invasion was successful. Please note that this is a manifestation of logic overpowering reality, but it was a possibility that Spruance could not afford to dismiss. His primary mission was to prevent the occupation of Midway. The balance he struck here is a masterpiece of operational expertise. . . .' Ryan paused for a moment. What was it that he'd just said? *Logic overcoming reality.* Hadn't he just come to the logical conclusion that the ULA wouldn't – no, no, a different situation entirely. He shook off the thought and kept going on the lessons from the Battle of Midway. He had the class going now, and ideas were crackling across the room like lightning.

'Perfect,' Cathy said as she pulled her mask down around her neck. She stood up from the stool and stretched her arms over her head. 'Nice one, folks.'

The patient was wheeled out to the recovery room while Lisa-Marie made a final check of her instruments. Cathy Ryan pulled off her mask and rubbed her nose. Then her hands went down to her belly. The little guy really was kicking up a storm.

'Football player?' Bernice asked.

'Feels like a whole backfield. Sally wasn't this active. I think this one's a boy,' Cathy judged, knowing that there was no such correlation. It was good enough that the baby was very active. That was always a positive sign. She smiled, mostly to herself, at the miracle and the magic of motherhood. Right there inside her was a brand-new human being waiting to be born, and by the feel of it, rather impatient. 'Well. I have a family to talk to.'

She walked out of the operating room, not bothering to change out of her greens. It always looked more dramatic to keep them on. The waiting room was a mere fifty feet away. The Jeffers family – the father and one of their daughters – was waiting on the inevitable couch, staring at the inevitable magazines but not reading them. The moment she came through the swinging door, both leaped to their feet. She gave them her best smile, always the quickest way to convey the message.

'Okay?' the husband asked, his anxiety a physical thing.

'Everything went perfectly,' Cathy said. 'No problems at all. She'll be fine.'

'When will she be able –'

'A week. We have to be patient on this. You'll be able to see her in about an hour and a half. Now, why don't you get yourselves something to eat.

There's no sense having a healthy patient if the family is worn out, I –'

'Doctor Ryan,' the public address speaker said. 'Doctor Caroline Ryan.'

'Wait a minute.' Cathy walked to the nurses' station and lifted the phone. 'This is Doctor Ryan.'

'Cathy, this is Gene in the ER. I've got a major eye trauma. Ten-year-old black male, he took his bike through a store window,' the voice said urgently. 'His left eye is badly lacerated.'

'Send him up to six.' Cathy hung up and went back to the Jeffers family. 'I have to run, there's an emergency case coming up. Your wife will be fine. I'll be seeing you tomorrow.' Cathy walked as quickly as she could to the OR.

'Heads up, we have an emergency coming in from ER. Major eye trauma to a ten-year-old.' Lisa-Marie was already moving. Cathy walked to the wall phone and punched the number for surgeons' lounge. 'This is Ryan in Wilmer six. Where's Bernie?'

'I'll get him.' A moment later: 'Doctor Katz.'

'Bernie, I have a major eye trauma coming into six. Gene Wood in ER says it's a baddie.'

'On the way.' Cathy Ryan turned.

'Terri?'

'All ready,' the anesthesiologist assured her.

'Give me another two minutes,' Lisa-Marie said.

Cathy went into the scrub room to rewash her hands. Bernie Katz arrived before she started. He was a thoroughly disreputable-looking man, only an inch taller than Cathy Ryan, with longish hair and a Bismarck moustache. He was also one of the best surgeons at Hopkins.

'You'd better lead on this one,' she said. 'I haven't done a major trauma in quite a while.'

'No problem. How's the baby coming?'

'Great.' A new sound arrived, the high-pitched shrieks of a child in agony. The doctors moved into the OR. They watched dispassionately as two orderlies were strapping the child down. *Why weren't you in school?* Cathy asked him silently. The left side of the boy's face was a mess. The reconstructive teams would have to work on that later. Eyes came first. The child had already tried to be brave, but the pain was too great for that. Terri did the first medication, with both orderlies holding the child's arm in place. Cathy and Bernie hovered over the kid's face a moment later.

'Bad,' Dr Katz observed. He looked to the circulating nurse. 'I have a procedure scheduled for one o'clock. Have to bump it. This one's going to take some time.'

'All ready on this side,' the scrub nurse said.

'Two more minutes,' the anesthesiologist advised. You had to be careful medicating kids.

'Gloves,' Cathy said. Bernie came over with them a moment later. 'What happened?'

563

'He was riding his bike down the sidewalk on Monument Street,' the orderly said. 'He hit something and went through an appliance-store window.'

'Why wasn't he in school?' she asked, looking back at the kid's left eye. She saw hours of work and an uncertain outcome.

'President's Day, Doc,' the orderly replied.

'Oh. That's right.' She looked at Bernie Katz. His grimace was visible around the mask.

'I don't know, Cathy.' He was examining the eye through the magnifying-glass headset. 'Must have been a cheap window – lots of slivers. I count five penetrations. Jeez, look at how that one's extended into the cornea. Let's go.'

The Chevvy pulled into one of Hopkins' high-rise parking garages. From the top level the driver had a perfect view of the door leading from the hospital to the doctors' parking area. The garage was guarded, of course, but there was plenty of traffic in and out, and it was not unusual for someone to wait in a car while another visited a family member inside. He settled back and lit a cigarette, listening to music on the car radio.

Ryan put roast beef on his hard roll and selected iced tea. The Officer and Faculty Club had an unusual arrangement for charging: he set his tray on a scale and the cashier billed him by weight. Jack paid up his two dollars and ten cents. The price for lunch was hardly exorbitant, but it did seem an odd way to set the price. He joined Robby Jackson in a corner booth.

'Mondays!' he observed to his friend.

'Are you kidding? I can relax today. I was up flying Saturday and Sunday.'

'I thought you liked that.'

'I do,' Robby assured him. 'But both days I got off before seven. I actually got to sleep until six this morning. I needed the extra two hours. How's the family?'

'Fine. Cathy had a big procedure today – had to be up there early. The one bad thing about being married to a surgeon, they always start early. Sometimes it's a little hard on Sally.'

'Yeah, early to bed, early to rise – might as well be dead,' Robby agreed. 'How's the baby coming?'

'Super.' Jack smiled. 'He's an active little bugger. I never figured how women can take that – having the kid kick and turn like that, I mean.'

'Mind if I join you?' Skip Tyler slipped into the booth.

'How are the twins?' Jack asked at once.

The reply was a low moan, and a look at the circles under Tyler's eyes provided the answer. 'The trick is getting both of them asleep. You just get one quieted down, then the other one goes off like a damned fire alarm. I don't know how Jean does it. Of course' – Tyler grinned – 'she can walk the floor with them. When I do it it's step-*thump*, step-*thump*.'

All three men laughed. Skip Tyler had never been the least sensitive about losing his leg.

'How's Jean holding up?' Robby asked.

'No problem – she sleeps when they do and I get to do all the housework.'

'Serves you right, turkey,' Jack observed. 'Why don't you give it a rest?'

'Can I help it if I'm hot-blooded?' Skip demanded.

'No, but your timing sucks,' Robby replied.

'My timing,' Tyler said with raised eyebrows, 'is perfect.'

'I guess that's one way to look at it,' Jack agreed.

'I heard you were out jogging this morning.' Tyler changed subjects.

'So did I.' Robby laughed.

'I'm still alive, guys.'

'One of my mids said tomorrow they're going to follow you around with an ambulance just in case.' Skip chuckled. 'I suppose it's nice for you to remember that most of the kids know CPR.'

'Why are Mondays always like this?' Jack asked.

Alex and Sean Miller made a final run along Route 50. They were careful to keep just under the speed limit. The State Police radar cars were out in force today for some reason or other. Alex assured his colleague that this would end around 4:30. Rush hour had too many cars on the road for efficient law enforcement. Two other men were in the back of the van, each with his weapon.

'Right about here, I think,' Miller said.

'Yeah, it's the best place,' Alex agreed.

'Escape route.' Sean clicked on a stopwatch.

'Okay.' Alex changed lanes and kept heading west. 'Remember, it's gonna be slower tonight.'

Miller nodded, getting the usual pre-op butterflies in his stomach. He ran through his plan, thinking over each contingency as he sat in the right-front seat of the van, watching the way traffic piled up at certain exits off the highway. The road was far better than the roads he was accustomed to in Ireland, but people drove on the wrong side here, he thought, though with pretty good traffic manners compared to Europe. Especially France and Italy . . . he shook off the thought and concentrated on the situation at hand.

Once the attack was completed, they would reach the getaway vehicles in under ten minutes. The way it was timed, Ned Clark would be waiting for them. Miller completed his mental run-through, satisfied that his plan, though a hasty one, was effective.

'You're early,' Breckenridge said.

'Yeah, well, I have a couple of mids coming in this afternoon to go over their term papers. Any problem?' Jack took the Browning from his briefcase.

The Sergeant Major grabbed a box of 9mm rounds. 'Nope. Mondays are supposed to be screwed up.'

Ryan walked to lane three and pulled the gun from the holster. First he ejected the empty clip and pulled the slide back. Next he checked the barrel for obstructions. He knew the weapon was fine mechanically, of course, but Breckenridge had range-safety rules that were inviolable. Even the Superintendent of the Academy had to follow them.

'Okay, Gunny.'

'I think today we'll try rapid fire.' The Sergeant Major clipped the appropriate target on the rack, and the motorized pulley took it fifty feet downrange. Ryan loaded five rounds into the clip.

'Get your ears on, Lieutenant.' Breckenridge tossed the muff-type protectors. Ryan put them on. He slid the clip into the pistol and thumbed down the slide release. The weapon was now 'in battery,' ready to fire. Ryan pointed it downrange and waited. A moment later the light over the target snapped on. Jack brought the gun up and set the black circle right on the top of his front sight blade before he squeezed. Rapid-fire rules gave him one second per shot. This was more time than it sounded like. He got the first round off a little late, but most people did. The gun ejected the spent case and Ryan pulled it down for the next shot, concentrating on the target and his sights. By the time he counted to five, the gun was locked open. Jack pulled off the ear protectors.

'You're getting there, Lieutenant,' Breckenridge said at the spotting scope. 'All in the black: a nine, four tens, one of 'em in the X-ring. Again.'

Ryan reloaded with a smile. He'd allowed himself to forget how much fun a pistol could be. This was a pure physical skill, a man's skill that carried the same sort of satisfaction as a just-right golf shot. He had to control a machine that delivered a .357-inch bullet to a precise destination. Doing this required coordination of eye and hand. It wasn't quite the same as using a shotgun or a rifle. Pistol was much harder than either of those, and hitting the target carried a subintellectual pleasure that was not easily described to someone who hadn't done it. His next five rounds were all tens. He tried the two-hand Weaver stance, and placed four out of five in the X-ring, a circle half the diameter of the ten-ring, used for tie-breaking in competition shoots.

'Not bad for a civilian,' Breckenridge said. 'Coffee?'

'Thanks, Gunny.' Ryan took the cup.

'I want you to concentrate a little more on your second round. You keep letting that one go off to the right some. You're rushing it a little.' The difference, Ryan knew, was barely two inches at fifty feet. Breckenridge was a stone perfectionist. It struck him that the Sergeant Major and Cathy had very similar personalities: either you were doing it exactly right or you were doing

566

it completely wrong. 'Doc, it's a shame you got hurt. You would have made a good officer, with the right sergeant to bring you along – they all need that of course.'

'You know something, Gunny? I met a couple of guys in London that you'd just love.' Jack slipped the magazine back into his automatic.

'Ryan is rather a clever lad, isn't he?' Owens handed the document back to Murray.

'Nothing really new in here,' Dan admitted, 'but at least it's well organized. Here's the other thing you wanted.'

'Oh, our friends in Boston. How is Paddy O'Neil doing?' Owens was more than just annoyed at this. Padraig O'Neil was an insult to the British parliamentary system, an elected mouthpiece for the Provisional IRA. In ten years of trying, however, neither Owens' Anti-Terror Branch nor the Royal Ulster Constabulary had ever linked him to an illegal act.

'Drinking a lot of beer, talking to a lot of folks, and raising a little money, just like always.' Murray sipped at his port. 'We have agents following him around. He knows they're there, of course. If he spits on the sidewalk, we'll put him on the next bird home. He knows that, too. He hasn't broken a single law. Even his driver – the guy's a teetotaller. I hate to say it, Jimmy, but the bum's clean, and he's making points.'

'Oh, yes, he's a charming one, Paddy is.' Owens flipped a page and looked up. 'Let me see that thing your Ryan fellow did again.'

'The guys at Five glommed your copy. I expect they'll give it to you tomorrow.'

Owens grunted as he flipped to the summary at the back of the document. 'Here it is. . . . Good God above!'

'What?' Murray snapped forward in his chair.

'The link, the bloody link. It's right here!'

'What are you talking about, Jimmy? I've read the thing twice myself.'

'"The fact that ULA personnel seem to have been drawn almost entirely from 'extreme' elements within the Provisional IRA itself,"' he read aloud, '"must have a significance beyond that established by existing evidence. It seems likely that since the ULA membership has been so recruited, some ULA 'defectors-in-place' remain within the Provisional IRA, serving as information sources to their actual parent organization. It follows that such information may be of an operational nature in addition to its obvious counterintelligence value." *Operational*,' Owens said quietly. 'We've always assumed that O'Donnell was simply trying to protect himself. . . but he could be playing another game entirely.'

'I still haven't caught up with you, Jimmy.' Murray set his glass down and frowned for a moment. 'Oh. Maureen Dwyer. You never did figure out that tip, did you?'

Owens was thinking about another case, but Murray's remark exploded like a flashbulb in front of his eyes. The detective just stared at his American colleague for a moment while his brain raced down a host of ideas.

'But why?' Murray asked. 'What do they gain?'

'They can do great embarrassment to the leadership, inhibit operations.'

'But what material good does that do for the ULA? O'Donnell's too professional to screw his old friends just for the hell of it. The INLA might, but they're just a bunch of damned-fool cowboys. The ULA is too sophisticated for that sort of crap.'

'Yes. We've just surmounted one wall to find another before us. Still, that's one more wall behind us. It gives us something to question young Miss Dwyer about, doesn't it?'

'Well, it's an idea to run down. The ULA has the Provisional IRA penetrated, and sometimes they feed information to you to make the Provos look bad.' Murray shook his head. *Did I just say that one terrorist outfit was trying to make another one look* bad? 'Do you have enough evidence to back that idea up?'

'I can name you three cases in the last year where anonymous tips gave us Provos who were at the top of our list. In none of the three did we ever learn who the source was.'

'But if the Provos suspect it – oh, scratch that idea. They want O'Donnell anyway, and that's straight revenge for all the people he did away with within the organization. Okay, embarrassing the Provisional IRA leadership may be an objective in itself – *if* O'Donnell was trying to recruit some new members. But you've already discarded that idea.'

Owens swore under his breath. Criminal investigation, he often said, was like doing a jigsaw puzzle when you didn't have all the pieces and never really knew their shapes. But telling that to his subordinates wasn't the same thing as experiencing it himself. If only they hadn't lost Sean Miller. Maybe they might have got something from him by now. His instinct told him that one small, crucial fact would make a complete picture of all the rubbish he was sorting through. Without that fact, his reason told Owens, everything he thought he knew was nothing more than speculation. But one thought kept repeating itself in his mind:

'Dan, if you wanted to embarrass the Provisionals' leadership politically, how and where would you do it?'

'Hello, this is Doctor Ryan.'

'This is Bernice Wilson at Johns Hopkins. Your wife asked me to tell you that she's in an emergency procedure and she'll be about a half hour late tonight.'

'Okay, thank you.' Jack replaced the phone. *Mondays*, he told himself. He went back to discussing the term paper projects with his two mids. His desk clock said four in the afternoon. Well, there was no hurry, was there?

The watch changed at Gate Three. The civilian guard was named Bob Riggs. He was retired Navy chief master at arms, past fifty, with a beer belly that made it hard for him to see his shoes. The cold affected him badly, and he spent as much time as possible in the guardhouse. He didn't see a man in his late thirties approach the opposite corner and disappear into a doorway. Neither did Sergeant Tom Cummings of the Marine guard force, who was checking some paperwork just after relieving the previous watch-stander. The Academy was good duty for the young Marine NCO. There were a score of good saloons within easy walking distance, and plenty of unattached womenfolk to be sampled, but the duty at Annapolis was pretty boring when you got down to it, and Cummings was young enough to crave some action. It had been a typical Monday. The previous guard had issued three parking citations. He was already yawning.

Fifty feet away, an elderly lady approached the entrance to the apartment building. She was surprised to see a handsome young man there and dropped her shopping bag while fumbling for her key.

'Can I help you with that, now?' he asked politely. His accent made him sound different, but rather kind, the lady thought. He held the bag while she unlocked the door.

'I'm afraid I'm a little early – waiting to meet my young lady, you see,' he explained with a charming smile. 'I'm sorry if I startled you, ma'am – just trying to keep out of this bitter wind.'

'Would you like to wait inside the door?' she offered.

'That's very kind indeed, ma'am, but no. I might miss her and it's a bit of a surprise, you see. Good day to you.' His hand relaxed around the knife in his coat pocket.

Sergeant Cummings finished going over the papers and walked outside. He noticed the man in the doorway for the first time. Looked like he was waiting for someone, the Sergeant judged, and trying to keep out of the cold north wind. That seemed sensible enough. The Sergeant checked his watch. Four-fifteen.

'I think that does it,' Bernie Katz said.

'We did it,' Cathy Ryan agreed. There were smiles all around the OR. It had taken over five hours, but the youngster's eye was back together. He might need another operation, and certainly he'd wear glasses for the rest of his life, but that was better than having only one eye.

'For somebody who hasn't done one of these in four months, not bad, Cath. This kid will have both his eyes. You want to tell the family? I have to go to the john.'

The boy's mother was waiting exactly where the Jeffers family had been, the same look of anxiety on her face. Beside her was someone with a camera.

'We saved the eye,' Cathy said at once. After she sat down beside the woman, the photographer – he said he was from the *Baltimore Sun* – fired away with his Nikon for several minutes. The surgeon explained the procedure to the mother for several minutes, trying to calm her down. It wasn't easy, but Cathy'd had lots of practice.

Finally someone from Social Services arrived, and Cathy was able to head for the locker room. She pulled off her greens, tossing them in the hamper. Bernie Katz was sitting on the bench, rubbing his neck.

'I could use some of that myself,' Cathy observed. She stood there in her Gucci underwear and stretched. Katz turned to admire the view.

'Getting pretty big, Cath. How's the back?'

'Stiff. Just like it was with Sally. Avert your gaze, Doctor, you're a married man.'

'Can I help it if pregnant women look sexy?'

'I'm glad I look it, 'cause I sure as hell don't feel like it at the moment.' She dropped to the bench in front of her locker. 'I didn't think we could do that one, Bernie.'

'We were lucky,' Katz admitted. 'Fortunately the dear Lord looks after fools, drunks, and little children. Some of the time, anyway.'

Cathy pulled open the locker. In the mirror she had inside, she saw that her hair did indeed look like the Medusa's. She made a face at herself. 'I need another vacation.'

'But you just had one,' Katz observed.

'Right,' Dr Ryan snorted. She slid her legs into her pants and reached for her blouse.

'And when that foetus decides to become a baby, you'll have another.'

The jacket came next. 'Bernie, if you were in OB, your patients would kill you for that sort of crap.'

'What a loss to medicine that would be,' Katz thought aloud.

Cathy laughed. 'Nice job, Bern. Kiss Annie for me.'

'Sure, and you take it a little easy, eh, or I'll tell Madge North to come after you.'

'I see her Friday, Bernie. She says I'm doing fine.' Cathy breezed out the door. She waved to her nurses, complimenting them yet again for a superb job in the OR. The lift was next. Already she had her car keys in her hand.

The green Porsche was waiting for her. Cathy unlocked the door and tossed her bag in the back before settling in the driver's seat. The six-cylinder engine started in an instant. The tachometer needle swung upwards to the idle setting. She let the engine warm up for a minute while she buckled her seat belt and slipped off the parking brake. The throaty rumble of the engine echoed down the concrete walls of the parking garage. When the temperature needle started to move, she shifted into reverse. A moment later she dropped the gear lever into first and moved towards Broadway. She checked the clock on the dashboard and winced – worse, she had to make a stop at the store on the way home. Well, she did have her 911 to play catch-up with.

'The target is moving,' a voice said into a radio three levels up. The message was relayed by telephone to Alex's safehouse, then by radio again.

'About bloody time,' Miller growled a few minutes later. 'Why the hell is she late?' The last hour had been infuriating for him. First thirty minutes of waiting for her to be on time, then another thirty minutes while she wasn't. He told himself to relax. She had to be at the day-care centre to pick up the kid.

'She's a doc. It happens, man,' Alex said. 'Let's roll.'

The pickup car led off first, followed by the van. The Ford would be at the 7-Eleven across from Giant Steps in exactly thirty minutes.

'He must be waiting for somebody pretty,' Riggs said when he got back into the guard shack.

'Still there?' Cummings was surprised. Three weeks before Breckenridge had briefed the guard force about the possible threat to Dr Ryan. Cummings knew that the history teacher always went out this gate – he was late today, though. The Sergeant could see that the light in his office was still on. Though the duty here was dull Cummings was serious about it. Three months in Beirut had taught him everything he would ever need to know about that. He walked outside and took a place on the other side of the road.

Cummings watched the cars leaving. Mostly they were driven by civilians, but those driven by naval officers got a regulation Marine salute. The wind only got colder. He wore a sweater under his blouse. This kept his torso warm, but the white kid gloves that went with the dress-blue uniform were the next thing to useless. He made a great show of clapping his hands together as he turned around periodically. He never stared at the apartment building, never acted as though he knew anybody were there. It was getting dark now, and it wasn't all that easy to see him anyway. But somebody was there.

'That was fast,' the man in the pickup car said. He checked his watch. She'd just knocked five minutes off her fastest time. *Damn*, he thought, *must be nice to have one of those little Porsches*. He checked the tag: CR-SRGN. Yep, that was the one. He grabbed the radio.

'Hi, Mom, I'm home,' he said.

'It's about time,' a male voice answered. The van was half a mile away, sitting on Joyce Lane, west of Ritchie Highway.

He saw the lady come out of the day-care centre less than two minutes later. She was in a hurry.

'Rolling.'

'Okay,' came the answer.

'Come on, Sally, we're late. Buckle up.' Cathy Ryan hated to be late. She restarted the engine. She hadn't been this late in over a month, but she could still make it home before Jack if she hustled.

The rush hour was under way in earnest, but the Porsche was small, fast, and agile. In a minute from sitting in the car park she was doing sixty-five, weaving through traffic like a race driver at Daytona.

For all their preparation, Alex almost missed her. An eighteen-wheeler was labouring up the hill in the right lane when the distinctive shape of the Porsche appeared next to it. Alex floored the van and darted out onto the road, causing the semi to jam his brakes and horn at the same time. Alex didn't look back. Miller got out of the right-front seat and went back to the window on the sliding door.

'Whooee, this lady's in a hurry tonight!'

'Can you catch her?' Miller asked.

Alex just smiled. 'Watch.'

'Damn, look at that Porsche!' Trooper First Class Sam Waverly was driving J-30, a State Police car coming off an afternoon of pursuit-radar work on US Route 50. He and Larry Fontana of J-19 were heading back to the Annapolis police barracks off Rowe Boulevard after a long day's work when they saw the green sports car take the entrance ramp off Ritchie Highway. Both troopers were driving about sixty-five miles per hour, a privilege that accrued only to police officers. Their cars were unmarked. This made them and their radar guns impossible to spot until it was too late. They usually worked in pairs, and took turns, with one working his radar gun and the other a quarter mile down the road to wave the speeders over for their tickets.

'Another one!' Fontana said over the radio. A van swerved into the highway's right lane, forcing somebody in a Pontiac to jam on his brakes. 'Let's get 'em.' They were both young officers and while, contrary to legend, the State Police didn't assign ticket quotas to its officers, everyone knew that one sure way to promotion was to write a lot of them. It also made the roads safer, and that was their mission as state troopers. Neither officer really enjoyed giving out traffic citations, but they enjoyed responding to major accidents far less.

'Okay, I got the Porsche.'

'You get all the fun,' Fontana noted. He'd got a quick look at the driver.

It was harder than one might imagine. First they had to clock the speeding vehicles to establish how far over the limit they were going – the greater the speed, the greater the fine, of course – then they had to close and switch on their lights to pull them over. Both subject vehicles were two hundred yards ahead of the police cruisers now.

Cathy checked her clock again. She'd managed to cut nearly ten minutes off her trip time. Next she checked her rearview mirror for a police car. She didn't want to get a ticket. There was nothing that looked like a cop car, only ordinary cars and trucks. She had to slow as the traffic became congested approaching the Severn River bridge. She debated getting over into the left lane, but decided against it. Sometimes it was hard to get back into the right lane in time to take the Route 2 exit. Beside her, Sally was craning her neck to see over the dash, as usual, and playing with the seat-belt buckle. Cathy didn't say anything this time, but concentrated on the traffic as she eased off the pedal.

Miller slipped the door latch and moved the door an inch backwards. Another man took hold of the door as he knelt and thumbed the safety forward on his weapon.

He couldn't get her for speeding now, Trooper Waverly noted sourly. She'd slowed before he could establish her speed. He was a hundred yards back. Fontana could, however, ticket the van for improper lane-changing, and one out of two wasn't bad. Waverly checked his mirror. J-19 was catching up, about to pull even with his J-30. There was something odd about the black van, he saw . . . like the side door wasn't quite right.

'Now!' Alex called.

Cathy Ryan noted that a van was pulling up on her left side. She took a casual look in time to see the van's door slide back. There was a man kneeling, holding something. There came a chilling moment of realization. She stomped her foot on the brake a fraction of a second before she saw the white flash.

'What!' Waverly saw a foot-long tongue of flame spit out from the side of the van. The windshield of the Porsche went cloudy and the car swerved sideways, straightened out, then slammed into the bridge's concrete work at over fifty miles per hour. Instantly cars in both lanes slammed on their brakes. The van kept going.

'Larry, shots fired – shots fired from the van. The Porsche was hit!' Waverly flipped on his lights and stood on his brakes. The police car skidded right and nearly slid sideways into the wrecked Porsche. 'Get the van, get the van!'

'I'm on him,' Fontana replied. He suddenly realized that the gout of flame he'd seen could only mean some kind of machine gun. 'Holy shit,' he said to himself.

Waverly returned his attention to the Porsche. Steam poured from the rear engine compartment. 'J-30, Annapolis, officer reports shots fired – looked like automatic weapons fire – and a PI accident westbound Route 50 on Severn River bridge. Appears to be serious PI. J-19 in pursuit of vehicle 2. Stand by.'

'Standing by,' the dispatcher acknowledged. *What the hell* . . .

Waverly grabbed his fire extinguisher and ran the fifteen feet to the wreck. Glass and metal were scattered as far as he could see. The engine, thank God, wasn't on fire. He checked the passenger compartment next.

'Oh, Jesus!' He ran back to his car. 'J-30, Annapolis. Call fireboard, officer requests helicopter response. Serious PI, two victims, a white female adult and a white female child, repeat we have a serious PI accident westbound Route 50 east side of Severn River bridge. Officer requests helicopter response.'

'J-19, Annapolis,' Fontana called in next. 'I am in pursuit of a dark van, with handicap tag number Henry Six-Seven-Seven-Two. I am westbound on Route 50 just west of the Severn River bridge. Shots fired from this vehicle. Officer requests assistance,' he said coolly. He decided against turning his lights on for the moment. *Holy Shit.* . . .

'You get her?' Alex called back.

Miller was breathing heavily. He wasn't sure – he wasn't sure about his shots. The Porsche had slowed suddenly just as he squeezed the trigger, but he saw the car hit the bridge and spring up into the air like a toy. No way they could walk away from that sort of accident, he was sure of that.

'Yes.'

'Okay, let's boogie.' Alex didn't let his emotions interfere with his work. This job meant weapons and money for his movement. It was too bad about the woman and the kid, but it wasn't his fault that they made the wrong kind of enemies.

The Annapolis dispatcher was already on his UHF radio to the State Police helicopter. Trooper-1, a Bell JetRanger-II was just lifting off from a refuelling stop at Baltimore-Washington International Airport.

'Roger that,' the helicopter pilot replied, turning south and twisting the throttle control to full power. The para-medic in the left seat leaned forward to change the transponder 'squawk' setting from 1200 to 5101. This would inform air traffic controllers that the helicopter was on an emergency medivac mission.

'Trooper-1, J-30, we are en route to your position, ETA four minutes.'

Waverly didn't acknowledge. He and two civilians were prying the driver's side window off the car with a tyre iron. The driver and passenger were both unconscious, and there was blood all over the interior of the car. She was probably pretty, Waverly thought, looking at the driver, but her head was covered with glistening blood. The child lay like a broken doll, half on the seat, half on the floor. His stomach was a tight cold ball just below his pounding heart. *Another dead kid*, he thought. *Please, God, not another one.*

'Trooper-2, Annapolis,' came the next call to the dispatcher.

'Annapolis, Trooper-2, where are you?'

'We are over Mayo Beach, northbound. I copied your medivac call. I have the Governor and Attorney General aboard. Can we help? Over.'

The dispatcher made a quick decision. Trooper-1 would be at the accident scene in three more minutes. J-19 needed backup in a hurry. This was real luck. Already he had six state vehicles converging on the area, plus three more from the Anne Arundel County Police station at Edgewater. 'Trooper-2, contact J-19.'

'Trooper-2, J-19, please advise your location,' the radio squawked in Fontana's car.

'Westbound Route 50, just passing Rowe Boulevard. I am in pursuit of a dark van with a handicap tag. J-30 and I observed automatic weapons fire from this vehicle, repeat automatic weapons fire. I need some help, people.'

It was easy to spot. The Sergeant flying Trooper-2 saw the other helicopter circling over the accident to the east, and Route 50 was nearly bare of cars from west of the accident to Rowe Boulevard. The police car and the van were on the back edge of the moving traffic.

'What gives?' the Governor asked from the back. The paramedic in the left-front seat filled them in as the pilot continued his visual search for. . . there! *Okay, sucker. . . .*

'J-19, this is Trooper-2, I got you and the subject car visual.' The pilot dropped altitude to five hundred feet. 'Trooper-2, Annapolis, I got 'em. Black, or maybe blue van westbound on 50, with an unmarked car in pursuit.'

Alex was wondering who the car was. It was unmarked, but a cheap-body car, with dull, monocolour paintwork. *Uh-oh.*

'That's a cop behind us!' he shouted. One of Miller's men looked out the window. Unmarked cars were nothing new where they came from.

'Get rid of him!' Alex snarled.

Fontana held at fifty yards from the van. This was far enough, he thought, to keep himself out of danger. The trooper was listening to continuous chatter on his radio as additional cars announced that they were inbound on the call. The distraction of the radio made him a second late on seeing the van's door fly open. Fontana blanched and hit the brakes.

Miller handled this one too. The moment the door was open, he levelled his machine gun and loosed ten rounds at the police car. He saw it dip when the driver tried to panic-stop, swerve sideways in the road, and flip over. He was too excited even to smile, though inwardly he was awash with glee. The door came back shut as Alex changed lanes.

Fontana felt the bullet hit his chest before he realized that the car's windshield was shattering around him. His right arm jerked down, turning the car too rapidly to the right. The locked-up rear wheels gave the car a broadside skid, a tyre blew out, and the car flipped over. Fontana watched in fascination the world rotate around him as the car's top crumpled. Like most policemen he never bothered with his seat belt, and he fell on his neck. The collapsing car top broke it. It didn't matter. A car that had been following his crashed into the police cruiser, finishing the work begun by Miller's submachine gun.

'Shit!' the pilot of Trooper-2 cursed. 'Trooper-2, Annapolis, J-19 is wrecked with serious PI on 50 west of the Route 2 exit. Where the hell are the other cars!'

'Trooper-2, advise condition of J-19.'

'He's dead, man – I'm on that fucking van! Where's the goddamned backup!'

'Trooper-2, be advised we have eleven cars converging. We have a roadblock setting up now on 50 at South Haven Road. There are three cars westbound on 50 about half a mile back of you and two more eastbound approaching the exit to General's Highway.'

'Roger that, I am on the van,' the pilot responded.

'Come on, Alex!' Miller shouted.

'Almost there, man,' the black man said, changing to the right lane exit. About a mile ahead he saw the blue and red flashing lights of two police cars coming east towards him, but there was no eastbound exit here. *Tough luck, pigs*. He didn't feel very happy about doing the Porsche, but a dead cop was always something to feel good about. 'Here we go!'

'Annapolis, Trooper-2,' the pilot called, 'the subject van is turning north off of Route 50.' It took a moment to register. 'Oh, no!' He gave a quick order. The eastbound police cars slowed, then darted across the grass median strip into the westbound lanes. These were clear, blocked by a second major accident, but the median was uneven. One car bogged down in the grass and mud while the other bounded up onto the pavement and ran the wrong way on the highway towards the exit.

Alex hit the traffic light exactly right, crossing West Street and heading north. His peripheral vision caught a county police car stuck in the rush-hour traffic on West Street two hundred yards to his right, despite his lights and siren. *Too late, pig*. He proceeded two hundred yards and turned left.

The Sergeant flying Trooper-2 started cursing, oblivious to the Governor and Attorney General in the back. As he watched, the van pulled into the hundred-acre car park that surrounded Annapolis Mall. The vehicle proceeded towards the inner ring of parking spaces as three cars turned off West Street in pursuit.

'Son of a *bitch*!' He pushed down on his collective control and drove at the car park.

Alex pulled into a handicap parking slot and stopped the van. His passengers were ready, and opened the doors as soon as the vehicle stopped. They walked slowly and normally to the entrance to the mall. The driver looked up in surprise when he heard the whine and flutter of the helicopter. It hovered at about a hundred feet. Alex made sure his hat was in place and waved as he went through the door.

The helicopter pilot looked at the paramedic in the left seat, whose hand was clenched in rage at his shoulder-holstered .357 revolver while the pilot needed both of his on the controls.

'They're gone,' the paramedic said quietly over the intercom.

'What do you mean they're gone!' the Attorney General demanded.

Below them, a county and a State Police car screeched to a halt outside the entrance. But inside those doors were about three thousand shoppers, and the police didn't know what the suspects looked like. The officers stood there, guns drawn, not knowing what to do next.

Alex and his men were inside a public rest room. Two members of Alex's organization were waiting there with shopping bags. Each man from the van got a new coat. They broke up into pairs and walked out into the shopping concourse, heading for an exit at the west end of the mall. They took their time. There was no reason to hurry.

'He waved at us,' the Governor said. 'Do something!'

'What?' the pilot asked. 'What do you want us to do? Who do we stop? They're gone, they might as well be in California now.'

The Governor was slow to catch on, though faster than the Attorney General, who was still blubbering. What had begun as a routine political meeting in Salisbury, on Maryland's eastern shore, had turned into an exciting pursuit, but one with a most unsatisfactory ending. He'd watched one of his state troopers killed right before his eyes, and neither he nor his people could do a single thing about it. The Governor swore, finally. The voters would have been shocked at his language.

Trooper-1 was sitting on the Severn River bridge, its rotor turning rapidly to stay above the concrete barriers. The paramedic, Trooper Waverly, and a motorist who turned out to be a volunteer fireman, were loading the two accident victims into Stokes litters for transport on the helicopter. The other motorist who had assisted was standing alone by the police car, over a puddle of his own vomit. A fire engine was pulling up to the scene, and two more state troopers were preparing to get traffic moving, once the helicopter took off. The highway was already backed up at least four miles. As they prepared to start directing traffic, they heard on their radios what had happened to J-19 and its driver. The police officers exchanged looks, but no words. They would come later.

As first officer on the scene, Waverly took the driver's bag and started looking for identification. He had lots of forms to fill out, and people to notify. Inside the bag, he saw, was some kind of finger painting. He looked up as the little girl's litter was loaded into the top rack of the helicopter's passenger bay. The paramedic went in behind it, and less than thirty seconds later, Waverly's face stung with the impact of gravel, thrown up by the helicopter's rotor. He watched it lift into the air, and whispered a prayer for the little girl who'd done a painting of something that looked like a blue cow. *Back to work*, he told himself. The bag had a red address book. He checked the driver's licence to get a name, then looked in the book under the same letter. Someone with the first name of Jack, but no last name written in, had a number designated 'work'. It was probably her husband's. Somebody had to call him.

'Baltimore Approach, this is Trooper-1 on a medivac inbound to Baltimore.'

'Trooper-1, roger, you are cleared for direct approach, come left to course three-four-seven and maintain current altitude,' the air controller at Baltimore-Washington International responded. The 5101 squawk number was clear on his scope, and medical emergencies had unconditional priority.

'Hopkins Emergency, this is Trooper-1, inbound with a white female child accident victim.'

'Trooper-1, Hopkins. Divert to University. We're full up here.'

'Roger that. University, Trooper-1, do you copy? Over.'

'Trooper-1, this is University, we copy, and we're ready for you.'

'Roger that, ETA five minutes. Out.'

'Gunny, this is Cummings at Gate Three,' the Sergeant called on the telephone.

'What is it, Sergeant?' Breckenridge asked.

'There's this guy, he's been standing on the corner across the street for about forty-five minutes. It just feels funny, you know? He's off the grounds, but it doesn't feel right.'

'Call the cops?' the Sergeant Major asked.

'What for?' Cummings asked reasonably. 'He ain't even spit far as I can tell.'

'Okay, I'll walk on up.' Breckenridge stood. He was bored anyway. The Sergeant Major donned his cap and walked out of the building, heading north across the campus. It took five minutes, during which he saluted six officers and greeted a larger number of mids. He didn't like the cold. It had never been like this during his childhood on a Mississippi dirt farm. But spring was coming. He was careful not to look too obviously out of the gate as he crossed the street.

He found Cummings in the guardhouse, standing inside the door. A good young sergeant, Cummings was. He had the new look of the Corps. Breckenridge was built along the classic John Wayne lines, with broad shoulders and imposing bulk. Cummings was a black kid, a runner who had the frame of a Frank Shorter. The boy could run all day, something that the Gunny had never been able to do. But more than all of that, Cummings was a lifer. He understood what the Marine Corps was all about. Breckenridge had taken the young man under his wing, imparting a few important lessons along the way. The Sergeant Major knew that he would soon be part of the Corps' past. Cummings was its future, and he told himself that the future looked pretty good.

'Hey, Gunny,' the Sergeant greeted him.

'The guy in the doorway?'

'He's been there since a little after four. He don't live here.' Cummings paused for a moment. He was, after all, only a 'buck' sergeant with no rockers under his stripes, talking to a man whom generals addressed with respect. 'It just feels funny.'

'Well, let's give him a few minutes,' Breckenridge thought aloud.

'God, I hate grading quizzes.'

'So go easy on the boys and girls,' Robby chuckled.

'Like you do?' Ryan asked.

'I teach a difficult, technical subject. I have to give quizzes.'

'Engineers! Shame you can't read and write as well as you multiply.'

'You must have taken a tough-pill this afternoon, Jack.'

'Yeah, well –' The phone rang. Jack picked it up. 'Doctor Ryan. Yes – who?' His face changed, his voice became guarded.

'Yes, that's right.' Robby saw his friend go stiff in the chair. 'Are you sure? Where are they now? Okay – ah, okay, thank you . . . I, uh, thank you.' Jack stared at the phone for a second or two before hanging it up.

'What's the matter, Jack?' Robby asked.

It took him a moment to answer. 'That was the police. There's been an accident.'

'Where are they?' Robby said immediately.

'They flew them – they flew them to Baltimore.' Jack stood shakily. 'I have to get there.' He looked down at his friend. 'God, Robby. . . .'

Jackson was on his feet in an instant. 'Come on, I'll take you up there.'

'No, I'll –'

'Stuff it, Jack. I'm driving.' Robby got his coat and tossed Jack's over the desk. 'Move it, boy!'

'They took them by helicopter. . . .'

'Where? Where to, Jack?'

'University,' he said.

'Get it together, Jack.' Robby grabbed his arm. 'Settle down some.' The flyer led his friend down the stairs and out of the building. His red Corvette was parked a hundred yards away.

'Still there,' the civilian guard reported when he came back in.

'Okay,' Breckenridge said, standing. He looked at the pistol holster hanging in the corner, but decided against that. 'This is what we're going to do.'

Ned Clark hadn't liked the mission from the first moment. Sean was too eager on this one. But he hadn't said so. Sean had masterminded the prison break that had made him a free man. If nothing else, Ned Clark was loyal to the Cause. He was exposed here and didn't like that either. His briefing

580

had told him that the guards at the Academy gate were lax, and he could see that they were unarmed. They had no authority at all off the grounds of the school.

But it was taking too long. His target was thirty minutes late. He didn't smoke, didn't do anything to make himself conspicuous, and he knew that he'd be hard to spot. The doorway of the tired old apartment building had no light – one of Alex's people had taken care of that with a pellet gun the previous night.

Ought to call this one off, Clark told himself. But he didn't want to do that. He didn't want to fail Sean. He saw a pair of men leave the Academy. Bootnecks, bloody Marines in their Sunday clothes. They looked so pretty without their guns, so vulnerable.

'So the Captain, he says,' the big one was saying loudly, 'get that goddamned gook off my chopper!' And the other one started laughing.

'I love it!'

'How about a couple of beers?' the big one said next. They crossed the street, heading his way.

'Okay by me, Gunny. You buyin'?'

'My turn, isn't it? I have to get some money first.' The big one reached in his pocket for some keys and turned towards Clark. 'Excuse me, sir, can I help you?' His hand came out of his pocket without any keys.

Clark reacted quickly, but not quickly enough. The right hand inside his overcoat started moving up, but Breckenridge's own right grabbed it like a vice.

'I asked if I could help you, sir,' the Sergeant Major said pleasantly. 'What do you have in that hand?' Clark tried to move, but the big man pushed him against the brick wall.

'Careful, Tom,' Breckenridge warned.

Cummings' hand searched downwards and found the metallic shape of a pistol. 'Gun,' he said sharply.

'It better not go off,' the Gunny announced, his left arm across Clark's throat. 'Let the man have it, sonny, real careful, like.'

Clark was amazed at his stupidity, letting them get so close to him. His head tried to turn to look up the street, but the man waiting for him in the car was around the corner. Before he could think of anything to do, the black man had disarmed him and was searching his pockets. Cummings removed the knife next.

'Talk to me,' Breckenridge said. Clark didn't say anything, and the forearm slid roughly across his throat. '*Please* talk to me, *sir*.'

'Get your bloody hands off of me! Who do you think you are?'

'Where you from, boy?' Breckenridge didn't need an answer to that one. The Sergeant wrenched Clark's arm out of the pocket and twisted it behind his back. 'Okay, sonny, we're going to walk through that gate over yonder, and you're gonna sit down and be a good boy while we call the police. If you make any trouble, I'm going to tear this arm off and shove it right up your ass. Let's go, boy.'

The driver who'd been waiting for Clark was standing at the far corner. He took one look at what had happened and walked to his car. Two minutes later he was blocks away.

Cummings handcuffed the man to a chair while Breckenridge established that he carried no identification – aside from an automatic pistol, which was ID enough. First he called his captain, then the Annapolis City police. It started there, but, though the Gunny didn't know, it wouldn't stop there.

15

Shock and Trauma

If Jack had ever doubted that Robby Jackson really was a fighter pilot, this would have cured him. Jackson's personal toy was a two-year-old Chevrolet Corvette, painted candy-apple red, and he drove it with a sense of personal invincibility. The flyer raced out the Academy's west gate, turned left, and found his way to Rowe Boulevard. The traffic problems on Route 50 west were immediately apparent, and he changed lanes to head east. In a minute he was streaking across the Severn River bridge. Jack was too engrossed in his thoughts to see much of anything, but Robby saw what looked like the remains of a Porsche on the other side of the roadway. Jackson's blood went cold as he turned away. He cast the thoughts aside and concentrated on his driving, pushing the Corvette past eighty. There were too many cops on the other side of the road for him to worry about a ticket. He took the Ritchie Highway exit a minute later and curved around north towards Baltimore. Rush-hour traffic was heavy, though most of it was heading in the other direction. This gave him gaps to exploit, and the pilot used every one. He worked up and down through the gears, rarely touching the brakes.

To his right, Jack simply stared straight ahead, not seeing much of anything. He managed to wince when Robby paused behind two tractor-trailers running side by side – then shot up right between them with scant inches of clearance on either side. The outraged screams of the two diesel horns faded irrelevantly behind the racing 'Vette, and Jack returned to the emptiness of his thoughts.

Breckenridge allowed his captain, Mike Peters, to handle the situation. He was a pretty good officer, the Sergeant Major thought, who had the common sense to let his NCOs run things. He'd managed to get to the guard shack about two minutes ahead of the Annapolis City police, long enough for Breckenridge and Cummings to fill him in.

'So what gives, gentlemen?' the responding officer asked. Captain Peters nodded for Breckenridge to speak.

'Sir, Sergeant Cummings here observed this individual to be standing over at the corner across the street. He did not look like a local resident, so we kept an eye on him. Finally Cummings and I walked over and asked if we might be of assistance to him. He tried to pull this on us' – the Gunny lifted the pistol carefully, so as not to disturb the fingerprints – 'and he had this knife in his pocket. Carrying a concealed weapon is a violation of local law, so Cummings and I made a citizen's arrest and called you. This character does not have any identification on him, and he declined to speak with us.'

'What kind of gun is that?' the cop asked.

'It's a FN nine-millimetre,' Breckenridge answered. 'It's the same as the Browning Hi-Power, but a different trademark, with a thirteen-round magazine. The weapon was loaded, with a live round in the chamber. The hammer was down. The knife is a cheap piece of shit. Punk knife.'

The cop had to smile. He knew Breckenridge from the department firearms training unit.

'Can I have your name, please,' the cop said to Eamonn Clark. The 'suspect' just stared at him. 'Sir, you have a number of constitutional rights which I am about to read to you, but the law does not allow you to withhold your identity. You have to tell me your name.'

The cop stared at Clark for another minute. At last he shrugged and pulled a card from his clipboard. 'Sir, you have the right to remain silent. . . .' He read the litany off the card. 'Do you understand these rights?'

Still Clark didn't say anything. The police officer was getting irritated. He looked at the other three men in the room. 'Gentlemen, will you testify that I read this individual his rights?'

'Yes, sir, we certainly will,' Captain Peters said.

'If I may make a suggestion, officer,' Breckenridge said. 'You might want to check this boy out with the FBI.'

'How come?'

'He talks funny,' the Sergeant Major explained. 'He don't come from here.'

'Great – two crazy ones in one day.'

'What do ya mean?' Breckenridge asked.

'Little while ago a car got machine-gunned on 50, sounds like some kind of drug hit. A trooper got killed by the same bunch a few minutes later. The bad guys got away.' The cop leaned down to look Clark in the face. 'You better start talkin', sir. The cops in this town are in a mean mood tonight. What I'm tellin' you, man, is that we don't want to put up with some unnecessary shit. You understand me?'

Clark didn't understand. In Ireland carrying a concealed weapon was a serious crime. In America it was rather less so since so many citizens owned guns. Had he said he was waiting for someone and carried a gun because he was afraid of street criminals, he might have got out on the street before identification procedures were complete. Instead, his intransigence was only making the policeman angry and ensuring that the identification procedures would be carried out in full before he was arraigned.

Captain Peters and Sergeant Major Breckenridge exchanged a meaningful look.

'Officer,' the Captain said, 'I would most strongly recommend that you check this character's ID with the FBl. We've, uh, we had a sort of an informal warning about terrorist activity a few weeks back. This is still your jurisdiction since he was arrested in the city, but. . . .'

'I hear you, Cap'n,' the cop said. He thought for a few seconds and concluded that there was something more here than met the eye. 'If you gentlemen will come to the station with me, we'll find out who Mr Doe here really is.'

Ryan charged through the entrance of the Shock-Trauma Centre and identified himself at the reception desk, whose occupant directed him to a waiting room where, she said firmly, he would be notified as soon as there was anything to report. The sudden change from action to inaction disoriented Jack enormously. He stood at the entrance to the waiting room for some minutes, his mind a total blank as it struggled with the situation. By the time Robby arrived from parking his car, he found his friend sitting on the cracked vinyl of an old sofa, mindlessly reading through a brochure whose stiff paper had become as soft as chamois from the numberless hands of parents, wives, husbands, and friends of the patients who had passed through this building.

The brochure explained in bureaucratic prose how the Maryland Institute for Emergency Medical Services was the first and best organization of its kind, devoted exclusively to the most sophisticated emergency care for trauma victims. Ryan knew all this. Johns Hopkins managed the more recent paediatric unit and provided many of the staff surgeons for eye injuries. Cathy had spent some time doing that during her residency, an intense two months that she'd been happy to leave behind. Jack wondered if she were now being treated by a former colleague. *Would he recognize her? Would it matter?*

The Shock-Trauma Centre – so known to everyone but the billing department – had begun as the dream of a brilliant, aggressive, and supremely arrogant heart surgeon who had bludgeoned his way through a labyrinth of bureaucratic empires to build this 21st-century emergency room.

It had blossomed into a dazzling, legendary success. Shock-Trauma was the leading edge of emergency medical technology. It had already pioneered many techniques for critical care, and in doing so had overthrown many historical precepts of conventional medicine – which had not endeared its founder to his medical brethren. That would have been true in any field, and Shock-Trauma's founder had not helped the process with his brutally outspoken opinions. His greatest – but unacknowledged – crime, of course, was being right in nearly all details. And while this prophet was without honour in the mainstream of his profession, its younger members were easier to convert. Shock-Trauma attracted the best young surgical talent in the world, and only the finest of them were chosen.

But will they be good enough? Ryan asked himself.

He lost all track of time, waiting, afraid to look at his watch, afraid to speculate on the significance of time's flight. Alone, completely alone in his circumscribed world, he reflected that God had given him a wife he loved and a child he treasured more than his own life; that his first duty as husband and father was to protect them from an often hostile world; that he had failed; that, because of this, their lives were now in strangers' hands. All his knowledge, all his skills were useless now. It was worse than impotence, and some evil agency in his mind kept repeating over and over the thoughts that made him cringe as he retreated farther and farther into catatonic numbness. For hours he stared at the floor, then the wall, unable even to pray as his mind sought the solace of emptiness.

Jackson sat beside his friend, silent, in his own private world. A naval aviator, he had seen close friends vanish from a trivial mistake or a mechanical glitch – or seemingly nothing at all. He'd felt death's cold hand brush his own shoulder less than a year before. But this wasn't a danger to a mature man who had freely chosen a dangerous profession. This was a young wife and an innocent child whose lives were at risk. He couldn't joke about how 'old Dutch' would luck this one out. He knew nothing at all he could say, no encouragement he could offer other than just sitting there, and though he gave no sign of it, Robby was sure that Jack knew his friend was close at hand.

After two hours Jackson quietly left the waiting room to call his wife and check discreetly at the desk. The receptionist fumbled for the names, then identified them as: a Female, Blonde, Age Thirty or so, Head; and a Female, Blonde, Age Four or so, Flailed Chest. The pilot was tempted to throttle the receptionist for her coldness, but his discipline was sufficient to allow him to turn away without a word. Jackson rejoined Ryan a moment later, and together they stared at the wall through the passage of time. It started to rain outside, a cold rain that perfectly matched what they both felt.

Special Agent Shaw was walking through the door of his Chevy Chase home when the phone rang. His teenage daughter answered it and just held it out to him. This sort of thing was not the least unusual.

'Shaw here.'

'Mr Shaw, this is Nick Capitano from the Annapolis office. The city police here have in custody a man with a pistol, a knife, but no ID. He refuses to talk at all, but earlier he did speak to a couple of Marines, and he had an accent.'

'That's nice, he has an accent. What kind?' Shaw asked testily.

'Maybe Irish,' Capitano replied. 'He was apprehended just outside Gate Three of the US Naval Academy. There's a Marine here who says that some teacher named Ryan works there, and he got some sort of warning from the Anti-Terrorism Office.'

What the hell? 'Have you ID'd the suspect yet?'

'No, sir. The local police just fingerprinted him, and they faxed a copy of the prints and photo to the Bureau. The suspect refuses to say anything. He just isn't talking at all, sir.'

'Okay.' Shaw thought for a moment. *So much for dinner.* 'I'll be back in my office in thirty minutes. Have them send a copy the mug shot and the prints there. You stay there, and have somebody find Doctor Ryan and stay with him.'

'Right.'

Shaw hung up and dialled his office at the Bureau. 'Dave, Bill. Call London, and tell Dan Murray I want him in his office in half an hour. We may have something happening over here.'

''Bye, Daddy,' his daughter said. Shaw hadn't even had time to take off his coat.

He was at his desk twenty-seven minutes later. First he called Nick Capitano in Annapolis.

'Anything new?'

'No, sir. The security detail at Annapolis can't find this Ryan guy. His car is parked on the Academy grounds, and they've got people looking for him. I've asked the Anne Arundel County Police to send a car to his home in case he got a ride – car broke down, or something like that. Things are a little wild here at the moment. Something crazy happened about the same time this John Doe gunman got picked up. A car got hosed down with a machine gun just outside the city.'

'What the hell was that?'

'The State Police are handling it. We haven't been called in,' Capitano explained.

'Get a man over there!' Shaw said at once. A secretary came into the office and handed him a folder. Inside was a facsimile copy of the suspect's mug shot. It showed full face and profile.

'Hold it!' He caught the secretary before the door was closed. 'I want this faxed to London right now.'

'Yes, sir.'

Shaw next dialled the tie line to the embassy in London.

'I just got to sleep,' the voice answered after the first ring.

'Hi, Dan. I just missed dinner. It's a tough world. I have a photo being faxed to you now.' Shaw filled Murray in on what had happened.

586

'Oh, my God.' Murray gulped down some coffee. 'Where's Ryan?'

'We don't know. Probably just wandering around somewhere. His car's still parked in Annapolis – at the Academy, I mean. The security guys are looking for him. He's gotta be all right, Dan. If I read this right, the suspect in Annapolis was probably waiting for him.'

The photograph of Eamonn Clark was already in the embassy. The Bureau's communications unit worked on the same satellite net used by the intelligence services. The embassy communications officers were actually employees of the National Security Agency, which never slept. The facsimile had arrived with a FLASH-priority header, and a messenger ran it up to the Legal Attaché's office. But the door was locked. Murray had to set the phone down to open it.

'I'm back,' Murray said. He opened the folder. The photo had suffered somewhat from twice being broken into electronic bits and broadcast, but for all of that it was recognizable. 'This one's familiar. I can't put a name on him, but he's a bad guy.'

'How fast can you ID him?'

'I can call Jimmy Owens real quick. You in your office?'

'Yeah,' Shaw answered.

'I'll be back.' Murray changed buttons on his phones. He didn't have Owens' home number memorized and had to look it up.

'Yes?'

'Hi, Jimmy, it's Dan.' Murray's voice was actually chipper now. *Have I got something for you.*

Owens didn't know that yet. 'Do you know what time it is?'

'Our guys have somebody in custody that you may be interested in.'

'Who?' Owens asked.

'I got a picture but no name. He was arrested in Annapolis, outside the Naval Academy –'

'Ryan?'

'Maybe.' Murray was worried about that.

'Meet me at the Yard,' Owens said.

'On the way.' Murray headed downstairs for his car.

It was easier for Owens. His house was always watched by a pair of armed detectives in a police car. All he had to do was step outside and wave, and the Land-Rover came to his door. He beat Murray by five minutes. By the time the FBI agent arrived, Owens had already consumed a cup of tea. He poured two more.

'This guy look familiar?' The FBI agent tossed the photo over. Owens' eyes went wide.

'Ned Clark,' he breathed. 'In America, you say?'

'I thought he looked familiar. He got picked up in Annapolis.'

'This is one of the lads who broke out of Long Kesh, a very bad boy with several murders to his name. Thank you, Mr Murray.'

'Thank the Marines.' Murray grabbed a cup of tea. He really needed the caffeine. 'Can I make a call?' Within a minute he was back to FBI headquarters. The desk phone was on speaker so that Owens could listen in.

'Bill, the suspect is one Ned Clark, a convicted murderer who escaped from prison last year. He used to be a big-time assassin with the Provos.'

'I got some bad news, Dan,' Shaw replied. 'It appears that there was an attack on this Ryan fellow's family. The State Police are investigating what looks like a machine-gun attack on a car belonging to Doctor Caroline Ryan, MD. The suspects were in a van and made a clean escape after killing a state trooper.'

'Where is Jack Ryan?' Murray asked.

'We don't know yet. He was seen leaving the Naval Academy grounds in the car of a friend. The troopers are looking for the car now.'

'What about his family?' It was Owens this time.

'They were flown to the Shock-Trauma Centre in Baltimore. The local police have been notified to keep an eye on the place, but it's usually guarded anyway. As soon as we find Ryan we'll put some people with him. Okay, on this Clark kid, I'll have him in federal custody by tomorrow morning. I expect that Mr Owens wants him back?'

'Yes.' Owens leaned back in his chair. He had his own call to make now. As often happened in police work, there was bad news to accompany the good.

'Mr Ryan?' It was a doctor. Probably a doctor. He wore a pink paper gown and strange-looking pink booties over what were probably sneakers. The gown was bloodstained. He couldn't be much over thirty, Ryan judged. The face was tired and dark. DR BARRY SHAPIRO, the name tag announced, DEPUTY TRAUMA-SURGEON-IN-CHIEF. Ryan tried to stand but found that his legs would not work. The doctor waved for him to remain seated. He came over slowly and fell into the chair next to the sofa.

What news do you bring me? Ryan thought. His mind both screamed for information and dreaded learning what had happened to his family.

'I'm Barry Shapiro. I've been working on your daughter.' He spoke quickly, with a curious accent that Ryan noted but discarded as irrelevant. 'Okay, your wife is fine. She had a broken and lacerated upper left arm and a nasty cut on her head. When the helicopter paramedic saw the head wound – heads bleed a lot – he brought her here as a precaution. We ran a complete head protocol on her, and she's fine. A mild concussion, but nothing to worry about. She'll be fine.'

'She's pregnant. Do –'

'We noticed.' Shapiro smiled. 'No problem with that. The pregnancy has not been compromised in any way.'

'She's a surgeon. Will there be any permanent damage?'

'Oh? I didn't know that. We don't bother very much with patient identification,' Shapiro explained. 'No, there should be no problem. The damage to her arm is extensive but routine. It should heal completely.'

Ryan nodded, afraid to ask the next question. The doctor paused before going on. *Does the bad news come next. . . .*

'Your daughter is a very sick little girl.'

Jack nearly choked with his next breath. The iron fist that had clutched his stomach relaxed a millimetre. *At least she's alive. Sally's alive!*

'Apparently she wasn't wearing her seat belt. When the car hit she was thrown forward, very hard.' Jack nodded. Sally liked to play with her seat belt buckle – *we thought it was cute*, Ryan reminded himself bitterly. 'Okay, tib and fib are broken in both legs, along with the left femur. All of the left-side ribs are broken, and six on the right side – a classic flailed chest. She can't breathe for herself, but she's on a respirator; that is under control. She arrived with extensive internal injuries and haemorrhaging, severe damage to the liver and spleen, and the large bowel. Her heart stopped right after she got here, probably – almost certainly – from loss of blood volume. We got it restarted at once and immediately started replacing the blood loss.' Shapiro went on quickly. 'That problem is also behind us.

'Doctor Kinter and I have been working on her for the best part of five hours. We had to remove the spleen – that's okay, you can live without a spleen.' Shapiro didn't say that the spleen was an important part of the body's defence against infections. 'The liver had a moderately extensive stellate fracture and damage to the main artery that feeds blood into the organ. We had to remove about a quarter of the liver – again no problem with that – and I think we fixed the arterial damage, and I think the repair will hold. The liver is important. It has a great deal to do with blood formation and the body's biochemical balance. You can't live without it. If liver function is maintained . . . she'll probably make it. The damage to the bowel was easy to repair. We removed about thirty centimetres. The legs are immobilized. We'll repair them later. The ribs – well, that's painful but not life-threatening. And the skull is relatively minor. I guess her chest took the main impact. She has a concussion, but there's no sign of intercranial bleeding.' Shapiro rubbed his hands over his heavily-bearded face.

'The whole thing revolves around her liver function. If the liver continues to work, she will probably recover fully. We're keeping a very close watch on her blood chemistry, and we'll know something in, oh, maybe eight or nine hours.'

'Not till then?' Ryan's face twisted into an agonized mass. The fist tightened its grip yet again. *She still might die. . . ?*

'Mr Ryan,' Shapiro said slowly, 'I know what you are going through. If it hadn't been for the helicopter bringing your little girl in, well, right now I'd be telling you that she had died. Another five minutes getting here – maybe not that long – and she would not have made it this far. That's how close it was. But she *is* alive now, and I promise you that we're doing our very best to keep her that way. And our best is the best there is. My team of doctors and nurses is the best of its kind in the world – period. Nobody comes close. If there's a way, we'll find it.' *And if there's not*, he didn't say, *we won't.*

'Can I see them?'

'No.' Shapiro shook his head. 'Right now both of them are in the CCRU – the Critical Care Recovery Unit. We keep that as clean as an OR. The smallest infection can be lethal for a trauma patient. I'm sorry, but it would be too dangerous to them. My people are watching them constantly. A nurse – an experienced trauma nurse – is with each of them every second with a team of doctors and nurses thirty feet away.'

'Okay.' He almost gasped the word. Ryan leaned his head back against the wall and closed his eyes. *Eight more hours? But you have no choice. You have to wait. You have to do what they say.* 'Okay.'

Shapiro left and Jackson followed after him, catching him by the lift.

'Doc, can't Jack see his little girl? She –'

'Not a chance.' Shapiro half fell against the wall and let out a long breath. 'Look, right now the little girl – what's her name anyway?'

'Sally.'

'Okay, right now she's in a bed, stark naked, with IV tubes running into both arms and one leg. Her head's partially shaved. She's wired up to a half-dozen monitors, and we have an Engstrom respirator breathing for her. Her legs are wrapped – all you can see of her is one big bruise from her hips to the top of her head.' Shapiro looked down at the pilot. He was too tired to show any emotion. 'Look, she might die. I don't think so, but there's no way we can be sure. With liver injuries, you can't tell until the blood-chemistry readings come in, you just can't. If she does die, would you want your friend to see her like that? Would you want him to remember her like that, for the rest of his life?'

'I guess not.' Jackson said quietly, surprised at how much he wanted this little girl to live. His wife could not have children, and somehow Sally had become like their own. 'What are her chances?'

'I'm not a bookie, I don't quote odds. Numbers don't mean a thing in a case like this. Sorry, but either she makes it or she doesn't. Look, that wasn't a song and dance I gave – Jack, you said? She could not be in a better place.' Shapiro's eyes focused on Jackson's chest. He jabbed a finger at the wings of gold. 'You a pilot?'

'Yeah. Fighters.'

'Phantoms?'

'No, the F-14. Tomcat.'

'I fly.' Shapiro smiled. 'I used to be a flight surgeon in the Air Force. Last year I got a sailplane. Nice and peaceful up there. When I can get away from this mad-house, I go up every time I can. No phones. No hassles. Just me and the clouds.' The doctor was not talking to Jackson so much as himself. Robby set his hand on the surgeon's arm.

'Doc, tell you what – you save that little girl, and I'll get you a checkride in any bird you want. Ever been up in a T-38?'

'What's that?' Shapiro was too tired to remember that he'd seen them before.

'A spiffy little supersonic trainer. Two seats, dual controls, and she handles like a wet dream. I can disguise you as one of ours and get you up, no sweat. Ever been past mach-1?'

'No. Can you do some aerobatics?' Shapiro smiled like a tired little boy.

'Sure, Doc.' Jackson grinned, knowing that he could do manoeuvres to make a quail lose its lunch.

'I'll take you up on that. We work the same way with every patient, but I'll take you up on that anyway. Keep an eye on your friend. He looks a little rocky. That's normal. This sort of thing can be harder on the family than it is on the victims. If he doesn't come around some, tell the receptionist. We have a staff psychiatrist who specializes in working with – the *other* victims, he calls 'em.' Yet another new idea at Shock-Trauma was a specialist in helping people cope with the injuries to family and friends.

'Cathy's arm. She's an eye surgeon, lots of fine work, you know? You sure there's no problem with that?'

Shapiro shook his head. 'No big deal. It was a clean break to the humerus. Must have been a jacketed slug. The bullet went in clean, went out clean. Pretty lucky, really.'

Robby's hand clamped shut on the doctor's arm as the lift arrived. *'Bullet?'*

'Didn't I say that? God, I must be tireder than I thought. Yeah, it was a gunshot wound, but very clean. Hell, I wish they were all that clean. A nine-millimetre, maybe a thirty-eight, about that size. I have to get back to work.' The doctor went into the lift.

'Shit,' Jackson said to the wall. He turned when he heard a man with an English accent – two of them, it turned out – whom the receptionist directed to the waiting room. Robby followed them in.

The taller one approached Ryan and said, 'Sir John?'

Ryan looked up. *Sir John?* Robby thought. The Brit drew himself to attention and went on briskly.

'My name is Geoffrey Bennett. I am Chargé d'Affaires at the British Embassy.' He produced an envelope from his pocket and handed it to Ryan. 'I am directed by Her Majesty to deliver this personally into your hand and to await your reply.'

Jack blinked his eyes a few times, then tore open the envelope and extracted a yellow message form. The cable was brief, kind, and to the point. *What time is it over there?* Ryan wondered. *Two in the morning? Three? Something like that.* That meant that she'd been awakened with the news, probably, and cared enough to send a personal message. And was waiting for a reply.

How about that.

Ryan closed his eyes and told himself that it was time to return to the world of the living. Too drained for the tears he needed to shed, he swallowed a few times and rubbed his hands across his face before standing.

'Please tell Her Majesty that I am most grateful for her concern. My wife is expected to recover fully, but my daughter is in critical condition and we will

591

have no definitive word on her for another eight or nine hours. Please tell Her Majesty that . . . that I am deeply touched by her concern, and that all of us value her friendship very highly indeed.'

'Thank you, Sir John.' Bennett made some notes. 'I will cable your reply immediately. If you have no objection, I will leave a member of the embassy staff here with you.' Jack nodded, puzzled, as Bennett made his exit.

Robby took all this in with a raised eyebrow and a dozen unasked questions. *Who was this guy?* He introduced himself as Edward Wayson, and took a seat in the corner facing the doorway. He looked over at Jackson. Their eyes met briefly and each man evaluated the other. Wayson had cool, detached eyes, and a wispy smile at the corners of his mouth. Robby gave him a closer look. There was a slight bulge under his left arm. Wayson affected to read a paperback novel, which he held in his left hand, but his eyes kept flickering to the door every few seconds, and his right hand stayed free in his lap. He caught Jackson's glance and nodded. So, Robby concluded, a spook, or at least a security officer. *So that's what this is all about.* The realization came as a blast of cold air. The pilot's hands flexed as he considered the type of person who would deliberately attempt to murder a woman and her child.

Five minutes later three State Police officers made their belated arrival. They talked to Ryan for ten minutes. Jackson watched with interest and saw his friend's face go pale with anger as he stammered answers to numerous questions. Wayson didn't look but heard it all.

'You were right, Jimmy,' Murray said. He was standing at the window, watching the early morning traffic negotiate the corner of Broadway and Victoria streets.

'Paddy O'Neil in Boston likes to say what wonderful chaps Sinn Fein are,' Owens said speculatively. 'And our friend O'Donnell decides to embarrass them. We could not have known, Dan. A possibility of a suspicion is not evidence and you know it. There was no basis in fact for giving them a more serious warning than what you did. And you *did* warn then, Dan.'

'She's a pretty little girl. Gave me a hug and a kiss before they flew home.' Murray looked at his watch again and subtracted six hours. 'Jimmy, there are times. . . . Fifteen years ago we arrested this – this person who went after kids, little boys. I interrogated him. Sang like a canary, he couldn't be happier with himself. He copped to six cases, gave me all the details with a big shit-eatin' grin. It was right after the Supreme Court struck down all the death-penalty laws, so he knew that he'd live to a ripe old age. Do you know how close I came to –' He stopped for a moment before going on. 'Sometimes we're too damned civilized.'

'The alternative, Dan, is to become like them.'

'I know that's true, Jimmy, but I just don't like it right now.'

When Barry Shapiro next checked his watch it was five in the morning. *No wonder I feel so tired*, he thought. *Twenty hours on duty. I'm too old for this.* He was senior staff. He was supposed to know better.

The first sign was staying on duty too long, taking on too much personal responsibility, taking too keen an interest in patients who in the final analysis were nothing more or less than bruised and broken pieces of meat. Some of them died. No matter how great his skill, how refined his technique, how determined the efforts of his team, some would always die. And when you got this tired, you couldn't sleep. Their injuries – and worse, their faces – were too fresh in your memory, too haunting to go away. Doctors need sleep more than most men. Persistent loss of sleep was the last and most dangerous warning. That was when you had to leave – or risk a breakdown, as had happened all too often to the Shock-Trauma staffers.

It was their grimmest institutional joke: how their patients arrived with broken bodies and mostly went home whole – but the staff doctors and nurses who came in with the greatest energy and highest personal ideals would so often leave broken in spirit. It was the ultimate irony of his profession that success would engender the expectation of still greater success; the failure in this most demanding of medical disciplines could leave almost as much damage on the practitioner as the patient. Shapiro was cynic enough to see the humour of it.

The surgeon re-read the print-out that the blood-analyser unit had spat out a minute before, and handed it back to the nurse-practitioner. She attached it to the child's chart, then sat back down, stroking her dirty hair outside the oxygen mask.

'Her father is downstairs. Get relief here and go down and tell him. I'm going upstairs for a smoke.' Shapiro left the CCRU and got his overcoat, fishing in his pockets for his cigarettes.

He wandered down the hall to the fire stairs, then climbed slowly up the six flights to the roof. *God*, he thought. *Dear God, I'm tired.* The roof was flat, covered with tar and gravel, spotted here and there with the UHF antennae for the centre's SYSCOM communications net, and a few air-conditioning condensers. Shapiro lit a cigarette in the lee of the stairway tower, cursing himself for his inability to break the noxious habit. He rationalized that, unlike most of his colleagues, he never saw the degenerative effects of smoking. Most of his patients were too young for chronic diseases. Their injuries resulted from the miracles of a technical society: automobiles, motorcycles, firearms, and industrial machinery.

Shapiro walked to the edge of the roof, rested his foot on the parapet as though on a bar rail, and blew smoke into the early-morning air. It wafted away to appear and disappear as a gentle morning breeze carried it past the rooftop lights. The doctor stretched his tired arms and neck. The night's rain had washed the sky clean of its normal pollution, and he could see stars overhead in the pre-dawn darkness.

Shapiro's curious accent resulted from his background. His early childhood had been spent in the Williamsburg section of New York, the son of a rabbi who had taken his family to South Carolina. Barry had had good private schooling there, but emerged from it with a mixture of Southern drawl and New York quip. It was further damaged by a prairie twang acquired during his medical training at Baylor University in Texas. His father was a distinguished man of letters in his own right, a frequent lecturer at the University of South Carolina at Columbia. An expert in 19th-century American literature, Rabbi Shapiro's speciality was the work of Edgar Allan Poe. Barry Shapiro loathed Poe. A scribbler of death and perversity, the surgeon called him whenever the subject came up, and he'd been surprised to learn that Poe had died in Baltimore long before, after falling asleep, drunk, in a gutter; and that Poe's home was only a few blocks from the University Hospital complex, a demi-shrine for the local literati.

It seemed to the surgeon that everything about Poe was dark and twisted, always expecting the inevitability of death – violent, untimely death, Shapiro's own very personal enemy. He had come to think of Poe as the embodiment of that enemy, sometimes beaten, sometimes not. It was not something he talked about to the staff psychiatrist, who also kept a close eye on the hospital staff – but now, alone, he looked north to the Poe house.

'You son of a bitch,' he whispered. To himself. To Poe. To no one. '*You son of a bitch!* Not this time – you don't get this one! This one goes home.' He flicked the cigarette away and watched the point of orange light fall all the way to the shining, empty street. He turned back to the stairs. It was time to get some sleep.

16

Objectives and Patriots

Like most professional officers, Lieutenant Commander Robby Jackson had little use for the press. The irony of it was that Jack had tried many times to tell him that his outlook was wrong, that the press was as important to the preservation of American democracy as the Navy was. Now, as he watched, reporters were hounding his friend with questions that alternated between totally inane and intrusively personal. Why did everyone need to know how Jack felt about his daughter's condition? What would any normal person feel about having his child hovering near death – did they need such feelings explained? How was Jack supposed to know who'd done the shooting – if the police didn't know, how could he?

'And what's *your* name?' one finally asked Robby. He gave the woman his name and rank, but not his serial number.

'What are you doing here?' she persisted.

'We're friends. I drove him up here.' *You dumbass.*

'And what do you think of all this?'

'What do you think I think? If that was your friend's little girl up there, what the hell would you think?' the pilot snapped back at her.

'Do you know who did it?'

'I fly airplanes for a living, I'm not a cop. Ask them.'

'They're not talking.'

Robby smiled thinly. 'Well, score one for the good guys. Lady, why don't you leave that man alone? If you were going through what he is, do you think you would want a half-dozen strangers asking you these kind of questions? That's a human being over there, y'know? And he's my friend and I don't like what you people are doing to him.'

'Look, Commander, we know that his wife and daughter were attacked by terrorists –'

'Says who?' Jackson demanded.

'Who else would it be? Do you think we're stupid?' Robby didn't answer that. 'This is news – it's the first attack by a foreign terrorist group on American soil, if we're reading this right. That is important. The people have a right to know what happened and why,' the reporter said reasonably.

She's right, Robby admitted reluctantly to himself. He didn't like it, but she was right. *Damn.*

'Would it make you feel any better to know that I do have a kid about that age? Mine's a boy,' she said. The reporter actually seemed sympathetic.

Jackson searched for something to dislike about her. 'Answer me this: if you have a chance to interview the people who do this, would you do it?'

'That's my job. We need to know where they're coming from.'

'Where they're comin' from, lady, is they kill people for the fun of it. It's all part of their game.' Robby remembered intelligence reports he'd seen while in the Eastern Med. 'Back a couple of years ago – you never heard this from me, okay?'

'Off the record,' she said solemnly.

'I was on a carrier off Beirut, okay? We had intelligence reports – and pictures – of people from Europe who flew in to do some killing. They were mainly kids, musta been from good families – I mean, from the way they dressed. No shit, this is for real, I saw the friggin' pictures. They joined up with some of the crazies, got guns, and just started blasting away, at random, for the pure hell of it. They shot from those high-rise hotels and office buildings into the streets. With a rifle you can hit from a thousand yards away.

Something moves – boom, they blast it with automatic weapons fire. Then they got to go home. They were killing people, for fun! Maybe some of them grew up to be real terrorists, I don't know. It was pretty sickening stuff, not the sort of thing you forget. That's the kind of people we're talking about here, okay?

'I don't give a good goddamn about their point of view, lady! When I was a little kid in Alabama, we had problems with people like that, those assholes in the Klan. I don't give a damn about their point of view, either. The only good thing about the Klan was they were idiots. The terrorists we got running around now are a lot more efficient. Maybe that makes them more legitimate in your eyes, but not mine.'

'That thing in Beirut never made the papers,' the reporter said.

'I know for a fact that one reporter saw it. Maybe he figured that nobody would believe it. I don't know that I would have without the photos. But I saw 'em. You got my word on that, lady.'

'What kind of pictures?'

'That I can't say – but they were good enough to see their shiny young faces.' The photos had been made by US and Israeli reconnaissance aircraft.

'So what do you do about it?'

'If you could arrange to have all these bastards in one place, I think we and the Marines could figure something out,' Robby replied, voicing a wish common to professional soldiers throughout the world. 'We might even invite you newsies to the wake. Who the hell is that?' Two new people came into the room.

Jack was too tired to be fully coherent. The news that Sally was out of immediate danger had been like a giant weight leaving his shoulders, and he was waiting for the chance to see his wife, who would soon be moved to a regular hospital floor. A few feet away, Wayson, the British security officer, watched with unconcealed contempt, refusing even to give his name to the reporters who asked. The State Police officers were unable to keep the press away, though hospital personnel flatly refused to let the TV equipment in the front door, and were able to make that stick. The question that kept repeating was, Who did it? Jack said he didn't know, though he thought he did. It was probably the people he'd decided not to worry about.

It could have been worse, he told himself. At least it was now probable that Sally would be alive at the end of the week. His daughter was not dead because of his misjudgment. That was some consolation.

'Mr Ryan?' one of the new visitors asked.

'Yeah?' Jack was too exhausted to look up. He was awake only because of adrenalin now. His nerves were too ragged to allow him sleep, much as he needed it.

'I'm Special Agent Ed Donoho, Boston Field Office of the FBI. I have somebody who wants to say something to you.'

Nobody ever said that Paddy O'Neil was stupid, Donoho thought. As soon as the report had made the Eleven O'Clock News, the man from Sinn Fein had asked his FBI 'escort' if he might fly down to Baltimore. Donoho was in no position to deny him the right, and had been co-opted into bringing the man himself on the first available plane into BWI.

'Mr Ryan,' O'Neil said with a voice that dripped sympathy, 'I understand that the condition of your child has been upgraded. I hope that my prayers had something to do with it, and . . .'

It took Ryan over ten seconds to recognize the face that he'd seen a few days before on TV. His mouth slowly dropped open as his eyes widened. For some reason he didn't hear what the man was saying. The words came through his ears, but, as though they were in some unknown tongue, his brain did not assemble them into speech. All he saw was the man's throat, five feet away. *Just about five feet*, was what his brain told him.

'Uh-oh,' Robby said on the other side of the room. He stood as his friend went beet-red. Two seconds later, Ryan's face was as pale as the collar on his white cotton shirt. Jack's feet shifted, sliding straight beneath his body as he leaned forward on the couch.

Robby pushed past the FBI agent as Ryan launched himself from the couch, hands stretching out for O'Neil's neck. Jackson's shoulder caught his friend's chest, and the pilot wrapped Jack up in a bear hug, trying to push him backwards as three photographers recorded the scene. Jack didn't make a sound, but Robby knew exactly what he wanted to do. Jackson had leverage going for him, and pushed Ryan back, hurling him onto the couch. He turned quickly.

'Get that asshole outa here before *I* kill him!' Jackson was four inches shorter than the Irishman, but his rage was scarcely less than Ryan's. 'Get that terrorist bastard out of here!'

'Officer!' Special Agent Donoho pointed to a state trooper, who grabbed O'Neil and dragged him from the room in an instant. For some reason the reporters followed as O'Neil loudly protested his innocence.

'Are you out of your fucking mind!' Jackson snarled at the FBI agent.

'Cool down, Commander. I'm on your side, okay? Cool it down some.'

Jackson sat down beside Ryan, who was breathing like a horse at the end of a race while he stared at the floor. Donoho sat down on the other side.

'Mr Ryan, I couldn't keep him from coming down. I'm sorry, but we can't do that. He wanted to tell you – shit, all the way down on the plane, he told me that his outfit had nothing to do with this; that it would be a disaster for them. He wanted to extend his sympathy, I guess.' The agent hated himself for saying that, even though it was true enough. He hated himself even more because he'd almost started to like Paddy O'Neil over the past week. The front man for Sinn Fein was a person of considerable charm, a man with a gift for presenting his point of view in a reasonable way. Ed Donoho asked himself why he'd been assigned to this job. *Why couldn't they have picked an Italian?* He knew the answer to that, of course, but just because there was a reason didn't mean that he had to like it. 'I'll make sure he doesn't bother you anymore.'

'You do that,' Robby said.

Donoho went back into the hall, and unsurprisingly found O'Neil giving his spiel to the reporters. *Mr Ryan is distraught*, he was saying, *as any family man would be in similar circumstances*. His first exposure to the man the previous week had given him a feeling of distaste. Then he'd started to admire his skill and charm. Now Donoho's reaction to the man's words was one of loathing. An idea blinked on in his head. He wondered if the Bureau would approve and decided it was worth the risk. First the agent grabbed a state trooper by the arm and made sure that the man wouldn't get close to Ryan again. Next he got hold of a photographer and talked to him briefly. Together they found a doctor.

'No, absolutely not,' the surgeon replied to the initial request.

'Hey, Doc,' the photojournalist said. 'My wife's pregnant with our first. If it'll help this guy, I'm for it. This one doesn't make the papers. You got my word, Doc.'

'I think it'll help,' the FBI agent said. 'I really do.'

Ten minutes later Donoho and the photographer stripped off their scrub clothing. The FBI agent took the film cassette and tucked it in his pocket. Before he took O'Neil back to the airport, he made a call to headquarters in Washington, and two agents drove out to Ryan's home on Peregrine Cliff. They didn't have any problem with the alarm system.

Jack had been awake for more than twenty-four hours now. If he'd been able to think about it, he would have marvelled at the fact that he was awake and functional, though the latter observation would have been a matter of dispute to anyone who saw him walking. He was alone now. Robby was off attending to something that he couldn't remember.

He would have been alone in any case. Twenty minutes earlier, Cathy had been moved into the main University Hospital complex, and Jack had to go see her. He walked like a man facing execution down a drab corridor of glazed institutional brick. He turned a corner and saw what room it had to be. A pair of state troopers were standing there. They watched him approach, and Jack watched their eyes for a sign that they knew all of this was his fault, that his wife and daughter had nearly died because he'd decided that there was nothing to worry about. Not once in his life had Jack experienced failure, and its bitter taste made him think that the whole world would hold him in the same contempt he felt for himself.

You're so fucking smart.

It seemed to his senses that he did not so much approach the door – it approached him, looming ever larger in his sight. Behind the door was the woman he loved. The woman who had nearly died because of his confidence in himself. What would she say to him? Did he dare to find out? Jack stood at the door for a moment. The troopers tried not to stare at him. Perhaps they felt sympathy, Jack thought, knowing that he didn't deserve it. The doorknob was cold, accusing metal in his hand as he entered the room.

Cathy was lying in her single-bed room. Her arm was in a cast. An enormous purple bruise covered the right side of her face and there was a bandage over half her forehead. Her eyes were open but almost lifeless, staring at a television that wasn't on. Jack moved towards her as though asleep. A nurse had set a chair alongside the bed. He sat in it, and took his wife's hand while he tried to think of something he could say to the wife he had failed. Her face turned towards his. Her eyes were blackened and full of tears.

'I'm sorry, Jack,' she whispered.

'What?'

'I knew she was fooling with the seat belt, but I didn't do anything because I was in a hurry – and then that truck came, and I didn't have time to – if I had made sure she was strapped in, Sally would be fine . . . but I was in a hurry,' she finished, and looked away. 'Jack, I'm so sorry.'

My God, she thinks it's her fault . . . what do I say now?

'She's going to be okay, babe,' Ryan managed to say, stunned at what he'd just heard. He held Cathy's hand to his face and kissed it. 'And so are you. That's the only thing that matters now.'

'But –' She stared at the far wall.

'No "buts."'

Her face turned back. Cathy tried to smile but tears were rolling from her eyes. 'I talked to Doctor Ellingstone at Hopkins – he came over and saw Sally. He says – he says she'll be okay. He says that Shapiro saved her life.'

'I know.'

'I haven't even seen her – I remember seeing the bridge and then I woke up two hours ago, and – oh, Jack!' Her hand closed on his like a claw. He leaned forward to kiss her, but before their lips touched, both started weeping.

'It's okay, Cathy,' Jack said, and he started to believe that it really was, or at least that it would be so again. His world had not ended, not quite.

But someone else's will, Ryan told himself. The thought was a quiet, distant one, voiced in a part of his mind that was already looking at the future while the present occupied his sight. Seeing his wife weeping tears caused by someone else started a cold rage in him which only that someone's death could ever warm.

The time for grief was already ending, carried away by his own tears. Though it had not yet happened, Ryan's intellect was already beginning to think of the time when his emotions would be at rest – most of them. One would remain. He would control it, but it would also control him. He would not feel like a whole man again until he was purged of it.

One can only weep for so long; it is as though each tear carries a finite amount of emotion away with it. Cathy stopped first. She used her hand to wipe her husband's face. She managed a real smile now. Jack hadn't shaved. It was like rubbing sandpaper.

'What time is it?'

'Ten-thirty.' Jack didn't have to check his watch.

'You need sleep, Jack,' she said. 'You have to stay healthy, too.'

'Yeah.' Jack rubbed his eyes.

'Hi, Cathy,' Robby said as he came through the door. 'I've come to take him away from you.'

'Good.'

'We're checked into the Holiday Inn over on Lombard Street.'

'We? Robby, you don't –'

'Stuff it, Jack,' Robby said. 'How are you, Cathy?'

'I have a headache you wouldn't believe.'

'Good to see you smile,' Robby said softly. 'Sissy'll be up after lunch. Is there anything she can get for you?'

'Not right now. Thanks, Rob.'

'Hang in there, Doc.' Robby took Jack's arm and hauled him to his feet. 'I'll have him back to you later today.'

Twenty minutes later Robby led Jack into their motel room. He pulled a pill container from his pocket. 'The doc said you should take one of these.'

'I don't take pills.'

'You're taking one of these, sport. It's a nice yellow one. That's not a request, Jack, it's an order. You need sleep. Here.' Robby tossed them over and stared until Jack swallowed one. Ryan was asleep in ten minutes. Jackson made certain that the door was secured before settling down on the other bed. The pilot dreamed of seeing the people who had done all this. They were in an airplane. Four times he fired a missile into their bird and watched their bodies spill out of the hole it made so that he could blast them with his cannon before they fell into the sea.

The Patriots Club was a bar across the street from Broadway Station in one of South Boston's Irish enclaves. Its name harked back not to the revolutionaries of the 1770s, but rather to the owner's image of himself. John Donoho had served in the First Marine Division on the bitter retreat from the Chosin Reservoir. Wounded twice, he'd never left his squad on the long, cold march to the port of Hungnam. He still walked with a slight limp from the four toes that frostbite had taken from his right foot. He was prouder of this than of his several decorations, framed under a Marine Corps standard behind the bar. Anyone who entered the bar in a Marine uniform always got his first drink free, along with a story or two about the Old Corps, which Corporal John Donoho, USMC (ret.), had served at the ripe age of eighteen.

He was also a professional Irishman. Every year he took an Aer Lingus flight from Boston's Logan International Airport to the old sod, to brush up on his roots and his accent, and sample the better varieties of whiskey that somehow were never exported to America in quantity. Donoho also tried to keep current on the happenings in the North, 'the Six Counties,' as he called them, to maintain his spiritual connection with the rebels who laboured courageously to free their people from the British yoke. Many a dollar had been raised in his bar, to aid those in the north, many a glass raised to their health and to the Cause.

'Hello, Johnny!' Paddy O'Neil called from the door.

'And good evening to you, Paddy!' Donoho was already drawing a beer when he saw his nephew follow O'Neil through the door. Eddie was his dead brother's only son, a good boy, educated at Notre Dame, where he'd played second string on the football team before joining up with the FBI. It wasn't quite as good as being a Marine, but Uncle John knew that it paid a lot better. He'd heard that Eddie was following O'Neil around, but was vaguely sad to see that it was true. Perhaps it was to protect Paddy from a Brit assassin, the owner rationalized.

John and Paddy had a beer together before the latter joined a small group waiting for him in the back room. His nephew stayed alone at the end of the bar, where he drank a cup of coffee and kept an eye on things. After ten minutes O'Neil went back to give his talk. Donoho went to say hello to his nephew.

'Hi, Uncle John,' Eddie greeted him.

'Have you set the date yet, now?' John asked, affecting an Irish accent, as he usually did when O'Neil was around.

'Maybe next September,' the younger man allowed.

'And what would your father say, you living with the girl for almost a year? And the good fathers at Notre Dame?'

'Probably the same thing they'd say to you for raising money for terrorists,' the young agent replied. Eddie was sick and tired of being told how to live his life.

'I don't want to hear any of that in my place.' He'd heard that line before, too.

'That's what O'Neil does, Uncle John.'

'They're freedom fighters. I know they bend some of our laws from time to time, but the English laws they break are no concern of mine – or yours,' John Donoho said firmly.

'You watch TV?' the agent didn't need an answer to that. A wide-screen TV in the opposite corner was used for baseball and football games. The bar's name had also made it an occasional watering hole for the New England Patriots football players. Uncle John's interest in TV was limited to the Patriots, Red Sox, Celtics, and Bruins. His interest in politics was virtually nil. He voted for Teddy Kennedy every six years and considered himself a staunch proponent of national defence. 'I want to show you a couple of pictures.'

He set the first one on the bar. 'This is a little girl named Sally Ryan. She lives in Annapolis.'

His uncle picked it up and smiled. 'I remember when my Kathleen looked like that.'

'Her father is a teacher at the Naval Academy, used to be a Marine lieutenant. He went to Boston College. His father was a cop.'

'Sounds like a good Irishman. Friend of yours?'

'Not exactly,' Eddie said. 'Paddy and I met him earlier today. This is what his daughter looked like then.' The second photo was laid on the bar.

'Jesus, Mary, and Joseph.' It wasn't easy to discern that there was a child under all the medical equipment. Her feet stuck out from heavy wrappings. An inch-wide plastic pipe was in her mouth, and what parts of her body were visible formed a horribly discoloured mass that the photographer had recorded with remarkable skill.

'She's the lucky one, Uncle John. The girl's mother was there too.' Two more photos went onto the bar.

'What happened, car accident – what are you showing me?' John Donoho asked. He really didn't know what this was all about.

'She's a surgeon – she's pregnant, too, the pictures don't show that. Her car was machine-gunned yesterday, right outside of Annapolis, Maryland. They killed a State Police officer a few minutes later.' Another picture went down.

'What? Who did it?' the older man asked.

'Here's the father, Jack Ryan.' It was the same picture that the London papers had used, Jack's graduation shot from Quantico. Eddie knew that his uncle always looked at Marine dress blues with pride.

'I've seen him before somewhere . . .'

'Yeah. He stopped a terrorist attack over in London a few months back. It looks like he offended the terrorists enough that they came after him and his family. The Bureau is working on that.'

'Who did it?'

The last photo went down on the bar. It showed Ryan's hands less than a foot from Paddy O'Neil, and a black man holding him back.

'Who's the jig?' John asked. His nephew almost lost his temper.

'Goddammit, Uncle John! That *man* is a Navy fighter pilot.'

'Oh.' John was briefly embarrassed. He had little use for blacks, though one who wore a Marine uniform into his bar got his first drink free, too. It was different with the ones in uniform, he told himself. Anyone who served the flag as he had done was okay in his book, John Donoho always said. *Some of my best friends in the Corps.* . . He remembered how Navy strike aircraft had supported his outfit all the way back to the sea, holding the Chinese back with rockets and napalm. Well, maybe this one was different, too. He stared at the rest of the picture for a few seconds. 'So, you say Paddy had something to do with this?'

'I've been telling you for years who the bastard fronts for. If you don't believe me, maybe you want to ask Mr Ryan here. It's bad enough that O'Neil spits on our whole country every time he comes over here. His friends damned near killed this whole family yesterday. We got one of 'em. Two Marine guards at the Naval Academy grabbed him, waiting to shoot Ryan. His name's Eamonn Clark, and we know that he used to work for the Provisional Wing of the IRA – we *know* it, Uncle John, he's a convicted murderer. They caught him with a loaded pistol in his pocket. You still think they're good guys? Dammit, they're going after Americans now! If you don't believe me, believe this!' Eddie Donoho rearranged the photos on the wooden surface. 'This little girl, and her mother, and a kid not even born yet almost died yesterday. This state trooper did. He left a wife and a kid behind. That friend of yours in the back room raises the money to buy the guns, he's connected with the people who did this.'

'But why?'

'Like I said, this girl's dad got in the way of a murder over in London. I guess the people he stopped wanted to get even with him – not just him, though, they went for his whole family,' the agent explained slowly.

'The little girl didn't –'

'Goddammit,' Eddie swore again. 'That's why they're called terrorists!' It was getting through. He could see that he was finally getting the message across.

'You're sure that Paddy is part of this?' his uncle asked.

'He's never lifted a gun that we know of. He's their mouthpiece, he comes over here and raises money so that they can do things like this at home. Oh, he never gets his hands bloody. He's too smart for that. But this is what the money goes for. We are absolutely sure of that. And now they're playing their games over here.' Agent Donoho knew that the money-raising was secondary to the psychological reasons for coming over, but now wasn't the time to clutter the issue with details. He watched his uncle stare at the photos of the little girl. His face showed the confusion that always accompanies a completely new thought.

'You're sure? Really sure?'

'Uncle John, we have over thirty agents on the case now, plus the local police. You bet we're sure. We'll get 'em, too. The Director's put the word out on this case. We want 'em. Whatever it takes, we'll get these bastards,' Edward Michael Donoho, Jr., said with cold determination.

John Donoho looked at his nephew, and for the first time he saw a man. Eddie's FBI post was a source of family pride, but John finally knew why this was so. He wasn't a kid anymore. He was a man with a job about which he was deadly serious. More than the photographs, it was this that decided things. John had to believe what he'd been told.

The owner of the Patriots Club stood up straight and walked down the bar to the folding gate. He lifted it and made for the back room, with his nephew trailing behind.

'But our boys are fighting back,' O'Neil was telling the fifteen men in the room. 'Every day they fight back to – joining us, Johnny?'

'Out,' Donoho said quietly.

'What – I don't understand, John,' O'Neil said, genuinely puzzled.

'You must think I'm pretty stupid. I guess maybe I was. Leave.' The voice was more forceful now, and the feigned accent was gone. 'Get out of my club and don't ever come back.'

'But, Johnny – what are you talking about?'

Donoho grabbed the man by his collar and lifted him off his chair. O'Neil's voice continued to protest as he was propelled all the way out the front door. Eddie Donoho waved to his uncle as he followed his charge out onto the street.

'What was that all about?' one of the men from the back room asked. Another of them, a reporter for the *Boston Globe*, started making notes as the bar owner stumbled through what he had finally learned.

To this point no police agency had implicated any terrorist group by name, and in fact neither had Special Agent Donoho done so. His instructions from Washington on that score had been carefully given and carefully followed. But in the translation through Uncle John and a reporter, the facts got slightly garbled – as surprised no one – and within hours the story was on the AP wire that the attack on Jack Ryan and his family had been made by the Provisional Wing of the Irish Republican Army.

Sean Miller's mission in America had been fully accomplished by an agency of the United States government.

Miller and his party were already back home. As many people in this line of work had done before, Sean reflected on the value of rapid international air travel. In this case it had been off to Mexico from Washington's Dulles International, from there to the Netherlands Antilles, to Schiphol International Airport on a KLM flight, and then to Ireland. All one needed were correct travel documents and a little money. The travel documents in question were already destroyed, and the money untraceable cash. He sat across from Kevin O'Donnell's desk, drinking water to compensate for the dehydration normal to flying.

'What about Eamonn?' One rule of ULA operations was that no overseas telephone calls ever came to his house.

'Alex's man says he was picked up.' Miller shrugged. 'It was a risk I felt worth taking. I selected Ned for it because he knows very little about us.' He knew that O'Donnell had to agree with that. Clark was one of the new men brought into the Organization, and more of an accident than a recruit. He'd come south because one of his friends from the H-blocks had come. O'Donnell had thought him of possible use, since they had no experienced work-alone assassins. But Clark was stupid. His motivations came from emotion rather than ideology. He was, in fact, a typical Provisional IRA thug, little different from those in the UVF for that matter, useful in the same sense that a trained dog was useful, Kevin told himself. He knew but a few names and faces within the Organization. Most damning of all, he had failed. Clark's one redeeming characteristic was his doglike loyalty. He hadn't broken in Long Kesh prison and he probably wouldn't break now. He lacked the imagination.

'Very well,' Kevin O'Donnell said after a moment's reflection. Clark would be remembered as a martyr, gaining greater respect in failure than he had managed to earn in success. 'The rest?'

'Perfect. I saw the wife and child die, and Alex's people got us away cleanly.' Miller smiled and poured some whiskey to follow his litre of ice water.

'They're not dead, Sean,' O'Donnell said.

'What?' Miller had been on an airplane less than three hours after the shooting, and hadn't seen or heard a snippet of news since. He listened to his boss's explanation in incredulous silence.

'But it doesn't matter,' O'Donnell concluded. He explained that, too. The AP story that had originated in the *Boston Globe* had been picked up by the *Irish Times* of Dublin. 'It was a good plan after all, Sean. Despite everything that went wrong, the mission is accomplished.'

Sean didn't allow himself to react. Two operations in a row had gone wrong for him. Before the fiasco in London, he'd never failed at all. He'd written that off to random chance, pure luck, nothing more. He didn't even think of that in this case. Two in a row, that wasn't luck. He knew that Kevin would not tolerate a third failure. The young operations officer took a deep breath and told himself to be objective. He'd allowed himself to think of Ryan as a personal target, not a political one. That had been his first mistake. Though Kevin hadn't said it, losing Ned had been a serious mistake. Miller reviewed his plan, rethinking every aspect of the operation. Just going after the wife and child would have been simple thuggery, and he'd never approved of that; it was not professional. Just going after Ryan himself, however, would not have carried the same political impact, which was the whole point of the operation. The rest of the family was – had been – necessary. So his objectives had been sound enough, but . . .

'I should have taken more time on this one,' he said finally. 'I tried to be too dramatic. Perhaps we should have waited.'

'Yes,' his boss agreed, pleased that Sean saw his errors.

'Any help we can give you,' Owens said, 'is yours. You know that, Dan.'

'Yeah, well, this has attracted some high-level interest.' Murray held a cable from Director Emil Jacobs himself. 'Well, it was only a matter of time. It had to happen sooner or later.' *And if we don't bag these sons of bitches,* he thought, *it'll happen again. The ULA just proved that terrorists could operate in the US.* The emotional shock of the event had come as a surprise to Murray. As a professional in the field, he knew that it was mere luck that it hadn't happened already. The inept domestic terrorist groups had set off some bombs and murdered a few people, but the Bureau had experienced considerable success running them to ground. None of them had ever got much in the way of foreign support. But that had changed, too. The helicopter pilot had identified one of the escaping terrorists as black, and there weren't many of them in Ireland.

It was a new ball game, and for all his experience in the FBI, Murray was worried about how well the Bureau would be able to handle it. Director Jacobs was right on one thing: this was a top-priority mission. Bill Shaw would run the case personally, and Murray knew him to be one of the best intellects in the business. The thirty agents initially assigned to the case would treble in the next few days, to demonstrate that America was too dangerous a place for terrorists. In his heart, Murray knew that this was impossible. No place was too dangerous, certainly no democracy.

But the Bureau did have formidable resources, and it wouldn't be the only agency involved.

17

Recriminations and Decisions

Ryan awoke to find Robby waving a cup of coffee under his nose. Jack had managed to sleep without dreams this time, and the oblivion of undisturbed slumber had worked wonders on him.

'Sissy was over the hospital earlier. She says Cathy looks all right, considering. It's all set up so you can get in to see Sally. She'll be asleep, but you can see her.'

'Where is she?'

'Sissy? She's out runnin' some errands.'

'I need a shave.'

'Me, too. She's getting what we need. First I'm gonna get some food in ya,' Robby said.

'I owe you, man,' Jack said as he stood.

'Give it a rest, Jack. That's what the Lord put us here for, like my pappy says. Now, eat!' Robby commanded.

Jack realized that he'd not eaten anything for a long time, and once his stomach reminded itself of this, it cried out for nourishment. Within five minutes he'd disposed of two eggs, bacon, hash-browns, four slices of toast, and two cups of coffee.

'Shame they don't have grits here,' Robby observed. A knock came to the door. The pilot answered it. Sissy breezed in with a shopping bag in one hand and Jack's briefcase in the other.

'You better freshen up, Jack,' she said. 'Cathy looks better than you do.'

'Nothing unusual about that,' Jack replied – cheerfully, he realized with surprise. Sissy had baited him into it.

'Robby?'

'Yeah?'

'What the hell are grits?'

'YOU don't want to know,' Cecilia Jackson answered.

'I'll take your word for it.' Jack walked into the bathroom and started the shower. By the time he got out, Robby had shaved, leaving the razor and cream on the sink. Jack scraped his beard away and patched the bloody spots with toilet paper. A new toothbrush was sitting there too, and Ryan emerged from the room looking and feeling like a human being.

'Thanks, guys,' he said.

'I'll take you home tonight,' Robby said. 'I have to teach class tomorrow. You don't. I fixed it with the department.'

'Okay.'

Sissy left for home. Jack and Robby walked over to the hospital. Visiting hours were under way and they were able to walk right up to Cathy's room.

'Well, if it isn't our hero!' Joe Muller was Cathy's father. He was a short, swarthy man – Cathy's hair and complexion came from her mother, now dead. A senior VP with Merrill Lynch, he was a product of the Ivy League, and had started in the brokerage business much as Ryan had, though his brief stint in the military had been two years of drafted service in the Army that he'd long since put behind him. He'd once had big plans for Jack and had never forgiven him for leaving the business. Muller was a passionate man who was also well aware of his importance in the financial community. He and Jack hadn't exchanged a civil word in over three years. It didn't look to Jack as though that was going to change.

'Daddy,' Cathy said, 'we don't need that.'

'Hi, Joe.' Ryan held out his hand. It hung there for five seconds, all by itself. Robby excused himself out the door, and Jack went to kiss his wife. 'Lookin' better, babe.'

'What do you have to say for yourself?' Muller demanded .

'The guy who wanted to kill me was arrested yesterday. The FBI has him,'

Jack said carefully. He amazed himself by saying it so calmly. Somehow it seemed a trivial matter compared with his wife and daughter.

'This is all your fault, you know.' Muller had been rehearsing this for hours.

'I know,' Jack conceded the point. He wondered how much more he could back up.

'Daddy –' Cathy started to say.

'You keep out of this,' Muller said to his daughter, a little too sharply for Jack.

'You can say anything you want to me, but don't snap at her,' he warned.

'Oh, you want to protect her, eh? So where the hell were you yesterday!'

'I was in my office, just like you were.'

'You had to stick your nose in where it didn't belong, didn't you? You had to play hero – and you damned near got your family killed,' Muller went on through his lines.

'Look, Mr Muller.' Jack had told himself all these things before. He could accept the punishment from himself. But not from his father-in-law. 'Unless you know of a company on the exchange that makes a time machine, we can't very well change that, can we? All we can do now is help the authorities find the people who did this.'

'Why didn't you think about all this before, dammit!'

'Daddy, that's enough!' Cathy rejoined the conversation.

'Shut up – this is between us!'

'If you yell at her again, mister, you'll regret it.' Jack needed a release. He hadn't protected his family the previous day, but he could now.

'Calm down, Jack.' His wife didn't know that she was making things worse, but Jack took the cue after a moment. Muller didn't.

'You're a real big guy now, aren't you?'

Keep going, Joe, and you might find out. Jack looked over to his wife and took a deep breath. 'Look, if you came down here to yell at me, that's fine, we can do that by ourselves, okay? – but that's your daughter over there, and maybe she needs you, too.' He turned to Cathy. 'I'll be outside if you need me.'

Ryan left the room. There were still two very serious state troopers at the door, and another at the nurses' station down the hall. Jack reminded himself that a trooper had been killed, and that Cathy was the only thing they had that was close to being a witness. She was safe, finally. Robby waved to his friend from down the hall.

'Settle down, boy,' the pilot suggested.

'He has a real talent for pissing me off,' Jack said after another deep breath.

'I know he's an asshole, but he almost lost his kid. Try to remember that. Taking it out on him doesn't help things.'

'It might,' Jack said with a smile, thinking about it. 'What are you, a philosopher?'

'I'm a PK, Jack. Preacher's Kid. You can't imagine the stuff I used to hear from the parlour when people came over to talk with the old man. He isn't so much mad at you as scared by what almost happened,' Robby said.

'So am I, pal.' Ryan looked down the hall.

'But you've had more time to deal with it.'

'Yeah.' Jack was quiet for a moment. 'I still don't like the son of a bitch.'

'He gave you Cathy, man. That's something.'

'Are you sure you're in the right line of work? How come you're not a chaplain?'

'I am the voice of reason in a chaotic world. You don't accomplish as much when you're pissed off. That's why we train people to be professionals. If you want to get the job done, emotions don't help. You've already gotten even with the man, right?'

'Yeah. If he'd had his way, I'd be living up in Westchester County, taking the train in every day, and – crap!' Jack shook his head. 'He still makes me mad.'

Muller came out of the room just then. He looked around for a moment, spotted Jack, and walked down. 'Stay close,' Ryan told his friend.

'You almost killed my little girl.' Joe's mood hadn't improved.

Jack didn't reply. He'd told himself that about a hundred times, and was just starting to consider the possibility that he was a victim, too.

'You ain't thinking right, Mr Muller,' Robby said.

'Who the hell are you!'

'A friend,' Robby replied. He and Joe were about the same height, but the pilot was twenty years younger. The look he gave the broker communicated this rather clearly. The voice of reason didn't like being yelled at. Joe Muller had a talent for irritating people. On Wall Street he could get away with it, and he assumed that meant that he could do it anywhere he liked. He was a man who had not learned the limitations of his power.

'We can't change what has happened,' Jack offered. 'We can work to see that it doesn't happen again.'

'If you'd done what I wanted, this never would have happened!'

'If I'd done what *you* wanted, I'd be working with you every day, moving money from Column A to Column B and pretending it was important, like all the other Wall Street wimps – and hating it, and turning into another miserable bastard in the financial world. I proved that I could do that as well as you, but I made my pile, and so now I do something I like. At least we're trying to make the world a better place instead of trying to take it over with leveraged buyouts. It's not my fault that you don't understand that. Cathy and I are doing what we like to do.'

'Something you *like*,' Muller snapped, rejecting the concept that making money wasn't something to be enjoyed in and of itself. 'Make the world a better place, eh?'

'Yeah, because I'm going to help catch the bastards who did this.'

'And how is a punk history teacher going to do that!'

Ryan gave his father-in-law his best smile. 'That's something I can't tell you, Joe.'

The stockbroker swore and stalked away. *So much for reconciliation*, Jack told himself. He wished it had gone otherwise. His estrangement with Joe Muller was occasionally hard on Cathy.

'Back to the Agency, Jack?' Robby asked.

'Yeah.'

Ryan spent twenty minutes with his wife, long enough to learn what she'd told the police and to make sure that she really was feeling better. She was dozing off when he left. Next he went across the street to the Shock-Trauma Centre.

Getting into scrubs reminded him of the only other time he'd done so, the night Sally was born. A nurse took him into the Critical Care Recovery Unit, and he saw his little girl for the first time in thirty-six hours, a day and a half that had stretched into an eternity. It was a thoroughly ghastly experience. Had he not been told positively that her survival chances were good, he might have broken down on the spot. The bruised little shape was unconscious from the combination of drugs and injuries. He watched and listened as the respirator breathed for her. She was being fed from bottles and tubes that ran into her veins. A doctor explained that her condition looked far worse than it was. Sally's liver was functioning well, under the circumstances. In two or three more days the broken legs would be set.

'Is she going to be crippled?' Jack asked quietly.

'No, there's no reason to worry about that. Kids' bones – what we say is, if the broken pieces are in the same room, they'll heal. It looks far worse than it is. The trick with cases like this is getting them through the first hour – in her case, the first twelve or so. Once we get kids through the initial crisis, once we get the system working again, they heal fast. You'll have her home in a month. In two months, she'll be running around like it never happened. As crazy as that sounds, it's true. Nothing heals like a kid. She's a very sick little girl right now, but she's going to get well. Hey, I was here when she arrived.'

'What's your name?'

'Rich Kinter. Barry Shapiro and I did most of the surgery. It was close – God, it was so close! But we won. Okay? We won. You will be taking her home.'

'Thanks – that doesn't cover it, Doc.' Jack stumbled over a few more words, not knowing what to say to the people who had saved his daughter's life.

Kinter shook his head. 'Bring her back sometime and we're even. We have a party for ex-patients every few months. Mr Ryan, there is nothing you can do that comes close to what we all feel when we see our little patients come back – walk back. That's why we're here, man, to make sure they come back for cake and juice. Just let us bounce her on our knees after she's better.'

'Deal.' Ryan wondered how many people were alive because of the people in this room. He was certain that this surgeon could be a rich man in private practice. Jack understood him, understood why he was here, and knew that his father-in-law wouldn't. He sat for a few minutes at Sally's side, listening to the machine breathe for her through the plastic tube. The nurse-practitioner overseeing the case smiled at him around her mask. He kissed Sally's bruised forehead before leaving. Jack felt better now, better about almost everything. But one item remained. The people who had done this to his little girl.

'It had wheelchair tags,' the clerk in the 7-Eleven was saying, 'but the dude who drove it didn't look crippled or anything.'

'You remember what he looked like?' Special Agent Nick Capitano and a major from the Maryland State Police were interviewing the witness.

'Yeah, he was 'bout as black as me. Tall dude. He wore sunglasses, the mirror kind. Had a beard, too. There was always at least one other dude in the truck, but I never got a look at him – black man, that's all I can say.'

'What did he wear?'

'Jeans and a brown leather jacket, I think. You know, like a construction worker.'

'Shoes or boots?' the major asked.

'Never did see that,' the clerk said after a moment.

'How about jewellery, T-shirt with a pattern, anything special or different about him?'

'No, nothin' I remember.'

'What did he do here?'

'He always bought a six-pack of Coke Classic. Once or twice he got some Twinkies, but he always got hisself the Cokes.'

'What did he sound like? Anything special?'

The clerk shook her head. 'Nah, just a dude, y'know?'

'Do you think you could recognize him again?' Capitano asked.

'Maybe – we get a lot of folks through here, lotta regulars, lotta strangers, y'know?'

'Would you mind looking through some pictures?' the agent went on.

'Gotta clear it with the boss. I mean, I need the job, but you say this chump tried to kill a little girl – yeah, sure, I'll help ya.'

'We'll clear it with the boss,' the Major assured her. 'You won't lose pay over it.'

'Gloves,' she said, looking up. 'Forgot to say that. He wore work gloves. Leather ones, I think.' *Gloves*, both men wrote in their notebooks.

'Thank you, ma'am. We'll call you tonight. A car will pick you up tomorrow morning so you can look at some pictures for us,' the FBI agent said.

'Pick me up?' The clerk was surprised.

'You bet.' Manpower was not a factor on this case. The agent who picked her up would pick her brain again on the drive into D.C. The two investigators left. The Major drove his unmarked State Police car.

Capitano checked his notes. This wasn't bad for a first interview. He, the Major, and fifteen others had spent the day interviewing people in stores and shops up and down five miles of Ritchie Highway. Four people thought they remembered the van, but this was the first person who had seen one of its occupants closely enough for a description. It wasn't much, but it was a start. They already had the shooter ID'd. Cathy Ryan had recognized Sean Miller's face – thought she did, the agent corrected himself. If it had been Miller, he had a beard now, on the brown side of black and neatly trimmed. An artist would try to recreate that.

Twenty more agents and detectives had spent their day at the three local airports, showing photos to every ticket agent and gate clerk. They'd come up blank, but they hadn't had a description of Miller then. Tomorrow they would try again. A computer check was being made of international flights that connected to flights to Ireland, and domestic flights that connected to international ones. Capitano was happy that he didn't have to run all of those down. It would take weeks, and the chance of getting an ID from an airport worker diminished measurably every hour.

The van had been identified for more than a day, off the FBI's computer. It had been stolen a month before in New York City, repainted – professionally, by the look of it – and given new tags. Several sets of them, since the handicap tags found on it yesterday had been stolen less than two days before from a nursing home's van in Hagerstown, Maryland, a hundred miles away. Everything about the crime said it was a professional job from start to finish. Switching cars at the shopping centre had been a brilliant finale to a perfectly planned and executed operation. Capitano and the Major were able to restrain their admiration, but they had to make an objective assessment of the people they were after. These weren't common thugs. They were professionals in every perverted sense of the word.

'You suppose they got the van themselves?' Capitano asked the Major.

The State Police investigator grunted. 'There's some outfit in Pennsylvania that steals them from all over the Northeast, paints them, reworks the interior, and sells 'em. You guys are looking for them, remember?'

'I've heard a few things about the investigation, but that's not my territory. It's being looked at. Personally, I think they did it themselves. Why risk a connection with somebody else?'

'Yeah,' the Major agreed reluctantly. The van had already been checked out by state and federal forensic experts. Not a single fingerprint had been found. The vehicle had been thoroughly cleaned, down to the knobs on the window handles. The technicians found nothing that could lead them to the criminals. Now the dirt and fabric fibres vacuumed from the van's carpet were being analysed in Washington, but this was the sort of clue that worked reliably only on TV. If the people had been smart enough to clean out the van, they were almost certainly smart enough to burn the clothing they'd worn. Everything was being checked out anyway, because even the smartest people did make mistakes.

'You heard anything on the ballistics yet?' the Major asked, turning the car onto Rowe Boulevard.

'Oughta be waiting for us.' They'd found almost twenty nine-millimetre cartridge cases to go along with the two usable bullets recovered from the Porsche, and the one that had gone through Trooper Fontana's chest and lodged in the back seat of his wrecked car. These had gone directly to the FBI laboratory in Washington for analysis. The evidence would tell them that the weapon was a sub-machine gun, which they already knew, but might give them a type, which they didn't yet know. The cartridge cases were Belgian-made, from the Fabrique Nationale at Liège. They might be able to identify the lot number, but FN made so many millions such rounds per year, which were shipped and reshipped all over the world, that the lead was a slim one. Very often such shipments simply disappeared, mainly from sloppy – or creative – bookkeeping.

'How many black groups are known to have contact with these ULA characters?'

'None,' Capitano replied. 'That's something we are going to have to establish.'

'Great.'

Ryan arrived home to find an unmarked car and a liveried State Police cruiser in his driveway. Jack's own FBI interview wasn't a long one. It hadn't taken long to confirm the fact that he quite simply knew nothing about the attempt on his family or himself.

'Any idea where they are?' he asked finally.

'We're checking airports,' the agent answered. 'If these guys are as smart as they look, they're long gone.'

'They're smart, all right,' Ryan noted sourly. 'What about the one you caught?'

'He's doing one hell of a good imitation of a clam. He has a lawyer now, of course, and the lawyer is telling him to keep his mouth shut. You can depend on lawyers for that.'

'Where'd the lawyer come from?'

'Public defender's office. It's a rule, remember. You hold a suspect for any length of time, he has to have a lawyer. I don't think it matters. He probably isn't talking to the lawyer either. We have him on a state weapons violation and federal immigration laws. He goes back to the UK as soon as the paperwork gets done . Maybe two weeks or so, depending on if the attorney contests things.' The agent closed his notebook. 'You never know, maybe he'll start talking, but don't count on it. The word we get from the Brits is that he's not real bright anyway. He's the Irish version of a street hood, very good with weapons but a little slow upstairs.'

'So if he's dumb, how come –'

'How come he's good at what he does? How smart do you have to be to kill somebody? Clark's a sociopathic personality. He has very little in the way of feelings. Some people are like that. They don't relate to the people around them as being real people. They see them as objects, and since they're only objects, whatever happens to them is not important. Once I met a hit man who killed four people – just the ones we know about – and didn't bat an eye, far as I could tell; but he cried like a baby when we told him his cat died. People like that don't even understand why they get sent to prison; they really don't understand,' he concluded. 'Those are the scary ones.'

'No,' Ryan said. 'The scary ones are the ones with brains, the ones who believe in it.'

'I haven't met one of those yet,' he admitted.

'I have.' Jack walked him to the door and watched him pull away. The house was an empty, quiet place without Sally running around, without the TV on, without Cathy talking about her friends at Hopkins. For several minutes Jack wandered around aimlessly, as though expecting to find someone. He didn't want to sit down, because that would somehow be an admission that he was all alone. He walked into the kitchen and started to fix a drink, but before he was finished, he dumped it all down the sink. He didn't want to get drunk. It was better to keep his mind unimpaired. Finally he lifted the phone and dialled.

'Yes,' a voice answered.

'Admiral, Jack Ryan.'

'I understand that your girl's going to be all right,' James Greer said. 'I'm glad to hear that, son.'

'Thank you, sir. Is the Agency involved in this?'

'This is an unsecure line, Jack,' the Admiral replied.

'I want in,' Ryan said.

'Be here tomorrow morning.'

Ryan hung up and went looking for his briefcase. He opened it and took out the Browning automatic pistol. After setting it on the kitchen table, he got out his shotgun and cleaning kit. He spent the next hour cleaning and oiling first the pistol, then the shotgun. When he was satisfied, he loaded both.

He left for Langley at five the next morning. Ryan had managed to get four more hours of sleep before rising and going through the usual morning ritual of coffee and breakfast. His early departure allowed him to miss the worst of the traffic, though the George Washington Parkway was never really free of the government workers heading to and from the agencies that were always more or less awake. After getting into the CIA building, he reflected that he had never called here and found Admiral Greer absent. *Well*, he told himself, *that's one thing in this world that I can depend on.* A security officer escorted him to the seventh floor.

'Good morning, sir,' Jack said on entering the room.

'You look better than I expected,' the DDI observed.

'It's an illusion mostly, but I can't solve my problem by hiding in a corner, can I? Can we talk about what's going on?'

'Your Irish friends have gotten a lot of attention. The President himself wants action on this. We've never had international terrorists play games in our country – at least, not things that ever made the press,' Greer said cryptically. 'It is now a high-priority case. It's getting a lot of resources.'

'I want to be one of them,' Ryan said simply.

If you think that you can be part of an operation –'

'I know better than that, Admiral.'

Greer smiled at the younger man . 'That's good to see, son. I thought you were smart. So what do you want to do for us?'

'We both know that the bad guys are part of the network. The data you let me look at was pretty limited. Obviously you're going to be trying to collate data on all the groups, searching for leads on the ULA. Maybe I can help.'

'What about your teaching?'

'I can be here when I'm not teaching. There isn't much to hold me at home at the moment, sir.'

'It isn't good practice to use people who are personally involved in the investigation,' Greer pointed out.

'This isn't the FBI, sir. I'm not going out into the field. You just told me that. I know you want me back here on a permanent basis, Admiral. If you really want me, let me start off doing something that's important to both of us.' Jack paused, searching for another point. 'If I'm good enough, let's find out now.'

'Some people aren't going to like it.'

'There's things happening to me that I don't like very much, sir, and I have to live with it. If I can't fight back somehow, I might as well stay at home. You're the only chance I have to do something to protect my family, sir.'

Greer turned to refill his coffee cup from the drip machine behind his desk. He'd liked Jack almost from the first moment he'd met him. This was a young man accustomed to having his way, though he was not arrogant about it. That was a point in his favour: Ryan knew what he wanted, but wasn't overly pushy. He wasn't a person driven by ambition, another point in his favour. Finally, he had a lot of raw talent to be shaped and trained and directed. Greer was always looking for talent. The Admiral turned back.

'Okay, you're on the team. Marty's coordinating the information. You'll work directly with him. I hope you don't talk in your sleep, son, because you're going to see stuff that you're not even allowed to dream about.'

'Sir, there's only one thing that I'm going to dream about.'

It had been a very busy month for Dennis Cooley. The death of an earl in East Anglia had forced his heirs to sell off a massive collection of books to pay the death duties, and Cooley had used up nearly all of his available capital to secure no less than twenty-one items for his shop. But it was worth it: among them was a rare first-folio of Marlowe's plays. Better still, the dead earl had been assiduous in protecting his treasures. The books had been deep-frozen several times to kill off the insects that desecrated these priceless relics of the past. The Marlowe was in remarkably good shape, despite the waterstained cover that had put off a number of less perceptive buyers. Cooley was stooped over his desk, reading the first act of *The Jew of Malta*, when the bell rang.

'Is that the one I heard about?' his visitor asked at once.

'Indeed.' Cooley smiled to cover his surprise. He hadn't seen this particular visitor for some time, and was somewhat disturbed that he'd come back so soon. 'Printed in 1633, forty years after Marlowe's death. Some parts of the text are suspect, of course, but this is one of the few surviving copies of the first printed edition.'

'It's quite authentic?'

'Of course,' Cooley replied, slightly put off at the question. 'In addition to my own humble expertise, it has authentication papers from Sir Edmund Grey of the British Museum.'

'One cannot argue with that,' the customer agreed.

'I'm afraid I have not yet decided upon a price for it.' *Why are you here?*

'Price is not an object. I understand that you may wish to enjoy it for yourself, but I must have it.' This told Cooley why he was here. He leaned to look over Cooley's shoulder at the book. 'Magnificent,' he said, placing a small envelope in the book dealer's pocket.

'Perhaps we can work something out,' Cooley allowed. 'In a few weeks, perhaps.' He looked out the window. A man was window-shopping at the jewellery store on the opposite side of the arcade. After a moment he straightened up and walked away.

'Sooner than that, please,' the man insisted.

Cooley sighed. 'Come and see me next week and we may be able to discuss it. I do have other customers, you know.'

'But none more important, I hope.'

Cooley blinked twice. 'Very well.'

Geoffrey Watkins continued to browse the shop for another few minutes. He selected a Keats that had also come from the dead earl's estate and paid six hundred pounds for it before leaving. On leaving the arcade he failed to notice a young lady at the news-stand outside and could not have known that another was waiting at the arcade's other end. The one who followed him was dressed in a manner guaranteed to garner attention, including orange hair that would have fluoresced if the sun had been out. She followed him west for two blocks and kept going in that direction when he crossed the street. Another police officer was on the walk down Green Park.

That night the daily surveillance reports came to Scotland Yard where, as always, they were put on computer. The operation being run was a joint venture between the Metropolitan Police and the Security Service, once known as MI-5. Unlike the American FBI, the people at 'Five' did not have the authority to arrest suspects, and had to work through the police to bring a case to a conclusion. The marriage was not entirely a happy one. It meant that James Owens had to work closely with David Ashley. Owens entirely concurred with his FBI colleague's assessment of the younger man: 'a snotty bastard.'

'Patterns, patterns, patterns,' Ashley said, sipping his tea while he looked at the print-out. They had identified a total of thirty-nine people who knew, or might have known, information common to the ambush on The Mall and Miller's transport to the Isle of Wight. One of them had leaked the information. Every one of them was being watched. Thus far they had discovered a closet homosexual, two men and one woman who were having affairs not of state, and a man who got considerable enjoyment watching pornographic movies in the Soho cinemas. Financial records got from Inland Revenue showed nothing particularly interesting, nor did living habits. There was the usual spread of hobbies, taste in theatrical plays and television shows. Several of the people had wide collections of friends. A few had none at all. The investigations were grateful for these sad, lonely people – many of the other people's friends had to be checked out, too, and this took time and manpower. Owens viewed the entire operation as something necessary but rather distasteful. It was the police equivalent of peering through windows. The tapes of telephone conversations – especially those between lovers – made him squirm on occasion. Owens was a man who appreciated the individual's need for privacy. No one's life could survive this sort of scrutiny. He told himself that one person's life wouldn't, and that was the point of the exercise.

'I see Mr Watkins visited a rare bookshop this afternoon,' Owens noted, reading over his own print-out.

'Yes. He collects them. So do I,' Ashley said. 'I've been in that shop once or twice myself. There was an estate sale recently. Perhaps Cooley bought a few things that Geoffrey wants for himself.' The security officer made a mental note to look at the shop for himself. 'He was in there for ten minutes, spoke with Dennis –'

'You know him?' Owens looked up.

'One of the best men in the trade,' Ashley said. He smiled at his own choice of words: *the trade*. 'I bought a Brontë there for my wife, for Christmas two years ago, I think. He's a fat little poof, but he's quite knowledgeable. So Geoffrey spoke with him for about ten minutes, made a purchase, and left. I wonder what he bought.' Ashley rubbed his eyes. He'd been on a strict regime of fourteen-hour days for longer than he cared to remember.

'The first new person Watkins has seen in several weeks,' Owens noted. He thought about it for a moment. There were better leads than this to follow up on, and his manpower was limited.

'So can we deal on this immigration question?' the public defender asked.

'Not a chance,' Bill Shaw said from the other side of the table. *You think we're going to give him political asylum?*

'You're not offering us a thing,' the lawyer observed. 'I bet I can beat the weapons charge, and there's no way you can make the conspiracy stick.'

'That's fine, counsellor. If it will make you any happier we'll cut him loose and give him a plane ticket, and even an escort, home.'

'To a maximum-security prison.' The public defender closed his file folder on the case of Eamonn Clark. 'You're not giving me anything to deal with.'

'If he cops to the gun charge and conspiracy, and if he helps us, he gets to spend a few years in a much nicer prison. But if you think we're going to let a convicted murderer just walk, mister, you are kidding yourself. What do you think you have to deal with?'

'You might be surprised,' the attorney said cryptically.

'Oh, yeah? I'm willing to bet that he hasn't said anything to you either,' the agent challenged the young attorney, and watched closely for his reaction. Bill Shaw, too, had passed the bar exam, though he devoted his legal expertise to the safety of society rather than the freedom of criminals.

'Conversations between attorney and client are privileged.' The lawyer had been practicing for exactly two and a half years. His understanding of his job was limited largely to keeping the police away from his charges. At first he'd been gratified that Clark hadn't said much of anything to the police and FBI, but he was surprised that Clark wouldn't even talk to him. After all, maybe he could cut a deal, despite what this FBI fellow said. But he had nothing to deal with, as Shaw had just told him. He waited a few moments for a reaction from the agent and got nothing but a blank stare. The public defender admitted defeat to himself. Well, there hadn't been much of a chance on this.

'That's what I thought.' Shaw stood. 'Tell your client that unless he opens up by the day after tomorrow, he's flying home to finish out a life sentence. Make sure you tell him that. If he wants to talk after he gets back, we'll send people to him. They say the beer's pretty good over there, and I wouldn't

618

mind flying over myself to find out.' The only thing the Bureau could use over Clark was fear. The mission he'd been part of had hurt the Provos, and young, dumb Ned might not like the reception he got. He'd be safer in a US penitentiary than he would be in a British one, but Shaw doubted that he understood this, or that he'd crack in any case. Maybe after he got back, something might be arranged.

The case was not going well; not that he'd expected otherwise. This sort of thing either cracked open immediately, or took months – or years. The people they were after were too clever to have left an immediate opening to be exploited. What remained to him and his men was the day-by-day grind. But that was the textbook definition of investigative police work. Shaw knew this well enough: he had written one of the standard texts.

18

Lights

Ashley entered the bookshop at four in the afternoon. A true bibliophile, he paused on opening the door to appreciate the aroma.

'Is Mr Cooley in today?' he asked the clerk.

'No, sir,' Beatrix replied. 'He's abroad on business. May I help you?'

'Yes. I understand that you've made some new acquisitions.'

'Ah, yes. Have you heard about the Marlowe first folio?' Beatrix looked remarkably like a mouse. Her hair was exactly the proper drab shade of brown and ill-kept. Her face was puffy, whether from too much food or too much drink, Ashley couldn't say. Her eyes were hidden behind thick glasses. She dressed in a way that fitted the store exactly – everything she had on was old and out of date. Ashley remembered buying his wife the Brontë here, and wondered if those three sad, lonely sisters had looked like this girl. It was too bad, really. With a little effort she might actually have been attractive.

'A Marlowe?' the man from 'Five' asked. 'First folio, you said?'

'Yes, sir, from the collection of the late Earl of Crundale. As you know, Marlowe's plays were not actually printed until forty years after his death.' She went on, displaying something that her appearance didn't begin to hint at. Ashley listened with respect. The mouse knew her business as well as an Oxford don.

'How do you find such things?' Ashley asked when she'd finished her discourse.

She smiled. 'Mr Dennis can smell them. He is always travelling, working with other dealers and lawyers and such. He's in Ireland today, for example. It's amazing how many books he manages to obtain over there. Those horrid people have the most marvellous collections.' Beatrix did not approve of the Irish.

'Indeed,' David Ashley observed. He didn't react to this bit of news at all. At least not physically, but a switch in the back of his head flipped on. 'Well, that is one of the contributions our friends across the water have made. A few rather good writers, and whiskey.'

'And bombers,' Beatrix observed. 'I shouldn't want to travel there so much myself.'

'Oh, I take my holiday there quite often. The fishing is marvellous.'

'That's what Lord Louis Mountbatten thought,' the clerk observed.

'How often does Dennis go over?'

'At least once a month.'

'Well, on this Marlowe you have – may I see it?' Ashley asked with an enthusiasm that was only partially feigned.

'By all means.' The girl took the volume from a shelf and opened it with great care. 'As you see, though the cover is in poor condition, the pages are in a remarkable state of preservation.'

Ashley hovered over the book, his eyes running down the opened page. 'Indeed they are. How much for this one?'

'Mr Dennis hasn't set a price yet. I believe another customer is already very interested in it, however.'

'Do you know who that is?'

'No, sir, I don't, and I wouldn't be able to reveal his name in any case. We respect our customers' confidentiality,' Beatrix said primly.

'Quite so. That is entirely proper,' Ashley agreed. 'So when will Mr Cooley be back? I want to talk to him about this myself.'

'He'll be back tomorrow afternoon.'

'Will you be here also?' Ashley asked with a charming smile.

'No, I'll be at my other job.'

'Too bad. Well, thank you very much for showing me this.' Ashley made for the door.

'My pleasure, sir.'

The security officer walked out of the arcade and turned right. He waited for the afternoon traffic to clear before crossing the street. He decided to walk back to Scotland Yard instead of taking a cab, and went downhill along St James's Street, turning left to go around the Palace to the east, then down Marlborough Road to The Mall.

It happened right there, he thought. *The getaway car turned here to make its escape. The ambush was a mere hundred yards west of where I'm standing now.* He stood and looked for a few seconds, remembering.

The personality of a security officer is much the same all over the world. They do not believe in coincidences, though they do believe in accidents. They lack any semblance of a sense of humour where their work is concerned. This comes from the knowledge that only the most trusted of people have the ability to be traitors; before betraying their countries, they must first betray the people who trust them. Beneath all his charm, Ashley was a man who hated traitors beyond all things, who suspected everyone and trusted no one.

Ten minutes later Ashley got past the security checkpoint at Scotland Yard and took the elevator to James Owens' office.

'That Cooley chap,' he said.

'Cooley?' Owens was puzzled for a moment. 'Oh, the book dealer Watkins visited yesterday. Is that where you were?'

'A fine little shop. Its owner is in Ireland today,' Ashley said deadpan.

Commander Owens nodded thoughtfully at that. What had been unimportant changed with a word. Ashley outlined what he had learned over several minutes. It wasn't even a real lead yet, but it was something to be looked at. Neither man said anything about how significant it might be – there had been many such things to run down, all of which to date had ended at blank walls. Many of the walls had also been checked out in every possible detail. The investigation wasn't at a standstill. People were still out on the street, accumulating information – none of which was the least useful to the case. This was something new to be looked at, nothing more than that; but for the moment that was enough.

It was eleven in the morning at Langley. Ryan was not admitted to the meetings between CIA and FBI people coordinating information on the case. Marty Cantor had explained to him that the FBI might be uneasy to have him there. Jack didn't mind. He'd get the information summaries after lunch, and that was enough for the moment. Cantor would come away both with the information FBI had developed, plus the thoughts and ideas of the chief investigators. Ryan didn't want that. He preferred to look at the raw data. His unprejudiced outsider's perspective had worked before and it might work again, he thought – hoped.

The wonderful world of the international terrorist, Murray had said to him outside the Old Bailey. It wasn't very wonderful, Jack thought, but it was a fairly complete world, including all of what the Greeks and Romans thought the civilized world was. He was going over satellite reconnaissance data at the moment. The bound report he was looking at contained no less than sixteen maps. In addition to the cities and roads shown on them were little red triangles designating suspected terrorist training camps in four countries. These were being photographed on almost a daily basis by the photoreconnaissance satellites (Jack was not allowed to know their number) orbiting the globe. He concentrated on the ones in Libya. They did have that report from an Italian agent that Sean Miller had been seen leaving a freighter in Bengazi harbour. The freighter had been of Cypriot registry, owned by a network of corporations sufficiently complex that it didn't really matter, since the ship was under charter to yet another such network. An American destroyer had photographed the ship in what certainly seemed a chance encounter in the Straits of Sicily. The ship was old but surprisingly well maintained, with modern radar and radio gear. She was regularly employed on runs from Eastern European ports to Libya and Syria, and was known to carry arms and military equipment from the East Bloc to client states on the Mediterranean. This data had already been set aside for further use.

Ryan found that the CIA and National Reconnaissance Office were looking at a number of camps in the North African desert. A simple graph accompanied the dated photos of each, and Ryan was looking for a camp whose apparent activity had changed the day that Miller's ship had docked at Bengazi. He was disappointed to find that four had done so. One was known to be used by the Provisional Wing of the IRA – this datum had come from the interrogation of a convicted bomber. The other three were unknowns. The people there – aside from the maintenance staff provided by the Libyan armed forces – could be identified from the photos as Europeans from their fair skin, but that was all. Jack was disappointed to see that you couldn't recognize a face from these shots, just colour of skin, and if the sun was right, colour of hair. You could also determine the make of a car or truck, but not its identifying tag numbers. Strangely, the clarity of the photos was better at night. The cooler night air was less roiled and did not interfere with imaging as much as in the shimmering heat of the day.

The pictures in the heavy binder that occupied his attention were of camps 11-5-04, 11-5-18, and 11-5-20. Jack didn't know how the number designators had been arrived at and didn't really care. The camps were all pretty much the same; only the spacing of the huts distinguished one from another.

Jack spent the best part of an hour looking over the photos, and concluded that this miracle of modern technology told him all sorts of technical things, none of which were pertinent to his purpose. Whoever ran those camps knew enough to keep people out of sight when a reconsat was overhead – except for one which was not known to have photographic capability. Even then, the number of people visible was almost never the same, and the actual occupancy of the camps was therefore a matter for uncertain estimation. It was singularly frustrating.

Ryan leaned back and lit another low-tar cigarette bought from the kiosk on the next floor down. It went well with the coffee that was serving to keep him awake. He was up against another blank wall. It made him think of the computer games he occasionally played at home when he was tired of writing – Zork and Ultima. The business of intelligence analysis was so often like those computer 'head games'. You had to figure things out, but you never quite knew what it was that you were figuring out. The patterns you had to deduce could be very different from anything one normally dealt with, and the difference could be significant or mere happenstance.

Two of the suspected ULA camps were within forty miles of the known IRA outpost. *Less than an hour's drive*, Jack thought. *If they only knew.* He would have settled for having the Provos clean out the ULA, as they evidently wanted to do. There were indications that the Brits were thinking along similar lines. Jack wondered what Mr Owens thought of that one and concluded that he probably didn't know. It was a surprising thought that he now had information that some experienced players did not. He went back to the pictures.

One, taken a week after Miller had been seen in Bengazi, showed a car – it looked like a Toyota Land Cruiser – about a mile from 11-5-18, heading away. Ryan wondered where it was going. He wrote down the date and time on the bottom of the photo and checked the cross-reference table in the front. Ten minutes later he found the same car, the next day, at Camp 11-5-09, a PIRA camp forty miles from 11-5-18.

Jack told himself not to get overly excited: 11-5-18 could belong to the Red Army Faction of West Germany, Italy's resurgent Red Brigades, or any number of other organizations with which the PIRA cross-pollinated. He still made some notes. It was a 'datum', a bit of information that was worth checking out.

Next he checked the occupancy graph for the camp. This showed the number of camp buildings occupied at night, and went back for over two years. He compared it with a list of known ULA operations, and discovered . . . nothing, at first. The instances where the number of occupied buildings blipped up did not correlate with the organization's known activities . . . but there was some sort of pattern, he saw.

What kind of pattern? Jack asked himself. Every three months or so the occupancy went up by one. Regardless of the number of the people at the camp, the number of huts being used went up by one, for a period of three days. Ryan swore when he saw that the pattern didn't quite hold. Twice in two years the number didn't change. *And what does* that *mean?*

'You are in a maze of twisty passages, all alike,' Jack murmured to himself. It was a line from one of his computer games. Pattern-recognition was not one of his strong points. Jack left the room to get a can of Coke, but more to clear his head. He was back in five minutes.

He pulled the occupancy graphs from the three 'unknown' camps to compare the respective levels of activity. What he really needed to do was to make Xerox copies of the graphs, but CIA had strict rules on the use of copying machines. Doing it would take time that he didn't want to lose at the moment. The other two camps showed no recognizable pattern at all, while Camp 18 did seem to lean in that direction. He spent an hour doing this. By the end of it he had all three graphs memorized. He had to get away from it. Ryan tucked the graphs back where they belonged and returned to examining the photographs themselves.

Camp 11-5-20, he saw, showed a girl in one photo. At least there was someone there wearing a two-piece bathing suit. Jack stared at the image for a few seconds, then turned away in disgust. He was playing voyeur, trying to discern the figure of someone who was probably a terrorist. There were no such attractions at camps -04 and -18, and he wondered at the significance of this until he remembered that only one satellite was giving daylight photos with people in them. Ryan made a note to himself to check at the Academy's library for a book on orbital mechanics. He decided that he needed to know how often a single satellite passed over a given spot in a day.

'You're not getting anywhere,' he told himself aloud.

'Neither is anybody else,' Marty Cantor said. Ryan spun around.

'How did you get in here?' Jack demanded.

'I'll say one thing for you, Jack, when you concentrate you really concentrate. I've been standing here for five minutes.' Cantor grinned. 'I like your intensity, but if you want an opinion, you're pushing a little hard, fella.'

'I'll survive.'

'You say so,' Cantor said dubiously. 'How do you like our photo album?'

'The people who do this full-time must go nuts.'

'Some do,' Cantor agreed.

'I might have something worth checking out,' Jack said, explaining his suspicions on Camp -18.

'Not bad. By the way, number -20 may be *Action Directe*, the French group that's picked up lately. DGSE – the French foreign intelligence service – thinks they have a line on it.'

'Oh. That may explain one of the photos.' Ryan flipped to the proper page.

'Thank God Ivan doesn't know what that bird does,' Cantor nodded. 'Hmm. We may be able to ID from this.'

'How?' Jack asked. 'You can't make out her face.'

'You can tell her hair length, roughly. You can also tell the size of her tits.' Cantor grinned ear to ear.

'What?'

'The guys in photointerpretation are – well, they're very technical. For cleavage to show up in these photos, a girl has to have C-cup breasts – at least that's what they told me once. I'm not kidding, Jack. Somebody actually worked the math out, because you can identify people from a combination of factors like hair colour, length, and bust size. *Action Directe* has lots of female operatives. Our French colleagues might find this interesting.' *If they're willing to deal*, he didn't say.

'What about -18?'

'I don't know. We've never really tried to identify that one. The thing about the car may count against it, though.'

'Remember that our ULA friends have the Provos infiltrated,' Jack said.

'You're still on that, eh? Okay, it's something to be considered,' Cantor conceded. 'What about this pattern thing you talked about?'

'I haven't got anything to point to yet,' Jack admitted.

'Let's see the graph.'

Jack unfolded it from the back of the binder. 'Every three months, mostly, the occupancy rate picks up.'

Cantor frowned at the graph for a moment. Then he flipped through the photographs. On only one of the dates did they have a daylight photo that showed anything. Each of the camps had what looked like a shooting range. In the photo Cantor selected, there were three men standing near it.

'You might have something, Jack.'

'What?' Ryan had looked at the photo and made nothing of it.

'What's the distinguishing feature of the ULA?'

'Their professionalism,' Ryan answered.

'Your last paper on them said they were more militarily organized than some of the others, remember? Every one of them, as far as we can tell, is skilled with weapons.'

'So?'

'Think!' Cantor snapped. Ryan gave him a blank look. 'Periodic weapons-refresher training, maybe?'

'Oh. I hadn't thought of that. How come nobody ever –'

'Do you know how many satellite photos come through here? I can't say exactly, but you may safely assume that it's a fairly large number, thousands per month. Figure it takes a minimum of five minutes to examine each one. Mostly we're interested in the Russians – missile silos, factories, troop movements, tank parks, you name it. That's where most of the analytical talent goes, and they can't keep up with what comes in. The guys we have on this stuff here are technicians, not analysts.' Cantor paused. 'Camp -18 looks interesting enough that we might try to figure a way to check it out, see who really lives there. Not bad.'

'He's violated security,' Kevin O'Donnell said by way of greeting. He was quiet enough that no one in the noisy pub would have heard him.

'Perhaps this is worth it,' Cooley replied. 'Instructions?'

'When are you going back?'

'Tomorrow morning, the early flight.'

O'Donnell nodded, finishing off his drink. He left the pub and walked directly to his car. Twenty minutes later he was home. Ten minutes after that, his operations and intelligence chiefs were in his study.

'Sean, how did you like working with Alex's organization?'

'They're like us, small but professional. Alex is a very thorough technician, but an arrogant one. He hasn't had a great deal of formal training. He's clever, very clever. And he's hungry, as they say over there. He wants to make his mark.'

'Well, he may just have his chance next summer.' O'Donnell paused, holding up the letter Cooley had delivered. 'It would seem that His Royal Highness will be visiting America next summer. The Treasure Houses exhibit was such a success that they are going to stage another one. Nearly ninety percent of the works of Leonardo Da Vinci belong to the Royal Family, and they'll be sending them over to raise money for some favoured charities. The show opens in Washington on August the first, and the Prince of Wales will be going over to start things off. This will not be announced until July, but here is his itinerary, including the proposed security arrangements. It is as yet undecided whether or not his lovely bride will accompany His Highness, but we will proceed on the assumption that she will.'

'The child?'

'I rather suspect not, but we will allow for that possibility also.' He handed the letter to Joseph McKenney. The intelligence officer for the ULA skimmed over the data.

'The security at the official functions will be airtight. The Americans have had a number of incidents, and they've learned from each of them,' McKenney said. Like all intelligence officers, he saw his potential opponents as overwhelmingly powerful. 'But if they go forward with this one . . .'

'Yes,' O'Donnell said. 'I want you two to work together on this. We have plenty of time and we'll use all of it.' He took the letter back and reread it before giving it to Miller. After they left, he wrote his instructions for their agent in London.

At the airport the next morning Cooley saw his contact and walked into the coffee shop. He was early for his flight, seasoned traveller that he was, and had a cup while he waited for it to be announced. Finished, he walked outside. His contact was just walking in. The two men brushed by each other, and the message was passed, just as was taught in every spy school in the world.

'He does travel about a good deal,' Ashley observed. It had taken Owens' detectives less than an hour to find Cooley's travel agent and to get a record of his trips for the past three years. Another pair was assembling a biographical file on the man. It was strictly routine work. Owens and his men knew better than to get excited about a new lead. Enthusiasm all too easily got in the way of objectivity. His car – parked at Gatwick Airport – had considerable mileage on the clock for its age, that was explained by his motoring about buying books. This was the extent of the data assembled in eighteen hours. They would patiently wait for more.

'How often does he travel to Ireland?'

'Quite frequently, but he does business in English-language books, and we are the only two countries in Europe that speak English, aren't we?' Ashley, too, was able to control himself.

'America?' Owens asked.

'Once a year, looks like. I rather suspect it's to an annual trade show. I can check that myself.'

'They speak English, too.'

Ashley grinned. 'Shakespeare didn't live or print books there. There aren't many examples of American publishing old enough to excite a person like Cooley. What he might do is buy up books of ours that have found their way across the water, but more likely he's looking for buyers. No, Ireland fits beautifully with his cover – excuse me, if it is that. My own dealer, Samuel Pickett and Sons, travels there often also . . . but not as much, I should think,' he added.

'Perhaps his biography will tell us something,' Owens noted.

'One can hope.' Ashley was looking for a light at the end of this tunnel, but saw only more tunnel.

'It's okay, Jack,' Cathy said.

He nodded. Ryan knew that his wife was right. The nurse-practitioner had positively beamed at the news she gave them on their arrival. Sally was bouncing back like any healthy child should. The healing process had already begun.

Yet there was a difference between the knowledge of the mind and the knowledge of the heart. Sally had been awake this time. She was unable to speak, of course, with the respirator hose in her mouth, but the murmurs that tried to come out could only have meant: *It hurts*. The injuries inflicted on the body of his child did not appear any less horrific, despite his knowledge that they would heal. If anything they seemed worse now that she was occasionally conscious. The pain would eventually go away – but his little girl was in pain now. Cathy might be able to tell herself that only the living could feel pain, that it was a positive sign for all the discomfort it gave. Jack could not. They stayed until she dozed off again. He took his wife outside.

'How are you?' he asked her.

'Better. You can take me home tomorrow night.'

Jack shook his head. He hadn't thought about that. Stupid, Ryan told himself. Somehow he'd assumed that Cathy would stay here, close to Sally.

'The house is pretty empty without you, babe,' he said after a moment.

'It'll be empty without her,' his wife answered, and the tears started again. She buried her face in her husband's shoulder. 'She's so little . . .'

'Yeah.' Jack thought of Sally's face, the two little blue eyes surrounded by a sea of bruises, the hurt there, the pain there. 'She's going to get better, honey, and I don't want to hear any more of that "it's my fault" crap.'

'But it is!'

'No, it isn't. Do you know how lucky I am to have you both alive? I saw the FBI's data today. If you hadn't stomped on the brakes when you did, you'd both be dead.' The supposition was that this had thrown off Miller's aim by a few inches. At least two rounds had missed Cathy's head by a whisker, the forensic experts said. Jack could close his eyes and recite that information word for word. 'You saved her life and yours by being smart.'

It took Cathy a moment to react. 'How did you find that out?'

'CIA. They're cooperating with the police. I asked to be part of the team and they let me join up.'

'But –'

'A lot of people are working on this, babe. I'm one of them,' Jack said quietly. 'The only thing that matters now is finding them.'

'Do you think . . .'

'Yeah, I do.' *Sooner or later.*

Bill Shaw had no such hopes at the moment. The best potential lead they had was the identity of the black man who'd driven the van. This was being kept out of the media. As far as the TV and newspapers were concerned, all the suspects were white. The FBI hadn't so much lied to the press as allowed them to draw a false conclusion from the partial data that had been released – as happened frequently enough. It might keep the suspect from being spooked. The only person who'd seen him at close range was the 7-Eleven clerk. She had spent several hours going over pictures of blacks thought to be members of revolutionary groups and come up with three possibles. Two of these were in prison, one for bank robbery, the other for interstate transport of explosives. The third had dropped out of sight seven years before. He was only a picture to the Bureau. The name they had for him was known to be an alias, and there were no fingerprints. He'd cut himself loose from his former associates – a smart move, since most of them had been arrested and convicted for various criminal acts – and simply disappeared. The best bet, Shaw told himself, was that he was now part of society, living a normal life somewhere with his past activities no more than a memory.

The agent looked over the file once again. 'Constantine Duppens,' his alias had been. Well-spoken on the few occasions when he'd spoken at all, the informant had said of him. Educated, probably. Attached to the group the Bureau had been watching, but never really part of it, the file went on. He'd never participated in a single illegal act, and had drifted away when the leaders of the little band had started talking about supporting themselves with bank robberies and drug trafficking. Maybe a dilettante, Shaw thought, a student with a radical streak who'd gotten a look at one of the groups and recognized them for what they were – what Shaw thought they were: ineffective dolts, street hoods with a smattering of Marxist garbage or pseudo-Hitlerism.

A few fringe groups occasionally managed to set off a bomb somewhere, but these cases were so rare, so minor, that the American people scarcely knew that they'd happened at all. When a group robbed a bank or armoured car to support itself, the public remembered that one need not be politically motivated to rob a bank; greed was enough. From a high of fifty-one terrorist incidents in 1982, the number had been slashed to seven in 1985. The Bureau had managed to run down many of these amateurish groups, preventing more than twenty incidents the previous year, with good intelligence followed by quick action. Fundamentally, the small cells of crazies had been done in by their own amateurism.

America didn't have any ideologically motivated terrorist groups, at least not in the European sense. There were the Armenian groups whose main objective was murdering Turkish diplomats, and the white-supremacist people in the Northwest, but in both cases the only ideology was hatred – of Turks, blacks, Jews, or whatever. These were vicious but not really dangerous to society, since they lacked a shared vision of their political objective. To be really effective, the members of such a group had to believe in something more than the negativity of hate. The most dangerous terrorists were the idealists, of course, but America was a hard place to see the benefits of Marxism or Nazism. When even welfare families had colour televisions, how much attraction could there be to collectivism? When the country lacked a system of class distinctions, what group could one hate with conviction? And so most of the small groups found that they were guerrilla fish swimming not in a sea of peasants, but rather a sea of apathy. Not a single group had been able to overcome that fact before being penetrated and destroyed by the Bureau – then to learn that their destruction was granted but a few column inches on page eleven, their defiant manifesto not printed at all. They were judged by faceless editors not to be newsworthy. In so many ways this was the perfect conclusion to a terrorist trial.

In that sense the FBI was a victim of its own success. So well had the job been done that the possibility of terrorist activity in America was not a matter of general public concern. Even the Ryan Case, as it was now being called, was regarded as nothing more than a nasty crime, not a harbinger of something new in America. To Shaw it was both. As a matter of institutional policy, the FBI regarded terrorism as a crime without any sort of political dimension that might lend a perverted respectability to the perpetrators. The importance of this distinction was not merely semantic. Since by their nature, terrorists struck at the foundations of civilized society, to grant them the thinnest shred of respectability was the equivalent of a suicide note for the targeted society. The Bureau recognized, however, that these were not mere criminals chasing after money. Their objective was far more dangerous than that. For this reason, crimes that otherwise would have been in the domain of local police departments were immediately taken under charge by the federal government.

Shaw returned to the photo of 'Constantine Duppens' one more time. It was expecting too much for a convenience-store clerk to remember one face from the hundred she saw every day, or at least to remember it well enough to pick out a photo that might be years old. She'd certainly tried to help, and had agreed to tell no one of what she'd done. They had a description of the suspect's clothing – almost certainly burned – and the van, which they had. It was being dismantled piece by piece not far from Shaw's office. The forensic experts had identified the type of gun used. For the moment, that was all they had. All Inspector Bill Shaw could do was wait for his agents in the field to come up with something new. A paid informant might overhear something, or a new witness might turn up, or maybe the forensics team would discover something unexpected in the van. Shaw told himself to be patient. Despite twenty-two years in the FBI, patience was something he still had to force on himself.

'Aw, I was starting to like the beard,' a co-worker said.

'Damned thing itched too much.' Alexander Constantine Dobbens was back at his job. 'I was spending half my time just scratching my face.'

'Yeah, same thing when I was on subs,' his roommate agreed. 'Different when you're young.'

'Speak for yourself, grandpop!' Dobbens laughed. 'You old married turkey. Just because you're chained doesn't mean I have to be.'

'You oughta settle down, Alex.'

'The world is full of interesting things to do, and I haven't done them all yet.' *Not hardly.* He was a field engineer for Baltimore Gas and Electric Company and usually worked nights. The job forced him to spend much of his time on the road, checking equipment and supervising line crews. Alex was a popular fellow who didn't mind getting his hands dirty, who actually enjoyed the physical work that many engineers were too proud to do. A man of the people, he called himself. His pro-union stance was a source of irritation to management, but he was a good engineer, and being black didn't hurt either. A man who was a good engineer, popular with his people, *and* black was fireproof. He'd done a good deal of minority recruiting, moreover, having brought a dozen good workers into the company. A few of them had shaky backgrounds, but Alex had brought them around.

It was often quiet working nights, and as was usually the case, Alex got the first edition of the *Baltimore Sun*. The case was already off the front page, now back in the local news section. The FBI and State Police, he read, were continuing to investigate the case. He was still amazed that the woman and kid had survived – testimony, his training told him, to the efficacy of seat belts, not to mention the work of the Porsche engineers. *Well*, he decided, *that's okay.* Killing a little kid and a pregnant woman wasn't exactly something to brag about. They had wasted the state trooper, and that was enough for him. Losing that Clark boy to the cops continued to rankle Dobbens, though. *I told the dumb fuck that the man was too exposed there, but no, he wanted to waste the whole family at once.* Alex knew why that was so, but saw it as a case of zeal overcoming realism. *Damned political-science majors, they think you can make something happen if you wish hard enough.* Engineers knew different.

Dobbens took comfort from the fact that all the known suspects were white. Waving to the helicopter had been his mistake. Bravado had no place in revolutionary activity. It was his own lesson to be learned, but this one hadn't hurt anyone. The gloves and hat had denied the pigs a description. The really funny thing was that despite all the screwups, the operation had been a success. That IRA punk, O-something, had been booted out of Boston with his honky tail between his legs. At least the operation had been politically sound. And that, he told himself, was the real measure of success.

From his point of view, success meant earning his spurs. He and his people had provided expert assistance to an established revolutionary group. He could now look to his African friends for funding. They really weren't African to his way of thinking, but they liked to call themselves that. There were ways to hurt America, to get attention in a way that no revolutionary group ever had. What, for example, if he could turn out the lights in fifteen states at once? Alex Dobbens knew how. The revolutionary had to know a way of hitting people where they lived, and what better way, he thought, than to make unreliable something that they took for granted? If he could demonstrate that the corrupt government could not even keep their lights on reliably, what doubts might he put in people's heads next? America was a society of things, he thought. What if those things stopped working? What then would people think? He didn't know the answer to that, but he knew that something would change, and change was what he was after.

19

Tests and Passing Grades

'He's an odd duck,' Owens observed. The dossier was the result of three weeks of work. It could have gone faster, of course, but when you don't want the news of an inquiry to reach its subject, you have to be more circumspect.

Dennis Cooley was a Belfast native, born to a middle-class Catholic family, although neither of his deceased parents had been churchgoers, something decidedly odd in a region where religion defines both life and death. Dennis had attended church – a necessity for one who'd been educated at the parish school – until university, then stopped at once and never gone back. No criminal record at all. None. Not even a place in a suspected associates file. As a university student he'd hung around the fringes of a few activist groups, but never joined, evidently preferring his studies in literature. He'd graduated with the highest honours. A few courses in Marxism, a few more in economics, always with a teacher whose leanings were decidedly left of centre, Owens saw. The police commander snorted to himself. There were enough of those at the London School of Economics, weren't there?

For two years all they had were tax records. He'd worked in his father's bookshop, and so far as the police were concerned, simply did not exist. That was a problem with police work – you noticed only the criminals. A few very discreet inquiries made in Belfast hadn't turned up anything. All sorts of people had visited the shop, even soldiers of the British Army, who'd arrived there about the time Cooley had graduated from university. The shop's window had been smashed once or twice by marauding bands of Protestants – the reason the Army had been called in in the first place – but nothing more serious than that. Young Dennis hadn't frequented the local pubs enough that anyone had noticed, hadn't belonged to any church organization, nor any political club, nor any sports association. 'He was always reading something,' someone had told one of the detectives. *There's a bloody revelation*, Owens told himself. *A bookshop owner who reads. . . .*

Then his parents had died in a car accident.

Owens was struck by the fact that they'd died in a completely ordinary way. A lorry's brakes had failed and smashed into their Mini one Saturday afternoon. It was hard to remember that some people in Ulster actually died 'normally', and were just as dead as those blown up or shot by the terrorists who prowled the night. Dennis Cooley had taken the insurance settlement and continued to operate the store as before after the quiet, ill-attended funeral ceremony at the local church. Some years later he'd sold out and moved to London, first setting up a shop in Knightsbridge and soon thereafter taking over a shop in the arcade where he continued to do business.

Tax records showed that he made a comfortable living. A check of his flat showed that he lived within his means. He was well-regarded by his fellow dealers. His one employee, Beatrix, evidently liked working with him part-time. Cooley had no friends, still didn't frequent local pubs – rarely drank at all, it seemed – lived alone, had no known sexual preferences, and travelled a good deal on business.

'He's a bloody cipher, a zero,' Owens said.

'Yes,' Ashley replied. 'At least it explains where Geoff met him – he was a lieutenant with one of the first regiments to go over, and probably wandered into the shop once or twice. You know what a talker Geoff Watkins is. They probably started talking books – can't have been much else. I doubt that Cooley has any interest beyond that.'

'Yes, I believe he's what the Yanks call a nerd. Or at least it's an image he's cultivating. What about his parents?'

Ashley smiled. 'They are remembered as the local Communists. Nothing serious, but decidedly bolshie until the Hungarian uprising of 1956. That seems to have disenchanted them. They remained outspokenly left-wing, but their political activities effectively ended then. Actually they're remembered as rather pleasant people, but a little odd. Evidently they encouraged the local children to read – made good business sense, if nothing else. Paid their bills on time. Other than that, nothing.'

'This girl Beatrix?'

'Somehow she got an education from our state schools. Didn't attend university, but self-taught in literature and the history of publishing. Lives with her elderly father – he's a retired RAF sergeant. She has no social life. She probably spends her evenings watching the telly and sipping Dubonnet. She rather intensely dislikes the Irish, but doesn't mind working with "Mr Dennis" because he's an expert in his field. Nothing there at all.'

'So, we have a dealer in rare books with a Marxist family, but no known ties with any terrorist group,' Owens summarized. 'He was in university about the same time as our friend O'Donnell, wasn't he?'

'Yes, but nobody remembers if they ever met. In fact, they lived only a few streets apart, but again no one remembers if Kevin ever frequented the bookshop.' Ashley shrugged. 'That goes back before O'Donnell attracted any serious attention, remember. If there were a lead of some sort then, it was never documented. They shared this economics teacher. That might have been a useful lead, but the bloke died two years ago – natural causes. Their fellow students have scattered to the four winds, and we've yet to find one who knew both of them.'

Owens walked to the corner of his office to pour a cup of tea. *A bloke with a Marxist background who attended the same school at the same time as O'Donnell.* Despite the total lack of a connection with a terrorist group, it was enough to follow up. If they could find something to suggest that Cooley and O'Donnell knew each other, then Cooley was the likely bridge between Watkins and the ULA. That did not mean there was any evidence to suggest the link was real, but in several months they had discovered nothing else even close.

'Very well, David, what do you propose to do?'

'We'll plant microphones in his shop and his home, and tap all of his telephone calls, of course. When he travels, he'll have a companion.'

Owens nodded approval. That was more than he could do legally, but the Security Service didn't operate under the same rules as did the Metropolitan Police. 'How about watching his shop?'

'Not easy, when you remember where it is. Still, we might try to get one of our people hired in one of the neighbouring shops.'

'The one opposite his is a jewellery establishment, isn't it?'

'Nicholas Reemer and Sons,' Ashley nodded. 'Owner and two employees.'

Owens thought about that. 'I could find an experienced burglary detective, someone knowledgeable in the field. . . .'

'Morning, Jack,' Cantor said.

'Hi, Marty.'

Ryan had given up on the satellite photographs weeks before. Now he was trying to find patterns within the terrorist network. Which group had connections with which other? Where did their arms come from? Where did they train? Who helped with the training? Who provided the money? Travel documents? What countries did they use for safe transits?

The problem with these questions was not a lack of information, but a glut of it. Literally thousands of CIA field officers and their agents, plus those of every other Western intelligence service, were scouring the world for such information. Many of the agents – foreign nationals recruited and paid by the Agency – would make reports on the most trivial encounter in the hope of delivering The One Piece of information that would crack open Abu Nidal, or Islamic Jihad, or one of the other high-profile groups, for a substantial reward. The result was thousands of communiqués, most of them full of worthless garbage that was indistinguishable from the one or two nuggets of real information. Jack had not realized the magnitude of the problem. The people working on this were all talented, but they were being overwhelmed by a sea of raw intelligence data that had to be graded, collated, and cross-referenced before proper analysis could begin. The difficulty of finding any single organization was inversely proportional to its size, and some of these groups were composed of a mere handful of people – in extreme cases composed of family members only.

'Marty,' Jack said, looking away from the papers on his desk, 'this is the closest thing to impossible I've ever seen.'

'Maybe, but I've come to deliver a well-done,' Cantor replied.

'What?'

'Remember that satellite photo of the girl in the bikini? The French think they've ID'd her: Françoise Theroux. Long, dark hair, a striking figure, and she was thought to be out of the country when the photo was made. That confirms that the camp belongs to *Action Directe*.'

'So who's the girl?'

'An assassin,' Marty replied. He handed Jack a photograph taken at closer range. 'And a good one. Three suspected kills, two politicians and an industrialist, all with a pistol at close range. Imagine how it's done: you're a middle-aged man walking down the street; you see a pretty girl; she smiles at you, maybe asks for directions or something; you stop, and the next thing you know, there's a pistol in her hand. Goodbye, Charlie.'

Jack looked at the photograph. She didn't look dangerous – she looked like every man's fantasy. 'Like we used to say in college, not the sort of girl you'd kick out of bed. Jesus, what sort of world do we live in, Marty?'

'You know that better than I do. Anyway, we've been asked to keep an eye on the camp. If we spot her there again, the French want us to real-time the photo to them.'

'They're going to go in after her?'

'They didn't say, but you might recall that the French have troops in Chad, maybe four hundred miles away. Airborne units, with helicopters.'

Jack handed the picture back. 'What a waste.'

'Sure is.' Cantor pocketed the photo and the issue. 'How's it going with your data?'

'So far I have a whole lot of nothing. The people who do this full-time . . .'

'Yeah, for a while there they were working around the clock. We had to make them stop, they were burning out. Computerizing it was a little helpful. Once we had the head of one group turn up at six airports in one day, and we knew the data was for crap, but every so often we get a live one. We missed that guy by a half hour outside Beirut last March. Thirty goddamned minutes,' Cantor said. 'You get used to it.'

Thirty minutes, Jack thought. *If I'd left my office thirty minutes earlier, I'd be dead. How am I supposed to get used to that?*

'What would you have done to him?'

'We wouldn't have read him his constitutional rights,' Cantor replied. 'So, any connections that you've been able to find?'

Ryan shook his head. 'This ULA outfit is so goddamned small. I have sixteen suspected contacts between the IRA and other groups. Some of them could be our boys, but how can you tell? The reports don't have pictures, the written descriptions could be anybody. Even when we have a reported IRA contact with a bunch they're not supposed to be talking to – one that might actually be the ULA – then, (A) our underlying information could easily be wrong, and (B) it could be the first time they talked with the IRA! Marty, how in the hell is somebody supposed to make any sense out of this garbage?'

'Well, the next time you hear somebody ask what the CIA is doing about terrorism – you won't be able to tell him.' Cantor actually smiled at that. 'These people we're looking for aren't dumb. They know what'll happen if they get caught. Even if we don't do it ourselves – which we might not want to do – we can always tip the Israelis. Terrorists are tough, nasty bastards, but they can't stand up to real troops and they know it.

'That's the frustrating part. My brother-in-law's an Army major, part of the Delta Force down at Fort Bragg. I've seen them operate. They could take out this camp you looked at in under two minutes, kill everybody there, and be gone before the echo fades. They're deadly and efficient, but without the right information, they don't know *where* to be deadly and efficient *at*. Same with police work. Do you think the Mafia could survive if the cops knew exactly where and when they did their thing? How many bank robberies would be successful if the SWAT team was waiting inside the doors? But you gotta know where the crooks are. It's all about intelligence, and intelligence comes down to a bunch of faceless bureaucrats sifting through all this crap. The people who gather the intel give it to us, and we process it and give it to the operations teams. The battle is fought here, too, Jack. Right here in this building, by a bunch of GS-9s and -10s who go home to their families every night.'

But the battle is being lost, Jack told himself. *It sure as hell isn't being won.*

'How's the FBI doing?' he asked.

'Nothing new. The black guy – well, he might as well not exist so far as anyone can tell. They have a crummy picture that's several years old, an alias with no real name or prints to check, and about ten lines of description that mainly says he's smart enough to keep his mouth shut. The Bureau's checking through people who used to be in the radical groups – funny how they have mostly settled down – without any success so far.'

'How about the bunch who flew over there two years back?' Not so long ago members of several radical American groups had flown to Libya to meet with 'progressive elements' of the third-world community. The echoes of that event still reverberate through the antiterrorism community.

'You've noticed that we don't have any pictures from Bengazi, right? Our agent got picked up – one of those horrible accidents. It cost us the photos and it cost him his neck. Fortunately they never found out he was working for us. We know some of the names of the people who were there, but not all.'

'Passport records?'

Cantor leaned against the doorframe. 'Let's say Mr X flew to Europe, and America on vacation – we're talking tens of thousands of people per month. He makes contact with someone on the other side, and they get him the rest of the way without going through the usual immigration-control procedures. It's easy – hell, the Agency does it all the time. If we had a name we could see if he was out of the country at the right time. That would be a start – but we don't have a name to check.'

'We don't have anything!' Ryan snapped.

'Sure we do. We have all that' – he waved at the documents on Ryan's desk – 'and lots more where that came from. Somewhere in there is the answer.'

'You really believe that?'

'Every time we crack one of these things, we find that all the information was under our nose for months. The oversight committees in Congress always hammer us on that. Sitting in that pile right now, Jack, is a crucial lead. That's almost a statistical certainty. But you probably have two or three hundred such reports sitting there, and only one matters.'

'I didn't expect miracles, but I did expect to make some progress,' Jack said quietly, the magnitude of the problem finally sinking in.

'You did. You saw something that no one else did. You may have found Françoise Theroux. And now if a French agent sees something that might be useful to us, maybe they'll pass it along. You didn't know this, but the intel business is like the old barter economy. We give them, and then they give us, or we'll never give to them again. If this pans out, they'll owe us big-time. They really want that gal. She popped a close friend of their President, and he took it personally.

'Anyway, you get a well-done from the Admiral and the DGSE. The boss says you should take it a little easier, by the way.'

'I'll take it easy when I find the bastards.' Ryan replied.

'Sometimes you have to back off. You look like hell. You're tired. Fatigue makes for errors. We don't like errors. No more late hours, Jack, that comes from Greer, too. You're out of here by six.' Cantor left, denying Jack a chance to object.

Ryan turned back toward his desk, but stared at the wall for several minutes. Cantor was right. He was working so late that half the time he couldn't drive up to Baltimore to see how his daughter was doing. He rationalized that his wife was with her every day, frequently spending the night at Hopkins to be close to their daughter. *Cathy has her job and I have mine.*

So, he told the wall, *at least I managed to get something right.* He remembered that it had been an accident, that Marty had made the real connection; but it was also true that he'd done what an analyst was supposed to do, find something odd and bring it to someone's attention. He could feel good about that. He'd found a terrorist maybe, but certainly not the right one.

It's a start. His conscience wondered what the French would do if they found that pretty girl, and how he'd feel about it if he found out. It would be better, he decided, if terrorists were ugly, but pretty or not, their victims were just as dead. He promised himself that he wouldn't go out of his way to find out if anyone got her. Jack went back into the pile, looking for that one piece of hard information. The people he was looking for were somewhere in the pile. He had to find them.

'Hello, Alex,' Miller said as he entered the car.

'How was the trip?' He still had his beard, Dobbens saw. Well, nobody had gotten much of a look at him. This time he'd flown to Mexico, driven across the border, then taken a domestic flight into DC, where Alex had met him.

'Your border security over here's a bloody joke.'

'Would it make you happy if they changed it?' Alex inquired. 'Let's talk business.' The abruptness of his tone surprised Miller.

Aren't you a proud one, with one whole operation under your belt, Miller thought. 'We have another job for you.'

'You haven't paid me for the last one yet, boy.'

Miller handed over a passbook. 'Numbered account, Bahamian bank. I believe you'll find the amount correct.'

Alex pocketed the book. 'That's more like it. Okay, we have another job. I hope you don't expect to go with it as fast as before.'

'We have several months to plan it,' Miller replied.

'I'm listening.' Alex sat through ten minutes of information.

'Are you out of your fucking mind?' Dobbens asked when he was finished.

'How hard would it be to gather the information we need?'

'That's not the problem, Sean. The problem is getting your people in and out. No way I could handle that.'

'That is my concern.'

'Bullshit! If my people are involved, it's my concern, too. If that Clark turkey broke to the cops, it would have burned a safehouse – and me!'

'But he didn't break, did he? That's why we chose him.'

'Look, what you do with your people, I don't give a rat's ass. What happens to my people, I do. That last little game we played for you was bush league, Sean.'

Miller figured out what 'bush league' meant from context. 'The operation was politically sound, and you know it. Perhaps you've forgotten that the objective is always political. Politically, the operation was a complete success.'

'I don't need you to tell me that!' Alex snapped back in his best intimidating tone. Miller was a proud little twerp, but Alex figured he could pinch his head off with one good squeeze. 'You lost a troop because you were playing this personal, not professional – and I know what you're thinking. It was our first big play, right? Well, son, I think we proved that we got our shit together, didn't we? And I warned you up front that your man was too exposed. If you'd listened to me, you wouldn't have a man on the inside. I know your background is pretty impressive, but this is my turf, and I know it.'

Miller knew that he had to accept that. He kept his face impassive. 'Alex, if we were in any way displeased, we would not have come back to you. Yes, you do have your shit together,' *you bloody nigger*, he didn't say. 'Now, can you get us the information we need?'

'Sure, for the right price. You want us in the op?'

'We don't know yet,' Miller replied honestly. *Of course the only issue here is money. Bloody Americans.*

'If you want us in, I'm part of the planning. Number one, I want to know how you get in and out. I might have to go with you. If you shitcan my advice this time, I walk and I take my people with me.'

'It's a little early to be certain, but what we hope to arrange is really quite simple. . . .'

'You think you can set that up?' For the first time since he'd arrived, Sean had Alex nodding approval. 'Slick. I'll give you that. It's slick. Now let's talk price.'

Sean wrote a figure on a piece of paper and handed it to Alex. 'Fair enough?' People interested in money were easy to impress.

'I sure would like an account at your bank, brother.'

'If this operation comes off, you will.'

'You mean that?'

Miller nodded emphatically. 'Direct access. Training facilities, help with travel documents, the lot. Your skill in helping us last time attracted attention. Our friends like the idea of an active revolutionary cell in America.' *If they really want to do business with you, it's their problem.* 'Now, how quickly can you get the information?'

'End of the week good enough?'

'Can you do it that fast without attracting attention?'

'Let me worry about that,' Alex replied with a smile.

'Anything new at your end?' Owens asked.

'Not much,' Murray admitted. 'We have plenty of forensic evidence, but only one witness who got a clear look at one face, and she can't give us a real ID.'

'The local help?'

'That's who we almost ID'd. Nothing yet. Maybe they've learned from the ULA. No manifesto, no announcement claiming credit for the job. The people we have inside some other radical groups – that is, those that still exist – have drawn a big blank. We're still working on it and we have a lot of money out on the street, but so far we haven't got anything to show for it.' Murray paused. 'That'll change. Bill Shaw is a genius, one of the real brains we have in the Bureau. They switched him over from counterintelligence to terrorism a few years back, and he's done really impressive work. What's new on your end?'

'I can't go into specifics yet,' Owens said. 'But we might have a small break. We're trying to decide now if it's real or not. That's the good news. The bad is that His Royal Highness is travelling to America this coming summer. A number of people were informed of his itinerary, including six on our list of possible suspects.'

'How the hell did you let that happen, Jimmy?'

'No one asked me, Dan,' Owens replied sourly. 'In several cases, if the people hadn't been informed it would have told them that something odd was happening – you can't simply stop trusting people, can you? For the rest, it was just another balls-up. Some secretary put out the plans on the normal list without consulting the security officers.' This wasn't a new story for either man. There was always someone who didn't get the word.

'Super. So call it off. Let him get the flu or something when the time comes,' Murray suggested.

'His Highness won't do that. He's become quite adamant on the subject. He won't allow a terrorist threat to affect his life in any way.'

Murray grunted. 'You gotta admire the kid's guts, but –'

'Quite so,' Owens agreed. He didn't really care for having his next king referred to as the kid, but he'd long since got used to the American way of expressing things. 'It doesn't make our job any easier.'

'How firm are the travel plans?' Murray asked, getting back to business.

'Several items on the itinerary are tentative, of course, but most are set in stone. Our security people will be meeting with yours in Washington. They're flying over next week.'

'Well, you know that you'll get all the cooperation you want, Secret Service, the Bureau, local police, everything. We'll take good care of him for you,' Murray assured him. 'He and his wife are pretty popular back home. Will they be taking the baby with them?'

'No. We were able to prevail on him about that.'

'Okay. I'll call Washington tomorrow and get things rolling. What's happening with our friend Ned Clark?'

'Nothing as yet. His colleagues are evidently giving him rather a bad time, but he's too bloody stupid to break.'

Murray nodded. He knew the type.

Well, they wanted me to take off early, Ryan thought. He decided to accept an invitation to a lecture at Georgetown University. Unfortunately, it was something of a disappointment. Professor David Hunter was Columbia's *enfant terrible*, America's ranking authority on political affairs in Eastern Europe. His book of the previous year, *Revolution Postponed*, had been a penetrating study of the political and economic problems of the Soviet's unsteady empire, and Ryan, like others, had been eager to hear his new information on the subject. The speech had turned out to be little more than a rehash of the book, with the rather startling suggestion at the end that the NATO countries should be more aggressive in trying to separate the Soviet Union from her captives. Ryan considered that to be lunacy, even if it did guarantee lively discussions at the reception.

At the end of the talk, Ryan moved quickly to the reception. He'd skipped dinner to make it here on time. There was a wide table of hors d'oeuvres, and Jack filled his plate as patiently as he could before drifting off to a sedate corner by the elevators. He let others form knots of conversation around Professor Hunter. On the whole, it was nice to be back at Georgetown, if only for a few hours. The 'Galleria' in the Intercultural Center was quite a contrast to the CIA institutional drab. The four-storey atrium of the language building was lined with the glass windows of offices, and a pair of potted trees reached toward the glass roof. The plaza outside was paved with bricks, and known to the students as Red Square. To the west was the old quadrangle, and the cemetery where rested the priests who had taught here for nearly two hundred years. It was a thoroughly civilized setting, except for the discordant shriek of jets coming out of National Airport, a few miles downriver. Someone jostled Ryan just as he was finishing his snacks.

'Excuse me, Doctor.' Ryan turned to see a man shorter than himself. He had a florid complexion and was dressed in a cheap-looking suit. His blue eyes seemed to sparkle with amusement. His voice had a pronounced accent. 'Did you enjoy the lecture?'

'It was interesting,' Ryan said diffidently.

'So. I see that capitalists can lie as well as we poor socialists.' The man had a jolly, overpowering laugh, but Jack decided that his eyes were sparkling with something other than amusement. They were measuring eyes, playing yet another variation of the game he'd been part of in England. Already Ryan disliked him.

'Have we met?'

'Sergey Platonov.' They shook hands after Ryan set his plate on a table. 'I am Third Secretary of the Soviet Embassy. Perhaps my photograph at Langley does not do me justice.'

A Russian – Ryan tried not to look too surprised – *who knows I've been working at CIA.* Third Secretary could easily mean that he was KGB, perhaps a diplomatic intelligence specialist, or maybe a member of the CPSU's Foreign Department – as though it made a difference. A 'legal' intelligence officer with a diplomatic cover. *What do I do now?* For one thing, he knew that he'd have to write up a contact report for CIA tomorrow, explaining how they'd met and what they'd talked about, perhaps an hour's work. It took an effort to remain polite.

'You must have the wrong guy, Mr Platonov. I'm a history teacher. I work at the Naval Academy in Annapolis. I was invited to this because I got my degree here.'

'No, no.' The Russian shook his head. 'I recognize you from the photograph on your book jacket. You see, I purchased ten copies of it last summer.'

'Indeed.' Jack was surprised again and unable to conceal it. 'My publisher and I thank you, sir.'

'Our Naval Attaché was much taken by it, Doctor Ryan. He felt that it should be brought to the attention of the Frunze Academy, and, I think, the Grechko Naval Academy in Leningrad.' Platonov applied his considerable charm. Ryan knew it for what it was, but . . . 'To be honest, I merely skimmed the book myself. It seemed quite well organized, and the Attaché said that your analysis of the way decisions are made in the heat of battle was highly accurate.'

'Well.' Jack tried not to be overly flattered, but it was hard. Frunze was *the* Soviet staff academy, the finishing school for young field-grade officers who were tagged for stardom. The Grechko Academy was only slightly less prestigious.

'Sergey Nikolay'ch,' boomed a familiar voice, 'it is not *kulturny* to prey upon the vanity of helpless young authors.' Father Timothy Riley joined them. A short, plump Jesuit priest, Riley had headed the history department at Georgetown while Ryan had gotten his doctorate. He was a brilliant intellect with a series of books to his credit, including two penetrating works on the history of Marxism – neither of which, Ryan was certain, had found their way into the library at Frunze. 'How's the family, Jack?'

'Cathy's back to work, Father. They moved Sally over to Hopkins. With luck we'll have her home early next week.'

'She will recover fully, your little daughter?' Platonov asked. 'I read about the attack on your family in the newspaper.'

'We think so. Except for losing her spleen, there seems to be no permanent damage. The docs say she's recovering nicely, and with her at Hopkins, Cathy's able to see her every day,' Ryan said more positively than he felt. Sally was a different child. Her legs weren't fully healed yet, but worst of all, his bouncing little girl was a sad thing now. She'd learned a lesson that Ryan had hoped to hold off for at least ten more years – that the world is a dangerous place even when you have a mother and a father to take care of you. A hard lesson for a child, it was harder still for a parent. *But she's alive*, Jack told himself, unaware of the expression on his face. *With time and love, you can recover from anything, except death.* The doctors and nurses at Hopkins were taking care of her like one of their own. That was a tangible advantage of having a doctor in the family.

'A terrible thing.' Platonov shook his head in what seemed to be genuine disgust. 'A terrible thing to attack innocent people for no reason.'

'Indeed, Sergey,' Riley said in the astringent voice that Ryan had known so well. When he wanted, 'Father Tim' had a tongue that could saw through wood. 'I seem to recall that V. I. Lenin said the purpose of terrorism is to terrorize, and that sympathy in a revolutionary is as reprehensible as cowardice on the field of battle.'

'Those were hard times, good Father,' Platonov said smoothly. 'My country has no business with those IRA madmen. They are not revolutionaries, however much they pretend to be. They have no revolutionary ethic. It is madness, what they do. The working classes should be allies, contesting together against the common enemy that exploits them both, instead of killing one another. Both sides of the conflict are victimized by bosses who play them off against each other, but instead of recognizing this they kill one another like mad dogs, and with as little point. They are bandits, not revolutionaries,' he concluded with a distinction lost on the other two.

'Maybe so, but if I ever get my hands on them, I'll give them a lesson in revolutionary justice.' It was good to let his hatred out in the open for once.

'You have no sympathy for them, either of you?' Platonov baited them. 'After all, you are both related to the victims of British imperialism. Did not both your families flee to America to escape it?'

Ryan was caught very short by that remark. It seemed an incredible thing to say until he saw that the Russian was watching for his reaction.

'Or perhaps the direct victim of Soviet imperialism,' Jack responded with his own look. 'Those two guys in London had Kalashnikov rifles. So did the ones who attacked my wife,' he lied. 'You don't buy one of those at the local hardware store. Whether you choose to admit it or not, most of the terrorists over there profess to be Marxists. That makes them your allies, not mine, and it makes it appear more than a coincidence that they use Soviet arms.'

'Do you know how many countries manufacture weapons of Soviet design? It is sadly inevitable that some will fall into the wrong hands.'

'In any case, my sympathy for their aim is, shall we say, limited by their choice of technique. You can't build a civilized country on a foundation of murder,' Ryan concluded. 'Much as some people have tried.'

'It would be well if the world worked in more peaceful ways.' Platonov ignored the implicit comment on the Soviet Union. 'But it is an historical fact that nations are born in blood, even yours. As countries grow, they mature beyond such conduct. It is not easy, but I think we can all see the value of peaceful coexistence. For myself, Doctor Ryan, I can sympathize with your feelings. I have two fine sons. We once had a daughter also, Nadia. She died long ago, at age seven, from leukemia. I know it is a hard thing to see your child in pain, but you are more fortunate than I. Your daughter will live.' He allowed his voice to soften. 'We disagree on many things, but no man can fail to love his children.

'So.' Platonov changed gears smoothly. 'What did you really think of Professor Hunter's little speech? Should America seek to foment counter-revolution in the socialist states of Europe?'

'Why don't you ask the State Department? That's not my part of the world, remember? I teach naval history. But if you want a personal opinion, I don't see how we can encourage people to rebel if we have no prospect of helping them directly when your country reacts.'

'Ah, good. You understand that we must act to protect our fraternal socialist brothers from aggression.'

The man was good, Ryan saw, but he'd had a lot of practice at this. 'I wouldn't call the encouragement of people to seek their own freedom a form of aggression, Mr Platonov. I was a stockbroker before I got my history degree, and that doesn't make me much of a candidate for sympathizing with your political outlook. What I am saying is that your country used military force to crush democratic feelings in Czechoslovakia and Hungary. To encourage people toward their own suicide is both immoral and counterproductive.'

'Ah, but what does your government think?' the Russian asked with another jolly laugh.

'I'm a historian, not a soothsayer. In this town they all work for the *Post*. Ask them.'

'In any case,' the Russian went on, 'our Naval Attaché is most interested to meet you and discuss your book. We are having a reception at the embassy on the twelfth of next month. The good Father is coming, he can watch over your soul. Might you and your wife attend?'

'For the next few weeks I plan to be at home with my family. My girl needs me there for a while.'

The diplomat was not to be put off. 'Yes, I can understand that. Some other time, perhaps?'

'Sure, give me a call sometime this summer.' *Are you kidding?*

'Excellent. Now if you will excuse me, I wish to speak to Professor Hunter.' The diplomat shook hands again and walked off to the knot of historians who were hanging on Hunter's every word.

Ryan turned to Father Riley, who'd watched the exchange in silence while sipping at his champagne.

'Interesting guy, Sergey,' Riley said. 'He loves to hit people for reactions. I wonder if he really believes in his system or if he's just playing the game for points. . . ?'

Ryan had a more immediate question. 'Father, what in the hell was that all about?'

Riley chuckled. 'You're being checked out, Jack.'

'Why?'

'You don't need me to answer that. You're working at CIA. If I guess right, Admiral Greer wants you on his personal staff. Marty Cantor is taking a job at the University of Texas next year, and you're one of the candidates for his job. I don't know if Sergey's aware of that, but you probably looked like the best target of opportunity in the room, and he wanted to get a feel for you. Happens all the time.'

'Cantor's job? But – nobody told me that!'

'The world's full of surprises. They probably haven't finished the full background check on you yet, and they won't pop the offer until they do. I presume the information you're looking at is still pretty limited?'

'I can't discuss that, Father.'

The priest smiled. 'Thought so. The work you've done over there has impressed the right people. If I have things right, they're going to bring you along like a good welterweight prospect.' Riley got another glass of champagne. 'If I know James Greer, he'll just sort of ease you into it. What did it, you see, was that Canary Trap thing. It really impressed some folks.'

'How do you know about all this?' Ryan asked, shocked at what he'd just heard.

'Jack, how do you think you got over there in the first place? Who do you think got you that Center for Strategic and International Studies fellowship?

The people there liked your work, too. Between what I said and what they said, Marty thought you were worth a look last summer, and you worked out better than anyone expected. There are some people around town who respect my opinion.'

'Oh.' Ryan had to smile. He'd allowed himself to forget the first thing about the Society of Jesus: they know everyone, from whom they can learn nearly everything. The President of the university belonged to both the Cosmos and University clubs, with which came access to the most important ears and mouths in Washington. That's how it would start. Occasionally a man would need advice on something, and being unable to consult the people he worked with, he might try to discuss it with a clergyman. No one was better qualified for this than a Jesuit, meticulously educated, well versed in the ways of the world, but not spoiled by it – most of the time. Like any clergyman, each was a good listener. So effective was the Society at gathering information that the State Department's code-breakers had once been tasked to break the Jesuits' own cipher system; the assignment had started a small revolt in the 'Black Chamber' . . . until they'd realized what sort of information was finding its way to them.

When Saint Ignatius Loyola had founded the order, the ex-soldier set it on a path to do only two things: to send out missionaries and to build schools. Both had been done extraordinarily well. The influence passed on by the schooling would never be lost on the men who'd graduated. It wasn't Machiavellian, not really. The colleges and universities plied its students with philosophy and ethics and theology – all required courses – to mute their baser tendencies and sharpen their wits. For centuries the Jesuits had built 'men for others', and wielded a kind of invisible temporal power, mainly for the good. Father Riley's intellectual credentials were widely known, and his opinions would be sought, just as from any distinguished academic, added to which was his moral authority as a graduate theologian.

'We're good security risks, Jack,' Riley said benignly. 'Can you imagine one of us being a Communist agent? So, are you interested in the job?'

'I don't know.' Ryan looked at his reflection in a window. 'It would mean more time away from the family. We're expecting another one this summer, you know.'

'Congratulations, that's good news. I know you're a family man, Jack. The job would mean some sacrifices, but you're a good man for it.'

'Think so?' *I haven't exactly set the world on fire yet.*

'I'd rather see people like you over there than some others I know. Jack, you're plenty smart enough. You know how to make decisions, but more importantly, you're a pretty good fellow. I know you're ambitious, but you've got ethics, values. I'm one of those people who thinks that still matters for something in the world, regardless of how nasty things get.'

'They get pretty nasty, Father,' Ryan said after a moment.

'How close are you to finding them?'

'Not very close at –' Jack stopped himself too late. 'You did that one pretty well.'

'I didn't mean it that way,' Father Tim said very sincerely. 'It would be a better world if they were off the street. There must be something wrong with the way they think. It's hard to understand how anyone could deliberately hurt a child.'

'Father, you really don't have to understand them. You just have to know where to find them.'

'That's work for the police, and the courts, and a jury. That's why we have laws, Jack,' Riley said gently.

Ryan turned to the window again. He examined his own image and wondered what it was that he saw. 'Father, you're a good man, but you've never had kids of your own. I can forgive somebody who comes after me, maybe, but not anyone who tries to hurt my little girl. If I find him – hell, I won't. But I sure would like to,' Jack told the image of himself. *Yes*, agreed.

'It's not a good thing, hate. It might do things to you that you'll regret, things that can change you from the person you are.'

Ryan turned back, thinking about the person he'd just looked at. 'Maybe it already has.'

20

Data

It was a singularly boring tape. Owens was used to reading police reports, transcripts of interrogations, and, worst of all, intelligence documents, but the tape was even more boring than that. The microphone which the Security Service had hidden in Cooley's shop was sound-activated and sensitive enough to pick up any noise. The fact that Cooley hummed a lot made Owens regret this feature. The detective whose job it was to listen to the unedited tape had included several minutes of the awful, atonal noise to let his commander know what he had to suffer through. The bell finally rang.

Owens heard the clatter, made metallic by the recording system, of the door opening and closing, then the sound of Cooley's swivel chair scraping across the floor. It must have had a bad wheel, Owens noted.

'Good morning, sir!' It was Cooley's voice.

'And to you,' said the second. 'Well, have you finished the Milton?'

'Yes, I have.'

'So what's the price?'

Cooley didn't say it aloud, but Ashley had told Owens that the shop owner never spoke a price. He handed it to his customers on a file card. That, Owens thought, was one way to keep from haggling.

'That is quite steep, you know,' Watkins' voice observed.

'I could get more, but you are one of our better clients,' Cooley replied.

The sigh was audible on the tape. 'Very well, it is worth it.'

The transaction was made at once. They could hear the rasping sound of new banknotes being counted.

'I may soon have something new from a collection in Kerry,' Cooley said next.

'Oh?' There was interest in the reply.

'Yes, a signed first edition of *Great Expectations*. I saw it on my last trip over. Might you be interested in that?'

'Signed, eh?'

'Yes, sir, "Boz" himself. I realize that the Victorian period is rather more recent than most of your acquisitions, but the author's signature. . . .'

'Indeed. I would like to see it, of course.'

'That can be arranged.'

'At this point,' Owens told Ashley, 'Watkins leaned over, and our man in the jewellery shop lost sight of him.'

'So he could have passed a message.'

'Possibly.' Owens switched off the tape machine. The rest of the conversation had no significance.

'The last time he was in Ireland, Cooley didn't go to County Kerry. He was in Cork the whole time. He visited three dealers in rare books, spent the night in a hotel, and had a few pints at a local pub,' Ashley reported.

'A pub?'

'Yes, he drinks in Ireland, but not in London.'

'Did he meet anyone there?'

'Impossible to tell. Our man wasn't close enough. His orders were to be discreet, and he did well not to be spotted.' Ashley was quiet for a moment as he tried to pin down something on the tape. 'It sounded to me as though he paid cash for the book.'

'He did, and it's out of pattern. Like most of us he uses cheques and credit cards for the majority of his transactions, but not for this. His bank records show no cheques to this shop, though he does occasionally make large cash withdrawals. They may or may not match with his purchases there.'

'How very odd,' Ashley thought aloud. 'Everyone – well, someone must know that he goes there.'

'Cheques have dates on them,' Owens suggested.

'Perhaps.' Ashley wasn't convinced, but he'd done enough investigations of this kind to know that you never got all the answers. Some details were always left hanging. 'I took another look at Geoff's service record last night. Do you know that when he was in Ireland, he had four men killed in his platoon?'

'What? That makes him a fine candidate for our investigation!' Owens didn't think this was good news.

'That's what I thought,' Ashley agreed. 'I had one of our chaps in Germany – his former regiment's assigned to the BAOR at the moment – interview one of Watkins's mates. Had a platoon in the same company, the chap's a half-colonel now. He said that Geoff took it quite hard, that he was quite vociferous on the point that they were in the wrong place, doing the wrong thing, and losing people in the process. Rather puts a different spin on things, doesn't it?'

'Another lieutenant with the solution to the problem.' Owens snorted.

'Yes – we leave and let the bloody Irish sort things out. That's not exactly a rare sentiment in the Army, you know.'

It wasn't exactly a rare sentiment throughout England, Commander Owens knew. 'Even so, it's not much of a basis for motive, is it?'

'Better than nothing at all.'

The cop grunted agreement. 'What else did the Colonel tell your bloke?'

'Obviously Geoff had a rather busy tour of duty in the Belfast area. He and his men saw a lot. They were there when the Army was welcomed in by the Catholics, and they were there when the situation reversed. It was a bad time for everyone,' Ashley added unnecessarily.

'It's still not very much. We have a former subaltern, now in the striped-pants brigade, who didn't like being in Northern Ireland; he happens to buy rare books from a bloke who grew up there and now runs a completely legit-imate business in central London. You know what my solicitor would say: pure coincidence. We don't have one single thing that can remotely be called evidence. The background of each man is pure enough to qualify him for sainthood.'

'These are the people we've been looking for,' Ashley insisted.

'I know that.' Owens almost surprised himself when he said it for the first time. His professionalism told him that this was a mistake, but his instincts told him otherwise. It wasn't a new feeling for the Commander of C-13, but one that always made him uneasy. If his instincts were wrong, he was looking in the wrong place, at the wrong people. But his instincts were almost never wrong. 'You know the rules of the game, and by those rules, I don't even have enough to go to the Commissioner. He'd boot me out of the office, and be right to do so. We have nothing but unsupported suspicions.' The two men stared at each other for several seconds.

'I never wanted to be a policeman.' Ashley smiled and shook his head.

'I didn't get my wish, either. I wanted to be an engine driver when I was six, but my father said there were enough railway people in the family. So I became a copper.' Both men laughed. There wasn't anything else to do.

'I'll increase the surveillance on Cooley's trips abroad. I don't think there's much more to be done on your side,' Ashley said finally.

'We have to wait for them to make a mistake. Sooner or later they all do, you know.'

'But soon enough?' That was the question.

'Here we are,' Alex said.

'How did you get these?' Miller asked in amazement.

'Routine, man. Power companies shoot aerial photographs of their territory all the time. They help us plan the surveys we have to do. And here –' he reached into his briefcase ' – is a topographic map. There's your target, boy.' Alex handed him a magnifying glass borrowed from his company. It was a colour shot, taken on a bright sunny day. You could tell the makes of the cars. It must have been done the previous summer – the grass had just been cut. . . .

'How tall is the cliff?'

'Enough that you don't want to fall off it. Tricky, too. I forget what it's made of, sandstone or something crumbly, but you want to be careful with it. See that fence here? The man knows to keep away from the edge. We have the same problem at our reactor plant at Calvert Cliff. It's the same geological structure, and a lot of work went into giving the plant a solid foundation.'

'Only one road in,' Miller noted.

'Dead end, too. That *is* a problem. We have these gullies here and here. Notice that the power line comes in cross country, from this road over here. It looks like there was an old farm road that connected with this one, but they let it go to seed. That's going to be helpful.'

'How? No one can use it.'

'I'll tell you later. Friday, you and me are going fishing.'

'What?' Miller looked up in surprise.

'You want to eyeball the cliff, right? Besides, the blues are running. I love bluefish.'

Breckenridge had silhouette targets up, finally. Jack's trips to the range were less frequent now, mainly in the mornings before class. If nothing else, the incident outside the gate had told the Marine and civilian guards that their jobs were valuable. Two Marines and one of the civilians were also firing their service pieces. They didn't just shoot to qualify now. They were all shooting for scores. Jack hit the button to reel his target in. His rounds were all clustered in the centre of the target.

'Pretty good, Doc.' The Sergeant Major was standing behind him. 'If you want, we can run a competition string. I figure you'll qualify for a medal now.'

Ryan shook his head. He still had to shower after his morning jog. 'I'm not doing this for score, Gunny.'

'When does the little girl come home?'

'Next Wednesday, I hope.'

'That's good, sir. Who's going to look after her?'

'Cathy's taking a few weeks off.'

'My wife asked if y'all might need any help,' Breckenridge said.

Jack turned in surprise. 'Sissy – Commander Jackson's wife – will be over most of the time. Please thank your wife for us, Gunny, that's damned nice of her.'

'No big deal. Any luck finding the bastards?' Ryan's day-hops to CIA were not much of a secret.

'Not yet.'

'Good morning, Alex,' the field superintendent said. 'You're staying in a little late. What can I do for you?' Bert Griffin was always in early, but he rarely saw Dobbens before he went home at seven every morning.

'I've been looking over the specifications on that new Westinghouse transformer.'

'Getting dull working nights?' Griffin asked with a smile. This was a fairly easy time of year for the utility company. In the summer, with all the air conditioners up and running, things would be different, of course. Spring was the time of year for new ideas.

'I think we're ready to give it a try.'

'Have they ironed the bugs out?'

'Pretty much, enough for a field test, I think.'

'Okay.' Griffin sat back in his chair. 'Tell me about it.'

'Mainly, sir, I'm worried about the old ones. The problem's only going to get worse as we start retiring the old units. We had that chemical spill last month –'

'Oh, yeah.' Griffin rolled his eyes. Most of the units in use contained PBBs, polybrominated biphenyls, as a cooling element within the power transformer. These were dangerous to the linemen, who were supposed to wear protective clothing when working on them, but, despite company rules, often didn't bother. PBBs were a serious health hazard to the men. Even worse, the company had to dispose of the toxic liquid periodically. It was expensive and ran the risk of spills, the paperwork for which was rapidly becoming as time-consuming as that associated with the company's nuclear reactor plant. Westinghouse was experimenting with a transformer that used a completely inert chemical in place of the PBBs. Though expensive, it held great promise for long-term economics – and would help get the environmentalists off their backs, which was even more attractive than the monetary savings. 'Alex, if you can get those babies up and working, I will personally get you a new company car!'

'Well, I want to try one out. Westinghouse will lend us one for free.'

'This is really starting to sound good,' Griffin noted. 'But have they really ironed the bugs out yet?'

'They say so, except for some occasional voltage fluctuations. They're not sure what causes that, and they want to do some field tests.'

'How bad are the fluctuations?'

'Marginal.' Alex pulled out a pad and read off the numbers. 'It seems to be an environmental problem. Looks like it only happens when the ambient air temperature changes rapidly. If that's the real cause, it shouldn't be too hard to beat.'

Griffin considered that for a few seconds. 'Okay, where do you want to set it up?'

'I have a spot picked out down in Anne Arundel County, south of Annapolis.'

'That's a long ways away. Why there?'

'It's a dead-end line. If the transformer goes bad, it won't hurt many houses. The other thing is, one of my crews is only twenty miles away, and I've been training them on the new unit. We'll set up the test instrumenta-tion, and I can have them check it every day for the first few months. If it works out, we can make our purchase order in the fall and start setting them up next spring.'

'Okay. Where exactly is this?'

Dobbens unfolded his map on Griffin's table. 'Right here.'

'Expensive neighbourhood,' the field superintendent said dubiously.

'Aw, come on, boss!' Alex snorted. 'How would it look in the papers if we did all our experiments on poor folk? Besides' – he smiled – 'all those environmental freaks are rich, aren't they?'

Dobbens had chosen his remark with care. One of Griffin's personal hobbyhorses was the 'Park Avenue Environmentalist'. The field superinten-dent owned a small farm, and didn't like having some condo-owning dilet-tante tell him about nature.

'Okay, you can run with it. How soon can you set it up?'

'Westinghouse can have the unit to us the end of next week. I can have it up and running three days after that. I want my crew to check the lines – in fact, I'll be going down myself to set it up if you don't mind.'

Griffin nodded approval. 'You're my kind of engineer, son. Most of the schoolboys we get now are afraid to get their hands dirty. You'll keep me posted?'

'Yes, sir.'

'Keep up the good work, Alex. I've been telling management about you.'

'I appreciate that, Mr Griffin.'

Dobbens left the building and drove home in his two-year-old company Plymouth. Most of the rush-hour traffic was heading in while he headed out. He was home in under an hour. Sean Miller was just waking up, drinking tea and watching television. Alex wondered how anyone could start the day with tea. He made some instant coffee for himself.

'Well?' Miller asked.

'No problem.' Alex smiled, then stopped. It occurred to him that he'd miss his job. After all the talk in college about bringing Power to the People, he'd realized with surprise after starting with BG&E that a utility company engineer did exactly that. In a funny sort of way, he was now serving the ordinary people, though not in a manner that carried much significance. Dobbens decided that it was good training for his future ambitions. He'd remember that even those who served humbly still served. An important lesson for the future. 'Come on, we'll talk about it in the boat.'

Wednesday was a special day. Jack was away from both his jobs, carrying the bear while Cathy wheeled their daughter out. The bear was a gift from the midshipmen of his history classes, an enormous monster that weighed sixty pounds and was nearly five feet tall, topped off with a Smokey Bear hat – actually that of a Marine drill instructor courtesy of Breckenridge and the guard detail. A police officer opened the door for the procession. It was a windy March day, but the family wagon was parked just outside. Jack scooped up his daughter in both arms while Cathy thanked the nurses. He made sure she was in her safety seat and buckled the belt himself. The bear had to go in the back.

'Ready to go home, Sally?'

'Yes.' Her voice was listless. The nurses reported that she still cried out in her sleep. Her legs were fully healed, finally. She could walk again, badly and awkwardly, but she could walk. Except for the loss of her spleen, she was whole again. Her hair was trimmed short to compensate for what had been shaved, but that would grow out soon enough. Even the scars, the surgeons said, would fade, and the pediatricians assured him that in a few months the nightmares would end. Jack turned to run his hand along the little face, and got a smile for his efforts. It wasn't the smile he was accustomed to getting. Behind his own smile, Ryan's mind boiled with rage yet again, but he told himself that this wasn't the time. Sally needed a father now, not an avenger.

'We have a surprise waiting for you,' he said.

'What?' Sally asked.

'If I told you, it wouldn't be a surprise,' her father pointed out.

'*Daddy!*' For a moment his little girl was back.

'Wait and see.'

'What's that?' Cathy asked on getting in the car.

'The surprise.'

'What surprise?'

'See,' Jack told his daughter. 'Mommy doesn't know either.'

'Jack, what's going on?'

'Doctor Schenk and I had a little talk last week,' was all Ryan would say. He released the parking brake and headed off onto Broadway.

'I want my bear,' Sally said.

'He's too big to sit there, honey,' Cathy responded.

'But you can wear his Smokey hat. He said it was okay.' Jack handed it back. The wide-brimmed campaign hat dropped over her head.

'Did you thank the people for the bear?' Cathy asked.

'You bet.' Ryan smiled for a moment. 'Nobody flunks this term. But don't tell anybody that.' Jack had a reputation as a tough marker. That might not survive this semester. *Principles be damned*, he told himself. The mids in his class had sent Sally a steady stream of flowers, toys, puzzles, and cards that had entertained his little girl, then circulated around the pediatric floor and brightened the days of fifty more sick kids. Smokey Bear was the crowning achievement. The nurses had told Cathy that it had made a difference. The monster toy had often sat at the top of Sally's bed, with the little girl clinging to it. It would be a tough act to follow, but Jack had that one figured out. Skip Tyler was making the final arrangements now.

Jack took his time, driving as though he were carrying a cargo of cracked eggs. His recent habits at CIA made him yearn for a cigarette, but he knew that he'd have to stop that now, with Cathy home all the time. He was careful to avoid the route Cathy had taken the day that – His hands tightened on the wheel as they had for weeks now. He knew he had to stop thinking about it so much. It had become an obsession, and that wasn't going to help anything.

The scenery had changed since the . . . accident. What had been bare trees now had the green edges of buds and leaves with the beginning of spring. Horses and cows were out on the farms. Some calves and colts were visible, and Sally's nose pressed against the car window as she looked at them. As it did every year, life was renewing itself, Ryan told himself. His family was whole again, and he'd keep it that way. The last turn onto Falcon's Nest Road finally came. Jack noted that the utility trucks were still around, and he wondered briefly what they had been up to as he turned left into his driveway.

'Skip's here?' Cathy asked.

'Looks like it,' Jack replied with a suppressed grin.

'They're home,' Alex said.

'Yeah,' Louis noted. Both men were perched at the top of the utility pole, ostensibly stringing new power lines to accommodate the experiment transformer. 'You know, the day after the job,' the lineman said, 'there was a picture of the lady in the papers. Some kid went through a window and got his face all cut up. It was a little brother, Alex. The lady saved his eyes, man.'

'I remember, Louis.' Alex raised his camera and snapped off a string of shots.

'An' I don't like fucking with kids, man,' Louis said. 'A cop's a different thing,' he added defensively. He didn't have to say that so was the kid's father. That was business. Like Alex, he had a few remaining scruples, and hurting children was not something he could do without some internal turmoil.

'Maybe we were all lucky.' Alex knew objectively that this was a stupid way for a revolutionary to think. Sentimentality had no place in his mission; it got in the way of what he had to do, prolonging the task and causing more deaths in the process. He also knew that the taboos against injuring children were part of the genetic programming of any human being. Mankind had progressed in its knowledge since Marx and Lenin. So whenever possible he'd avoid injuring kids. He rationalized that this would enhance his sympathy in the community he was seeking to liberate.

'Yeah.'

'So what have you seen?'

'They got a maid – black o'course. Fine-lookin' woman, drives a Chevy. There's somebody else in there now. He's a white dude, big guy, an' he walks funny.'

'Right.' Alex made note of the former and dismissed the latter. The man was probably a family friend.

'The cops – state cops – are back here every two hours minimum. One of them asked me what we were doing yesterday afternoon. They're keeping an eye on this place. There's an extra phone line into the house – gotta be for an alarm company. So they got a house alarm and the cops are always close.'

'Okay. Keep your eyes open but don't be too obvious.'

'You got it.'

'Home,' Ryan breathed. He stopped the car and got out, walking around to Sally's door. He saw that the little girl wasn't playing with the seat-buckle. He took care of it himself, then lifted his daughter out of the car. She wrapped her arms around his neck, and for a moment life was perfect again. He carried Sally to the front door, both arms clasping her to his chest.

'Welcome back.' Skip had the door open already.

'Where's my surprise?' Sally demanded.

'Surprise?' Tyler was taken aback. 'I don't know about any surprise.'

'Daddy!' Her father got an accusing look.

654

'Come on in,' Tyler said.

Mrs Hackett was there, too. She'd gotten lunch ready for everyone. A single mother of two sons, she worked hard to support them. Ryan set his girl down, and she walked to the kitchen. Skip Tyler and her father watched her stiff legs negotiate the distance.

'God, it's amazing how kids heal,' Tyler observed.

'What?' Jack was surprised.

'I broke a leg playing ball once – damned if I bounced back that fast. Come on,' Tyler beckoned Jack out the door. First he checked out the stuffed animal in the car. 'I heard it was some kind of bear. That one must have played in Chicago!'

Then they went into the trees north of Ryan's house. Here they found the surprise, tied to a tree. Jack loosed the chain and picked him up.

'Thanks for bringing him over.'

'Hey, no big deal. It's good to see her home, pal.'

The two men walked back into the house. Jack peeked around the corner and saw that Sally was already demolishing a peanut-butter sandwich.

'Sally . . .' he said. His wife was already looking at him with an open mouth. His daughter's head came around just as Jack set the puppy on the floor.

It was a black Labrador, just old enough to be separated from his mother. The puppy needed a single look to know to whom he belonged. He scampered across the floor, mostly sideways, with his tail gyrating wildly. Sally was on the floor, and grabbed him. A moment later, the dog was cleaning her face.

'She's too little for a puppy,' Cathy said.

'Okay, you can take him back this afternoon,' Jack replied quietly. The remark got him an angry look. His daughter squealed when the dog started chewing on the heel of one shoe. 'She's not big enough for a pony yet, but I think this is just the right thing.'

'You train it!'

'That'll be easy. He comes from good stock. Champion Chesapeake's Victor Hugo Black for a father, would you believe? The Lab's got a soft mouth, and they like kids,' Jack went on. 'I've already scheduled him for classes.'

'Classes in what?' Cathy was really befuddled now.

'The breed is called the Labrador *Retriever*,' Jack noted. 'How big does it get?'

'Oh, maybe seventy pounds.'

'That's bigger than she is!'

'Yeah, they love to swim, too. He can look after her in the pool.'

'We don't have a pool.'

'They start in three weeks.' Jack smiled again. 'Doctor Schenk also said that swimming is good therapy for this kind of injury.'

'You've been busy,' his wife observed. She was smiling now.

655

'I was going to get a Newfoundland, but they're just too big – one-fifty.' Jack didn't say that his first wish had been to get a dog big and tough enough to tear the head off anyone who came close to his daughter, but that his common sense had prevented it.

'Well, there's your first job,' Cathy pointed. Jack got a paper towel to clean up the puddle on the tile. Before he could do it, his daughter nearly strangled him with a ferocious hug. It was all he could do to control himself, but he had to. Sally would not have understood why her daddy was crying. The world was back in its proper shape. *Now if we can just keep it that way.*

'I'll have the pictures tomorrow. I wanted to get them done before the trees fill in. When they do, you won't be able to see the house from the road very well.' Alex summarized the results of his reconnaissance.

'What about the alarm?'

Alex read off the data from his notes.

'How the bloody hell did you get that?'

Dobbens chuckled as he popped open the beer. 'It's easy. If you want the data for any kind of burglar alarm, you call the company that did it and say you work for an insurance company. You give them a policy number – you make that up, of course – and they give you all the information you want. Ryan has a perimeter system, and a backup intruder system "with keys", which means that the alarm company has keys to the house. Somewhere on the property they have infrared beams. Probably on the driveway in the trees. This guy isn't dumb, Sean.'

'It doesn't matter.'

'Okay, I'm just telling you. One more thing.'

'Yes?'

'The kid doesn't get hurt this time, not the wife either if we can help it.'

'That is not part of the plan,' Miller assured him. *You bloody wimp.* Sean had learned a new word in America. *What sort of revolutionary do you think you are?* he didn't say.

'That's from my people,' Alex continued, telling only part of the truth. 'You gotta understand, Sean, child abuse looks bad over here. It's not the kind of image we want to have, you dig?'

'And you want to come out with us?'

Dobbens nodded. 'It might be necessary.'

'I think we can avoid that. It just means eliminating all the people who see your faces.'

You're a cold little cocksucker, Dobbens thought, though his words made perfect sense. Dead men told no tales.

'Very well. All we have to do now is find a way to make the security people relax a bit,' the Irishman said. 'I'd prefer to avoid brute force.'

'I've been thinking about that.' Alex took a moment before going on. 'How do armies succeed?'

656

'What do you mean?' Miller asked.

'I mean, the great plans, the ones that really work. They all work because you show the other guy something he expects to see, right? You make him go for the fake, but it's gotta be a really good fake. We have to make them look for the wrong thing in the wrong place, and they have to put the word out.'

'And how do we do that?' After two minutes: 'Ah.'

Alex retired to his bedroom a few minutes later, leaving Miller in front of the television to go over his material. On the whole, it had been a very useful tip. The plan was already beginning to take shape. It would require a lot of people, but that came as no surprise.

Curiously, his respect for Alex was now diminished. The man was competent, certainly, even brilliant in his plan for a diversion – but that absurd sentimentality! It was not that Miller revelled in the idea of hurting children, but if that was what the revolution took, then it was a necessary price to pay. Besides, it got people's attention. It told them that he and his organization were serious. Until Alex got over that, he'd never be successful. But that wasn't Miller's problem. Part One of the operation was now outlined in his mind. Part Two was already drawn up, already had been aborted once. *But not this time*, Miller promised himself.

By noon the following day, Alex had handed him the photos and driven him to an outlying station of the DC Metro. Miller took the subway train to National Airport to catch the first of four flights that would take him home.

Jack walked into Sally's bedroom just before eleven. The dog – his daughter had named him Ernie – was an invisible shape in the corner. This was one of the smartest things he had ever done. Sally was too much in love with Ernie to dwell on her injuries, and she chased after him as fast as her weakened legs would allow. That was enough to make her father overlook the chewed shoes and occasional mistakes with which the dog was littering the house. In a few weeks she'd be back to normal. Jack adjusted the covers slightly before leaving. Cathy was already in bed when he got there.

'Is she okay?'

'Sleeping like an angel,' Jack replied as he slid in beside her.

'And Ernie?'

'He's in there somewhere. I could hear his tail hitting the wall.' He wrapped his arms around her. It was hard getting close to her now. He ran one hand down to her abdomen, feeling the shape of his unborn child. 'How's the next one?'

'Quiet, finally. God, he's an active one. Don't wake him up.'

It struck Jack as an absurd idea that babies were awake before they were born, but you couldn't argue with a doctor. 'He?'

'That's what Madge says.'

'What's she say about you?' He felt her ribs next. They were too prominent. His wife had always been slender, but this was too much.

'I'm gaining the weight back,' Cathy answered. 'You don't have to worry. Everything's fine.'

'Good.' He kissed her.

'Is that all I get?' he heard from the darkness.

'You think you can handle more?'

'Jack, I don't have to go to work tomorrow,' she pointed out.

'Some of us do,' he protested, but soon found that his heart wasn't in it.

21

Plans

'He is thorough,' O'Donnell observed. Miller had returned with the aerial photographs that Dobbens had copied, topographic maps, and photos of Ryan's home from the land and water sides. Added to these were typed notes of the observations made by his people and other data thought to be of interest.

'Unfortunately he allows his personal feelings to interfere with his activities,' Miller observed coolly.

'And you don't, Sean?' O'Donnell chided gently.

'It won't happen again,' his operations officer promised.

'That's good. The important thing about mistakes is that we learn from them. So let's go over your proposed operation.'

Sean took out two other maps and spent twenty minutes running through his ideas. He concluded with Dobbens' suggestion for a diversion.

'I like it.' He turned to his intelligence chief. 'Joseph?'

'The opposition will be formidable, of course, but the plan allows for that. The only thing that worries me is that it will take nearly all of our people to do it.'

'Nothing else looks feasible,' Miller replied. 'It's not so much a question of getting close enough, but of leaving the area after the mission is accomplished. Timing is crucial –'

'And when timing is crucial, simplicity is a must.' O'Donnell nodded. 'Is there anything else that the opposition might try?'

'I think not,' McKenney said. 'This is the worst-case expectation.'

'Helicopters,' Miller said. 'They nearly did for us the last time. No real problem if we're prepared for it, but we must be prepared.'

'Very well,' O'Donnell said. 'And the second part of the operation?'

'Obviously we need to know where all the targets will be,' McKenney said. 'When do you want me to activate our people?' On orders, the intelligence chief's penetration agents had been quiescent for some weeks.

'Not just yet,' the Commander replied thoughtfully. 'Again a question of timing. Sean?'

'I think we should wait until the mission is fully accomplished before moving.'

'Yes, it proved to be a good idea the last time,' the Commander agreed. 'How many people are needed for your operation?'

'No less than fifteen. I think we can depend on Alex for three trained men, himself included. More than that – no, we should limit his participation as much as possible.'

'Agreed,' McKenney said.

'And training?' O'Donnell asked.

'The most we've ever done.'

'To start when?'

'A month beforehand,' Miller answered. 'Any more time would be a waste of resources. For the moment I have quite a lot of work to do.'

'So here are the plans,' Murray said. 'You can either let them stay at your embassy or we'll put them in Blair House, right across the street from the President.'

'With all due respect to your Secret Service chaps –' The head of the Diplomatic Protection Group didn't have to go on. Their safety was his responsibility and he wouldn't trust it to foreigners any more than he had to.

'Yeah, I understand. They'll get a full security detail from the Secret Service plus a couple of FBI liaison people and the usual assistance from the local police. Finally we'll have two HRT groups on alert the whole time they're over, one in DC, and a backup team at Quantico.'

'How many people know?' Ashley asked.

'The Secret Service and Bureau police are already fully briefed. When your advance men go over, they ought to have most of the events scouted for you already. The local cops will not be notified until they have to know.'

'You said most of the locations have been scouted, but not all?' Owens asked.

'Do you want us to check out the unannounced points this early, too?'

'No.' The man from DPG shook his head. 'It's bad enough that the public functions have to be exposed this early. It's still not official that they're going, you know. The element of surprise is our best defence.'

Owens looked at his colleague, but didn't react. The head of the DPG was on his suspects list, and his orders were not to allow anyone to know the details of his investigation. Owens thought him to be in the clear, but his detectives had discovered a few irregularities in the man's personal life that had somehow got past all the previous security screenings. Until it was certain that he was not a possible blackmail risk, he would not be allowed to know that some possible suspects had already seen the itinerary. The Commander of C-13 gave Murray an ironic look.

'I think you're overdoing this, gentlemen, but that's your business,' the FBI man said as he stood. 'Your people are flying over tomorrow?'

'That's right.'

'Okay, Chuck Avery of the Secret Service will meet your people at Dulles. Tell them not to be bashful about asking for things. You will have our total cooperation.' He watched them leave. Five minutes later Owens was back.

'What gives, Jimmy?' Murray wasn't surprised.

'What further progress have you made on the lads who attacked Ryan?'

'Not a thing for the past two weeks,' Murray admitted. 'You?'

'We have a possible link – let me be precise, we suspect that there might be a possible link.'

The FBI man grinned. 'Yeah, I know what that's like. Who is it?'

'Geoffrey Watkins.' That got a reaction.

'The foreign-service guy? Damn! Anybody else on the list that I know?'

'The chap you were just talking to. Ashley's people discovered that he's not entirely faithful to his wife.'

'Boys or girls?' Murray took a cue from the way Owens had said that. 'You mean that he doesn't know, Jimmy?'

'He doesn't know that the itinerary has been leaked, possibly to the wrong people. Watkins is among them, but so is our DPG friend.'

'Oh, that's real good! The plans may be leaked, and you can't tell the head of the security detail because he may be the one –'

'It's most unlikely, but we must allow for the possibility.'

'Call the trip off, Jimmy. If you have to break his leg, call it the hell off.'

'We can't. He won't. I spoke with His Highness the day before yesterday and told him the problem. He refuses to allow his life to be managed that way.'

'Why are you telling me this?' Murray rolled his eyes.

'I must tell someone, Dan. If I can't tell my lads, then . . .' Owens waved his hands.

'You want us to call the trip off for you, is that it?' Murray demanded. He knew that Owens couldn't answer that one. 'Let's spell this one out nice and clear. You want our people to be alert to the chance that an attack is a serious possibility, and that one of the good guys might be a bad guy.'

'Correct.'

'This isn't going to make our folks real happy.'

'I'm not terribly keen on it myself, Dan,' Owens replied.

'Well, it gives Bill Shaw something else to think about.' Another thought struck him. 'Jimmy, that's one expensive piece of live bait you have dangling on the hook.'

'He knows that. It's our job to keep the sharks away, isn't it?'

Murray shook his head. The ideal solution would be to find a way to cancel the trip, thereby handing the problem back to Owens and Ashley. That meant involving the State Department. The boys at Foggy Bottom would spike that idea, Murray knew. You couldn't un-invite a future chief of state because the FBI and Secret Service didn't think they could guarantee his safety – the reputation of American law-enforcement would be laid open to ridicule, they'd say, knowing that his protection wasn't the responsibility of the people at State.

'What do you have on Watkins?' he asked after a moment. Owens outlined his 'evidence'.

'That's all?'

'We're still digging, but so far there is nothing more substantive. It could all be coincidence, of course. . . .'

'No, it sounds to me like you're right.' Murray didn't believe in coincidences either. 'But there's nothing that I could take to a grand jury at home. Have you thought about flushing the game?'

'You mean running through a change in the schedule? Yes, we have. But then what? We could do that, see if Watkins goes to the shop, and arrest both men there – if we can confirm that what is happening is what we think it to be. Unfortunately, that means throwing away the only link we've ever had with the ULA, Dan. At the moment, we're watching Cooley as closely as we dare. He's still travelling. If we can find out whom he's contacting, then perhaps we can wrap up the entire operation. What you suggest is an option but not the best one. We do have time, you know. We have several months before we need to do something as drastic as that.'

Murray nodded, not so much in agreement as in understanding. The possibility of finding and destroying O'Donnell's bunch had been tantalizing to Scotland Yard. Bagging Cooley now would quash that. It wasn't something that they'd simply toss off. He knew that the Bureau would think much the same way.

'Jack, I want you to come along with me,' Marty Cantor said. 'No questions.'

'What?' Ryan asked, and got an accusing look. 'All right, all right.' He took the files he was working on and locked them in his file cabinet, then grabbed his jacket. Cantor led him around the corner to the elevator. After arriving on the first floor, he walked rapidly west into the annex behind the headquarters building. Once in the new structure, they passed through five security checkpoints. This was an all-time record for Ryan, and he wondered if Cantor had had to reprogramme the pass-control computer to get him into this building. After ten minutes he was on the fourth floor in a room identified only by its number.

'Jack, this is Jean-Claude. He's one of our French colleagues.'

Ryan shook hands with a man twenty years older than himself, whose face was the embodiment of civilized irony. 'What gives, Marty?'

'Professor Ryan,' Jean-Claude said. 'I am informed that you are the man we must thank.'

'What for –' Ryan stopped. *Uh-oh.* The Frenchman led him to a TV monitor.

'Jack, you never saw this,' Cantor said as a picture formed on the screen. It had to be satellite photography. Ryan knew it at once from the viewing angle, which changed very slowly.

'When?' he asked.

'Last night, our time, about three A.M. local.'

'Correct.' Jean-Claude nodded, his eyes locked on the screen.

It was Camp-20, Ryan thought. The one that belonged to *Action Directe*. The spacing of the huts was familiar. The infrared picture showed that three of the huts had their heaters on. The brightness of the heat signals told him that ground temperature must have been about freezing. South of the camp, behind a dune, two vehicles were parked. Jack couldn't tell if they were jeeps or small trucks. On closer inspection, faint figures were moving on the cold background: men. From the way they moved: soldiers. He counted eight of them split into two equal groups. Near one of the huts was a brighter light. There appeared to be a man standing there. *Three in the morning, when one's body functions are at the lowest ebb.* One of the camp guards was smoking on duty, doubtlessly trying to stay awake. That was a mistake, Ryan knew. The flare of the match would have destroyed his night vision. *Oh, well. . . .*

'Now,' Jean-Claude said.

There was a brief flash from one of the eight intruders; it was strange to see but not hear it. Ryan couldn't tell if the guard moved as a result, but his cigarette did, flying perhaps two yards, after which both images remained stationary. *That's a kill*, he told himself. *Dear God, what am I watching?* The eight pale shapes closed on the camp. First they entered the guard hut – it was always the same one. A moment later they were back outside. Next, they redeployed into the two groups of four, each group heading toward one of the 'lighted' huts.

'Who are the troops?' Jack asked.

'Paras,' Jean-Claude answered simply.

Some of the men reappeared thirty seconds later. After another minute, the rest emerged – more than had gone in, Ryan saw. Two seemed to be carrying something. Then something else entered the picture. It was a bright glow that washed out other parts of the picture, but the new addition was a helicopter, its engines blazing in the infrared picture. The picture quality deteriorated and the camera zoomed back. Two more helicopters were in the area. One landed near the vehicles, and the jeeps were driven into it. After that helicopter lifted off, the other skimmed the ground, following the vehicle tracks for several miles and erasing them with its downdraft. By the time the satellite lost visual lock with the scene, everyone was gone. The entire exercise had taken less than ten minutes.

'Quick and clean,' Marty breathed.

'You got her?' Jack had to ask.

'Yes,' Jean-Claude replied. 'And five others, four of them alive. We removed all of them, and the camp guards who, I regret to say, did not survive the evening.' The Frenchman's regrets were tossed in for good manners only. His face showed what he really felt.

'Any of your people hurt?' Cantor asked.

An amused shake of his head: 'No. They were all asleep, you see. One slept with a pistol next to his cot, and made the mistake of reaching for it.'

'You pulled everybody out, even the camp guards?'

'Of course. All are now in Chad. The living are being questioned.'

'How did you arrange the satellite coverage?' Jack asked.

This answer came with a Gallic shrug. 'A fortunate coincidence.'

Right, Jack thought. *Some coincidence. I just watched the instant-replay of the death of three or four people. Terrorists*, he corrected himself. *Except for the camp guards, who only helped terrorists. The timing could not have been an accident. The French wanted us to know that they were in counter-terrorist operations for real.*

'Why am I here?'

'But you made this possible,' Jean-Claude said. 'It is my pleasure to give you the thanks of my country.'

'What's going to happen to the people you captured?' Jack wanted to know.

'Do you know how many people they have assassinated? For those crimes they will answer. Justice, that will happen to them.'

'You wanted to see a success, Jack,' Cantor said. 'You just did.'

Ryan thought that one over. Removing the bodies of the camp guards told him how the operation would end. No one was supposed to know what had happened. Sure, some bullet holes were left behind, and a couple of blood-stains, but no bodies. The raiders had quite literally covered their tracks. The whole operation was 'deniable'. There was nothing left behind that would point to the French. In that sense it had been a perfect covert operation. And if that much effort had gone into making it so, then there was little reason to suspect that the *Action Directe* people would ever face a jury. *You wouldn't go to that much trouble and then go through the publicity of a trial*, Ryan told himself. *Goodbye, Françoise Theroux. . . .*

I condemned these people to death, *he realized finally. Just the one of them was enough to trouble his conscience. He remembered the police-style photograph he'd seen of her face and the fuzzy satellite image of a girl in a bikini.*

663

'She's murdered at least three people,' Cantor said, reading Jack's face.

'Professor Ryan, she has no heart, that one. No feelings. You must not be misled by her face,' Jean-Claude advised. 'They cannot all look like Hitler.'

But that was only part of it, Ryan knew. Her looks merely brought into focus that hers was a human life whose term was now unnaturally limited. *As she has limited those of others*, Jack told himself. He admitted to himself that he would have no qualms at all if her name had been Sean Miller.

'Forgive me,' he said. 'It must be my romantic nature.'

'But of course,' the Frenchman said generously. 'It is something to be regretted, but those people made their choice, Professor, not you. You have helped to avenge the lives of many innocent people, and you have saved those of people you will never know. There will be a formal note of thanks – a secret one, of course – for your assistance.'

'Glad to help, Colonel,' Cantor said. Hands were shaken all around, and Marty led Jack back to the headquarters building.

'I don't know that I want to see anything like that again,' Ryan said in the corridor. 'I mean, I don't want to know their faces. I mean – hell, I don't know what I mean. Maybe – It's just . . . different when you're detached from it, you know? It was too much like watching a ball game on TV, but it wasn't a ball game. Who was that guy, anyway?'

'Jean-Claude's the head of the DGSE's Washington Station, and he was the liaison man. We got the first new picture of her a day and a half ago. They had the operation all ready to roll, and he got things going inside of six hours. Impressive performance.'

'I imagine they wanted us to be impressed. They're not bringing 'em in, are they?'

'No. I seriously doubt those people are going back to France to stand trial. Remember the problem they had the last time they tried a public trial of *Action Directe* members? The jurors started getting midnight phone calls, and the case got blown away. Maybe they don't want to put up with the hassle again.' Cantor frowned. 'Well, it's not our call to make. Their system isn't the same as ours. All we did was forward information to an ally.'

'An American court could call that accessory to murder.'

'Possibly,' Cantor admitted. 'Personally, I prefer, what Jean-Claude called it.'

'Then why are you leaving in August?' Ryan asked.

Cantor delivered his answer without facing him. 'Maybe you'll find out someday, Jack.'

Back alone in his office, Ryan couldn't get his mind off what he'd seen. Five thousand miles away, agents of the DGSE's 'action' directorate were now questioning that girl. If this had been a movie, their techniques would be brutal. What they used in real life, Ryan didn't want to know. He told himself that the members of *Action Directe* had brought it on themselves. First, they had made a conscious choice to be what they were. Second, in subverting the French legal system the previous year, they'd given their enemies an excuse to bypass whatever constitutional guarantees . . . but was that truly an excuse?

'What would Dad think?' he murmured to himself. Then the next question hit him. Ryan lifted his phone and punched in the right number.

'Cantor.'

'Why, Marty?'

'Why what, Jack?'

'Why did you let me see that?'

'Jean-Claude wanted to meet you, and he also wanted you to see what your data accomplished.'

'That's bull, Marty! You let me into a real-time satellite display – okay, taped, but essentially the same thing. There can't be many people cleared for that. I don't need-to-know how good the real-time capability is. You could have told him I wasn't cleared for it and that would have been that.'

'Okay, you've had some time to think it over. Tell me what you think.'

'I don't like it.'

'Why?' Cantor asked.

'It broke the law.'

'Not ours. Like I told you twenty minutes ago, all we did was provide intelligence information to a friendly foreign nation.'

'But they used it to kill people.'

'What do you think intel is *for*, Jack? What should they have done? No, answer this first: what if they were foreign nationals who had murdered French nationals in – in Liechtenstein, say, and then boogied back to their base?'

'That's not the same thing. That's more . . . more like an act of war – like doing the guards at the camp. The people they *were* after were their own citizens who committed crimes in their own country, and – and are subject to French law.'

'And what if it had been a different camp? What if those paratroopers had done a job for us, or the Brits, and taken out your ULA friends?'

'That's different!' Ryan snapped back. *But why?* he asked himself a moment later. 'It's personal. You can't expect me to feel the same way about that.'

'Can't I?' Cantor hung up the phone.

Ryan stared at the telephone receiver for several seconds before replacing it in the cradle. What was Marty trying to tell him? Jack reviewed the events in his own mind, trying to come to a conclusion that made sense.

Did any of it make sense? Did it make sense for political dissidents to express themselves with bombs and machine guns? Did it make sense for small nations to use terrorism as a short-of-war weapon to change the policies of larger ones? Ryan grunted. That depended on which side of the issue you were on – or at least there were people who thought that way. Was this something completely new?

It was, and it wasn't. State-sponsored terrorism, in the form of the Barbary pirates, had been America's first test as a nation. The enemy objective then had been simple greed. The Barbary states demanded tribute before they would give right of passage to American-flag trading ships, but it had finally been decided that enough was enough. Preble took the infant U.S. Navy to the Mediterranean Sea to put an end to it – no, to put an end to America's victimization by it, Jack corrected himself.

God, it was even the same place, Ryan thought. 'To the shores of Tripoli,' the Marine Hymn said, where First Lieutenant Presley O'Bannon, USMC, had attacked the fort at Derna. Jack wondered if the place still existed. Certainly the problem did.

The violence hadn't changed. What had changed were the rules under which the large nations acted, and the objectives of their enemies. Two hundred years earlier when a small nation offended a larger one, ships and troops would settle matters. No longer was this simple wog-bashing, though. The smaller countries now had arsenals of modern weapons that could make such punitive expeditions too expensive for societies that had learned to husband the lives of their young men. A regiment of troops could no longer settle matters, and moving a whole army was no longer such a simple thing. Knowing this, the small country could inflict wounds itself, or even more safely, sponsor others to do so – 'deniably' – in order to move its larger opponent in the desired direction. There wasn't even much of a hurry. Such low-level conflict could last years, so small were the expenditures of resources and so different the perceived value of the human lives taken and lost.

What was new, then, was not the violence, but the safety of the nation that either performed or sponsored it. Until that changed, the killing would never stop.

So, on the international level, terrorism was a form of war that didn't even have to interrupt normal diplomatic relations. America itself had embassies in some of the nations, even today. Nearer to home, however, it was being treated as a crime. He'd faced Miller in the Old Bailey, Ryan remembered, not a military court-martial. *They can even use that against us.* It was a surprising realization. *They can fight their kind of war, but we can't recognize it as such without giving up something our society needs. If we treat terrorists as politically motivated activists, we give them an honour they don't deserve. If we treat them as soldiers, and kill them as such, we both give them legitimacy and violate our own laws.* By a small stretch of the imagination, organized crime could be thought of as a form of terrorism, Ryan knew. The terrorists' only weakness was their negativity. They were a political movement with nothing to offer other than their conviction that their parent society was unjust. So long as the people in that society felt otherwise, it was the terrorists who were alienated from it, not the population as a whole. The democratic processes that benefited the terrorists were also their worst

666

political enemy. Their prime objective, then, had to be the elimination of the democratic process, converting justice to injustice in order to arouse members of the society to sympathy with the terrorists.

The pure elegance of the concept was stunning. Terrorists could fight a war and be protected by the democratic processes of their enemy. If those processes were obviated, the terrorists would win additional political support, but so long as those processes were not obviated, it was extremely difficult for them to lose. They could hold a society hostage against itself and its most important precepts, daring it to change. They could move around at will, taking advantage of the freedom that defined a democratic state, and get all the support needed from a nation-state with which their parent society was unwilling or unable to deal effectively.

The only solution was international cooperation. The terrorists had to be cut off from support. Left to their own resources, terrorists would become little more than an organized-crime network. . . . But the democracies found it easier to deal with their domestic problems singly than to band together and strike a decisive blow at those who tormented them, despite all the rhetoric to the contrary. Had that just changed? The CIA had given data on terrorists to someone else, and action had been taken as a result. What he had seen earlier, therefore, was a step in the right direction, even if it wasn't necessarily the right kind of step. Ryan told himself that he'd just witnessed one of the world's many imperfections, but at least one aimed in the proper direction. That it had disturbed him was a consequence of his civilization. That he was now rationalizing it was a result of . . . what?

Cantor walked into Admiral Greer's office.

'Well?' the DDI asked.

'We'll give him a high B, maybe an A-minus. It depends on what he learns from it.'

'Conscience attack?' the DDI asked.

'Yeah.'

'It's about time he found out what the game's really like. Everybody has to learn that. He'll stay,' Greer said.

'Probably.'

The pickup truck tried to pull into the driveway that passed under the Hoover building, but a guard waved him off. The driver hesitated, partly in frustration, partly in rage while he tried to figure something else out. The heavy traffic didn't help. Finally he started circling the block until he was able to find a way into a public parking garage. The attendant held up his nose at the plebian vehicle – he was more accustomed to Buicks and Cadillacs – and burned rubber on the way up the ramp to show his feelings.

The driver and his son didn't care. They walked downhill and across the street, going by foot on the path denied their truck. Finally they got to the door and walked in.

The agent who had desk duty noted the entrance of two people somewhat disreputably dressed, the elder of whom had something wrapped in his leather jacket and tucked under his arm. This got the agent's immediate and full attention. He waved the visitors over with his left hand. His right was somewhere else.

'Can I help you, sir?'

'Hi,' the man said. 'I got something for you.' The man raised the jacket and pulled out a submachine gun. He quickly learned that this wasn't the way to get on the FBI's good side.

The desk agent snatched the weapon and yanked it off the desk, standing and reaching for his service revolver. The panic button under the desk was already pushed, and two more agents in the room converged on the scene. The man behind the desk immediately saw that the gun's bolt was closed – the gun was safe, and there wasn't a magazine in the pistol grip.

'I found it!' the kid announced proudly.

'What?' one of the arriving agents said.

'And I figured I'd bring it here,' the lad's father said.

'What the hell?' the desk agent observed.

'Let's see it.' A supervisor agent arrived next. He came from a surveillance room whose TV cameras monitored the entrance. The man behind the desk rechecked to make sure the weapon was safe, then handed it across.

It was an Uzi, the 9mm Israeli submachine gun used all over the world because of its quality, balance, and accuracy. The cheap-looking (the Uzi is anything but cheap, though it does look that way) metal stampings were covered with red-brown rust, and water dripped from the receiver. The agent pulled open the bolt and stared down the barrel. The gun had been fired and not cleaned since. It was impossible to tell how long ago that had been, but there weren't all that many FBI cases pending in which a weapon of this type had been used.

'Where did you find this, sir?'

'In a quarry, about thirty miles from here,' the man said.

'*I* found it!' the kid pointed out.

'That's right, he found it,' his father conceded. 'I figured this was the place to bring it.'

'You thought right, sir. Will both of you come with me, please?'

The agent on the desk gave both of them 'visitor' passes. He and the other two agents on entrance-guard duty went back to work, wondering what the hell that had been all about.

On the building's top floor, those few people in the corridor were surprised to see a man walking around with a machine gun, but it would not have been in keeping with Bureau chic to pay too much attention – the man with the

668

gun did have an FBI pass, and he was carrying it properly. When he walked into an office, however, it did get a reaction from the first secretary he saw.

'Is Bill in?' the agent asked.

'Yes, I'll –' Her eyes didn't leave the gun.

The man waved her off, motioned for the visitors to follow him, and walked towards Shaw's office. The door was open. Shaw was talking with one of his people. Special Agent Richard Alden went straight to Shaw's desk and set the gun on the blotter.

'Christ, Richie!' Shaw looked up at the agent, then back down at the gun. 'What's this?'

'Bill, these two folks just walked in the door downstairs and gave it to us. I thought it might be interesting.'

Shaw looked at the two people with visitor passes and invited them to sit on the couch against the wall. He called for two more agents to join them, plus someone from the ballistics laboratory. While things were being organized, his secretary got a cup of coffee for the father and a Dr Pepper for the son.

'Could I have your names, please?'

'I'm Robert Newton and this here's my son Leon.' He gave his address and phone number without being asked.

'And where did you find the gun?' Shaw asked while his subordinates were taking notes.

'It's called Jones Quarry. I can show you on a map.'

'What were you doing there?'

'I was fishing. I found it,' Leon reminded them.

'I was getting in some firewood,' his father said.

'This time of year?'

'Beats doing it during the summer, when it's hot, man,' Mr Newton pointed out reasonably. 'Also lets the wood season some. I'm a construction worker. I walk iron, and it's a little slow right now, so I went out for some wood. The boy's off from school today, so I brought him along. While I cut the wood, Leon likes to fish. There's some big ones in the quarry,' he added with a wink.

'Oh, okay.' Shaw grinned. 'Leon, you ever catch one?'

'No, but I got close last time,' the youngster responded.

'Then what?'

Mr Newton nodded for his son.

'My hook got caught on sumthin' heavy, you know, an' I pulled and pulled and pulled. It come loose, and I tried real hard, but I couldn't reel it up. So I called my daddy.'

'I reeled it in,' Mr Newton explained. 'When I saw it was a gun, I almost crapped my drawers. The hook was snagged on the trigger guard. What kinda gun is that, anyway?'

'Uzi. It's made in Israel, mostly,' the ballistics expert said, looking up from the weapon. 'It's been in the water at least a month.'

Shaw and another agent shared a look at that bit of news.

'I'm afraid I handled it a lot,' Newton said. 'Hope I didn't mess up any fingerprints.'

'Not after being in the water, Mr Newton,' Shaw replied. 'And you brought it right here?'

'Yeah, we only got it, oh' – he checked his watch – 'an hour and a half ago. Aside from handling it, we didn't do anything. It didn't have no magazine in it.'

'You know guns?' the ballistics man asked.

'I spent a year in Nam. I was a grunt with the 173rd Airborne. I know M-16s pretty good.' Newton smiled. 'And I used to do a little hunting, mostly birds and rabbits.'

'Tell us about the quarry,' Shaw said.

'It's off the main road, back maybe three-quarters of a mile, I guess. Lots of trees back there. That's where I get my firewood. I don't really know who owns it. Lots of cars go back there. You know, it's a parking spot for kids on Saturday nights, that sorta place.'

'Have you ever heard shooting there?'

'No, except during hunting season. There's squirrels in there, lotsa squirrels. So what's with the gun? Does it mean anything to y'all?'

'It might. It's the kind of gun used in the murder of a police officer, and –'

'Oh, yeah! That lady and her kid over Annapolis, right?' He paused for a moment. 'Damn.'

Shaw looked at the boy. He was about nine, the agent thought, and the kid had smart eyes, scanning the items Shaw had on his walls, the memorabilia from his many cases and posts. 'Mr Newton, you have done us a very big favour.'

'Oh, yeah?' Leon responded. 'What you gonna do with the gun?'

The ballistics expert answered. 'First we'll clean it and make sure it's safe. Then we'll fire it.' He looked at Shaw. 'You can forget any other forensic stuff. The water in the quarry must be chemically active. This corrosion is pretty fierce.' He looked at Leon. 'If you catch any fish there, son, you be sure you don't eat them unless your dad says it's all right.'

'Okay,' the boy assured him.

'Fibers,' Shaw said.

'Yeah, maybe that. Don't worry. If they're there, we'll find 'em. What about the barrel?'

'Maybe,' the man replied. 'By the way, this gun comes from Singapore. That makes it fairly new. The Israelis just licensed them to make the piece eighteen months ago. It's the same outfit that makes the M-16 under licence from Colt's.' He read off the number. It would be telexed to the FBI's Legal Attaché in Singapore in a matter of minutes. 'I want to get to work on this right now.'

'Can I watch?' Leon asked. 'I'll keep out of the way.'

'Tell you what,' Shaw said. 'I want to talk to your dad a little longer. How about I have one of our agents take you through our museum. You can see how we caught all the old-time bad guys. If you wait outside, somebody will come and take you around.'

'Okay!'

'We can't talk about this, right?' Mr Newton asked after his son had left.

'That's correct, sir.' Shaw paused. 'That's important for two reasons. First, we don't want the perpetrators to know that we've had a break in the case – and this could be a major break, Mr Newton; you've done something very important. The other reason is to protect you and your family. The people involved in this are very dangerous. Put it this way: you know that they tried to kill a pregnant woman and a four-year-old girl.'

That got the man's attention. Robert Newton, who had five children, three of them girls, didn't like hearing that.

'Now, have you ever seen people around the quarry?' Shaw asked.

'What do you mean?'

'Anybody.'

'There's maybe two or three other folks who cut wood back there. I know the names – I mean their first names, y'know? And like I said, kids like to go parking back there.' He laughed. 'Once I had to help one out. I mean, the road's not all that great, and this one kid was stuck in the mud, and. . .' Newton's voice trailed off. His face changed. 'Once, it was a Tuesday . . . I couldn't work that day 'cause the crane was broke, and I didn't much feel like sitting around the house, y'know? So I went out to chop some wood. There was this van coming outa the road. He was having real trouble in the mud. I had to wait like ten minutes 'cause he blocked the whole road, slippin' and slidin', like.'

'What kind of van?'

'Dark, mostly. The kind with the sliding door – musta been customized some, it had that dark stuff on the windows, y'know?'

Bingo! Shaw told himself. 'Did you see the driver or anybody inside?'

Newton thought for a moment. 'Yeah . . . it was a black dude. He was – yeah, I remember, he was yellin', like. I guess he was pissed at getting stuck like that. I mean, I couldn't hear him, but you could tell he was yelling, y'know? He had a beard, and a leather jacket like the one I wear to work.'

'Anything else about the van?'

'I think it made a noise, like it had a big V-8. Yeah, it must have been a custom van to have that.'

Shaw looked at his men, too excited to smile as they scribbled their notes.

'The papers said all the crooks were white,' Newton said.

'The papers don't always get things right,' Shaw noted.

'You mean the bastard who killed that cop was black?' Newton didn't like that. So was he. 'And he tried to do that family, too. . . . Shit!'

'Mr Newton, that is secret. Do you understand me? You can't tell anybody about that, not even your son – was he there then?'

'Nah, he was in school.'

'Okay, you can't tell anyone. That is to protect you and your family. We're talking about some very dangerous people here.'

'Okay, man.' Newton looked at the table for a moment. 'You mean we got people running around with machine guns, killing people – here? Not in Lebanon and like that, but here?'

'That's about the size of it.'

'Hey, man, I didn't spend a year in the Nam so we could have that shit where I live.'

Several floors downstairs, two weapons experts had already detail-stripped the Uzi. A small vacuum cleaner was applied to every part in the hope there might be cloth fibers that matched those taken from the van. A final careful look was taken at the parts. The damage from water immersion had done no good to the stampings, made mostly of mild steel. The stronger, corrosion-resistant ballistic steel of the barrel and bolt were in somewhat better shape. The lab chief reassembled the gun himself, just to show his technicians that he still knew how. He took his time, oiling the pieces with care, finally working the action to make sure it functioned properly.

'Okay,' he said to himself. He left the weapon on the table, its bolt closed on an empty chamber. Next he pulled an Uzi magazine from a cabinet and loaded twenty 9 millimetre rounds. This he stuck in his pocket.

It always struck visitors as somewhat incongruous. The technicians usually wore white laboratory coats, like doctors, when they fired the guns. The man donned his ear protectors, stuck the muzzle into the slot, and fired a single round to make certain that the gun really worked. It did. Then he held the trigger down, emptying the magazine in a brief span of seconds. He pulled out the magazine, checked that the weapon was safe, and handed it to his assistant.

'I'm going to wash my hands. Let's get those bullets checked out.' The chief ballistics technician was a fastidious person.

By the time he was finished drying his hands, he had a collection of twenty spent bullets. The metal jacket on each showed the characteristic marks made by the rifling of the machine gun's barrel. The marks were roughly the same on each bullet, but slightly different, since the gun barrel expanded when it got hot.

He took a small box from the evidence case. This bullet had gone completely through the body of a police officer, he remembered. It seemed such a puny thing to have taken a life, he thought, not even an ounce of lead and steel, hardly deformed at all from its deadly passage. It was hard not to dwell on such thoughts. He placed it on one side of the comparison microscope and took another from the set he'd just fired. Then he removed his glasses and bent down to the eyepieces. The bullets were. . . close. They'd definitely been fired by the same kind of gun. . . . He switched samples. Closer. The third bullet was closer still. He carefully rotated the sample, comparing it with the round that was kept in the evidence case, and it . . .

'We got a match.' He backed away from the 'scope and another technician bent down to check.

'Yeah, that's a match. One hundred percent,' the man agreed. The boss ordered his men to check other rounds and walked to the phone.

'Shaw.'

'It's the same gun. One-hundred-percent sure. I have a match on the round that killed the trooper. They're checking the ones from the Porsche now.'

'Good work, Paul!'

'You bet. I'll be back to you in a little while.'

Shaw replaced the phone and looked at his people. 'Gentlemen, we just had a break in the Ryan case.'

22

Procedures

Robert Newton took the agents to the quarry that night. By dawn the next day a full team of forensic experts was sifting through every speck of dirt at the site. A pair of divers went into the murky water, and ten agents were posted in the woods to watch for company. Another team located and interviewed Newton's fellow woodcutters. More spoke with the residents of the farms near the road leading back into the woods. Dirt samples were taken to be matched with those vacuumed from the van. The tracks were photographed for later analysis.

The ballistics people had already made further tests on the Uzi. The ejected cartridge cases were compared with those recovered from the van and the crime scene, and showed perfect matches in extractor marks and firing-pin penetrations. The match of the gun with the crime and the van was now better than one hundred percent. The serial number had been confirmed with the factory in Singapore, and records were being checked to determine where the gun had been shipped. The name of every arms dealer in the world was in the Bureau's computer.

The whole purpose of the FBI's institutional expertise was to take a single piece of information and develop it into a complete criminal case. What it could not entirely prevent was having someone see them. Alex Dobbens drove past the quarry road on his way to work every day. He saw a pair of vehicles pulling out onto the highway from the dirt and gravel path. Though both the car and van from the FBI laboratory were unmarked, they had federal licence plates, and that was all he needed to see.

Dobbens was not an excitable man. His professional training permitted him to look at the world as a collection of small, discrete problems, each of which had a solution; and if you solved enough of the small ones, then the large ones would similarly be solved, one at a time. He was also a meticulous person. Everything he did was part of a larger plan, both part of, and isolated from, the next planned step. It was not something that his people had easily come to understand, but it was hard to argue with success, and everything Dobbens did was successful. This had earned him respect and obedience from people who had once been too passionate for what Alex deemed their mission in life.

It was unusual, Dobbens thought, for two cars at once to come out of that road. It was out of the ordinary realm of probability that both should have government licence plates. Therefore he had to assume that somehow the feds had learned that he'd used the quarry for weapons training. How had it been blown? he wondered. A hunter, perhaps, one of the rustics who went in there after squirrels and birds? Or one of the people who chopped wood, maybe? Or some kid from a nearby farm? How big a problem was this?

He'd taken his people to shoot there only four times, the most recent being when the Irish had come over. *Hmm, what does that tell me?* he asked the road in front of his car. *That was weeks ago.* Each time, they'd done all the shooting during rush hour, mostly in the morning. Even this far from DC, there were a lot of cars and trucks on the road in the morning and late afternoon, enough to add quite a bit of noise to the environment. It was therefore unlikely that anyone had heard them. *Okay.*

Every time they had shot there, Alex had been assiduous about picking up the brass, and he was certain that they'd left nothing behind, not even a cigarette butt, to prove that they'd been there. They could not avoid leaving tire marks, but one of the reasons he'd picked the place was that kids went back there to park on weekends – there were plenty of tire marks.

They had dumped the gun there, he remembered, but who could have discovered that? The water in the quarry was over eight feet deep – he'd checked – and looked about as uninviting as a rice paddy, murky from dirt that washed in, and whatever kind of scum it was that formed on the surface. Not a place to go swimming. They had dumped only the gun that had been fired, but as unlikely as it seemed, he had to assume they'd found it. How that had happened didn't matter for the moment. *Well, we have to dispose of the others too, now,* Alex told himself. *You can always get new guns.*

What is the most the cops can learn? he asked himself. He was well versed on police procedures. It seemed only reasonable that he should know his enemy, and Alex owned a number of texts on investigative techniques, the books used to train cops in their various academies, like Snyder's *Homicide Investigation* and the *Law Enforcement Bible*. He and his people studied them as carefully as the would-be cops with their shiny young faces. . . .

There could be no fingerprints on the gun. After being in water, the skin oil that makes the marks would long since have been gone. Alex had handled and cleaned it, but he didn't need to worry about that.

The van was gone. It had been stolen to begin with, then customized by one of Alex's own people, and had used four different sets of tags. The tags were long gone, underneath a telephone/power pole in Anne Arundel County. If something had resulted from that, he'd have known it long before now, Alex thought. The van itself had been fully sanitized, everything had been wiped clean, the dirt from the quarry road . . . that was something to think about, but the van still led to a dead end. They'd left nothing in it to connect it with his group.

Had any of his people talked, perhaps a man with an aching conscience because of the kid who'd almost died? Again, had that happened, he would have awakened this afternoon to see a badge and gun in front of his face. So that was out. Probably. He'd talk to his people about that, remind them that they could never talk with anyone about what they did.

Might his face have been seen? Alex chided himself again for having waved at the helicopter. But he'd been wearing a hat, sunglasses, and a beard, all of which were now gone, along with the jacket, jeans, and boots that he'd worn. He still had the work gloves, but they were so common an item that you could buy them in any hardware store. *So dump 'em and buy another pair, asshole!* he said to himself. *Make sure they're the same colour, and keep the sales receipt.*

His mind ran through the data again. He might even be overreacting, he thought. The feds could be investigating some totally unrelated thing, but it was stupid to take any unnecessary risks. Everything that they'd used at the quarry would be disposed of. He'd make a complete list of possible connections and eliminate every one of them. They'd never go back there again. Cops had their rules and procedures, and he'd unhesitatingly copied the principle to deny its advantage to his opponents. He had established the rules for himself after seeing what catastrophes resulted from having none. The radical groups he'd hovered around in his college days had died because of their arrogance and stupidity, their underestimation of the skill of their enemies. Fundamentally, they'd died because they were unworthy of success. *Victory comes only to those prepared to make it, and take it,* Alex thought.

He was even able to keep from congratulating himself on spotting the feds. It was simple prudence, not genius. His route had been chosen with an eye to taking note of such things. He already had another promising site for weapons training.

'Erik Martens,' Ryan breathed. 'We meet again.'

All of the FBI's data had been forwarded to the Central Intelligence Agency's working group within hours of its receipt. The Uzi that had been recovered – Ryan marvelled at how that had happened! – had, he saw, been fabricated in Singapore, at a plant that also made a version of the M-16 rifle that he'd carried in the Corps, and a number of other military arms, both East and West, for sale to third-world countries . . . and other interested parties. From his work the previous summer, Ryan knew that there were quite a few such factories, and quite a few governments whose only measure for the legitimacy of an arms purchaser was his credit rating. Even those who paid lip-service to such niceties as 'end-user certificates' often turned a blind eye to the reputation of a dealer who never quite proved to be on the wrong side of the shadowy line that was supposed to distinguish the honest from the others. Since it was the dealer's government that generally made this determination, yet another variable was added to an already inexact equation.

Such was the case with Mr Martens. A very competent man in his business, a man with remarkable connections, Martens had once worked with the CIA-backed UNITA rebels in Angola until a more regular pipeline had been established. His principal asset, however, was his ability to obtain items for the South African government. His last major coup had been obtaining the manufacturing tools and dies for the Milan antitank missile, a weapon that could not be legally shipped to the Afrikaner government due to the Western embargo. After three months' creative effort on his part, the government's own armaments factories would be making it themselves. His fee for that had doubtless been noteworthy, Ryan knew, though the CIA had been unable to ascertain just how noteworthy. The man owned his own business jet, a Grumman G-3 with intercontinental range. To make sure that he could fly it anywhere he wished, Martens had obtained weapons for a number of black African nations, and even missiles for Argentina. He could go to any corner of the world and find a government that was in his debt. The man would have been a sensation on Wall Street or any other marketplace, Ryan smiled to himself. He could deal with anyone, could market weapons the way that people in Chicago traded wheat futures.

The Uzis from Singapore had come to him. Everyone loved the Uzi. Even the Czechs had tried to copy it, but without great commercial success. The Israelis sold them by the thousands to military and security forces, always – most of the time – following the rules that the United States insisted upon. Quite a few had found their way to South Africa, Ryan read, until the

676

embargo had made it rather more difficult. *Is that the reason they finally let someone make the gun under licence?* Jack wondered. *Let someone else broaden the market for you, and just keep the profits. . . .*

The shipment had been five thousand units . . . about two million dollars, wholesale. Not very much, really, enough to equip a city police force or a regiment of paratroopers, depending on the receiving government's orientation. Large enough to show a profit for Mr Martens, small enough not to attract a great deal of attention. One truckload, Ryan wondered, maybe two? The pallets of boxes would be tucked into a corner of his warehouse, technically supervised by his government, but more likely in fact to be Martens' private domain. . . .

That's what Sir Basil Charleston told me at the dinner, Ryan reminded himself. *You didn't pay enough attention to that South African chap. . . .* So the Brits think he deals to terrorists . . . directly? No, his government wouldn't tolerate that. *Probably wouldn't*, Ryan corrected himself. The guns might find their way to the African National Congress, which might not be very good news for the government they were pledged to destroy. So now Ryan had to find an intermediary. It took thirty minutes to get that file, involving a call to Marty Cantor.

The file was a disaster. Martens had eight known and fifteen suspected intermediary agents . . . one or two in every country he sold to – of course! Ryan punched Cantor's number again.

'I take it we've never talked to Martens?' Ryan asked.

'Not for a few years. He ran some guns into Angola for us, but we didn't like the way he handled things.'

'How so?'

'The man's something of a crook,' Cantor replied. 'That's not terribly unusual in the arms business, but we try to avoid the type. We set up our own pipeline after the Congress took away the restriction on those operations.'

'I got twenty-three names here,' Ryan said.

'Yeah, I'm familiar with the file. We thought he was passing arms to an Iranian-sponsored group last November, but it turned out he wasn't. It took us a couple of months to clear him. It would have been a whole lot easier if we'd been able to talk to him.

'Stone wall,' Marty said. 'Every time they try to talk with him, some big ol' Afrikaner soldier says no. You can't blame them, really, if the West treats them like pariahs, they're sure as hell going to act like pariahs. The other thing to remember is, pariahs stick together.'

'So we don't know what we need to know about this guy and we're not going to find out.'

'I didn't say that exactly.'

'Then we're sending people in to check a few things out?' Ryan asked hopefully.

'I didn't say that either.'

'Dammit, Marty!'

'Jack, you are not cleared to know anything about field operations. In case you haven't noticed, not one of the files you've seen tells you how the information gets in here.'

Ryan had noticed that. Informants weren't named, meeting places weren't specified; and the methods used to pass the information were nowhere to be found. 'Okay, may I safely assume that we will, by some unknown means, get more data on this gentleman?'

'You may safely assume that the possibility is being considered.'

'He may be the best lead we have,' Jack pointed out.

'I know.'

'This can be pretty frustrating stuff, Marty,' Ryan said, getting that off his chest.

'Tell me about it,' Cantor chuckled. 'Wait till you get involved with something really important – sorry, but you know what I mean. Like what the Politburo people really think about something, or how powerful and accurate their missiles are, or whether they have somebody planted in this building.'

'One problem at a time.'

'Yeah, that must be nice, sport, just to have one problem at a time.'

'When can I expect something on Martens?' Ryan asked.

'You'll know when it comes in,' Cantor promised. ' 'Bye.'

'Great.' Jack spent the rest of the day and part of another looking through the list of people Martens had dealt with. It was a relief to have to go back to teaching class the next two days, but he did find one possible connection. The Mercury motors found on the Zodiac used by the ULA had probably – the bookkeeping had broken down in Europe – gone through a Maltese dealer with whom Martens had done a little business.

The good news of the spring was that Ernie was a quick study. The dog got the hang of relieving himself outside within the first two weeks, which relieved Jack of a message from his daughter. 'Daaaaddy, there's a little proooblem . . .' invariably followed by a question from his wife: 'Having fun, Jack?' In fact, even his wife admitted that the dog was working out nicely. Ernie could only be separated from their daughter with a hard tug on his leash. He now slept in her bed, except when he patrolled the house every few hours. It was somewhat unnerving at first to see the dog – rather, to see a black mass darker than the night a few inches from one's face – when Ernie seemed to be reporting that everything was clear before he headed back to Sally's room for two more hours of protective slumber. He was still a puppy, with impossibly long legs and massive webbed feet, and he still liked to chew things. When that had included the leg of one of Sally's Barbie dolls, it resulted in a furious scolding from his owner that ended when he started licking Sally's face by way of contrition.

Sally was finally back to normal. As the doctors had promised her parents, her legs were fully healed, and she was running around now as she had before. This day would mark her return to Giant Steps. Her way of knocking glasses off tables as she ran past them was the announcement that things were right again, and her parents were too pleased by this to bring themselves to scold the girl for her unladylike behaviour. For her part, Sally endured an abnormally large number of spontaneous hugs which she didn't really understand. She'd been sick and she was now better. She'd never really known that an attack had happened, Jack was slow to realize. The handful of times she referred to it, it had always been 'the time the car broke'. She still had to see the doctors every few weeks for tests. She both hated and dreaded these, but children adapt to a changing reality far more readily than their parents.

One of these changes was her mother. The baby was really growing now. Cathy's petite frame seemed poorly suited to such abuse. After every morning shower, she looked at herself, naked, in a full-length mirror that hung on the back of the closet door and came away with an expression that was both proud and mournful as her hands traced over the daily alterations.

'It's going to get worse,' her husband told her as he emerged from the shower next.

'Thanks, Jack, I really need to hear that.'

'Can you see your feet?' he asked with a grin.

'No, but I can feel them.' They were swelling, too, along with her ankles.

'You look great to me, babe.' Jack stood behind her, reaching his arms around to hold her bulging abdomen. He rested his cheek on the top of her head. 'Love ya.'

'That's easy for you to say!' She was still looking in the mirror. Jack saw her face in the glass, a tiny smile on her lips. An invitation? He moved his hands upward to find out. 'Ouch! I'm sore.'

'Sorry.' He softened his grip to provide nothing more than support. 'Humph. Has something changed here?'

'It took you this long to notice?' The smile broadened a tad. 'It's a shame that I have to go through this for that to happen.'

'Have you ever heard me complain? Everything about you has always been A-plus. I guess pregnancy drops you to a B-minus. But only in one subject,' he added.

'You've been teaching too long, Professor.' Her teeth were showing now. Cathy leaned back, rubbing her skin against her husband's hairy chest. For some reason she loved to do that.

'You're beautiful,' he said. 'You glow.'

'Well, I have to glow my way to work.' Jack didn't move his hands. 'I have to get dressed, Jack.'

'"How do I love thee, let me count the ways . . ."' he murmured into her damp hair. 'One. . . two. . . three. . .'

'Not *now*, you lecher!'

'Why?' His hands moved very gently.

'Because I have to operate in three hours, and you have to go to spook city.' She didn't move, though. There weren't all that many moments that they could be alone.

'I'm not going there today. I got stuck with a seminar at the Academy. I'm afraid the department is a little miffed with me.' He kept looking in the mirror. Her eyes were closed now. *Screw the department* . . . 'God, I love you!'

'Tonight, Jack.'

'Promise?'

'You've sold me on the idea, okay? Now I –' She reached up to grab his hands, pulled them downward, and pressed them against the taut skin of her belly.

He – the baby was definitely a he, insofar as that was what they called him – was wide awake, rolling and kicking, pushing at the dark envelope that defined his world.

'Wow,' his father observed. Cathy's hands were over his, moving them about every few seconds to follow the movements of the baby. 'What does that feel like?'

Her head leaned back a fraction. 'It feels good – except when I'm trying to sleep or when he kicks my bladder during a procedure.'

'Was Sally this – this strong?'

'I don't think so.' She didn't say that it wasn't the sort of thing you remember in terms of strength. It was just the singular feeling that your baby is alive and healthy, something that no man would ever understand. Not even Jack. Cathy Ryan was a proud woman. She knew that she was one of the best eye surgeons around. She knew that she was attractive, and worked hard to keep herself that way; even now, mis-shapen by her pregnancy, she knew that she was carrying it well. She could tell that from her husband's biological reaction, in the small of her back. But more than that, she knew that she was a woman, doing something that Jack could neither duplicate nor fully comprehend. *Well*, she told herself, *Jack does things I don't much understand either.* 'I have to get dressed.'

'Okay.' Jack kissed the base of her neck. He took his time. It would have to last until this evening. 'I'm up to eleven,' he said as he stepped back.

She turned. 'Eleven what?'

'Counting the ways,' Jack laughed.

'You turkey!' She swung her bra at him. '*Only* eleven?'

'It's early. My brain isn't fully functional yet.'

'I can tell it doesn't have enough of a blood supply.' The funny thing, she thought, was that Jack didn't think he was very good-looking. She liked the strong jaw, except when he forgot to shave it, and his kind, loving eyes. She looked at the scars on his shoulder, and remembered her horror as she'd watched her husband run into harm's way, then her pride in him for what he had accomplished. Cathy knew that Sally had almost died as a direct result, but there was no way Jack could have foreseen it. It was her fault, too, she knew, and Cathy promised herself that Sally would never play with her seat belt again. Each of them had paid a price for the turns their lives had taken. Sally was almost fully recovered from hers, as was she. Cathy knew it wasn't true of her husband, who'd been awake through it all while she slept.

When that happened, at least I had the blessing of unconsciousness. Jack had to live through it. He's still paying that price for it, she thought. *Working two jobs now, his face always locked into a frown of concentration, worrying over something he can't talk about.* She didn't know exactly what he was doing, but she was certain that it was not yet done.

The medical profession had unexpectedly given her a belief in fate. Some people simply had their time. If it was not yet that time, chance or a good surgeon would save the life in question, but if the time had come, all the skilled people in the world could not change it. Caroline Ryan, MD, knew that this was a strange way for a physician to think, and she balanced the belief with the professional certainty that she was the instrument which would thwart the force that ruled the world – but she had also chosen a field in which life-and-death was rarely the issue. Only she knew that. A close friend had gone into pediatric oncology, the treatment of children stricken with cancer. It was a field that cried out for the best people in medicine, and she'd been tempted, but she knew that the effect on her humanity would be intolerable. How could she carry a child within her while she watched other children die? How could she create life while she was unable to prevent its loss? Her belief in fate could never have made that leap of imagination, and the fear of what it might have done to her psyche had turned her to a field that was demanding in a different way. It was one thing to put your life on the line – quite another to wager your soul.

Jack, she knew, had the courage to face up to that. This, too, had its price. The anguish she occasionally saw in him could only be that kind of question. She was sure that his unspoken work at CIA was aimed at finding and killing the people who had attacked her. She felt it necessary, and she would shed no tears for those who had nearly killed her little girl, but it was a task which, as a physician, she could not herself contemplate. Clearly it wasn't easy for her man. Something had just happened a few days ago. He was struggling with whatever it was, unable to discuss it with anyone while he tried to retain the rest of his world in an undamaged state, trying to love his family while he laboured . . . to bring others to their death? It could not have come easily to him. Her husband was a genuinely good man, in so many ways the ideal man – *at least for me*, she thought. He'd fallen in love with her at first meeting, and she could recount every step of their courtship. She remembered his clumsy – in retrospect, hilarious – proposal of marriage, the terror in his eyes as she'd hesitated over the answer, as though he felt himself unworthy of her; the idiot. Most of all, she remembered the look on his face when Sally had been born. The man who had turned his back on the dog-eat-dog world of investments – the world that since the death of her mother had made her father into a driven, unhappy man – who had returned to teaching eager young minds, was now trapped in something he didn't like. But she knew that he was doing his best, and she knew just how good his best was. She'd just experienced that. Cathy wished that she could share it, as he occasionally had to share with her the depression following a failed procedure. As much as she had needed him a few painful weeks past, now he needed her. She couldn't do that – or could she?

'What's been bothering you? Can I help?'

'I can't really talk about it,' Jack said as he knotted his tie. 'It was the right thing, but not something you can feel very good about.'

'The people who –'

'No, not them. If it was them . . .' He turned to face his wife. 'If it was them, I'd be all smiles. There's been a break. The FBI – I shouldn't be telling you this, and it doesn't go any farther than this room – they found the gun. That might be important, but we don't know for sure yet. The other thing – well, I can't talk about that at all. Sorry. I wish I could.'

'You haven't done anything wrong?' His face changed at that question.

'No. I've thought that one over the past few days. Remember the time you had to take that lady's eye out? It was necessary, but you still felt pretty bad about it. Same thing.' He looked in the mirror. *Sort of the same thing.*

'Jack, I love you and I believe in you. I know that you'll do the right thing.'

'I'm glad, babe, because sometimes I'm not so sure.' He held out his arms and she came to him. At some French military base in Chad, another young woman was experiencing something other than a loving embrace, Ryan thought. *Whose fault is that? One thing for sure, she isn't the same as my wife. She's not like this girl of mine.*

He felt her against himself, felt the baby move again, and finally he was sure. As his wife had to be protected, so did all the other wives, and all the children, and all the living people who were judged as mere abstractions by the ones who trained in those camps. Because they weren't abstractions, they were real. It was the terrorists who had cast themselves out of the civilized community and had to be hunted down one way or another. *If we can do it by civilized rules, well and good – but if not, then we have to do the best we can, and rely on our consciences to keep us from going over the edge.* He thought that he could trust his conscience. He was holding it in his arms. Jack kissed his wife gently on the cheek.

'Thanks. That's twelve.'

The seminar led to the final two weeks of classes which led in turn to final exams and Commissioning Week: yet another class of midshipmen graduated to join the fleet, and the Corps. The plebes were plebes no longer, and were finally able to smile in public once or twice per day. The campus became quiet, or nearly so, as the underclassmen went home for brief vacations before taking cruises with the fleet, and preparing for Plebe Summer, the rough initiation for a new class of mids. Ryan was incongruously trapped in his real job for a week, finishing up a mountain of paperwork. Neither the Academy's history department nor the CIA was very happy with him now. His attempt to serve two masters had not been a total success. Both jobs, he realized, had suffered somewhat, and he knew that he'd have to choose between them. It was a decision that he consciously tried to avoid while the proof of its necessity piled up around him.

'Hey, Jack!' Robby came in wearing his undress whites.

'Grab a seat, Commander. How's the flying business?'

'No complaints. The kid is back in the saddle,' Jackson said, sitting down. 'You should have been up in the Tomcat with me last week. Oh, man, I'm finally back in the groove. I was hassling with a guy in an A4 playing aggressor, and I ruined his day. It was so fine.' He grinned like a lion surveying a herd of crippled antelope. 'I'm ready!'

'When do you leave?'

'I report for duty 5 August. I guess I'll be heading out of here on the first.'

'Not before we have you and Sissy over for dinner.' Jack checked his calendar. 'The thirtieth is a Friday. Seven o'clock. Okay?'

'Aye aye, sir.'

'What's Sissy going to do down there?'

'Well, they have a little symphony in Norfolk. She's going to be their number-two piano soloist, plus doing her teachin' on the side.'

'You know they have the in-vitro centre down there. Maybe you guys can have a kid after all.'

'Yeah, Cathy told her about that. We're thinking about it, but – well, Sissy's had a lot of disappointments, you know?'

'You want Cathy to talk to her about it some more?'

Robby thought about that. 'Yeah, she knows how. How's she making out with this one?'

'She's bitching about her figure a lot,' Jack chuckled. 'Why is it that they never understand how pretty they look pregnant?'

'Yeah.' Robby grinned his agreement, wondering if Sissy would ever look the same way to him. Jack felt guilty for touching a sensitive topic, and changed the subject.

'By the way, what's with all the boats? I saw a bunch of yardbirds parked on the waterfront this morning.'

'That's "moored", you dumb jarhead,' Robby corrected his friend. 'They're replacing the pilings over at the naval station across the river. It's supposed to take two months. Something went wrong with the old ones – the preservative didn't work or some such bullcrap. Your basic government-contractor screwup. No big deal. The job's supposed to be finished in time for the next school year – not that I care one way or another, of course. By that time, boy, I'll be spending my mornings at twenty-five thousand feet, back where I belong. What are you going to be doing?'

'What do you mean?'

'Well, you're either gonna be here or at Langley, right?'

Ryan looked out the window. 'Damned if I know, Rob, we got a baby on the way and a bunch of other things to think about.'

'You haven't found 'em yet?'

Jack shook his head. 'We thought we had a break, but it didn't work out. These guys are pros, Robby.'

Jackson reacted with surprising passion. 'Bullshit, man! Professionals don't hurt kids. Hey, they want to take a shot at a soldier or a cop, okay, I can understand that – it ain't right, but I can understand it, okay? – soldiers and cops have guns to shoot back with, and they got training. So it's an even match, surprise on one side and procedure on the other, and that makes it a fair game. Going after noncombattants, they're just fucking street hoods, Jack. Maybe they're clever, but they sure as hell ain't professionals! Professionals got balls. Professionals put it on the line for real.'

Jack shook his head. Robby was wrong, but he knew of no way to persuade his friend otherwise. His code was that of the warrior, who had to live by civilized rules. Rule Number One was: You don't deliberately harm the helpless. It was bad enough when that happened by accident. To do so on purpose was cowardly, beneath contempt; those who did so merited only death. They were beyond the pale.

'They're playing a goddamned game, Jack,' the pilot went on. 'There's even a song about it. I heard it at Riordan's on St Patrick's Day. "I've learned all my heroes and wanted the same/To try out my hand at the patriot game." Something like that.' Jackson shook his head in disgust. 'War isn't a game, it's a profession. They play their little *games*, and call themselves patriots, and go out and kill little kids. Bastards. Jack, out in the fleet, when I'm driving Tomcat, we play *our* games with the Russians. Nobody gets killed, because both sides are professionals. I don't much like the Russians, but the boys that fly the Bears know their stuff. We know our stuff, and both sides respect the other. There's rules, and both sides play by 'em. That's the way it's supposed to be.'

'The world isn't that simple, Robby,' Jack said quietly.

'Well, it damned well ought to be!' Jack was surprised at how worked up his friend was about this. 'You tell those guys at CIA: find 'em for us, then get somebody to give the order, and I'll escort the strike in.'

'The last two times we did that we lost people,' Ryan pointed out.

'We take our chances. That's what they pay us for, Jack.'

'Yeah, but before you toss the dice again, we want you over for dinner.'

Jackson grinned sheepishly. 'I won't bring my soap box with me, I promise. Dressy?'

'Robby, am I ever dressy?'

'I told 'em it wasn't dressy,' Jack said afterward.

'Good,' his wife agreed.

'I thought you'd say that.' He looked up at his wife, her skin illuminated by moonlight. 'You really are pretty.'

'You keep saying that –'

'Don't move. Just stay where you are.' He ran his hand across her flanks.

'Why?'

'You said this is the last time for a while. I don't want it to be over yet.'

'The next time you can be on top,' she promised.

'It'll be worth waiting for, but you won't be as beautiful as you are now.'

'I don't feel beautiful at the moment.'

'Cathy, you are talking to an expert,' her husband pronounced. 'I am the one person in this house who can give out a dispassionate appraisal of the pulchritude of any female human being, living or dead, and *I* say that you are beautiful. End of discussion.'

Cathy Ryan took her own appraisal. Her belly was disfigured by gross-looking stretch marks, her breasts were bloated and sore, her feet and ankles swollen, and her legs were knotting up from her current position. 'Jack, you are a dope.'

'She never listens,' he told the ceiling.

'It's just pheromones,' she explained. 'Pregnant women smell different and it must tickle your fancy somehow or other.'

'Then how come you're beautiful when my nose is stuffy? Answer me that!'

She reached down to twist her fingers in the hair on his chest. Jack started squirming. It tickled. 'Love is blind.'

'When I kiss you, my eyes are always open.'

'I didn't know that!'

'I know,' Jack laughed quietly. 'Your eyes are always closed. Maybe your love is blind, but mine isn't.' He ran his fingertips over her abdomen. It was still slick from the baby oil she used to moisturize her skin. Jack found this a little kinky. His fingertips traced circles on the taut, smooth surface.

'You're a throwback. You're something out of a thirties movie.' She started squirming now. 'Stop that.'

'Errol Flynn never did this in the movies,' Jack noted, without stopping that.

'They had censors then.'

'Spoilsports. Some people are just no fun.' His hands expanded their horizons. The next target was the base of her neck. It was a long reach, but worth the effort. She was shivering now. 'Now, I, on the other hand . . .'

'Mmmmm.'

'I thought so.'

'Uh-oh. He's awake again.'

Jack felt him almost as soon as his wife. He – she, it – was rotating. Jack wondered how a baby could do that, without anything to latch on to, but the evidence was clear, his hands felt a lump shift position. The lump was his child's head, or the opposite end. Moving. Alive. Waiting to be born. He looked up to see his wife, smiling down at him and knowing what he felt.

'You're beautiful, and I love you very much. Whether you like it or not.' He was surprised to find that there were tears in his eyes. He was even more surprised by what happened next.

'Love you, too, Jack – again?'

'Maybe that wasn't the last time for a while after all. . .'

23

Movement

'We got these last night.' Priorities had changed somewhat at CIA. Ryan could tell. The man going over the photos with him was going gray, wore rimless glasses and a bow tie. Garters on his sleeves would not have seemed out of place. Marty stood in the corner and kept his mouth shut. 'We figure it's one of these three camps, right?'

'Yeah, the others are identified.' Ryan nodded. This drew a snort.

'You say so, son.'

'Okay, these two are active, this one as of last week, and this one two days ago.'

'What about -20, the *Action Directe* camp?' Cantor asked.

'Shut down ever since the Frenchies went in. I saw the tape of that.' The man smiled in admiration. 'Anyway, here.'

It was one of the rare daylight photographs, even in colour. The firing range adjacent to the camp had six men standing in line. The angle prevented them from seeing if the men held guns or not.

'Weapons training?' Ryan asked cautiously.

'Either that or they're taking a leak by the numbers.' This was humour.

'Wait a minute, you said these came in last night.'

'Look at the sun angle,' the man said derisively.

'Oh. Early morning.'

'Around midnight our time. Very good,' the man observed. *Amateurs*, he thought. *Everybody thinks he can read a recon photo!* 'You can't see any guns, but see these little points of light here? That might be sunlight reflecting off ejected cartridge brass. Okay, we have six people here. Probably Northern Europeans because they're so pale – see this one here with the sunburn, his arm looks a little pink? All appear to be male, from the short hair and style of dress. Okay, now the question is, who the hell are they?'

'They're not *Action Directe*,' Marty said.

'How do you know that?' Ryan asked.

'The ones who got picked up are no longer with us. They were given trials by military tribunal and executed two weeks ago.'

'Jesus!' Ryan turned away. 'I didn't want to know that, Marty.'

'Those who asked had clergy in attendance. I thought that was decent of our colleagues.' He paused for a moment, then went on: 'It turns out that French law allows for that sort of trial under very special circumstances. So despite what we both thought all the time, it was all done by the book. Feel better?'

'Some,' Ryan admitted on reflection. It might not have made a great deal of difference to the terrorists, but at least the formality of law had been observed, and that was one of the things 'civilization' meant.

'Good. A couple sang like canaries beforehand, too. DGSE was able to bag two more members outside of Paris' – this hasn't made the papers yet – 'plus a barnful of guns and explosives. They may not be out of business, but they've been hurt.'

'All right,' the man in the bow tie acknowledged. 'And this is the guy who tumbled to it?'

'All because he likes to see tits from three hundred miles away,' Cantor replied.

'How come nobody else saw that first?' Ryan would have preferred that someone else had done all this.

'Because there aren't enough people in my section. I just got authority to hire ten new ones. I've already got them picked out. They're people who're leaving the Air Force. Pros.'

'Okay, what about the other camp?'

'Here.' A new photo came into view. 'Pretty much the same thing. We have two people visible –'

'One's a girl,' Ryan said at once.

'One appears to have shoulder-length hair,' the photo expert agreed. He went on: 'That doesn't necessarily mean it's a girl.' Jack thought about that, looking at the figure's stance and posture.

'If we assume it's a girl, what does that tell us?' he asked Marty.

'You tell me.'

'We have no indication that the ULA has female members, but we know that the PIRA does. This is the camp – remember that jeep that was driving from one to the other and was later seen parked at this camp?' Ryan paused before going on. *Oh, what the hell* . . . He grabbed the photo of the six people on the gun range. 'This is the one.'

'And what the hell are you basing that on?' the photo-intel man asked.

'Call it a strong hunch,' Ryan replied.

'That's fine. The next time I go to the track I'll bring you along to pick my horses for me. Listen, the thing about these photos is, what you see is all you got. If you read too much into these photos, you end up making mistakes. Big ones. What you have here is six people lined up, *probably* firing guns. That's all.'

'Anything else?' Cantor asked.

'We'll have a night pass at about 2200 local time – this afternoon our time. I'll have the shots to you right after they come in.'

'Very good. Thanks,' Cantor said. The man left the room to go back to his beloved photo equipment.

'I believe you call that sort of person an empiricist,' Ryan observed after a moment.

Cantor chuckled. 'Something like that. He's been in the business since we had U-2s flying over Russia. He's a real expert. The important thing about that is, he doesn't say he's sure about something until he's *really* sure. What he said's true, you can easily read too much into these things.'

'Fine, but you agree with me.'

'Yeah.' Cantor sat on the desk next to Ryan and examined the photo through a magnifying glass.

The six men lined up on the firing line were not totally clear. The hot air rising off the desert even in early morning was disturbed enough to ruin the clarity of the image. It was like looking through the shimmering mirage on a flat highway. The satellite camera had a very high 'shutter' speed – actually the photoreceptors were totally electronic – that cancelled most of the distortion, but all they really had was a poorly focused, high-angle image that showed man-shapes. You could tell what they were wearing – tan short-sleeved shirts and long pants – and the colour of their hair with total certainty. A glimmer off one man's wrist seemed to indicate a watch or bracelet. The face of one man was darker than it should have been – his uncovered forearm was quite pale – and that probably indicated a short beard. . . . *Miller has a beard now*, Ryan reminded himself.

'Damn, if this was only a little better . . .'

'Yeah,' Marty agreed. 'But what you see here is the result of thirty years of work and God only knows how much money. In cold climates it comes out a little better, but you can't ever recognize a face.'

'This is it, Marty. This is the one. We have to have something that confirms that, or at least confirms something.'

''Fraid not. Our French colleagues asked the people they captured. The answer they got was that the camps are totally isolated from one another. When the groups meet, it's almost always on neutral ground. They didn't even know for sure that there was a camp here.'

'*That* tells us something!'

'The thing about the car? It could have been somebody from the Army, you know. The guy who oversees the guards, maybe. It didn't have to be one of the players who drove from this one to the Provisionals' camp. In fact, there is ample reason to believe that it wasn't. Compartmentalization is a logical security measure. It makes sense for the camps to be isolated from one another. These people know about the importance of security, and even if they didn't before, the French op was a gilt-edge reminder.'

Ryan hadn't thought about that. The raid on the *Action Directe* camp had to have an effect on the others, didn't it?

'You mean we shot ourselves in the foot?'

'No, we sent a message that was worth sending. So far as we can determine, nobody knows what actually happened there. We have reason to believe that the suspicion on the ground is that a rival outfit settled a score – not all of these groups like each other. So, if nothing else, we've fostered some suspicions among the groups themselves, and vis-à-vis their hosts. That sort of thing could break some information loose for us, but it'll take time to find out.'

'Anyway, now that we know that this camp is likely to be the one we want, what are we going to do about it?'

'We're working on that. I can't say anymore.'

'Okay.' Ryan gestured to his desk. 'You want some coffee, Marty?'

Cantor's face took on a curious expression. 'No, I'm off coffee for a while.'

What Cantor didn't say was that a major operation had been laid on. It was fairly typical in that very few of the participants actually knew what was going on. A Navy carrier battle group centred on USS *Saratoga* was due to sail west out of the Mediterranean Sea, and would pass north of the Gulf of Sidra in several days. As was routine, the formation was being trailed by a Soviet AGI – a fishing trawler that gather electronic intelligence instead of mackerel – which would give information to the Libyans. When the carrier was directly north of Tripoli, in the middle of the night, a French-controlled agent would interrupt electrical power to some radar installations soon after the carrier started conducting nighttime flight operations. This was expected to get some people excited, although the carrier group Commander had no idea that he was doing anything other than routine flight ops. It was hoped that the same team of French commandos that had raided Camp -20 would also be able to slip into Camp -18. Marty couldn't tell Ryan any of this, but it was a measure of how well *Action Directe* had been damaged that the French were willing to give the Americans such cooperation. While it hadn't exactly been the first example of international cooperation, it was one of three such operations that had actually been successful. The CIA had helped to avenge the murder of a friend of the French President. Whatever the differences between the two countries, debts of honour were still paid in full. It appealed to Cantor's sense of propriety, but was something known to only twenty people within the Agency. The op was scheduled to run in four days. A senior case officer from the Operations Directorate was even now working with the French paratroopers who, he reported, were eager to demonstrate their prowess yet again. With luck, the terrorist group that had had the temerity to commit murder within the United States and the United Kingdom would be hurt by the troops of yet another nation. If successful, the precedent would signal a new and valuable development in the struggle against terrorism.

Dennis Cooley was working on his ledger book. It was early. The shop wasn't open for business yet, and this was the time of day for him to set his accounts straight. It wasn't very hard. His shop didn't have all that many transactions. He hummed away to himself, not knowing what annoyance this habit caused for the man listening to the microphone planted behind one of his bookshelves. Abruptly his humming stopped and his head came up. What was wrong. . .

The little man nearly leaped from his chair when he smelled the acrid smoke. He scanned the room for several seconds before looking up. The smoke was coming from the ceiling light fixture. He darted to the wall switch and slapped his hand on it. A blue flash erupted from the wall, giving him a powerful electric shock that numbed his arm to the elbow. He stared at his arm in surprise, flexing his fingers and looking at the smoke that seemed to be trailing off. He didn't wait to see it stop. Cooley had a fire extinguisher in the back room. He got it and came back, pulled the safety pin, and aimed the device at the switch. No smoke there anymore. Next he stood on his chair to get close to the ceiling fixture, but already the smoke was nearly gone. The smell remained. Cooley stood on the chair for over a minute, his knees shaking as the chair moved slightly under him, holding the extinguisher and trying to decide what to do. Call the fire brigade? But there wasn't any fire – was there? All his valuable books. . . . He'd been trained in many things, but fighting fires was not one of them. He was breathing heavily now, nearly panicked until he finally decided that there wasn't anything to be panicked about. He turned to see three people staring at him through the glass with curious expressions.

He lowered the extinguisher with a shamefaced grin and gestured comically to the spectators. The light was off. The switch was off. The fire, if it had been a fire, was gone. He'd call the building's electrician. Cooley opened the door to explain what was wrong to his fellow shop owners. One remarked that the wiring in the arcade was horribly out of date. It was something Cooley hadn't ever thought about. Electricity was electricity. You flipped the switch and the light went on, and that was that. It annoyed him that something so reliable, wasn't. A minute later he called the building manager, who promised that an electrician would be there in half an hour.

The man arrived forty minutes later, apologizing for being held up in traffic. He stood for a moment, admiring the bookshelves.

'Smells like a wire burned out,' he judged next. 'You're lucky, sir. That frequently causes a fire.'

'How difficult will it be to fix?'

'I expect that I'll have to replace the wiring. Ought to have been done years ago. This old place – well, the electric service is older than I am, and that's too old by half.' He smiled.

Cooley showed him to the fuse box in the back room, and the man went to work. Dennis was unwilling to use his table lamp, and sat in the semi-darkness while the tradesman went to work.

The electrician flipped off the outside master switch and examined the fuse box. It still had the original inspection tag, and when he rubbed off the dust, he read off the date: 1919. The man shook his head in amazement. Almost seventy bloody years! He had to remove some items to get at the wall, and was surprised to see that there was some recent plasterwork. It was as good a place to start as any. He didn't want to damage the wall any more than he had to. With hammer and chisel he broke into the plaster, and there was the wire. . . .

But it wasn't the right one, he thought. It had plastic insulation, not the gutta-percha used in his grandfather's time. It wasn't in quite the right place, either. Strange, he thought. He pulled on the wire. It came out easily.

'Mr Cooley, sir?' he called. The shop owner appeared a moment later. 'Do you know what this is?'

'Bloody hell!' the detective said in the room upstairs. 'Bloody fucking hell!' He turned to his companion, a look of utter shock on his face. 'Call Commander Owens!'

'I've never seen anything like this.' He cut off the end and handed it over. The electrician did not understand why Cooley was so pale.

Neither had Cooley, but he knew what it was. The end of the wire showed nothing, just a place where the polyvinyl insulation stopped, without the copper core that one expects to see in electrical circuitry. Hidden in the end was a highly sensitive microphone. The shop owner composed himself after a moment, though his voice was somewhat raspy.

'I have no idea. Carry on.'

'Yes, sir.' The electrician resumed his search for the power line.

Cooley had already lifted his telephone and dialed a number.

'Hello?'

'Beatrix?'

'Good morning, Mr Dennis. How are you today?'

'Can you come into the shop this morning? I have a small emergency.'

'Certainly.' She lived only a block from Holloway Road tube station. The Piccadilly Line ran almost directly to the shop. 'I can be there in fifteen minutes.'

'Thank you, Beatrix. You're a love,' he added before he hung up. By this time Cooley's mind was racing at mach-1. There was nothing in the shop or his home that could incriminate him. He lifted the phone again and hesitated. His instructions under these circumstances were to call a number he had memorized – but if there were a microphone in his office, his phone. . . and his home phone. . . Cooley was sweating now despite the cool temperature. He commanded himself to relax. He'd never said anything compromising on either phone – had he? For all his expertise and discipline, Cooley had never faced danger, and he was beginning to panic. It took all of his concentration to focus on his operational procedures, the things he had learned and practiced for years. Cooley told himself that he had never deviated from them. Not once. He was sure of that. By the time he stopped shaking, the bell rang.

It was Beatrix, he saw. Cooley grabbed his coat.

'Will you be back later?'

'I'm not sure. I'll call you.' He went right out the door, leaving his clerk with a very curious look.

It had taken ten minutes to locate James Owens, who was in his car south of London. The Commander gave immediate orders to shadow Cooley and to arrest him if it appeared that he was attempting to leave the country. Two men were already watching the man's car and were ready to trail him. Two more were sent to the arcade, but the detectives arrived just as he walked out of the arcade, and were on the wrong side of the street. One hopped out of the car and followed, expecting him to turn onto Berkeley Street toward his travel agent. Instead, Cooley ducked into the tube station. The detective was caught off guard and raced down the entrance on his side of the street. The crowd of morning commuters made spotting his short target virtually impossible. In under a minute, the officer was sure that his quarry had caught a train that he had been unable to get close to. Cooley had escaped.

The detective ran back to the street and put out a radio call to alert the police at Heathrow airport, where this underground line ended – Cooley always flew, unless he drove his own car – and to get cars to all the underground stations on the Piccadilly Line. There simply wasn't enough time.

Cooley got off at the next station, as his training had taught him, and took a cab to Waterloo Station. There he made a telephone call.

'Five-five-two-nine,' the voice answered.

'Oh, excuse me, I was trying to get six-six-three-zero. Sorry.' There followed two seconds of hesitation on the other side of the connection.

'Oh . . . That's quite all right,' the voice assured him in a tone that was anything but all right.

Cooley replaced the phone and walked to a train. It was everything he could do not to look over his shoulder.

'This is Geoffrey Watkins,' he said as he lifted the phone.

'Oh, I beg your pardon,' the voice said. 'I was trying to get Mr Titus. Is this six-two-nine-one?' *All contacts are broken until further notice*, the number told him. *Not known if you are in danger. Will advise if possible.*

'No, this is six-two-one-nine,' he answered. Understood. Watkins hung the phone up and looked out his window. His stomach felt as though a ball of refrigerated lead had materialized there. He swallowed twice, then reached for his tea. For the rest of the morning, it was hard to concentrate on the Foreign Office white paper he was reading. He needed two stiff drinks with lunch to settle himself down.

By noon, Cooley was in Dover, aboard a cross-channel ferry. He was fully alert now, and sat in a corner seat on the upper deck, looking over the newspaper in his hands to see if anyone was watching him. He'd almost boarded the hovercraft to Calais, but decided against it at the last moment. He had enough cash for the Dover-Dunkerque ferry, but not the more expensive hovercraft, and he didn't want to leave a paper trail behind. It was only two and a quarter hours in any case. Once in France, he could catch a train to Paris, then start flying. He started to feel secure for the first time in hours, but was able to suppress it easily enough. Cooley had never known this sort of fear before, and it left a considerable aftertaste. The quiet hatred that had festered for years now ate at him like an acid. They had made him run. *They* had spied on *him!* Because of all his training, all the precautions that he'd followed assiduously, and all the professional skill that he'd employed, Cooley had never seriously considered the possibility that he would be turned. He had thought himself too skilful for that. That he was wrong enraged him, and for the first time in his life, he wanted to lash out at himself. He'd lost his bookshop and with it all the books he loved, and this, too, had been taken from him by the bloody Brits! He folded the paper neatly and set it down in his lap while the ferry pulled into the English Channel, placid with the summer sun overhead. His bland face stared out at the water with a gaze as calm as a man in contemplation of his garden while he fantasized images of blood and death.

Owens was as furious as anyone had ever seen him. The surveillance of Cooley had been so easy, so routine – but that was no excuse, he told his men. That harmless-looking little poof, as Ashley had called him, had slipped away from his shadowers as adroitly as someone trained at Moscow Centre itself. There were men at every international airport in Britain clutching pictures of Cooley, and if he used his credit card to purchase any kind of ticket, the computers would notify Scotland Yard at once, but Owens had a sickening feeling that the man was already out of the country. The Commander of C-13 dismissed his people.

Ashley was in the room, too, and his people had been caught equally off guard. He and Owens shared a look of anger mixed with despair.

A detective had left the tape of a phone call to Geoffrey Watkins made less than an hour after Cooley disappeared. Ashley played it. It lasted all of twenty seconds. And it wasn't Cooley's voice. If it had been, they would have arrested Watkins then and there. For all their effort, they still did not have a single usable piece of evidence on Geoffrey Watkins.

'There is a Mr Titus in the building. The voice even gave the correct number. By all rights it could have been a simple wrong number.'

'But it wasn't, of course.'

'That is how it's done, you know. You have pre-set messages that are constructed to sound entirely harmless. Whoever trained these blokes knew what they were about. What about the shop?'

'The girl Beatrix knows absolutely nothing. We have people searching the shop at this moment, but so far they've found nothing but old bloody books. Same story as his flat.' Owens stood and spoke in a voice full of perverse wonder. 'An electrician.... Months of work, gone because he yanks the wrong wire.'

'He'll turn up. He could not have had a great deal of cash. He must use his credit card.'

'He's out of the country already. Don't say he isn't. If he's clever enough for what we know he's done –'

'Yes.' Ashley nodded reluctant agreement. 'One doesn't always win, James.'

'It is so nice to hear that!' Owens snapped out his reply. 'These bastards have outguessed us every step of the way. The Commissioner is going to ask me how it is that we couldn't get our thumbs out in time, and there is no answer to that question.'

'So what's the next step, then?'

'At least we know what he looks like. We . . . we share what we know with the Americans, all of it. I have a meeting scheduled with Murray this evening. He's hinted that they have something operating that he's not able to talk about, doubtless some sort of CIA op.'

'Agreed. Is it here or there?'

'There.' Owens paused. 'I am getting sick of this place.'

'Commander, you should measure your successes against your failures,' Ashley said. 'You're the best man we've had in this office in some years.'

Owens only grunted at that remark. He knew it was true. Under his leadership, C-13 had scored major coups against the Provisionals. But in this job, as in so many others, the question one's superiors always asked was, *What have you accomplished today?* Yesterday was ancient history.

'Watkins' suspected contact has flown,' he announced three hours later.

'What happened?' Murray closed his eyes halfway through the explanation and shook his head sadly. 'We had the same sort of thing happen to us,' he said after Owens finished. 'A renegade CIA officer. We were watching his place, and let things settle into a comfortable routine, and then – zip! He snookered the surveillance team. He turned up in Moscow a week later. It happens, Jimmy.'

'Not to me,' Owens almost snarled. 'Not until now, that is.'

'What's he look like?' Owens handed a collection of photographs across the desk. Murray flipped through them. 'Mousy little bastard, isn't he? Almost bald.' The FBI man considered this for a moment, then lifted his phone and punched in four numbers. 'Fred? Dan. You want to come down to my office for a minute?'

The man arrived a minute later. Murray didn't identify him as a member of the CIA and Owens didn't ask. He didn't have to. He'd given over two copies of each photo.

Fred – one of the men from 'down the hall' – took his photos and looked at them. 'Who's he supposed to be?'

Owens explained briefly, ending, 'He's probably out of the country by now.'

'Well, if he turns up in any of our nets, we'll let you know,' Fred promised, and left.

'Do you know what they're up to?' Owens asked Murray.

'No. I know something is happening. The Bureau and the Agency have a joint task force set up, but it's compartmented, and I don't need to know all of it yet.'

'Did your lads have a part in the raid on *Action Directe*?'

'I don't know what you're talking about,' Murray said piously. *How the hell did you hear about that, Jimmy?*

'I thought as much,' Owens replied. *Bloody security!* 'Dan, we are concerned here with the personal safety of –'

Murray held his hands up like a man at bay. 'I know, I know. And you're right, too. We ought to cut your people in on this. I'll call the Director myself.'

The phone rang. It was for Owens.

'Yes?' The Commander of C-13 listened for a minute before hanging up. 'Thank you.' A sigh. 'Dan, he's definitely on the continent. He used a credit card to purchase a railway ticket. Dunkerque to Paris, three hours ago.'

'Have the French pick him up?'

'Too late. The train arrived twenty minutes ago. He's completely gone now. Besides, we have nothing to arrest him for, do we?'

'And Watkins has been warned off.'

'Unless that was a genuinely wrong number, which I rather doubt, but try to prove *that* in a court of law!'

'Yeah.' Judges didn't understand any instinct but their own.

'And don't tell me that you can't win them all! That's what they pay me to do.' Owens looked down at the rug, then back up. 'Please forgive me for that.'

'Aah!' Murray waved it off. 'You've had bad days before. So have I. It's part of the business we're in. What we both need at a time like this is a beer. Come on downstairs, and I'll treat you to a burger.'

'When will you call your Director?'

'It's lunchtime over there. He always has a meeting going over lunch. We'll let it wait a few hours.'

Ryan had lunch with Cantor that day in the CIA cafeteria. It could have been the eating place in any other government building. The food was just as unexciting. Ryan decided to try the lasagna, but Marty stuck with fruit salad and cake. It seemed an odd diet until Jack watched him take a tablet before eating. He washed it down with milk.

'Ulcers, Marty?'

'What makes you say that?'

'I'm married to a doc, remember? You just took a Tagamet. That's for ulcers.'

'This place gets to you after a while,' Cantor explained. 'My stomach started acting up last year and didn't get any better. Everyone in my family comes down with it sooner or later. Bad genes, I guess. The medication helps some, but the doctor says that I need a less stressful environment.' A snort.

'You do work long hours,' Ryan observed.

'Anyway, my wife got offered a teaching position at the University of Texas – she's a mathematician. And to sweeten the deal they offered me a place in the Political Science Department. The pay's better than it is here, too. I've been here twelve years,' he said quietly. 'Long time.'

'So what do you feel bad about? Teaching's great. I love it, and you'll be good at it. You'll even have a good football team to watch.'

'Yeah, well, she's already down there, and I leave in a few weeks. I'm going to miss this place.'

'You'll get over it. Imagine being able to walk into a building without getting permission from a computer. Hey, I walked away from my first job.'

'But this one's important.' Cantor drank his milk and looked across the table. 'What are you going to do?'

'Ask me after the baby is born.' Ryan didn't want to dwell on this question.

'The Agency needs people like you, Jack. You've got a feel for things. You don't think and act like a bureaucrat. You say what you think. Not everyone in this building does that, and that's why the Admiral likes you.'

'Hell, I haven't talked to him since –'

'He knows what you're doing.' Cantor smiled.

'Oh.' Ryan understood. 'So that's it.'

'That's right. The old man really wants you, Jack. You still don't know how important that photo you tripped over was, do you?'

'All I did was show it to you, Marty,' Ryan protested. 'You're the one who really made the connection.'

'You did exactly the right thing, exactly what an analyst is supposed to do. There was more brains in that than you know. You have a gift for this sort of work. If you can't see it, I can.' Cantor examined the lasagna and winced. How could anybody eat that greasy poison? 'Two years from now you'll be ready for my job.'

'One bridge at a time, Marty.' They let it go at that.

An hour later Ryan was back in his office. Cantor came in.

'Another pep talk?' Jack smiled. *Full-court press time.*

'We have a picture of a suspected ULA member and it's only a week old. We got it in from London a couple of hours ago.'

'Dennis Cooley.' Ryan examined it and laughed. 'He looks like a real wimp. What's the story?'

Cantor explained. 'Bad luck for the Brits, but maybe good luck for us. Look at the picture again and tell me something important.'

'You mean . . . he's lost most of his hair. Oh! We can ID the guy if he turns up at one of the camps. None of the other people are bald.'

'You got it. And the boss just cleared you for something. There's an op laid on for Camp -18.'

'What kind?'

'The kind you watched before. Is that still bothering you?'

'No, not really.' *What bothers me is that it* doesn't *bother me*, Ryan thought. *Maybe it should. . . .* 'Not with these guys, it doesn't. When?'

'I can't tell you, but soon.'

'So why did you let me know – nice one, Marty. Not very subtle, though. Does the Admiral want me to stay that bad?

'Draw your own conclusions.'

An hour after that the photo expert was back. Another satellite had passed over the camp at 2208 local time. The infrared image showed eight people standing at line on the firing range. Bright tongues of flame marked two of the shapes. They were firing their weapons at night, and there were now at least eight of them there.

'What happened?' O'Donnell asked. He'd met Cooley at the airport. A cutout had gotten word out that Cooley was on the run, but the reason for it had had to wait until now.

'There was a bug in my shop.'

'You're sure?' O'Donnell asked.

Cooley handed it over. The wire had been in his pocket for thirty hours. O'Donnell pulled the Toyota Land Cruiser over to examine it.

'Marconi makes these for intelligence use. Quite sensitive. How long might it have been there?'

Cooley could not remember having anyone go into his back room unsupervized. 'I've no idea.'

O'Donnell put the vehicle back into gear, heading out into the desert. He pondered the question for over a mile. Something had gone wrong? but what. . . ?

'Did you ever think you were being followed?'

'Never.'

'How closely did you check, Dennis?' Cooley hesitated, and O'Donnell took this for an answer. 'Dennis, did you ever break trade craft – *ever*?'

'No, Kevin, of course not. It isn't possible that – for God's sake, Kevin, it's been weeks since I've been in contact with Watkins.'

'Since your last trip to Cork.' O'Donnell squinted in the bright sun.

'Yes, that's right. You had a security man watching me then – was there anyone following me?'

'If there were, he must have been a damnably clever one, and he could not have been too close. . . .' The other possibility that O'Donnell was considering, of course, was that Cooley had turned traitor. *But if he'd done that, he wouldn't have come here, would he?* the chief of the ULA thought. *He knows me, knows where I live, knows McKenney, knows Sean Miller, knows about the fishing fleet at Dundalk.* O'Donnell realized that Cooley knew quite a lot. No, if he'd gone tout, he wouldn't be here. Cooley was sweating despite the air conditioning in the car. Dennis didn't have the belly to risk his life that way. He could see that.

'So, Dennis, what are we to do with you?'

Cooley's heart was momentarily irregular, but he spoke with determination. 'I want to be part of the next op.'

'Sorry?' O'Donnell's head came around in surprise.

'The fucking Brits – Kevin, they came after me!'

'That is something of an occupational hazard, you know.'

'I'm quite serious,' Cooley insisted.

It wouldn't hurt to have another man. . . . 'Are you in shape for it?'

'I will be.'

The chief made his decision. 'Then you can start this afternoon.'

'What is it, then?'

O'Donnell explained.

'It would seem that your hunch was correct, Doctor Ryan,' the man with the rimless glasses said the next afternoon. 'Maybe I will take you to the track.'

He was standing outside of the huts, a dumpy little man with a head that shone from the sunlight reflecting off his sweaty, hairless dome. Camp -18 was the one.

'Excellent,' Cantor observed. 'Our English friends have really scored on this one. Thanks,' he said to the photo expert.

'When's the op?' Ryan asked after he left.

'Early morning, day after tomorrow. Our time . . . eight in the evening, I think.'

'Can I watch in real time?'

'Maybe.'

'This is a secret that's hard to keep,' he said.

'Most of the good ones are,' Cantor agreed. 'But –'

'Yeah, I know.' Jack put his coat on and locked up his files. 'Tell the Admiral that I owe him one.'

Driving home, Ryan thought about what might be happening. He realized that his anticipation was not very different from . . . Christmas? No, that was not the right way to think about this. He wondered how his father had felt right before a big arrest after a lengthy investigation. He forgot about it, as he was supposed to do with everything that he saw at Langley.

There was a strange car parked in front of the house when he got there, just beyond the nearly completed swimming pool. On inspection he saw that it had diplomatic tags. He went inside to find three men talking to his wife. He recognized one but couldn't put a name on him.

'Hello, Doctor Ryan, I'm Geoffrey Bennett from the British Embassy. We met before at –'

'Yeah, I remember now. What can we do for you?'

'Their Royal Highnesses will be visiting the States in a few weeks. I understand that you offered an invitation when you met, and they wish to see if it remains open.'

'Are you kidding?'

'They're not kidding, Jack, and I already said yes,' his wife informed him. Even Ernie was wagging his tail in anticipation.

'Of course. Please tell them that we'd be honoured to have them down. Will they be staying the night?'

'Probably not. It was hoped that they could come in the evening.'

'For dinner? Fine. What day?'

'Friday, 30th July.'

'Done.'

'Excellent. I hope you won't mind if our security people – plus your Secret Service chaps – conduct a security sweep in the coming week.'

'Do I have to be home for that?'

'I can do it, Jack. I'm off work now, remember?'

'Oh, of course,' Bennett said. 'When is the baby due?'

'First week of August – that might be a problem for this,' Cathy realized belatedly.

'If something unexpected happens, you may be sure that Their Highnesses will understand. One more thing. This is a private matter, not one of the public events for the trip. We must ask that you keep this entirely confidential.'

'Sure, I understand,' Ryan said.

'If they're going to be here for dinner, is there anything we shouldn't serve?' Cathy asked.

'What do you mean?' Bennett responded.

'Well, some people are allergic to fish, for example.'

'Oh, I see. No, I know of nothing along those lines.'

'Okay, the basic Ryan dinner,' Jack said. 'I – uh-oh.'

'What's the matter?' Bennett asked.

'We're having company that night.'

'Oh,' Cathy nodded. 'Robby and Sissy.'

'Can't you cancel?'

'It's a going-away party. Robby – he's a Navy fighter pilot, we both teach at the Academy – is transferring back to the fleet. Would they mind?'

'Doctor Ryan, His Highness –'

'His Highness is a good guy. So's Robby. He was there that night we met. I can't cancel him out, Mr Bennett. He's a friend. The good news is, His Highness will like him. He used to fly fighter planes, too, right?'

'Well, yes, but –'

'Do you remember the night we met? Without Robby I might not have gotten through it. Look, this guy's a lieutenant commander in the United States Navy who happens to fly a forty-million-dollar fighter airplane. He probably is not a security risk. His wife plays one hell of a piano.' Ryan saw that he hadn't quite gotten through yet. 'Mr Bennett, check Rob out through your attaché and ask His Highness if it's all right.'

'And if he objects?'

'He won't. I've met him. Maybe he's a better guy than you give him credit for,' Jack observed. *He won't object, you dummy. It's the security pukes who'll throw a fit.*

'Well.' That remark took him somewhat aback. 'I cannot fault your sense of loyalty, Doctor. I will pass this through His Highness's office. But I must insist that you do not tell Commander Jackson anything.'

'You have my word.' Jack nearly laughed. He couldn't wait to see the look on Robby's face. This would finally even the score for that kendo match.

'Contraction peaks,' Jack said that night. They were practicing the breathing exercises in preparation for the delivery. His wife started panting. Jack knew that this was a serious business. It merely looked ridiculous. He checked the numbers on his digital watch. 'Contraction ends. Deep, cleansing breath. I figure steaks on the grill, baked potatoes, and fresh corn on the cob, with a nice salad.'

'It's too plain,' Cathy protested.

'Everywhere they go over here, people will be hitting them with that fancy French crap. Somebody ought to give them a decent American meal. You know I do a mean steak on the grill, and your spinach salad is famous from here to across the road.'

'Okay.' Cathy started laughing. It was becoming uncomfortable for her to do so. 'If I stand over a stove for more than a few minutes, I get nauseous anyway.'

'It must be tough, being pregnant.'

'You should try it,' she suggested.

Her husband went on: 'It's the *only* hard thing women have to do, of course.'

'*What!*' Cathy's eyes nearly popped out.

'Look at history. Who has to go out and kill the buffalo? The man. Who has to carry the buffalo back? The man. Who has to drive off the bear? The man. We do all the hard stuff. I still have to take out the garbage every night! Do I ever complain about that?' He had her laughing again. He'd read her mood right. She didn't want sympathy. She was too proud of herself for that.

'I'd hit you on the head, but there's no sense in breaking a perfectly good club over something worthless.'

'Besides, I was there the last time, and it didn't look all that hard.'

'If I could move, Jack, I'd kill you for that one!'

He moved from opposite his wife to beside her. 'Nah, I don't think so. I want you to form a picture in your mind.'

'Of what?'

'Of the look on Robby's face when he gets here for dinner. I'm going to jiggle the time a little.'

'I'll bet you that Sissy handles it better than he does.'

'How much?'

'Twenty.'

'Deal.' He looked at his watch. 'Contraction begins. Deep breath.' A minute later, Jack was amazed to see that he was breathing the same way as his wife. That got them both laughing.

Connections Missed and Made

There were no new pictures of Camp -18 the day of the raid. A sandstorm had swept over the area at the time of the satellite pass, and the cameras couldn't penetrate it, but a geosynchronous weather satellite showed that the storm had left the site. Ryan was cued after lunch that day that the raid was on, and spent his afternoon in fidgety anticipation. Careful analysis of the existing photos showed that between twelve and eighteen people were at the camp, over and above the guard force. If the higher number were correct, and the official estimate of the ULA's size was also accurate, that represented more than half of its membership. Ryan worried a little about that. If the French were sending in only eight paratroopers . . . but then he remembered his own experiences in the Marine Corps. They'd be hitting the objective at three in the morning. Surprise would be going for them. The assault team would have its weapons loaded and locked – and aimed at people who were asleep. The element of surprise, in the hands of elite commandos, was the military equivalent of a Kansas tornado. Nothing could stand up to it.

They're in their choppers now, Ryan thought. He remembered his own experience in the fragile, ungainly aircraft. *There you are, all your equipment packed up, clean utilities, your weapons ready, and despite it all you're as vulnerable as a baby in the womb.* He wondered what sort of men they were, and realized that they wouldn't be too very different from the Marines he'd served with: all would be volunteers, doubly so since you also had to volunteer for parachute training. They'd opted a third time to be part of the antiterror teams. It would be partly for the extra pay they got and partly for the pride that always came with membership in a small, very special force – like the Marine Corps' Force Recon – but mostly they'd be there because they knew that this was a mission worth doing. To a man, professional soldiers despised terrorists, and each would dream about getting them in an even-up-battle – the idea of the Field of Honor had never died for the real professionals. It was the place where the ultimate decision was made on the basis of courage and skill, on the basis of manhood itself, and it was this concept that marked the professional soldier as a romantic, a person who truly believed in the rules.

They'd be nervous in their helicopter. Some would fidget and be ashamed of it. Others would make a great show of sharpening their knives. Some would joke quietly. Their officers and sergeants would sit quietly, setting an example and going over the plans. All would look about the helicopter and silently hate being trapped within it. For a moment Jack was there with them.

'Good luck, guys,' he whispered to the wall. '*Bonne chance*.'

The hours crept by. It seemed to Ryan that the numbers on his digital watch were reluctant to change at all, and it was impossible for him to concentrate on his work. He was going over the photos of the camp again, counting the man-figures, examining the ground to predict for himself how the final approach would be made. He wondered if their orders were to take the terrorists alive. He couldn't decide on that question. From a legal perspective, he didn't think it really mattered. If terrorism were the modern manifestation of piracy – the analogy seemed apt enough – then the ULA was fair game for any nation's armed forces. On the other hand, taken alive, they could be put on trial and displayed. The psychological impact on other such groups might be real. If it didn't put the fear of God in them, it would at least get their attention. It would frighten them to know that they were not safe even in their most remote, most secure sanctuary. Some members might drift away, and maybe one or two of them would talk. It didn't take much intelligence information to hammer them. Ryan had seen that clearly enough. You needed to know where they were, that was all. With that knowledge you could bring all the forces of a modern nation to bear, and for all their arrogance and brutality, they couldn't hope to stand up to that.

Marty came into the office. 'Ready to go over?'

'Hell, yes!'

'Did you have dinner?'

'No. Maybe later.'

'Yeah.' Together they walked to the annex. The corridors were nearly empty now. For the most part, CIA worked like any other place. At five the majority of the workers departed for home and dinner and evening television.

'Okay, Jack, this is real-time. Remember that you can't discuss any aspect of this.' Cantor looked rather tired, Jack thought.

'Marty, if this op is successful, I will tell my wife that the ULA is out of business. She has a right to know that much.'

'I can understand that. Just so she doesn't know how it happens.'

'She wouldn't even be interested,' Jack assured him as they entered the room with the TV monitor. Jean-Claude was there again.

'Good evening, Mr Cantor, Professor Ryan,' the DGSE officer greeted them both.

'How's the op going?'

'They are under radio silence,' the Colonel replied.

'What I don't understand is how they can do it the same way twice,' Ryan went on.

'There is a risk. A little disinformation has been used,' Jean-Claude said cryptically. 'In addition, your carrier now has their full attention.'

'*Saratoga* has an alpha-strike up,' Marty explained. 'Two fighter squadrons and three attack ones, plus jamming and radar coverage. They're patrolling that "Line of Death" right now. According to our electronic listening people, the Libyans are going slightly ape. Oh, well.'

'The satellite comes over the horizon in twenty-four minutes,' the senior technician reported. 'Local weather looks good. We ought to get some clear shots.'

Ryan wished he had a cigarette. They made the waiting easier, but every time Cathy smelled them on his breath, there was hell to pay. At this point the raiding force would be crawling across the last thousand yards. Ryan had done the drill himself. They'd come away with bloody hands and knees, sand rubbed into the wounds. It was an incredibly tiring thing to do, made more difficult still by the presence of armed soldiers at the objective. You had to time your moves for when they were looking the other way, and you had to be quiet. They'd be carrying the bare minimum of gear, their personal weapons, maybe some grenades, a few radios, slinking across the ground the way a tiger did, watching and listening.

Everyone was staring at the blank TV monitor now, each of them bewitched by his imagination's picture of what was happening.

'Okay,' the technician said, 'cameras coming on line, attitude and tracking controls in automatic, programming telemetry received. Target acquisition in ninety seconds.

The TV picture lit up. It showed a test pattern. Ryan hadn't seen one of those in years.

'Getting a signal.'

Then the picture appeared. Disappointingly, it was in infrared again. Somehow Ryan had expected otherwise. The low-angle showed very little of the camp. They could discern no movement at all. The technician frowned and increased the viewing field. Nothing more, not even the helicopters.

The viewing angle changed slowly, and it was hard to believe that the reconnaissance satellite was racing along at over eighteen thousand miles per hour. Finally they could see all of the huts. Ryan blinked. Only one was lit up on the infrared picture. *Uh-oh.* Only one hut – the guards' one – had had its heater on. What did that mean? *They're gone – nobody's home . . . and the assault force isn't there either.*

Ryan said what the others didn't want to say: 'Something's gone wrong.'

'When can they tell us what happened?' Cantor asked.

'They cannot break silence for several hours.'

Two more hours followed. They were spent in Marty's office. Food was sent up. Jean-Claude didn't say anything, but he was clearly disappointed by it. Cantor didn't touch his at all. The phone rang. The Frenchman took the call, and spoke in his native tongue. The conversation lasted four or five minutes. Jean-Claude hung up and turned.

'The assault force came upon a regular army unit a hundred kilometres from the camp, apparently a mechanized unit on an exercise. This was not expected. Coming in low, they encountered them quite suddenly. It opened fire on the helicopters. Surprise was lost, and they had to turn back.' Jean-Claude didn't have to explain that, at best, operations like this were successful barely more than half the time.

'I was afraid of that.' Jack stared at the floor. He didn't need to have anyone tell him that the mission could not be repeated. They had run a serious risk, trying a covert mission the same way twice. There would be no third attempt. 'Are your people safe?'

'Yes, one helicopter was damaged, but managed to return to base. No casualties.'

'Please thank your people for trying, Colonel.' Cantor excused himself and walked to his private bathroom. Once in there, he threw up. His ulcers were bleeding again. Marty tried to stand, but found himself faint. He fell against the door with a hard rap on the head.

Jack heard the noise and went to see what it was. It was hard to open the door, but he finally saw Marty lying there. Ryan's first instinct was to tell Jean-Claude to call for a doctor, but Jack himself didn't know how to do that here. He helped Marty to his feet and led him back into his office, setting him in a chair.

'What's the matter?'

'He just tossed up blood – how do you call . . .' Ryan said the hell with it and dialled Admiral Greer's line.

'Marty's collapsed – we need a doctor here.'

'I'll take care of it. Be there in two minutes,' the Admiral answered.

Jack went into the bathroom and got a glass of water and some toilet paper. He used this to wipe Cantor's mouth, then held up the glass. 'Wash your mouth out.'

'I'm okay,' the man protested.

'Bullshit,' Ryan replied. 'You jerk. You've been working too damned late, trying to finish up all your stuff before you leave, right?'

'Got – got to.'

'What you got to do, Marty, is get the hell out of here before it eats you up.'

Cantor gagged again.

You weren't kidding, Marty, Jack thought. *The war is being fought here, too, and you're one of the casualties. You wanted that mission to score as much as I did.*

'What the hell!' Greer entered the room. He even looked a little dishevelled.

'His ulcers let go,' Jack explained. 'He's been puking blood.'

'Aw, Jesus, Marty!' the Admiral said.

Ryan hadn't known that there was a medical dispensary at Langley. Someone identifying himself as a paramedic arrived next. He examined

705

Cantor quickly, then he and a security guard loaded the man on a wheelchair. They took him out, and the three men left behind stared at each other.

'How hard is it to die from ulcers?' Ryan asked his wife just before midnight.

'How old is he?' she asked. Jack told her. Cathy thought about it for a moment. 'It can happen, but it's fairly rare. Somebody at work?'

'My supervisor at Langley. He's been on Tagamet, but he vomited blood tonight.'

'Maybe he tried going without it. That's one of the problems. You give people medications, and as soon as they start feeling better, they stop taking the meds. Even smart people,' Cathy noted. 'Is it *that* stressful over there?'

'I guess it was for him.'

'Super.' It was the kind of remark that should have been followed by a roll-over, but Cathy hadn't been able to do that for some time. 'He'll probably be all right. You really have to work at it to be in serious trouble from ulcers nowadays. Are you sure you want to work there?'

'No. They want me, but I won't decide until you lose a little weight.'

'You'd better not be that far away when I go into labour.'

'I'll be there when you need me.'

'Almost got 'em,' Murray reported.

'The same mob who raided *Action Directe*, eh? Yes, I've heard that was a nicely run mission. What happened?' Owens asked.

'The assault group was spotted seventy miles out and had to turn back. On reexamination of the photos, it may be that our friends were already gone anyway.'

'Marvellous. I see our luck is holding. Where did they go, you reckon?'

Murray grunted. 'I've got to make the same assumption you have, Jimmy.'

'Quite.' He looked out the window. The sun would be rising soon. 'Well, we've cleared the DPG man and told him the story.'

'How'd he take it?'

'He immediately offered his resignation, but the Commissioner and I prevailed upon him to withdraw it. We all have our little foibles,' Owens said generously. 'He's very good at what he does. You'll be pleased to learn that his reaction was precisely the same as yours. He said we should arrange for His Highness to fall off one of his polo ponies and break his leg. Please don't quote either of us on that!'

'It's a hell of a lot easier to protect cowards, isn't it? It's the brave ones who complicate our lives. You know something? He's going to be a good king for you someday. If he lives long enough,' Murray added. It was impossible not to like the kid, he thought. And his wife was dynamite. 'Well, if it makes you feel any better, the security on 'em in the States will be *tight*. Just like what we give the President. Even some of the same people are involved.'

That's supposed to make me feel happy? Owens asked himself silently, remembering how close several American Presidents had come to death at the hands of madmen, not to mention John F. Kennedy. It could be, of course, that the ULA was back wherever it lived, but all his instincts told him otherwise. Murray was a close friend, and he also knew and respected the Secret Service agents who'd formed the security detail. But the security of Their Highnesses was properly the responsibility of the Yard, and he didn't like the fact that it was now largely in others' hands. Owens had been professionally offended the last time the American President had been in the UK, when the Secret Service had made a big show of shoving the locals as far aside as they dared. Now he understood them a little better.

'How much is the rent?' Dobbens asked.

'Forty-fifty a month,' the agent answered. 'That's furnished.'

'Uh-huh.' The furnishings weren't exactly impressive, Alex saw. They didn't have to be.

'When can my cousin move in?'

'It's not for you?'

'No, it's my cousin. He's in the same business I am,' Alex explained. 'He's new to the area. I'll be responsible for the rent, of course. A three-month deposit, you said?'

'Okay.' The agent had specified two months' rent up-front.

'Cash all right?' Dobbens asked.

'Sure. Let's go back to the office and get the paperwork done.'

'I'm running a little late, I'm afraid. Don't you have the contract with you?'

The agent nodded. 'Yeah, I can do it right here.' He walked out to his car and came back with a clipboard and a boilerplate rental contract. He didn't know that he was condemning himself to death, that no one else from his office had seen this man's face.

'My mail goes to a box – I get it on the way into work.' That took care of the address.

'What sort of work, did you say?'

'I work at the Applied Physics Laboratory, electrical engineer. I'm afraid I can't be more specific than that. We do a lot of government work, you understand.' Alex felt vaguely sorry for the man. He was pleasant enough, and hadn't given him a runaround like many real estate people did. It was too bad. *That's life.*

'You always deal in cash?'

'That's one way to make sure you can afford it,' Alex chuckled.

'Could you sign here, please?'

'Sure thing.' Alex did so with his own pen, left-handed as he'd practised. 'And that's thirteen-fifty.' He counted off the bills.

'That was easy,' the agent said as he handed over the keys and the receipt.

'It sure was. Thank you, sir.' Alex shook his hand. 'He'll probably be moving in next week, certainly by the week after that.'

The two men walked out to their cars. Alex wrote down the agent's tag number: he drove his own car, not one belonging to the brokerage. Alex noted his description anyway, just to be sure that his people didn't kill the wrong man. He was glad he hadn't drawn a woman agent. Alex knew that he'd have to overcome that prejudice sooner or later, but for the moment it was an issue he was just as happy to avoid. He followed the agent for a few blocks, then turned off and doubled back to the house.

It wasn't exactly perfect, but close enough. Three small bedrooms. The eat-in kitchen was all right, though, as was the living room. Most important, it had a garage, and sat on nearly an acre of ground. The lot was bordered by hedges, and sat in a semirural working-class neighbourhood where the houses were separated by about fifty feet. It would do just fine as a safehouse.

Finished, he drove to Washington National Airport, where he caught a flight to Miami. There was a three-hour layover until he took another aeroplane to Mexico City. Miller was waiting for him in the proper hotel.

'Hello, Sean.'

'Hello, Alex. Drink?'

'What do you have?'

'Well, I brought a bottle of decent whiskey, or you can have some of the local stuff. The beer isn't bad, but I personally stop short of drinking something with a worm in the bottle.'

Alex selected a beer. He didn't bother with a glass.

'So?'

Dobbens drained the beer in one long pull. It was good to be able to relax – really relax. Play-acting all the time at home could be a strain. 'I got the safehouse all set up. Did that this morning. It'll do fine for what we want. What about your people?'

'They're on the way. They'll arrive as planned.'

Alex nodded approval as he got a second beer. 'Okay, let's see how the operation's going to run.'

'In a very real sense, Alex, you inspired this.' Miller opened his briefcase and extracted the maps and charts. They went on the coffee table. Alex didn't smile. Miller was trying to stroke him, and Dobbens didn't like being stroked. He listened for twenty minutes.

'Not bad, that's pretty fair, but you're going to have to change a few things.'

'What?' Miller asked. He was already angered by Dobbens' tone.

'Look, man, there's going to be at least fifteen security guys right here.' Alex tapped the map. 'And you're going to have to do them right quick, y'know? We're not talking street cops here. These guys are trained and well-armed. They're not exactly dumb, either. If you want this to work, man, you have to land the first punch harder. Your timing is off some, too. No, we have to tighten this up some, Sean.'

'But they'll be in the wrong place!' Miller objected as dispassionately as he could manage.

'And you want them to be running around loose? No way, boy! You'd better think about taking them out in the first ten seconds. Hey, think of them as soldiers. This ain't no snatch-and-run job. We're talking combat here.'

'But if the security is going to be as tight as you say –'

'I can handle that, man. Don't you pay attention to what I'm doing? I can put your shooters in exactly the right spot at exactly the right time.'

'And how the hell will you do that!' Miller was unable to calm himself any more. There was just something about Alex that set him off.

'It's easy, man.' Dobbens smiled. He enjoyed showing this hotshot how things were done. 'All you gotta do . . .'

'And you really think you can get past them just like that!' Miller snapped after he finished.

'Easy. I can write my own work orders, remember?'

Miller struggled with himself again, and this time he won. He told himself to view Alex's idea dispassionately. He hated admitting to himself that the plan made sense. This amateur black was telling him how to run an op, and the fact that he was right just made it worse.

'Hey, man, it's not just better, it's easier to do.' Alex backed off somewhat. Even arrogant whities needed their pride. This boy was used to having his own way. He was smart enough, Dobbens admitted to himself, but too inflexible. Once he got himself set on an idea, he didn't want to change a thing. He never would have made a good engineer, Alex knew. 'Remember the last op we ran for you? Trust me, man. I was right then, wasn't I?'

For all his technical expertise, Alex did not have tremendous skills for handling people. The last remark almost set Miller off again, but the Irishman took a deep breath as he continued to stare at the map. *Now I know why the Yanks love their niggers so much.*

'Let me think about it.'

'Sure. Tell you what. I'm going to get some sleep. You can pray over the map all you want.'

'Who else besides the security and the targets?'

Alex stretched. 'Maybe they're going to cater it. Hell – I don't know. I imagine they'll have their maid. I mean, you don't have that kind of company without one servant, right? She doesn't get hurt either, man. She's a sister, handsome woman. And remember what I said about the lady and the kid. If it's necessary, I can live with it, but if you pop 'em for fun, Sean, you'll answer to me. Let's try to keep this one professional. You have three legitimate political targets. That's enough. The rest are bargaining chips, we can use 'em to show goodwill. That might not be important to you, boy, but it's fucking well important to me. You dig?'

'Very well, Alex.' Sean decided then and there that Alex would not see the end of this operation. It shouldn't be too hard to arrange. With his absurd sentimentality, he was unfit to be a revolutionary. *You'll die a brave death. At least we can make a martyr of you.*

Two hours later Miller admitted to himself that this was unfortunate. The man did have a flair for operations.

The security people were late enough that Ryan pulled into the driveway right behind them. There were three of them, led by Chuck Avery of the Secret Service.

'Sorry, we got held up,' Avery said as he shook hands. 'This is Bert Longley and Mike Keaton, two of our British colleagues.'

'Hello, Mr Longley,' Cathy called from the door.

His eyes went wide as he saw her condition. 'My goodness, perhaps we should bring a physician in with us! I'd no idea you were so far along.'

'Well, this one will be part English.' Jack explained. 'Come on in.'

'Mr Longley arranged our escort when you were in the hospital,' Cathy told her husband. 'Nice to see you again.'

'How are you feeling?' Longley asked.

'A little tired, but okay,' Cathy allowed.

'Have you cleared the problem about Robby?' Jack asked.

'Yes, we have. Please excuse Mr Bennett. I'm afraid he took his instructions a bit too literally. We have no problems with a naval officer. In fact, His Highness is looking forward to meeting him. So, may we look around?'

'If it's all right with you, I want to see that cliff of yours,' Avery said.

'Follow me, gentlemen.' Jack let the three through the sliding-glass doors onto the deck that faced Chesapeake Bay.

'Magnificent!' Longley observed.

'The only thing we did wrong is that the living and dining room aren't separated, but that's how the design was drawn, and we couldn't figure a graceful way to change it. But all those windows do give us a nice view, don't they?'

'Indeed, also one that gives our chaps good visibility,' Keaton observed, surveying the area.

Not to mention decent fields of fire, Ryan thought.

'How many people will you be bringing?' Jack asked.

'I'm afraid that's not something we can discuss,' Longley replied.

'More than twenty?' Jack persisted. 'I plan to have coffee and sandwiches for your troops. Don't worry, I haven't even told Robby.'

'Enough for twenty will be more than ample,' Avery said after a moment. 'Just coffee will be fine.' They'd be drinking a lot of coffee, the Secret Service man thought.

'Okay, let's see the cliff.' Jack went down the steps from the deck to the grass. 'You want to be very careful here, gentlemen.'

'How unstable is it?' Avery asked.

'Sally has been past where the fence is twice. Both times she got smacked for it. The problem's erosion. The cliff's made out of something real soft – sandstone, I think. I've been trying to stabilize it. The state conservation people talked me into planting this damned kudzu, and – stop right there!'

Keaton had stepped over the low fence.

'Two years ago I watched a twenty-square-foot piece drop off. That's why I planted these vines. You don't think somebody's going to climb that, do you?'

'It's one possibility,' Longley answered.

'You'd think different if you looked at it from a boat. The cliff won't take the weight. A squirrel can make it up, but that's all.'

'How high is it?' Avery asked.

'Forty-three feet over there, almost fifty here. The kudzu vines just make it worse. The damned stuff's nearly impossible to kill, but if you try grabbing onto it, you're in for a big surprise. Like I said, if you want to check it, do it from a boat,' Ryan said.

'We'll do that,' Avery replied.

'Coming in, that driveway must be three hundred yards,' Keaton said.

'Just over four hundred, counting the curves. It cost an arm and a leg to pave it.'

'What about the swimming pool people?' It was Longley this time.

'The pool's supposed to be finished next Wednesday.'

Avery and Keaton walked around the north side of the house. There were trees twenty yards from there, and a swarm of brambles that went on forever. Ryan had planted a long row of shrubs to mark the border. Sally didn't go in there either.

'This looks pretty secure,' Avery said. 'There's two hundred yards of open space between the road and the trees, then more open ground between the pool and the house.'

'Right.' Ryan chuckled. 'You can set up your heavy machine guns in the treeline and put the mortars over by the pool.'

'Doctor Ryan, we are quite serious about this,' Longley pointed out.

'I'm sure. But it's an unannounced trip, right? They can't –' Jack stopped short. He didn't like the look on their faces.

Avery said, 'We always assume that the other side knows what we're up to.'

'Oh.' *Is that all of it, or is there more?* He knew it wouldn't do any good to ask. 'Well, speaking as a has-been Marine, I wouldn't want to hit this place cold. I know a little about how you guys are trained. I wouldn't want to mess with you.'

'We try,' Avery assured him, still looking around. The way the driveway came through the trees, he could use his communications van to block vehicles out entirely. He reminded himself that there would be ten people from his agency, six Brits, a liaison guy from the Bureau, and probably two or three State Police for traffic control on the road. Each of his men would have both a service revolver and a submachine gun. They practised at least once a week.

Avery still was not happy, not with the possibility of an armed terrorist group running around loose. But all the airports were being watched, all the local police forces alerted. There was only one road in here. The surrounding terrain would be difficult even for a platoon of soldiers to penetrate without making all kinds of noise, and as nasty as terrorists were, they'd never fought a set-piece battle. This wasn't London, and the potential targets weren't driving blithely about with a single armed guard.

'Thank you, Doctor Ryan. We will check the cliff out from the water side. If you see a Coast Guard cutter, that'll be us.'

'You know how to get to the station at Thomas Point? You take Forest Drive east to Arundel-on-the-Bay and hang a right. You can't miss it.'

'Thanks, we'll do that.'

The real estate agent came out of the office just before ten. It was his turn to shut down. In his briefcase was an envelope for the bank's night depository and some contracts he'd go over the next morning before going into work. He set the case on the seat beside him and started the car. Two headlights pulled right in behind him.

'Can I talk to you?' a voice called in the darkness. The agent turned to see a shape coming toward him.

'I'm afraid we're closed. The office opens at –' He saw that he was looking at a gun.

'I want your money, man. Just be cool, and everything'll be okay,' the gunman said. There was no sense terrifying the man. He might do something crazy, and he might get lucky.

'But I don't have any –'

'The briefcase and the wallet. Slow and easy and you'll be home in half an hour.'

The man got his wallet first. It took three attempts to loose the button on his hip pocket, and his hands were quivering as he handed it over. The briefcase came next.

'It's just cheques – no cash.'

'That's what they all say. Lie down on the seat and count to one hundred. Don't stick your head up till you finish, and everything'll be just fine. Out loud, so's I can hear you.' *Let's see, the heart's right about there. . . .* He reached his gun hand inside the open window. The man got to seven. When it went off, the sound of the silenced automatic was further muffled by being inside the car. The body jerked a few times, but not enough to require a second round. The gunman opened the door and wound up the

712

window, then killed the engine and the lights before going back to his car. He pulled back onto the road and drove at the legal limit. Ten minutes later the empty briefcase and wallet were tossed into a shopping centre dumpster. He got back onto the highway and drove in the opposite direction. It was dangerous to hold on to the gun, but that had to be disposed of more carefully. The gunman drove the car back to where it belonged – the family that owned it was on vacation – and walked two blocks to get his own. *Alex was right*, as always, the gunman thought. *If you plan everything, think it all out, and most important, don't leave any evidence behind, you can kill all the people you want. Oh*, he remembered, *one more thing: you don't talk about it.*

'Hi, Ernie,' Jack said quietly. The dog showed up as a dark spot on the light-coloured carpet in the living room. It was four in the morning. Ernie had heard a noise and come out of Sally's room to see what it was. One thing about dogs, they never slept the way people did. Ernie looked at him for several minutes, his tail gyrating back and forth until he got a scratch between his ears, then he moved off, back to Sally's room. It was amazing, Jack thought. The dog had entirely supplanted AG Bear. He found it hard to believe that anything could do that.

They're coming back, aren't they? he asked the night. Jack rose off the leather couch and walked to the windows. It was a clear night. Out on the Chesapeake Bay, he could see the running lights of ships plying their way to or from the Port of Baltimore, and the more ornate displays of tug-barge combinations that plodded along more slowly.

He didn't know how he could have been so slow on the uptake. Perhaps because the activity at Camp -18 almost tracked with the pattern that he'd tried repeatedly to discern. It was about the right time for them to show up for refresher training. But it was equally likely that they were planning something big. *Like maybe right here. . . .*

'Jesus. You were too close to the problem, Jack,' he whispered. It was public knowledge – had been for a couple of weeks – that they were coming over, and the ULA had already demonstrated its ability to operate in America, he remembered. *And we're bringing known targets into our home! Real smart, Jack.* In retrospect it was amazing enough. They'd accepted the backwards invitation without the first thought . . . and even when the security people had been here the previous day, he'd made jokes. *You asshole!*

He thought over the security provisions, taking himself back again to his time in the Corps. As an abstract battle problem, his house was a tough objective. You couldn't do anything from the east – the cliff was a more dangerous obstacle than a minefield. North and south, the woods were so thick and tangled that even the most skilled commando types would be hard-pressed to come through without making a horrendous racket – and they sure as hell couldn't practise that kind of skill in a barren, treeless

713

desert! So they had to come from the west. *How many people did Avery say – well, he didn't say, but I got the impression of about twenty.* Twenty security people, armed and trained. He remembered the days from the Basic Officer's Course at Quantico, and the nights. Twenty-two years old, invincible and immortal, drinking beer at local bars. There'd been one night at a place called the Command Post, the one with a picture of Patton on the wall, when he'd started talking to a couple of instructors from the FBI Academy, just south of the Marine base. They were every bit as proud as his brother Marines. *They never bothered to say 'we are the best'. They simply assumed that everyone knew it. Just like us.* The next day he'd accepted the invitation to shoot on their range and settle a gentlemanly wager. It had cost him ten dollars to learn that one of them was the chief firearms instructor. *God, I wonder if Breckenridge could beat him!* The Secret Service wouldn't be very difficult, given their mission. *Would you want to tangle with them? Hell, no!*

If I assume that the ULA is as smart as it seems to be . . . and it is an unannounced trip, a private sort of thing. . . . They won't know to come here, and even if they did, if they're too smart to take this one . . . it should be safe, shouldn't it?

But that was a word whose meaning was forever changed. Safe. It was something no longer real.

Jack walked around the fireplace into the house's bedroom wing. Sally was sleeping, with Ernie curled up on the foot of the bed. His head came up when Jack entered the room, as if to say, 'Yes?'

His little girl was lying there, at peace, dreaming a child's dreams while her father contemplated the nightmare that still hovered over his family, the one he'd allowed himself to forget for a few hours. He straightened the covers and patted the dog on the head before leaving the room.

Jack wondered how public figures did it. They lived with the nightmare all the time. He remembered congratulating the Prince for not letting such a threat dominate his life: *Well done, old boy, that'll show them! Be a fearless target!* It was a very different thing when you were yourself the target, Ryan admitted to the night, when your family was the target. You put on the brave face, and followed your instructions, and wondered if every car on the street could hold a man with a machine gun who was bent on making *your* death into a very special political statement. You could keep your mind off it during the day when you had work to do, but at night, when the mind wanders and dreams begin . . .

The dualism was incredible. You couldn't dwell on it, but neither could you allow yourself to forget it. You couldn't let your life be dominated by fear, but you couldn't ever lapse into a feeling of security. A sense of fatalism would have helped, but Ryan was a man who had always deemed himself the master of his fate. He would not admit that anything else could be true. He wanted to lash out, if not at *them*, then at destiny, but both were as far

714

beyond his reach as the ships whose lights passed miles from his windows. The safety of his family had almost been assured –

We came so close! he cried silently to the night.

They'd almost done it. They'd almost won that one battle, and they had helped others win another. He *could* fight back, and he knew that he could do it best by working at that desk in Langley, by joining the team full-time. He would not be the master of his fate, but at least he could play a part. He had played a part. It had been important enough – if only an accident – to Françoise Theroux, that pretty, malignant thing now dead. And so the decision was made. The people with guns would play their part, and the man behind the desk would play his. Jack would miss the Academy, miss the eager young kids, but that was the price he'd have to pay for getting back into the game. Jack got a drink of water before going back to bed.

Plebe Summer started on schedule. Jack watched with impassive sympathy as the recently graduated high school seniors were introduced to the rigours of military life. The process was consciously aimed at weeding out the weak as early as possible, and so it was largely in the hands of upperclassmen who had only recently been through the same thing. The new youngsters were at the debatable mercy of the older ones, running around with their closely cropped hair to the double-time cadence of students only two years their senior.

'Morning, Jack!' Robby came over to watch with him from the parking lot.

'You know, Rob, Boston College was never like this.'

'If you think this is a Plebe Summer,' Jackson snorted, 'you should have seen what it was like when I was here!'

'I bet they've been saying that for a hundred years,' Jack suggested.

'Probably so.' The white-clad plebes passed like a herd of buffalo, all gasping for air on the hot, humid morning. 'We kept better formations, though.'

'The first day?'

'The first few days were a blur,' Jackson admitted.

'Packing up?'

Jackson nodded. 'Most of the gear's already in boxes. I have to get my relief settled in.'

'Me, too.'

'You're leaving?' Robby was surprised.

'I told Admiral Greer that I wanted in.'

'Admiral – oh, the guy at CIA. You're going to do it, eh? How did the department take it?'

'I think you can say that they managed to restrain their tears. The boss isn't real happy about all the time I missed this year. So it looks like we're both having a going-away dinner.'

'Jeez, it's this Friday, isn't it?'

'Yeah. Can you show up about eight-fifteen?'

'You got it. You said not dressy, right?'

'That's right.' Jack smiled. *Gotcha.*

The RAF VC-10 aircraft touched down at Andrews Air Force Base at eight in the evening and taxied to the same terminal used by Air Force One. The reporters noted that security was very tight, with what looked to be a full company of Air Police in view, plus the plainclothes Secret Service agents. They told themselves that security at this particular part of the base was always strict. The plane came to a halt at exactly the right place, and the stairs were rolled to the forward door, which opened after a moment.

At the foot of the stairs waited the Ambassador and officials from the State Department. Inside the aircraft, security men made a final check out the windows. Finally His Highness appeared in the doorway, joined by his young wife, waving to the distant spectators, and descending the stairs gingerly despite legs that were stiff from the flight. At the bottom a number of military officers from two nations saluted, and the State Department protocol officer curtsied. This would earn her a reprimand from the *Washington Post*'s arbiter of manners in the morning edition. The six-year-old granddaughter of the base commander presented Her Highness with a dozen yellow roses. Strobes flashed, and both royal personages smiled dutifully at the cameras while they took the time to say something pleasant to everyone in the receiving line. The Prince shared a joke with a naval officer who had once commanded him, and the Princess said something about the oppressive, muggy weather that had persisted into the evening. The Ambassador's wife pointed out that the climate here was such that Washington DC had once been considered a hazardous-duty station. The malaria mosquitoes were long gone, but the climate hadn't changed very much. Fortunately, everyone had air conditioning. Reporters noted the colour, style, and cut of the Princess's outfit, especially her 'daring' new hat. She stood with the poise of a professional model while her husband looked as casual as a Texas cowboy, as incongruous as that might have seemed, one hand in his pocket and a relaxed grin on his face. The Americans who'd never met the couple before found him wonderfully easygoing, and of course every man there had long since fallen in love with the Princess, along with most of the Western world.

The security people saw none of this. They all had their backs to the scene, their eyes scanning the crowd, their faces stamped into the same serious expression while each with various degrees of emphasis thought: *Please, God, not while I'm on duty.* Every one had a radio earpiece constantly providing information that their brains monitored while their eyes were otherwise occupied.

Finally they moved to the embassy's Rolls-Royce, and the motorcade formed up. Andrews had a number of gates, and the one they took had been decided upon only an hour before. The route into town was its own traffic jam of marked and unmarked cars. Two additional Rolls-Royce automobiles, of exactly the same model and colour, were dispersed through the procession, each with a lead and chase-car, and a helicopter was overhead. If anyone had taken the time to count the firearms present, the total would have been nearly a hundred. The arrival had been timed to allow swift passage through Washington, and twenty-five minutes later the motorcade got to the British Embassy. A few minutes after that, Their Highnesses were safely in the building, and for the moment the responsibility of someone else. Most of the local security people dispersed, heading back to their homes or stations, but ten men and women stayed around the building, most invisibly hidden in cars and vans, while a few extra uniformed police walked the perimeter.

'America,' O'Donnell said. 'The land of opportunity.' The television news coverage came on at eleven, and had tape of the arrival.

'What do you suppose they're doing now?' Miller asked.

'Working on their jet lag, I imagine,' his chief observed. 'Getting a good night's sleep. So, all ready here?'

'Yes, the safehouse is all prepared for tomorrow. Alex and his people are ready, and I've gone over the changes in the plan.'

'They're from Alex, too?'

'Yes, and if I hear one more bit of advice from that arrogant bastard –'

'He is one of our revolutionary brethren,' O'Donnell noted with a smile. 'But I know what you mean.'

'Where's Joe?'

'Belfast. He'll run Phase Two.'

'The timing is all set?'

'Yes. Both brigade commanders, and the whole Army Council. We should be able to get them all. . . .' O'Donnell finally revealed his plan in toto. McKenney's penetration agents either worked closely with all of the senior PIRA people or knew those who did. On command from O'Donnell, they would assassinate them all, completely removing the Provisional's military leadership. There would be no one left to run the Organization . . . except one man whose masterstroke mission would catapult him back to respectability with rank-and-file Provos. With his hostages, he'd get the release of all the men 'behind the wire' even if it meant mailing the Prince of Wales to Buckingham Palace one cubic centimetre at a time. O'Donnell was certain of this. For all the brave, pious talk in Whitehall, it was centuries since an English king had faced death, and the idea of martyrdom sat better with revolutionaries than with those in power. Public

717

pressure would see to that. They would *have* to negotiate to save the life of the heir to the throne. The scope of this operation would enliven the Movement, and Kevin Joseph O'Donnell would lead a revolution reborn in boldness and blood. . . .

'Changing of the guard, Jack?' Marty observed. He, too, had packed up his things. A security officer would check the box before he left.

'How are you feeling?'

'Better, but you can get tired of watching daytime TV.'

'Taking all your pills?' Ryan asked.

'I'll never forget again, Mom,' was the answer.

'I see there's nothing new on our friends.'

'Yeah. They dropped back into that black hole they live in. The FBI is worried that they're over here, of course, but there hasn't even been a hint of it. Of course, whenever anybody's felt secure dealing with these bastards, they've gotten bit on the ass. Still, about the only outfit that isn't on alert is the Delta Force. All kinds of assets are standing by. If they're over here and they show anybody a whisker, the whole world is going to come crashing in on them. "Call in the whole world." We used to say that in Vietnam.' Cantor grunted. 'I'll be in Monday and Tuesday. You don't have to say goodbye yet. Have a good weekend.'

'You too, pal. ' Ryan walked out, with a new security pass hanging around his neck and his jacket draped over his shoulder. It was hot outside, and his Rabbit didn't have air conditioning. The drive home along Route 50 was complicated by all the people heading to Ocean City for the weekend, anything to get away from the heat that had covered the area like an evil spell for two weeks. They were in for a surprise, Jack thought. A cold front was supposed to come through.

'Howard County Police,' the Desk Sergeant said. 'Can I help you?'

'This is 911, right?' It was a male voice.

'Yes, sir. What seems to be the problem?'

'Hey, uh, my wife said I shouldn't get involved, you know, but –'

'Can you give me your name and phone number, please?'

'No way – look, this house, uh, down the street. There's people there with guns, you know? Machine guns.'

'Say that again.' The Sergeant's eyes narrowed.

'Machine guns – no shit, I saw an M-60 machine gun, like in the Army – y'know, thirty caliber, feeds off a belt, heavy bitch to pack along, a real friggin' machine gun. I saw some other stuff, too.'

'Where?'

The voice became rapid. 'Eleven-sixteen Green Cottage Lane. There's maybe – I mean I saw four of 'em, one black and three white. They were unloading the guns from a van. It was three in the morning. I had to get up an' take a leak, and I looked out the bathroom window, y'know? The garage door was open, and the light was on, and when they passed the gun across, it was in the light, like, and I could tell it was a sixty. Hey, I used to carry one in the Army, y'know? Anyway, that's it, man, you wanna do something about it, that's your lookout.' The line clicked off. The Sergeant called his captain at once.

'What is it?' The Sergeant handed over his notes. 'Machine gun? M-60?'

'He said it was – he said it was a thirty-caliber that feeds off a belt. That's the M-60. That alert we got from the FBI, Captain . . .'

'Yeah.' The Station Commander had visions of promotion dangling before his eyes – but also visions of his men in a pitched battle where the perpetrators had better weapons. 'Get a car out there. Tell them to keep out of sight and take no action. I'm going to request a SWAT callup and get hold of the feds.'

Less than a minute later a police car was heading to the area. The responding officer was a six-year veteran of the county police who very much wanted to be a seven-year veteran. It took him almost ten minutes to reach the scene. He parked his car a block away, behind a large shrub, and was able to watch the house without exposing himself as a police officer. The shotgun that usually hung under the dashboard was in his sweating hands now, with a double-ought buck round chambered. Another car was four minutes behind his, and two more officers joined him. Then the whole world really did seem to arrive. First a patrol sergeant, then a lieutenant, then two captains, and finally, two agents from the FBI's Baltimore office. The officer who had first responded was now one of the Indians in a tribe top-heavy with chiefs.

The FBI Special Agent in Charge for the Baltimore office set up a radio link with the Washington headquarters, but left the operation in the hands of the local police. The county police had its own SWAT team, like most local forces did, and they quickly went to work. The first order of business was to evacuate the people from the area's homes. To everyone's relief, they were able to do that from the rear in every case. The people removed from their homes were immediately interviewed. Yes, they had seen people in that house. Yes, they were mostly white, but there had been at least one black person. No, they hadn't seen any guns – in fact, they hardly saw the people at all. One lady thought they had a van, but if so, it was usually kept in the garage. The interviews went on while the SWAT team moved in. The neighbourhood houses were all of the same style and design, and the men made a quick check through one to establish its layout. Another set up a scope-sighted rifle in the house directly across the street and used his sight to examine the target home's windows.

The SWAT team might have waited, but the longer they did that, the greater was the risk of alerting their quarry. They moved in slowly and carefully, skillfully using cover and concealment until they were within fifty feet of the target house. Anxious, sharp eyes scanned the windows for movement and saw none. *Could they all be asleep?* The team leader went in first, sprinting across the yard and stopping under a window. He held up a stick-on microphone and attached it to the corner of the window, listening to an earpiece for a sign of occupancy. The second-in-command watched the man's head cock almost comically to one side, then he spoke into a radio that all his team members could hear: 'The TV's on. No conversation, I – something else, can't make it out.' He motioned for his team to approach, one at a time, while he crouched under the window, gun at the ready. Three minutes later the team was ready.

'Team leader,' the radio crackled. 'This is Lieutenant Haber. We have a young man here who says a van went tearing out of that house about quarter to five – that's about the time the police radio call went out.'

The team leader waved acknowledgment and treated the message as something that mattered not a bit. The team executed a forced entry manoeuvre. Two simultaneous shotgun blasts blew the hinges off the windowless side door and it hadn't even hit the floor before the team leader was through the opening, training his gun around the kitchen. Nothing. They proceeded through the house in movements that looked like a kind of evil ballet. The entire exercise was over in a minute. The radio message went out: 'The building is secure.'

The team leader emerged on the front porch, his shotgun pointed at the floor, and pulled off his black mask before he waved the others in. His hands moved back and forth across his chest in the universal wave-off signal. The Lieutenant and the senior FBI agent ran across the street as he wiped the sweat away from his eyes.

'Well?'

'You're gonna love it,' the team leader said. 'Come on.' The living room had a small-screen colour TV on, sitting on a table. The floor was covered with wrappers from McDonald's, and the kitchen sink held what looked like fifty neatly stacked paper cups. The master bedroom – it was a few square feet larger than the other two – was the armoury. Sure enough, there was an American M-60 machinegun, with two 250-round ammo boxes, along with a dozen AK-47 assault rifles, three of them stripped down for cleaning, and a bolt-action rifle with a telescopic sight. On the oaken dresser, however, was a scanner radio. Its indicator lights skipped on and off. One of them was on the frequency of the Howard County Police. Unlike the FBI, the local police did not use secure – that is, scrambled – radio circuits. The FBI agent walked out to his vehicle and got Bill Shaw on the radio.

'So they monitored the police call and split,' Shaw said after a couple of minutes.

'Looks like it. The locals have a description of the van out. At least they bugged out so fast that they had to leave a bunch of weapons behind. Maybe they're spooked. Anything new coming in at your end?'

'Negative.' Shaw was in the FBI's emergency command centre, Room 5005 of the J. Edgar Hoover Building. He knew of the French attempt to hit their training camp. *Twice now they've escaped by sheer luck.* 'Okay, I'll get talking to the State Police forces. The forensic people are on the way. Stay put and coordinate with the locals.'

'Right. Out.'

The security people were already setting up. Discreetly, he saw, their cars were by the pool, which had been filled up only a couple of days before and there was a van which evidently contained special communications gear. Jack counted eight people in the open, two of them with Uzis. Avery was waiting for him when he pulled into the carport.

'Good news for a change – well, good and bad.'

'How so?' Ryan asked.

'Somebody phoned the cops and said he saw some people with guns. They rolled on it real quick. The suspects split – they were monitoring the police radio – but we captured a bunch of guns. Looks like our friends had a safehouse set up. Unfortunately for them it didn't quite work out. We may have 'em on the run. We know what kind of car they're using, and the local cops have this area completely sealed off, and we're sweeping the whole state. The Governor has even authorized the use of helicopters from the National Guard to help with the search.'

'Where were they?'

'Howard County, a little community south of Columbia. We missed them by a whole five minutes, but we have them moving and out in the open. Just a matter of time.'

'I hope the cops are careful,' Ryan said.

'Yes, sir.'

'Any problems here?'

'No, everything's going just fine. Your guests should be here about quarter to eight. What's for dinner?' Avery asked.

'Well, I picked up some fresh white corn on the way home – you passed the place coming in. Steaks on the grill, baked potatoes, and Cathy's spinach salad. We'll give 'em some good, basic American food.' Jack opened the hatch on the Rabbit and pulled out a bag of freshly picked corn.

Avery grinned. 'You're making me hungry.'

'I got a caterer coming in at six-thirty. Cold cuts and rolls. I'm not going to let you guys work all that time without food, okay?' Ryan insisted. 'You can't stay alert if you're hungry.'

'We'll see. Thanks.'

'My dad was a cop.'

'By the way, I tried the lights around the pool, but they don't work.'

'I know, the electricity's been acting up the last couple of days. The power company says they have a new transformer up, and it needs work – something like that.' Ryan shrugged. 'Evidently it damaged the breaker on the pool line, but so far nothing's gone bad in the house. You weren't planning to go swimming, were you?'

'No. We wanted to use one of the plugs here, but it's out too.'

'Sorry. Well, I have some stuff to do.'

Avery watched him leave, and went over his own deployment plans one last time. A pair of State Police cars would be a few hundred yards down the road to stop and check anyone coming back here. The bulk of his men would be covering the road. Two would watch each side of the clearing – the woods looked too inhospitable to penetrate, but they'd watch them anyway. This was called Team One. The second team would consist of six men. There would be three people in the house. Three more, one of them a communicator in the radio van, in the trees by the pool.

The speed trap was well known to the locals. Every weekend a car or two was set up on this stretch of Interstate 70. There had even been something about it in the local paper. But people from out of state didn't read that, of course. The trooper had his car just behind a small crest, which allowed cars heading up to Pennsylvania to fly by, right past his radar gun before they knew it. The pickings were so good that he never bothered chasing after anyone who did under sixty-five, and at least twice a night he nailed people for doing over eighty.

Be on the lookout for a black van, make and year unknown, the all-points call had said a few minutes before. The trooper estimated that there were at least five thousand such vans in the state of Maryland, and they'd all be on the road on a Friday night. Somebody else would have to worry about that. *Approach with extreme caution.*

His patrol car rocked like a boat crossing a wake as a vehicle zoomed past. The radar gun readout said 83. Business. The trooper dropped his car into gear and started moving after it before he saw that it was a black van. *Approach with extreme caution. . . . They didn't give a tag number. . . .*

'Hagerstown, this is Eleven. I am following a van, black in colour, that I clocked at eighty-three. I am westbound on I-70, about three miles east of exit thirty-five.'

'Eleven, get the tag number but do not – repeat *do not* – attempt to apprehend. Get the number, back off, and stay in visual contact. We'll get some backup for you.'

'Roger. Moving in now.' *Damn.*

He floored his accelerator and watched his speedometer go to ninety. The

722

van had slowed a little, it seemed. He was now two hundred yards back. His eyes squinted. He could see the plate but not the number. He closed the distance more slowly now. At fifty yards he could make out the plate – it was a handicap one. The trooper lifted his radio microphone to call in the tag numbers when the rear doors flew open.

It all hit him in a moment: *This was how Larry Fontana got it!* He slammed on his brakes and tried to turn the wheel, but the microphone cable got caught on his arm. The police officer cringed and slid down behind the dashboard as the car slowed, and then he saw the flash, a sun-white tongue of flame that reached directly at him. As soon as he understood what that was, he heard the impacting rounds. One of his tires blew, and his radiator exploded, sending a shower of steam and water into the air. More rounds walked up the hood into the right side of the car, and the trooper dived under the steering wheel while the car bounced up and down on the flattened tire. Then the noise stopped. The State Police officer stuck his head up and saw the van was a hundred yards away, accelerating up the hill. He tried to make a call on the radio, but it didn't work. He discovered soon after that two bullets had blasted through the car's battery, now leaking acid on the pavement. He stood there for several minutes, wondering why he was alive, before another police car arrived.

The trooper was shaking badly enough that he had to hold the microphone in both hands. 'Hagerstown, the bastard machine-gunned my car! It's a Ford van, looks like an eighty-four, handicap tag Nancy two-two-nine-one, last seen westbound on I-70 east of exit thirty – fi-five.'

'Were you hit?'

'Negative, but the car's b-beat to shit. They used a goddamned machine gun on me!'

That really got things rolling. The FBI was again notified, and every available State Police helicopter converged on the Hagerstown area. For the first time, the choppers held men with automatic weapons. In Annapolis, the Governor wondered if he should use National Guard units. An infantry company was put on alert – it was already engaged in its weekend drill – but for the moment, he limited the Guard's active involvement to helicopter support of the State Police. The hunt was on in the central Maryland hill country. Warnings went out over commercial radio and TV stations for people to be on the alert. The President was spending the weekend in the country, and that was another major complication. Marines at nearby Camp David and a few other highly secret defence installations tucked away in the rolling hills hung up their usual dress blues and pistol belts. They substituted M-16 rifles and camouflage greens.

25

Rendezvous

They arrived exactly on time. A pair of State Police cars remained on the road, and three more loaded with security people accompanied the Rolls up the driveway to the Ryan house. The chauffeur, one of the security force, pulled right to the front and jumped out to open the passenger door. His Highness came out first, and helped his wife. The security people were already swarming all over the place. The leader of the British contingent conferred with Avery, and the detail dispersed to their predetermined stations. As Jack came down the steps to greet his guests, he had the feeling that his home had been subjected to an armed invasion.

'Welcome to Peregrine Cliff.'

'Hello, Jack!' The Prince took his hand. 'You're looking splendid.'

'You, too, sir.' He turned to the Princess, whom he'd never actually met. 'Your Highness, this is a great pleasure.'

'And for us, Doctor Ryan.'

He led them into the house. 'How's your trip been so far?'

'Awfully hot,' the Prince answered. 'Is it always like this in the summer?'

'We've had two pretty bad weeks,' Jack answered. The temperature had hit ninety-five a few hours earlier. 'They say that's going to change by tomorrow. It isn't supposed to go much past eighty for the next few days.' This did not get an enthusiastic response.

Cathy was waiting inside with Sally. The weather was especially hard on her, this close to delivery. She shook hands, but Sally remembered how to curtsy from England, and performed a beautiful one, accompanied by a giggle.

'Are you quite all right?' Her Highness asked Cathy.

'Fine, except for the heat. Thank God for air conditioning!'

'Can we show you around?' Jack led the party into the living/dining room.

'The view is marvellous,' the Prince observed.

'Okay, the first thing is, nobody wears a coat in my house,' Ryan pronounced. 'I think you call this "Planter's Rig" over in England.'

'Excellent idea,' said the Prince. Jack took his jacket and hung it in the foyer closet next to his old Marine parka, then got rid of his own. By this time Cathy had everyone seated. Sally perched next to her mother, her feet high off the floor as she tried to keep her dress down on her knees. Cathy found it almost impossible to sit comfortably.

'How much longer?' the Princess asked.

'Eight days – of course with number two, that means any time.'

'I shall find that out myself in seven more months.'

'Really? Congratulations!' Both women beamed.

'Way to go, sir,' Ryan observed.

'Thank you, Jack. How have you been?'

'I suppose you know the work I'm doing?'

'Yes, I heard last night from one of our security people. I've been told that you located and identified a terrorist camp that has since been . . . neutralized,' the Prince said quietly.

Ryan nodded discreetly. 'I'm afraid that I'm not able to discuss that.'

'I quite understand. And how has your little girl been since . . .'

'Sally?' Jack turned. 'How's my little girl?'

'I'm a *big* girl!' she replied forcefully.

'What do you think?'

'I think you've been damned lucky.'

'I'd settle for a little bit more. I presume you've heard?'

'Yes.' He paused. 'I hope your chaps are careful.'

Jack voiced agreement, then rose as he heard a car pull up. He opened the door to see Robby and Sissy Jackson getting out of the pilot's Corvette. The Secret Service's communications van moved to block the driveway behind them. Robby stormed up the steps.

'What gives? Who's here, the President?'

Cathy must have warned them, Jack saw. Sissy was dressed in a simple but very nice blue dress, and Robby had a tie on. Too bad.

'Come on in and join the party,' Jack said with a nasty grin.

Robby looked at the two men by the pool, their jackets unbuttoned, and gave Jack a puzzled look, but followed. As they came around the brick fireplace, the pilot's eyes went wide.

'Commander Jackson, I presume.' His Highness rose.

'Jack,' Robby whispered. 'I'm going to kill you!' Louder: 'How do you do, sir. This is my wife, Cecilia.' As usually happened, the people immediately split into male and female groups.

'I understand you're a naval aviator.'

'Yes, sir. I'm going back to a fleet squadron now. I fly the F-14.' Robby struggled to keep his voice under control. He was successful, mostly.

'Yes, the Tomcat. I've flown the Phantom. Have you?'

'I have a hundred twenty hours in them, sir. My squadron transitioned into fourteens a few months after I joined up. I was just getting the Phantom figured out when they took 'em away. I – uh – sir, aren't you a naval officer also?'

'Yes, Commander, I have the rank of captain,' His Highness answered.

'Thank you. Now I know what to call you, Captain,' Robby said with visible relief. 'That's okay, isn't it?'

'Of course. You know, it does get rather tiresome when people act so awkwardly around one. This friend of yours here actually read me off some months ago.'

Robby smiled finally. 'You know Marines, sir. Long on mouth and short on brains.'

Jack realized that it was going to be that kind of night. 'Can I get anyone something to drink?'

'I gotta fly tomorrow, Jack,' Robby answered. He checked his watch. 'I'm under the twelve-hour rule.'

'You really take that so seriously?' the Prince asked.

'You bet you do, Captain, when the bird costs thirty or forty mil. If you break one, booze better not be the reason. I've been through that once.'

'Oh? What happened?'

'An engine blew when I put her in burner. I tried to get back but I lost hydraulic pressure five miles from the boat and had to punch out. That's twice I've ejected, and that's by-God enough.'

'Oh?' This question got Robby started on how his test-pilot days at Pax River had ended. *There I was at ten thousand* . . . Jack went into the kitchen to get everyone some iced tea. He found two security types, an American and a Brit.

'Everything okay?' Ryan asked.

'Yeah. It looks like our friends got spotted near Hagerstown. They blasted a State Police car and split. The trooper's okay, they missed this one. Anyway, they were last seen heading west.' The Secret Service agent seemed very pleased by that. Jack looked outside to see another one standing on the outside deck.

'You sure it's them?'

'It was a van, and it had handicap tags. They usually fall into patterns,' the agent explained. 'Sooner or later it catches up with them. The area's been sealed off. We'll get 'em.'

'Good.' Jack lifted a tray of glasses.

By the time he got back, Robby was discussing some aspect of flying with the Prince. He could tell since it involved elaborate hand movements.

'So if you fire the Phoenix inside that radius, he just can't evade it. The missile can pull more gees than any pilot can,' Jackson concluded.

'Ah, yes, the same thing with the Sparrow, isn't it?'

'Right, Cap'n, but the radius is smaller.' Robby's eyes really lit up. 'Have you ever been up in a Tomcat?'

'No, I wish I could.'

'For crying out loud, that's no big deal. Hell, we take *civilians* up all the time – I mean it has to be cleared and all that, but we've even had Hollywood actors up. Getting you a hop ought to be a snap. I mean, it's not like you're a security risk, is it?' Robby laughed and grabbed a glass of tea. 'Thanks, Jack. Captain, if you've got the time, I've got the bird.'

'I'd love to be there. We do have a little free time. . . .'

726

'Then let's do it,' Jackson said.

'I see you two are getting along.'

'Indeed,' the Prince replied. 'I've wanted to meet an F-14 pilot for years. Now, you say that telescopic camera arrangement is really effective?'

'Yes, sir! It's not that big a deal. It's a ten-power lens on a dinky little TV camera. You can identify your target fifty miles out, and it's Phoenix time. If you play it right, you can splash the guy before he knows you're in the same country, and that's the idea, isn't it?'

'So you try to avoid the dogfight?'

'ACM, you mean – air-combat manoeuvring, Jack,' Robby explained to the ignorant bystander. 'That'll change when we get the new engines, Cap'n, but, yeah, the farther away you can take him, the better, right? Sometimes you have to get wrapped up in the fur-ball, but if you do that you're giving away your biggest advantage. Our mission is to engage the other guy as far from the boat as we can. That's why we call it the Outer Air Battle.'

'It would have been rather useful in the Falklands,' His Highness observed.

'That's right. If you engage the enemy over your own decks, he's already won the biggest part of the battle. We want to start scoring three hundred miles out, and hammer their butts all the way in. If your navy'd had a full-size carrier, that useless little war never would have happened. Excuse me, sir. That wasn't your fault.'

'Can I show you around the house?' Jack asked. It always seemed to happen. You worked to have one of your guests meet another, and all of a sudden you were cut out of the conversation.

'How old is it, Jack?'

'We moved in a few months before Sally was born.'

'The woodwork is marvellous. Is that the library down there?'

'Yes, sir.' The way the house was laid out, you could look down from the living room into the library. The master bedroom was perched over it. There had been a rectangular hole in the wall, which allowed someone in there to see into the living room, but Ryan had placed a print over it. The picture was mounted on a rail and could be slid aside, Jackson noticed. The purpose of that was clear enough. Jack led them to his library next. Everyone liked the fact that the only window was over his desk and looked out over the bay.

'No servants, Jack?'

'No, sir. Cathy's talking about getting a nanny, but she hasn't sold me on that idea yet. Is everyone ready for dinner?'

The response was enthusiastic. The potatoes were already in the oven, and Cathy was ready to start the corn. Jack took the steaks from the refrigerator and led the menfolk outside.

'You'll like this, Cap'n. Jack does a mean steak.'

'The secret's in the charcoal,' Ryan explained. He had six gorgeous-looking sirloins, and a hamburger for Sally. 'It helps to have good meat, too.'

'I know it's too late to ask, Jack, but where do you get those?'

'One of my old stock clients has a restaurant-supply business. These are Kansas City strips.' Jack transferred them to the grill with a long-handled fork. A gratifying sizzle rose to their ears. He brushed some sauce on the meat.

'The view is spectacular,' His Highness observed.

'It's nice to be able to watch the boats go by,' Jack agreed. 'Looks a little thin now, though.'

'They must be listening to the radio,' Robby observed. 'There's a severe-thunderstorm warning on for tonight.'

'I didn't hear that.'

'It's the leading edge of that cold front. They developed pretty fast over Pittsburgh. I'm going up tomorrow, like I said, and I called Pax Weather right before we left. They told me that the storms look pretty ferocious on radar. Heavy rain and gusts. Supposed to hit around ten or so.'

'Do you get many of those here?' His Highness asked.

'Sure do, Captain. We don't get tornadoes like in the Midwest, but the thunder-boomers we get here'll curl your hair. I was bringing a bird back from Memphis last – no, two years ago, and it was like being on a pogo stick. You just don't have control of the airplane. Those suckers can be scary. Down at Pax, they're taking all the birds they can inside the hangars, and they'll be tying the rest down tight.'

'It'll be worth it to cool things off,' Jack said as he turned the steaks.

'Roger that. It's just your basic thunderstorm, Captain. We get the big ones three or four times a year. It'll knock down some trees, but as long as you're not in the air or out in a small boat, it's no big deal. Down in Alabama with this kind of storm coming across, we'd be sweating tornadoes. Now that's scary!'

'You've seen one?'

'More 'n one, Cap'n. You get those mostly in the spring down home. When I was ten or so, I watched one come across the road, pick up a house like it was part of a Christmas garden, and drop it a quarter mile away. They're weird, though. It didn't even take the weather-vane off my pappy's church. They're like that. It's something to see, all right – but you want to do it from a safe distance.'

'Turbulence is the main flying hazard, then?'

'Right. But the other thing is water. I know of cases where jets have ingested enough water through the intakes to snuff the engines right out.' Robby snapped his fingers. 'All of a sudden you're riding in a glider. Definitely not fun. So you keep away from them when you can.'

'And when you can't?'

'Once, Cap'n, I had to land on a carrier in one – at night. That's about as close as I've come to wetting my pants since I was two.' He even threw in a shudder.

'Your Highness, I have to thank you for getting all of this out of Robby. I've known him for over a year and he's never admitted to being mildly nervous up there.' Jack grinned.

I didn't want to spoil the image,' Jackson explained. 'You have to put a gun to Jack's head to get him aboard a plane, and I didn't want to scare him any more than he already is.' *Zing!* And Robby took the point.

It helped that the deck was now in the shade, and there was a slight northerly breeze. Jack manipulated the steaks over the coals. There were a few boats out on the bay, but most of them seemed to be heading back to harbour. Jack nearly jumped out of his skin when a jet fighter screamed past the cliff. He turned in time to see the white-painted aircraft heading south.

'Robby, what the hell is that all about? They've been doing that for two weeks.'

Jackson watched the plane's double tail vanish in the haze. 'They're testing a new piece of gear on the F-18. What's the big deal?'

'The noise!' Ryan flipped the steaks over.

Robby laughed. 'Aw, Jack, that's not noise. That's the sound of freedom.'

'Not bad, Commander,' His Highness judged.

'Well, how about the sound of dinner?' Ryan asked.

Robby grabbed the platter, and Jack piled the meat on it. The salads were already on the table. Cathy made a superb spinach salad, with homemade dressing. Jack noted that Sissy was bringing the corn and potatoes out, wearing an apron to protect her dress. He distributed the steaks and put Sally's hamburger on a roll. Next he got their daughter in a booster seat. The one awkward thing was that nobody was drinking. He'd gotten four bottles of a choice California red to go with the steaks, but it seemed that everyone was in a teetotaling mood.

'Jack, the electricity is acting up again,' his wife reported. 'For a while there I didn't think we'd get the corn finished.'

The Secret Service agent stood in the middle of the road, forcing the van to stop.

'Yes, sir?' the driver said.

'What are you doing here?' The agent's coat was unbuttoned. No gun was visible, but the driver knew it was there somewhere. He counted six more men within ten yards of the van and another four readily visible.

'Hey, I just told the cop.' The man gestured backward. The two State Police cars were only two hundred yards away.

'Could you tell me, please?'

'There's a problem with the transformer at the end of the road. I mean, you can see this is a BG and E truck, right?'

'Could you wait here, please?'

'Okay with me, man.' The driver exchanged a look with the man in the right-front seat. The agent returned with another. This one held a radio.

'What seems to be the problem?'

The driver sighed. 'Third time. There's a problem with the electrical trans-former at the end of the road. Have the people here been complaining about the electricity?'

'Yeah,' the second man, Avery, said. 'I noticed, too. What gives?'

The man in the right seat answered. 'I'm Alex Dobbens, field engineer. We have a new, experimental transformer on this line. There's a test monitor on the box, and it's been sending out some weird signals, like the box is going to fail. We're here to check it out.'

'Could we see some ID, please?'

'Sure.' Alex got out of the truck and walked around. He handed over his BG&E identification card. 'What the hell's going on here?'

'Can't say.' Avery examined the pass and handed it back. 'You have a work order?'

Dobbens gave the man his clipboard. 'Hey, if you want to check it out, you can call that number up top. That's the field-operations office at company headquarters in Baltimore. Ask for Mr Griffin.'

Avery talked into his radio, ordering his men to do just that. 'Do you mind if we look at the truck?'

'Be my guest,' Dobbens replied. He led the two agents around. He noted also that four men were keeping a very close eye on things, and that they were widely separated, with their hands free. Others were scattered across the yard. He yanked open the sliding door and waved the two agents inside.

The agents saw a mass of tools and cables and test equipment. Avery let his subordinate do the searching. 'Do you have to go back there now?'

'The transformer might go out, man. I could let it, but the folks in the neighbourhood might be upset if the lights went off. People are like that, you know? Do you mind if I ask who you are?'

'Secret Service.' Avery held up his ID. Dobbens was taken aback.

'Jeez! You mean the President's back there?'

'I can't say,' Avery replied. 'What's the problem with the transformer – you said it was new?'

'Yeah, it's an experimental model. It uses an inert cooling agent instead of PBBs, and it has a built-in surge-suppressor. That's probably the problem. It looks like the unit's temperature-sensitive for some reason. We've adjusted it several times, but we can't seem to get it dialled in right. I've been on the project for a couple of months. Usually I let my people do it, but this time the boss wanted me to eyeball it myself.' He shrugged. 'It's my project.'

The other agent came out of the van and shook his head. Avery nodded. Next the chief agent called the radio van, whose occupants had called Baltimore Gas & Electric and confirmed what Alex had told them.

'You want to send a guy to watch us?' Dobbens asked.

'No, that's okay. How long will it take?' Avery asked.

'Your guess is as good as mine, sir. It's probably something simple, but we haven't figured it out yet. The simple ones are the ones that kill you.'

'There's a storm coming in. I wouldn't want to be up on a pole in one of those,' the agent observed.

'Yeah, well, while we're sitting here, we're not getting much work done. Everything okay with you guys?'

'Yeah, go ahead.'

'You really can't tell me who's in the neighbourhood?'

Avery smiled. 'Sorry.'

'Well, I didn't vote for him anyway.' Dobbens laughed.

'Hold it!' the second agent called.

'What's the matter?'

'That left-front tire.' The man pointed.

'Goddammit, Louis!' Dobbens growled at the driver. The steel belt was showing on part of the tire.

'Hey, boss, it's not my fault. They were supposed to change it this morning. I wrote it up Wednesday,' the driver protested. 'I got the order slip right here.'

'All right, just take it easy.' Dobbens looked over to the agent. 'Thanks, pal.'

'Can't you change it?'

'We don't have a jack. Somebody lifted it. That's a problem with company trucks. Something is always missing. It'll be all right. Well, we got a transformer to fix. See ya.' Alex reboarded the truck and waved as the vehicle pulled off.

'Good one, Louis.'

The driver smiled. 'Yeah, I thought the tire was a nice touch. I counted fourteen.'

'Right. Three in the trees. Figure four more in the house. They're not our problem.' He paused, looking at the clouds that were building on the horizon. 'I hope Ed and Willy made out all right.'

'They did. All they had to do was hose down one pigmobile and switch cars. The pigs here were more relaxed than I expected,' Louis observed.

'Why not? They think we're someplace else.' Alex opened a tool box and removed his transceiver. The agent had seen it and not questioned it. He couldn't tell that the frequency range had been altered. There were no guns in the van, of course, but radios were far deadlier. He radioed what he'd learned and got an acknowledgement. Then he smiled. The agents hadn't even asked about the two extension ladders on the roof. He checked his watch. Rendezvous was scheduled in ninety minutes. . . .

'The problem is, there really isn't a civilized way to eat corn on the cob,' Cathy said. 'Not to mention buttering it.'

'It was excellent, though,' the Prince noted. 'From a local farm, Jack?'

'Picked 'em off the stalk this afternoon,' Ryan confirmed. 'That's the best way to get it.'

Sally'd become a slow eater of late. She was still labouring at her food, but nobody seemed anxious to leave the table.

'Jack, Cathy, that was a wonderful dinner,' His Highness pronounced.

His wife agreed. 'And no after-dinner speechmaking!'

'I guess all that formal stuff gets to be tiresome,' Robby noted, trying to ask a question that he couldn't voice: *What's it like to be a prince?*

'It wouldn't be so bad if the speeches could be original, but I've been listening to the same one for years!' he said wryly. 'Excuse me. I musn't say such things, even around friends.'

'It's not all that different at a History Department meeting,' Jack said.

At Quantico, Virginia, the phone rang. The FBI's Hostage Rescue Team had its own private building, located at the end of the long line of firing ranges that served the Bureau's training centre. An engineless DC sat behind it, and was used to practise assault techniques on hijacked aircraft. Down the hill was the 'Hostage House' and other facilities used every day for the team members to hone their skills. Special Agent Gus Werner picked up the phone.

'Hi, Gus,' Bill Shaw said.

'Have they found 'em yet?' Werner asked. He was thirty-five, a short, wiry man with red hair and a brushy moustache that never would have been allowed under Hoover's directorship.

'No, but I want you to assemble an advance team and fly them up. If something breaks, we may have to move fast.'

'Fair enough. Where are we going, exactly?'

'Hagerstown, the State Police barracks. S-A-C Baltimore will be waiting for you.'

'Okay, I'll take six men. We can probably get moving in thirty or forty minutes, as soon as the chopper gets here. Buzz me if anything happens.'

'Will do. See ya.' Shaw hung up.

Werner switched buttons on the phone and alerted the helicopter crew. Next he walked across the building to the classroom on the far side. The five men of his ready-response group were lounging about, mostly reading. They'd been on alert status for several days. This had increased their training routines somewhat, but it was mainly to defend against boredom that came from waiting for something that probably wouldn't happen. Nighttimes were devoted to reading and television. The Red Sox were playing the Yankees on TV. These were not Brooks Brothers FBI agents. The men were in baggy jumpsuits lavishly equipped with pockets. In addition to being experienced field agents, nearly all were veterans of combat or peacetime military service, and each man was a match-quality marksman who fired several boxes of ammunition per week.

'Okay, listen up,' Werner said. 'They want an advance team in Hagerstown. The chopper'll be here in half an hour.

'There's a severe thunderstorm warning,' one objected lightly.

'So take your airsick pills,' Werner advised.

'They find 'em yet?' another asked.

'No, but people are getting a little nervous.'

'Right.' The questioner was a long-rifleman. His custom-made sniper rifle was already packed in a foam-lined case. The team's gear was in a dozen duffle bags. The men buttoned their shirts. Some headed off to the bathroom for a preflight pitstop. None were especially excited. Their job involved far more waiting than doing. The Hostage Rescue Team had been in existence for years, but it had yet to rescue a single hostage. Instead its members were mainly used as a special SWAT team, and they had earned a reputation as awesome as it was little known, except within the law-enforcement community.

'Wow,' Robby said. 'Here it comes. This one's going to be a beauty.' In the space of ten minutes, the wind had changed from gentle breezes to gusts that made the high-ceilinged house resonate.

'It was a dark and stormy night,' Jack chuckled. He went into the kitchen. Three agents were making sandwiches to take out to the men by the road. 'I hope you guys have raincoats.'

'We're used to it,' one assured him.

'At least it will be a warm rain,' his British colleague thought. 'Thank you very much for the food and coffee.' The first rumble of distant thunder rolled through the house.

'Don't stand under any trees,' Jack suggested. 'Lightning can ruin your whole day.' He returned to the dining room. Conversation was still being made around the table. Robby was back to discussing flying. The current war-story was about catapults.

'You never get used to the thrill,' he was saying. 'In a couple of seconds you go from a standstill to a hundred fifty knots.'

'And if something goes wrong?' the Princess asked.

'You go swimming,' Robby answered.

'Mr Avery,' the hand-held radio squawked.

'Yeah,' he answered.

'Washington's on the line.'

'Okay, I'll be there in a minute.' Avery walked down the driveway toward the communications van. Longley, the leader of the British contingent, tagged along. Both had left their raincoats there anyway, and they'd need them in a few minutes. They could see lightning flashes a few miles away, and the jagged strokes of light were approaching fast.

'So much for the weather,' Longley said.

'I was hoping it would miss us.' The wind lashed at them again, blowing dust from the ploughed field on the other side of Falcon's Nest Road. They passed the two men carrying a covered plate of sandwiches. A black puppy trotted along behind in the hope that they'd drop one.

'This Ryan fellow's a decent chap, isn't he?'

'He's got a real nice kid. You can tell a lot about a man from his kids,' Avery thought aloud. They got to the van just as the first sprinkles started. The Secret Service agent got on the radiophone.

'Avery here.'

'Chuck, this is Bill Shaw at the Bureau. I just got a call from our forensics people at that house in Howard County.'

'Okay.'

At the other end of the connection, Shaw was looking at a map and frowning. 'They can't find any prints, Chuck. They have guns, they have ammo, some of the guns were being cleaned, but no prints. Not even on the hamburger wrappers. Something feels bad.'

'What about the car that got shot up in western Maryland?'

'Nothing, not a damned thing. Like the bad guys jumped in a hole and pulled it in behind them.'

That was all Shaw had to say. Chuck Avery had been a Secret Service agent all of his adult life, and was normally on the Presidential detail. He thought exclusively in terms of threats. This was an inevitable consequence of his job. He guarded people whom other people wanted to kill. It had given him a limited and somewhat paranoid outlook on life. Avery's mind reviewed his threat briefing. *The enemy here is extremely clever. . . .*

'Thanks for the tip, Bill. We'll keep our eyes open.' Avery got into his coat and picked up his radio. 'Team One, this is Avery. Heads up. Assemble at the entrance. We have a possible new threat.' *The full explanation will have to wait.*

'What's the matter?' Longley asked.

'There's no real evidence at the house, the lab people haven't found any prints.'

'They couldn't have had time to wipe everything before they left.' Longley didn't need much of a hint either. 'It might all have been planned to –'

'Exactly. Let's get out and talk to the troops. First thing, I'm going to get the perimeter spread out some. Then I'll call for more police backup.' The rain was pelting the van now. 'I guess we're all going to get wet.'

'I want two more people at the house,' Longley said.

'Agreed, but let's brief the people first.' He slid the door open and both men went back up the driveway.

The agents on perimeter duty came together where the driveway met the road. They were alert, but it was hard to see with the wind-driven rain in their faces and the stinging dust blowing from the field on the other side of the road. Several were trying to finish sandwiches. One agent did a head count and came up one short. He sent a fellow agent to fetch the man whose radio was evidently out. Ernie tagged along with him; this agent had given him half a sandwich.

'You want to retire to the living room?' Cathy waved at the seats a few feet away. 'I'd like to clear these dishes away.'

'I'll do it, Cath,' Sissy Jackson said. 'You go sit down.' She went into the kitchen and got the apron. Ryan knew for certain that Cathy had warned the Jacksons – Sissy at least, since she was wearing what on further inspection seemed an expensive dress. Everyone stood, and Robby walked off to the bathroom for a head call.

'Here we go,' Alex said. He was at the wheel now. 'All ready?'

'Go!' O'Donnell said. Like Alex, he wanted to be out in front with his troops. 'Thank God for the weather!'

'Right,' Alex agreed. He flipped the van's headlights to high-beam. He saw two groups of agents, standing a few yards apart.

The security force saw the approaching lights, and, being trained men, they kept a close eye on it despite knowing who it was and what it had been doing. Thirty yards from them there was a flash and a bang. Some men reached instinctively for their guns, then stopped when they saw that the vehicle's left-front tire had blown and was fluttering on the road as the driver struggled to get the truck back under control. It stopped right in front of the driveway. No one had commented on the ladders before. No one noticed their absence now. The driver got out and looked at the wheel.

'Aw, shit!'

Two hundred yards away, Avery saw the truck sitting on the road, and his instincts set off an alarm. He started running.

The van's door slid back, revealing four men with automatic weapons.

The agents a few feet away reacted in a moment, but too late. Barely had the door moved when the first weapon fired . A cylindrical silencer hung on the muzzle, which muffled the noise, but not the tongue of white flame that hovered in the darkness, and five men were down in the first second. The other gunmen had already joined in, and the first group of agents was wiped out without having fired a single return shot. The terrorists leaped out of the side and back doors of the van and engaged the second group. One Secret Service agent got his Uzi up and fired a short burst that killed the first man out of the back of the van, but the man behind him killed the agent with his weapon. Two more of the guards were now dead, and the other four of the group dropped to the ground and tried to return fire.

'What the hell is that?' Ryan said. The sound was hard to distinguish through the noise of the rain and the recurring thunder. Heads throughout the room turned. There was a British security officer in the kitchen and two Secret Service agents on the deck outside the room. Their heads had already turned, and one man was reaching for his radio.

Avery's service revolver was out. As team leader he didn't bother carrying anything but his Smith & Wesson .357 Magnum. His other hand was in any case busy with his radio.

'Call Washington, we are under attack! We need backup right the hell now! Unknown gunmen on the west perimeter. Officers down, officers need help!'

Alex reached back into the truck and pulled out an RPG-7 rocket launcher. He could just make out the two State Police cars two hundred yards down the road. He couldn't see the cops, but they had to be there. He elevated the weapon to the proper mark on the steel sight and squeezed the trigger, adding yet another thundering noise to the flashing sky. The round fell a few feet short of the target, but its explosion lanced hot fragments through one gas tank. It exploded, bathing both cars in burning fuel.

'Hot damn!'

Behind him, the gunmen had spread out and flanked the Secret Service officers. Only one was still shooting back. Two more of the ULA shooters were down, Alex saw, but the rest closed in on the agent from behind and finished him with a barrage of fire.

'Oh, God!' Avery saw it, too. He and Longley looked at each other and each knew what the other thought. *They won't get them, not while I'm alive.*

'Shaw.' The radio-telephone circuit crackled with static.

'We are under attack. We have officers down,' the wall speaker said. 'Unknown number of – it sounds like a fucking war out there! We need help and we need it now.'

'Okay, stand by, we're working on it.' Shaw gave quick orders and phone lines started lighting up. The first calls to go out went to the nearest state and county police stations. Next, the Hostage Rescue Team group on alert in Washington was ordered out. Their Chevy Suburban was sitting in the garage. He checked the wall clock and called Quantico on the direct line.

'The chopper's just landing now,' Gus Werner answered.

'Do you know where the Ryan house is?' Shaw asked.

'Yeah, it's on the map. That's where our visitors are now, right?'

'It's under attack. How fast can you get there?'

'What's the situation?' Werner watched his men out the window, loading their gear into the helicopter.

'Unknown – we just rolled the team from here, but you may be the first ones in. The communications guy just called in, says they're under attack, officers down.'

'If there's any additional information, get it to us. We'll be up in two minutes.' Werner ran outside to his men. He had to shout at them to be heard under the turning rotor, then ran back to the building, where the watch officers were ordered to summon the rest of the team to the HRT headquarters. By the time he got back in the chopper, his men had their weapons out of their duffles. Then the helicopter lifted off into the approaching storm.

Ryan noted the flurry of activity outside as the British officer from the kitchen ran outside and conferred briefly with the Secret Service agents. He was just coming back inside when a series of lightning flashes illuminated the deck. One of the agents turned and brought his gun out – then fell backward. The glass behind him shattered. The other two men both dived for the deck. One rose up to fire and fell beside his comrade. The last came inside and shouted for everyone to lie flat. Jack had barely enough time to be horrified when another window shattered and the last security man was down. Four armed figures appeared where the broken glass was. They were all dressed in black, except for the mud on their boots and chests. One pulled off his mask. It was Sean Miller.

Avery and Longley were alone, lying in the middle of the yard. The Brit watched as a number of armed men checked the bodies of the fallen agents. Then they formed into two groups and started moving toward the house.

'We're too bloody exposed here,' Longley said. 'If we're to do any good at all, we must be back in the trees.'

'You go first.' Avery held his revolver in both hands and sighted on a black-clad figure visible only when the lightning flashed. They were still over a hundred yards away, very long range for a handgun. The next flash gave him a target, and Avery fired, missing and drawing a storm of fire at himself. Those rounds missed, too, but the sound of thuds in the wet ground was far too close. The fire shifted. Perhaps they saw Longley running back to the trees. Avery fired another carefully aimed shot and saw a man go down with a leg wound. The return fire was more accurate this time. The Secret Service agent emptied his gun. He thought he might have hit another of them when everything stopped.

Longley made it to the trees and looked back. Avery's prone figure didn't move despite the gunmen fifty yards away. The British security officer shouted a curse and gathered the remaining people. The FBI liaison agent had only his revolver, the three British officers had automatic pistols, and the one Secret Service agent had an Uzi with two spare magazines. Even if there weren't people to protect, there wasn't anyplace to run.

'So we meet again,' Miller said. He held an Uzi submachine gun and bent down to pick up another from one of the fallen guards. Five more men came in behind them. They spread out in a semicircle to cover Ryan and his guests. 'Get up! Hands where we can see them.'

Jack stood, with the Prince next to him. Cathy came up next, holding Sally in her arms, and finally Her Highness. Three men spun around when the kitchen door swung open. It was Sissy Jackson, trying to hold some plates while a gunman held on to her arm. Two plates fell to the floor and broke when he jerked her arm up.

They have a maid, Miller remembered, seeing the dark dress and the apron. *Black, handsome woman.* He was smiling now. The disgrace of his failed missions was far behind him. He had all his targets before him, and in his hands was the instrument to eliminate them.

'You get over here with the rest,' he ordered.

'What the hell –'

'Move, nigger!' Another of the gunmen, the shortest of the bunch, roughly propelled her toward the others. Jack's eyes fixed on him for a moment – where had he seen that face before. . . .

'You trash!' Sissy's eyes flared in outrage at that, her fear momentarily forgotten as she wheeled to snap back at the man.

'You should be more careful who you work for,' Miller said. He gestured with his weapon. 'Move.'

'What are you going to do?' Ryan asked.

'Why spoil the surprise?'

Forty feet away, Robby was in the worst part of the house to hear anything. He'd been washing his hands, ignoring the thunder when the gunfire had erupted at the home's deck. Jackson slipped out of the bathroom and peered down the corridor to the living room, but saw nothing. What he heard was enough. He turned and went upstairs to the master bedroom. His first instinct was to call the police on the telephone, but the line was dead. His mind searched for something else to do. This wasn't like flying a fighter plane.

Jack has guns. . . but where the hell does he keep them. . . ? It was dark in the bedroom and he didn't dare to flip on a light.

Outside, the line of gunmen advanced toward the woods. Longley deployed his men to meet them. His military service was too far in the past, and his

738

work as a security officer hadn't prepared him for this sort of thing, but he did his best. They had good cover in the trees, some of which were thick enough to stop a bullet. He ordered his only automatic weapon to the left.

'FBI, this is Patuxent River Approach. Squawk four-zero-one-niner, over.'

Aboard the helicopter, the pilot turned the transponder wheels until the proper code number came up. Next he read off the map coordinates of his destination. He knew what it looked like from aerial photographs, but they'd been taken in daylight. Things could look very different at night, and there was also the problem of controlling the aircraft. He was flying with a forty-knot crosswind, and weather conditions deteriorated with every mile. In the back the HRT members were trying to get into their night-camouflage clothing.

'Four-zero-one-niner, come left to heading zero-two-four. Maintain current altitude. Warning, it looks like a pretty strong thunder cell is approaching your target,' the controller said. 'Recommend you do not exceed one thousand feet. I'll try to steer you around the worst of it.'

'Roger.' The pilot grimaced. It was plain that the weather ahead was even worse than he'd feared. He lowered his seat as far as it would go, pulled his belts tighter, and turned on his storm lights. The only other thing he could do was sweat, and that came automatically. 'You guys in back, strap down tight!'

O'Donnell called for his men to stop. The treeline was a hundred yards ahead, and he knew that it held guns. One group moved left, the other right. They'd attack by echelons, with each group alternately advancing and providing fire support for the other. All his men wore black and carried submachine guns, except for one man who trailed a few yards behind the rest. He found himself wishing that they'd brought heavier weapons. There was still much to do, including removing the bodies of his fallen men. One was dead and two more wounded. But first – he lifted his radio to order one of his squads in.

On O'Donnell's right, the single remaining Secret Service agent tucked his left side against an oak tree and shouldered his Uzi. For him and his comrades in the trees, there was no retreat. The black metal sights were hard to use in the dark, and his targets were nearly invisible. Lightning again played a part, strobe-lighting the lawn for an instant that showed the green grass and black-clad men. He selected a target and fired a short burst, but missed. Both groups of attackers returned fire, and the agent cringed as he heard a dozen rounds hit the tree. The whole countryside seemed alive with the flashes of gunfire. The Secret Service agent came around again and fired. The group that had been approaching him directly was running to his left into the brambles. He was going to be flanked – but then they reappeared, firing their weapons into the bushes, and there were flashes firing *out*. Everyone was surprised by that, and suddenly no one had control of the situation.

O'Donnell had planned to advance his teams on either side of the clearing, but unexpectedly there was fire coming from the woodline to the south, and one of his squads was exposed and flanked from two directions. He evaluated the new tactical situation in an instant and started giving orders.

Ryan watched in mute rage. The gunmen knew exactly what they were doing, and that reduced his number of options to exactly zero. There were six guns on him and his guests, and not a chance that he could do anything about it. To his right, Cathy held on to their daughter, and even Sally kept quiet. Neither Miller nor his men made any unnecessary sound.

'Sean, this is Kevin,' Miller's radio crackled with static. 'We have opposition in the treeline. Do you have them?'

'Yes, Kevin, the situation is under control.'

'I need help out here.'

'We're coming.' Miller pocketed his radio. He pointed to his comrades. 'You three, get them ready. If they resist, kill them all. You two come with me.' He led them out the broken glass doors and disappeared.

'Come on.' The remaining three gunmen had their masks off now. Two were tall, about Ryan's height, one with blond hair, the other black. The other was short and going bald – *I know you, but from where?* He was the most frightening. His face was twisted with emotions that Jack didn't want to guess at. Blondie threw him a bundle of rope. An instant later it was plain that it was a collection of smaller pieces already cut and meant to tie them up.

Robby, where the hell are you? Jack looked over to Sissy, who was thinking the same thing. She nodded imperceptibly, and there was still hope in her eyes. The short one noticed.

'Don't worry,' Shorty said. 'You'll get paid.' He set his weapon on the dinner table and moved forward while Blondie and Blackie backed off to cover them all. Dennis Cooley took the rope to the Prince first, yanking his hands down behind his back.

There! Robby looked up. Jack had set his shotgun on the top shelf of the walk-in closet, along with a box of shells. He had to reach to get them, and when he did so, a holstered pistol dropped to the floor. Jackson winced at the sound it made, but grabbed it from the holster and tucked it into his belt. Next he checked the shotgun, pulling back the bolt – there was a round in the chamber and the gun was on safe. *Okay.* He filled his pockets with additional rounds and went back into the bedroom.

Now what? This wasn't like flying his F-14, with radar to track targets a hundred miles away and a wingman to keep the bandits off his tail.

The picture . . . You had to kneel on the bed to see out of it – *Why the hell did Jack arrange his furniture like this!* the pilot raged. He set the shotgun down and used both hands to slide the picture aside. He moved it only a few inches, barely enough to see out. *How many . . . one, two . . . three. Are there any others. . . ? What if I leave one alive. . . ?*

As he watched, Jack was being tied up. The Prince – *the Captain,* Robby thought – already was tied, and was sitting with his back to the pilot. The short one finished Jack next and pushed him back onto the couch. Jackson next watched the man put hands on his wife.

'What are you going to do with us?' Sissy asked.

'Shut up, nigger!' Shorty replied.

Even Robby knew that this was a trivial thing to get angry about; the problem at hand was far worse than some white asshole's racist remark, but his blood turned to fire as he watched the woman he loved being handled by that . . . *little white shit!*

Use your head, boy, something in the back of his brain said. *Take your time. You have to get it right on the first try. Cool down.*

Longley was beginning to hope. There were friendlies in the trees to his left. Perhaps they'd come from the house, he thought. At least one of them had an automatic weapon, and he counted three of the terrorists dead, or at least not moving on the grass. He had fired five rounds and missed with every one – the range was just too great for a pistol in the dark – but they'd stopped the terrorists cold. And help was coming. It had to be. The radio van was empty, but the FBI agent to his right had been there. All they had to do was wait, hold on for a few more minutes. . . .

'I got flashes on the ground ahead,' the pilot said. 'I –'

Lightning revealed the house for a brief moment in time. They couldn't see people on the ground, but that was the right house, and there were flashes that had to be gunfire, half a mile off as the helicopter buffeted through the wind and rain. It was about all the pilot could see. His instrument lights were turned up full-white, and the lightning had decorated his vision with a stunning collection of blue and green spots.

'Jesus,' Gus Werner said over the intercom. 'What are we getting into?'

'In Vietnam,' the pilot replied coolly, 'we called it a hot LZ.' *And I was scared then, too.*

'Get Washington.' The copilot switched frequencies on the radio and waved to the agent in the back while both men orbited the helicopter. 'This is Werner.'

741

'Gus, this is Bill Shaw. Where are you?'

'We have the house in sight, and there's a goddamned battle going on down there. Do you have contact with our people?'

'Negative, they're off the air. The DC team is still thirty minutes away. The state and county people are close but not there yet. The storm's knocking trees down all over the place and traffic is tied up something fierce. You're the man on the scene, Gus, you'll have to call it.'

The mission of the Hostage Rescue Team was to take charge of an existing situation, stabilize it, and rescue the hostages – peacefully if possible, by force if not. They were not assault troops; they were special agents of the FBI. But there were brother agents down there.

'We're going in now. Tell the police that federal officers are on the scene. We'll try to keep you informed.'

'Right. Be careful, Gus.'

'Take us in,' Werner told the pilot.

'Okay. I'll skirt the house first, then come around in and land you to windward. I can't put you close to the house. The wind's too bad, I might lose it down there.'

'Go.' Werner turned. Somehow his men had all their gear on. Each carried an automatic pistol. Four had MP-5 machine guns, as did he. The long-rifleman and his spotter would be the first men out the door. 'We're going in.' One of the men gave a thumbs-up that looked a lot jauntier than anyone felt.

The helicopter lurched toward the ground when a sudden downdraft hammered at it. The pilot wrenched upward on his collective and bottomed the aircraft out a scant hundred feet from the trees. The house was only a few hundred yards away now. They skimmed over the southern edge of the clearing, allowing everyone a close look at the situation.

'Hey, the spot between the house and the cliff might be big enough after all,' the pilot said. He increased power as the chopper swept to windward.

'Helicopter!' someone screamed to O'Donnell's right. The chief looked up, and there it was, a spectral shape and a fluttering sound. That was a hazard he'd prepared for.

Back near the road, one of his men pulled the cover off a Redeye missile launcher purchased along with the rest of their weapons.

'I have to use landing lights – my night vision is wasted,' the pilot said over the intercom. He turned the aircraft half a mile west of the Ryan house. He planned to head straight past the house; then he'd drop and turn into the wind and slide up behind what he hoped was a wind shadow in its lee. *God*, he thought, *this is like Vietnam.* From the pattern of the flashes on the ground, it seemed that the house was in friendly hands. The pilot reached down and flipped on his landing lights. It was a risk, but one he had to accept.

Thank God I can see again, he told himself. The ground was visible through a shimmering curtain of rain. He realized that the storm was still worsening. He had to approach from windward. Flying into the rain would reduce his visibility to a few feet. At least this way he could see a couple of hundred or so – *what the hell!*

He saw a man standing all alone in the centre of the field, aiming something. The pilot pushed down on the collective just as a streak of red light rocketed toward the helicopter, his eyes locked on what could only be a surface-to-air missile. The two seconds it took seemed to stretch into an hour as the missile passed through his rotor blades and disappeared overhead – he immediately pulled back on the control, but there was no time to recover from his evasion manoeuvre. The helicopter slammed into the middle of a ploughed field, four hundred yards from the Ryan house. It wouldn't move again until a truck came to collect the wreckage.

Miraculously, only two men were hurt. Werner was one of them. It felt as though he'd been shot in the back. The rifleman pulled the door open and ran out with his spotter behind. The others went next, one of them helping Werner while another hobbled on a sprained ankle.

The Princess was next. She was taller than Cooley, and managed a look that contained more than mere contempt. The little man spun her around roughly to tie her hands.

'We have big plans for you,' he promised when he finished.

'You little scum, I bet you don't even know how,' Sissy said. It earned her a vicious slap. Robby watched, waiting for the blond-haired one to get in the clear. Finally he did, moving back toward the others. . . .

26

The Sound of Freedom

Pellets fired from a shotgun disperse radially at a rate of one inch per yard of linear travel. A lightning flash blazed through the windows, and Ryan cringed on hearing the thunder immediately after – then realized it had followed too quickly to be thunder. The shot pattern had missed his head by three feet, and before he understood what had passed by him, Blondie's head snapped back, exploding into a cloud of red as his body fell backward to crash against a table leg. Blackie was looking out the window in the corner and turned to see his comrade go down without knowing how or why. His eyes searched frantically for a second, then a red circle the size of a 45-rpm record appeared in his chest and he was flung against the wall. Shorty was tying up Cathy's hands and concentrating a little too much. He hadn't recognized the first shot for what it was. He did with the second – too late.

The Prince sprang at him, knocking him down with a lowered shoulder before himself falling on the floor. Jack leaped over the coffee table and kicked wildly at Shorty's head. He connected, but lost his balance doing so and fell backward. Shorty was stunned for a moment, then shook it off and moved toward the dinner table, where his gun was. Ryan lurched to his feet too, and threw himself on the terrorist's legs. The Prince was back up now. Shorty threw a wild punch at him and tried to kick Ryan off his legs – then stopped when the warm muzzle of a shotgun pressed against his nose.

'You hold it right there, sucker, or I'll blow your head off.'

Cathy already had the ropes shucked off her hands, and untied Jack first. He went over to Blondie. The body was still twitching. Blood was still pumping from the surreal nightmare that had been a human face thirty seconds before. Jack took the Uzi from his hands, and a spare magazine. The Prince did the same with Blackie, whose body was quite still.

'Robby,' Jack said as he examined the safety-selector switch on the gun. 'Let's get the hell away from here.'

'Second the motion, Jack, but where to?' Jackson pushed Shorty's head against the floor. The terrorist's eyes crossed almost comically on the business end of the Remington shotgun. 'I expect he might know something useful. How'd you plan to get away, boy?'

'No.' It was all Cooley could muster at the moment. He realized that he was, after all, the wrong man for this kind of job.

'That the way it is?' Jackson asked, his voice a low, angry rasp. 'You listen to me, boy. That lady over there, the one you called *niggah* – that's my wife, boy, that's my lady. I saw you hit her. So, I already got one good reason to kill you, y'dig?' Robby smiled wickedly, and let the shotgun trace a line down to Shorty's crotch. 'But I ain't gonna kill ya'. I'll do somethin' lots worse –

'I'll make a girl outa you, punk.' Robby pushed the muzzle against the man's zipper. 'Think fast, boy.'

Jack listened to his friend in amazement. Robby never talked like this. But it was convincing. Jack believed that he'd do it.

So did Cooley: 'Boats . . . boats at the base of the cliff.'

'That's not even clever. Say goodbye to 'em, boy.' The angle of the shotgun changed fractionally.

'*Boats! Two boats at the base of the cliff.* There are two ladders –'

'How many watching them?' Jack demanded.

'One, that's all.'

Robby looked up. 'Jack?'

'People, I suggest we go steal some boats. That firefight outside is getting closer.' Jack ran to his closet and got coats for everyone. For Robby he picked up his old Marine field jacket that Cathy hated so much. 'Put this on, that white shirt is too damned visible.'

'Here.' Robby handed over Jack's automatic. 'I got a box of rounds for the shotgun.' He started transferring them from his pants to the jacket pockets and then hefted the last Uzi over his shoulder. 'We're leaving friendlies behind, Jack,' he added quietly.

Ryan didn't like it either, 'I know, but if they get him, they win – and this ain't no place for women and kids, man.'

'Okay, you're the Marine.' Robby nodded. That was that.

'Let's get outta here. I have the point. I'm going to take a quick look-see. Rob, you take Shorty for now. Prince, you take the women.' Jack reached down and grabbed Dennis Cooley by the throat. 'You screw up, you're dead. No fartin' around with him, Robby, just waste him.'

'That's a roge.' Jackson backed away from the terrorist. 'Up slow, punk.'

Jack led them through the shattered doors. The two dead agents lay crumpled on the wood deck, and he hated himself for not doing something about it, but Ryan was proceeding on some sort of automatic control that the Marine Corps had programmed into him ten years before. It was a combat situation, and all the lectures and field exercises were flooding back into his consciousness. In a moment he was drenched by the falling sheets of rain. He trotted down the stairs and looked around the house.

Longley and his men were too busy dealing with the threat to their front to notice what was approaching from behind. The British security officer fired four rounds at an advancing black figure and had the satisfaction of seeing him react from at least one hit when a hammering impact hurled him against a tree. He rebounded off the rough bark and half turned to see yet another black-clad shape holding a gun ten feet away. The gun flashed again. Within seconds the woodline was quiet.

'Dear God,' the rifleman muttered. Running in a crouch, he passed the bodies of five agents, but there wasn't time for that. He and his spotter went down next to a bush. The rifleman activated his night scope and tracked on the woodline a few hundred yards ahead. The green picture he got on the imaging tube showed men dressed in dark clothes heading into the woodline.

'I count eleven,' the spotter said.

'Yeah,' the rifleman agreed. His bolt-action sniper rifle was loaded with .308 caliber match rounds. He could hit a moving three-inch target the first time, every time, at over two hundred yards, but his mission for the moment was reconnaissance, to gather information and forward it to the team leader. Before the team could act, they had to know what the hell was going on, and all they had now was chaos.

'Werner, this is Paulson. I count what looks like eleven bad guys moving into the trees between us and the house. They appear to be armed with light automatic weapons.' He pivoted the rifle around. 'Looks like six of them down in the yard. Lots of good guys down – Jesus, I hope there's ambulances on the way.'

'Do you see any friendlies around?'

'Negative. Recommend that you move in from the other side. Can you give me a backup here?'

'Sending one now. When he gets there, move in carefully. Take your time, Paulson.'

'Right.'

To the south, Werner and two other men advanced along the treeline. Their night-camouflage clothing was a hatchwork of light green, designed by computer, and even in the lightning they were nearly invisible.

Something had just happened. Jack saw a sudden flurry of fire, then nothing. Despite what he'd told Robby, he didn't like running away from the scene. But what else could he do? There was an unknown number of terrorists out there. He had only three armed men to protect three women and a child, with their backs to a cliff. Ryan swore and returned to the others.

'Okay, Shorty, show me the way down,' Ryan said, pressing the muzzle of his Uzi against the man's chest.

'Right there.' The man pointed, and Ryan swore again.

In all the time they'd lived here, Jack's only concern with the cliff was to keep away from it, lest it crumble under him or his daughter. The view from his house was magnificent enough, but the cliff's height meant that from the house there was an unseen dead zone a thousand yards wide which the terrorists had used to approach. And they'd used ladders to climb up – *of course, that's what ladders are for!* Their placements were marked the way it said in every field manual in the world, with wooden stakes wrapped with white gauze bandaging, to be seen easily in the dark.

'Okay, people,' Ryan began, looking around. 'Shorty and I go first. Your Highness, you come next with the women. Robby, stay ten yards back and cover the rear.'

'I am adept with light weapons,' the Prince said.

Jack shook his head emphatically. 'No, if they get you, they win. If something goes wrong, I'm depending on you to take care of my wife and kid, sir. If something happens, go south. About half a mile down you'll find a gully. Take that inland and don't stop till you find a hard surface road. It's real thick cover, you should be okay. Robby, if anything gets close, blast it.'

'But what if –'

'But, hell! Anything that moves is the enemy.' Jack looked around one last time. *Give me five trained men, maybe Breckenridge and four others, and I could set up one pisser of an ambush . . . and if pigs had wings . . .* 'Okay, Shorty, you go down first. If you fuck us up, the first thing happens, I'll cut you in half. Do you believe me?'

'Yes.'

'Then move.'

Cooley moved to the ladder and proceeded down backward, with Ryan several feet above him. The aluminium rungs were slippery with the rain, but at least the wind was blocked by the body of the cliff. The extension ladder – *how the hell did they get that here?* – wobbled under him. Ryan tried to keep an eye on Shorty and slipped once halfway down. Above him, the second group was beginning its descent. The Princess had taken charge of Sally, and was coming down with Ryan's daughter between her body and the ladder to keep her from falling. He could hear his little girl whimpering anyway. Jack had to ignore it. There wasn't room in his consciousness for anger or pity now. He had to do this one right the first time. There would be no second. A flash of lightning revealed the two boats a hundred yards to the north. Ryan couldn't tell if anyone was there or not. Finally they reached the bottom. Cooley moved a few feet to the north and Ryan jumped down the next few feet, gun at the ready.

'Let's just stay put for a minute.'

The Prince arrived next, then the women. Finally Robby started down, his Marine parka making him invisible against the black sky. He came down quickly, also jumping the last five feet.

'They got to the house just as I started down. Maybe this'll slow them some.' He held the white-wrapped stakes. It might make the ladders harder to find.'

'Good one, Rob.' Jack turned. The boats were out there, invisible again in the rain and shadows. Shorty had said that only one man was guarding them. *What if he's lying?* Ryan asked himself. *Is this guy willing to die for his cause? Will he sacrifice himself to shout a warning and get us killed? Does it make a difference – do we have a choice? No!*

'Move out, Shorty.' Ryan gestured with his gun. 'Just remember who dies first.'

It was high tide, and the water came to within a few feet of the base of the cliff. The sand was wet and hard under his feet as Ryan stayed three feet behind the terrorist. *How far were they – a hundred yards? How far can one hundred yards be?* Ryan asked himself. He was discovering that now. The people behind him kept close to the kudzu covered cliff. That made them extremely hard to see, though if there was someone in the boat, he'd know that people were coming toward him.

Krak!

Everyone's heart stopped for a moment. A lightning stroke had shattered a tree on the cliff's edge not two hundred yards behind them. For a brief instant he saw the boats again – and there was a man in each.

'Just one, eh?' Jack muttered. Shorty hesitated, then proceeded, hands at his side. With the return of darkness, he again lost sight of the boats, and Jack reasoned that everyone's night vision was equally ruined by the lightning. His mind returned to the image he'd just seen. The man in the near boat was standing at the near side, amidships, and appeared to be holding a weapon – one that needed two hands. Ryan was enraged that Shorty had lied to him. It seemed absurd as he watched the emotion flare and fade in his consciousness.

'What's the password?'

'There isn't one,' Dennis Cooley replied, his voice unsteady as he contemplated the situation from rather a different perspective. He was between the loaded guns of two sides, each of which was likely to shoot. Cooley's mind was racing, too, looking for something he could do to turn the tables.

Was he telling the truth now? Ryan wondered, but there wasn't time to puzzle that one out. 'Keep moving.'

The boat reappeared now. At first it was just something different from the darkness and the beach. In five more yards it was a shape. The rain was pouring down hard enough to distort everything he saw, but there was a white, almost rectangular shape ahead. Ryan guessed the range at fifty yards. He prayed for the lightning to hold off now. If they were lighted, the men in the boats might be able to recognize a face, and if they saw that Shorty was in front . . .

How do I do this. . . ?

You can be a policeman or a soldier, but not both. *Joe Evans' words at the Tower came back, and told him what he had to do.*

Forty yards to go. There were rocks on the beach, too, and Jack had to be careful not to trip over one. He reached forward with his left hand and unscrewed the bulky silencer. He stuck it in his belt. He didn't like what it did to the gun's balance.

Thirty yards. He searched for and found the stock release switch on the Uzi. Jack extended the stock, planting the metal buttplate in his armpit and snugging the weapon in tight. *Just a few more seconds . . .*

Twenty-five yards. He could see the boat clearly now, twenty feet or so, with a blunt bow, and another just like it perhaps twenty yards beyond. There was definitely a man in the near boat, standing amidships on its port side, looking straight at the people approaching him. Jack's right thumb pushed the Uzi's selector switch all the way forward, to full automatic fire, and he tightened his fist on the pistol grip. He hadn't fired an Uzi since a brief familiarization at Quantico. It was small but nicely balanced. The black metal sights were nearly useless in the dark, though, and what he had to do . . .

Twenty yards. *The first burst has to be right on, Jack, right the hell on . . .*

Ryan took half a step to his right and dropped to one knee. He brought the weapon up, placing the front sight low and left of his target before he held the trigger down for a four-round burst. The gun jerked up and to the right as the bullets left, tracing a diagonal line across the target's outline. The man dropped instantly from sight, and Ryan was again dazzled, this time by his own muzzle flashes. Shorty had dived to the ground at the sound.

'*Come on!*' Ryan yanked Cooley up and threw him forward, but Jack stumbled in the sand and recovered to see that the terrorist was indeed running for the boat – *where there was a gun to turn against them all!* He was yelling something Ryan couldn't understand.

Jack had nearly caught up when Shorty got there first –

And died. The man in the other boat fired a long, wild burst in their direction just as Cooley was leaping aboard. Ryan saw his head snap over and Shorty fell into the boat like a sack of groceries. Jack knelt at the gunnel and fired his own burst, and the other man went down. Hit or not, Ryan couldn't tell. It was just like the exercises at Quantico, he told himself, total chaos, and the side that makes the fewest mistakes wins.

'Get aboard!' He stayed up, holding his gun on the other boat. He didn't turn his head, but felt the others board. Lightning flashed, and Ryan saw the man he'd shot, three red spots on his chest, his eyes and mouth open in surprise. Shorty was beside him, the side of his head horribly opened. Between the two it seemed a gallon of blood had been poured onto the fibreglass deck. Robby finally arrived and jumped aboard. A head appeared in the other boat, and Ryan fired again, then clambered aboard.

'Robby, get us the hell outta here!' Jack moved on hands and knees to the other side, making sure that everyone's head was down.

Jackson moved into the driver's seat and searched for the ignition. It was set up just like a car, and the keys were in. He turned them, and the engine coughed to life as yet another burst of fire came from the other boat. Ryan heard the sound of bullets hitting the fibreglass. Robby cringed but didn't move as his hand found the shift lever. Jack brought the gun up and fired again.

'Men on the cliff!' the Prince shouted.

O'Donnell gathered his men quickly and gave out new orders. All the security men were dead, he was sure, but that helicopter had probably landed to the west. He didn't think the missile had hit, thought it was impossible to be sure.

'Thanks for the help, Sean, they were better than I expected. You have them in the house?'

'I left Dennis and two others. I think we should leave.'

'You got that right!' Alex said. He pointed west. 'I think we have some more company.'

'Very well. Sean, you collect them and bring them to the cliff.'

Miller got his two men and ran back to the house. Alex and his man tagged along. The front door was open, and all five raced inside, turned around the fireplace, and stopped cold.

Paulson, his spotter, and another agent were running too. He led them along the woodline to where the driveway turned, and dropped again, setting his rifle up on the bipod. There were sirens in the distance now, and he wondered what had taken so goddamned long as he tracked his night-sight in a search for targets. He caught a glimpse of men running around the northern side of the house.

'Something feels wrong about this,' the sniper said.

'Yeah,' his spotter agreed. 'They sure as hell didn't plan to leave by the road – but what else is there?'

'Somebody better find out,' Paulson thought aloud, and got on his radio.

Werner struggled forward on the south side of the yard, trying his best to ignore his throbbing back as he led his group forward. The radio squawked again, and he ordered his other team to advance with extreme caution.

'Well, where are they, man?' Alex asked.

Miller looked around in stunned amazement. Two of his men were dead on the floor, their guns were gone – and so were . . .

'*Where the hell are they!*' Alex repeated.

'Search the house!' Miller screamed. He and Alex stayed in the room. The black man looked at him with an unforgiving stare.

'Did I go through all this to watch you fuck up again?' The three men returned a few seconds later and reported the house empty. Miller had already determined that his men's guns were gone. Something had gone wrong. He took his people outside.

Paulson had a new spot and finally could see his targets again. He counted twelve, then more joined from the house. They seemed to be confused as he watched the images on his night-sight gesture at one another. Some men were talking while others just milled around waiting for orders. Several appeared to be hurt, but he couldn't tell for sure.

'They're gone.' Alex said it before Miller had a chance.

O'Donnell couldn't believe it. Sean explained in a rapid, halting voice while Dobbens looked on.

'Your boy fucked up,' Dobbens said.

750

It was just too much. Miller slipped his own Uzi behind his back and retrieved the one he'd taken from the Secret Service agent. He brought it up in one smooth motion and fired into Alex's chest from a distance of three feet. Louis looked at his fallen boss for a second, then tried to bring his pistol up, but Miller cut him down, too.

'What the hell!' the spotter said.

Paulson flipped the rifle's safety off and centred his sight on the man who had just fired, killing two men – but whom had he killed? He could shoot only to save the lives of friendlies, and the dead men had almost certainly been bad guys. There weren't any hostages to be saved, as far as he could tell. *Where the hell are they?* One of the men near the cliff's edge appeared to shout something, and the others ran to join him. The marksman had his choice of targets, but without positive identification, he couldn't dare to fire a shot.

'Come on, baby,' Jackson said to the engine. The motor was still cold and ran unevenly as he shifted to reverse. The boat moved slowly backward, away from the beach. Ryan had his Uzi trained on the other boat. The man there appeared again, and Ryan fired three rounds before the gun stopped. He cursed and switched magazines before firing a number of short bursts again to keep his head down.

'Men on the cliff,' the Prince repeated. He'd taken the shotgun and had it aimed, but didn't fire. He didn't know who it was up there, and the range was too great in any case. Then flashes appeared. Whoever it was, they were firing at the boat. Ryan turned when he heard bullets hitting the water, and two thudded into the boat itself. Sissy Jackson screamed and grabbed at herself, while the Prince fired three rounds back.

Robby had the boat thirty yards from the beach now, and savagely brought the wheel around as he shifted the selector back into drive. When he rammed the throttle forward, the engine coughed again for one long, terrible moment, but then it caught and the boat surged forward.

'*All right!*' the aviator hooted. 'Jack – where to? How about Annapolis?'

'Do it!' Ryan agreed. He looked aft. There were men coming down the ladder. Some were still shooting at them but missing wildly. Next he saw that Sissy was holding her foot.

'Cathy, see if you can find a first-aid kit,' His Highness said. He'd already inspected the wound, but was now in the stern, facing aft with the shotgun at the ready. Jack saw a white plastic box under the driver's seat and slid it toward his wife.

'Rob, Sissy took a round in the foot,' Jack said.

'I'm okay, Rob,' his wife said at once. She didn't sound okay.

'How is it, Sis?' Cathy asked, moving to take a look.

'It hurts, but it's no big deal,' she said through her teeth, trying to smile.

'You sure you're okay, honey?' Robby asked.

'Just *go*, Robby!' she gasped. Jack moved aft and looked. The bullet had gone straight through the top of her foot, and her light-coloured shoe was bathed in dark blood. He looked around to see if anyone else was hurt, but aside from the mere terror that each felt, everyone else seemed all right.

'Commander, do you want me to take the wheel for you?' the Prince asked.

'Okay, Cap'n, come on forward.' Robby slid away from the controls as His Highness joined him. 'Your course is zero-three-six magnetic. Watch it, it's going to get rough when we're out of the cliff's lee, and there's lot of merchant traffic out there.' They could already see four feet of chop building a hundred yards ahead, driven by the gusting winds.

'Right. How do I know when we've arrived at Annapolis?' the Prince settled behind the wheel and started checking out the controls.

'When you see the lights on the Bay Bridges, call me. I know the harbour, I'll take her in.'

The Prince nodded agreement. He throttled back to half power as they entered the heavy chop, and kept moving his eyes from the compass to the water. Jackson moved to check his wife.

Sissy waved him away. 'You worry about *them*!'

In another moment they were roller-coasting over four- and five-foot waves. The boat was a nineteen-foot cathedral-hull lake boat of a type favoured by local fishermen for her good calm-seas speed and shallow draft. Her blunt nose didn't handle the chop very well. They were taking water over the bow, but the forward snap-on cover was in place, and the windshield deflected most of the water over the side. That water which did get into the back emptied down a self-bailing hole next to the engine box. Ryan had never been in a boat like this, but knew what it was. Its hundred-fifty-horse engine drove an inboard-outdrive transmission whose movable propeller eliminated the need for a rudder. The bottom and sides of the boat were filled with foam for positive flotation. You could fill it with water and it wouldn't sink – but more to the point, the fibreglass and the foam would probably stop the bullets from a submachine gun. Jack checked his fellow passengers again. His wife was ministering to Sissy. The Princess held his daughter. Except for himself, Robby, and the Prince at the wheel, everyone's head was down. He started to relax slightly. They were away, and their fate was back in their own hands. Jack promised himself that this would never change again.

'They're coming after us,' Robby said as he fed two rounds into the bottom of the shotgun. ' 'Bout three hundred yards back. I saw them in the lightning, but they'll lose us in this rain if we're lucky.'

'What would you call the visibility?'

752

'Except for the lightning' – Robby shrugged – 'maybe a hot hundred yards, tops. We're not leaving a wake for them to follow, and they don't know where we're going.' He paused. 'God, I wish we had a radio! We could get the Coast Guard in on this, or maybe somebody else, and set up a nice little trap for them.'

Jack sat all the way down, facing aft on the opposite side of the engine box from his friend. He saw that his daughter was asleep in the arms of the Princess. *It must be nice to be a kid*, he reflected.

'Count your blessings, Commander.'

'Bet your ass, boy! I guess I picked a good time to take a leak.'

Ryan grunted agreement. 'I didn't know you could handle a shotgun.'

'Back when I was a kid, the Klan had this little hobby. They'd get boozed up every Tuesday night and burn down a nigger church – just to keep us in line, y'know? Well, one night, the sheetheads decided to burn my pappy's church. We got word – a liquor-store owner called; not all red-necks are assholes. Anyway, Pappy and me were waiting for them. Didn't kill any, but we must have scared them as white as their sheets. I blew the radiator right out of one car.' Robby chuckled at the memory. 'They never did come back for it. The cops didn't arrest anybody, but that's the last time anybody tried to burn a church in our town, so I guess they learned their lesson.' He paused again. When he went on, his voice was more sober. 'That's the first time I ever killed a man, Jack. Funny, it doesn't feel like anything, not anything at all.'

'It will tomorrow.'

Robby looked over at his friend. 'Yeah.'

Ryan looked aft, his hands tight on the Uzi. There was nothing to be seen. The sky and water merged into an amorphous grey mass, and the wind-driven rain stung at his face. The boat surged up and down on the breaking swells, and for a moment Jack wondered why he wasn't seasick. Lightning flashed again, and still he saw nothing, as though they were under a grey dome on a sparkling, uneven floor.

They were gone. After the sniper team reported that all the terrorists had disappeared over the cliff, Werner's men searched the house and found nothing but dead men. The second HRT group was now on the scene, plus over twenty police, and another crowd of firemen and para-medics. Three of the Secret Service agents were still alive, plus a terrorist who'd been left behind. All were being transported to hospitals. That made for seventeen security people dead, and a total of four terrorists, two of them apparently killed by their own side.

'They all crowded into the boat and took off that way,' Paulson said. 'I could have taken a few out, but there just wasn't any way to figure who was who.' He'd done the right thing. The sniper knew it, and so did Werner. You don't shoot without knowing what your target is.

753

'So now what the hell do we do?' This question came from a captain of the State Police. It was a rhetorical question insofar as there was no immediate answer.

'Do you suppose the good guys got away?' Paulson asked. 'I didn't see anything that looked like a friendly, and the way the bad guys were acting . . . something went wrong,' he said. 'Something went wrong for everybody.'

Something went wrong, all right, Werner thought. *A goddamned battle was fought here. Twenty-some people dead and nobody in sight.*

'Let's assume that the friendlies escaped somehow – no, let's just assume that the bad guys got away in a boat. Okay. Where would they go?' Werner asked.

'Do you know how many boatyards there are around here?' the State Police Captain asked. 'Jesus, how many houses with private slips? Hundreds – we can't check them all out!'

'Well, we have to do something!' Werner snapped back, his anger amplified by his sprained back. A black dog came up to them. He looked as confused as everyone else.

'I think they lost us.'

'Could be,' Jackson replied. The last lightning flash had revealed nothing. 'The bay's right big, and visibility isn't worth a damn – but the way the rain's blowing, they can see better than we can. Twenty yards, maybe, just enough to matter.'

'How about we go farther east?' Jack asked.

'Into the main ship channel? It's a Friday night. There'll be a bunch of ships coming out of Baltimore, knocking down ten-twelve knots, and as blind as we are.' Robby shook his head. 'Uh-uh, we didn't make it this far to get run down by some Greek rustbucket. This is hairy enough.'

'Lights ahead,' the Prince reported.

'We're home, Jack!' Robby went forward. The lights of the twin Chesapeake Bay Bridges winked at them unmistakably in the distance. Jackson took the wheel, and the Prince took up his spot in the stern. All were long since soaked through by the rain, and they shivered in the wind. Jackson brought the boat around to the west. The wind was on the bow now, coming straight down the Severn River valley, as it usually did here. The waves moderated somewhat as he steered past the Annapolis town harbour. The rain was still falling in sheets, and Robby navigated the boat mostly by memory.

The lights along the Naval Academy's Sims Drive were a muted, linear glow through the rain and Robby steered for them, barely missing a large can buoy as he fought the boat through the wind. In another minute they could see the line of grey YPs – Yard Patrol boats – still moored to the concrete seawall while their customary slips were being renovated across the river. Robby stood to see better, and brought the boat in between a pair of the wood-hulled training craft. He actually wanted to enter the Academy yacht basin, but it was too full at the moment. Finally he nosed the boat to the seawall, holding her to the concrete with engine power.

'Y'all stop that!' A Marine came into view. His white cap had a plastic cover over it, and he wore a raincoat. 'Y'all can't tie up here.'

'This is Lieutenant Commander Jackson, son,' Robby replied. 'I work here. Stand by. Jack, you get the bowline.'

Ryan ducked under the windshield and unsnapped the bow cover. A white nylon line was neatly coiled in the right place, and Ryan stood as Robby used engine power to bring the boat's port side fully against the seawall. Jack jumped up and tied the line off. The Prince did the same at the stern. Robby killed the engine and went up to face the Marine.

'You recognize me, son?'

The Marine saluted. 'Beg pardon, Commander, but –' He flashed his light into the boat. 'Holy Christ!'

About the only good thing that could be said about the boat was that the rain had washed most of the blood down the self-bailing hole. The Marine's mouth dropped open as he saw two bodies, three women, one of them apparently shot, and a sleeping child. Next he saw a machine gun draped around Ryan's neck. A dull, wet evening of walking guard came to a screeching end.

'You got a radio, Marine?' Robby asked. He held it up and Jackson snatched it away. It was a small Motorola CC unit like those used by police. 'Guardroom, this is Commander Jackson.'

'Commander? This is Sergeant Major Breckenridge. I didn't know you had the duty tonight, sir. What can I do for you?'

Jackson took a long breath. 'I'm glad it's you, Gunny. Listen up: Alert the command duty officer. Next, I want some armed Marines on the seawall west of the yacht basin *immediately*! We got big trouble here, Gunny, so let's shag it!'

'Aye aye, sir!' The radio squawked. Orders had been given. Questions could wait.

'What's your name, son?' Robby asked the Marine next.

'Lance Corporal Green, sir!'

'Okay, Green, help me get the womenfolk out of the boat.' Robby reached out his hand. 'Let's go, ladies.'

Green leaped down and helped Sissy out first, then Cathy, then the Princess, who was still holding Sally. Robby got them all behind the wood hull of one of the YPs.

'What about them, sir?' Green gestured at the bodies.

'They'll keep. Get back up here, Corporal!'

Green gave the bodies a last look. 'Reckon so,' he muttered. He already had his raincoat open and the flap loose on his holster.

'What's going on here?' a woman's voice asked. 'Oh, it's you, Commander.'

'What are you doing here, Chief?' Robby asked her.

'I have the duty section out keeping an eye on the boats, sir. The wind could beat 'em to splinters on this seawall if we don't –' Chief Bosun's Mate Mary Znamirowski looked at everyone on the dock. 'Sir, what the hell . . .'

'Chief, I suggest you get your people together and put them under cover. No time for explanations.'

A pickup truck came next. It halted in the parking lot just behind them. The driver jumped out and sprinted toward them with three others trailing behind. It was Breckenridge. The Sergeant Major gave the women a quick look, then turned to Jackson and asked the night's favourite question –

'What the hell is going on, sir?'

Robby gestured to the boat. Breckenridge gave it a quick look that lingered into four or five questions. 'Christ!'

'We were at Jack's place for dinner,' Robby explained. 'And some folks crashed the party. They were after him –' Jackson gestured to the Prince of Wales, who turned and smiled. Breckenridge's eyes went wide in recognition. His mouth flapped open for a moment, but he recovered and did what Marines always do when they don't know what else – he saluted, just as prescribed in the *Guide Book*. Robby went on: 'They killed a bunch of security troops. We got lucky. They planned to escape by boat. We stole one and came here, but there's another boat out there, full of the bastards. They might have followed us.'

'Armed with what?' the Sergeant Major asked.

'Like this, Gunny.' Ryan held up his Uzi.

The Sergeant Major nodded and reached into his coat. His hand came out with a radio. 'Guardroom, this is Breckenridge. We have a Class-One Alert: Wake up all the people. Call Captain Peters. I want a squad of riflemen on the seawall in five minutes. Move out!'

'Roger,' the radio answered. 'Class-One Alert.'

'Let's get the women the hell outta here,' Ryan urged.

'Not yet, sir,' Breckenridge replied. He looked around, his professional eye making a quick evaluation. 'I want some more security here first. Your friends might have landed upriver and be coming overland – that's how I'd do it. In ten minutes I'll have a platoon of riflemen sweepin' the grounds, maybe a full squad here in five. If my people ain't too drunked out,' he concluded quietly, reminding Ryan that it was indeed a Friday night – Saturday morning – and Annapolis had many bars. 'Cummings and Foster, look after the ladies. Mendoza, get on one of these boats and keep a lookout. Y'all heard the man, so stay awake!'

Breckenridge walked up and down the seawall for a minute, checking fields of view and fields of fire. The .45 Colt automatic looked small in his hands. They could see in his face that he didn't like the situation, and wouldn't until he had more people here and the civilians tucked safely away. Next he checked the women out.

756

'You ladies all right – oh, sorry, Mrs Jackson. We'll get you to the sick bay real quick, ma'am.'

'Any way to turn the lights off?' Ryan asked.

'Not that I know of – I don't like being under 'em either. Settle down, Lieutenant, we got all this open ground behind us, so nobody's going to sneak up this way. Soon as I get things organized, we'll get the ladies off to the dispensary and put a guard on 'em. You ain't as safe as I'd like, but we're gettin' there. How did you get away?'

'Like Robby said, we got lucky. He did two of them with the shotgun. I got one in the boat. The other one got popped by his own man.' Ryan shivered, this time not from wind or rain. 'It was kinda hairy there for a while.'

'I believe it. These guys any good?'

'The terrorists? You tell me. They had surprise going for them before, and that counts for a lot.'

'We'll see about that.' Breckenridge nodded.

'There's a boat out there!' It was Mendoza, up on one of the YPs.

'Okay, boys,' the Sergeant Major breathed, holding his .45 up alongside his head. 'Just wait a couple of minutes, till we get some real weapons here.'

'They're coming in slow,' the Marine called.

Breckenridge's first look was to make sure the women were safely behind cover. Then he ordered everyone to spread out and pick an open spot between the moored boats. 'And for Christ's sake keep your damned heads down!'

Ryan picked a spot for himself. The others did the same, at intervals of from ten to over a hundred feet apart. He felt the reinforced-concrete seawall with his hand. He was sure it would stop a bullet. The four sailors from the YP duty section stayed with the women, with a Marine on either side. Breckenridge was the only one moving, crouching behind the seawall, following the white shape of the moving boat. He got to Ryan.

'There, about eighty yards out, going left to right. They're trying to figure things out, too. *Just give me a couple more minutes, people,*' he whispered.

'Yeah.' Ryan thumbed off the safety, one eye above the lip of the concrete. It was just a white outline, but he could hear the muted sputter of the engine. The boat turned in toward where Robby had tied up the one they'd stolen. It was their first real mistake, Jack thought.

'Great.' The Sergeant Major levelled his automatic, shielded by the stern of a boat. 'Okay, gentlemen. Come on if you're coming. . . .'

Another pickup truck approached on Sims Drive. It came up without lights and stopped right by the women. Eight men jumped off the back. Two Marines ran along the seawall, and were illuminated by a light between two of the moored YPs. Out on the water, the small boat lit up with muzzle flashes, and both Marines went down. Bullets started hitting the moored boats around them. Breckenridge turned and yelled.

'*Fire!*' The area exploded with noise. Ryan spotted on the flashes and depressed his trigger with care. The submachine gun fired four rounds before locking open on an empty magazine. He cursed and stared stupidly at the weapon before he realized that he had a loaded pistol in his belt. He got the Browning up and fired a single shot before he realized that the target wasn't there anymore. The noise from the boat's motor increased dramatically.

'Cease fire! Cease fire! They're buggin' out.' Breckenridge called. 'Anybody hit?'

'Over here!' someone called to the right, where the women were.

Ryan followed the Sergeant Major over. Two Marines were down, one with a flesh wound in the arm, but the other had taken a round right through the hip and was screaming like a banshee. Cathy was already looking at him.

'Mendoza, what's happening?' Breckenridge called.

'They're heading out – wait – yeah, they're moving east!'

'Move your hands, soldier,' Cathy was saying. The Private First-Class had taken a painful hit just below the belt on his left side. 'Okay, okay, you're going to be all right. It hurts, but we can fix it.' Breckenridge reached down to take the man's rifle. He tossed it to Sergeant Cummings.

'Who's in command here?' demanded Captain Mike Peters.

'I guess I am,' Robby said.

'Christ, Robby, what's going on?'

'What the hell does it look like!'

Another truck arrived, carrying another six Marines. They took one collective look at the wounded men and yanked at the charging handles on their rifles.

'Goddammit, Robby – sir!' Captain Peters yelled.

'Terrorists. They tried to get us at Jack's place. They were trying to get – well, look!'

'Good evening, Captain,' the Prince said after checking his wife. 'Did we get any? I didn't have a clear shot.' His voice showed real disappointment at that.

'I don't know, sir,' Breckenridge answered. 'I saw some rounds go short, and pistol stuff won't penetrate a boat like that.' Another series of lightning flashes illuminated the area.

'I see 'em, they're going out to the bay!' Mendoza called.

'Damn!' Breckenridge growled. 'You four, get the ladies over to the dispensary.' He bent down to help the Princess to her feet as Robby lifted his wife. 'You want to give the little girl to the Private, ma'am? They're going to take you to the hospital and get you all dried off.'

Ryan saw that his wife was still trying to help one of the wounded Marines, then looked at the patrol boat in front of him. 'Robby?'

'Yeah, Jack?'

'Does this boat have a radar?'

Chief Znamirowski answered. 'They all do, sir.'

A Marine lowered the tailgate on the one pickup and helped Jackson load his wife aboard. 'What are you thinking, Jack?'

'How fast are they?'

'About thirteen – I don't think they're fast enough.'

Chief Bosun's Mate Znamirowski looked over the seawall at the boat Robby had steered in. 'In the seas we got now, you bet I can catch one of those little things! But I need someone to work the radar. I don't have an operator in my section right now.'

'I can do that,' the Prince offered. He was tired of being a target, and no one would keep him out of this. 'It would be a pleasure in fact.'

'Robby, you're senior here,' Jack said.

'Is it legal?' Captain Peters asked, fingering his automatic.

'Look,' Ryan said quickly, 'we just had an armed attack by *foreign* nationals on a US government reservation – that's an act of war and posse commitatus doesn't apply.' *At least I don't think it does*, he thought. 'Can you think of a good reason not to go after them?'

He couldn't. 'Chief Z, you have a boat ready?' Jackson asked.

'Hell, yes, we can take the seventy-six-boat.'

'Crank her up! Captain Peters, we need some Marines.'

'Sar-Major Breckenridge, secure the area, and bring along ten men.'

The Sergeant Major had left the officers to their arguments while getting the civilians loaded onto the truck. He grabbed Cummings.

'Sergeant, take charge of the civilians, get 'em to sick bay, and put a guard on 'em. Beef up the guard force, but your primary mission is to take care of these people here. Their safety is your responsibility – and you ain't relieved till I relieve you! Got it?'

'Aye, Gunny.'

Ryan helped his wife to the truck. 'We're going after them.'

'I know. Be careful, Jack. Please.'

'I will, but we're going to get 'em this time, babe.' He kissed his wife. There was a funny sort of look on her face, something more than concern. 'Are you okay?'

'I'll be fine. You worry about you. Be careful!'

'Sure, babe. I'll be back.' *But they won't!* Jack turned away to jump aboard the boat. He went inside the deckhouse and found the ladder to the bridge.

'I am Chief Znamirowski, and I have the conn,' she announced. Mary Znamirowski didn't look like a chief bosun's mate, but the young seaman – was seawoman the proper term for her? Jack wondered – on the wheel jumped as though she were. 'Starboard back two thirds, port back one third, left full rudder.'

'Stern line is in,' a seaman – this one was a man – reported.

'Very well,' she acknowledged, and continued her terse commands to get the YP away from the dock. Within seconds they were clear of the seawall and the other boats.

'Right full rudder, all ahead full! Come to the new course one-three-five.'
She turned. 'How's the radar look?'

The Prince was looking over the controls on the unfamiliar set. He found the clutter-suppression switch and bent down to the viewing hood. 'Ah! Target bearing one-one-eight, range thirteen hundred, target course north-easterly, speed . . . about eight knots.'

'That's about right, it can get choppy by the point,' Chief Z thought. 'What's our mission, Commander?'

'Can we stay with them?'

'They shot up *my* boats! I'll ram the turkeys if you want, sir,' the chief replied. 'I can give you thirteen knots as long as you want. I doubt they can do more than ten in the seas we got.'

'Okay. I want us to follow as close as we can without being spotted.'

'The chief opened one of the pilothouse doors and looked at the water. 'We'll close to three hundred. Anything else?'

'Go ahead and close up. For the rest of it, I am open to ideas,' Robby replied.

'How about we see where they're going?' Jack suggested. 'Then we can call in the cavalry.'

'That makes sense. If they try to run for shore . . . Christ, I'm a fighter pilot, not a cop.' Robby lifted the radio microphone. The set showed the boat's call sign: NAEF. 'Naval Station Annapolis, this is November Alfa Echo Foxtrot. Do you read? Over.' He had to repeat the call twice more before getting an acknowledgement.

'Annapolis, give me a phone patch to the Superintendent.'

'He just called us, sir. Stand by.' A few clicks followed, plus the usual static. 'This is Admiral Reynolds, who is this?'

'Lieutenant Commander Jackson, sir, aboard the seventy-six boat. We are one mile southeast of the Academy in pursuit of the boat that just shot up our waterfront.'

'Is that what happened? All right, who do you have aboard?'

'Chief Znamirowski and the duty boat section, Captain Peters and some Marines, Doctor Ryan, and, uh, Captain Wales, sir, of the Royal Navy,' Robby answered.

'Is *that* where he is? I have the FBI on the other phone – Christ, Robby! Okay, the civilians are under guard at the hospital, and the FBI and police are on the way here. Repeat your situation and then state your intentions.'

'Sir, we are tracking the boat that attacked the dock. Our intentions are to close and track by radar to determine its destination, then call in the proper law-enforcement agencies, sir.' Robby smiled into the mike at his choice of words. 'My next call is to Coast Guard Baltimore, sir. Looks like they're heading in that direction at the moment.'

'Roger that. Very well, you may continue the mission, but the safety of your guests is your responsibility. Do not, repeat do not take any unnecessary chances. Acknowledge.'

'Yes, sir, we will not take any unnecessary chances.'

'Use your head, Commander, and report as necessary. Out.'

'Now there's a vote of confidence,' Jackson thought aloud. 'Carry on.'

'Left fifteen degrees rudder,' Chief Z ordered, rounding Greenbury Point. 'Come to new course zero-two-zero.'

'Target bearing zero-one-four, range fourteen hundred, speed still eight knots,' His Highness told the quarter-master on the chart table. 'They took a shorter route around this point.'

'No problem,' the chief noted, looking at the radar plot. 'We have deep water all the way up from here.'

'Chief Z, do we have any coffee aboard?'

'I got a pot in the galley, sir, but I don't have anybody to work it.'

'I'll take care of that,' Jack said. He went below, then to starboard and below again. The galley was a small one, but the coffee machine was predictably of the proper size. Ryan got it started and went back topside. Breckenridge was passing out life jackets to everyone aboard, which seemed a sensible enough precaution. The Marines were deployed on the bridgewalk outside the pilothouse.

'Coffee in ten minutes,' he announced.

'Say again, Coast Guard,' Robby said into the microphone.

'November Alfa Echo Foxtrot, this is Coast Guard Baltimore, do you read? Over.'

'That's better.'

'Can you tell us what's going on?'

'We are tracking a small boat, about a twenty-footer – with ten or more armed terrorists aboard.' He gave position, course, and speed. 'Acknowledge that.'

'Roger, you say a boat full of bad guys and machine guns. Is this for real? Over.'

'That's affirmative, son. Now let's cut the crap and get down to it.'

The response was slightly miffed. 'Roger that, we have a forty-one boat about to leave the dock and a thirty-two-footer'll be about ten minutes behind it. These are small harbour-patrol boats. They are not equipped to fight a surface gun action, mister.'

'We have ten Marines aboard,' Jackson replied. 'Do you request assistance?'

'Hell, yes – that's affirmative, Echo Foxtrot. I have the police and the FBI on the phone, and they are heading to this area.'

'Okay, have your forty-one boat call us when they clear the dock. Let's have your boat track from in front and we'll track from behind. If we can figure where the target is heading, I want you to call in the cops.'

'We can do that easy enough. Let me get some things rolling here, Navy. Stand by.'

'A ship,' the Prince said.

'It's gotta be,' Ryan agreed. 'The same way they did it when they rescued that Miller bastard. . . . Robby, can you get the Coast Guard to give us a list of the ships in the harbour?'

Werner and both Hostage Rescue groups were already moving. He wondered what had gone wrong – and right – tonight, but that would be determined later. For the moment he had agents and police heading toward the Naval Academy to protect the people he was supposed to have rescued, and his men were split between an FBI Chevy Suburban and two State Police cars, all heading north on Ritchie Highway toward Baltimore. If only they could use helicopters, he thought, but the weather was too bad, and everyone had had enough of that for one night. They were back to being a SWAT team, a purpose for which they were well suited. Despite everything that had gone wrong tonight, they now had a large group of terrorists flushed and in the open. . . .

'Here's the list of the ships in port,' the Coast Guard Lieutenant said over the radio. 'We had a lot of them leave Friday night, so the list isn't too long. I'll start off at the Dundalk Marine Terminal. *Nissan Courier*, Japanese registry, she's a car carrier out of Yokohama delivering a bunch of cars and trucks. *Wilhelm Schörner*, West German registry, a container boat out of Bremen with general cargo. *Costanza*, Cypriot registry, out of Valetta, Malta –

'Bingo!' Ryan said.

'– scheduled to sail in about five hours, looks like. *George McReady*, American, arrived with cargo of lumber from Portland, Oregon. That's the last one there.'

'Tell me about the *Costanza*,' Robby said, looking at Jack.

'She arrived in ballast and loaded up a cargo mainly of farm equipment and some other stuff. Sails before dawn, supposed to be headed back for Valetta.'

'That's probably our boy,' Jack said quietly.

'Stand by, Coast Guard.' Robby turned away from the radio. 'How do you know, Jack?'

'I don't *know*, but it's a solid guess. When these bastards pulled the rescue on Christmas Day, they were probably picked up in the Channel by a Cypriot-registered ship. We think their weapons get to them through a Maltese dealer who works with a South African, and a lot of terrorists move back and forth through Malta – the local government's tight with a certain country due south of there. The Maltese don't get their own hands dirty, but they're real good at looking the other way if the money's right.' Robby nodded and keyed his mike.

762

'Coast Guard, have you gotten things straightened out with the local cops?'

'That's a roge, Navy.'

'Tell them that we believe the target's objective is the *Costanza*.'

'Roger that. We'll have our thirty-two boat stake her out and call in the cops.'

'Don't let them see you, Coast Guard!'

'Understood, Navy. We can handle that part easy enough. Stand by.... Navy, be advised that our forty-one boat reports radar contact with you and the target, rounding Bodkin Point. Is this correct? Over.'

'Yes!' called the Quartermaster at the chart table. He was making a precise record of the course tracks from the radar plot.

'That's affirm, Coast Guard. Tell your boat to take station five hundred yards forward of the target. Acknowledge.'

'Roger, five-zero-zero yards. Okay, let's see if we can get the cops moving. Stand by.'

'We got 'em,' Ryan thought aloud.

'Uh, Lieutenant, keep your hands still, sir.' It was Breckenridge. He reached into Ryan's belt and extracted the Browning automatic. Jack was surprised to see that he'd stuck it in there with the hammer back and safety off. Breckenridge lowered the hammer and put the pistol back where it was. 'Let's try to think "safe", sir, okay? Otherwise you might lose something important.'

Ryan nodded rather sheepishly. 'Thanks, Gunny.'

'Somebody has to protect the lieutenants.' Breckenridge turned. 'Okay, Marines – let's stay awake out there!'

'You got a man on the Prince?' Jack asked.

'Even before the Admiral said so.' The Sergeant Major gestured to where a corporal was standing, rifle in hand, three feet from His Highness, with orders to stay between him and the gunfire.

Five minutes later a trio of State Police cars drove without lights to Berth Six of the Dundalk Marine Terminal. The cars were parked under one of the gantry cranes used for transferring cargo containers, and five officers walked quietly to the ship's accommodation ladder. A crewman stationed there stopped them – or tried to. A language barrier prevented proper communications. He found himself accompanying the troopers, with his hands cuffed behind his back. The senior police officer bounded up three more ladders and arrived at the bridge.

'What is this!'

'And who might you be?' the cop inquired from behind a shotgun.

'I am the master of this ship!' Captain Nikolai Frenza proclaimed.

'Well, Captain, I am Sergeant William Powers of the Maryland State Police, and I have some questions for you.'

763

'You have no authority on my ship!' Frenza answered. His accent was a mixture of Greek and some other tongue. 'I will talk to the Coast Guard and no one else.'

'I want to make this real clear.' Powers walked the fifteen feet to the Captain, his hands tight around the Ithaca 12-gauge shotgun. 'That shore you're tied to is the State of Maryland, and this shotgun says I got all the authority I need. Now we have information that a boatload of terrorists is coming here, and the word is they've killed a bunch of people, including three state troopers.' He planted the muzzle against Frenza's chest. 'Captain, if they do come here, or if you fuck with me any more tonight, *you are in a whole shitpot full of trouble – do you understand me*!'

The man wilted before his eyes, Powers saw. *So the information is correct. Good.*

'You would be well advised to cooperate, 'cause pretty soon we're going to have more cops here 'n you ever saw. You just might need some friends, mister. If you have something to tell me, I want to hear it right now.'

Frenza hesitated, his eyes shifting toward the bow and back. He was in deep trouble, more than his advance payment would ever cover. 'There are four of them aboard. They are forward, starboard side, near the bow. We didn't know –'

'Shut up.' Powers nodded to a corporal, who got on his portable radio. 'What about your crew?'

'The crew is below, preparing to take the ship to sea.'

'Sarge, the Coast Guard says they're three miles off and heading in.'

'All right.' Powers pulled a set of handcuffs from his belt. He and his men took the four men standing bridge watch and secured them to the ship's wheel and two other fittings. 'Captain, if you or your people make any noise at all, I'll come back here and splatter you all over this ship. I am not kidding.'

Powers took his men down to the main deck and forward on the port side. The *Costanza*'s superstructure was all aft. Forward of it, the deck was a mass of cargo containers, each the size of a truck-trailer, piled three and four-high. Between each pile was an artificial alleyway, perhaps three feet wide, which allowed them to approach the bow unobserved. The Sergeant had no SWAT experience, but all of his men had shotguns and he did know something of infantry tactics.

It was like walking alongside a building, except that the street was made of rusty steel. The rain had abated, finally, but it still made noise, clattering on the metal container boxes. They passed the last of these to find that the ship's forward hold was open and a crane was hanging over the starboard side. Powers peeked around the corner and saw two men standing at the far side of the deck. They appeared to be looking southeast, toward the entrance to the harbour. There was no easy way to approach. He and his men crouched and went straight toward them. They'd gotten halfway when one turned.

'Who are you?'

'State Police!' Powers noted the accent and brought his gun up, but he tripped on a deck fitting and his first shot went into the air. The man on the starboard side came up with a pistol and fired, also missing, then ducked behind the container. The fourth state trooper went forward around the deck and hatch and fired at the container edge, covering his comrades. Powers heard a flurry of conversation and the sound of running feet. He took a deep breath and ran to the starboard side.

No one was in sight. The men who'd run aft were nowhere to be seen. There was an accommodation ladder leading from an opening in the rail down to the water, and nothing else but a radio that someone had dropped.

'Oh, shit.' The tactical situation was lousy. He had armed criminals close by but out of sight and a boatload of others on the way. He sent one of his men to the port side to watch that line of approach, and another to train his shotgun down the starboard side. Then he got on the radio and learned that plenty more help was on the way. Powers decided to sit tight and take his chances. He'd known Larry Fontana, helped carry his coffin out of the church, and he was damned if he'd pass up the chance to get the people who'd killed him.

A State Police car had taken the lead. The FBI was now on the Francis Scott Key Bridge, crossing over Baltimore Harbour. The next trick was to get from the expressway to the marine terminal. A trooper said he knew a shortcut, and he led the procession of three cars. A twenty-foot boat was going under the bridge at that very moment.

'Target coming right, appears to be heading towards a ship tied to the quay, bearing three-five-two,' His Highness reported.

'That's it,' Ryan said. 'We got 'em.'

'Chief, let's close up some.' Jackson ordered.

'They might spot us, sir – the rain's slacking off. If they're heading to the north, I can close up on their port side. They're heading for that ship – you want us to hit them right when they get there?' Chief Znamirowski asked.

'That's right.'

'Okay. I'll get somebody on the searchlight. Captain Peters, you'll want to get your Marines on the starboard side. Looks like surface action starboard,' Chief Z noted. Navy regulations prohibited her from serving on a combatant ship, but she'd beaten the game after all!

'Right.' Peters gave the order and Breckenridge got the Marines in place. Ryan left the pilothouse and went to the main deck aft. He had already come to his decision. Sean Miller was out there.

'I hear a boat,' one of the troopers said quietly.

'Yeah.' Powers fed a round into his shotgun. He looked aft. There were people there with guns. He heard footsteps behind him – more police!

'Who's in charge here?' a corporal asked.

'I am,' Powers replied. 'You stay here. You two, move aft. If you see a head come out from behind a container, blow it the hell off.'

'I see it!' So did Powers. A white fibreglass boat appeared a hundred yards off, coming slowly up to the ship's ladder.

'Jesus.' It seemed full of people, and every one, he'd been told, had an automatic weapon. Unconsciously he felt the steel plating on the ship's side. He wondered if it would stop a bullet. Most troopers now wore protective body armour, but Powers didn't. The Sergeant flipped off the safety on his shotgun. It was just about time.

The boat approached like a car edging into a parking space. The helmsman nosed the boat to the bottom of the accommodation ladder and someone in the bow tied it off. Two men got out onto the small lower platform. They helped someone off the boat, then started to carry him up the metal staircase. Powers let them get halfway.

'*Freeze!* State Police!' He and two others pointed shotguns straight down at the boat. 'Move and you're dead,' he added, and was sorry for it. It sounded too much like TV.

He saw heads turn upward, a few mouths open in surprise. A few hands moved, too, but before anything that looked like a weapon moved in his direction, a two-foot searchlight blazed down on the boat from seaward.

Powers was thankful for the light. He saw their heads snap around, then up at him. He could see their expressions now. They were trapped and knew it.

'Hi, there.' A voice came across the water. It was a woman's voice on a loudspeaker. 'If anybody moves, I have ten Marines to blow you to hell-and-gone. Make my day,' the voice concluded. Sergeant Powers winced at that.

Then another light came on. 'This is the US Coast Guard. You are all under arrest.'

'Like hell!' Powers screamed. 'I got 'em!' It took another minute to establish what was going on to everyone's satisfaction. The big, grey Navy patrol boat came right alongside the smaller boat, and Powers was relieved to see ten rifles pointed at his prisoners.

'Okay, let's put all the guns down, people, and come up one at a time.' His head jerked around as a single pistol shot rang out, followed by a pair of shotgun blasts. The Sergeant winced, but ignored it as best he could and kept his gun zeroed on the boat.

'I seen one!' a trooper said. 'About a hundred feet back of us!'

'Cover it,' Powers ordered. 'Okay, you people get the hell up here and flat down on the deck.'

The first two arrived, carrying a third man who was wounded in the chest. Powers got them stretched out, facedown on the deck, forwards of the front rank of containers. The rest came up singly. By the time the last was up, he'd counted twelve, several more of them hurt. They'd left behind a bunch of guns and what looked like a body.

'Hey, Marines, we could use a hand here!'

It was all the encouragement he needed. Ryan was standing on the YP's afterdeck, and jumped down. He slipped and fell on the deck. Breckenridge arrived immediately behind him and looked at the body the terrorists had left behind. A half-inch hole had been drilled in the man's forehead.

'I thought I got off one good round. Lead on, Lieutenant.' He gestured at the ladder. Ryan charged up the steps, pistol in hand. Behind him, Captain Peters was screaming something at him, but Jack simply didn't care.

'Careful, we have bad guys down that way in the container stacks,' Powers warned.

Jack went around the front rank of metal boxes and saw the men facedown on the deck, hands behind their necks, with a pair of troopers standing over them. In a moment there were six Marines there, too.

Captain Peters came up and went to the police Sergeant, who seemed to be in command.

'We have at least two more, maybe four, hiding in the container rows,' Powers said.

'Want some help flushing them out?'

'Yeah, let's go do it.' Powers grinned in the darkness. He assembled all of his men, leaving Breckenridge and three Marines to guard the men on the deck. Ryan stayed there, too. He waited for the others to move aft.

Then he started looking at faces.

Miller was looking, too, still hoping to find a way out. He turned his head to the left and saw Ryan staring at him from twenty feet away. They recognized each other in an instant, and Miller saw something, a look that he had always reserved for his own use.

I am Death, Ryan's face told him.

I have come for you!

It seemed to Ryan that his body was made of ice. His fingers flexed once around the butt of his pistol as he walked slowly to port, his eyes locked on Miller's face. He still looked like an animal to Jack, but he was no longer a predator on the loose. Jack reached him and kicked Miller's leg. He gestured with the pistol for him to stand, but didn't say a word.

You don't talk to snakes. You kill snakes.

'Lieutenant . . .' Breckenridge was a little slow to catch on.

Jack pushed Miller back against the metal wall of a container, his forearm across the man's neck. He savoured the feel of the man's throat on his wrist.

This is the little bastard who nearly killed my family. Though he didn't know it, his face showed no emotion at all.

Miller looked into his eyes and saw . . . nothing. For the first time in his life, Sean Miller knew fear. He saw his own death, and remembered the long-past lessons in Catholic school, remembered what the sisters had taught him, and his fear was that they might have been right. His face broke out in a sweat and his hands trembled as, despite all his contempt for religion, he feared the eternity in hell that surely awaited him.

Ryan saw the look in Miller's eyes, and knew it for what is was. *Goodbye, Sean. I hope you like it there....*

'Lieutenant!'

Jack knew that he had little time. He brought up the pistol and forced it into Miller's mouth as his eyes bored in on Sean's. He tightened his finger on the trigger just as he'd been taught. A gentle squeeze, so you never know when the trigger will break....

But nothing happened, and a massive hand came down on the gun.

'He ain't worth it, Lieutenant, he just ain't worth it.' Breckenridge withdrew his hand, and Ryan saw that the gun's hammer was down. He'd have to cock it before the weapon could fire. 'Think, son.'

The spell was broken. Jack swallowed twice and took a breath. What he saw now was something less monstrous than before. Fear had given Miller the humanity that he'd lacked before. He was no longer an animal, after all. He was a human being, an evil example of what could happen when a man lost something that all men needed. Miller's breath was coming in gasps as Ryan pulled the gun out of his mouth. He gagged, but couldn't bend over with Jack's arm across his throat. Ryan backed away and the man fell to the deck. The Sergeant Major put his hand on Ryan's right arm, forcing the gun downward.

'I know what you're thinking, what he did to your little girl, but it isn't worth what you'd have to go through. I could tell the cops you shot him when he tried to run. My boys would back me up. You'd never go to trial, but it ain't worth what it would do to you, son. You're not cut out to be a murderer,' Breckenridge said gently. 'Besides, look what you did to him. I don't know what that is down there, but it's not a man, not anymore.'

Jack nodded, as yet unable to speak. Miller was still on all fours, looking down at the deck, unable to meet Ryan's eyes. Jack could feel his body again; the blood coursing through his veins told him that he was alive and whole. *I've won*, he thought, as his mind regained control of his emotions. *I've won. I've defeated him and I haven't destroyed myself doing it.* His hands relaxed around the pistol grip.

'Thanks, Gunny. If you hadn't –'

'If you'd really wanted to kill him, you would have remembered to cock it. Lieutenant, I had you figured out a long time ago.' Breckenridge nodded to reinforce his words. 'Back on the deck, you,' he told Miller, who slowly complied.

'Before any of you people think you're lucky, I got a hot flash for you,' the Sergeant Major said next. 'You have committed murder in a place that has a gas chamber. You can die by the numbers over here, people. Think about it.'

The Hostage Rescue Team arrived next. They found the Marines and state troopers on the deck, working their way aft. It took a few minutes to determine that no one was in the container stacks. The remaining four ULA members had used an alleyway to head aft, and were probably in the superstructure. Werner took over. He had a solid perimeter. Nobody was going anywhere. Another group of FBI agents went forward to collect the terrorists.

Three TV news trucks arrived on the scene, adding their lights to the ones turning night into day on the dock. The police were keeping them back, but already live broadcasts were being sent worldwide. A colonel of the State Police was giving out a press release at the moment. The situation, he told the cameras, was under control, thanks to a little luck and a lot of good police work.

By this time all the terrorists forward were handcuffed and had been searched. The agents read off their constitutional rights while three of their number went into the boat to collect their weapons and other evidence. The Prince finally came up the ladder, with a heavy guard. He came to where the terrorists were sitting, now. He looked at them for a minute or so but didn't say a word. He didn't have to.

'Okay, we have things contained aft. There seems to be four of them. That's what the crew says,' one of the HRT people said. 'They're below somewhere, and we'll have to talk them out. It shouldn't be too hard, and we have all the time in the world.'

'How do we get these characters off?' Sergeant Powers asked.

'We haven't worked that out yet, but let's get the civilians off. We'd prefer you did it from here. It might be a little dangerous to use the aft ladder. That means the Marines, too. Thanks for the assist, Captain.'

'I hope we didn't screw anything up, joining in, I mean.'

The agent shook his head. 'You didn't break any laws that I know of. We got all the evidence we need, too.'

'Okay, then we head back to Annapolis.'

'Fine. There'll be a team of agents waiting to interview you there. Please thank the boat crew for us.'

'Sar-Major, let's get the people moving.'

'Okay, Marines, saddle up,' Breckenridge called. Two minutes later everyone was aboard the patrol boat, heading out of the harbour. The rain had finally ended and the sky was clearing, the cooler Canadian air finally breaking the heat wave that had punished the area. The Marines took the opportunity to climb into the boat's bunks. Chief Znamirowski and her crew handled the driving. Ryan and the rest congregated in the galley and started drinking the coffee that no one had touched to this point.

'Long day,' Jackson said. He checked his watch. 'I'm supposed to fly in a few hours. Well, I was, anyway.'

'Looks like we finally won a round,' Captain Peters observed.

'It wasn't cheap.' Ryan stared into his cup.

'It's never cheap, sir,' Breckenridge said after a few seconds.

The boat rumbled with increased engine power. Jackson lifted a phone and asked why they were speeding up. He smiled at the answer, but said nothing.

Ryan shook his head to clear it and went topside. Along the way he found a crewman's pack of cigarettes on a table and stole one. He proceeded out onto the fantail. Baltimore Harbour was already low on the horizon, and the boat was turning south toward Annapolis, chugging along at thirteen knots – about fifteen miles per hour, but on a boat it seemed fast enough. The smoke he blew out made its own trail as he stared aft. *Was Breckenridge right?* he asked the sky. The answer came in a moment. *He got one part right. I'm not cut out to be a murderer. Maybe he was right on the other part, too. I sure hope so. . . .*

'Tired, Jack?' the Prince asked, standing beside him.

'I ought to be, but I guess I'm still too pumped up.'

'Indeed,' His Highness observed quietly. 'I wanted to ask them why. When I went up to look at them, I wanted –'

'Yeah.' Ryan took a last drag and flipped the butt over the side. 'You could ask, but I doubt the answer would mean much of anything.'

'Then how are we supposed to solve the problem?'

We did solve my *problem*, Jack thought. *They won't be coming after my family anymore. But that's not the answer you want, is it?* 'I guess maybe it comes down to justice. If people believe in their society, they don't break its rules. The trick's making them believe. Hell, we can't always accomplish that.' Jack turned. 'But you try your best, and you don't quit. Every problem has a solution if you work at it long enough. You have a pretty good system over there. You just have to make it work for everybody, and do it well enough that they believe. It's not easy, but I think you can do it. Sooner or later, civilization always wins over barbarism.' *I just proved that, I think.* I hope.

The Prince of Wales looked aft for a moment. 'Jack, you're a good man.'

'So are you, pal. That's why we'll win.'

It was a grisly scene, but not one to arouse pity in any of the men who surveyed it. Geoffrey Watkins' body was quite warm, and his blood was still dripping from the ceiling. After the photographer finished up, a detective took the gun from his hands. The television remained on, and 'Good Morning, Britain' continued to run its live report from America. All the terrorists were now in custody. *That's what must have done it*, Murray thought.

'Bloody fool,' Owens said. 'We didn't have a scrap of usable evidence.'

'We do now.' A detective held three sheets of paper in his hand. 'This is quite a letter, Commander.' He slid the sheets into a plastic envelope.

Sergeant Bob Highland was there, too. He was still learning to walk again, with a leg brace and a cane, and looked down at the body of the man whose information had almost made orphans of his children. Highland didn't say a word.

'Jimmy, you've closed the case,' Murray observed.

'Not the way I would have liked,' Owens replied. 'But now I suppose Mr Watkins is answering to a higher authority.'

The boat arrived in Annapolis forty minutes later. Ryan was surprised when Chief Znamirowski passed the line of moored boats and proceeded straight to Hospital Point. She conned the boat expertly alongside the seawall, where a couple of Marines were waiting. Ryan and everyone but the boat's crew jumped off.

'All secure,' Sergeant Cummings reported to Breckenridge. 'We got a million cops and feds here, Gunny. Everybody's just fine.'

'Very well, you're relieved.'

'Doctor Ryan, will you come along with me? You want to hustle, sir,' the young Sergeant said. He led off at a slow trot.

It was well that the pace was an easy one. Ryan's legs were rubbery with fatigue as the Sergeant led him up the hill and into the old Academy hospital.

'Hold it!' A federal agent took the pistol from Ryan's belt. 'I'll keep this for you, if that's okay?'

'Sorry,' Jack said with embarrassment.

'It's all right. You can go in.' There was no one in sight. Sergeant Cummings motioned for him to follow.

'Where is everybody?'

'Sir, your wife's in the delivery room at the moment.' Cummings turned to grin at him.

'Nobody told me!' Ryan said in alarm.

'She said not to worry you, sir.' They reached the proper floor. Cummings pointed. 'Down there. Don't toss your cookies, Doc.'

Jack ran down the corridor. A corpsman stopped him and waved Ryan into a dressing room, where Ryan tore off his clothes and got into surgical greens. It took a few minutes. Ryan was clumsy from fatigue. He walked to the waiting room and saw that all his friends were there. Then the corpsman walked him into the delivery room.

'I haven't done this in a long time,' the doctor was saying.

'It's been a few years for me, too,' Cathy reproached him. 'You're supposed to inspire confidence in your patient.' Then she started blowing again, fighting off the impulse to push. Jack grabbed her hand.

'Hi, babe.'

'Your timing is pretty good,' the doctor observed.

'Five minutes earlier would have been better. Are you all right?' she asked. As it had been the last time, her face was bathed in sweat, and very tired. And she looked beautiful.

'It's all over. *All* over,' he repeated. 'I'm fine, how about you?'

'Her water broke two hours ago, and she'd be in a hurry if we weren't all waiting for you to get back from your boat ride. Otherwise everything looks good,' the doctor answered. He seemed far more nervous than the mother. 'Are you ready to push?'

'Yes!'

Cathy squeezed his hand. Her eyes closed and she summoned her strength for the effort. Her breath came out slowly.

'There's the head. Everything's fine. One more push and we're home,' the doctor said. His gloved hands were poised to make the catch.

Jack turned as the rest of the newborn appeared. His position allowed him to tell even before the doctor did. The infant had already started screaming, as a healthy baby should. *And that, too*, Jack thought, *is the sound of freedom.*

'Boy,' John Patrick Ryan Sr told his wife just before he kissed her, 'I love you.'

The nearest corpsman assisted the doctor as he clamped off the cord and swaddled the infant in a white blanket to take him away a few feet. The placenta came next with an easy push.

'A little tearing,' the doctor reported. He reached for a painkiller before he started the stitching.

'I can tell,' Cathy replied with a slight grimace. 'Is he okay?'

'Looks okay to me,' the corpsman said. 'Eight pounds even, and all the pieces in the right places. Airway's fine, and the kid's got a great little heart.'

Jack picked up his son, a small, noisy package of red flesh with an absurd little button of a nose.

'Welcome to the world. I'm your father,' he said quietly. *And your father isn't a murderer. That might not sound like much, but it's a lot more than most people think.* He cradled the newborn to his chest for a moment and reminded himself that there really was a God. After a moment he looked down at his wife. 'Do you want to see your son?'

'I'm afraid he doesn't have much of a mother left.'

'She looks pretty good to me.' Jack placed his son in Cathy's arms. 'Are you all right?'

'Except for Sally, I think I have everything here that I need, Jack.'

'Finished,' the doctor said. 'I may not be much of an OB, but I do one hell of a good stitch.' He looked up to see the usual aftermath of a birth, and he wondered why he'd decided against obstetrics. It had to be the happiest discipline of them all. But the hours were lousy, he reminded himself.

The corpsman reclaimed the infant, and took John Patrick Ryan Jr to the nursery, where he'd be the only baby for a while. It would give the pediatric people something to do.

Jack watched his wife drift off to sleep after – he checked his watch – a twenty-three-hour day. She needed it. So did he, but not quite yet. He kissed his wife one more time before another corpsman wheeled her away to the recovery room. There was one thing left for him to do.

Ryan walked out to the waiting room to announce the birth of his son, a handsome young man who would have two complete, but very different, sets of godparents.